SNOPES

SNOPES

THE HAMLET, THE TOWN,
THE MANSION

WILLIAM FAULKNER

INTRODUCTION BY GEORGE GARRETT

THE MODERN LIBRARY

NEW YORK

CONTENTS

INTRODUCTION

*A*t the living center of the life work of William Faulkner are the novels and stories which deal with Yoknapatawpha County, that imaginary and deeply imagined place, at once based on and derived from his real home country, Lafayette County, Mississippi; but nevertheless independent with its own myths and legends, its own long and shadowy history, its diverse populations, its places much like places he had known and yet altogether his own invention. And at the heart of the fictional accounting of Yoknapatawpha County stands this trilogy—*The Hamlet* (1940), *The Town* (1957), and *The Mansion* (1959)—here joined together, as he had always hoped and planned they would be, as one continuous and sequential narrative.

Since constant change, the overwhelming and universal energy of change (for the better and for the worse) is an almost obsessive theme in Faulkner's fiction, the story of the Snopes family, from the Civil War until nearly the here and now, is itself constantly changing. There is consistency, to be sure, even though the books were written years apart, interrupted by other books and projects and at otherwise very busy times of his life. Faulkner and his later editors—Saxe Commins for *The Town* and Albert Erskine for *The Mansion*—made a serious effort to reduce and to modify, if not to eliminate discrepancies in the individual novels and, indeed, with many other bits and pieces of the Snopes story as it had emerged, early and late, in other novels and in many of the short stories. The author's note at the outset of *The Mansion* is a kind of credo celebrating his "hopes that his entire life's work is part of a living literature, and since 'living' is motion, and 'motion' is change and alteration and therefore the only alternative to motion is un-motion, stasis, death, there will be found discrepancies and contradictions in the thirty-four-year progress of this particular chronicle. . . ."

Even so, Faulkner was perfectly consistent about his aims in the reconciliation of the Snopes material: that consistency should, in fact, work backward from the latest version. Thus a given detail in *The Mansion* can be taken as the authentic version, but by and large the factual details of the story need not match each other exactly. As he wrote to Albert Erskine: "What I am trying to say is, the essential truth of these people and their doings, is the thing; the facts are not too important."

One of the deepest sources of Faulkner's art and vision is to be found in his habitual conservation of literary material, a kind of routine recycling that allowed him (and his readers) to review and renew events, characters, places, and things—the whole experience of a story from a variety of different angles and points of view. A visionary writer by nature, he was also continually revising, in the context of new work as if freshly remembered, stories he had already told. He was thinking about the Snopes material in the early 1920s, and already by 1926, he was writing some versions of it. Because of the hypnotic impact and signature of his style (*styles*, plural, would be more accurate), it is easy to miss the wild variety of his work. As an ever-exploring craftsman Faulkner was relentlessly, extravagantly innovative. Among all of his novels no two are constructed in exactly the same manner or told in precisely the same way or from the same points of view. Each is a new artistic adventure, making new and sometimes surprising demands on the reader. (Faulkner is not, not even at his most complex, "hard" to read, but he insistently invites the reader to a deeper engagement in the experience of the story. To that extent he honors his readers, allowing them to bring as much as they can to the shared experience.) What relates each of the Yoknapatawpha novels, and especially the Snopes trilogy to each other, among other things, is his habit of returning to old stories and reclaiming them for a new look. He invites his reader to remember as well as to encounter events.

The Snopes trilogy, though its forward motion and action, events and plot are riddled with remembering, moves inexorably and chronologically ahead, from the late nineteenth and early twentieth century rural world of Frenchman's Bend in *The Hamlet* through the first quarter, and then some, of our century in the county seat of Jefferson in *The Town*, ending there in 1948 in *The Mansion*. We move from the timeless world of poor farmers and sharecroppers, the "Peasants," a world not essentially different from the rural life of all recorded history, into our own times. The world that we know comes alive, comes to be before our eyes. The automobile replaces the mule and wagon. The Memphis airport—a hundred driving miles away, not the railroad—becomes the link to the larger, wider world. And yet the past, the world of *The Hamlet* vividly endures, linked by characters and by stories about them, stories they tell. The past persists and is forever modified by the memories and myths, the speculation and the insatiable curiosity of the central characters, some of whom are, appropriately, the chief tellers of the tale. *The Hamlet*, though it has many tales told in the quoted words of its chief characters— especially the wonderful V. K. Ratliff, itinerant salesman of sewing machines and the true custodian and preserver of the county's history and news (which become history and legend soon enough)—has an overall, omniscient narrator possessed of a kind of collective voice, a master of many voices and moods. And points of view. There are virtuoso moments as, for example, in the first chapter of Book Three, "The Long Summer," the narrator gently, even sympathetically inhabits the consciousness of Ike Snopes, the idiot in love with a cow, and even, for a moment, presents reality from the cow's point of view. Mostly the narrator offers a collective point of view (not altogether unlike that of Ratliff) or limits his focus to a deeply sympathetic, yet utterly unsentimental version of the vision of a single character. Sometimes the narrator indulges himself and talks to us in rich mouthfuls of words, as if words were paint to be flung against his canvas. Sometimes this is for fun as when the fart of an old horse, in the opening sentence of Book Three, is described as "the rich sonorous organ-tone of its entrails." But the same high style is used to enhance events and to lift the ordinary to the level of the uncommon. See for yourself how Eula Varner is perceived and presented to us in Book Two.

The Town is entirely told by three voices: first by Charles Mallison, who was not yet born when half the events of the story took palce and calls himself, in the second paragraph of the first chapter, the collective point of view of the town of Jefferson; by the highly educated (Harvard and Heidelberg) lawyer, Gavin Stevens, an indefatigable talker who can manage some stylish mouthfuls on his own; and by his friend Ratliff, a patient listener who has learned some wisdom. The three, taken together, tell the whole story and very gradually begin to sound more and more like each other as they influence each other. In *The Mansion* the original third-person narrator returns now to share the telling with the same three monologists from *The Town*.

Clearly, then, one of the things that the whole Snopes trilogy is "about" is story-telling, how stories come to be and come to us and how the sum and substance of them become our history; how history is made. In a larger sense the history of Yoknapatawpha County becomes, as Faulkner planned and hoped, by action, event, allusion, and echo, a version of the history of the world. In that sense the cumulative story of that one place is the story of every place.

The surface of these novels, this trilogy, is complex, often intricate. But the tale, itself, is passionately simple. It follows the almost uninterrupted rise of Flem Snopes, from poverty and obscurity to power, first in the county and later in the town where he manages also to acquire the patina of respectability, if not honor, peaking as a bank president and a deacon of the Baptist Church—a paradigm, then, of the American dream of upward mobility, except for the undeniable fact that each and every step of the way has been achieved by every conceivable kind and form of merciless double-dealing—from simple scams worked on the illusions of simple people (never forget that Ratliff, too, falls victim at the end of *The Hamlet* and learns a lot thereby) to overt acts of blackmail and extortion, larceny, grand and petty. Nothing is too small for the ruthless, greedy attention of Flem Snopes; and, until the very end of the trilogy he is secure in his shamelessness. Most of the swarming Snopes clan—though not all by any means; bear in mind the honorable and successful Wall Street Panic Snopes—are up to no good most of the time, fascinating and repulsive and often as funny as can be. But Flem is the master Snopes, identified like his aristocratic counterpart, Jason Compson, who has a significant cameo role, as a true son of Satan, a banal and evil man.

All by himself, Flem Snopes would be worth a trilogy or more, but the two women in his life (never mind how and why; read and find out), the fabulous Eula Varner Snopes, heir to Lillith and Helen of Troy, and her daughter, Linda, are equally remarkable creations, both doomed and tragic figures, though with a difference; the first raised to mysterious and mythical proportion, both biblical and classical, by all her beholders and a multitude of admirers; the latter more "real" to those close around her (thus to readers also).

The only two characters in the trilogy of whom we are not invited to share the inner experience of consciousness are Flem and Eula. Mysterious to others, they become the occasion for steady and unrelenting speculation. We know them only from their works and ways. They keep their secrets to the end. They remain always able to surprise us, and everyone else, fictional and real, for as long as they live. Nevertheless, we notice, suddenly and briefly, some special truths about the. In *The Town* we learn in one flashing moment, when Eula confronts her profoundly romantic admirer, Gavin Stevens, that, mythical creature or not, she can be coldly pragmatic and ruthlessly single-minded when she thinks she has to be. She is something more and different, in truth, than anyone had imagined her to be. Flem's nefarious career, in all three novels, is so marked by success that we tend not to notice his few failures or the true source of his power over others. His powers work, like those of any confidence man, only by appealing to the greed of others. When as in the case in the first chapter of *The Town*, the two black men, Tom Tom and Tomey's Turl, set against each other and sorely abused by Snopes, manage to get together, swallow their pride, and come to "complete federation," Snopes is beaten. We know then that he is not invulnerable.

There are so many things to celebrate about this magnificent trilogy. I have elected here to speak, in awe and honor, about only a couple of things. One is the rich variety of Faulkner's method, his endlessly inventive ways and means of telling stories. He has opened up new territories for all the writers who have come and will come after him. He has changed our ways of thinking about the power and glory of fiction. He has challenged writers and readers alike, all over the world, to bring and to give to the experience of his art nothing less than the best they have. He has demonstrated that they (we) will be well rewarded.

And I have stressed his magical capacity at characterization. The events, outrageous or quotidian, that occur in these novels are perfectly presented, executed with a timing and finesse that the finest athletes could envy. But they work, they capture our attention and sustain our involvement because they happen to characters we can care about and believe in. He presents the surface—Flem's bow tie, Ratliff's blue shirt, Stevens' corncob pipe—directly and engages us with an intense physicality. Their flesh and bones seem real enough to suffer or rejoice, and the world they move in is not so much described as felt. And, above all, no matter how foolish or flawed they may be, no matter how educated or ignorant, they are blessed with the equality of an inner life and being that renders even the least of them worthy of full attention. All of this is clear, at once poetic and explicit, in the final pages of *The Mansion* when both Stevens and Ratliff unknowingly echo the prayer of the preacher Goodyhay—"Save us, Christ, the poor sons of bitches." And the classic poor s.o.b. Mink Snopes has a final and authentic vision of himself among the dead, "himself among them, equal to any, good, as any, brave as any, being inextricable from, anonymous with all of them. . . ." Faulkner has been sometimes faulted for giving deep thoughts and feelings to common characters, but that criticism can come only from a different vision of mankind, a vision as cold and mechanical as that of Flem Snopes. Faulkner's inclusive, democratic vision of the equality of human souls shines through all his characters and makes them matter. There is much laughter in the Snopes trilogy, but there are tears also.

A great deal has been written by scholars and critics about Faulkner and about this trilogy. Some of it is extremely valuable to a fuller and deeper appreciation of his work. But my strong suggestion to readers coming to these novels for the first time (and there will be generations of you) is to plunge in and fare forward, allowing the experience of the story to happen as it does, without any additional mediation or guidance. Experience the story before turning to or trusting the opinions and judgments of others, myself included.

The one big exception to this rule is the biography by Joseph Blotner, preferably the revised, one-volume version of 1984, wherein the story of the creation of the Snopes novels and the public reception of each as it first appeared is followed closely and accurately and does not in any way lessen the original impact. It also seems to me likely that the words and thoughts of Faulkner, himself, about these books, to be found in the *Selected Letters of William Faulkner* (1977) can only serve to enhance the reader's experience.

—GEORGE GARRETT

WILLIAM FAULKNER

William Faulkner was born in New Albany, Mississippi, on September 25, 1897. His family was rooted in local history: his great-grandfather, a Confederate colonel and state politician, was assassinated by a former partner in 1889, and his grandfather was a wealthy lawyer who owned a railroad. When Faulkner was five his parents moved to Oxford, Mississippi, where he received a desultory education in local schools, dropping out of high school in 1915. Rejected for pilot training in the U.S. Army, he passed himself off as British and joined the Canadian Royal Air Force in 1918, but the war ended before he saw any service. After the war, he took some classes at the University of Mississippi and worked for a time at the university post office. Mostly, however, he educated himself by reading promiscuously.

Faulkner had begun writing poems when he was a schoolboy, and in 1924 he published a poetry collection, *The Marble Faun*, at his own expense. His literary aspirations were fueled by his close friendship with Sherwood Anderson, whom he met during a stay in New Orleans. Faulkner's first novel, *Soldiers' Pay*, was published in 1926, followed a year later by *Mosquitoes*, a literary satire. His next book, *Flags in the Dust*, was heavily cut and rearranged at the publisher's insistence and appeared finally as *Sartoris* in 1929. In the meantime he had completed *The Sound and the Fury*, and when it appeared at the end of 1929 he had finished *Sanctuary* and was ready to begin writing *As I Lay Dying*. That same year he married Estelle Oldham, whom he had courted a decade earlier.

Although Faulkner gained literary acclaim from these and subsequent novels— *Light in August* (1932), *Pylon* (1935), *Absalom, Absalom!* (1936), *The Unvanquished* (1938), *The Wild Palms* (1939),

The Hamlet (1940), and *Go Down, Moses* (1942)—and continued to publish stories regularly in magazines, he was unable to support himself solely by writing fiction. He worked as a screenwriter for MGM, Twentieth Century-Fox, and Warner Brothers, forming a close relationship with director Howard Hawks, with whom he worked on *To Have and Have Not, The Big Sleep*, and *Land of the Pharaohs*, among other films. In 1944 all but one of Faulkner's novels were out of print, and his personal life was at low ebb due in part to his chronic heavy drinking. During the war he had been discovered by Sartre and Camus and others in the French literary world. In the postwar period his reputation rebounded, as Malcolm Cowley's anthology *The Portable Faulkner* brought him fresh attention in America, and the immense esteem in which he was held in Europe consolidated his worldwide stature.

Faulkner wrote seventeen books set in the mythical Yoknapatawpha County, home of the Compson family of *The Sound and the Fury*. "No land in all fiction lives more vividly in its physical presence than this county of Faulkner's imagination," Robert Penn Warren wrote in an essay on Cowley's anthology. "The descendants of the old families, the descendants of bushwhackers and carpetbaggers, the swamp rats, the Negro cooks and farm hands, the bootleggers and gangsters, tenant farmers, college boys, county-seat lawyers, county storekeepers, peddlers—all are here in their fullness of life and their complicated interrelations." In 1950 Faulkner was awarded the Nobel Prize for Literature. In later books—*Intruder in the Dust* (1948), *Requiem for a Nun* (1951), *A Fable* (1954), *The Town* (1957), *The Mansion* (1959), and *The Reivers* (1962)—he continued to explore what he had called "the problems of the human heart in conflict with itself," but did so in the context of Yoknapatawpha's increasing connection with the modern world. He died of a heart attack on July 6, 1962.

SNOPES

THE HAMLET

TO PHIL STONE

CONTENTS

BOOK ONE

FLEM

CHAPTER ONE

*F*renchman's Bend was a section of rich river-bottom country lying twenty miles southeast of Jefferson. Hill-cradled and remote, definite yet without boundaries, straddling into two counties and owning allegiance to neither, it had been the original grant and site of a tremendous pre-Civil War plantation, the ruins of which—the gutted shell of an enormous house with its fallen stables and slave quarters and overgrown gardens and brick terraces and promenades—were still known as the Old Frenchman's place, although the original boundaries now existed only on old faded records in the Chancery Clerk's office in the county courthouse in Jefferson, and even some of the once-fertile fields had long since reverted to the cane-and-cypress jungle from which their first master had hewed them.

He had quite possibly been a foreigner, though not necessarily French, since to the people who had come after him and had almost obliterated all trace of his sojourn, anyone speaking the tongue with a foreign flavor or whose appearance or even occupation was strange, would have been a Frenchman regardless of what nationality he might affirm, just as to their more urban coevals (if he had elected to settle in Jefferson itself, say) he would have been called a Dutchman. But now nobody knew what he had actually been, not even Will Varner, who was sixty years old and now owned a good deal of his original grant, including the site of his ruined mansion. Because he was gone now, the foreigner, the Frenchman, with his family and his slaves and his magnificence. His dream, his broad acres were parcelled out now into small shiftless mortgaged farms for the directors of Jefferson banks to squabble over before selling finally to Will Varner, and all that remained of him was the river bed which his slaves had straightened for almost ten miles to keep his land from flooding and the skeleton of the tremendous house which his heirs-at-large had been pulling down and chopping up—walnut newel posts and stair spindles, oak floors which fifty years later would have been almost priceless, the very clapboards themselves—for thirty years now for firewood. Even his name was forgotten, his pride but a legend about the land he had wrested from the jungle and tamed as a monument to that appellation which those who came after him in battered wagons and on muleback and even on foot, with flintlock rifles and dogs and children and home-made whiskey stills and Protestant psalm-books, could not even read, let alone pronounce, and which now had nothing to do with any once-living man at all—his dream and his pride now dust with the lost dust of his anonymous bones, his legend but the stubborn tale of the money he buried somewhere about the place when Grant overran the country on his way to Vicksburg.

The people who inherited from him came from the northeast, through the Tennessee mountains by stages marked by the bearing and raising of a generation of children. They came from the Atlantic seaboard and before that, from England and the Scottish and Welsh Marches, as some of the names would indicate—Turpin and Haley and Whittington, McCallum and Murray and Leonard and Little-john, and other names like Riddup and Armstid and Doshey which could have come from nowhere since certainly no man would deliberately select one of them for his own. They brought no slaves and no Phyfe and Chippendale highboys; indeed, what they did bring most of them could (and did) carry in their hands. They took up land and built one- and two-room cabins and never painted them, and married one another and produced children and added other rooms one by one to the original cabins and did not paint them either, but that was all. Their descendants still planted cotton in the bottom land and corn along the edge of the hills and in the secret coves in the hills made whiskey of the corn and sold what they did not drink. Federal officers went into the country and vanished. Some garment which the missing man had worn might be seen—a felt hat, a broad-cloth coat, a pair of city shoes or even his pistol—on a child or an old man or woman. County officers did not bother them at all save in the heel of election years. They supported their own churches and schools, they married and committed infrequent adulteries and more frequent homicides among themselves and were their own courts judges and executioners. They were Protestants and Democrats and prolific; there was not one Negro landowner in the entire section. Strange Negroes would absolutely refuse to pass through it after dark.

Will Varner, the present owner of the Old Frenchman place, was the chief man of the country. He was the largest landholder and beat supervisor in one county and Justice of the Peace in the next and election commissioner in both, and hence the fountainhead if not of law at least of advice and suggestion to a countryside which would have repudiated the term constituency if they had ever heard it, which came to him, not in the attitude of *What must I do* but *What do you think you think you would like for me to do if you was able to make me do it.* He was a farmer, a usurer, a veterinarian; Judge Benbow of Jefferson once said of him that a milder-mannered man never bled a mule or stuffed a ballot box. He owned most of the good land in the country and held mortgages on most of the rest. He owned the store and the cotton gin and the combined grist mill and blacksmith shop in the village proper and it was considered, to put it mildly, bad luck for a man of the neighborhood to do his trading or gin his cotton or grind his meal or shoe his stock anywhere else. He was thin as a fence rail and almost as long, with reddish-gray hair and moustaches and little hard bright innocently blue eyes; he looked like a Methodist Sunday School superintendent who on week days conducted a railroad passenger train or vice versa and who owned the church or perhaps the railroad or perhaps both. He was shrewd secret and merry, of a Rabelaisian turn of mind and very probably still sexually lusty (he had fathered sixteen children to his wife, though only two of them remained at home, the others scattered, married and buried, from El Paso to the Alabama line) as the spring of his hair which even at sixty was still more red than gray, would indicate. He was at once active and lazy; he did nothing at all (his son managed all the family business) and spent all his time at it, out of the house and gone before the son had come down to breakfast even, nobody knew where save that he and the old fat white horse which he rode might be seen anywhere within the surrounding ten miles at any time, and at least once every month during the spring and summer and early fall, the old

white horse tethered to an adjacent fence post, he would be seen by
someone sitting in a home-made chair on the jungle-choked lawn
of the Old Frenchman's homesite. His blacksmith had made the
chair for him by sawing an empty flour barrel half through the middle and trimming out the sides and nailing a seat into it and Varner
would sit there chewing his tobacco or smoking his cob pipe, with a
brusque word for passers cheerful enough but inviting no company,
against his background of fallen baronial splendor. The people (those
who saw him sitting there and those who were told about it) all
believed that he sat there planning his next mortgage foreclosure in
private, since it was only to an itinerant sewing-machine agent
named Ratliff—a man less than half his age—that he ever gave a reason: "I like to sit here. I'm trying to find out what it must have felt
like to be the fool that would need all this"—he did not move, he
did not so much as indicate with his head the rise of old brick and
tangled walks topped by the columned ruin behind him—"just to eat
and sleep in." Then he said—and he gave Ratliff no further clue to
which might have been the truth—"For a while it looked like I was
going to get shut of it, get it cleared up. But by God folks have got
so lazy they wont even climb a ladder to pull off the rest of the boards
It looks like they will go into the woods and even chop up a tree
before they will reach above eyelevel for a scantling of pine kindling.
But after all, I reckon I'll just keep what there is left of it, just to
remind me of my one mistake. This is the only thing I ever bought in
my life I couldn't sell to nobody."

The son, Jody, was about thirty, a prime bulging man, slightly
thyroidic, who was not only unmarried but who emanated a quality
of invincible and inviolable bachelordom as some people are said
to breathe out the odor of sanctity or spirituality. He was a big man,
already promising a considerable belly in ten or twelve years,
though as yet he still managed to postulate something of the trig
and unattached cavalier. He wore, winter and summer (save that in
the warm season he dispensed with the coat) and Sundays and week
days, a glazed collarless white shirt fastened at the neck with a heavy
gold collar-button beneath a suit of good black broadcloth. He put
on the suit the day it arrived from the Jefferson tailor and wore it
every day and in all weathers thereafter until he sold it to one of the

family's Negro retainers, so that on almost any Sunday night one whole one or some part of one of his old suits could be met—and promptly recognised—walking the summer roads, and replaced it with the new succeeding one. In contrast to the unvarying overalls of the men he lived among he had an air not funereal exactly but ceremonial—this because of that quality of invincible bachelorhood which he possessed: so that, looking at him you saw, beyond the flabbiness and the obscuring bulk, the perennial and immortal Best Man, the apotheosis of the masculine Singular, just as you discern beneath the dropsical tissue of the '09 halfback the lean hard ghost which once carried a ball. He was the ninth of his parents' sixteen children. He managed the store of which his father was still titular owner and in which they dealt mostly in foreclosed mortgages, and the gin, and oversaw the scattered farm holdings which his father at first and later the two of them together had been acquiring during the last forty years.

One afternoon he was in the store, cutting lengths of plowline from a spool of new cotton rope and looping them in neat seaman-like bights onto a row of nails in the wall, when at a sound behind him he turned and saw, silhouetted by the open door, a man smaller than common, in a wide hat and a frock coat too large for him, standing with a curious planted stiffness. "You Varner?" the man said, in a voice not harsh exactly, or not deliberately harsh so much as rusty from infrequent use.

"I'm one Varner," Jody said, in his bland hard quite pleasant voice. "What can I do for you?"

"My name is Snopes. I heard you got a farm to rent."

"That so?" Varner said, already moving so as to bring the other's face into the light. "Just where did you hear that?" Because the farm was a new one, which he and his father had acquired through a fore-closure sale not a week ago, and the man was a complete stranger. He had never even heard the name before.

The other did not answer. Now Varner could see his face—a pair of eyes of a cold opaque gray between shaggy graying irascible brows and a short scrabble of iron-gray beard as tight and knotted as a sheep's coat. "Where you been farming?" Varner said.

"West." He did not speak shortly. He merely pronounced the one word with a complete inflectionless finality, as if he had closed a door behind himself.

"You mean Texas?"

"No."

"I see. Just west of here. How much family you got?"

"Six." Now there was no perceptible pause, nor was there any hurrying on into the next word. But there was something. Varner sensed it even before the lifeless voice seemed deliberately to compound the inconsistency: "Boy and two girls. Wife and her sister."

"That's just five."

"Myself," the dead voice said.

"A man dont usually count himself among his own field hands," Varner said. "Is it five or is it seven?"

"I can put six hands into the field."

Now Varner's voice did not change either, still pleasant, still hard: "I dont know as I will take on a tenant this year. It's already almost first of May. I figure I might work it myself, with day labor. If I work it at all this year."

"I'll work that way," the other said. Varner looked at him.

"Little anxious to get settled, aint you?" The other said nothing. Varner could not tell whether the man was looking at him or not. "What rent were you aiming to pay?"

"What do you rent for?"

"Third and fourth," Varner said. "Furnish out of the store here. No cash."

"I see. Furnish in six-bit dollars."

"That's right," Varner said pleasantly. Now he could not tell if the man were looking at anything at all or not.

"I'll take it," he said.

Standing on the gallery of the store, above the half dozen overalled men sitting or squatting about it with pocket knives and slivers of wood, Varner watched his caller limp stiffly across the porch, looking neither right nor left, and descend and from among the tethered teams and saddled animals below the gallery choose a gaunt saddleless mule in a worn plow bridle with rope reins and lead it to the steps and mount awkwardly and stiffly and ride away, still without once looking to either side. "To hear that ere foot, you'd think he weighed two hundred pounds," one of them said. "Who's he, Jody?"

Varner sucked his teeth and spat into the road. "Name's Snopes," he said.

"Snopes?" a second man said. "Sho now. So that's him." Now not only Varner but all the others looked at the speaker—a gaunt man in absolutely clean though faded and patched overalls and even freshly shaven, with a gentle, almost sad face until you unravelled what were actually two separate expressions—a temporary one of static peace and quiet overlaying a constant one of definite even though faint harriedness, and a sensitive mouth which had a quality of adolescent freshness and bloom until you realised that this could just as well be the result of a lifelong abstinence from tobacco—the face of the breathing archetype and protagonist of all men who marry young and father only daughters and are themselves but the eldest daughter of their own wives. His name was Tull. "He's the fellow that wintered his family in a old cottonhouse on Ike McCaslin's place. The one that was mixed up in that burnt barn of a fellow named Harris over in Grenier County two years ago."

"Huh?" Varner said. "What's that? Burnt barn?"

"I never said he done it," Tull said. "I just said he was kind of involved in it after a fashion you might say."

"How much involved in it?"

"Harris had him arrested into court."

"I see," Varner said. "Just a pure case of mistaken identity. He just hired it done."

"It wasn't proved," Tull said. "Leastways, if Harris ever found any proof afterward, it was too late then. Because he had done left the country. Then he turned up at McCaslin's last September. Him and his family worked by the day, gathering for McCaslin, and McCaslin let them winter in a old cottonhouse he wasn't using. That's all I know. I aint repeating nothing."

"I wouldn't," Varner said. "A man dont want to get the name of a idle gossip." He stood above them with his broad bland face, in his dingy formal black-and-white—the glazed soiled white shirt and the bagging and uncared-for trousers—a costume at once ceremonial

and negligee. He sucked his teeth briefly and noisily. "Well well
well," he said. "A barn burner. Well well well."

That night he told his father about it at the supper table. With the
exception of the rambling half-log half-sawn plank edifice known as
Littlejohn's hotel, Will Varner's was the only house in the country
with more than one storey. They had a cook too, not only the only
Negro servant but the only servant of any sort in the whole district.
They had had her for years yet Mrs Varner still said and apparently
believed that she could not be trusted even to boil water unsuper-
vised. He told it that evening while his mother, a plump cheery
bustling woman who had borne sixteen children and already outlived
five of them and who still won prizes for preserved fruits and vegetables at the annual County Fair, bustled back and forth between
dining room and kitchen, and his sister, a soft ample girl with definite
breasts even at thirteen and eyes like cloudy hothouse grapes and a
full damp mouth always slightly open, sat at her place in a kind of
sullen bemusement of rife young female flesh, apparently not even
having to make any effort not to listen.

"You already contracted with him?" Will Varner said.

"I hadn't aimed to at all till Vernon Tull told me what he did. Now
I figure I'll take the paper up there tomorrow and let him sign."

"Then you can point out to him which house to burn too. Or are
you going to leave that to him?"

"Sho," Jody said. "We'll discuss that too." Then he said—and now
all levity was gone from his voice, all poste and riposte of humor's
light whimsy, tierce quarto and prime: "All I got to do is find out for
sho about that barn. But then it will be the same thing, whether he
actually did it or not. All he'll need will be to find out all of a sudden at gathering time that I think he did it. Listen. Take a case like
this." He leaned forward now, over the table, bulging, protuberant,
intense. The mother had bustled out, to the kitchen, where her brisk
voice could be heard scolding cheerfully at the Negro cook. The
daughter was not listening at all. "Here's a piece of land that the folks
that own it hadn't actually figured on getting nothing out of this late
in the season. And here comes a man and rents it on shares that the
last place he rented on a barn got burnt up. It dont matter whether
he actually burnt that barn or not, though it will simplify matters if

I can find out for sho he did. The main thing is, it burnt while he was there and the evidence was such that he felt called on to leave the country. So here he comes and rents this land we hadn't figured on nothing out of this year nohow and we furnish him outen the store all regular and proper. And he makes his crop and the landlord sells it all regular and has the cash waiting and the fellow comes in to get his share and the landlord says, 'What's this I heard about you and that barn?' That's all. 'What's this I just heard about you and that barn?' " They stared at one another—the slightly protuberant opaque eyes and the little hard blue ones. "What will he say? What can he say except 'All right. What do you aim to do?' "

"You'll lose his furnish bill at the store."

"Sho. There aint no way of getting around that. But after all, a man that's making you a crop free gratis for nothing, at least you can afford to feed him while he's doing it.—Wait," he said. "Hell fire, we wont even need to do that; I'll just let him find a couple of rotten shingles with a match laid across them on his doorstep the morning after he finishes laying-by and he'll know it's all up then and aint nothing left for him but to move on. That'll cut two months off the furnish bill and all we'll be out is hiring his crop gathered." They stared at one another. To one of them it was already done, accomplished: he could actually see it; when he spoke it was out of a time still six months in the future yet: "Hell fire, he'll have to! He cant fight it! He dont dare!"

"Hmph," Will said. From the pocket of his unbuttoned vest he took a stained cob pipe and began to fill it. "You better stay clear of them folks."

"Sho now," Jody said. He took a toothpick from the china receptacle on the table and sat back. "Burning barns aint right. And a man that's got habits that way will just have to suffer the disadvantages of them."

He did not go the next day nor the one after that either. But early in the afternoon of the third day, his roan saddle horse hitched and waiting at one of the gallery posts, he sat at the roll-top desk in the rear of the store, hunched, the black hat on the back of his head and one broad black-haired hand motionless and heavy as a ham of meat on the paper and the pen in the other tracing the words of the con-

tract in his heavy deliberate sprawling script. An hour after that and
five miles from the village, the contract blotted and folded neatly into
his hip pocket, he was sitting the horse beside a halted buckboard in
the road. It was battered with rough usage and caked with last winter's dried mud, it was drawn by a pair of shaggy ponies as wild and
active-looking as mountain goats and almost as small. To the rear of
it was attached a sheet-iron box the size and shape of a dog kennel
and painted to resemble a house, in each painted window of which a
painted woman's face simpered above a painted sewing machine, and
Varner sat his horse and glared in shocked and outraged consternation at its occupant, who had just said pleasantly, "Well, Jody, I hear
you got a new tenant."

"Hell fire!" Varner cried. "Do you mean he set fire to another
one? even after they caught him, he set fire to *another* one?"

"Well," the man in the buckboard said, "I dont know as I would go
on record as saying he set ere a one of them afire. I would put it that
they both taken fire while he was more or less associated with them.
You might say that fire seems to follow him around, like dogs follows
some folks." He spoke in a pleasant, lazy, equable voice which you
did not discern at once to be even more shrewd than humorous. This
was Ratliff, the sewing-machine agent. He lived in Jefferson and he
travelled the better part of four counties with his sturdy team and the
painted dog kennel into which an actual machine neatly fitted. On
successive days and two counties apart the splashed and battered
buckboard and the strong mismatched team might be seen tethered
in the nearest shade and Ratliff's bland affable ready face and his neat
tieless blue shirt one of the squatting group at a crossroads store,
or—and still squatting and still doing the talking apparently though
actually doing a good deal more listening than anybody believed
until afterward—among the women surrounded by laden clothes-
lines and tubs and blackened wash pots beside springs and wells, or
decorous in a splint chair on cabin galleries, pleasant, affable, courteous, anecdotal and impenetrable. He sold perhaps three machines
a year, the rest of the time trading in land and livestock and second-
hand farming tools and musical instruments or anything else which
the owner did not want badly enough, retailing from house to house
the news of his four counties with the ubiquity of a newspaper and

carrying personal messages from mouth to mouth about weddings
and funerals and the preserving of vegetables and fruit with the reli-
ability of a postal service. He never forgot a name and he knew
everyone, man mule and dog, within fifty miles. "Just say it was following along behind the wagon when Snopes druv up to the house
De Spain had give him, with the furniture piled into the wagon bed
like he had druv up to the house they had been living in at Harris's or
wherever it was and said 'Get in here' and the cookstove and beds
and chairs come out and got in by their selves. Careless and yet good
too, tight, like they was used to moving and not having no big help at
it. And Ab and that big one, Flem they call him—there was another
one too, a little one; I remember seeing him once somewhere. He
wasn't with them. Leastways he aint now. Maybe they forgot to tell
him when to get outen the barn.—setting on the seat and them two
hulking gals in the two chairs in the wagon bed and Miz Snopes and
her sister, the widow, setting on the stuff in back like nobody cared
much whether they come along or not either, including the furniture. And the wagon stops in front of the house and Ab looks at it and
says, 'Likely it aint fitten for hawgs.' "

Sitting the horse, Varner glared down at Ratliff in protuberant and
speechless horror. "All right," Ratliff said. "Soon as the wagon
stopped Miz Snopes and the widow got out and commenced to
unload. Them two gals aint moved yet, just setting there in them two
chairs, in their Sunday clothes, chewing sweet gum, till Ab turned
round and cussed them outen the wagon to where Miz Snopes and
the widow was wrastling with the stove. He druv them out like a pair
of heifers just a little too valuable to hit hard with a stick, and then
him and Flem set there and watched them two strapping gals take a
wore-out broom and a lantern outen the wagon and stand there
again till Ab leant out and snicked the nigh one across the stern with
the end of the reins. 'And then you come back and help your maw
with that stove,' he hollers after them. Then him and Flem got outen
the wagon and went up to call on De Spain."

"To the barn?" Varner cried. "You mean they went right straight
and—"

"No no. That was later. The barn come later. Likely they never
knowed just where it was yet. The barn burnt all regular and in due

course; you'll have to say that for him. This here was just a call, just pure friendship, because Snopes knowed where his fields was and all he had to do was to start scratching them, and it already the middle of May. Just like now," he added in a tone of absolutely creamlike innocence. "But then I hear tell he always makes his rent contracts later than most." But he was not laughing. The shrewd brown face was as bland and smooth as ever beneath the shrewd impenetrable eyes.

"Well?" Varner said violently. "If he sets his fires like you tell about it, I reckon I dont need to worry until Christmas. Get on with it. What does he have to do before he starts lighting matches? Maybe I can recognise at least some of the symptoms in time."

"All right," Ratliff said. "So they went up the road, leaving Miz Snopes and the widow wrastling at the cookstove and them two gals standing there now holding a wire rat-trap and a chamber pot, and went up to Major de Spain's and walked up the private road where that pile of fresh horse manure was and the nigger said Ab stepped in it on deliberate purpose. Maybe the nigger was watching them through the front window. Anyway Ab tracked it right across the front porch and knocked and when the nigger told him to wipe it offen his feet, Ab shoved right past the nigger and the nigger said he wiped the rest of it off right on that ere hundred-dollar rug and stood there hollering 'Hello. Hello, De Spain' until Miz de Spain come and looked at the rug and at Ab and told him to please go away. And then De Spain come home at dinner time and I reckon maybe Miz de Spain got in behind him because about middle of the afternoon he rides up to Ab's house with a nigger holding the rolled-up rug on a mule behind him and Ab setting in a chair against the door jamb and De Spain hollers 'Why in hell aint you in the field?' and Ab says, he dont get up or nothing, 'I figger I'll start tomorrow. I dont never move and start to work the same day,' only that aint neither here nor there; I reckon Miz de Spain had done got in behind him good because he just set on the horse a while saying 'Confound you Snopes, confound you Snopes' and Ab setting there saying 'If I had thought that much of a rug I dont know as I would keep it where folks coming in would have to tromp on it.' " Still he was not laughing. He just sat there in the buckboard, easy and relaxed, with his shrewd intelligent eyes in his smooth brown face, well-shaved and clean in his perfectly clean faded shirt, his voice pleasant and drawling and anecdotal, while Varner's suffused swollen face glared down at him.

"So after a while Ab hollers back into the house and one of them strapping gals comes out and Ab says, 'Take that ere rug and wash it.' And so next morning the nigger found the rolled-up rug throwed onto the front porch against the door and there was some more tracks across the porch too only it was just mud this time and it was said how when Miz de Spain unrolled the rug this time it must have been hotter for De Spain than before even—the nigger said it looked like they had used brickbats instead of soap on it—because he was at Ab's house before breakfast even, in the lot where Ab and Flem was hitching up to go to the field sho enough, setting on the mare mad as a hornet and cussing a blue streak, not at Ab exactly but just sort of at all rugs and all horse manure in general and Ab not saying nothing, just buckling hames and choke strops until at last De Spain says how the rug cost him a hundred dollars in France and he is going to charge Ab twenty bushels of corn for it against his crop that Ab aint even planted yet. And so De Spain went back home. And maybe he felt it was all neither here nor there now. Maybe he felt that long as he had done something about it Miz de Spain would ease up on him and maybe come gathering time he would a even forgot about that twenty bushels of corn. Only that never suited Ab. So here, it's the next evening I reckon, and Major laying with his shoes off in the barrel-stave hammock in his yard and here comes the bailiff hemming and hawing and finally gets it out how Ab has done sued him—"

"Hell fire," Varner murmured. "Hell fire."

"Sho," Ratliff said. "That's just about what De Spain hisself said when he finally got it into his mind that it was so. So it come Sat-dy and the wagon druv up to the store and Ab got out in that preacher's hat and coat and tromps up to the table on that clubfoot where Uncle Buck McCaslin said Colonel John Sartoris his-self shot Ab for trying to steal his clay-bank riding stallion during the war, and the Judge said, 'I done reviewed your suit, Mr Snopes, but I aint been able to find nothing nowhere in the law bearing on rugs, let alone horse manure. But I'm going to accept it because twenty bushels is too much for you to have to pay because a man as busy as you seem to stay aint going to have time to make twenty bushels of corn. So I am going to charge you ten bushels of corn for ruining that rug.' "

"And so he burnt it," Varner said. "Well well well."

"I dont know as I would put it just that way," Ratliff said, repeated. "I would just put it that that same night Major de Spain's barn taken fire and was a total loss. Only somehow or other De Spain got there on his mare about the same time, because somebody heard him passing in the road. I dont mean he got there in time to put it out but he got there in time to find something else already there that he felt entitled to consider enough of a foreign element to justify shooting at it, setting there on the mare and blasting away at it or them three or four times until it run into a ditch on him where he couldn't follow on the mare. And he couldn't say neither who it was because any animal can limp if it wants to and any man is liable to have a white shirt, with the exception that when he got to Ab's house (and that couldn't a been long, according to the gait the fellow heard him passing in the road) Ab and Flem wasn't there, wasn't nobody there but the four women and De Spain never had time to look under no beds and such because there was a cypress-roofed corn crib right next to that barn. So he rid back to where his niggers had done fetched up the water barrels and was soaking tow-sacks to lay on the crib, and the first person he see was Flem standing there in a white-colored shirt, watching it with his hands in his pockets, chewing tobacco. 'Evening,' Flem says. 'That ere hay goes fast' and De Spain setting on the horse hollering 'Where's your paw? Where's that—' and Flem says, 'If he aint here somewhere he's done went back home. Me and him left at the same time when we see the blaze.' And De Spain knowed where they had left from too and he knowed why too. Only that wasn't neither here nor there neither because, as it was just maintained, any two fellows anywhere might have a limp and a white shirt between them and it was likely the coal oil can he seen one of them fling into the fire when he shot the first time. And so here the next morning he's setting at breakfast with a right smart of his eyebrows and hair both swinged off when the nigger comes in and says it's a fellow to see him and he goes to the office and it's Ab, already in the preacher hat and coat and the wagon done already loaded again too, only Ab aint brought that into the house where it could be seen. 'It looks like me and you aint going to get along together,' Ab says, 'so I reckon we better quit trying before we have a misunderstanding over something. I'm moving this morning.' And De Spain says, 'What about your contract?' And Ab says, 'I done cancelled it.' and De Spain setting there saying 'Cancelled. Cancelled' and then he says, 'I would cancel it and a hundred more like it and throw in that barn too just to know for sho if it was you I was shooting at last night.' And Ab says, 'You might sue me and find out. Justices of the Peace in this country seems to be in the habit of finding for plaintiffs.' "

"Hell fire," Varner said quietly again. "Hell fire."

"So Ab turned and went stomping out on that stiff foot and went back "

"And burnt the tenant house," Varner said.

"No no. I aint saying he might not a looked back at it with a certain regret, as the fellow says, when he druv off. But never nothing else taken all of a sudden on fire. Not right then, that is. I dont—"

"That's so," Varner said. "I recollect you did say he had to throw the balance of the coal oil into the fire when De Spain started shooting at him. Well well well," he said, bulging, slightly apoplectic. "And now, out of all the men in this country, I got to pick him to make a rent contract with." He began to laugh. That is, he began to say "Ha. Ha. Ha." rapidly, but just from the teeth, the lungs: no higher, nothing of it in the eyes. Then he stopped. "Well, I cant be setting here, no matter how pleasant it is. Maybe I can get there in time to get him to cancel with me for just a old cottonhouse."

"Or at least maybe for a empty barn," Ratliff called after him.

An hour later Varner was sitting the halted horse again, this time before a gate, or a gap that is, in a fence of sagging and rusted wire. The gate itself or what remained of it lay unhinged to one side, the interstices of the rotted palings choked with grass and weeds like the ribs of a forgotten skeleton. He was breathing hard but not because he had been galloping. On the contrary, since he had approached near enough to his destination to believe he could have seen smoke if there had been smoke, he had ridden slower and slower. Nevertheless he now sat the horse before the gap in the fence, breathing hard through his nose and even sweating a little, looking at the sagging broken-backed cabin set in its inevitable treeless and grassless plot and weathered to the color of an old beehive, with that expression of tense and rapid speculation of a man approaching a dud howitzer shell. "Hell fire," he said again quietly. "Hell fire. He's been here three days now and he aint even set the gate up. And I dont even dare to mention it to him. I dont even dare to act like I knowed there was even a fence to hang it to." He twitched the reins savagely. "Come up!" he said to the horse. "You hang around here very long standing still and you'll be a-fire too."

The path (it was neither road nor lane: just two parallel barely discernible tracks where wagon wheels had run, almost obliterated by this year's grass and weeds) went up to the sagging and stepless porch of the perfectly blank house which he now watched with wire-taut wariness, as if he were approaching an ambush. He was watching it with such intensity as to be oblivious to detail. He saw suddenly in one of the sashless windows and without knowing when it had come there, a face beneath a gray cloth cap, the lower jaw moving steadily and rhythmically with a curious sidewise thrust, which even as he shouted "Hello!" vanished again. He was about to shout again when he saw beyond the house the stiff figure which he recognised even though the frock coat was missing now, doing something at the gate to the lot. He had already begun to hear the mournful measured plaint of a rusted well-pulley, and now he began to hear two flat meaningless loud female voices. When he passed beyond the house he saw it—the narrow high frame like an epicene gallows, two big absolutely static young women beside it, who even in that first glance postulated that immobile dreamy solidarity of statuary (this only emphasised by the fact that they both seemed to be talking at once and to some listener—or perhaps just circumambience—at a considerable distance and neither listening to the other at all) even though one of them had hold of the well-rope, her arms extended at full reach, her body bent for the down pull like a figure in a charade, a carved piece symbolising some terrific physical effort which had died with its inception, though a moment later the pulley began again its rusty plaint but stopped again almost immediately, as did the voices also when the second one saw him, the first one paused now in the obverse of the first attitude, her arms stretched downward on the rope and the two broad expressionless faces turning slowly in unison as he rode past.

He crossed the barren yard littered with the rubbish—the ashes, the shards of pottery and tin cans—of its last tenants. There were two women working beside the fence too and they were all three aware of his presence now because he had seen one of the women look around. But the man himself (Durn little clubfooted murderer, Varner thought with that furious helpless outrage) had not looked up nor even paused in whatever it was he was doing until Varner rode directly up behind him. The two women were watching him now. One wore a faded sunbonnet, the other a shapeless hat which at one time must have belonged to the man and holding in her hand a rusted can half full of bent and rusted nails. "Evening," Varner said, realising too late that he was almost shouting. "Evening, ladies." The man turned, deliberately, holding a hammer—a rusted head from which both claws had been broken, fitted onto an untrimmed stick of stove wood—and once more Varner looked down into the cold impenetrable agate eyes beneath the writhen overhang of brows.

"Howdy," Snopes said.

"Just thought I'd ride up and see what your plans were," Varner said, too loud still; he could not seem to help it. I got too much to think about to have time to watch it, he thought, beginning at once to think, Hell fire. Hell fire, again, as though proving to himself what even a second's laxity of attention might bring him to.

"I figure I'll stay," the other said. "The house aint fitten for hogs. But I reckon I can make out with it."

"But look here!" Varner said. Now he was shouting; he didn't care. Then he stopped shouting. He stopped shouting because he stopped speaking because there was nothing else to say, though it was going through his mind fast enough: Hell fire. Hell fire. Hell fire. I dont dare say Leave here, and I aint got anywhere to say Go there. I dont even dare to have him arrested for barn-burning for fear he'll set my barn a-fire. The other had begun to turn back to the fence when Varner spoke. Now he stood half-turned, looking up at Varner not courteously and not exactly patiently, but just waiting. "All right," Varner said. "We can discuss the house. Because we'll get along all right. We'll get along. Anything that comes up, all you got to do is come down to the store. No, you dont even need to do that: just send me word and I'll ride right up here as quick as I can get here. You understand? Anything, just anything you dont like—"

"I can get along with anybody," the other said. "I been getting along with fifteen or twenty different landlords since I started farming. When I cant get along with them, I leave. That all you wanted?"

All, Varner thought. All. He rode back across the yard, the littered grassless desolation scarred with the ashes and charred stick-ends and blackened bricks where pots for washing clothes and scalding hogs had sat. I just wish I never had to have but just the little I do want now, he thought. He had been hearing the well-pulley again. This time it did not cease when he passed, the two broad faces, the one motionless, the other pumping up and down with metronome-like regularity to the wheel's not-quite-musical complaint, turning slowly again as though riveted and synchronised to one another by a mechanical arm as he went on beyond the house and into the imperceptible lane which led to the broken gate which he knew would still be lying there in the weeds when he saw it next. He still had the contract in his pocket, which he had written out with that steady and deliberate satisfaction which, it now seemed to him, must have occurred in another time, or more likely, to another person altogether. It was still unsigned. I could put a fire-clause in it, he thought. But he did not even check the horse. Sho, he thought. And then I could use it to start shingling the new barn. So he went on. It was late, and he eased the horse into a rack which it would be able to hold nearly all the way home, with a little breathing on the hills, and he was travelling at a fair gait when he saw suddenly, leaning against a tree beside the road, the man whose face he had seen in the window of the house. One moment the road had been empty, the next moment the man stood there beside it, at the edge of a small copse— the same cloth cap, the same rhythmically chewing jaw materialised apparently out of nothing and almost abreast of the horse, with an air of the complete and purely accidental which Varner was to remember and speculate about only later. He had almost passed the other before he pulled the horse up. He did not shout now and now his big face was merely bland and extremely alert. "Howdy," he said. "You're Flem, aint you? I'm Varner."

"That so?" the other said. He spat. He had a broad flat face. His eyes were the color of stagnant water. He was soft in appearance like Varner himself, though a head shorter, in a soiled white shirt and cheap gray trousers.

"I was hoping to see you," Varner said. "I hear your father has had a little trouble once or twice with landlords. Trouble that might have been serious." The other chewed. "Maybe they never treated him right; I dont know about that and I dont care. What I'm talking about is a mistake, any mistake, can be straightened out so that a man can still stay friends with the fellow he aint satisfied with. Dont you agree to that?" The other chewed steadily. His face was as blank as a pan of uncooked dough. "So he wont have to feel that the only thing that can prove his rights is something that will make him have to pick up and leave the country next day," Varner said. "So that there wont come a time some day when he will look around and find out he has run out of new country to move to." Varner ceased. He waited so long this time that the other finally spoke, though Varner was never certain whether this was the reason or not:

"There's a right smart of country."

"Sho," Varner said pleasantly, bulging, bland. "But a man dont want to wear it out just moving through it. Especially because of a matter that if it had just been took in hand and straightened out to begin with, wouldn't have amounted to nothing. That could have been straightened out in five minutes if there had just been some other fellow handy to take a hold of a fellow that was maybe a little high-tempered to begin with say, and say to him, 'Hold up here, now; that fellow dont aim to put nothing on you. All you got to do is consult with him peaceable and it will be fixed up. I know that to be a fact because I *got his promise to that effect.*' " He paused again. "Especially if this here fellow we are speaking of, that could take a hold of him and tell him that, was going to get a benefit out of keeping him quiet and peaceable." Varner stopped again. After a while the other spoke again:

"What benefit?"

"Why, a good farm to work. Store credit. More land if he felt he could handle it."

"Aint no benefit in farming. I figure on getting out of it soon as I can."

"All right," Varner said. "Say he wanted to take up some other line, this fellow we're speaking of. He will need the good will of the folks he aims to make his money off of to do it. And what better way—"

"You run a store, dont you?" the other said.

"—better way—" Varner said. Then he stopped. "What?" he said. "I hear you run a store."

Varner stared at him. Now Varner's face was not bland. It was just completely still and completely intent. He reached to his shirt pocket and produced a cigar. He neither smoked nor drank himself, being by nature so happily metabolised that, as he might have put it himself, he could not possibly have felt better than he naturally did. But he always carried two or three. "Have a cigar," he said.

"I dont use them," the other said.

"Just chew, hah?" Varner said.

"I chew up a nickel now and then until the suption is out of it. But I aint never lit a match to one yet."

"Sho now," Varner said. He looked at the cigar; he said quietly: "And I just hope to God you and nobody you know ever will." He put the cigar back into his pocket. He expelled a loud hiss of breath. "All right," he said. "Next fall. When he has made his crop." He had never been certain just when the other had been looking at him and when not, but now he watched the other raise his arm and with his other hand pick something infinitesimal from the sleeve with infinitesimal care. Once more Varner expelled his breath through his nose. This time it was a sigh. "All right," he said. "Next week then. You'll give me that long, wont you? But you got to guarantee it." The other spat.

"Guarantee what?" he said.

Two miles further on dusk overtook him, the shortening twilight of late April, in which the blanched dogwoods stood among the darker trees with spread raised palms like praying nuns; there was the evening star and already the whippoorwills. The horse, travelling supperward, was going well in the evening's cool, when Varner pulled it to a stop and held it for a full moment. "Hell fire," he said. "He was standing just exactly where couldn't nobody see him from the house."

CHAPTER TWO

1

$\mathcal{R}$atliff, the sewing-machine agent, again approaching the village, with a used music box and a set of brand-new harrow teeth still fastened together by the factory shipping wire in the dog-kennel box in place of the sewing machine, saw the old white horse dozing on three legs at a fence post and, an instant later, Will Varner himself sitting in the home-made chair against the rise of shaggy lawns and overgrown gardens of the Old Frenchman place.

"Evening, Uncle Will," he said in his pleasant, courteous, even deferent voice. "I hear you and Jody got a new clerk in the store." Varner looked at him sharply, the reddish eyebrows beetling a little above the hard little eyes.

"So that's done spread," he said. "How far you been since yesterday?"

"Seven-eight miles," Ratliff said.

"Hah," Varner said. "We been needing a clerk." That was true. All they needed was someone to come and unlock the store in the morning and lock it again at night—this just to keep stray dogs out, since even tramps, like stray Negroes, did not stay in Frenchman's Bend after nightfall. In fact, at times Jody Varner himself (Will was never there anyhow) would be absent from the store all day. Customers would enter and serve themselves and each other, putting the price of the articles, which they knew to a penny as well as Jody himself did, into a cigar box inside the circular wire cage which protected the cheese, as though it—the cigar box, the worn bills and thumb-polished coins—were actually baited.

"At least you can get the store swept out every day," Ratliff said. "Aint everybody can get that included into a fire insurance policy."

"Hah," Varner said again. He rose from the chair. He was chewing tobacco. He removed from his mouth the chewed-out wad which resembled a clot of damp hay, and threw it away and wiped his palm on his flank. He approached the fence, where at his direction the blacksmith had contrived a clever passage which (neither the blacksmith nor Varner had ever seen one before or even imagined one) operated exactly like a modern turnstile, by the raising of a chained pin instead of inserting a coin. "Ride my horse on back to the store," Varner said. "I'll drive your rig. I want to sit down and ride."

"We can tie the horse behind the buckboard and both ride in it," Ratliff said.

"You ride the horse," Varner said. "That's close as I want you right now. Sometimes you are a little too smart to suit me."

"Why, sho, Uncle Will," Ratliff said. So he cramped the buckboard's wheel for Varner to get in, and himself mounted the horse. They went on, Ratliff a little behind the buckboard, so that Varner talked to him over his shoulder, not looking back:

"This here fire-fighter—"

"It wasn't proved," Ratliff said mildly. "Of course, that's the trouble. If a fellow's got to choose between a man that is a murderer and one he just thinks maybe is, he'll choose the murderer. At least then he will know exactly where he's at. His attention aint going to wander then."

"All right, all right," Varner said. "This here victim of libel and mis-statement then. What do you know about him?"

"Nothing to mention," Ratliff said. "Just what I hear about him. I aint seen him in eight years. There was another boy then, besides Flem. A little one. He would be about ten or twelve now if he was there. He must a been mislaid in one of them movings."

"Has what you have heard about him since them eight years ago caused you to think he might have changed his habits any?"

"Sho now," Ratliff said. What dust the three horses raised blew lightly aside on the faint breeze, among the dogfennel and bitterweed just beginning to bloom in the roadside ditches. "Eight years. And before that it was fifteen more pretty near I never saw him. I growed up next to where he was living. I mean, he lived for about two years on the same place where I growed up. Him and my pap was both renting from Old Man Anse Holland. Ab was a horse-trader then. In fact, I was there the same time the horse-trading give out on him and left him just a farmer. He aint naturally mean. He's just soured."

"Soured," Varner said. He spat. His voice was now sardonic, almost contemptuous: "Jody came in last night, late. I knowed it soon as I saw him. It was exactly like when he was a boy and had done something he knowed I was going to find out about tomorrow and so he would figure he better tell me first himself. 'I done hired a clerk,' he says. 'What for?' I says. 'Dont Sam shine your shoes on Sunday no more to suit you?' and he hollers, 'I had to! I had to hire him! I had to, I tell you!' And he went to bed without eating no supper. I dont know how he slept; I never listened to see. But this morning he seemed to feel a little better about it. He seemed to feel consider-able better about it. 'He might even be useful,' he says. 'I dont doubt it,' I says. 'But there's a law against it. Besides, why not just tear them down instead? You could even sell the lumber then.' And he looked at me a while longer. Only he was just waiting for me to stop; he had done figured it all out last night. 'Take a man like that,' he says. 'A man that's independent about protecting his-self, his own rights and interests. Say the advantages of his own rights and interests is another fellow's advantage and interest too. Say his benefits is the same benefits as the fellow that's paying some of his kinfolks a salary to protect his business; say it's a business where now and then (and you know it as well as I do,' Jody says) '—say benefits is always com-ing up that the fellow that's going to get the benefits just as lief not be actively mixed up in himself, why, a fellow that independent—' "

"He could have said 'dangerous' with the same amount of breath," Ratliff said.

"Yes," Varner said. "Well?"

Ratliff didn't answer. Instead, he said: "That store aint in Jody's name, is it?" Only he answered this himself, before the other could have spoken: "Sho now. Why did I need to ask that? Besides, it's just Flem that Jody's mixed up with. Long as Jody keeps him, maybe old Ab will—"

"Out with it," Varner said. "What do you think about it?"

"You mean what I really think?"

"What in damnation do you think I am talking about?"

"I think the same as you do," Ratliff said quietly. "That there aint but two men I know can risk fooling with them folks. And just one of them is named Varner and his front name aint Jody."

"And who's the other one?" Varner said.

"That aint been proved yet neither," Ratliff said pleasantly.

2

Besides Varner's store and cotton gin and the combined grist mill and blacksmith shop which they rented to the actual smith, and the schoolhouse and the church and the perhaps three dozen dwellings within sound of both bells, the village consisted of a livery barn and lot and a contiguous shady though grassless yard in which sat a sprawling rambling edifice partly of sawn boards and partly of logs, unpainted and of two storeys in places and known as Littlejohn's hotel, where behind a weathered plank nailed to one of the trees and lettered ROOMS AND BORD drummers and livestock-traders were fed and lodged. It had a long veranda lined with chairs. That night after supper, the buckboard and team in the stable, Ratliff was sitting here with five or six other men who had drifted in from the adjacent homes within walking distance. They would have been there on any other night, but this evening they were gathered even before the sun was completely gone, looking now and then toward the dark front of Varner's store as people will gather to look quietly at the cold embers of a lynching or at the propped ladder and open window of an elopement, since the presence of a hired white clerk in the store of a man still able to walk and with intellect still sound enough to make money mistakes at least in his own favor, was as unheard of as the presence of a hired white woman in one of their own kitchens. "Well," one said, "I dont know nothing about that one Varner hired. But blood's thick. And a man that's got kinfolks that stays mad enough all the time to set fire to a man's barn—"

"Sho now," Ratliff said. "Old man Ab aint naturally mean. He's just soured."

For a moment nobody spoke. They sat or squatted along the veranda, invisible to one another. It was almost full dark, the departed sun a pale greenish stain in the northwestern sky. The whippoor-wills had begun and fireflies winked and drifted among the trees beyond the road.

"How soured?" one said after a while.

"Why, just soured," Ratliff said pleasantly, easily, readily. "There was that business during the War. When he wasn't bothering nobody, not harming or helping either side, just tending to his own business, which was profit and horses—things which never even heard of such a thing as a political conviction—when here comes somebody that never even owned the horses even and shot him in the heel. And that soured him. And then that business of Colonel Sar-toris's main-law, Miss Rosa Millard, that Ab had done went and formed a horse- and mule-partnership with in good faith and honor, not aiming to harm nobody blue or gray but just keeping his mind fixed on profit and horses, until Miz Millard had to go and get her-self shot by that fellow that called his-self Major Grumby, and then Colonel's boy Bayard and Uncle Buck McCaslin and a nigger caught Ab in the woods and something else happened, tied up to a tree or something and maybe even a double bridle rein or maybe even a heated ramrod in it too though that's just hearsay. Anyhow, Ab had to withdraw his allegiance to the Sartorises, and I hear tell he skulked for a considerable back in the hills until Colonel Sartoris got busy enough building his railroad for it to be safe to come out. And that soured him some more. But at least he still had horse-trading left to fall back on. Then he run into Pat Stamper. And Pat eliminated him from horse-trading. And so he just went plumb curdled."

"You mean he locked horns with Pat Stamper and even had the bridle left to take back home?" one said. Because they all knew Stam-per. He was a legend, even though still alive, not only in that coun-try but in all North Mississippi and West Tennessee—a heavy man with a stomach and a broad pale expensive Stetson hat and eyes the color of a new axe blade, who travelled about the country with a wagon carrying camping equipment and played horses against horses as a gambler plays cards against cards, for the pleasure of beating a worthy opponent as much as for gain, assisted by a Negro hostler

who was an artist as a sculptor is an artist, who could take any piece
of horseflesh which still had life in it and retire to whatever closed
building or shed was empty and handy and then, with a quality of
actual legerdemain, reappear with something which the beast's own
dam would not recognise, let alone its recent owner; the two of them,
Stamper and the Negro, working in a kind of outrageous rapport like
a single intelligence possessing the terrific advantage over common
mortals of being able to be in two places at once and directing two
separate sets of hands and fingers at the same time.

"He done better than that," Ratliff said. "He come out exactly
even. Because if it was anybody that Stamper beat, it was Miz Snopes.
And even she never considered it so. All she was out was just having
to make the trip to Jefferson herself to finally get the separator and
maybe she knowed all the time that sooner or later she would have to
do that. It wasn't Ab that bought one horse and sold two to Pat Stamper. It was Miz Snopes. Her and Pat just used Ab to trade through."

Once more for a moment no one spoke. Then the first speaker
said: "How did you find all this out? I reckon you was there too."

"I was," Ratliff said. "I went with him that day to get the separator.
We lived about a mile from them. My pap and Ab were both renting from Old Man Anse Holland then, and I used to hang around
Ab's barn with him. Because I was a fool about a horse too, same as
he was. And he wasn't curdled then. He was married to his first wife
then, the one he got from Jefferson, that one day her pa druv up in
a wagon and loaded her and the furniture into it and told Ab that if
he ever crossed Whiteleaf Bridge again he would shoot him. They
never had no children and I was just turning eight and I would go
down to his house almost every morning and stay all day with him,
setting on the lot fence with him while the neighbors would come up
and look through the fence at whatever it was he had done swapped
some more of Old Man Anse's bob-wire or busted farm tools for this
time, and Ab lying to just exactly the right amount about how old it
was and how much he give for it. He was a fool about a horse; he
admitted it, but he wasn't the kind of a fool about a horse Miz Snopes
claimed he was that day when we brought Beasley Kemp's horse
home and turned it into the lot and come up to the house and Ab
taken his shoes off on the gallery to cool his feet for dinner and Miz

Snopes standing in the door shaking the skillet at him and Ab saying, 'Now Vynie, now Vynie. I always was a fool about a good horse and you know it and aint a bit of use in you jawing about it. You better thank the Lord that when He give me a eye for horseflesh He give me a little judgment and gumption with it.'

"Because it wasn't the horse. It wasn't the trade. It was a good trade because Ab had just give Beasley a straight stock and a old wore-out sorghum mill of Old Man Anse's for the horse, and even Miz Snopes had to admit that that was a good swap for anything that could get up and walk from Beasley's lot to theirn by itself, because like she said while she was shaking the skillet at him, he couldn't get stung very bad in a horse-trade because he never had nothing of his own that anybody would want to swap even a sorry horse for. And it wasn't because Ab had left the plow down in the far field where she couldn't see it from the house and had snuck the wagon out the back way with the plow stock and the sorghum mill in it while she still thought he was in the field. It was like she knowed already what me and Ab didn't: that Pat Stamper had owned that horse before Beasley got it and that now Ab had done caught the Pat Stamper sickness just from touching it. And maybe she was right. Maybe to himself Ab did call his-self the Pat Stamper of the Holland farm or maybe even of all Beat Four, even if maybe he was fairly sho that Pat Stamper wasn't going to walk up to that lot fence and challenge him for it. Sho, I reckon while he was setting there on the gallery with his feet cooling and the sidemeat plopping and spitting in the kitchen and us waiting to eat it so we could go back down to the lot and set on the fence while the folks would come up and look at what he had brung home this time, I reckon maybe Ab not only knowed as much about horse-trading as Pat Stamper, but he owned head for head of them with Old Man Anse himself. And I reckon while we would be setting there, just moving enough to keep outen the sun, with that empty plow standing in the furrow down in the far field and Miz Snopes watching him outen the back window and saying to herself, 'Horse-trader! Setting there bragging and lying to a passel of shiftless men with the weeds and morning glories climbing so thick in the cotton and corn I am afraid to tote his dinner down to him for fear of snakes'; I reckon Ab would look at whatever it was he had just traded the mailbox or some more of Old Man Anse's bob-wire or some of the winter corn for this time, and he would say to his-self, 'It's not only mine, but before God it's the prettiest drove of a horse I ever see.'

"It was fate. It was like the Lord Himself had decided to buy a horse with Miz Snopes's separator money. Though I will admit that when He chose Ab He picked out a good quick willing hand to do His trading for Him. The morning we started, Ab hadn't planned to use Beasley's horse a-tall because he knowed it probably couldn't make that twenty-eight-mile trip to Jefferson and back in one day. He aimed to go up to Old Man Anse's lot and borrow a mule to work with hisn and he would a done it except for Miz Snopes. She kept on taunting him about swapping for a yard ornament, about how if he could just git it to town somehow maybe he could swap it to the livery stable to prop up in front for a sign. So in a way it was Miz Snopes herself that put the idea in Ab's head of taking Beasley's horse to town. So when I got there that morning we hitched Beasley's horse into the wagon with the mule. We had done been feeding it for two-three days now by forced draft, getting it ready to make the trip, and it looked some better now than when we had brung it home. But even yet it didn't look so good. So Ab decided it was the mule that showed it up, that when it was the only horse or mule in sight it looked pretty good and that it was standing by something else on four legs that done the damage. 'If it was just some way to hitch the mule under the wagon, so it wouldn't show but could still pull, and just leave the horse in sight,' Ab says. Because he wasn't soured then. But we had done the best we could with it. Ab thought about mixing a right smart of salt in some corn so it would drink a lot of water so some of the ribs wouldn't show so bad at least, only we knowed it wouldn't never get to Jefferson then, let alone back home, besides having to stop at every creek and branch to blow it up again. So we done the best we could. That is, we hoped for the best. Ab went to the house and come back in his preacher's coat (it's the same one he's still got; it was Colonel Sartoris's that Miss Rosa Millard give him, it would be thirty years ago) and that twenty-four dollars and sixty-eight cents Miz Snopes had been saving on for four years now, tied up in a rag, and we started out.

"We wasn't even thinking about horse-trading. We was thinking about horse all right, because we was wondering if maybe we wasn't fixing to come back home that night with Beasley's horse in the wagon and Ab in the traces with the mule. Yes sir, Ab eased that team outen the lot and on down the road easy and careful as ere a horse and mule ever moved in this world, with me and Ab walking up every hill that tilted enough to run water offen it, and we was aiming to do that right in to Jefferson. It was the weather, the hot day; it was the middle of July. Because here we was about a mile from White- leaf store, with Beasley's horse kind of half walking and half riding on the double tree and Ab's face looking worrieder and worrieder every time it failed to lift its feet high enough to step, when all of a sud- den that horse popped into a sweat. It flung its head up like it had been touched with a hot poker and stepped up into the collar, touch- ing the collar for the first time since the mule had taken the weight of it when Ab shaken out the whip in the lot, and so we come down the hill and up to Whiteleaf store with that horse of Beasley's eyes rolling white as darning eggs and its mane and tail swirling like a grass fire. And I be dog if it hadn't not only sweated itself into as pretty a dark blood bay as you ever saw, but even its ribs didn't seem to show so much. And Ab that had been talking about taking the back road so we wouldn't have to pass the store at all, setting there on the wagon seat like he would set on the lot fence back home where he knowed he was safe from Pat Stamper, telling Hugh Mitchell and the other fellows on the gallery that that horse come from Kentucky. Hugh Mitchell never even laughed. 'Sho now,' he says. 'I wondered what had become of it. I reckon that's what taken it so long; Ken- tucky's a long walk. Herman Short swapped Pat Stamper a mule and buggy for that horse five years ago and Beasley Kemp give Herman eight dollars for it last summer. What did you give Beasley? Fifty cents?'

"That's what did it. It wasn't what the horse had cost Ab because you might say all it had cost Ab was the straight stock, since in the first place the sorghum mill was wore out and in the second place it wasn't Ab's sorghum mill nohow. And it wasn't the mule and buggy of Herman's. It was them eight cash dollars of Beasley's, and not that Ab held them eight dollars against Herman, because Herman had

done already invested a mule and buggy in it. And besides, the eight
dollars was still in the country and so it didn't actually matter
whether it was Herman or Beasley that had them. It was the fact that
Pat Stamper, a stranger, had come in and got actual Yoknapatawpha
County cash dollars to rattling around loose that way. When a man
swaps horse for horse, that's one thing and let the devil protect him if
the devil can. But when cash money starts changing hands, that's
something else. And for a stranger to come in and start that cash
money to changing and jumping from one fellow to another, it's like
when a burglar breaks into your house and flings your things ever
which way even if he dont take nothing. It makes you twice as mad.
So it was not just to unload Beasley Kemp's horse back onto Pat
Stamper. It was to get Beasley Kemp's eight dollars back outen Pat
someway. And that's what I meant about it was pure fate that had
Pat Stamper camped outside Jefferson right by the road we would
have to pass on that day we went to get Miz Snopes's milk separator; camped right there by the road with that nigger magician on
the very day when Ab was coming to town with twenty-four dollars
and sixty-eight cents in his pocket and the entire honor and pride
of the science and pastime of horse-trading in Yoknapatawpha
County depending on him to vindicate it.

    "I dont recollect just when and where we found out Pat was in Jef-
ferson that day. It might have been at Whiteleaf store. Or it might
have just been that in Ab's state it was not only right and natural that
Ab would have to pass Stamper to get to Jefferson, but it was fore-
ordained and fated that he would have to. So here we come, easing
them eight dollars of Beasley Kemp's up them long hills with Ab and
me walking and Beasley's horse laying into the collar the best it could
but with the mule doing most of the pulling and Ab walking on his
side of the wagon and cussing Pat Stamper and Herman Short and
Beasley Kemp and Hugh Mitchell; and we went down the hills with
Ab holding the wagon braked with a sapling pole so it wouldn't shove
Beasley's horse through the collar and turn it wrong-side-out like a
sock, and Ab still cussing Pat Stamper and Herman and Beasley and
Mitchell, until we come to the Three Mile Bridge and Ab turned the
team outen the road and druv into the bushes and taken the mule out
and knotted up one rein so I could ride and give me the quarter and

told me to ride for town and get a dime's worth of saltpeter and a nickel's worth of tar and a number ten fish hook and hurry back.

"So we didn't get into town until after dinner time. We went straight to Pat's camp and druv in with that horse of Beasley's laying into the collar now sho enough, with its eyes looking nigh as wild as Ab's and foaming a little at the mouth where Ab had rubbed the salt-peter into its gums and a couple of as pretty tarred bob-wire cuts on its chest as you could want, and another one where Ab had worked that fish hook under its hide where he could touch it by drooping one rein a little, and Pat's nigger running up to catch the head-stall before the horse run right into the tent where Pat slept and Pat his-self coming out with that ere cream-colored Stetson cocked over one eye and them eyes the color of a new plow point and just about as warm and his thumbs hooked into his waist band. 'That's a pretty lively horse you got there,' he says.

" 'You damn right,' Ab says. 'That's why I got to get shut of it. Just consider you done already trimmed me and give me something in place of it I can get back home without killing me and this boy both.' Because that was the right system: to rush right up and say he had to trade instead of hanging back for Pat to persuade him. It had been five years since Pat had seen the horse, so Ab figured that the chance of his recognising it would be about the same as a burglar recognis-ing a dollar watch that happened to get caught for a minute on his vest button five years ago. And Ab wasn't trying to beat Pat bad. He just wanted to recover that eight dollars' worth of the honor and pride of Yoknapatawpha County horse-trading, doing it not for profit but for honor. And I believe it worked. I still believe that Ab fooled Pat, and that it was because of what Pat aimed to trade Ab and not because Pat recognised Beasley's horse, that Pat refused to trade any way except team for team. Or I dont know: maybe Ab was so busy fooling Pat that Pat never had to fool Ab at all. So the nigger led the span of mules out and Pat standing there with his thumbs in his pants-top, watching Ab and chewing tobacco slow and gentle, and Ab standing there with that look on his face that was desperate but not scared yet, because he was realising now he had got in deeper than he aimed to and that he would either have to shut his eyes and bust on through, or back out and quit, get back in the wagon and go on before Beasley's horse even give up to the fish hook. And then Pat Stamper showed how come he was Pat Stamper. If he had just started in to show Ab what a bargain he was getting, I reckon Ab would have backed out. But Pat didn't. He fooled Ab just exactly as one first-class burglar would fool another first-class burglar by purely and simply refusing to tell him where the safe was at.

" 'I already got a good mule,' Ab says. 'It's just the horse I dont want. Trade me a mule for the horse.'

" 'I dont want no wild horse neither,' Pat says. 'Not that I wont trade for anything that walks, provided I can trade my way. But I aint going to trade for that horse alone because I dont want it no more than you do. What I am trading for is that mule. And this here team of mine is matched. I aim to get about three times as much for them as a span as I would selling them single.'

" 'But you would still have a team to trade with,' Ab says.

" 'No,' Pat says. 'I aim to get more for them from you than I would if the pair was broken. If it's a single mule you want, you better try somewhere else.'

"So Ab looked at the mules again. They looked just exactly right. They didn't look extra good and they didn't look extra bad. Neither one of them looked quite as good as Ab's mule, but the two of them together looked just a little mite better than just one mule of anybody's. And so he was doomed. He was doomed from the very minute Hugh Mitchell told him about that eight dollars. I reckon Pat Stamper knowed he was doomed the very moment he looked up and seen that nigger holding Beasley's horse back from running into the tent. I reckon he knowed right then he wouldn't even have to try to trade Ab: all he would have to do would be just to say No long enough. Because that's what he done, leaning there against our wagon bed with his thumbs hooked into his pants, chewing his tobacco and watching Ab go through the motions of examining them mules again. And even I knowed that Ab had done traded, that he had done walked out into what he thought was a spring branch and then found out it was quicksand, and that now he knowed he couldn't even stop long enough to turn back. 'All right,' he says. 'I'll take them.'

"So the nigger put the new team into the harness and we went on

to town. And them mules still looked all right. I be dog if I didn't
begin to think that Ab had walked into that Stamper quicksand and
then got out again, and when we had got back into the road and
beyond sight of Stamper's tent, Ab's face begun to look like it would
while he would set on the lot fence at home and tell folks how he was
a fool about a horse but not a durn fool. It wasn't easy yet, it was just
watchful, setting there and feeling out the new team. We was right at
town now and he wouldn't have much time to feel them out in, but
we would have a good chance on the road back home. 'By God,' Ab
says. 'If they can walk home at all, I have got that eight dollars back,
damn him.'

"But that nigger was a artist. Because I swear to God them mules
looked all right. They looked exactly like two ordinary, not extra
good mules you might see in a hundred wagons on the road. I had
done realised how they had a kind of jerky way of starting off, first
one jerking into the collar and then jerking back and then the other
jerking into the collar and then jerking back, and even after we was in
the road and the wagon rolling good one of them taken a spell of
some sort and snatched his-self crossways in the traces like he aimed
to turn around and go back, maybe crawling right across the wagon
to do it, but then Stamper had just told us they was a matched team;
he never said they had ever worked together as a matched team, and
they was a matched team in the sense that neither one of them
seemed to have any idea as to just when the other one aimed to start
moving. But Ab got them straightened out and we went on, and we
was just starting up that big hill onto the Square when they popped
into a sweat too, just like Beasley's horse had done just beyond
Whiteleaf. But that was all right, it was hot enough; that was when I
first noticed that that rain was coming up; I mind how I was watching a big hot-looking bright cloud over to the southwest and thinking how it was going to rain on us before we got home or to
Whiteleaf either, when all of a sudden I realised that the wagon had
done stopped going up the hill and was starting down it backwards
and I looked around just in time to see both of them mules this time
crossways in the traces and kind of glaring at one another across the
tongue and Ab trying to straighten them out and glaring too, and
then all of a sudden they straightened out and I mind how I was

thinking what a good thing it was they was pointed away from the wagon when they straightened out. Because they moved at the same time for the first time in their lives, or for the first time since Ab owned them anyway, and here we come swurging up that hill and into the Square like a roach up a drainpipe, with the wagon on two wheels and Ab sawing at the reins and saying 'Hell fire, hell fire' and folks, ladies and children mostly, scattering and screeching and Ab just managed to swing them into the alley behind Cain's store and stopped them by locking our nigh wheel with another wagon's and the other team (they was hitched) holp to put the brakes on. So it was a good crowd by then, helping us to get untangled, and Ab led our team over to Cain's back door and tied them snubbed up close to a post, with folks still coming up and saying, 'It's that team of Stamper's,' and Ab breathing hard now and looking a right smart less easy in the face and most all-fired watchful. 'Come on,' he says. 'Let's get that damn separator and get out of here.'

"So we went in and give Cain Miz Snopes's rag and he counted the twenty-four sixty-eight and we got the separator and started back to the wagon, to where we had left it. Because it was still there; the wagon wasn't the trouble. In fact, it was too much wagon. I mind how I could see the bed and the tops of the wheels where Ab had brought it up close against the loading platform and I could see the folks from the waist up standing in the alley, twice or three times as many of them now, and I was thinking how it was too much wagon and too much folks; it was like one of these here pictures that have printed under them, *What's wrong with this picture?* and then Ab begun to say 'Hell fire, hell fire' and begun to run, still toting his end of the separator, up to the edge of the platform where we could see under it. The mules was all right too. They was laying down. Ab had snubbed them up pretty close to the same post, with the same line through both bits, and now they looked exactly like two fellows that had done hung themselves in one of these here suicide packs, with their heads snubbed up together and pointing straight up and their tongues hanging out and their eyes popping and their necks stretched about four foot and their legs doubled back under them like shot rabbits until Ab jumped down and cut them down with his pocket knife. A artist. He had give them just exactly to the inch of

whatever it was to get them to town and off the Square before it
played out.

"So Ab was desperate. I can see him now, backed off in a corner
behind Cain's plows and cultivators, with his face white and his voice
shaking and his hand shaking so he couldn't hardly hand me the six
bits outen his pocket. 'Go to Doc Peabody's,' he says, 'and get me a
bottle of whiskey. Hurry.' He was desperate. It wasn't even quicksand
now. It was a whirlpool and him with just one jump left. He drunk
that pint of whiskey in two drinks and set the empty bottle down in
the corner careful as a egg and we went back to the wagon. The mules
was still standing up this time and we loaded the separator in and he
eased them away careful, with folks still telling each other it was that
team of Stamper's. Ab's face was red instead of white now and the sun
was gone but I dont think he even noticed it. And we hadn't et too,
and I dont believe he knowed that either. And I be dog if it didn't
seem like Pat Stamper hadn't moved either, standing there at the gate
to his rope stock pen, with that Stetson cocked and his thumbs still
hooked in the top of his pants and Ab sitting in the wagon trying to
keep his hands from shaking and the team Stamper had swapped him
stopped now with their heads down and their legs spraddled and
breathing like a sawmill. 'I come for my team,' Ab says.

" 'What's the matter?' Stamper says. 'Dont tell me these are too
lively for you too. They dont look it.'

" 'All right,' Ab says. 'All right. I got to have my team. I got four
dollars. Make your four-dollar profit and give me my team.'

" 'I aint got your team,' Stamper says. 'I didn't want that horse neither. I told you that. So I got shut of it.'

"Ab set there for a while. It was cooler now. A breeze had got up
and you could smell the rain in it. 'But you still got my mule,' Ab
says. 'All right. I'll take it.'

" 'For what?' Stamper says. 'You want to swap that team for your
mule?' Because Ab wasn't trading now. He was desperate, sitting
there like he couldn't even see, with Stamper leaning easy against the
gate post and looking at him for a minute. 'No,' Stamper says. 'I dont
want them mules. Yours is the best one. I wouldn't trade that way,
even swap.' He spit, easy and careful. 'Besides, I done included your
mule into another team. With another horse. You want to look at it?'

" 'All right,' Ab says. 'How much?'

" 'Dont you even want to see it first?' Stamper says.

" 'All right,' Ab says. So the nigger led out Ab's mule and a horse, a little dark brown horse; I remember how even with it clouded up and no sun, how that horse shined—a horse a little bigger than the one we had traded Stamper, and hog fat. That's just exactly how it was fat: not like a horse is fat but like a hog: fat right up to its ears and looking tight as a drum; it was so fat it couldn't hardly walk, putting its feet down like they didn't have no weight nor feeling in them at all. 'It's too fat to last,' Ab says. 'It wont even get me home.'

" 'That's what I think myself,' Stamper says. 'That's why I want to get shut of it.'

" 'All right,' Ab says. 'I'll have to try it.' He begun to get outen the wagon.

" 'Try it?' Stamper says. Ab didn't answer. He got outen the wagon careful and went to the horse, putting his feet down careful and stiff too, like he never had no weight in his feet too, like the horse. It had a hackamore on and Ab taken the rope from the nigger and started to get on the horse. 'Wait,' Stamper said. 'What are you fixing to do?'

" 'Going to try it,' Ab says. 'I done swapped a horse with you once today.' Stamper looked at Ab a minute. Then spit again and kind of stepped back.

" 'All right, Jim,' he says to the nigger. 'Help him up.' So the nigger holp Ab onto the horse, only the nigger never had time to jump back like Stamper because soon as Ab's weight come onto the horse it was like Ab had a live wire in his britches. The horse made one swirl, it looked round as a ball, without no more front or back end than a Irish potato. It throwed Ab hard and Ab got up and went back to the horse and Stamper says, 'Help him up, Jim,' and the nigger holp Ab up again and the horse slammed him off again and Ab got up with his face just the same and went back and taken the rope again when Stamper stopped him. It was just exactly like Ab wanted that horse to throw him, hard, like the ability of his bones and meat to stand that ere hard ground was all he had left to pay for something with life enough left to get us home. 'Are you trying to kill yoursel'?' Stamper says.

" 'All right,' Ab says. 'How much?'

" 'Come into the tent,' Stamper says.

"So I waited in the wagon. It was beginning to blow a little now, and we hadn't brought no coats with us. But we had some croker sacks in the wagon Miz Snopes had made us bring along to wrap the separator in and I was wrapping it in the sacks when the nigger come outen the tent and when he lifted up the flap I seen Ab drinking outen the bottle. Then the nigger led up a horse and buggy and Ab and Stamper come outen the tent and Ab come to the wagon, he didn't look at me, he just lifted the separator outen the sacks and went and put it into the buggy and him and Stamper went and got into it and drove away, back toward town. The nigger was watching me. 'You fixing to get wet fo you get home,' he said.

" 'I reckon so,' I said.

" 'You want to eat a snack of dinner until they get back?' he said. 'I got it on the stove.'

" 'I reckon not,' I said. So he went back into the tent and I waited in the wagon. It was most sholy going to rain, and that soon. I mind how I thought that anyway we would have the croker sacks now to try to keep dry under. Then Ab and Stamper come back and Ab never looked at me that time either. He went back into the tent and I could see him drinking outen the bottle again and this time he put it into his shirt. And then the nigger led our mule and the new horse up and put them in the wagon and Ab come out and got in. Stamper and the nigger both holp him now.

" 'Dont you reckon you better let that boy drive?' Stamper says.

" 'I'll drive,' Ab says. 'Maybe I cant swap a horse with you, but by God I can still drive it.'

" 'Sho now,' Stamper says. 'That horse will surprise you.'

"And it did," Ratliff said. He laughed, for the first time, quietly, invisible to his hearers though they knew exactly how he would look at the moment as well as if they could see him, easy and relaxed in his chair, with his lean brown pleasant shrewd face, in his faded clean blue shirt, with that same air of perpetual bachelorhood which Jody Varner had, although there was no other resemblance between them and not much here, since in Varner it was a quality of shabby and fustian gallantry where in Ratliff it was that hearty celibacy as of a lay brother in a twelfth-century monastery—a gardener, a pruner of

vines, say. "That horse surprised us. The rain, the storm, come up
before we had gone a mile and we rode in it for two hours, hunched
under the croker sacks and watching that new shiny horse that was so
fat it even put its feet down like it couldn't even feel them, that every
now and then, even during the rain, would give a kind of flinching
jerk like when Ab's weight had come down onto its back at Stamper's camp, until we found a old barn to shelter under. I did, that is,
because Ab was laying out in the wagon bed by then, flat on his back
with the rain popping him in the face and me on the seat driving now
and watching that shiny black horse turning into a bay horse.
Because I was just eight then, and me and Ab had done all our horse-
trading up and down that lane that run past his lot. So I just drove
under the first roof I come to and shaken Ab awake. The rain had
cooled him off by then and he waked up sober. And he got a heap
soberer fast. 'What?' he says. 'What is it?'

" 'The horse!' I hollered. 'He's changing color!'

"He was sober then. We was both outen the wagon then and Ab's
eyes popping and a bay horse standing in the traces where he had
went to sleep looking at a black one. He put his hand out like he
couldn't believe it was even a horse and touched it at a spot where the
reins must every now and then just barely touched it and just about
where his weight had come down on it when he was trying to ride it
at Stamper's, and next I knowed that horse was plunging and swurging. I dodged just as it slammed into the wall behind me; I could even
feel the wind in my hair. Then there was a sound like a nail jabbed
into a big bicycle tire. It went *whishhhhhhhhh* and then the rest of that
shiny fat black horse we had got from Pat Stamper vanished. I dont
mean me and Ab was standing there with just the mule left. We had
a horse too. Only it was the same horse we had left home with that
morning and that we had swapped Beasley Kemp the sorghum mill
and the straight stock for two weeks ago. We even got our fish hook
back, with the barb still bent where Ab had bent it and the nigger had
just moved it a little. But it wasn't till next morning that Ab found the
bicycle pump valve under its hide just inside the nigh foreshoulder—
the one place in the world where a man might own a horse for twenty
years and never think to look at it.

"Because we never got home till well after sunup the next day, and

my pap was waiting at Ab's house, considerable mad. So I didn't stay
long, I just had time to see Miz Snopes standing in the door where I
reckon she had been setting all night too, saying, 'Where's my separator?' and Ab saying how he had always been a fool about a horse
and he couldn't help it and then Miz Snopes begun to cry. I had been
hanging around them a heap by now, but I never had seen her cry
before. She looked like the kind of somebody that never had done
much crying to speak of nohow, because she cried hard, like she
didn't know just how to do it, like even the tears never knowed just
exactly what they was expected to do, standing there in a old wrapper, not even hiding her face, saying, 'Fool about a horse, yes! But
why the horse? why the horse?'

"So me and Pap went on. He had my arm a right smart twisted
up in his hand, but when I begun to tell him about what happened
yesterday, he changed his mind about licking me. But it was almost
noon before I got back down to Ab's. He was setting on the lot fence
and I clumb up and set by him. Only the lot was empty. I couldn't see
his mule nor Beasley's horse neither. But he never said nothing and
I never said nothing, only after a while he said, 'You done had breakfast?' and I said I had and he said, 'I aint et yet.' So we went to the
house then, and sho enough, she was gone. And I could imagine it—
Ab setting there on that fence and her coming down the hill in her
sunbonnet and shawl and gloves too and going into the stable and
saddling the mule and putting the halter on Beasley's horse and Ab
setting there trying to decide whether to go and offer to help her or
not.

"So I started the fire in the stove. Ab wasn't much of a hand at
cooking, so by the time he got his breakfast started it was so late we
just decided to cook enough for breakfast and dinner too and we et
it and I washed the dishes and we went back to the lot. The middle
buster was still setting down yonder in the far field, but there wasn't
nothing to pull it with nohow now lessen he walked up to Old Man
Anse's and borrowed a span of mules, which would be just like going
up to a rattlesnake and borrowing a rattle: but then, I reckon he felt
he had stood all the excitement he could for the rest of that day at
least. So we just set on the fence and looked at that empty lot. It
never had been a big lot and it would look kind of crowded even with

just one horse in it. But now it looked like all Texas; and sho enough, I hadn't hardly begun to think about how empty it was when he clumb down offen the fence and went across and looked at a shed that was built against the side of the barn and that would be all right if it was just propped up and had a new roof on it. 'I think next time I will trade for a mare and build me up a brood herd and raise mules,' he says. 'This here will do all right for colts with a little fixing up.' Then he come back and we set on the fence again, and about middle of the afternoon a wagon druv up. It was Cliff Odum, it had the side-boards on it and Miz Snopes was on the seat with Cliff, coming on past the house, toward the lot. 'She aint got it,' Ab says. 'He wouldn't dicker with her.' We was behind the barn now and we watched Cliff back his wagon up against a cut bank by the gate and we watched Miz Snopes get out and take off her shawl and gloves and come across the lot and into the cow shed and lead the cow back and up onto the cut bank behind the wagon and Cliff said, 'You come hold the team. I'll get her in the wagon.' But she never even stopped. She faced the cow into the tail gate and got behind it and laid her shoulder against its hams and hove that cow into the wagon before Cliff could have got out. And Cliff put up the tail gate and Miz Snopes put her shawl and gloves back on and they got into the wagon and they went on.

"So I built him another fire to cook his supper and then I had to go home; it was almost sundown then. When I come back the next morning I brung a pail of milk. Ab was in the kitchen, still cooking breakfast. 'I am glad you thought about that,' he says when he seen the milk. 'I was aiming to tell you yesterday to see if you could borrow some.' He kept on cooking breakfast because he hadn't expected her that soon, because that would make two twenty-eight-mile trips in not much more than twenty-four hours. But we heard the wagon again and this time when she got out she had the separator. When we got to the barn we could see her toting it into the house. 'You left that milk where she will see it, didn't you?' Ab says.

" 'Yes sir,' I says.

" 'Likely she will wait to put on her old wrapper first,' Ab says. 'I wish I had started breakfast sooner.' Only I dont think she even waited that long, because it seemed like we begun to hear it right

away. It made a fine high sound, good and strong, like it would separate a gallon of milk in no time. Then it stopped. 'It's too bad she
aint got but the one gallon,' Ab says.

" 'I can bring her another one in the morning,' I said. But he
wasn't listening, watching the house.

" 'I reckon you can go now and look in the door,' he says. So I
went and did. She was taking Ab's breakfast offen the stove, onto two
plates. I didn't know she had even seen me till she turned and handed
the two plates to me. Her face was all right now, quiet. It was just
busy.

" 'I reckon you can eat something more too,' she said. 'But eat it
out yonder. I am going to be busy in here and I dont want you and
him in my way.' So I taken the plates back and we set against the
fence and et. And then we heard the separator again. I didn't know
it would go through but one time. I reckon he didn't neither.

" 'I reckon Cain showed her,' he says, eating. 'I reckon if she wants
it to run through more than once, it will run through more than
once.' Then it stopped and she come to the door and hollered to us
to bring the dishes up so she could wash them and I taken the plates
back and set them on the step and me and Ab went back and set on
the fence. It looked like it would have held all Texas and Kansas too.
'I reckon she just rode up to that damn tent and said, Here's your
team. You get my separator and get it quick because I got to catch a
ride back home.', he said. And then we heard it again, and that
evening we walked up to Old Man Anse's to borrow a mule to finish
the far piece with, but he never had none to spare now. So as soon
as Old Man Anse had finished cussing, we come on back and set on
the fence. And sho enough, we could hear the separator start up
again. It sounded strong as ever, like it could make the milk fly, like it
didn't give a whoop whether that milk had been separated once or a
hundred times. 'There it goes again,' Ab says. 'Dont forget that other
gallon tomorrow.'

" 'No sir,' I says. We listened to it. Because he wasn't curdled then.

" 'It looks like she is fixing to get a heap of pleasure and satisfaction outen it,' he says."

3

He halted the buckboard and sat for a moment looking down at the same broken gate which Jody Varner had sat the roan horse and looked at nine days ago—the weed-choked and grass-grown yard, the weathered and sagging house—a cluttered desolation filled already, even before he reached the gate and stopped, with the loud flat sound of two female voices. They were young voices, talking not in shouts or screams but with an unhurried profundity of volume the very apparent absence from which of any discernible human speech or language seemed but natural, as if the sound had been emitted by two enormous birds; as if the aghast and amazed solitude of some inaccessible and empty marsh or desert were being invaded and steadily violated by the constant bickering of the two last survivors of a lost species which had established residence in it—a sound which stopped short off when Ratliff shouted. A moment later the two girls came to the door and stood, big, identical, like two young tremendous cows, looking at him.

"Morning, ladies," he said. "Where's your paw?"

They continued to contemplate him. They did not seem to breathe even, though he knew they did, must; bodies of that displacement and that apparently monstrous, that almost oppressive, wellness, would need air and lots of it. He had a fleeting vision of them as the two cows, heifers, standing knee-deep in air as in a stream, a pond, nuzzling into it, the level of the pond fleeing violently and silently to one inhalation, exposing in astounded momentary amaze the teeming lesser subaerial life about the planted feet. Then they spoke exactly together, like a trained chorus: "Down to the field."

Sho now, he thought, moving on: Doing what? Because he did not believe that the Ab Snopes he had known would have more than two mules. And one of these he had already seen standing idle in the lot beyond the house; and the other he knew to be tied at this moment to a tree behind Varner's store eight miles away, because only three hours ago he had left it there, tied where for six days now he had watched Varner's new clerk ride up each morning and tie it. For an

instant he actually halted the buckboard again. By God, he thought
quietly, This would be exactly the chance he must have been waiting on for twenty-three years now to get his-self that new un-Stam-
pered start. So when he came in sight of the field and recognised the
stiff, harsh, undersized figure behind a plow drawn by two mules, he
was not even surprised. He did not wait until he had actually recognised the mules to be a pair which until a week ago at least had
belonged to Will Varner: he merely changed the tense of the possessing verb: Not *had* belonged, he thought. They still do. By God,
he has done even better than that. He aint even trading horses now.
He has done swapped a man for a span of them.

He halted the buckboard at the fence. The plow had reached the
far end of the field. The man turned the team, their heads tossing
and yawing, their stride breaking as he sawed them about with
absolutely needless violence. Ratliff watched soberly. Just like always,
he thought. He still handles a horse or a mule like it had done already
threatened him with its fist before he even spoke to it. He knew that
Snopes had seen and even recognised him too, though there was no
sign of it, the team straightened out now and returning, the delicate
mule-legs and narrow deer-like feet picking up swiftly and nervously,
the earth shearing dark and rich from the polished blade of the plow.
Now Ratliff could even see Snopes looking directly at him—the cold
glints beneath the shaggy ill-tempered brows as he remembered
them even after eight years, the brows only a little grayer now—
though once more the other merely swung the team about with that
senseless savageness, canting the plow onto its side as he stopped it.
"What you doing here?" he said.

"Just heard you were here and stopped by," Ratliff said "It's been a
while, aint it? Eight years."

The other grunted. "It dont show on you, though. You still look
like butter wouldn't melt in your mouth."

"Sho now," Ratliff said. "Speaking of mouths." He reached
beneath the seat cushion and produced a pint bottle filled apparently
with water. "Some of McCallum's best," he said. "Just run off last
week. Here." He extended the bottle. The other came to the fence.
Although they were now not five feet apart, still all that Ratliff could
see were the two glints beneath the fierce overhang of brow.

"You brought it to me?"

"Sholy," Ratliff said. "Take it."

The other did not move. "What for?"

"Nothing," Ratliff said. "I just brought it. Try a sup of it. It's good."

The other took the bottle. Then Ratliff knew that something had gone out of the eyes. Or maybe they were just not looking at him now. "I'll wait till tonight," Snopes said. "I dont drink in the sun any more."

"How about in the rain?" Ratliff said. And then he knew that Snopes was not looking at him, although the other had not moved, no change in the harsh knotted violent face as he stood holding the bottle. "You ought to settle down pretty good here," Ratliff said. "You got a good farm now, and Flem seems to taken hold in the store like he was raised store-keeping." Now the other did not seem to be listening either. He shook the bottle and raised it to the light as though testing the bead. "I hope you will," Ratliff said.

Then he saw the eyes again, fierce and intractable and cold. "What's it to you if I do or dont?"

"Nothing," Ratliff said, pleasantly, quietly. Snopes stooped and hid the bottle in the weeds beside the fence and returned to the plow and raised it.

"Go on to the house and tell them to give you some dinner," he said.

"I reckon not," Ratliff said. "I got to get on to town."

"Suit yourself," the other said. He looped the single rein about his neck and gave another savage yank on the inside line; again the team swung with yawing heads, already breaking stride even before they had come into motion. "Much obliged for the bottle," he said.

"Sho now," Ratliff said. The plow went on. Ratliff watched it. He never said, Come back again, he thought. He lifted his own reins. "Come up, rabbits," he said. "Let's hit for town."

CHAPTER THREE

1

On the Monday morning when Flem Snopes came to clerk in Varner's store, he wore a brand-new white shirt. It had not even been laundered yet; the creases where the cloth had lain bolted on a shelf, and the sun-browned streaks repeated zebra-like on each successive fold, were still apparent. And not only the women who came to look at him, but Ratliff himself (he did not sell sewing machines for nothing. He had even learned to operate one quite well from demonstrating them, and it was even told of him that he made himself the blue shirts which he wore) knew that the shirt had been cut and stitched by hand and by a stiff and unaccustomed hand too. He wore it all that week. By Saturday night it was soiled, but on the following Monday he appeared in a second one exactly like it, even to the zebra-stripes. By the second Saturday night that one was soiled too, in exactly the same places as the other. It was as though its wearer, entering though he had into a new life and milieu already channelled to compulsions and customs fixed long before his advent, had nevertheless established in it even on that first day his own particular soiling groove.

He rode up on a gaunt mule, on a saddle which was recognised at once as belonging to the Varners, with a tin pail tied to it. He hitched the mule to a tree behind the store and untied the pail and came and mounted to the gallery, where already a dozen men, Ratliff among them, lounged. He did not speak. If he ever looked at them individually, that one did not discern it—a thick squat soft man of no establishable age between twenty and thirty, with a broad still face containing a tight seam of mouth stained slightly at the corners with tobacco, and eyes the color of stagnant water, and projecting from

among the other features in startling and sudden paradox, a tiny
predatory nose like the beak of a small hawk. It was as though the
original nose had been left off by the original designer or craftsman
and the unfinished job taken over by someone of a radically different school or perhaps by some viciously maniacal humorist or perhaps by one who had had only time to clap into the center of the face
a frantic and desperate warning.

He entered the store, carrying the pail, and Ratliff and his companions sat and squatted about the gallery all that day and watched
not only the village proper but all the countryside within walking distance come up singly and in pairs and in groups, men women and
children, to make trivial purchases and look at the new clerk and go
away. They came not belligerently but completely wary, almost decorous, like half-wild cattle following word of the advent of a strange
beast upon their range, to buy flour and patent medicine and plow
lines and tobacco and look at the man whose name a week ago they
had never heard, yet with whom in the future they would have to
deal for the necessities of living, and then depart as quietly as they
had come. About nine oclock Jody Varner rode up on his roan saddle horse and entered the store. They could hear the bass murmur of
his voice inside, though for all the answer he got he might have been
talking to himself. He came out at noon and mounted and rode away,
though the clerk did not follow him. But they had known anyway
what the tin pail would contain, and they began to disperse noonward too, looking into the store as they passed the door, seeing nothing. If the clerk was eating his lunch, he had hidden to do it. Ratliff
was back on the gallery before one oclock, since he had had to walk
only a hundred yards for his dinner. But the others were not long
after him, and for the rest of that day they sat and squatted, talking
quietly now and then about nothing at all, while the rest of the people within walking distance came and bought in nickels and dimes
and went away.

By the end of that first week they had all come in and seen him,
not only all those who in future would have to deal through him for
food and supplies but some who had never traded with the Varners
and never would—the men, the women, the children—the infants
who had never before crossed the doorsteps beyond which they had

been born, the sick and the aged who otherwise might never have crossed them but once more—coming on horses and mules and by wagonsful. Ratliff was still there, the buckboard still containing the music box and the set of virgin harrow teeth standing, a plank propping its tongue and the sturdy mismatched team growing vicious with idleness, in Mrs Littlejohn's lot, watching each morning as the clerk would ride up on the mule, on the borrowed saddle, in the new white shirt growing gradually and steadily a little more and more soiled with each sunset, with the tin pail of lunch which no man had ever yet seen him eating, and hitch the mule and unlock the store with the key which they had not quite expected him to have in his possession for a few days yet at least. After the first day or so he would even have the store open when Ratliff and the others arrived. Jody Varner would appear on the horse about nine oclock and mount the steps and jerk his head bluffly at them and enter the store, though after the first morning he remained only about fifteen minutes. If Ratliff and his companions had hoped to divine any hidden undercurrent or secret spark between the younger Varner and the clerk, they were disappointed. There would be the heavy bass matter-of-fact murmur, still talking apparently to itself for all the audible answer it ever got, then he and the clerk would come to the door and stand in it while Varner finished his instructions and sucked his teeth and departed; when they looked toward the door, it would be empty.

Then at last, on Friday afternoon, Will Varner himself appeared. Perhaps it was for this Ratliff and his companions had been waiting. But if it was, it was doubtless not Ratliff but the others who even hoped that anything would divulge here. So it was very likely Ratliff alone who was not surprised, since what did divulge was the obverse of what they might have hoped for; it was not the clerk who now discovered at last whom he was working for, but Will Varner who discovered who was working for him. He came up on the old fat white horse. A young man squatting on the top step rose and descended and took the reins and tied the horse and Varner got down and mounted the steps, speaking cheerily to their deferential murmur, to Ratliff by name: "Hell fire, aint you gone back to work yet?" Two more of them vacated the knife-gnawed wooden bench, but Varner did not approach it at once. Instead, he paused in front of the open door in almost exactly the same attitude of the people themselves, lean, his neck craned a little like a turkey as he looked into the store, though only for an instant because almost at once he shouted, "You there. What's your name? Flem. Bring me a plug of my tobacco. Jody showed you where he keeps it." He came and approached the group, two of whom vacated the knife-gnawed wooden bench for him, and he sat down and took out his knife and had already begun his smoking-car story in his cheerful drawling bishop's voice when the clerk (Ratliff had not heard his feet at all) appeared at his elbow with the tobacco. Still talking, Varner took the plug and cut off a chew and shut the knife with his thumb and straightened his leg to put the knife back into his pocket, when he stopped talking and looked sharply upward. The clerk was still standing at his elbow. "Hey?" Varner said. "What?"

"You aint paid for it," the clerk said. For an instant Varner did not move at all, his leg still extended, the plug and the severed chew in one hand and the knife in the other just about to enter his pocket. None of them moved in fact, looking quietly and attentively at their hands or at wherever their eyes had been when Varner interrupted himself. "The tobacco," the clerk said.

"Oh," Varner said. He put the knife into his pocket and drew from his hip a leather purse about the size and shape and color of an eggplant and took a nickel from it and gave it to the clerk. Ratliff had not heard the clerk come out and he did not hear him return. Now he saw why. The clerk wore also a new pair of rubber-soled tennis shoes. "Where was I?" Varner said.

"The fellow had just begun to unbutton his over-halls," Ratliff said mildly.

The next day Ratliff departed. He was put into motion not by the compulsion of food, earning it. He could have passed from table to table in that country for six months without once putting his hand into his pocket. He was moved by his itinerary, his established and nurtured round of newsmongering, the pleasure of retailing it, not the least nor stalest of which present stock he had spent the last two weeks actually watching. It was five months before he saw the village again. His route embraced four counties. It was absolutely rigid, flexible only within itself. In ten years he had not once crossed the boundaries of these four, yet one day in this summer he found himself in Tennessee. He found himself not only on foreign soil but shut away from his native state by a golden barrier, a wall of neatly accumulating minted coins.

During the spring and summer he had done a little too well. He had oversold himself, selling and delivering the machines on notes against the coming harvest, employing what money he collected or sold the exchanged articles for which he accepted as down-payments, to make his own down-payments to the Memphis wholesaler on still other machines, which he delivered in turn on new notes, countersigning them, until one day he discovered that he had almost sold himself insolvent on his own bull market. The wholesaler made demand upon him for his (the wholesaler's) half of the outstanding twenty-dollar notes. Ratliff in his turn made a swift canvass of his own debtors. He was affable, bland, anecdotal and apparently unhurried as ever but he combed them thoroughly, not to be denied, although the cotton had just begun to bloom and it would be months yet before there would be any money in the land. He collected a few dollars, a set of used wagon harness, eight White Leghorn hens. He owed the wholesaler $120.00. He called on the twelfth customer, a distant kinsman, and found that he had departed a week ago with a string of mules to sell at the mule curb-market at Columbia, Tennessee.

He followed at once in the buckboard, with the wagon harness and the hens. He not only saw a chance to collect his note, provided he got there before someone sold the kinsman some mules in his own turn, but he might even borrow enough to appease the wholesaler. He reached Columbia four days later, where, after the first amazed moment or so, he looked about him with something of the happy surmise of the first white hunter blundering into the idyllic solitude of a virgin African vale teeming with ivory, his for the mere shooting and fetching out. He sold a machine to the man whom he asked the whereabouts of his cousin, he went with the kinsman to pass the night at the home of the kinsman's wife's cousin ten miles from Columbia and sold a machine there. He sold three in the first four days; he remained a month and sold eight in all, collecting $80.00 in down-payments, with the $80.00 and the wagon harness and the eight hens he bought a mule, took the mule to Memphis and sold it at curb auction for $135.00, gave the wholesaler $120.00 and the new notes for a quit-claim on the old ones in Mississippi, and reached home at gathering-time with $2.53 in cash and full title to the twelve twenty-dollar notes which would be paid as the cotton was ginned and sold.

When he reached Frenchman's Bend in November, it had returned to normal. It had acquiesced to the clerk's presence even if it had not accepted him, though the Varners seemed to have done both. Jody had used to be in the store at some time during the day and not far from it at any time. Ratliff now discovered that for months he had been in the habit of sometimes not appearing at all, customers who had traded there for years, mostly serving themselves and putting the correct change into the cigar box inside the cheese cage, now having to deal for each trivial item with a man whose name they had not even heard two months ago, who answered Yes and No to direct questions and who apparently never looked directly or long enough at any face to remember the name which went with it, yet who never made mistakes in any matter pertaining to money. Jody Varner had made them constantly. They were usually in his own favor to be sure, letting a customer get away with a spool of thread or a tin of snuff now and then, but getting it back sooner or later. They had come to expect mistakes of him, just as they knew he would correct them when caught with a bluff, hearty amiability, making a joke of it, which sometimes left the customer wondering just a little about the rest of the bill. But they expected this too, because he would give them credit for food and plow-gear when they needed it, long credit, though they knew they would pay interest for that which on its face looked like generosity and openhandedness, whether that interest showed in the final discharge or not. But the clerk never made mistakes.

"Nonsense," Ratliff said. "Somebody's bound to catch him sooner or later. There aint a man woman or child in twenty-five miles that dont know what's in that store and what it cost as well as Will or Jody Varner either."

"Hah," the other said—a sturdy short-legged black-browed ready-faced man named Odum Bookwright. "That's it."

"You mean aint nobody ever caught him *once* even?"

"No," Bookwright said. "And folks dont like it. Otherwise, how can you tell?"

"Sho," Ratliff said. "How can you?"

"There was that credit business too," another said—a lank man with a bulging dreamy scant-haired head and pale myopic eyes named Quick, who operated a sawmill. He told about it: how they had discovered almost at once that the clerk did not want to credit anyone with anything. He finally flatly refused further credit to a man who had been into and out of the store's debt at least once a year for the last fifteen, and how that afternoon Will Varner himself came galloping up on the old fat grumble-gutted white horse and stormed into the store, shouting loud enough to be heard in the blacksmith shop across the road: "Who in hell's store do you think this is, anyway?"

"Well, we know whose store it is yet, anyway," Ratliff said.

"Or whose store some folks still thinks it is yet," Bookwright said. "Anyhow, he aint moved into Varner's house yet."

Because the clerk now lived in the village. One Saturday morning someone noticed that the saddled mule was not hitched behind the store. The store remained open until ten and later on Saturdays and there was always a crowd about it and several men saw him put out the lamps and lock the door and depart, on foot. And the next morning he who had never been seen in the village between Saturday night and Monday morning appeared at the church, and those who saw him looked at him for an instant in incredulous astonishment. In addition to the gray cloth cap and the gray trousers, he wore not only a clean white shirt but a necktie—a tiny machine-made black bow which snapped together at the back with a metal fastener. It was not two inches long and with the exception of the one which Will Varner himself wore to church it was the only tie in the whole Frenchman's Bend country, and from that Sunday morning until the day he died he wore it or one just like it (it was told of him later, after he had become president of his Jefferson bank, that he had them made for him by the gross)—a tiny viciously depthless cryptically balanced splash like an enigmatic punctuation symbol against the expanse of white shirt which gave him Jody Varner's look of ceremonial hetero-

doxy raised to its tenth power and which postulated to those who had
been present on that day that quality of outrageous overstatement
of physical displacement which the sound of his father's stiff foot
made on the gallery of the store that afternoon in the spring. He
departed on foot; he came to the store the next morning still walking and still wearing the tie. By nightfall the countryside knew that
since the previous Saturday he had boarded and lodged in the home
of a family living about a mile from the store.

Will Varner had long since returned to his old idle busy cheerful
existence—if he had ever left it. The store had not seen him since the
Fourth of July. And now that Jody no longer came in, during the
dead slack days of August while the cotton ripened and there was
nothing for anyone to do, it had actually seemed as if not only the
guiding power but the proprietorial and revenue-deriving as well was
concentrated in that squat reticent figure in the steadily-soiling white
shirts and the minute invulnerable bow, which in those abeyant days
lurked among the ultimate shadows of the deserted and rich-odored
interior with a good deal of the quality of a spider of that bulbous
blond omnivorous though non-poisonous species.

Then in September something happened. It began rather, though
at first they did not recognise it for what it was. The cotton had
opened and was being picked. One morning the first of the men to
arrive found Jody Varner already there. The gin was unlocked and
Trumbull, Varner's blacksmith, and his apprentice and the Negro
fireman were overhauling the machinery, getting it ready for the season's run, and presently Snopes came out of the store and went across
to the gin and entered it and passed from sight and so, for the
moment, from remembering too. It was not until the store closed
that afternoon that they realised that Jody Varner had been inside it
all day. But even then they attached little importance to this. They
thought that without doubt Jody himself had sent the clerk to super-
intend the opening of the gin, which Jody himself had used to do, out
of laziness, assuming himself the temporary onus of tending store
so he could sit down. It took the actual firing-up of the gin and the
arrival of the first loaded wagons to disabuse them. Then they saw
that it was Jody who was now tending store again, fetching and carrying for the nickels and dimes, while the clerk sat all day long on the

stool behind the scale-beam as the wagons moved in turn onto it and so beneath the suction pipe. Jody had used to do both. That is, he was mostly behind the scales, letting the store take care of itself, as it always had, though now and then, just to rest himself, he would keep a wagon standing upon the scales, blocking them for fifteen minutes or even forty-five minutes, while he was in the store; maybe there would not even be any customers during that time, just loungers, listeners for him to talk to. But that was all right. Things got along just as well. And now that there were two of them, there was no reason why one should not remain in the store while the other did the weighing, and there was no reason why Jody should not have designated the weighing to the clerk. The cold surmise which now began to dawn upon them was that—

"Sho," Ratliff said. "I know. That Jody should have stayed there a-tall. Just who it was that told him to stay there." He and Bookwright looked at each other. "It wasn't Uncle Will. That store and that gin had been running themselves at the same time for nigh forty years all right, with just one fellow between them. And a fellow Uncle Will's age aint likely to change his notions. Sho now. All right. Then what?"

They could watch them both from the gallery. They would come in on their laden wagons and draw into line, mule-nose to tail gate, beside the road, waiting for their turn to move onto the scales and then under the suction pipe, and dismount and wrap the reins about a stanchion and cross to the gallery, from which they could watch the still, impenetrable, steadily-chewing face throned behind the scale-beam, the cloth cap, the minute tie, while from within the store they could hear now and then the short surly grunts with which Varner answered when his customers forced him to speak at all. Now and then they would even go in themselves and buy sacks or plugs of tobacco or tins of snuff which they did not actually need yet, or maybe just to drink from the cedar water bucket. Because there was something in Jody's eyes that had not been there before either—a shadow, something between annoyance and speculation and purest foreknowledge, which was not quite bafflement yet but was certainly sober. This was the time they referred to later, two and three years later, when they told one another: "That was when he passed Jody," though it was Ratliff who amended it: "You mean, that was when Jody begun to find it out."

But that was to be sometime in the future yet. Now they just watched, missing nothing. During that month the air was filled from daylight until dark with the whine of the gin; the wagons stood in line for the scales and moved up one by one beneath the suction pipe. Now and then the clerk would cross the road to the store, the cap, the trousers, even the tie wisped with cotton; the men lounging upon the gallery while they waited their turns at the suction pipe or the scales would watch him enter the store now and a moment later hear his voice this time, murmuring, matter-of-fact, succinct. But Jody Varner would not come to the door with him to stand for a moment as before, and they would watch the clerk return to the gin—the thick squat back, shapeless, portentous, without age. After the crops were in and ginned and sold, the time came when Will Varner made his yearly settlement with his tenants and debtors. He had used to do this alone, not even allowing Jody to help him. This year he sat at the desk with the iron cash box while Snopes sat on a nail keg at his knee with the open ledgers. In the tunnel-like room lined with canned food and cluttered with farming implements and now crowded with patient earth-reeking men waiting to accept almost without question whatever Varner should compute he owed them for their year's work, Varner and Snopes resembled the white trader and his native parrot-taught headman in an African outpost.

That headman was acquiring the virtues of civilization fast. It was not known what the Varners paid him, except that Will Varner had never been known to pay very much for anything. Yet this man who five months ago was riding eight miles back and forth to work on a plow mule and a cast-off saddle with a tin pail of cold turnip greens or field pease tied to it, was now not only sleeping in a rented bed and eating from a furnished table like a drummer, he had also made a considerable cash loan, security and interest not specified, to a resident of the village, and before the last of the cotton was ginned it was generally known that any sum between twenty-five cents and ten dollars could be borrowed from him at any time, if the borrower agreed to pay enough for the accommodation. In the next spring Tull, in Jefferson with a drove of cattle for shipping on the railroad, came to see Ratliff, who was sick in bed in the house which he owned and which his widowed sister kept for him, with a recurrent old gall-bladder trouble. Tull told him of a considerable herd of scrub cattle which had passed the winter in pasture on the farm which Snopes's father had rented from the Varners for another year—a herd which, by the time Ratliff had been carried to a Memphis hospital and operated on and returned home and once more took an interest in what went on about him, had increased gradually and steadily and then overnight vanished, its disappearance coincident with the appearance of a herd of good Herefords in a pasture on another place which Varner owned and kept himself as his home farm, as though transmogrified, translated complete and intact save for their altered appearance and obviously greater worth, it only later becoming known that the cattle had reached the pasture via a foreclosed lien nominally held by a Jefferson bank. Bookwright and Tull both came to see him and told him of this.

"Maybe they was in the bank vault all the time," Ratliff said weakly. "Who did Will say they belonged to?"

"He said they was Snopes's," Tull said. "He said, 'Ask that son-of-a-gun of Jody's.' "

"And did you?" Ratliff said.

"Bookwright did. And Snopes said, 'They're in Varner's pasture.' And Bookwright said, 'But Will says they are yourn.' And Snopes turned his head and spit and says, 'They're in Varner's pasture.' "

And Ratliff, ill, did not see this either. He only heard it second hand, though by that time he was mending, well enough to muse upon it, speculate, curious, shrewd, and inscrutable himself, sitting up now in a chair propped with pillows in a window where he could watch the autumn begin, feel the bright winy air of October noons: How one morning in that second spring a man named Houston, heeled by a magnificent grave blue-ticked Walker hound, led a horse up to the blacksmith shop and saw, stooping over the forge and trying to start a fire in it with liquid from a rusty can, a stranger—a young, well-made, muscle-bound man who, turning, revealed an open equable face beginning less than an inch below his hairline, who said, "Howdy. I cant seem to get this here fire started. Every-

time I put this here coal oil onto it, it just goes further out. Watch."
He prepared to pour from the can again.

"Hold on," Houston said. "Is that coal oil you've got?"

"It was setting on that ere ledge yonder," the other said. "It looks
like the kind of a can coal oil would be in. It's a little rusty, but I never
heard tell of even rusty coal oil that wouldn't burn before." Houston came and took the can from him and sniffed it. The other
watched him. The splendid hound sat in the doorway and watched
them both. "It dont smell exactly like coal oil, does it?"

"---t," Houston said. He set the can back on the sooty ledge above
the forge. "Go on. Haul that mud out. You'll have to start over.
Where's Trumbull?" Trumbull was the smith who had been in the
shop for almost twenty years, until this morning.

"I dont know," the other said. "Wasn't nobody here when I come."

"What are you doing here? Did he send you?"

"I dont know," the other said. "It was my cousin hired me. He told
me to be here this morning and get the fire started and tend to the
business till he come. But everytime I put that ere coal oil—"

"Who is your cousin?" Houston said. At that moment a gaunt
aged horse came up rapidly, drawing a battered and clattering buggy
one of whose wheels was wired upright by two crossed slats, which
looked as if its momentum alone held it intact and that the instant it
stopped it would collapse into kindling. It contained another
stranger—a frail man none of whose garments seemed to belong to
him, with a talkative weasel's face—who halted the buggy, shouting
at the horse as if they were a good-sized field apart, and got out of the
buggy and came into the shop, already (or still) talking.

"Morning, morning," he said, his little bright eyes darting. "Want
that horse shod, hey? Good, good: save the hoof and save all. Good-
looking animal. Seen a considerable better one in a field a piece back.
But no matter; love me, love my horse, beggars cant be choosers, if
wishes was horseflesh we'd all own thoroughbreds. What's the matter?" he said to the man in the apron. He paused, though still he
seemed to be in violent motion, as though the attitude and position
of his garments gave no indication whatever of what the body within
them might be doing—indeed, if it were still inside them at all. "Aint

you got that fire started yet? Here." He darted to the ledge; he seemed to translate himself over beneath it without increasing his appearance of violent motion at all, and had taken the can down and sniffed at it and then prepared to empty it onto the coals in the forge before anyone could move. Then Houston intercepted him at the last second and took the can from him and flung it out the door.

"I just finished taking that damn hog piss away from him," Houston said. "What the hell's happened here? Where's Trumbull?"

"Oh, you mean the fellow that used to be here," the newcomer said. "His lease has done been cancelled. I'm leasing the shop now. My name's Snopes. I. O. Snopes. This here's my young cousin, Eck Snopes. But it's the old shop, the old stand; just a new broom in it."

"I dont give a damn what his name is," Houston said. "Can he shoe a horse?" Again the newcomer turned upon the man in the apron, shouting at him as he had shouted at the horse:

"All right. All right. Get that fire started." After watching a moment, Houston took charge and they got the fire going. "He'll pick it up though," the newcomer said. "Just give him time. He's handy with tools, even though he aint done no big sight of active blacksmithing. But give a dog a good name and you dont need to hang him. Give him a few days to practise up and he'll shoe a horse quick as Trumbull or any of them."

"I'll shoe this one," Houston said. "Just let him keep pumping that bellows. He looks like he ought to be able to do that without having to practise." Nevertheless, the shoe shaped and cooled in the tub, the newcomer darted in again. It was as if he took not only Houston but himself too by complete surprise—that weasel-like quality of existing independent of his clothing so that although you could grasp and hold that you could not restrain the body itself from doing what it was doing until the damage had been done—a furious already dissipating concentration of energy vanishing the instant after the intention took shape, the newcomer darting between Houston and the raised hoof and clapping the shoe onto it and touching the animal's quick with the second blow of the hammer on the nail and being hurled, hammer and all, into the shrinking-tub by the plunging horse which Houston and the man in the apron finally backed into a corner and held while Houston jerked nail and shoe free and flung them into the corner and backed the horse savagely out of the shop, the hound rising and resuming its position quietly at proper heeling distance behind the man. "And you can tell Will Varner—if he cares a damn, which evidently he dont," Houston said, "that I have gone to Whiteleaf to have my horse shod."

The shop and the store were just opposite, only the road between. There were several men already on the gallery, who watched Houston, followed by the big quiet regal dog, lead the horse away. They did not even need to cross the road to see one of the strangers, because presently the smaller and older one crossed to the store, in the clothes which would still appear not to belong to him on the day they finally fell off his body, with his talkative pinched face and his bright darting eyes. He mounted the steps, already greeting them. Still talking, he entered the store, his voice voluble and rapid and meaningless like something talking to itself about nothing in a deserted cavern. He came out again, still talking: "Well, gentlemen, off with the old and on with the new. Competition is the life of trade, and though a chain aint no stronger than its weakest link, I dont think you'll find the boy yonder no weak reed to have to lean on once he catches onto it. It's the old shop, the old stand; it's just a new broom in it and maybe you cant teach a old dog new tricks but you can teach a new young willing one anything. Just give him time; a penny on the waters pays interest when the flood turns. Well, well; all pleasure and no work, as the fellow says, might make Jack so sharp he might cut his-self. I bid you good morning, gentlemen." He went on and got into the buggy, still talking, now to the man in the shop and now to the gaunt horse, all in one breath, without any break to indicate to the hearers which he addressed at any time. He drove away, the men on the gallery looking after him, completely expressionless. During the day they crossed to the shop, one by one, and looked at the second stranger—the quiet empty open face which seemed to have been a mere afterthought to the thatching of the skull, like the binding of a rug, harmless. A man brought up a wagon with a broken hound. The new smith even repaired it, though it took him most of the forenoon, working steadily but in a dreamlike state in which what actually lived inside him apparently functioned somewhere else, paying no heed to and having no interest in, not even in the money he would earn, what his hands were doing; busy, thick-moving, getting nowhere seemingly though at last the job was finished. That afternoon Trumbull, the old smith, appeared. But if they had waited about the store to see what would happen when he arrived who until last night anyway must have still believed himself the incumbent, they were disappointed. He drove through the village with his wife, in a wagon loaded with household goods. If he even looked toward his old shop nobody saw him do it—an old man though still hale, morose and efficient, who would have invited no curiosity even before yesterday. They never saw him again.

A few days later they learned that the new smith was living in the house where his cousin (or whatever the relationship was: nobody ever knew for certain) Flem lived, the two of them sleeping together in the same bed. Six months later the smith had married one of the daughters of the family where the two of them boarded. Ten months after that he was pushing a perambulator (once—or still—Will Varner's, like the cousin's saddle) about the village on Sundays, accompanied by a five- or six-year-old boy, his son by a former wife which the village did not know either he had ever possessed—indicating that there was considerably more force and motion to his private life, his sex life anyway, than would appear on the surface of his public one. But that all appeared later. All they saw now was that they had a new blacksmith—a man who was not lazy, whose intentions were good and who was accommodating and unfailingly pleasant and even generous, yet in whom there was a definite limitation of physical co-ordination beyond which design and plan and pattern all vanished, disintegrated into dead components of pieces of wood and iron straps and vain tools.

Two months later Flem Snopes built a new blacksmith shop in the village. He hired it done, to be sure, but he was there most of the day, watching it going up. This was not only the first of his actions in the village which he was ever seen in physical juxtaposition to, but the first which he not only admitted but affirmed, stating calmly and flatly that he was doing it so that people could get decent work done again. He bought completely new equipment at cost price through the store and hired the young farmer who during the slack of planting and harvesting time had been Trumbull's apprentice. Within a month the new shop had got all the trade which Trumbull had had and three months after that Snopes had sold the new shop—smith clientele and goodwill and new equipment—to Varner, receiving in return the old equipment in the old shop, which he sold to a junk man, moved the new equipment to the old shop and sold the new building to a farmer for a cowshed, without even having to pay himself to have it moved, leaving his kinsman now apprentice to the new smith—at which point even Ratliff had lost count of what profit Snopes might have made. But I reckon I can guess the rest of it, he told himself, sitting, a little pale but otherwise well, in his sunny window. He could almost see it—in the store, at night, the door barred on the inside and the lamp burning above the desk where the clerk sat, chewing steadily, while Jody Varner stood over him, in no condition to sit down, with a good deal more in his eyes than had been in them last fall, shaking, trembling, saying in a shaking voice: "I want to make one pure and simple demand of you and I want a pure and simple Yes and No for a answer: How many more is there? How much longer is this going on? Just what is it going to cost me to protect one goddamn barn full of hay?"

2

He had been sick and he showed it as, the buckboard once more with a new machine in the dog-kennel box and the little sturdy team fat and slick with the year's idleness hitched in an adjacent alley, he sat at the counter of a small side-street restaurant in which he owned a sleeping partner's half interest, with a cup of coffee at his hand and in his pocket a contract to sell fifty goats to a Northerner who had recently established a goat-ranch in the western part of the county. It was actually a subcontract which he had purchased at the rate of twenty-five cents a goat from the original contractor who held his from the Northerner at seventy-five cents a goat and was about to fail to complete. Ratliff bought the subcontract because he happened to know of a herd of some fifty-odd goats in a little-travelled section near Frenchman's Bend village which the original contractor had failed to find and which Ratliff was confident he could acquire by offering to halve his profit with the owner of them.

He was on his way to Frenchman's Bend now, though he had not started yet and did not know just when he would start. He had not seen the village in a year now. He was looking forward to his visit not only for the pleasure of the shrewd dealing which far transcended mere gross profit, but with the sheer happiness of being out of bed and moving once more at free will, even though a little weakly, in the sun and air which men drank and moved in and talked and dealt with one another—a pleasure no small part of which lay in the fact that he had not started yet and there was absolutely nothing under heaven to make him start until he wanted to. He did not still feel weak, he was merely luxuriating in that supremely gutful lassitude of convalescence in which time, hurry, doing, did not exist, the accumulating seconds and minutes and hours to which in its well state the body is slave both waking and sleeping, now reversed and time now the lip-server and mendicant to the body's pleasure instead of the body thrall to time's headlong course. So he sat, thin, the fresh clean blue shirt quite loose upon him now, yet looking actually quite well, the smooth brown of his face not pallid but merely a few shades lighter, cleaner-looking; emanating in fact a sort of delicate robustness like some hardy odorless infrequent woodland plant blooming into the actual heel of winter's snow, nursing his coffee cup in one thin hand and telling three or four listeners about his operation in that shrewd humorous voice which would require a good deal more than just illness to other than merely weaken its volume a little, when two men entered. They were Tull and Bookwright. Bookwright had a stock whip rolled about its handle and thrust into the back pocket of his overalls.

"Howdy, boys," Ratliff said. "You're in early."

"You mean late," Bookwright said. He and Tull went to the counter.

"We just got in last night with some cattle to ship today," Tull said. "So you was in Memphis. I thought I'd missed you."

"We all missed him," Bookwright said. "My wife aint mentioned nobody's new sewing machine in almost a year. What was it that Memphis fellow cut outen you anyway?"

"My pocketbook," Ratliff said. "I reckon that's why he put me to sleep first."

"He put you to sleep first to keep you from selling him a sewing machine or a bushel of harrow teeth before he could get his knife open," Bookwright said. The counterman came and slid two plates of bread and butter before them.

"I'll have steak," Tull said.

"I wont," Bookwright said. "I been watching the dripping sterns of steaks for two days now. Let alone running them back out of corn fields and vegetable patches. Bring me some ham and a half a dozen fried eggs." He began to eat the bread, wolfing it. Ratliff turned slightly on his stool to face them.

"So I been missed," he said. "I would a thought you folks would a had so many new citizens in Frenchman's Bend by now you wouldn't a missed a dozen sewing-machine agents. How many kinfolks has Flem Snopes brought in to date? Is it two more, or just three?"

"Four," Bookwright said shortly, eating.

"Four?" Ratliff said. "That's that blacksmith—I mean, the one that uses the blacksmith shop for his address until it's time to go back home and eat again—what's his name? Eck. And that other one, the contractor, the business executive—"

"He's going to be the new school professor next year," Tull said mildly. "Or so they claim."

"No no," Ratliff said. "I'm talking about them Snopeses. That other one. I.O. That Jack Houston throwed into the water tub that day in the blacksmith shop."

"That's him," Tull said. "They claim he's going to teach the school next year. The teacher we had left all of a sudden just after Christmas. I reckon you never heard about that neither."

But Ratliff wasn't listening to this. He wasn't thinking about the other teacher. He stared at Tull, for the moment surprised out of his own humorous poise. "What?" he said. "Teach the school? That fellow? That Snopes? The one that came to the shop that day that Jack Houston— Here, Odum," he said; "I been sick, but sholy it aint affected my ears that much."

Bookwright didn't answer. He had finished his bread; he leaned and took a piece from Tull's plate. "You aint eating it," he said. "I'll tell him to bring some more in a minute."

"Well," Ratliff said. "I'll be damned. By God, I knowed there was something wrong with him soon as I saw him. That was it. He was standing in front of the wrong thing—a blacksmith shop or a plowed field. But teaching the school. I just hadn't imagined that yet. But that's it, of course. He has found the one and only place in the world or Frenchman's Bend either where he not only can use them proverbs of hisn all day long but he will be paid for doing it. Well," he said. "So Will Varner has caught that bear at last. Flem has grazed up the store and he has grazed up the blacksmith shop and now he is starting in on the school. That just leaves Will's house. Of course, after that he will have to fall back on you folks, but that house will keep him occupied for a while because Will—"

"Hah!" Bookwright said shortly. He finished the slice of bread he had taken from Tull's plate and called to the counterman: "Here. Bring me a piece of pie while I'm waiting."

"What kind of pie, Mr Bookwright?" the counterman said.

"Eating pie," Bookwright said.

"—because Will might be a little hard to dislodge outen the actual house," Ratliff went on. "He might even draw the line there altogether. So maybe Flem will have to start in on you folks sooner than he had figured on—"

"Hah," Bookwright said again, harsh and sudden. The counterman slid the pie along to him. Ratliff looked at him.

"All right," Ratliff said. "Hah what?"

Bookwright sat with the wedge of pie poised in his hand before his mouth. He turned his fierce dark face toward Ratliff. "I was sitting on the sawdust pile at Quick's mill last week. His fireman and another nigger were shovelling the chips over toward the boiler, to fire with. They were talking. The fireman wanted to borrow some money, said Quick wouldn't let him have it. 'Go to Mr Snopes at the store,' the other nigger says. 'He will lend it to you. He lent me five dollars over two years ago and all I does, every Saturday night I goes to the store and pays him a dime. He aint even mentioned that five dollars.' " Then he turned his head and bit into the pie, taking a little less than half of it. Ratliff watched him with a faint quizzical expression which was almost smiling.

"Well well well," he said. "So he's working the top and the bottom both at the same time. At that rate it will be a while yet before he has to fall back on you ordinary white folks in the middle." Bookwright took another huge bite of the pie. The counterman brought his and Tull's meal and Bookwright crammed the rest of the pie into his mouth. Tull began to cut his steak neatly into bites as though for a child to eat it. Ratliff watched them. "Aint none of you folks out there done nothing about it?" he said.

"What could we do?" Tull said. "It aint right. But it aint none of our business."

"I believe I would think of something if I lived there," Ratliff said.

"Yes," Bookwright said. He was eating his ham as he had the pie. "And wind up with one of them bow ties in place of your buckboard and team. You'd have room to wear it."

"Sho now," Ratliff said. "Maybe you're right." He stopped looking at them now and raised his spoon, but lowered it again. "This here cup seems to have a draft in it," he said to the counterman. "Maybe you better warm it up a little. It might freeze and bust, and I would have to pay for the cup too." The counterman swept the cup away and refilled it and slid it back. Ratliff spooned sugar into it carefully, his face still wearing that faint expression which would have been called smiling for lack of anything better. Bookwright had mixed his six eggs into one violent mess and was now eating them audibly with a spoon. He and Tull both ate with expedition, though Tull even contrived to do that with almost niggling primness. They did not talk, they just cleaned their plates and rose and went to the cigar case and paid their bills.

"Or maybe them tennis shoes," Bookwright said. "He aint wore them in a year now.—No," he said. "If I was you I would go out there nekkid in the first place. Then you wont notice the cold coming back."

"Sho now," Ratliff said mildly. After they left he drank his coffee again, sipping it without haste, talking again to the three or four listeners, finishing the story of his operation. Then he rose too and paid for his coffee, scrupulously, and put on his overcoat. It was now March but the doctor had told him to wear it, and in the alley now he stood for a while beside the buckboard and the sturdy little horses overfat with idleness and sleek with new hair after their winter coats, looking quietly at the dog-kennel box where, beneath the cracked paint of their fading and incredible roses, the women's faces smiled at him in fixed and sightless invitation. It would need painting again this year; he must see to that. It will have to be something that will burn, he thought. And in his name. Known to be in his name. Yes, he thought, if my name was Will Varner and my partner's name was Snopes I believe I would insist that some part of our partnership at least, that part of it that will burn anyway, would be in his name. He walked on slowly, buttoned into the overcoat. It was the only one in sight. But then the sick grow well fast in the sun; perhaps when he returned to town he would no longer need it. And soon he would not need the sweater beneath it either—May and June, the summer, the long good days of heat. He walked on, looking exactly as he always had save for the thinness and the pallor, pausing twice to tell two different people that yes, he felt all right now, the Memphis doctor had evidently cut the right thing out whether by accident or design, crossing the Square now beneath the shaded marble gaze of the Confederate soldier, and so into the courthouse and the Chancery Clerk's office, where he found what he sought—some two hundred acres of land, with buildings, recorded to Flem Snopes.

Toward the end of the afternoon he was sitting in the halted buckboard in a narrow back road in the hills, reading the name on a mailbox. The post it sat on was new, but the box was not. It was battered and scarred; at one time it had apparently been crushed flat as though by a wagon wheel and straightened again, but the crude lettering of the name might have been painted on it yesterday. It seemed to shout at him, all capitals, MINKSNOPES, sprawling, without any spacing between the two words, trailing off and uphill and over the curve of the top to include the final letters. Ratliff turned in beside it—a rutted lane now, at the end of it a broken-backed cabin of the same two rooms which were scattered without number through these remote hill sections which he travelled. It was built on a hill; below it was a foul muck-trodden lot and a barn leaning away downhill as though a human breath might flatten it. A man was emerging from it, carrying a milk pail, and then Ratliff knew that he was being watched from the house itself though he had seen no one. He pulled the team up. He did not get down. "Howdy," he said. "This Mr Snopes? I brought your machine."

"Brought my what?" the man in the lot said. He came through the gate and set the pail on the end of the sagging gallery. He was slightly less than medium height also but thin, with a single line of heavy eyebrow. But it's the same eyes, Ratliff thought.

"Your sewing machine," he said pleasantly. Then he saw from the corner of his eye a woman standing on the gallery—a big-boned hard-faced woman with incredible yellow hair, who had emerged with a good deal more lightness and quickness than the fact that she was barefoot would have presaged. Behind her were two towheaded children. But Ratliff did not look at her. He watched the man, his expression bland courteous and pleasant.

"What's that?" the woman said. "A sewing machine?"

"No," the man said. He didn't look at her either. He was approaching the buckboard. "Get on back in the house." The woman paid no attention to him. She came down from the gallery, moving again with that speed and co-ordination which her size belied. She stared at Ratliff with pale hard eyes.

"Who told you to bring it here?" she said.

Now Ratliff looked at her, still bland, still pleasant. "Have I done made a mistake?" he said. "The message come to me in Jefferson, from Frenchman's Bend. It said Snopes. I taken it to mean you, because if your . . . cousin?" Neither of them spoke, staring at him. "Flem. If Flem had wanted it, he would have waited till I got there. He knowed I was due there tomorrow. I reckon I ought to made sho." The woman laughed harshly, without mirth.

"Then take it on to him. If Flem Snopes sent you word about anything that cost more than a nickel it wasn't to give away. Not to his kinfolks anyhow. Take it on to the Bend."

"I told you to go in the house," the man said. "Go on." The woman didn't look at him. She laughed harshly and steadily, staring at Ratliff.

"Not to give away," she said. "Not the man that owns a hundred

head of cattle and a barn and pasture to feed them in his own name."
The man turned and walked toward her. She turned and began to
scream at him, the two children watching Ratliff quietly from behind
her skirts as if they were deaf or as if they lived in another world from
that in which the woman screamed, like two dogs might. "Deny it if
you can!" she cried at the man. "He'd let you rot and die right here
and glad of it, and you know it! Your own kin you're so proud of
because he works in a store and wears a necktie all day! Ask him to
give you a sack of flour even and see what you get. Ask him! Maybe
he'll give you one of his old neckties someday so you can dress like
a Snopes too!" The man walked steadily toward her. He did not even
speak again. He was the smaller of the two of them; he walked
steadily toward her with a curious sidling deadly, almost deferential,
air until she broke, turned swiftly and went back toward the house,
the herded children before her still watching Ratliff over their shoulders. The man approached the buckboard.

"You say the message came from Flem?" he said.

"I said it come from Frenchman's Bend," Ratliff said. "The name
mentioned was Snopes."

"Who was it seems to done all this mentioning about Snopes?"

"A friend," Ratliff said pleasantly. "He seems to made a mistake. I
ask you to excuse it. Can I follow this lane over to the Whiteleaf
Bridge road?"

"If Flem sent you word to leave it here, suppose you leave it."

"I just told you I thought I had made a mistake and ask you to
excuse it," Ratliff said. "Does this lane—"

"I see," the other said. "That means you aim to have a little cash
down. How much?"

"You mean on the machine?"

"What do you think I am talking about?"

"Ten dollars," Ratliff said. "A note for twenty more in six months.
That's gathering-time."

"Ten dollars? With the message you got from—"

"We aint talking about messages now," Ratliff said. "We're talking
about a sewing machine."

"Make it five."

"No," Ratliff said pleasantly.

"All right," the other said, turning. "Fix up your note." He went back to the house. Ratliff got out and went to the rear of the buckboard and opened the dog kennel's door and drew from beneath the new machine a tin dispatch box. It contained a pen, a carefully corked ink bottle, a pad of note forms. He was filling in the note when Snopes returned, reappeared at his side. As soon as Ratliff's pen stopped Snopes slid the note toward himself and took the pen from Ratliff's hand and dipped it and signed the note, all in one continuous motion, without even reading it, and shoved the note back to Ratliff and took something from his pocket which Ratliff did not look at yet because he was looking at the signed note, his face perfectly expressionless. He said quietly,

"This is Flem Snopes's name you have signed."

"All right," the other said. "Then what?" Ratliff looked at him. "I see. You want my name on it too, so one of us anyway cant deny it has been signed. All right." He took the note and wrote again on it and passed it back. "And here's your ten dollars. Give me a hand with the machine." But Ratliff did not move again, because it was not money but another paper which the other had given him, folded, dog-eared and soiled. Opened, it was another note. It was dated a little more than three years ago, for ten dollars with interest, payable on demand one year after date of execution, to *Isaac Snopes or bearer*, and signed *Flem Snopes*. It was indorsed on the back (and Ratliff recognised the same hand which had just signed the two names to the first note) to *Mink Snopes*, by *Isaac Snopes (X) his mark*, and beneath that and still in the same hand and blotted (or dried at least), to *V. K. Ratliff*, by *Mink Snopes*, and Ratliff looked at it quite quietly and quite soberly for almost a minute. "All right," the other said. "Me and Flem are his cousins. Our grandma left us all three ten dollars a piece. We were to get it when the least of us—that was him—come twenty-one. Flem needed some cash and he borrowed his from him on this note. Then he needed some cash a while back and I bought Flem's note from him. Now if you want to know what color his eyes are or anything else, you can see for yourself when you get to Frenchman's Bend. He's living there now with Flem."

"I see," Ratliff said. "Isaac Snopes. He's twenty-one, you say?"

"How could he have got that ten dollars to lend Flem if he hadn't been?"

"Sho," Ratliff said. "Only this here aint just exactly a cash ten dollars—"

"Listen," the other said. "I dont know what you are up to and I dont care. But you aint fooling me any more than I am fooling you. If you were not satisfied Flem is going to pay that first note, you wouldn't have taken it. And if you aint afraid of that one, why are you afraid of this one, for less money, on the same machine, when this one has been collectible by law for more than two years? You take these notes on to him down yonder. Just hand them to him. Then you give him a message from me. Say 'From one cousin that's still scratching dirt to keep alive, to another cousin that's risen from scratching dirt to owning a herd of cattle and a hay barn. To owning cattle and a hay barn.' Just say that to him. Better keep on saying it over to yourself on the way down there so you will be sure not to forget it."

"You dont need to worry," Ratliff said. "Does this road lead over to Whiteleaf Bridge?"

He spent that night in the home of kin people (he had been born and raised not far away) and reached Frenchman's Bend the next afternoon and turned his team into Mrs Littlejohn's lot and walked down to the store, on the gallery of which apparently the same men who had been there when he saw it last a year ago were still sitting, including Bookwright. "Well, boys," he said. "A quorum as usual, I see."

"Bookwright says it was your pocketbook that Memphis fellow cut outen you," one said. "No wonder it taken you a year to get over it. I'm just surprised you didn't die when you reached back and found it gone."

"That's when I got up," Ratliff said. "Otherwise I'd a been laying there yet." He entered the store. The front of it was empty but he did not pause, not even long enough for his contracted pupils to have adjusted themselves to the obscurity, as he might have been expected to. He went on to the counter, saying pleasantly, "Howdy, Jody. Howdy, Flem. Dont bother; I'll get it myself." Varner, standing beside the desk at which the clerk sat, looked up.

"So you got well, hah," he said.

"I got busy," Ratliff said, going behind the counter and opening the store's single glassed-in case which contained a jumble of shoe-strings and combs and tobacco and patent medicines and cheap candy. "Maybe that's the same thing." He began to choose sticks of the striped gaudy candy with care, choosing and rejecting. He did not once look toward the rear of the store, where the clerk at the desk had never looked up at all. "You know if Uncle Ben Quick is at home or not?"

"Where would he be?" Varner said. "Only I thought you sold him a sewing machine two-three years back."

"Sho," Ratliff said, rejecting a stick of candy and substituting another one for it. "That's why I want him to be at home: so his folks can look after him when he faints. I'm going to buy something from him this time."

"What in thunder has he got you had to come all the way out here to buy?"

"A goat," Ratliff said. He was counting the candy sticks into a sack now.

"A what?"

"Sho," Ratliff said. "You wouldn't think it, would you? But there aint another goat in Yoknapatawpha and Grenier County both except them of Uncle Ben's."

"No I wouldn't," Varner said. "But what's curiouser than that is what you want with it."

"What does a fellow want with a goat?" Ratliff said. He moved to the cheese cage and put a coin into the cigar box. "To pull a wagon with. You and Uncle Will and Miss Maggie all well, I hope."

"Ah-h-h!" Varner said. He turned back to the desk. But Ratliff had not paused to see him do it. He returned to the gallery, offering his candy about.

"Doctor's orders," he said. "He'll probably send me another bill now for ten cents for advising me to eat a nickel's worth of candy. I dont mind that though. What I mind is the order he give me to spend so much time setting down." He looked now, pleasant and quizzical, at the men sitting on the bench. It was fastened against the wall, directly beneath one of the windows which flanked the door, a little longer than the window was wide. After a moment a man on one end of the bench rose.

"All right," he said. "Come on and set down. Even if you wasn't sick you will probably spend the next six months pretending like you was."

"I reckon I got to get something outen that seventy-five dollars it cost me," Ratliff said. "Even if it aint no more than imposing on folks for a while. Only you are fixing to leave me setting in a draft. You folks move down and let me set in the middle." They moved and made room for him in the middle of the bench. He sat now directly before the open window. He took a stick of his candy himself and began to suck it, speaking in the weak thin penetrating voice of recent illness: "Yes sir. I'd a been in that bed yet if I hadn't a found that pocketbook gone. But it wasn't till I got up that I got sho enough scared. I says to myself, here I been laying on my back for a year now and I bet some enterprising fellow has done come in and flooded not only Frenchman's Bend but all Yoknapatawpha County too with new sewing machines. But the Lord was watching out for me. I be dog if I had hardly got outen bed before Him or somebody had done sent me a sheep just like He done to save Isaac in the Book. He sent me a goat-rancher."

"A what?" one said.

"A goat-rancher. You never heard of a goat-rancher. Because wouldn't nobody in this country think of it. It would take a Northerner to do that. This here one thought of it away up yonder in Massachusetts or Boston or Ohio and here he come all the way down to Mississippi with his hand grip bulging with greenback money and bought him up two thousand acres of as fine a hill-gully and rabbit-grass land as ever stood on one edge about fifteen miles west of Jefferson and built him a ten-foot practically waterproof fence around it and was just getting ready to start getting rich, when he run out of goats."

"Shucks," another said. "Never nobody in the world ever run out of goats."

"Besides," Bookwright said, suddenly and harshly, "if you want to tell them folks at the blacksmith shop about it too, why dont we all just move over there."

"Sho now," Ratliff said. "You fellows dont know how good a man's voice feels running betwixt his teeth until you have been on your back where folks that didn't want to listen could get up and go away and you couldn't follow them." Nevertheless he did lower his voice a little, thin, clear, anecdotal, unhurried: "This one did. You got to keep in mind he is a Northerner. They does things different from us. If a fellow in this country was to set up a goat-ranch, he would do it purely and simply because he had too many goats already. He would just declare his roof or his front porch or his parlor or wherever it was he couldn't keep the goats out of a goat-ranch and let it go at that. But a Northerner dont do it that way. When he does something, he does it with a organised syndicate and a book of printed rules and a gold-filled diploma from the Secretary of State at Jackson saying for all men to know by these presents, greeting, that them twenty thousand goats or whatever it is, is goats. He dont start off with goats or a piece of land either. He starts off with a piece of paper and a pencil and measures it all down setting in the library—so many goats to so many acres and so much fence to hold them. Then he writes off to Jackson and gets his diploma for that much land and fence and goats and he buys the land first so he can have something to build the fence on, and he builds the fence around it so nothing cant get outen it, and then he goes out to buy some things not to get outen the fence. So everything was going just fine at first. He picked out land that even the Lord hadn't never thought about starting a goat-ranch on and bought it without hardly no trouble at all except finding the folks it belonged to and making them understand it was actual money he was trying to give them, and that fence practically taken care of itself because he could set in one place in the middle of it and pay out the money for it. And then he found he had done run out of goats. He combed this country up and down and backwards and forwards to find the right number of goats to keep that gold diploma from telling him to his face he was lying. But he couldn't do it. In spite of all he could do, he still lacked fifty goats to take care of the rest of that fence. So now it aint a goat-ranch; it's a insolvency. He's either got to send that diploma back, or get them fifty goats from somewhere. So here he is, done come all the way down here from Boston, Maine, and paid for two thousand acres of

land and built forty-four thousand feet of fence around it, and now
the whole blame pro-jeck is hung up on that passel of goats of Uncle
Ben Quick's because they aint another goat betwixt Jackson and the
Tennessee line apparently."

"How do you know?" one said.

"Do you reckon I'd a got up outen bed and come all the way out
here if I hadn't?" Ratliff said.

"Then you better get in that buckboard right now and go and
make yourself sure," Bookwright said. He was sitting against a
gallery post, facing the window at Ratliff's back. Ratliff looked at him
for a moment, pleasant and inscrutable behind his faint constant
humorous mask.

"Sho," he said. "He's had them goats a good while now. I reckon
he'll be still telling me I cant do this and must do that for the next
six months, not to mention sending me bills for it"—changing the
subject so smoothly and completely that, as they realised later, it was
as if he had suddenly produced a signboard with Hush in red letters
on it, glancing easily and pleasantly upward as Varner and Snopes
came out. Snopes did not speak. He went on across the gallery and
descended the steps. Varner locked the door. "Aint you closing early,
Jody?" Ratliff said.

"That depends on what you call late," Varner said shortly. He
went on after the clerk.

"Maybe it is getting toward supper time," Ratliff said.

"Then if I was you I'd go eat it and then go and buy my goats,"
Bookwright said.

"Sho now," Ratliff said. "Uncle Ben might have a extra dozen or
so by tomorrow. Howsomedever—" He rose and buttoned the overcoat about him.

"Go buy your goats first," Bookwright said. Again Ratliff looked
at him, pleasant, impenetrable. He looked at the others. None of
them were looking at him.

"I figure I can wait," he said. "Any of you fellows eating at Mrs
Littlejohn's?" Then he said, "What's that?" and the others saw what
he was looking at—the figure of a grown man but barefoot and in
scant faded overalls which would have been about right for a fourteen-year-old boy, passing in the road below the gallery, dragging

behind him on a string a wooden block with two snuff tins attached to its upper side, watching over his shoulder with complete absorption the dust it raised. As he passed the gallery he looked up and Ratliff saw the face too—the pale eyes which seemed to have no vision in them at all, the open drooling mouth encircled by a light fuzz of golden virgin beard.

"Another one of them," Bookwright said, in that harsh short voice. Ratliff watched the creature as it went on—the thick thighs about to burst from the overalls, the mowing head turned backward over its shoulder, watching the dragging block.

"And yet they tell us we was all made in His image," Ratliff said.

"From some of the things I see here and there, maybe he was," Bookwright said.

"I dont know as I would believe that, even if I knowed it was true," Ratliff said. "You mean he just showed up here one day?"

"Why not?" Bookwright said. "He aint the first."

"Sho," Ratliff said. "He would have to be somewhere." The creature, opposite Mrs Littlejohn's now, turned in the gate.

"He sleeps in her barn," another said. "She feeds him. He does some work. She can talk to him somehow."

"Maybe she's the one that was then," Ratliff said. He turned; he still held the end of the stick of candy. He put it into his mouth and wiped his fingers on the skirt of his overcoat. "Well, how about supper?"

"Go buy your goats," Bookwright said. "Wait till after that to do your eating."

"I'll go tomorrow," Ratliff said. "Maybe by then Uncle Ben will have another fifty of them even." Or maybe the day after tomorrow, he thought, walking on toward the brazen sound of Mrs Littlejohn's supper-bell in the winy chill of the March evening. So he will have plenty of time. Because I believe I done it right. I had to trade not only on what I think he knows about me, but on what he must figure I know about him, as conditioned and restricted by that year of sickness and abstinence from the science and pastime of skullduggery. But it worked with Bookwright. He done all he could to warn me. He went as far and even further than a man can let hisself go in another man's trade.

So tomorrow he not only did not go to see the goat-owner, he drove six miles in the opposite direction and spent the day trying to sell a sewing machine he did not even have with him. He spent the night there and did not reach the village until midmorning of the second day, halting the buckboard before the store, to one of the gallery posts of which Varner's roan horse was tied. So he's even riding the horse now, he thought. Well well well. He did not get out of the buckboard. "One of you fellows mind handing me a nickel's worth of candy?" he said. "I might have to bribe Uncle Ben through one of his grandchillen." One of the men entered the store and fetched out the candy. "I'll be back for dinner," he said. "Then I'll be ready for another needy young doc to cut at again."

His destination was not far: a little under a mile to the river bridge, a little more than a mile beyond it. He drove up to a neat well-kept house with a big barn and pasture beyond it; he saw the goats. A hale burly old man was sitting in his stocking feet on the veranda, who roared, "Howdy, V. K. What in thunder are you fellows up to over at Varner's?"

Ratliff did not get out of the buckboard. "So he beat me," he said.

"Fifty goats," the other roared. "I've heard of a man paying a dime to get shut of two or three, but I never in my life heard of a man buying fifty."

"He's smart," Ratliff said. "If he bought fifty of anything he knowed beforehand he was going to need exactly that many."

"Yes, he's smart. But fifty goats. Hell and sulphur. I still got a passel left, bout one hen-house full, say. You want them?"

"No," Ratliff said. "It was just them first fifty."

"I'll give them to you. I'll even pay you a quarter to get the balance of them outen my pasture."

"I thank you," Ratliff said. "Well, I'll just charge this to social overhead."

"Fifty goats," the other said. "Stay and eat dinner."

"I thank you," Ratliff said. "I seem to done already wasted too much time eating now. Or sitting down doing something, anyway." So he returned to the village—that long mile then the short one, the small sturdy team trotting briskly and without synchronization. The roan horse still stood before the store and the men still sat and squatted about the gallery, but Ratliff did not stop. He went on to Mrs Littlejohn's and tied his team to the fence and went and sat on the veranda, where he could see the store. He could smell food cooking in the kitchen behind him and soon the men on the store's gallery began to rise and disperse, noonward, though the saddled roan still stood there. Yes, he thought, He has passed Jody. A man takes your wife and all you got to do to ease your feelings is to shoot him. But your horse.

Mrs Littlejohn spoke behind him: "I didn't know you were back. You going to want some dinner, aint you?"

"Yessum," he said. "I want to step down to the store first. But I wont be long." She went back into the house. He took the two notes from his wallet and separated them, putting one into his inside coat pocket, the other into the breast pocket of his shirt, and walked down the road in the March noon, treading the noon-impacted dust, breathing the unbreathing suspension of the meridian, and mounted the steps and crossed the now deserted gallery stained with tobacco and scarred with knives. The store, the interior, was like a cave, dim, cool, smelling of cheese and leather; it needed a moment for his eyes to adjust themselves. Then he saw the gray cap, the white shirt, the minute bow tie. The face looked up at him, chewing. "You beat me," Ratliff said. "How much?" The other turned his head and spat into the sand-filled box beneath the cold stove.

"Fifty cents," he said.

"I paid twenty-five for my contract," Ratliff said. "All I aim to get is seventy-five. I could tear the contract up and save hauling them to town."

"All right," Snopes said. "What'll you give?"

"I'll trade you this for them," Ratliff said. He drew the first note from the pocket where he had segregated it. And he saw it—an instant, a second of a new and completer stillness and immobility touch the blank face, the squat soft figure in the chair behind the desk. For that instant even the jaw had stopped chewing, though it began again almost at once. Snopes took the paper and looked at it. Then he laid it on the desk and turned his head and spat into the sand-box.

"You figure this note is worth fifty goats," he said. It was not a question, it was a statement.

"Yes," Ratliff said. "Because there is a message goes with it. Do you want to hear it?"

The other looked at him, chewing. Otherwise he didn't move, he didn't even seem to breathe. After a moment he said, "No." He rose, without haste. "All right," he said. He took his wallet from his hip and extracted a folded paper and gave it to Ratliff. It was Quick's bill-of-sale for the fifty goats. "Got a match?" Snopes said. "I dont smoke." Ratliff gave him the match and watched him set fire to the note and hold it, blazing, then drop it still blazing into the sand-box and then crush the carbon to dust with his toe. Then he looked up; Ratliff had not moved. And now just for another instant Ratliff believed he saw the jaw stop. "Well?" Snopes said. "What?" Ratliff drew the second note from his pocket. And then he knew that the jaw had stopped chewing. It did not move at all during the full minute while the broad impenetrable face hung suspended like a balloon above the soiled dog-eared paper, front back then front again. The face looked at Ratliff again with no sign of life in it, not even breathing, as if the body which belonged to it had learned somehow to use over and over again its own suspirations. "You want to collect this too," he said. He handed the note back to Ratliff. "Wait here," he said. He crossed the room to the rear door and went out. What, Ratliff thought. He followed. The squat reluctant figure was going on, in the sunlight now, toward the fence to the livery lot. There was a gate in it. Ratliff watched Snopes pass through the gate and go on across the lot, toward the barn. Then something black blew in him, a suffocation, a sickness, nausea. They should have told me! he cried to himself. Somebody should have told me! Then, remembering: Why, he did! Bookwright did tell me. He said Another one. It was because I have been sick, was slowed up, that I didn't— He was back beside the desk now. He believed he could hear the dragging block long before he knew it was possible, though presently he did hear it as Snopes entered and turned, moving aside, the block thumping against the wooden step and the sill, the hulking figure in the bursting overalls blotting the door, still looking back over its shoulder, entering, the block thumping and scraping across the floor until it caught and lodged behind the counter leg where a three-year-old child would have stooped and lifted it clear though the idiot himself merely stood jerking fruitlessly at the string and beginning a wet whimpering moaning at once pettish and concerned and terrified and amazed until Snopes kicked the block free with his toe. They came on to the desk where Ratliff stood—the mowing and bobbing head, the eyes which at some instant, some second once, had opened upon, been vouchsafed a glimpse of, the Gorgon-face of that primal injustice which man was not intended to look at face to face and had been blasted empty and clean forever of any thought, the slobbering mouth in its mist of soft gold hair. "Say what your name is," Snopes said. The creature looked at Ratliff, bobbing steadily, drooling. "Say it," Snopes said, quite patiently. "Your name."

"Ike H-mope," the idiot said hoarsely.

"Say it again."

"Ike H-mope." Then he began to laugh, though almost at once it stopped being laughing and Ratliff knew that it had never been laughing, cachinnant, sobbing, already beyond the creature's power to stop it, galloping headlong and dragging breath behind it like something still alive at the galloping heels of a cossack holiday, the eyes above the round mouth fixed and sightless.

"Hush," Snopes said. "Hush." At last he took the idiot by the shoulder, shaking him until the sound began to fall, bubbling and gurgling away. Snopes led him toward the door, pushing him on ahead, the other moving obediently, looking backward over his shoulder at the block with its two raked snuff tins dragging at the end of the filthy string, the block about to lodge again behind the same counter leg though this time Snopes kicked it free before it stopped. The hulking shape—the backlooking face with its hanging mouth and pointed faun's ears, the bursting overalls drawn across the incredible female thighs—blotted the door again and was gone. Snopes closed the door and returned to the desk. He spat again into the sand-box. "That was Isaac Snopes," he said. "I'm his guardian. Do you want to see the papers?"

Ratliff didn't answer. He looked down at the note where he had laid it on the desk when he returned from the door, with that same faint, quizzical, quiet expression which his face had worn when he looked at his coffee cup in the restaurant four days ago. He took up the note, though he did not look at Snopes yet. "So if I pay him his ten dollars myself, you will take charge of it as his guardian. And if I collect the ten dollars from you, you will have the note to sell again. And that will make three times it has been collected. Well well well." He took another match from his pocket and extended it and the note to Snopes. "I hear tell you said once you never set fire to a piece of money. This here's your chance to see what it feels like." He watched the second note burn too and drift, still blazing, onto the stained sand in the box, curling into carbon which vanished in its turn beneath the shoe.

He descended the steps, again into the blaze of noon upon the pocked quiet dust of the road; actually it was not ten minutes later. Only thank God men have done learned how to forget quick what they aint brave enough to try to cure, he told himself, walking on. The empty road shimmered with mirage, the pollen-roiled chiaroscuro of spring. Yes, he thought, I reckon I was sicker than I knowed. Because I missed it, missed it clean. Or maybe when I have et I will feel better. Yet, alone in the dining room where Mrs Littlejohn had set a plate for him, he could not eat. He could feel what he had thought was appetite ebbing with each mouthful becoming heavy and tasteless as dirt. So at last he pushed the plate aside and onto the table he counted the five dollars profit he had made—the thirty-seven-fifty he would get for the goats, less the twelve-fifty his contract had cost him, plus the twenty of the first note. With a chewed pencil stub he calculated the three years' interest on the ten-dollar note, plus the principal (that ten dollars would have been his commission on the machine, so it was no actual loss anyway) and added to the five dollars the other bills and coins—the frayed banknotes, the worn coins, the ultimate pennies. Mrs Littlejohn was in the kitchen, where she cooked what meals she sold and washed the dishes too, as well as caring for the rooms in which they slept who ate them. He put the money on the table beside the sink. "That what's-his-name, Ike. Isaac. They tell me you feed him some. He dont need money. But maybe——"

"Yes," she said. She dried her hands on her apron and took the money and folded the bills carefully about the silver and stood holding it. She didn't count it. "I'll keep it for him. Dont you worry. You going on to town now?"

"Yes," he said. "I got to get busy. No telling when I will run into another starving and eager young fellow that aint got no way to get money but to cut meat for it." He turned, then paused again, not quite looking back at her, with that faint quizzical expression on his face that was smiling now, sardonic, humorous. "I got a message I would like to get to Will Varner. But it dont matter especially."

"I'll give it to him," Mrs Littlejohn said. "If it aint too long I will remember it."

"It dont matter," Ratliff said. "But if you happen to think of it. Just tell him Ratliff says it aint been proved yet neither. He'll know what it means."

"I'll try to remember it," she said.

He went out to the buckboard and got into it. He would not need the overcoat now, and next time he would not even have to bring it along. The road began to flow beneath the flickering hooves of the small hickory-tough horses. I just never went far enough, he thought. I quit too soon. I went as far as one Snopes will set fire to another Snopes's barn and both Snopeses know it, and that was all right. But I stopped there. I never went on to where that first Snopes will turn around and stomp the fire out so he can sue that second Snopes for the reward and both Snopeses know that too.

3

Those who watched the clerk now saw, not the petty dispossession of a blacksmith, but the usurpation of an heirship. At the next harvest the clerk not only presided at the gin scales but when the yearly settling of accounts between Varner and his tenants and debtors occurred, Will Varner himself was not even present. It was Snopes who did what Varner had never even permitted his son to do—sat alone at the desk with the cash from the sold crops and the account-books before him and cast up the accounts and charged them off and apportioned to each tenant his share of the remaining money, one or two of them challenging his figures as they had when he first entered the store, on principle perhaps, the clerk not even listening, just waiting in his soiled white shirt and the minute tie, with his steady thrusting tobacco and his opaque still eyes which they never knew whether or not were looking at them, until they would finish, cease; then, without speaking a word, taking pencil and paper and proving to them that they were wrong. Now it was not Jody Varner who would come leisurely to the store and give the clerk directions and instructions and leave him to carry them out; it was the ex-clerk who would enter the store, mounting the steps and jerking his head at the men on the gallery exactly as Will Varner himself would do, and enter the store, from which presently the sound of his voice would come, speaking with matter-of-fact succinctness to the bull-goaded bafflement of the man who once had been his employer and who still seemed not to know just exactly what had happened to him. Then Snopes would depart, to be seen no more that day, for Will Varner's old fat white horse had a companion now. It was the roan which Jody had used to ride, the white and the roan now tied side by side to the same fence while Varner and Snopes examined fields of cotton and corn or herds of cattle or land boundaries, Varner cheerful as a cricket and shrewd and bowel-less as a tax-collector, idle and busy and Rabelaisian; the other chewing his steady tobacco, his hands in the pockets of the disreputable bagging gray trousers, spitting now and then his contemplative bullet-like globules of chocolate saliva. One morning he came to the village carrying a brand-new straw suitcase. That evening he carried it up to Varner's house. A month after that Varner bought a new runabout buggy with bright red wheels and a fringed parasol top, which, the fat white horse and the big roan in new brass-studded harness and the wheels glinting in vermilion and spokeless blurs, swept all day long along back country roads and lanes while Varner and Snopes sat side by side in outrageous paradox above a spurting cloud of light dust, in a speeding aura of constant and invincible excursion. And one afternoon in that same summer Ratliff again drove up to the store, on the gallery of which was a face which he did not recognise for a moment because he had only seen it once before and that two years ago, though only for a moment for almost at once he said, "Howdy. Machine still running good?" and sat looking with an expression quite pleasant and

absolutely impenetrable at the fierce intractable face with its single
eyebrow, thinking *Fox? cat? oh yes, mink.*

"Howdy," the other said. "Why not? Aint you the one that claims
not to sell no other kind?"

"Sholy," Ratliff said, still quite pleasant, impenetrable. He got out
of the buckboard and tied it to a gallery post and mounted the steps
and stood among the four men who sat and squatted about the
gallery. "Only it aint quite that, I would put it. I would say, folks
named Snopes dont buy no other kind." Then he heard the horse
and turned his head and saw it, coming up fast, the fine hound running easily and strongly beside it as Houston pulled up, already dismounting, and dropped the loose reins over its head as a Western
rider does and mounted the steps and stopped before the post against
which Mink Snopes squatted.

"I reckon you know where that yearling is," Houston said.

"I can guess," Snopes said.

"All right," Houston said. He was not shaking, trembling, any
more than a stick of dynamite does. He didn't even raise his voice.
"I warned you. You know the law in this country. A man must keep
his stock up after ground's planted, or take the consequences."

"I would have expected you to have fences that would keep a yearling up," Snopes said. Then they cursed each other, hard and brief
and without emphasis, like blows or pistol-shots, both speaking at
the same time and neither moving, the one still standing in the middle of the steps, the other still squatting against the gallery post. "Try
a shotgun," Snopes said. "That might keep it up." Then Houston
went on into the store and those on the gallery stood or squatted quietly, the man with his single eyebrow no less quiet than any, until
Houston came out again and passed without looking at any of them
and mounted and galloped off, the hound following again, strong,
high-headed, indefatigable, and after another moment or so Snopes
rose too and went up the road on foot. Then one leaned and spat
carefully over the gallery-edge, into the dust, and Ratliff said,

"I dont quite understand about that fence. I gathered it was
Snopes's yearling in Houston's field."

"It was," the man who had spat said. "He lives on a piece of what used to be Houston's land. It belongs to Will Varner now. That is, Varner foreclosed on it about a year ago."

"That is, it was Will Varner Houston owed the money to," a second said. "It was the fences on that he was talking about."

"I see," Ratliff said. "Just conversational remarks. Unnecessary."

"It wasn't losing the land that seems to rile Houston," a third said. "Not that he dont rile easy."

"I see," Ratliff said again. "It's what seems to happened to it since. Or who it seems Uncle Will has rented it to. So Flem's got some more cousins still. Only this here seems to be a different kind of Snopes like a cotton-mouth is a different kind of snake." So that wasn't the last time this one is going to make his cousin trouble, he thought. But he did not say it, he just said, absolutely pleasant, easy, inscrutable: "I wonder where Uncle Will and his partner would be about now. I aint learned the route good yet like you folks."

"I passed them two horses and the buggy tied to the Old French-man fence this morning," the fourth man said. He too leaned and spat carefully over the gallery-edge. Then he added, as if in trivial after-thought: "It was Flem Snopes that was setting in the flour barrel."

BOOK TWO

EULA

CHAPTER ONE

$\mathcal{W}$hen Flem Snopes came to clerk in her father's store, Eula Varner was not quite thirteen. She was the last of the sixteen children, the baby, though she had overtaken and passed her mother in height in her tenth year. Now, though not yet thirteen years old, she was already bigger than most grown women and even her breasts were no longer the little, hard, fiercely-pointed cones of puberty or even maidenhood. On the contrary, her entire appearance suggested some symbology out of the old Dionysic times—honey in sunlight and bursting grapes, the writhen bleeding of the crushed fecundated vine beneath the hard rapacious trampling goat-hoof. She seemed to be not a living integer of her contemporary scene, but rather to exist in a teeming vacuum in which her days followed one another as though behind sound-proof glass, where she seemed to listen in sullen bemusement, with a weary wisdom heired of all mammalian maturity, to the enlarging of her own organs.

Like her father, she was incorrigibly lazy, though what was in him a constant bustling cheerful idleness was in her an actual force impregnable and even ruthless. She simply did not move at all of her own volition, save to and from the table and to and from bed. She was late in learning to walk. She had the first and only perambulator the countryside had ever seen, a clumsy expensive thing almost as large as a dog-cart. She remained in it long after she had grown too large to straighten her legs out. When she reached the stage where it almost took the strength of a grown man to lift her out of it, she was graduated from it by force. Then she began to sit in chairs. It was not that she insisted upon being carried when she went anywhere. It was rather as though, even in infancy, she already knew there was nowhere she wanted to go, nothing new or novel at the end of any progression, one place like another anywhere and everywhere. Until

she was five and six, when she did have to go anywhere because her
mother declined to leave her at home while she herself was absent,
she would be carried by their Negro manservant. The three of them
would be seen passing along the road—Mrs Varner in her Sunday
dress and shawl, followed by the Negro man staggering slightly
beneath his long, dangling, already indisputably female burden like a
bizarre and chaperoned Sabine rape.

She had the usual dolls. She would place them in chairs about the
one in which she sat, and they would remain so, none with either
more or less of the semblance of life than any other. Finally her father
had his blacksmith make her a miniature of the perambulator in
which she had spent her first three years. It was crude and heavy also,
but it was the only doll perambulator anyone in that country had ever
seen or even heard of. She would place all the dolls in it and sit in a
chair beside it. At first they decided it was mental backwardness, that
she merely had not yet reached the maternal stage of female adult-
hood in miniature, though they soon realised that her indifference to
the toy was that she would have to move herself to keep it in motion.

She grew from infancy to the age of eight in the chairs, moving
from one to another about the house as the exigencies of sweeping
and cleaning house and eating meals forced her to break cover. At
her mother's insistence, Varner continued to have the blacksmith
make miniatures of housekeeping implements—little brooms and
mops, a small actual stove—hoping to make a sport, a game, of utility, all of which, singly and collectively, was apparently no more to
her than the tot of cold tea to the old drunkard. She had no play-
mates, no inseparable girl companion. She did not want them. She
never formed one of those violent, sometimes short-lived intimacies
in which two female children form embattled secret cabal against
their masculine coevals and the mature world too. She did nothing.
She might as well still have been a foetus. It was as if only half of her
had been born, that mentality and body had somehow become either
completely separated or hopelessly involved; that either only one of
them had ever emerged, or that one had emerged, itself not accompanied by, but rather pregnant with, the other. "Maybe she's fixing to
be a tomboy," her father said.

"When?" Jody said—a spark, a flash, even though born of enraged exasperation. "At the rate she's going at it, there aint a acorn that will fall in the next fifty years that wont grow up and rot down and be burnt for firewood before she'll ever climb it."

When she was eight, her brother decided she should start to school. Her parents had intended that she should start someday, perhaps mainly because Will Varner was, with the nominal designation of Trustee, the principal mainstay and arbiter of the school's existence. It was, as the other parents of the countryside considered it, actually another Varner enterprise, and sooner or later Varner would have insisted that his daughter attend it, for a while at least, just as he would have insisted upon collecting the final odd cents of an interest calculation. Mrs Varner did not particularly care whether the daughter went to school or not. She was one of the best housewives in the county and was indefatigable at it. She derived an actual physical pleasure which had nothing at all to do with mere satisfaction in husbandry and fore-handedness, from the laying-away of ironed sheets and the sight of packed shelves and potato cellars and festooned smoke-house rafters. She did not read herself, though at the time of her marriage she had been able to read a little. She did not practise it much then and during the last forty years she had lost even that habit, preferring now to be face to face with the living breath of event, fiction or news either, and being able to comment and moralise upon it. So she saw no need for literacy in women. Her conviction was that the proper combining of food ingredients lay not on any printed page but in the taste of the stirring spoon, and that the housewife who had to wait until she had been to school to know how much money she had left after subtracting from it what she had spent, would never be a housewife.

It was the brother, Jody, who emerged almost violently in her eighth summer as erudition's champion, and three months later came bitterly to regret it. He did not regret that it had been himself who had insisted that she go to school. His regret was that he was still convinced, and knew that he would remain convinced, of the necessity of that for which he now paid so dear a price. Because she refused to walk to school. She did not object to attending it, to being in school, she just declined to walk to it. It was not far. It was not a half mile from the Varner home. Yet during the five years she attended it, which, if it had been computed in hours based upon what she accomplished while there, would have been measured not in years or even months but in days, she rode to and from it. While other children living three and four and five times the distance walked back and forth in all weathers, she rode. She just calmly and flatly refused to walk. She did not resort to tears and she did not even fight back emotionally, let alone physically. She just sat down, where, static, apparently not even thinking, she emanated an outrageous and immune perversity like a blooded and contrary filly too young yet to be particularly valuable, though which in another year or so would be, and for which reason its raging and harried owner does not dare whip it. Her father immediately and characteristically washed his hands of the business. "Let her stay at home then," he said. "She aint going to lift her hand here either, but at least maybe she will learn something about housekeeping from having to move from one chair to another to keep out of the way of it. All we want anyway is to keep her out of trouble until she gets old enough to sleep with a man without getting me and him both arrested. Then you can marry her off. Maybe you can even find a husband that will keep Jody out of the poorhouse too. Then we will give them the house and store and the whole shebang and me and you will go to that world's fair they are talking about having in Saint Louis, and if we like it by God we will buy a tent and settle down there."

But the brother insisted that she go to school. She still declined to walk there, sitting supine and female and soft and immovable and not even thinking and apparently not even listening either, while the battle between her mother and brother roared over her tranquil head. So at last the Negro man who had used to carry her when her mother went visiting would bring up the family surrey and drive her the half mile to school and would be waiting there with the surrey at noon and at three oclock when school dismissed. This lasted about two weeks. Mrs Varner stopped it because it was too wasteful, like firing up a twenty-gallon pot to make a bowl of soup would be wasteful. She delivered an ultimatum; if Jody wanted his sister to go to school, he would have to see that she got there himself. She suggested that, since he rode his horse to and from the store every day anyhow, he might carry Eula to and from school behind him, the daughter sitting there again, neither thinking nor listening while this roared and concussed to the old stalemate, sitting on the front porch in the mornings with the cheap oilcloth book-satchel they had bought her until her brother rode the horse up to the gallery-edge and snarled at her to come and mount behind him. He would carry her to the school and go and fetch her at noon and carry her back afterward and be waiting when school was out for the day. This lasted for almost a month. Then Jody decided that she should walk the two hundred yards from the schoolhouse to the store and meet him there. To his surprise, she agreed without protest. This lasted for exactly two days. On the second afternoon the brother fetched her home at a fast single-foot, bursting into the house and standing over his mother in the hall and trembling with anger and outrage, shouting. "No wonder she agreed so easy and quick to walk to the store and meet me!" he cried. "If you could arrange to have a man standing every hundred feet along the road, she would walk all the way home! She's just like a dog! Soon as she passes anything in long pants she begins to give off something. You can smell it! You can smell it ten feet away!"

"Fiddlesticks," Mrs Varner said. "Besides, dont worry me with it. It was you insisted she had to go to school. It wasn't me. I raised eight other daughters, I thought they turned out pretty well. But I am willing to agree that maybe a twenty-seven-year-old bachelor knows more about them than I do. Anytime you want to let her quit school, I reckon your pa and me wont object. Did you bring me that cinnamon?"

"No," Jody said. "I forgot it."

"Try to remember it tonight. I'm already needing it."

So she no longer began the homeward journey at the store. Her brother would be waiting for her at the schoolhouse. It had been almost five years now since this sight had become an integral part of the village's life four times a day and five days a week—the roan horse bearing the seething and angry man and the girl of whom, even at nine and ten and eleven, there was too much—too much of leg, too much of breast, too much of buttock; too much of mammalian female meat which, in conjunction with the tawdry oilcloth receptacle that was obviously a grammar-grade book-satchel, was a travesty

and paradox on the whole idea of education. Even while sitting
behind her brother on the horse, the inhabitant of that meat seemed
to lead two separate and distinct lives as infants in the act of nursing
do. There was one Eula Varner who supplied blood and nourishment
to the buttocks and legs and breasts; there was the other Eula Varner
who merely inhabited them, who went where they went because it
was less trouble to do so, who was comfortable there but in their
doings she intended to have no part, as you are in a house which you
did not design but where the furniture is all settled and the rent paid
up. On the first morning Varner had put the horse into a fast trot,
to get it over with quick, but almost at once he began to feel the
entire body behind him, which even motionless in a chair seemed to
postulate an invincible abhorrence of straight lines, jigging its com-
ponent boneless curves against his back. He had a vision of himself
transporting not only across the village's horizon but across the
embracing proscenium of the entire inhabited world like the sun
itself, a kaleidoscopic convolution of mammalian ellipses. So he
would walk the horse. He would have to, his sister clutching the
cross of his suspenders or the back of his coat with one hand and
holding the book-satchel with the other, passing the store where the
usual quota of men would be squatting and sitting, past Mrs Littlejohn's veranda where there would usually be an itinerant drummer or
horse-trader—and Varner now believing, convinced, that he knew
why they were there too, the real reason why they had driven twenty
miles from Jefferson—and so up to the school where the other children in overalls and coarse calico and cast-off adult shoes as often as
not when they wore shoes at all, were already gathered after walking three and four and five times the distance. She would slide off the
horse and her brother would sit for a moment longer, seething,
watching the back which already used its hips to walk with as women
used them, and speculate with raging impotence whether to call the
school-teacher (he was a man) outside at once and have it out with
him, warn or threaten or even use his fists, or whether to wait until
that happened which he, Varner, was convinced must occur. They
would repeat that at one oclock and in the reverse direction at twelve
and three, Varner riding on a hundred yards up the road to where,
hidden by a copse, a fallen tree lay. The Negro manservant had felled

it one night while he sat the horse and held the lantern; he would ride up beside it, snarling fiercely to her the third time she mounted from it: "God damn it, cant you try to get on it without making it look like the horse is twenty feet tall?"

He even decided one day that she should not ride astride anymore. This lasted one day, until he happened to look aside and so behind him and saw the incredible length of outrageously curved dangling leg and the bare section of thigh between dress and stocking-top looking as gigantically and profoundly naked as the dome of an observatory. And his rage was only intensified by the knowledge that she had not deliberately exposed it. He knew that she simply did not care, doubtless did not even know it was exposed, and if she had known, would not have gone to the trouble to cover it. He knew that she was sitting even on the moving horse exactly as she would in a chair at home, and, as he knew, inside the schoolhouse itself, so that he wondered at times in his raging helplessness how buttocks as constantly subject to the impact of that much steadily increasing weight could in the mere act of walking seem actually to shout aloud that rich mind- and will-sapping fluid softness; sitting, even on the moving horse, secret and not even sullen, bemused with that whatever it was which had nothing to do with flesh, meat, at all; emanating that outrageous quality of being, existing, actually on the outside of the garments she wore and not only being unable to help it but not even caring.

She attended the school from her eighth year until shortly after Christmas in her fourteenth. She would undoubtedly have completed that year and very probably the next one or two, learning nothing, except that in January of that year the school closed. It closed because the teacher vanished. He disappeared overnight, with no word to anyone. He neither collected his term's salary nor removed his meagre and monklike personal effects from the fireless rented lean-to room in which he had lived for six years.

His name was Labove. He came from the adjoining county, where Will Varner himself had discovered him by sheer chance. The incumbent, the Professor at that time, was an old man bibulous by nature, who had been driven still further into his cups by the insubordination of his pupils. The girls had respect neither for his ideas and information nor for his ability to convey them; the boys had no respect for his capacity, not to teach them but to make them obey and behave or even be civil to him—a condition which had long since passed the stage of mere mutiny and had become a kind of bucolic Roman holiday, like the baiting of a mangy and toothless bear.

Thus everyone, including the Professor, knew that he would not be there next term. But nobody minded especially whether the school functioned next year or not. They owned it. They had built the schoolhouse themselves and paid the teacher and sent their children to it only when there was no work for them to do at home, so it only ran between harvest-time and planting—from mid-October through March. Nothing had been done yet about replacing the Professor until one day in the summer Varner happened to make a business trip into the next county, was benighted, and was invited to pass the night in a bleak puncheon-floored cabin on a barren little hill farm. When he entered the house he saw, sitting beside the cold hearth and sucking a foul little clay pipe, an incredibly old woman wearing a pair of stout-looking man's shoes slightly unorthodox or even a little bizarre in appearance. But Varner paid no attention to them until he heard a clattering scraping noise behind him and turned and saw a girl of about ten, in a tattered though quite clean gingham dress and a pair of shoes, exactly like those of the old lady—if anything, even a little larger. Before he departed the next morning Varner had seen three more pairs of the same shoes, by which time he had discovered that they resembled no other shoes he had ever seen or even heard of. His host told him what they were.

"What?" Varner said. "Football shoes?"

"It's a game," Labove said. "They play it at the University." He explained. It was the eldest son. He was not at home now, off working at a sawmill to earn money to return to the University, where he had been for one summer normal term and then half of the following academic term. It was then that the University played the game out of which the shoes had come. The son had wanted to learn to be a school-teacher, or so he said when he left for the University the first time. That is, he wanted to go to the University. The father saw no point in it. The farm was clear and would belong to the son someday and it had always made them a living. But the son insisted. He could work at mills and such and save enough to attend the summer terms and learn to be a teacher anyway, since this was all they taught in the summer sessions. He would even be back home in the late summer in time to help finish the crop. So he earned the money— "Doing harder work than farming too," the elder Labove said. "But he was almost twenty-one. I couldn't have stood in his way even if I would have."—and enrolled for the summer session, which would last eight weeks and so would have had him back home in August but did not do so. When September arrived, he still had not returned. They did not know for certain where he was, though they were not worried so much as annoyed, concerned, even a little outraged that he should have deserted them with the remaining work on the crop—the picking and ginning of the cotton, the gathering and cribbing of the corn—to be done. In mid-September the letter came. He was going to stay on longer at the University, through the fall. He had a job there; they must gather the crops without him. He did not say what kind of a job it was and the father took it for granted as being another sawmill, since he would never have associated any sort of revenue-producing occupation with going to school, and they did not hear from him again until in October, when the first package arrived. It contained two pair of the curious cleated shoes. A third pair came early in November. The last two came just after Thanksgiving, which made five pair, although there were seven in the family. So they all used them indiscriminately, anyone who found a pair available, like umbrellas, four pair of them that is, Labove explained. The old lady (she was the elder Labove's grandmother) had fastened upon the first pair to emerge from the box and would let no one else wear them at all. She seemed to like the sound the cleats made on the floor when she sat in a chair and rocked. But that still left four pair. So now the children could go shod to school, removing the shoes when they reached home for whoever else needed to go outdoors. In January the son came home. He told them about the game. He had been playing it all that fall. They let him stay at the University for the entire fall term for playing it. The shoes were provided them free of charge to play it in.

"How did he happen to get six pairs?" Varner asked.

Labove did not know that. "Maybe they had a heap of them on

hand that year," he said. They had also given the son a sweater at the University, a fine heavy warm dark blue sweater with a big red M on the front of it. The great-grandmother had taken that too, though it was much too big for her. She would wear it on Sundays, winter and summer, sitting beside him on the seat of the churchward wagon on the bright days, the crimson accolade of the color of courage and fortitude gallant in the sun, or on the bad days, sprawled and quiet but still crimson, still brave, across her shrunken chest and stomach as she sat in her chair and rocked and sucked the dead little pipe.

"So that's where he is now," Varner said. "Playing the football."

No, Labove told him. He was at the sawmill now. He had calculated that by missing the current summer term and working instead, he could save enough money to stay on at the University even after they stopped letting him stay to play the football, thus completing a full year in the regular school instead of just the summer school in which they only taught people how to be school-teachers.

"I thought that's what he wanted to be," Varner said.

"No," Labove said. "That was all he could learn in the summer school. I reckon you'll laugh when you hear this. He says he wants to be Governor."

"Sho now," Varner said.

"You'll laugh, I reckon."

"No," Varner said. "I aint laughing. Governor. Well well well. Next time you see him, if he would consider putting off the governor business for a year or two and teach school, tell him to come over to the Bend and see me."

That was in July. Perhaps Varner did not actually expect Labove to come to see him. But he made no further effort to fill the vacancy, which he certainly could not have forgotten about. Even apart from his obligation as Trustee, he would have a child of his own ready to start to school within another year or so. One afternoon in early September he was lying with his shoes off in the barrel-stave hammock slung between two trees in his yard, when he saw approaching on foot across the yard the man whom he had never seen before but knew at once—a man who was not thin so much as actually gaunt, with straight black hair coarse as a horse's tail and high Indian cheekbones and quiet pale hard eyes and the long nose of thought but with the slightly curved nostrils of pride and the thin lips of secret and ruthless ambition. It was a forensic face, the face of invincible conviction in the power of words as a principle worth dying for if necessary. A thousand years ago it would have been a monk's, a militant fanatic who would have turned his uncompromising back upon the world with actual joy and gone to a desert and passed the rest of his days and nights calmly and without an instant's self-doubt battling, not to save humanity about which he would have cared nothing, for whose sufferings he would have had nothing but contempt, but with his own fierce and unappeasable natural appetites.

"I came to tell you I cant teach for you this year," he said. "I haven't got time. I've got things fixed now so I can stay at the University the whole year."

Varner did not rise. "That's just one year. What about next year?"

"I have arranged about the sawmill too. I am going back to it next summer. Or something else."

"Sho," Varner said. "I been thinking about it some myself. Because the school here dont need to open until first of November. You can stay at Oxford until then and play your game. Then you can come and open the school and get it started. You can bring your books here from the University and keep up with the class and on the day you have to play the game again you can go back to Oxford and play it and let them find out whether you have kept up in the books or not or whether you have learned anything or whatever they would need to know. Then you could come back to the school; even a day or two wont matter. I will furnish you a horse that can make the trip in eight hours. It aint but forty miles to Oxford from here. Then when the time comes for the examination in January your pa was telling me about, you can shut up the school here and go back and stay until you are through with them. Then you can close the school here in March and go back for the rest of the year, until the last of next October if you wanted. I dont reckon a fellow that really wanted to would have much trouble keeping up with his class just forty miles away. Well?"

For some time now Varner knew that the other no longer saw him though he had not moved and his eyes were still open. Labove stood quite still, in a perfectly clean white shirt which had been washed so

often that it now had about the texture of mosquito netting, in a coat
and trousers absolutely clean too and which were not mates and the
coat a little too small for him and which Varner knew were the only
ones he owned and that he owned them only because he believed,
or had been given to understand, that one could not wear overalls
to a University classroom. He stood there enveloped in no waking
incredulous joy and hope but in that consuming fury, the gaunt body
not shaped by the impact of its environment but as though shrunken
and leaned by what was within it, like a furnace. "All right," he said.
"I'll be here the first of November." He was already turning away.

"Dont you want to know what your pay will be?"

"All right," Labove said, pausing. Varner told him. He (Varner)
had not moved in the hammock, his home-knit socks crossed at the
ankles.

"That game," he said. "Do you like to play it?"

"No," Labove said.

"I hear it aint much different from actual fighting."

"Yes," Labove said, again shortly, paused, courteous and waiting,
looking at the lean shrewd shoeless old man prone and profoundly
idle in the hammock, who seemed to have laid upon him already the
curse of his own invincible conviction of the absolute unimportance
of this or any other given moment or succession of them, holding
him there and forcing him to spend time thinking about what he had
never told anyone and did not intend to talk about since it did not
matter now. It began just before the end of the summer term a year
ago. He had intended to return home at the end of the term, as he
had told his father he would, to help finish the crop. But just before
the term ended he found a job. It was practically dropped into his lap.
There would be two or three weeks yet before the cotton would be
ready to pick and gin and he was already settled where he could stay
on until the middle of September at little additional expense. So
most of what the work would bring him would be clear profit. He
took the job. It was grading and building a football field. He didn't
know then what a football field was and he did not care. To him it
was merely an opportunity to earn so much additional money each
day and he did not even stop his shovel when he would speculate now
and then with cold sardonicism on the sort of game the preparation

of ground for which demanded a good deal more care and expense both than the preparing of that same ground to raise a paying crop on; indeed, to have warranted that much time and money for a crop, a man would have had to raise gold at least. So it was still sardonicism and not curiosity when in September and before the field was finished, it began to be used, and he discovered that the young men engaged upon it were not even playing the game but just practising. He would watch them at it. He was probably watching them more closely or at least more often than he was aware and with something in his face, his eyes, which he did not know was there too, because one afternoon one of them (he had already discovered that the game had a paid teacher) said to him, "You think you can do it better, do you? All right. Come here." That night he sat on the front steps of the coach's house in the dry dusty September darkness, still saying No quietly and patiently.

"I aint going to borrow money just to play a game on," he said.

"You wont have to, I tell you!" the coach said. "Your tuition will be paid. You can sleep in my attic and you can feed my horse and cow and milk and build the fires and I will give you your meals. Dont you understand?" It could not have been his face because that was in darkness, and he did not believe it had been in his voice. Yet the coach said, "I see. You dont believe it."

"No," he said. "I dont believe anybody will give me all that just for playing a game."

"Will you try it and see? Will you stay here and do it until somebody comes to you and asks you for money?"

"Will I be free to go when they do?"

"Yes," the coach said. "You have my word." So that night he wrote his father he would not be home to help finish the harvest and if they would need an extra hand in his place he would send money. And they gave him a uniform and on that afternoon, as on the one before when he had still worn the overalls in which he had been working, one of the other players failed to rise at once and they explained that to him—how there were rules for violence, he trying patiently to make this distinction, understand it: "But how can I carry the ball to that line if I let them catch me and pull me down?"

He didn't tell this. He just stood beside the hammock, in the clean unmatching garments, composed and grave, answering Yes or No briefly and quietly to Varner's questions while it recapitulated, ran fast and smooth and without significance now in his memory, finished and done and behind him, meaning nothing, the fall itself going fast, dreamlike and telescoped. He would rise in the icy attic at four oclock and build fires in the houses of five different faculty members and return to feed and milk. Then the lectures, the learning and wisdom distilled of all man had ever thought, plumbed, the ivied walls and monastic rooms impregnated with it, abundant, no limit save that of the listener's capacity and thirst; the afternoons of practice (soon he was excused from this on alternate days, which afternoons he spent raking leaves in the five yards), the preparing of coal and wood against tomorrow's fires. Then the cow again and then in the overcoat which the coach had given him he sat with his books beneath the lamp in his fireless garret until he went to sleep over the printed page. He did this for five days, up to the Saturday's climax when he carried a trivial contemptible obloid across fleeing and meaningless white lines. Yet during these seconds, despite his contempt, his ingrained conviction, his hard and spartan heritage, he lived, fiercely free—the spurning earth, the shocks, the hard breathing and the grasping hands, the speed, the rocking roar of massed stands, his face even then still wearing the expression of sardonic not-quite-belief. And the shoes. Varner was watching him, his hands beneath his head. "Them shoes," Varner said. It was because I never did really believe it was going to last until the next Saturday, Labove could have answered. But he did not, he just stood, his hands quiet at his sides, looking at Varner. "I reckon they always had a plenty of them on hand," Varner said.

"They bought them in lots. They kept all sizes on hand."

"Sho now," Varner said. "I reckon all a fellow had to do was just to say his old pair didn't fit good or had got lost."

Labove did not look away. He stood quietly facing the man in the hammock. "I knew what the shoes cost. I tried to get the coach to say what a pair was worth. To the University. What a touchdown was worth. Winning was worth."

"I see. You never taken a pair except when you beat. And you sent five pairs home. How many times did you play?"

"Seven," Labove said. "One of them nobody won."

"I see," Varner said. "Well, I reckon you want to get on back home before dark. I'll have that horse ready by November."

Labove opened the school in the last week of October. Within that week he had subdued with his fists the state of mutiny which his predecessor had bequeathed him. On Friday night he rode the horse Varner had promised him the forty-odd miles to Oxford, attended morning lectures and played a football game in the afternoon, slept until noon Sunday and was on his pallet bed in the unheated lean-to room in Frenchman's Bend by midnight. It was in the house of a widow who lived near the school. He owned a razor, the unmatching coat and trousers he stood in, two shirts, the coach's overcoat, a Coke, a Blackstone, a volume of Mississippi Reports, an original Horace and a Thucydides which the classics professor, in whose home he had built the morning fires, had given him at Christmas, and the brightest lamp the village had ever seen. It was nickel, with valves and pistons and gauges; as it sat on his plank table it obviously cost more than everything else he owned lumped together and people would come in from miles away at night to see the fierce still glare it made.

By the end of that first week they all knew him—the hungry mouth, the insufferable humorless eyes, the intense ugly blue-shaved face like a composite photograph of Voltaire and an Elizabethan pirate. They called him Professor too even though he looked what he was—twenty-one—and even though the school was a single room in which pupils ranging in age from six to the men of nineteen whom he had had to meet with his fists to establish his professorship, and classes ranging from bald abc's to the rudiments of common fractions were jumbled together. He taught them all and everything. He carried the key to the building in his pocket as a merchant carries the key to his store. He unlocked it each morning and swept it, he divided the boys by age and size into water-carrying and wood-cutting details and by precept, bullying, ridicule and force saw that they did it, helping them at times not as an example but with a kind of contemptuous detached physical pleasure in burning up his excess energy. He would ruthlessly keep the older boys after school, standing before the door and barring it and beating them to the open windows when they broke for these. He forced them to climb with him to the roof and replace shingles and such which heretofore Varner, as Trustee, had seen to after the teacher had nagged and complained to him enough. At night passers would see the fierce dead glare of the patent lamp beyond the lean-to window where he would be sitting over the books which he did not love so much as he believed that he must read, compass and absorb and wring dry with something of that same contemptuous intensity with which he chopped firewood, measuring the turned pages against the fleeing seconds of irrevocable time like the implacable inching of a leaf worm.

Each Friday afternoon he would mount the wiry strong hammerheaded horse in Varner's lot and ride to where the next day's game would be played or to the railroad which would get him there, sometimes arriving only in time to change into his uniform before the whistle blew. But he was always back at the school on Monday morning, even though on some occasions it meant he had spent only one night—Saturday—in bed between Thursday and Monday. After the Thanksgiving game between the two State colleges, his picture was in a Memphis paper. He was in the uniform and the picture (to the people in the village, and for that reason) would not have looked like him. But the name was his and that would have been recognised, except that he did not bring the paper back with him. They did not know what he did on those week-ends, except that he was taking work at the University. They did not care. They had accepted him, and although his designation of professor was a distinction, it was still a woman's distinction, functioning actually in a woman's world like the title of reverend. Although they would not have actually forbidden him the bottle, they would not have drunk with him, and though they were not quite as circumspect in what they said before him as they would have been with the true minister, if he had responded in kind he might have found himself out of a position when the next term began and he knew it. This distinction he accepted in the spirit offered and even met it more than halfway, with that same grim sufficiency, not pride quite and not quite actual belligerence, grave and composed.

He was gone for a week at the time of the mid-term examinations at the University. He returned and hounded Varner into clearing a basketball court. He did a good deal of the work himself, with the older boys, and taught them the game. At the end of the next year the team had beaten every team they could find to play against and in the third year, himself one of the players, he carried the team to Saint Louis, where, in overalls and barefoot, they won a Mississippi Valley tournament against all comers.

When he brought them back to the village, he was through. In three years he had graduated, a master of arts and a bachelor of laws. He would leave the village now for the last time—the books, the fine lamp, the razor, the cheap reproduction of an Alma-Tadema picture which the classics professor had given him on the second Christmas—to return to the University to his alternating academic and law classes, one following another from breakfast time to late afternoon. He had to read in glasses now, leaving one class to walk blinking painfully against the light to the next, in the single unmatching costume he owned, through throngs of laughing youths and girls in clothes better than he had ever seen until he came here, who did not stare through him so much as they did not see him at all any more than they did the poles which supported the electric lights which until he arrived two years ago he had never seen before either. He would move among them and look with the same expression he would wear above the cleat-spurned fleeing lines of the football field, at the girls who had apparently come there to find husbands, the young men who had come there for what reason he knew not.

Then one day he stood in a rented cap and gown among others and received the tightly-rolled parchment scroll no larger than a rolled calendar yet which, like the calendar, contained those three years—the spurned cleat-blurred white lines, the nights on the tireless horse, the other nights while he had sat in the overcoat and with only the lamp for heat, above spread turning pages of dead verbiage. Two days after that he stood with his class before the Bench in an actual courtroom in Oxford and was admitted to the Bar, and it was finished. He made one that night at a noisy table in the hotel dining room, at which the Judge presided, flanked by the law professors and the other legal sponsors. This was the anteroom to that world he had been working to reach for three years now—four, counting that first one when he could not yet see his goal. He had only to sit with that fixed expression and wait until the final periphrase died, was blotted by the final concussion of palms, and rise and walk out of the room and on, his face steady in the direction he had chosen to set it, as it had been for three years now anyway, not faltering, not looking back. And he could not do it. Even with that already forty miles of start toward freedom and (he knew it, said it) dignity and self-respect, he could not do it. He must return, drawn back into the radius and impact of an eleven-year-old girl who, even while sitting with veiled eyes against the sun like a cat on the schoolhouse steps at recess and eating a cold potato, postulated that ungirdled quality of the very goddesses in his Homer and Thucydides: of being at once corrupt and immaculate, at once virgins and the mothers of warriors and of grown men.

On that first morning when her brother had brought her to the school, Labove had said to himself: No. No. Not here. Dont leave her here. He had taught the school for only one year, a single term of five months broken by the weekly night ride to Oxford and return and the two-weeks' gap of the mid-term examinations in January, yet he had not only extricated it from the chaos in which his predecessor had left it, he had even coerced the curriculum itself into something resembling order. He had no assistant, there was not even a partition in the single room, yet he had segregated the pupils according to capacity into a routine which they not only observed but had finally come to believe in. He was not proud of it, he was not even satisfied. But he was satisfied that it was motion, progress, if not toward increasing knowledge to any great extent, at least toward teaching order and discipline. Then one morning he turned from the crude blackboard and saw a face eight years old and a body of fourteen with the female shape of twenty, which on the instant of crossing the threshold brought into the bleak, ill-lighted, poorly-heated room dedicated to the harsh functioning of Protestant primary education a moist blast of spring's liquorish corruption, a pagan triumphal prostration before the supreme primal uterus.

He took one look at her and saw what her brother would doubtless be the last to discern. He saw that she not only was not going to study, but there was nothing in books here or anywhere else that she would ever need to know, who had been born already completely equipped not only to face and combat but to overcome anything the future could invent to meet her with. He saw a child whom for the next two years he was to watch with what he thought at first was only rage, already grown at eight, who apparently had reached and passed puberty in the foetus, who, tranquil bemused and not even sullen, obedient to whatever outside compulsion it had been had merely transferred from one set of walls to another that quality of static waiting through and beneath the accumulating days of burgeoning and unhurryable time until whatever man it was to be whose name and face she probably had neither seen nor heard yet, would break into and disperse it. For five years he was to watch her, fetched each morning by the brother and remain just as he had left her, in the same place and almost in the same position, her hands lying motionless for hours on her lap like two separate slumbering bodies. She would answer "I dont know" when her attention was finally attracted at last, or, pressed, "I never got that far." It was as if her muscles and flesh too were even impervious to fatigue and boredom or as if, the drowsing maidenhead symbol's self, she possessed life but not sentience and merely waited until the brother came, the jealous seething eunuch priest, and removed her.

She would arrive each morning with the oilcloth satchel in which if she carried anything else beside the baked sweet potatoes which she ate at recess, Labove did not know it. By merely walking down the aisle between them she would transform the very wooden desks and benches themselves into a grove of Venus and fetch every male in the room, from the children just entering puberty to the grown men of nineteen and twenty, one of whom was already a husband and father, who could turn ten acres of land between sunup and sundown, springing into embattled rivalry, importunate each for precedence in immolation. Sometimes on Friday nights there would be parties in the schoolhouse, where the pupils would play the teasing games of adolescence under his supervision. She would take no part in them, yet she would dominate them. Sitting beside the stove exactly as she had sat during the hours of school, inattentive and serene amid the uproar of squeals and trampling feet, she would be assaulted simultaneously beneath a dozen simultaneous gingham or calico dresses in a dozen simultaneous shadowy nooks and corners. She was neither at the head nor at the foot of her class, not because she declined to study on the one hand and not because she was Varner's daughter on the other and Varner ran the school, but because the class she was in ceased to have either head or foot twenty-four hours after she entered it. Within the year there even ceased to be any lower class for her to be promoted from, for the reason that she would never be at either end of anything in which blood ran. It would have but one point, like a swarm of bees, and she would be that point, that center, swarmed over and importuned yet serene and intact and apparently even oblivious, tranquilly abrogating the whole long sum of human thinking and suffering which is called knowledge, education, wisdom, at once supremely unchaste and inviolable: the queen, the matrix.

He watched that for two years, still with what he thought was only rage. He would graduate at the end of the second year, take his two degrees. He would be done then, finished. His one reason for having taken the school would be cancelled and discharged. His aim and purpose would be gained at the price it had cost him, not the least of which was riding that horse forty miles at night to and from the University, since after his dirt-farmer tradition and heritage, he did not ride a horse for fun. Then he could go on, quit the village and never lay eyes upon it again. For the first six months he believed he was going to do that and for the next eighteen he still told himself he was. This was especially easy not only to tell himself but to believe too while he was away from the village during the last two months of the spring term at the University and the following eight weeks of the summer term into which he was crowding by sections his fourth academic year, then the eight weeks of what the school called his vacation, which he spent at the sawmill although he did not need the money now, he could graduate without it, but it would be that much more in his pocket when he passed through the last door and faced the straight hard road with nothing between him and his goal save himself; then the six fall weeks when each Saturday afternoon the spurned white lines fled beneath him and the hysteric air screamed and roared and he for those fleet seconds and despite himself did live, fierce, concentrated, even though still not quite believing it.

Then one day he discovered that he had been lying to himself for almost two years. It was after he had returned to the University in the second spring and about a month before he would graduate. He had not formally resigned from the school, though when he left the village a month ago he believed it was for the last time, considering it understood between Varner and himself that he was teaching the school only to enable himself to finish at the University. So he believed he had quitted the village for the last time. The final examinations were only a month away, then the Bar examination and the door would be open to him. There was even the promise of a position in the profession he had chosen. Then one afternoon, he had no warning at all, he had entered the dining room of his boarding house for the evening meal when the landlady came and said, "I have a treat for you. My sister's husband brought them to me," and set a dish before him. It was a single baked sweet potato, and while the landlady cried, "Why, Mr Labove, you are sick!" he managed to rise and leave the room. In his room at last it seemed to him that he must go at once, start now, even on foot. He could see her, even smell her, sitting there on the school steps, eating the potato, tranquil and chewing and with that terrible quality of being not only helplessly and unawares on the outside of her clothing, but of being naked and not even knowing it. He knew now that it was not on the school steps but in his mind that she had constantly been for two years now, that it had not been rage at all but terror, and that the vision of that gate which he had held up to himself as a goal was not a goal but just a point to reach, as the man fleeing a holocaust runs not for a prize but to escape destruction.

But he did not really give up then, though for the first time he said the words, I will not back. It had not been necessary to say them before because until now he had believed he was going on. But at least he could still assure himself aloud that he would not, which was something and which got him on through the graduation and the Bar initiation and banquet too. Just before the ceremony he had been approached by one of his fellow neophytes. After the banquet they were going to Memphis, for further and informal celebrating. He knew what that meant: drinking in a hotel room and then, for some of them at least, a brothel. He declined, not because he was a virgin and not because he did not have the money to spend that way but because up to the very last he still believed, still had his hill-man's purely emotional and foundationless faith in education, the white magic of Latin degrees, which was an actual counterpart of the old monk's faith in his wooden cross. Then the last speech died into the final clapping and scraping of chairs; the door was open and the road waited and he knew he would not take it. He went to the man who had invited him to Memphis and accepted. He descended with the group from the train in the Memphis station and asked quietly how to find a brothel. "Hell, man," the other said. "Restrain yourself. At least let's go through the formality of registering at the hotel." But he would not. He went alone to the address given him. He knocked firmly at the equivocal door. This would not help him either. He did not expect it to. His was that quality lacking which no man can ever be completely brave or completely craven: the ability to see both sides of the crisis and visualise himself as already vanquished—itself inherent with its own failure and disaster. At least it wont be my virginity that she is going to scorn, he told himself. The next morning he borrowed a sheet of cheap ruled tablet paper (the envelope was pink and had been scented once) from his companion of the night, and wrote Varner that he would teach the school for another year.

He taught it for three more years. By then he was the monk indeed, the bleak schoolhouse, the little barren village, was his mountain, his Gethsemane and, he knew it, his Golgotha too. He was the virile anchorite of old time. The heatless lean-to room was his desert cell, the thin pallet bed on the puncheon floor the couch of stones on which he would lie prone and sweating in the iron winter nights, naked, rigid, his teeth clenched in his scholar's face and his legs haired-over like those of a faun. Then day would come and he could rise and dress and eat the food which he would not even taste. He had never paid much attention to what he ate anyway, but now he would not always know that he had eaten it. Then he would go and unlock the school and sit behind his desk and wait for her to walk down the aisle. He had long since thought of marrying her, waiting until she was old enough and asking for her in marriage, attempting to, and had discarded that. In the first place, he did not want a wife at all, certainly not yet and probably not ever. And he did not want her as a wife, he just wanted her one time as a man with a gangrened hand or foot thirsts after the axe-stroke which will leave him comparatively whole again. But he would have paid even this price to be free of his obsession, only he knew that this could never be, not only because her father would never agree to it, but because of her, that quality in her which absolutely abrogated the exchange value of any single life's promise or capacity for devotion, the puny asking-price of any one man's reserve of so-called love. He could almost see the husband which she would someday have. He would be a dwarf, a gnome, without glands or desire, who would be no more a physical factor in her life than the owner's name on the fly-leaf of a book. There it was again, out of the books again, the dead defacement of type which had already betrayed him: the crippled Vulcan to that Venus, who would not possess her but merely own her by the single strength which power gave, the dead power of money, wealth, gewgaws, baubles, as he might own, not a picture, statue: a field, say. He saw it: the fine land rich and fecund and foul and eternal and impervious to him who claimed title to it, oblivious, drawing to itself tenfold the quantity of living seed its owner's whole life could have secreted and compounded, producing a thousandfold the harvest he could ever hope to gather and save.

So that was out. Yet still he stayed on. He stayed for the privilege of waiting until the final class was dismissed and the room was empty so that he could rise and walk with his calm damned face to the bench and lay his hand on the wooden plank still warm from the impact of her sitting or even kneel and lay his face to the plank, wallowing his face against it, embracing the hard unsentient wood, until the heat was gone. He was mad. He knew it. There would be times now when he did not even want to make love to her but wanted to hurt her, see blood spring and run, watch that serene face warp to the indelible mark of terror and agony beneath his own; to leave some indelible mark of himself on it and then watch it even cease to be a face. Then he would exorcise that. He would drive it from him, whereupon their positions would reverse. It would now be himself importunate and prostrate before that face which, even though but fourteen years old, postulated a weary knowledge which he would never attain, a surfeit, a glut of all perverse experience.

He would be as a child before that knowledge. He would be like a young girl, a maiden, wild distracted and amazed, trapped not by the seducer's maturity and experience but by blind and ruthless forces inside herself which she now realised she had lived with for years without even knowing they were there. He would grovel in the dust before it, panting: "Show me what to do. Tell me. I will do anything you tell me, anything, to learn and know what you know." He was mad. He knew it. He knew that sooner or later something was going to happen. And he knew too that, whatever it would be, he would be the vanquished, even though he did not know yet what the one crack in his armor was and that she would find it unerringly and instinctively and without ever being aware that she had been in deadly danger. Danger? he thought, cried. Danger? Not to her: to me. I am afraid of what I might do, not because of her because there is nothing I or any man could do to her that would hurt her. It's because of what it will do to me.

Then one afternoon he found his axe. He continued to hack in almost an orgasm of joy at the dangling nerves and tendons of the gangrened member long after the first bungling blow. He had heard no sound. The last footfall had ceased and the door had closed for the last time. He did not hear it open again, yet something caused him to raise his wallowing face from the bench. She was in the room again, looking at him. He knew that she not only recognised the place at which he knelt, but that she knew why. Possibly at that instant he believed she had known all the time, because he knew at once that she was neither frightened nor laughing at him, that she simply did not care. Nor did she know that she was now looking at the face of a potential homicide. She merely released the door and came down the aisle toward the front of the room where the stove sat. "Jody aint come yet," she said. "It's cold out there. What are you doing down there?"

He rose. She came steadily on, carrying the oilcloth satchel which she had carried for five years now and which he knew she had never opened outside of the schoolhouse save to put into it the cold potatoes. He moved toward her. She stopped, watching him. "Dont be afraid," he said. "Dont be afraid."

"Afraid?" she said. "Of what?" She took one step back, then no

more, watching his face. She was not afraid. She aint got that far
either, he thought; and then something furious and cold, of repudiation and bereavement both, blew in him though it did not show in
his face which was even smiling a little, tragic and sick and damned.

"That's it," he said. "That's the trouble. You are not afraid. That's
what you have got to learn. That's one thing I am going to teach you,
anyway." He had taught her something else, though he was not to
find it out for a minute or so yet. She had indeed learned one thing
during the five years in school and was presently to take and pass an
examination on it. He moved toward her. She still stood her ground.
Then he had her. He moved as quickly and ruthlessly as if she had a
football or as if he had the ball and she stood between him and the
final white line which he hated and must reach. He caught her, hard,
the two bodies hurling together violently because she had not even
moved to avoid him, let alone to begin resisting yet. She seemed to
be momentarily mesmerised by a complete inert soft surprise, big,
immobile, almost eye to eye with him in height, the body which
seemed always to be on the outside of its garments, which without
even knowing it apparently had made a priapic hullabaloo of that to
which, at the price of three years of sacrifice and endurance and fla-
gellation and unceasing combat with his own implacable blood, he
had bought the privilege of dedicating his life, as fluid and muscleless
as a miraculous intact milk.

Then the body gathered itself into furious and silent resistance
which even then he might have discerned to be neither fright nor
even outrage but merely surprise and annoyance. She was strong. He
had expected that. He had wanted that, he had been waiting for it.
They wrestled furiously. He was still smiling, even whispering.
"That's it," he said. "Fight it. Fight it. That's what it is: a man and a
woman fighting each other. The hating. To kill, only to do it in such
a way that the other will have to know forever afterward he or she is
dead. Not even to lie quiet dead because forever afterward there will
have to be two in that grave and those two can never again lie quiet
anywhere together and neither can ever lie anywhere alone and be
quiet until he or she is dead." He held her loosely, the better to feel
the fierce resistance of bones and muscles, holding her just enough to
keep her from actually reaching his face. She had made no sound,

although her brother, who was never late in calling for her, must by now be just outside the building. Labove did not think of this. He would not have cared probably. He held her loosely, still smiling, whispering his jumble of fragmentary Greek and Latin verse and American-Mississippi obscenity, when suddenly she managed to free one of her arms, the elbow coming up hard under his chin. It caught him off-balance; before he regained it her other hand struck him a full-armed blow in the face. He stumbled backward, struck a bench and went down with it and partly beneath it. She stood over him, breathing deep but not panting and not even dishevelled.

"Stop pawing me," she said. "You old headless horseman Ichabod Crane."

After the sound of her feet and the closing door had ceased, he could hear the cheap clock which he had brought back with him from his room at the University, loud in the silence, with a tinny sound like minute shot being dropped into a can, though before he could begin to get up the door opened again and, sitting on the floor, he looked up at her as she came back down the aisle. "Where's my—" she said. Then she saw it, the book-satchel, and lifted it from the floor and turned again. He heard the door again. So she hasn't told him yet, he thought. He knew the brother too. He would not have waited to take her home first, he would have come in at once, vindicated at last after five years of violent and unsupported conviction. That would be something, anyway. It would not be penetration, true enough, but it would be the same flesh, the same warm living flesh in which the same blood ran, under impact at least—a paroxysm, an orgasm of sorts, a katharsis, anyway—something. So he got up and went to his desk and sat down and squared the clock-face (it sat at an oblique angle, so he could see it from the point before the recitation bench where he usually stood) toward him. He knew the distance between the school and the Varner home and he had ridden that horse back and forth to the University enough to calculate time in horse-distance. He will gallop back too, he thought. So he measured the distance the minute hand would have to traverse and sat watching it as it crept toward the mark. Then he looked up at the only comparatively open space in the room, which still had the stove in it, not to speak of the recitation bench. The stove could not be moved, but the bench could. But even then. . . . Maybe he had better meet the brother outdoors, or someone might get hurt. Then he thought that that was exactly what he wanted: for somebody to get hurt, and then he asked himself quietly, Who? and answered himself: I dont know. I dont care. So he looked back at the clock-face. Yet even when a full hour had passed he still could not admit to himself that the final disaster had befallen him. He is lying in ambush for me with the pistol, he thought. But where? What ambush? What ambush could he want better than here? already seeing her entering the room again tomorrow morning, tranquil, untroubled, not even remembering, carrying the cold potato which at recess she would sit on the sunny steps and eat like one of the unchaste and perhaps even anonymously pregnant immortals eating bread of Paradise on a sunwise slope of Olympus.

So he rose and gathered up the books and papers which, with the clock, he carried to his barren room each afternoon and fetched back the next morning, and put them into the desk drawer and closed it and with his handkerchief he wiped off the desk top, moving without haste yet steadily, his face calm, and wound the clock and set it back on the desk. The overcoat which the football coach had given him six years ago hung on its nail. He looked at it for a moment, though presently he went and got it and even put it on and left the room, the now deserted room in which there were still and forever would be too many people; in which, from that first day when her brother had brought her into it, there had been too many people, who would make one too many forever after in any room she ever entered and remained in long enough to expel breath.

As soon as he emerged, he saw the roan horse tied to the post before the store. Of course, he thought quietly. Naturally he would not carry a pistol around with him, and it would not do him any good hidden under a pillow at home. Of course. That's it. That's where the pistol will be; telling himself that perhaps the brother even wanted witnesses, as he himself wanted them, his face tragic and calm now, walking on down the road toward the store. That will be proof, he cried silently. Proof in the eyes and beliefs of living men that that happened which did not. Which will be better than nothing, even though I am not here to know men believe it. Which will be fixed in the beliefs of living men forever and ever ineradicable, since one of the two alone who know different will be dead.

It was a gray day, of the color and texture of iron, one of those windless days of a plastic rigidity too dead to make or release snow even, in which even light did not alter but seemed to appear complete out of nothing at dawn and would expire into darkness without gradation. The village was lifeless—the shuttered and silent gin and blacksmith shop, the weathered store; the motionless horse alone postulating life and that not because it moved but because it resembled something known to be alive. But they would be inside the store. He could see them—the heavy shoes and boots, the overalls and jumper coats bulging over the massed indiscriminate garments beneath—planted about the box of pocked sand in which the stove, squatting, radiated the strong good heat which had an actual smell, masculine, almost monastic—a winter's concentration of unwomaned and deliberate tobacco-spittle annealing into the iron flanks. The good heat: he would enter it, not out of the bleak barren cold but out of life, mounting steps and walking through a door and out of living. The horse raised its head and looked at him as he passed it. But not you, he said to it. You've got to stand outside, stand here and remain intact for the blood to contrive to run through. I dont. He mounted the steps, crossing the heel-gnawed planks of the gallery. On the closed door was tacked a paper placard advertising a patent medicine, half defaced—the reproduction of a portrait, smug, bearded, successful, living far away and married, with children, in a rich house and beyond the reach of passion and blood's betrayal and not even needing to be dead to be embalmed with spaced tacks, ubiquitous and immortal in ten thousand fading and tattered effigies on ten thousand weathered and paintless doors and walls and fences in all the weathers of rain and ice and summer's harsh heat, about the land.

Then, with his hand already on the knob to turn it, he stopped. Once—it was one of the football trips of course, he had never ridden in a train otherwise save on that night visit to Memphis—he had descended onto a bleak station platform. There was a sudden commotion about a door. He heard a man cursing, shouting, a Negro ran out the door, followed by a shouting white man. The Negro turned, stooping, and as the onlookers scattered the white man shot the Negro in the body with a blunt pistol. He remembered how the Negro, clutching his middle, dropped onto his face then suddenly flopped over onto his back, actually appearing to elongate himself, to add at least a yard to his stature; the cursing white man was overpowered and disarmed, the train whistled once and began to draw away, a uniformed trainman breaking out of the crowd and running to overtake it and still looking back from the moving step. And he remembered how he shoved himself up, instinctively using his football tactics to make a place, where he looked down upon the Negro lying rigid on his back, still clutching his middle, his eyes closed and his face quite peaceful. Then there was a man—a doctor or an officer, he did not know—kneeling over the Negro. He was trying to draw the Negro's hands away. There was no outward show of resistance; the forearms and hands at which the doctor or officer was tugging merely seemed to have become iron. The Negro's eyes did not open nor his peaceful expression alter; he merely said: "Look out, white folks. I aready been shot." But they unclasped his hands at last, and he remembered the peeling away of the jumper, the overalls, a ragged civilian coat beneath which revealed itself to have been a long overcoat once, the skirts cut away at the hips as with a razor; beneath that a shirt and a pair of civilian trousers. The waist of them was unbuttoned and the bullet rolled out onto the platform, bloodless. He released the doorknob and removed the overcoat and hung it over his arm. At least I wont make a failure with one of us, he thought, opening the door, entering. At first he believed the room was empty. He saw the stove in its box of pocked sand, surrounded by the nail kegs and upended boxes; he even smelled the rank scorch of recent spitting. But no one sat there, and when a moment later he saw the brother's thick humorless surly face staring at him over the desk, for an instant he felt rage and outrage. He believed that Varner had cleared the room, sent them all away deliberately in order to deny him that last vindication, the ratification of success which he had come to buy with his life; and suddenly he knew a furious disinclination, even a raging refusal, to die at all. He stooped quickly aside, already dodging, scrabbling about him for some weapon as Varner's face rose still further above the desk top like a bilious moon.

"What in hell are you after?" Varner said. "I told you two days ago that window sash aint come yet."

"Window sash?" Labove said.

"Nail some planks over it," Varner said. "Do you expect me to make a special trip to town to keep a little fresh air out of your collar?"

Then he remembered it. The panes had been broken out during the Christmas holidays. He had nailed boards over them at the time. He did not remember doing it. But then he did not remember being told about the promised sash two days ago, let alone asking about it. And now he stopped remembering the window at all. He rose quietly and stood, the overcoat over his arm; now he did not even see the surly suspicious face anymore. Yes, he thought quietly; Yes. I see. She never told him at all. She didn't even forget to. She doesn't even know anything happened that was worth mentioning. Varner was still talking; apparently someone had answered him:

"Well, what do you want, then?"

"I want a nail," he said.

"Get it, then." The face had already disappeared beyond the desk. "Bring the hammer back."

"I wont need the hammer," he said. "I just want a nail."

The house, the heatless room in which he had lived for six years now with his books and his bright lamp, was between the store and the school. He did not even look toward it when he passed. He returned to the schoolhouse and closed and locked the door. With a fragment of brick he drove the nail into the wall beside the door and hung the key on the nail. The schoolhouse was on the Jefferson road. He already had the overcoat with him.

CHAPTER TWO

1

*T*hrough that spring and through the long succeeding summer of her fourteenth year, the youths of fifteen and sixteen and seventeen who had been in school with her and others who had not, swarmed like wasps about the ripe peach which her full damp mouth resembled. There were about a dozen of them. They formed a group, close, homogeneous, and loud, of which she was the serene and usually steadily and constantly eating axis, center. There were three or four girls in the group, lesser girls, though if she were deliberately using them for foils, nobody knew it for certain. They were smaller girls, even though mostly older. It was as though that abundance which had invested her cradle, not content with merely overshadowing them with the shape of features and texture of hair and skin, must also dwarf and extinguish them ultimately with sheer bulk and mass.

They were together at least once a week and usually oftener. They would meet at the church on Sunday mornings and sit together in two adjacent pews which presently became their own by common consent of the congregation and authorities, like a class or an isolation place. They met at the community parties which would be held in the now empty schoolhouse, which was to be used for nothing else for almost two years before another teacher was installed. They arrived in a group, they chose one another monotonously in the two-sing games, the boys clowning and ruthless, loud. They might have been a masonic lodge set suddenly down in Africa or China, holding a weekly meeting. They departed together, walking back down the star- or moonlit road in a tight noisy clump, to leave her at her father's gate before dispersing. If the boys had been sparring for opportunities to walk home with her singly, nobody knew that either because she was never known to walk home singly from anywhere or to walk anywhere anyhow when she could help it.

They would meet again at the singings and baptisings and picnics about the country. It was election year and after the last of the planting and the first of the laying-by of the crops, there were not only the first-Sunday all-day singings and baptisings, but the vote-rousing picnics as well. The Varner surrey would be seen now week after week among the other tethered vehicles at country churches or on the edge of groves within which the women spread a week's abundance of cold food on the long plank tables while the men stood beneath the raised platforms on which the candidates for the county offices and the legislature and Congress spoke, and the young people in groups or pairs moved about the grove or, in whatever of seclusion the girls could be enticed into, engaged in the clumsy horseplay of adolescent courtship or seduction. She listened to no speeches and set no tables and did no singing. Instead, with those two or three or four lesser girls she sat, nucleus of that loud frustrated group; the nucleus, the center, the centrice; here as at the school parties of last year, casting over them all that spell of incipient accouchement while refusing herself to be pawed at, preserving even within that aura of license and invitation in which she seemed to breathe and walk—or sit rather—a ruthless chastity impervious even to the light precarious balance, the actual overlapping, of Protestant religious and sexual excitement. It was as if she really knew what instant, moment, she was reserved for, even if not his name and face, and was waiting for that moment rather than merely for the time for the eating to start, as she seemed to be.

They would meet again at the homes of the girls. This would be by prearrangement without doubt, and doubtless contrived by the other girls, though if she were aware that they invited her so that the boys would come, nobody ever divined this from her behavior either. She would make visits of overnight or of two and three days with them. She was not allowed to attend the dances which would be held in the village schoolhouse or in other schoolhouses or country stores at night. She had never asked permission; it had rather been violently refused her by her brother before anyone knew whether she was going to ask it or not. The brother did not object to the house visits though. He even fetched her back and forth on the horse as he had used to do to and from the school and for the same reason he would not let her walk from the school to the store to meet him, still seething and grimly outraged and fanatically convinced of what he believed he was battling against, riding for miles, the oilcloth book-satchel containing the nightgown and the toothbrush which her mother compelled her to bring held in the same hand which clutched the cross of his suspenders, the soft mammalian rubbing against his back and the steady quiet sound of chewing and swallowing in his ear, stopping the horse at last before the house she had come to visit and snarling at her, "Cant you stop eating that damn potato long enough to get down and let me go back to work?"

In early September the annual County Fair was held in Jefferson. She and her parents went to town and lived for four days in a board-ing house. The youths and the three girls were already there wait-ing for her. While her father looked at livestock and farm tools and her mother bustled cheerful and martinettish among ranked cans and jars and decorated cakes, she moved all day long in the hem-length-ened dresses she had worn last year to school and surrounded by her loud knot of loutish and belligerent adolescents, from shooting gallery to pitch game to pop stand, usually eating something, or time after time without even dismounting and still eating, rode, her long Olympian legs revealed halfway to the thigh astride the wooden horses of merry-go-rounds.

By her fifteenth year they were men. They were the size of men and doing the work of grown men at least—eighteen and nineteen and twenty, who in that time and country should have been think-ing of marriage and, for her sake anyway, looking toward other girls; for their own sakes, almost any other girl. But they were not thinking of marriage. There were about a dozen of them too, who at some moment, instant, during that second spring which her brother still could not definitely put his finger on, had erupted into her placid orbit like a stampede of wild cattle, trampling ruthlessly aside the children of last summer's yesterday. Luckily for her brother, the pic-nics were not as frequent this year as during the election summer, because he went with the family now in the surrey—the humorless seething raging man in his hot bagging broadcloth and collarless glazed shirt who now, as if in a kind of unbelieving amazement, did not even snarl at her anymore. He had nagged Mrs Varner into making her wear corsets. He would grasp her each time he saw her outside the house, in public or alone, and see for himself if she had them on.

Although the brother declined to attend the singings and baptisings, he had badgered the parents into standing in his stead then. So the young men had what might be called a free field only on Sundays. They would arrive in a body at the church, riding up on horses and mules taken last night from the plow and which would return to the plow with tomorrow's sun, and wait for the Varner surrey to arrive. That was all the adolescent companions of last year ever saw of her now—that glimpse of her between the surrey and the church door as she moved stiff and awkward in the corset and the hem-lengthened dress of last year's childhood, seen for an instant then hidden by the crowding surge of those who had dispossessed them. Within another year it would be the morning's formal squire in a glittering buggy drawn by a horse or mare bred for harness, and the youths of this year would be crowded aside in their turn. But that would be next year; now it was a hodge-podge though restrained into something like decorum or at least discretion by the edifice and the day, a leashed turmoil of lust like so many lowering dogs after a scarce-fledged and apparently unawares bitch, filing into the church to sit on a back bench where they could watch the honey-colored head demure among those of her parents and brother.

After church the brother would be gone, courting himself, it was believed, and through the long drowsing afternoons the trace-galled mules would doze along the Varner fence while their riders sat on the veranda, doggedly and vainly sitting each other out, crass and loud and baffled and raging not at one another but at the girl herself who apparently did not care whether they stayed or not, apparently not even aware that the sitting-out was going on. Older people, passing, would see them—the half dozen or so bright Sunday shirts with pink or lavender sleeve-garters, the pomaded hair above the shaved sun-burned necks, the polished shoes, the hard loud faces, the eyes filled with the memory of a week of hard labor in fields behind them and knowledge of another week of it ahead; among them the girl, the centrice here too—the body of which there was simply too much dressed in the clothing of childhood, like a slumberer washed out of Paradise by a night flood and discovered by chance passers and covered hurriedly with the first garment to hand, still sleeping. They would sit leashed and savage and loud and wild at the vain galloping seconds while the shadows lengthened and the frogs and whippoorwills began and the fireflies began to blow and drift above the creek. Then Mrs Varner would come bustling out, talking, and still talking herd them all in to eat the cold remains of the heavy noon meal beneath the bug-swirled lamp, and they would give up. They would depart in a body, seething and decorous, to mount the patient mules and horses and ride in furious wordless amity to the creek ford a half mile away and dismount and hitch the horses and mules and with bare fists fight silently and savagely and wash the blood off in the water and mount again and ride their separate ways, with their skinned knuckles and split lips and black eyes and for the time being freed even of rage and frustration and desire, beneath the cold moon, across the planted land.

By the third summer the trace-galled mules had given way to the trotting horses and the buggies. Now it was the youths, the outgrown and discarded of last year, who waited about the churchyard on Sunday mornings to watch in impotent and bitter turn their own dispossession—the glittering buggy powdered only lightly over with dust, drawn by a bright mare or horse in brass-studded harness, driven by the man who owned them both—a man grown in his own right and never again to be haled from an attic bed in an iron dawn to milk cows or break land not his own, by a father who still held over him legally and sometimes physically too the power to bind and loose. Beside him would be the girl who last year, after a fashion at least, had been their own and who had outgrown them, escaped them like the dead summer itself, who had learned at last to walk without proclaiming the corsets beneath the dresses of silk in which she looked, not like a girl of sixteen dressed like twenty, but a woman of thirty dressed in the garments of her sixteen-year-old sister.

At one time in the spring, for an afternoon and evening, to be exact, there were four buggies. The fourth one belonged to a drummer, rented. He appeared in the village by accident one day, having lost his way and blundered upon Frenchman's Bend to ask directions without even knowing there was a store there, in a battered rig which a Jefferson livery stable rented to travelling men. He saw the store and stopped and tried to sell the clerk, Snopes, a bill of goods and got nowhere quickly. He was a youngish city man with city ways and assurance and insistence. He had presently wormed from the usual loungers on the gallery who the actual owner of the store was and where he lived, and went on to Varner's house and doubtless knocked and was or was not admitted, since that was all they knew then. Two weeks later he was back, in the same rig. This time he did not even try to sell the Varners anything; it was learned later that he had taken supper at the Varner house. That was Tuesday. On Friday he returned. He was now driving the best turnout which the Jefferson stable had—a runabout and a fair horse—and he not only wore a necktie, he had on the first white flannel trousers Frenchman's Bend ever saw. They were the last ones too, and they were not there long: he ate supper with the Varners and that evening he drove the daughter to a dance in a schoolhouse about eight miles away, and vanished. Someone else brought the daughter home and at daylight the next morning the hostler found the rented horse and buggy tied to the stable door in Jefferson and that afternoon the night station agent told of a frightened and battered man in a pair of ruined ice-cream pants who had bought a ticket on the early train. The train was going south, though it was understood that the drummer lived in Memphis, where it was later learned he had a wife and family, but about this nobody in Frenchman's Bend either knew or cared.

That left three. They were constant, almost in rotation, week and week and Sunday and Sunday about, last summer's foreclosed bankrupts waiting at the church to watch him of that morning lift her out of the buggy. They still waited there to look at her exposed leg when she got back into it, or, a lowering clot further along the road, they would stand suddenly out of the undergrowth as the buggy swept past to shout vicious obscenity after it out of the spinning and choking dust. At some time during the afternoon one or two or three of them would pass the Varner house, to see without looking at them the horse and buggy hitched to the fence and Will Varner napping in his wooden hammock in its small grove in the yard and the closed blinds of the parlor windows beyond, shuttered after the local fashion, against the heat. They would lurk in the darkness, usually with a jug of white hill whiskey, just beyond the light-radius of the homes or stores or school buildings within the lamplit doors and windows of which the silhouettes of dancing couples moved athwart the whine and squeal of fiddles. Once they charged yelling from a clump of shadow beside the moonlit road, upon the moving buggy, the mare rearing and plunging, the driver standing up in the buggy and slashing at them with the whip and laughing at them as they ducked and dodged. Because it was not the brother, it was this dead last summer's vain and raging jetsam, who divined or at least believed that there had never been but one buggy all the time. It was almost a year now since Jody had ceased to wait for her in the hall until she came out, dressed, the buggy waiting, to grasp her arm and exactly as he would have felt the back of a new horse for old saddle sores, grimly explore with his hard heavy hand to see if she had the corset on or not.

This buggy belonged to a man named McCarron who lived about twelve miles from the village. He was the only child of a widow, herself the only child of a well-to-do landowner. Motherless, she had eloped at nineteen with a handsome, ready-tongued, assured and pleasant man who had come into the country without specific antecedents and no definite past. He had been there about a year. His occupation seemed to be mainly playing poker in the back rooms of country stores or the tack rooms of stables, and winning, though perfectly honestly; there had never been any question of that. All the women said he would make a poor husband. The men said that only a shotgun would ever make him a husband of any sort, and most of them would have declined him as a son-in-law even on those terms, because he had that about him which loved the night—not the night's shadows, but the bright hysteric glitter-glare which made them, the perversity of unsleeping. Nevertheless, Alison Hoake climbed out a second-storey window one night. There was no ladder, no drainpipe, no rope of knotted sheets. They said she jumped and McCarron caught her in his arms and they vanished for ten days and returned, McCarron walking, his fine teeth exposed though the rest of his face took no part in the smile, into the room where old Hoake had sat for ten days now with a loaded shotgun across his lap.

To everyone's surprise, he made not only a decent husband, but son-in-law too. He knew little about farming and did not pretend to like it, nevertheless he served as his father-in-law's overseer, carrying out the old man's verbatim instructions like a dictaphone record would have of course, but having himself the gift of getting along well with, and even dominating somewhat, all men not as ready of tongue as he, though it was actually his jolly though lightly-balanced temper and his reputation as a gambler which got him the obedience of the Negro field hands even more than his position as the son-in-law or even his proved prowess with a pistol. He even stayed home at night and quit the poker-playing. In fact, later nobody could decide for certain if the cattle-buying scheme had not been the father-in-law's instead of his. But within a year, by which time he was a father himself, he was buying up cattle and taking them in droves overland to the railroad and Memphis every two or three months. This went on for ten years, by which time the father-in-law had died and left the property to his grandson. Then McCarron made his last trip. Two nights later one of his drovers galloped up to the house and waked his wife. McCarron was dead, and the countryside never did know much about that either, shot in a gambling house apparently. His wife left the nine-year-old boy with the Negro servants and went in the farm wagon and fetched her husband's body home and buried it on the oak and cedar knoll beside her father and mother. Shortly after that a rumor, a tale of a brief day or two, went about that a woman had shot him. But that died; they only said to one another, "So that's what he was doing all the time," and there remained only the legend of the money and jewels he was supposed to have won during the ten years and fetched home at night and, with his wife's help, bricked up in one of the chimneys of the house.

The son, Hoake, at twenty-three looked older. This was his father's assurance in his face which was bold and handsome too. It was also a little swaggering and definitely spoiled though not vain so much as intolerant, which his father's face had not been. It also lacked humor and equability and perhaps intelligence too, which his father's face had not lacked, but which that of the man who sat for ten days after his daughter's elopement with a loaded shotgun on his lap, probably did. He grew up with a Negro lad for his sole companion. They slept in the same room, the Negro on a pallet on the floor, until he was ten years old. The Negro was a year older. When they were six and seven, he conquered the Negro with his fists in fair fight. Afterward he would pay the Negro out of his pocket money at a standard rate fixed between them, for the privilege of whipping the Negro, not severely, with a miniature riding crop.

At fifteen his mother sent him to a military boarding school. Precocious, well-co-ordinated and quick to learn whatever he saw was to his benefit, he acquired enough credits in three years to enter college. His mother chose an agricultural college. He went there and spent a whole year in the town without even matriculating while his mother believed he was passing his freshman work. The next fall he did matriculate, remained five months and was given the privilege of withdrawing from the school following a scandalous denouement involving the wife of a minor instructor. He returned home and spent the next two years ostensibly overseeing the plantation which his mother now ran. This meant that he spent some part of the day riding about it in the dress boots of his military school days which still fitted his small feet and which were the first riding boots the countryside had ever seen. Five months ago he happened by chance to ride through Frenchman's Bend village and saw Eula Varner. This was he against whom, following the rout of the Memphis drummer, the youths of last summer's trace-galled mules rose in embattled concert to defend that in which apparently they and the brother both had no belief, even though they themselves had failed signally to disprove it, as knights before them have probably done. A scout of two or three would lurk about the Varner fence to watch the buggy depart and find which road it would take. They would follow or precede it to whatever plank-trampling fiddle-impregnated destination, to wait there with the jug of raw whiskey and follow it back home or toward home—the long return through night-time roads across the mooned or unmooned sleeping land, the mare's feet like slow silk in the dust as a horse moves when the reins are wrapped about the upright whip in its dashboard socket, the fords into which the unguided mare would step gingerly down and stop unchidden and drink, nuzzling and blowing among the broken reflections of stars, raising its dripping muzzle and maybe drinking again or maybe just blowing into the water as a thirst-quenched horse will. There would be no voice, no touch of rein to make it move on; anyway, it would be standing there too long, too long, too long. One night they charged the moving buggy from the roadside shadows and were driven off by the whip because they had no concerted plan but were moved by a spontaneous combustion of rage and grief. A week after that, the horse and buggy tied to the Varner fence, they burst with yells and banging pans around the corner of the dark veranda, McCarron presently strolling composedly out, not from the porch but from the clump of trees where Varner's wooden hammock hung, and called upon two or three of them by name and cursed them in a pleasant, drawling, conversational voice and dared any two of them to meet him down the road. They could see the pistol hanging in his hand against his flank.

Then they gave him formal warning. They could have told the brother but they did not, not because the brother would more than likely have turned upon the informers with physical violence. Like the teacher Labove, they would have welcomed that, they would have accepted that with actual joy. As with Labove, it would at least have been the same living flesh warm under furious impact, bruising, scoriating, springing blood, which, like Labove, was what they actually desired now whether they knew it or not. It was because they were already insulated against acceptance of the idea of telling him by the fact that their rage would be wasted then upon the agent of their vengeance and not the betrayer; they would have met the profferer of a mortal affronting and injury with their hands bound up in boxing gloves. So they sent McCarron a formal warning in writing with their names signed. One of them rode the twelve miles to his mother's house one night and fastened the notice to the door. The next afternoon McCarron's Negro, a grown man too now, brought the five separate answers and escaped from them at last, bloody about the head but not seriously hurt.

Yet for almost another week he foiled them. They were trying to take him when he was in the buggy alone, either before he had reached the Varner house or after he had left it. But the mare was too fast for them to overtake, and their spiritless plow-animals would not stand ground and halt the mare, and they knew from the previous attempt that if they tried to stop the mare on foot, he would ride them down, standing up in the buggy with the slashing whip and his hard bare jeering teeth. Besides, he had the pistol, they had learned enough about him to know that he had never been without it since he turned twenty-one. And there was still the matter to be settled between him and the two who had beaten his Negro messenger.

So they were forced at last to ambush him at the ford with Eula in the buggy when the mare stopped to drink. Nobody ever knew exactly what happened. There was a house near the ford, but there were no yells and shouts this time, merely abrasions and cuts and missing teeth on four of the five faces seen by daylight tomorrow. The fifth one, the other of the two who had beaten the Negro, still lay unconscious in the nearby house. Someone found the butt of the buggy whip. It was clotted with dried blood and human hair and later, years later, one of them told that it was the girl who had wielded it, springing from the buggy and with the reversed whip beating three of them back while her companion used the reversed pistol-butt against the wagon-spoke and the brass knuckles of the other two. That was all that was ever known, the buggy reaching the Varner house not especially belated. Will Varner, in his nightshirt and eating a piece of cold peach pie with a glass of buttermilk in the kitchen, heard them come up from the gate and onto the veranda, talking quietly, murmuring as she and her young men did about what her father believed was nothing, and on into the house, the hall, and on to the kitchen door. Varner looked up and saw the bold handsome face, the pleasant hard revelation of teeth which would have been called smiling at least, though it was not particularly deferent, the swelling eye, the long welt down the jaw, the hanging arm flat against the side. "He bumped into something," the daughter said.

"I see he did," Varner said. "He looks like it kicked him too."

"He wants some water and a towel," she said. "It's over yonder," she said, turning; she did not come into the kitchen, the light. "I'll be back in a minute." Varner heard her mount the stairs and move about in her room overhead but he paid no further attention. He looked at McCarron and saw that the exposed teeth were gritted rather than smiling, and he was sweating. After he saw that, Varner paid no more attention to the face either.

"So you bumped into something," he said. "Can you get that coat off?"

"Yes," the other said. "I did it catching my mare. A piece of scantling."

"Serve you right for keeping a mare like that in a woodshed," Varner said. "This here arm is broke."

"All right," McCarron said. "Aint you a veterinary? I reckon a man aint so different from a mule."

"That's correct," Varner said. "Usually he aint got quite as much sense." The daughter entered. Varner had heard her on the stairs again, though he did not notice that she now wore another dress from that in which she had left the house. "Fetch my whiskey jug," he said. It was beneath his bed, where it stayed. She fetched it down. McCarron sat now with his bared arm flat on the kitchen table. He fainted once, erect in the chair, but not for long. After that it was only the fixed teeth and the sweat until Varner had done. "Pour him another drink and go wake Sam to drive him home," Varner said. But McCarron would not, either be driven home or go to bed where he was. He had a third drink from the jug and he and the girl went back to the veranda and Varner finished his pie and milk and carried the jug back upstairs and went to bed.

It was not the father and not even the brother, who for five or six years now had actually been supported upright and intact in breathing life by an idea which had not even grown through the stage of suspicion at all but had sprung fullblown as a conviction only the more violent for the fact that the most unremitting effort had never been able to prove it, whom divination descended upon. Varner took a drink himself from the jug and shoved it back under the bed where a circle of dust marked the place where it had sat for years, and went to sleep. He entered his accustomed state of unsnoring and child-like slumber and did not hear his daughter mount the stairs, to remove this time the dress which had her own blood on it. The mare, the buggy, was gone by then, though McCarron fainted in it again before he reached home. The next morning the doctor found that, although the break had been properly set and splinted, nevertheless it had broken free since, the two bone-ends telescoping, and so had to be set again. But Varner did not know that—the father, the lean pleasant shrewd unillusioned man asleep in the bed above the whiskey jug twelve miles away, who, regardless of what error he might have made in the reading of the female heart in general and his daughter's in particular, had been betrayed at the last by failing to anticipate that she would not only essay to, but up to a certain point actually support, with her own braced arm from underneath, the injured side.

Three months later, when the day came for the delicate buggies and the fast bright horses and mares to be seen no more along the Varner fence, Will Varner himself was the last to discover it. They and the men who drove them were gone, vanished overnight, not only from Frenchman's Bend but from the country itself. Although one of the three knew certainly one who was guilty, and the other two knew collectively two who were not, all three of them fled, secretly and by back roads probably, with saddle-bags or single hurried portmanteaus for travelling fast. One of them went because of what he believed the Varner men would do. The other two fled because they knew that the Varners would not do it. Because the Varners too would know by now from the one incontrovertible source, the girl herself, that two of them were not guilty, and so those two would thus be relegated also to the flotsam of a vain dead yesterday of passionate and eternal regret and grief, along with the impotent youths who by badgering them also, along with him who had been successful, had conferred upon them likewise blindly and unearned the accolade of success. By fleeing too, they put in a final and despairing bid for the guilt they had not compassed, the glorious shame of the ruin they did not do.

So when the word went quietly from house to house about the country that McCarron and the two others had vanished and that Eula Varner was in what everyone else but her, as it presently appeared, called trouble, the last to learn of it was the father—this man who cheerfully and robustly and undeviatingly declined to accept any such theory as female chastity other than as a myth to hoodwink young husbands with just as some men decline to believe in free tariff or the efficacy of prayer; who, as it was well known, had

spent and was still spending no inconsiderable part of his time proving to himself his own contention, who at the present moment was
engaged in a liaison with the middle-fortyish wife of one of his own
tenants. He was too old, he told her baldly and plainly, to be tomcatting around at night, about his own house or any other man's. So
she would meet him in the afternoons, on pretence of hunting hen-
nests, in a thicket beside the creek near her house, in which sylvan
Pan-hallowed retreat, the fourteen-year-old boy whose habit it was
to spy on them told, Varner would not even remove his hat. He was
the last to hear about it, waked where he slept in his sock feet in the
wooden hammock, by the peremptory voice of his wife, hurrying,
lean, loose-jointed and still not quite awake, in his stockings across
the yard and into the hall where Mrs Varner, in a loose old wrapper
and the lace boudoir cap in which she took her afternoon naps,
shouted at him in an immediate irate voice above the uproar of his
son's voice from the daughter's room upstairs: "Eula's got a baby. Go
up there and knock that fool in the head."

"Got a what?" Varner said. But he did not pause. He hurried on,
Mrs Varner following, up the stairs and into the room in which for
the last day or two the daughter had remained more or less constantly, not even coming down for meals, suffering from what, if
Varner had thought about it at all, he would have judged merely a
stomach disorder from eating too much, possibly accumulated and
suddenly and violently retroactive after sixteen years of visceral for-
bearance and outragement. She sat in a chair beside the window in
her loosened hair and a bright near-silk negligee she had ordered
recently from a Chicago mail-order house. Her brother stood over
her, shaking her arm and shouting: "Which one was it? Tell me
which one!"

"Stop shoving me," she said. "I dont feel good." Again Varner did
not pause. He came between them and thrust Jody back.

"Let her alone," he said. "Get on out of here." Jody turned on
Varner his suffused face.

"Let her alone?" he said. He laughed fiercely, with no mirth, his
eyes pale, popping and enraged. "That's what's the matter now! She's
done been let alone too damn much already! I tried. I knowed what
was coming. I told both of you five years ago. But no. You both knew

better. And now see what you got! See what's happened! But I'll make her talk. By God, I'll find out who it was. And then I—"

"All right," Varner said. "What's happened?" For a moment, a minute almost, Jody appeared to be beyond speech. He glared at Varner. He looked as though only a supreme effort of will kept him from bursting where he stood.

"And he asks me what's happened," he said at last, in an amazed and incredulous whisper. "He asks me what's happened." He whirled; he jerked one hand upward in a gesture of furious repudiation and, Varner following, rushed upon Mrs Varner, who had just reached the door, her hand upon her fleshy now heaving breast and her mouth open for speech as soon as breath returned. Jody weighed two hundred pounds and Mrs Varner, although not much over five feet tall, weighed almost as much. Yet he managed somehow to run past her in the door, she grasping at him as Varner, eel-like, followed. "Stop the fool!" she shouted, following again as Varner and Jody thundered back down the stairs and into the ground-floor room which Varner still called his office though for the last two years now the clerk, Snopes, had slept on a cot in it, where Varner now overtook Jody bending over the open drawer of the clumsy (and now priceless, though Varner did not know it) walnut secretary which had belonged to Varner's grandfather, scrabbling a pistol from among the jumble of dried cotton bolls and seed pods and harness buckles and cartridges and old papers which it contained. Through the window beside the desk the Negress, the cook, could be seen running across the back yard toward her cabin, her apron over her head, as Negroes do when trouble starts among the white people. Sam, the man, was following, though slower, looking back at the house, when both Varner and Jody saw him at the same time.

"Sam! Saddle my horse!" Jody roared.

"You Sam!" Varner shouted. They both grasped the pistol now, the four hands now apparently hopelessly inextricable in the open drawer. "Dont touch that horse! Come back here this minute!" Mrs Varner's feet were now pounding in the hall. The pistol came free of the drawer, they stepped back, their hands locked and tangled, to see her now in the door, her hand still at her heaving breast, her ordinarily cheerful opinionated face suffused and irate.

"Hold him till I get a stick of stove wood," she gasped. "I'll fix him. I'll fix both of them. Turning up pregnant and yelling and cursing here in the house when I am trying to take a nap!"

"All right," Varner said. "Go and get it." She went out; she seemed to have been sucked violently out of the door by her own irate affrontment. Varner wrenched the pistol free and hurled Jody (he was quite strong, incredibly wiry and quick for all his sixty years, though he had cold intelligence for his ally where the son had only blind rage) back into the desk and went and threw the pistol into the hall and slammed the door and turned the key and came back, panting a little but not much. "What in hell are you trying to do?" he said.

"Nothing!" Jody cried. "Maybe you dont give a damn about your name, but I do. I got to hold my head up before folks even if you aint."

"Hah," Varner said. "I aint noticed you having any trouble holding it up. You have just about already got to where you cant get it far enough down to lace your own shoes." Jody glared at him, panting.

"By God," he said, "maybe she wont talk but I reckon I can find somebody that will. I'll find all three of them. I'll—"

"What for? Just out of curiosity to find out for certain just which of them was and wasn't diddling her?" Again for a long moment Jody could not speak at all. He stood against the desk, huge, bull-goaded, impotent and outraged, actually suffering, not from lese-Varner but from frustration. Mrs Varner's heavy stockinged feet pounded again in the hall; she began now to hammer at the door with the stick of wood.

"You, Will!" she shouted. "Open this door!"

"You mean you aint going to do *nothing?*" Jody said. "Not anything?"

"Do what?" Varner said. "To who? Dont you know them damn tomcats are halfway to Texas now? Where would you be about now, if it was you? Where would I be, even at my age, if I was footloose enough to prowl any roof I wanted to and could get in when I did? I know damn well where, and so would you—right where they are and still lathering horsemeat." He went to the door and unlocked it, though the steady irate tattoo of Mrs Varner's stick was so loud that she apparently did not hear the key turn at all. "Now you go on out to the barn and set down until you cool off. Make Sam dig you some worms and go fishing. If this family needs any head-holding-up done, I'll tend to it myself." He turned the knob. "Hell and damnation, all this hullabaloo and uproar because one confounded running bitch finally foxed herself. What did you expect—that she would spend the rest of her life just running water through it?"

That was Saturday afternoon. On the next Monday morning the seven men squatting about the gallery of the store saw the clerk, Snopes, coming on foot down the road from Varner's house, followed by a second man who was carrying a suitcase. The clerk not only wore the gray cloth cap and the minute tie but a coat too, and then they saw that the suitcase which the second man carried was the straw one which Snopes had carried new to Varner's house one afternoon a year ago and left there. Then they began to look at the man who was carrying it. They saw that the clerk was heeled as by a dog by a man a little smaller than himself but shaped exactly like him. It was as though the two of them were merely graded by perspective. At first glance even the two faces were identical, until the two of them mounted the steps. Then they saw that the second face was a Snopes face right enough, differing from the other only by that unpredictable variation within the iron kinship to which they had become accustomed—in this case a face not smaller than the other exactly but closer, the features plucked together at the center of it not by some inner impulse but rather from the outside, as though by a single swift gesture of the fingers of one hand; a face quick and bright and not derisive exactly, but profoundly and incorrigibly merry behind the bright, alert, amoral eyes of a squirrel or a chipmunk.

They mounted the steps and crossed the gallery, carrying the suitcase. Snopes jerked his head at them exactly as Will Varner himself did it, chewing; they entered the store. After a while three more men came out of the blacksmith shop opposite, so there were a dozen of them about within sight of the gallery when, an hour later, the Varner surrey came up. The Negro, Sam, was driving. Beside him in front was the tremendous battered telescope bag which Mr and Mrs Varner had made their honeymoon to Saint Louis with and which all travelling Varners had used since, even the daughters mar-

rying, sending it back empty, when it would seem to be both symbol
and formal notice of moonset, the mundane return, the valedictory
of bright passion's generous impulsive abandon, as the printed card
had been of its hopeful dawn. Varner, in the back seat with his daughter, called a general greeting, short, perfectly inflectionless, unread-
able. He did not get out, and those on the gallery looked quietly once
and then away from the calm beautiful mask beside him beneath the
Sunday hat, the veil, above the Sunday dress, even the winter coat,
seeing without looking at him as Snopes came out of the store, carrying the straw suitcase, and mounted to the front seat beside the
telescope bag. The surrey moved on. Snopes turned his head once
and spat over the wheel. He had the straw suitcase on his knees like
the coffin of a baby's funeral.

The next morning Tull and Bookwright returned from Jefferson,
where they had delivered another drove of cattle to the railroad. By
that night the countryside knew the rest of it—how on that Monday
afternoon Varner and his daughter and his clerk had visited his bank,
where Varner had cashed a considerable check. Tull said it was for
three hundred dollars. Bookwright said that meant a hundred and
fifty then, since Varner would discount even his own paper to himself
fifty percent. From there they had gone to the courthouse, to the
Chancery Clerk's office, where a deed to the Old Frenchman place
was recorded to Flem and Eula Varner Snopes. A Justice of the Peace
had a desk in the Circuit Clerk's office, where they bought the
license.

Tull blinked rapidly, telling it. He coughed. "The bride and
groom left for Texas right after the ceremony," he said.

"That makes five," a man named Armstid said. "But they say Texas
is a big place."

"It's beginning to need to be," Bookwright said. "You mean six."

Tull coughed. He was still blinking rapidly. "Mr Varner paid for
it too," he said.

"Paid for what too?" Armstid said.

"The wedding license," Tull said.

2

She knew him well. She knew him so well that she never had to look at him anymore. She had known him ever since her fourteenth summer, when the people said that he had "passed" her brother. They did not say it to her. She would not have heard them. She would not have cared. She saw him almost every day, because in her fifteenth summer he began to come to the house itself, usually after supper, to sit with her father on the veranda, not talking but listening, spitting his tobacco neatly over the railing. Sometimes on Sunday afternoons he would come and squat against a tree beside the wooden hammock where her father lay in his stockings, still not talking and still chewing; she would see him there from where she sat on the veranda surrounded by her ravening crowd of that year's Sunday beaux. By then she had learned to recognise the mute hissing of his tennis shoes on the veranda planks; without rising or even turning her head she would call toward the interior of the house: "Papa, here's that man," or, presently, "the man,"—"papa, here's the man again," though sometimes she said Mr Snopes, saying it exactly as she would have said Mr Dog.

In the next summer, her sixteenth, she not only did not look at him, she never saw him again because he now lived in the same house, eating at the same table, using her brother's saddle horse to attend to his and her father's interminable business. He would pass her in the hall where her brother held her, dressed to go out to the waiting buggy, while his hard raging hand explored to see if she had the corset on, and she would not see him. She faced him across the table to eat twice a day because she ate her own breakfast in the kitchen, at whatever midmorning hour her mother finally got her up, though once she was awake it was no further trouble to get her down to the table; harried at last from the kitchen by the Negress or her mother, the last half-eaten biscuit in her hand and her face unwashed and looking, in the rich deshabille of her loose hair and the sloven and not always clean garments she had groped into between bed and breakfast table, as if she had just been surprised from a couch of illicit love by a police raid, she would meet and pass him returning to his

noon meal, in the hall, and he had never been. And so one day they
clapped her into her Sunday clothes and put the rest of her things—
the tawdry mail-order negligees and nightgowns, the big cheap
flimsy shoes and what toilet things she had—into the tremendous
bag and took her to town in the surrey and married her to him.

Ratliff was in Jefferson that Monday afternoon too. He saw the
three of them cross the Square from the bank to the courthouse and
followed them. He walked past the door to the Chancery Clerk's
office and saw them inside; he could have waited and seen them go
from there to the Circuit Clerk's office and he could have witnessed
the marriage, but he did not. He did not need to. He knew what was
happening now and he had already gone on to the station, there waiting an hour before the train was due, and he was not wrong; he saw
the straw suitcase and the big telescope bag go into the vestibule, in
that juxtaposition no more paradoxical and bizarre; he saw the calm
beautiful mask beneath the Sunday hat once more beyond a moving
window, looking at nothing, and that was all. If he had lived in
Frenchman's Bend itself during that spring and summer, he would
have known no more—a little lost village, nameless, without grace,
forsaken, yet which wombed once by chance and accident one blind
seed of the spendthrift Olympian ejaculation and did not even know
it, without tumescence conceived, and bore—one bright brief summer, concentric, during which three fairly well-horsed buggies stood
in steady rotation along a picket fence or spun along adjacent roads
between the homes and the crossroads stores and the schoolhouses
and churches where people gathered for pleasure or at least for
escape, and then overnight and simultaneously were seen no more;
then eccentric: buggies gone, vanished—a lean, loose-jointed, cot-
ton-socked, shrewd, ruthless old man, the splendid girl with her
beautiful masklike face, the froglike creature which barely reached
her shoulder, cashing a check, buying a license, taking a train—a
word, a single will to believe born of envy and old deathless regret,
murmured from cabin to cabin above the washing pots and the
sewing, from wagon to horseman in roads and lanes or from rider
to halted plow in field furrows; the word, the dream and wish of all
male under sun capable of harm—the young who only dreamed yet
of the ruins they were still incapable of; the sick and the maimed

sweating in sleepless beds, impotent for the harm they willed to do; the old, now-glandless earth-creeping, the very buds and blossoms, the garlands of whose yellowed triumphs had long fallen into the profitless dust, embalmed now and no more dead to the living world if they were sealed in buried vaults, behind the impregnable matronly calico of others' grandchildren's grandmothers—the word, with its implications of lost triumphs and defeats of unimaginable splendor—and which best: to have that word, that dream and hope for future, or to have had need to flee that word and dream, for past. Even one of the actual buggies remained. Ratliff was to see it, discovered a few months afterward, standing empty and with propped shafts in a stable shed a few miles from the village, gathering dust; chickens roosted upon it, steadily streaking and marring the once-bright varnish with limelike droppings, until the next harvest, the money-time, when the father of its late driver sold it to a Negro farmhand, after which it would be seen passing through the village a few times each year, perhaps recognised, perhaps not, while its new owner married and began to get a family and then turn gray, spilling children, no longer glittering, its wheels wired upright in succession by crossed barrel staves until staves and delicate wheels both vanished, translated apparently in motion at some point into stout, not new, slightly smaller wagon wheels, giving it a list, the list too interchangeable, ranging from quarter to quarter between two of its passing appearances behind a succession of spavined and bony horses and mules in wire- and rope-patched harness, as if its owner had horsed it ten minutes ago out of a secret boneyard for this particular final swan-song's apotheosis which, woefully misinformed as to its own capacities, was each time not the last.

But when he at last turned his little tough team toward Frenchman's Bend again, Bookwright and Tull had long since returned home and told it. It was now September. The cotton was open and spilling into the fields; the very air smelled of it. In field after field as he passed along the pickers, arrested in stooping attitudes, seemed fixed amid the constant surf of bursting bolls like piles in surf, the long, partly-filled sacks streaming away behind them like rigid frozen flags. The air was hot, vivid and breathless—a final fierce concentration of the doomed and dying summer. The feet of the small

horses twinkled rapidly in the dust and he sat, loose and easy to the
motion, the reins loose in one hand, inscrutable of face, his eyes
darkly impenetrable, quizzical and bemused, remembering, still seeing them—the bank, the courthouse, the station; the calm beautiful
mask seen once more beyond a moving pane of glass, then gone. But
that was all right, it was just meat, just gal-meat he thought, and God
knows there was a plenty of that, yesterday and tomorrow too. Of
course there was the waste, not wasted on Snopes but on all of them,
himself included—Except was it waste? he thought suddenly, seeing
the face again for an instant as though he had recalled not only the
afternoon but the train too—the train itself, which had served its day
and schedule and so, despite the hard cars, the locomotive, no more
existed. He looked at the face again. It had not been tragic, and now
it was not even damned, since from behind it there looked out only
another mortal natural enemy of the masculine race. And beautiful:
but then, so did the highwayman's daggers and pistols make a pretty
shine on him; and now as he watched, the lost calm face vanished. It
went fast; it was as if the moving glass were in retrograde, it too
merely a part, a figment, of the concentric flotsam and jetsam of the
translation, and there remained only the straw bag, the minute tie,
the constant jaw:

*Until at last, baffled, they come to the Prince his-self. 'Sire,' they says.
'He just wont. We cant do nothing with him.'*

'What?' the Prince hollers.

*'He says a bargain is a bargain. That he swapped in good faith and
honor, and now he has come to redeem it, like the law says. And we cant find
it,' they says. 'We done looked everywhere. It wasn't no big one to begin with
nohow, and we was specially careful in handling it. We sealed it up in a
asbestos matchbox and put the box in a separate compartment to itself. But
when we opened the compartment, it was gone. The matchbox was there and
the seal wasn't broke. But there wasn't nothing in the matchbox but a little kind of dried-up smear under one edge. And now he has come to redeem
it. But how can we redeem him into eternal torment without his soul?'*

*'Damn it,' the Prince hollers. 'Give him one of the extra ones. Aint there
souls turning up here every day, banging at the door and raising all kinds of
hell to get in here, even bringing letters from Congressmen, that we never
even heard of? Give him one of them.'*

'We tried that,' they says. 'He wont do it. He says he dont want no more and no less than his legal interest according to what the banking and the civil laws states in black and white is hisn. He says he has come prepared to meet his bargain and signature, and he sholy expects you of all folks to meet yourn.'

'Tell him he can go then. Tell him he had the wrong address. That there aint nothing on the books here against him. Tell him his note was lost—if there ever was one. Tell him we had a flood, even a freeze.'

'He wont go, not without his—'

'Turn him out. Eject him.'

'How?' they says. 'He's got the law.'

'Oho,' the Prince says. 'A sawmill advocate. I see. All right,' he says. 'Fix it. Why bother me?' And he set back and raised his glass and blowed the flames offen it like he thought they was already gone. Except they wasn't gone.

'Fix what?' they says.

'His bribe!' the Prince hollers. 'His bribe! Didn't you just tell me he come in here with his mouth full of law? Did you expect him to hand you a wrote-out bill for it?'

'We tried that,' they says. 'He wont bribe.'

Then the Prince set up there and sneered at them with his sharp bitter tongue and no talkback, about how likely what they thought was a bribe would be a cash discount with maybe a trip to the Legislature throwed in, and them standing there and listening and taking it because he was the Prince. Only there was one of them that had been there in the time of the Prince's pa. He used to dandle the Prince on his knee when the Prince was a boy; he even made the Prince a little pitchfork and learned him how to use it practising on Chinees and Dagoes and Polynesians, until his arms would get strong enough to handle his share of white folks. He didn't appreciate this and he drawed his-self up and he looked at the Prince and he says,

'Your father made, unreproved, a greater failure. Though maybe a greater man tempted a greater man.'

'Or you have been reproved by a lesser,' the Prince snaps back. But he remembered them old days too, when the old fellow was smiling fond and proud on his crude youthful inventions with BB size lava and brimstone and such, and bragging to the old Prince at night about how the boy done that day, about what he invented to do to that little Dago or Chinee that even the *grown folks hadn't thought of yet. So he apologised and got the old fellow smoothed down, and says, 'What did you offer him?'*

'The gratifications.'

'And——?'

'He has them. He says that for a man that only chews, any spittoon will do.'

'And then?'

'The vanities.'

'And——?'

'He has them. He brought a gross with him in the suitcase, specially made up for him outen asbestos, with unmeltable snaps.'

'Then what does he want?' the Prince hollers. 'What does he want? Paradise?' And the old one looks at him and at first the Prince thinks it's because he aint forgot that sneer. But he finds out different.

'No,' the old one says. 'He wants hell.'

And now for a while there aint a sound in that magnificent kingly hall hung about with the proud battle-torn smokes of the old martyrs but the sound of frying and the faint constant screams of authentic Christians. But the Prince was the same stock and blood his pa was. In a flash the sybaritic indolence and the sneers was gone; it might have been the old Prince hisself that stood there. 'Bring him to me,' he says. 'Then leave us.'

So they brought him in and went away and closed the door. His clothes was still smoking a little, though soon he had done brushed most of it off. He come up to the Throne, chewing, toting the straw suitcase.

'Well?' the Prince says.

He turned his head and spit, the spit frying off the floor quick in a little blue ball of smoke. 'I come about that soul,' he says.

'So they tell me,' the Prince says. 'But you have no soul.'

'Is that my fault?' he says.

'Is it mine?' the Prince says. 'Do you think I created you?'

'Then who did?' he says. And he had the Prince there and the Prince knowed it. So the Prince set out to bribe him hisself. He named over all the temptations, the gratifications, the satieties; it sounded sweeter than music the way the Prince fetched them up in detail. But he didnt even stop chewing, standing there holding the straw suitcase. Then the Prince said, 'Look yonder,' pointing at the wall, and there they was, in order and rite for him to watch, watching hisself performing them all, even the ones he hadn't even *thought about inventing to his-self yet, until they was done, the last unimaginable one. And he just turned his head and spit another scorch of tobacco onto the floor and the Prince flung back on the Throne in very exasperation and baffled rage.*

'Then what do you want?' the Prince says. 'What do you want? Paradise?'

'I hadn't figured on it,' he says. 'Is it yours to offer?'

'Then whose is it?' the Prince says. And the Prince knowed he had him there. In fact, the Prince knowed he had him all the time, ever since they had told him how he had walked in the door with his mouth already full of law; he even leaned over and rung the fire-bell so the old one could be there to see and hear how it was done, then he leaned back on the Throne and looked down at him standing there with his straw suitcase, and says, 'You have admitted and even argued that I created you. Therefore your soul was mine all the time. And therefore when you offered it as security for this note, you offered that which you did not possess and so laid yourself liable to—

'I have never disputed that,' he says.

'—criminal action. So take your bag and—' the Prince says. 'Eh?' the Prince says. 'What did you say?'

'I have never disputed that,' he says.

'What?' the Prince says. 'Disputed what?' Except that it dont make any noise, and now the Prince is leaning forward, and now he feels that ere hot floor under his knees and he can feel his-self grabbing and hauling at his throat to get the words out like he was digging potatoes outen hard ground. 'Who are you?' he says, choking and gasping and his eyes a-popping up at him setting there with that straw suitcase on the Throne among the bright, crown-shaped flames. 'Take Paradise!' the Prince screams. 'Take it! Take it!' And the wind roars up and the dark roars down and the Prince scrabbling across the floor, clawing and scrabbling at that locked door, screaming. . . .

BOOK THREE

THE LONG SUMMER

CHAPTER ONE

1

Sitting in the halted buckboard, Ratliff watched the old fat white horse emerge from Varner's lot and come down the lane beside the picket fence, surrounded and preceded by the rich sonorous organ-tone of its entrails. So he's back to the horse again, he thought. He's got to straddle his legs at least once to keep on moving. So he had to pay that too. Not only the deed to the land and the two-dollar wedding license and them two tickets to Texas and the cash, but the riding in that new buggy with somebody to do the driving, to get that patented necktie out of his store and out of his house. The horse came up and stopped, apparently of its own accord, beside the buckboard in which Ratliff sat neat, decorous, and grave like a caller in a house of death.

"You must have been desperate," he said quietly. He meant no insult. He was not even thinking of Varner's daughter's shame or of his daughter at all. He meant the land, the Old Frenchman place. He had never for one moment believed that it had no value. He might have believed this if anyone else had owned it. But the very fact that Varner had ever come into possession of it and still kept it, apparently making no effort to sell it or do anything else with it, was proof enough for him. He declined to believe that Varner ever had been or ever would be stuck with anything; that if he acquired it, he got it cheaper than anyone else could have, and if he kept it, it was too valuable to sell. In the case of the Old Frenchman place he could not see why this was so, but the fact that Varner had bought it and still had it was sufficient. So when Varner finally did let it go, Ratliff believed it was because Varner had at last got the price for which he had been holding it for twenty years, or at least some sufficient price, whether it was in money or not. And when he considered who Varner had relinquished possession to, he believed that the price had been necessity and not cash.

Varner knew that Ratliff was thinking it. He sat the old horse and looked down at Ratliff, the little hard eyes beneath their bushy rust-colored brows glinting at the man who was a good deal nearer his son in spirit and intellect and physical appearance too than any of his own get. "So you think pure liver aint going to choke that cat," he said.

"Maybe with that ere little piece of knotted-up string in it?" Ratliff said.

"What little piece of knotted-up string?"

"I dont know," Ratliff said.

"Hah," Varner said. "You going my way?"

"I reckon not," Ratliff said. "I'm going to mosey down to the store." Unless maybe he even feels he can set around it too again now, he thought.

"So am I," Varner said. "I got that damn trial this morning. That damn Jack Houston and that What's-his-name. Mink. About that durned confounded scrub yearling."

"You mean Houston sued him?" Ratliff said. "*Houston?*"

"No no. Houston just kept the yearling up. He kept it up all last summer and Snopes let him pasture and feed it all winter, and it run in Houston's pasture all this spring and summer too. Then last week for some reason he decided to go and get it. I reckon he figured to beef it. So he went to Houston's with a rope. He was in Houston's pasture, trying to catch it, when Houston come up and stopped him. He finally had to draw his pistol, he claims. He says Snopes looked at the pistol and said, 'That's what you'll need. Because you know I aint got one.' And Houston said all right, they would lay the pistol on a fence post and back off one post apiece on each side and count three and run for it."

"Why didn't they?" Ratliff said.

"Hah," Varner said shortly. "Come on. I want to get it over with. I got some business to tend to."

"You go on," Ratliff said. "I'll mosey on slow. I aint got no yearling calf nor trial neither today."

So the old fat clean horse (it looked always as if it had just come back from the dry-cleaner's; you could almost smell the benzine) moved on again, with a rich preliminary internal chord, going on along the gapped and weathered picket fence. Ratliff sat in the still-motionless buckboard and watched it and the lean, loose-jointed figure which, with the exception of the three-year runabout interval, had bestridden it, the same saddle between them, for twenty-five years, thinking how if, as dogs do, the white horse or his own two either had snuffed along that fence for yellow-wheeled buggies now, they would not have found them, thinking: *And all the other two-legged feice in this country between thirteen and eighty can pass here now without feeling no urge to stop and raise one of them against it.* And yet those buggies were still there. He could see them, sense them. Something was; it was too much to have vanished that quickly and completely—the air polluted and rich and fine which had flowed over and shaped that abundance and munificence, which had done the hydraulic office to that almost unbroken progression of chewed food, which had held intact the constant impact of those sixteen years of sitting down: so why should not that body at the last have been the unscalable sierra, the rosy virginal mother of barricades for no man to conquer scot-free or even to conquer at all, but on the contrary to be hurled back and down, leaving no scar, no mark of himself (*That ere child aint going to look no more like nobody this country ever saw than she did,* he thought.)—the buggy merely a part of the whole, a minor and trivial adjunct, like the buttons on her clothing, the clothes themselves, the cheap beads which one of the three of them had given her. That would never have been for him, not even at the prime summer peak of what he and Varner both would have called his tomcatting's heyday. He knew that without regret or grief, he would not have wanted it to be (*It would have been like giving me a pipe organ, that never had and never would know any more than how to wind up the second-hand music box I had just swapped a mailbox for,* he thought.) and he even thought of the cold and froglike victor without jealousy: and this not because he knew that, regardless of whatever Snopes had expected or would have called what it was he now had, it would not be victory. What he felt was outrage at the waste, the useless squandering; at a situation intrinsically and inherently wrong by any economy, like building a log dead-fall and baiting it with a freshened heifer to catch a rat; or no, worse: as though the gods themselves had funnelled all the concentrated bright wet-slanted unparadised June onto a dung-heap, breeding pismires. Beyond the white horse, beyond the corner of the picket fence, the faint, almost overgrown lane turned off which led to the Old Frenchman place. The horse attempted to turn into it until Varner hauled it roughly back. Not to mention the poorhouse, Ratliff thought. But then, he wouldn't have been infested. He shook his own reins slightly. "Boys," he said, "advance."

The team, the buckboard, went on in the thick dust of the spent summer. Now he could see the village proper—the store, the blacksmith shop, the metal roof of the gin with a thin rapid shimmer of exhaust above the stack. It was now the third week in September; the dry, dust-laden air vibrated steadily to the rapid beat of the engine, though so close were the steam and the air in temperature that no exhaust was visible but merely a thin feverish shimmer of mirage. The very hot, vivid air, which seemed to be filled with the slow laborious plaint of laden wagons, smelled of lint; wisps of it clung among the dust-stiffened roadside weeds and small gouts of cotton lay imprinted by hoof- and wheel-marks into the trodden dust. He could see the wagons too, the long motionless line of them behind the patient, droop-headed mules, waiting to advance a wagon-length at a time, onto the scales and then beneath the suction pipe where Jody Varner would now be again, what with a second new clerk in the store—the new clerk exactly like the old one but a little smaller, a little compacter, as if they had both been cut with the same die but in inverse order to appearance, the last first and after the edges of the die were dulled and spread a little—with his little, full, bright-pink mouth like a kitten's button and his bright, quick, amoral eyes like a chipmunk and his air of merry and incorrigible and unflagging conviction of the inherent constant active dishonesty of all men, including himself.

Jody Varner was at the scales; Ratliff craned his turkey's neck in passing and saw the heavy bagging broadcloth, the white collarless shirt with a yellow halfmoon of sweat at each armpit, the dusty, lint-wisped black hat. So I reckon maybe everybody is satisfied now, he thought. Or everybody except one, he added to himself because before he reached the store Will Varner came out of it and got onto the white horse which someone had just untied and held for him, and on the gallery beyond Ratliff now saw the eruption of men whose laden wagons stood along the road opposite, waiting for the scales, and as he drove up to the gallery in his turn, Mink Snopes and the other Snopes, the proverbist, the school-teacher (he now wore a new frock coat which, for all its newness, looked no less like it belonged to him than the old one in which Ratliff had first seen him did) came down the steps. Ratliff saw the intractable face now cold and still with fury behind the single eyebrow; beside it the rodent's face of the teacher, the two of them seeming to pass him in a whirling of flung unco-ordinated hands and arms out of the new, black, swirling frock coat, the voice that, also like the gestures, seemed to be not servant but master of the body which supplied blood and wind to them:

"Be patient; Caesar never built Rome in one day; patience is the horse that runs steadiest; justice is the right man's bread but poison for the evil man if you give it time. I done looked the law up; Will Varner has misread it pure and simple. We'll take a appeal. We will—" until the other turned his furious face with its single violent emphasis of eyebrow upon him and said fiercely: "---t!" They went on. Ratliff moved up to the gallery. While he was tying his team, Houston came out, followed by the big hound, and mounted and rode away. Ratliff mounted to the gallery where now at least twenty men were gathered, Bookwright among them.

"The plaintiff seems to had legal talent," he said. "What was the verdict?"

"When Snopes pays Houston three dollars pasturage, he can get his bull," Quick said.

"Sho now," Ratliff said. "Wasn't his lawyer even allowed nothing by the court?"

"The lawyer was fined what looked like the considerable balance of one uncompleted speech," Bookwright said. "If that's what you want to know."

"Well well," Ratliff said. "Well well well. So Will couldn't do nothing to the next succeeding Snopes but stop him from talking. Not that any more would have done any good. Snopes can come and

Snopes can go, but Will Varner looks like he is fixing to snopes forever. Or Varner will Snopes forever—take your pick. What is it the
fellow says? off with the old and on with the new; the old job at the
old stand, maybe a new fellow doing the jobbing but it's the same
old stern getting reamed out?" Bookwright was looking at him.

"If you would stand closer to the door, he could hear you a heap
better," he said.

"Sholy," Ratliff said. "Big ears have little pitchers, the world beats
a track to the rich man's hog-pen but it aint every family has a new
lawyer, not to mention a prophet. Waste not want not, except that a
full waist dont need no prophet to prophesy a profit and just whose."
Now they were all watching him—the smooth, impenetrable face
with something about the eyes and the lines beside the mouth which
they could not read.

"Look here," Bookwright said. "What's the matter with you?"

"Why, nothing," Ratliff said. "What could be wrong with nothing
nowhere nohow in this here best of all possible worlds? Likely the
same folks that sells him the neckties will have a pair of long black
stockings too. And any sign-painter can paint him a screen to set up
alongside the bed to look like looking up at a wall full of store shelves
of canned goods—"

"Here," Bookwright said.

"—so he can know to do what every man and woman that ever
seen her between thirteen and Old Man Hundred-and-One McCallum has been thinking about for twenty-nine days now. Of course, he
could fix it with a shed roof to climb up on and a window to crawl
through too. But that aint necessary; that aint his way. No sir. This
here man aint no trifling eave-cat. This here man—" A little boy of
eight or ten came up, trotting, in overalls, and mounted the steps and
gave them a quick glance out of eyes as blue and innocent as peri-
winkles and trotted intently into the store. "—this here man that all
he needs is just to set back there in the store until after a while one
comes in to get a nickel's worth of lard, not buy it: come and ax Mr
Snopes for it, and he gives it to her and writes in a book about it and
her not knowing no more about what he wrote in that book and why
than she does how that ere lard got into that tin bucket with the picture of a hog on it that even she can tell is a hog, and he puts the

bucket back and puts the book away and goes and shuts the door and puts the bar up and she has done already went around behind the counter and laid down on the floor because maybe she thinks by now that's what you have to do, not to pay for the lard because that's done already been wrote down in the book, but to get out of that door again—" The new clerk appeared suddenly among them. He bounced out of the store, his features all seeming to hasten into the center of his face in a fierce depthless glare of bright excitement, the little periwinkle-eyed boy trotting intently around him and on down the steps without waiting.

"All right, boys," the clerk said rapidly, tensely. "He's started. You better hurry. I cant go this time. I got to stay here. Kind of make a swing around from the back so old Littlejohn cant see you. She's done already begun to look cross-eyed." Five or six men had already risen, with a curious, furtive, defiant sort of alacrity. They began to leave the gallery. The little boy was now trotting indefatigably along the fence which enclosed the end of Mrs Littlejohn's lot.

"What's this?" Ratliff said.

"Come on, if you aint seen it yet," one of the departing men said.

"Seen what?" Ratliff said. He looked about at the ones who had not risen. Bookwright was one of them. He was whittling steadily and deeply into a stick of white pine, his face lowered.

"Go on, go on," a second said behind the man who had paused on the steps. "It'll be over before we get there." The group went on then. Ratliff watched them too hurry along Mrs Littlejohn's lot fence after the little boy, still with that curiously furtive defiance.

"What's this you all have got here now?" he said.

"Go and see it," Bookwright said harshly. He did not look up from his knife. Ratliff looked at him.

"Have you seen it?"

"No."

"You going to?"

"No."

"You know what it is?"

"Go on and see it," Bookwright said again, harshly and violently.

"It looks like I'll have to, since aint nobody going to tell me," Ratliff said. He moved toward the steps. The group was now well

on ahead, hurrying along the fence. Ratliff began to descend. He was
still talking. He continued to talk as he went down the steps, not
looking back; nobody could have told whether he was actually talking to the men behind him or not, if he was talking to anyone or not:
"—goes and puts the bar up on the inside and comes back and this
here black brute from the field with the field sweat still drying on her
that she dont know it's sweat she smells because she aint never
smelled nothing else, just like a mule dont know it's mule he smells
for the same reason, and the one garment to her name and that's the
one she's laying there on the floor behind the counter in and looking up past him at them rows of little tight cans with fishes and dev-
ils on them that she dont know what's on the inside either because
she aint never had the dime or the fifteen cents that even if he was
to give her the nickel, not to mention the lard she come after, she
would have after the next two or three times she come after lard, but
just heard somewhere one day the name of what folks said was inside
them, laying there and looking up at them every time his head would
get out of the way long enough, and says, 'Mr Snopes, whut you ax
fer dem sardines?' "

2

As winter became spring and the spring itself advanced, he had less
and less of darkness to flee through and from. Soon it was dark only
when he left the barn, backed carefully, with one down-groping foot,
from the harness-room where his quilt-and-straw bed was, and
turned his back on the long rambling loom of the house where last
night's new drummer-faces snored on the pillows of the beds which
he had now learned to make as well as Mrs Littlejohn could; by April
it was the actual thin depthless suspension of false dawn itself, in
which he could already see and know himself to be an entity solid and
cohered in visibility instead of the uncohered all-sentience of fluid
and nerve-springing terror alone and terribly free in the primal
sightless inimicality. That was gone now. Now the terror existed only
during that moment after the false dawn, that interval's second

between it and the moment which birds and animals know: when the night at last succumbs to day; and then he would begin to hurry, trot, not to get there quicker but because he must get back soon, without fear and calmly now in the growing visibility, the gradation from gray through primrose to the morning's ultimate gold, to the brow of the final hill, to let himself downward into the creekside mist and lie in the drenched myriad waking life of grasses and listen for her approach.

Then he would hear her, coming down the creekside in the mist. It would not be after one hour, two hours, three; the dawn would be empty, the moment and she would not be, then he would hear her and he would lie drenched in the wet grass, serene and one and indivisible in joy, listening to her approach. He would smell her; the whole mist reeked with her; the same malleate hands of mist which drew along his prone drenched flanks palped her pearled barrel too and shaped them both somewhere in immediate time, already married. He would not move. He would lie amid the waking instant of earth's teeming minute life, the motionless fronds of water-heavy grasses stooping into the mist before his face in black, fixed curves, along each parabola of which the marching drops held in minute magnification the dawn's rosy miniatures, smelling and even tasting the rich, slow, warm barn-reek milk-reek, the flowing immemorial female, hearing the slow planting and the plopping suck of each deliberate cloven mud-spreading hoof, invisible still in the mist loud with its hymeneal choristers.

Then he would see her; the bright thin horns of morning, of sun, would blow the mist away and reveal her, planted, blond, dew-pearled, standing in the parted water of the ford, blowing into the water the thick, warm, heavy, milk-laden breath; and lying in the drenched grasses, his eyes now blind with sun, he would wallow faintly from thigh to thigh, making a faint, thick, hoarse moaning sound. Because he cannot make one with her through the day's morning and noon and evening. It is not that he must return to work. There is no work, no travail, no muscular and spiritual reluctance to overcome, constantly war against; yesterday was not, tomorrow is not, today is merely a placid and virginal astonishment at the creeping ridge of dust and trash in front of the broom, at sheets com-

ing smooth and taut at certain remembered motions of the hands—
a routine grooved, irkless; a firm gentle compelling hand, a voice to
hold and control him through joy out of kindness as a dog is taught
and held.

It is because he can go no further. He tried it. It was the third time
he lay and waited for her; the mist blew away and he saw her and this
time there was no today even—no beds to return to, no hand, no
voice: he repudiated fidelity and even habit. He rose and approached
her, speaking to her, his hand extended. She raised her head and
looked at him and scrambled up the further bank, out of the water.
He followed, stepping gingerly down into the water, and began to
cross, lifting his feet high at each step, moaning a little, urgent and
concerned yet not to alarm her more. He fell once, at full length into
the water, making no effort to catch himself, vanishing completely
with one loud cry and rising again, streaming, his breath already
indrawn to cry again. But he stopped the cry, speaking to her instead,
and climbed out onto the bank and approached her again, his hand
extended. This time she ran, rushed on a short distance and turned,
her head lowered; she whirled and rushed away again before his hand
touched her, he following, speaking to her, urgent and cajoling.
Finally she broke back past him and went back to the ford. She ran
faster than he could; trotting, moaning, he watched the vain stippling
of leaf-shadows as they fled across the intact and escaping shape of
love as she recrossed the creek and galloped on up the path for a
short way, where once more she stopped to graze.

He ceased to moan. He hurried back to the creek and began to
cross it, lifting his feet high out of the water at each step as if he
expected each time to find solidity there, or perhaps at each step did
not know whether he would or not. This time he did not fall. But as
soon as he climbed the bank, she moved again, on up the path, not
galloping now but purposefully, so that he once more had to run,
once more steadily losing ground, moaning again now with that
urgent and now alarmed and bewildered amazement. She was now
retracing the path by which she had appeared that morning and all
the other mornings. Probably he did not even know it, was paying no
attention at all to where he was going, seeing nothing but the cow;
perhaps he did not even realise they were in the lot, even when she

went on across it and entered the milking shed which she had left less than an hour ago, though he probably knew generally where she would come from each morning, since he knew most of the adjacent countryside and was never disoriented: objects became fluid in darkness but they did not alter in place and juxtaposition. Perhaps he did not even comprehend that she was in her stable, in any stable, but only that she had stopped at last, ceased to flee at last, because at once he stopped the alarmed and urgent moaning and followed her into the shed, speaking to her again, murmurous, drooling, and touched her with his hand. She whirled; possibly he saw, not that she could not, but only that she did not flee. He touched her again, his hand, his voice, thin and hungry with promise. Then he was lying on his back, her heels were still thudding against the plank wall beside his head and then the dog was standing over him and an instant later the man was hauling him savagely to his feet by the slack of his shirt. Then he was outside the shed while Houston still clutched him by the shirt and cursed in what he could not know was not rage but angry exasperation. The dog stood a few feet away, watching.

"Ike H-mope," he said. "Ike H-mope."

"Ike hell," Houston said, cursing, shaking him. "Go on!" he said. "Git!" He spoke to the dog. "Take him out of here. Easy, now." Now the dog shouted at him. It did not move yet, it merely shouted once; it was as if it said "Boo!" and, still moaning, trying now to talk to the man with his blasted eyes, he moved on toward the still-open gate which he had just entered. Now the dog moved too, just behind him. He looked back at the shed, the cow; he tried again to speak to the man with his eyes, moaning, drooling, when the dog shouted at him again, once, taking one pace toward him but no more, whereupon he gave the dog one terrified glance and broke, trotting toward the gate. The dog shouted again, three times in rapid succession, and he cried now, hoarse and abject, running now, the thick reluctant hips working with a sort of abject and hopeless unco-ordination. "Easy, now!" Houston shouted. He did not hear. He heard only the feet of the dog just behind him. He ran heavily, bellowing.

So now he can go no further. He can lie in the grass and wait for her and hear her and then see her when the mist parts, and that is all. So he would rise from the grass and stand, still swaying faintly from side to side and making the faint, hoarse sound. Then he would turn and mount the hill, stumbling a little because his eyes were still full of sun yet. But his bare feet would know the dust of the road, and in it again, he would begin to trot again, hurrying, still moaning, his shadow shortening on the dust ahead and the mounting sun warm on his back and already drying the dust on his damp overalls; and so back to the house, the littered rooms and the unmade beds. Soon he would be sweeping again, stopping only occasionally to make the hoarse sound of bafflement and incredulous grieving, then watching again with peaceful and absorbed astonishment the creeping ridge of dust and trash before the moving broom. Because even while sweeping he would still see her, blond among the purpling shadows of the pasture, not fixed amid the suppurant tender green but integer of spring's concentrated climax, by it crowned, garlanded.

He was upstairs sweeping when he saw the smoke. He knew exactly where it was—the hill, the sedge-and-brier overgrown hill beyond the creek. Although it was three miles away, he can even see her backing away before the flames and hear her bellowing. He began to run where he stood, carrying the broom. He ran blundering at the wall, the high small window through which he had seen the smoke, which he could not have passed through even if he could have taken the eighteen-foot drop to the earth, as a moth or a trapped bird might. Then the corridor door was facing him and without pausing he ran to it and through it, still carrying the broom, and on down the corridor toward the stairs, when Mrs Littlejohn emerged from a second bedroom and stopped him. "You, Isaac," she said. "You, Isaac." She did not raise her voice and she did not touch him, yet he stopped, moaning, the empty eyes striving at her, picking his feet up in turn like a cat standing on something hot. Then she put her hand out and took him by the shoulder and turned him and he went obediently back up the corridor and into the room again, moaning; he even made a stroke or two with the broom before he saw the smoke again through the window. This time he found the corridor door almost at once, though he did not approach it. Instead he stood for a moment, looking at the broom in his hands, whimpering, then at the bed, smooth and neat where he had just made it up, and he stopped whimpering and went to the bed and turned the covers back and put the broom into it, the straw end on the pillow like a face, and drew the covers up smooth again, tucking them about the broom with that paradoxical unco-ordinated skill and haste, and left the room.

He made no sound now. He did not move on tiptoe, yet he went down the corridor with astonishing silence and celerity; he had reached the stairs and begun to descend before Mrs Littlejohn could have emerged from the other room. At first three years ago, he would not try to descend them. He had ascended them alone; nobody ever knew if he had walked or crawled up, or if perhaps he had mounted them without realising he was doing so, altering his position in altitude, depth perception not functioning in reverse. Mrs Littlejohn had gone to the store. Someone passing the house heard him and when she returned there were five or six people in the hall, looking up at where he clung to the rail at the top step, his eyes shut, bellowing. He still clung to the rail, bellowing and tugging back, when she tried to break his grip and draw him downward. He stayed upstairs three days while she carried food to him and people would come in from miles away and say, "Aint you got him down yet?" before she finally coaxed him to attempt to descend. And even then it took several minutes, while faces gathered in the lower hall to watch as the firm, gentle, unremitting hand, the cold, grim, patient voice, drew him, clinging to the rail and bellowing, step by step downward. For a while after that he would fall down them each time he tried to descend. He would know he was going to fall; he would step blindly and already moaning onto nothing and plunge, topple, sprawling and bumping, terrified not by pain but by amazement, to lie at last on the floor of the lower hall, bellowing, his blasted eyes staring aghast and incredulous at nothing.

But at last he learned to negotiate them. Now he merely slowed a little before stepping, not confidently quite but not with alarm, off onto that which at each successive step, was not quite space; was almost nothing but at each advancing instant, not quite was, and hurried on through the lower hall and into the back yard, where he paused again and began to sway from side to side and moan, his empty face now filled with baffled bewilderment. Because he could not see the smoke from here and now all he remembers is the empty dawn-hill from which he will let himself downward into the creek-side mist to wait for her, and it is wrong now. Because he stands in sun, visible—himself, earth, trees, house—already cohered and fixed in visibility; no darkness to flee through and from, and this is wrong. So he stood, baffled, moaning and swaying for a time, then he moved again, across the yard to the lot gate. He had learned to open it too. He turned the catch and the gate vanished from between its two posts; he passed through and after a moment he found the gate where it had swung to against the fence and closed it and turned the latch and went on across the sun-glared lot, moaning, and entered the hallway of the stable.

Because of his sun-contracted pupils, he could not see at once. But then, it always was dark when he entered the stable on his way to bed, so at once he ceased to moan and went straight to the door to the harness-room, moving now with actual assurance, and grasped the door-jamb with both hands and raised his foot to the step, and, his down-groping foot already on the ground, he backed out of darkness and into visibility, turning, visibility roaring soundless down about him, establishing him intact and cohered in it and already trotting, running, toward the crest where he will let himself downward into the creekside mist to lie and wait for her, on across the lot and through the spread place in the wire fence. His overalls snagged on the wire but he ripped free, making no sound now, and into the road, running, his thick female thighs working, his face, his eyes, urgent and alarmed.

When he reached the hill three miles away, he was still trotting; when he turned from the road and mounted to the crest of the hill and saw the smoke beyond the creek, he made the hoarse, aghast sound again and ran on down the hill and through the now-dry grass in which at dawn he had lain, and to the creek, the ford. He did not hesitate. He ran full-tilt off the bank and onto the rimpled water, continuing to run even after he began to fall, plunging face-down into the water, completely submerged, and rose, streaming, knee-deep, bellowing. He lifted one foot above the surface and stepped forward as though onto a raised floor and took another step running before he fell. This time his outflung hands touched the further bank and this time when he rose he actually heard the cow's voice, faint and terrified, from beyond the smokepall on the other hill. He raised one foot above the surface and ran again. When he fell this time he lay on dry land. He scrambled up and ran in his sodden overalls, across the pasture and on up the other hill, on whose crest the smokepall lay without wind, grading from blue to delicate mauve and lilac and then copper beneath the meridional sun.

A mile back he had left the rich, broad, flat river-bottom country and entered the hills—a region which topographically was the final blue and dying echo of the Appalachian Mountains. Chickasaw Indians had owned it, but after the Indians it had been cleared where possible for cultivation, and after the Civil War, forgotten save by small peripatetic sawmills which had vanished too now, their sites marked only by the mounds of rotting sawdust which were not only their gravestones but the monuments of a people's heedless greed. Now it was a region of scrubby second-growth pine and oak among which dogwood bloomed until it too was cut to make cotton spindles, and old fields where not even a trace of furrow showed any more, gutted and gullied by forty years of rain and frost and heat into plateaus choked with rank sedge and briers loved of rabbits and quail coveys, and crumbling ravines striated red and white with alternate sand and clay. It was toward one of these plateaus that he now ran, running in ashes without knowing it since the earth here had had time to cool, running among the blackened stubble of last year's sedge dotted with small islands of this year's incombustible green and the blasted heads of tiny blue-and-white daisies, and so onto the crest of the hill, the plateau.

The smoke lay like a wall before him; beyond it he could hear the steady terrified bellowing of the cow. He ran into the smoke and toward the voice. The earth was now hot to his feet. He began to snatch them quickly up; he cried once himself, hoarse and amazed, whereupon, as though in answer, the smoke, the circumambience itself, screamed back at him. The sound was everywhere, above and beneath, funnelling downward at him; he heard the hooves and as he paused, his breath indrawn, the horse appeared, materialised furiously out of the smoke, monstrous and distorted, wild-eyed and with tossing mane, bearing down upon him. He screamed too. For an instant they yelled face to face, the wild eyes, the yellow teeth, the long gullet red with ravening gleeful triumph, stooping at him and then on as the horse swerved without breaking, the wind, the fierce dragon-reek of its passage, blasting at his hair and garments; it was gone. He ran again toward the cow's voice. When he heard the horse behind him again he did not even look back. He did not even scream again. He just ran, running, as again the earth, the smoke, filled and became thunderous with the hard, rapid hoofbeats and again the intolerable voice screamed down at him and he flung both arms about his head and fell sprawling as the wind, the dragon-reek, blasted at him again as the maddened horse soared over his prone body and vanished once more.

He scrambled up and ran. The cow was quite near now and now he saw the fire—a tender, rosy, creeping thread low in the smoke between him and the location of the cow's voice. Each time his feet touched the earth now he gave a short shriek like an ejaculation, trying to snatch his foot back before it could have taken his weight, then turning immediately in aghast amazement to the other foot which he had for the moment forgotten, so that presently he was not progressing at all but merely moving in one spot, like a dance, when he heard the horse coming at him again. He screamed. His voice and that of the horse became one voice, wild, furious and without hope, and he ran into and through the fire and burst into air, sun, visibility again, shedding flames which sucked away behind him like a tattered garment. The cow stood at the edge of a ravine about ten feet away, facing the fire, her head lowered, bellowing. He had just time to reach her and turn, his body intervened and his arms about his head, as the frantic horse burst out of the smoke and bore down upon them.

It did not even swerve. It took off almost without gathering, at full stride. The teeth, the wild eyes, the long red gullet, stooped at him, framed out of a swirled rigidity of forelock and mane, the entire animal floating overhead in monstrous deliberation. The air was filled with furious wings and the four crescent-glints of shod hooves as, still screaming, the horse vanished beyond the ravine's lip, sucking first the cow and then himself after it as though by the violent vacuum of its passing. Earth became perpendicular and fled upward—

the yawn of void without even the meretricious reassurance of graduated steps. He made no sound as the three of them plunged down
the crumbling sheer, at the bottom of which the horse rolled to its
feet without stopping and galloped on down the ditch and where he,
lying beneath the struggling and bellowing cow, received the violent
relaxing of her fear-constricted bowels. Overhead, in the down draft
of the ravine, the last ragged flame tongued over the lip, tip-curled,
and vanished, swirled off into the windless stain of pale smoke on the
sunny sky.

At first he couldn't do anything with her at all. She scrambled to
her feet, facing him, her head lowered, bellowing. When he moved
toward her, she whirled and ran at the crumbling sheer of the slope,
scrambling furiously at the vain and shifting sand as though in a blind
paroxysm of shame, to escape not him alone but the very scene of the
outragement of privacy where she had been sprung suddenly upon
and without warning from the dark and betrayed and outraged by
her own treacherous biological inheritance, he following again,
speaking to her, trying to tell her how this violent violation of her
maiden's delicacy is no shame, since such is the very iron imperish-
able warp of the fabric of love. But she would not hear. She continued to scrabble at the shifting rise, until at last he set his shoulder to
her hams and heaved forward. Striving together, they mounted for
a yard or so up the slope, the sand shifting and fleeing beneath their
feet, before momentum and strength were spent and, locked
together and motionless, they descended once more to the floor of
the ditch, planted and fixed ankle-deep in a moving block of sand like
two effigies on a float. Again, his shoulder to her hams, they rushed
at the precipice and up it for a yard or more before the treacherous
footing completely failed. He spoke to her, exhortative; they made a
supreme effort. But again the earth fled upward; footing, sand and all
plucked violently from beneath them and rushed upward into the
pale sky still faintly stained with smoke, and once more they lay inextricable and struggling on the floor of the ravine, he once more
underneath, until, bellowing and never ceasing her mad threshing,
the cow scrambled up and galloped on down the ditch as the horse
had done, vanishing before he could get to his feet to follow.

The ravine debouched onto the creek. Almost at once he was in the pasture again, though possibly he did not realise it, seeing only the cow as she galloped on ahead. Possibly at the moment he did not even recognise the ford at once, even when the cow, slowing, walked down into the water and stopped and drank and he ran up, slowing too, moaning, urgent but not loud, not to send her once more into flight. So he approaches the bank, stilling his voice now, picking his feet up and putting them down again in one spot, his singed and scorched face urgent and tense. But she does not move, and at last he steps down into the water, onto the water, forgetting again that it will give under his weight, crying once again not so much in surprise as in alarm lest he alarm her, and steps again forward onto the receptive solid, and touches her. She does not even stop drinking; his hand has lain on her flank for a second or two before she lifts her dripping muzzle and looks back at him, once more maiden meditant, shame-free.

Houston found them there. He came across the pasture on the horse, bareback, galloping, the hound following, and saw the thick squatting shape in the water behind the cow, clumsily washing her legs with a broken willow branch. "Is she all right?" he shouted, speaking to the horse to slow it since he did not even have a hackamore: "Whoa. Whoa. Ho now. Ho now, damn you.—Why in hell didn't you try to catch the horse?" he shouted. "He might have broke—" Then the other, squatting in the water, turned his scorched face and Houston recognised him. He began to curse, checking the horse with his hand in its mane, already flinging his leg over and sliding down before the horse stopped, cursing with that fretted exasperation which was not anger, rage. He came to the creek, the hound following, and stooped and caught up a dried limb left from last winter's flood water and slashed the cow savagely with it and flung the broken end after her as she sprang forward and scrambled up the further bank. "Git!" Houston shouted. "Git on home, you damn whore!" The cow galloped on a few steps, then stopped and began to graze. "Take her home," Houston said to the dog. Without moving, only raising its head, the hound bayed once. The cow jerked her head up and trotted again, and he in the creek made again his faint hoarse sound, rising too as the hound rose. But the dog did not even cross the creek, it did not even hurry; it merely followed the bank until it came opposite the cow and bayed again, once, contemptuous and peremptory. This time the cow went off at a gallop, back up the creek toward the lot, the hound following on its side of the creek. They went out of sight so. Twice more at intervals the hound bayed, one time, as though it merely shouted "Boo!" each time the cow prepared to stop.

He stood in the water, moaning. Now he actually bellowed himself, not loud, just amazed. When Houston and the dog came up he had looked around, at first at the dog. His mouth had opened to cry then, but instead there had come into his face an expression almost intelligent in its foolish fatuity, which, when Houston began to curse, faded and became one of incredulity, amazement, and which was still incredulous and bereft as he stood in the water, moaning, while Houston on the bank looked at the stained foul front of his overalls, cursing with that baffled exasperation, saying, "Jesus Christ. Jesus Christ.—Come here," he said. "Get out of there"; gesturing his arm savagely. But the other did not move, moaning, looking away up the creek where the cow had gone, until Houston came to the edge and leaned and caught him by the strap of his overalls and drew him roughly out of the water and, his nose wrinkled fiercely and still cursing, unfastened the straps and snatched the overalls down about his hips. "Step out!" Houston said. But he did not move until Houston jerked him, stumbling, out of the overalls, to stand in his shirt and nothing else, moaning faintly, though when Houston picked up the overalls gingerly by the strap and flung them into the creek, he cried again, once, hoarse, abject, not loud. "Go on," Houston said. "Wash them." He made violent washing motions in pantomime. But the other only looked at Houston, moaning, until Houston found another stick and twisted it into the overalls and soused and walloped them violently in the water, cursing steadily, and drew them out and, still using the stick, scrubbed them front-down on the grass. "There," he said. "Now git! Home! Home!" he shouted. "Stay there! Let her alone!" He had stopped moaning to watch Houston. Now he began to moan again, drooling, while Houston glared at him in baffled and raging exasperation. Then Houston took a handful of coins from his pocket and chose a fifty-cent piece and came and put it into his shirt pocket and buttoned the flap and went back to the horse, speaking to it until he touched it, grasped it by the mane, and vaulted onto its back. He had stopped moaning now, he just watched as, again without seeming to gather itself, just as when it had soared above him and the cow on the edge of the ravine an hour ago, the horse made two short circles under Houston's hand and then took the creek cleanly, already galloping, and was gone.

Then he began to moan again. He stood for a while, moaning, looking down at the shirt pocket which Houston had buttoned, fumbling at it. Then he looked at his soaked and wadded overalls on the ground beside him. After a while he stooped and picked them up. One leg was turned wrong-side-outward. He tried patiently for a while to put them on so, moaning. Then presently they came straight again and he got into them and fastened the straps and went to the creek and crossed, moving gingerly, raising his foot at each step as if he were mounting onto a raised floor, and climbed out and went back to the place where he had lain at each dawn for three months now, waiting for her. It was the same spot; he would return as exactly to it each time as a piston to its cylinder-head, and he stood there for a time, fumbling at the buttoned pocket, moaning. Then he went on up the hill; his feet knew the dust of the road again though perhaps he himself was unaware of it, possibly it was pure instinct functioning in the desolation of bereavement which carried him back toward the house which he had left that morning, because twice more in the first mile he stopped and fumbled at the buttoned pocket. Apparently he was not trying to unbutton the pocket without being able to do it, because presently he had the coin in his hand, looking at it, moaning. He was standing then on a plank bridge over a narrow, shallow, weed-choked ditch. He made no false motion with the hand which held the coin, he had made no motion of any kind, he was standing perfectly still at the moment, yet suddenly his palm was empty. The coin rang dully once on the dusty planks and perhaps glinted once, then vanished, though who to know what motion, infinitesimal and convulsive, of supreme repudiation there might have been, its impulse gone, vanished with the movement, because he even ceased to moan as he stood looking at his empty palm with quiet amazement, turning the hand over to look at the back, even raising and opening the other hand to look into it. Then—it was an effort almost physical, like childbirth—he connected two ideas, he progressed backward into time and recaptured an image by logical retrogression and fumbled into the shirt pocket again, peering into it, though only for a moment, as if he actually did not expect to find the coin there, though it was doubtless pure instinct which caused him to look down at the dusty planks on which he stood. And he was not moaning. He made no sound at all. He just stood there, looking at the planks, lifting his feet in turn; when he stepped off the bridge and into the ditch, he fell. You could not have told if he did step off intentionally or if he fell off, though it was doubtless a continuation of the instinct, the inherited constant awareness of gravity, which caused him to look under the bridge for the coin—if he were looking for it as he squatted in the weeds, bobbing his head faintly yet still making no sound. From then on he made no sound at all. He squatted for a time, pulling at the weeds, and now even the paradoxical dexterity was missing from his movements, even the dexterity which caused his hands to function at other times as though in spite of him; watching him you would have said he did not want to find the coin. And then you would have said, known, that he did not intend to find it; when after a time a wagon came up the road and crossed the bridge and the driver spoke to him, when he raised his face it was not even empty, it was unfathomable and profoundly quiet; when the man spoke his name, he did not even reply with the one sound which he knew, or at least was ever known to make, and that infallibly when anyone spoke to him.

He did not move until the wagon was out of sight, though he was not watching it. Then he rose and climbed back into the road. He was already trotting, back in the direction from which he had just come, treading his own tracks into the hot dust of the road beneath the May noon, back to where he would leave the road to mount the hill, and crossed the hill again and trotted down the slope to the creek. He passed the place where he would lie in the wet grass each dawn without even looking at it and turned on up the creek, trotting. It was then about two oclock Saturday afternoon. He could not have known that at that hour and day Houston, a childless widower who lived alone with the hound and a Negro man to cook for them both, would already be sitting on the gallery of Varner's store three miles away; he could not have thought that maybe Houston would not be at home. Certainly he did not pause to find out. He entered the lot, trotting, he went straight to the closed door of the shed. There was a halter hanging from a nail beside it. Perhaps he merely put his hand on the halter by chance in fumbling at the latch. But he put it on the cow properly, as he had seen it done.

At six oclock that afternoon they were five miles away. He did not know it was that distance. It did not matter; there is no distance in either space or geography, no prolongation of time for distance to exist in, no muscular fatigue to establish its accomplishment. They are moving not toward a destination in space but a destination in time, toward the pinnacle-keep of evening where morning and after-noon become one; the sleight hand of May shapes them both, not in the immediate, the soon, but in the now as, facing her, braced against the pull of the rope, he speaks to her implacable and com-pelling while she tugs back, shaking her head against the rope and bellowing. She had been doing this for the last half hour, drawn backward and barnward by the discomfort of her bag. But he held her, slacking the rope gradually until his other hand touched her, first her head then her neck, speaking to her until the resistance went out of her and she moved on again. They were in the hills now, among pines. Although the afternoon wind had fallen, the shaggy crests still made a constant murmuring sound in the high serene air. The trunks and the massy foliage were the harps and strings of afternoon; the barred inconstant shadow of the day's retrograde flowed steadily over them as they crossed the ridge and descended into shadow, into the azure bowl of evening, the windless well of night; the portcullis of sunset fell behind them. At first she would not let him touch her bag at all. Even then she kicked him once, but only because the hands were strange and clumsy. Then the milk came down, warm among his fingers and on his hands and wrists, making a thin sharp hissing on the earth.

There was a moon at that time. It waned nightly westward; juxta-posed to it, each dawn the morning star burned in fierce white period to the night, and he would smell the waking's instant as she would rise, hindquarters first, backing upward out of invisibility, attenuat-ing then disseminating out of the nest-form of sleep, the smell of milk. Then he would rise too and tie the rope-end to a swinging branch and seek and find the basket by the smell of the feed which it contained last night, and depart. From the edge of the woods he would look back. She would be still invisible, but he could hear her; it is as though he can see her—the warm breath visible among the tearing roots of grass, the warm reek of the urgent milk a cohered shape amid the fluid and abstract earth.

The barn is less than a half mile away. Soon it looms, forthright and square upon the scroll and cryptogram of heaven. The dog meets him at the fence, not barking, furrowing invisibility somewhere between sight and sound, moving completely in neither. On the first morning it rushed at him, yapping furiously. He stopped then. Perhaps he remembered that other dog five miles away, but only for a moment, since such is succeeding's success, such is that about victory which out-odors the betraying stink of all past defeats: so that now it comes up to him already fawning, invisible and fluid about his walking legs, its warm wet limber tongue shaping for him out of invisibility his own swinging hand.

In the ammoniac density of the barn, filled with the waking dawn-sounds of horses and cattle, he cannot even sense space. But he does not hesitate. He finds the crib door and enters; his sightless hand which knows and remembers finds the feed-box. He sets the basket down and begins to fill it, working steadily and fast, spilling half of what his cupped hands raise, as on the two preceding mornings establishing between feed-box and basket the agent of his own betrayal. When he rises and faces the door, he can see it now, gray, lighter in tone yet paradoxically no more luminous, as if a rectangle of opaque glass had been set into nothing's self while his back was turned, to further confound obscurity. And now he becomes aware of the birds. The cattle-sounds are louder now, constant; he can actually see the dog waiting in the stable door and he knows that he should hurry, since he knows that soon someone will come to feed and milk. So he leaves the crib, pausing for a moment in the door before descending as though he were listening, breathing in the reek, the odor of cows and mares as the successful lover does that of a room full of women, his the victor's drowsing rapport with all anonymous faceless female flesh capable of love walking the female earth.

He and the dog recross the lot together in the negative dawn-wash cacophonous and loud with birds. He can see the fence now, where the dog leaves him. He climbs through the fence, hurrying now, carrying the basket awkwardly before him in both arms, leaving in the wet grass a dark fixed wake. Now he watches the recurrence of that which he discovered for the first time three days ago: that dawn, light, is not decanted onto earth from the sky, but instead is from the earth itself suspired. Roofed by the woven canopy of blind annealing grass-roots and the roots of trees, dark in the blind dark of time's silt and rich refuse—the constant and unslumbering anonymous worm-glut and the inextricable known bones—Troy's Helen and the nymphs and the snoring mitred bishops, the saviors and the victims and the kings—it wakes, upseeping, attritive in uncountable creeping channels: first, root; then frond by frond, from whose escaping tips like gas it rises and disseminates and stains the sleep-fast earth with drowsy insect-murmur; then, still upward-seeking, creeps the knitted bark of trunk and limb where, suddenly louder leaf by leaf and dispersive in diffusive sudden speed, melodious with the winged and jeweled throats, it upward bursts and fills night's globed negation with jonquil thunder. Far below, the gauzy hemisphere treads with herald-cock, and sty and pen and byre salute the day. Vanes on steeples groove the southwest wind, and fields for plowing, since sunset married to the bedded and unhorsed plow, spring into half-furrowed sight like the slumbering half-satiate sea. Then the sun itself: within the half-mile it overtakes him. The silent copper roar fires the drenched grass and flings long before him his shadow prone for the vain eluded treading; the earth mirrors his antic and constant frustration which soars up the last hill and, motionless in the void, hovers until he himself crests over, whereupon it drops an invisible bridge across the ultimate ebb of night and, still preceding him, leaps visible once more across the swale and touches the copse itself, shortening into the nearing leafy wall, head: shoulders: hips: and then the trotting legs, until at last it stands upright upon the mazy whimple of the windy leaves for one intact inconstant instant before he runs into and through it.

She stands as he left her, tethered, chewing. Within the mild enormous moist and pupilless globes he sees himself in twin miniature mirrored by the inscrutable abstraction; one with that which Juno might have looked out with, he watches himself contemplating what those who looked at Juno saw. He sets the basket before her. She begins to eat. The shifting shimmer of incessant leaves gives to her a quality of illusion as insubstantial as the prone negative of his late hurrying, but this too is not so: one blond touch stipulates and affirms both weight and mass out of the flowing shadow-maze; a hand's breadth of contact shapes her solid and whole out of the infinity of hope. He squats beside her and begins to draw the teats.

They eat from the basket together. He has eaten feed before—hulls and meal, and oats and raw corn and silage and pig-swill, never much at one time but more or less constantly while he is awake as birds do, eating not even very much of the filled plate which Mrs Littlejohn would set for him, leaving it less than half-emptied, then an hour later eating something else, anything else, things which the weary long record of shibboleth and superstition had taught his upright kind to call filth, neither liking nor disliking the taste of any thing save that of certain kinds of soil and the lime in old plaster and the dissolved ink in chewed newspapers and the formic acid of stinging ants, making but one discrimination: he is herbivorous, even the life he eats is the life of plants. Then he removed the basket. It was not empty. It contained yet almost to the measured ounce exactly half of the original feed, but he takes it away from her, drags it from beneath the swinging muzzle which continues to chew out of the center of surprise, and hangs it over a limb, who is learning fast now, who has learned success and then precaution and secrecy and how to steal and even providence; who has only lust and greed and bloodthirst and a moral conscience to keep him awake at night, yet to acquire.

They go first to the spring. He found it on the first day—a brown creep of moisture in a clump of alder and beech, sunless, which wandered away without motion among the unsunned roots of other alders and willows. He cleaned it out and scooped a basin for it, which now at each return of light stood full and clear and leaf by leaf repeating until they lean and interrupt the green reflections and with their own drinking faces break each's mirroring, each face to its own shattered image wedded and annealed. Then he rises and takes up the rope, and they go on across the swale, toward the woods, and enter them.

Dawn is now over. It is now bald and forthright day. The sun is well up the sky. The air is still loud with birds, but the cries are no longer the mystery's choral strophe and antistrophe rising vertical among the leafed altars, but are earth-parallel, streaking the lateral air in prosaic busy accompaniment to the prosaic business of feeding. They dart in ceaseless arrowings, tinted and electric, among the pines whose shaggy crests murmur dry and incessant in the high day wind. Now he slacks the rope; from now until evening they will advance only as the day itself advances, no faster. They have the same destination: sunset. They pursue it as the sun itself does and within the compass of one single immutable horizon. They pace the ardent and unheeding sun, themselves unheeding and without ardor among the shadows of the soaring trunks which are the sun-geared ratchet-spokes which wheel the axled earth, powerful and without haste, up out of the caverns of darkness, through dawn and morning and mid-morning, and on toward and at last into the slowing neap of noon, the flood, the slack of peak and crown of light garlanding all within one single coronet the fallen and unregenerate seraphim. The sun is a yellow column, perpendicular. He bears it on his back as, stooping with that thick, reluctant unco-ordination of thigh and knee, he gathers first the armful of lush grass, then the flowers. They are the bright blatant wild daisies of flamboyant summer's spendthrift beginning. At times his awkward and disobedient hand, instead of breaking the stem, merely shuts about the escaping stalk and strips the flower-head into a scatter of ravished petals. But before he reaches the windless noon-bound shade in which she stands, he has enough of them. He has more than enough; if he had only gathered two of them, there would have been too many: he lays the plucked grass before her, then out of the clumsy fumbling of the hands there emerges, already in dissolution, the abortive diadem. In the act of garlanding, it disintegrates, rains down the slant of brow and chewing head; fodder and flowers become one inexhaustible rumination. From the sidling rhythm of the jaws depends one final blossom.

That afternoon it rained. It came without warning and it did not last long. He watched it for some time and without alarm, wanton and random and indecisive before it finally developed, concentrated, drooping in narrow unperpendicular bands in two or three different places at one time, about the horizon, like gauzy umbilical loops from the bellied cumulae, the sun-belled ewes of summer grazing up the wind from the southwest. It was as if the rain were actually seeking the two of them, hunting them out where they stood amid the shade, finding them finally in a bright intransigent fury. The pine-snoring wind dropped, then gathered; in an anticlimax of complete vacuum the shaggy pelt of earth became overblown like that of a receptive mare for the rampant crash, the furious brief fecundation which, still rampant, seeded itself in flash and glare of noise and fury and then was gone, vanished; then the actual rain, from a sky already breaking as if of its own rich over-fertile weight, running in a wild lateral turmoil among the unrecovered leaves, not in drops but in needles of fiery ice which seemed to be not trying to fall but, immune to gravity, earthless, were merely trying to keep pace with the windy uproar which had begotten and foaled them, striking in thin brittle strokes through his hair and shirt and against his lifted face, each brief lance already filled with the glittering promise of its imminent cessation like the brief bright saltless tears of a young girl over a lost flower; then gone too, fled north and eastward beyond the chromatic arch of its own insubstantial armistice, leaving behind it the spent confetti of its carnival to gather and drip leaf by leaf and twig by twig then blade by blade of grass, to gather in murmurous runnels, releasing in mirrored repetition the sky which, glint by glint of fallen gold and blue, the falling drops had prisoned.

It was over at last. He takes up the rope again and they move out from beneath the tree and go on, moving no faster than before but for the first time since they entered the woods, with purpose. Because it is nearing sunset. Although the rain had not seemed to last long, yet now it is as if there had been something in that illogical and harmless sound and fury which abrogated even the iron schedule of grooved and immutable day as the abrupt unplumbable tantrum of a child, the very violence of which is its own invincible argument against protraction, can somehow seem to set the clock up. He is soaking wet. His overalls are heavy and dank and cold upon him— the sorry refuse, the scornful lees of glory—a lifeless chill which is no kin to the vivid wet of the living water which has carried into and still retains within the very mud, the boundless freedom of the golden air as that same air glitters in the leaves and branches which globe in countless minute repetition the intact and iridescent cosmos. They walk in splendor. Joined by the golden skein of the wet grass rope, they move in single file toward the ineffable effulgence, directly into the sun. They are still pacing it. They mount the final ridge. They will arrive together. At the same moment all three of them cross the crest and descend into the bowl of evening and are extinguished.

The rapid twilight effaces them from the day's tedious recording. Original, in the womb-dimension, the unavoidable first and the inescapable last, eyeless, they descend the hill. He finds the basket by smell and lifts it down from the limb and sets it before her. She nuzzles into it, blowing the sweet breath-reek into the sweetish reek of feed until they become indistinguishable with that of the urgent and unimpatient milk as it flows among and about his fingers, hands, wrists, warm and indivisible as the strong inexhaustible life ichor itself, inherently, of itself, renewing. Then he leaves the invisible basket where he can find it again at dawn, and goes to the spring. Now he can see again. Again his head interrupts, then replaces as once more he breaks with drinking the reversed drinking of his drowned and fading image. It is the well of days, the still and insatiable aperture of earth. It holds in tranquil paradox of suspended precipitation dawn, noon, and sunset; yesterday, today, and tomorrow—star-spawn and hieroglyph, the fierce white dying rose, then gradual and invincible speeding up to and into slack-flood's coronal of nympholept noon. Then ebb's afternoon, until at last the morning, noon, and afternoon flow back, drain the sky and creep leaf by voiceless leaf and twig and branch and trunk, descending, gathering frond by frond among the grass, still creeping downward in drowsy insect murmurs, until at last the complete all of light gathers about that still and tender mouth in one last expiring inhalation. He rises. The swale is constant with random and erratic fireflies. There is the one fierce evening star, though almost at once the marching constellations mesh and gear and wheel strongly on. Blond too in that gathered last of light, she owns no dimension against the lambent and undimensional grass. But she is there, solid amid the abstract earth. He walks lightly upon it, returning, treading lightly that frail inextricable canopy of the subterrene slumber—Helen and the bishops, the kings and the graceless seraphim. When he reaches her, she has already begun to lie down—first the forequarters, then the hinder ones, lowering herself in two distinct stages into the spent ebb of evening, nestling back into the nest-form of sleep, the mammalian attar. They lie down together.

3

It was after sunset when Houston returned home and missed the cow. He was a widower, without family. Since the death of his wife three or four years ago, the cow was the only female creature on the place, obviously. He even had a man cook, a Negro, who did the milking too, but on this Saturday the Negro had asked permission to attend a picnic of his race, promising to be back in plenty of time to milk and get supper too—a statement in which Houston naturally put no credence at all. Indeed, except for a certain monotonous recapitulation about the promise which finally began to impinge on him, he might not have returned home at all that night and so would not have missed the cow until the next day.

As it was, he returned home just after sunset, not for food, the presence or lack of which meant nothing to him, but to milk the cow, the prospect and necessity of which had been facing him and drawing nearer and nearer all afternoon. Because of this, he had drunk a little more than his customary Saturday afternoon quantity, which (a man naturally of a moody, though robustly and healthily so, habit) in conjunction with the savage fixation about females which the tragic circumstances of his bereavement had created in him, and the fact that not only must he return and establish once more physical contact with the female world which three years ago he had abjured but the time this would require would be that (the hour between sunset and dark) one of the entire day's hierarchy which he could least bear—when the presence of his dead wife and sometimes even that of the son which they had never had, would be everywhere about the house and the place—left him in no very predictable frame of mind when he went to the cowshed and found the cow gone.

He thought at first that she had merely continued to bump and butt at the door until the latch turned and allowed it to open. But even then he was surprised that the discomfort of her bag had not fetched her, waiting and even lowing, at the lot gate before he arrived. But she was not there, and cursing her (and himself for having neglected to close the gate which led to the creek pasture) he called the hound and took the path back to the creek. It was not yet full dark. He could (and did) see tracks, though when he did notice the prints of the man's bare feet, the cow's prints superposed, so he merely took the two sets of tracks to be six hours apart and not six feet. But primarily he did not bother with the tracks because he was convinced he knew where the cow was, even when the hound turned from the creek at the ford and bore away up the hill. He shouted it angrily back. Even when it paused and looked back at him in grave and intelligent surprise, he still acted out of that seething conviction born of drink and exasperation and the old strong uncompromising grief, shouting at the dog until it returned and then actually kicking it toward the ford and then following it across, where it now heeled him, puzzled and gravely alert, until he kicked at it again and drove it out ahead.

She was not in the pasture. Now he knew that she was not, and therefore had been led away; it was as though his very savageness toward the dog had recalled him to something like sanity. He recrossed the creek. He had in his hip pocket the weekly county paper which he had taken from his mailbox on his way to the village early in the afternoon. He rolled it into a torch. By its light he saw the prints of the idiot's feet and those of the cow where they had turned away at the ford and mounted the hill to the road, where the torch burned out, leaving him standing there in the early starlight (the moon had not risen yet) cursing again in that furious exasperation which was not rage but savage contempt and pity for all blind flesh capable of hope and grief.

He was almost a mile from his horse. What with the vain quartering of the pasture, he had already walked twice that distance, and he was boiling with that helpless rage at abstract circumstance which feeds on its own impotence, has no object to retaliate upon; it seemed to him that once more he had been victim of a useless and elaborate practical joke at the hands of the prime maniacal Risibility, the sole purpose of which had been to leave him with a mile's walk in darkness. But even if he could not actually punish, hurt, the idiot, at least he could put the fear, if not of God, at least of cow-stealing and certainly of Jack Houston, into him, so that in any event he, Houston, would not leave home each time from now on wondering whether or not the cow would be there when he returned. Yet, mounted at last and in motion again and the cool wind of motion drawing about him, he found that the grim icy rage had given way to an even more familiar sardonic humor, a little clumsy and heavy-footed perhaps, but indomitable and unconquerable above even the ruthless grief: so that long before he reached the village he knew exactly what he would do. He would cure the idiot forever more of coveting cows by the immemorial and unfailing method: he would make him feed and milk her, he would return home and ride back tomorrow morning and make him feed and milk again and then lead the cow back on foot to where he had found her. So he did not stop at Mrs Littlejohn's house at all. He turned into the lane and went on toward the lot; it was Mrs Littlejohn who spoke to him from the dense moonshade beside the fence: "Who's that?"

He stopped the horse. She aint even saw the dog, he thought. That was when he knew he was not going to say anything else to her either. He could see her now, tall, tall like a chimney and with little more shape, standing at the fence. "Jack Houston," he said.

"What you want?" she said.

"Thought I'd water my horse at your trough."

"Aint there water at the store any more?"

"I come from home."

"Oh," she said. "Then you aint—" She spoke in a harsh rush, stopping. Then he knew he was going to say more. He was saying it:

"He's all right. I saw him."

"When?"

"Before I left home. He was there this morning and again this evening. In my pasture. He's all right. I reckon he's taking a Saturday holiday too."

She grunted. "That nigger of yours go to the picnic?"

"Yessum."

"Then come on in and eat. There's some cold supper left."

"I done et." He began to turn the horse. "I wouldn't worry. If he's still there, I'll tell him to get to hell on home."

She grunted again. "I thought you was going to water your horse."

"That's a fact," he said. So he rode into the lot. He had to dismount and open the gate and close it and then open it and close it again in order to do so, and then mount again. She was still standing beside the fence but when he called goodnight in passing she did not answer.

He returned home. The moon was now high and full above the trees. He stabled the horse and crossed the blanched lot, passing the moony yawn of the empty cowshed, and went on to the dark and empty and silver-roofed house and undressed and lay on the monk-like iron cot where he now slept, the hound on the floor beside it, the moony square of the window falling across him as it had used to fall across both of them when his wife was alive and there was a bed there in place of the cot. He was not cursing now, and it was still not rage when at sunup he sat the horse in the road where he had lost the tracks last night. He looked down at the dust blandly inscrutable with the wheel- and hoof- and human-prints of a whole Saturday afternoon, where the very virginity of the idiot at hiding had seemed to tap at need an inexhaustible reservoir of cleverness as one who has never before needed courage can seem at need to find it, cursing, not with rage but with that savage contempt and pity for the weak, nerve-raddled, yet curiously indestructible flesh already doomed and damned before it saw light and breathed.

By that time the owner of the barn had already found in the crib the telltale ridge of spilled feed beginning at the feed-box and ending in a shelving crescent about the shape of the absent basket; presently he even discovered it was his own basket which was gone. He tracked the feet across the lot and lost them. But there was nothing else missing, not a great quantity of feed and the basket was an old one. He gathered up the spilled feed and put it back into the box and soon even his first burst of impotent wrath at the moral outrage, the crass violation of private property, evaporated, recurring only once or twice during the day as angry and exasperated puzzlement: so that on the second morning when he entered the crib and saw the mute ridge of spilled feed ending in that empty embracing crescent, he experienced a shocking bewilderment followed by a furious and blazing wrath like that of a man who, leaping to safety from in front of a runaway, slips on a banana skin. For that moment his state of mind was homicidal. He saw in this second flagrant abrogation of the ancient biblical edict (on which he had established existence, integrity, all) that man must sweat or have not, the same embattled moral point which he had fought singly and collectively with his five children for more than twenty years and in which battle, by being victorious, he had lost. He was a man past middle age, who with nothing to start with but sound health and a certain grim and puritanical affinity for abstinence and endurance, had made a fair farm out of the barren scrap of hill land which he had bought at less than a dollar an acre and married and raised a family on it and fed and clothed them all and even educated them after a fashion, taught them at least hard work, so that as soon as they became big enough to resist him, boys and girls too, they left home (one was a professional nurse, one a ward-heeler to a minor county politician, one a city barber, one a prostitute; the oldest had simply vanished completely) so that there now remained the small neat farm which likewise had been worked to the point of mute and unflagging mutual hatred and resistance but which could not leave him and so far had not been able to eject him but which possibly knew that it could and would outlast him, and his wife who possibly had the same, perhaps not hope for resisting, but maybe staff and prop for bearing and enduring.

He ran out of the barn, shouting her name. When she appeared in the kitchen door, he shouted at her to come and milk and ran on into the house and reappeared with a shotgun, and ran past her again in the barn, cursing her for her slowness, and bridled one of the mules and took up the gun and followed the tracks once more across the lot, to where they disappeared at the fence. But this time he did not quit, and presently he found them again—the dark, drag-

ging wake still visible in the dew-heavy grass of his hayfield, crossing the field and entering the woods. Then he did lose them. But still
he did not quit. He was too old for this, too old certainly for such
prolonged and panting rage and thirst for blood. He had eaten no
breakfast yet, and at home there was that work waiting, the constant
and unflagging round of repetitive nerve-and-flesh wearing labor by
which alone that piece of earth which was his mortal enemy could
fight him with, which he had performed yesterday and must perform
again today and again tomorrow and tomorrow, alone and unassisted
or else knock under to that very defeat which had been his barren
victory over his children;—this until the day came when (he knew
this too) he would stumble and plunge, his eyes still open and his
empty hands stiffening into the shape of the plow-handles, into the
furrow behind the plow, or topple into the weedy ditch, still clutching the brush-hook or the axe, this final victory marked by a ceno-
taph of coiling buzzards on the sky until some curious stranger
happened there and found and buried what was left of him. Yet he
went on. After a while he even found the tracks again, three of them
in a sandy ditch where a branch ran, coming upon them more or less
by chance since the last one he had seen was a mile away; he could
have had no reason to believe they were even the right ones, though
as it happened they were. But he did not for one moment doubt that
they were the right ones. About the middle of the morning he even
discovered whom the cow belonged to. He met Houston's Negro,
also on a mule, in the woods. He told the Negro violently, even
swinging the gun toward him, that he had seen no stray cow, there
was no stray cow about there, and that this was his land although he
owned nothing within three miles of where he stood unless it might
have been the temporarily hidden feed-basket, and ordered the
Negro to get off it and stay off.

He returned home. He had not given up; he now knew not only
what he intended to do, but how to do it. He saw before him not
mere revenge and reprisal, but redress. He did not want to surprise
the thief; he wanted now to capture the cow and either collect a
reward from its owner for returning it, or if the owner refused, resort
to his legal rights and demand a pound fee on the cow as a stray—
this, this legal dollar which would be little enough compensation, not

for the time he had spent recovering the cow, but for the time he had lost from the endless round of that labor which he could not have hired done in his place, not because he could not pay for it but because no man in that country, white or black, would work for him at any price, and which he durst not permit to get the ascendancy of him or he would be lost. He did not even go to the house. He went straight to the field and put the mule into the plow which he had left in the furrow last night and plowed until his wife rang the bell at noon; he returned to the field after dinner and plowed on until dark.

He was in the barn, the mule already saddled and waiting in its stall, before moonset the next morning. He saw against the pallid lift of dawn the thick, bearlike figure enter with the basket and followed by his own dog, and enter the crib and then emerge, carrying the basket in both arms as a bear does, and hurry back across the lot, the dog still following. When he saw the dog he was suffused again by that almost unbearable rage. He had heard it on the first morning, but its uproar had ceased by the time he came good awake; now he understood why he had not heard it on the second and third mornings, and he knew now that even if the man did not look back and see him, if he now appeared from the barn the dog in all likelihood would bark at him. So when he did feel it safe to come out of the barn, there was nothing in sight but the dog, which stood peering through the fence after the thief, remaining unaware of his presence until he had actually kicked it, savage and raging, toward the house.

But the thief's dark wake lay again upon the dew-pearled grass of the pasture, though when he reached the woods he discovered that he had made the same error of underestimation which Houston had made: that there is perhaps something in passion too, as well as in poverty and innocence, which cares for its own. So he spent another half morning, breakfastless, seething with incredulous outrage, riding the green and jocund solitudes of the May woods, while behind him the dark reminder of his embattled and unremitting fields stood higher and higher in despotic portent. This time he even found the trail again—the stain of wasted milk on the earth (so close he was), the bent grass where the basket had sat while the cow fed from it. He should have found the basket itself hanging on the limb, since nobody had tried to conceal it. But he did not look that high, since he now had the cow's trail. He followed it, calm and contained and rigidly boiling, losing it and finding it and losing it again, on through the morning and into the access of noon—that concentration of light and heat which he could seem to feel raising not only the temperature of his blood but that of the very abstract conduits and tubes through which the current of his wrath had to flow. That afternoon though he discovered that the sun had nothing to do with it. He also stood beneath a tree while the thunderstorm crashed and glared and the furious cold rain drove at that flesh which cringed and shivered only on the outside, then galloped on in tearful and golden laughter across the glittering and pristine earth. He was then seven miles from home. There was an hour more of daylight. He had done perhaps four of the miles and the evening star had risen, when it occurred to him that the fugitives might just possibly return to the place where he had found the milkstain on the earth. He went back there without hope. He was not even raging anymore.

He reached home about midnight, on foot, leading the mule and the cow. At first he had been afraid that the thief himself would escape. Then he had expected him to. Then for that half mile between the barn and the place where he had found them, he tried to drive away the creature which had started up from beside the cow with a hoarse, alarmed cry which he recognised, which still followed, moaning and blundering along in the darkness behind even when he would turn—a man too old for this, spent not so much by the long foodless day as by constant and unflagging rage—and shout at it, cursing. His wife was waiting at the lot gate with a lighted lantern. He entered, he handed the two halter-reins carefully to her and went and closed the gate carefully and stooped as an old man stoops and found a stick and then sprang, ran at the idiot, striking at it, cursing in a harsh spent panting voice, the wife following, calling him by name. "You stop!" she cried. "Stop it! Do you want to kill yourself?"

"Hah!" he said, panting, shaking. "I aint going to die for a few more miles yet. Go get the lock." It was a padlock. It was the only lock of any sort on the place. It was on the front gate, where he had put it the day after his last child left home. She went and got it while he still tried to drive the idiot from the lot. But he could not overtake the creature. It moved awkwardly and thickly, moaning and bubbling, but he could neither overtake it nor frighten it. It was somewhere behind him, just outside the radius of the lantern which his wife held, even while he locked the piece of chain through the door of the stall into which he had put the cow. The next morning when he unlocked the chain, the creature was inside the stall with the cow. It had even fed the cow, climbing back out and then back into the stall to do it, and for that five miles to Houston's place it still followed, moaning and slobbering, though just before they reached the house he looked back, and it was gone. He did not know just when it disappeared. Later, returning, with Houston's dollar in his pocket, he examined the road to see just where it had vanished. But he found no trace.

The cow was in Houston's lot less than ten minutes. Houston was at the house at the time; his immediate intention was to send the cow on by his Negro. But he countermanded this in the next breath and sent the man instead to saddle his horse, during which time he stood waiting, cursing again with that savage and bleak contempt which was not disgust nor rage. Mrs Littlejohn was putting her horse into the buggy when he led the cow into the lot, so he did not need to tell her himself, after all. They just looked at one another, not man and woman but two integers which had both reached the same ungendered peace even if by different roads. She drew the clean, knotted rag from her pocket. "I dont want money," he said roughly. "I just dont want to see her again."

"It's his," she said, extending the rag. "Take it."

"Where'd he get money?"

"I dont know. V. K. Ratliff gave it to me. It's his."

"I reckon it is, if Ratliff gave it up. But I still dont want it."

"What else could he do with it?" she said. "What else did he ever want?"

"All right," Houston said. He took the rag. He did not open it. If he had asked how much was in it, she could not have told him since she had never counted it either. Then he said, furious and still out of his calm rigid face: "God damn it, keep them both away from my place. Do you hear?"

That lot was beyond the house from the road; the rear wall of the stable was not in sight from either. It was not directly in view from anywhere in the village proper, and on this September forenoon Ratliff realised that it did not need to be. Because he was walking in a path, a path which he had not seen before, which had not been there in May. Then that rear wall came into his view, the planks nailed horizontally upon it, that plank at head-height prized off and leaning, the projecting nails faced carefully inward, against the wall and no more motionless than the row of backs, the row of heads which filled the gap. He knew not only what he was going to see but that, like Bookwright, he did not want to see it, yet, unlike Bookwright, he was going to look. He did look, leaning his face in between two other heads; and it was as though it were himself inside the stall with the cow, himself looking out of the blasted tongueless face at the row of faces watching him who had been given the wordless passions but not the specious words. When they looked around at him, he already held the loose plank, holding it as if he were on the point of striking at them with it. But his voice was merely sardonic, mild even, familiar, cursing as Houston had: not in rage and not even in outraged righteousness.

"I notice you come to have your look too," one said.

"Sholy," Ratliff said. "I aint cussing you folks. I'm cussing all of us," lifting the plank and fitting it back into the orifice. "Does he—What's his name? that new one? Lump.—does he make you pay again each time, or is it a general club ticket good for every performance?" There was a half-brick on the ground beside the wall. With it he drove the nails back while they watched him, the brick splitting and shaling, crumbling away onto his hands in fine dust—a dry, arid, pallid dust of the color of shabby sin and shame, not splendid, not magnificent like blood, and fatal. "That's all," he said. "It's over. This here engagement is completed." He did not wait to see if they were departing. He crossed the lot in the bright hazy glare of the September noon, and the back yard. Mrs Littlejohn was in the kitchen. Again like Houston, he did not need to tell her.

"What do you think I think when I look out that window and watch them sneaking up along that fence?" she said.

"Only all you done was think," he said. "That new clerk," he said. "That Snopes encore. Launcelot," he said. "Lump. I remember his ma." He remembered her in life, as well as from inquiry—a thin, eager, plain woman who had never had quite enough to eat and showed it and did not even know that she had actually never had enough to eat, who taught school. Out of a moil of sisters and brothers fathered by a congenital failure who between a constant succession of not even successful petty-mercantile bankruptcies, begot on his whining and sluttish wife still more children whom he could not quite clothe and feed. Out of this, through one summer term at the State Teacher's College and into a one-room country school, and out of the school before the first year was done and into marriage with a man under indictment then because of a drummer's sample-case of shoes, all for the right foot, which had vanished from a railway baggage-room. And who brought with her into that marriage, as sole equipment and armament, the ability to wash and feed and clothe a swarm of brothers and sisters without ever enough food or clothing or soap to do it with, and a belief that there was honor and pride and salvation and hope too to be found for man's example between the pages of books, and who bore one child and named it Launcelot, flinging this quenchless defiance into the very jaws of the closing trap, and died. "Launcelot!" Ratliff cried. He did not even curse: not that Mrs Littlejohn would have minded, or perhaps even have heard him. "Lump! Just think of his shame and horror when he got big enough to realise what his ma had done to his family's name and pride so that he even had to take Lump for folks to call him in place of it! He pulled that plank off! At just exactly the right height! Not child-height and not woman-height: man-height! He just keeps that little boy there to watch and run to the store and give the word when it's about to start. Oh, he aint charging them to watch it yet, and that's what's wrong. That's what I dont understand. What I am afraid of. Because if he, Lump Snopes, Launcelot Snopes . . . I said encore," he cried. "What I was trying to say was echo. Only what I meant was forgery." He ceased, having talked himself wordless, mute into baffled and aghast outrage, glaring at the man-tall, man-grim woman in the faded wrapper who stared as steadily back at him.

"So that's it," she said. "It aint that it is, that itches you. It's that somebody named Snopes, or that particular Snopes, is making something out of it and you dont know what it is. Or is it because folks come and watch? It's all right for it to be, but folks mustn't know it, see it."

"Was," he said. "Because it's finished now. I aint never disputed I'm a pharisee," he said. "You dont need to tell me he aint got nothing else. I know that. Or that I can sholy leave him have at least this much. I know that too. Or that besides, it aint any of my business. I know that too, just as I know that the reason I aint going to leave him have what he does have is simply because I am strong enough to keep him from it. I am stronger than him. Not righter. Not any better, maybe. But just stronger."

"How are you going to stop it?"

"I dont know. Maybe I even cant. Maybe I dont even want to. Maybe all I want is just to have been righteouser, so I can tell myself I done the right thing and my conscience is clear now and at least I can go to sleep tonight." But he seemed to be at no loss as to what to do next. He did stand for a time on Mrs Littlejohn's front steps, but he was only canvassing the possibilities—or rather, discarding the faces as he called them up: the fierce intractable one barred with the single eyebrow; the high one ruddy and open and browless as a segment of watermelon above the leather blacksmith's apron; that third one which did not belong to the frock coat so much as it appeared to be attached to it like a toy balloon by its string, the features of which seemed to be in a constant state of disorganised flight from about the long, scholarly, characterless nose as if the painted balloon-face had just been fetched in out of a violent and driving rain—Mink, Eck, I. O.; and then he began to think Lump again, cursing, driving his mind back to the immediate problem with an almost physical effort, though actually standing quite still on the top step, his face familiar and enigmatic, quiet, actually almost smiling, bringing the three possible faces once more into his mind's eye and watching them elide once more—the one which would not stay at all; the second which would never even comprehend what he was talking about; the third which in that situation would be like one of the machines in railway waiting-rooms, into which you could insert the copper coin or lead slug of impulse to action, and you would get something back in return, you would not know what, except that it would not be worth quite as much as the copper or the slug. He even thought of the older one, or at least the first one: Flem, thinking how this was probably the first time anywhere where breath inhaled and suspired and men established the foundations of their existences on the currency of coin, that anyone had ever wished Flem Snopes were here instead of anywhere else, for any reason, at any price.

It was now nearing noon, almost an hour since he had seen the man he sought emerge from the store. He made inquiries at the store; ten minutes later he turned from a lane, through a gate in a new wire fence. The house was new, one-storey, paintless. There were a few of the summer's flowers blooming on dustily into the summer's arid close, all red ones—cannas and geraniums—in a raw crude bed before the steps and in rusted cans and buckets along the edge of the porch. The same little boy was in the yard beyond the house, and a big, strong, tranquil-faced young woman opened the door to him, an infant riding her hip and another child peering from behind her skirt. "He's in his room, studying," she said. "Just walk right in."

The room also was unpainted, of tongue-and-groove planking; it looked and was as air-tight as a strong-box and not much larger, though even then he remarked how the odor of it was not a bachelor-uncle smell but was curiously enough that of a closet in which a middle-aged widow kept her clothes. At once he saw the frock coat lying across the bed's foot, because the man (he really was holding a book, and he wore spectacles) in the chair had given the opening door one alarmed look and sprang up and snatched up the coat and began to put it on. "Never mind," Ratliff said. "I aint going to stay long. This here cousin of yours. Isaac." The other finished getting into the coat, buttoning it hurriedly about the paper dickey he wore in place of a shirt (the cuffs were attached to the coat sleeves themselves) then removing the spectacles with that same flustered haste, as if he had hurried into the coat in order to remove the spectacles, so that for that reason Ratliff noticed that the frames had no lenses in them. The other was watching him with that intentness which he had seen before, which (the concentration and intelligence both) seemed actually to be no integral part either of the organs or the process behind them, but seemed rather to be a sort of impermanent fungus-growth on the surface of the eyeballs like the light down which children blow from the burrs of dandelion blooms. "About that cow," Ratliff said.

Now the features fled. They streamed away from the long nose which burlesqued ratiocination and firmness and even made a sort of crass Roman holiday of rationalised curiosity, fluid and flowing even about the fixed grimace of glee. Then Ratliff saw that the eyes were not laughing but were watching him and that there was something intelligently alert, or at least competent, behind them, even if it were not firm. "Aint he a sight now?" Snopes cackled, chortled. "I done often thought, since Houston give him that cow and Mrs Littlejohn located them in that handy stall, what a shame it is some of his folks aint running for office. Bread and circuses, as the fellow says, makes hay at the poll-box. I dont know of no cheaper way than Lump's got to get a man—"

"Beat," Ratliff said. He did not raise his voice, and he did not speak further than that one word. The other face did not change either: the long, still nose, the fixed grimace, the eyes which partook of the life of neither. After a moment Snopes said:

"Beat?"

"Beat," Ratliff said.

"Beat," the other said. If it were not intelligence, Ratliff told himself, it was a good substitute. "Except as it happens, I ain't—"

"Why?" Ratliff said. "When Caesar's wife goes up to Will Varner next month to get that ere school job again, and he aint pure as a marble monument, what do you think is going to happen?" The face did not actually alter because the features were in a constant state of flux, having no relation to one another save that the same skull bore them, the same flesh fed them.

"Much obliged," Snopes said. "What do you figure we better do?"

"We aint going to do nothing," Ratliff said. "I dont want to teach school."

"But you'll help. After all, we was getting along all right until you come into it."

"No," Ratliff said harshly. "Not me. But I aim to do this much. I am going to stay here until I see if his folks are doing something about it. About letting them folks hang around that crack and watch, any-how."

"Sholy," Snopes said. "That ere wont do. That's it. Flesh is weak, and it wants but little here below. Because sin's in the eye of the beholder; cast the beam outen your neighbors' eyes and out of sight is out of mind. A man cant have his good name drug in the alleys. The Snopes name has done held its head up too long in this country to have no such reproaches against it like stock-diddling."

"Not to mention that school," Ratliff said.

"Sholy. We'll have a conference. Family conference. We'll meet at the shop this afternoon."

When Ratliff reached the shop that afternoon, they were both there—the smith's apprentice and the school-teacher, and a third man: the minister of the village church—a farmer and a father; a harsh, stupid, honest, superstitious and upright man, out of no seminary, holder of no degrees, functioning neither within nor without any synod but years ago ordained minister by Will Varner as he decreed his school teachers and commissioned his bailiffs. "It's all right," I. O. said when Ratliff entered. "Brother Whitfield has done solved it. Only—"

"I said I knowed of a case before where it worked," the minister corrected. Then he told them—or the teacher did, that is:

"You take and beef the critter the fellow has done formed the habit with, and cook a piece of it and let him eat it. It's got to be a authentic piece of the same cow or sheep or whatever it is, and the fellow has got to know that's what he is eating; he cant be tricked nor forced to eating it, and a substitute wont work. Then he'll be all right again and wont want to chase nothing but human women. Only—" and now Ratliff noticed it—something in the diffusive face at once speculative and annoyed: "—only Mrs Littlejohn wont let us have the cow. You told me Houston give it to him."

"No I didn't," Ratliff said. "You told me that."

"But didn't he?"

"Mrs Littlejohn or Houston or your cousin will be the one to tell you that."

"Well, no matter. Anyway, she wont. And now we got to buy it from her. And what I cant understand is, she says she dont know how much, but that you do."

"Oh," Ratliff said. But now he was not looking at Snopes. He was looking at the minister. "Do you know it will work, Reverend?" he said.

"I know it worked once," Whitfield said.

"Then you have knowed it to fail."

"I never knowed it to be tried but that once," Whitfield said.

"All right," Ratliff said. He looked at the two others—cousins, nephew and uncle, whatever they were. "It will cost you sixteen dollars and eighty cents."

"Sixteen dollars and eighty cents?" I. O. said. "Hell fire." The little quick pale eyes darted from face to face between them. Then he turned to the minister. "Look here. A cow is a heap of different things besides the meat. Yet it's all that same cow. It's got to be, because it's some things that cow never even had when it was born, so what else can it be but the same thing? The horns, the hair. Why couldn't we take a little of them and make a kind of soup; we could even take a little of the actual living blood so it wouldn't be no technicality in it—"

"It was the meat, the flesh," the minister said. "I taken the whole cure to mean that not only the boy's mind but his insides too, the seat of passion and sin, can have the proof that the partner of his sin is dead."

"But sixteen dollars and eighty cents," I. O. said. He looked at Ratliff. "I dont reckon you aim to put up none of it."

"No," Ratliff said.

"And Mink aint, not to mention after that law verdict Will Varner put on him this morning," the other said fretfully. "And Lump. If anything, Lump is going to be put out considerable with what after all wasn't a whole heap of your business," he told Ratliff. "And Flem aint in town. So that leaves me and Eck here. Unless Brother Whitfield would like to help us out for moral reasons. After all, what reflects on one, reflects on all the members of a flock."

"But he dont," Ratliff said. "He cant. Come to think of it, I've heard of this before myself. It's got to be done by the fellow's own

blood kin, or it wont work." The little bright quick eyes went constantly between his face and the minister's.

"You never said nothing about that," he said.

"I just told you what I know happened," Whitfield said. "I dont
know how they got the cow."

"But sixteen-eighty," I. O. said. "Hell fire." Ratliff watched him—
the eyes which were much shrewder than they appeared—not intelligent; he revised that: shrewd. Now he even looked at his cousin or
nephew for the first time. "So it's me and you, Eck." And the cousin
or nephew spoke for the first time.

"You mean we got to buy it?"

"Yes," I. O. said. "You sholy wont refuse a sacrifice for the name
you bear, will you?"

"All right," Eck said. "If we got to." From beneath the leather
apron he produced a tremendous leather purse and opened it and
held it in one grimed fist as a child holds the paper sack which it is
about to inflate with its breath. "How much?"

"I'm a single man, unfortunately," I. O. said. "But you got three
children—"

"Four," Eck said. "One coming."

"Four. So I reckon the only way to figure it is to divide it according to who will get the most benefits from curing him. You got yourself and four children to consider. That will be five to one. So that
will be I pay the one-eighty and Eck pays the fifteen because five
goes into fifteen three times and three times five is fifteen dollars.
And Eck can have the hide and the rest of the beef."

"But a beef and hide aint worth fifteen dollars," Eck said. "And
even if it was, I dont want it. I dont want fifteen dollars worth of
beef."

"It aint the beef and the hide. That's just a circumstance. It's the
moral value we are going to get out of it."

"How do I need fifteen dollars worth of moral value when all you
need is a dollar and eighty cents?"

"The Snopes name. Cant you understand that? That aint never
been aspersed yet by no living man. That's got to be kept pure as a
marble monument for your children to grow up under."

"But I still dont see why I got to pay fifteen dollars, when all you got to pay is—"

"Because you got four children. And you make five. And five times three is fifteen."

"I aint got but three yet," Eck said.

"Aint that just what I said? five times three? If that other one was already here, it would make four, and five times four is twenty dollars, and then I wouldn't have to pay anything."

"Except that somebody would owe Eck three dollars and twenty cents change," Ratliff said.

"What?" I. O. said. But he immediately turned back to his cousin or nephew. "And you got the meat and the hide," he said. "Cant you even try to keep from forgetting that?"

CHAPTER TWO

1

*T*he woman Houston married was not beautiful. She had neither wit nor money. An orphan, a plain girl, almost homely and not even very young (she was twenty-four) she came to him out of the home of the remote kinswoman who had raised her, with the domestic skill of her country heritage and blood and training and a small trunk of neat, plain, dove-colored clothes and the hand-stitched sheets and towels and table-linen which she had made herself and an infinite capacity for constancy and devotion, and no more. And they were married and six months later she died and he grieved for her for four years in black, savage, indomitable fidelity, and that was all.

They had known one another all their lives. They were both only children, born of the same kind of people, on farms not three miles apart. They belonged to the same country congregation and attended the same one-room country school, where, although five years his junior, she was already one class ahead of him when he entered and, although he failed twice during the two years he attended it, she was still one class ahead of him when he quit, vanished, not only from his father's house but from the country too, fleeing even at sixteen the immemorial trap, and was gone for thirteen years and then as suddenly returned, knowing (and perhaps even cursing himself) on the instant he knew he was going to return, that she would still be there and unmarried; and she was.

He was fourteen when he entered the school. He was not wild, he was merely unbitted yet; not high-spirited so much as possessed of that strong lust, not for life, not even for movement, but for that fetterless immobility called freedom. He had nothing against learning; it was merely the confinement, the regimentation, which it entailed.

He could competently run his father's farm, and his mother had taught him to write his name before she died at last and so gave up trying to compel his father to send him to the school which for four years at least he had contrived to avoid by playing his mother's spoiling fondness against the severity of his father's pride; he really enjoyed the increasing stint of responsibility and even work which his father set him as a training for manhood. But at last he outgeneralled himself with his own strategy: finally even his father admitted that there was nothing else about the farm for him to learn. So he entered school, not a paragon but a paradox. He was competent for citizenship before he could vote and capable of fatherhood before he learned to spell. At fourteen he was already acquainted with whiskey and was the possessor of a mistress—a Negro girl two or three years his senior, daughter of his father's renter—and so found himself submitting to be taught his abc's four and five and six years after his coevals and hence already too big physically for where he was; bulging in Lilliput, inevitably sophisticated, logically contemptuous, invincibly incorrigible, not deliberately intending to learn nothing but merely convinced that he would not, did not want and did not believe he needed to.

Afterward, it seemed to him that the first thing he saw when he entered the room was that bent, demure, simply-brown and straight-haired head. Still later, after he believed he had escaped, it seemed to him that it had been in his life always, even during those five years between his birth and hers; and not that she had contrived somehow to exist during those five years, but that he himself had not begun to exist until she was born, the two of them chained irrevocably from that hour and onward forever, not by love but by implacable constancy and invincible repudiation—on the one hand, that steadfast and undismayable will to alter and improve and remake; on the other, that furious resistance. It was not love—worship, prostration—as he knew it, as passion had manifested heretofore in an experience limited to be sure, yet not completely innocent. He would have accepted that, taken it as his due, calling himself submitting to it as he called himself submitting when he was really using that same quality which he called proffered slavedom in all the other women—his mother and his mistress—so far in his life. What he did not com-

prehend was that until now he had not known what true slavery
was—that single constant despotic undeviating will of the enslaved
not only for possession, complete assimilation, but to coerce and
reshape the enslaver into the seemliness of his victimization. She did
not even want him yet, not because she was too young yet but
because apparently she had not found even in him the one suitable. It
was as though she had merely elected him out of all the teeming
earth, not as one competent to her requirements, but as one possessing the possibilities on which she would be content to establish the
structure of her life.

She was trying to get him through school. Not out of it and apparently not even educated, any wiser; apparently just through it, grade
by grade in orderly progression and at the appointed times for
advancing from one to the next as people commonly do. At one time
the thought occurred to him that what she perhaps wanted was to get
him on and into the class of his age, where he should have been; that
if she could do that, perhaps she would let him alone, to fail or not
fail as his nature and character dictated. Perhaps she would have. Or
perhaps she, who was fond enough to attempt it at all, was also wise
enough to know that he not only would never reach the grade where
he should have been but he would not even keep up with the one
where he was, and more: that where he was did not even matter, that
even failing did not matter so long as she had a hand too in the failing.

It was a feud, a gage, wordless, uncapitulating, between that
unflagging will not for love or passion but for the married state, and
that furious and as unbending one for solitariness and freedom. He
was going to fail that first year. He expected to. Not only himself
but the whole school knew it. She never even spoke directly to him,
she would pass him on the playground without even looking at him,
apparently ever seeing him, yet there would be, mute and inevitable
on his desk, the apple or the piece of cake from her lunch-box, and
secret in one of his books the folded sheet of problems solved or
spelling corrected or sentences written out in the round, steadfast
child's hand—the reward and promise which he spurned, the assistance which he repudiated, raging not because his integrity and gulli-
bility had been attempted but because he could neither publicly

express the scorn of the repudiation nor be sure that the private exposition—the wanton destruction of the food or the paper—had even registered upon that head bent, decorous, intent, in profile or three-quarters and sometimes in full rear, which he had never yet heard even pronounce his name. Then one day a boy not a third his size chanted a playground doggerel at him—not that Lucy Pate and Jack Houston were sweethearts, but that Lucy Pate was forcing Jack Houston to make the rise to the second grade. He struck the child as he would one of his own size, was immediately swarmed over by four older boys and was holding his furious own when his assailants gave back and she was beside him, flailing at his enemies with her school-satchel. He struck her as blindly and furiously as he had the little boy and flung her away. For the next two minutes he was completely berserk. Even after he was down, the four of them had to bind him up with a piece of fence wire in order to turn him loose and run.

So he won that first point. He failed. When he entered school the next fall, in the same grade and surrounded (a giant knee-deep in midgets) by a swarm of still smaller children, he believed that he had even escaped. The face was still there to be sure, and it looked no smaller, no more distant. But he now believed he saw it from beyond the additional abyss of yet another intervening grade. So he believed that he had taken the last point too, and the game; it was almost two months before he discovered that she too had failed in her last year's examinations.

Now something very like panic took possession of him. Because he also discovered that the scale and tone of the contest between them had altered. It was no more deadly; that was impossible. It had matured. Up to now, for all its deadly seriousness, it had retained something of childhood, something both illogical and consistent, both reasonable and bizarre. But now it had become a contest between adults; at some instant during that summer in which they had not even seen one another except among the congregation at church, the ancient worn glove of biological differentiation had been flung and raised. It was as if, mutually unaware yet at the same moment, they had looked upon the olden Snake, had eaten of the Tree with the will and capacity for assimilation but without the equipment, even if the lack of equipment were not true in his case.

There were no more apples and cake now, there was only the paper, correct, inescapable and implacable, in the book or in his overcoat pocket or in the mailbox before his gate; he would submit his own blank paper at the written monthly tests and receive back that one bearing a perfect grade and written in that hand, even to the signature, which was coming more and more to look like his own. And always there was the face which still never addressed him nor even looked at him, bent, in profile or three-quarters, sober and undismayable. He not only looked at it all day, he carried it home with him at night, waking from sleep to meet it, still serene, still steadfast. He would even try to efface and exorcise it beyond that of the Negress paramour but it still remained, constant, serene, not reproachful nor even sad nor even angry, but already forgiving him before forgiveness had been dared or earned; waiting, tranquil, terrifying. Once during that year the frantic thought occurred to him of escaping her forever by getting beyond the reach of her assistance, of applying himself and making up the lost years, overhauling the class where he should have been. For a short time he even attempted it. But there was the face. He knew he could never pass it, not that it would hold him back, but he would have to carry it on with him in his turn, just as it had held him somehow in abeyance during those five years before she was even born; not only would he never pass it, he would not even ever overtake it by that one year, so that regardless of what stage he might reach it would still be there, one year ahead of him, inescapable and impervious to passing. So there was but one alternative. That was the old one: the movement not in retrograde since he could retrograde no further than the grade in which he already was, but of braking, clapping the invincible spike-heels of immobility into the fleeing and dizzy scope.

He did that. His mistake was in assuming a limitation to female ruthlessness. He watched his blank monthly test papers vanish into the teacher's hands and then return to him, perfectly executed even to his own name at the top, while the months passed and the final examination for promotion or not arrived. He submitted the blank sheets bearing nothing but his name and the finger-smudges where he had folded them and closed for the last time the books which he had not even managed to soil and walked out of the room, free save for the minor formality of being told by the teacher that he had failed. His conviction of freedom lasted through the afternoon and through supper and into the evening itself. He was undressing for bed, one leg already out of his trousers; without pause or falter he put the leg back into the trousers, already running, barefoot and shirtless, out of the house where his father was already asleep. The schoolhouse was not locked, though he had to break a lock to get into the teacher's desk. Yet all three of his papers were there, even to the same type of foolscap which he had submitted in blank—arithmetic, geography, the paragraph of English composition which, if he had not known he had submitted a blank one and if it had not been that he could neither pronounce nor recognise some of the words and could not understand all of what the ones he did know were talking about, he could not have sworn himself he had not written.

He returned home and got a few clothes and the pistol which he had owned for three years now, and waked his father, the two of them meeting for the last time in life in the summer lamplit midnight room—the determined and frightened youth and the fierce thin wiry man almost a head shorter, unshaven, with a wild flurry of gray hair, in a calf-length nightshirt, who gave him the contents of the worn wallet from the trousers flung across a nearby chair and, in iron spectacles now, wrote out the note for the amount, with interest, and made the son sign it. "All right," he said. "Go then, and be damned to you. You certainly ought to be enough kin to me to take care of yourself at sixteen. I was. But I'll bet you the same amount, by God, that you'll be hollering for help before six months." He went back past the schoolhouse and restored the papers, including the new set of blank ones; he would have repaired the broken lock if he could. And he even paid the bet, although he did not lose it. He sent the money back out of three times that sum won at dice one Saturday night a year later in the railroad construction camp in Oklahoma where he was a time-keeper.

He fled, not from his past, but to escape his future. It took him twelve years to learn you cannot escape either of them. He was in El Paso then, which was one end of his run as a locomotive fireman well up the service list toward an engine of his own, where he lived in the neat, small, urban house which he had rented for four years now, with the woman known to the neighborhood and the adjacent grocers and such as his wife, whom he had taken seven years ago out of a Galveston brothel. He had been a Kansas wheat-hand, he had herded sheep in New Mexico, he was again with a construction gang in Arizona and west Texas and then a longshoreman on the Galveston docks; if he were still fleeing, he did not know it because it had been years now since he had even remembered that he had forgotten the face. And when he proved that at least you cannot escape either past or future with nothing better than geography, he did not know that. (Geography: that paucity of invention, that fatuous faith in distance of man, who can invent no better means than geography for escaping; himself of all, to whom, so he believed he believed, geography had never been merely something to walk upon but was the very medium which the fetterless to- and fro-going required to breathe in.) And if he were merely being consistent in escaping from one woman by violating the skirts of another, as with his mother and the Negro girl of his adolescence, he did not know that, taking almost by force out of the house at daybreak the woman whom he had never seen until the previous midnight; there was a scene by gaslight between him and the curl-papered landlady as violent as if he were ravishing from the house an only daughter with an entailed estate.

They lived together for seven years. He went back to railroading and stuck with it and even came at last into the hierarchical current of seniority; he was mentally and spiritually, and with only an occasional aberration, physically faithful to her who in her turn was loyal, discreet, undemanding, and thrifty with his money. She bore his name in the boarding houses where they lived at first, then in the rented house in El Paso which they called home and were furnishing as they were able to buy furniture. Although she had never suggested it, he even thought of marrying her, so had the impact of the West which was still young enough then to put a premium on individuality, softened and at last abolished his inherited southern-provincial-Protestant fanaticism regarding marriage and female purity, the biblical Magdalen. There was his father, to be sure. He had not seen him since the night he left home and he did not expect to see him again. He did not think of his father as being dead, being any further removed than the old house in Mississippi where he had seen him last; he simply could not visualise them meeting anywhere else except in Mississippi, to which he could only imagine himself returning as an old man. But he knew what his father's reaction to his marriage with a once-public woman would be, and up to this time, with all that he had done and failed to do, he had never once done anything which he could not imagine his father also doing, or at least condoning. Then he received the message that his father was dead (He received at the same time an offer from a neighbor for the farm. He did not sell it. At the time he did not comprehend why.) and so that was removed. But it had never actually existed anyway. He had already settled that as a matter purely between him and himself, long ago one night while the dim engine rocked through the darkness over the clucking rail-joints: "Maybe she was not much once, but neither was I. And for a right smart while now she has been better than I know myself to have been." Perhaps they would have a child after a while. He thought of waiting for that, letting that be the sign. At first that eventuality had never occurred to him—here again was the old mystical fanatic Protestant; the hand of God lying upon the sinner even after the regeneration: the Babylonian interdict by heaven forever against reproduction. He did not know just how much time, just what span of chastity, would constitute purgatorium and absolution, but he would imagine it—some instant, mystical still, when the blight of those nameless and faceless men, the scorched scars of merchandised lust, would be effaced and healed from the organs which she had prostituted.

But that time was past now, not the mystic moment when the absolvement would be discharged, but the hour, the day before the elapse of which he had thought she would have told him she was pregnant and they would have married. It was long past now. It would never be. And one night in that twelfth year, in the boarding house at the other end of his run where he spent the alternate nights, he took out the three-year-old offer for the farm and he knew why he had not accepted it. I'm going home, he told himself—no more than that, not why; not even seeing the face which up to the day he entered school he could not even have described and which now he could not even remember. He made his run back to El Paso the next day and drew the seven years' accumulation out of the bank and divided it into two equal parts. The woman who had been his wife for seven years glanced once at the money and then stood cursing him. "You are going to get married," she said. There were no tears; she just cursed him. "What do I want with money? Look at me. Do you think I will lack money? Let me go with you. There will be some town, some place close where I can live. You can come when you want to. Have I ever bothered you?"

"No," he said. She cursed him, cursing them both. If she would just touch me, hit me, make me mad enough to hit her, he thought. But that did not happen either. It was not him she cursed, any more than she could curse the woman she had never seen and whose face even he could not quite recall. So he divided his half of the money again—that money which he had been lucky with: not lucky in the winning or earning or finding, but lucky in having the vices and desiring the pleasures which left a fair balance of it after they had been fed and satisfied—and returned to Mississippi. But even then, it apparently took him still another year to admit that he did not want to escape that past and future. The countryside believed he had come back to sell the farm. Yet the weeks passed, and he did not. Spring came and he had made no preparations either to rent it or work it himself. He merely continued to live in the old pre-Civil War house which, although no mansion, owning no columns, had been too big for three, while month after month passed, still apparently on that vacation from the Texas railroad his father had already told them he worked for, alone, without companionship, meeting (when he met them at all) the contemporaries who remembered him from youth over casual drinks or cards and that not often. Occasionally he would be seen at the picnics during the summer, and each Saturday afternoon he would make one of the group on the gallery of Varner's store, talking a little, answering questions rather, about the West, not secret and reserved so much as apparently thinking in another tongue from that in which he listened and would presently have to answer. He was bitted now, even if it did not show so much yet. There was still the mark of space and solitude in his face, but fading a little, rationalised and corrupted even into something consciously alert even if it was not fearful; the beast, prime solitary and sufficient out of the wild fields, drawn to the trap and knowing it to be a trap, not comprehending why it was doomed but knowing it was, and not afraid now—and not quite wild.

They were married in January. His part of the Texas money was gone then, though the countryside still believed he was rich, else he could not have lived for a year without working and would not have married a penniless orphan. Since he had arrived home solvent, the neighborhood would be unalterably convinced forever that he was wealthy, just as it had been unalterably convinced at first that only beggary had brought him home. He borrowed money from Will Varner, on a portion of the land, to build the new house on a new site nearer the road. He bought the stallion too then, as if for a wedding present to her, though he never said so. Or if that blood and bone and muscles represented that polygamous and bitless masculinity which he had relinquished, he never said that. And if there were any among his neighbors and acquaintances—Will Varner or Ratliff perhaps—who discerned that this was the actual transference, the deliberate filling of the vacancy of his abdication, they did not say it either.

Three months after the marriage the house was finished and they moved into it, with a Negro woman to cook although the only other hired cook, white or black, in the country was Varner's. Then the countryside would call, the men to the lot to look at the stallion, the women to the house, the new bright rooms, the new furniture and equipment and devices for saving steps and labor whose pictures they would dream over in the mail-order catalogues. They would watch her moving among the new possessions, busy, indefatigable, in the plain, neat garments, the plain and simple hair, the plain face blooming now with something almost like beauty—not amazement at luck, not particularly vindication of will and faith, but just serene, steadfast and boldly rosy when they would remark how the house had been completed exactly in time to catch the moon's full of April through the window where the bed was placed.

Then the stallion killed her. She was hunting a missing hen-nest in the stable. The Negro man had warned her: "He's a horse, missy. But he's a man horse. You keep out of there." But she was not afraid. It was as if she had recognised that transubstantiation, that duality, and thought even if she did not say it: Nonsense. I've married him now. He shot the stallion, running first into the stall with the now frenzied animal with nothing but an open pocket knife, until the Negro grappled with him and persuaded him to wait for the pistol to be fetched from the house, and for four years and two months he had lived in the new house with the hound and the Negro man to cook for them. He sold the mare which he had bought for her, and the cow he owned then, and discharged the woman cook and gave away the chickens. The new furniture had been bought on installment. He moved it all into the barn at the old place where he was born and notified the merchant to come and get it. Then he had only the stove, the kitchen table he ate from, and the cot he had substituted for the bed beneath the window. The moon was full on that first night he slept on the cot too, so he moved the cot into another room and then against a north wall where the moon could not possibly reach him, and two nights later he even went and spent one night in the old house. But there he lost everything, not only peace but even fibred and durable grief for despair to set its teeth into.

So he returned to the new house. The moon was waning then and would return only at monthly intervals, so that left only that single hour between sunset and full dark between its fulls, and weariness was an antidote for that. And weariness was cheap: he not only had the note he had given Will Varner for the loan, but there had been some trouble with the installment people who did not want to take the furniture back. So he farmed again, finding gradually how much he had forgotten about it. Thus, at times he would have actually forgotten that hour he dreaded until he would find himself entering it, walking into it, finding it suddenly upon him, drowning him with suffocation. Then that stubborn part of her and sometimes even of the son which perhaps next year they would have had would be everywhere about the house he had built to please her even though it was empty now of all the objects she had touched and used and looked at except the stove and the kitchen table and the one garment—not a nightgown or an undergarment, but the gingham dress which resembled the one in which he had first seen her that day at the school—and the window itself, so that even on the hottest evenings of summer he would sit in the sweltering kitchen while the Negro man cooked supper, drinking whiskey from a stone jug and tepid water from the cedar bucket and talking louder and louder, profane, intolerant, argumentative, with no challenge to be rebutted and no challenger to be vanquished and overcome.

But sooner or later the moon would wax again. There would be nights which were almost blank ones. Yet sooner or later that silver and blanched rectangle of window would fall once more, while night waxed into night then waned from night, as it had used to fall across the two of them while they observed the old country belief that the full moon of April guaranteed the fertilising act. But now there was no body beside his own for the moon to fall upon, and nothing for another body to have lain beside his own upon. Because the cot was too narrow for that and there was only the abrupt downward sheer of inky shadow in which only the invisible hound slept, and he would lie rigid, indomitable, and panting. "I dont understand it," he would say. "I dont know why. I wont ever know why. But You cant beat me. I am strong as You are. You cant beat me."

He was still alive when he left the saddle. He had heard the shot, then an instant later he knew he must have felt the blow before he heard it. Then the orderly sequence of time as he had known it for thirty-three years became inverted. He seemed to feel the shock of the ground while he knew he was still falling and had not yet reached it, then he was on the ground, he had stopped falling, and remembering what he had seen of stomach-wounds he thought: If I dont get the hurting started quick, I am going to die. He willed to start it, and for an instant he could not understand why it did not start. Then he saw the blank gap, the chasm somewhere between vision and where his feet should have been, and he lay on his back watching the ravelled and shattered ends of sentience and will projecting into the gap, hair-light and worm-blind and groping to meet and fuse again, and he lay there trying to will the sentience to meet and fuse. Then he saw the pain blast like lightning across the gap. But it came from the other direction: not from himself outward, but inward toward himself out of all the identifiable lost earth. Wait, wait, he said. Just go slow at first, and I can take it. But it would not wait. It roared down and raised him, tossed and spun. But it would not wait for him. It would not wait to hurl him into the void, so he cried, "Quick! Hurry!" looking up out of the red roar, into the face which with his own was wedded and twinned forever now by the explosion of that ten-gauge shell—the dead who would carry the living into the ground with him; the living who must bear about the repudiating earth with him forever, the deathless slain—then, as the slanted barrels did not move: "God damn it, couldn't you even borrow two shells, you fumbling ragged—" and put the world away. His eyes, still open to the lost sun, glazed over with a sudden well and run of moisture which flowed down the alien and unremembering cheeks too, already drying, with a newness as of actual tears.

2

That shot was too loud. It was not only too loud for any shot, it was too loud for any sound, louder than any sound needed to be. It was as though the very capacity of space and echo for reproducing noise were leagued against him too in the vindication of his rights and the liquidation of his injuries, building up and building up about the thicket where he crouched and the dim faint road which ran beside it long after the gun-butt had shocked into his shoulder and the black powder smoke had reeked away and the horse had whirled, galloping, the empty stirrups clashing against the empty saddle. He had not fired the gun in four years; he had not even been certain that either two of the five shells he owned would explode. The first one had not; it was the second one—the vain click louder than thunderbolt, the furious need to realign and find the second trigger, then the crash which after the other deafening click he did not hear at all, the reek and stink of powder pressing him backward and downward into the thicket until for an instant he was physically off-balance, so that even if he could have made a second shot it would have been too late and the hound too was gone, leaving him betrayed here too, crouching behind the log, panting and trembling.

Then he would have to finish it, not in the way he wanted to but in the way he must. It was no blind, instinctive, and furious desire for flight which he had to combat and curb. On the contrary. What he would have liked to do would be to leave a printed placard on the breast itself: *This is what happens to the men who impound Mink Snopes's cattle*, with his name signed to it. But he could not, and here again, for the third time since he had pulled the trigger, was that conspiracy to frustrate and outrage his rights as a man and his feelings as a sentient creature. He must rise and quit the thicket and do what he had next to do, not to finish it but merely to complete the first step of what he had started, put into motion, who realised now that he had known already, before he heard the horse and raised the gun, that that would happen which had happened: that he had pulled trigger on an enemy but had only slain a corpse to be hidden. So he sat up behind the log and shut his eyes and counted slowly until the shaking stopped and the sound of the galloping horse and even the outrageous and incredible shot had died out of his ears and he could rise, carrying the slanted gun still loaded with the shell which had failed to explode, and emerge from the thicket, already hurrying. But even then it would be dusk before he reached home.

It was dusk. He emerged from the bottom and looked up the slope of his meagre and sorry corn and saw it—the paintless two-room cabin with an open hallway between and a lean-to kitchen, which was not his, on which he paid rent but not taxes, paying almost as much in rent in one year as the house had cost to build; not old, yet the roof of which already leaked and the weather-stripping had already begun to rot away from the wall planks and which was just like the one he had been born in which had not belonged to his father either, and just like the one he would die in if he died indoors—which he probably would even if in his clothes, repudiated without warning at some instant between bed and table or perhaps the door itself, by his unflagging furious heart-muscles—and it was just like the more than six others he had lived in since his marriage and like the twice that many more he knew he would live in before he did die and although he paid rent on this one he was unalterably convinced that his cousin owned it and he knew that this was as near as he would ever come to owning the roof over his head. Then he saw the two children in the yard before it, who even as he saw them, stood quickly up, watching him, then turned and scuttled toward the house. Then it seemed to him that he could see her also, standing in the open hallway almost exactly where she had stood eight hours before and watched his back where he sat over the cold hearth, oiling the gun with the bacon-drippings which was the only thing he owned that could be used for oil, which would not lubricate but in contact with the metal would congeal into a substance like soap, inherent with its own salty corrosion; standing there as if in all that time she had not moved, once more framed by an opening, though without the lamp, as she was standing in the savage lamplight, above the loud harsh voices of invisible men, in the open door of the mess-hall in that south Mississippi convict camp where he first saw her nine years ago. He stopped looking at the house; he had only glanced at it as it was, and mounted through the yellow and stunted stand of his corn, yellow and stunted because he had had no money to buy fertilizer to put beneath it and owned neither the stock nor the tools to work it properly with and had had no one to help him with what he did own in order to gamble his physical strength and endurance against his body's livelihood not only with ordinary climate but with the incredible spring of which the dry summer was the monstrous abortion, which had rained every day from the middle of May into July, as if the zodiac too had stacked cards against him. He mounted on among the bitten and fruitless stalks, carrying the gun which looked too big for him to carry or aim or dare to fire, which he had acquired seven years ago at the sacrifice of actual food and had acquired at all only because no other man would want it since it carried a shell too big to shoot at anything but a wild goose or a deer and too costly to shoot at anything but a man.

He did not look toward the house again. He went on past it and entered the rotting lattice which enclosed the well and leaned the gun against the wall and removed his shoes and drew a bucket of water and began to wash the shoes. Then he knew that she was behind him. He didn't look back, sitting on the rotted bench, small, in a faded clean shirt and patched overalls, tipping the bucket over the shoe and scrubbing at it with a corn cob. She began to laugh, harshly and steadily. "I told you this morning," she said. "I said, if you do, if you left here with that gun, I was going." He didn't look up, crouched over the wet shoe into which he had slipped his hand like a shoe-last, scrubbing at it with the cob. "Never you mind where. Dont you worry about where when they come for you." He didn't answer. He finished the first shoe and set it down and slipped his hand into the second one and tipped water from the bucket over it and began to scrub it. "Because it wont be far!" she cried suddenly, yet without raising her voice at all. "Because when they come to hang you, I'm going to be where I can see it!" Now he rose. He set the unfinished second shoe carefully down and laid the cob beside it and rose, small, almost a half head shorter than she, barefoot, moving toward her, not fast, sidling a little, his head bent and apparently not even looking at her as she stood in the gaping and broken entrance— the bleached hair darkening again at the roots since it had been a year now since there had been any money to buy more dye, the harshly and steadily laughing face watching him with a curious and expectant glitter in the eyes. He struck her across the mouth. He watched his hand, almost labored, strike across the face which did not flinch, beneath the eyes which did not even blink. "You damned little murdering bastard," she said past the bright sudden blood. He struck her again, the blood smearing between mouth and palm and then renewed, striking again with that slow gathering which was not deliberation but extreme and patiently indomitable and implacable weariness, and again. "Go," he said. "Go. Go."

He followed her, across the yard and into the hallway, though he did not enter the room. From the door he could see her, although the room itself was almost completely dark, against the small high square of the dusk-faint window. Then the match spurted and glared and steadied above the wick, and now she was framed in an opening by shadeless light and surrounded by the loud soundless invisible shades of the nameless and numberless men—that body which, even when he was actually looking at them, at times to him had never borne children, was anterior even to the two-dollar marriage which had not sanctified but sanctioned them, which each time he approached it, it was not garments intervening but the cuckolding shades which had become a part of his past too, as if he and not she had been their prone recipient; which despite the soiled and shapeless garments concealing it he would contemplate even from the cold star-less night-periphery beyond both hatred and desire and tell himself: It's like drink. It's like dope to me. Then he saw the faces of the two children also, in the same flare of match and wick as if she had touched that single match to all three of them at the same time. They were sitting on the floor in the corner, not crouched, not hiding, just sitting there in the dark as they had been sitting doubtless ever since he had watched them scuttle toward the house when he came out of the bottom, looking at him with that same quality which he himself possessed: not abject but just still, with an old tired wisdom, acceptance of the immitigable discrepancy between will and capability due to that handicap of physical size in which none of the three of them had had any choice, turning from him to look without curiosity at the blood on their mother's face and watching quietly as she took a garment from a nail in the wall and spread it on the pallet bed and wrapped the other objects—the other garments, the single pair of half-size shoes which either child wore indiscriminately in cold weather, the cracked hand-glass, the wooden comb, the handleless brush—into it. "Come," she said. He moved aside and they passed him, the children huddled against her skirt and for a moment hidden from him as they emerged from the room, then visible again, moving on up the hallway before her, he following, keeping that same distance, stopping again at the entrance while they crossed the porch and descended the warped and rotting steps. When she paused on the ground beyond the steps he moved again, again with that invincible, that weary implacability, until he saw and stopped also and watched the larger child hurry across the yard, soundless and incorporeal in the dusk which was almost night now, and snatch something from the ground and return, clasping the object—a wooden block with the tops of four snuff tins nailed to it like wheels—to its breast. They went on. He did not follow further. He did not even appear to be looking at them as they passed through the broken gate.

He returned to the house and blew out the lamp, whereupon the dark became complete, as if the puny vanishing flame had carried along with it all that remained of day, so that when he returned to the well, it was by touch alone that he found the cob and the unfinished shoe and finished cleaning it. Then he washed the gun. When he first got it, when the gun was new, or new at least to him, he had had a cleaning rod for it. He had made it himself, of cane, chosen carefully and trimmed and scraped carefully and eyed neatly at the tip to take the greasy rag, and during the first year or so, when he had had money to buy powder and shot and caps to load the shells with and could hunt a little now and then, he had been no less particular in the care of the cleaning rod than of the gun because he had only bought the gun but the rod he had made. But the rod was gone now, he did not remember when nor know where, vanished along with the other accumulations of his maturity which had been dear to him too once, which he had shed somehow and somewhere along the road between the attaining of manhood and this hour when he found himself with nothing but an empty and foodless house which did not actually belong to him, and the gun, and that irremediable instant when the barrels had come level and true and his will had told his finger to contract, which nothing but his own death would ever efface from his memory. So he tipped water from the bucket over the gun and removed his shirt and wiped it dry and picked up the shoes and returned to the house and, without lighting the lamp again, stood in the dark at the cold stove and ate with his fingers from the pot of cold peas which sat on it and went and lay down, still in his overalls, on the pallet bed in the room which was empty at last even of the loud shades, lying flat on his back in the darkness with his eyes open and his arms straight beside him, thinking of nothing. Then he heard the hound.

At first he did not move; except for his regular and unhurried breathing, he might have been the corpse his attitude resembled, lying perfectly still while the first cry died away and the myriad night-silence came down and then indrew and the second cry came, ringing, deep, resonant and filled with grief. He did not move. It was as though he had been expecting it, waiting for it; had lain down and composed and emptied himself, not for sleep but to gather strength and will as distance runners and swimmers do, before assuming the phase of harried and furious endeavor which his life was about to enter, lying there for perhaps ten minutes while the long cries rang up from the dark bottom, as if he knew that those ten minutes were to be the last of peace. Then he rose. Still in the dark, he put on the still-damp shirt and the shoes he had just washed and from a nail behind the door he took down the new plow-line still looped in the coils in which his cousin, Varner's clerk, had knotted it two weeks ago, and left the house.

The night was moonless. He descended through the dry and invisible corn, keeping his bearing on a star until he reached the trees, against the black solidity of which fireflies winked and drifted and from beyond which came the booming and grunting of frogs and the howling of the dog. But once among them, he could not even see the sky anymore, though he realised then what he should have before: that the hound's voice would guide him. So he followed it, slipping and plunging in the mud and tripping and thrashing among the briers and tangled undergrowth and blundering against invisible tree trunks, his arm crooked to shield his face, sweating, while the steady cries of the dog drew nearer and nearer and broke abruptly off in mid-howl. He believed for an instant that he actually saw the phosphorescent glints of eyes although he had no light to reflect them, and suddenly and without knowing that he was going to do it, he ran toward where he had seen the eyes. He struck the next tree a shocking blow with his shoulder; he was hurled sideways but caught balance again, still plunging forward, his hands extended. He was falling now. If there's a tree in front of me now, he thought, it will be all. He actually touched the dog. He felt its breath and heard the click of its teeth as it slashed at him, springing away, leaving him on his hands and knees in the mud while the noise of its invisible flight crashed and ceased.

He was kneeling at the brink of the depression. He had only to rise and, half stooping, his arm still crooked to fend his face, step down into the ankle-deep ooze of sunless mud and rotting vegetation and follow it for another step or so to reach the brush-pile. He thrust the coiled plow-line into the bib of his overalls and stooped and began to drag away the slimed and rotten branches. Something gave a choked, infant-like cry, scrabbling among the sticks; it sprawled frantically across his foot as he kicked at it, telling himself: It's just a possum. It aint nothing but a possum, stooping again to the tangle of foul and sweating wood, lifting it away until he reached the body. He wiped his hands free of mud and slime on his shirt and overalls and took hold of the shoulders and began to walk backward, dragging it along the depression. It was not a ditch, it was an old logging road, choked with undergrowth and almost indistinguishable now, about two feet below the flat level of the bottom. He followed it for

better than a mile, dragging the body which outweighed him by fifty
pounds, pausing only to wipe his sweating hands from time to time
on his shirt and to establish his whereabouts anew whenever he could
find enough visible sky to distinguish the shapes of individual trees
against.

Then he turned and dragged the body up out of the depression
and went on for a hundred yards, still walking backward. He seemed
to know exactly where he was, he did not even look over his shoulder
until he released the body at last and stood erect and laid his hand
upon what he sought—the shell of a once-tremendous pin oak, topless and about ten feet tall, standing in the clearing which the lightning bolt or age or decay or whatever it had been, had created. Two
years ago he had lined a wild bee into it; the sapling which he had cut
and propped against the shell to reach the honey was still in place.
He took the plow-line from his breast and knotted one end about the
body and removed his shoes and with the other end of the rope
between his teeth, he climbed the sapling and straddled the rim of
the shell and hand over hand hauled up the body which was half
again as large as he, dragging it bumping and scraping up the trunk,
until it lay like a half-filled sack across the lip. The knot in the rope
had slipped tight. At last he took his knife and cut the rope and tumbled the body over into the shell. But it stopped almost at once, and
only when it was too late did he realise that he should have reversed
it. He shoved at it, probing about the shoulders, but it was not hung,
it was wedged by one twisted arm. So he tied one end of the rope
about the stub of a limb just below his foot and took a turn of the
rope about his wrist and stood up on the wedged shoulders and
began to jump up and down, whereupon without warning the body
fled suddenly beneath him, leaving him dangling on the rope. He
began to climb it, hand over hand, rasping off with his knuckles the
rotten fibre of the wall so that a faint, constant, dry powder of decay
filled his nostrils like snuff. Then he heard the stub crack, he felt the
rope slip free and he leaped upward from nothing and got the fin-
gertips of one hand over the lip. But when his weight came down on
it, a whole shard of the rotten shell carried away and he flung the
other hand up but the shell crumbled beneath that one also and he
climbed interminably, furiously perpetual and without gain, his

mouth open for his panting breath and his eyes glaring at the remote
September sky which had long since turned past midnight, until at
last the wood stopped crumbling, leaving him dangling by his hands,
panting, until he could pull himself up once more and straddle the
rim. After a while he climbed down and lifted the propped sapling
onto his shoulder and carried it fifteen or twenty yards beyond the
edge of the clearing and returned and got his shoes. When he
reached home dawn had already begun. He took off the muddy shoes
and lay down on the pallet bed. Then, as if it had waited for him to
lie down, the hound began to howl again. It seemed to him that he
had even heard the intake of breath before the first cry came up from
the bottom where it was still night, measured, timbrous, and prolonged.

His days and nights were now reversed. He would emerge from
the bottom with the morning star or perhaps the actual sun and
mount through the untended and abortive corn. He did not wash the
shoes now. He would not always remove them, and he would make
no fire but would eat standing from the pot of cold peas on the stove
while they lasted and drank down to its dregs the pot of cold, stale
coffee while it lasted, and when they were gone he would eat hands-
full of raw meal from the almost empty barrel. For during the first
day or so he would be hungry, since what he was doing now was
harder than any work he had ever done, besides the excitement, the
novelty. But after that it was not new anymore, and by then he
realised it could have but one ending and so it would last forever, and
he stopped being hungry. He would merely rouse, wake, to tell himself, You got to eat, and eating the raw meal (presently there was
nothing in the barrel but the dried cake on the sides which he would
scrape off with a knife-blade) which he did not want and apparently
did not even need, as if his body were living on the incorrigible sin-
gleness of his will like so much fatty tissue. Then he would lie down
on the pallet bed in his overalls and shoes on which the freshest and
most recent caking of mud had not even begun to dry, still chewing
and with the lengthening stubble about his mouth still full of meal
grains and, as though in a continuation of the lying down, plunge not
into oblivion but into an eyeless and tongueless interval of resting
and recuperation like a man stepping deliberately into a bath, to

wake as though to an alarm clock at the same afternoon hour, the continuity unbroken between the lying down and the opening of eyes again, since it was only the body which bore and would bear the burden which needed the rest. He would build a fire in the stove then, although there was nothing to cook save the scrapings from the meal barrel. But it was the hot drink he wanted, though there was no more coffee either. So he would fill the pot with water and heat it and drink the hot water sweetened with sugar, then in the splint chair on the porch he would watch the night, the darkness, emerge from the bottom and herd, drive, the sun gradually up the slope of the corn-patch which even in dusk stood no less barren and yellow than in sunlight, and at last take the house itself. Then the hound would begin and he would sit there for perhaps ten or fifteen minutes longer, as the holder of the annual commuter's ticket sits on his accustomed bench and continues to read his paper after the train has already whistled for the stop.

On the second afternoon when he waked a little boy was sitting on the front steps—the round-headed periwinkle-eyed son of his kinsman who operated Varner's blacksmith shop—though at the first sound of his feet on the floor the boy moved, so that when he reached the porch the boy was already on the ground beyond it and several feet away, looking back at him. "Uncle Lump says for you to come to the store," the boy said. "He says it's important." He didn't answer. He stood there with last night's mud now dried on the shoes and overalls and (so still had been his sleep) this morning's meal grains still clinging in the stubble around his mouth, until the boy turned and began to walk away and then began to run, looking back for an instant from the edge of the woods, then running on, vanishing. Still he didn't move and still there was nothing in his face. If it had been money, he could have brought it, he thought. Because it aint money. Not from them. And on the third morning he knew suddenly that someone was standing in the door watching him. He knew, even in the midst of the unreality which was not dream but a barren place where his mind, his will, stood like an unresting invincible ungrazing horse while the puny body which rode it renewed its strength, that it was not the boy now and that it was still morning, that he had not been asleep that long. They were hid here, watching me when I come up out of the bottom, he thought, trying to speak aloud to wake himself as he might have knelt to shake his own shoulder: Wake up. Wake up: until he waked, knowing at once that it was too late, not even needing the position of the window's shadow on the floor to tell him it was that same automatic hour of afternoon. He did not hurry. He started the fire and set the pot on to heat and scooped a handfull of meal scrapings from the barrel and ate it, chewing the splinters out of it, spitting them, rubbing them from his lips with his hand. In doing so, he discovered the meal already clinging in his beard and he ate that too, wiping the grains from either side with his fingers across his chewing mouth. Then he drank the cup of sweetened water and went out into the yard. The tracks were there. He knew the sheriff's—the heavy, deep, deliberate prints, even in the rainless summer's parched earth, of those two hundred and forty pounds of flesh which wore the metal shield smaller than a playing card, on which he had gambled not only his freedom but perhaps his obliteration too, followed by those of its satellites. He saw the prints of the hands and the crawling knees where one of them had searched back and forth beneath the floor while he was sleeping on top of it; he found leaning against the wall inside the stable his own shovel with which they had cleared away the year's accumulation of mule-droppings to examine the earth beneath, and he found among the trees above the cabin the place where the surrey had stood. And still there was nothing in his face—no alarm, no terror, no dread; not even contempt or amusement—only the cold and incorrigible, the almost peaceful, intractability.

He returned to the house and took the shotgun from its corner. It was covered now almost completely over with a thin, snuff-colored frost of rust, as though the very tedious care of that first night's wiping had overreached itself, had transferred the water from the gun to the shirt then back from the shirt to the gun again. And it did not breech, break, but opened slowly to steady force, exposing the thick, chocolate-colored soap-like mass of congealed animal fat, so that at last he dismantled it and boiled water in the coffee pot and scalded the grease away and laid the dismembered sections along the edge of the back porch where the sun fell on them as long as there was sun. Then he reassembled it and loaded it with two of the three remain-

ing shells and leaned it against the wall beside the chair, and again he
watched the night emerge from the bottom and mount through the
bitten corn, taking corn, taking the house itself at last and, still rising, become as two up-opening palms releasing the westward-flying
ultimate bird of evening. Below him, beyond the corn, the fireflies
winked and drifted against the breast of darkness; beyond, within, it
the steady booming of the frogs was the steady pulse and beat of the
dark heart of night, so that at last when the unvarying moment
came—that moment as unvarying from one dusk to the next as the
afternoon's instant when he would awake—the beat of that heart
seemed to fall still too, emptying silence for the first deep cry of
strong and invincible grief. He reached his hand backward and took
up the gun.

This time he used the hound's voice for a bearing from the start.
When he entered the bottom he thought about wind and paused to
test it. But there was no wind, so he went straight on toward the
howling, not fast now since he was trying for silence, yet not slow
either since this would not take long and then he could return home
and lie down before midnight, long before midnight, telling himself
as he moved cautiously and steadily toward the howling: Now I can
go back to sleeping at night again. The howling was quite near now.
He slanted the gun forward, his thumb on the two hammers. Then
the dog's voice stopped, again in mid-howl; again for an instant he
saw the two yellow points of eyes before the gun-muzzle blotted
them. In the glare of the explosion he saw the whole animal sharp
in relief, leaping. He saw the charge strike and hurl it backward into
the loud welter of following darkness. By an actual physical effort
he restrained his finger before it contracted on the second trigger
and with the gun still at his shoulder he crouched, holding his breath
and glaring into the sightless dark while the tremendous silence
which had been broken three nights ago when the first cry of the
hound reached him and which had never once been restored,
annealed, even while he slept, roared down about him and, still roaring, began to stiffen and set like cement, not only in his hearing but
in his lungs, his breathing, inside and without him too, solidifying
from tree-trunk to tree-trunk, among which the shattered echoes of
the shot died away in strangling murmurs, caught in that cooling

solidity before they had had time to cease. With the gun still cocked and presented, he advanced toward the place where he had seen the dog fall, panting through his bared clenched teeth, feeling about with his feet in the undergrowth. Then he realised suddenly that he had already passed the spot and that he was still advancing. He knew that he was about to start running and then he was running, blindly in the pitch darkness, speaking, hissing to himself: Stop. Stop. You'll bust your damn brains out. He stopped, panting. He got his bearings anew on a patch of sky, yet he forced himself to remain motionless until even the panting stopped. Then he let the hammer of the gun down and went on, walking now. Now he had the booming of the frogs to guide him, blending and fading then rising again in choral climax, each separate voice not a single note but an octave, almost a chord, in bass, growing louder and louder and nearer and nearer, then ceasing abruptly too into a second of frozen immobility followed by a swift random patter of small splashes like hands striking the water, so that when he saw the water it was already shattered into fluid ceaseless gleams across which reflected stars slid and vanished and recovered. He flung the gun. For an instant he saw it, spinning slowly. Then it splashed, not sinking but disintegrating among that shattered scurrying of broken stars.

When he reached home, it was not even midnight yet. Now he removed not only the shoes but the overalls too which had not passed his knees in seventy-two hours, and lay down on the pallet. But at once he knew he was not going to sleep, not because of the seventy-two hours' habit of reversed days and nights, not because of any twitching and jerking of spent and ungovernable nerves and muscles, but because of that silence which the first gunshot had broken and the second one had made whole again. So he lay again, rigid and composed on his back, his arms at his sides and his eyes open in the darkness and his head and lungs filled with that roaring silence across which the random and velvet-shod fireflies drifted and winked and beyond which the constant frogs pulsed and beat, until the rectangle of sky beyond the oblique door of the room and the open end of the hallway began to turn gray and then primrose, and already he could see three buzzards soaring in it. Now I must get up, he told himself; I will have to start staying up all day if I aim to begin sleep-

ing again at night. Then he began to say, Wake up. Wake up, until he
waked at last, with the yellow square of window-shaped sun lying
once more on the floor where each unvarying afternoon it would lie.
Resting upon the quilt not an inch from his face was a folded scrap of
brown paper; when he rose, he found in the dust at the doorsill the
print of the little boy's naked foot. The note was in pencil, on a scrap
torn from a paper sack, unsigned: *Come on in here your wifes got some
money for you* He stood, unshaven, in his shirt, blinking at it. Now I
can go, he thought, and something began to happen in his heart. He
raised his head, blinking almost painfully, looking for the first time in
three days beyond the desolate and foodless cabin which symbolised
the impasse his life had reached, into the limitless freedom of the
sunny sky. He spoke aloud. "Now I can—" he said. Then he saw the
buzzards. At dawn he had seen three. Now he might possibly have
counted them, though he did not. He just watched the black concentric spiraling as if they followed an invisible funnel, disappearing
one by one below the trees. He spoke aloud again. "It's the dog," he
said, knowing it was not the dog. And it didn't matter. Because I'll
be gone then, he thought. It was not that something lifted from his
heart; it was as though he had become aware for the first time of the
weight which lay on it.

It was almost sunset when, shaved and with the shoes and overalls washed again, he mounted to the empty gallery and entered the
store. His kinsman was behind the open candy case, in the act of
putting something into his mouth.

"Where—" he said.

The cousin closed the case, chewing. "You durned fool, I sent
word to you two days ago to get away from there before that pussel-
gutted Hampton come prowling around here with that surrey full
of deputies. A nigger grabbling in that slough found that durn gun
before the water even quit shaking."

"It's not mine," he said. "I have no gun. Where—"

"Hell fire, everybody knows it's yours. There aint another one of
them old hammer-lock ten-gauge Hadleys in this country but that
one. That's why I never told no lie about it, let alone that durn
Hampton sitting right out there on that bench when the nigger come
up the steps with it. I says, 'Sure it's Mink's gun. He's been hunting

for it ever since last fall.' Then I turns to the nigger. 'What the hell you mean, you black son of a bitch,' I says, 'borrowing Mr Snopes's gun last fall to go squirl hunting and letting it fall in that ere slough and claiming you couldn't find it?' Here." The cousin stooped beneath the counter and rose and laid the gun on the counter. It had been wiped off save for a patch of now-dried mud on the stock.

He did not even look at it. "It's not mine," he said. "Where is—"

"But that's all right now. I fixed that in time. What Hampton expected was for me to deny it was yours. Then he would a had you. But I fixed that. I throwed the suspicion right onto the nigger fore Hampton could open his mouth. I figger about tonight or maybe tomorrow night I'll take a few of the boys and go to the nigger's house with a couple of trace chains or maybe a little fire under his feet. And even if he dont confess nothing, folks will hear that he has done been visited at night and there's too many votes out here for Hampton to do nothing else but take him on in and send him to the penitentiary, even if he cant quite risk hanging him, and Hampton knows it. So that's all right. Besides, what I sent you that first message for was about your wife."

"Yes," he said. "Where—"

"She's going to get you in trouble. She's done already got you in trouble. That's how come that durn vote-sucking sheriff noseying around out here. His nigger found the horse, with him and the dog both missing, but that was all right until folks begun to remember how she turned up here that same night, with them two kids and that bundle of clothes and blood still running out of her busted mouth until folks couldn't help but know you had run her out of the house. And even that might have been all right if she hadn't started in telling everybody that would listen that you never done it. Just a horse with a empty saddle; no body and no blood neither found yet, and here she is trying to help you by telling everybody she meets that you never done something that nobody knows for sure has even been done yet. Why in hell aint you got out of here? Didn't you have sense enough to do that the first day?"

"On what?" he said.

The cousin had been blinking rapidly at him. Now the little eyes stopped blinking. "On what?" he said. The other did not answer. He had not moved since he entered, small, immobile, in the middle of the floor opposite the entrance, through which the dying sunlight stained him from head to foot with a thin wash like diluted blood. "You mean you aint got any money? You mean to stand there and tell me he never had nothing in his pocket? Because I dont believe it. By God, I know better. I saw inside his purse that same morning. He never carried a cent less than fifty . . ." The voice ceased, died. Then it spoke in a dawning incredulous amazement and no louder than a whisper: "Do you mean to tell me you never even looked? *never even looked?*" The other did not answer. He might not have even heard, motionless, looking at nothing while the last of the copper light, mounting like rising water up his body, gathered for an instant in concentrated and dying crimson upon the calm and unwavering and intractable mask of his face, and faded, and the dusk, the twilight, gathered along the ranked shelves and in the shadowy corners and the old strong smells of cheese and leather and kerosene, condensed and thickened among the rafters above his head like the pall of oblivion itself. The cousin's voice seemed to emerge from it, sourceless, unlocatable, without even the weight of breath to give it volume: "Where did you put him?" and again, the cousin outside the counter now, facing him, almost breast to breast with him, the fierce repressed breathing murmuring on his face now: "By God, he had at least fifty dollars. I know. I seen it. Right here in this store. Where did you—"

"No," he said.

"Yes."

"No." Their faces were not a foot apart, their breathing steady and audible. Then the other face moved back, larger than his, higher than his, beginning to become featureless in the fading light.

"All right," the cousin said. "I'm glad you dont need money. Because if you come to me expecting any, you'd just have to keep on expecting. You know what Will Varner pays his clerks. You know about how much any man working for Will Varner's wages could get ahead in ten years, let alone two months. So you wont even need that ten dollars your wife's got. So that'll be just fine, wont it?"

"Yes," he said. "Where—"

"Staying at Will Varner's." He turned at once and went toward the door. As he passed out of it the cousin spoke again out of the shadows behind him: "Tell her to ask Will or Jody to lend her another ten to go with that one she's already got."

Although it was not quite dark yet, there was already a light in the Varner house. He could see it even at this distance, and it was as if he were standing outside of himself, watching the distance steadily shorten between himself and the light. And then that's all, he thought. All them days and nights that looked like they wasn't going to have no end, come down to the space of a little piece of dusty road between me and a lighted door. And when he put his hand on Varner's gate, it was as if she had been waiting, watching the road for him. She came out of the front door, running, framed again for an instant by the lighted doorway as when he had first seen her that night at the lumber camp to which, even nine years afterward, he did not like to remember how, by what mischance, he had come. The feeling was no less strong now than it had ever been. He did not dread to remember it nor did he try not to, and not in remorse for the deed he had done, because he neither required nor desired absolution for that. He merely wished he did not have to remember the fiasco which had followed the act, contemptuous of the body or the intellect which had failed the will to do, not writhing with impotent regret on remembering it and not snarling, because he never snarled; but just cold, indomitable, and intractable. He had lived in a dozen different sorry and ill-made rented cabins as his father had moved from farm to farm, without himself ever having been more than fifteen or twenty miles away from any one of them. Then suddenly and at night he had had to leave the roof he called home and the only land and people and customs he knew, without even time to gather up anything to take with him, if there had been anything to take, nor to say farewell to anyone if there had been anyone to say farewell to, to find himself weeks later and still on foot, more than two hundred miles away. He was seeking the sea; he was twenty-three then, that young. He had never seen it; he did not know certainly just where it was, except that it was to the south. He had never thought of it before and he could not have said why he wanted to go to it—what of repudiation of the land, the earth, where his body or intellect had faulted somehow to the cold undeviation of his will to do—seeking

what of that iodinic proffer of space and oblivion of which he had
no intention of availing himself, would never avail himself, as if, by
deliberately refusing to cut the wires of remembering, to punish that
body and intellect which had failed him. Perhaps he was seeking only
the proffer of this illimitable space and irremediable forgetting along
the edge of which the contemptible teeming of his own earth-kind
timidly seethed and recoiled, not to accept the proffer but merely to
bury himself in this myriad anonymity beside the impregnable haven
of all the drowned intact golden galleons and the unattainable deathless seamaids. Then, almost there and more than twenty-four hours
without food, he saw a light and approached it and heard the loud
voices and saw her framed in the open door, immobile, upright and
unlistening, while those harsh loud manshouts and cries seemed to
rise toward her like a roaring incense. He went no further. The next
morning he was at work there, an axeman, without even knowing
whom he was working for, asking only incidentally of the foreman
who hired him and who told him bluntly that he was too small, too
light, to swing his end of a cross-cut saw, what his wage would be. He
had never seen convicts' stripes before either, so it was not with that
first light but only after several succeeding ones that he learned
where he was—a tract of wild-catted virgin timber in process of
being logged by a roaring man of about fifty who was no taller than
he was, with strong, short iron-gray hair and a hard prominent belly,
who through political influence or bribery or whatever got his convict labor from the State for the price of their board and keep; a widower who had lost his wife years ago at the birth of their first child
and now lived openly with a magnificent quadroon woman most of
whose teeth were gold and who superintended the kitchen where
other convicts did the actual work, in a separate house set among the
plank-and-canvas barracks in which the convicts lived. The woman
in the lighted door was that child. She lived in the same house with
her father and the quadroon, in a separate wing with an entrance of
its own, and her hair was black then—a splendid heavy mane of it
which whatever present one out of foremen and armed guards and
convict laborers, and himself in his turn, after his summons came and
he had long since discovered the reason for the separate entrance,
contributed to keep cut almost man-short with razors. It was strong

and short and not fine, either in the glare of that first evening's lamp or in the next day's sunlight when, the axe lifted for the stroke, he turned and she was sitting a big, rangy, well-kept horse behind and above him, in overalls, looking at him not brazenly and not speculatively, but intently and boldly, as a bold and successful man would. That was what he saw: the habit of success—that perfect marriage of will and ability with a single undiffused object—which set her not as a feminine garment but as one as masculine as the overalls and her height and size and the short hair; he saw not a nympholept but the confident lord of a harem. She did not speak that time. She rode on, and now he discovered that that separate entrance was not used only at night. Sometimes she would ride past on the horse and stop and speak briefly to the foreman and ride on; sometimes the quadroon would appear on the horse and speak a name to the foreman and return, and the foreman would call that name and the man would drop his axe or saw and follow the horse. Then he, still swinging his axe and not even looking up, would seem to follow and watch that man enter the private door and then watch him emerge later and return to work—the nameless, the identical, highwayman, murderer, thief, among whom there appeared to be no favorites and no jealousy. That was to be his alone, apparently. But even before his summons came, he was resigned to the jealousy and cognizant of his fate. He had been bred by generations to believe invincibly that to every man, whatever his past actions, whatever depths he might have reached, there was reserved one virgin, at least for him to marry; one maidenhead, if only for him to deflower and destroy. Yet he not only saw that he must compete for mere notice with men among whom he saw himself not only as a child but as a child of another race and species, but that when he did approach her at last he would have to tear aside not garments alone but the ghostly embraces of thirty or forty men; and this not only once but each time and hence (he foresaw even then his fate) forever: no room, no darkness, no desert even ever large enough to contain the two of them and the constant stallion-ramp of those inexpugnable shades. Then his turn, his summons came at last, as he had known it would. He obeyed it with foreknowledge but without regret. He entered not the hot and quenchless bed of a barren and lecherous woman, but the fierce simple cave of a lioness—a tumescence which surrendered nothing and asked no quarter, and which made a monogamist of him forever, as opium and homicide do of those whom they once accept. That was early one afternoon, the hot sun of July falling through the shadeless and even curtainless windows open to all outdoors, upon a bed made by hand of six-inch unplaned timbers cross-braced with light steel cables, yet which nevertheless would advance in short steady skidding jerks across the floor like a light and ill-balanced rocking chair. Five months later they were married. They did not plan it. Never at any time afterward did he fail to affirm, even to himself, that the marriage had been no scheme or even intention of hers. What did it was the collapse of her father's enterprise, which even he had been able to see was inherent with its own inevitable bankruptcy which the crash of each falling tree brought one stick nearer. Afterward it seemed to him that that afternoon's bedding had been the signal for that entire furious edifice of ravished acres and shotgun houses and toiling men and mules which had been erected overnight and founded on nothing, to collapse overnight into nothing, back into the refuse—the sawdust heaps, the lopped dead limbs and tree-butts and all the grief of wood—of its own murdering. He had most of his five months' pay. They walked to the nearest county-seat and bought a license; the Justice of the Peace who sold it to them removed his chew of tobacco and, holding it damp in his hand, called in two passing men and pronounced them man and wife. They returned to his native country, where he rented a small farm on shares. They had a second-hand stove, a shuck mattress on the floor, the razor with which he still kept her hair cut short, and little else. At that time they needed little else. She said: "I've had a hundred men, but I never had a wasp before. That stuff comes out of you is rank poison. It's too hot. It burns itself and my seed both up. It'll never make a kid." But three years afterward it did. Five years later it had made two; and he would watch them as they approached across whatever sorry field or patch, fetching his cold meagre dinner or the jug of fresh water, or as they played with blocks of wood or rusted harness buckles or threadless and headless plow-bolts which even he could no longer use, in the dust before whatever rented porch he sat on while the sweat cooled out of him, and in a resurgence of the old hot quick invincible fury still as strong and fierce and brief as on the first time, he would think, By God, they better be mine. Then, quieter, on the pallet bed where she would already be asleep although his own spent body had not yet ceased to jerk and twitch, he would think how, even if they were not, it was the same thing. They served to shackle her too, more irrevocably than he himself was shackled, since on her fate she had even put the seal of a formal acquiescence by letting her hair grow out again and dyeing it.

She came down the walk, running heavily but fast. She reached it before he had finished opening it, flinging both him and the gate back as she ran through it and caught him by the front of his overalls. "No!" she cried, though her voice still whispered: "No! Oh God, what do you mean? You cant come in here!"

"I can go anywhere I want to," he said. "Lump said—" Then he tried to wrench free, but she had already released him and caught his arm and was hurrying, almost dragging him along the fence, away from the light. He wrenched at her grip again, setting his feet. "Wait," he said.

"You fool!" she said, in that harsh panting whisper: "You fool! Oh, God damn you! God damn you!" He began to struggle, with a cold condensed fury which did not seem quite able or perhaps ready to emerge yet from his body. Then he lashed suddenly out, still not at her but to break her grip. But she held him, with both hands now, as they faced each other. "Why didn't you go that night? God, I thought of course you were going to get out as soon as I left!" She shook him savagely, with no more effort than if he were a child. "Why didn't you? Why in hell didn't you?"

"On what?" he said. "Where? Lump said—"

"I know you didn't have any money, like I know you haven't had anything to eat except the dust in that barrel. You could have hidden! In the woods—anywhere, until I would have time to—God damn you! God damn you! If they would just let me do the hanging!" She shook him, her face bent to his, her hard, hot, panting breath on his face. "Not for killing him, but for doing it when you had no money to get away on if you ran, and nothing to eat if you stayed. If they'd just let me do it: hang you just enough to take you down and bring you to and hang you again just enough to cut you down and bring you to—" He slashed out again, viciously. But she had already released him, standing on one foot now, the other foot angled upward from the knee to meet her reaching hand. She took something from her shoe and put it into his hand. He knew at once what it was—a banknote, folded and refolded small and square and still warm with body-heat. And it was just one note. It's one dollar, he thought, knowing it was not. It was I. O. and Eck, he told himself, knowing it was not, just as he knew there was but one man in the country who would have ten dollars in one bill—or at the most, two men; now he even heard what his cousin had said as he walked out of the store fifteen minutes ago. He didn't even look toward his hand.

"Did you sell Will something for it, or did you just take it out of his pants while he was asleep? Or was it Jody?"

"What if I did? What if I can sell enough more of it tonight to get ten more? Only for God's sake dont go back to the house. Stay in the woods. Then tomorrow morning—" He did not move; she saw only the slight jerk of his hand and wrist—no coin to ring against his thumbnail or to make any sound among the dust-stiffened road-side weeds where gouts of dusty cotton clung. When he went on, she began to run after him. "Mink!" she said. He walked steadily on. She was at his shoulder, running, though he continued to walk. "For God's sake," she said. "For God's sake." Then she caught his shoulder and swung him to face her. This time he slashed free and sprang into the weeds, stooping, and rose with a stick lifted in his hand and walked toward her again with that patient and implacable weariness, until she turned. He lowered the stick, but he continued to stand there until he could no longer distinguish her, even against the pale dust of the road. Then he tossed the stick into the weeds and turned. The cousin was standing behind him. If the other had been smaller or he larger he would have stepped on him, walked him down. The other stepped aside and turned with him, the faint rasp of the repressed breathing at his shoulder.

"So you throwed that away too," the cousin said. He didn't answer. They went on side by side in the thick, ankle-deep dust. Their feet made no sound in it. "He had at least fifty dollars. I tell you I saw it. And you expect me to believe you aint got it." He didn't answer. They walked steadily on, not fast, like two people walking without destination or haste, for pleasure or exercise. "All right. I'm going to do what wouldn't no other man living do: I'm going to give you the benefit of the doubt that you aint got it, actually never looked. Now where did you put him?" He didn't answer nor pause. The cousin caught him by the shoulder, stopping him; now there was in the fierce baffled breathing, the whispering voice, not only the old amazement but a sort of cold and desperate outrage, like one trying to reach through a fleeing crisis to the comprehension of an idiot: "Are you going to let that fifty dollars lay there for Hampton and them deputies to split up between them?"

He struck the hand off. "Let me alone," he said.

"All right. I'll do this. I'll give you twenty-five dollars now. I'll go with you, all you got to do is hand me the wallet, sight unseen. Or hand me his pants, if you dont want to take it out of them. You wont even touch or even see the money." He turned to go on again. "All right. If you are too puke-stomached to do it yourself, tell me where it is. When I come back, I'll give you ten dollars, though a fellow that just throwed away a ten-dollar bill dont—" He walked on. Again the hand caught his shoulder and swung him about; the tense fierce voice murmured from nowhere and everywhere out of the breathless dark: "Wait. Listen. Listen good. Suppose I look up Hampton; he's been around here all day; he's probably still somewhere here tonight. Suppose I tell him I done recollected a mistake, that that gun wasn't lost last fall because you come in the store and bought a nickel's worth of powder just last week. Then you can explain how you was aiming to swap Houston the powder for the pound-fee on that yearling—"

This time he did not fling the hand off. He merely began to walk toward the other with that patient and invincible weariness which the other did not recognise, walking steadily toward the cousin as the other gave ground. His voice was not loud either; it was flat, absolutely toneless: "I ask you to let me alone," he said. "I dont tell you; I ask you to let me alone. Not for my sake. Because I'm tired. I ask you to let me alone." The other backed away before him, moving slightly faster, so that the distance between them increased. When he stopped, it continued to increase until he could no longer see the other and only the whisper, furious and outraged, came back:

"All right, you durn little tight-fisted murderer. See if you get away with it."

Approaching the village again, his feet made no sound in the dust and, in the darkness, seemingly no progress either, though the light in Mrs Littlejohn's kitchen window just beyond the store's dark bulk—the only light anywhere—drew steadily nearer. Just beyond it the lane turned off which led to his cabin four miles away. *That's where I would have kept straight on, to Jefferson and the railroad,* he thought; and suddenly, now that it was too late, now that he had lost all hope of alternative between planned and intelligent escape and mere blind desperate harried fleeing and doubling through the swamp and jungle of the bottom like a spent and starving beast cut off from its den, he knew that for three days now he had not only hoped but had actually believed that opportunity to choose would be given him. And he had not only lost that privilege of choice, but due to the blind mischance which had permitted his cousin either to see or guess what was in the wallet, even the bitter alternative was deferred for another night. It began to seem to him now that that puny and lonely beacon not only marked no ultimate point for even desperate election but was the period to hope itself, and that all which remained to him of freedom lay in the shortening space between it and his advancing foot. *I thought that when you killed a man, that finished it,* he told himself. *But it dont. It just starts then.*

When he reached home, he did not enter it. Instead, he went around to the woodpile and got his axe and stood for a moment to examine the stars. It was not much past nine; he could allow himself until midnight. Then he circled the house and entered the corn-patch. Halfway down the slope he paused, listening, then he went on. He did not enter the bottom either; he stepped behind the first tree large enough to conceal him and leaned the axe carefully against it where he could find it again and stood there, motionless, breathing quietly, and listened to the heavy body running with hurried and cautious concern among the clashing cornstalks, the tense and hurried panting drawing rapidly nearer, then the quick indraw of breath when the other ran past the tree, checking, as he stepped out from behind it and turned back up the slope.

They went back through the corn, in single file and five feet apart.

He could hear the clumsy body behind him stumbling and thrashing among the sibilant rows, and the breathing fierce, outraged, and
repressed. His own passage made no noise, even in the trigger-set
dryness of the corn, as if his body had no substance. "Listen," the
cousin said. "Let's look at this thing like two reasonable . . ." They
emerged from the corn and crossed the yard and entered the house,
still five feet apart. He went on to the kitchen and lit the lamp and
squatted before the stove, preparing to start the fire. The cousin
stood in the door, breathing heavily and watching while the other
coaxed the chips into a blaze and took the coffee-pot from the stove
and filled it from the water pail and set it back. "Aint you even got
nothing to eat?" the cousin said. The other did not answer. "You got
some feed corn, aint you? We could parch some of that." The fire
was burning well now. The other laid his hand on the pot, though
of course it had not even begun to be warm yet. The cousin watched
the back of his head. "All right," he said. "Let's go get some of it."
    The other removed his hand from the pot. He did not look back.
"Get it," he said. "I'm not hungry." The cousin breathed in the door,
watching the still, slanted face. His breath made a faint, steady, rasping sound.
    "All right," he said. "I'll go to the barn and get some." He left the
door and walked heavily down the hallway and onto the back porch
and stepped down to the earth, already running. He ran frantically in
the blind darkness and on tiptoe, around toward the front of the
house and stopped, peering around the corner toward the front door,
holding his breath, then ran again, on to the steps, where he could
see into the hallway lighted faintly by the lamp in the kitchen, and
paused again for an instant, crouched, glaring. The son of a bitch
tricked me, he thought; He went out the back: and ran up the steps,
stumbling heavily and recovering, and thundered down the hall to
the kitchen door and saw, in the instant of passing it, the other standing beside the stove as he had left him, his hand again on the coffee-
pot. The murdering little son of a bitch, he thought. I wouldn't have
believed it. I wouldn't have believed a man would have to go through
all this even for five hundred dollars.
    But when he stood in the door again, save for the slightly
increased rasp and tempo of his breathing, he might never have left

it. He watched the other fetch to the stove a cracked china cup, a thick glass tumbler, a tin can containing a little sugar, and a spoon; when he spoke, he might have been talking to his employer's wife over a tea-table: "It's done made up its mind at last to get hot, has it?" The other did not answer. He filled the cup from the pot and spooned sugar into it and stirred it and stood beside the stove, turned three quarters from the cousin, his head bent, sipping from the cup. After a moment the cousin approached and filled the tumbler and put sugar into it and sipped, wry-faced, his features all seeming to flee from the tumbler's rim, upward, gathering, eyes, nose, even mouth, toward his forehead, as if the skin in which they were embedded was attached to his skull only at one point somewhere in the back. "Listen," the cousin said. "Just try to look at this thing like two reasonable people. There's that fifty dollars laying out there, not belonging to nobody. And you cant go and get it without taking me, because I aint going to let you. And I cant go get it without taking you, because I dont know where it's at. Yet here we are, setting around this house while every minute we waste is bringing that durn sheriff and them deputies just that much closer to finding it. It's just a matter of pure and simple principle. Aint no likes and dislikes about it. If I had my way, I'd keep all of it myself, the same as you would. But you cant and I cant. Yet here we are, setting here—" The other tilted the cup and drained it.

"What time is it?" he said. From the creased bulge of his waistband the cousin wrenched a dollar watch on a thong of greasy leather and looked at it and prized it back into the fob-pocket.

"Twenty-eight past nine. And it aint going to stay that forever. And I got to open the store at six oclock in the morning. And I got to walk five miles tonight before I can go to bed. But never mind that. Dont pay no attention to that, because there aint nothing personal in this because it is a pure and simple business matter. Think about your—" The other set the empty cup on the stove.

"Checkers?" he said.

"—self. You got—What?" The cousin stopped talking. He watched the other cross the room and lift from among the shadows in the corner a short, broad piece of plank. From the shelf above it he took another tin can and brought them to the table. The board was marked off with charcoal into alternate staggered squares; the can contained a handful of small china- and glass-fragments in two colors, apparently from a broken plate and a blue glass bottle. He laid the board beside the lamp and began to oppose the men. The cousin watched him, the tumbler arrested halfway to his mouth. For an instant he ceased to breathe. Then he breathed again. "Why, sholy," he said. He set the glass on the stove and drew up a chair opposite. Sitting, he seemed to be on the point of enveloping not only the chair but the table too in a collapsing mass of flabby and badly-filled flesh, like a collapsing balloon. "We'll play a nickel a game against that fifty dollars," he said. "All right?"

"Move," the other said. They began to play—the one with a cold and deadly deliberation and economy of moves, the other with a sort of clumsy speed and dash. It was that amateurish, that almost child-like, lack of premeditation and plan or even foresight of one who, depending on manipulation and not intellect in games of chance, finds himself involved in one where dexterity cannot avail, yet nevertheless attempting to cheat even at bald and simple draughts with an incredible optimism, an incorrigible dishonesty long since become pure reflex and probably now beyond his control, making his dashing and clumsy moves then withdrawing his closed fist to sit watching with his little intent unwinking eyes the still, wasted, down-looking face opposite, talking steadily about almost everything except money and death, the fist resting on the table-edge still closed about the pawn or the king's crown which it had palmed. The trouble with checkers is, he thought, It aint nothing but checkers. At the end of an hour he was thirteen games ahead.

"Make it a quarter," he said.

"What time is it?" the other said. The cousin wrung the watch from his waistband again and returned it.

"Four minutes to eleven."

"Move," the other said. They played on. The cousin was not talking now. He was keeping score now with a chewed pencil stub on the edge of the board. Thus when, thirty minutes later, he totted up the score, the pencil presented to his vision not a symbol but a sum complete with decimal and dollar mark, which seemed in the next instant to leap upward and strike comprehension with an impact almost audible; he became dead still, for an instant he did not breathe indeed, thinking rapidly: Hell fire. Hell fire. Of course he never caught me. He didn't want to. Because when I have won all of his share, he'll figure he wont need to risk going where it's at. So now he had to completely reverse his entire tactics. And now for the first time the crawling hands on the face of the watch which he now produced without being asked and laid face-up beside the board, assumed a definite significance. Because this here just cant go on forever, he thought in a resurgence of the impotent rage. It just cant. A man just cant be expected to go through much more of this even for all of fifty dollars. So he reversed himself. Whereupon it was as if even dishonesty had foresworn him. He would make the dashing, clumsy, calculated moves; he would sit back with his own pawn or king's crown in his fist now. Only now the other's thin hard hand would be gripping that wrist while the cold, flat, dead voice demonstrated how a certain pawn could not possibly have arrived at the square on which it suddenly appeared to be, and lived, or even rapping the knuckles of that gripped hand on the table until it disgorged. Yet he would attempt it again, with that baffled and desperate optimism and hope, and be caught again and then try it again, until at the end of the next hour his movements on the board were not even childlike, they were those of an imbecile or a blind person. And he was talking again now: "Listen. There's that fifty dollars that dont belong to nobody because he never had no kin, nobody to claim it. Just laying out there for the first man that comes along to—"

"Move," the other said. He moved a pawn. "No," the other said. "Jump." He made the jump. The other moved a second pawn.

"—and here you are needing money to keep from being hung maybe and you cant go and get it because I wont leave. And me that cant get up and go on home and get to bed so I can get up, and go to work tomorrow because you wont show me where that money's at—"

"Move," the other said. The cousin moved a pawn. "No," the other said. "Jump." The cousin took the jump. Then he watched the gaunt black-haired fingers holding the scrap of blue glass clear the board in five jumps.

"And now it's after midnight. It will be light in six hours. And Hampton and them durn deputies—" The cousin ceased. The other was now standing, looking down at him; the cousin rose quickly. They stared at one another across the table. "Well?" the cousin said. His breath began to make the harsh, tense, rasping sound again, not triumphant yet. "Well?" he said. "Well?" But the other was not looking at him, he was looking down, the face still, wasted, seemingly without life.

"I ask you to go," the other said. "I ask you to leave me alone."

"Sholy," the cousin said, his voice no louder than the other's. "Quit now? after I done gone through all this?" The other turned toward the door. "Wait," the cousin said. The other did not pause. The cousin blew out the lamp and overtook the other in the hallway. He was talking again, whispering now. "If you'd just listened to me six hours ago. We'd a done had it and been back, in bed, instead of setting up here half the night. Dont you see how it was tit for tat all the time? You had me and I had you, and couldn't neither— Where we going?" The other didn't answer. He went steadily on across the yard, toward the barn, the cousin following; again he heard just behind him the tense, fierce adenoidal breathing, the whispering voice: "Hell fire, maybe you dont want me to have half of it and maybe I dont want nobody to have half of it neither. But hell fire, aint just half of it better than to think of that durn Hampton and them deputies—" He entered the barn and opened the door to the crib and stepped up into it, the cousin stopping just outside the door behind him, and reached down from its nail in the wall a short, smooth white-oak stick eyed at the end with a loop of hemp rope— a twister which Houston had used with his stallion, which Snopes had found when he rented the foreclosed portion of Houston's farm from the Varners—and turned and struck all in one motion and dropped the cudgel and caught the heavy body as it fell so that its own weight helped to carry it into the crib and all he needed to do was to drag it on in until the feet cleared the door. He unbuckled a hame-string and the check-rein from his plow gear and bound the other's hands and feet and tore a strip from the tail of his shirt and made a gag with it.

When he reached the bottom, he could not find the tree behind which he had left the axe. He knew what was wrong. It was as though with the cessation of that interminable voice he had become aware not of silence but of elapsed time, that on the instant it had ceased he had retraced and resumed at the moment it began in the store at six oclock in the afternoon, and now he was six hours late. You're trying too hard, he told himself. You got to slow up. So he held himself still for the space of a hundred, trying to orient himself by looking back up the slope, to establish whether he was above or below the tree, to the right or left of it. Then he went back halfway through the corn and looked back at the bottom from there, trying to recognise by its shape and position the tree where he had left the axe, standing in the roar not of silence now but of time's friction. He thought of starting from some point which he knew was below the tree he sought and searching each tree as he came to it. But the sound of time was too loud, so when he began to move, to run, it was toward neither the bottom nor the cabin but across the slope, quartering, out of the corn and on into the road a half mile beyond his house.

He ran for another mile and came to another cabin, smaller and shabbier than his. It belonged to the Negro who had found the gun. There was a dog here, a mongrel terrier, a feice, not much larger than a cat and noisy as a calliope; at once it came boiling out from beneath the house and rushed toward him in shrill hysteria. He knew it and it should know him; he spoke to it to quiet it but it continued to yap, the sound seeming to come from a dozen different points out of the darkness before him until he ran suddenly at it, whereupon the shrill uproar faded rapidly back toward the house. He continued to run, on toward the woodpile which he knew too; the axe was there. As he caught it up a voice said from the dark cabin: "Who there?" He didn't answer. He ran on, the terrier still yapping behind him though from beneath the house now. Now he was in corn again, better than his. He ran on through it, descending, toward the bottom.

Before entering the bottom, he stopped and took his bearings on a star. He did not expect to find the tree from this point, it was the old sunken road he aimed for; once in that, he could orient himself again. His surest course, even though it would be longer, would be to skirt the bottom until he reached country he knew in the dark and strike in for the tree from there, but when he examined the sky to fix his bearing, he thought, It's after one oclock.

Yet, thirty minutes later, he had not found the road. He had been able to see the sky only intermittently, and not always the star he guided by then. But he believed he had not deviated much. Also, he had cautioned himself: You will expect to come onto it before you do; you will have to watch for that. But in this time he had travelled twice the distance in which he should have found it. When he realised, admitted at last that he was lost, it was with neither alarm nor despair, but rage. It was as though, like the cousin and his dishonesty two or three hours ago, ruthlessness likewise had repudiated the disciple who had flagged for a moment in ruthlessness; that it was that humanity which had caused him to waste three hours in hope that the cousin would tire and go away instead of striking the other over the head when he ran past the tree where he had lost the axe, which had brought him to this.

His first impulse was to run, not in panic but to keep ahead of that avalanche of accumulating seconds which was now his enemy. But he quelled it, holding himself motionless, his spent body shaking faintly and steadily with exhaustion, until he was satisfied his muscles would not be able to take him by surprise and run with him. Then he turned deliberately and carefully until he believed he was facing his back trail and the direction from which he had come, and walked forward. After a while he came to an opening in which he could see the sky. The star on which he had fixed his course when he entered the bottom was directly in front of him. And now it's after two oclock, he thought.

Now he began to run, or as fast as he dared, that is. He could not help himself. I got to find the road now, he thought. If I try to go back and start over, it will be daylight before I get out of the bottom. So he hurried on, stumbling and thrashing among the briers and undergrowth, one arm extended to fend himself from the trees, voiceless, panting, blind, the muscles about his eyelids strained and aching against the flat impenetrable face of the darkness, until suddenly there was no earth under his feet; he made another stride, running upon nothing, then he was falling and then he was on his back, panting. He was in the road. But he did not know where. But I aint

crossed it, he thought. I am still on the west side of it. And now it's
past two oclock.

Now he was oriented again. By turning his back on the road and
holding a straight course, he would reach the edge of the bottom.
Then he would be able to ascertain where he was. When he found
himself falling, he had flung the axe away. He hunted for it on his
hands and knees and found it and climbed out of the road and went
on. He did not run now. Now he knew that he dared not lose himself again. When, an hour later, he emerged from the bottom, it was
at the corner of a corn-patch. It was his own; the bizarre erst-fluid
earth became fixed and stable in the old solid dimensions and juxta-
positions. He saw the squat roof-line of his own house, and running
again, stumbling a little among the rows of whispering stalks, panting through his dry lips and his dry clenched teeth, he saw and recognised the tree behind which he had left the axe, and again it was as if
he had retraced and resumed at some dead point in time and only
time was lost. He turned and approached it, he was about to pass it
when a thicker shadow detached itself from the other shadow, rising
without haste, and the cousin's voice said, weakly and harshly: "Forgot your durned axe, hah? Here it is. Take it."

He had stopped with no sound, no ejaculation, no catch of breath.
Except I better not use the axe, he thought, still, immobile, while
the other breathed harshly above him and the harsh, weak, outraged
voice went on: "You durn little fratricidal murderer, if I hadn't just
about stood all one man can stand, for twenty-five dollars or twenty-
five thousand either, I'd be a good mind to knock you in the head
with it and tote you out and throw you into Hampton's surrey myself.
And by God it aint your fault it wasn't Hampton instead of me sitting
here waiting for you. Hell fire, you hadn't hardly got started good
chuckling over them other twenty-five dollars you thought you had
just got before Hampton and the whole durn mess of them was in
that crib, untying me and throwing water in my face. And I lied for
you again. I told them you had knocked me in the head and tied me
up and robbed me and lit out for the railroad. Now just how much
longer do you figure I aim to keep telling lies just to save your neck?
Hah?—Well? What are we waiting for? For Hampton?"

"Yes," he said. "All right." But not the axe, he thought. He turned and went on, into the trees. The other followed him, right at his heels now, the fierce adenoidal breath, the weak, outraged voice almost over his head, so that when he stooped and groped with his hand about the ground at his feet, the other walked into him.

"What the hell you doing now? Have you lost the durn axe again? Find it and give it to me and then get on and show me where it's at before not only sunup but ever durn vote-sucking—" His hand touched and found a stick large enough. I cant see this time, so I got to be ready to hit twice, he thought, rising. He struck toward the harsh, enraged voice, recovering and striking again though one blow had been enough.

He knew where he was now. He needed no guide, though presently he knew that he had one and he went quite fast now, nosing into the thin taint of air, needing to go fast now. Because it's more than three oclock now, he thought, thinking: I had forgot that. It's like just about everything was in cahoots against one man killing another. Then he knew that he smelled it, because now there was no focal point, no guiding point, it was everywhere; he saw the opening, the topless shell of the blasted oak rising against the leaf-frayed patch of rainless sky. He squared himself away for proper distance by touching his hand against the shell and swung the axe. The entire head sank helve-deep into the rotten pith. He wrenched at it, twisting it free, and raised it again. Then—there was no sound, the darkness itself merely sighed and flowed behind him, and he tried to turn but it was too late— something struck him between the shoulders. He knew at once what it was. He was not surprised even, feeling the breath and hearing the teeth as he fell, turning, trying to raise the axe, hearing the teeth again at his throat and feeling the hot breath-reek as he hurled the hound temporarily back with his forearm and got onto his knees and got both hands on the axe. He could see its eyes now as it leaped the second time. They seemed to float toward him interminably. He struck at them, striking nothing; the axe-head went into the ground, almost snatching him after it onto his face. This time when he saw the eyes, he was on his feet. He rushed at them, the axe lifted. He went charging on even after the eyes vanished, crashing and plunging in the undergrowth, stopping at last, the axe raised and poised, panting, listening, seeing and hearing nothing. He returned to the tree.

At the first stroke of the axe, the dog sprang again. He was expecting it. He did not bury the head this time and he had the axe raised and ready as he whirled. He struck at the eyes and felt the axe strike and leap spinning from his hands, and he sprang toward where the animal thrashed and groaned in the underbrush, leaping toward the sound, stamping furiously about him, pausing crouched, to listen, leaping toward another sound and stamping again, but again in vain. Then he got down on his hands and knees and crawled in widening circles about the tree, hunting the axe. When he found it at last he could see, above the jagged top of the shell, the morning star.

He chopped again at the base of the shell, stopping after each blow to listen, the axe already poised, his feet and knees braced to whirl. But he heard nothing. Then he began to chop steadily, the axe sinking helve-deep at each stroke as though into sand or sawdust. Then the axe sank, helve and all, into the rotten wood, he knew now it was not imagination he had smelled and he dropped the axe and began to tear at the shell with his hands, his head averted, his teeth bared and clenched, his breath hissing through them, freeing one arm momentarily to fling the hound back though it surged against him again, whimpering, and then thrust its head into the growing orifice out of which the foul air seemed to burst with an audible sound. "Get back, God damn you!" he panted as though he were speaking to a man, trying again to hurl the hound away; "give me room!" He dragged at the body, feeling it slough upon its bones as though it were too large for itself. Now the hound had its entire head and shoulders in the opening, howling.

When the body came suddenly free, he went over backward, lying on his back in the mud, the body across his legs, while the hound stood over it, howling. He got up and kicked at it. It moved back, but when he stooped and took hold of the legs and began to walk backward, the hound was beside him again. But it was intent on the body, and as long as they were in motion, it did not howl. But when he stopped to get his breath, it began to howl again and again he braced himself and kicked at it and this time as he did so he discovered that he was actually seeing the animal and that dawn had come, the animal visible now, gaunt, thin, with a fresh bloody gash across its face, howling. Watching it, he stooped and groped until his hand found a stick. It was foul with slime but still fairly sound. When the hound raised its head to howl again, he struck. The dog whirled; he saw the long scar of the gunshot running from its shoulder to its flank as it sprang at him. This time the stick took it fairly between the eyes. He picked up the ankles, facing forward now, and tried to run.

When he came out of the undergrowth and onto the river bank, the east was turning red. The stream itself was still invisible—a long bank of mist like cotton batting, beneath which the water ran. He stooped; once more he raised the body which was half again his size, and hurled it outward into the mist and, even as he released it, springing after it, catching himself back just before he followed it, seeing at the instant of its vanishing the sluggish sprawl of three limbs where there should have been four, and recovering balance to turn, already running as the pattering rush of the hound whispered behind him and the animal struck him in the back. It did not pause. On his hands and knees he saw it in midair like a tremendous wing-less bird soar out and vanish into the mist. He got to his feet and ran. He stumbled and fell once and got up, running. Then he heard the swift soft feet behind him and he fell again and on his hands and knees again he watched it soar over him and turn in midair so that it landed facing him, its eyes like two cigar-coals as it sprang at him before he could rise. He struck at its face with his hands and got up and ran. They reached the stump together. The hound leaped at him again, slashing at his shoulder as he ducked into the opening he had made and groped furiously for the missing arm, the hound still slash-ing at his back and legs. Then the dog was gone. A voice said: "All right, Mink. We've got him. You can come out now."

The surrey was waiting among the trees behind his house, where he had found the marks of it two days ago. He sat with a deputy in the back seat, their inside wrists manacled together. The sheriff rode beside the other deputy, who drove. The driver swung the team around to return to Varner's store and the Jefferson highroad, but the sheriff stopped him. "Wait," the sheriff said and turned in the front seat—a tremendous man, neckless, in an unbuttoned waistcoat and a collarless starched shirt. In his broad heavy face his small, cold, shrewd eyes resembled two bits of black glass pressed into uncooked dough. He addressed both of them. "Where does this road come out at the other end?"

"Into the old Whiteleaf Bridge road," the deputy said. "That's fourteen miles. And you are still nine miles from Whiteleaf store then. And when you reach Whiteleaf store, you are still eight miles from Jefferson. It's just twenty-five miles by Varner's."

"I reckon we'll skip Varner's this time," the sheriff said. "Drive on, Jim."

"Sure," the deputy said. "Drive on, Jim. It wouldn't be our money we saved, it would just be the county's." The sheriff, turning to face forward again, paused and looked at the deputy. They looked at one another. "I said all right, didn't I?" the deputy said. "Drive on."

Through the rest of that morning and into noon they wound among the pine hills. The sheriff had a shoe box of cold food and even a stone jug of buttermilk wrapped in wet gunnysacks. They ate without stopping save to let the team drink at a branch which crossed the road. Then the road came down out of the hills and in the early afternoon they passed Whiteleaf store in the long broad rich flat-lands lush with the fine harvest, the fired and heavy corn and the cot-ton-pickers still moving through the spilling rows, and he saw the men squatting and sitting on the gallery beneath the patent medicine and tobacco posters stand suddenly up. "Well, well," the deputy said. "There are folks here too that act willing to believe their name is Houston for maybe ten or fifteen minutes anyway."

"Drive on," the sheriff said. They went on, pacing in the thick, soft dust the long, parched summer afternoon, though actually they could not keep pace with it and presently the fierce sun slanted into the side of the surrey where he sat. The sheriff spoke now without turning his head or removing his cob pipe: "George, swap sides with him. Let him ride in the shade."

"I'm all right," he said. "It dont bother me." After a while it did not bother him, or it was no worse for him than for the others, because the road approached the hills again, rising and winding again as the long shadows of the pines wheeled slowly over the slow surrey in the now slanting sun; soon Jefferson itself would appear beyond the final valley, with the poised fierce ball of the sun dropping down beyond it, shining from directly ahead and almost level into the surrey, upon all their faces. There was a board on a tree, bearing a merchant's name above the legend *Jefferson 4 mi*, drawing up and then past, yet with no semblance of motion, and he moved his feet slightly and braced his inside elbow for the coming jerk and gathered and hurled himself feet foremost out of the moving surrey, snapping his arm and shoulder forward against the expected jerk but too late, so that even as his body swung out and free of the wheel his head slipped down into the V of the stanchion which supported the top and the weight and momentum of his whole body came down on his vised neck. In a moment now he would hear the bone, the vertebrae, and he wrenched his body again, kicking backward now toward where he believed the moving wheel would be, thinking, If I can just hook my foot in them spokes, something will have to give; lashing with his foot toward the wheel, feeling each movement of his body travel back to his neck as though he were attempting, in a cold fury of complete detachment, to see which would go first: the living bone or the dead metal. Then something struck him a terrific blow at the base of his neck and ceased to be a blow and became instead a pressure, rational and furious with deadly intent. He believed he heard the bone and he knew he heard the deputy's voice: "Break! God damn it, break! Break!" and he felt the surge of the surrey and he even seemed to see the sheriff leaning over the seat-back and grappling with the raging deputy; choking, gasping, trying to close his mouth and he could not, trying to roll his head from beneath the cold hard blow of the water and there was a bough over his head against the sunny sky, with a faint wind in the leaves, and the three faces. But after a while he could breathe again all right, and the faint wind of motion had dried the water from his face and only his shirt was a little damp, not a cool wind yet but just a wind free at last of the unendurable sun, blowing out of the beginning of dusk, the surrey moving now beneath an ordered overarch of sun-shot trees, between the clipped and tended lawns where children shrieked and played in bright small garments in the sunset and the ladies sat rocking in the fresh dresses of afternoon and the men coming home from work turned into the neat painted gates, toward plates of food and cups of coffee in the long beginning of twilight.

They approached the jail from the rear and drove into the enclosed yard. "Jump," the sheriff said. "Lift him out."

"I'm all right," he said. But he had to speak twice before he made any sound, and even then it was not his voice. "I can walk."

After the doctor had gone, he lay on his cot. There was a small, high, barred window in the wall, but there was nothing beyond the window save twilight. Then he smelled supper cooking somewhere—ham and hot bread and coffee—and suddenly a hot, thin, salty liquid began to run in his mouth, though when he tried to swallow, it was so painful that he sat up, swallowing the hot salt, moving his neck and head rigidly and gingerly to ease the swallowing. Then a loud trampling of feet began beyond the barred door, coming rapidly nearer, and he rose and went to it and looked through the bars into the common room where the Negro victims of a thousand petty white man's misdemeanors ate and slept together. He could see the head of the stairs; the trampling came from it and he watched a disorderly clump of heads in battered hats and caps and bodies in battered overalls and broken shoes erupt and fill the foul barren room with a subdued uproar of scuffling feet and mellow witless singsong voices—the chain gang which worked on the streets, seven or eight of them, in jail for vagrancy or razor fights or shooting dice for ten or fifteen cents, freed of their shovels and rock hammers for ten hours at least. He held to the bars and looked at them. "It—" he said. His voice made no sound at all. He put his hand to his throat and spoke again, making a dry, croaking sound. The Negroes fell completely still, looking at him, their eyeballs white and still in the already fading faces. "I was all right," he said, "until it started coming to pieces. I could have handled that dog." He held his throat, his voice harsh and dry and croaking. "But the son of a bitch started coming to pieces on me."

"Who him?" one of the Negroes said. They whispered among themselves, murmuring. The white eyeballs rolled at him.

"I was all right," he said. "But the son of a bitch—"

"Hush, white man," the Negro said. "Hush. Dont be telling us no truck like that."

"I would have been all right," he said, harsh, whispering. Then his voice failed altogether again and he held to the bars with one hand, holding his throat with the other, while the Negroes watched him, huddled, their eyeballs white and still in the failing light. Then with one accord they turned and rushed toward the stairs and he heard the slow steps too and then he smelled the food, and he clung to the bars, trying to see the stairhead. Are they going to feed them niggers before they do a white man? he thought, smelling the coffee and the ham.

3

That was the fall before the winter from which the people as they became older were to establish time and date events. The summer's rainless heat—the blazing days beneath which even the oak leaves turned brown and died, the nights during which the ordered stars seemed to glare down in cold and lidless amazement at an earth being drowned in dust—broke at last, and for the three weeks of Indian summer the ardor-wearied earth, ancient Lilith, reigned, throned and crowned amid the old invincible courtesan's formal defunction. Through these blue and drowsy and empty days filled with silence and the smell of burning leaves and woodsmoke, Ratliff, passing to and fro between his home and the Square, would see the two small grimed hands, immobile and clasping loosely the bars of the jail window at a height not a great deal above that at which a child would have held them. And in the afternoons he would watch his three guests, the wife and the two children, entering or leaving the jail on their daily visit. On the first day, the day he had brought her home with him, she had insisted on doing some of the housework, all of it which his sister would permit, sweeping and washing dishes and chopping wood for fires which his nieces and nephews had heretofore done (and incidentally, in doing so, gaining their juvenile contempt too), apparently oblivious of the sister's mute and outraged righteousness, big yet not fat, actually slender as Ratliff realised at last in a sort of shocked and sober . . . not pity: rather, concern; usually barefoot, with the untidy mass of bleached hair long since turning back to dark at the roots, and the cold face in which there was something of a hard not-quite-lost beauty, though it may have been only an ingrained and ineradicable self-confidence or perhaps just toughness. Because the prisoner had refused not only bond (if he could have made one) but counsel. He had stood between two officers—small, his face like a mask of intractability carved in wood, wasted and almost skeleton-thin—before the committing magistrate, and he might not even have been present, hearing or perhaps not hearing himself being arraigned, then at a touch from one of the officers turning back toward the jail, the cell. So the case was pretermitted from sheer desuetude of physical material for formal suttee, like a half-cast play, through the October term of court, to the spring term next May; and perhaps three afternoons a week Ratliff would watch his guests as, the children dressed in cast-off garments of his nephews and nieces, the three of them entered the jail, thinking of the four of them sitting in the close cell rank with creosote and old wraiths of human excreta—the sweat, the urine, the vomit discharged of all the old agonies: terror, impotence, hope. Waiting for Flem Snopes, he thought. For Flem Snopes.

Then the winter, the cold, came. By that time she had a job. He had known as well as she that the other arrangement could not last, since in a way it was his sister's house, even if only by a majority of voting strength. So he was not only not surprised, he was relieved when she came and told him she was going to move. Then, as soon as she told him she was going to leave, something happened to him. He told himself that it was the two children. "That's all right about the job," he said. "That's fine. But you dont need to move. You'll have to pay board and lodging if you move. And you will need to save. You will need money."

"Yes," she said harshly. "I'll need money."

"Does he still think—" He stopped himself. He said, "You aint heard yet when Flem will be back, have you?" She didn't answer. He didn't expect her to. "You will need to save all you can," he said. "So you stay here. Pay her a dollar a week board for the children if that would make you feel better about it. I dont reckon a kid would eat more than four bits' worth in seven days. But you stay here."

So she stayed. He had given up his room to them and he slept with his oldest nephew. Her job was in a rambling shabby side-street boarding house with an equivocal reputation, named the Savoy Hotel. Her work began at daybreak and ended sometime after dark, sometimes well after dark. She swept and made the beds and did some of the cooking, since there was a Negro porter who washed the dishes and kept up the fires. She had her meals there and received three dollars a week. "Only she's going to keep her heels blistered running barefooted in and out of them horse-traders' and petty juries' and agents for nigger insurance's rooms all night long," a town wit said. But that was her affair. Ratliff knew nothing about that and cared less and, to his credit, believed even still less than that. So now he would not see her at all save on Sunday afternoons as, the children in the new overcoats which he had bought for them and the woman in his old one which she had insisted on paying him fifty cents for, they would enter the gate to the jail or perhaps emerge from it. That was when it occurred to him how not once had any of his kin—old Ab or the schoolmaster or the blacksmith or the new clerk—come in to see him. And if all the facts about that business was knowed, he thought, There's one of them that ought to be there in that cell too. Or in another one just like it, since you cant hang a man twice— granted of course that a Snopes carries the death penalty even for another Snopes.

There was snow on Thanksgiving and though it did not remain two days, it was followed early in December by an iron cold which locked the earth in a frozen rigidity, so that after a week or so actual dust blew from it. Smoke turned white before it left the chimney, unable to rise, becoming the same color as the misty sky itself in which all day long the sun stood pale as an uncooked biscuit and as heatless. Now they dont even need to have to not come in to see him, Ratliff told himself. For a man to drive them twenty miles in from Frenchman's Bend just on a errand of mercy, even a Snopes dont have to excuse himself from it. There was a windowpane now between the bars and the hands; they were not visible now, even if anyone had paused along before the jail to look for them. Instead he would be walking fast when he passed, hunched in his overcoat, holding his ears in turn with his yarn-mitted hands, his breath wisping about the crimson tip of his nose and his watering eyes and into the empty Square across which perhaps one country wagon moved, its occupants wrapped in quilts with a lighted lantern on the seat between them while the frosted windows of the stores seemed to stare at it without comprehension or regret like the faces of cataracted old men.

Christmas passed beneath that same salt-colored sky, without even any surface softening of the iron ground, but in January a wind set up out of the northwest and blew the sky clear. The sun drew shadows on the frozen ground and for three days patches of it thawed a little at noon, for an inch or so, like a spreading of butter or axle-grease; and toward noon people would emerge, like rats or roaches, Ratliff told himself, amazed and tentative at the sun or at the patches of earth soft again out of an old, almost forgotten time, capable again of taking a footprint. "It wont freeze again tonight," they told one another. "It's clouding up from the southwest. It will rain and wash the frost out of the ground and we will be all right again." It did rain. The wind moved counter-clockwise into the east. "It will go through to the northwest again and freeze again. Even that would be better than snow," they told one another, even though the rain had already begun to solidify and by nightfall had become snow, falling for two days and dissolving into the mud as it fell until the mud itself froze at last and still the snow fell and stopped too finally and the windless iron cold came down upon it without even a heatless wafer of sun to preside above a dead earth cased in ice; January and then February, no movement anywhere save the low constant smoke and the infrequent people unable to stand up on the sidewalks creeping townward or homeward in the middle of the streets where no horse could have kept its feet, and no sound save the chopping of axes and the lonely whistles of the daily trains and Ratliff would seem to see them, black, without dimension and unpeopled and plumed with fading vapor, rushing without purpose through the white and rigid solitude. At home now, sitting over his own fire on those Sunday afternoons, he would hear the woman arrive for the children after dinner and put the new overcoats on them above the outgrown garments in which regardless of temperature they had gone to Sunday school (his sister saw to that) with the nephew and nieces who had discarded them; and he would think of the four of them sitting, huddled still in the coats, about the small ineffective sheet-iron stove which did not warm the cell but merely drew from the walls like tears the old sweat of the old agonies and despairs which had harbored there. Later they would return. She would never stay for supper, but once a month she would bring to him the eight dollars she had saved out of her twelve-dollar salary, and the other coins and bills (once she had nine dollars more) which he never asked how she had come by. He was her banker. His sister may or may not have known this, though she probably did. The sum mounted up. "But it will take a lot of weeks," he said. She didn't answer. "Maybe he might answer a letter," he said. "After all, blood is blood."

The freeze could not last forever. On the ninth of March it even snowed again and this snow even went away without turning to ice. So people could move about again, and one Saturday he entered the restaurant of which he was half owner and saw Bookwright sitting again before a plate containing a mass of jumbled food a good deal of which was eggs. They had not seen one another in almost six months. No greeting passed between them. "She's back home again," Bookwright said. "Got in last week."

"She gets around fast," Ratliff said. "I just saw her toting a scuttle of ashes out of the back door of the Savoy Hotel five minutes ago."

"I mean the other one," Bookwright said, eating. "Flem's wife. Will drove over to Mottstown and picked them up last week."

"Them?"

"Not Flem. Her and the baby."

So he has already heard, Ratliff thought. Somebody has done already wrote him. He said: "The baby. Well well. February, January, December, November, October, September, August. And some of March. It aint hardly big enough to be chewing tobacco yet, I reckon."

"It wouldn't chew," Bookwright said. "It's a girl."

So for a while he didn't know what to do, though it did not take him long to decide. Better now, he told himself. Even if she was ever hoping without knowing she was. He waited at home the next afternoon until she came for the children. "His wife's back," he said. For just an instant she did not move at all. "You never really expected nothing else, did you?" he said.

"No," she said.

Then even that winter was over at last. It ended as it had begun, in rain, not cold rain but loud fierce gusts of warm water washing out of

the earth the iron enduring frost, the belated spring hard on its
bright heels and all coming at once, pell mell and disordered, fruit
and bloom and leaf, pied meadow and blossoming wood and the long
fields shearing dark out of winter's slumber, to the shearing plow.
The school was already closed for the planting year when he passed
it and drove up to the store and hitched his team to the old familiar
post and mounted among the seven or eight men squatting and
lounging about the gallery as if they had not moved since he had
looked back last at them almost six months ago. "Well, men," he said.
"School's already closed I see. Chillen can go to the field now and
give you folks a chance to rest."

"It's been closed since last October," Quick said. "Teacher quit."

"I. O.? Quit?"

"His wife come in one day. He looked up and saw her and lit out."

"His what?" Ratliff said.

"His wife," Tull said. "Or so she claimed. A kind of big gray-
colored woman with a—"

"Ah shucks," Ratliff said. "He aint married. Aint he been here
three years? You mean his mother."

"No, no," Tull said. "She was young all right. She just had a kind
of gray color all over. In a buggy. With a baby about six months old."

"A baby?" Ratliff said. He looked from face to face among them,
blinking. "Look here," he said. "What's all this anyway? How'd he
get a wife, let alone a baby six months old? Aint he been right here
three years? Hell a mile, he aint been out of hearing long enough to
done that."

"Wallstreet says they are his," Tull said.

"Wallstreet?" Ratliff said. "Who's Wallstreet?"

"That boy of Eck's."

"That boy about ten years old?" Ratliff blinked at Tull now. "They
never had that panic until a year or two back. How'd a boy ten years
old get to be named Wall street?"

"I dont know," Tull said.

"I reckon it's his all right," Quick said. "Leastways he taken one
look at that buggy and he aint been seen since."

"Sho now," Ratliff said. "A baby is one thing in pants that will make any man run, provided he's still got room enough to start in. Which it seems I. O. had."

"He needed room," Bookwright said in his harsh, abrupt voice. "This one could have held him, provided somebody just throwed I. O. down first and give it time to get a hold. It was bigger than he was already."

"It might hold him yet," Quick said.

"Yes," Tull said. "She just stopped long enough to buy a can of sardines and crackers. Then she druv on down the road in the same direction somebody told her I. O. had been going. He was walking. Her and the baby both et the sardines."

"Well, well," Ratliff said. "Them Snopeses. Well, well—" He ceased. They watched quietly as the Varner surrey came up the road, going home. The Negro was driving; in the back seat with her mother, Mrs Flem Snopes sat. The beautiful face did not even turn as the surrey drew abreast of the store. It passed in profile, calm, oblivious, incurious. It was not a tragic face: it was just damned. The surrey went on.

"Is he really waiting in that jail yonder for Flem Snopes to come back and get him out?" the fourth man said.

"He's still in jail," Ratliff said.

"But is he waiting for Flem?" Quick said.

"No," Ratliff said. "Because Flem aint corning back here until that trial is over and finished." Then Mrs Littlejohn stood on her veranda, ringing the dinner bell, and they rose and began to disperse. Ratliff and Bookwright descended the steps together.

"Shucks," Bookwright said. "Even Flem Snopes aint going to let his own blood cousin be hung just to save money."

"I reckon Flem knows it aint going to go that far. Jack Houston was shot from in front, and everybody knows he never went anywhere without that pistol, and they found it laying there in the road where they found the marks where the horse had whirled and run, whether it had dropped out of his hand or fell out of his pocket when he fell or not. I reckon Flem had done inquired into all that. And so he aint coming back until it's all finished. He aint coming back here where Mink's wife can worry him or folks can talk about him for leaving his cousin in jail. There's some things even a Snopes wont do. I dont know just exactly what they are, but they's some somewhere."

Then Bookwright went on, and he untied the team and drove the buckboard on into Mrs Littlejohn's lot and unharnessed and carried the harness into the barn. He had not seen it since that afternoon in September either, and something, he did not know what, impelled and moved him; he hung the gear up and went on through the dim high ammoniac tunnel, between the empty stalls, to the last one and looked into it and saw the thick, female, sitting buttocks, the shapeless figure quiet in the gloom, the blasted face turning and looking up at him, and for a fading instant there was something almost like recognition even if there could have been no remembering, in the devastated eyes, and the drooling mouth slacking and emitting a sound, hoarse, abject, not loud. Upon the overalled knees Ratliff saw the battered wooden effigy of a cow such as children receive on Christmas.

He heard the hammer before he reached the shop. The hammer stopped, poised; the dull, open, healthy face looked up at him without either surprise or interrogation, almost without recognition. "Howdy, Eck," Ratliff said. "Can you pull the old shoes off my team right after dinner and shoe them again? I got a trip to make tonight."

"All right," the other said. "Any time you bring them in."

"All right," Ratliff said. "That boy of yours. You changed his name lately, aint you?" The other looked at him, the hammer poised. On the anvil the ruby tip of the iron he was shaping faded slowly. "Wall street."

"Oh," the other said. "No, sir. It wasn't changed. He never had no name to speak of until last year. I left him with his grandma after my first wife died, while I was getting settled down; I was just sixteen then. She called him after his grandpa, but he never had no actual name. Then last year after I got settled down and sent for him, I thought maybe he better have a name. I. O. read about that one in the paper. He figured if we named him Wallstreet Panic it might make him get rich like the folks that run that Wallstreet panic."

"Oh," Ratliff said. "Sixteen. And one kid wasn't enough to settle you down. How many did it take?"

"I got three."

"Two more beside Wallstreet. What—"

"Three more besides Wall," the other said.

"Oh," Ratliff said. The other waited a moment. Then he raised the hammer again. But he stopped it and stood looking at the cold iron on the anvil and laid the hammer down and turned back to the forge. "So you had to pay all that twenty dollars," Ratliff said. The other looked back at him. "For that cow last summer."

"Yes. And another two bits for that ere toy one."

"You bought him that too?"

"Yes. I felt sorry for him. I thought maybe any time he would happen to start thinking, that ere toy one would give him something to think about."

BOOK FOUR

THE PEASANTS

CHAPTER ONE

1

A little while before sundown the men lounging about the gallery of the store saw, coming up the road from the south, a covered wagon drawn by mules and followed by a considerable string of obviously alive objects which in the levelling sun resembled varisized and -colored tatters torn at random from large billboards—circus posters, say—attached to the rear of the wagon and inherent with its own separate and collective motion, like the tail of a kite.

"What in the hell is that?" one said.

"It's a circus," Quick said. They began to rise, watching the wagon. Now they could see that the animals behind the wagon were horses. Two men rode in the wagon.

"Hell fire," the first man—his name was Freeman—said. "It's Flem Snopes." They were all standing when the wagon came up and stopped and Snopes got down and approached the steps. He might have departed only this morning. He wore the same cloth cap, the minute bow tie against the white shirt, the same gray trousers. He mounted the steps.

"Howdy, Flem," Quick said. The other looked briefly at all of them and none of them, mounting the steps. "Starting you a circus?"

"Gentlemen," he said. He crossed the gallery; they made way for him. Then they descended the steps and approached the wagon, at the tail of which the horses stood in a restive clump, larger than rabbits and gaudy as parrots and shackled to one another and to the wagon itself with sections of barbed wire. Calico-coated, smallbodied, with delicate legs and pink faces in which their mismatched eyes rolled wild and subdued, they huddled, gaudy motionless and alert, wild as deer, deadly as rattlesnakes, quiet as doves. The men

259

stood at a respectful distance, looking at them. At that moment Jody
Varner came through the group, shouldering himself to the front of it.

"Watch yourself, doc," a voice said from the rear. But it was
already too late. The nearest animal rose on its hind legs with lightning rapidity and struck twice with its forefeet at Varner's face, faster
than a boxer, the movement of its surge against the wire which held
it travelling backward among the rest of the band in a wave of thuds
and lunges. "Hup, you broom-tailed hay-burning sidewinders," the
same voice said. This was the second man who had arrived in the
wagon. He was a stranger. He wore a heavy densely black moustache,
a wide pale hat. When he thrust himself through and turned to herd
them back from the horses they saw, thrust into the hip pockets of his
tight jeans pants, the butt of a heavy pearl-handled pistol and a florid
carton such as small cakes come in. "Keep away from them, boys," he
said. "They've got kind of skittish, they aint been rode in so long."

"Since when have they been rode?" Quick said. The stranger
looked at Quick. He had a broad, quite cold, wind-gnawed face and
bleak cold eyes. His belly fitted neat and smooth as a peg into the
tight trousers.

"I reckon that was when they were rode on the ferry to get across
the Mississippi River," Varner said. The stranger looked at him. "My
name's Varner," Jody said.

"Hipps," the other said. "Call me Buck." Across the left side of his
head, obliterating the tip of that ear, was a savage and recent gash
gummed over with a blackish substance like axle-grease. They
looked at the scar. Then they watched him remove the carton from
his pocket and tilt a gingersnap into his hand and put the gingersnap
into his mouth, beneath the moustache.

"You and Flem have some trouble back yonder?" Quick said. The
stranger ceased chewing. When he looked directly at anyone, his
eyes became like two pieces of flint turned suddenly up in dug earth.

"Back where?" he said.

"Your nigh ear," Quick said.

"Oh," the other said. "That." He touched his ear. "That was my
mistake. I was absent-minded one night when I was staking them
out. Studying about something else and forgot how long the wire
was." He chewed. They looked at his ear. "Happen to any man care-

less around a horse. Put a little axle-dope on it and you wont notice it tomorrow though. They're pretty lively now, lazing along all day doing nothing. It'll work out of them in a couple of days." He put another gingersnap into his mouth, chewing. "Dont you believe they'll gentle?" No one answered. They looked at the ponies, grave and noncommittal. Jody turned and went back into the store. "Them's good, gentle ponies," the stranger said. "Watch now." He put the carton back into his pocket and approached the horses, his hand extended. The nearest one was standing on three legs now. It appeared to be asleep. Its eyelid drooped over the cerulean eye; its head was shaped like an ironing-board. Without even raising the eyelid it flicked its head, the yellow teeth cropped. For an instant it and the man appeared to be inextricable in one violence. Then they became motionless, the stranger's high heels dug into the earth, one hand gripping the animal's nostrils, holding the horse's head wrenched half around while it breathed in hoarse, smothered groans. "See?" the stranger said in a panting voice, the veins standing white and rigid in his neck and along his jaw. "See? All you got to do is handle them a little and work hell out of them for a couple of days. Now look out. Give me room back there." They gave back a little. The stranger gathered himself then sprang away. As he did so, a second horse slashed at his back, severing his vest from collar to hem down the back exactly as the trick swordsman severs a floating veil with one stroke.

"Sho now," Quick said. "But suppose a man dont happen to own a vest."

At that moment Jody Varner, followed by the blacksmith, thrust through them again. "All right, Buck," he said. "Better get them on into the lot. Eck here will help you." The stranger, the severed halves of the vest swinging from either shoulder, mounted to the wagon seat, the blacksmith following.

"Get up, you transmogrified hallucinations of Job and Jezebel," the stranger said. The wagon moved on, the tethered ponies coming gaudily into motion behind it, behind which in turn the men followed at a respectful distance, on up the road and into the lane and so to the lot gate behind Mrs Littlejohn's. Eck got down and opened the gate. The wagon passed through but when the ponies saw the

fence the herd surged backward against the wire which attached it
to the wagon, standing on its collective hind legs and then trying to
turn within itself, so that the wagon moved backward for a few feet
until the Texan, cursing, managed to saw the mules about and so lock
the wheels. The men following had already fallen rapidly back.
"Here, Eck," the Texan said. "Get up here and take the reins." The
blacksmith got back in the wagon and took the reins. Then they
watched the Texan descend, carrying a looped-up blacksnake whip,
and go around to the rear of the herd and drive it through the gate,
the whip snaking about the harlequin rumps in methodical and pis-
tol-like reports. Then the watchers hurried across Mrs Littlejohn's
yard and mounted to the veranda, one end of which overlooked the
lot.

"How you reckon he ever got them tied together?" Freeman said.

"I'd a heap rather watch how he aims to turn them loose," Quick
said. The Texan had climbed back into the halted wagon. Presently
he and Eck both appeared at the rear end of the open hood. The
Texan grasped the wire and began to draw the first horse up to the
wagon, the animal plunging and surging back against the wire as
though trying to hang itself, the contagion passing back through the
herd from animal to animal until they were rearing and plunging
again against the wire.

"Come on, grab a holt," the Texan said. Eck grasped the wire also.
The horses laid back against it, the pink faces tossing above the back-
surging mass. "Pull him up, pull him up," the Texan said sharply.
"They couldn't get up here in the wagon even if they wanted to."
The wagon moved gradually backward until the head of the first
horse was snubbed up to the tail-gate. The Texan took a turn of the
wire quickly about one of the wagon stakes. "Keep the slack out of
it," he said. He vanished and reappeared, almost in the same second,
with a pair of heavy wire-cutters. "Hold them like that," he said, and
leaped. He vanished, broad hat, flapping vest, wire-cutters and all,
into a kaleidoscopic maelstrom of long teeth and wild eyes and slashing feet, from which presently the horses began to burst one by one
like partridges flushing, each wearing a necklace of barbed wire. The
first one crossed the lot at top speed, on a straight line. It galloped
into the fence without any diminution whatever. The wire gave,

recovered, and slammed the horse to earth where it lay for a moment, glaring, its legs still galloping in air. It scrambled up without having ceased to gallop and crossed the lot and galloped into the opposite fence and was slammed again to earth. The others were now freed. They whipped and whirled about the lot like dizzy fish in a bowl. It had seemed like a big lot until now, but now the very idea that all that fury and motion should be transpiring inside any one fence was something to be repudiated with contempt, like a mirror trick. From the ultimate dust the stranger, carrying the wire-cutters and his vest completely gone now, emerged. He was not running, he merely moved with a light-poised and watchful celerity, weaving among the calico rushes of the animals, feinting and dodging like a boxer until he reached the gate and crossed the yard and mounted to the veranda. One sleeve of his shirt hung only at one point from his shoulder. He ripped it off and wiped his face with it and threw it away and took out the paper carton and shook a gingersnap into his hand. He was breathing only a little heavily. "Pretty lively now," he said. "But it'll work out of them in a couple of days." The ponies still streaked back and forth through the growing dusk like hysterical fish, but not so violently now.

"What'll you give a man to reduce them odds a little for you?" Quick said. The Texan looked at him, the eyes bleak, pleasant and hard above the chewing jaw, the heavy moustache. "To take one of them off your hands?" Quick said.

At that moment the little periwinkle-eyed boy came along the veranda, saying, "Papa, papa; where's papa?"

"Who you looking for, sonny?" one said.

"It's Eck's boy," Quick said. "He's still out yonder in the wagon. Helping Mr Buck here." The boy went on to the end of the veranda, in diminutive overalls—a miniature replica of the men themselves.

"Papa," he said. "Papa." The blacksmith was still leaning from the rear of the wagon, still holding the end of the severed wire. The ponies, bunched for the moment, now slid past the wagon, flowing, stringing out again so that they appeared to have doubled in number, rushing on; the hard rapid light patter of unshod hooves came out of the dust. "Mamma says to come on to supper," the boy said.

The moon was almost full then. When supper was over and they had gathered again along the veranda, the alteration was hardly one of visibility even. It was merely a translation from the lapidary-dimensional of day to the treacherous and silver receptivity in which the horses huddled in mazy camouflage, or singly or in pairs rushed, fluid, phantom, and unceasing, to huddle again in mirage-like clumps from which came high abrupt squeals and the vicious thudding of hooves.

Ratliff was among them now. He had returned just before supper. He had not dared take his team into the lot at all. They were now in Bookwright's stable a half mile from the store. "So Flem has come home again," he said. "Well, well, well. Will Varner paid to get him to Texas, so I reckon it aint no more than fair for you fellows to pay the freight on him back." From the lot there came a high thin squeal. One of the animals emerged. It seemed not to gallop but to flow, bodiless, without dimension. Yet there was the rapid light beat of hard hooves on the packed earth.

"He aint said they was his yet," Quick said.

"He aint said they aint neither," Freeman said.

"I see," Ratliff said. "That's what you are holding back on. Until he tells you whether they are his or not. Or maybe you can wait until the auction's over and split up and some can follow Flem and some can follow that Texas fellow and watch to see which one spends the money. But then, when a man's done got trimmed, I dont reckon he cares who's got the money."

"Maybe if Ratliff would leave here tonight, they wouldn't make him buy one of them ponies tomorrow," a third said.

"That's a fact," Ratliff said. "A fellow can dodge a Snopes if he just starts lively enough. In fact, I dont believe he would have to pass more than two folks before he would have another victim intervened betwixt them. You folks aint going to buy them things sho enough, are you?" Nobody answered. They sat on the steps, their backs against the veranda posts, or on the railing itself. Only Ratliff and Quick sat in chairs, so that to them the others were black silhouettes against the dreaming lambence of the moonlight beyond the veranda. The pear tree across the road opposite was now in full and frosty bloom, the twigs and branches springing not outward from the limbs but standing motionless and perpendicular above the horizontal boughs like the separate and upstreaming hair of a drowned woman sleeping upon the uttermost floor of the windless and tideless sea.

"Anse McCallum brought two of them horses back from Texas once," one of the men on the steps said. He did not move to speak. He was not speaking to anyone. "It was a good team. A little light. He worked it for ten years. Light work, it was."

"I mind it," another said. "Anse claimed he traded fourteen rifle cartridges for both of them, didn't he?"

"It was the rifle too, I heard," a third said.

"No, it was just the shells," the first said. "The fellow wanted to swap him four more for the rifle too, but Anse said he never needed them. Cost too much to get six of them back to Mississippi."

"Sho," the second said. "When a man dont have to invest so much into a horse or a team, he dont need to expect so much from it." The three of them were not talking any louder, they were merely talking among themselves, to one another, as if they sat there alone. Ratliff, invisible in the shadow against the wall, made a sound, harsh, sardonic, not loud.

"Ratliff's laughing," a fourth said.

"Dont mind me," Ratliff said. The three speakers had not moved. They did not move now, yet there seemed to gather about the three silhouettes something stubborn, convinced, and passive, like children who have been chidden. A bird, a shadow, fleet and dark and swift, curved across the moonlight, upward into the pear tree and began to sing; a mockingbird.

"First one I've noticed this year," Freeman said.

"You can hear them along Whiteleaf every night," the first man said. "I heard one in February. In that snow. Singing in a gum."

"Gum is the first tree to put out," the third said. "That was why. It made it feel like singing, fixing to put out that way. That was why it taken a gum."

"Gum first to put out?" Quick said. "What about willow?"

"Willow aint a tree," Freeman said. "It's a weed."

"Well, I dont know what it is," the fourth said. "But it aint no weed. Because you can grub up a weed and you are done with it. I been grubbing up a clump of willows outen my spring pasture for fifteen years. They are the same size every year. Only difference is, it's just two or three more trees every time."

"And if I was you," Ratliff said, "that's just exactly where I would be come sunup tomorrow. Which of course you aint going to do. I reckon there aint nothing under the sun or in Frenchman's Bend neither that can keep you folks from giving Flem Snopes and that Texas man your money. But I'd sholy like to know just exactly who I was giving my money to. Seems like Eck here would tell you. Seems like he'd do that for his neighbors, dont it? Besides being Flem's cousin, him and that boy of his, Wallstreet, helped that Texas man tote water for them tonight and Eck's going to help him feed them in the morning too. Why, maybe Eck will be the one that will catch them and lead them up one at a time for you folks to bid on them. Aint that right, Eck?"

The other man sitting on the steps with his back against the post was the blacksmith. "I dont know," he said.

"Boys," Ratliff said, "Eck knows all about them horses. Flem's told him, how much they cost and how much him and that Texas man aim to get for them, make off of them. Come on, Eck. Tell us." The other did not move, sitting on the top step, not quite facing them, sitting there beneath the successive layers of their quiet and intent concentrated listening and waiting.

"I dont know," he said. Ratliff began to laugh. He sat in the chair, laughing while the others sat or lounged upon the steps and the railing, sitting beneath his laughing as Eck had sat beneath their listening and waiting. Ratliff ceased laughing. He rose. He yawned, quite loud.

"All right. You folks can buy them critters if you want to. But me, I'd just as soon buy a tiger or a rattlesnake. And if Flem Snopes offered me either one of them, I would be afraid to touch it for fear it would turn out to be a painted dog or a piece of garden hose when I went up to take possession of it. I bid you one and all goodnight." He entered the house. They did not look after him, though after a while they all shifted a little and looked down into the lot, upon the splotchy, sporadic surge and flow of the horses, from among which from time to time came an abrupt squeal, a thudding blow. In the pear tree the mockingbird's idiot reiteration pulsed and purled.

"Anse McCallum made a good team outen them two of hisn," the first man said. "They was a little light. That was all."

When the sun rose the next morning a wagon and three saddled mules stood in Mrs Littlejohn's lane and six men and Eck Snopes's son were already leaning on the fence, looking at the horses which huddled in a quiet clump before the barn door, watching the men in their turn. A second wagon came up the road and into the lane and stopped, and then there were eight men beside the boy standing at the fence, beyond which the horses stood, their blue-and-brown eyeballs rolling alertly in their gaudy faces. "So this here is the Snopes circus, is it?" one of the newcomers said. He glanced at the faces, then he went to the end of the row and stood beside the blacksmith and the little boy. "Are them Flem's horses?" he said to the blacksmith.

"Eck dont know who them horses belong to any more than we do," one of the others said. "He knows that Flem come here on the same wagon with them, because he saw him. But that's all."

"And all he will know," a second said. "His own kin will be the last man in the world to find out anything about Flem Snopes's business."

"No," the first said. "He wouldn't even be that. The first man Flem would tell his business to would be the man that was left after the last man died. Flem Snopes dont even tell himself what he is up to. Not if he was laying in bed with himself in a empty house in the dark of the moon."

"That's a fact," a third said. "Flem would trim Eck or any other of his kin quick as he would us. Aint that right, Eck?"

"I dont know," Eck said. They were watching the horses, which at that moment broke into a high-eared, stiff-kneed swirl and flowed in a patchwork wave across the lot and brought up again, facing the men along the fence, so they did not hear the Texan until he was among them. He wore a new shirt and another vest a little too small for him and he was just putting the paper carton back into his hip pocket.

"Morning, morning," he said. "Come to get an early pick, have you? Want to make me an offer for one or two before the bidding starts and runs the prices up?" They had not looked at the stranger long. They were not looking at him now, but at the horses in the lot, which had lowered their heads, snuffing into the dust.

"I reckon we'll look a while first," one said.

"You are in time to look at them eating breakfast, anyhow," the Texan said. "Which is more than they done without they staid up all night." He opened the gate and entered it. At once the horses jerked their heads up, watching him. "Here, Eck," the Texan said over his shoulder, "two or three of you boys help me drive them into the barn." After a moment Eck and two others approached the gate, the little boy at his father's heels, though the other did not see him until he turned to shut the gate.

"You stay out of here," Eck said. "One of them things will snap your head off same as a acorn before you even know it." He shut the gate and went on after the others, whom the Texan had now waved fanwise outward as he approached the horses which now drew into a restive huddle, beginning to mill slightly, watching the men. Mrs Littlejohn came out of the kitchen and crossed the yard to the wood-pile, watching the lot. She picked up two or three sticks of wood and paused, watching the lot again. Now there were two more men standing at the fence.

"Come on, come on," the Texan said. "They wont hurt you. They just aint never been in under a roof before."

"I just as lief let them stay out here, if that's what they want to do," Eck said.

"Get yourself a stick—there's a bunch of wagon stakes against the fence yonder—and when one of them tries to rush you, bust him over the head so he will understand what you mean." One of the men went to the fence and got three of the stakes and returned and distributed them. Mrs Littlejohn, her armful of wood complete now, paused again halfway back to the house, looking into the lot. The little boy was directly behind his father again, though this time the father had not discovered him yet. The men advanced toward the horses, the huddle of which began to break into gaudy units turning inward upon themselves. The Texan was cursing them in a loud steady cheerful voice. "Get in there, you banjo-faced jack rabbits. Dont hurry them, now. Let them take their time. Hi! Get in there. What do you think that barn is—a law court maybe? Or maybe a church and somebody is going to take up a collection on you?" The animals fell slowly back. Now and then one feinted to break from the huddle, the Texan driving it back each time with skillfully thrown bits of dirt. Then one at the rear saw the barn door just behind it but before the herd could break the Texan snatched the wagon stake from Eck and, followed by one of the other men, rushed at the horses and began to lay about the heads and shoulders, choosing by unerring instinct the point animal and striking it first square in the face then on the withers as it turned and then on the rump as it turned further, so that when the break came it was reversed and the entire herd rushed into the long open hallway and brought up against the further wall with a hollow, thunderous sound like that of a collapsing mine-shaft. "Seems to have held all right," the Texan said. He and the other man slammed the half-length doors and looked over them into the tunnel of the barn, at the far end of which the ponies were now a splotchy phantom moiling punctuated by crackings of wooden partitions and the dry reports of hooves which gradually died away. "Yep, it held all right," the Texan said. The other two came to the doors and looked over them. The little boy came up beside his father now, trying to see through a crack, and Eck saw him.

"Didn't I tell you to stay out of here?" Eck said. "Dont you know them things will kill you quicker than you can say scat? You go and get outside of that fence and stay there."

"Why dont you get your paw to buy you one of them, Wall?" one of the men said.

"Me buy one of them things?" Eck said. "When I can go to the river anytime and catch me a snapping turtle or a moccasin for nothing? You go on, now. Get out of here and stay out." The Texan had entered the barn. One of the men closed the doors after him and put the bar up again and over the top of the doors they watched the Texan go on down the hallway, toward the ponies which now huddled like gaudy phantoms in the gloom, quiet now and already beginning to snuff experimentally into the long lipworn trough fastened against the rear wall. The little boy had merely gone around behind his father, to the other side, where he stood peering now through a knot-hole in a plank. The Texan opened a smaller door in the wall and entered it, though almost immediately he reappeared.

"I dont see nothing but shelled corn in here," he said. "Snopes said he would send some hay up here last night."

"Wont they eat corn either?" one of the men said.

"I dont know," the Texan said. "They aint never seen any that I know of. We'll find out in a minute though." He disappeared, though they could still hear him in the crib. Then he emerged once more, carrying a big double-ended feed-basket, and retreated into the gloom where the parti-colored rumps of the horses were now ranged quietly along the feeding-trough. Mrs Littlejohn appeared once more, on the veranda this time, carrying a big brass dinner bell. She raised it to make the first stroke. A small commotion set up among the ponies as the Texan approached but he began to speak to them at once, in a brisk loud unemphatic mixture of cursing and cajolery, disappearing among them. The men at the door heard the dry rattling of the corn-pellets into the trough, a sound broken by a single snort of amazed horror. A plank cracked with a loud report; before their eyes the depths of the hallway dissolved in loud fury, and while they stared over the doors, unable yet to begin to move, the entire interior exploded into mad tossing shapes like a downrush of flames.

"Hell fire," one of them said. "Jump!" he shouted. The three turned and ran frantically for the wagon, Eck last. Several voices from the fence were now shouting something but Eck did not even hear them until, in the act of scrambling madly at the tail-gate, he looked behind him and saw the little boy still leaning to the knot-hole in the door which in the next instant vanished into matchwood, the knot-hole itself exploding from his eye and leaving him, motionless in the diminutive overalls and still leaning forward a little until he vanished utterly beneath the towering parti-colored wave full of feet and glaring eyes and wild teeth which, overtopping, burst into scattering units, revealing at last the gaping orifice and the little boy still standing in it, unscathed, his eye still leaned to the vanished knot-hole.

"Wall!" Eck roared. The little boy turned and ran for the wagon. The horses were whipping back and forth across the lot, as if while in the barn they had once more doubled their number; two of them rushed up quartering and galloped all over the boy again without touching him as he ran, earnest and diminutive and seemingly without progress, though he reached the wagon at last, from which Eck, his sunburned skin now a sickly white, reached down and snatched the boy into the wagon by the straps of his overalls and slammed him face down across his knees and caught up a coiled hitching-rope from the bed of the wagon.

"Didn't I tell you to get out of here?" Eck said in a shaking voice. "Didn't I tell you?"

"If you're going to whip him, you better whip the rest of us too and then one of us can frail hell out of you," one of the others said.

"Or better still, take the rope and hang that durn fellow yonder," the second said. The Texan was now standing in the wrecked door of the barn, taking the gingersnap carton from his hip pocket. "Before he kills the rest of Frenchman's Bend too."

"You mean Flem Snopes," the first said. The Texan tilted the carton above his other open palm. The horses still rushed and swirled back and forth but they were beginning to slow now, trotting on high, stiff legs, although their eyes were still rolling whitely and various.

"I misdoubted that damn shell corn all along," the Texan said. "But at least they have seen what it looks like. They cant claim they aint got nothing out of this trip." He shook the carton over his open hand. Nothing came out of it. Mrs Littlejohn on the veranda made the first stroke with the dinner bell; at the sound the horses rushed again, the earth of the lot becoming vibrant with the light dry clatter of hooves. The Texan crumpled the carton and threw it aside. "Chuck wagon," he said. There were three more wagons in the lane now and there were twenty or more men at the fence when the Texan, followed by his three assistants and the little boy, passed through the gate. The bright cloudless early sun gleamed upon the pearl butt of the pistol in his hip pocket and upon the bell which Mrs Littlejohn still rang, peremptory, strong, and loud.

When the Texan, picking his teeth with a splintered kitchen match, emerged from the house twenty minutes later, the tethered wagons and riding horses and mules extended from the lot gate to Varner's store, and there were more than fifty men now standing along the fence beside the gate, watching him quietly, a little covertly, as he approached, rolling a little, slightly bowlegged, the high heels of his carved boots printing neatly into the dust. "Morning, gents," he said. "Here, bud," he said to the little boy, who stood slightly behind him, looking at the protruding butt of the pistol. He took a coin from his pocket and gave it to the boy. "Run to the store and get me a box of gingersnaps." He looked about at the quiet faces, protuberant, sucking his teeth. He rolled the match from one side of his mouth to the other without touching it. "You boys done made your picks, have you? Ready to start her off, hah?" They did not answer. They were not looking at him now. That is, he began to have the feeling that each face had stopped looking at him the second before his gaze reached it. After a moment Freeman said:

"Aint you going to wait for Flem?"

"Why?" the Texan said. Then Freeman stopped looking at him too. There was nothing in Freeman's face either. There was nothing, no alteration, in the Texan's voice. "Eck, you done already picked out yours. So we can start her off when you are ready."

"I reckon not," Eck said. "I wouldn't buy nothing I was afraid to walk up and touch."

"Them little ponies?" the Texan said. "You helped water and feed them. I bet that boy of yours could walk up to any one of them."

"He better not let me catch him," Eck said. The Texan looked about at the quiet faces, his gaze at once abstract and alert, with an impenetrable surface quality like flint, as though the surface were impervious or perhaps there was nothing behind it.

"Them ponies is gentle as a dove, boys. The man that buys them will get the best piece of horseflesh he ever forked or druv for the money. Naturally they got spirit; I aint selling crowbait. Besides, who'd want Texas crowbait anyway, with Mississippi full of it?" His stare was still absent and unwinking; there was no mirth or humor in his voice and there was neither mirth nor humor in the single guffaw which came from the rear of the group. Two wagons were now drawing out of the road at the same time, up to the fence. The men got down from them and tied them to the fence and approached. "Come up, boys," the Texan said. "You're just in time to buy a good gentle horse cheap."

"How about that one that cut your vest off last night?" a voice said. This time three or four guffawed. The Texan looked toward the sound, bleak and unwinking.

"What about it?" he said. The laughter, if it had been laughter, ceased. The Texan turned to the nearest gatepost and climbed to the top of it, his alternate thighs deliberate and bulging in the tight trousers, the butt of the pistol catching and losing the sun in pearly gleams. Sitting on the post, he looked down at the faces along the fence which were attentive, grave, reserved and not looking at him. "All right," he said. "Who's going to start her off with a bid? Step right up; take your pick and make your bid, and when the last one is sold, walk in that lot and put your rope on the best piece of horse-flesh you ever forked or druv for the money. There aint a pony there that aint worth fifteen dollars. Young, sound, good for saddle or work stock, guaranteed to outlast four ordinary horses; you couldn't kill one of them with a axle-tree—" There was a small violent commotion at the rear of the group. The little boy appeared, burrowing among the motionless overalls. He approached the post, the new and unbroken paper carton lifted. The Texan leaned down and took it and tore the end from it and shook three or four of the cakes into the boy's hand, a hand as small and almost as black as that of a coon. He held the carton in his hand while he talked, pointing out the horses with it as he indicated them. "Look at that one with the three stocking-feet and the frost-bit ear; watch him now when they pass again. Look at that shoulder-action; that horse is worth twenty dollars of any man's money. Who'll make me a bid on him to start her off?" His voice was harsh, ready, forensic. Along the fence below him the men stood with, buttoned close in their overalls, the tobacco-sacks and worn purses, the sparse silver and frayed bills hoarded a coin at a time in the cracks of chimneys or chinked into the logs of walls. From time to time the horses broke and rushed with purposeless violence and huddled again, watching the faces along the fence with wild mismatched eyes. The lane was full of wagons now. As the others arrived they would have to stop in the road beyond it and the occupants came up the lane on foot. Mrs Littlejohn came out of her kitchen. She crossed the yard, looking toward the lot gate. There was a blackened wash pot set on four bricks in the corner of the yard. She built a fire beneath the pot and came to the fence and stood there for a time, her hands on her hips and the smoke from the fire drifting blue and slow behind her. Then she turned and went back into the house. "Come on, boys," the Texan said. "Who'll make me a bid?"

"Four bits," a voice said. The Texan did not even glance toward it.

"Or, if he dont suit you, how about that fiddle-head horse without no mane to speak of? For a saddle pony, I'd rather have him than that stocking-foot. I heard somebody say fifty cents just now. I reckon he meant five dollars, didn't he? Do I hear five dollars?"

"Four bits for the lot," the same voice said. This time there were no guffaws. It was the Texan who laughed, harshly, with only his lower face, as if he were reciting a multiplication table.

"Fifty cents for the dried mud offen them, he means," he said. "Who'll give a dollar more for the genuine Texas cockle-burrs?" Mrs Littlejohn came out of the kitchen, carrying the sawn half of a wooden hogshead which she set on a stump beside the smoking pot, and stood with her hands on her hips, looking into the lot for a while without coming to the fence this time. Then she went back into the house. "What's the matter with you boys?" the Texan said. "Here, Eck, you been helping me and you know them horses. How about making me a bid on that wall-eyed one you picked out last night? Here. Wait a minute." He thrust the paper carton into his other hip pocket and swung his feet inward and dropped, cat-light, into the lot. The ponies, huddled, watched him. Then they broke before him and slid stiffly along the fence. He turned them and they whirled and rushed back across the lot; whereupon, as though he had been waiting his chance when they should have turned their backs on him, the Texan began to run too, so that when they reached the opposite side of the lot and turned, slowing to huddle again, he was almost upon them. The earth became thunderous; dust arose, out of which the animals began to burst like flushed quail and into which, with that apparently unflagging faith in his own invulnerability, the Texan rushed. For an instant the watchers could see them in the dust—the pony backed into the angle of the fence and the stable, the man facing it, reaching toward his hip. Then the beast rushed at him in a sort of fatal and hopeless desperation and he struck it between the eyes with the pistol-butt and felled it and leaped onto its prone head. The pony recovered almost at once and pawed itself to its knees and heaved at its prisoned head and fought itself up, dragging the man with it; for an instant in the dust the watchers saw the man free of the earth and in violent lateral motion like a rag attached to the horse's head. Then the Texan's feet came back to earth and the dust blew aside and revealed them, motionless, the Texan's sharp heels braced into the ground, one hand gripping the pony's forelock and the other its nostrils, the long evil muzzle wrung backward over its scarred shoulder while it breathed in labored and hollow groans. Mrs Littlejohn was in the yard again. No one had seen her emerge this time. She carried an armful of clothing and a metal-ridged washboard and she was standing motionless at the kitchen steps, looking into the lot. Then she moved across the yard, still looking into the lot, and dumped the garments into the tub, still looking into the lot. "Look him over, boys," the Texan panted, turning his own suffused face and the protuberant glare of his eyes toward the fence. "Look him over quick. Them shoulders and—" He had relaxed for an instant apparently. The animal exploded again; again for an instant the Texan was free of the earth, though he was still talking: "—and legs you whoa I'll tear your face right look him over quick boys worth fifteen dollars of let me get a holt of who'll make me a bid whoa you blare-eyed jack rabbit, whoa!" They were moving now—a kaleidoscope of inextricable and incredible violence on the periphery of which the metal clasps of the Texan's suspenders sun-glinted in ceaseless orbit, with terrific slowness across the lot. Then the broad clay-colored hat soared deliberately outward; an instant later the Texan followed it, though still on his feet, and the pony shot free in mad, staglike bounds. The Texan picked up the hat and struck the dust from it against his leg, and returned to the fence and mounted the post again. He was breathing heavily. Still the faces did not look at him as he took the carton from his hip and shook a cake from it and put the cake into his mouth, chewing, breathing harshly. Mrs Littlejohn turned away and began to bail water from the pot into the tub, though after each bucketful she turned her head and looked into the lot again. "Now, boys," the Texan said. "Who says that pony aint worth fifteen dollars? You couldn't buy that much dynamite for just fifteen dollars. There aint one of them cant do a mile in three minutes; turn them into pasture and they will board themselves; work them like hell all day and every time you think about it, lay them over the head with a single-tree and after a couple of days every jack rabbit one of them will be so tame you will have to put them out of the house at night like a cat." He shook another cake from the carton and ate it. "Come on, Eck," he said. "Start her off. How about ten dollars for that horse, Eck?"

"What need I got for a horse I would need a bear-trap to catch?" Eck said.

"Didn't you just see me catch him?"

"I seen you," Eck said. "And I dont want nothing as big as a horse if I got to wrastle with it every time it finds me on the same side of a fence it's on."

"All right," the Texan said. He was still breathing harshly, but now there was nothing of fatigue or breathlessness in it. He shook another cake into his palm and inserted it beneath his moustache. "All right. I want to get this auction started. I aint come here to live, no matter how good a country you folks claim you got. I'm going to give you that horse." For a moment there was no sound, not even that of breathing except the Texan's.

"You going to give it to me?" Eck said.

"Yes. Provided you will start the bidding on the next one." Again there was no sound save the Texan's breathing, and then the clash of Mrs Littlejohn's pail against the rim of the pot.

"I just start the bidding," Eck said. "I dont have to buy it lessen I aint over-topped." Another wagon had come up the lane. It was battered and paintless. One wheel had been repaired by crossed planks bound to the spokes with baling wire and the two underfed mules wore a battered harness patched with bits of cotton rope; the reins were ordinary cotton plow-lines, not new. It contained a woman in a shapeless gray garment and a faded sunbonnet, and a man in faded and patched though clean overalls. There was not room for the wagon to draw out of the lane so the man left it standing where it was and got down and came forward—a thin man, not large, with something about his eyes, something strained and washed-out, at once vague and intense, who shoved into the crowd at the rear, saying,

"What? What's that? Did he give him that horse?"

"All right," the Texan said. "That wall-eyed horse with the scarred neck belongs to you. Now. That one that looks like he's had his head in a flour barrel. What do you say? Ten dollars?"

"Did he give him that horse?" the newcomer said.

"A dollar," Eck said. The Texan's mouth was still open for speech; for an instant his face died so behind the hard eyes.

"A dollar?" he said. "One dollar? Did I actually hear that?"

"Durn it," Eck said. "Two dollars then. But I aint—"

"Wait," the newcomer said. "You, up there on the post." The Texan looked at him. When the others turned, they saw that the woman had left the wagon too, though they had not known she was there since they had not seen the wagon drive up. She came among them behind the man, gaunt in the gray shapeless garment and the sunbonnet, wearing stained canvas gymnasium shoes. She overtook the man but she did not touch him, standing just behind him, her hands rolled before her into the gray dress.

"Henry," she said in a flat voice. The man looked over his shoulder.

"Get back to that wagon," he said.

"Here, missus," the Texan said. "Henry's going to get the bargain of his life in about a minute. Here, boys, let the missus come up close where she can see. Henry's going to pick out that saddle-horse the missus has been wanting. Who says ten—"

"Henry," the woman said. She did not raise her voice. She had not once looked at the Texan. She touched the man's arm. He turned and struck her hand down.

"Get back to that wagon like I told you." The woman stood behind him, her hands rolled again into her dress. She was not looking at anything, speaking to anyone.

"He aint no more despair than to buy one of them things," she said. "And us not but five dollars away from the poorhouse, he aint no more despair." The man turned upon her with that curious air of leashed, of dreamlike fury. The others lounged along the fence in attitudes gravely inattentive, almost oblivious. Mrs Littlejohn had been washing for some time now, pumping rhythmically up and down above the washboard in the sud-foamed tub. She now stood erect again, her soap-raw hands on her hips, looking into the lot.

"Shut your mouth and get back in that wagon," the man said. "Do you want me to take a wagon stake to you?" He turned and looked up at the Texan. "Did you give him that horse?" he said. The Texan was looking at the woman. Then he looked at the man; still watching him, he tilted the paper carton over his open palm. A single cake came out of it.

"Yes," he said.

"Is the fellow that bids in this next horse going to get that first one too?"

"No," the Texan said.

"All right," the other said. "Are you going to give a horse to the man that makes the first bid on the next one?"

"No," the Texan said.

"Then if you were just starting the auction off by giving away a horse, why didn't you wait till we were all here?" The Texan stopped looking at the other. He raised the empty carton and squinted carefully into it, as if it might contain a precious jewel or perhaps a deadly insect. Then he crumpled it and dropped it carefully beside the post on which he sat.

"Eck bids two dollars," he said. "I believe he still thinks he's bidding on them scraps of bob-wire they come here in instead of on one of the horses. But I got to accept it. But are you boys—"

"So Eck's going to get two horses at a dollar a head," the newcomer said. "Three dollars." The woman touched him again. He flung her hand off without turning and she stood again, her hands rolled into her dress across her flat stomach, not looking at anything.

"Misters," she said, "we got chaps in the house that never had shoes last winter. We aint got corn to feed the stock. We got five dollars I earned weaving by firelight after dark. And he aint no more despair."

"Henry bids three dollars," the Texan said. "Raise him a dollar, Eck, and the horse is yours." Beyond the fence the horses rushed suddenly and for no reason and as suddenly stopped, staring at the faces along the fence.

"Henry," the woman said. The man was watching Eck. His stained and broken teeth showed a little beneath his lip. His wrists dangled into fists below the faded sleeves of his shirt too short from many washings.

"Four dollars," Eck said.

"Five dollars!" the husband said, raising one clenched hand. He shouldered himself forward toward the gatepost. The woman did not follow him. She now looked at the Texan for the first time. Her eyes were a washed gray also, as though they had faded too like the dress and the sunbonnet.

"Mister," she said, "if you take that five dollars I earned my chaps a-weaving for one of them things, it'll be a curse on you and yours during all the time of man."

"Five dollars!" the husband shouted. He thrust himself up to the post, his clenched hand on a level with the Texan's knees. He opened it upon a wad of frayed banknotes and silver. "Five dollars! And the man that raises it will have to beat my head off or I'll beat hisn."

"All right," the Texan said. "Five dollars is bid. But dont you shake your hand at me."

At five oclock that afternoon the Texan crumpled the third paper carton and dropped it to the earth beneath him. In the copper slant of the leveling sun which fell also upon the line of limp garments in Mrs Littlejohn's back yard and which cast his shadow and that of the post on which he sat long across the lot where now and then the ponies still rushed in purposeless and tireless surges, the Texan straightened his leg and thrust his hand into his pocket and took out a coin and leaned down to the little boy. His voice was now hoarse, spent. "Here, bud," he said. "Run to the store and get me a box of gingersnaps." The men still stood along the fence, tireless, in their overalls and faded shirts. Flem Snopes was there now, appeared suddenly from nowhere, standing beside the fence with a space the width of three or four men on either side of him, standing there in his small yet definite isolation, chewing tobacco, in the same gray trousers and minute bow tie in which he had departed last summer but in a new cap, gray too like the other, but new, and overlaid with a bright golfer's plaid, looking also at the horses in the lot. All of them save two had been sold for sums ranging from three dollars and a half to eleven and twelve dollars. The purchasers, as they had bid them in, had gathered as though by instinct into a separate group on the other side of the gate, where they stood with their hands lying upon the top strand of the fence, watching with a still more sober intensity the animals which some of them had owned for seven and eight hours now but had not yet laid hands upon. The husband, Henry, stood beside the post on which the Texan sat. The wife had gone back to the wagon, where she sat gray in the gray garment, motionless, looking at nothing still; she might have been something inanimate which he had loaded into the wagon to move it somewhere, waiting now in the wagon until he should be ready to go on again, patient, insensate, timeless.

"I bought a horse and I paid cash for it," he said. His voice was harsh and spent too, the mad look in his eyes had a quality glazed now and even sightless. "And yet you expect me to stand around here till they are all sold before I can get my horse. Well, you can do all the expecting you want. I'm going to take my horse out of there and go home." The Texan looked down at him. The Texan's shirt was blotched with sweat. His big face was cold and still, his voice level.

"Take your horse then." After a moment Henry looked away. He stood with his head bent a little, swallowing from time to time.

"Aint you going to catch him for me?"

"It aint my horse," the Texan said in that flat still voice. After a while Henry raised his head. He did not look at the Texan.

"Who'll help me catch my horse?" he said. Nobody answered. They stood along the fence, looking quietly into the lot where the ponies huddled, already beginning to fade a little where the long shadow of the house lay upon them, deepening. From Mrs Littlejohn's kitchen the smell of frying ham came. A noisy cloud of sparrows swept across the lot and into a chinaberry tree beside the house, and in the high soft vague blue swallows stooped and whirled in erratic indecision, their cries like strings plucked at random. Without looking back, Henry raised his voice: "Bring that ere plowline." After a time the wife moved. She got down from the wagon and took a coil of new cotton rope from it and approached. The husband took the rope from her and moved toward the gate. The Texan began to descend from the post, stiffly, as Henry put his hand on the latch. "Come on here," he said. The wife had stopped when he took the rope from her. She moved again, obediently, her hands rolled into the dress across her stomach, passing the Texan without looking at him.

"Dont you go in there, missus," he said. She stopped, not look-

ing at him, not looking at anything. The husband opened the gate
and entered the lot and turned, holding the gate open but without
raising his eyes.

"Come on here," he said.

"Dont you go in there, missus," the Texan said. The wife stood
motionless between them, her face almost concealed by the sunbonnet, her hands folded across her stomach.

"I reckon I better," she said. The other men did not look at her
at all, at her or Henry either. They stood along the fence, grave and
quiet and inattentive, almost bemused. Then the wife passed through
the gate; the husband shut it behind them and turned and began to
move toward the huddled ponies, the wife following in the gray and
shapeless garment within which she moved without inference of
locomotion, like something on a moving platform, a float. The
horses were watching them. They clotted and blended and shifted
among themselves, on the point of breaking though not breaking yet.
The husband shouted at them. He began to curse them, advancing,
the wife following. Then the huddle broke, the animals moving with
high, stiff knees, circling the two people who turned and followed
again as the herd flowed and huddled again at the opposite side of the
lot.

"There he is," the husband said. "Get him into that corner." The
herd divided; the horse which the husband had bought jolted on stiff
legs. The wife shouted at it; it spun and poised, plunging, then the
husband struck it across the face with the coiled rope and it whirled
and slammed into the corner of the fence. "Keep him there now," the
husband said. He shook out the rope, advancing. The horse watched
him with wild, glaring eyes; it rushed again, straight toward the wife.
She shouted at it and waved her arms but it soared past her in a long
bound and rushed again into the huddle of its fellows. They followed
and hemmed it again into another corner; again the wife failed to
stop its rush for freedom and the husband turned and struck her with
the coiled rope. "Why didn't you head him?" he said. "Why didn't
you?" He struck her again; she did not move, not even to fend the
rope with a raised arm. The men along the fence stood quietly, their
faces lowered as though brooding upon the earth at their feet. Only
Flem Snopes was still watching—if he ever had been looking into the

lot at all, standing in his little island of isolation, chewing with his characteristic faint sidewise thrust beneath the new plaid cap.

The Texan said something, not loud, harsh and short. He entered the lot and went to the husband and jerked the uplifted rope from his hand. The husband whirled as though he were about to spring at the Texan, crouched slightly, his knees bent and his arms held slightly away from his sides, though his gaze never mounted higher than the Texan's carved and dusty boots. Then the Texan took the husband by the arm and led him back toward the gate, the wife following, and through the gate which he held open for the woman and then closed. He took a wad of banknotes from his trousers and removed a bill from it and put it into the woman's hand. "Get him into the wagon and get him on home," he said.

"What's that for?" Flem Snopes said. He had approached. He now stood beside the post on which the Texan had been sitting. The Texan did not look at him.

"Thinks he bought one of them ponies," the Texan said. He spoke in a flat still voice, like that of a man after a sharp run. "Get him on away, missus."

"Give him back that money," the husband said, in his lifeless, spent tone. "I bought that horse and I aim to have him if I got to shoot him before I can put a rope on him." The Texan did not even look at him.

"Get him on away from here, missus," he said.

"You take your money and I take my horse," the husband said. He was shaking slowly and steadily now, as though he were cold. His hands open and shut below the frayed cuffs of his shirt. "Give it back to him," he said.

"You dont own no horse of mine," the Texan said. "Get him on home, missus." The husband raised his spent face, his mad glazed eyes. He reached out his hand. The woman held the banknote in her folded hands across her stomach. For a while the husband's shaking hand merely fumbled at it. Then he drew the banknote free.

"It's my horse," he said. "I bought it. These fellows saw me. I paid for it. It's my horse. Here." He turned and extended the banknote toward Snopes. "You got something to do with these horses. I bought one. Here's the money for it. I bought one. Ask him." Snopes took the banknote. The others stood, gravely inattentive, in relaxed attitudes along the fence. The sun had gone now; there was nothing save violet shadow upon them and upon the lot where once more and for no reason the ponies rushed and flowed. At that moment the little boy came up, tireless and indefatigable still, with the new paper carton. The Texan took it, though he did not open it at once. He had dropped the rope and now the husband stooped for it, fumbling at it for some time before he lifted it from the ground. Then he stood with his head bent, his knuckles whitening on the rope. The woman had not moved. Twilight was coming fast now; there was a last mazy swirl of swallows against the high and changing azure. Then the Texan tore the end from the carton and tilted one of the cakes into his hand; he seemed to be watching the hand as it shut slowly upon the cake until a fine powder of snuff-colored dust began to rain from his fingers. He rubbed the hand carefully on his thigh and raised his head and glanced about until he saw the little boy and handed the carton back to him.

"Here, bud," he said. Then he looked at the woman, his voice flat, quiet again. "Mr Snopes will have your money for you tomorrow. Better get him in the wagon and get him on home. He dont own no horse. You can get your money tomorrow from Mr Snopes." The wife turned and went back to the wagon and got into it. No one watched her, nor the husband who still stood, his head bent, passing the rope from one hand to the other. They leaned along the fence, grave and quiet, as though the fence were in another land, another time.

"How many you got left?" Snopes said. The Texan roused; they all seemed to rouse then, returning, listening again.

"Got three now," the Texan said. "Swap all three of them for a buggy or a—"

"It's out in the road," Snopes said, a little shortly, a little quickly, turning away. "Get your mules." He went on up the lane. They watched the Texan enter the lot and cross it, the horses flowing before him but without the old irrational violence, as if they too were spent, vitiated with the long day, and enter the barn and then emerge, leading the two harnessed mules. The wagon had been backed under the shed beside the barn. The Texan entered this and came out a moment later, carrying a bedding-roll and his coat, and led the mules back toward the gate, the ponies huddled again and watching him with their various unmatching eyes, quietly now, as if they too realised there was not only an armistice between them at last but that they would never look upon each other again in both their lives. Someone opened the gate. The Texan led the mules through it and they followed in a body, leaving the husband standing beside the closed gate, his head still bent and the coiled rope in his hand. They passed the wagon in which the wife sat, her gray garment fading into the dusk, almost the same color and as still, looking at nothing; they passed the clothesline with its limp and unwinded drying garments, walking through the hot vivid smell of ham from Mrs Littlejohn's kitchen. When they reached the end of the lane they could see the moon, almost full, tremendous and pale and still lightless in the sky from which day had not quite gone. Snopes was standing at the end of the lane beside an empty buggy. It was the one with the glittering wheels and the fringed parasol top in which he and Will Varner had used to drive. The Texan was motionless too, looking at it.

"Well well well," he said. "So this is it."

"If it dont suit you, you can ride one of the mules back to Texas," Snopes said.

"You bet," the Texan said. "Only I ought to have a powder puff or at least a mandolin to ride it with." He backed the mules onto the tongue and lifted the breast-yoke. Two of them came forward and fastened the traces for him. Then they watched him get into the buggy and raise the reins.

"Where you heading for?" one said. "Back to Texas?"

"In this?" the Texan said. "I wouldn't get past the first Texas saloon without starting the vigilance committee. Besides, I aint going to waste all this here lace-trimmed top and these spindle wheels just on Texas. Long as I am this far, I reckon I'll go on a day or two and look-see them northern towns. Washington and New York and Baltimore. What's the short way to New York from here?" They didn't know. But they told him how to reach Jefferson.

"You're already headed right," Freeman said. "Just keep right on up the road past the schoolhouse."

"All right," the Texan said. "Well, remember about busting them ponies over the head now and then until they get used to you. You wont have any trouble with them then." He lifted the reins again. As he did so Snopes stepped forward and got into the buggy.

"I'll ride as far as Varner's with you," he said.

"I didn't know I was going past Varner's," the Texan said.

"You can go to town that way," Snopes said. "Drive on." The Texan shook the reins. Then he said,

"Whoa." He straightened his leg and put his hand into his pocket. "Here, bud," he said to the little boy, "run to the store and— Never mind. I'll stop and get it myself, long as I am going back that way. Well, boys," he said. "Take care of yourselves." He swung the team around. The buggy went on. They looked after it.

"I reckon he aims to kind of come up on Jefferson from behind," Quick said.

"He'll be lighter when he gets there," Freeman said. "He can come up to it easy from any side he wants."

"Yes," Bookwright said. "His pockets wont rattle." They went back to the lot; they passed on through the narrow way between the two lines of patient and motionless wagons, which at the end was completely closed by the one in which the woman sat. The husband was still standing beside the gate with his coiled rope, and now night had completely come. The light itself had not changed so much; if anything, it was brighter but with that other-worldly quality of moonlight, so that when they stood once more looking into the lot, the splotchy bodies of the ponies had a distinctness, almost a brilliance, but without individual shape and without depth—no longer horses, no longer flesh and bone directed by a principle capable of calculated violence, no longer inherent with the capacity to hurt and harm.

"Well, what are we waiting for?" Freeman said. "For them to go to roost?"

"We better all get our ropes first," Quick said. "Get your ropes everybody." Some of them did not have ropes. When they left home that morning, they had not heard about the horses, the auction. They had merely happened through the village by chance and learned of it and stopped.

"Go to the store and get some then," Freeman said.

"The store will be closed now," Quick said.

"No it wont," Freeman said. "If it was closed, Lump Snopes would a been up here." So while the ones who had come prepared got their ropes from the wagons, the others went down to the store. The clerk was just closing it.

"You all aint started catching them yet, have you?" he said. "Good; I was afraid I wouldn't get there in time." He opened the door again and amid the old strong sunless smells of cheese and leather and molasses he measured and cut off sections of plow-line for them and in a body and the clerk in the center and still talking, voluble and unlistened to, they returned up the road. The pear tree before Mrs Littlejohn's was like drowned silver now in the moon. The mockingbird of last night, or another one, was already singing in it, and they now saw, tied to the fence, Ratliff's buckboard and team.

"I thought something was wrong all day," one said. "Ratliff wasn't there to give nobody advice." When they passed down the lane, Mrs Littlejohn was in her back yard, gathering the garments from the clothesline; they could still smell the ham. The others were waiting at the gate, beyond which the ponies, huddled again, were like phantom fish, suspended apparently without legs now in the brilliant treachery of the moon.

"I reckon the best way will be for us all to take and catch them one at a time," Freeman said.

"One at a time," the husband, Henry, said. Apparently he had not moved since the Texan had led his mules through the gate, save to lift his hands to the top of the gate, one of them still clutching the coiled rope. "One at a time," he said. He began to curse in a harsh, spent monotone. "After I've stood around here all day, waiting for that—" He cursed. He began to jerk at the gate, shaking it with spent violence until one of the others slid the latch back and it swung open and Henry entered it, the others following, the little boy pressing close behind his father until Eck became aware of him and turned.

"Here," he said. "Give me that rope. You stay out of here."

"Aw, paw," the boy said.

"No sir. Them things will kill you. They almost done it this morning. You stay out of here."

"But we got two to catch." For a moment Eck stood looking down at the boy.

"That's right," he said. "We got two. But you stay close to me now. And when I holler run, you run. You hear me?"

"Spread out, boys," Freeman said. "Keep them in front of us." They began to advance across the lot in a ragged crescent-shaped line, each one with his rope. The ponies were now at the far side of the lot. One of them snorted; the mass shifted within itself but without breaking. Freeman, glancing back, saw the little boy. "Get that boy out of here," he said.

"I reckon you better," Eck said to the boy. "You go and get in the wagon yonder. You can see us catch them from there." The little boy turned and trotted toward the shed beneath which the wagon stood. The line of men advanced, Henry a little in front.

"Watch them close now," Freeman said. "Maybe we better try to get them into the barn first—" At that moment the huddle broke. It parted and flowed in both directions along the fence. The men at the ends of the line began to run, waving their arms and shouting. "Head them," Freeman said tensely. "Turn them back." They turned them, driving them back upon themselves again; the animals merged and spun in short, huddling rushes, phantom and inextricable. "Hold them now," Freeman said. "Dont let them get by us." The line advanced again. Eck turned; he did not know why—whether a sound, what. The little boy was just behind him again.

"Didn't I tell you to get in that wagon and stay there?" Eck said.

"Watch out, paw!" the boy said. "There he is! There's ourn!" It was the one the Texan had given Eck. "Catch him, paw!"

"Get out of my way," Eck said. "Get back to that wagon." The line was still advancing. The ponies milled, clotting, forced gradually backward toward the open door of the barn. Henry was still slightly in front, crouched slightly, his thin figure, even in the mazy moonlight, emanating something of that spent fury. The splotchy huddle of animals seemed to be moving before the advancing line of men like a snowball which they might have been pushing before them by some invisible means, gradually nearer and nearer to the black yawn of the barn door. Later it was obvious that the ponies were so intent upon the men that they did not realise the barn was even behind them until they backed into the shadow of it. Then an indescribable sound, a movement desperate and despairing, arose among them; for an instant of static horror men and animals faced one another, then the men whirled and ran before a gaudy vomit of long wild faces and splotched chests which overtook and scattered them and flung them sprawling aside and completely obliterated from sight Henry and the little boy, neither of whom had moved though Henry had flung up both arms, still holding his coiled rope, the herd sweeping on across the lot, to crash through the gate which the last man through it had neglected to close, leaving it slightly ajar, carrying all of the gate save the upright to which the hinges were nailed with them, and so among the teams and wagons which choked the lane, the teams springing and lunging too, snapping hitch-reins and tongues. Then the whole inextricable mass crashed among the wagons and eddied and divided about the one in which the woman sat, and rushed on down the lane and into the road, dividing, one half going one way and one half the other.

The men in the lot, except Henry, got to their feet and ran toward the gate. The little boy once more had not been touched, not even thrown off his feet; for a while his father held him clear of the ground in one hand, shaking him like a rag doll. "Didn't I tell you to stay in that wagon?" Eck cried. "Didn't I tell you?"

"Look out, paw!" the boy chattered out of the violent shaking. "There's ourn! There he goes!" It was the horse the Texan had given them again. It was as if they owned no other, the other one did not exist; as if by some absolute and instantaneous rapport of blood they had relegated to oblivion the one for which they had paid money. They ran to the gate and down the lane where the other men had disappeared. They saw the horse the Texan had given them whirl and dash back and rush through the gate into Mrs Littlejohn's yard and run up the front steps and crash once on the wooden veranda and vanish through the front door. Eck and the boy ran up onto the veranda. A lamp sat on a table just inside the door. In its mellow light they saw the horse fill the long hallway like a pinwheel, gaudy, furious and thunderous. A little further down the hall there was a varnished yellow melodeon. The horse crashed into it; it produced a single note, almost a chord, in bass, resonant and grave, of deep and sober astonishment; the horse with its monstrous and antic shadow whirled again and vanished through another door. It was a bedroom; Ratliff, in his underclothes and one sock and with the other sock in his hand and his back to the door, was leaning out the open window facing the lane, the lot. He looked back over his shoulder. For an instant he and the horse glared at one another. Then he sprang through the window as the horse backed out of the room and into the hall again and whirled and saw Eck and the little boy just entering the front door, Eck still carrying his rope. It whirled again and rushed on down the hall and onto the back porch just as Mrs Littlejohn, carrying an armful of clothes from the line and the washboard, mounted the steps.

"Get out of here, you son of a bitch," she said. She struck with the washboard; it divided neatly on the long mad face and the horse whirled and rushed back up the hall, where Eck and the boy now stood.

"Get to hell out of here, Wall!" Eck roared. He dropped to the floor, covering his head with his arms. The boy did not move, and for the third time the horse soared above the unwinking eyes and the unbowed and untouched head and onto the front veranda again just as Ratliff, still carrying the sock, ran around the corner of the house and up the steps. The horse whirled without breaking or pausing. It galloped to the end of the veranda and took the railing and soared outward, hobgoblin and floating, in the moon. It landed in the lot still running and crossed the lot and galloped through the wrecked gate and among the overturned wagons and the still intact one in which Henry's wife still sat, and on down the lane and into the road.

A quarter of a mile further on, the road gashed pallid and moony between the moony shadows of the bordering trees, the horse still galloping, galloping its shadow into the dust, the road descending now toward the creek and the bridge. It was of wood, just wide enough for a single vehicle. When the horse reached it, it was occupied by a wagon coming from the opposite direction and drawn by two mules already asleep in the harness and the soporific motion. On the seat were Tull and his wife, in splint chairs in the wagon behind them sat their four daughters, all returning belated from an all-day visit with some of Mrs Tull's kin. The horse neither checked nor swerved. It crashed once on the wooden bridge and rushed between the two mules which waked lunging in opposite directions in the traces, the horse now apparently scrambling along the wagon-tongue itself like a mad squirrel and scrabbling at the end-gate of the wagon with its forefeet as if it intended to climb into the wagon while Tull shouted at it and struck at its face with his whip. The mules were now trying to turn the wagon around in the middle of the bridge. It slewed and tilted, the bridge-rail cracked with a sharp report above the shrieks of the women; the horse scrambled at last across the back of one of the mules and Tull stood up in the wagon and kicked at its face. Then the front end of the wagon rose, flinging Tull, the reins now wrapped several times about his wrist, backward into the wagon bed among the overturned chairs and exposed stockings and under-garments of his women. The pony scrambled free and crashed again on the wooden planking, galloping again. The wagon lurched again; the mules had finally turned it on the bridge where there was not room for it to turn and were now kicking themselves free of the traces. When they came free, they snatched Tull bodily out of the wagon. He struck the bridge on his face and was dragged for several feet before the wrist-wrapped reins broke. Far up the road now, distancing the frantic mules, the pony faded on. While the five women still shrieked above Tull's unconscious body, Eck and the little boy came up, trotting, Eck still carrying his rope. He was panting. "Which way'd he go?" he said.

In the now empty and moon-drenched lot, his wife and Mrs Littlejohn and Ratliff and Lump Snopes, the clerk, and three other men raised Henry out of the trampled dust and carried him into Mrs Littlejohn's back yard. His face was blanched and stony, his eyes were closed, the weight of his head tautened his throat across the protruding larynx; his teeth glinted dully beneath his lifted lip. They carried him on toward the house, through the dappled shade of the chinaberry trees. Across the dreaming and silver night a faint sound like remote thunder came and ceased. "There's one of them on the creek bridge," one of the men said.

"It's that one of Eck Snopes's," another said. "The one that was in the house." Mrs Littlejohn had preceded them into the hall.

When they entered with Henry, she had already taken the lamp from the table and she stood beside an open door, holding the lamp high.

"Bring him in here," she said. She entered the room first and set the lamp on the dresser. They followed with clumsy scufflings and pantings and laid Henry on the bed and Mrs Littlejohn came to the bed and stood looking down at Henry's peaceful and bloodless face. "I'll declare," she said. "You men." They had drawn back a little, clumped, shifting from one foot to another, not looking at her nor at his wife either, who stood at the foot of the bed, motionless, her hands folded into her dress. "You all get out of here, V. K.," she said to Ratliff. "Go outside. See if you cant find something else to play with that will kill some more of you."

"All right," Ratliff said. "Come on boys. Aint no more horses to catch in here." They followed him toward the door, on tiptoe, their shoes scuffling, their shadows monstrous on the wall.

"Go get Will Varner," Mrs Littlejohn said. "I reckon you can tell him it's still a mule." They went out; they didn't look back. They tiptoed up the hall and crossed the veranda and descended into the moonlight. Now that they could pay attention to it, the silver air seemed to be filled with faint and sourceless sounds—shouts, thin and distant, again a brief thunder of hooves on a wooden bridge, more shouts faint and thin and earnest and clear as bells; once they even distinguished the words: "Whooey. Head him."

"He went through that house quick," Ratliff said. "He must have found another woman at home." Then Henry screamed in the house behind them. They looked back into the dark hall where a square of light fell through the bedroom door, listening while the scream sank into a harsh respiration: "Ah. Ah. Ah" on a rising note about to become screaming again. "Come on," Ratliff said. "We better get Varner." They went up the road in a body, treading the moon-blanched dust in the tremulous April night murmurous with the moving of sap and the wet bursting of burgeoning leaf and bud and constant with the thin and urgent cries and the brief and fading bursts of galloping hooves. Varner's house was dark, blank and without depth in the moonlight. They stood, clumped darkly in the silver yard and called up at the blank windows until suddenly someone was standing in one of them. It was Flem Snopes's wife. She was in a white garment; the heavy braided club of her hair looked almost black against it. She did not lean out, she merely stood there, full in the moon, apparently blank-eyed or certainly not looking downward at them—the heavy gold hair, the mask not tragic and perhaps not even doomed: just damned, the strong faint lift of breasts beneath marblelike fall of the garment; to those below what Brunhilde, what Rhinemaiden on what spurious river-rock of papier-mâché, what Helen returned to what topless and shoddy Argos, waiting for no one. "Evening, Mrs Snopes," Ratliff said. "We want Uncle Will. Henry Armstid is hurt at Mrs Littlejohn's." She vanished from the window. They waited in the moonlight, listening to the faint remote shouts and cries, until Varner emerged, sooner than they had actually expected, hunching into his coat and buttoning his trousers over the tail of his nightshirt, his suspenders still dangling in twin loops below the coat. He was carrying the battered bag which contained the plumber-like tools with which he drenched and wormed and blistered and floated or drew the teeth of horses and mules; he came down the steps, lean and loose-jointed, his shrewd ruthless head cocked a little as he listened also to the faint bell-like cries and shouts with which the silver air was full.

"Are they still trying to catch them rabbits?" he said.

"All of them except Henry Armstid," Ratliff said. "He caught his."

"Hah," Varner said. "That you, V. K.? How many did you buy?"

"I was too late," Ratliff said. "I never got back in time."

"Hah," Varner said. They moved on to the gate and into the road again. "Well, it's a good bright cool night for running them." The moon was now high overhead, a pearled and mazy yawn in the soft sky, the ultimate ends of which rolled onward, whorl on whorl, beyond the pale stars and by pale stars surrounded. They walked in a close clump, tramping their shadows into the road's mild dust, blotting the shadows of the burgeoning trees which soared, trunk branch and twig against the pale sky, delicate and finely thinned. They passed the dark store. Then the pear tree came in sight. It rose in mazed and silver immobility like exploding snow; the mockingbird still sang in it. "Look at that tree," Varner said. "It ought to make this year, sho."

"Corn'll make this year too," one said.

"A moon like this is good for every growing thing outen earth," Varner said. "I mind when me and Mrs Varner was expecting Eula. Already had a mess of children and maybe we ought to quit then. But I wanted some more gals. Others had done married and moved away, and a passel of boys, soon as they get big enough to be worth anything, they aint got time to work. Got to set around store and talk. But a gal will stay home and work until she does get married. So there was a old woman told my mammy once that if a woman showed her belly to the full moon after she had done caught, it would be a gal. So Mrs Varner taken and laid every night with the moon on her nekid belly, until it fulled and after. I could lay my ear to her belly and hear Eula kicking and scrouging like all get-out, feeling the moon."

"You mean it actually worked sho enough, Uncle Will?" the other said.

"Hah," Varner said. "You might try it. You get enough women showing their nekid bellies to the moon or the sun either or even just to your hand fumbling around often enough and more than likely after a while there will be something in it you can lay your ear and listen to, provided something come up and you aint got away by that time. Hah, V. K.?" Someone guffawed.

"Dont ask me," Ratliff said. "I cant even get nowhere in time to buy a cheap horse." Two or three guffawed this time. Then they began to hear Henry's respirations from the house: "Ah. Ah. Ah." and they ceased abruptly, as if they had not been aware of their closeness to it. Varner walked on in front, lean, shambling, yet moving quite rapidly, though his head was still slanted with listening as the faint, urgent, indomitable cries murmured in the silver lambence, sourceless, at times almost musical, like fading bell-notes; again there was a brief rapid thunder of hooves on wooden planking.

"There's another one on the creek bridge," one said.

"They are going to come out even on them things, after all," Varner said. "They'll get the money back in exercise and relaxation. You take a man that aint got no other relaxation all year long except dodging mule-dung up and down a field furrow. And a night like this one, when a man aint old enough yet to lay still and sleep, and yet he aint young enough anymore to be tomcatting in and out of other folks' back windows, something like this is good for him. It'll make him sleep tomorrow night anyhow, provided he gets back home by then. If we had just knowed about this in time, we could have trained up a pack of horse-dogs. Then we could have held one of these field trials."

"That's one way to look at it, I reckon," Ratliff said. "In fact, it might be a considerable comfort to Bookwright and Quick and Freeman and Eck Snopes and them other new horse-owners if that side of it could be brought to their attention, because the chances are aint none of them thought to look at it in that light yet. Probably there aint a one of them that believes now there's any cure a-tall for that Texas disease Flem Snopes and that Dead-eye Dick brought here."

"Hah," Varner said. He opened Mrs Littlejohn's gate. The dim light still fell outward across the hall from the bedroom door; beyond it, Armstid was saying "Ah. Ah. Ah" steadily. "There's a pill for every ill but the last one."

"Even if there was always time to take it," Ratliff said.

"Hah," Varner said again. He glanced back at Ratliff for an instant, pausing. But the little hard bright eyes were invisible now; it was only the bushy overhang of the brows which seemed to concentrate downward toward him in writhen immobility, not frowning but with a sort of fierce risibility. "Even if there was time to take it. Breathing is a sight-draft dated yesterday."

At nine oclock on the second morning after that, five men were sitting or squatting along the gallery of the store. The sixth was Ratliff. He was standing up, and talking: "Maybe there wasn't but one of them things in Mrs Littlejohn's house that night, like Eck says. But it was the biggest drove of just one horse I ever seen. It was in my room and it was on the front porch and I could hear Mrs Littlejohn hitting it over the head with that washboard in the back yard all at the same time. And still it was missing everybody everytime. I reckon that's what that Texas man meant by calling them bargains: that a man would need to be powerful unlucky to ever get close enough to one of them to get hurt." They laughed, all except Eck himself. He and the little boy were eating. When they mounted the steps, Eck had gone on into the store and emerged with a paper sack, from which he took a segment of cheese and with his pocket knife divided it carefully into two exact halves and gave one to the boy and took a handful of crackers from the sack and gave them to the boy, and now they squatted against the wall, side by side and, save for the difference in size, identical, eating.

"I wonder what that horse thought Ratliff was," one said. He held a spray of peach bloom between his teeth. It bore four blossoms like miniature ballet skirts of pink tulle. "Jumping out windows and running indoors in his shirt-tail? I wonder how many Ratliffs that horse thought he saw."

"I dont know," Ratliff said. "But if he saw just half as many of me as I saw of him, he was sholy surrounded. Everytime I turned my head, that thing was just running over me or just swirling to run back over that boy again. And that boy there, he stayed right under it one time to my certain knowledge for a full one-and-one-half minutes without ducking his head or even batting his eyes. Yes sir, when I looked around and seen that varmint in the door behind me blaring its eyes at me, I'd a made sho Flem Snopes had brought a tiger back from Texas except I knowed that couldn't no just one tiger completely fill a entire room." They laughed again, quietly. Lump Snopes, the clerk, sitting in the only chair tilted back against the door-facing and partly blocking the entrance, cackled suddenly.

"If Flem had knowed how quick you fellows was going to snap them horses up, he'd a probably brought some tigers," he said. "Monkeys too."

"So they was Flem's horses," Ratliff said. The laughter stopped. The other three had open knives in their hands, with which they had been trimming idly at chips and slivers of wood. Now they sat apparently absorbed in the delicate and almost tedious movements of the knife-blades. The clerk had looked quickly up and found Ratliff watching him. His constant expression of incorrigible and mirthful disbelief had left him now; only the empty wrinkles of it remained about his mouth and eyes.

"Has Flem ever said they was?" he said. "But you town fellows are smarter than us country folks. Likely you done already read Flem's mind." But Ratliff was not looking at him now.

"And I reckon we'd a bought them," he said. He stood above them again, easy, intelligent, perhaps a little sombre but still perfectly impenetrable. "Eck here, for instance. With a wife and family to support. He owns two of them, though to be sho he never had to pay money for but one. I heard folks chasing them things up until midnight last night, but Eck and that boy aint been home a-tall in two days." They laughed again, except Eck. He pared off a bite of cheese and speared it on the knife-point and put it into his mouth.

"Eck caught one of hisn," the second man said.

"That so?" Ratliff said. "Which one was it, Eck? The one he give you or the one you bought?"

"The one he give me," Eck said, chewing.

"Well, well," Ratliff said. "I hadn't heard about that. But Eck's still one horse short. And the one he had to pay money for. Which is pure proof enough that them horses wasn't Flem's because wouldn't no man even give his own blood kin something he couldn't even catch." They laughed again, but they stopped when the clerk spoke. There was no mirth in his voice at all.

"Listen," he said. "All right. We done all admitted you are too smart for anybody to get ahead of. You never bought no horse from Flem or nobody else, so maybe it aint none of your business and maybe you better just leave it at that."

"Sholy," Ratliff said. "It's done already been left at that two nights ago. The fellow that forgot to shut that lot gate done that. With the exception of Eck's horse. And we know that wasn't Flem's, because that horse was give to Eck for nothing."

"There's others besides Eck that aint got back home yet," the man with the peach spray said. "Bookwright and Quick are still chasing theirs. They was reported three miles west of Burtsboro Old Town at eight oclock last night. They aint got close enough to it yet to tell which one it belongs to."

"Sholy," Ratliff said. "The only new horse-owner in this country that could a been found without bloodhounds since whoever it was left that gate open two nights ago, is Henry Armstid. He's laying right there in Mrs Littlejohn's bedroom where he can watch the lot so that any time the one he bought happens to run back into it, all he's got to do is to holler at his wife to run out with the rope and catch it—" He ceased, though he said, "Morning, Flem," so immediately afterward and with no change whatever in tone, that the pause was not even discernible. With the exception of the clerk, who sprang up, vacated the chair with a sort of servile alacrity, and Eck and the little boy who continued to eat, they watched above their stilled hands as Snopes in the gray trousers and the minute tie and the new cap with its bright overplaid mounted the steps. He was chewing; he already carried a piece of white pine board; he jerked his head at them, looking at nobody, and took the vacated chair and opened his knife and began to whittle. The clerk now leaned in the opposite side of the door, rubbing his back against the facing. The expression of merry and invincible disbelief had returned to his face, with a quality watchful and secret.

"You're just in time," he said. "Ratliff here seems to be in a considerable sweat about who actually owned them horses." Snopes drew his knife-blade neatly along the board, the neat, surgeon-like sliver curling before it. The others were whittling again, looking carefully at nothing, except Eck and the boy, who were still eating, and the clerk rubbing his back against the door-facing and watching Snopes with that secret and alert intensity. "Maybe you could put his mind at rest." Snopes turned his head slightly and spat, across the gallery and the steps and into the dust beyond them. He drew the knife back and began another curling sliver.

"He was there too," Snopes said. "He knows as much as anybody else." This time the clerk guffawed, chortling, his features gathering toward the center of his face as though plucked there by a hand. He slapped his leg, cackling.

"You might as well to quit," he said. "You cant beat him."

"I reckon not," Ratliff said. He stood above them, not looking at any of them, his gaze fixed apparently on the empty road beyond Mrs Littlejohn's house, impenetrable, brooding even. A hulking, half-grown boy in overalls too small for him, appeared suddenly from nowhere in particular. He stood for a while in the road, just beyond spitting-range of the gallery, with that air of having come from nowhere in particular and of not knowing where he would go next when he should move again and of not being troubled by that fact. He was looking at nothing, certainly not toward the gallery, and no one on the gallery so much as looked at him except the little boy, who now watched the boy in the road, his periwinkle eyes grave and steady above the bitten cracker in his halted hand. The boy in the road moved on, thickly undulant in the tight overalls, and vanished beyond the corner of the store, the round head and the unwinking eyes of the little boy on the gallery turning steadily to watch him out of sight. Then the little boy bit the cracker again, chewing. "Of course there's Mrs Tull," Ratliff said. "But that's Eck she's going to sue for damaging Tull against that bridge. And as for Henry Armstid—"

"If a man aint got gumption enough to protect himself, it's his own look-out," the clerk said.

"Sholy," Ratliff said, still in that dreamy, abstracted tone, actually speaking over his shoulder even. "And Henry Armstid, that's all right because from what I hear of the conversation that taken place, Henry had already stopped owning that horse he thought was his before that Texas man left. And as for that broke leg, that wont put him out none because his wife can make his crop." The clerk had ceased to rub his back against the door. He watched the back of Ratliff's head, unwinking too, sober and intent; he glanced at Snopes who, chewing, was watching another sliver curl away from the advancing knife-blade, then he watched the back of Ratliff's head again.

"It wont be the first time she has made their crop," the man with the peach spray said. Ratliff glanced at him.

"You ought to know. This wont be the first time I ever saw you in their field, doing plowing Henry never got around to. How many days have you already given them this year?" The man with the peach spray removed it and spat carefully and put the spray back between his teeth.

"She can run a furrow straight as I can," the second said.

"They're unlucky," the third said. "When you are unlucky, it dont matter much what you do."

"Sholy," Ratliff said. "I've heard laziness called bad luck so much that maybe it is."

"He aint lazy," the third said. "When their mule died three or four years ago, him and her broke their land working time about in the traces with the other mule. They aint lazy."

"So that's all right," Ratliff said, gazing up the empty road again. "Likely she will begin right away to finish the plowing; that oldest gal is pretty near big enough to work with a mule, aint she? or at least to hold the plow steady while Mrs Armstid helps the mule?" He glanced again toward the man with the peach spray as though for an answer, but he was not looking at the other and he went on talking without any pause. The clerk stood with his rump and back pressed against the door-facing as if he had paused in the act of scratching, watching Ratliff quite hard now, unwinking. If Ratliff had looked at Flem Snopes, he would have seen nothing below the down-slanted peak of the cap save the steady motion of his jaws. Another sliver was curling with neat deliberation before the moving knife. "Plenty of time now because all she's got to do after she finishes washing Mrs Littlejohn's dishes and sweeping out the house to pay hers and Henry's board, is to go out home and milk and cook up enough vittles to last the children until tomorrow and feed them and get the littlest ones to sleep and wait outside the door until that biggest gal gets the bar up and gets into bed herself with the axe—"

"The axe?" the man with the peach spray said.

"She takes it to bed with her. She's just twelve, and what with this country still more or less full of them uncaught horses that never belonged to Flem Snopes, likely she feels maybe she cant swing a mere washboard like Mrs Littlejohn can. —and then come back and wash up the supper dishes. And after that, not nothing to do until morning except to stay close enough where Henry can call her until it's light enough to chop the wood to cook breakfast and then help Mrs Littlejohn wash the dishes and make the beds and sweep while watching the road. Because likely any time now Flem Snopes will get back from wherever he has been since the auction, which of course is to town naturally to see about his cousin that's got into a little legal trouble, and so get that five dollars. 'Only maybe he wont give it back to me,' she says, and maybe that's what Mrs Littlejohn thought too, because she never said nothing. I could hear her—"

"And where did you happen to be during all this?" the clerk said.

"Listening," Ratliff said. He glanced back at the clerk, then he was looking away again, almost standing with his back to them. "—could hear her dumping the dishes into the pan like she was throwing them at it. 'Do you reckon he will give it back to me?' Mrs Armstid says. 'That Texas man give it to him and said he would. All the folks there

saw him give Mr Snopes the money and heard him say I could get it
from Mr Snopes tomorrow.' Mrs Littlejohn was washing the dishes
now, washing them like a man would, like they was made out of iron.
'No,' she says. 'But asking him wont do no hurt.'—'If he wouldn't
give it back, it aint no use to ask,' Mrs Armstid says.—'Suit yourself,'
Mrs Littlejohn says. 'It's your money.' Then I couldn't hear nothing
but the dishes for a while. 'Do you reckon he might give it back to
me?' Mrs Armstid says. 'That Texas man said he would. They all
heard him say it.'—'Then go and ask him for it,' Mrs Littlejohn says.
Then I couldn't hear nothing but the dishes again. 'He wont give it
back to me,' Mrs Armstid says.—'All right,' Mrs Littlejohn says.
'Dont ask him, then.' Then I just heard the dishes. They would have
two pans, both washing. 'You dont reckon he would, do you?' Mrs
Armstid says. Mrs Littlejohn never said nothing. It sounded like she
was throwing the dishes at one another. 'Maybe I better go and talk
to Henry,' Mrs Armstid says.—'I would,' Mrs Littlejohn says. And I
be dog if it didn't sound exactly like she had two plates in her hands,
beating them together like these here brass bucket-lids in a band.
'Then Henry can buy another five-dollar horse with it. Maybe he'll
buy one next time that will out and out kill him. If I just thought he
would, I'd give him back that money, myself.'—'I reckon I better talk
to him first,' Mrs Armstid says. And then it sounded just like Mrs
Littlejohn taken up the dishes and pans and all and throwed the
whole business at the cookstove—" Ratliff ceased. Behind him the
clerk was hissing "Psst! Psst! Flem. Flem!" Then he stopped, and all
of them watched Mrs Armstid approach and mount the steps, gaunt
in the shapeless gray garment, the stained tennis shoes hissing faintly
on the boards. She came among them and stood, facing Snopes but
not looking at anyone, her hands rolled into her apron.

"He said that day he wouldn't sell Henry that horse," she said in
a flat toneless voice. "He said you had the money and I could get it
from you." Snopes raised his head and turned it slightly again and
spat neatly past the woman, across the gallery and into the road.

"He took all the money with him when he left," he said. Motionless, the gray garment hanging in rigid, almost formal folds like drap-
ery in bronze, Mrs Armstid appeared to be watching something near
Snopes's feet, as though she had not heard him, or as if she had quit-

ted her body as soon as she finished speaking and although her body, hearing, had received the words, they would have no life nor meaning until she returned. The clerk was rubbing his back steadily against the door-facing again, watching her. The little boy was watching her too with his unwinking ineffable gaze, but nobody else was. The man with the peach spray removed it and spat and put the twig back into his mouth.

"He said Henry hadn't bought no horse," she said. "He said I could get the money from you."

"I reckon he forgot it," Snopes said. "He took all the money away with him when he left." He watched her a moment longer, then he trimmed again at the stick. The clerk rubbed his back gently against the door, watching her. After a time Mrs Armstid raised her head and looked up the road where it went on, mild with spring dust, past Mrs Littlejohn's, beginning to rise, on past the not-yet-bloomed (that would be in June) locust grove across the way, on past the schoolhouse, the weathered roof of which, rising beyond an orchard of peach and pear trees, resembled a hive swarmed about by a cloud of pink-and-white bees, ascending, mounting toward the crest of the hill where the church stood among its sparse gleam of marble headstones in the sombre cedar grove where during the long afternoons of summer the constant mourning doves called back and forth. She moved; once more the rubber soles hissed on the gnawed boards.

"I reckon it's about time to get dinner started," she said.

"How's Henry this morning, Mrs Armstid?" Ratliff said. She looked at him, pausing, the blank eyes waking for an instant.

"He's resting, I thank you kindly," she said. Then the eyes died again and she moved again. Snopes rose from the chair, closing his knife with his thumb and brushing a litter of minute shavings from his lap.

"Wait a minute," he said. Mrs Armstid paused again, half-turning, though still not looking at Snopes nor at any of them. Because she *cant possibly actually believe it*, Ratliff told himself. *Any more than I do.* Snopes entered the store, the clerk, motionless again, his back and rump pressed against the door-facing as though waiting to start rubbing again, watched him enter, his head turning as the other passed him like the head of an owl, the little eyes blinking rapidly now. Jody Varner came up the road on his horse. He did not pass but instead turned in beside the store, toward the mulberry tree behind it where he was in the habit of hitching his horse. A wagon came up the road, creaking past. The man driving it lifted his hand; one or two of the men on the gallery lifted theirs in response. The wagon went on. Mrs Armstid looked after it. Snopes came out of the door carrying a small striped paper bag and approached Mrs Armstid. "Here," he said. Her hand turned just enough to receive it. "A little sweetening for the chaps," he said. His other hand was already in his pocket, and as he turned back to the chair, he drew something from his pocket and handed it to the clerk, who took it. It was a five-cent piece. He sat down in the chair and tilted it back against the door again. He now had the knife in his hand again, already open. He turned his head slightly and spat again, neatly past the gray garment, into the road. The little boy was watching the sack in Mrs Armstid's hand. Then she seemed to discover it also, rousing.

"You're right kind," she said. She rolled the sack into the apron, the little boy's unwinking gaze fixed upon the lump her hands made beneath the cloth. She moved again. "I reckon I better get on and help with dinner," she said. She descended the steps, though as soon as she reached the level earth and began to retreat, the gray folds of the garment once more lost all inference and intimation of locomotion, so that she seemed to progress without motion like a figure on a retreating and diminishing float; a gray and blasted tree-trunk moving, somehow intact and upright, upon an unhurried flood. The clerk in the doorway cackled suddenly, explosively, chortling. He slapped his thigh.

"By God," he said, "you cant beat him."

Jody Varner, entering the store from the rear, paused in midstride like a pointing bird-dog. Then, on tiptoe, in complete silence and with astonishing speed, he darted behind the counter and sped up the gloomy tunnel, at the end of which a hulking, bear-shaped figure stooped, its entire head and shoulders wedged into the glass case which contained the needles and thread and snuff and tobacco and the stale gaudy candy. He snatched the boy savagely and viciously out; the boy gave a choked cry and struggled flabbily, cramming a final handful of something into his mouth, chewing. But he ceased to struggle almost at once and became slack and inert save for his jaws. Varner dragged him around the counter as the clerk entered, seemed to bounce suddenly into the store with a sort of alert concern. "You, Saint Elmo!" he said.

"Aint I told you and told you to keep him out of here?" Varner demanded, shaking the boy. "He's damn near eaten that candy-case clean. Stand up!" The boy hung like a half-filled sack from Varner's hand, chewing with a kind of fatalistic desperation, the eyes shut tight in the vast flaccid colorless face, the ears moving steadily and faintly to the chewing. Save for the jaw and the ears, he appeared to have gone to sleep chewing.

"You, Saint Elmo!" the clerk said. "Stand up!" The boy assumed his own weight, though he did not open his eyes yet nor cease to chew. Varner released him. "Git on home," the clerk said. The boy turned obediently to re-enter the store. Varner jerked him about again.

"Not that way," he said. The boy crossed the gallery and descended the steps, the tight overalls undulant and reluctant across his flabby thighs. Before he reached the ground, his hand rose from his pocket to his mouth; again his ears moved faintly to the motion of chewing.

"He's worse than a rat, aint he?" the clerk said.

"Rat, hell," Varner said, breathing harshly. "He's worse than a goat. First thing I know, he'll graze on back and work through that lace leather and them hame-strings and lap-links and ring-bolts and eat me and you and him all three clean out the back door. And then be damned if I wouldn't be afraid to turn my back for fear he would cross the road and start in on the gin and the blacksmith shop. Now you mind what I say. If I catch him hanging around here one more time, I'm going to set a bear-trap for him." He went out onto the gallery, the clerk following. "Morning, gentlemen," he said.

"Who's that one, Jody?" Ratliff said. Save for the clerk in the background, they were the only two standing, and now, in juxtaposition, you could see the resemblance between them—a resemblance intangible, indefinite, not in figure, speech, dress, intelligence; certainly not in morals. Yet it was there, but with this bridgeless difference, this hallmark of his fate upon him: he would become an old man;

Ratliff, too: but an old man who at about sixty-five would be caught and married by a creature not yet seventeen probably, who would for the rest of his life continue to take revenge upon him for her whole sex; Ratliff, never. The boy was moving without haste up the road. His hand rose again from his pocket to his mouth.

"That boy of I. O.'s," Varner said. "By God, I've done everything but put out poison for him."

"What?" Ratliff said. He glanced quickly about at the faces; for an instant there was in his own not only bewilderment but something almost like terror. "I thought—the other day you fellows told me— You said it was a woman, a young woman with a baby—Here now," he said. "Wait."

"This here's another one," Varner said. "I wish to hell he couldn't walk. Well, Eck, I hear you caught one of your horses."

"That's right," Eck said. He and the little boy had finished the crackers and cheese and he had sat for some time now, holding the empty bag.

"It was the one he give you, wasn't it?" Varner said.

"That's right," Eck said.

"Give the other one to me, paw," the little boy said.

"What happened?" Varner said.

"He broke his neck," Eck said.

"I know," Varner said. "But how?" Eck did not move. Watching him, they could almost see him visibly gathering and arranging words, speech. Varner, looking down at him, began to laugh steadily and harshly, sucking his teeth. "I'll tell you what happened. Eck and that boy finally run it into that blind lane of Freeman's, after a chase of about twenty-four hours. They figured it couldn't possibly climb them eight-foot fences of Freeman's so him and the boy tied their rope across the end of the lane, about three feet off the ground. And sho enough, soon as the horse come to the end of the lane and seen Freeman's barn, it whirled just like Eck figured it would and come helling back up that lane like a scared hen-hawk. It probably never even seen the rope at all. Mrs Freeman was watching from where she had run up onto the porch. She said that when it hit that rope, it looked just like one of these here great big Christmas pinwheels. But the one you bought got clean away, didn't it?"

"That's right," Eck said. "I never had time to see which way the other one went."

"Give him to me, paw," the little boy said.

"You wait till we catch him," Eck said. "We'll see about it then."

That afternoon Ratliff sat in the halted buckboard in front of Bookwright's gate. Bookwright stood in the road beside it. "You were wrong," Bookwright said. "He come back."

"He come back," Ratliff said. "I misjudged his . . . nerve aint the word I want, and sholy lack of it aint. But I wasn't wrong."

"Nonsense," Bookwright said. "He was gone all day yesterday. Nobody saw him going to town or coming back, but that's bound to be where he was at. Aint no man, I dont care if his name is Snopes, going to let his own blood kin rot in jail."

"He wont be in jail long. Court is next month, and after they send him to Parchman, he can stay outdoors again. He will even go back to farming, plowing. Of course it wont be his cotton, but then he never did make enough out of his own cotton to quite pay him for staying alive."

"Nonsense," Bookwright said. "I dont believe it. Flem aint going to let him go to the penitentiary."

"Yes," Ratliff said. "Because Flem Snopes has got to cancel all them loose-flying notes that turns up here and there every now and then. He's going to discharge at least some of them notes for good and all." They looked at one another—Ratliff grave and easy in the blue shirt, Bookwright sober too, black-browed, intent.

"I thought you said you and him burned them notes."

"I said we burned two notes that Mink Snopes gave me. Do you think that any Snopes is going to put all of anything on one piece of paper that can be destroyed by one match? Do you think there is any Snopes that dont know that?"

"Oh," Bookwright said. "Hah," he said, with no mirth. "I reckon you gave Henry Armstid back his five dollars too." Then Ratliff looked away. His face changed—something fleeting, quizzical, but not smiling, his eyes did not smile; it was gone.

"I could have," he said. "But I didn't. I might have if I could just been sho he would buy something this time that would sho enough kill him, like Mrs Littlejohn said. Besides, I wasn't protecting a

Snopes from Snopeses; I wasn't even protecting a people from a
Snopes. I was protecting something that wasn't even a people, that
wasn't nothing but something that dont want nothing but to walk
and feel the sun and wouldn't know how to hurt no man even if it
would and wouldn't want to even if it could, just like I wouldn't
stand by and see you steal a meat-bone from a dog. I never made
them Snopeses and I never made the folks that cant wait to bare
their backsides to them. I could do more, but I wont. I wont, I tell
you!"

"All right," Bookwright said. "Hook your drag up; it aint nothing
but a hill. I said it's all right."

2

The two actions of Armstid pl. vs. Snopes, and Tull pl. vs. Eckrum
Snopes (and anyone else named Snopes or Varner either which Tull's
irate wife could contrive to involve, as the village well knew) were
accorded a change of venue by mutual agreement and arrangement
among the litigants. Three of the parties did, that is, because Flem
Snopes flatly refused to recognise the existence of the suit against
himself, stating once and without heat and first turning his head
slightly aside to spit, "They wasn't none of my horses," then fell to
whittling again while the baffled and helpless bailiff stood before the
tilted chair with the papers he was trying to serve.

"What a opportunity for that Snopes family lawyer this would a
been," Ratliff said when told about it. "What's his name? that quick-
fatherer, the Moses with his mouth full of mottoes and his coat-tail
full of them already half-grown retroactive sons? I dont understand
yet how a man that has to spend as much time as I do being constantly reminded of them folks, still cant keep the names straight.
I. O. That he never had time to wait. This here would be probably
the one tried case in his whole legal existence where he wouldn't be
bothered with no narrow-ideaed client trying to make him stop talking, and the squire presiding himself would be the only man in company with authority to tell him to shut up."

So neither did the Varner surrey nor Ratliff's buckboard make one among the wagons, the buggies, and the saddled horses and mules which moved out of the village on that May Saturday morning, to converge upon Whiteleaf store eight miles away, coming not only from Frenchman's Bend but from other directions too since by that time, what Ratliff had called 'that Texas sickness,' that spotted corruption of frantic and uncatchable horses, had spread as far as twenty and thirty miles. So by the time the Frenchman's Bend people began to arrive, there were two dozen wagons, the teams reversed and eased of harness and tied to the rear wheels in order to pass the day, and twice that many saddled animals already standing about the locust grove beside the store and the site of the hearing had already been transferred from the store to an adjacent shed where in the fall cotton would be stored. But by nine oclock it was seen that even the shed would not hold them all, so the palladium was moved again, from the shed to the grove itself. The horses and mules and wagons were cleared from it; the single chair, the gnawed table bearing a thick Bible which had the appearance of loving and constant use of a piece of old and perfectly-kept machinery and an almanac and a copy of Mississippi Reports dated 1881 and bearing along its opening edge a single thread-thin line of soilure as if during all the time of his possession its owner (or user) had opened it at only one page though that quite often, were fetched from the shed to the grove; a wagon and four men were dispatched and returned presently from the church a mile away with four wooden pews for the litigants and their clansmen and witnesses; behind these in turn the spectators stood—the men, the women, the children, sober, attentive, and neat, not in their Sunday clothes to be sure, but in the clean working garments donned that morning for the Saturday's diversion of sitting about the country stores or trips into the county seat, and in which they would return to the field on Monday morning and would wear all that week until Friday night came round again. The Justice of the Peace was a neat, small, plump old man resembling a tender caricature of all grandfathers who ever breathed, in a beautifully laundered though collarless white shirt with immaculate starch-gleaming cuffs and bosom, and steel-framed spectacles and neat, faintly curling white hair. He sat behind the table and looked at them—at the gray woman in the gray sunbonnet and dress, her clasped and motionless hands on her lap resembling a gnarl of pallid and drowned roots from a drained swamp; at Tull in his faded but absolutely clean shirt and the overalls which his womenfolks not only kept immaculately washed but starched and ironed also, and not creased through the legs but flat across them from seam to seam, so that on each Saturday morning they resembled the short pants of a small boy, and the sedate and innocent blue of his eyes above the month-old corn-silk beard which concealed most of his abraded face and which gave him an air of incredible and paradoxical dissoluteness, not as though at last and without warning he had appeared in the sight of his fellow-men in his true character, but as if an old Italian portrait of a child saint had been defaced by a vicious and idle boy; at Mrs Tull, a strong, full-bosomed though slightly dumpy woman with an expression of grim and seething outrage which the elapsed four weeks had apparently neither increased nor diminished but had merely set, an outrage which curiously and almost at once began to give the impression of being directed not at any Snopes or at any other man in particular but at all men, all males, and of which Tull himself was not at all the victim but the subject, who sat on one side of her husband while the biggest of the four daughters sat on the other as if they (or Mrs Tull at least) were not so much convinced that Tull might leap up and flee, as determined that he would not; and at Eck and the little boy, identical save for size, and Lump the clerk in a gray cap which someone actually recognised as being the one which Flem Snopes had worn when he went to Texas last year, who between spells of rapid blinking would sit staring at the Justice with the lidless intensity of a rat—and into the lens-distorted and irisless old-man's eyes of the Justice there grew an expression not only of amazement and bewilderment but, as in Ratliff's eyes while he stood on the store gallery four weeks ago, something very like terror.

"This—" he said. "I didn't expect—I didn't look to see—. I'm going to pray," he said. "I aint going to pray aloud. But I hope—" He looked at them. "I wish . . . Maybe some of you all anyway had better do the same." He bowed his head. They watched him, quiet and grave, while he sat motionless behind the table, the light morning wind moving faintly in his thin hair and the shadow-stipple of windy leaves gliding and flowing across the starched bulge of bosom and the gleaming bone-buttoned cuffs, as rigid and almost as large as sections of six-inch stovepipe, at his joined hands. He raised his head. "Armstid against Snopes," he said. Mrs Armstid spoke. She did not move, she looked at nothing, her hands clasped in her lap, speaking in that flat, toneless and hopeless voice:

"That Texas man said —"

"Wait," the Justice said. He looked about at the faces, the blurred eyes fleeing behind the thick lenses. "Where is the defendant? I dont see him."

"He wouldn't come," the bailiff said.

"Wouldn't come?" the Justice said. "Didn't you serve the papers on him?"

"He wouldn't take them," the bailiff said. "He said—"

"Then he is in contempt!" the Justice cried.

"What for?" Lump Snopes said. "Aint nobody proved yet they was his horses." The Justice looked at him.

"Are you representing the defendant?" he said. Snopes blinked at him for a moment.

"What's that mean?" he said. "That you aim for me to pay whatever fine you think you can clap onto him?"

"So he refuses to defend himself," the Justice said. "Dont he know that I can find against him for that reason, even if pure justice and decency aint enough?"

"It'll be pure something," Snopes said. "It dont take no mind-reader to see how your mind is—"

"Shut up, Snopes," the bailiff said. "If you aint in this case, you keep out of it." He turned back to the Justice. "What you want me to do: go over to the Bend and fetch Snopes here anyway? I reckon I can do it."

"No," the Justice said. "Wait." He looked about at the sober faces again with that bafflement, that dread. "Does anybody here know for sho who them horses belonged to? Anybody?" They looked back at him, sober, attentive—at the neat immaculate old man sitting with his hands locked together on the table before him to still the trembling. "All right, Mrs Armstid," he said. "Tell the Court what happened." She told it, unmoving, in the flat, inflectionless voice,

looking at nothing, while they listened quietly, coming to the end
and ceasing without even any fall of voice, as though the tale mattered nothing and came to nothing. The Justice was looking down
at his hands. When she ceased, he looked up at her. "But you haven't
showed yet that Snopes owned the horses. The one you want to sue
is that Texas man. And he's gone. If you got a judgment against him,
you couldn't collect the money. Dont you see?"

"Mr Snopes brought him here," Mrs Armstid said. "Likely that
Texas man wouldn't have knowed where Frenchman's Bend was if
Mr Snopes hadn't showed him."

"But it was the Texas man that sold the horses and collected the
money for them." The Justice looked about again at the faces. "Is
that right? You, Bookwright, is that what happened?"

"Yes," Bookwright said. The Justice looked at Mrs Armstid again,
with that pity and grief. As the morning increased the wind had risen,
so that from time to time gusts of it ran through the branches overhead, bringing a faint snow of petals, prematurely bloomed as the
spring itself had condensed with spendthrift speed after the hard
winter, and the heavy and drowsing scent of them, about the motionless heads.

"He give Mr Snopes Henry's money. He said Henry hadn't
bought no horse. He said I could get the money from Mr Snopes
tomorrow."

"And you have witnesses that saw and heard him?"

"Yes, sir. The other men that was there saw him give Mr Snopes
the money and say that I could get it—"

"And you asked Snopes for the money?"

"Yes, sir. He said that Texas man taken it away with him when he
left. But I would . . ." She ceased again, perhaps looking down at her
hands also. Certainly she was not looking at anyone.

"Yes?" the Justice said. "You would what?"

"I would know them five dollars. I earned them myself, weaving at
night after Henry and the chaps was asleep. Some of the ladies in Jefferson would save up string and such and give it to me and I would
weave things and sell them. I earned that money a little at a time and
I would know it when I saw it because I would take the can outen

the chimney and count it now and then while it was making up to enough to buy my chaps some shoes for next winter. I would know it if I was to see it again. If Mr Snopes would just let—"

"Suppose there was somebody seen Flem give that money back to that Texas fellow," Lump Snopes said suddenly.

"Did anybody here see that?" the Justice said.

"Yes," Snopes said, harshly and violently. "Eck here did." He looked at Eck. "Go on. Tell him." The Justice looked at Eck; the four Tull girls turned their heads as one head and looked at him, and Mrs Tull leaned forward to look past her husband, her face cold, furious, and contemptuous, and those standing shifted to look past one another's heads at Eck sitting motionless on the bench.

"Did you see Snopes give Armstid's money back to the Texas man, Eck?" the Justice said. Still Eck did not answer nor move. Lump Snopes made a gross violent sound through the side of his mouth.

"By God, I aint afraid to say it if Eck is. I seen him do it."

"Will you swear that as testimony?" Snopes looked at the Justice. He did not blink now.

"So you wont take my word," he said.

"I want the truth," the Justice said. "If I cant find that, I got to have sworn evidence of what I will have to accept as truth." He lifted the Bible from the two other books.

"All right," the bailiff said. "Step up here." Snopes rose from the bench and approached. They watched him, though now there was no shifting nor craning, no movement at all among the faces, the still eyes. Snopes at the table looked back at them once, his gaze traversing swiftly the crescent-shaped rank; he looked at the Justice again. The bailiff grasped the Bible; though the Justice did not release it yet.

"You are ready to swear you saw Snopes give that Texas man back the money he took from Henry Armstid for that horse?" he said.

"I said I was, didn't I?" Snopes said. The Justice released the Bible.

"Swear him," he said.

"Put your left hand on the Book raise your right hand you solemnly swear and affirm—" the bailiff said rapidly. But Snopes had already done so, his left hand clapped onto the extended Bible and the other hand raised and his head turned away as once more his gaze went rapidly along the circle of expressionless and intent faces, saying in that harsh and snarling voice:

"Yes. I saw Flem Snopes give back to that Texas man whatever money Henry Armstid or anybody else thinks Henry Armstid or anybody else paid Flem for any of them horses. Does that suit you?"

"Yes," the Justice said. Then there was no movement, no sound anywhere among them. The bailiff placed the Bible quietly on the table beside the Justice's locked hands, and there was no movement save the flow and recover of the windy shadows and the drift of the locust petals. Then Mrs Armstid rose; she stood once more (or still) looking at nothing, her hands clasped across her middle.

"I reckon I can go now, cant I?" she said.

"Yes," the Justice said, rousing. "Unless you would like—"

"I better get started," she said. "It's a right far piece." She had not come in the wagon, but on one of the gaunt and underfed mules. One of the men followed her across the grove and untied the mule for her and led it up to a wagon, from one hub of which she mounted. Then they looked at the Justice again. He sat behind the table, his hands still joined before him, though his head was not bowed now. Yet he did not move until the bailiff leaned and spoke to him, when he roused, came suddenly awake without starting, as an old man wakes from an old man's light sleep. He removed his hands from the table and, looking down, he spoke exactly as if he were reading from a paper:

"Tull against Snopes. Assault and—"

"Yes!" Mrs Tull said. "I'm going to say a word before you start." She leaned, looking past Tull at Lump Snopes again. "If you think you are going to lie and perjure Flem and Eck Snopes out of—"

"Now, mamma," Tull said. Now she spoke to Tull, without changing her position or her tone or even any break or pause in her speech:

"Dont you say hush to me! You'll let Eck Snopes or Flem Snopes or that whole Varner tribe snatch you out of the wagon and beat you half to death against a wooden bridge. But when it comes to suing them for your just rights and a punishment, oh no. Because that wouldn't be neighborly. What's neighborly got to do with you lying flat on your back in the middle of planting time while we pick splinters out of your face?" By this time the bailiff was shouting,

"Order! Order! This here's a law court!" Mrs Tull ceased. She sat back, breathing hard, staring at the Justice, who sat and spoke again as if he were reading aloud:

"—assault and battery on the person of Vernon Tull, through the agency and instrument of one horse, unnamed, belonging to Eckrum Snopes. Evidence of physical detriment and suffering, defendant himself. Witnesses, Mrs Tull and daughters—"

"Eck Snopes saw it too," Mrs Tull said, though with less violence now. "He was there. He got there in plenty of time to see it. Let him deny it. Let him look me in the face and deny it if he—"

"If you please, ma'am," the Justice said. He said it so quietly that Mrs Tull hushed and became quite calm, almost a rational and composed being. "The injury to your husband aint disputed. And the agency of the horse aint disputed. The law says that when a man owns a creature which he knows to be dangerous and if that creature is restrained and restricted from the public commons by a pen or enclosure capable of restraining and restricting it, if a man enter that pen or enclosure, whether he knows the creature in it is dangerous or not dangerous, then that man has committed trespass and the owner of that creature is not liable. But if that creature known to him to be dangerous ceases to be restrained by that suitable pen or enclosure, either by accident or design and either with or without the owner's knowledge, then that owner is liable. That's the law. All necessary now is to establish first, the ownership of the horse, and second, that the horse was a dangerous creature within the definition of the law as provided."

"Hah," Mrs Tull said. She said it exactly as Bookwright would have. "Dangerous. Ask Vernon Tull. Ask Henry Armstid if them things was pets."

"If you please, ma'am," the Justice said. He was looking at Eck. "What is the defendant's position? Denial of ownership?"

"What?" Eck said.

"Was that your horse that ran over Mr Tull?"

"Yes," Eck said. "It was mine. How much do I have to p——"

"Hah," Mrs Tull said again. "Denial of ownership. When there were at least forty men—fools too, or they wouldn't have been there. But even a fool's word is good about what he saw and heard. —at least forty men heard that Texas murderer give that horse to Eck Snopes. Not sell it to him, mind; give it to him."

"What?" the Justice said. "Gave it to him?"

"Yes," Eck said. "He give it to me. I'm sorry Tull happened to be using that bridge too at the same time. How much do I——"

"Wait," the Justice said. "What did you give him? a note? a swap of some kind?"

"No," Eck said. "He just pointed to it in the lot and told me it belonged to me."

"And he didn't give you a bill of sale or a deed or anything in writing?"

"I reckon he never had time," Eck said. "And after Lon Quick forgot and left that gate open, never nobody had time to do no writing even if we had a thought of it."

"What's all this?" Mrs Tull said. "Eck Snopes has just told you he owned that horse. And if you wont take his word, there were forty men standing at that gate all day long doing nothing, that heard that murdering card-playing whiskey-drinking antichrist—" This time the Justice raised one hand, in its enormous pristine cuff, toward her. He did not look at her.

"Wait," he said. "Then what did he do?" he said to Eck. "Just lead the horse up and put the rope in your hand?"

"No," Eck said. "Him nor nobody else never got no ropes on none of them. He just pointed to the horse in the lot and said it was mine and auctioned off the rest of them and got into the buggy and said good-bye and druv off. And we got our ropes and went into the lot, only Lon Quick forgot to shut the gate. I'm sorry it made Tull's mules snatch him outen the wagon. How much do I owe him?" Then he stopped, because the Justice was no longer looking at him and, as he realised a moment later, no longer listening either. Instead, he was sitting back in the chair, actually leaning back in it for the first time, his head bent slightly and his hands resting on the table before him, the fingers lightly overlapped. They watched him quietly for almost a half-minute before anyone realised that he was looking quietly and steadily at Mrs Tull.

"Well, Mrs Tull," he said, "by your own testimony, Eck never owned that horse."

"What?" Mrs Tull said. It was not loud at all. "What did you say?"

"In the law, ownership cant be conferred or invested by word-of-mouth. It must be established either by recorded or authentic document, or by possession or occupation. By your testimony and his both, he never gave that Texas man anything in exchange for that horse, and by his testimony the Texas man never gave him any paper to prove he owned it, and by his testimony and by what I know myself from these last four weeks, nobody yet has ever laid hand or rope either on any one of them. So that horse never came into Eck's possession at all. That Texas man could have given that same horse to a dozen other men standing around that gate that day, without even needing to tell Eck he had done it; and Eck himself could have transferred all his title and equity in it to Mr Tull right there while Mr Tull was lying unconscious on that bridge just by thinking it to himself, and Mr Tull's title would be just as legal as Eck's."

"So I get nothing," Mrs Tull said. Her voice was still calm, quiet, though probably no one but Tull realised that it was too calm and quiet. "My team is made to run away by a wild spotted mad-dog, my wagon is wrecked; my husband is jerked out of it and knocked unconscious and unable to work for a whole week with less than half of our seed in the ground, and I get nothing."

"Wait," the Justice said. "The law—"

"The law," Mrs Tull said. She stood suddenly up—a short, broad, strong woman, balanced on the balls of her planted feet.

"Now, mamma," Tull said.

"Yes, ma'am," the Justice said. "Your damages are fixed by statute. The law says that when a suit for damages is brought against the owner of an animal which has committed damage or injury, if the owner of the animal either cant or wont assume liability, the injured or damaged party shall find recompense in the body of the animal. And since Eck Snopes never owned that horse at all, and since you just heard a case here this morning that failed to prove that Flem

Snopes had any equity in any of them, that horse still belongs to that Texas man. Or did belong. Because now that horse that made your team run away and snatch your husband out of the wagon, belongs to you and Mr Tull."

"Now, mamma!" Tull said. He rose quickly. But Mrs Tull was still quiet, only quite rigid and breathing hard, until Tull spoke. Then she turned on him, not screaming: shouting; presently the bailiff was banging the table-top with his hand-polished hickory cane and roaring "Order! Order!" while the neat old man, thrust backward in his chair as though about to dodge and trembling with an old man's palsy, looked on with amazed unbelief.

"The horse!" Mrs Tull shouted. "We see it for five seconds, while it is climbing into the wagon with us and then out again. Then it's gone, God dont know where and thank the Lord He dont! And the mules gone with it and the wagon wrecked and you laying there on the bridge with your face full of kindling-wood and bleeding like a hog and dead for all we knew. And he gives us the horse! Dont you hush me! Get on to that wagon, fool that would sit there behind a pair of young mules with the reins tied around his wrist! Get on to that wagon, all of you!"

"I cant stand no more!" the old Justice cried. "I wont! This court's adjourned! Adjourned!"

There was another trial then. It began on the following Monday and most of those same faces watched it too, in the county court-house in Jefferson when the prisoner entered between two officers and looking hardly larger than a child, in a suit of brand-new over-alls, thin, almost frail-looking, the sombre violent face thin in repose and pallid from the eight months in jail, and was arraigned and then plead by the counsel appointed him by the Court—a young man graduated only last June from the State University's law school and admitted to the Bar, who did what he could and overdid what he could not, zealous and, for all practical purposes and results, ignored, having exhausted all his challenges before the State had made one and in despite of which seeing himself faced by an authenticated jury in almost record time as if the State, the public, all rational mankind, possessed an inexhaustible pool of interchangeable faces and names all cradling one identical conviction and intention, so that his very challenges could have been discharged for him by the janitor who opened the courtroom, by merely counting off the first members of the panel corresponding to that number. And, if the defendant's counsel had any detachment and objectivity left at all by then, he probably realised soon that it was not his client but himself who was embattled with that jury. Because his client was paying no attention whatever to what was going on. He did not seem to be interested in watching and listening to it as someone else's trial. He sat where they had placed him, manacled to one of the officers, small, in the new iron-hard board-stiff overalls, the back of his head toward the Bar and what was going on there and his upper body shifting constantly until they realised that he was trying to watch the rear of the room, the doors and who entered them. He had to be spoken to twice before he stood up and plead and continued to stand, his back completely turned to the Court now, his face sombre, thin, curiously urgent and quite calm and with something else in it which was not even just hope but was actual faith, looking not at his wife who sat on the bench just behind him but out into the crowded room, among the ranked and intent faces some of which, most of which, he knew, until the officer he was handcuffed to pulled him down again. And he sat that way through the rest of the brief and record day-and-a-quarter of his trial, the small, neatly-combed, vicious and ironlike incorrigible head turning and craning constantly to see backward past the bulk of the two officers, watching the entrance while his attorney did what he could, talked himself frantic and at last voiceless before the grave impassivity of the jury which resembled a conclave of grown men self-delegated with the necessity (though for a definitely specified and limited time) of listening to prattle of a licensed child. And still the client listened to none of it, watching constantly the rear of the room while toward the end of the first day the faith went out of his face, leaving only the hope, and at the beginning of the second day the hope was gone too and there was only the urgency, the grim and intractable sombreness, while still he watched the door. The State finished in midmorning of the second day. The jury was out twenty minutes and returned with a ballot of murder in the second degree; the prisoner stood again and was sentenced by the Court to be transported to the State Penal Farm and there remain until he died. But he was not listening to that either; he had not only turned his back to the Court to look out into the crowded room, he was speaking himself even before the Judge had ceased, continuing to speak even while the Judge hammered the desk with his gavel and the two officers and three bailiffs converged upon the prisoner as he struggled, flinging them back and for a short time actually successful, staring out into the room. "Flem Snopes!" he said. "Flem Snopes! Is Flem Snopes in this room? Tell that son of a bitch——"

CHAPTER TWO

1

*R*atliff stopped the buckboard at Bookwright's gate. The house was dark, but at once three or four of Bookwright's dogs came yelling out from beneath it or behind it. Armstid swung his legs stiffly out and prepared to get down. "Wait," Ratliff said. "I'll go get him."

"I can walk," Armstid said harshly.

"Sholy," Ratliff said. "Besides, them dogs knows me."

"They'll know me, after the first one runs at me once," Armstid said.

"Sholy," Ratliff said. He was already out of the buckboard. "You wait here and hold the team." Armstid swung his leg back into the buckboard, not invisible even in the moonless August darkness, but on the contrary, because of his faded overalls, quite distinct against the buckboard's dark upholstery; it was only his features beneath his hatbrim which could not be distinguished. Ratliff handed him the reins and turned past the metal mailbox on its post in the starlight, toward the gate beyond it and the mellow uproar of the dogs. When he was through the gate he could see them—a yelling clump of blackness against the slightly paler earth which broke and spread fan-wise before him, braced, yelling, holding him bayed—three black-and-tan hounds whose tan the starlight had transposed to black too so that, not quite invisible but almost and without detail, they might have been the three intact carbons of burned newspaper-sheets standing upright from the earth, yelling at him. He shouted at them. They should have recognised him already by smell. When he shouted, he knew that they already had, because for perhaps a second they hushed, then as he moved forward they retreated before him, keeping the same distance, baying. Then he saw Bookwright, pale too in overalls against the black house. When Bookwright shouted at the hounds, they did hush.

"Git," he said. "Shut up and git." He approached, becoming black in his turn against the paler earth, to where Ratliff waited. "Where's Henry?" he said.

"In the buggy," Ratliff said. He turned back toward the gate.

"Wait," Bookwright said. Ratliff stopped. The other came up beside him. They looked at one another, each face invisible to the other. "You aint let him persuade you into this, have you?" Bookwright said. "Between having to remember them five dollars every time he looks at his wife maybe, and that broke leg, and that horse he bought from Flem Snopes with it he aint even seen again, he's plumb crazy now. Not that he had far to go. You aint just let him persuade you?"

"I dont think so," Ratliff said. "I know I aint," he said. "There's something there. I've always knowed it. Just like Will Varner knows there is something there. If there wasn't, he wouldn't never bought it. And he wouldn't a kept it, selling the balance of it off and still keeping that old house, paying taxes on it when he could a got something for it, setting there in that flour-barrel chair to watch it and claiming he did it because it rested him to set there where somebody had gone to all that work and expense just to build something to sleep and eat and lay with his wife in. And I knowed it for sho when Flem Snopes took it. When he had Will Varner just where he wanted him, and then he sold out to Will by taking that old house and them ten acres that wouldn't hardly raise goats. And I went with Henry last night. I saw it too. You dont have to come in, if you feel uncertain. I'd rather you wouldn't."

"All right," Bookwright said. He moved on. "That's all I wanted to know." They returned to the buckboard. Henry moved to the middle of the seat and they got in. "Dont let me crowd your leg," Bookwright said.

"There aint anything wrong with my leg," Armstid said in that harsh voice. "I can walk as far as you or any man any day."

"Sholy," Ratliff said quickly, taking the reins. "Henry's leg is all right now. You cant even notice it."

"Let's get on," Bookwright said. "Wont nobody have to walk for a while, if that team can."

"It's shorter through the Bend," Ratliff said. "But we better not go that way."

"Let them see," Armstid said. "If anybody here is afraid, I dont need no help. I can—"

"Sholy," Ratliff said. "If folks sees us, we might have too much help. That's what we want to dodge." Armstid hushed. He said no more from then on, sitting between them in an immobility which was almost like a temperature, thinner, as though it had not been the sickness (after being in bed about a month, he had got up one day and broken the leg again; nobody ever knew how, what he had been doing, trying to do, because he never talked about it) but impotence and fury which had wasted him.

Ratliff asked neither advice nor directions; there was little anybody could have told him about the back roads and lanes of that or any of the other country he travelled. They passed nobody; the dark and sleeping land was empty, the scattered and remote homesteads indicated only by the occasional baying of dogs. The lanes he followed ran pale between the broad spread of fields felt rather than seen, where the corn was beginning to fire and the cotton to bloom, then into tunnels of trees rising and feathered lushly with summer's full leaf against the sky of August heavy and thick with stars. Then they were in the old lane which for years now had been marked by nothing save the prints of Varner's old white horse and, for a brief time, by the wheels of the parasol-topped runabout—the old scar almost healed now, where nearly fifty years ago a courier (perhaps a neighbor's slave flogging a mule taken out of the plow) had galloped with the news of Sumter, where perhaps the barouche had moved, the women swaying and pliant in hooped crinoline beneath parasols, the men in broadcloth riding the good horses at the wheels, talking about it, where the son and perhaps the master himself had ridden into Jefferson with his pistols and his portmanteau and a body-servant on the spare horse behind, talking of regiments and victory; where the Federal patrols had ridden the land peopled by women and Negro slaves about the time of the battle of Jefferson.

There was nothing to show of that now. There was hardly a road; where the sand darkened into the branch and then rose again, there was no trace left of the bridge. Now the scar ran straight as a plumb-

line along a shaggy hedgerow of spaced cedars decreed there by the
same nameless architect who had planned and built the house for its
nameless master, now two and three feet thick, the boughs interlocked and massed now. Ratliff turned in among them. He seemed to
know exactly where he was going. But then Bookwright remembered
that he had been here last night.

Armstid didn't wait for them. Ratliff tied the team hurriedly and
they overtook him—a shadow, still faintly visible because of his overalls faded pale with washing, hurrying stiffly on through the undergrowth. The earth yawned black before them, a long gash: a ravine,
a ditch. Bookwright remembered that Armstid had been here for
more than one night, nevertheless the limping shadow seemed about
to hurl itself into the black abyss. "You better help him," Bookwright
said. "He's going to break—"

"Hush!" Ratliff hissed. "The garden is just up the hill yonder."

"—break that leg again," Bookwright said, quieter now. "Then
we'll be into it."

"He'll be all right," Ratliff whispered. "It's been this way every
night. Just dont push him too close. But dont let him get too far
ahead. Once last night while we were laying there I had to hold him."
They went on, just behind the figure which moved now in absolute
silence and with surprising speed. They were in a ravine massed with
honeysuckle and floored with dry sand in which they could hear the
terrific laboring of the lame leg. Yet still they could hardly keep up
with him. After about two hundred yards Armstid turned to climb up
out of the ravine. Ratliff followed him. "Careful now," he whispered
back to Bookwright. "We're right at it." But Bookwright was watching Armstid. He wont never make it, he thought. He wont never
climb that bank. But the other did it, dragging the stiffened and
once-fragile and hence maybe twice-fragile leg at the almost sheer
slope, silent and unaided and emanating that trigger-like readiness to
repudiate assistance and to deny that he might possibly need it. Then
on hands and knees Bookwright was crawling after the others in a
path through a mass of man-tall briers and weeds and persimmon
shoots, overtaking them where they lay flat at the edge of a vague
slope which rose to the shaggy crest on which, among oaks, the shell
of the tremendous house stood where it had been decreed too by the

imported and nameless architect and its master whose anonymous dust lay with that of his blood and of the progenitors of saxophone players in Harlem honkytonks beneath the weathered and illegible headstones on another knoll four hundred yards away, with its broken roof and topless chimneys and one high rectangle of window through which he could see the stars in the opposite sky. The slope had probably been a rose-garden. None of them knew or cared, just as they, who had seen it, walked past and looked at it perhaps a hundred times, did not know that the fallen pediment in the middle of the slope had once been a sundial. Ratliff reached across Armstid's body and gripped his arm, then, above the sound of their panting breath, Bookwright heard the steady and unhurried sigh of a shovel and the measured thud of spaded earth somewhere on the slope above them. "There!" Ratliff whispered.

"I hear somebody digging," Bookwright whispered. "How do I know it's Flem Snopes?"

"Hasn't Henry been laying here every night since ten days ago, listening to him? Wasn't I right here last night with Henry myself, listening to him? Didn't we lay right here until he quit and left and then we crawled up there and found every place where he had dug and then filled the hole back up and smoothed the dirt to hide it?"

"All right," Bookwright whispered. "You and Armstid have been watching somebody digging. But how do I know it is Flem Snopes?"

"All right," Armstid said, with a cold restrained violence, almost aloud; both of them could feel him trembling where he lay between them, jerking and shaking through his gaunt and wasted body like a leashed dog. "It aint Flem Snopes then. Go on back home."

"Hush!" Ratliff hissed. Armstid had turned, looking toward Bookwright. His face was not a foot from Bookwright's, the features more indistinguishable than ever now.

"Go on," he said. "Go on back home."

"Hush, Henry!" Ratliff whispered. "He's going to hear you!" But Armstid had already turned his head, glaring up the dark slope again, shaking and trembling between them, cursing in a dry whisper. "If you knowed it was Flem, would you believe then?" Ratliff whispered across Armstid's body. Bookwright didn't answer. He lay there too, with the others, while Armstid's thin body shook and jerked beside him, listening to the steady and unhurried whisper of the shovel and to Armstid's dry and furious cursing. Then the sound of the shovel ceased. For a moment nobody moved. Then Armstid said,

"He's done found it!" He surged suddenly and violently between them. Bookwright heard or felt Ratliff grasp him.

"Stop!" Ratliff whispered. "Stop! Help hold him, Odum!" Bookwright grasped Armstid's other arm. Between them they held the furious body until Armstid ceased and lay again between them, rigid, glaring, cursing in that dry whisper. His arms felt no larger than sticks; the strength in them was unbelievable. "He aint found it yet!" Ratliff whispered at him. "He just knows it's there somewhere; maybe he found a paper somewhere in the house telling where it is. But he's got to hunt to find it same as we will. He knows it's somewhere in that garden, but he's got to hunt to find it same as us. Aint we been watching him hunting for it?" Bookwright could hear both the voices now speaking in hissing whispers, the one cursing, the other cajoling and reasoning while the owners of them glared as one up the starlit slope. Now Ratliff was speaking to him. "You dont believe it's Flem," he said. "All right. Just watch." They lay in the weeds; they were all holding their breaths now, Bookwright too. Then he saw the digger—a shadow, a thicker darkness, moving against the slope, mounting it. "Watch," Ratliff whispered. Bookwright could hear him and Armstid where they lay glaring up the slope, breathing in hissing exhalations, in passionate and dying sighs. Then Bookwright saw the white shirt; an instant later the figure came into complete relief against the sky as if it had paused for a moment on the crest of the slope. Then it was gone. "There!" Ratliff whispered. "Wasn't that Flem Snopes? Do you believe now?" Bookwright drew a long breath and let it out again. He was still holding Armstid's arm. He had forgotten about it. Now he felt it again under his hand like a taut steel cable vibrating.

"It's Flem," he said.

"Certainly it's Flem," Ratliff said. "Now all we got to do is find out tomorrow night where it's at and—"

"Tomorrow night, hell!" Armstid said. He surged forward again, attempting to rise. "Let's get up there now and find it. That's what we got to do. Before he—" They both held him again while Ratliff argued with him, sibilant and expostulant. They held him flat on the ground again at last, cursing.

"We got to find where it is first," Ratliff panted. "We got to find exactly where it is the first time. We aint got time just to hunt. We got to find it the first night because we cant afford to leave no marks for him to find when he comes back. Cant you see that? that we aint going to have but one chance to find it because we dont dare be caught looking?"

"What we going to do?" Bookwright said.

"Ha," Armstid said. "Ha." It was harsh, furious, restrained. There was no mirth in it. "What *we* going to do. I thought you had gone back home."

"Shut up, Henry," Ratliff said. He rose to his knees, though he still held Armstid's arm. "We agreed to take Odum in with us. At least let's wait till we find that money before we start squabbling over it."

"Suppose it aint nothing but Confederate money," Bookwright said.

"All right," Ratliff said. "What do you reckon that old Frenchman did with all the money he had before there was any such thing as Confederate money? Besides, a good deal of it was probably silver spoons and jewelry."

"You all can have the silver spoons and jewelry," Bookwright said. "I'll take my share in money."

"So you believe now, do you?" Ratliff said. Bookwright didn't answer.

"What we going to do now?" he said.

"I'm going up the bottom tomorrow and get Uncle Dick Bolivar," Ratliff said. "I ought to get back here a little after dark. But then we cant do anything here until after midnight, after Flem has done got through hunting it."

"And finding it tomorrow night," Armstid said. "By God, I aint—"They were all standing now. Armstid began to struggle, sudden and furious, to free his arm. But Ratliff held him. He flung both arms around Armstid and held him until he stopped struggling.

"Listen," Ratliff said. "Flem Snopes aint going to find it. If he knowed where to look, do you think he'd a been here digging for it every night for two weeks? Dont you know folks have been looking for that money for thirty years? That every foot of this whole place has been turned over at least ten times? That there aint a piece of land in this whole country that's been worked as much and as often as this here little shirt-tail of garden? Will Varner could have raised cotton or corn either in it so tall he would have to gather it on horseback just by putting the seed in the ground. The reason aint nobody found it yet is it's buried so deep aint nobody had time to dig that far in just one night and then get the hole filled back up where Will Varner wouldn't find it when he got out here at daylight to sit in that flour-barrel chair and watch. No sir. There aint but one thing in this world can keep us from finding it." Armstid had ceased. He and Bookwright both looked toward Ratliff's indistinguishable face. After a while Armstid said harshly:

"And what's that?"

"That's for Flem Snopes to find out somebody else is hunting for it," Ratliff said.

It was about midnight the next night when Ratliff turned his buckboard into the cedars again. Bookwright now rode his horse, because there were already three people in the buckboard, and again Armstid did not wait for Ratliff to tie the team. He was out as soon as the buckboard stopped; he dragged a shovel dashing and clanging out of the dog-kennel box, making no effort whatever to be quiet, and was gone limping terrifically into the darkness before Ratliff and Bookwright were on the ground. "We might as well go back home," Bookwright said.

"No, no," Ratliff said. "He aint never there this late. But we better catch up with Henry anyway." The third man in the buckboard had not moved yet. Even in the obscurity his long white beard had a faintly luminous quality, as if it had absorbed something of the starlight through which Ratliff had fetched him and were now giving it back to the dark. Ratliff and Bookwright helped him, groping and fumbling, out of the buckboard, and carrying the other shovel and the pick and half-carrying the old man, they hurried down into the ravine and then ran, trying to overtake the sound of Armstid's limping progress. They never overtook him. They climbed up out of the ditch, carrying the old man bodily now, and even before they reached the foot of the garden they could hear the sound of Armstid's rapid shovel up the slope. They released the old man, who sank to the ground between them, breathing in reedy gasps, and as one Ratliff and Bookwright glared up the dark slope toward the hushed furious sound of the shovel. "We got to make him stop until Uncle Dick can find it," Ratliff said. They ran toward the sound, shoulder to shoulder in the stumbling dark, among the rank weeds. "Here, Henry!" Ratliff whispered. "Wait for Uncle Dick." Armstid didn't pause, digging furiously, flinging the dirt and thrusting the shovel again all in one motion. Ratliff grasped at the shovel. Armstid jerked it free and whirled, the shovel raised like an axe, their faces invisible to one another, strained, spent. Ratliff had not had his clothes off in three nights, but Armstid had probably been in his for the whole two weeks.

"Touch it!" Armstid whispered. "Touch it!"

"Wait now," Ratliff said. "Give Uncle Dick a chance to find where it's at."

"Get away," Armstid said. "I warn you. Get outen my hole." He resumed his furious digging. Ratliff watched him for a second.

"Come on," he said. He turned, running, Bookwright behind him. The old man was sitting up when they reached him. Ratliff plunged down beside him and began to scrabble among the weeds for the other shovel. It was the pick he found first. He flung it away and plunged down again; he and Bookwright found the shovel at the same time. Then they were standing, struggling for the shovel, snatching and jerking at it, their breathing harsh and repressed, hearing even above their own breathing the rapid sound of Armstid's shovel up the slope. "Leave go!" Ratliff whispered. "Leave go!" The old man, unaided now, was struggling to get up.

"Wait," he said. "Wait." Then Ratliff seemed to realise what he was doing. He released the shovel; he almost hurled it at Bookwright.

"Take it," he said. He drew a long shuddering breath. "God," he whispered. "Just look at what even the money a man aint got yet will do to him." He stooped and jerked the old man to his feet, not with intentional roughness but merely out of his urgency. He had to hold him up for a moment.

"Wait," the old man said in a reedy, quavering voice. He was

known through all that country. He had no kin, no ties, and he ante-
dated everyone; nobody knew how old he was—a tall thin man in a
filthy frock coat and no shirt beneath it and a long, perfectly white
beard reaching below his waist, who lived in a mud-daubed hut in the
river bottom five or six miles from any road. He made and sold nos-
trums and charms, and it was said of him that he ate not only frogs
and snakes but bugs as well—anything that he could catch. There
was nothing in his hut but his pallet bed, a few cooking vessels, a
tremendous Bible and a faded daguerreotype of a young man in a
Confederate uniform which was believed by those who had seen it to
be his son. "Wait," he said. "There air anger in the yearth. Ye must
make that ere un quit a-bruisin hit."

"That's so," Ratliff said. "It wont work unless the ground is quiet.
We got to make him stop." Again when they stood over him, Henry
continued to dig; again when Ratliff touched him he whirled, the
shovel raised, and stood cursing them in a spent whisper until the old
man himself walked up and touched his shoulder.

"Ye kin dig and ye kin dig, young man," the reedy voice said. "For
what's rendered to the yearth, the yearth will keep until hit's ready
to reveal hit."

"That's right, Henry," Ratliff said. "We got to give Uncle Dick
room to find where it is. Come on, now." Armstid lowered the shovel
and came out of his pit (it was already nearly a foot deep). But he
would not relinquish the shovel; he still held to it until the old man
drove them back to the edge of the garden and produced from the
tail-pocket of his frock coat a forked peach branch, from the butt-end
of which something dangled on a length of string; Ratliff, who had
seen it before at least, knew what it was—an empty cloth tobacco-
sack containing a gold-filled human tooth. He held them there for
ten minutes, stooping now and then to lay his hand flat on the earth.
Then, with the three of them clumped and silent at his heels, he went
to the weed-choked corner of the old garden and grasped the two
prongs of the branch in his hands, the string and the tobacco-sack
hanging plumblike and motionless before him, and stood for a time,
muttering to himself.

"How do I—" Bookwright said.

"Hush," Ratliff said. The old man began to walk, the three of them following. They moved like a procession, with something at once outrageously pagan and orthodoxly funereal about them, slowly back and forth across the garden, mounting the slope gradually in overlapping traverses. Suddenly the old man stopped; Armstid, limping just behind him, bumped into him.

"There's somebody agin it," he said. He didn't look back. "It aint you," he said, and they all knew he was talking to Ratliff. "And it aint that cripple. It's that other one. That black one. Let him get offen this ground and quieten hit, or you can take me on back home."

"Go back to the edge," Ratliff said quietly over his shoulder to Bookwright. "It'll be all right then."

"But I—" Bookwright said.

"Get off the garden," Ratliff said. "It's after midnight. It'll be daylight in four hours." Bookwright returned to the foot of the slope. That is, he faded into the darkness, because they did not watch him; they were moving again now, Armstid and Ratliff close at the old man's heels. Again they began to mount the slope in traverses, passing the place where Henry had begun to dig, passing the place where Ratliff had found signs of the other man's excavation on the first night Armstid had brought him here; now Ratliff could feel Armstid beginning to tremble again. The old man stopped. They did not bump into him this time, and Ratliff did not know that Bookwright was behind him again until the old man spoke:

"Tech my elbers," he said. "Not you," he said. "You that didn't believe." When Bookwright touched them, inside the sleeves the arms—arms thin and frail and dead as rotten sticks—were jerking faintly and steadily; when the old man stopped suddenly again and Bookwright blundered into him, he felt the whole thin body straining backward. Armstid was cursing steadily in his dry whisper. "Tech the peach fork," the old man panted. "You that didn't believe." When Bookwright touched it, it was arched into a rigid down-pointing curve, the string taut as wire. Armstid made a choked sound; Bookwright felt his hand on the branch too. The branch sprang free; the old man staggered, the fork lying dead on the ground at his feet until Armstid, digging furiously with his bare hands, flung it away.

They turned as one and plunged back down the slope to where they had left the tools. They could hardly keep up with Armstid. "Dont let

him get the pick," Bookwright panted. "He will kill somebody with it."
But Armstid was not after the pick. He went straight to where he had
left his shovel when the old man produced the forked branch and
refused to start until he put the shovel down, and snatched it up and
ran back up the slope. He was already digging when Ratliff and Bookwright reached him. They all dug then, frantically, hurling the dirt
aside, in each other's way, the tools clashing and ringing together,
while the old man stood above them behind the faint gleam of his
beard in the starlight and his white brows above the two caverns from
which, even if they had paused to look, they could not have told
whether his eyes even watched them or not, musing, detached, without interest in their panting frenzy. Suddenly the three of them
became frozen in the attitudes of digging for perhaps a second. Then
they leaped into the hole together; the six hands at the same instant
touched the object—a heavy solid sack of heavy cloth through which
they all felt the round milled edges of coins. They struggled for it, jerking it back and forth among them, clutching it, gripping it, panting.

"Stop it!" Ratliff panted. "Stop it! Aint we all three partners
alike?" But Armstid clung to it, trying to jerk it away from the others,
cursing. "Let go, Odum," Ratliff said. "Let him have it." They
turned it loose. Armstid clutched it to himself, stooping, glaring at
them as they climbed out of the hole. "Let him keep it," Ratliff said.
"Dont you know that aint all?" He turned quickly away. "Come on,
Uncle Dick," he said. "Get your—" He ceased. The old man was
standing motionless behind them, his head turned as if he were listening toward the ditch from which they had come. "What?" Ratliff
whispered. They were all three motionless now, rigid, still stooped
a little as when they had stepped away from Armstid. "Do you hear
something?" Ratliff whispered. "Is somebody down there?"

"I feel four bloods lust-running," the old man said. "Hit's four sets
of blood here lusting for trash." They crouched, rigid. But there was
no sound.

"Well, aint it four of us here?" Bookwright whispered.

"Uncle Dick dont care nothing about money," Ratliff whispered.
"If somebody's hiding there—" They were running. Armstid was the
first to start, still carrying his shovel. Again they could hardly keep up
with him as they went plunging down the slope.

"Kill him," Armstid said. "Watch every bush and kill him."

"No," Ratliff said. "Catch him first." When he and Bookwright reached the ditch, they could hear Armstid beating along the edge of it, making no effort whatever to be quiet, slashing at the dark undergrowth with the axe-like shovel-edge with the same fury he had dug with. But they found nothing, nobody.

"Maybe Uncle Dick never heard nothing," Bookwright said.

"Well, whatever it was is gone, anyway," Ratliff said. "Maybe it—" He ceased. He and Bookwright stared at one another; above their held breaths they heard the horse. It was in the old road beyond the cedars; it was as if it had been dropped there from the sky in full gallop. They heard it until it ceased into the sand at the branch. After a moment they heard it again on the hard ground beyond, fainter now. Then it ceased altogether. They stared at one another in the darkness, across their held breaths. Then Ratliff exhaled. "That means we got till daylight," he said. "Come on."

Twice more the old man's peach branch sprang and bent; twice more they found small bulging canvas bags solid and unmistakable even in the dark. "Now," Ratliff said, "we got a hole a piece and till daylight to do it in. Dig, boys."

When the east began to turn gray, they had found nothing else. But digging three holes at once, as they had been doing, none of them had been able to go very deep. And the bulk of the treasure would be deep; as Ratliff had said, if it were not it would have been found ten times over during the last fifty years since there probably were not many square feet of the ten acres which comprised the old mansion-site which had not been dug into between some sunset and dawn by someone without a light, trying to dig fast and dig quiet at the same time. So at last he and Bookwright prevailed on Armstid to see a little of reason, and they desisted and filled up the holes and removed the traces of digging. Then they opened the bags in the gray light. Ratliff's and Bookwright's contained twenty-five silver dollars each. Armstid refused to tell what his contained or to let anyone see it. He crouched over it, his back toward them, cursing them when they tried to look. "All right," Ratliff said. Then a thought struck him. He looked down at Armstid. "Of course aint nobody fool enough to try to spend any of it now."

"Mine's mine," Armstid said. "I found it. I worked for it. I'm going to do any God damn thing I want to with it."

"All right," Ratliff said. "How are you going to explain it?"

"How am I—" Armstid said. Squatting, he looked up at Ratliff. They could see one another's faces now. All three of them were strained, spent with sleeplessness and fatigue.

"Yes," Ratliff said. "How are you going to explain to folks where you got it? Got twenty-five dollars all coined before 1861?" He quit looking at Armstid. He and Bookwright looked at one another quietly in the growing light. "There was somebody in the ditch, watching us," he said. "We got to buy it."

"We got to buy it quick," Bookwright said. "Tomorrow."

"You mean today," Ratliff said. Bookwright looked about him. It was as though he were waking from an anaesthetic, as if he saw the dawn, the earth, for the first time.

"That's right," he said. "It's already tomorrow now."

The old man lay under a tree beside the ditch, asleep, flat on his back, his mouth open, his beard dingy and stained in the increasing dawn; they hadn't even missed him since they really began to dig. They waked him and helped him back to the buckboard. The dog-kennel box in which Ratliff carried the sewing machines had a pad-locked door. He took a few ears of corn from the box, then he stowed his and Bookwright's bags of coins beneath the odds and ends of small and still-frozen traded objects at the back of it and locked it again.

"You put yours in here too, Henry," he said. "What we want to do now is to forget we even got them until we find the rest of it and get it out of the ground." But Armstid would not. He climbed stiffly onto the horse behind Bookwright, unaided, repudiating the aid which had not even been offered yet, clutching his bag inside the bib of his patched and faded overalls, and they departed. Ratliff fed his team and watered them at the branch; he too was on the road before the sun rose. Just before nine oclock he paid the old man his dollar fee and put him down where the five-mile path to his hut entered the river bottom, and turned the wiry and indefatigable little horses back toward Frenchman's Bend. There was somebody hid in that ditch, he thought. We got to buy it damn quick.

Later it seemed to him that, until he reached the store, he had not actually realised himself how quick they would have to buy it. Almost as soon as he came in sight of the store, he saw the new face among the familiar ones along the gallery and recognised it—Eustace Grimm, a young tenant-farmer living ten or twelve miles away in the next county with his wife of a year, to whom Ratliff intended to sell a sewing machine as soon as they had finished paying for the baby born two months ago; as he tied his team to one of the gallery posts and mounted the heel-gnawed steps, he thought, Maybe sleeping rests a man, but it takes staying up all night for two or three nights and being worried and scared half to death during them, to sharpen him. Because as soon as he recognised Grimm, something in him had clicked, though it would be three days before he would know what it was. He had not had his clothes off in more than sixty hours; he had had no breakfast today and what eating he had done in the last two days had been more than spotty—all of which showed in his face. But it didn't show in his voice or anywhere else, and nothing else but that showed anywhere at all. "Morning, gentlemen," he said.

"Be durn if you dont look like you aint been to bed in a week, V. K.," Freeman said. "What you up to now? Lon Quick said his boy seen your team and buckboard hid out in the bottom below Armstid's two mornings ago, but I told him I didn't reckon them horses had done nothing to have to hide from. So it must be you."

"I reckon not," Ratliff said. "Or I'd a been caught too, same as the team. I used to think I was too smart to be caught by anybody around here. But I dont know now." He looked at Grimm, his face, except for the sleeplessness and fatigue, as bland and quizzical and impenetrable as ever. "Eustace," he said, "you're strayed."

"It looks like it," Grimm said. "I come to see—"

"He's paid his road-tax," Lump Snopes, the clerk, sitting as usual in the single chair tilted in the doorway, said. "Do you object to him using Yoknapatawpha roads too?"

"Sholy not," Ratliff said. "And if he'd a just paid his poll-tax in the right place, he could drive his wagon through the store and through Will Varner's house too." They guffawed, all except Lump.

"Maybe I will yet," Grimm said. "I come up here to see—" He ceased, looking up at Ratliff. He was perfectly motionless, squatting, a sliver of wood in one hand and his open and arrested knife in the other. Ratliff watched him.

"Couldn't you see him last night either?" he said.

"Couldn't I see who last night?" Grimm said.

"How could he have seen anybody in Frenchman's Bend last night when he wasn't in Frenchman's Bend last night?" Lump Snopes said. "Go on to the house, Eustace," he said. "Dinner's about ready. I'll be along in a few minutes."

"I got—" Grimm said.

"You got twelve miles to drive to get home tonight," Snopes said. "Go on, now." Grimm looked at him a moment longer. Then he rose and descended the steps and went on up the road. Ratliff was no longer watching him. He was looking at Snopes.

"Eustace eating with you during his visit?" he said.

"He happens to be eating at Winterbottom's where I happen to be boarding," Snopes said harshly. "Where a few other folks happens to be eating and paying board too."

"Sho now," Ratliff said. "You hadn't ought to druv him away like that. Likely Eustace dont get to town very often to spend a day or two examining the country and setting around store."

"He'll have his feet under his own table tonight," Snopes said. "You can go down there and look at him. Then you can be in his back yard even before he opens his mouth."

"Sho now," Ratliff said, pleasant, bland, inscrutable, with his spent and sleepless face. "When you expecting Flem back?"

"Back from where?" Snopes said, in that harsh voice. "From laying up yonder in that barrel-slat hammock, taking time about with Will Varner, sleeping? Likely never."

"Him and Will and the womenfolks was in Jefferson yesterday," Freeman said. "Will said they was coming home this morning."

"Sho now," Ratliff said. "Sometimes it takes a man even longer than a year to get his new wife out of the idea that money was just made to shop with." He stood above them, leaning against a gallery post, indolent and easy, as if he had not ever even heard of haste. So Flem Snopes has been in Jefferson since yesterday, he thought. And Lump Snopes didn't want it mentioned. And Eustace Grimm—again his mind clicked; still it would be three days before he would know what had clicked, because now he believed he did know, that he saw the pattern complete—and Eustace Grimm has been here since last night, since we heard that galloping horse anyway. Maybe they was both on the horse. Maybe that's why it sounded so loud. He could see that too—Lump Snopes and Grimm on the single horse, fleeing, galloping in the dark back to Frenchman's Bend where Flem Snopes would still be absent until sometime in the early afternoon. And Lump Snopes didn't want that mentioned either, he thought, and Eustace Grimm had to be sent home to keep folks from talking to him. And Lump Snopes aint just worried and mad: he's scared. They might even have found the hidden buckboard. They probably had, and so knew at least one of those who were digging in the garden; now Snopes would not only have to get hold of his cousin first through his agent, Grimm, he might even then become involved in a bidding contest for the place against someone who (Ratliff added this without vanity) had more to outbid him with; he thought, musing, amazed as always though still impenetrable, how even a Snopes was not safe from another Snopes. Damn quick, he thought. He stood away from the post and turned back toward the steps. "I reckon I'll get along," he said. "See you boys tomorrow."

"Come home with me and take dinner," Freeman said.

"Much obliged," Ratliff said. "I ate breakfast late at Bookwright's. I want to collect a machine note from Ike McCaslin this afternoon and be back here by dark." He got into the buckboard and turned the team back down the road. Presently they had fallen into their road gait, trotting rapidly on their short legs in the traces though their forward motion was not actually fast, on until they had passed Varner's house, beyond which the road turned off to McCaslin's farm and so out of sight from the store. They entered this road galloping, the dust bursting from their shaggy backs in long spurts where the whip slashed them. He had three miles to go. After the first half mile it would be all winding and little-used lane, but he could do it in twenty minutes. And it was only a little after noon, and it had probably been at least nine oclock before Will Varner got his wife away from the Jefferson church-ladies' auxiliary with which she was affiliated. He made it in nineteen minutes, hurtling and bouncing among the ruts ahead of his spinning dust, and slowed the now-lathered

team and swung them into the Jefferson highroad a mile from the
village, letting them trot for another half mile, slowing, to cool them
out gradually. But there was no sign of the surrey yet, so he went on
at a walk until he reached a crest from which he could see the road
for some distance ahead, and pulled out of the road into the shade
of a tree and stopped. Now he had had no dinner either. But he was
not quite hungry, and although after he had put the old man out and
turned back toward the village this morning he had had an almost
irresistible desire to sleep, that was gone too now. So he sat in the
buckboard, lax now, blinking painfully against the glare of noon,
while the team (he never used check-reins) nudged the lines slack
and grazed over the breast-yoke. People would probably pass and see
him there; some might even be going toward the village, where they
might tell of seeing him. But he would take care of that when it arose.
It was as though he said to himself, Now I got a little while at least
when I can let down.

Then he saw the surrey. He was already in the road, going at that
road-gait which the whole countryside knew, full of rapid little
hooves which still did not advance a great deal faster than two big
horses could have walked, before anyone in the surrey could have
seen him. And he knew that they had already seen and recognised
him when, still two hundred yards from it, he pulled up and sat in the
buckboard, affable, bland and serene except for his worn face, until
Varner stopped the surrey beside him. "Howdy, V. K.," Varner said.

"Morning," Ratliff said. He raised his hat to the two women in the
back seat. "Mrs Varner. Mrs Snopes."

"Where you headed?" Varner said. "Town?" Ratliff told no lie; he
attempted none, smiling a little, courteous, perhaps even a little deferential.

"I come out to meet you. I want to speak to Flem a minute." He
looked at Snopes for the first time. "I'll drive you on home," he said.

"Hah," Varner said. "You had to come two miles to meet him and
then turn around and go two miles back, to talk to him."

"That's right," Ratliff said. He was still looking at Snopes.

"You got better sense than to try to sell Flem Snopes anything,"
Varner said. "And you sholy aint fool enough by God to buy anything from him, are you?"

"I dont know," Ratliff said in that same pleasant and unchanged and impenetrable voice out of his spent and sleepless face, still looking at Snopes. "I used to think I was smart, but now I dont know. I'll bring you on home," he said. "You wont be late for dinner."

"Go on and get out," Varner said to his son-in-law. "He aint going to tell you till you do." But Snopes was already moving. He spat outward over the wheel and turned and climbed down over it, backward, broad and deliberate in the soiled light-gray trousers, the white shirt, the plaid cap; the surrey went on. Ratliff cramped the wheel and Snopes got into the buckboard beside him and he turned the buckboard and again the team fell into their tireless and familiar roadgait. But this time Ratliff reined them back until they were walking and held them so while Snopes chewed steadily beside him. They didn't look at one another again.

"That Old Frenchman place," Ratliff said. The surrey went on a hundred yards ahead, pacing its own dust, as they themselves were now doing. "What are you going to ask Eustace Grimm for it?" Snopes spat tobacco juice over the moving wheel. He did not chew fast nor did he seem to find it necessary to stop chewing in order to spit or speak either.

"He's at the store, is he?" he said.

"Aint this the day you told him to come?" Ratliff said. "How much are you going to ask him for?" Snopes told him. Ratliff made a short sound, something like Varner's habitual ejaculation. "Do you reckon Eustace Grimm can get his hands on that much money?"

"I dont know," Snopes said. He spat over the moving wheel again. Ratliff might have said, Then you dont want to sell it; Snopes would have answered, I'll sell anything. But they did not. They didn't need to.

"All right," Ratliff said. "What are you going to ask me for it?" Snopes told him. It was the same amount. This time Ratliff used Varner's ejaculation. "I'm just talking about them ten acres where that old house is. I aint trying to buy all Yoknapatawpha County from you." They crossed the last hill; the surrey began to move faster, drawing away from them. The village was not far now. "We'll let this one count," Ratliff said. "How much do you want for that Old Frenchman place?" His team was trying to trot too, ahead of the buckboard's light weight. Ratliff held them in, the road beginning to curve to pass the schoolhouse and enter the village. The surrey had already vanished beyond the curve.

"What do you want with it?" Snopes said.

"To start a goat-ranch," Ratliff said. "How much?" Snopes spat over the moving wheel. He named the sum for the third time. Ratliff slacked off the reins and the little strong tireless team began to trot, sweeping around the last curve and past the empty schoolhouse, the village now in sight, the surrey in sight too, already beyond the store, going on. "That fellow, that teacher you had three-four years ago. Labove. Did anybody ever hear what become of him?"

A little after six that evening, in the empty and locked store, Ratliff and Bookwright and Armstid bought the Old Frenchman place from Snopes. Ratliff gave a quit-claim deed to his half of the side-street lunch-room in Jefferson. Armstid gave a mortgage on his farm, including the buildings and tools and live-stock and about two miles of three-strand wire fence; Bookwright paid his third in cash. Then Snopes let them out the front door and locked it again and they stood on the empty gallery in the fading August afterglow and watched him depart up the road toward Varner's house—two of them did, that is, because Armstid had already gone ahead and got into the buckboard, where he sat motionless and waiting and emanating that patient and seething fury. "It's ours now," Ratliff said. "And now we better get on out there and watch it before somebody fetches in Uncle Dick Bolivar some night and starts hunting buried money."

They went first to Bookwright's house (he was a bachelor) and got the mattress from his bed and two quilts and his coffee-pot and skillet and another pick and shovel, then they went to Armstid's home. He had but one mattress too, but then he had a wife and five small children; besides, Ratliff, who had seen the mattress, knew that it would not even bear being lifted from the bed. So Armstid got a quilt and they helped him fill an empty feed sack with shucks for a pillow and returned to the buckboard, passing the house in the door of which his wife still stood, with four of the children huddled about her now. But she still said nothing, and when Ratliff looked back from the moving buckboard, the door was empty.

When they turned from the old road and drove up through the shaggy park to the shell of the ruined house, there was still light enough for them to see the wagon and mules standing before it, and at that moment a man came out of the house itself and stopped, looking at them. It was Eustace Grimm, but Ratliff never knew if Armstid recognised him or even bothered to try to, because once more before the buckboard had even stopped Armstid was out of it and snatched the other shovel from beneath Bookwright's and Ratliff's feet and rushed with his limping and painful fury toward Grimm, who moved swiftly too and put the wagon between Armstid and himself, standing there and watching Armstid across the wagon as Armstid slashed across the wagon at him with the shovel. "Catch him!" Ratliff said. "He'll kill him!"

"Or break that damn leg again," Bookwright said. When they overtook him, he was trying to double the wagon, the shovel raised and poised like an axe. But Grimm had already darted around to the other side, where he now saw Ratliff and Bookwright running up, and he sprang away from them too, watching them, poised and alert. Bookwright caught Armstid from behind in both arms and held him.

"Get away quick, if you dont want anything," Ratliff told Grimm.

"No, I dont want anything," Grimm said.

"Then go on while Bookwright's got him." Grimm moved toward the wagon, watching Armstid with something curious and veiled in his look.

"He's going to get in trouble with that sort of foolishness," he said.

"He'll be all right," Ratliff said. "You just get on away from here." Grimm got into the wagon and went on. "You can let him go now," Ratliff said. Armstid flung free of Bookwright and turned toward the garden. "Wait, Henry," Ratliff said. "Let's eat supper first. Let's get our beds into the house." But Armstid hurried on, limping in the fading light toward the garden. "We ought to eat first," Ratliff said. Then he let out a long breath like a sigh; he and Bookwright ran side by side to the rear of the sewing-machine box, which Ratliff unlocked, and they snatched out the other shovels and picks and ran down the slope and into the old garden where Armstid was already digging. Just before they reached him he stood up and began to run toward the road, the shovel raised, whereupon they too saw that

Grimm had not departed but was sitting in the wagon in the road, watching them across the ruined fence of iron pickets until Armstid had almost reached it. Then he drove on.

They dug all that night, Armstid in one hole, Ratliff and Bookwright working together in another. From time to time they would stop to rest while the summer constellations marched overhead. Ratliff and Bookwright would move about to flex their cramped muscles, then they would squat (They did not smoke; they could not risk showing any light. Armstid had probably never had the extra nickel or dime to buy tobacco with.) and talk quietly while they listened to the steady sound of Armstid's shovel below them. He would be digging when they stopped; he would still be digging, unflagging and tireless, when they started again, though now and then one of them would remember him and pause to see him sitting on the side of his pit, immobile as the lumps of earth he had thrown out of it. Then he would be digging again before he had actually had time to rest; this until dawn began and Ratliff and Bookwright stood over him in the wan light, arguing with him. "We got to quit," Ratliff said. "It's already light enough for folks to see us." Armstid didn't pause.

"Let them," he said. "It's mine now. I can dig all day if I want."

"All right," Ratliff said. "You'll have plenty of help then." Now Armstid paused, looking up at him out of his pit. "How can we dig all night and then set up all day to keep other folks out of it?" Ratliff said. "Come on now," he said. "We got to eat and then sleep some." They got the mattress and the quilts from the buckboard and carried them into the house, the hall in whose gaping door-frames no doors any longer hung and from whose ceiling depended the skeleton of what had been once a crystal chandelier, with its sweep of stairs whose treads had long since been prized off and carried away to patch barns and chicken-houses and privies, whose spindles and walnut railings and newel-posts had long ago been chopped up and burned as firewood. The room they chose had a fourteen-foot ceiling. There were the remains of a once-gilt filigree of cornice above the gutted windows and the ribbed and serrated grin of lathing from which the plaster had fallen, and the skeleton of another prismed chandelier. They spread the mattress and the quilts upon the dust of plaster, and Ratliff and Bookwright returned to the buckboard and got the food they had brought, and the two sacks of coins. They hid the two sacks in the chimney, foul now with bird-droppings, behind the mantel in which there were still wedged a few shards of the original marble. Armstid didn't produce his bag. They didn't know what he had done with it. They didn't ask.

They built no fire. Ratliff would probably have objected, but nobody suggested it; they ate cold the tasteless food, too tired to taste it; removing only their shoes stained with the dampening earth from the deepening pits, they lay among the quilts and slept fitfully, too tired to sleep completely also, dreaming of gold. Toward noon jagged scraps and flecks of sun came through the broken roof and the two rotted floors overhead and crept eastward across the floor and the tumbled quilts and then the prone bodies and the slack-mouthed upflung faces, whereupon they turned and shifted or covered their heads and faces with their arms, as though, still sleeping, they fled the weightless shadow of that for which, awake, they had betrayed themselves. They were awake at sunset without having rested. They moved stiffly about, not talking, while the coffee-pot boiled on the broken hearth; they ate again, wolfing the cold and tasteless food while the crimson glow from the dying west faded in the high ruined room. Armstid was the first one to finish. He put his cup down and rose, turning first onto his hands and knees as an infant gets up, dragging his stiff twice-broken leg painfully beneath him, and limped toward the door. "We ought to wait till full dark," Ratliff said, to no one; certainly no one answered him. It was as if he spoke to himself and had answered himself. He rose too. Bookwright was already standing. When they reached the garden, Armstid was already in his pit, digging.

They dug through that brief summer night as through the previous one while the familiar stars wheeled overhead, stopping now and then to rest and ease their muscles and listen to the steady sigh and recover of Armstid's shovel below them; they prevailed upon him to stop at dawn and returned to the house and ate—the canned salmon, the sidemeat cold in its own congealed grease, the cold cooked bread—and slept again among the tumbled quilts while noon came and the creeping and probing golden sun at whose touch they turned and shifted as though in impotent nightmare flight from that impalpable and weightless burden. They had finished the bread that morning. When the others waked at the second sunset, Ratliff had the coffee-pot on the fire and was cooking another batch of cornbread in the skillet. Armstid would not wait for it. He ate his portion of meat alone and drank his coffee and got to his feet again as small children do, and went out. Bookwright was standing also. Ratliff, squatting beside the skillet, looked up at him. "Go on then," he said. "You dont need to wait either."

"We're down six foot," Bookwright said. "Four foot wide and near ten foot long. I'll start where we found the third sack."

"All right," Ratliff said. "Go on and start." Because something had clicked in his mind again. It might have been while he was asleep, he didn't know. But he knew that this time it was right. Only I dont want to look at it, hear it, he thought, squatting, holding the skillet steady over the fire, squinting his watering eyes against the smoke which the broken chimney no longer drew out of the house, I dont dare to. Anyway, I dont have to yet. I can dig again tonight. We even got a new place to dig. So he waited until the bread was done. Then he took it out of the skillet and set it near the ashes and sliced some of the bacon into the skillet and cooked it; he had his first hot meal in three days, and he ate it without haste, squatting, sipping his coffee while the last of the sunset's crimson gathered along the ruined ceiling and died from there too, and the room had only the glow of the dying fire.

Bookwright and Armstid were already digging. When he came close enough to see, Armstid unaided was three feet down and his pit was very nearly as long as the one Ratliff and Bookwright had dug together. He went on to where Bookwright had started the new pit and took up his shovel (Bookwright had fetched it for him) and began to dig. They dug on through that night too, beneath the marching and familiar stars, stopping now and then to rest although Armstid did not stop when they did, squatting on the lip of the new excavation while Ratliff talked, murmurous, not about gold, money, but anecdotal, humorous, his invisible face quizzical, bemused, impenetrable. They dug again. Daylight will be time enough to look at it, he thought. Because I done already looked at it, he thought. I looked at it three days ago. Then it began to be dawn. In the wan beginning of that light he put his shovel down and straightened up. Bookwright's pick rose and fell steadily in front of him; twenty feet beyond, he could now see Armstid waist-deep in the ground as if he had been cut in two at the hips, the dead torso, not even knowing it was dead, laboring on in measured stoop and recover like a metronome as Armstid dug himself back into that earth which had produced him to be its born and fated thrall forever until he died. Ratliff climbed out of the pit and stood in the dark fresh loam which they had thrown out of it, his muscles flinching and jerking with fatigue, and stood looking quietly at Bookwright until Bookwright became aware of him and paused, the pick raised for the next stroke, and looked up at him. They looked at each other—the two gaunt, unshaven, weary faces. "Odum," Ratliff said, "who was Eustace Grimm's wife?"

"I dont know," Bookwright said.

"I do," Ratliff said. "She was one of them Calhoun County Dosheys. And that aint right. And his ma was a Fite. And that aint right either." Bookwright quit looking at him. He laid the pick down carefully, almost gently, as if it were a spoon level-full of soup or of that much nitro-glycerin, and climbed out of the pit, wiping his hands on his trousers.

"I thought you knew," he said. "I thought you knew everything about folks in this country."

"I reckon I know now," Ratliff said. "But I reckon you'll still have to tell me."

"Fite was his second wife's name. She wasn't Eustace's ma. Pa told me about it when Ab Snopes first rented that place from the Varners five years ago."

"All right," Ratliff said. "Tell me."

"Eustace's ma was Ab Snopes's youngest sister." They looked at one another, blinking a little. Soon the light would begin to increase fast.

"Sholy now," Ratliff said. "You finished?"

"Yes," Bookwright said. "I'm finished."

"Bet you one of them I beat you," Ratliff said. They mounted the slope and entered the house, the room where they slept. It was still dark in the room, so while Ratliff fumbled the two bags out of the chimney, Bookwright lit the lantern and set it on the floor and they squatted facing each other across the lantern, opening the bags.

"I reckon we ought to knowed wouldn't no cloth sack . . ." Bookwright said. "After fifty years . . ." They emptied the bags onto the floor. Each of them took up a coin, examined it briefly, then set them one upon the other like a crowned king in checkers, close to the lantern. Then one by one they examined the other coins by the light of the dingy lantern. "But how did he know it would be us?" Bookwright said.

"He didn't," Ratliff said. "He didn't care. He just come out here every night and dug for a while. He knowed he couldn't possibly dig over two weeks before somebody saw him." He laid his last coin down and sat back on his heels until Bookwright had finished. "1891," he said.

"1901," Bookwright said. "I even got one that was made last year. You beat me."

"I beat you," Ratliff said. He took up the two coins and they put the money back into the bags. They didn't hide them. They left each bag on its owner's quilt and blew out the lantern. It was lighter now and they could see Armstid quite well where he stooped and rose and stooped in his thigh-deep pit. The sun would rise soon; already there were three buzzards soaring against the high yellow-blue. Armstid did not even look up when they approached; he continued to dig even while they stood beside the pit, looking down at him. "Henry," Ratliff said. Then Ratliff leaned down and touched his shoulder. He whirled, the shovel raised and turned edgewise and glinting a thin line of steel-colored dawn as the edge of an axe would.

"Get out of my hole," he said. "Get outen it."

2

The wagons containing the men, the women and the children approaching the village from that direction, stopped, and the men who had walked up from the store to stand along Varner's fence, watched, while Lump and Eck Snopes and Varner's Negro, Sam, loaded the furniture and the trunks and the boxes into the wagon backed up to the edge of the veranda. It was the same wagon drawn by the same mules which had brought Flem Snopes back from Texas in April, and the three men came and went between it and the house, Eck or the Negro backing clumsily through the door with the burden between them and Lump Snopes scuttling along beside it in a constant patter of his own exhortations and commands, holding to it, to be sure, but carrying no weight, to load that into the wagon and return, pausing at the door and stepping aside as Mrs Varner bustled out with another armful of small crocks and hermetic jars of fruit and vegetables. The watchers along the fence checked the objects off—the dismantled bed, the dresser, the washstand with its flowered matching bowl and ewer and slop-jar and chamber-pot, the trunk which doubtless contained the wife's and the child's clothing, the wooden box which the women at least knew doubtless contained dishes and cutlery and cooking vessels, and lastly a tightly roped mass of brown canvas. "What's that?" Freeman said. "It looks like a tent."

"It is a tent," Tull said. "Eck brought it out from the express office in town last week."

"They aint going to move to Jefferson and live in a tent, are they?" Freeman said.

"I dont know," Tull said. At last the wagon was loaded; Eck and the Negro bumped through the door for the last time, Mrs Varner bustled out with the final hermetic jar; Lump Snopes re-entered the house and emerged with the straw suitcase which they all knew, then Flem Snopes and then his wife came out. She was carrying the baby which was too large to have been born at only seven months but which had certainly not waited until May, and stood there for a moment. Olympus-tall, a head taller than her mother or husband either, in a tailored suit despite the rich heat of summer's full maturing, whose complexion alone showed that she was not yet eighteen since the unseeing and expressionless mask-face had no age, while the women in the wagons looked at her and thought how that was the first tailored suit ever seen in Frenchman's Bend and how she had got some clothes out of Flem Snopes anyway because it would not be Will Varner that bought them now, and the men along the fence looked at her and thought of Hoake McCarron and how any one of them would have bought the suit or anything else for her if she had wanted it.

Mrs Varner took the child from her and they watched her sweep the skirts inward into one hand with the gesture immemorial and female and troubling, and climb the wheel to the seat where Snopes already sat with the reins, and lean down and take the child from Mrs Varner. The wagon moved, lurched into motion, the team swinging to cross the yard toward the open gate into the lane, and that was all. If farewell was said, that was it, the halted wagons along the road creaking into motion again though Freeman and Tull and the other four men merely turned, relaxed again, their backs against the picket fence now, their faces identically grave, a little veiled and perhaps even sober, not quite watching the laden wagon as it turned out of the lane and approached and then was passing them—the plaid cap, the steady and deliberate jaw, the minute bow and the white shirt; the other face calm and beautiful and by its expression carven or even corpse-like, looking not at them certainly and maybe not at anything they knew. "So long, Flem," Freeman said. "Save me a steak when you get your hand in at cooking." He didn't answer. He might not have heard even. The wagon went on. Watching it, not moving yet, they saw it turn into the old road which until two weeks ago had been marked only by the hooves of Varner's fat white horse for more than twenty years.

"He'll have to drive three extra miles to get back into the road to town that way," Tull said in an anxious voice.

"Maybe he aims to take them three miles on into town with him and swap them to Grover Cleveland Winbush for the other half of that restaurant," Freeman said.

"Maybe he'll swap them to Ratliff and Bookwright and Henry Armstid for something else," a third man—his name was Winbush also, a brother of the other one—said. "He'll find Ratliff in town too."

"He'll find Henry Armstid without having to go that far," Freeman said.

That road was no longer a fading and almost healed scar. It was rutted now, because there had been rain a week ago, and now the untroubled grass and weeds of almost fifty years bore four distinct paths: the two outer ones where iron wheel-rims had run, the two inner ones where the harnessed teams had walked daily since that first afternoon when the first ones had turned into it—the weathered and creaking wagons, the plow-galled horses and mules, the men and women and children entering another world, traversing another land, moving in another time, another afternoon without time or name.

Where the sand darkened into the shallow water of the branch and then lightened and rose again, the countless overlapping prints of rims and iron shoes were like shouts in a deserted church. Then the wagons would begin to come into sight, drawn up in line at the roadside, the smaller children squatting in the wagons, the women still sitting in the splint chairs in the wagon beds, holding the infants and nursing them when need arose, the men and larger children standing quietly along the ruined and honeysuckle-choked iron fence, watching Armstid as he spaded the earth steadily down the slope of the old garden. They had been watching him for two weeks. After the first day, after the first ones had seen him and gone home with the news of it, they began to come in by wagon and on horse-and mule-back from as far away as ten and fifteen miles, men, women and children, octogenarian and suckling, four generations in one battered and weathered wagon bed still littered with dried manure or hay and grain chaff, to sit in the wagons and stand along the fence with the decorum of a formal reception, the rapt interest of a crowd watching a magician at a fair. On the first day, when the first one descended and approached the fence, Armstid climbed out of his pit and ran at him, dragging the stiffened leg, the shovel raised, cursing in a harsh, light, gasping whisper, and drove the man away. But soon he quit that; he appeared to be not even aware of them where they stood along the fence, watching him spading himself steadily back and forth across the slope with that spent and unflagging fury. But none of them attempted to enter the garden again, and now it was only the half-grown boys who ever bothered him.

Toward the middle of the afternoon the ones who had come the long distances would begin to depart. But there were always some who would remain, even though it meant unharnessing and feeding and perhaps even milking in the dark. Then, just before sunset, the last wagon would arrive—the two gaunt, rabbit-like mules, the braced and dishing and ungreased wheels—and they would turn along the fence and watch quietly while the woman in the gray and shapeless garment and the faded sunbonnet got down and lifted from beneath the seat a tin pail and approached the fence beyond which the man still had not looked up nor faltered in his metronome-like labor. She would set the pail in the corner of the fence and stand for a time, motionless, the gray garment falling in rigid carven folds to her stained tennis shoes, her hands clasped and rolled into her apron, against her stomach. If she were looking at the man, they could not tell it; if she were looking at anything, they did not know it. Then she would turn and go back to the wagon (she had feeding and milking to do too, as well as the children's supper to get) and mount to the seat and take up the rope reins and turn the wagon and drive away. Then the last of the watchers would depart, leaving Armstid in the middle of his fading slope, spading himself into the waxing twilight with the regularity of a mechanical toy and with something monstrous in his unflagging effort, as if the toy were too light for what it had been set to do, or too tightly wound. In the hot summer mornings, squatting with slow tobacco or snuff-sticks on the gallery of Varner's store, or at quiet crossroads about the land in the long slant of afternoon, they talked about it, wagon to wagon, wagon to rider, rider to rider or from wagon or rider to one waiting beside a mailbox or a gate: "Is he still at it?"

"He's still at it."

"He's going to kill himself. Well, I dont know as it will be any loss."

"Not to his wife, anyway."

"That's a fact. It will save her that trip every day toting food to him. That Flem Snopes."

"That's a fact. Wouldn't no other man have done it."

"Couldn't no other man have done it. Anybody might have fooled Henry Armstid. But couldn't nobody but Flem Snopes have fooled Ratliff."

Now though it was only a little after ten, so not only had the day's quota all arrived, they were still there, including even the ones who, like Snopes, were going all the way in to Jefferson, when he drove up.

He did not pull out of the road into line. Instead, he drove on past the halted wagons while the heads of the women holding the nursing children turned to look at him and the heads of the men along the fence turned to watch him pass, the faces grave, veiled too, still looking at him when he stopped the wagon and sat, chewing with that steady and measured thrust and looking over their heads into the garden. Then the heads along the ruined fence turned as though to follow his look, and they watched two half-grown boys emerge from the undergrowth on the far side of the garden and steal across it, approaching Armstid from behind. He had not looked up nor even ceased to dig, yet the boys were not within twenty feet of him when he whirled and dragged himself out of the trench and ran at them, the shovel lifted. He said nothing; he did not even curse now. He just ran at them, dragging his leg, stumbling among the clods he had dug while the boys fled before him, distancing him. Even after they had vanished in the undergrowth from which they had come, Armstid continued to run until he stumbled and fell headlong and lay there for a time, while beyond the fence the people watched him in a silence so complete that they could hear the dry whisper of his panting breath. Then he got up, onto his hands and knees first as small children do, and picked up the shovel and returned to the trench. He did not glance up at the sun, as a man pausing in work does to gauge the time. He came straight back to the trench, hurrying back to it with that painful and laboring slowness, the gaunt unshaven face which was now completely that of a madman. He got back into the trench and began to dig.

Snopes turned his head and spat over the wagon wheel. He jerked the reins slightly. "Come up," he said.

THE TOWN

TO PHIL STONE

He did half the laughing for thirty years

ONE

CHARLES MALLISON

I wasn't born yet so it was Cousin Gowan who was there and big enough to see and remember and tell me afterward when I was big enough for it to make sense. That is, it was Cousin Gowan plus Uncle Gavin or maybe Uncle Gavin rather plus Cousin Gowan. He—Cousin Gowan—was thirteen. His grandfather was Grandfather's brother, so by the time it got down to us, he and I didn't know what cousin to each other we were. So he just called all of us except Grandfather "cousin" and all of us except Grandfather called him "cousin" and let it go at that.

They lived in Washington, where his father worked for the State Department, and all of a sudden the State Department sent his father to China or India or some far place, to be gone two years; and his mother was going too, so they sent Gowan down to stay with us and go to school in Jefferson until they got back. "Us" was Grandfather and Mother and Father and Uncle Gavin then. So this is what Gowan knew about it until I got born and big enough to know about it too. So when I say "we" and "we thought" what I mean is Jefferson and what Jefferson thought.

At first we thought that the water tank was only Flem Snopes's monument. We didn't know any better then. It wasn't until afterward that we realised that that object low on the sky above Jefferson, Mississippi, wasn't a monument at all. It was a footprint.

One day one summer he drove up the southeast road into town in a two-mule wagon containing his wife and baby and a small assortment of house-furnishings. The next day he was behind the counter of a small back-alley restaurant which belonged to V. K. Ratliff. That is, Ratliff owned it with a partner, since he—Ratliff—had to spend most of his time in his buckboard (this was before he owned the

Model T Ford) about the county with his demonstrator sewing machine for which he was the agent. That is, we thought Ratliff was still the other partner until we saw the stranger in the other greasy apron behind the counter—a squat uncommunicative man with a neat minute bow tie and opaque eyes and a sudden little hooked nose like the beak of a small hawk; a week after that, Snopes had set up a canvas tent behind the restaurant and he and his wife and baby were living in it. And that was when Ratliff told Uncle Gavin:

"Just give him time. Give him six months and he'll have Grover Cleveland" (Grover Cleveland Winbush was the partner) "out of that cafe too."

That was the first summer, the first Summer of the Snopeses, Uncle Gavin called it. He was in Harvard now, working for his M.A. After that he was going to the University of Mississippi law school to get ready to be Grandfather's partner. But already he was spending the vacations helping Grandfather be City Attorney; he had barely seen Mrs Snopes yet, so he not only didn't know he would ever go to Germany to enter Heidelberg University; he didn't even know yet that he would ever want to: only to talk about going there some day as a nice idea to keep in mind or to talk about.

He and Ratliff talked together a lot. Because although Ratliff had never been to school anywhere much and spent his time travelling about our county selling sewing machines (or selling or swapping or trading anything else for that matter), he and Uncle Gavin were both interested in people—or so Uncle Gavin said. Because what I always thought they were mainly interested in was curiosity. Until this time, that is. Because this time it had already gone a good deal further than just curiosity. This time it was alarm.

Ratliff was how we first began to learn about Snopes. Or rather, Snopeses. No, that's wrong: there had been a Snopes in Colonel Sartoris's cavalry command in 1861 in that part of it whose occupation had been raiding Yankee picket-lines for horses. Only this time it was a Confederate picket which caught him—that Snopes—raiding a Confederate horse-line and, it was believed, hung him. Which was evidently wrong too, since (Ratliff told Uncle Gavin) about ten years ago Flem and an old man who seemed to be his father appeared suddenly from nowhere one day and rented a little farm from Mr Will

Varner who just about owned the whole settlement and district called Frenchman's Bend, about twenty miles from Jefferson. It was a farm so poor and small and already worn out that only the most trifling farmers would undertake it, and even they stayed only one year. Yet Ab and Flem rented it and evidently (this is Ratliff) he or Flem or both of them together found it—

"Found what?" Uncle Gavin said.

"I don't know," Ratliff said. "Whatever it was Uncle Billy and Jody had buried out there and thought was safe."—because that winter Flem was the clerk in Uncle Billy's store. And what they found on that farm must have been a good one, or maybe they didn't even need it any more; maybe Flem found something else the Varners thought was hidden and safe under the counter of the store itself. Because in another year old Ab had moved into Frenchman's Bend to live with his son and another Snopes had appeared from somewhere to take over the rented farm; and in two years more still another Snopes was the official smith in Mr Varner's blacksmith shop. So there were as many Snopeses in Frenchman's Bend as there were Varners; and five years after that, which was the year Flem moved to Jefferson, there were even more Snopeses than Varners because one Varner was married to a Snopes and was nursing another small Snopes at her breast.

Because what Flem found that last time was inside Uncle Billy's house. She was his only daughter and youngest child, not just a local belle but a belle throughout that whole section. Nor was it just because of old Will's land and money. Because I saw her too and I knew what it was too, even if she was grown and married and with a child older than I was and I only eleven and twelve and thirteen. ("Oh ay," Uncle Gavin said. "Even at twelve dont think you are the first man ever chewed his bitter thumbs for a reason such as her.") She wasn't too big, heroic, what they call Junoesque. It was that there was just too much of what she was for any one human female package to contain, and hold: too much of white, too much of female, too much of maybe just glory, I dont know: so that at first sight of her you felt a kind of shock of gratitude just for being alive and being male at the same instant with her in space and time, and then in the next second and forever after a kind of despair because you knew that there never would be enough of any one male to match and hold and deserve her; grief forever after because forever after nothing less would ever do.

That was what he found this time. One day, according to Ratliff, Frenchman's Bend learned that Flem Snopes and Eula Varner had driven across the line into the next county the night before and bought a license and got married; the same day, still according to Ratliff, Frenchman's Bend learned that three young men, three of Eula's old suitors, had left the country suddenly by night too, for Texas it was said, or anyway west, far enough west to be farther than Uncle Billy or Jody Varner could have reached if they had needed to try. Then a month later Flem and Eula also departed for Texas (that bourne, Uncle Gavin said, in our time for the implicated, the insolvent or the merely hopeful), to return the next summer with a girl baby a little larger than you would have expected at only three months—

"And the horses," Uncle Gavin said. Because we did know about that, mainly because Flem Snopes had not been the first to import them. Every year or so someone brought into the county a string of wild unbroken plains ponies from somewhere in the west and auctioned them off. This time the ponies arrived, in the charge of a man who was obviously from Texas, at the same time that Mr and Mrs Snopes returned home from that state. This string however seemed to be uncommonly wild, since the resultant scattering of the untamed and untamable calico-splotched animals covered not just Frenchman's Bend but the whole east half of the county too. Though even to the last, no one ever definitely connected Snopes with their ownership. "No, no," Uncle Gavin said. "You were not one of the three that ran from the smell of Will Varner's shotgun. And dont tell me Flem Snopes traded you one of those horses for your half of that restaurant because I wont believe it. What was it?"

Ratliff sat there with his bland brown smoothly shaven face and his neat tieless blue shirt and his shrewd intelligent gentle eyes not quite looking at Uncle Gavin. "It was that old house," he said. Uncle Gavin waited. "The Old Frenchman place." Uncle Gavin waited. "That buried money." Then Uncle Gavin understood: not an old pre-Civil War plantation house in all Mississippi or the South either but had its legend of the money and plate buried in the flower garden from Yankee raiders—in this particular case, the ruined mansion which in the old time had dominated and bequeathed its name to the whole section known as Frenchman's Bend, which the Varners now owned. "It was Henry Armstid's fault, trying to get even with Flem for that horse that Texas man sold him that broke his leg. No," Ratliff said, "it was me too as much as anybody else, as any of us. To figger out what Flem was doing owning that old place that anybody could see wasn't worth nothing. I dont mean why Flem bought it. I mean, why he even taken it when Uncle Billy give it to him and Eula for a wedding gift. So when Henry taken to following and watching Flem and finally caught him that night digging in that old flower garden, I dont reckon Henry had to persuade me very hard to go back the next night and watch Flem digging myself."

"So when Flem finally quit digging and went away, you and Henry crawled out of the bushes and dug too," Uncle Gavin said. "And found it. Some of it. Enough of it. Just exactly barely enough of it for you to hardly wait for daylight to swap Flem Snopes your half of that restaurant for your half of the Old Frenchman place. How much longer did you and Henry dig before you quit?"

"I quit after the second night," Ratliff said. "That was when I finally thought to look at the money."

"All right," Uncle Gavin said. "The money."

"They was silver dollars me and Henry dug up. Some of them was pretty old. One of Henry's was minted almost thirty years ago."

"A salted gold mine," Uncle Gavin said. "One of the oldest tricks in the world, yet you fell for it. Not Henry Armstid: you."

"Yes," Ratliff said. "Almost as old as that handkerchief Eula Varner dropped. Almost as old as Uncle Billy Varner's shotgun." That was what he said then. Because another year had passed when he stopped Uncle Gavin on the street and said, "With the court's permission, Lawyer, I would like to take a exception. I want to change that-ere to 'still.' "

"Change what-ere to 'still'?" Uncle Gavin said.

"Last year I said 'That handkerchief Miz Flem Snopes dropped.' I want to change that 'dropped' to 'still dropping.' They's one feller I know still following it."

Because in six months Snopes had not only eliminated the partner

from the restaurant, Snopes himself was out of it, replaced behind
the greasy counter and in the canvas tent too by another Snopes
accreted in from Frenchman's Bend into the vacuum behind the first
one's next advancement by that same sort of osmosis by which,
according to Ratliff, they had covered Frenchman's Bend, the chain
unbroken, every Snopes in Frenchman's Bend moving up one step,
leaving that last slot at the bottom open for the next Snopes to
appear from nowhere and fill, which without doubt he had already
done though Ratliff had not yet had time to go out there and see.

And now Flem and his wife lived in a small rented house in a back
street near the edge of town, and Flem was now superintendent of
the town power-plant which pumped the water and produced the
electricity. Our outrage was primarily shock; shock not that Flem had
the job, we had not got that far yet, but shock that we had not known
until now that the job existed; that there was such a position in Jefferson as superintendent of the power-plant. Because the plant—the
boilers and the engines which ran the pump and dynamo—was operated by an old saw-mill engineer named Harker, and the dynamos
and the electric wiring which covered the town were cared for by a
private electrician who worked on a retainer from the town—a condition which had been completely satisfactory ever since running
water and electricity first came to Jefferson. Yet suddenly and without warning, we needed a superintendent for it. And as suddenly and
simultaneously and with that same absence of warning, a country
man who had not been in town two years now, and (we assumed) had
probably never seen an electric light until that first night two years
ago when he drove in, was that superintendent.

That was the only shock. It wasn't that the country man was Flem
Snopes. Because we had all seen Mrs Snopes by now, what few times
we did see her which was usually behind the counter in the restaurant
in another greasy apron, frying the hamburgers and eggs and ham
and the tough pieces of steak on the grease-crusted kerosene griddle,
or maybe once a week on the Square, always alone; not, as far as we
knew, going anywhere: just moving, walking in that aura of decorum
and modesty and solitariness ten times more immodest and a hundred times more disturbing than one of the bathing suits young
women would begin to wear about 1920 or so, as if in the second just

before you looked, her garments had managed in one last frantic pell-mell scurry to overtake and cover her. Though only for a moment because in the next one, if only you followed long enough, they would wilt and fail from that mere plain and simple striding which would shred them away like the wheel of a constellation through a wisp and cling of trivial scud.

And we had known the mayor, Major de Spain, longer than that. Jefferson, Mississippi, the whole South for that matter, was still full at that time of men called General or Colonel or Major because their fathers or grandfathers had been generals or colonels or majors or maybe just privates, in Confederate armies, or who had contributed to the campaign funds of successful state governors. But Major de Spain's father had been a real major of Confederate cavalry, and De Spain himself was a West Pointer who had gone to Cuba as a second lieutenant with troops and came home with a wound—a long scar running from his hair through his left ear and down his jaw, which could have been left by the sabre or gun-rammer we naturally assumed some embattled Spaniard had hit him with, or by the axe which political tactics during the race for mayor claimed a sergeant in a dice game had hit him with.

Because he had not been long at home and out of his blue Yankee coat before we realised that he and Jefferson were incorrigibly and invincibly awry to one another, and that one of them was going to have to give. And that it would not be him: that he would neither flee Jefferson nor try to alter himself to fit Jefferson, but instead would try to wrench Jefferson until the town fitted him, and—the young people hoped—would succeed.

Until then, Jefferson was like all the other little Southern towns: nothing had happened in it since the last carpetbagger had given up and gone home or been assimilated into another unregenerate Mississippian. We had the usual mayor and board of aldermen who seemed to the young people to have been in perpetuity since the Ark or certainly since the last Chickasaw departed for Oklahoma in 1820, as old then as now and even now no older: old Mr Adams the mayor with a long patriarchal white beard, who probably seemed to young people like Cousin Gowan older than God Himself, until he might actually have been the first man; Uncle Gavin said there were more

than just boys of twelve and thirteen like Cousin Gowan that
referred to him by name, leaving off the last s, and to his old fat wife
as "Miss Eve Adam," fat old Eve long since free of the danger of
inciting a snake or anything else to tempt her.

So we were wondering just what axe Lieutenant de Spain would
use to chop the corners off Jefferson and make it fit him. One day
he found it. The city electrician (the one who kept the town's gen-
erators and dynamos and transformers working) was a genius. One
afternoon in 1904 he drove out of his back yard into the street in the
first automobile we had ever seen, made by hand completely, engine
and all, from magneto coil to radius rod, and drove into the Square
at the moment when Colonel Sartoris the banker's surrey and
blooded matched team were crossing it on the way home. Although
Colonel Sartoris and his driver were not hurt and the horses when
caught had no scratch on them and the electrician offered to repair
the surrey (it was said he even offered to put a gasoline engine in it
this time), Colonel Sartoris appeared in person before the next meeting of the board of aldermen, who passed an edict that no gasoline-
propelled vehicle should ever operate on the streets of Jefferson.

That was De Spain's chance. It was more than just his. It was the
opportunity which that whole contemporary generation of young
people had been waiting for, not just in Jefferson but everywhere,
who had seen in that stinking noisy little home-made self-propelled
buggy which Mr Buffaloe (the electrician) had made out of odds and
ends in his back yard in his spare time, not just a phenomenon but an
augury, a promise of the destiny which would belong to the United
States. He—De Spain—didn't even need to campaign for mayor: all
he needed was to announce. And the old dug-in city fathers saw that
too, which was why they spooked to the desperate expedient of creating or exhuming or repeating (whichever it was) the story of the
Cuban dice game and the sergeant's axe. And De Spain settled that
once and for all not even as a politician; Caesar himself couldn't have
done it any neater.

It was one morning at mail-time. Mayor Adams and his youngest
son Theron who was not as old as De Spain and not even very much
bigger either, mainly just taller, were coming out of the post office
when De Spain met them. That is, he was already standing there

with a good crowd watching, his finger already touching the scar when Mr Adams saw him. "Good morning, Mister Mayor," he said. "What's this I hear about a dice game with an axe in it?"

"That's what the voters of the city of Jefferson would like to ask you, sir," Mr Adams said. "If you know of any proof to the contrary nearer than Cuba, I would advise you to produce it."

"I know a quicker way than that," De Spain said. "Your Honor's a little too old for it, but Theron there's a good-sized boy now. Let him and me step over to McCaslin's hardware store and get a couple of axes and find out right now if you are right."

"Aw now, Lieutenant," Theron said.

"That's all right," De Spain said. "I'll pay for both of them."

"Gentlemen," Theron said. And that was all of that. In June De Spain was elected mayor. It was a landslide because more than just he had won, been elected. The new age had entered Jefferson; he was merely its champion, the Godfrey de Bouillon, the Tancred, the Jefferson Richard Lion-heart of the twentieth century.

He wore that mantle well. No: it wasn't a mantle: it was a banner, a flag and he was carrying it, already out in front before Jefferson knew we were even ready for it. He made Mr Buffaloe City Electrician with a monthly salary, though his first official act was about Colonel Sartoris's edict against automobiles. We thought of course that he and his new aldermen would have repealed it for no other reason than that one old mossback like Colonel Sartoris had told another old mossback like Mayor Adams to pass it, and the second old mossback did. But they didn't do that. Like I said, it was a landslide that elected him; it was like that axe business with old Mayor Adams and Theron in front of the post office that morning had turned on a light for all the other young people in Jefferson. I mean, the ones who were not yet store- and gin-owners and already settled lawyers and doctors, but were only the clerks and bookkeepers in the stores and gins and offices, trying to save enough to get married on, who all went to work to get De Spain elected mayor. And not only did that, but more: before they knew it or even intended it, they had displaced the old dug-in aldermen and themselves rode into office as the city fathers on Manfred de Spain's coat-tails or anyway axe. So you would have thought the first thing they would have done would be to throw out forever that automobile law. Instead, they had it copied out on a piece of parchment like a diploma or a citation and framed and hung on the wall in a lighted glass case in the hall of the Courthouse, where pretty soon people were coming in automobiles from as far away as Chicago to laugh at it. Because Uncle Gavin said this was still that fabulous and legendary time when there was still no paradox between an automobile and mirth, before the time when every American had to have one and they were killing more people than wars did.

He—De Spain—did even more than that. He himself had brought into town the first real automobile—a red E.M.F. roadster, and sold the horses out of the livery stable his father had left him and tore out the stalls and cribs and tack-rooms and established the first garage and automobile agency in Jefferson, so that now all his aldermen and all the other young people to whom neither of the banks would lend one cent to buy a motor vehicle with, no matter how solvent they were, could own them too. Oh yes, the motor age had reached Jefferson and De Spain led it in that red roadster: that vehicle alien and debonair, as invincibly and irrevocably polygamous and bachelor as De Spain himself. And would ever be, living alone in his late father's big wooden house with a cook and a houseman in a white coat; he led the yearly cotillion and was first on the list of the ladies' german; if café society—not the Social Register nor the Four Hundred: Café Society—had been invented yet and any of it had come to Jefferson, he would have led it; born a generation too soon, he would have been by acclamation ordained a high priest in that new national religious cult of Cheesecake as it translated still alive the Harlows and Grables and Monroes into the hierarchy of American cherubim.

So when we first saw Mrs Snopes walking in the Square giving off that terrifying impression that in another second her flesh itself would burn her garments off, leaving not even a veil of ashes between her and the light of day, it seemed to us that we were watching Fate, a fate of which both she and Mayor de Spain were victims. We didn't know when they met, laid eyes for the first time on each other. We didn't need to. In a way, we didn't want to. We assumed of course that he was slipping her into his house by some devious means or method at night, but we didn't know that either. With any else but them, some of us—some boy or boys or youths—would have lain in ambush just to find out. But not with him. On the contrary, we were on his side. We didn't want to know. We were his allies, his confederates; our whole town was accessory to that cuckolding—that cuckolding which for any proof we had, we had invented ourselves out of whole cloth; that same cuckoldry in which we would watch De Spain and Snopes walking amicably together while (though we didn't know it yet) De Spain was creating, planning how to create, that office of power-plant superintendent which we didn't even know we didn't have, let alone needed, and then get Mr Snopes into it. It was not because we were against Mr Snopes; we had not yet read the signs and portents which should have warned, alerted, sprung us into frantic concord to defend our town from him. Nor were we really in favor of adultery, sin: we were simply in favor of De Spain and Eula Snopes, for what Uncle Gavin called the divinity of simple unadulterated uninhibited immortal lust which they represented; for the two people in each of whom the other had found his single ordained fate; each to have found out of all the earth that one match for his mettle; ours the pride that Jefferson would supply their battleground.

Even Uncle Gavin; Uncle Gavin also. He said to Ratliff: "This town aint that big. Why hasn't Flem caught them?"

"He dont want to," Ratliff said. "He dont need to yet."

Then we learned that the town—the mayor, the board of aldermen, whoever and however it was done—had created the office of power-plant superintendent, and appointed Flem Snopes to fill it.

At night Mr Harker, the veteran saw-mill engineer, ran the power-plant, with Tomey's Turl Beauchamp, the Negro fireman, to fire the boilers as long as Mr Harker was there to watch the pressure gauges, which Tomey's Turl either could not or would not do, apparently simply declining to take seriously any connection between the firebox below the boiler and the little dirty clock-face which didn't even tell the hour, on top of it. During the day the other Negro fireman, Tom Tom Bird, ran the plant alone, with Mr Buffaloe to look in now and then, though as a matter of routine since Tom Tom not only fired the boilers, he was as competent to read the gauges and keep the bearings of the steam engine and the dynamos cleaned and oiled as Mr Buffaloe and Mr Harker were: a completely satisfactory arrangement since Mr Harker was old enough not to mind or possibly even prefer the night shift, and Tom Tom—a big bull of a man weighing two hundred pounds and sixty years old but looking about forty and married about two years ago to his fourth wife: a young woman whom he kept with the strict jealous seclusion of a Turk in a cabin about two miles down the railroad track from the plant— declined to consider anything but the day one. Though by the time Cousin Gowan joined Mr Harker's night shift, Mr Snopes had learned to read the gauges and even fill the oil cups too.

This was about two years after he became superintendent. Gowan had decided to go out for the football team that fall and he got the idea, I dont reckon even he knew where, that a job shovelling coal on a power-plant night shift would be the exact perfect training for dodging or crashing over enemy tacklers. Mother and Father didn't think so until Uncle Gavin took a hand. (He had his Harvard M.A. now and had finished the University of Mississippi law school and passed his bar and Grandfather had begun to retire and now Uncle Gavin really was the city attorney; it had been a whole year now— this was in June, he had just got home from the University and he hadn't seen Mrs Snopes yet this summer—since he had even talked of Heidelberg as a pleasant idea for conversation.)

"Why not?" he said. "Gowan's going on thirteen now: it's time for him to begin to stay out all night. And what better place can he find than down there at the plant where Mr Harker and the fireman can keep him awake?"

So Gowan got the job as Tomey's Turl's helper and at once Mr Harker began to keep him awake talking about Mr Snopes, talking about him with the kind of amoral amazement with which you would recount having witnessed the collision of a planet. According to Mr Harker, it began last year. One afternoon Tom Tom had finished cleaning his fires and was now sitting in the gangway smoking his pipe, pressure up and the safety-valve on the middle boiler blowing off, when Mr Snopes came in and stood there for a while, chewing tobacco and looking up at the whistling valve.

"How much does that whistle weigh?" he said.

"If you talking about that valve, about ten pounds," Tom Tom said.

"Solid brass?" Mr Snopes said.

"All except that little hole it's what you call whistling through," Tom Tom said. And that was all then, Mr Harker said; it was two months later when he, Mr Harker, came on duty one evening and found the three safety-valves gone from the boilers and the vents stopped with one-inch steel screw plugs capable of a pressure of a thousand pounds and Tomey's Turl still shovelling coal into the fire-boxes because he hadn't heard one of them blow off yet.

"And them three boiler heads you could poke a hole through with a sody straw," Mr Harker said. "When I seen the gauge on the first boiler I never believed I would live to reach the injector.

"So when I finally got it into Turl's head that that 100 on that dial meant where Turl wouldn't only lose his job, he would lose it so good wouldn't nobody never find the job nor him again neither, I finally got settled down enough to inquire where them safety-valves had went to.

" 'Mr Snopes took um off,' he says.

" 'What in hell for?'

" 'I dont know. I just telling you what Tom Tom told me. He say Mr Snopes say the shut-off float in the water tank aint heavy enough. Say that tank start leaking some day, so he going to fasten them three safety-valves on the float and weight it heavier.'

" 'You mean,' I says. That's as far as I could get. 'You mean—'

" 'That's what Tom Tom say. I don't know nothing about it.'

"Anyhow they was gone; whether they was in the water tank or not, was too late to find out now. Until then, me and Turl had been taking it pretty easy after the load went off and things got kind of quiet. But you can bet we never dozed none that night. Me and him spent the whole of it time about on the coal pile where we could watch them three gauges all at once. And from midnight on, after the load went off, we never had enough steam in all them three boilers put together to run a peanut parcher. And even when I was home in bed, I couldn't go to sleep. Time I shut my eyes I would begin to see a steam gauge about the size of a washtub, with a red needle big as a coal scoop moving up toward a hundred pounds, and I would wake myself up hollering and sweating.

"So come daylight enough to see; and I never sent Turl neither: I clumb up there myself and looked at that float. And there wasn't no safety-valves weighting it neither and maybe he hadn't aimed for them to be fastened to it where the first feller that looked in could a reached them. And even if that tank is forty-two foot deep I still could a opened the cock and dreened it. Only I just work there, Mr Snopes was the superintendent, and it was the day shift now and Tom Tom could answer whatever questions Joe Buffaloe would want to know in case he happened in and seen them thousand-pound screw plugs where safety-valves was supposed to been.

"So I went on home and that next night I couldn't hardly get Turl to run them gauge needles up high enough to turn the low-pressure piston, let alone move the dynamos; and the next night, and the next one, until about ten days when the express delivered a box; Tom Tom had waited and me and him opened the box (It was marked C.O.D. in big black paint but the tag itself had been wrenched off and gone temporarily. 'I know where he throwed it,' Tom Tom said.) and taken them screw plugs out of the vents and put the three new safety-valves back on; and sho enough Tom Tom did have the crumpled-up tag: Mister Flem Snopes Power-plant Jefferson Miss C.O.D. twenty-three dollars and eighty-one cents."

And now there was some of it which Mr Harker himself didn't know until Uncle Gavin told him after Tom Tom told Uncle Gavin: how one afternoon Tom Tom was smoking his pipe on the coal pile when Mr Snopes came in carrying in his hand what Tom Tom thought at first was a number-three mule shoe until Mr Snopes took it into a corner behind the boilers where a pile of discarded fittings— valves, rods, bolts and such—had been accumulating probably since the first light was turned on in Jefferson; and, kneeling (Mr Snopes), tested every piece one by one into two separate piles in the gangway behind him. Then Tom Tom watched him test with the magnet every loose piece of metal in the whole boiler room, sorting the mere iron from the brass. Then Snopes ordered Tom Tom to gather up the separated brass and bring it to the office.

Tom Tom gathered the brass into a box. Snopes was waiting in the office, chewing tobacco. Tom Tom said he never stopped chewing even to spit. "How do you and Turl get along?" he said.

"I tend to my business," Tom Tom said. "What Turl does with his aint none of mine."

"That aint what Turl thinks," Mr Snopes said. "He wants me to give him your day shift. He claims he's tired of firing at night."

"Let him fire as long as I is, and he can have it," Tom Tom said.

"Turl dont aim to wait that long," Mr Snopes said. Then he told Tom Tom: how Turl was planning to steal iron from the plant and lay it on Tom Tom and get him fired. That's right. That's what Tom Tom told Uncle Gavin Mr Snopes called it: iron. Maybe Mr Snopes hadn't heard of a magnet himself until just yesterday and so he thought that Tom Tom had never heard of one and so didn't know what he was doing. I mean, not of magnets nor brass either and couldn't tell brass from iron. Or maybe he just thought that Tom Tom, being a Negro, wouldn't care. Or maybe that, being a Negro, whether he knew or not or cared or not, he wouldn't have any part of what a white man was mixed up in. Only we had to imagine this part of it of course. Not that it was hard to do: Tom Tom standing there about the size and shape and color (disposition too) of a Black Angus bull, looking down at the white man. Turl on the contrary was the color of a saddle and even with a scoop full of coal he barely touched a hundred and fifty pounds. "That's what he's up to," Mr Snopes said. "So I want you to take this stuff out to your house and hide it and dont breathe a word to nobody. And soon as I get enough evidence on Turl, I'm going to fire him."

"I knows a better way than that," Tom Tom said.

"What way?" Snopes said. Then he said: "No no, that wont do. You have any trouble with Turl and I'll fire you both. You do like I say. Unless you are tired of your job and want Turl to have it. Are you?"

"Aint no man complained about my pressure yet," Tom Tom said.

"Then you do like I tell you," Snopes said. "You take that stuff home with you tonight. Dont let nobody see you, even your wife. And if you dont want to do it, just say so. I reckon I can find somebody that will."

So Tom Tom did. And each time the pile of discarded fittings accumulated again, he would watch Snopes test out another batch of brass with his magnet for Tom Tom to take home and hide.

Because Tom Tom had been firing boilers for forty years now, ever since he became a man, and these three for the twenty they had been there, since it was he who built the first fires beneath them. At first he had fired one boiler and he had got five dollars a month for it. Now he had the three and he got sixty dollars a month, and now he was sixty and he owned his little cabin and a little piece of corn land and a mule and wagon to ride to church in twice each Sunday, with a gold watch and the young wife who was the last new young wife he would probably have too.

Though all Mr Harker knew at this time was that the junked metal would accumulate slowly in the corner behind the boilers, then suddenly disappear overnight; now it became his nightly joke to enter the plant with his busy bustling air and say to Turl: "Well, I notice that-ere little engine is still running. There's a right smart of brass in them bushings and wrist-pins, but I reckon they're moving too fast to hold that magnet against. But I reckon we're lucky, at that. I reckon he'd sell them boilers too if he knowed any way you and Tom Tom could keep up steam without them."

Though he—Mr Harker—did tell what came next, which was at the first of the year, when the town was audited: "They come down here, two of them in spectacles. They went over the books and poked around ever where, counting ever thing in sight and writing it down. Then they went back to the office and they was still there at six oclock when I come on. It seems there was something a little out; it seems there was some old brass fittings wrote down in the books, except that that brass seemed to be missing or something. It was on the books all right, and the new valves and truck that had replaced it was there. But be durn if they could find a one of them old fittings except one busted bib that had done got mislaid beyond magnet range you might say under a work bench some way or other. It was right strange. So I went back with them and held the light while they looked again in all the corners, getting a right smart of sut and grease and coal-dust on them white shirts. But that brass just naturally seemed to be plumb gone. So they went away.

"And the next morning they come back. They had the city clerk with them this time and they beat Mr Snopes down here and so they had to wait until he come in in his check cap and his chew of tobacco, chewing and looking at them while they hemmed and hawed until they told him. They was right sorry; they hemmed and hawed a right smart being sorry, but there wasn't nothing else they could do except come back on him being as he was the superintendent; and did he want me and Turl and Tom Tom arrested right now or would tomorrow do? And him standing there chewing, with his eyes looking like two gobs of cup grease on a hunk of raw dough, and them still telling him how sorry they was.

" 'How much does it come to?' he says.

" 'Two hundred and eighteen dollars and fifty-two cents, Mr Snopes.'

" 'Is that the full amount?'

" 'We checked our figgers twice, Mr Snopes.'

" 'All right,' he says. And he reaches down and hauls out the money and pays the two hundred and eighteen dollars and fifty-two cents in cash and asks for a receipt."

Only by the next summer Gowan was Turl's student fireman, so now Gowan saw and heard it from Turl at first hand; it was evening when Mr Snopes stood suddenly in the door to the boiler room and crooked his finger at Turl and so this time it was Turl and Snopes facing one another in the office.

"What's this trouble about you and Tom Tom?" he said.

"Me and which?" Turl said. "If Tom Tom depending on me for his trouble, he done quit firing and turned waiter. It takes two folks to have trouble and Tom Tom aint but one, I dont care how big he is."

"Tom Tom thinks you want to fire the day shift," Mr Snopes said.

Turl was looking at everything now without looking at anything. "I can handle as much coal as Tom Tom," he said.

"Tom Tom knows that too," Mr Snopes said. "He knows he's getting old. But he knows there aint nobody else can crowd him for his job but you." Then Mr Snopes told him how for two years now Tom Tom had been stealing brass from the plant and laying it on Turl to get him fired; how only that day Tom Tom had told him, Mr Snopes, that Turl was the thief.

"That's a lie," Turl said. "Cant no nigger accuse me of stealing something I aint, I dont care how big he is."

"Sho," Mr Snopes said. "So the thing to do is to get that brass back."

"Not me," Turl said. "That's what they pays Mr Buck Connor for." Buck Connors was the town marshall.

"Then you'll go to jail sho enough," Snopes said. "Tom Tom will say he never even knowed it was there. You'll be the only one that knew that. So what you reckon Mr Connor'll think? You'll be the one that knowed where it was hid at, and Buck Connor'll know that even a fool has got more sense than to steal something and hide it in his own corn crib. The only thing you can do is, get that brass back. Go out there in the daytime, while Tom Tom is here at work, and get that brass and bring it to me and I'll put it away to use as evidence on Tom Tom. Or maybe you dont want that day shift. Say so, if you dont. I can find somebody else."

Because Turl hadn't fired any boilers forty years. He hadn't done anything at all that long, since he was only thirty. And if he were a hundred, nobody could accuse him of having done anything that would aggregate forty years net. "Unless tomcatting at night would add up that much," Mr Harker said. "If Turl ever is unlucky enough to get married he would still have to climb in his own back window or he wouldn't even know what he come after. Aint that right, Turl?"

So, as Mr Harker said, it was not Turl's fault so much as Snopes's mistake. "Which was," Mr Harker said, "when Mr Snopes forgot to remember in time about that young light-colored new wife of Tom Tom's. To think how he picked Turl out of all the Negroes in Jefferson, that's prowled at least once—or tried to—every gal within ten miles of town, to go out there to Tom Tom's house knowing all the time how Tom Tom is right here under Mr Snopes's eye wrestling coal until six oclock a m and then with two miles to walk down the railroad home, and expect Turl to spend his time out there" (Gowan was doing nearly all the night firing now. He had to; Turl had to get some sleep, on the coal pile in the bunker after midnight. He was losing weight too, which he could afford even less than sleep.) "hunting anything that aint hid in Tom Tom's bed. And when I think about Tom Tom in here wrestling them boilers in that-ere same amical cuckolry like what your uncle says Miz Snopes and Mayor de Spain walks around in, stealing brass so he can keep Turl from getting his job away from him, and all the time Turl is out yonder tending by daylight to Tom Tom's night homework, sometimes I think I will jest die."

He was spared that; we all knew it couldn't last much longer. The question was, which would happen first: if Tom Tom would catch Turl, or if Mr Snopes would catch Turl, or if Mr Harker really would burst a blood vessel. Mr Snopes won. He was standing in the office door that evening when Mr Harker, Turl and Gowan came on duty; once more he crooked his finger at Turl and once more they stood facing each other in the office. "Did you find it this time?" Mr Snopes said.

"Find it which time?" Turl said.

"Just before dark tonight," Mr Snopes said. "I was standing at the corner of the crib when you crawled out of that corn patch and climbed in that back window." And now indeed Turl was looking everywhere fast at nothing. "Maybe you are still looking in the wrong place," Mr Snopes said. "If Tom Tom had hid that iron in his bed, you ought to found it three weeks ago. You take one more look. If you dont find it this time, maybe I better tell Tom Tom to help you." Turl was looking fast at nothing now.

"I'm gonter have to have three or four extra hours off tomorrow night," he said. "And Tom Tom gonter have to be held right here unto I gets back."

"I'll see to it," Snopes said.

"I mean held right here unto I walks in and touches him," Turl said. "I dont care how late it is."

"I'll see to that," Snopes said.

Except that it had already quit lasting any longer at all; Gowan and Mr Harker had barely reached the plant the next evening when Mr Harker took one quick glance around. But before he could even speak Mr Snopes was standing in the office door, saying, "Where's Tom Tom?" Because it wasn't Tom Tom waiting to turn over to the night crew: it was Tom Tom's substitute, who fired the boilers on Sunday while Tom Tom was taking his new young wife to church; Gowan said Mr Harker said,

"Hell fire," already moving, running past Mr Snopes into the office and scrabbling at the telephone. Then he was out of the office again, not even stopping while he hollered at Gowan: "All right, Otis"—his nephew or cousin or something who had inherited the saw mill, who would come in and take over when Mr Harker wanted a night off—"Otis'll be here in fifteen minutes. Jest do the best you can until then."

"Hold up," Gowan said. "I'm going too."

"Durn that," Mr Harker said, still running, "I seen it first:" on out the back where the spur track for the coal cars led back to the main line where Tom Tom would walk every morning and evening between his home and his job, running (Mr Harker) in the moonlight now because the moon was almost full. In fact, the whole thing was full of moonlight when Mr Harker and Turl appeared peacefully at the regular hour to relieve Tom Tom's substitute the next evening:

"Yes sir," Mr Harker told Gowan, "I was jest in time. It was Turl's desperation, you see. This would be his last go-round. This time he was going to have to find that brass, or come back and tell Mr Snopes he couldn't; in either case that country picnic was going to be over. So I was jest in time to see him creep up out of that corn patch and cross the moonlight to that back window and tomcat through it; jest exactly time enough for him to creep across the room to the bed and likely fling the quilt back and lay his hand on meat and say, 'Honey-bunch, lay calm. Papa's done arrived.' " And Gowan said how even twenty-four hours afterward he partook for the instant of Turl's horrid surprise, who believed that at that moment Tom Tom was two miles away at the power plant waiting for him (Turl) to appear and relieve him of the coal scoop—Tom Tom lying fully dressed beneath the quilt with a naked butcher knife in his hand when Turl flung it back.

"Jest exactly time enough," Mr Harker said. "Jest exactly as on time as two engines switching freight cars. Tom Tom must a made his jump jest exactly when Turl whirled to run, Turl jumping out of the house into the moonlight again with Tom Tom and the butcher knife riding on his back so that they looked jest like—what do you call them double-jointed half-horse fellers in the old picture books?"

"Centaur," Gowan said.

"—looking jest like a centawyer running on its hind legs and trying to ketch up with itself with a butcher knife about a yard long in one of its extry front hoofs until they run out of the moonlight again into the woods. Yes sir, Turl aint even half as big as Tom Tom, but he sho toted him. If you'd a ever bobbled once, that butcher knife would a caught you whether Tom Tom did or not, wouldn't it?"

"Tom Tom a big buck man," Turl said. "Make three of me. But I toted him. I had to. And whenever I would fling my eye back and see the moon shining on that butcher knife I could a picked up two more like him without even slowing down." Turl said how at first he just ran; it was only after he found himself—or themselves—among the trees that he thought about trying to rake Tom Tom off against the trunk of one. "But he helt on so tight with that one arm that whenever I tried to bust him against a tree I busted myself too. Then we'd bounce off and I'd catch another flash of moonlight on that nekkid blade and all I could do was just run.

" 'Bout then was when Tom Tom started squalling to let him down. He was holding on with both hands now, so I knowed I had done outrun that butcher knife anyway. But I was good started then; my feets never paid Tom Tom no more mind when he started squalling to stop and let him off than they done me. Then he grabbed my head with both hands and started to wrenching it around like I was a runaway bareback mule, and then I seed the ditch too. It was about forty foot deep and it looked a solid mile across but it was too late then. My feets never even slowed up. They run as far as from here to that coal pile yonder out into nekkid air before we even begun to fall. And they was still clawing moonlight when me and Tom Tom hit the bottom."

The first thing Gowan wanted to know was, what Tom Tom had used in lieu of the dropped butcher knife. Turl told that. Nothing. He and Tom Tom just sat in the moonlight on the floor of the ditch and talked. And Uncle Gavin explained that: a sanctuary, a rationality of perspective, which animals, humans too, not merely reach but earn by passing through unbearable emotional states like furious rage or furious fear, the two of them sitting there not only in Uncle Gavin's amicable cuckoldry but in mutual and complete federation too: Tom Tom's home violated not by Tomey's Turl but by Flem Snopes; Turl's life and limbs put into frantic jeopardy not by Tom Tom but by Flem Snopes.

"That was where I come in," Mr Harker said.

"You?" Gowan said.

"He holp us," Turl said.

"Be durn if that's so," Mr Harker said. "Have you and Tom Tom both already forgot what I told you right there in that ditch last night? I never knowed nothing and I dont aim to know nothing, I dont give a durn how hard either one of you try to make me."

"All right," Gowan said. "Then what?" Turl told that: how he and Tom Tom went back to the house and Tom Tom untied his wife where he had tied her to a chair in the kitchen and the three of them hitched the mule to the wagon and got the brass out of the corn crib and loaded it to haul it away. There was near a half-ton of it; it took them the rest of the night to finish moving it.

"Move it where?" Gowan said. Only he said he decided to let Mr Snopes himself ask that; it was nearing daylight now and soon Tom Tom would come up the spur track from the main line, carrying his lunch pail to take over for the day shift; and presently there he was, with his little high hard round intractable cannon-ball head, when they all turned and there was Mr Snopes too standing in the boiler-room door. And Gowan said that even Mr Snopes seemed to know he would just be wasting his time crooking his finger at anybody this time; he just said right out to Turl:

"Why didn't you find it?"

"Because it wasn't there," Turl said.

"How do you know it wasn't there?" Mr Snopes said.

"Because Tom Tom said it wasn't," Turl said.

Because the time for wasting time was over now. Mr Snopes just looked at Tom Tom a minute. Then he said: "What did you do with it?"

"We put it where you said you wanted it," Tom Tom said.

"We?" Mr Snopes said.

"Me and Turl," Tom Tom said. And now Mr Snopes looked at Tom Tom for another minute. Then he said:

"Where I said I wanted it when?"

"When you told me what you aimed to do with them safety-valves," Tom Tom said.

Though by the time the water in the tank would begin to taste brassy enough for somebody to think about draining the tank to clean it, it wouldn't be Mr Snopes. Because he was no longer super-intendent now, having resigned, as Mr de Spain would have said when he was still Lieutenant de Spain, "for the good of the service." So he could sit all day now on the gallery of his little back-street rented house and look at the shape of the tank standing against the sky above the Jefferson roof-line—looking at his own monument, some might have thought. Except that it was not a monument: it was a footprint. A monument only says *At least I got this far* while a foot-print says *This is where I was when I moved again.*

"Not even now?" Uncle Gavin said to Ratliff.

"Not even now," Ratliff said. "Not catching his wife with Manfred de Spain yet is like that twenty-dollar gold piece pinned to your undershirt on your first maiden trip to what you hope is going to be a Memphis whorehouse. He dont need to unpin it yet."

TWO

GAVIN STEVENS

*H*e hadn't unpinned it yet. So we all wondered what he was using to live on, for money, sitting (apparently) day long day after day through the rest of that summer on the flimsy porch of that little rented house, looking at his water tank. Nor would we ever know, until the town would decide to drain the tank and clean it and so rid the water of the brassy taste, exactly how much brass he had used one of the Negro firemen to blackmail the other into stealing for him and which the two Negroes, confederating for simple mutual preservation, had put into the tank where he could never, would never dare, recover it.

And even now we don't know whether or not that brass was all. We will never know exactly how much he might have stolen and sold privately (I mean before he thought of drafting Tom Tom or Turl to help him) either before or after someone—Buffaloe probably, since if old Harker had ever noticed those discarded fittings enough to miss any of them he would probably have beat Snopes to the market; very likely, for all his pretence of simple spectator enjoyment, his real feeling was rage at his own blindness—notified somebody at the city hall and had the auditors in. All we knew was that one day the three safety-valves were missing from the boilers; we had to assume, imagine, what happened next: Manfred de Spain—it would be Manfred—sending for him and saying, "Well, Bud," or Doc or Buster or whatever Manfred would call his . . . you might say foster husband; who knows? maybe even Superintendent: "Well, Superintendent, this twenty-three dollars and eighty-one cents' worth of brass"—naturally he would have looked in the catalogue before he sent for him— "was missing during your regime, which you naturally wish to keep spotless as Caesar's wife: which a simple C.O.D. tag addressed to you will do." And that, according to Harker, the two auditors hemmed and hawed around the plant for two days before they got up nerve enough to tell Snopes what amount of brass they thought to the best of their knowledge was missing, and that Snopes took the cash out of his pocket and paid them.

That is, disregarding his salary of fifty dollars a month, the job cost Snopes two hundred and forty-two dollars and thirty-three cents out of his own pocket or actual cash money you might say. And even if he had saved every penny of his salary, less that two-hundred-plus-dollar loss, and assuming there had been two hundred dollars more of brass for him to have stolen successfully during that time, that was still not enough for him to support his family on very long. Yet for two years now he had been sitting on that little front gallery, looking (as far as we knew) at that water tank. So I asked Ratliff.

"He's farming," Ratliff said. "Farming?" I said (all right, cried if you like). "Farming what? Sitting there on that gallery from sunup to sundown watching that water tank?"

Farming Snopeses, Ratliff said. Farming Snopeses: the whole rigid hierarchy moving intact upward one step as he vacated ahead of it except that one who had inherited into the restaurant was not a Snopes. Indubitably and indefensibly not a Snopes; even to impugn him so was indefensible and outrageous and forever beyond all pale of pardon, whose mother, like her incredible sister-by-marriage a generation later, had, must have, as the old bucolic poet said, cast a leglin girth herself before she married whatever Snopes was Eck's titular father.

That was his name: Eck. The one with the broken neck; he brought it to town when he moved in as Flem's immediate successor, rigid in a steel brace and leather harness. Never in the world a Snopes. Ratliff told it; it happened at the saw mill. (You see, even his family—Flem—knew he was not a Snopes: sending, disposing of him into a sawmill where even the owner must be a financial genius to avoid bankruptcy and there is nothing for a rogue at all since all to steal is lumber, and to embezzle a wagonload of planks is about like embezzling an iron safe or a—yes: that dammed water tank itself.)

So Flem sent Eck to Uncle Billy Varner's saw mill (it was that I suppose or chloroform or shoot him as you do a sick dog or a

wornout mule) and Ratliff told about it: one day Eck made the
proposition that for a dollar each, he and one of the Negro hands
(one of the larger ones and of course the more imbecilic) would pick
up a tremendous cypress log and set it onto the saw-carriage. And
they did (didn't I just say that one was not even a Snopes and the
other already imbecile), had the log almost safely on, when the
Negro slipped, something, anyway went down; whereupon all Eck
had to do was let go his end and leap out from under. But not he: no
Snopes nor no damned thing else, bracing his shoulder under and
holding his end up and even taking the shock when the Negro's end
fell to the ground, still braced under it until it occurred to someone
to drag the Negro out.

And still without sense enough to jump, let alone Snopes enough,
not even knowing yet that even Jody Varner wasn't going to pay him
anything for saving even a Varner Negro: just standing there holding
that whole damned log up, with a little blood already beginning to
run out of his mouth, until it finally occurred again to them to shim
the log up with another one and pull him from under too, where he
could sit hunkered over under a tree, spitting blood and complaining
of a headache. ("Don't tell me they gave him the dollar," I said—all
right: cried—to Ratliff. "Don't tell me that!")

Never in this world a Snopes: himself and his wife and son living
in the tent behind the restaurant and Eck in his turn in the greasy
apron and the steel-and-leather neck harness (behind the counter,
frying on the crusted grill the eggs and meat which, because of the
rigid brace, he couldn't even see to gauge the doneness, cooking, as
the blind pianist plays, by simple ear), having less business here than
even in the saw mill since at the saw mill all he could do was break his
own bones where here he was a threat to his whole family's long tradition of slow and invincible rapacity because of that same incredible
and innocent assumption that all people practise courage and honesty for the simple reason that if they didn't everybody would be
frightened and confused; saying one day, not even privately but right
out loud where half a dozen strangers not even kin by marriage to
Snopeses heard him: "Aint we supposed to be selling beef in these
here hamburgers? I don't know jest what this is yet but it aint no
beef."

So of course they—when I say "they" I mean Snopeses; when you say "Snopeses" in Jefferson you mean Flem Snopes—fired him. They had to; he was intolerable there. Only of course the question rose immediately: where in Jefferson, not in the Jefferson economy but in the Snopes (oh yes, when you say Snopes in Jefferson you mean Flem Snopes) economy would he not be intolerable, would Snopeses be safe from him? Ratliff knew that too. I mean everybody in Jefferson knew because within twenty-four hours everybody in Jefferson had heard about that hamburger remark and naturally knew that something would have to be done about Eck Snopes and done quick and so of course (being interested) as soon as possible, almost as soon in fact as Flem himself knew, what and where. I mean, it was Ratliff who told me. No: I mean it had to be Ratliff who told me: Ratliff with his damned smooth face and his damned shrewd bland innocent intelligent eyes, too damned innocent, too damned intelligent:

"He's night watchman now down at Renfrow's oil tank at the deepo. Where it won't be no strain on his neck like having to look down to see what that was he jest smelled burning. He won't need to look up to see whether the tank's still there or not, he can jest walk up and feel the bottom of it. Or even set there in his chair in the door and send that boy to look. That horse boy," Ratliff said.

"That what boy?" I said, cried.

"That horse boy," Ratliff said. "Eck's boy. Wallstreet Panic. The day that Texas feller arctioned off them wild Snopes ponies, I was out there. It was jest dust-dark and we had done et supper at Miz Littlejohn's and I was jest undressing in my room to go to bed when Henry Armstid and Eck and that boy of hisn went in the lot to ketch their horses; Eck had two: the one the Texas feller give him to get the arction started off, and the one Eck felt he had to at least bid on after having been give one for nothing, and won it. So when Henry Armstid left the gate open and the whole herd stampeded over him and out of it, I reckon the hardest instantaneous decision Eck ever had to make in his life was to decide which one of them horses to chase: the one the Texas man give him, which represented the most net profit if he caught it, or the one that he already had five or six dollars of his own money invested in; that is, was a hundred-plus percent of a free horse worth more than just a hundred percent of a six-dollar horse? That is, jest how far can you risk losing a horse that no matter what you get for him you will still have to subtract six dollars from it, to jest catch one that will be all net profit?

"Or maybe he decided him and that boy better split up after both of them while he figgered it out. Anyway, the first I knowed, I had done took off my britches and was jest leaning out of the window in my shirttail trying to see what was going on, when I heerd a kind of sound behind me and looked over my shoulder and there was one of them horses standing in the door looking at me and standing in the hall behind him with a piece of plow-line was that boy of Eck's. I reckon we both moved at the same moment: me out of the window in my shirttail and the horse swirling to run on down the hall, me realizing I never had no britches on and running around the house toward the front steps jest about the time the horse met Miz Little-john coming onto the back gallery with a armful of washing in one hand and the washboard in the other; they claimed she said 'git out of here you son of a bitch' and split the washboard down the center of its face and throwed the two pieces at it without even changing hands, it swirling again to run back up the hall jest as I run up the front steps, and jumped clean over that boy still standing in the hall with his plow-line without touching a hair, on to the front gallery again and seen me and never even stopped: jest swirled and run to the end of the gallery and jumped the railing and back into the lot again, looking jest like a big circus-colored hawk, sailing out into the moonlight and across the lot again in about two jumps and out the gate that still hadn't nobody thought to close yet; I heerd him once more when he hit the wooden bridge jest this side of Bookwright's turn-off. Then that boy come out of the house, still toting the plow-line. 'Howdy, Mr Ratliff,' he says. 'Which way did he go?'—Except you're wrong."

Horse boy, dog boy, cat boy, monkey boy, elephant boy: anything but Snopes boy. And then suppose, just suppose; suppose and tremble: one generation more removed from Eck Snopes and his innocence; one generation more until that innocent and outrageous belief that courage and honor are practical has had time to fade and cool so that merely the habit of courage and honor remain; add to that

then that generation's natural heritage of cold rapacity as instinctive
as breathing and tremble at that prospect: the habit of courage and
honor compounded by rapacity or rapacity raised to the absolute *nth*
by courage and honor: not horse boy but a lion or tiger boy: Genghis
Khan or Tamerlane or Attila in the defenseless midst of indefensible
Jefferson. Then Ratliff was looking at me. I mean, he always was. I
mean I discovered with a kind of terror that for a second I had forgot it. "What?" I said. "What did you say?"

"That you're wrong. About Eck's night watchman job at the oil
tank. It wasn't Manfred de Spain this time. It was the Masons."

"What?" I said, cried.

"That's right. Eck was one of the biggest ones of Uncle Billy
Varner's Frenchman's Bend Masons. It was Uncle Billy sent word in
to the Masons in Jefferson to find Eck a good light broke-neck job."

"That bad?" I said. "That bad? The next one in the progression so
outrageous and portentous and terrifying that Will Varner himself
had to use influence twenty-two miles away to save Frenchman's
Bend?" Because the next one after Eck behind the restaurant counter
was I.O., the blacksmith-cum-schoolmaster-cum-bigamist, or multi-
plied by bigamy—a thin undersize voluble weasel-faced man talking
constantly in a steady stream of worn saws and proverbs usually having no connection with one another nor application to anything else,
who even with the hammer would not have weighed as much as the
anvil he abrogated and dispossessed; who (Ratliff of course, Ratliff
always) entered Frenchman's Bend already talking, or rather
appeared one morning already talking in Varner's blacksmith shop
which an old man named Trumbull had run man and boy for fifty
years.

But no blacksmith, I.O. He merely held the living. It was the other
one, our Eck, his cousin (whatever the relationship was, unless simply being both Snopes was enough until one proved himself unworthy, as Eck was to do, like two Masons from that moment to apostasy
like Eck's, forever sworn to show a common front to life), who did
the actual work. Until one day, one morning perhaps the curate, Eck,
was not there or perhaps it simply occurred to the vicar, the high
priest, for the first time that his actually was the right and the authority to hold a communion service and nobody could really prevent

him: that morning, Jack Houston with his gaited stallion until
Snopes quicked it with the first nail; whereupon Houston picked
Snopes up and threw him hammer and all into the cooling tub and
managed somehow to hold the plunging horse and wrench the shoe
off and the nail out at the same time, and led the horse outside and
tied it and came back and threw Snopes back into the cooling tub
again.

And no schoolmaster either. He didn't merely usurp that as a position among strangers, he actually stole it as a vocation from his own
kin. Though Frenchman's Bend didn't know that yet. They knew
only that he was hardly out of the blacksmith shop (or dried again
out of the cooling tub where Houston had flung him) when he was
installed as teacher ("Professor," the teacher was called in Frenchman's Bend, provided of course he wore trousers) in the one-room
schoolhouse which was an integer of old Varner's princedom—integer not because old Varner or anyone else in Frenchman's Bend considered that juvenile education filled any actual communal lack or
need, but simply because his settlement had to have a going schoolhouse to be complete as a freight train has to have a caboose to be
complete.

So I.O. Snopes was now the schoolmaster; shortly afterward he
was married to a Frenchman's Bend belle and within a year he was
pushing a homemade perambulator about the village and his wife
was already pregnant again; here, you would have said, was a man not
merely settled but doomed to immobilization, until one day in the
third year a vast gray-colored though still young woman, accompanied by a vast gray-colored five-year-old boy, drove up to Varner's
store in a buggy—

"It was his wife," Ratliff said.

"His wife?" I said, cried. "But I thought—"

"So did we," Ratliff said. "Pushing that-ere homemade buggy with
two of them in it this time, twins, already named Bilbo and Vardaman, besides the first one, Clarence. Yes sir, three chaps already
while he was waiting for his other wife with that one to catch up with
him—a little dried-up feller not much bigger than a crawfish, and
that other wife—no, I mean the one he had now in Frenchman's
Bend when that-ere number-one one druv up—wasn't a big girl nei-

ther—Miz Vernon Tull's sister's niece by marriage she was—yet he
got onto her too them same big gray-colored kind of chaps like the
one in the buggy with his ma driving up to the store and saying to
whoever was setting on the gallery at the moment: 'I hear I.O.
inside.' (He was. We could all hear him.) 'Kindly step in and tell him
his wife's come.'

"That was all. It was enough. When he come to the Bend that day
three years ago he had a big carpet-bag, and in them three years he
had probably accumulated some more stuff; I mean besides them
three new chaps. But he never stopped for none of it. He jest stepped
right out of the back door of the store. And Flem had done long since
already sold old man Trumbull back to Varner for the blacksmith,
but now they was needing a new professor too or anyhow they would
as soon as I.O. could get around the first corner out of sight where he
could cut across country. Which he evidently done; never nobody
reported any dust-cloud travelling fast along a road nowhere. They
said he even stopped talking, though I doubt that. You got to draw
the line somewhere, aint you?"

You have indeed. Though I.O. didn't. That is, he was already talking when he appeared in his turn behind the restaurant counter in
the greasy apron, taking your order and cooking it wrong or cooking the wrong thing not because he worked so fast but simply
because he never stopped talking long enough for you to correct or
check him, babbling that steady stream of confused and garbled
proverbs and metaphors attached to nothing and going nowhere.

And the wife, I mean the number-one wife, what might be called
the original wife, who was number one in the cast even though she
was number two on the stage. The other one, the number two in the
cast even though she was number one on the stage, the Tull's wife's
sister's niece wife, who foaled the second set of what Ratliff called
gray-colored chaps, Clarence and the twins Vardaman and Bilbo,
remained in Frenchman's Bend. It was the original one, who
appeared in Frenchman's Bend sitting in the buggy and left Frenchman's Bend in the buggy, still sitting, and appeared in Jefferson five
years later still sitting, translated, we knew not how, and with no
interval between from the buggy where Ratliff had seen her twenty-
two miles away that day five years ago, to the rocking chair on the

front gallery of the boarding house where we saw her now, still at
that same right angle enclosing her lap as if she had no movable
hinge at the hips at all—a woman who gave an impression of specific density and immobility like lead or uranium, so that whatever
force had moved her from the buggy to that chair had not been
merely human, not even ten I.O.s.

Because Snopes was moving his echelons up fast now. That one—
I.O. and the vast gray-colored sitting wife and that vast gray-colored
boy (his name was Montgomery Ward)—did not even pause at the
tent behind the restaurant where Eck and his wife and two sons now
("Why not?" Ratliff said. "There's a heap of more things beside frying a hamburger you dont really have to look down for.") were still
living. They—the I.O.s—by-passed it completely, the wife already
sitting in the rocking chair on the boarding house's front gallery—a
big more-or-less unpainted square building just off the Square where
itinerant cattle drovers and horse- and mule-traders stopped and
where were incarcerated, boarded and fed, juries and important witnesses during court term, where she would sit rocking steadily—not
doing anything, not reading, not particularly watching who passed in
or out of the door or along the street: just rocking—for the next five
years while and then after the place changed from a boarding house
to a warren, with nailed to one of the front veranda posts a pine
board lettered terrifically by hand:

ƧNOPEƧ HOTEL

And now Eck, whose innocence or honesty or both had long since
eliminated him from the restaurant into his night watchman's chair
beside the depot oil tank, had vacated his wife and sons (Wallstreet
Panic: oh yes, I was like Ratliff: I couldn't believe that one either,
though the younger one, Admiral Dewey, we both could) from the
tent behind it. In fact, the restaurant was not sold lock stock barrel
and goodwill, but gutted, moved intact even to the customers and
without even a single whole day's closure, into the new boarding
house where Mrs Eck was now the landlady; moved intact past the
rocking figure on the gallery which continued to rock there through
mere legend and into landmark like the effigy signs before the old-

time English public houses, so that country men coming into town and inquiring for the Snopes hotel were told simply to walk in that direction until they came to a woman rocking, and that was it.

And now there entered that one, not whose vocation but at least the designation of whose vocation, I.O. Snopes had usurped. This was the actual Snopes schoolmaster. No: he looked like a schoolmaster. No: he looked like John Brown with an ineradicable and unhidable flaw: a tall gaunt man in a soiled frock coat and string tie and a wide politician's hat, with cold furious eyes and the long chin of a talker: not that verbal diarrhea of his cousin (whatever kin I.O. was; they none of them seemed to bear any specific kinship to one another; they were just Snopeses, like colonies of rats or termites are just rats and termites) but a kind of unerring gift for a base and evil ratiocination in argument, and for correctly reading the people with whom he dealt: a demagogue's capacity for using people to serve his own appetites, all clouded over with a veneer of culture and religion; the very names of his two sons, Byron and Virgil, were not only instances but warnings.

And no schoolmaster himself either. That is, unlike his cousin, he was not even with us long enough to have to prove he was not. Or maybe, coming to us in the summer and then gone before the summer was, he was merely between assignments. Or maybe taking a busman's holiday from a busman's holiday. Or maybe in and about the boarding house and the Square in the mere brief intervals from his true bucolic vocation whose stage and scene were the scattered country churches and creeks and horse-ponds where during the hot summer Sundays revival services and baptisings took place: himself (he had a good baritone voice and probably the last working pitch pipe in north Mississippi) setting the tune and lining out the words, until one day a posse of enraged fathers caught him and a fourteen-year-old girl in an empty cotton house and tarred and feathered him out of the country. There had been talk of castration also though some timid conservative dissuaded them into holding that as a promise against his return.

So of him there remained only the two sons, Byron and Virgil. Nor was Byron with us long either, gone to Memphis now to attend business college. To learn book-keeping; we learned with incredulity

that Colonel Sartoris himself was behind that: Colonel Sartoris himself in the back room of the bank which was his office—an
incredulity which demanded, compelled inquiry while we remembered what some of us, the older ones, my father among them, had
not forgot: the original Ab Snopes, the (depending on where you
stand) patriot horse raider or simple horse thief who had been
hanged (not by a Federal provost-marshal but by a Confederate one,
the old story was) while a member of the cavalry command of old
Colonel Sartoris, the real colonel, father of our present banker–hon-
orary colonel who had been only an uncommissioned A.D.C. on his
father's staff, back in that desperate twilight of 1864-65 when more
people than men named Snopes had to choose not survival with
honor but simply between empty honor and almost as empty survival.

The horse which came home to roost. Oh yes, we all said that, all
us wits: we would not have missed that chance. Not that we believed
it or even disbelieved it, but simply to defend the old Colonel's memory by being first to say aloud among ourselves what we believed the
whole Snopes tribe was long since chortling over to one another.
Indeed, no Confederate provost-marshal hanged that first Ab
Snopes, but Snopeses themselves had immolated him in that skeleton, to put, as the saying is, that monkey on the back of Ab's commander's descendant as soon as the lineage produced a back
profitable to the monkey; in this case, the new bank which our
Colonel Sartoris established about five years ago.

Not that we really believed that, of course. I mean, our Colonel
Sartoris did not need to be blackmailed with a skeleton. Because we
all in our country, even half a century after, sentimentalise the heroes
of our gallant lost irrevocable unreconstructible debacle, and those
heroes were indeed ours because they were our fathers and grandfathers and uncles and great-uncles when Colonel Sartoris raised the
command right here in our contiguous counties. And who with more
right to sentimentalise them than our Colonel Sartoris, whose father
had been the Colonel Sartoris who had raised and trained the command and saved its individual lives when he could in battle and even
defended them or at least extricated them from their own simple
human lusts and vices while idle between engagements; Byron

Snopes was not the first descendant of those old company and battalion and regimental names who knew our Colonel Sartoris's
bounty.

But the horse which at last came home to roost sounded better.
Not witty, but rather an immediate unified irrevocably scornful front
to what the word Snopes was to mean to us, and to all others, no
matter who, whom simple juxtaposition to the word irrevocably
smirched and contaminated. Anyway, he (it: the horse come to roost)
appeared in good time, armed and girded with his business-college
diploma; we would see him through, beyond, inside the grillework
which guarded our money and the complex records of it whose custodian Colonel Sartoris was, bowed (he, Snopes, Byron) over the
book-keeper's desk in an attitude not really of prayer, obeisance; not
really of humility before the shine, the blind glare of the blind
money, but rather of a sort of respectful unhumble insistence, a deferent invincible curiosity and inquiry into the mechanics of its
recording; he had not entered crawling into the glare of a mystery
so much as, without attracting any attention to himself, he was trying
to lift a corner of its skirt.

Using, since he was the low last man in that hierarchy, a long cane
fishing-pole until he could accrete close enough for the hand to
reach; using, to really mix, really confuse our metaphor, an humble
cane out of that same quiver which had contained that power-plant
superintendency, since Colonel Sartoris had been of that original
group of old Major de Spain's bear and deer hunters when Major de
Spain established his annual hunting camp in the Big Bottom shortly
after the war; and when Colonel Sartoris started his bank five years
ago, Manfred de Spain used his father's money to become one of the
first stockholders and directors.

Oh yes: the horse home at last and stabled. And in time of course
(we had only to wait, never to know how of course even though we
watched it, but at least to know more or less when) to own the stable,
Colonel Sartoris dis-stabled of his byre and rick in his turn as Ratliff
and Grover Cleveland Winbush had been dis-restauranted in theirs.
We not to know how of course since that was none of our business;
indeed, who to say but there was not one among us but did not want
to know: who, already realising that we would never defend Jefferson

from Snopeses, let us then give, relinquish Jefferson to Snopeses, banker mayor aldermen church and all, so that, in defending themselves from Snopeses, Snopeses must of necessity defend and shield us, their vassals and chattels, too.

The quiver borne on Manfred de Spain's back, but the arrows drawn in turn by the hand, that damned incredible woman, that Frenchman's Bend Helen, Semiramis—no: not Helen nor Semiramis: Lilith: the one before Eve herself whom earth's Creator had perforce in desperate and amazed alarm in person to efface, remove, obliterate, that Adam might create a progeny to populate it; and we were in my office now where I had not sent for him nor even invited him: he had just followed, entered, to sit across the desk in his neat faded tieless blue shirt and the brown smooth bland face and the eyes watching me too damned shrewd, too damned intelligent.

"You used to laugh at them too," he said.

"Why not?" I said. "What else are we going to do about them? Of course you've got the best joke: you dont have to fry hamburgers any more. But give them time; maybe they have got one taking a correspondence-school law course. Then I wont have to be acting city attorney any more either."

"I said 'too,' " Ratliff said.

"What?" I said.

"At first you laughed at them too," he said. "Or maybe I'm wrong, and this here is still laughing?"—looking at me, watching me, too damned shrewd, too damned intelligent. "Why dont you say it?"

"Say what?" I said.

" 'Get out of my office, Ratliff,' " he said.

"Get out of my office, Ratliff," I said.

THREE

CHARLES MALLISON

*M*aybe it was because Mother and Uncle Gavin were twins, that Mother knew what Uncle Gavin's trouble was just about as soon as Ratliff did.

We were all living with Grandfather then. I mean Grandfather was still alive then and he and Uncle Gavin had one side of the house, Grandfather in his bedroom and what we all called the office downstairs, and Uncle Gavin on the same side upstairs, where he had built an outside stairway so he could go and come from the side yard, and Mother and Father and Cousin Gowan on the other side while Gowan was going to the Jefferson high school while he was waiting to enter the prep school in Washington to get ready for the University of Virginia.

So Mother would sit at the end of the table where Grandmother used to sit, and Grandfather opposite at the other end, and Father on one side and Uncle Gavin and Gowan (I wasn't born then and even if I had been I would have been eating in the kitchen with Aleck Sander yet) on the other and, Gowan said, Uncle Gavin not even pretending any more to eat: just sitting there talking about Snopeses like he had been doing now through every meal for the last two weeks. It was almost like he was talking to himself, like something wound up that couldn't even run down, let alone stop, like there wasn't anybody or anything that wished he would stop more than he did. It wasn't snarling. Gowan didn't know what it was. It was like something Uncle Gavin had to tell, but it was so funny that his main job in telling it was to keep it from being as funny as it really was, because if he ever let it be as funny as it really was, everybody and himself too would be laughing so hard they couldn't hear him. And Mother not eating either now: just sitting there perfectly still, watching

Uncle Gavin, until at last Grandfather took his napkin out of his collar and stood up and Father and Uncle Gavin and Gowan stood up
too and Grandfather said to Mother like he did every time:

"Thank you for the meal, Margaret," and put the napkin on the
table and Gowan went and stood by the door while he went out like
I was going to have to do after I got born and got big enough. And
Gowan would have stood there while Mother and Father and Uncle
Gavin went out too. But not this time. Mother hadn't even moved,
still sitting there and watching Uncle Gavin; she was still watching
Uncle Gavin when she said to Father:

"Dont you and Gowan want to be excused too?"

"Nome," Gowan said. Because he had been in the office that day
when Ratliff came in and said,

"Evening, Lawyer. I just dropped in to hear the latest Snopes
news," and Uncle Gavin said:

"What news?" and Ratliff said:

"Or do you jest mean what Snopes?" and sat there too looking at
Uncle Gavin, until at last he said, "Why dont you go on and say it?"
and Uncle Gavin said,

"Say what?" and Ratliff said,

" 'Get out of my office, Ratliff.' " So Gowan said,

"Nome."

"Then maybe you'll excuse me," Uncle Gavin said, putting his
napkin down. But still Mother didn't move.

"Would you like me to call on her?" she said.

"Call on who?" Uncle Gavin said. And even to Gowan he said it
too quick. Because even Father caught on then. Though I dont know
about that. Even if I had been there and no older than Gowan was,
I would have known that if I had been about twenty-one or maybe
even less when Mrs Snopes first walked through the Square, I not
only would have known what was going on, I might even have been
Uncle Gavin myself. But Gowan said Father sounded like he had just
caught on. He said to Uncle Gavin:

"I'll be damned. So that's what's been eating you for the past two
weeks." Then he said to Mother: "No, by Jupiter. My wife call on
that—"

"That what?" Uncle Gavin said, hard and quick. And still Mother hadn't moved: just sitting there between them while they stood over her.

" 'Sir,' " she said.

"What?" Uncle Gavin said.

" 'That what, sir?' " she said. "Or maybe just 'sir' with an inflection."

"You name it then," Father said to Uncle Gavin. "You know what. What this whole town is calling her. What this whole town knows about her and Manfred de Spain."

"What whole town?" Uncle Gavin said. "Besides you? you and who else? The same ones that probably rake Maggie here over the coals too without knowing any more than you do?"

"Are you talking about my wife?" Father said.

"No," Uncle Gavin said. "I'm talking about my sister and Mrs Snopes."

"Boys, boys, boys," Mother said. "At least spare my nephew." She said to Gowan: "Gowan, dont you really want to be excused?"

"Nome," Gowan said.

"Damn your nephew," Father said. "I'm not going to have his aunt—"

"Are you still talking about your wife?" Uncle Gavin said. This time Mother stood up too, between them while they both leaned a little forward, glaring at each other across the table.

"That really will be all now," Mother said. "Both of you apologise to me." They did. "Now apologise to Gowan." Gowan said they did that too.

"But I'll still be damned if I'm going to let—" Father said.

"Just the apology, please," Mother said. "Even if Mrs Snopes is what you say she is, as long as I am what you and Gavin both agree I am since at least you agree on that, how can I run any risk sitting for ten minutes in her parlor? The trouble with both of you is, you know nothing about women. Women are not interested in morals. They aren't even interested in unmorals. The ladies of Jefferson dont care what she does. What they will never forgive is the way she looks. No: the way the Jefferson gentlemen look at her."

"Speak for your brother," Father said. "I never looked at her in her life."

"Then so much the worse for me," Mother said, "with a mole for a husband. No: moles have warm blood; a Mammoth Cave fish—"

"Well, I *will* be damned," Father said. "That's what you want, is it? A husband that will spend every Saturday night in Memphis chasing back and forth between Gayoso and Mulberry Street—"

"Now I will excuse you whether you want to be or not," Mother said. So Uncle Gavin went out and on upstairs toward his room and Mother rang the bell for Guster and Gowan stood at the door again for Mother and Father and then Mother and Gowan went out to the front gallery (it was October, still warm enough to sit outside at noon) and she took up the sewing basket again and Father came out with his hat on and said,

"Flem Snopes's wife, riding into Jefferson society on Judge Lemuel Stevens's daughter's coat-tail," and went on to town to the store; and then Uncle Gavin came out and said:

"You'll do it, then?"

"Of course," Mother said. "Is it that bad?"

"I intend to try to not let it be," Uncle Gavin said. "Even if you aren't anything but just a woman, you must have seen her. You must have."

"Anyway, I have watched men seeing her," Mother said.

"Yes," Uncle Gavin said. It didn't sound like an out-breathe, like talking. It sounded like an in-breathe: "Yes."

"You're going to save her," Mother said, not looking at Uncle Gavin now: just watching the sock she was darning.

"Yes!" Uncle Gavin said, fast, quick: no in-breathe this time, so quick he almost said the rest of it before he could stop himself, so that all Mother had to do was say it for him:

"—from Manfred de Spain."

But Uncle Gavin had caught himself by now; his voice was just harsh now. "You too," he said. "You and your husband too. The best people, the pure, the unimpugnable. Charles who by his own affirmation has never even looked at her; you by that same affirmation not only Judge Stevens's daughter, but Caesar's wife."

"Just what—" Mother said, then Gowan said she stopped and looked at him. "Dont you really want to be excused a little while? As a personal favor?" she said.

"Nome," Gowan said.

"You cant help it either, can you?" she said. "You've got to be a man too, haven't you?" She just talked to Uncle Gavin then: "Just what is it about this that you cant stand? That Mrs Snopes may not be chaste, or that it looks like she picked Manfred de Spain out to be unchaste with?"

"Yes!" Uncle Gavin said. "I mean no! It's all lies—gossip. It's all—"

"Yes," Mother said. "You're right. It's probably all just that. Saturday's not a very good afternoon to get in the barbershop, but you might think about it when you pass."

"Thanks," Uncle Gavin said. "But if I'm to go on this crusade with any hope of success, the least I can do is look wild and shaggy enough to be believed. You'll do it, then?"

"Of course," Mother said.

"Thank you," Uncle Gavin said. Then he was gone.

"I suppose I could be excused now," Gowan said.

"What for now?" Mother said. She was still watching Uncle Gavin, down the walk and into the street now. "He should have married Melisandre Backus," she said. Melisandre Backus lived on a plantation about six miles from town with her father and a bottle of whiskey. I dont mean he was a drunkard. He was a good farmer. He just spent the rest of his time sitting on the gallery in summer and in the library in winter with the bottle, reading Latin poetry. Miss Melisandre and Mother had been in school together, at high school and the Seminary both. That is, Miss Melisandre was always four years behind Mother. "At one time I thought he might; I didn't know any better then."

"Cousin Gavin?" Gowan said. "Him married?"

"Oh yes," Mother said. "He's just too young yet. He's the sort of man doomed to marry a widow with grown children."

"He could still marry Miss Melisandre," Gowan said.

"It's too late," Mother said. "He didn't know she was there."

"He sees her every day she comes in to town," Gowan said.

"You can see things without looking at them, just like you can hear things without listening," Mother said.

"He sure didn't just do that when he saw Mrs Snopes that day,"

Gowan said. "Maybe he's waiting for her to have another child besides Linda and for them to grow up?"

"No no," Mother said. "You don't marry Semiramis: you just commit some form of suicide for her. Only gentlemen with as little to lose as Mr Flem Snopes can risk marrying Semiramis.—It's too bad you are so old too. A few years ago I could have made you come with me to call on her. Now you'll have to admit openly that you want to come; you may even have to say 'Please.' "

But Gowan didn't. It was Saturday afternoon and there was a football game and though he hadn't made the regular team yet you never could tell when somebody that had might break a leg or have a stroke or even a simple condition in arithmetic. Besides, he said Mother didn't need his help anyway, having the whole town's help in place of it; he said they hadn't even reached the Square the next morning on the way to church when the first lady they met said brightly:

"What's this I hear about yesterday afternoon?" and Mother said just as brightly:

"Indeed?" and the second lady they met said (she belonged to the Byron Society and the Cotillion Club too):

"I always say we'd all be much happier to believe nothing we don't see with our own eyes, and only half of that," and Mother said still just as brightly:

"Indeed?" They—the Byron Society and the Cotillion Club, both when possible of course though either alone in a pinch—seemed to be the measure. Now Uncle Gavin stopped talking about Snopeses. I mean, Gowan said he stopped talking at all. It was like he didn't have time any more to concentrate on talk in order to raise it to conversation, art, like he believed was everybody's duty. It was like he didn't have time to do anything but wait, to get something done that the only way he knew to get it done was waiting. More than that, than just waiting: not only never missing a chance to do things for Mother, he even invented little things to do for her, so that even when he would talk a little, it was like he was killing two birds with the same stone.

Because when he talked now, in sudden spells and bursts of it that sometimes never had any connection at all with what Father and Mother and Grandfather might have been talking about the minute before, it wouldn't even be what he called BB-gun-conversation. It would be the most outrageous praise, praise so outrageous that even Gowan at just thirteen years old could tell that. It would be of Jefferson ladies that he and Mother had known all their lives, so that whatever ideas either one of them must have had about them, the other must have known it a long time by now. Yet all of a sudden every few days during the next month Uncle Gavin would stop chewing fast over his plate and drag a fresh one of them by the hair you might say into the middle of whatever Grandfather and Mother and Father had been talking about, talking not to Grandfather or Father or Gowan, but telling Mother how good or pretty or intelligent or witty somebody was that Mother had grown up with or anyway known all her life.

Oh yes, members of the Byron Society and the Cotillion Club or maybe just one of them (probably only Mother knew it was the Cotillion Club he was working for) at a pinch, so that each time they would know that another new one had called on Mrs Flem Snopes. Until Gowan would wonder how Uncle Gavin would always know when the next one had called, how to scratch her off the list that hadn't or add her onto the score that had or whatever it was he kept. So Gowan decided that maybe Uncle Gavin watched Mrs Snopes's house. And it was November now, good fine hunting weather, and since Gowan had finally given up on the football team, by rights he and Top (Top was Aleck Sander's older brother except that Aleck Sander wasn't born yet either. I mean, he was Guster's boy and his father was named Top too so they called him Big Top and Top Little Top) would have spent every afternoon after school with the beagles Uncle Gavin gave them after rabbits. But instead, Gowan spent every afternoon for almost a week in the big ditch behind Mr Snopes's house, not watching the house but to see if Uncle Gavin was hid somewhere in the ditch too watching to see who called on Mrs Snopes next. Because Gowan was only thirteen then; he was just watching for Uncle Gavin; it wasn't until later that he said how he realised that if he had tried harder or longer, he might have caught Mr de Spain climbing in or out of the back window like most of Jefferson was convinced he was doing, and then he really would have had something he could have sold for a dollar or two to a lot of people in town.

But if Uncle Gavin was hid somewhere in that ditch too, Gowan never caught him. Better still, Uncle Gavin never caught Gowan in it. Because if Mother had ever found out Gowan was hiding in that ditch behind Mr Snopes's house because he thought Uncle Gavin was hidden in it too, Gowan didn't know what she might have done about Uncle Gavin but he sure knew what would have happened to him. And worse: if Mr Snopes had ever found out Gowan thought Uncle Gavin might be hiding in that ditch spying on his house. Or worse still: if the town ever found out Gowan was hiding in that ditch because he thought Uncle Gavin was.

Because when you are just thirteen you dont have sense enough to realise what you are doing and shudder. Because even now I can remember some of the things Aleck Sander and I did for instance and never think twice about it, and I wonder how any boys ever live long enough to grow up. I remember, I was just twelve; Uncle Gavin had just given me my shotgun; this was after (this is how Father put it) Mrs Snopes had sent him to Heidelberg to finish his education and he had been in the War and then come back home and got himself elected County Attorney in his own right; there were five of us; me and three other white boys and Aleck Sander, hunting rabbits one Saturday. It was cold, one of the coldest spells we ever had; when we came to Harrykin Creek it was frozen over solid and we begun talk about how much we would take to jump into it. Aleck Sander said he would do it if each one of us would give him a dollar so we said we would and sure enough, before we could have stopped him, Aleck Sander hauled off and jumped into the creek, right through the ice, clothes and all.

So we got him out and built a fire while he stripped off and wrapped up in our hunting coats while we tried to dry his clothes before they froze solid too and got him dressed again at last and then he said, "All right. Now pay me my money."

We hadn't thought about that. Back then, no Jefferson, Mississippi boy or anywhere else in Mississippi that I know of, ever had a whole dollar at one time very often, let alone four at the same time. So we had to trade with him. Buck Connors and Aleck Sander traded first: if Buck jumped through the ice, Aleck Sander would let him off his dollar. So Buck did, and while we dried him off I said,

"If that's what we got to do, let's all jump in at once and get it over with," and we even started for the creek when Aleck Sander said No, that we were all white boys taking advantage of him because he was a Negro by asking him to let us do the same thing he did. So we had to trade again. Ashley Holcomb was next. He climbed up a tree until Aleck Sander said he was high enough and shut his eyes and jumped out of it, and Aleck Sander let him off his dollar. Then I was next, and somebody said how, because Aleck Sander's mother was our cook and Aleck Sander and I had more or less lived together ever since we were born, that Aleck Sander would probably let me off light. But Aleck Sander said No, he had thought of that himself and for that very reason he was going to have to be harder on me than on Ashley and so the tree I would jump out of would be over a brier patch. And I did; it was like jumping into cold fire streaking my hands and face and tearing my britches though my hunting coat was brand new almost (Uncle Gavin had mailed it to me from Germany the day he got Mother's cable that I was born; it was the best hunting coat in Jefferson everybody said when I finally got big enough to wear it) so it didn't tear except for one pocket.

So that left only John Wesley Roebuck and maybe all of a sudden Aleck Sander realised that here was his last dollar going because John Wesley suggested everything but Aleck Sander still said No. Finally John Wesley offered to do all of them: jump through the ice then out of Ashley's tree and then out of mine but Aleck Sander still said No. So this is how they finally traded though in a way that still wasn't fair to Aleck Sander because old man Ab Snopes had already shot John Wesley in the back once about two years ago and so John Wesley was used to it, which may have been one of the reasons why he agreed to the trade. This was it. John Wesley borrowed my hunting coat to put on top of his because we had already proved that mine was the toughest, and he borrowed Ashley's sweater to wrap around his head and neck, and we counted off twenty-five steps for him and Aleck Sander put one shell in his gun and somebody, maybe me, counted One Two Three slow and when whoever it was said One John Wesley broke and ran and when whoever it was said Three Aleck Sander shot John Wesley in the back and John Wesley gave me and Ashley back the sweater and my hunting coat and (it was late by then) we went home. Except that I had to run all the way (it was cold, the coldest spell I ever remember) because we had to burn up my hunting coat because it would be easier to explain no hunting coat at all than one with the back full of Number Six shot.

Then we found out how Uncle Gavin would find out which one called next. It was Father did the scoring for him. I dont mean Father was Uncle Gavin's spy. The last thing Father was trying to do was to help Uncle Gavin, ease Uncle Gavin's mind. If anything, he was harder against Uncle Gavin even than he had thought he was that first day against Mother going to call on Mrs Snopes; it was like he was trying to take revenge on Mother and Uncle Gavin both: on Uncle Gavin for even wanting Mother to call on Mrs Snopes, and on Mother for saying right out loud in front of Uncle Gavin and Gowan both that she not only was going to do it, she didn't see any harm in it. In fact, Gowan said it was Father's mind that Mrs Snopes seemed to stay on now, more than on Uncle Gavin's. Almost any time now Father would walk in rubbing his hands and saying "oh you kid" or "twenty-three skiddoo" and they knew that he had just seen Mrs Snopes again on the street or had just heard that another Cotillion or Byron Society member had called on her; if they had invented wolf whistles then, Father would have been giving one.

Then it was December; Mother had just told how the Cotillion Club had finally voted to send Mr and Mrs Snopes an invitation to the Christmas Ball and Grandfather had got up and put his napkin down and said, "Thank you for the meal, Margaret," and Gowan went and held the door for him to go out, then Father said:

"Dance? Suppose she dont know how?" and Gowan said,

"Does she have to?" and now they all stopped; he said they all stopped at exactly the same time and looked at him and he said that even if Mother and Uncle Gavin were brother and sister one was a woman and the other was a man and Father wasn't any kin to either one of them. Yet he said they all three looked at him with exactly the same expression on their faces. Then Father said to Mother:

"Hold him while I look at his teeth again. You told me he wasn't but thirteen."

"What have I said?" Gowan said.

"Yes," Father said. "What were we saying? Oh yes, dancing the

Christmas Cotillion." He was talking to Uncle Gavin now. "Well by godfrey, that puts you one up on Manfred de Spain, dont it? He's a lone orphan; he hasn't got a wife or a twin sister who was one of the original founders of Jefferson literary and snobbery clubs; all he can do to Flem Snopes's wife is—" Gowan said how until now Mother was always between Father and Uncle Gavin, with one hand on each of their chests to hold them apart. He said that now Mother and Uncle Gavin were both at Father, with Mother holding one hand on Father's mouth and reaching for his, Gowan's, ears with the other, and she and Uncle Gavin both saying the same thing, only Uncle Gavin was just using another set of words for it:

"Dont you dare!"

"Go on. Say it."

So Father didn't. But even he didn't anticipate what Uncle Gavin would do next: try to persuade Mother to make the Cotillion committee not invite Mr de Spain to the ball at all. "Hell fire," Father said. "You cant do that."

"Why cant we?" Mother said.

"He's the mayor!" Father said.

"The mayor of a town is a servant," Mother said. "He's the head servant of course: the butler. You dont invite a butler to a party because he's a butler. You invite him in spite of it."

But Mayor de Spain got his invitation too. Maybe the reason Mother didn't stop it like Uncle Gavin wanted her to, was simply for that reason she had already given, explained, described: that she and the Cotillion Club didn't have to invite him because he was Mayor, and so they invited him just to show it, prove it. Only Father didn't think that was the reason. "No sir," he said. "You damned gals aint fooling me or anybody else. You want trouble. You want something to happen. You like it. You want two red-combed roosters strutting at one another, provided one of you hens is the reason for it. And if there's anything else you can think of to shove them in to where one of them will have to draw blood in self-defense, you'll do that too because every drop of that blood or every black eye or every public-torn collar or split or muddy britches is another item of revenge on that race of menfolks that holds you ladies thralled all day long day after day with nothing to do between meals but swap gos-

sip over the telephone. By godfrey," he said, "if there wasn't any club
to give a Christmas dance two weeks from now, you all would probably organise one just to invite Mrs Snopes and Gavin and Manfred
de Spain to it. Except you are wasting your time and money this trip.
Gavin dont know how to make trouble."

"Gavin's a gentleman," Mother said.

"Sure," Father said. "That's what I said: it aint that he dont want
to make trouble: he just dont know how. Oh, I dont mean he wont
try. He'll do the best he knows. But he just dont know how to make
the kind of trouble that a man like Manfred de Spain will take seriously."

But Mr de Spain did the best he could to teach Uncle Gavin how.
He began the day the invitations were sent out and he got his after
all. When he bought that red E.M.F. the first thing he did was to
have a cut-out put on it and until he got elected mayor the first time
you could hear him all the way to the Square the moment he left
home. And soon after that Lucius Hogganbeck got somebody (it was
Mr Roth Edmonds and maybe Mr de Spain too since Lucius's father,
old Boon Hogganbeck, had been Mr Roth's father's, Mr McCaslin
Edmonds, and his uncle's, Uncle Ike McCaslin, and old Major de
Spain's huntsman-doghandler-manFriday back in the time of Major
de Spain's old hunting camp) to sign a note for him to buy a Model T
Ford and set up in the jitney passenger-hauling business, and he had
a cut-out too and on Sunday afternoons half the men in Jefferson
would slip off from their wives and go out to a straight stretch of road
about two miles from town (even two miles back in town you could
hear them when the wind was right) and Mr de Spain and Lucius
would race each other. Lucius would charge his passengers a nickel
a head to ride in the race, though Mr de Spain carried his free.

Though the first thing Mr de Spain did after he got to be mayor
was to have an ordinance passed that no cut-out could be opened
inside the town limits. So it had been years now since we had heard
one. Then one morning we did. I mean we—Grandfather and
Mother and Father and Uncle Gavin and Gowan—did, because it
was right in front of our house. It was just about the time everybody
would be going to school or to work and Gowan knew which car it
was even before he got to the window because Lucius's Ford made a

different sound, and besides nobody but the mayor would have risked that cut-out with the cut-out law in force. It was him: the red car just going out of sight and the cut-out off again as soon as he had passed the house; and Uncle Gavin still sitting at the table finishing his breakfast just as if there hadn't been any new noise at all.

And as Gowan reached the corner on the way home from school at noon, he heard it again; Mr de Spain had driven blocks out of his way to rip past our house again in second gear with the cut-out wide open; and again while Mother and Father and Grandfather and Uncle Gavin and he were still sitting at the table finishing dinner, with Mother sitting right still and not looking at anything and Father looking at Uncle Gavin and Uncle Gavin sitting there stirring his coffee like there wasn't a sound anywhere in the world except maybe his spoon in the cup.

And again about half-past five, about dark, when the storekeepers and doctors and lawyers and mayors and such as that would be going home at the end of the day to eat supper all quiet and peaceful, without having to go back to town until tomorrow morning; and this time Gowan could even see Uncle Gavin listening to the cut-out when it passed the house. I mean, this time Uncle Gavin didn't mind them seeing that he heard it, looking up from the paper a little and holding the paper in front of him until the sound went on and then quit off when Mr de Spain passed the end of our yard and picked up his foot; Uncle Gavin and Grandfather both looking up while it passed though all Grandfather did yet was just to frown a little and Uncle Gavin not even doing that: just waiting, almost peaceful, so that Gowan could almost hear him saying *That's all at last. He had to make the fourth run past to get back home.*

And it was all, through supper and afterward when they went to the office where Mother would sit in the rocking chair always sewing something though it seemed to be mostly darning socks and Gowan's stockings and Grandfather and Father would sit across the desk from one another playing checkers and sometimes Uncle Gavin would come in too with his book when he wouldn't feel like trying again to teach Mother to play chess until I got born next year and finally got big enough so he could begin to try to teach me. And now it was already past the time when the ones going to the picture show would have gone to it, and the men just going back to town after supper to loaf in Christian's drugstore or to talk with the drummers in the Holston House lobby or drink some more coffee in the café, and anybody would have thought he was safe. Only this time it wasn't even Father. It was Grandfather himself jerking his head up and saying:

"What the devil's that? That's the second time today."

"It's the fifth time today," Father said. "His foot slipped."

"What?" Grandfather said.

"He was trying to mash on the brake to go quiet past the house," Father said. "Only his foot slipped and mashed on the cut-out instead."

"Telephone Connors," Grandfather said. That was Mr Buck Connors. "I wont have it."

"That's Gavin's job," Father said. "He's the acting City Attorney when you're in a checker game. He's the one to speak to the marshal. Or better still, the mayor. Aint that right, Gavin?" And Gowan said they all looked at Uncle Gavin, and that he himself was ashamed, not of Uncle Gavin: of us, the rest of them. He said it was like watching somebody's britches falling down while he's got to use both hands trying to hold up the roof: you are sorry it is funny, ashamed you had to be there watching Uncle Gavin when he never even had any warning he would need to try to hide his face's nakedness when that cut-out went on and the car ripped slow in second gear past the house again after you would have thought that anybody would have had the right to believe that other time before supper would be the last one at least until tomorrow, the cut-out ripping past and sounding just like laughing, still sounding like laughing even after the car had reached the corner where Mr de Spain would always lift his foot off the cut-out. Because it was laughing: it was Father sitting at his side of the checker board, looking at Uncle Gavin and laughing.

"Charley!" Mother said. "Stop it!" But it was already too late. Uncle Gavin had already got up, quick, going toward the door like he couldn't quite see it, and on out.

"What the devil's this?" Grandfather said.

"He rushed out to telephone Buck Connors," Father said. "Since this was the fifth time today, he must have decided that fellow's foot never slipped at all." Now Mother was standing right over Father with the stocking and the darning egg in one hand and the needle in the other like a dagger.

"Will you please hush, dearest?" she said. "Will you please shut your gee dee mouth?—I'm sorry, Papa," she said to Grandfather. "But he—" Then she was at Father again: "Will you? Will you now?"

"Sure, kid," Father said. "I'm all for peace and quiet too." Then Mother was gone too and then it was bedtime and then Gowan told how he saw Uncle Gavin sitting in the dark parlor with no light except through the hall door, so that he couldn't read if he tried. Which Gowan said he wasn't: just sitting there in the half-dark, until Mother came down the stairs in her dressing gown and her hair down and said,

"Why dont you go to bed? Go on now. Go on," and Gowan said, "Yessum," and she went on into the parlor and stood beside Uncle Gavin's chair and said,

"I'm going to telephone him," and Uncle Gavin said,

"Telephone who?" and Mother came back and said,

"Come on now. This minute," and waited until Gowan went up the stairs in front of her. When he was in bed with the light off she came to the door and said good night and all they would have to do now would be just to wait. Because even if five was an odd number and it would take an even number to make the night whole for Uncle Gavin, it couldn't possibly be very long because the drugstore closed as soon as the picture show was out, and anybody still sitting in the Holston House lobby after the drummers had all gone to bed would have to explain it to Jefferson some time or other, no matter how much of a bachelor he was. And Gowan said he thought how at least Uncle Gavin and he had their nice warm comfortable familiar home to wait in, even if Uncle Gavin was having to sit up in the dark parlor by himself, instead of having to use the drugstore or the hotel to put off finally having to go home as long as possible.

And this time Gowan said Mr de Spain opened the cut-out as soon as he left the Square; he could hear it all the way getting louder and louder as it turned the two corners into our street, the ripping loud and jeering but at least not in second gear this time, going fast past the house and the dark parlor where Uncle Gavin was sitting, and on around the other two corners he would have to turn to get back into the street he belonged in, dying away at last until all you could hear was just the night and then Uncle Gavin's feet coming quiet up the stairs. Then the hall light went out, and that was all.

All for that night, that day I mean. Because even Uncle Gavin didn't expect it to be completely all. In fact, the rest of them found out pretty quick that Uncle Gavin didn't aim for it to be all; the next morning at breakfast it was Uncle Gavin himself that raised his head first and said: "There goes Manfred back to our salt-mine," and then to Gowan: "Mr de Spain has almost as much fun with his automobile as you're going to have with one as soon as your Cousin Charley buys it, doesn't he?" Whenever that would be because Father said almost before Uncle Gavin could finish getting the words out:

"Me own one of those stinking noisy things? I wouldn't dare. Too many of my customers use horses and mules for a living." But Gowan said that if Father ever did buy one while he was there, he would find something better to do with it besides running back and forth in front of the house with the cut-out open.

And again while he was on the way home at noon to eat dinner, and again while they were sitting at the table. Nor was it just Gowan who found out Uncle Gavin didn't aim for that to be all because Mother caught Gowan almost before Uncle Gavin turned his back. Gowan didn't know how she did it. Aleck Sander always said that his mother could see and hear through a wall (when he got bigger he said Guster could smell his breath over the telephone) so maybe all women that were already mothers or just acting like mothers like Mother had to while Gowan lived with us, could do that too and that was how Mother did it: stepping out of the parlor just as Gowan put his hand in his pocket.

"Where is it?" Mother said. "What Gavin just gave you. It was a box of tacks; wasn't it a box of tacks? To scatter out there in the street where he will run over them? Wasn't it? Acting just like a high-school sophomore. He should marry Melisandre Backus before he ruins the whole family."

"I thought you said it's too late for that," Gowan said. "That the one that marries Cousin Gavin will have to be a widow with four children."

"Maybe I meant too early," Mother said. "Melisandre hasn't even got the husband yet." Then she wasn't seeing Gowan. "Which is exactly what Manfred de Spain is acting like," she said. "A high-school sophomore." Gowan said she was looking right at him but she wasn't seeing him at all, and all of a sudden he said she was pretty, looking just like a girl. "No: exactly what we are all acting like," and now she was seeing him again. "But dont you dare let me see you doing it, do you hear? Dont you dare!"

"Yessum," Gowan said. It was no trouble. All he and Top had to do after school was just divide the tacks into their hands and kind of fool around out in the middle of the street like they were trying to decide what to do next while the tacks dribbled down across the tracks of the automobile; Mr de Spain had made nine trips by now so Gowan said he almost had two ruts. Only he and Top had to stay out in the cold now because they wanted to see it. Top said that when the wheels blew up, they would blow the whole automobile up. Gowan didn't think so, but he didn't know either and Top might be partly right, enough right anyway to be worth watching.

So they had to stand behind the big jasmine bush and it began to get dark and it got colder and colder and Guster opened the kitchen door and begun to holler for Top then after awhile she came to the front door and hollered for both of them; it was full dark and good and cold now when at last they saw the lights coming, they reached the corner of the yard and the cut-out went on and the car ripped slow and loud past and they listened and watched both but nothing happened, nothing at all, it just went on and even the cut-out went back off; Gowan said how maybe it would take a little time for the tacks to finally work in and blow the wheels up and they waited for that too but nothing happened. And now it had been long enough for him to be home.

And after supper, all of them in the office again, but not anything at all this time, not even anything passed the house so Gowan thought maybe it hadn't blown up until after he was home and now Uncle Gavin never would know when it would be safe to come out of the dark parlor and go upstairs to bed; so that he, Gowan, made a chance to whisper to Uncle Gavin: "Do you want me to go up to his house and look?" Only Father said,

"What? What're you whispering about?" so that didn't do any

good either. And the next morning nothing happened either, the cut-out ripping slow past the house like next time it was coming right through the dining room itself. And twice more at noon and that afternoon when Gowan got home from school Top jerked his head at him and they went to the cellar; Top had an old rake-head with a little of the handle still in it so they built a fire behind the stable and burned the handle out and when it was dark enough Gowan watched up and down the street while Top scraped a trench across the tire rut and set the rake teeth-up in it and scattered some leaves over to hide it and they watched from behind the jasmine bush again while the car ripped past. And nothing happened though when the car was gone they went and saw for themselves where the wheels had mashed right across the rake.

"We'll try it once more," Gowan said. And they did: the next morning: and nothing. And that afternoon Top worked on the rake a while with an old file and then Gowan worked on it a while even after they both knew they would still be working on it that way when the Cotillion Club would be planning next year's Christmas Ball. "We need a grindstone," Gowan said.

"Unk Noon," Top said.

"We'll take the gun like we are going rabbit hunting," Gowan said. So they did: as far as Uncle Noon Gatewood's blacksmith shop on the edge of town. Uncle Noon was big and yellow; he had a warped knee that just seemed to fit exactly into the break of a horse's forearm and pastern; he would pick up a horse's hind leg and set the foot inside the knee and reach out with one hand and take hold of the nearest post and if the post held, the horse could jerk and plunge all it wanted to and Uncle Noon and the horse might sway back and forth but the foot wouldn't move. He let Gowan and Top use his rock and while Top turned and tilted the water-can Gowan held the teeth one by one to the stone until they would have gone through almost anything that mashed against them, let alone an automobile.

And Gowan said they sure did have to wait for dark this time. For dark and late too, when they knew nobody would see them. Because if the sharpened rake worked, the car might not blow up so bad that Mr de Spain wouldn't have time to wonder what caused it and start looking around and find the rake. And at first it looked like it was going to be a good thing it was a long December night too because the ground was frozen so hard that they had to dig the trench through, not just a short trench like before to set the rake in but one long enough so they could tie a string to the rake and then snatch the rake back into the yard between the time the wheel blew up and Mr de Spain could begin to hunt for what caused it. But Gowan said at least tomorrow was Saturday so they would have all day to fix the rake so they could be behind the jasmine bush and see it by daylight.

So they were: already behind the bush with the rake-head fixed and the end of the string in Gowan's hand when they heard it coming and then saw it, then the cut-out came on and it came ripping past with the cut-out like it was saying HAhaHAhaHAha until they were already thinking they had missed this time too when the wheel said BANG and Gowan said he didn't have time to snatch the string because the string did the snatching, out of his hand and around the jasmine bush like the tail of a snake, the car saying HAhaHAha-clankHAhaHAhaclank every time the rake that seemed to be stuck to the wheel would wham against the mudguard again, until Mr de Spain finally stopped it. Then Gowan said the parlor window behind them opened, with Mother and Father standing in it until Mother said:

"You and Top go out and help him so you both will learn something about automobiles when your Cousin Charley buys one."

"Me buy one of those noisy stinking things?" Father said. "Why, I'd lose every horse and mule customer I've got—"

"Nonsense," Mother said. "You'd buy one today if you thought Papa would stand for it.—No," she said to Gowan. "Just you help Mr de Spain. I want Top in the house."

So Top went into the house and Gowan went out to the car where Mr de Spain was standing beside the crumpled wheel holding the rake-head in his hand and looking down at it with his lips poked out like he was kind of whistling a tune to himself, Gowan said. Then he looked around at Gowan and took out his knife and cut the string loose and put the rake-head into his overcoat pocket and begun to roll the string up, watching the string where it came jerking out of our yard, his mouth still pursed out like he was whistling to himself. Then Top came up. He was wearing the white jacket he wore when Mother would try to teach him to wait on the table, carrying a tray with a cup of coffee and the cream and sugar bowl. "Miss Maggie say would you care for a cup of coffee while you resting in the cold?" he said.

"Much obliged," Mr de Spain said. He finished rolling the string up and took the tray from Top and set it on the mudguard of the car and then handed the rolled-up string to Top. "Here's a good fish line for you," he said.

"It aint none of mine," Top said.

"It is now," Mr de Spain said. "I just gave it to you." So Top took the string. Then Mr de Spain told him to take off that clean white coat first and then he opened the back of the automobile and showed Gowan and Top the jack and tire tool and then he drank the coffee while Top crawled under the car and set the jack in place and he and Gowan wound up the wheel. Then Mr de Spain put down the empty cup and took off his overcoat and hunkered down by the crumpled wheel with the tire tool. Except that from then on Gowan said all he and Top learned was some curse-words they never had heard before, until Mr de Spain stood up and threw the tire tool at the wheel and said, to Gowan this time: "Run in the house and telephone Buck Connors to bring Jabbo here double quick." Only Father was there by that time.

"Maybe you've got too many experts," he said. "Come on in and have a drink. I know it's too early in the morning but this is Christmas."

So they all went into the house and Father telephoned Mr Connors to bring Jabbo. Jabbo was Uncle Noon Gatewood's son. He was going to be a blacksmith too until Mr de Spain brought that first red automobile to town and, as Uncle Noon said, "ruint him." Though Gowan said that never made much sense to him because Jabbo used to get drunk and wind up in jail three or four times a year while he was still only a blacksmith, while now, since automobiles had come to Jefferson, Jabbo was the best mechanic in the county and although he still got drunk and into jail as much as ever, he never stayed longer than just overnight any more because somebody with an automobile always needed him enough to pay his fine by morning.

Then they went into the dining room, where Mother already had the decanter and glasses set out. "Wait," Father said. "I'll call Gavin."

"He's already gone," Mother said right quick. "Sit down now and have your toddy."

"Maybe he hasn't," Father said, going out anyway.

"Please dont wait on them," Mother said to Mr de Spain.

"I don't mind waiting," Mr de Spain said. "It's too early in the morning to start drinking for the next few minutes." Then Father came back.

"Gavin says to please excuse him," Father said. "He seems to have heartburn these days."

"Tell him salt is good for heartburn," Mr de Spain said.

"What?" Father said.

"Tell him to come on," Mr de Spain said. "Tell him Maggie will set a salt-cellar between us." And that was all then. Mr Connors came with a shotgun and Jabbo in handcuffs and they all went out to the car while Mr Connors handed the shotgun to Jabbo to hold while he got out the key and unlocked the handcuffs and took the shotgun back. Then Jabbo picked up the tire tool and had the tire off in no time.

"Why dont you," Father said, "if you could just kind of embalm Jabbo a little—you know: so he wouldn't get cold or hungry—tie him on the back of the car like he was an extra wheel or engine, then every time you had a puncture or it wouldn't start, all you'd have to do would be to untie Jabbo and stand him up and unbalm him—is that the word? Unbalm?"

"When you get it patched," Mr de Spain said to Jabbo, "bring it on to my office."

"Yes sir," Jabbo said. "Mr Buck can bring the fining paper along with us."

"Thank your aunt for the coffee," Mr de Spain said to Gowan.

"She's my cousin," Gowan said. "And the toddy."

"I'll walk to town with you," Father said to Mr de Spain. That was Saturday. The Cotillion Ball would be Wednesday. On Monday and Tuesday and Wednesday Jefferson had the biggest run on flowers the town ever had, even when old General Compson died, who had not only been a Confederate brigadier, but for two days he had been Governor of Mississippi too. It wasn't through any of us that Mr de Spain found out what Uncle Gavin was planning to do, and decided

410

THE TOWN

that he—Mr de Spain—had better do it too. And it would be nice to
think that the same notion occurred to Uncle Gavin and Mr de Spain
at the same time. But that was too much to expect either.

So it was Mrs Rouncewell. She ran the flower shop; not, Uncle
Gavin said, because she loved flowers nor even because she loved
money but because she loved funerals; she had buried two husbands
herself and took the second one's insurance and opened the flower
shop and furnished the flowers for every funeral in Jefferson since;
she would be the one that told Mr de Spain how Uncle Gavin had
wanted to send Mrs Snopes a corsage to wear to the ball until
Mother told him that Mrs Snopes already had a husband and he
couldn't send one to her alone and Uncle Gavin said All right, did
Mother want him to send one to Mr Snopes too? And Mother said
he knew what she meant and Uncle Gavin said All right, he would
send one to each one of the Cotillion ladies. Until Mr de Spain had
to do the same thing, so that not just Mrs Snopes but all the ladies
of the Cotillion Club were going to get two corsages apiece.

Not to mention the rest of the town: not just the husbands and
beaus of the ladies in the Club, but the husbands and beaus of all the
other ladies who were invited; especially the husbands who were
already married because they wouldn't have had to send their wives
a corsage at all because their wives wouldn't have expected one
except for Uncle Gavin and Mr de Spain. But mainly Uncle Gavin
since he started the whole thing; to listen to them around the barbershop getting their hair cut for the dance, and in Mr Kneeland's
tailor shop renting the dress suits, you would have thought they were
going to lynch Uncle Gavin.

And one was more than just cussing Uncle Gavin: Mr Grenier
Weddel and Mrs Maurice Priest. But all that came out later; we
didn't hear about that until the day after the Ball. All we knew about
now was the corsage-run on Mrs Rouncewell, what Father called the
Rouncewell panic. ("I had to make that one myself," Father said. "It
was Gavin's by right; he should have done it but right now he aint
even as faintly close to humor as that one was." Because he was
cussing Uncle Gavin too, since now he would have to send Mother
a corsage that he hadn't figured on doing, since Uncle Gavin was,
which would make three she would get—that is, if the rest of the

men aiming to attend the Ball didn't panic too and decide they would all have to send the members a separate corsage.) Because by Monday night Mrs Rouncewell had run clean out of flowers; by the time the northbound train ran Tuesday afternoon all the towns up and down the road from Jefferson had been milked dry too; and early Wednesday morning a special hired automobile made a night emergency run from Memphis with enough flowers to make out so Mrs Rouncewell could begin to deliver the corsages, using her own delivery boy and Lucius Hogganbeck's jitney and even renting Miss Eunice Habersham's home-made truck that she peddled vegetables from to finish the deliveries in time, delivering five of them at our house which they all thought were for Mother until she read the names on the boxes and said:

"This one's not for me. It's for Gavin." And they all stood watching Uncle Gavin while he stood right still looking down at the box, his hand already raised toward the box and then his hand stopped too in midair. Until at last he broke the string and lifted the lid and moved the tissue paper aside and then Gowan said it was all of a sudden yet it wasn't fast either—moved the tissue paper back and put the lid back on and picked up the box. "Aren't you going to let us see it?" Mother said.

"No," Uncle Gavin said. But Gowan had already seen. It was the rake-head, with two flowers like a bouquet, all bound together with a band or strip of something that Gowan knew was thin rubber but it was another year or two until he was a good deal bigger and older that he knew what the thing was; and at the same time he realised what it was, he said he knew it had already been used; and at the same time he knew at least how Uncle Gavin was supposed to believe it had been used, which was the reason Mr de Spain sent it to him: that whether Uncle Gavin was right or not about how it had been used, he would never be sure and so forever afterward would have no peace about it.

And Gowan was just thirteen then; until that one, he wouldn't have thought that anybody could have paid him or even dragged him to a Cotillion Ball. But he said he had already had to see too much by now; he had to be there if there was going to be anything else, any more to it, even if he couldn't imagine what else there could be after this, what more could happen at just a dance. So he put on his blue Sunday suit and watched Mother with her hair all primped and Grandmother's best diamond earrings trying to make Father say which of her four corsages to carry: the one he gave her or to agree with the one of the other three that she thought went best with her dress; then he went across to Uncle Gavin's room where Uncle Gavin got out another white bow tie like his and put it on Gowan and a flower for his buttonhole too and they all went downstairs, the hack was waiting and they drove through the cold to the Square and the Opera House where the other hacks and now and then a car were pulling up for the other guests to get out crimped and frizzed in scarves and earrings and perfume and long white gloves like Mother or in claw-hammer coats and boiled shirts and white ties and yesterday's haircuts like Father and Uncle Gavin and (the white tie at least) Gowan, with the loafers, Negro and white boys too, hanging around the door to hear the music after the band started to play.

It was Professor Hardy, from Beale Street in Memphis. His band played at all the balls in north Mississippi and Gowan said how the hall was all decorated for Christmas and the Cotillion Club ladies and their escorts all lined up to receive the guests; he said you could smell all the corsages even before you began to climb the stairs and that when you got inside the ballroom it looked like you should have been able to see the smell from them too like mist in a swamp on a cold morning. And he said how Mr Snopes was there too, in a rented dress suit, and Jefferson probably thought at first that that rented dress suit was just the second footprint made on it, until they had time to realise that it wasn't any more just a footprint than that water tank was a monument: it was a red flag. No: it was that sign at the railroad crossing that says Look Out for the Locomotive.

And Gowan said how, since Mother was President of the Club that year, everybody (once Mrs Rouncewell finally realised that floral goldmine she had fallen into, there wasn't anybody in Jefferson in the dark any longer about Mr de Spain and Uncle Gavin and Mrs Snopes) expected her to give Uncle Gavin the first dance with Mrs Snopes. But she didn't. She sent Grenier Weddel; he was a bachelor too. And even after that she still kept the dances equal between Uncle Gavin and Mr de Spain until Mr de Spain ruined it. Because he was a bachelor. I mean, like Uncle Gavin said: that there are some men who are incorrigibly and invincibly bachelor no matter how often they marry, just as some men are doomed and emasculate husbands if they never find a woman to take them. And Mr de Spain was one of them. I mean the first kind: incorrigibly and invincibly bachelor and threat no matter what happened to him because Uncle Gavin said things, circumstance and conditions, didn't happen to people like Mr de Spain: people like him happened to circumstances and conditions.

This time he had help. I wasn't there to see it and I know now that Gowan didn't know what he was seeing either. Because after a while I got born and then big enough to see Mrs Snopes myself, and after a while more I was old enough to feel what Uncle Gavin and Mr de Spain (and all the other men in Jefferson, and Frenchman's Bend and everywhere else that ever saw her I reckon, the little cautious men who were not as brave and unlucky as Uncle Gavin and brave and lucky as Mr de Spain, though they probably called it being more sensible) felt just looking at her. And after a while more still and she was dead and Mr de Spain had left town wearing public mourning for her as if she had been his wife and Jefferson finally quit talking about her, my bet is there was more than me in Jefferson that even just remembering her could feel it still and grieve. I mean, grieve because her daughter didn't have whatever it was that she had; until you realised that what you grieved for wasn't that the daughter didn't have it too; grieved not that we didn't have it any more, but that we couldn't have it any more: that even a whole Jefferson full of little weak puny frightened men couldn't have stood more than one Mrs Snopes inside of just one one-hundred years. And I reckon there was a second or two at first when even Mr de Spain had time to be afraid. I reckon there was a second when even he said Hold on here; have I maybe blundered into something not just purer than me but even braver than me, braver and tougher than me because it is purer than me, cleaner than me? Because that was what it was.

Gowan said it was the way Mrs Snopes and Mr de Spain began to dance together. That is, the way that Mr de Spain all of a sudden began to dance with Mrs Snopes. Up to that time, Gowan said, Uncle Gavin and Mr de Spain and the other men Mother sent to write their names on Mrs Snopes's program had been taking turns all calm and peaceful. Then all of a sudden Gowan said everybody else stopped dancing and kind of fell back and he said he saw Mrs Snopes and Mr de Spain dancing together alone in a kind of aghast circle of people. And when I was old enough, fourteen or fifteen or sixteen, I knew what Gowan had seen without knowing what he was seeing: that second when Mr de Spain felt astonishment, amazement and unbelief and terror too at himself because of what he found himself doing without even knowing he was going to—dancing like that with Mrs Snopes to take revenge on Uncle Gavin for having frightened him, Mr de Spain, enough to make him play the sophomore tricks like the cut-out and the rake-head and the used rubber thing in a corsage; frightened at himself at finding out that he couldn't possibly be only what he had thought for all those years he was, if he could find himself in a condition capable of playing tricks like that; while Mrs Snopes was dancing that way, letting Mr de Spain get her into dancing that way in public, simply because she was alive and not ashamed of it like maybe right now or even for the last two weeks Mr de Spain and Uncle Gavin had been ashamed; was what she was and looked the way she looked and wasn't ashamed of it and not afraid or ashamed of being glad of it, nor even of doing this to prove it, since this appeared to be the only way of proving it, not being afraid or ashamed, that the little puny people fallen back speechless and aghast in a shocked circle around them, could understand; all the other little doomed mean cowardly married and unmarried husbands looking aghast and outraged in order to keep one another from seeing that what they really wanted to do was cry, weep because they were not that brave, each one knowing that even if there was no other man on earth, let alone in that ball room, they still could not have survived, let alone matched or coped with, that splendor, that splendid unshame.

It should have been Mr Snopes of course because he was the husband, the squire, the protector in the formal ritual. But it was Uncle Gavin and he wasn't any husband or squire or knight or defender or protector either except simply and quickly his own: who didn't really care even how badly Mrs Snopes got battered and bruised in the business provided there was enough of her left when he finally got the last spark of life trampled out of Mr de Spain. Gowan said how he stepped in and grabbed Mr de Spain by the shoulder and jerked, and now a kind of sound went up and then he said all the men were streaming across the floor toward the back stairs that led down into the back alley and now the ladies were screaming good only Gowan said that a lot of them were streaking after the men too so that he had to kind of burrow along among skirts and legs, down the back stairs; he said he could see Uncle Gavin through the legs just getting up from the alley and he, Gowan, pushed on through to the front and saw Uncle Gavin just getting up from the alley again with his face all bloody and two men helping him or anyway trying to, because he flung them off and ran at Mr de Spain again: and when I was older I knew that too: that Uncle Gavin wasn't trying any more to destroy or even hurt Mr de Spain because he had already found out by that time that he couldn't. Because now Uncle Gavin was himself again. What he was doing was simply defending forever with his blood the principle that chastity and virtue in women shall be defended whether they exist or not.

"Damn it," Mr de Spain said, "hold him, some of you fellows, and let me get out of here." So Father held Uncle Gavin and somebody brought Mr de Spain's hat and coat and he left; and Gowan said this was the time he expected to hear that cut-out again for sure. But he didn't. There was nothing: just Uncle Gavin standing there wiping the blood from his face on his handkerchief then on Father's.

"You fool," Father said. "Dont you know you cant fight? You dont know how."

"Can you suggest a better way to learn than the one I just tried?" Uncle Gavin said.

And at home too, in his bathroom, where he could take off his vest and collar and tie and shirt and hold a wet towel against the bleeding, when Mother came in. She had a flower in her hand, a red rose from one of the corsages. "Here," she said. "She sent it to you."

"You lie," Uncle Gavin said. "You did it."

"Lie yourself!" Mother said. "She sent it!"

"No," Uncle Gavin said.

"Then she should have!" Mother said; and now Gowan said she was crying, half way holding to Uncle Gavin and half way beating

him with both fists, crying: "You fool! You fool! They dont deserve
you! They aren't good enough for you! None of them are, no matter how much they look and act like a—like a—like a god damn
whorehouse! None of them! None of them!"

Only Mr Snopes left more footprints than them on Jefferson that
night; he left another bloody nose and two black eyes. That fourth
corsage Mother got that night was from Grenier Weddel. He was a
bachelor like Mr de Spain. I mean, he was the kind of bachelor that
Uncle Gavin said would still be one no matter how many times who
married him. Maybe that was why Sally Hampton turned him down.
Anyway, she sent his ring back and married Maurice Priest instead
and so when Uncle Gavin and Mr de Spain started what Father
called the Mrs Rouncewell panic that day, Grenier saw his chance
too and sent Mrs Priest not just what Father called a standard panic-
size corsage, but a triple one. Maybe that was why she didn't wear it
to the ball that night; it was too big to carry. Anyway she didn't but
anyway after Uncle Gavin and Mr de Spain got through with the
alley, Grenier and Maurice Priest went back there and Grenier came
out with one of the black eyes and Maurice went home with the
bloody nose and the next morning when Sally Parsons came to town
she had the other black eye. And maybe she didn't wear the corsage
in public but she sure did that eye. She was not only around town all
that morning, she came back that afternoon so everybody in Jefferson would have a chance to see it or at least hear about it. Gowan said
you would even have thought she was proud of it.

F O U R

V. K. Ratliff

*S*he was. His aunt (not his two uncles nor his grandpaw, but any of his womenfolks) could have told him why: proud she still had a husband that could and would black her eye; proud her husband had a wife that could still make him need to.

And Flem wasn't the first Snopes in Jefferson neither. The first one was Mink, that spent two and a half months in the Jefferson jail on his way to his permanent residence in the penitentiary at Parchman for killing Jack Houston. And he spent them two and a half months laboring under a mistake.

I dont mean a mistake in killing Houston. He knowed what he aimed to do then. Jack was a proud man to begin with, but solitary too: a bad combination; solitary because he had already lost his young wife that taken him a considerable getting to get in the first place, and that he hadn't even had her a whole year when he lost her; and too proud to let his-self get over it even after four years. Or maybe that was why: them six or seven months he had her measured against them six or seven or whatever they was years it had taken him to get her to marry him. And even then he had to lose her hard, the hardest way: that same blood stallion killed her with his feet in the stall one day that Mink shot Houston off of that morning—and that made him a little extra morose because he was unhappy. So between being proud to begin with and then unhappy on top of that, he was a little overbearing. But since most of the folks around Frenchman's Bend knowed he was proud and knowed how hard he had to work to persuade the folks that had raised Lucy Pate to let her marry him, he would a still been all right if he hadn't tangled with Mink Snopes.

417

Because Mink Snopes was mean. He was the only out-and-out mean Snopes we ever experienced. There was mad short-tempered barn-burners like old Ab, and there was the mild innocent ones like Eck that not only wasn't no Snopes, no matter what his maw said, he never had no more business being born into a Snopes nest than a sparrow would have in a hawk's nest; and there was the one pure out-and-out fool like I.O. But we never had run into one before that was just mean without no profit consideration or hope atall.

Maybe that was why he was the only mean Snopes: there wasn't no sign of any profit in it. Only he was bound or anyway must a had a little of his cousin I.O.'s foolishness too or he wouldn't have made his mistake. I mean, the mistake not of shooting Houston but of when he picked out to do it; picking out the time to do it while Flem was still off on his Texas honeymoon. Sholy he knowed that Flem hadn't got back yet. Or maybe the night before he had got the Snopes grapevine word that he had been waiting for, that Flem would reach Frenchman's Bend tomorrow, and it was only then that he taken that old wore-out ten-gauge britch-loader and hid in that thicket and bushwhacked Houston off the horse when he rid past. But then I dont know. Maybe by that time nothing else mattered to him but seeing Houston over the end of them barrels then feeling that stock jolt back against his shoulder.

Anyhow, that's what he done. And likely it wasn't until Houston was laying in the mud in the road and that skeered stallion with the loose reins and the empty saddle and flapping stirrups already tearing on to Varner's store to spread the news, that he realised with whatever horror it was, that he had done too soon something it was long since too late to undo. Which was why he tried to hide the body and then dropped the gun into that slough and come on to the store, hanging around the store ever day while the sheriff was still hunting for Houston, not to keep up with whether the sheriff was getting warm or not but waiting for Flem to get back from Texas and save him; right up to the time when Houston's hound led them to the body and some fish grabblers even found the gun in the slough that ever body knowed was hisn because wouldn't nobody else own it.

And that was when the rage and the outrage and the injustice and the betrayal must a got unbearable to him, when he decided or realized or whatever it was, that Flem by now must a heard about the killing and was deliberately keeping away from Frenchman's Bend or maybe even all Mississippi so he wouldn't have to help him, get him out of it. Not even despair: just simple anger and outrage: to show Flem Snopes that he never give a durn about him neither: handcuffed now and in the sheriff's surrey on the way in to the jail when he seen his chance right quick and wedged his neck tight into the V of the top stanchion and tried to fling his legs and body over the side until they caught him back.

But it was just the initial outrage and hurt and disappointment; it couldn't last. Which likely his good sense told him it wouldn't, and probably he was glad in a way he had got shut of it so calm good sense could come back. Which it did, since now all he had to do was just to be as comfortable as he could in jail and wait until Flem did get home since even Flem Snopes couldn't stay forever even on a honeymoon even in Texas.

So that's what he done. Up there on the top floor of the jail (since he was a authentic topclass murderer, he wouldn't have to go out and work on the streets like just a Negro crap-shooter), not even impatient for a long time: just standing there with his hands laying in the crossbars where he could watch the street and the sidewalk that Flem would come walking up from the Square; not impatient during all that first month and not even bad worried in the second one after the Grand Jury indicted him: just hollering down now and then to somebody passing if Flem Snopes was in town yet; not even until the end of the second month that he begun to think that maybe Flem hadn't got back yet and he would holler down to folks to send word out to Frenchman's Bend for Will Varner to come in and see him.

So it wasn't until just them two last weeks before Court and no Will Varner nor nobody else had come in to see him that he probably found out he simply could not believe that Flem Snopes hadn't got back to Frenchman's Bend; he just could not believe that, he dassent to believe that: only that the grown folks he had been hollering down to hadn't never delivered his message, not sleeping much at night now so that (that-ere top floor behind the barred window would be dark

and with the street light shining on it you could see the white blob
of his face and the two blobs of his hands gripping the bars) he had
plenty of time to stand there all night if necessary waiting for somebody to pass that he could trust would deliver his message: boys, a boy
like that Stevens boy, Lawyer Stevens's visiting nephew, that hadn't
been spoiled and corrupted yet by the world of growed-up men into
being his enemies, whispering down to them until they would stop
and look up at him; still whispering down at them even after they had
done broke and run: "Boys! Fellers! You, there. You want ten dollars?
Get word out to Frenchman's Bend, tell Flem Snopes his cousin Mink
Snopes says to hurry in here, hurry—"

And right up to that morning in court. As soon as they brung him
in the door, handcuffed, he started to craning his neck, looking at
all the faces, still craning his neck around at the folks still crowding
in long after they had run out of anything to set on and still at it
while they was choosing the jury, even trying to stand up on a chair
to see better until they would shove him down; still craning and darting his head while the clerk read the indictment and then said,
"Guilty or not guilty?" Only this time he had already stood up before
they could stop him, looking out over the crowd toward the last faces
at the clean back of the room and says:

"Flem!"

And now the Judge was banging his little mallet and the lawyer the
Court had appointed was up too and the bailiff hollering, "Order!
Order in the court!"

And Mink says again, "Flem! Flem Snopes!" Only this time the
Judge his-self leaned down toward him across the Bench and says,

"You there! Snopes!" until Mink finally turned and looked at him.
"Are you guilty or not guilty?"

"What?" Mink says.

"Did you kill Zack Houston or didn't you?" the Judge says.

"Dont bother me now," Mink says. "Cant you see I'm busy?"
turning his head again toward the faces come to see if maybe they
wouldn't hang him anyhow, no matter who said he was crazy, since
that was what he seemed to want his-self, having already tried it once
and so the Law wouldn't be doing no more than just accommodating
him, saying: "Somebody there! One of them automobiles! To run out

to Varner's store quick and get Flem Snopes. He will pay you, whatever you charge and whatever extry—ten dollars extry—twenty extry—"

Last summer Lawyer had to do something, he didn't know what. Now he had to do something, he didn't care what. I dont even think he especially hunted around for something. I think he just reached his hand and snatched something, the first nearest thing, and it just happened to be that old quick-vanishing power-plant brass that ever body in Jefferson, including Flem Snopes—sholy including Flem Snopes—had been trying out of pure and simple politeness to forget about.

When as acting City Attorney he drawed up the suit against Mayor de Spain's bonding company, charging malfeasance in office and criminal connivance or however they put it, naturally ever body thought all he aimed to do then was to walk in and lay the papers on Manfred de Spain's desk. But they was wrong; he never no more wanted to buy anything from De Spain than he did that night in the alley behind that Christmas Ball, when his brother-in-law told him he couldn't fight because he never knowed how—a piece of information already in Lawyer's possession, having already lived with hisself for more or less twenty-two or maybe twenty-three years. He didn't want nothing from De Spain because the only thing De Spain had that he wanted, Lawyer didn't know his-self that was what he wanted until his paw told him that last afternoon.

So Lawyer filed the suit. And the first thing was the pleasant young feller from the bonding company in his nice city suit getting off the morning train with his nice city suitcase, saying "Now, fellers, let's all have a drink of this-here nice city whiskey and see if we can jest all get together on this thing," then spending one quick horrified day, mostly on the long-distance telephone between talking with them two Negro firemen, Tom Tom Bird and Tomey's Turl Beauchamp, while waiting for Flem to get back from where he had went suddenly on a visit into the next county.

So on the third day the one come from the bonding company that was big enough in it to have the gray hair and come in a Pullman in striped britches and a gold watch chain big enough to boom logs with and gold eyeglasses and even a gold toothpick and the pigeon-tailed coat and the plug hat until by nightfall you couldn't even a got a glass of water in the Holston Hotel for ever porter and waiter hanging around his door to wait on him and he could a owned ever other Negro in Jefferson too by tomorrow if he had had anything he could a done with them, saying "Gentlemen. Gentlemen. Gentlemen." And the mayor coming in where they was all setting around the table, to stand there laughing at them for a while and then saying,

"You'll have to excuse me. Even the mayor of just Jefferson, Mississippi, has got to do a little work now and then." And Lawyer Stevens setting there calm and white in the face and looking exactly like he done that night when he told his brother-in-law: "Can you suh-jest a better way for me to learn how to fight than the one I just tried?"

And Flem Snopes hadn't got back yet and in fact they couldn't even locate him, like he had evidently went on a camping trip in the woods where there wasn't no telephone; and the big boss one, the one with the white vest and the gold toothpick, says: "Im sure Mr de Spain would resign. Why dont we jest let him resign and forget all this here unhappiness?" and Lawyer Stevens says, "He's a good mayor. We dont want him to resign," and the white vest says, "Then what do you want? You will have to prove our client's representative stole any brass and all you have is the word of them two nigras because Mr Snopes his-self has went out of town."

"That water tank aint went out of town," Lawyer says. "We can drain that water tank."

So what they called was a special meeting of the board of aldermen. What they got was like one of them mass carcasses to vote between two beauty queens, the courthouse bell beginning to ring about eight oclock like it actively was some kind of a night session of court, and the folks coming up the streets and gathering in the Square, laughing and making jokes back and forth, until they decided right quick that the mayor's office wouldn't hold even the start of it, so they moved into the courtroom upstairs like it was Court.

Because this was just January; that Christmas Ball wasn't barely three weeks old yet. Even when they chose sides it was still jest fun, because most of them had jest come to watch and listen anyhow, even after somebody beat the Judge's mallet on the table until they quit laughing and joking and hushed and one of the aldermen said, "I dont know how much it will cost to drain that tank, but I for one will be damned—"

"I do," Lawyer Stevens says. "I already asked. It will cost three hundred and eighty dollars to rig a auxiliary tank long enough to drain and then fill the other one up again and then dismantle the auxiliary and get shut of it. It wont cost nothing to send somebody down inside of it to look because I'll do that myself."

"All right," the alderman says. "Then I will still be damned—"

"All right," Lawyer says. "Then I will pay for it myself," and the old bonding feller, the white-vest one, saying "Gentlemen. Gentlemen. Gentlemen." And the young one, the first one, standing up now and hollering:

"Dont you see, Mr Stevens? Dont you see, Mr Stevens? If you find brass in the tank, there wont be no crime because the brass already belongs to the city?"

"I already thought of that too," Lawyer says. "The brass still belongs to the city even if we dont drain the tank. Only, where is it at?" and the little bonding feller saying:

"Wait! Wait! That aint what I meant. I mean if the brass aint missing there aint no crime because it wasn't never stole."

"Tom Tom Bird and Tomey's Turl Beauchamp says it was because they stole it," Lawyer says. Now they was two aldermen talking at once, saying:

"Hold up here; hold up here," until finally the loudest one, Henry Best, won:

"Then who are you charging, Gavin? Are them nigras under Manfred's bond too?"

"But there aint no crime! We know the brass is in that tank because that's where the nigras said they put it." The little bonding feller was hollering and all this time the big one, the white-vest one, still saying "Gentlemen. Gentlemen. Gentlemen," like a big bass drum a far piece off that never nobody paid any attention to nohow; until Henry Best hollered,

"Wait, god damn it," so loud that they did hush and Henry said: "Them nigras confessed they stole that brass, but there aint no evidence of theft until we drain that tank. So right now, they didn't steal no brass. And if we drain that damn tank and find brass in it, they did steal brass and are guilty of theft. Only, as soon as we find brass in that tank, they never stole any brass because the brass is not just once more in the possession of the city: it aint never been out of it. God damn it, Gavin, is that what you are trying to tell us? Then what the hell do you want? What in hell do you want?"

And Lawyer Stevens setting there calm and still, with his face still white and still as paper. And maybe he hadn't learned how to fight yet neither. But he still hadn't heard about no rule against trying. "That's right," he says. "If there is brass in that tank—valuable property of the city unlawfully constrained into that tank by the connivance and condonance of a employee of the city, a crime has been committed. If we find brass in that tank—valuable property belonging to the city unlawfully constrained into that tank with the connivance or condonance of a employee of the city, even if it is recovered, a attempt at a crime has been condoned by a employee of the city. But that tank *per se* and what brass may or may not *per se* be in it, is beside the point. What we have engaged the attention of this honorable bonding company about is, jest which malfeasance did our honorable mayor commit? Jest which crime, by who, did our chief servant of our city condone?" Because he didn't know either what he wanted. And even when next day his paw told him what his behavior looked like he wanted and for a minute Lawyer even agreed, that still wasn't it.

Because that was all they got then, which wasn't nothing to be settled jest off-hand by a passel of amateurs like a alderman board. It was something for a professional, a sho-enough active judge, whether they aimed to or not, they had done got themselves now to where they would have to have a court. Though I didn't know Judge Dukinfield was in the crowd until Henry Best stood up and looked out at us and hollered: "Judge Dukinfield, is Judge Dukinfield still here?" and Judge Dukinfield stood up in the back and says,

"Yes, Henry?"

"I reckon we'll have to have help, Judge," Henry says. "I reckon you heard as much of this as we done, and we all hope you made more sense out of it than we done—"

"Yes; all right," Judge Dukinfield says. "We will hold the hearing here in chambers tomorrow morning at nine. I dont believe either plaintiff or defendant will need more counsel than are represented tonight but they are welcome to bring juniors if they like—or should we say seconds?"

Then we all got up to leave, still laughing and talking and joking back and forth, still not taking no sides but jest mainly enjoying it, jest being in principle on whichever other side from them two foreign bonding fellers for the simple reason that they was foreigners, not even paying no attention to Lawyer's twin sister standing there by him now until you could almost hear her telling Henry Best: "Now you're satisfied; maybe you can let him alone now;" not even paying no attention when a boy—I didn't recognise who he was—come burrowing through and up to the table and handed Lawyer something and Lawyer taken it; not realising until tomorrow that something had happened between that meeting that night and the next morning that we never knowed about and it's my opinion we aint going to, just going on home or about our business until the Square was empty except for that one light in his and his paw's office over the hardware store where he was setting alone—provided it was him of course and providing he was alone—how does the feller say it? inviting his soul?

FIVE

GAVIN STEVENS

The poets are wrong of course. According to them I should even have known the note was on the way, let alone who it was from. As it was, I didnt even know who it was from after I read it. But then, poets are almost always wrong about facts. That's because they are not really interested in facts: only in truth: which is why the truth they speak is so true that even those who hate poets by simple natural instinct are exalted and terrified by it.

No: that's wrong. It's because you dont dare to hope, you are afraid to hope. Not afraid of the extent of hope of which you are capable, but that you—the frail web of bone and flesh snaring that fragile temeritous boundless aspirant sleepless with dream and hope—cannot match it; as Ratliff would say, Knowing always you wont never be man enough to do the harm and damage you would do if you were just man enough.—and, he might add, or maybe I do it for him, thank God for it. Ay, thank God for it or thank anything else for it that will give you any peace after it's too late; peace in which to coddle that frail web and its unsleeping ensnared anguish both on your knee and whisper to it: There, there, it's all right; I know you are brave.

The first thing I did on entering the office was to turn on all the lights; if it hadn't been January and the thermometer in the low thirties I would have propped the door to stand open too for that much more of a Mississippi gentleman's tender circumspection toward her good name. The second thing I did was to think *My God all the lights on for the whole town to see* because now I would have Grover Winbush (the night marshal) up the stairs as surely as if I had sent for him, since with the usual single desk lamp on he would have thought I was merely working and would let me alone, where with all of them burning like this he would come up certainly, not to surprise the intruder but to participate in the conversation.

So I should have leaped to turn them off again, knowing that once I moved, turned loose the chair arms I would probably bolt, flee, run home to Maggie who has tried to be my mother ever since ours died and some day may succeed. So I just sat there thinking how if there were only time and means to communicate, suggest, project onto her wherever she might be at this moment between her home and here, the rubber soles for silence and the dark enveloping night-blending cloak and scarf for invisibility; then in the next second thinking how the simple suggestion of secret shoes and concealing cloak would forever abrogate and render null all need for either since although I might still be I, she must forever be some lesser and baser other to be vulnerable to the base insult of secrecy and fearfulness and silence.

So when I heard her feet on the stairs I didn't even think *For God's sake take off your shoes or at least tiptoe.* What I thought was How can you move and make that little noise, with only the sound of trivial human feet: who should have moved like Wagner: not with but *in* the sonorous sweep of thunder or brass music, even the very limbs moving in tune with the striding other in a sound of tuned wind and storm and mighty harps. I thought *Since making this more or less secret date to meet me here at this hour of night is her idea, at least she will have to look at me.* Which she had never done yet. If she had ever even seen me yet while I was too busy playing the fool because of her to notice, buffoon for her, playing with tacks in the street like a vicious boy, using not even honest bribery but my own delayed vicious juvenility to play on the natural and normal savagery (plus curiosity; dont forget that) of an authentic juvenile—to gain what? for what? what did I want, what was I trying for: like the child striking matches in a haystack yet at the same time trembling with terror lest he does see holocaust.

You see? terror. I hadn't even taken time to wonder what in hell she wanted with me: only the terror after the boy put the note in my hand and I found privacy to open and read it and still (the terror) in the courage, desperation, despair—call it whatever you like and whatever it was and wherever I found it—to cross to the door and open it and think as I always had each time I was that near, either to dance with her or merely to challenge and give twenty or thirty pounds to an impugner of her honor: *Why, she can't possibly be this small, this little*, apparently standing only inches short of my own six feet, yet small, little; too small to have displaced enough of my peace to contain this much unsleep, to have disarranged this much of what I had at least thought was peace. In fact I might have said she stood almost eye to eye with me if she had looked at me that long, which she did not: that one quick unhasting blue (they were dark blue) envelopment and then no more; no more needing to look—if she ever had—at me, but rather instead one single complete perception to which that adjective complete were as trivial as the adjective dampness to the blue sea itself; that one single glance to add me up and then subtract and then dispense as if that calm unhasting blueness had picked me up whole and palped me over front and back and sides and set me down again. But she didn't sit down herself. She didn't even move yet. Then I realised suddenly that she was simply examining the office as women examine a room they have never seen before.

"Wont you sit down?" I said.

"All right," she said. And, sitting in that ordinary chair across the desk, she was still too small to hold, compass without one bursting seam all that unslumber, all that chewed anguish of the poet's bitter thumbs which were not just my thumbs but all male Jefferson's or actually all male earth's by proxy, that thumb being all men's fate who had earned or deserved the right to call themselves men; too small, too little to contain, bear those . . . I had, must have, seen her at least five years ago though it was only last summer that I must have looked at her; say only since last summer, since until then I had been too busy passing bar examinations to have had time to prone and supine myself for proper relinquishment; call it two hundred for round numbers from June to January with some (not much) out for sleeping—two hundred nights of fevered projection of my brother's mantle to defend and save her honor from its ravisher.

You see? It still had not once occurred to me to ask her what she wanted. I was not even waiting for her to tell me. I was simply waiting for those two hundred nights to culminate as I had spent at least some of them or some small part of them expecting when this moment came, if it did, would, was fated: I to be swept up as into storm or hurricane or tornado itself and tossed and wrung and wrenched and consumed, the light last final spent insentient husk to float slowing and weightless, for a moment longer during the long vacant rest of life, and then no more.

Only it didn't happen, no consumption to wrench, wring and consume me down to the ultimate last proud indestructible grateful husk, but rather simply to destroy me as the embalmer destroys with very intactness what was still life, was still life even though it was only the living worm's. Because she was not examining the office again because I realised now that she had never stopped doing it, examining it rapidly once more with that comprehensive female glance.

"I thought it would be all right here," she said. "Better here."

"Here?" I said.

"Do it here. In your office. You can lock the door and I dont imagine there'll be anybody high enough up this late at night to see in the window. Or maybe—" Because she was already up and probably for a moment I couldn't have moved, just watching as she went to the window and had already begun to pull down the shade.

"Here?" I said again, like a parrot. "Here? In here?" Now she was looking at me over her shoulder. That's right. She didn't even turn: just her head, her face to look back at me across her shoulder, her hands still drawing the shade down across the window in little final tucking tugs against the sill. No: not again. She never had looked at me but that once as she entered. She simply confronted me across her shoulder with that blue envelopment like the sea, not questioning nor waiting, as the sea itself doesn't need to question or wait but simply to be the sea. "Oh," I said. "And be quick, hurry too maybe since you haven't got much time, since you really ought to be in bed this minute with your husband, or is this one of Manfred's nights?" and she still watching me, though turned now, standing, perhaps leaning a little against the window-sill behind her, watching me quite grave, just a little curious. "But of course," I said. "Naturally it's one of Manfred's nights since it's Manfred you're saving: not Flem.—No, wait," I said. "Maybe I'm wrong; maybe it is both of them; maybe they both sent you: both of them that scared, that desperate; their mutual crisis and fear so critical as to justify even this last desperate gambit of your woman's—their mutual woman's—all?" And still she just watched me: the calm unfathomable serenely waiting blue, waiting not on me but simply on time. "I didn't mean that," I said. "You know I didn't. I know it's Manfred. And I know he didn't send you. Least of all, he." Now I could get up. "Say you forgive me first," I said.

"All right," she said. Then I went and opened the door. "Good night," I said.

"You mean you dont want to?" she said.

Now I could laugh too.

"I thought that was what you wanted," she said. And now she was looking at me. "What did you do it for?" Oh yes, I could laugh, with the door open in my hand and the cold dark leaning into the room like an invisible cloud and if Grover Winbush were anywhere on the Square now (which he would not be in this cold since he was not a fool about everything) he would not need merely to see all the lights. Oh yes, she was looking at me now: the sea which in a moment more would destroy me, not with any deliberate and calculated sentient wave but simply because I stood there in its insentient way. No: that was wrong too. Because she began to move.

"Shut the door," she said. "It's cold"—walking toward me, not fast. "Was that what you thought I came here for? Because of Manfred?"

"Didn't you?" I said.

"Maybe I did." She came toward me, not fast. "Maybe at first. But that doesn't matter. I mean, to Manfred. I mean that brass. He doesn't mind it. He likes it. He's enjoying himself. Shut the door before it gets so cold." I shut it and turned quickly, stepping back a little.

"Dont touch me," I said.

"All right," she said. "Because you cant. . . ." Because even she stopped then; even the insentient sea compassionate too but then I could bear that too; I could even say it for her:

"Manfred wouldn't really mind because just I cant hurt him, harm him, do any harm; not Manfred, not just me, no matter what I do. That he would really just as soon resign as not and the only reason he doesn't is just to show me I cant make him. All right. Agreed. Then why dont you go home? What do you want here?"

"Because you are unhappy," she said. "I dont like unhappy people. They're a nuisance. Especially when it can—"

"Yes," I said, cried, "this easy, at no more cost than this. When nobody will even miss it, least of all Manfred since we both agree that Gavin Stevens cant possibly hurt Manfred de Spain even by cuckolding him on his mistress. So you came just from compassion, pity: not even from honest fear or even just decent respect. Just compassion. Just pity." Then I saw all of it. "Not just to prove to me that having what I think I want wont make me happy, but to show me that what I thought I wanted is not even worth being unhappy over. Does it mean that little to you? I dont mean with Flem: even with Manfred?" I said, cried: "Dont tell me next that this is why Manfred sent you: to abate a nuisance!"

But she just stood there looking at me with that blue serene terrible envelopment. "You spend too much time expecting," she said. "Dont expect. You just are, and you need, and you must, and so you do. That's all. Dont waste time expecting," moving again toward me where I was trapped not just by the door but by the corner of the desk too.

"Dont touch me!" I said. "So if I had only had sense enough to have stopped expecting, or better still, never expected at all, never hoped at all, dreamed at all; if I had just had sense enough to say *I am, I want, I will and so here goes*—If I had just done that, it might have been me instead of Manfred? But dont you see? Cant you see? I wouldn't have been me then?" No: she wasn't even listening: just looking at me: the unbearable and unfathomable blue, speculative and serene.

"Maybe it's because you're a gentleman and I never knew one before."

"So is Manfred!" I said. "And that other one, that first one—your child's father—" *the only other one* I thought because, yes, oh yes, I knew now: Snopes himself was impotent. I even said it: "The only other one besides Manfred. Back there in Frenchman's Bend, that Ratliff told me about, that fought off the five or six men who tried to ambush you in the buggy that night, fought them off with the buggy whip and one hand because he had to use the other to shield you with, whipped them all off even with one arm broken where I couldn't even finish the fight I started myself with just one opponent?" And still not moving: just standing there facing me so that what I smelled was not even just woman but that terrible, that drowning envelopment. "Both alike," I said. "But not like me. All three gentlemen but only two were men."

"Lock the door," she said. "I've already drawn the shade. Stop being afraid of things," she said. "Why are you afraid?"

"No," I said, cried. I might—would—have struck her with my out-flung arm, but there was room: out of the trap now and even around her until I could reach the door knob and open it. Oh yes, I knew now. "I might buy Manfred from you but I wont buy Flem," I said. "Because it is Flem, isn't it? Isn't it?" But there was only the blue envelopment and the fading Wagner, trumpet and storm and rich brasses diminuendo toward the fading arm and hand and the rainbow-fading ring. "You told me not to expect: why dont you try it yourself? We've all bought Snopeses here, whether we wanted to or not; you of all people should certainly know that. I dont know why we bought them. I mean, why we had to: what coin and when and where we so recklessly and improvidently spent that we had to have Snopeses too. But we do. But nothing can hurt you if you refuse it, not even a brass-stealing Snopes. And nothing is of value that costs nothing so maybe you will value this refusal at what I value it cost me." She moved then and only then did I notice that she had evidently brought nothing with her: none of the scatter of gloves, bags, veils, this and that which women bring into a room with them so that the first minute of their quitting it is a problem resembling scavenging. "Dont worry about your husband," I said. "Just say I represent Jefferson and so Flem Snopes is my burden too. You see, the least I can do is to match you: to value him as highly as your coming here proves you do. Good night."

"Good night," she said. The cold invisible cloud leaned in again. Again I closed it.

V. K. Ratliff

So next morning first thing we heard was that Judge Dukinfield had recused his-self and designated Judge Stevens, Lawyer's paw, to preside in his stead. And they ought to rung the courthouse bell this time sholy, because whether or not it was a matter of communal interest and urgency last night, it was now. But it was to be in chambers this time and what Judge Dukinfield called his chamber wouldn't a helt us. So all we done this time was just to happen to be somewhere about the Square, in the store doors or jest looking by chance and accident out of the upstairs doctors' and suches' windows while old man Job, that had been Judge Dukinfield's janitor for longer than anybody in Jefferson, including Job and Judge Dukinfield too, knowed, in a old cast-off tailcoat of Judge Dukinfield's that he wore on Sundays, bustled in and out of the little brick house back of the courthouse that Judge Dukinfield called his chambers, sweeping and dusting it until it suited him enough to let folks in it.

Then we watched Judge Stevens cross the Square from his office and go through the door and then we watched the two bonding fellers come out of the hotel and cross the Square with their little lawyers' grips, the young one toting his own grip but Samson, the hotel porter, walking behind the white-vest one toting his, and Samson's least boy walking behind Samson toting what I reckon was the folded Memphis paper the white-vest one had been reading while they et breakfast and they, except Samson and his boy, went in too. Then Lawyer come up by his-self and went in, and sho enough before extra long we heard the car and then Mayor de Spain druv up and parked and got out and says,

"Morning, gentlemen. Any of you fellers looking for me? Excuse me a minute while I step inside and pass good morning with our out-of-town guests and I'll be right with you." Then he went in too and that was about all: Judge Stevens setting behind the desk with his glasses on and the paper open in his hand, and the two bonding fellers setting quiet and polite and anxious across from him, and Lawyer setting at one end of the table and Manfred de Spain that hadn't even set down: jest leaning against the wall with his hands in his pockets and that-ere dont-give-a-durn face of his already full of laughing even though it hadn't moved yet. Until Judge Stevens folded the paper up slow and deliberate and laid it to one side and taken off his glasses and folded them too and then laid his hands one in the other on the desk in front of him and says:

"The plaintiff in this suit has of this date withdrawn his charge and his bill of particulars. The suit—if it was a suit—no longer exists. The litigants—plaintiff, defendant and prisoner—if there was a prisoner—are discharged. With the Court's apologies to the gentlemen from Saint Louis that their stay among us was marred, and its hope and trust that their next one will not be, Court is adjourned. Good morning, gentlemen," and the two bonding fellers got up and begun to thank Judge Stevens for a little spell, until they stopped and taken up their grips and kind of tiptoed out; and now there wasn't nobody but just Lawyer still setting with his paper-colored face bent a little and Judge Stevens still setting there not looking at nothing in particular yet and Manfred de Spain still leaning with his feet crossed against the wall and his face still full of that laughing that was still jest waiting for a spell too. Then Judge Stevens was looking at him.

"Manfred," he says. "Do you want to resign?"

"Certainly, sir," De Spain says. "I'll be glad to. But not for the city: for Gavin. I want to do it for Gavin. All he's got to do is say Please."

And still Lawyer didn't move: jest setting there with that still paper-colored face like it was froze stiff and his hands too laying on the table in front of him: not clenched one inside the other like his paw's: jest laying there. Then Manfred begun to laugh, not loud, not even in no hurry: jest standing there laughing with his feet still crossed and his hands still in his pockets, jest laughing even while he turned and went across to the door and opened it and went out and closed it behind him. Which jest left Lawyer and his paw and that was when Lawyer said it.

"So you dont want him not to be mayor," Judge Stevens says. "Then what is it you do want? For him not to be alive? Is that it?"

That was when Lawyer said it: "What must I do now, Papa? Papa, what can I do now?"

So something happened somewhere between that board of aldermen meeting last night and that special court session this morning. Except that if we ever knowed what it was, it wasn't going to be Lawyer's fault. I mean, we might a knowed or anyway had a good idea what happened and where while them lights was burning in that upstairs office long after ever body else in Jefferson had done went home to bed; some day Lawyer his-self might tell it, probably would, would have to tell it to somebody jest to get some rest from it. What we wouldn't know would be jest how it happened. Because when Lawyer come to tell it, he wouldn't be having to tell what happened: he would be having to tell, to say, it wouldn't much matter what, to somebody, anybody listening, it wouldn't much matter who.

The only one of the whole three of them that understood her was Flem. Because needing or expecting to understand one another hadn't never occurred between her and Manfred de Spain. All the understanding one another they needed was you might say for both of them to agree on when and where next and jest how long away it would have to be. But apart from that, they never no more needed to waste time understanding one another than sun and water did to make rain. They never no more needed to be drawed together than sun and water needed to be. In fact, most of Manfred's work had already been done for him by that boy back in Frenchman's Bend— McCarron, who except that he come first, could a been Manfred's younger brother; who never even lived in Frenchman's Bend and nobody in Frenchman's Bend ever seen or heard of him before that summer, like he had been sent through Frenchman's Bend at the one exact moment to see her, like you might say Manfred de Spain had been sent through Jefferson at the one exact moment to see her.

And a heap of McCarron's work already done for him too because she done it: that night when them five Frenchman's Bend boys laid for them and bushwacked them in the buggy to drag him out of it and maybe beat him up or anyhow skeer him out of Frenchman's

Bend. And gradually the tale come out how, even with one arm broke, he fought them all off and got the buggy turned around and got her back home all safe except for a natural maiden swoon. Which aint quite right. Because them five boys (I knowed two of them) never told it, which you might say is proof. That after they broke his arm it was her that taken the loaded end of the buggy-whip and finished the last one or maybe two, and her that turned the buggy around in the road and got it away from there. Jest far enough; not back home yet: jest far enough; to as the feller says crown the triumph on the still-hot field of the triumph; right there on the ground in the middle of the dark road because somebody had to still hold that skeered horse, with the horse standing over them and her likely having to help hold him up too off of that broke arm; not jest her first time but the time she got that baby. Which folks says aint likely to happen jest the first time but between what did happen and what ought to happened, I dont never have trouble picking ought.

But Lawyer Stevens never understood her and never would: that he never had jest Manfred de Spain to have to cope with, he was faced with a simple natural force repeating itself under the name of De Spain or McCarron or whatever into ever gap or vacancy in her breathing as long as she breathed; and that wouldn't never none of them be him. And he never did realise that she understood him because she never had no way of telling him because she didn't know herself how she done it. Since women learn at about two or three years old and then forget it, the knowledge about their-selves that a man stumbles on by accident forty-odd years later with the same kind of startled amazement of finding a twenty-five-cent piece in a old pair of britches you had started to throw away. No, they dont forget it: they jest put it away until ten or twenty or forty years later the need for it comes up and they reach around and pick it out and use it and then hang it up again without no more remembering jest which one it was than she could remember today which finger it was she scratched with yesterday: only that tomorrow maybe she will itch again but she will find something to scratch that one with too.

Or I dont know, maybe he did understand all that and maybe he did get what he wanted. I mean, not what he wanted but what he knew he could have, the next best, like anything is better than nothing, even if that anything is jest a next-best anything. Because there was more folks among the Helens and Juliets and Isoldes and Guineveres than jest the Launcelots and Tristrams and Romeos and Parises. There was them others that never got their names in the poetry books, the next-best ones that sweated and panted too. And being the next-best to Paris is jest a next-best too, but it aint no bad next-best to be. Not ever body had Helen, but then not ever body lost her neither.

So I kind of happened to be at the deepo that day when Lucius Hogganbeck's jitney drove up and Lawyer got out with his grips and trunk and his ticket to Mottstown junction to catch the express from Memphis to New York and get on the boat that would take him to that German university he had been talking for two years now about what a good idea it would be to go to it providing you happened to want to go to a university in Germany like that one; until that morning yesterday or maybe it was the day before when he told his paw: "What must I do now, Papa? Papa, what can I do now?" It was still cold, so he taken his sister on into the waiting room and then he come back out where I was.

"Good," he says, brisk and chipper as you could want. "I was hoping to see you before I left, to pass the torch on into your active hand. You'll have to hold the fort now. You'll have to tote the load."

"What fort?" I says. "What load?"

"Jefferson," he says. "Snopeses. Think you can handle them till I get back?"

"Not me nor a hundred of me," I says. "The only thing to do is get completely shut of them, abolish them."

"No no," he says. "Say a herd of tigers suddenly appears in Yoknapatawpha County; wouldn't it be a heap better to have them shut up in a mule-pen where we could at least watch them, keep up with them, even if you do lose a arm or a leg ever time you get within ten feet of the wire, than to have them roaming and strolling loose all over ever where in the entire country? No, we got them now; they're ourn now; I dont know jest what Jefferson could a committed back there whenever it was, to have won this punishment, gained this right, earned this privilege. But we did. So it's for us to cope, to resist; us to endure, and (if we can) survive."

"But why me?" I says. "Why out of all Jefferson pick on me?"

"Because you're the only one in Jefferson I can trust," Lawyer says.

Except that that one dont really ever lose Helen, because for the rest of her life she dont never actively get rid of him. Likely it's because she dont want to.

CHARLES MALLISON

I remember how Ratliff once said that the world's Helens never really lose forever the men who once loved and lost them; probably because they—the Helens—dont want to.

I still wasn't born when Uncle Gavin left for Heidelberg, so as far as I know his hair had already begun to turn white when I first saw him. Because although I was born by then, I couldn't remember him when he came home from Europe in the middle of the War, to get ready to go back to it. He said that at first, right up to the last minute, he believed that as soon as he finished his Ph.D. he was going as a stretcher-bearer with the German army; almost up to the last second before he admitted to himself that the Germany he could have loved that well had died somewhere between the Liège and Namur forts and the year 1848. Or rather, the Germany which had emerged between 1848 and the Belgian forts he did not love since it was no longer the Germany of Goethe and Bach and Beethoven and Schiller. This is what he said hurt, was hard to admit, to admit even after he reached Amsterdam and could begin to really ask about the American Field Service of which he had heard.

But he said how we—America—were not used yet to European wars and still took them seriously; and there was the fact that he had been for two years a student in a German university. But the French were different: to whom another Germanic war was just the same old chronic nuisance; a nation of practical and practising pessimists who were willing to let anyone regardless of his politics, who wanted to, do anything—particularly one who was willing to do it free. So he— Uncle Gavin spent those five months with his stretcher just behind Verdun and presently was himself in a bed in an American hospital until he got over the pneumonia and could come home, in Jefferson again, waiting, he said, until we were in it, which would not be long.

And he was right: the Sartoris boys, Colonel Sartoris's twin grandsons, had already gone to England into the Royal Flying Corps and then it was April and then Uncle Gavin had his appointment as a Y.M.C.A. secretary, to go back to France with the first American troops; when suddenly there was Montgomery Ward Snopes, the first of what Ratliff called "them big gray-colored chaps of I.O.'s," the one whose mama was still rocking in the chair in the front window of the Snopes Hotel because it was still too cold yet to move back onto the front gallery. And Jackson McLendon had organized his Jefferson company and had been elected captain of it and Montgomery Ward could have joined them. But instead he came to Uncle Gavin, to go to France with Uncle Gavin in the Y.M.C.A.; and that was when Ratliff said what he did about sometimes the men that loved and lost Helen of Troy just thought they had lost her. Only he could have added, All her kinfolks too. Because Uncle Gavin did it. I mean, took Montgomery Ward.

"Confound it, Lawyer," Ratliff said. "It's a Snopes."

"Certainly," Uncle Gavin said. "Can you suggest a better place for a Snopes today than northwestern France? As far west of Amiens and Verdun as you can get him?"

"But why?" Ratliff said.

"I thought of that too," Uncle Gavin said. "If he had said he wanted to go in order to defend his country, I would have had Hub Hampton handcuff him hand and foot in jail and sit on him while I telephoned Washington. But what he said was, 'They're going to pass a law soon to draft us all anyhow, and if I go with you like you're going, I figger I'll get there first and have time to look around.'"

"To look around," Ratliff said. He and Uncle Gavin looked at one another. Ratliff blinked two or three times.

"Yes," Uncle Gavin said. Ratliff blinked two or three times again.

"To look around," he said.

"Yes," Uncle Gavin said. And Uncle Gavin took Montgomery Ward Snopes with him and that was the exact time when Ratliff said about the folks that thought they had finally lost Helen of Troy. But Gowan was still living with us; maybe because of the war in Europe the State Department still hadn't let his mother and father come back from China or wherever it was yet; at least once every week on the way home across the Square he would meet Ratliff, almost like Ratliff was waiting for him, and Gowan would tell Ratliff the news from Uncle Gavin and Ratliff would say:

"Tell him to watch close. Tell him I'm doing the best I can here."

"The best you can what?" Gowan said.

"Holding and toting," Ratliff said.

"Holding and toting what?" Gowan said. That was when Gowan said he first noticed that you didn't notice Ratliff hardly at all, until suddenly you did or anyway Gowan did. And after that, he began to look for him. Because the next time, Ratliff said:

"How old are you?"

"Seventeen," Gowan said.

"Then of course your aunt lets you drink coffee," Ratliff said. "What do you say—"

"She's not my aunt, she's my cousin," Gowan said. "Sure. I drink coffee. I dont specially like it. Why?"

"I like a occasional ice-cream cone myself," Ratliff said.

"What's wrong with that?" Gowan said.

"What say me and you step in the drugstore here and have a ice-cream cone?" Ratliff said. So they did. Gowan said Ratliff always had strawberry when they had it, and that he could expect Ratliff almost any afternoon now and now Gowan said he was in for it, he would have to eat the cone whether he wanted it or not, he and Ratliff now standing treat about, until finally Ratliff said, already holding the pink-topped cone in his brown hand:

"This here is jest about as pleasant a invention as any I know about. It's so pleasant a feller jest dont dare risk getting burnt-out on it. I cant imagine no tragedy worse than being burnt-out on strawberry ice cream. So what you say we jest make this a once-a-week habit and the rest of the time jest swapping news?"

So Gowan said all right and after that they would just meet in passing and Gowan would give Ratliff Uncle Gavin's last message: "He says to tell you he's doing the best he can too but that you were right: just one aint enough. One what?" Gowan said. "Aint enough for what?" But then Gowan was seventeen; he had a few other things to do, whether grown people believed it or not, though he didn't object to delivering the messages Mother said Uncle Gavin sent in his letters to Ratliff, when he happened to see Ratliff, or that is when Ratliff saw, caught him, which seemed to be almost every day so that he wondered just when Ratliff found time to earn a living. But he didn't always listen to all Ratliff would be saying at those times, so that afterward he couldn't even say just how it was or when that Ratliff put it into his mind and he even got interested in it like a game, a contest or even a battle, a war, that Snopeses had to be watched constantly like an invasion of snakes or wildcats and that Uncle Gavin and Ratliff were doing it or trying to because nobody else in Jefferson seemed to recognise the danger. So that winter when the draft finally came and got Byron Snopes out of Colonel Sartoris's bank, Gowan knew exactly what Ratliff was talking about when he said:

"I dont know how he will do it but I will lay a million to one he dont never leave the United States; I will lay a hundred to one he wont get further away from Mississippi than that first fort over in Arkansas where they first sends them; and if you will give me ten dollars I will give you eleven if he aint back here in Jefferson in three weeks." Gowan didn't do it but he said later he wished he had because Ratliff would have lost by two days and so Byron was back in the bank again. But we didn't know how and even Ratliff never found out how he did it until after he had robbed the bank and escaped to Mexico, because Ratliff said the reason Snopeses were successful was that they had all federated unanimously to remove being a Snopes from just a zoological category into a condition composed of success by means of the single rule and regulation and sacred oath of never to tell anybody how. The way Byron did it was to go to bed every night with a fresh plug of chewing tobacco taped into his left armpit until it ran his heart up to where the army doctor finally discharged him and sent him home.

So at least there was some fresh Snopes news to send Uncle Gavin, which was when Ratliff noticed that it had been months since Uncle Gavin had mentioned Montgomery Ward Snopes. Though by the time Uncle Gavin's letter got back saying *Don't mention that name to me again. I wont discuss it. I will not* we had some fresh Snopes news of our own to send him.

This time it was Eck. "Your uncle was right," Ratliff said.

"He's my cousin, I tell you," Gowan said.

"All right, all right," Ratliff said. "Eck wasn't a Snopes. That's why he had to die. Like there wasn't no true authentic room for Snopeses in the world and they made theirselves one by that pure and simple mutual federation, and the first time one slips or falters or fails in being Snopes, it dont even need the rest of the pack like wolves to finish him: simple environment jest watched its chance and taken it."

Eck was the one with the steel brace where a log broke his neck one time, the night watchman of the oil company's storage tank at the depot; I knew about this myself because I was almost four years old now. It was just dust-dark; we were at supper when there came a tremendous explosion, the loudest sound at one time that Jefferson ever heard, so loud that we all knew it couldn't be anything else but that German bomb come at last that we—Mayor de Spain—had been looking for ever since the Germans sank the *Lusitania* and we finally had to get into the War too. That is, Mayor de Spain had gone to West Point and had been a lieutenant in Cuba and when this one started he wanted to get into it too. But he couldn't maybe, so he tried to organize a Home Guard company, except that nobody but him took it very seriously. But at least he had an alarm system to ring the courthouse bell when a German attack came.

So when that tremendous big sound went off and the bell began to ring, we all knew what it was and we were all waiting for the next one to fall, until the people running out into the street hollering "Which way was it?" finally located it down toward the depot. It was the oil storage tank. It was a big round tank, about thirty feet long and ten feet deep, sitting on brick trestles. That is, it had been there because there wasn't anything there now, not even the trestles. Then about that time they finally got Mrs Nunnery to hush long enough to tell what happened.

She was Cedric Nunnery's mamma. He was about five years old. They lived in a little house just up the hill from the depot and finally they made her sit down and somebody gave her a drink of whiskey and she quit screaming and told how about five oclock she couldn't find Cedric anywhere and she came down to where Mr Snopes was

sitting in his chair in front of the little house about the size of a privy
that he called the office where he night-watched the tank, to ask him
if he had seen Cedric. He hadn't but he got up right away to help
her hunt, in all the box cars on the side track and in the freight warehouse and everywhere, hollering Cedric's name all around; only Mrs
Nunnery didn't remember which of them thought of the oil tank
first. Likely it was Mr Snopes since he was the one that knew it was
empty, though probably Mrs Nunnery had seen the ladder too still
leaning against it where Mr Snopes had climbed up to open the manhole in the top to let fresh air come in and drive the gas out.

And likely Mr Snopes thought all the gas was out by now, though
they probably both must have figured there would still be enough
left to fix Cedric when he climbed down inside. Because Mrs Nunnery said that's where they both thought Cedric was and that he was
dead; she said she was so sure that she couldn't even bear to wait and
see, she was already running—not running anywhere: just running—
when Mr Snopes came out of his little office with the lighted lantern
and still running while he was climbing up the ladder and still running when he swung the lantern over into the manhole; that is she
said she was still running when the explosion (she said she never even
heard it, she never heard anything, or she would have stopped)
knocked her down and the air all around her whizzing with pieces
of the tank like a swarm of bumblebees. And Mr Harker from the
power-plant that got there first and found her, said she begun to try
to run again as soon as he picked her up, shrieking and screaming
and thrashing around while they held her, until she sat down and
drank the whiskey and the rest of them walked and hunted around
among the scattered bricks from the trestles, still trying to find some
trace of Cedric and Mr Snopes, until Cedric came at a dead run up
the track from where he had been playing in a culvert about a half a
mile away when he heard the explosion.

But they never did find Mr Snopes until the next morning when
Tom Tom Bird, the day fireman at the power-plant, on his way in to
work from where he lived about two miles down the track, saw something hanging in the telegraph wires about two hundred yards from
where the tank had been and got a long pole and punched it down

and when he showed it to Mr Harker at the plant, it was Mr Snopes's steel neck-brace though none of the leather was left.

But they never did find anything of Mr Snopes, who was a good man, everybody liked him, sitting in his chair beside the office door where he could watch the tank or walking around the tank when he would let the coal oil run into the cans and drums and delivery tanks, with his neck and head stiff in the steel brace so he couldn't turn his head at all: he would have to turn all of himself like turning a wooden post. All the boys in town knew him because pretty soon they all found out that he kept a meal sack full of raw peanuts from the country and would holler to any of them that passed and give them a handful.

Besides, he was a Mason too. He had been a Mason such a long time that he was a good one even if he wasn't very high up in it. So they buried the neck-brace anyway, in a coffin all regular, with the Masons in charge of the funeral, and more people than you would have thought sent flowers, even the oil company too although Mr Snopes had ruined their tank for nothing because Cedric Nunnery wasn't even in it.

So they buried what they did have of him; there was the Baptist preacher too, and the Masons in their aprons dropping a pinch of dirt into the grave and saying "Alas my brother," and covered the raw red dirt with the flowers (one of the flower pieces had the Mason signs worked into it); and the tank was insured so when the oil company got through cussing Mr Snopes for being a grown man with no more sense than that, they even gave Mrs Snopes a thousand dollars to show they were sorry for her even if she had married a fool. That is, they gave the money to Mrs Snopes because their oldest boy, Wallstreet, wasn't but sixteen then. But he was the one that used it.

But that came later. All that happened now was that Mayor de Spain finally got to be a commanding officer long enough to ring his alarm bell at least, and we had some more fresh Snopes news to send Uncle Gavin. By "we" I mean me now. Gowan's mother and father had finally got home from China or wherever it was and now Gowan was in Washington (it was fall) for the last year anyway at the prep school getting ready for the University of Virginia next year and one afternoon Mother sent for me, into the parlor, and there was Ratliff in his neat faded blue tieless shirt and his smooth brown face, in the parlor like company (there was a tea tray and Ratliff had a teacup and a cucumber sandwich and I know now there were a lot of people in Jefferson, let alone in the county where Ratliff came from, that wouldn't have known what to do with a cup of tea at four oclock in the afternoon and maybe Ratliff never saw one before then either but you couldn't have told it by watching him) and Mother said,

"Make your manners to Mister Ratliff, bub. He's come to call on us," and Ratliff said,

"Is that what you call him?" and Mother said,

"No, we just call him whatever is handy yet," and Ratliff raid,

"Sometimes fellers named Charles gets called Chick when they gets to school." Then he said to me: "Do you like strawberry ice-cream cones?" and I said,

"I like any kind of ice-cream cones," and Ratliff said:

"Then maybe your cousin—" and stopped and said to Mother: "Excuse me, Miz Mallison; I done been corrected so many times that it looks like it may take me a spell yet." So after that it was me and Ratliff instead of Gowan and Ratliff, only instead of two cones, it cost Ratliff three now because when I went to town without Mother, Aleck Sander was with me. And I dont know how Ratliff did it and of course I cant remember when because I wasn't even five yet. But he had put into my mind too, just like into Gowan's, that idea of Snopeses covering Jefferson like an influx of snakes or varmints from the woods and he and Uncle Gavin were the only ones to recognise the danger and the threat and now he was having to tote the whole load by himself until they would finally stop the war and Uncle Gavin could get back home and help. "So you might just as well start listening now," he said, "whether you aint but five or not. You're going to have to hear a heap of it before you get old enough or big enough to resist."

It was November. Then that day, the courthouse bell rang again and all the church bells too this time, wild and frantic too in the middle of the week from the Sunday steeples and a few shotguns and pistols too like the old veterans that were still alive when they unveiled the Confederate monument that day except that the ones this time hadn't been to a war yet, so maybe what they were celebrating this time was that this one finally got over before they had to go to it. So now Uncle Gavin could come home where Ratliff himself could ask him what Montgomery Ward Snopes had done that his name must not be mentioned or discussed. That was when Ratliff told me, "You might as well get used to hearing it even if you aint but five." That was when he said: "What do you reckon it was he done? Your cousin has been watching Snopeses for going on ten years now; he even taken one all the way to France with him to keep his-self abreast and up-to-date. What you reckon a Snopes could a done after ten years to shock and startle him so much he couldn't bear even to discuss it?"

Or this was when he meant it because when Uncle Gavin came home it was for only two weeks. He was out of the uniform, the army, the Y.M.C.A. now but as soon as he was out they put him into some kind of board or committee or bureau for war rehabilitation in Europe because he had lived in Europe all that time, especially the two years as a student in Germany. And possibly the only reason he came home at all was that Grandfather had died during the last year of the war and he came home to see us as people do in bereavement. Though I believed then that the reason he came was to tell Ratliff what it was about Montgomery Ward Snopes that was too bad to write on paper. Which was when Ratliff said about all the listening I would have to do, meaning that with him, Ratliff, alone again to tote the load, anyway I could do that much.

It was one day; sometimes Mother let me go to town by myself now. I mean, when she wasn't noticing enough to say Come back here. No: I mean, when she found out I had now she didn't jump on me too hard.—it was one day, Ratliff's voice said, "Come here." He had traded off his buckboard and team and now he had a Model T, with the little painted house with the sewing machine in it fastened to the back in place of a back seat; what they call pickup trucks now though Ratliff and Uncle Noon Gatewood had made this one. He was sitting in it with the door already open and I got in and he shut the door and we drove right slow along the back streets around the edge of town. "How old did you say you was?" he said. I told him again: five. "Well, we cant help that, can we?"

"Cant help what?" I said. "Why?"

"Come to think of it, maybe you're right at that," he said. "So all we got to do now is jest take a short ride. So what happened to Montgomery Ward Snopes was, he quit the fighting army and went into business."

"What business?" I said.

"The . . . canteen business. Yes, the canteen business. That's what he done while he was with your cousin. They was at a town named Châlons, only your cousin had to stay in town to run the office, so he give Montgomery Ward, since he had the most spare time, the job of running the canteen at another little town not far away that would be more convenient for the soldiers—a kind of a shack with counters like a store where soldiers could buy the candy bars and sody pop and hand-knitted socks like your cousin told us about that time last week when they wasn't busy fighting, you remember? Except that after a while Montgomery Ward's canteen got to be jest about the most popular canteen the army or even the Y.M.C.A. either ever had in France or anywhere else; it got so popular that finally your cousin went his-self and looked at it and found that Montgomery Ward had cut off the back end and fixed it up as a new fresh entertainment room with a door in the back and a young French lady he happened to know in it, so that any time a soldier got tired of jest buying socks or eating chocolate bars he could buy a ticket from Montgomery Ward and go around through the back door and get his-self entertained.

"That was what your cousin found out. Only the army and the Y.M.C.A. had some kind of a rule against entertainment; they figgered that a soldier ought to be satisfied jest buying socks and sody pop in a canteen. Or maybe it was your cousin; likely it was him. Because if the army and the Y.M.C.A. had found out about that back room, they would a fired Montgomery Ward so hard he would likely a come back to Jefferson in handcuffs—providing he never stopped off at Leavenworth, Kansas, first. Which reminds me of something I may have said to your other cousin Gowan once when likely you wasn't present: about how some of the folks that lost Helen of Troy might some day wish they hadn't found her to begin with."

"Why?" I said. "Where was I if I wasn't there then?"

"It was your cousin. Montgomery Ward might have even saved enough out of the back-room entertainment tickets to bought hisself out of it. But he never needed to. He had your cousin. He was the hair-shirt of your cousin's lost love and devotion, whether he knowed it or not or cared or not. Or maybe it was Jefferson. Maybe your cousin couldn't bear the idea of Jefferson being represented in Leavenworth prison even for the reward of one Snopes less in Jefferson itself. So likely it was him, and afterwards saying, 'But dont never let me see your face again in France.'

"That is, dont never bring your face to me again. Because Montgomery Ward was the hair-shirt; likely your cousin taken the same kind of proud abject triumphant submissive horror in keeping up with his doings that them old hermits setting on rocks out in the hot sun in the desert use to take watching their blood dry up and their legs swivelling, keeping up from a distance while Montgomery Ward added more and more entertaining ladies to that-ere new canteen he set up in Paris—"

"They have chocolate bars and soda pop in canteens," I said. "Uncle Gavin said so. Chewing gum too."

"That was the American army," Ratliff said. "They had been in the war such a short time that likely they hadn't got used to it yet. This new canteen of Montgomery Ward's was you might say a French canteen, with only private American military connections. The French have been in enough wars long enough to find out that the best way to get shut of one is not to pay too much attention to it. In fact the French probably thought the kind of canteen Montgomery Ward was running this time was just about the most solvent and economical and you might say self-perpetuating kind he could a picked out, since, no matter how much money you swap for ice cream and chocolate candy and sody pop, even though the money still exists, that candy and ice cream and sody pop dont any more because it has been consumed and will cost some of that money to produce and replenish, where in jest strict entertainment there aint no destructive consumption at all that's got to be replenished at a definite production labor cost: only a normal natural general overall depreciation which would have took place anyhow."

"Maybe Montgomery Ward wont come back to Jefferson," I said.

"If I was him, I wouldn't," Ratliff said.

"Unless he can bring the canteen with him," I said.

"In that case I sholy wouldn't," Ratliff said.

"Is it Uncle Gavin you keep on talking about?" I said.

"I'm sorry," Ratliff said.

"Then why dont you say so?" I said.

"I'm sorry," Ratliff said. "Your uncle. It was your cousin Gowan (I'm right this time, aint I?) got me mixed up but I'll remember now. I promise it."

Montgomery Ward didn't come home for two years. Though I had to be older than that before I understood what Ratliff meant when he said Montgomery Ward had done the best he knew to bring an acceptable Mississippi version of his Paris canteen back home with him. He was the last Yoknapatawpha soldier to return. One of Captain McLendon's company was wounded in the first battle in which American troops were engaged and was back in uniform with his wound stripe in 1918. Then early in 1919 the rest of the company, except two dead from flu and a few in the hospital, were all home again to wear their uniforms too around the Square for a little while. Then in May one of Colonel Sartoris's twin grandsons (the other one had been shot down in July last year) got home from the British Air Force though he didn't have on a uniform at all: just a big low-slung racing car that made the little red E.M.F. that Mayor de Spain used to own look like a toy, driving it fast around town between the times when Mr Connors would have to arrest him for speeding, but mostly about once a week back and forth to Memphis while he was getting settled down again. That is, that's what Mother said he was trying to do.

Only he couldn't seem to either, like the war had been too much for him too. I mean, Montgomery Ward Snopes couldn't seem to settle down enough from it to come back home, and Bayard Sartoris came home all right but he couldn't settle down, driving the car so fast between Sartoris Station and Jefferson that finally Colonel Sartoris, who hated automobiles almost as much as Grandfather did, who wouldn't even lend the bank's money to a man who was going to buy one, gave up the carriage and the matched team, to ride back and forth into town with Bayard in the car, in hopes that maybe that would make Bayard slow it down before he killed himself or somebody else.

So when Bayard finally did kill somebody, as we (all Yoknapatawpha County grown folks) all expected he would, it was his grandfather. Because we didn't know that either: that Colonel Sartoris had a heart condition; Doctor Peabody had told him that three years ago, and that he had no business in an automobile at all. But Colonel Sartoris hadn't told anybody else, not even his sister, Mrs Du Pre that kept house for him: just riding in that car back and forth to town every day to keep Bayard slowed down (they even managed somehow to persuade Miss Narcissa Benbow to marry him in hopes maybe that would settle him down) until that morning they came over a hill at about fifty miles an hour and there was a Negro family in a wagon in the road and Bayard said, "Hold on, Grandfather," and turned the car off into the ditch; it didn't turn over or even wreck very bad: just stopped in the ditch with Colonel Sartoris still sitting in it with his eyes still open.

So now his bank didn't have a president any more. Then we found out just who owned the stock in it: that Colonel Sartoris and Major de Spain, Mayor de Spain's father until he died, had owned two of the three biggest blocks, and old man Will Varner out in Frenchman's Bend owned the other one. So we thought that maybe it wasn't just Colonel Sartoris's father's cavalry command that got Byron Snopes his job in the bank, but maybe old Will Varner had something to do with it too. Except that we never really believed that since we knew Colonel Sartoris well enough to know that any single one of those old cavalry raids or even just one night around a bivouac fire would have been enough.

Of course there was more of it, that much again and even more scattered around in a dozen families like the Compsons and Benbows and Peabodys and Miss Eunice Habersham and us and a hundred others that were farmers around in the county. Though it wasn't until Mayor de Spain got elected president of it to succeed Colonel Sartoris (in fact, because of that) that we found out that Mr Flem Snopes had been buying the stock in lots anywhere from one to ten shares for several years; this, added to Mr Varner's and Mayor de Spain's own that he had inherited from his father, would have been

enough to elect him up from vice president to president (There was
so much going on that we didn't even notice that when the dust
finally settled Mr Flem Snopes would be vice president of it too.)
even if Mrs Du Pre and Bayard's wife (Bayard had finally got himself killed testing an aeroplane at an Ohio testing field that they said
nobody else would fly and that Bayard himself didn't have any business in) hadn't voted theirs for him.

Because Mayor de Spain resigned from being mayor and sold his
automobile agency and became president of the bank just in time.
Colonel Sartoris's bank was a national bank because Ratliff said likely
Colonel Sartoris knew that would sound safer to country folks with
maybe an extra ten dollars to risk in a bank, let alone the female widows and orphans, since females never had much confidence in menfolks' doings about anything, let alone money, even when they were
not widows too. So with a change of presidents like that, Ratliff said
the government would have to send somebody to inspect the books
even if the regular inspection wasn't about due; the two auditors
waiting in front of the bank at eight o'clock that morning for somebody to unlock the door and let them in, which would have been
Byron Snopes except that he didn't show up. So they had to wait for
the next one with a key: which was Mr de Spain.

And by fifteen minutes after eight, which was about thirteen minutes after the auditors decided to start on the books that Byron kept,
Mr de Spain found out from the Snopes Hotel that nobody had seen
Byron since the southbound train at nine twenty-two last night, and
by noon everybody knew that Byron was probably already in Texas
though he probably wouldn't reach Mexico itself for another day yet.
Though it was not until two days later that the head auditor was
ready to commit himself roughly as to how much money was missing; by that time they had called a meeting of the bank's board of
directors and even Mr Varner that Jefferson never saw once in twelve
months had come in and listened to the head auditor for about a
minute and then said, "Police hell. Send somebody out home for my
pistol, then show me which way he went."

Which wasn't anything to the uproar Mr de Spain himself was
making, with all this time all Jefferson watching and listening, until

on the third day Ratliff said, though I didn't know what he meant then: "That's how much it was, was it? At least we know now jest how much Miz Flem Snopes is worth. Now your uncle wont need to worry about how much he lost when he gets home because now he can know exactly to the last decimal how much he saved." Because the bank itself was all right. It was a national bank, so whatever money Byron stole would be guaranteed whether they caught Byron or not. We were watching Mr de Spain. Since his father's money had helped Colonel Sartoris start it and Mr de Spain had himself been vice president of it, even if he had not been promoted president of it just ahead of when the auditors decided to look at Byron Snopes's books, we believed he would still have insisted on making good every cent of the money. What we expected to hear was that he had mortgaged his home, and when we didn't hear that, we just thought that he had made money out of his automobile agency that was saved up and put away that we didn't know about. Because we never expected anything else of him; when the next day they called another sudden meeting of the board of directors and announced the day after that that the stolen money had been made good by the voluntary personal efforts of the president, we were not even surprised. As Ratliff said, we were so unsurprised in fact that it was two or three days before anybody seemed to notice how at the same time they announced that Mr Flem Snopes was now the new vice president of it.

And now, it was another year, the last two Jefferson soldiers came home for good or anyway temporarily for good: Uncle Gavin finally came back from rehabilitating war-torn Europe to get elected County Attorney, and a few months later, Montgomery Ward Snopes too except that he was just temporarily at home for good, like Bayard Sartoris. He wasn't in uniform either but in a black suit and a black overcoat without any sleeves and a black thing on his head kind of drooping over one side like an empty cow's bladder made out of black velvet, and a long limp-ended bow tie; and his hair long and he had a beard and now there was another Snopes business in Jefferson. It had a name on the window that Ratliff didn't know either and when I went up to the office where Uncle Gavin was waiting for

the first of the year to start being County Attorney and told him, he
sat perfectly still for a good two seconds and then got up already
walking. "Show me," he said.

So we went back to where Ratliff was waiting for us. It was a store
on the corner by an alley, with a side door on the alley; the painter
was just finishing the curlicue letters; on the glass window that said

ATELIER MONTY

and inside, beyond the glass, Montgomery Ward still wearing the
French cap (Uncle Gavin said it was a Basque beret) but in his shirt-
sleeves. Because we didn't go in then; Uncle Gavin said, "Come on
now. Let him finish it first." Except Ratliff. He said,

"Maybe I can help him." But Uncle Gavin took hold of my arm
that time.

"If atelier means just a studio," I said, "why dont he call it that?"

"Yes," Uncle Gavin said. "That's what I want to know too." And
even though Ratliff went in, he hadn't seen anything either. And he
sounded just like me.

"Studio," he said. "I wonder why he dont just call it that?"

"Uncle Gavin didn't know either," I said.

"I know," Ratliff said. "I wasn't asking nobody yet. I was jest kind
of looking around for a place to jump." He looked at me. He blinked
two or three times. "Studio," he said. "That's right, you aint even up
that far yet. It's a photographing studio." He blinked again. "But
why? His war record has done already showed he aint a feller to be
satisfied with no jest dull run-of-the-mill mediocrity like us stay-
at-homes back here in Yoknapatawpha County has to get used to."

But that was all we knew then. Because the next day he had newspapers fastened on the window so you couldn't see inside and he kept
the door locked and all we ever saw would be the packages he would
get out of the post office from Sears and Roebuck in Chicago and
unlock the door long enough to take them inside.

Then on Thursday when the *Clarion* came out, almost half of the
front page was the announcement of the formal opening, saying
Ladies Especially Invited, and at the bottom: *Tea.* "What?" I said. "I
thought it was going to be a studio."

"It is," Uncle Gavin said. "You get a cup of tea with it. Only he's wasting his money. All the women in town and half the men will go once just to see why he kept the door locked." Because Mother had already said she was going.

"Of course you wont be there," she told Uncle Gavin.

"All right," he said. "Most of the men then." He was right. Montgomery Ward had to keep the opening running all day long to take care of the people that came. He would have had to run it in sections even with the store empty like he rented it. But now it wouldn't have held hardly a dozen at a time, it was so full of stuff, with black curtains hanging all the way to the floor on all the walls that when you drew them back with a kind of pulley it would be like you were looking through a window at outdoors that he said one was the skyline of Paris and another was the Seine river bridges and ks whatever they are and another was the Eiffel Tower and another Notre Dame, and sofas with black pillows and tables with vases and cups and something burning in them that made a sweet kind of smell; until at first you didn't hardly notice the camera. But finally you did, and a door at the back and Montgomery Ward said, he said it quick and he kind of moved quick, like he had already begun to move before he had time to decide that maybe he better not.

"That's the dark room. It's not open yet."

"I beg pardon?" Uncle Gavin said.

"That's the dark room," Montgomery Ward said. "It's not open yet."

"Are we expected to expect a dark room to be open to the public?" Uncle Gavin said. But Montgomery Ward was already giving Mrs Rouncewell another cup of tea. Oh yes, there was a vase of flowers too; in the *Clarion* announcement of the opening it said *Flowers by Rouncewell* and I said to Uncle Gavin, where else in Jefferson would anybody get flowers except from Mrs Rouncewell? and he said she probably paid for half the advertisement, plus a vase containing six overblown roses left over from another funeral, that she will probably take out in trade. Then he said he meant her trade and he hoped he was right. Now he looked at the door a minute, then he looked at Montgomery Ward filling Mrs Rouncewell's cup. "Beginning with tea," he said.

We left then. We had to, to make room. "How can he afford to keep on giving away tea?" I said.

"He wont after today," Uncle Gavin said. "That was just bait, ladies' bait. Now I'll ask you one: why did he have to need all the ladies in Jefferson to come in one time and look at his joint?" And now he sounded just like Ratliff; he kind of happened to be coming out of the hardware store when we passed. "Had your tea yet?" Uncle Gavin said.

"Tea," Ratliff said. He didn't ask it. He just said it. He blinked at Uncle Gavin.

"Yes," Uncle Gavin said. "So do we. The dark room aint open yet."

"Ought it to be?" Ratliff said.

"Yes," Uncle Gavin said. "So did we."

"Maybe I can find out," Ratliff said.

"Do you even hope so?" Uncle Gavin said.

"Maybe I will hear about it," Ratliff said.

"Do you even hope so?" Uncle Gavin said.

"Maybe somebody else will find out about it and maybe I will be standing where I can hear him," Ratliff said.

And that was all. Montgomery Ward didn't give away any more cups of tea but after a while photographs did begin to appear in the show window, faces that we knew—ladies with and without babies and high-school graduating classes and the prettiest girls in their graduation caps and gowns and now and then a couple just married from the country looking a little stiff and uncomfortable and just a little defiant and a narrow white line between his haircut and his sunburn; and now and then a couple that had been married fifty years that we had known all the time without really realising it until now how much alike they looked, not to mention being surprised, whether at being photographed or just being married that long.

And even when we begun to realise that not just the same faces but the same photographs of them had been in the same place in the window for over two years now, as if all of a sudden as soon as Montgomery Ward opened his atelier folks stopped graduating and getting married or staying married either, Montgomery Ward was still staying in business, either striking new pictures he didn't put in the window or maybe just selling copies of the old ones, to pay his rent and stay open. Because he was and maybe it was mostly dark-room work because it was now that we begun to realise that most of his business was at night like he did need darkness, his trade seeming to be mostly men now, the front room where he had had the opening dark now and the customers going and coming through the side door in the alley; and them the kind of men you wouldn't hardly think it had ever occurred to them they might ever need to have their picture struck. And his business was spreading too; in the second summer we begun to find out how people—men, the same kind of usually young men that his Jefferson customers were—were beginning to come from the next towns around us to leave or pick up their prints and negatives or whatever it was, by that alley door at night.

"No no," Uncle Gavin told Ratliff. "It cant be that. You simply just cant do that in Jefferson."

"There's folks would a said you couldn't a looted a bank in Jefferson too," Ratliff said.

"But she would have to eat," Uncle Gavin said. "He would have to bring her out now and then for simple air and exercise."

"Out where?" I said. "Bring who out?"

"It cant be liquor," Ratliff said. "At least that first suggestion of yours would a been quiet, which you cant say about peddling whiskey."

"What first suggestion?" I said. "Bring who out?" Because it wasn't whiskey or gambling either; Grover Cleveland Winbush (the one that owned the other half of Ratliff's cafe until Mr Flem Snopes froze him out too. He was the night marshal now.) had thought of that himself. He came to Uncle Gavin before Uncle Gavin had even thought of sending for him or Mr Buck Connors either, and told Uncle Gavin that he had been spending a good part of the nights examining and watching and checking on the studio and he was completely satisfied there wasn't any drinking or peddling whiskey or dice-shooting or card-playing going on in Montgomery Ward's dark room; that we were all proud of the good name of our town and we all aimed to keep it free of any taint of big-city corruption and misdemeanor and nobody more than him. Until for hours at night when he could have been sitting comfortably in his chair in the police station waiting for the time to make his next round, he would be hanging around that studio without once hearing any suspicion of dice or drinking or any one of Montgomery Ward's customers to come out smelling or even looking like he had had a drink. In fact, Grover Cleveland said, once during the daytime while it was not only his legal right but his duty to his job to be home in bed asleep, just like it was right now while he was giving up his rest to come back to town to make this report to Uncle Gavin as County Attorney, even though he had no warrant, not to mention the fact that by rights this was a job that Buck Connors himself should have done, he—Grover Cleveland—walked in the front door with the aim of walking right on into the dark room even if he had to break the door to do it since the reason the people of Jefferson appointed him night marshal was to keep down big-city misdemeanor and corruption like gambling and drinking, when to his surprise Montgomery Ward not only didn't try to stop him, he didn't even wait to be asked but instead opened the dark-room door himself and told Grover Cleveland to walk right in and look around.

So Grover Cleveland was satisfied, and he wanted the people of Jefferson to be too, that there was no drinking or gambling or any other corruption and misdemeanor going on in that back room that would cause the Christian citizens of Jefferson to regret their confidence in appointing him night marshal which was his sworn duty to do even if he didn't take any more pride in Jefferson's good name than just an ordinary citizen, and any time he could do anything else for Uncle Gavin in the line of his sworn duty, for Uncle Gavin just to mention it. Then he went out, pausing long enough in the door to say:

"Howdy, V.K.," before going on. Then Ratliff came the rest of the way in.

"He come hipering across the Square and up the stairs like maybe he had found something," Ratliff said. "But I reckon not. I dont reckon Montgomery Ward Snopes would have no more trouble easing him out of that studio than Flem Snopes done easing him out of the rest of our café."

"No," Uncle Gavin said. He said: "What did Grover Cleveland like for fun back then?"

"For fun?" Ratliff said. Then he said: "Oh. He liked excitement."

"What excitement?" Uncle Gavin said.

"The excitement of talking about it," Ratliff said.

"Of talking about what?" Uncle Gavin said.

"Of talking about excitement," Ratliff said. He didn't quite look at me. No: he didn't quite not look at me. No, that's wrong too because even watching him you couldn't have said that he had ever stopped looking at Uncle Gavin. He blinked twice. "Female excitement," he said.

"All right," Uncle Gavin said. "How?"

"That's right," Ratliff said. "How?"

Because I was only eight now, going on nine, and if Uncle Gavin and Ratliff who were three times that and one of them had been all the way to Europe and back and the other had left at least one footprint in every back road and lane and turn-row too probably in Yoknapatawpha County didn't know what it was until somebody came and told them, it wasn't any wonder that I didn't.

There was another what Ratliff called Snopes industry in town now too, though Uncle Gavin refused to call it that because he still refused to believe that Eck was ever a Snopes. It was Eck's boy, Wallstreet Panic, and from the way he began to act as soon as he reached Jefferson and could look around and I reckon find out for the first time in his life that you didn't actually have to act like a Snopes in order to breathe, whether his father was a Snopes or not he sure wasn't.

Because they said (he was about twelve when they moved in from Frenchman's Bend) how as soon as he got to town and found out about school, he not only made his folks let him go to it but he took his brother, Admiral Dewey, who wasn't but six, with him, the two of them starting out together in the kindergarten where the mothers brought the little children who were not big enough yet to stay in one place more than just half a day, with Wallstreet Panic sticking up out of the middle of them like a horse in a duck-pond.

Because he wasn't ashamed to enter the kindergarten: he was just ashamed to stay in it, not staying in it himself much longer than a half a day because in a week he was in the first grade and by Christ-

mas he was in the second and now Miss Vaiden Wyott who taught
the second grade began to help him, telling him what Wallstreet
Panic meant and that he didn't have to be named that, so that when
she helped him pass the third grade by studying with her the next
summer, when he entered the fourth grade that fall his name was just
Wall Snopes because she told him that Wall was a good family name
in Mississippi with even a general in it and that he didn't even need
to keep the Street if he didn't want to. And he said from that first
day and he kept right on saying it when people asked him why he
wanted to go to school so hard: "I want to learn how to count
money," so that when he heard about it, Uncle Gavin said:

"You see? That proves what I said exactly: no Snopes wants to
learn how to count money because he doesn't have to because you
will do that for him—or you had damn well better."

He, I mean Wall, was going to need to learn to count it. Even during that first winter while he was making up two grades he had a job.
The store next to the Snopes café that they lived behind in the tent
was a grocery store about the same class as the Snopes café. Every
morning Wall would get up before schooltime, as the days got
shorter he would get up in the dark, to build a fire in the iron stove
and sweep out the store and as soon as he got back after school in
the afternoon he would be the delivery boy too, using a wheelbarrow
until finally the owner of the store bought him a second-hand bicycle and took the money out of his pay each week.

And on Saturdays and holidays he would clerk in the store too,
and all that summer while Miss Wyott was helping him pass the third
grade; and even that wasn't enough: he got enough recommenda-
tions around the Square to get the delivery route for one of the
Memphis papers, only by that time he was so busy with his other
affairs that he made his brother the paper boy. And the next fall while
he was in the fourth grade he managed to get a Jackson paper too and
now he had two more boys besides Admiral Dewey working for him,
so that by that time any merchant or stock-trader or revival preacher
or candidate that wanted handbills put out always went to Wall
because he had an organization already set up.

He could count money and save it too. So when he was sixteen
and that empty oil tank blew his father away and the oil company

gave Mrs Snopes the thousand dollars, about a month later we found
out that Mrs Snopes had bought a half interest in the grocery store
and Wall had graduated from high school by now and he was a partner in the store. Though he was still the one that got up before daylight on the winter mornings to start the fire and sweep. Then he was
nineteen years old and his partner had sold the rest of the store to
Mrs Snopes and retired, and even if because of Wall's age the store
still couldn't be in his name, we knew who it really belonged to, with
a hired boy of his own now to come before daylight on the winter
mornings to build the fire and sweep.

And another one too, except that another Snopes industry
wouldn't be the right word for this one, because there wasn't any
profit in it. No, that's wrong; we worked at it too hard and Uncle
Gavin says that anything people work at as hard as all of us did at this
has a profit, is for profit whether you can convert that profit into dollars and cents or not or even want to.

The last Snopes they brought into Jefferson didn't quite make it. I
mean, this one came just so far, right up to in sight of the town clock
in fact, and then refused to go any farther; even, they said, threatening to go back to Frenchman's Bend, like an old cow or a mule that
you finally get right up to the open gate of the pen, but not a step
more.

He was the old one. Some folks said he was Mr Flem's father but
some said he was just his uncle: a short thick dirty old man with fierce
eyes under a tangle of eyebrows and a neck that would begin to swell
and turn red before, as Ratliff said, you had barely had time to cross
the first word with him. So they bought a little house for him about
a mile from town, where he lived with an old-maid daughter and the
twin sons named Vardaman and Bilbo that belonged to I.O. Snopes's
other wife, the one that Uncle Gavin called the number-two wife
that was different from the number-one one that rocked all day long
on the front gallery of the Snopes Hotel.

The house had a little piece of ground with it that old man Snopes
made into a truck garden and watermelon patch. The watermelon
patch was the industry. No, that's wrong. Maybe I mean the industry took place because of the watermelon patch. Because it was like

the old man didn't really raise the watermelons to sell or even just
to be eaten, but as a bait for the pleasure or sport or contest or maybe
just getting that mad, of catching boys robbing it; planting and cul-
tivating and growing watermelons just so he could sit ambushed with
a loaded shotgun behind a morning-glory vine on his back gallery
until he could hear sounds from the melon patch and then shooting
at it.

Then one moonlight night he could see enough too and this time
he actually shot John Wesley Roebuck with a load of squirrel shot,
and the next morning Mr Hub Hampton, the sheriff, rode out there
and told old Snopes that if he ever again let that shotgun off he
would come back and take it away from him and throw him in jail
to boot. So after that, old Snopes didn't dare use the gun. All he
could do now was to stash away piles of rocks at different places
along the fence, and just sit behind the vine with a heavy stick and a
flashlight.

That was how the industry started. Mr Hampton had passed the
word around town to all the mothers and fathers to tell their sons to
stay out of that damned patch now; that any time they wanted a
watermelon that bad, he, Mr Hampton, would buy them one,
because if they kept on making old man Snopes that mad, some day
he would burst a blood vessel and die and we would all be in jail. But
old Snopes didn't know that because Vardaman and Bilbo didn't tell
him. They would wait until he was in the house, lying down maybe
to take a nap after dinner, when they would run in and wake him,
yelling, hollering that some boys were in the patch, and he would
jump up yelling and cursing and grab up the oak cudgel and go tearing out to the patch, and nobody in it or near it except Vardaman and
Bilbo behind the corner of the house dying laughing, then dodging
and running and still laughing while the old man scrabbled up his
piled rocks to throw at them.

Because he never would catch on. No, that's wrong too: he always
caught on. The trouble was, he didn't dare risk doing nothing when
they would run in hollering "Grampaw! Grampaw! Chaps in the
melon patch!" because it might be true. He would have to jump up
and grab the stick and run out, knowing beforehand he probably
wouldn't find anybody there except Vardaman and Bilbo behind the

corner of the house that he couldn't even catch, throwing the rocks and cursing them until he would give out of rocks and breath both, then standing there gasping and panting with his neck as red as a turkey gobbler's and without breath any more to curse louder than whispering. That's what we—all the boys in Jefferson between six and twelve years old and sometimes even older—would go out there to hide behind the fence and watch. We never had seen anybody bust a blood vessel and die and we wanted to be there when it happened to see what it would look like.

This was after Uncle Gavin finally got home from rehabilitating Europe. We were crossing the Square when she passed us. I never could tell if she had looked at Uncle Gavin, though I know she never looked at me, let alone spoke when we passed. But then, that was all right; I didn't expect her either to or not to; sometimes she would speak to me but sometimes she never spoke to anybody and we were used to it. Like she did this time: just walking on past us exactly like a pointer dog walks just before it freezes onto the birds. Then I saw that Uncle Gavin had stopped and turned to look after her. But then I remembered he had been away since 1914 which was eight years ago now, so she was only about five or six when he saw her last.

"Who is that?" he said.

"Linda Snopes," I said. "You know: Mr Flem Snopes's girl." And I was still watching her too. "She walks like a pointer," I said. "I mean, a pointer that's just—"

"I know what you mean," Uncle Gavin said. "I know exactly what you mean."

EIGHT

GAVIN STEVENS

I knew exactly what he meant. She was walking steadily toward us, completely aware of us, yet not once had she looked at either of us, the eyes not hard and fixed so much as intent, oblivious; fixed and unblinking on something past us, beyond us, behind us, as a young pointer will walk over you if you dont move out of the way, during the last few yards before the actual point, since now it no longer needs depend on clumsy and fumbling scent because now it is actually looking at the huddled trigger-set covey. She went past us still walking, striding, like the young pointer bitch, the maiden bitch of course, the virgin bitch, immune now in virginity, not scorning the earth, spurning the earth, because she needed it to walk on in that immunity: just intent from earth and us too, not proud and not really oblivious: just immune in intensity and ignorance and innocence as the sleepwalker is for the moment immune from the anguishes and agonies of breath.

She would be thirteen, maybe fourteen now and the reason I did not know her and would not have known her was not because I had possibly not seen her in eight years and human females change so drastically in the years between ten and fifteen. It was because of her mother. It was as though I—you too perhaps—could not have believed but that a woman like that must, could not other than, produce an exact replica of herself. That Eula Varner—You see? Eula *Varner.* Never Eula Snopes even though I had—had had to—watched them in bed together. Eula Snopes it could never be simply because it must not simply because I would decline to have it so—that Eula Varner owed that much at least to the simple male hunger which she blazed into anguish just by being, existing, breathing; having been born, becoming born, becoming a part of Motion—that hunger which she herself could never assuage since there was but one of her to match with all that hungering. And that single *one* doomed to fade; by the fact of that mortality doomed not to assuage nor even negate the hunger; doomed never to efface the anguish and the hunger from Motion even by her own act of quitting Motion and so fill with her own absence from it the aching void where once had glared that incandescent shape.

That's what you thought at first, of course: that she must of necessity repeat herself, duplicate herself if she reproduced at all. Because immediately afterward you realised that obviously she must not, must not duplicate: very Nature herself would not permit that to occur, permit two of them in a place no larger than Jefferson, Mississippi, in one century, let alone in overlapping succession, within the anguished scope of a single generation. Because even Nature, loving concupiscent uproar and excitement as even Nature loves it, insists that it at least be reproductive of fresh fodder for the uproar and the excitement. Which would take time, the time necessary to produce that new crop of fodder, since she—Eula Varner—had exhausted, consumed, burned up that one of hers. Whereupon I would remember what Maggie said once to Gowan back there in the dead long time ago when I was in the throes of my own apprenticeship to holocaust: "You dont marry Helen and Semiramis; you just commit suicide for her."

Because she—the child—didn't look at all like her mother. And then in that same second I knew exactly whom she did resemble. Back there in that time of my own clowning belated adolescence (none the less either for being both), I remember how I could never decide which of the two unbearables was the least unbearable; which (as the poet has it) of the two chewed bitter thumbs was the least bitter for chewing. That is, whether Manfred de Spain had seduced a chaste wife, or had simply been caught up in passing by a rotating nympholept. This was my anguish. If the first was right, what qualities of mere man did Manfred have that I didn't? If the second, what blind outrageous fortune's lightning-bolt was it that struck Manfred de Spain that mightn't, shouldn't, couldn't, anyway didn't, have blasted Gavin Stevens just as well? Or even also (oh yes, it was that bad once, that comical once) I would even have shared her if I had to, couldn't have had her any other way.

That was when (I mean the thinking why it hadn't been me in Manfred's place to check that glance's idle fateful swing that day whenever that moment had been) I would say that she must be chaste, a wife true and impeachless. I would think *It's that damned child, that damned baby*—that innocent infant which, simply by innocently being, breathing, existing, lacerated and scoriated and reft me of peace: if there had only been no question of the child's paternity; or better still, no child at all. Thus I would even get a little relief from my chewed thumbs since I would need both of them for the moment to count with. Ratliff had told me how they departed for Texas immediately after the wedding and when they returned twelve months later, the child was already walking. Which (the walking at least) I did not believe, not because of the anguish, the jealousy, the despair, but simply because of Ratliff. In fact, it was Ratliff who gave me that ease of hope—or if you like, ease from anguish; all right: tears too, peaceful tears but tears, which are the jewel-baubles of the belated adolescence's clown-comedian—to paint with. Because even if the child had been only one day old, Ratliff would have invented the walking, being Ratliff. In fact, if there had been no child at all yet, Ratliff would have invented one, invented one already walking for the simple sake of his own paradox and humor, secured as he was from checkable facts by this much miles and time between Frenchman's Bend and Jefferson two years later. That was when I would rather believe it was Flem's own child; rather defilement by Manfred de Spain than promiscuity by Eula Varner—whereupon I would need only to taste that thumb again to realise that any other thumb was less bitter, no matter which: let her accept the whole earth's Manfred de Spains and refuse Gavin Stevens, than to accept one Flem Snopes and still refuse him.

So you see how much effort a man will make and trouble he will invent to guard and defend himself from the boredom of peace of mind. Or rather perhaps the pervert who deliberately infests himself with lice, not just for the simple pleasure of being rid of them again, since even in the folly of youth we know that nothing lasts; but because even in that folly we are afraid that maybe Nothing will last, that maybe Nothing will last forever, and anything is better than Nothing, even lice. So now, as another poet sings, That Fancy passed me by And nothing will remain; which, praise the gods, is a damned lie since, praise, O gods! Nothing cannot remain anywhere since nothing is vacuum and vacuum is paradox and unbearable and we will have none of it even if we would, the damned-fool poet's Nothing steadily and perennially full of perennially new and perennially renewed anguishes for me to measure my stature against whenever I need reassure myself that I also am Motion.

Because the second premise was much better. If I was not to have her, then Flem Snopes shall never have. So instead of the poet's Fancy passes by And nothing remaining, it is Remaining which will always remain, never to be completely empty of that olden anguish. So no matter how much more the blood will slow and remembering grow more lascerant, the blood at least will always remember that once it was that capable, capable at least of anguish. So that girl-child was not Flem Snopes's at all, but mine; my child and my grandchild both, since the McCarron boy who begot her (oh yes, I can even believe Ratliff when it suits me) in that lost time, was Gavin Stevens in that lost time; and, since remaining must remain or quit being remaining, Gavin Stevens is fixed by his own child forever at that one age in that one moment. So since the son is father to the man, the McCarron fixed forever and timeless in that dead youth as Gavin Stevens is of necessity now the son of Gavin Stevens's age, and McCarron's child is Gavin Stevens's grandchild.

Whether Gavin Stevens intended to be that father-grandfather or not, of course. But then neither did he dream that that one idle glance of Eula Varner's eye which didn't even mark him in passing would confer on him foster-uncleship over every damned Snopes wanting to claim it out of that whole entire damned connection she married into. I mean foster-uncleship in the sense that simple enragement and outrage and obsession *per se* take care of their own just as simple *per se* poverty and (so they say) virtue do of theirs. But foster-uncleship only to *he:* never *she*. So this was not the first time I ever thought how apparently all Snopeses are male, as if the mere and simple incident of woman's divinity precluded Snopesishness and made it paradox. No: it was rather as if *Snopes* were some profound and incontrovertible hermaphroditic principle for the furtherance of a race, a species, the principle vested always physically in the male, any anonymous conceptive or gestative organ drawn into that radius to conceive and spawn, repeating that male principle and then vanishing; the Snopes female incapable of producing a Snopes and hence harmless like the malaria-bearing mosquito of whom only the female is armed and potent, turned upside down and backward. Or even more than a mere natural principle: a divine one: the unsleeping hand of God Himself, unflagging and constant, else before now they would have owned the whole earth, let alone just Jefferson, Mississippi.

Because now Flem Snopes was vice president of what we still called Colonel Sartoris's bank. Oh yes, our banks have vice presidents the same as anybody else's bank. Only nobody in Jefferson ever paid any attention to just the vice president of a bank before; he—a bank vice president—was like someone who had gained the privilege of calling himself major or colonel by having contributed time or money or influence to getting a governor elected, as compared to him who had rightfully inherited his title from a father or grandfather who had actually ridden a horse at a Yankee soldier, like Manfred de Spain or our Colonel Sartoris.

So Flem was the first actual living vice president of a bank we had ever seen to notice. We heard he had fallen heir to the vice presidency when Manfred de Spain moved up his notch, and we knew why: Uncle Billy Varner's stock plus the odds and ends which (we now learned) Flem himself had been picking up here and there for some time, plus Manfred de Spain himself. Which was all right; it was done now; too late to help; we were used to our own Jefferson breed or strain of bank vice presidents and we expected no more of even a Snopes bank vice president than simple conformation to pattern.

Then to our surprise we saw that he was trying to be what he—a Snopes or anyway a Flem Snopes—thought a bank vice president was or should be. He began to spend most of the day in the bank. Not in the back office where Colonel Sartoris had used to sit and where

Manfred de Spain now sat, but in the lobby, standing a little back from the window watching the clients coming and going to leave their money or draw it out, still in that little cloth cap and the snap-on-behind bow tie he had come to town in thirteen years ago and his jaw still moving faintly and steadily as if he were chewing something though I anyway in my part of those thirteen years had never seen him spit.

Then one day we saw him at his post in the lobby and we didn't even know him. He was standing where he always stood, back where he would be out of the actual path to the window but where he could still watch it (watching how much money was going in or how much was coming out, we didn't know which; whether perhaps what held him thralled there was the simply solvency of the bank which in a way—by deputy, by proxy—was now his bank, his pride: that no matter how much money people drew out of it, there was always that one who had just deposited that zero-plus-one dollar into it in time; or whether he actually did believe in an inevitable moment when De Spain or whoever the designated job would belong to, would come to the window from the inside and say "Sorry, folks, you cant draw out any more money because there aint any more," and he—Flem simply wanted to prove to himself that he was wrong).

But this time we didn't know him. He still wore the little bow tie and his jaw was still pulsing faintly and steadily, but now he wore a hat, a new one of the broad black felt kind which country preachers and politicians wore. And the next day he was actually inside the cage where the money actually was and where the steel door opened into the concrete vault where it stayed at night; and now we realised that he was not watching the money any longer; he had learned all there was to learn about that. Now he was watching the records of it, how they kept the books.

And now we—some of us, a few of us—believed that he was preparing himself to show his nephew or cousin Byron how to really loot a bank. But Ratliff (naturally it was Ratliff) stopped that quick. "No no," he said, "he's jest trying to find out how anybody could think so light of money as to let a feller no brighter than Byron Snopes steal some of it. You boys have got Flem Snopes wrong. He's

got too much respect and reverence not jest for money, but for
sharpness too, to outrage and debase one of them by jest crude robbing and stealing the other one."

And as the days followed, he—Snopes—had his coat off too, in his
galluses now like he actually worked there, was paid money every
Saturday to stay inside the cage, except that he still wore the new hat,
standing now right behind the book-keepers while he found out for
himself how a bank was run. And now we heard how always when
people came in to pay off notes or the interest on them, and sometimes when they came to borrow the money too (except the old
short-tempered ones, old customers from back in Colonel Sartoris's
time, who would run Flem out of the back room without waiting for
De Spain to do it or even asking his—De Spain's—leave) he would be
there too, his jaw still faintly pulsing while he watched and learned;
that was when Ratliff said that all he—Snopes—needed to learn now
was how to write out a note so that the fellow borrowing the money
couldn't even read when it was due, let alone the rate of interest, like
Colonel Sartoris could write one (the tale, the legend was that once
the colonel wrote out a note for a country-man customer, a farmer,
who took the note and looked at it, then turned it upside down and
looked at it, then handed it back to the colonel and said, "What does
it say, Colonel? I cant read it," whereupon the colonel took it in his
turn, looked at it, turned it upside down and looked at it, then tore
it in two and threw it in the waste basket and said, "Be damned if I
can either, Tom. We'll try another one."), then he—Snopes—would
know all there was to learn about banking in Jefferson, and could
graduate.

Evidently he learned that too. One day he was not in the bank any
more, and the day after that, and the day after that. On the day the
bank first opened about twenty years ago Mrs Jennie Du Pre,
Colonel Sartoris' sister, had put a tremendous great rubber plant in
the corner of the lobby. It was taller than a man, it took up as much
room as a privy; it was in everybody's way and in summer they
couldn't even open the front door all the way back because of it. But
she wouldn't let the colonel nor the board of directors either remove
it, since she belonged to that school which believed that any room
inhabited by people had to have something green in it to absorb the

poison from the air. Though why it had to be that monstrous rubber plant, nobody knew, unless perhaps she believed that nothing less than rubber and that much of it would be tough and durable and resilient enough to cope with air poisoned by the anxiety or exultation over as much money as her brother's, a Sartoris, old Colonel Sartoris's son's bank would naturally handle.

So when the days passed and Snopes was no longer to be seen taking up room in the lobby while he watched the borrowing and the lending and the paying in and the drawing out (or who did each, and how much of each, which according to Ratliff was the real reason he was there, was what he was really watching), it was as if Mrs Du Pre's rubber tree had vanished from the lobby, abandoned it. And when still more days passed and we finally realised he was not coming back any more, it was like hearing that the rubber tree had been hauled away somewhere and burned, destroyed forever. It was as if the single aim and purpose of that long series of interlocked circumstances—the bank which a sentimentalist like Colonel Sartoris founded in order that, as Ratliff said, a feller no brighter than Byron Snopes could steal from it, the racing car which Bayard Sartoris drove too fast for our country roads (the Jefferson ladies said because he was grieving so over the death in battle of his twin brother that he too was seeking death though in my opinion Bayard liked war and now that there was no more war to go to, he was faced with the horrid prospect of having to go to work) until his grandfather took to riding with him in the hope that he would slow down: as a result of which, the normal check-up of the bank for re-organization revealed the fact that Byron Snopes had been robbing it: as a result of which, to save the good name of the bank which his father had helped to found, Manfred de Spain had to allow Flem Snopes to become vice president of it—the single result of all this apparently was to efface that checked cap from Flem Snopes and put that hot-looking black politician-preacher's hat on him in its stead.

Because he still wore the hat. We saw that about the Square every day. But never again in the bank, his bank, the one in which he was not only a director but in whose hierarchy he had an official designated place, second-in-command. Not even to deposit his own money in it. Oh yes, we knew that; we had Ratliff's word for that.

Ratliff had to know a fact like that by now. After this many years of working to establish and maintain himself as what he uniquely was in Jefferson, Ratliff could not afford, he did not dare, to walk the streets and not have the answer to any and every situation which was not really any of his business. Ratliff knew: that not only was Flem Snopes no longer a customer of the bank of which he was vice president, but that in the second year he had transferred his account to the other, rival bank, the old bank of Jefferson.

So we all knew the answer to that. I mean, we had been right all along. All except Ratliff of course, who had dissuaded us before against our mutually combined judgments. We had watched Flem behind the grille of his bank while he taught himself the intricacies of banking in order to plumb laboriously the crude and awkward method by which his cousin or nephew Byron had made his petty and unambitious haul; we had seen him in and out of the vault itself while he learned the tide-cycle, the rise and fall of the actual cash against the moment when it would be most worth pillaging; we believed now that when that moment came, Flem would have already arranged himself for his profit to be one hundred percent, that he himself was seeing to it in advance that he would not have to steal even one forgotten penny of his own money.

"No," Ratliff said. "No."

"In which case, he will defeat himself," I said. "What does he expect to happen when the other depositors, especially the ignorant ones that know too little about banks and the smart ones that know too much about Snopeses, begin to find out that the vice president of the bank doesn't even keep his own loose change in it?"

"No, I tell you," Ratliff said. "You folks—"

"So he's hoping—wishing—dreaming of starting a run on his own bank, not to loot it but to empty it, abolish it. All right. Why? For revenge on Manfred de Spain because of his wife?"

"No no, I tell you!" Ratliff said. "I tell you, you got Flem all wrong, all of you have. I tell you, he aint just got respect for money: he's got active" (he always said active for actual, though in this case I believe his choice was better than Webster's) "reverence for it. The last thing he would ever do is hurt that bank. Because any bank whether it's hisn or not stands for money, and the last thing he would ever do is to insult and degrade money by mishandling it. Likely the one and only thing in his life he is ashamed of is the one thing he wont never do again. That was that-ere power-plant brass that time. Likely he wakes up at night right now and writhes and squirms over it. Not because he lost by it because dont nobody know yet, nor never will, whether he actively lost or not because dont nobody know yet jest how much of that old brass he might a sold before he made the mistake of trying to do it wholesale by using Tom Tom Bird and Tomey Beauchamp. He's ashamed because when he made money that-a-way, he got his-self right down into the dirt with the folks that waste money because they stole it in the first place and aint got nowhere to put it down where they can risk turning their backs on it."

"Then what is he up to?" I said. "What is he trying to do?"

"I don't know," Ratliff said. And now he not only didn't sound like Ratliff, answering he didn't know to any question, he didn't even look like Ratliff: the customary bland smooth quizzical inscrutable face not quite baffled maybe but certainly questioning, certainly sober. "I jest dont know. We got to figger. That's why I come up here to see you: in case you did know. Hoping you knowed." Then he was Ratliff again, humorous, quizzical, invincibly . . . maybe the word I want is not optimism or courage or even hope, but rather of sanity or maybe even of innocence. "But naturally you dont know neither. Confound it, the trouble is we dont never know beforehand, to anticipate him. It's like a rabbit or maybe a bigger varmint, one with more poison or anyhow more teeth, in a patch or a brake: you can watch the bushes shaking but you cant see what it is or which-away it's going until it breaks out. But you can see it then, and usually it's in time. Of course you got to move fast when he does break out, and he's got the advantage of you because he's already moving because he knows where he's going, and you aint moving yet because you dont. But it's usually in time."

That was the first time the bushes shook. The next time was almost a year later; he came in, he said "Good morning Lawyer," and he was Ratliff again, bland, smooth, courteous, a little too damned intelligent. "I figgered you might like to hear the latest news first, being as you're a member of the family too by simple bad luck and exposure, you might say. Being as so far dont nobody know about it except the directors of the Bank of Jefferson."

"The Bank of Jefferson?" I said.

"That's right. It's that non-Snopes boy of Eck's, that other non-Snopes that blowed his-self up in that empty oil tank back while you was away at the war, wasting his time jest hunting a lost child that wasn't even lost, jest his maw thought he was—"

"Yes," I said. "Wallstreet Panic." Because I already knew about that: the non-Snopes son of a non-Snopes who had had the good fortune to discover (or be discovered by) a good woman early in life: the second-grade teacher who, obviously recognising that un-Snopes anomaly, not only told him what Wallstreet Panic meant, but that he didn't really have to have it for his name if he didn't want to; but if he thought a too-violent change might be too much, then he could call himself simply Wall Snopes since Wall was a good name, having been carried bravely by a brave Mississippi general at Chickamauga and Lookout Mountain, and though she didn't think that, being a non-Snopes, he would particularly need to remember courage, remembering courage never hurt anyone.

And how he had taken the indemnity money the oil company paid for his father's bizarre and needless and un-Snopesish death and bought into the little back-street grocery store where he had been the after-school-and-Saturday clerk and errand boy, and continued to save his money until, when the old owner died at last, he, Wallstreet, owned the store. And how he got married who was never a Snopes, never in this world a Snopes: doomed damned corrupted and self-convicted not merely of generosity but of taste; holding simple foolish innocent rewardless generosity, not to mention taste, even higher than his own repute when the town should learn he had actually proposed marriage to a woman ten years his senior.

That's what he did, not even waiting to graduate—the day, the moment when in the hot stiff brand-new serge suit, to walk sweating through the soundless agony of the cut flowers, across the highschool rostrum and receive his diploma from the hand of the principal—but only for the day when he knew he was done with the school, forever more beyond the range of its help or harm (he was nineteen. Seven years ago he and his six-year-old brother had entered the same kindergarten class. In this last year his grades had been such that they didn't even ask him to take the examinations.)— to leave the store of which he was now actual even if not titular proprietor, just in time to be standing at the corner when the dismissal bell rang, standing there while the kindergarten then the first-grade children streamed past him, then the second grade, standing there while the Lilliputian flow divided around them like a brook around two herons, while without even attempting to touch her in this all juvenile Jefferson's sight, he proposed to the second-grade teacher and then saw her, as another teacher did from a distance, stare at him and partly raise one defending hand and then burst into tears, right then in plain view of the hundred children who at one time within the last three or four years had been second-graders too, to whom she had been mentor, authority, infallible.

Until he could lead her aside, onto the vacating playground, himself to screen her while she used his handkerchief to regain composure, then, against all the rules of the school and of respectable decorum too, back into the empty room itself smelling of chalk and anguished cerebration and the dry inflexibility of facts, she leading the way, but not for the betrothing kiss, not to let him touch her even and least of all to remind him that she had already been twenty-two years old that day seven years ago and that twelve months from now he would discover that all Jefferson had been one year laughing at him. Who had been divinitive enough to see seven years beyond that wallstreet panic, but was more, much more than that: a lady, the tears effaced now and she once more the Miss Wyott, or rather the "Miss Vaiden" as Southern children called their teacher, telling him, feeding him none of those sorry reasons: saying simply that she was already engaged and some day she wanted him to know her fiancé because she knew they would be friends.

So that he would not know better until he was much older and had much more sense. Nor learning it then when it was too late because it was not too late, since didn't I just say that she was wise, more than just wise: divinitive? Also, remember her own people had come from the country (her own branch of it remained there where they had owned the nearest ford, crossing, ferry before Jefferson even became Jefferson) so without doubt she even knew in advance the girl, which girl even, since she seems to have taken him directly there, within the week, almost as though she said "This is she. Marry her" and within the month he didn't even know probably that he had not remarked that Miss Vaiden Wyott had resigned from the Jefferson school where she had taught the second grade for a decade, to accept a position in a school in Bristol, Virginia, since when that fall day came he was two months husband to a tense fierce not quite plain-faced girl with an ambition equal to his and a will if anything even more furious against that morass, that swamp, that fetid seethe from which her husband (she naturally believed) had extricated himself by his own suspenders and boot straps, herself clerking in the store now so that the mother-in-law could now stay at home and do the cooking and housework; herself, although at that time she didn't weigh quite a hundred pounds, doing the apprentice chores—sweeping, wrestling the barrels of flour and molasses, making the rounds of the town on the bicycle in which the telephone orders were delivered until they could afford to buy the second-hand Model T Ford—during the hours while the younger one, Admiral Dewey, was in school where it was she now, his sister-in-law, who made him go whether he would or not.

Yes, we all knew that; that was a part of our folklore, or Snopeslore, if you like: how Flem himself was anyway the second one to see that here was a young man who was going to make money by simple honesty and industry, and tried to buy into the business or anyway lend Wallstreet money to expand it; and we all knew who had refused the offer. That is, we liked to believe, having come to know Wallstreet a little now, that he would have declined anyway. But since we had come to know his wife, we knew that he was going to decline. And how he had learned to be a clerk and a partner the hard way, and he would have to learn to be a proprietor the hard way too: and sure enough in time he overbought his stock; and how he went to Colonel Sartoris's bank for help.

That was when we first realised that Flem Snopes actually was a member of the board of directors of a Jefferson bank. I mean, that a Flem Snopes actually could be. Oh, we had seen his name among the others on the annual bank report above the facsimile of Colonel Sartoris's illegible signature as president, but we merely drew the logical conclusion that that was simply old man Will Varner's voting proxy to save him a trip to town; all we thought was, "That means that Manfred de Spain will have Uncle Billy's stock too in case he ever wants anything."

And obviously we knew, believed, that Flem had tried again to buy into Wallstreet's business, save him with a personal private loan before he, as a director, blocked the loan from the bank. Because we thought we saw it all now; all we seemed to have missed was, what hold he could have had over the drummer to compel him to persuade Wallstreet to overbuy, and over the wholesale house in St. Louis to persuade it to accept the sale—very likely the same sign or hoodoo-mark he planned to use on the other bank, the Bank of Jefferson, to prevent them lending Wallstreet money after Colonel Sartoris's bank declined.

But there was never any question about which one of the Wall-street Snopeses had turned Flem down. Anybody could have seen her that morning, running, thin, not so much tense as fierce, still weighing less than a hundred pounds, even after six months of marriage looking still not so much like a nymph as like a deer, not around the Square as pedestrians walked but across it, through it, darting among the automobiles and teams and wagons, toward and into the bank (and how she knew, divined so quickly that he had been refused the loan we didn't know either, though on second thought that was obvious too: that simple automatic fierce Snopes antipathy which had reacted as soon as common sense told her it should not have taken the bank that long to say Yes, and that Flem Snopes was on the board of directors of it)—darting into the lobby already crying: "Where is he? Where is Wall?" and out again when they told her Gone, not at all desperate: just fierce and hurried, onto the street where someone else told her he went that way: which was the street leading to the back street leading to the rented house where Flem lived, who had no office nor other place of business, running now until she overtook him, in time. And anyone there could have seen that too: clinging to him in broad daylight when even sweethearts didn't embrace on the street by daylight and no lady anywhere at any time said God damn in public, crying (weeping too but no tears, as if the fierce taut irreconcilable face blistered and evaporated tears away as fast as they emerged onto it): "Dont you dare! Them damn Snopes! God damn them! God damn them!"

So we thought of course that her father, a small though thrifty farmer, had found the money somehow. Because Wallstreet saved his business. And he had not only learned about solvency from that experience, he had learned something more about success too. In another year he had rented (then bought it) the store next door and converted it into a warehouse, stock room, so he could buy in larger wholesale lots for less money; another few years and he had rented what had been the last livery stable in Jefferson for his warehouse and knocked down the wall between the two stores and now he had in Jefferson the first self-service grocery store we had ever seen, built on the pattern which the big chain grocery stores were to make nation-wide in the purveying of food; the street his store faced on made an L with the alley where the old Snopes restaurant had been so that the tent in which he had passed his first night in Jefferson was directly behind his store too; he either bought or rented that lot (there were more automobiles in Jefferson now) and made a parking lot and so taught the housewives of Jefferson to come to town and seek his bargains and carry them home themselves.

That is, we—or that is, I—thought that it was his father-in-law who had found the money to save him, until now. "Well, I'll be damned," I said. "So it was you."

"That's right," Ratliff said. "All I wanted was jest a note for it. But he insisted on making me a partner. And I'll tell you something else we're fixing to do. We're fixing to open a wholesale."

"A what?" I said.

"A wholesale company like the big ones in St. Louis, right here in Jefferson, so that instead of either having to pay high freight on a little shirttail full of stuff, or risk overloading on something perishable to save freight, a merchant anywhere in the county can buy jest what he needs at a decent price without having to add no freight a-tall."

"Well I'll be damned," I said. "Why didn't you think of that yourself years ago?"

"That's right," Ratliff said. "Why didn't you?"

"Well I'll be damned," I still said. Then I said: "Hell fire, are you still selling stock? Can I get in?"

"Why not?" he said. "Long as your name aint Snopes. Maybe you could even buy some from him if your name wasn't jest Flem Snopes. But you got to pass that-ere little gal first. His wife. You ought to stop in there sometime and hear her say Them goddamn Snopes once. Oh sho, all of us have thought that, and some of us have even said it out loud. But she's different. She means it. And she aint going to never let him change neither."

"Yes," I said. "I've heard about that. I wonder why she never changed their name."

"No no," he said. "You dont understand. She dont want to change it. She jest wants to live it down. She aint trying to drag him by the hair out of Snopes, to escape from Snopes. She's got to purify Snopes itself. She's got to beat Snopes from the inside. Stop in there and listen sometimes."

"A wholesale house," I said. "So that's why Flem—" But that was foolish, as Ratliff himself saw even before I said it.

"—why Flem changed his account from his own bank to the other one? No no. We aint using the banks here. We dont need them. Like Flem was the first feller in Jefferson to find out that. Wall's credit is too good with the big wholesalers and brokers we deal with. The way they figger, he aint cutting into nobody's private business: he's helping all business. We dont need no bank. But we—he—still aims to keep it homemade. So you see him if you want to talk about stock."

"I will," I said. "But what is Flem himself up to? Why did he pull his money out of De Spain's bank as soon as he got to be vice president of it? Because he's still that, so he still owns stock in it. But he doesn't keep his own money in it. Why?"

"Oh," he said, "is that what you're worried about? Why, we aint sho yet. All we're doing now is watching the bushes shake." Between the voice and the face there were always two Ratliffs: the second one offering you a fair and open chance to divine what the first one really meant by what it was saying, provided you were smart enough. But this time that second Ratliff was trying to tell me something which for whatever reason the other could not say in words. "As long as that little gal lives, Flem aint got no chance to ever get a finger-hold on Wall. So Eck Snopes is out. And I.O. Snopes never was in because I.O. never was worth nothing even to I.O., let alone for anybody else to take a cut of the profit. So that jest about exhausts all the Snopeses in reach that a earnest hardworking feller might make a forced share-crop on."

"There's that—" I said.

"All right," he said. "I'll say it for you. Montgomery Ward. The photograph gallery. If Flem aint been in that thing all the time from the very first, he dont never aim to be. And the fact that there aint been a new photograph in his show window in over a year now, let alone Jason Compson collecting his maw's rent prompt on time since the second month after Montgomery Ward opened up, is proof enough that Flem seen from the first day that there wasn't nothing there for him to waste his time on. So I cant think of but one Snopes object that he's got left."

"All right," I said. "I'll bite."

"That-ere twenty-dollar gold piece."

"What twenty-dollar gold piece?"

"Dont you remember what I said that day, about how when a country boy makes his first Sad-dy night trip to Memphis, that-ere twenty-dollar bill he wears pinned inside his undershirt so he can at least get back home?"

"Go on," I said. "You cant stop now."

"What's the one thing in Jefferson that Flem aint got yet? The one thing he might want. That maybe he's been working at ever since they taken Colonel Sartoris out of that wrecked car and he voted Uncle Billy Varner's stock to make Manfred de Spain president of that bank?"

"To be president of it himself," I said. "No!" I said. "It cant be! It must not be!" But he was just watching me. "Nonsense," I said.

"Why nonsense?" he said.

"Because, to use what you call that twenty-dollar gold piece, he's got to use his wife too. Do you mean to tell me you believe for one moment that his wife will side with him against Manfred de Spain?" But still he just looked at me. "Dont you agree?" I said. "How can he hope for that?"

Yes, he was just looking at me. "That would jest be when he finally runs out of the bushes," he said. "Out to where we can see him. Into the clearing. What's that clearing?"

"Clearing?" I said.

"That he was working toward?—All right," he said "That druv him to burrow through the bushes to get out of them?"

"Rapacity," I said. "Greed. Money. What else does he need? want? What else has ever driven him?"

But he just looked at me, and now I could actually watch that urgency fade until only the familiar face remained, bland, smooth, impenetrable and courteous. He drew out the dollar watch looped on a knotted shoelace between his button hole and his breast pocket. "I be dog if it aint almost dinner time," he said. "Jest about time to walk to it."

NINE

U. K. Ratliff

*B*ecause he missed it. He missed it completely.

TEN

CHARLES MALLISON

*T*hey finally caught Montgomery Ward Snopes. I mean, they caught Grover Cleveland Winbush. Like Ratliff said, anybody bootlegging anything that never had any more sense than to sell Grover Cleveland Winbush some of it deserved to be caught.

Except Uncle Gavin said that, even without Grover Cleveland, Montgomery Ward was bound to be caught sooner or later, since there simply wasn't any place in Jefferson, Mississippi, culture for a vocation or hobby or interest like the one Montgomery Ward had tried to establish among us. In Europe, yes; and maybe among the metropolitan rich or bohemians, yes too. But not in a land composed mainly of rural Baptists.

So they caught Grover Cleveland. It was one night, not very late. I mean, the stores were all closed but folks were still going home from the second running of the picture show; and some of them, I reckon anybody that passed and happened to look inside, saw the two fellows inside Uncle Willy Christian's drugstore working at the prescription case where Uncle Willy kept the medicines; and even though they were strangers—that is, nobody passing recognised them—the ones that looked in and saw them said the next day that they never thought anything of it, being that early and the lights on and Grover Cleveland not having anything to do as night marshal except to walk around the Square and look in the windows, that sooner or later he would have to see them if they never had any business there.

So it wasn't until the next morning when Uncle Willy opened up for business that he found out somebody had unlocked the store and not only unlocked the safe and took what money he had in it, they had broke open his pharmacy cabinet and stole all his morphine and

483

sleeping pills. That's what caused the trouble. Ratliff said they could have taken the money or for that matter all the rest of the store too except that prescription case, including the alcohol, because Walter Christian, the Negro janitor, had been taking the alcohol, a drink at a time ever since he and Uncle Willy both were boys and first started in the store, and Uncle Willy would have cussed and stomped around of course and even had the Law in, but that was all. But whoever touched that prescription cabinet with the morphine in it raised the devil himself. Uncle Willy was a bachelor, about sixty years old, and if you came in at the wrong time of day he even snarled at children too. But if you were careful to remember the right time of day he supplied the balls and bats for our baseball teams and after a game he would give the whole teams ice cream free whether they won or not. I mean, until one summer some of the church ladies decided to reform him. After that it was hard to tell when to speak to him or not. Then the ladies would give up for a while and it would be all right again.

Besides that, the federal drug inspectors had been nagging and worrying at him for years about keeping the morphine in that little flimsy wooden drawer that anybody with a screw-driver or a knife blade or maybe just a hair pin could prize open, even though it did have a key to it that Uncle Willy kept hidden under a gallon jug marked *Nux Vomica* on a dark shelf that nobody but him was even supposed to bother because it was so dark back there that even Walter never went back there since Uncle Willy couldn't have seen whether he had swept there or not even if he had; and each time Uncle Willy would have to promise the inspectors to lock the morphine up in the safe from now on.

So now he was going to have more trouble than ever explaining to the inspectors why he hadn't put the morphine in the safe like he promised; reminding them how, even if he had, the robbers would still have got it wasn't going to do any good now because, like Ratliff said, federal folks were not interested in whether anything worked or not, all they were interested in was that you did it exactly like their rules said to do it.

So Uncle Willy was the real cause of them catching Montgomery Ward Snopes. He was good and wild at first. He was so wild for a while that nobody could find out how much had been stolen or even what he was talking about, with more folks coming in from the street not so much to see where the robbery was but to watch Uncle Willy; until finally, it was Ratliff, of course, said: "Uncle Willy dont need no sheriff yet. What he needs first is Doc Peabody."

"Of course," Uncle Gavin said to Ratliff. "Why does it always have to be you?" He went back to where Skeets McGowan, Uncle Willy's clerk and soda-jerker, and two other boys were standing with their heads inside the open safe looking at where the money had been stolen from, and pulled Skeets out and told him to run upstairs quick and tell Doctor Peabody to hurry down. Then Uncle Gavin and the others kind of crowded Uncle Willy more or less quiet without actually holding him until Doctor Peabody came in with the needle already in his hand even and ran most of them out and rolled up Uncle Willy's sleeve then rolled it back down again and then Uncle Willy settled down into being just mad.

So he was the one responsible for catching Montgomery Ward. Or the two fellows that stole his morphine were. By this time we knew that several people passing from the picture show had seen the two fellows in the store, and now Uncle Willy wanted to know where Grover Cleveland Winbush was all that time. Yes sir, he wasn't wild now. He was just mad, as calm and steady and deadly about it as a horsefly. By that time, nine oclock in the morning, Grover Cleveland would be at home in bed asleep. Somebody said they would telephone out and wake him up and tell him to get on back to the Square fast as he could.

"Hell," Uncle Willy said. "That'll take too long. I'll go out there myself. I'd wake him up and get him back to town. He wont need to worry about quick because I'll tend to that. Who's got a car?"

Only Mr Buck Connors, the marshal, the chief of police, was there by this time. "Hold up now, Uncle Willy," he said. "There's a right way and a wrong way to do things. We want to do this one the right way. These folks have probably done already tromped up most of the evidence. But at least we can make an investigation according to police procedure regulations. Besides, Grover Cleveland was up all last night on duty. He's got to stay up again all night tonight. He's got to get his sleep."

"Exactly," Uncle Willy said. "Egg-zackly. Up all night, but not far enough up to see two damn scoundrels robbing my store in full view of the whole damn town. Robbed me of three hundred dollars' worth of valuable medicine, yet Grover Winbush—"

"How much cash did they get?" Mr Connors said.

"What?" Uncle Willy said.

"How much money was in the safe?"

"I dont know," Uncle Willy said. "I didn't count it.—Yet Grover Winbush that we pay a hundred and twenty-five a month just to wake up once an hour during the night and look around the Square, has got to get his sleep. If nobody's got a car here, get me a taxi. That son of a bitch has already cost me three hundred dollars; I aint going to stop at just one more quarter."

But they still held him hemmed off while somebody telephoned Grover Cleveland. And at first we thought that whoever telephoned and woke him up had scared him good too, until we learned the rest of it and realised all he needed for his scare was to hear that anything had happened anywhere in Jefferson last night that he would have seen if he had been where he was supposed to be or where folks thought he was. Because it wasn't hardly any time before Ratliff said:

"There he was. I jest seen him."

"Where?" somebody said.

"He jest snatched his head back in the alley yonder," Ratliff said. We all watched the alley. It led from a side street onto the Square where Grover Cleveland could have cut across lots from his boarding house. Then he stepped out of it, already walking fast. He didn't wear a uniform like Mr Connors; he wore ordinary clothes with usually his coattail hiked up over the handle of the pistol and the black-jack in his hip pocket, coming up the street fast, picking his feet up quick like a cat on a hot stove. And if you thought it would have been Mr Connors or even Mr Hampton, the sheriff, that did the investigating, you would have been wrong. It was Uncle Willy himself. At first Grover Cleveland tried to bluff. Then he fell back on lying. Then he just fell back.

"Howdy, son," Uncle Willy said. "Sorry to wake you up in the middle of the night like this, just to answer a few questions. The first one is, just where were you, roughly, more or less, at exactly half past ten oclock last night, more or less?"

"Who, me?" Grover Cleveland said. "Where I'm always at at that time of night: standing right across yonder in the station door where if anybody after the last picture show might need anything, like maybe losing their car key or maybe they find out they got a flat tire—"

"Well, well," Uncle Willy said. "And yet you never saw a light on in my store, and them two damned scoundrels—"

"Wait," Grover Cleveland said. "I'm wrong. When I seen the last picture show beginning to let out, I noticed the time, half past ten or maybe twenty-five to eleven, and I decided to go down and close up the Blue Goose and get that out of the way while I had time." The Blue Goose was a Negro café below the cotton gin. "I'm wrong," Grover Cleveland said. "That's where I was."

Uncle Willy never said anything. He just turned his head enough and hollered "Walter!" Walter came in. His grandfather had belonged to Uncle Willy's grandfather before the Surrender and he and Uncle Willy were about the same age and a good deal alike, except that instead of morphine Walter would go into the medicinal alcohol every time Uncle Willy put the key down and turned his back, and if anything Walter was a little more irascible and short-tempered. He came in from the back and said,

"Who calling me?"

"I am," Uncle Willy said. "Where were you at half past ten last night?"

"Who, me?" Walter said, exactly like Grover Cleveland did, except he said it like Uncle Willy had asked him where he was when Dr. Einstein first propounded his theory of relativity. "You talking about last night?" he said. "Where you reckon? At home in bed."

"You were at that damned Blue Goose café, where you are every night until Grover Winbush here comes in and runs all you niggers out and closes it up," Uncle Willy said.

"Then what you asking me, if you know so much?" Walter said.

"All right," Uncle Willy said. "What time last night did Mr Winbush close it?" Walter stood there, blinking. His eyes were always red. He made in an old-fashioned hand freezer the ice cream which Uncle Willy sold over his soda fountain. He made it in the cellar: a dark cool place with a single door opening onto the alley behind the store, sitting in the gloom and grinding the freezer, so that when you passed, about all you saw was his red eyes, looking not malevolent, not savage but just dangerous if you blundered out of your element and into his, like a dragon or a crocodile. He stood there, blinking. "What time did Grover Winbush close up the Blue Goose?" Uncle Willy said.

"I left before that," Walter said. Now suddenly, and we hadn't noticed him before, Mr Hampton was there, doing some of the looking too. He didn't blink like Walter. He was a big man with a big belly and little hard pale eyes that didn't seem to need to blink at all. They were looking at Grover Cleveland now.

"How do you know you did?" he said to Walter.

"Hell fire," Uncle Willy said. "He aint never left that damned place before they turned the lights out since they first opened the door."

"I know that," Mr Hampton said. He was still looking at Grover Cleveland with his little hard pale unblinking eyes. "I've been marshal and sheriff both here a long time too." He said to Grover Cleveland: "Where were you last night when folks needed you?" But Grover Cleveland still tried; you'll have to give him that, even if now even he never believed in it:

"Oh, you mean them two fellers in Uncle Willy's store about half past ten last night. Sure, I seen them. I naturally thought, taken for granted it was Uncle Willy and Skeets. So I. . . ."

"So you what?" Mr Hampton said.

"I . . . stepped back inside and . . . taken up the evening paper," Grover Cleveland said. "Yes, that's where I was: setting right there in the station reading the Memphis evening paper. . . ."

"When Whit Rouncewell saw them two fellows in here, he went back to the station looking for you," Mr Hampton said. "He waited an hour. By that time the lights were off in here but he never saw anybody come out the front door. And you never showed up. And Walter there says you never showed up at the Blue Goose either. Where were you last night, Grover?"

CHARLES MALLISON 489

So now there wasn't anywhere for him to go. He just stood there with his coattail hiked up over the handle of his pistol and blackjack like a little boy's shirttail coming out. Maybe that's what it was: Grover Cleveland was too old to look like a boy. And Uncle Willy and Mr Hampton and all the rest of us looking at him until all of a sudden we were all ashamed to look at him any more, ashamed to have to find out what we were going to find out. Except that Mr Hampton wasn't ashamed to. Maybe it was being sheriff so long had made him that way, learned him it wasn't Grover Cleveland you had to be ashamed of: it was all of us.

"One night Doc Peabody was coming back from a case about one oclock and he saw you coming out of that alley side door to what Montgomery Ward Snopes calls his studio. Another night I was going home late myself, about midnight, and I saw you going into it. What's going on in there, Grover?"

Grover Cleveland didn't move now either. It was almost a whisper: "It's a club."

Now Mr Hampton and Uncle Gavin were looking at each other. "Dont look at me," Uncle Gavin said. "You're the law." That was the funny thing: neither one of them paid any attention to Mr Connors, who was the marshal and ought to have been attending to this already. Maybe that was why.

"You're the County Attorney," Mr Hampton said. "You're the one to say what the law is before I can be it."

"What are we waiting for then?" Uncle Gavin said.

"Maybe Grover wants to tell us what it is and save time," Mr Hampton said.

"No, dammit," Uncle Gavin said. "Take your foot off him for a minute anyway." He said to Grover Cleveland: "You go on back to the station until we need you."

"You can read the rest of that Memphis paper," Mr Hampton said. "And we wont want you either," he said to Mr Connors.

"Like hell, Sheriff," Mr Connors said. "Your jurisdiction's just the county. What goes on in Jefferson is my jurisdiction. I got as much right—" He stopped then but it was already too late. Mr Hampton looked at him with the little hard pale eyes that never seemed to need to blink at all.

"Go on," Mr Hampton said. "Got as much right to see what Montgomery Ward Snopes has got hid as me and Gavin have. Why didn't you persuade Grover to take you into that club then?" But Mr Connors could still blink. "Come on," Mr Hampton said to Uncle Gavin, turning. Uncle Gavin moved too.

"That means you too," he said to me.

"That means all of you," Mr Hampton said. "All of you get out of Uncle Willy's way now. He's got to make a list of what's missing for the narcotics folks and the insurance too."

So we stood on the street and watched Mr Hampton and Uncle Gavin go on toward Montgomery Ward's studio. "What?" I said to Ratliff.

"I dont know," he said. "That is, I reckon I know. We'll have to wait for Hub and your uncle to prove it."

"What do you reckon it is?" I said.

Now he looked at me. "Let's see," he said. "Even if you are nine going on ten, I reckon you still aint outgrowed ice cream, have you. Come on. We wont bother Uncle Willy and Skeets now neither. We'll go to the Dixie Café." So we went to the Dixie Cafe and got two cones and stood on the street again.

"What?" I said.

"My guess is, it's a passel of French postcards Montgomery Ward brought back from the war in Paris. I reckon you dont know what that is, do you?"

"I dont know," I said.

"It's Kodak pictures of men and women together, experimenting with one another. Without no clothes on much." I dont know whether he was looking at me or not. "Do you know now?"

"I dont know," I said.

"But maybe you do?" he said.

That's what it was. Uncle Gavin said he had a big album of them, and that he had learned enough about photography to have made slides from some of them so he could throw them magnified on a sheet on the wall with a magic lantern in that back room. And he said how Montgomery Ward stood there laughing at him and Mr Hampton both. But he was talking mostly to Uncle Gavin.

"Oh sure," he said. "I dont expect Hub here—"

"Call me Mister Hampton," Mr Hampton said.

"—to know any better—"

"Call me Mister Hampton, boy," Mr Hampton said.

"Mister Hampton," Montgomery Ward said. "—but you're a lawyer; you dont think I got into this without reading a little law first myself, do you? You can confiscate these—all you'll find here; I dont guess Mister Hampton will let a little thing like law stop him from that—"

That was when Mr Hampton slapped him. "Stop it, Hub!" Uncle Gavin said. "You damned fool!"

"Let him go ahead," Montgomery Ward said. "Suing his bondsmen is easier than running a magic lantern. Safer too. Where was I? Oh yes. Even if they had been sent through the mail, which they haven't, that would just be a federal charge, and I dont see any federal dicks around here. And even if you tried to cook up a charge that I've been making money out of them, where are your witnesses? All you got is Grover Winbush, and he dont dare testify, not because he will lose his job because he'll probably do that anyway, but because the God-fearing Christian holy citizens of Jefferson wont let him because they cant have it known that this is what their police do when they're supposed to be at work. Let alone the rest of my customers, not to mention any names scattered around in banks and stores and gins and filling stations and farms too two counties wide in either direction—sure: I just thought of this too: come on, put a fine on me and see how quick it will be paid. . . ." and stopped and said with a kind of hushed amazement: "Sweet Christ." He was talking fast now: "Come on, lock me up, give me a thousand stamped envelopes and I'll make more money in three days than I made in the whole two years with that damned magic lantern." Now he was talking to Mr Hampton: "Maybe that's what you wanted, to begin with: not the postcards but the list of customers; retire from sheriff and spend all your time on the collections. Or no: keep the star to bring pressure on the slow payers—"

Only this time Uncle Gavin didn't have to say anything because this time Mr Hampton wasn't going to hit him. He just stood there with his little hard eyes shut until Montgomery Ward stopped. Then he said to Uncle Gavin:

"Is that right? We've got to have a federal officer? There's nothing on our books to touch him with? Come on, think. Nothing on the city books even?" Now it was Uncle Gavin who said By God.

"That automobile law," he said. "That Sartoris law," while Mr Hampton stood looking at him. "Hanging right there in that frame on the wall by your own office door? Didn't you ever look at it? That you cant drive an automobile on the streets of Jefferson—"

"What?" Montgomery Ward said.

"Louder," Uncle Gavin said. "Mr Hampton cant hear you."

"But that's just inside the city!" Montgomery Ward said. "Hampton's just County Sheriff; he cant make an arrest on just a city charge."

"So you say," Mr Hampton said; now he did put his hand on Montgomery Ward's shoulder; Uncle Gavin said if he had been Montgomery Ward, he'd just as soon Mr Hampton had slapped him again. "Tell your own lawyer, not ours."

"Wait!" Montgomery Ward said to Uncle Gavin. "You own a car too! So does Hampton!"

"We're doing this alphabetically," Uncle Gavin said. "We've passed the H's. We're in S now, and S-n comes before S-t. Take him on, Hub."

So Montgomery Ward didn't have anywhere to go then, he had run completely out; he just stood there now and Uncle Gavin watched Mr Hampton take his hand off Montgomery Ward and pick up the album of pictures and the envelopes that held the rest of them and carry them to the sink where Montgomery Ward really would develop a film now and then, and tumble them in and then start hunting among the bottles and cans of developer stuff on the shelf above it.

"What are you looking for?" Uncle Gavin said.

"Alcohol—coal oil—anything that'll burn," Mr Hampton said.

"Burn?" Montgomery Ward said. "Hell, man, those things are valuable. Look, I'll make a deal: give them back to me and I'll get to hell out of your damned town and it'll never see me again.—All right," he said. "I've got close to a hundred bucks in my pocket. I'll lay it on the table here and you and Stevens turn your backs and give me ten minutes—"

"Do you want to come back and hit him again?" Uncle Gavin said. "Dont mind me. Besides, he's already suggested we turn our backs so all you'll have to do is just swing your arm." But Mr Hampton just took another bottle down and took out the stopper and smelled. "You cant do that," Uncle Gavin said. "They're evidence."

"All we need is just one," Mr Hampton said.

"That depends," Uncle Gavin said. "Do you just want to convict him, or do you want to exterminate him?" Mr Hampton stopped, the bottle in one hand and the stopper in the other. "You know what Judge Long will do to the man that just owns one of these pictures." Judge Long was the Federal Judge of our district. "Think what he'll do to the man that owns a wheelbarrow full of them."

So Mr Hampton put the bottle back and after a while a deputy came with a suitcase and they put the album and the envelopes into it and locked it and Mr Hampton locked the suitcase in his safe to turn over to Mr Gombault, the U. S. marshal, when he got back to town, and they locked Montgomery Ward up in the county jail for operating an automobile contrary to law in the city of Jefferson, with Montgomery Ward cussing a while then threatening a while then trying again to bribe anybody connected with the jail or the town that would take the money. And we wondered how long it would be before he sent for Mr de Spain because of that connection. Because we knew that the last person on earth he would hope for help from would be his uncle or cousin Flem, who had already got shut of one Snopes through a murder charge so why should he balk at getting rid of another one with just a dirty postcard.

So even Uncle Gavin, that Ratliff said made a kind of religion of never letting Jefferson see that a Snopes had surprised him, didn't expect Mr Flem that afternoon when he walked into the office and laid his new black hat on the corner of the desk and sat there with the joints of his jaws working faint and steady like he was trying to chew without unclamping his teeth. You couldn't see behind Mr Hampton's eyes because they looked at you too hard; you couldn't pass them like you couldn't pass a horse in a lane that wasn't big enough for a horse and a man both but just for the horse. You couldn't see behind Mr Snopes's eyes because they were not really looking at you at all, like a pond of stagnant water is not looking at you. Uncle

Gavin said that was why it took him a minute or two to realise that he and Mr Snopes were looking at exactly the same thing: it just wasn't with the same eye.

"I'm thinking of Jefferson," Mr Snopes said.

"So am I," Uncle Gavin said. "Of that damned Grover Winbush and every other arrested adolescent between fourteen and fifty-eight in half of north Mississippi with twenty-five cents to pay for one look inside that album."

"I forgot about Grover Winbush," Mr Snopes said. "He wont only lose his job but when he does folks will want to know why and this whole business will come out." That was Mr Snopes's trouble. I mean, that was our trouble with Mr Snopes: there wasn't anything to see even when you thought he might be looking at you. "I dont know whether you know it or not. His ma lives out at Whiteleaf. He sends her a dollar's worth of furnish by the mail rider every Saturday morning."

"So to save one is to save both," Uncle Gavin said. "If Grover Winbush's mother is to keep on getting that dollar's worth of fat-back and molasses every Saturday morning, somebody will have to save your cousin, nephew—which is he, anyway?—too."

Like Ratliff said, Mr Snopes probably missed a lot folks said to him behind his back, but he never missed what folks didn't say to him to his face. Anyway, irony and sarcasm was not one of them. Or anyway it wasn't this time. "That's how I figgered it," he said. "But you're a lawyer. Your business is to know how to figger different."

Uncle Gavin didn't miss much of what wasn't quite said to his face either. "You've come to the wrong lawyer," he said. "This case is in federal court. Besides, I couldn't take it anyway; I draw a monthly salary to already be on the other side. Besides," he said (while he was just City Attorney he talked Harvard and Heidelberg. But after that summer he and I spent travelling about the county running for County Attorney, he began to talk like the people he would lean on fences or squat against the walls of country stores with, saying "drug" for "dragged" and "me and you" instead of "you and I" just like they did, even saying figgered just like Mr Snopes just said it), "let's you and me get together on this. I want him to go to the penitentiary."

And that's when Uncle Gavin found out that he and Mr Snopes were looking at exactly the same thing: they were just standing in different places because Mr Snopes said, as quick and calm as Uncle Gavin himself: "So do I." Because Montgomery Ward was his rival just like Wallstreet was, both of them alike in that there just wasn't room in Jefferson for either one of them and Mr Snopes too. Because according to Ratliff, Uncle Gavin was missing it. "So do I," Mr Snopes said. "But not this way. I'm thinking of Jefferson."

"Then it's just too bad for Jefferson," Uncle Gavin said. "He will get Judge Long and when Judge Long sees even one of those pictures, let alone a suitcase full of them, I will almost feel sorry even for Montgomery Ward. Have you forgotten about Wilbur Provine last year?"

Wilbur Provine lived in Frenchman's Bend too. Ratliff said he was really a Snopes; that when Providence realised that Eck Snopes was going to fail his lineage and tradition, it hunted around quick and produced Wilbur Provine to plug the gap. He ran a still in the creek bottom by a spring about a mile and a half from his house, with a path worn smooth as a ribbon and six inches deep from his back door to the spring where he had walked it twice a day for two years until they caught him and took him to federal court before Judge Long, looking as surprised and innocent as if he didn't even know what the word "still" meant while the lawyer questioned him, saying No, he never had any idea there was a still within ten miles, let alone a path leading from his back door to it because he himself hadn't been in that creek bottom in ten years, not even to hunt and fish since he was a Christian and he believed that no Christian should destroy God's creatures, and he had burned out on fish when he was eight years old and hadn't been able to eat it since

Until Judge Long himself asked him how he accounted for that path, and Wilbur blinked at Judge Long once or twice and said he didn't have any idea, unless maybe his wife had worn it toting water from the spring; and Judge Long (he had the right name, he was six and a half feet tall and his nose looked almost a sixth of that) leaning down across the bench with his spectacles at the end of his nose, looking down at Wilbur for a while, until he said:

"I'm going to send you to the penitentiary, not for making

whiskey but for letting your wife carry water a mile and a half from that spring." That was who Montgomery Ward would get when he came up for trial and you would have thought that everybody in Yoknapatawpha County, let alone just Jefferson, had heard the story by now. But you would almost thought Mr Snopes hadn't. Because now even the hinges of his jaws had quit that little faint pumping.

"I heard Judge Long gave him five years," he said. "Maybe them extra four years was for the path."

"Maybe," Uncle Gavin said.

"It was five years, wasn't it?" Mr Snopes said.

"That's right," Uncle Gavin said.

"Send that boy out," Mr Snopes said.

"No," Uncle Gavin said.

Now the hinges of Mr Snopes's jaws were pumping again. "Send him out," he said.

"I'm thinking of Jefferson too," Uncle Gavin said. "You're vice president of Colonel Sartoris's bank. I'm even thinking of you."

"Much obliged," Mr Snopes said. He wasn't looking at anything. He didn't waste any time but he wasn't hurrying either: he just got up and took the new black hat from the desk and put it on and went to the door and opened it and didn't quite stop even then, just kind of changing feet to step around the opening door and said, not to anybody any more than he had ever been looking at anybody: "Good day," and went out and closed the door behind him.

Then I said, "What—" and then stopped, Uncle Gavin and I both watching the door as it opened again, or began to, opening about a foot with no sound beyond it until we saw Ratliff's cheek and one of his eyes, then Ratliff came in, eased in, sidled in, still not making any sound.

"Am I too late, or jest too soon?" he said.

"Neither," Uncle Gavin said. "He stopped, decided not to. Something happened. The pattern went wrong. It started out all regular. You know: this is not just for me, and least of all for my kinsman. Do you know what he said?"

"How can I yet?" Ratliff said. "That's what I'm doing now."

"I said 'You and I should get together. I want him to go to the penitentiary.' And he said, 'So do I.'"

"All right," Ratliff said. "Go on."

" '—not for me, my kinsman,' " Uncle Gavin said. " 'For Jefferson.' So the next step should have been the threat. Only he didn't—"

"Why threat?" Ratliff said.

"The pattern," Uncle Gavin said. "First the soap, then the threat, then the bribe. As Montgomery Ward himself tried it."

"This aint Montgomery Ward," Ratliff said. "If Montgomery Ward had been named Flem, them pictures wouldn't a never seen Jefferson, let alone vice versa. But we dont need to worry about Flem being smarter than Montgomery Ward; most anybody around here is that. What we got to worry about is, who else around here may not be as smart as him too. Then what?"

"He quit," Uncle Gavin said. "He came right up to it. He even asked me to send Chick out. And when I said No, he just picked up his hat and said Much obliged and went out as if he had just stopped in here to borrow a match."

Ratliff blinked at Uncle Gavin. "So he wants Montgomery Ward to go to the penitentiary. Only he dont want him to go under the conditions he's on his way there now. Then he changed his mind."

"Because of Chick," Uncle Gavin said.

"Then he changed his mind," Ratliff said.

"You're right," Uncle Gavin said. "It was because he knew that by refusing to send Chick out I had already refused to be bribed."

"No," Ratliff said. "To Flem Snopes, there aint a man breathing that cant be bought for something; all you need to do is jest to find it. Only, why did he change his mind?"

"All right," Uncle Gavin said. "Why?"

"What was the conversation about jest before he told you to send Chick out?"

"About the penitentiary," Uncle Gavin said. "I just told you."

"It was about Wilbur Provine," I said.

Ratliff looked at me. "Wilbur Provine?"

"His still," I said. "That path and Judge Long."

"Oh," Ratliff said. "Then what?"

"That's all," Uncle Gavin said. "He just said 'Send that boy out' and I said—"

"That wasn't next," I said. "The next was what Mr Snopes said about the five years, that maybe the extra four years was for the path, and you said Maybe and Mr Snopes said again, 'It was five years, wasn't it?' and you said Yes and then he said to send me out."

"All right, all right," Uncle Gavin said. But he was looking at Ratliff. "Well?" he said.

"I dont know neither," Ratliff said. "All I know is, I'm glad I aint Montgomery Ward Snopes."

"Yes," Uncle Gavin said. "When Judge Long sees that suitcase."

"Sho," Ratliff said. "That's jest Uncle Sam. It's his Uncle Flem that Montgomery Ward wants to worry about, even if he dont know it yet. And us too. As long as all he wanted was jest money, at least you knowed which way to guess even if you knowed you couldn't guess first. But this time—" He looked at us, blinking.

"All right," Uncle Gavin said. "How?"

"You mind that story about how the feller found his strayed dog? He jest set down and imagined where he would be if he was that dog and got up and went and got it and brung it home. All right. We're Flem Snopes. We got a chance to get shut of our—what's that old-timey word? unsavory—unsavory nephew into the penitentiary. Only we're vice president of a bank now and we cant afford to have it knowed even a unsavory nephew was running a peep show of French postcards. And the judge that will send him there is the same judge that told Wilbur Provine he was going to Parchman not for making whiskey but for letting his wife tote water a mile and a half." He blinked at Uncle Gavin. "You're right. The question aint 'what' a-tall: it's jest 'how.' And since you wasn't interested in money, and he has got better sense than to offer it to Hub Hampton, we dont jest know what that 'how' is going to be. Unless maybe since he got to be a up-and-coming feller in the Baptist church, he is depending on Providence."

Maybe he was. Anyway, it worked. It was the next morning, about ten oclock; Uncle Gavin and I were just leaving the office to drive up to Wyott's Crossing where they were having some kind of a squabble over a drainage tax suit, when Mr Hampton came in. He was kind of blowing through his teeth, light and easy like he was whistling except that he wasn't making any noise and even less than that of tune. "Morning," he said. "Yesterday morning when we were in that studio and I was hunting through them bottles on that shelf for alcohol or something that would burn."

"All right," Uncle Gavin said.

"How many of them bottles and jugs did I draw the cork or unscrew the cap and smell? You were there. You were watching."

"I thought all of them," Uncle Gavin said. "Why?"

"So did I," Mr Hampton said. "I could be wrong." He looked at Uncle Gavin with his hard little eyes, making that soundless whistling between his teeth.

"You've prepared us," Uncle Gavin said. "Got us into the right state of nervous excitement. Now tell us."

"About six this morning, Jack Crenshaw telephoned me." (Mr Crenshaw was the Revenue field agent that did the moonshine still hunting in our district.) "He told me to come on to that studio as soon as I could. They were already inside, two of them. They had already searched it. Two of them gallon jugs on that shelf that I opened and smelled yesterday that never had nothing but Kodak developer in them, had raw corn whiskey in them this morning, though like I said I could have been wrong and missed them. Not to mention five gallons more of it in a oil can setting behind the heater, that I hadn't got around to smelling yesterday when you stopped me for the reason that I never seen it there when I looked behind the heater yesterday or I wouldn't been smelling at the bottles on that shelf for something to burn paper with. Though, as you say, I could be wrong."

"As you say," Uncle Gavin said.

"You may be right," Mr Hampton said. "After all, I've been having to snuff out moonshine whiskey in this county ever since I first got elected. And since 1919, I have been so in practice that now I dont even need to smell: I just kind of feel it the moment I get where some of it aint supposed to be. Not to mention that five-gallon coal oil can full of it setting where you would have thought I would have fell over it reaching my hand to that shelf."

"All right," Uncle Gavin said. "Go on."

"That's all," Mr Hampton said.

"How did he get in?" Uncle Gavin said.

"He?" Mr Hampton said.

"All right," Uncle Gavin said. "Take 'they' if you like it better."

"I thought of that too," Mr Hampton said. "The key. I said *the* key because even that fool would have more sense than to have a key to that place anywhere except on a string around his neck."

"That one," Uncle Gavin said.

"Yep," Mr Hampton said. "I dropped it into the drawer where I usually keep such, handcuffs and a extra pistol. Anybody could have come in while me and Miss Elma" (she was the office deputy, widow of the sheriff Mr Hampton had succeeded last time) "was out, and taken it."

"Or the pistol either," Uncle Gavin said. "You really should start locking that place, Hub. Some day you'll leave your star in there and come back to find some little boy out on the street arresting people."

"Maybe I should," Mr Hampton said. "All right," he said. "Somebody took that key and planted that whiskey. It could have been any of them—any of the folks that that damned Grover Winbush says was coming from four counties around to sweat over them damn pictures at night."

"Maybe it's lucky you at least had that suitcase locked up. I suppose you've still got that, since Mr Gombault hasn't got back yet?"

"That's right," Mr Hampton said.

"And Jack Crenshaw and his buddy are just interested in whiskey, not photography. Which means you haven't turned that suitcase over to anybody yet."

"That's right," Mr Hampton said.

"Are you going to?" Uncle Gavin said.

"What do you think?" Mr Hampton said.

"That's what I think too," Uncle Gavin said.

"After all, the whiskey is enough," Mr Hampton said. "And even if it aint, all we got to do is show Judge Long just any one of them photographs right before he pronounces sentence. Damn it," he said, "it's Jefferson. We live here. Jefferson's got to come first, even before the pleasure of crucifying that damned—"

"Yes," Uncle Gavin said. "I've heard that sentiment." Then Mr Hampton left. And all we had to do was just to wait, and not long. You never had to wonder about how much Ratliff had heard because you knew in advance he had heard all of it. He closed the door and stood just inside it.

"Why didn't you tell him yesterday about Flem Snopes?" he said.

"Because he let Flem Snopes or whoever it was walk right in his office and steal that key. Hub's already got about all the felonious malfeasance he can afford to compound," Uncle Gavin said. He finished putting the papers into the briefcase and closed it and stood up.

"You leaving?" Ratliff said.

"Yes," Uncle Gavin said. "Wyott's Crossing."

"You aint going to wait for Flem?"

"He wont come back here," Uncle Gavin said. "He wont dare. What he came here yesterday to try to bribe me to do is going to happen anyway without the bribe. But he dont dare come back here to find out. He will have to wait and see like anybody else. He knows that." But still Ratliff didn't move from the door.

"The trouble with us is, we dont never estimate Flem Snopes right. At first we made the mistake of not estimating him a-tall. Then we made the mistake of overestimating him. Now we're fixing to make the mistake of underestimating him again. When you jest want money, all you need to do to satisfy yourself is count it and put it where cant nobody get it, and forget about it. But this-here new thing he has done found out it's nice to have, is different. It's like keeping warm in winter or cool in summer, or peace or being free or contentment. You cant jest count it and lock it up somewhere safe and forget about it until you feel like looking at it again. You got to work at it steady, never to forget about it. It's got to be out in the open, where folks can see it, or there aint no such thing."

"No such thing as what?" Uncle Gavin said.

"This-here new discovery he's jest made," Ratliff said. "Call it civic virtue."

"Why not?" Uncle Gavin said. "Were you going to call it something else?" Ratliff watched Uncle Gavin, curious, intent; it was as if he were waiting for something. "Go on," Uncle Gavin said. "You were saying."

Then it was gone, whatever it had been. "Oh yes," Ratliff said. "He'll be in to see you. He'll have to, to make sho you recognize it

too when you see it. He may kind of hang around until middle of
the afternoon, to kind of give the dust a chance to settle. But he'll
be back then, so a feller can at least see jest how much he missed
heading him off."

So we didn't drive up to Wyott's then, and this time Ratliff was the
one who underestimated. It wasn't a half an hour until we heard his
feet on the stairs and the door opened and he came in. This time he
didn't take off the black hat: he just said "Morning, gentlemen" and
came on to the desk and dropped the key to Montgomery Ward's
studio on it and was going back toward the door when Uncle Gavin
said:

"Much obliged. I'll give it back to the sheriff. You're like me," he
said. "You dont give a damn about truth either. What you are interested in is justice."

"I'm interested in Jefferson," Mr Snopes said, reaching for the
door and opening it. "We got to live here. Morning, gentlemen."

ELEVEN

V. K. Ratliff

*A*nd still he missed it, even set—sitting right there in his own office and actively watching Flem rid Jefferson of Montgomery Ward. And still I couldn't tell him.

TWELVE

CHARLES MALLISON

*W*hatever it was Ratliff thought Mr Snopes wanted, I dont reckon that what Uncle Gavin took up next helped it much either. And this time he didn't even have Miss Melisandre Backus for Mother to blame it on because Miss Melisandre herself was married now, to a man, a stranger, that everybody but Miss Melisandre (we never did know whether her father, sitting all day long out there on that front gallery with a glass of whiskey-and-water in one hand and Horace or Virgil in the other—a combination which Uncle Gavin said would have insulated from the reality of rural north Mississippi harder heads than his—knew or not) knew was a big rich New Orleans bootlegger. In fact she still refused to believe it even when they brought him home with a bullet hole neatly plugged up in the middle of his forehead, in a bullet-proof hearse leading a cortege of Packards and Cadillac limousines that Hollywood itself, let alone Al Capone, wouldn't have been ashamed of.

No, that's wrong. We never did know whether she knew it or not too, even years after he was dead and she had all the money and the two children and the place which in her childhood had been just another Mississippi cotton farm but which he had changed with white fences and weather-vanes in the shape of horses so that it looked like a cross between a Kentucky country club and a Long Island race track, and plenty of friends who felt they owed it to her that she should know where all that money actually came from; and still, as soon as they approached the subject, she would change it— the slender dark girl still, even though she was a millionairess and the mother of two children, whose terrible power was that defenselessness and helplessness which conferred knighthood on any man who came within range, before he had a chance to turn and flee—chang-

504

ing the entire subject as if she had never heard her husband's name
or, in fact, as though he had never lived.

I mean, this time Mother couldn't even say "If he would only
marry Melisandre Backus, she would save him from all this," meaning Linda Snopes this time like she had meant Mrs Flem Snopes
before. But at least she thought about saying it because almost at
once she stopped worrying. "It's all right," she told Father. "It's the
same thing again: dont you remember? He never was really interested in Melisandre. I mean . . . you know: really interested. Books
and flowers. Picking my jonquils and narcissus as fast as they
bloomed, to send out there where that whole two-acre front yard was
full of jonquils, cutting my best roses to take out there and sit in that
hammock reading poetry to her. He was just forming her mind: that's
all he wanted. And Melisandre was only five years younger, where
with this one he is twice her age, practically her grandfather. Of
course that's all it is."

Then Father said: "Heh heh heh. Form is right, only it's on
Gavin's mind, not hers. It would be on mine too if I wasn't already
married and scared to look. Did you ever take a look at her? You're
human even if you are a woman." Yes, I could remember a heap of
times when Father had been born too soon, before they thought of
wolf whistles.

"Stop it," Mother said.

"But after all," Father said, "maybe Gavin should be saved from
those sixteen-year-old clutches. Suppose you speak to him; tell him
I am willing to make a sacrifice of myself on the family altar—"

"Stop it! Stop it!" Mother said. "Cant you at least be funny?"

"I'm worse than that, I'm serious," Father said. "They were at a
table in Christian's yesterday afternoon. Gavin just had a saucer of ice
cream but she was eating something in a dish that must have set him
back twenty or thirty cents. So maybe Gavin knows what he's doing
after all; she's got some looks of her own, but she still aint quite up
with her mother: you know—" using both hands to make a kind of
undulating hourglass shape in the air in front of him while Mother
stood watching him like a snake. "Maybe he's concentrating on just
forming her form first you might say, without bothering too much
yet about her mind. And who knows? Maybe some day she'll even

look at him like she was looking at that banana split or whatever it was when Skeets McGowan set it down in front of her."

But by that time Mother was gone. And this time she sure needed somebody like Miss Melisandre, with all her friends (all Jefferson for that matter) on the watch to tell her whenever Uncle Gavin and Linda stopped in Christian's drugstore after school while Linda ate another banana split or ice cream soda, with the last book of poetry Uncle Gavin had ordered for her lying in the melted ice cream or spilled Coca-Cola on the marble table top. Because I reckon Jefferson was too small for a thirty-five-year-old bachelor, even a Harvard M.A. and a Ph.D. from Heidelberg and his hair already beginning to turn white even at just twenty-five, to eat ice cream and read poetry with a sixteen-year-old high-school girl. Though if it had to happen, maybe thirty-five was the best age for a bachelor to buy ice cream and poetry for a sixteen-year-old girl. I told Mother that. She didn't sound like a snake because snakes cant talk. But if dentist's drills could talk she would have sounded just like one.

"There's no best or safe age for a bachelor anywhere between three and eighty to buy ice cream for a sixteen-year-old girl," she said. "Forming her mind," she said. But she sounded just like cream when she talked to Uncle Gavin. No: she didn't sound like anything because she didn't say anything. She waited for him to begin it. No: she just waited because she knew he would have to begin it. Because Jefferson was that small. No, I mean Uncle Gavin had lived in Jefferson or in little towns all his life, so he not only knew what Jefferson would be saying about him and Linda Snopes and those banana splits and ice-cream sodas and books of poetry by now, but that Mother had too many good friends to ever miss hearing about it.

So she just waited. It was Saturday. Uncle Gavin walked twice in and out of the office (we still called it that because Grandfather had, except when Mother could hear it. Though after a while even she stopped trying to call it the library) where Mother was sitting at the desk adding up something, maybe the laundry; he walked in and out twice and she never moved. Then he said:

"I was thinking—" Because they were like that. I mean, I thought the reason they were like that was because they were twins. I mean,

I assumed that because I didn't know any other twins to measure them against. She didn't even stop adding.

"Of course," she said. "Why not tomorrow?" So he could have gone out then, since obviously both of them knew what the other was talking about. But he said:

"Thank you." Then he said to me: "Aint Aleck Sander waiting for you outside?"

"Fiddlesticks," Mother said. "Anything he will learn about sixteen-year-old girls from you will probably be a good deal more innocent than what he will learn some day from sixteen-year-old girls. Shall I telephone her mother and ask her to let her come for dinner tomorrow, or do you want to?"

"Thank you," Uncle Gavin said. "Do you want me to tell you about it?"

"Do you want to?" Mother said.

"Maybe I'd better," Uncle Gavin said.

"Do you have to?" Mother said. This time Uncle Gavin didn't say anything Then Mother said: "All right. We're listening." Again Uncle Gavin didn't say anything. But now he was Uncle Gavin again. I mean, until now he sounded a good deal like I sounded sometimes. But now he stood looking at the back of Mother's head, with his shock of white hair that always needed cutting and the stained bitt of the corncob pipe sticking out of his breast pocket and the eyes and the face that you never did quite know what they were going to say next except that when you heard it you realised it was always true, only a little cranksided that nobody else would have said it quite that way.

"Well, well," he said, "if that's what a mind with no more aptitude for gossip and dirt than yours is inventing and thinking, just imagine what the rest of Jefferson, the experts, have made of it by now. By Cicero, it makes me feel young already; when I go to town this morning I believe I will buy myself a red necktie." He looked at the back of Mother's head. "Thank you, Maggie," he said. "It will need all of us of good will. To save Jefferson from Snopeses is a crisis, an emergency, a duty. To save a Snopes from Snopeses is a privilege, an honor, a pride."

"Especially a sixteen-year-old female one," Mother said.

"Yes," Uncle Gavin said. "Do you deny it?"

"Have I tried to?" Mother said.

"Yes, you have tried." He moved quick and put his hand on the top of her head, still talking. "And bless you for it. Tried always to deny that damned female instinct for uxorious and rigid respectability which is the backbone of any culture not yet decadent, which remains strong and undecadent only so long as it still produces an incorrigible unreconstructible with the temerity to assail and affront and deny it—like you—" and for a second both of us thought he was going to bend down and kiss her; maybe all three of us thought it. Then he didn't, or anyway Mother said:

"Stop it. Let me alone. Make up your mind: do you want me to telephone her, or will you do it?"

"I'll do it," he said. He looked at me. "Two red ties: one for you. I wish you were sixteen too. What she needs is a beau."

"Then if by being sixteen I'd have to be her beau, I'm glad I'm not sixteen," I said. "She's already got a beau. Matt Levitt. He won the Golden Gloves up in Ohio or somewhere last year. He acts like he can still use them. Would like to, too. No, much obliged," I said.

"What's that?" Mother said.

"Nothing," Uncle Gavin said.

"You never saw him box then," I said. "Or you wouldn't call him nothing. I saw him once. With Preacher Birdsong."

"And just which of your sporting friends is Preacher Birdsong?" Mother said.

"He aint sporting," I said. "He lives out in the country. He learned to box in France in the war. He and Matt Levitt—"

"Let me," Uncle Gavin said. "He—"

"Which he?" Mother said. "Your rival?"

"—is from Ohio," Uncle Gavin said. "He graduated from that new Ford mechanics' school and the company sent him here to be a mechanic in the agency garage—"

"He's the one that owns that yellow cut-down racer," I said.

"And Linda rides in it?" Mother said.

"—and since Jefferson is not that large and he has two eyes," Uncle Gavin said, "sooner or later he saw Linda Snopes, probably somewhere between her home and the school house; being male and about twenty-one, he naturally lost no time in making her acquaintance; the Golden Gloves reputation which he either really brought with him or invented somewhere en route has apparently eliminated what rivals he might have expected—"

"Except you," Mother said.

"That's all," Uncle Gavin said.

"Except you," Mother said.

"He's maybe five years her senior," Uncle Gavin said. "I'm twice her age."

"Except you," Mother said. "I dont think you will live long enough to ever be twice any woman's age, I dont care what it is."

"All right," Uncle Gavin said. "What was it I just said? To save Jefferson from a Snopes is a duty; to save a Snopes from a Snopes is a privilege."

"An honor, you said," Mother said. "A pride."

"All right," Uncle Gavin said. "A joy then. Are you pleased now?"

That was all, then. After a while Father came home but Mother didn't have much to tell him he didn't already know, so there wasn't anything for him to do except to keep on needing the wolf whistle that hadn't been invented yet; not until the next day after dinner in fact.

She arrived a little after twelve, just about when she could have got here after church if she had been to church. Which maybe she had, since she was wearing a hat. Or maybe it was her mother who made her wear the hat on account of Mother, coming up the street from the corner, running. Then I saw that the hat was a little awry on her head, as if something had pulled or jerked at it or it had caught on something in passing, and that she was holding one shoulder with the other hand. Then I saw that her face was mad. It was scared too, but right now it was mostly just mad as she turned in the gate, still holding her shoulder but not running now, just walking fast and hard, the mad look beginning to give way to the scared one. Then they both froze into something completely different because then the car passed, coming up fast from the corner—Matt Levitt's racer because there were other stripped-down racers around now but his was the only one with that big double-barrel brass horn on the hood that played two notes when he pressed the button, going past fast; and

suddenly it was like I had smelled something, caught a whiff of something for a second that even if I located it again I still wouldn't know
whether I had ever smelled it before or not; the racer going on and
Linda still walking rigid and fast with her hat on a little crooked and
still holding her shoulder and still breathing a little fast even if what
was on her face now was mostly being scared, on to the gallery where
Mother and Uncle Gavin were waiting.

"Good morning, Linda," Mother said. "You've torn your sleeve."

"It caught on a nail," Linda said.

"I can see," Mother said. "Come on up to my room and slip it off
and I'll tack it back for you."

"It's all right," Linda said. "If you've just got a pin."

"Then you take the needle and do it yourself while I see about
dinner," Mother said. "You can sew, cant you?"

"Yessum," Linda said. So they went up to Mother's room and
Uncle Gavin and I went to the office so Father could say to Uncle
Gavin:

"Somebody been mauling at her before she could even get here?
What's the matter, boy? Where's your spear and sword? Where's
your white horse?" Because Matt didn't blow the two-toned horn
when he passed that time so none of us knew yet what Linda was listening for, sitting at the dinner table with the shoulder of her dress
sewed back all right but looking like somebody about ten years old
had done it and her face still looking rigid and scared. Because we
didn't realise it then. I mean, that she was having to do so many
things at once: having to look like she was enjoying her dinner and
having to remember her manners in a strange house and with folks
that she didn't have any particular reason to think were going to like
her, and still having to wonder what Matt Levitt would do next without letting anybody know that's what was mainly on her mind. I
mean, having to expect what was going to happen next and then,
even while it was happening having to look like she was eating and
saying Yessum and Nome to what Mother was saying, and that cut-
down racer going past in the street again with that two-toned horn
blowing this time, blowing all the way past the house, and Father
suddenly jerking his head up and making a loud snuffing noise, saying, "What's that I smell?"

"Smell?" Mother said. "Smell what?"

"That," Father said. "Something we haven't smelled around here in . . . how long was it, Gavin?" Because I knew now what Father meant, even if I wasn't born then and Cousin Gowan just told me. And Mother knew too. I mean, she remembered, since she had heard the other one when it was Mr de Spain's cut-out. I mean, even if she didn't know enough to connect that two-toned horn with Matt Levitt, all she had to do was look at Linda and Uncle Gavin. Or maybe just Uncle Gavin's face was enough, which is what you get for being twins with anybody. Because she said,

"Charley," and Father said:

"Maybe Miss Snopes will excuse me this time." He was talking at Linda now. "You see, whenever we have a pretty girl to eat with us, the prettier she is, the harder I try to make jokes so they will want to come back again. This time I just tried too hard. So if Miss Snopes will forgive me for trying too hard to be funny, I'll forgive her for being too pretty."

"Good boy," Uncle Gavin said. "Even if that one wasn't on tip-toe, at least it didn't wear spikes like the joke did. Let's go out to the gallery where it's cool, Maggie."

"Let's," Mother said. Then we were all standing there in the hall, looking at Linda. It wasn't just being scared in her face now, of being a sixteen-year-old girl for the first time in the home of people that probably had already decided not to approve of her. I didn't know what it was. But Mother did, maybe because it was Mother she was looking at it with.

"I think it will be cooler in the parlor," Mother said. "Let's go there." But it was too late. We could hear the horn, not missing a note: da Da da Da da Da getting louder and louder then going past the house still not missing a note as it faded on, and Linda staring at Mother for just another second or two with the desperation. Because it—the desperation—went too; maybe it was something like despair for a moment, but then that was gone too and her face was just rigid again.

"I've got to go," she said. "I . . . excuse me, I've got. . . ." Then at least she kind of got herself together. "Thank you for my dinner, Mrs Mallison," she said. "Thank you for my dinner, Mr Mallison. Thank

you for my dinner, Mr Gavin," already moving toward the table
where she had put the hat and her purse. But then I hadn't expected
her to thank me for it.

"Let Gavin drive you home," Mother said. "Gavin—"

"No no," she said. "I dont—he dont—" Then she was gone, out
the front door and down the walk toward the gate, almost running
again, then through the gate and then she was running, desperate
and calm, not looking back. Then she was gone.

"By Cicero, Gavin," Father said. "You're losing ground. Last time
you at least picked out a Spanish-American War hero with an E.M.F.
sportster. Now the best you can do is a Golden Gloves amateur with
a homemade racer. Watch yourself, bud, or next time you'll have a
boy scout defying you to mortal combat with a bicycle."

"What?" Mother said.

"What would you do," Father said, "if you were a twenty-one-
year-old garage mechanic who had to work until six p.m., and a
white-headed old grandfather of a libertine was waylaying your girl
on her way home from school every afternoon and tolling her into
soda dens and plying her with ice cream? Because how could he
know that all Gavin wants is just to form her mind?"

Only it wasn't every afternoon any more. It wasn't any afternoon
at all. I dont know what happened, how it was done: whether she sent
word to Uncle Gavin not to try to meet her after school or whether
she came and went the back way where he wouldn't see her, or
whether maybe she stopped going to school at all for a while.
Because she was in high school and I was in grammar school so there
was no reason for me to know whether she was still going to school
or not.

Or whether she was still in Jefferson, for that matter. Because now
and then I would see Matt Levitt in his racer after the garage closed
in the afternoon, when Linda used to be with him, and now and then
at night going to and from the picture show. But not any more now.
He would be alone in the racer, or with another boy or man. But as
far as I knew, Matt never saw her any more than Uncle Gavin did.

And you couldn't tell anything from Uncle Gavin. It used to be
that on the way home from school I would see him and Linda inside
Christian's drugstore eating ice cream and when he or they saw me

he would beckon me in and we would all have ice cream. But that—
the fact that there was no longer any reason to look in Christian's
when I passed—was the only difference in him. Then one day—it
was Friday—he was sitting at the table inside waiting and watching
to beckon me inside, and even though there was no second dish on
the table I thought that Linda had probably just stepped away for a
moment, maybe to the perfume counter or the magazine rack, and
even when I was inside and he said, "I'm having peach. What do you
want?" I still expected Linda to step out from behind whatever for
the moment concealed her.

"Strawberry," I said. On the table was the last book—it was John
Donne—he had ordered for her.

"It will cost the same dime to mail it to her here in Jefferson that
it would cost if she were in Memphis," he said. "Suppose I stand the
ice cream and give you the dime and you take it by her house on the
way home."

"All right," I said. When Mr Snopes first came to Jefferson he
rented the house. Then he must have bought it because since he
became vice president of the bank they had begun to fix it up. It was
painted now and Mrs Snopes I reckon had had the wistaria arbor in
the side yard fixed up and when I came through the gate Linda called
me and I saw the hammock under the arbor. The wistaria was still
in bloom and I remember how she looked with her black hair under
it because her eyes were kind of the color of wistaria and her dress
almost exactly was: lying in the hammock reading and I thought
*Uncle Gavin didn't need to send this book because she hasn't finished the
other one yet.* Then I saw the rest of her school books on the ground
beneath the hammock and that the one she was reading was geometry and I wondered if knowing she would rather study geometry than
be out with him would make Matt Levitt feel much better than having her eat ice cream with Uncle Gavin.

So I gave her the book and went on home. That was Friday. The
next day, Saturday, I went to the baseball game and then I came back
to the office to walk home with Uncle Gavin. We heard the feet
coming up the outside stairs, more than two of them, making a kind
of scuffling sound and we could even hear hard breathing and something like whispering, then the door kind of banged open and Matt

Levitt came in, quick and fast, holding something clamped under his arm, and shoved the door back shut against whoever was trying to follow him inside, holding the door shut with his braced knee until he fumbled at the knob until he found how to shoot the bolt and lock it. Then he turned. He was good-looking. He didn't have a humorous or happy look, he had what Ratliff called a merry look, the merry look of a fellow that hadn't heard yet that they had invented doubt. But he didn't even look merry now and he took the book—it was the John Donne I had taken to Linda yesterday—and kind of shot it onto the desk so that the ripped and torn pages came scuttering and scattering out across the desk and some of them even on down to the floor.

"How do you like that?" Matt said, coming on around the desk where Uncle Gavin had stood up. "Dont you want to put up your dukes?" he said. "But that's right, you aint much of a fighter, are you? But that's O.K.; I aint going to hurt you much anyway: just mark you up a little to freshen up your memory." He didn't, he didn't seem to hit hard, his fists not travelling more than four or five inches it looked like, so that it didn't even look like they were drawing blood from Uncle Gavin's lips and nose but just instead wiping the blood onto them; two or maybe three blows before I could seem to move and grab up Grandfather's heavy walking stick where it still stayed in the umbrella stand behind the door and raise it to swing at the back of Matt's head as hard as I could.

"You, Chick!" Uncle Gavin said. "Stop! Hold it!" Though even with that, I wouldn't have thought Matt could have moved that fast. Maybe it was the Golden Gloves that did it. Anyway he turned and caught the stick and jerked it away from me almost before I knew it and naturally I thought he was going to hit me or Uncle Gavin or maybe both of us with it so I had already crouched to dive at his legs when he dropped the point of the stick like a bayoneted rifle, the point touching my chest just below the throat as if he were not holding me up but had really picked me up with the stick like you would a rag or a scrap of paper.

"Tough luck, kid," he said. "Nice going almost; too bad your uncle telegraphed it for you," and threw the stick into the corner and stepped around me toward the door, which was the first time I reckon that any of us realised that whoever it was he had locked out was still banging on it, and shot the bolt back and opened it, then stepped back himself as Linda came in, blazing; yes, that's exactly the word for it: blazing: and without even looking at Uncle Gavin or me, whirled onto her tiptoes and slapped Matt twice, first with her left hand and then the right, panting and crying at the same time:

"You fool! You ox! You clumsy ignorant ox! You clumsy ignorant stupid son of a bitch!" Which was the first time I ever heard a sixteen-year-old girl say that. No: the first time I ever heard any woman say that, standing there facing Matt and crying hard now, like she was too mad to even know what to do next, whether to slap him again or curse him again, until Uncle Gavin came around the desk and touched her and said,

"Stop it. Stop it now," and she turned and grabbed him, her face against his shirt where he had bled onto it, still crying hard, saying,

"Mister Gavin, Mister Gavin, Mister Gavin."

"Open the door, Chick," Uncle Gavin said. I opened it. "Get out of here, boy," Uncle Gavin said to Matt. "Go on." Then Matt was gone. I started to close the door. "You too," Uncle Gavin said.

"Sir?" I said.

"You get out too," Uncle Gavin said, still holding Linda where she was shaking and crying against him, his nose bleeding onto her too now.

THIRTEEN

GAVIN STEVENS

*G*o on," I said. "You get out too." So he did, and I stood there hold-ing her. Or rather, she was gripping me, quite hard, shuddering and gasping, crying quite hard now, burrowing her face into my shirt so that I could feel my shirt front getting wet. Which was what Ratliff would have called tit for tat, since what Victorians would have called the claret from my nose had already stained the shoulder of her dress. So I could free one hand long enough to reach around and over her other shoulder to the handkerchief in my breast pocket and do a little emergency work with it until I could separate us long enough to reach the cold-water tap.

"Stop it," I said. "Stop it now." But she only cried the harder, clutching me, saying,

"Mister Gavin. Mister Gavin. Oh, Mister Gavin."

"Linda," I said. "Can you hear me?" She didn't answer, just clutch-ing me; I could feel her nodding her head against my chest. "Do you want to marry me?" I said.

"Yes!" she said. "Yes! All right! All right!"

This time I got one hand under her chin and lifted her face by force until she would have to look at me. Ratliff had told me that McCarron's eyes were gray, probably the same hard gray as Hub Hampton's. Hers were not gray at all. They were darkest hyacinth, what I have always imagined that Homer's hyacinthine sea must have had to look like.

"Listen to me," I said. "Do you want to get married?" Yes, they dont need minds at all, except for conversation, social intercourse. And I have known some who had charm and tact without minds even then. Because when they deal with men, with human beings, all they need is the instinct, the instinct, the intuition before it became bat-

516

tered and dulled, the infinite capacity for devotion untroubled and unconfused by cold moralities and colder facts.

"You mean I dont have to?" she said.

"Of course not," I said. "Never if you like."

"I dont want to marry anybody!" she said, cried; she was clinging to me again, her face buried again in the damp mixture of blood and tears which seemed now to compose the front of my shirt and tie. "Not anybody!" she said. "You're all I have, all I can trust. I love you! I love you!"

FOURTEEN

CHARLES MALLISON

*W*hen he got home, his face was clean. But his nose and his lip still showed, and there wasn't anything he could have done about his shirt and tie. Except he could have bought new ones, since on Saturday the stores were still open. But he didn't. Maybe even that wouldn't have made any difference with Mother; maybe that's one of the other things you have to accept in being a twin. And yes sir, if dentist's drills could talk, that's exactly what Mother would have sounded like after she got done laughing and crying both and saying Damn you, Gavin, damn you, damn you, and Uncle Gavin had gone upstairs to put on a clean shirt and tie for supper.

"Forming her mind," Mother said.

It was like he could stand just anything except getting knocked down or getting his nose bloodied. Like if Mr de Spain hadn't knocked him down in the alley behind that Christmas dance, he could have got over Mrs Snopes without having to form Linda's mind. And like if Matt Levitt hadn't come into the office that afternoon and bloodied his nose again, he could have stopped there with Linda's mind without having to do any more to it.

So he didn't stop because he couldn't. But at least he got rid of Matt Levitt. That was in the spring. It was her last year in high school; she would graduate in May and any school afternoon I could see her walking along the street from school with a few books under her arm. But if any of them was poetry now I didn't know it, because when she came to Christian's drugstore now she wouldn't even look toward the door, just walking on past with her face straight in front and her head up a little like the pointer just a step or two from freezing on the game; walking on like she saw people, saw Jefferson, saw

518

the Square all right because at the moment, at any moment she had to walk on and among and through something and it might as well be Jefferson and Jefferson people and the Jefferson square as anything else, but that was all.

Because Uncle Gavin wasn't there somewhere around like an accident any more now. But then, if Uncle Gavin wasn't sitting on the opposite side of that marble-topped table in Christian's watching her eating something out of a tall glass that cost every bit of fifteen or twenty cents, Matt Levitt wasn't there either. Him and his cut-down racer both because the racer was empty now except for Matt himself after the garage closed on week days, creeping along the streets and across the Square in low gear, paralleling but a little behind where she would be walking to the picture show now with another girl or maybe two or three of them, her head still high and not once looking at him while the racer crept along at her elbow almost, the cut-out going chuckle-chuckle-chuckle, right up to the picture show and the two or three or four girls had gone into it. Then the racer would dash off at full speed around the block, to come rushing back with the cut-out as loud as he could make it, up the alley beside the picture show and then across in front of it and around the block and up the alley again, this time with Otis Harker, who had succeeded Grover Cleveland Winbush as night marshal after Grover Cleveland retired after what Ratliff called his eye trouble, waiting at the corner yelling at Matt at the same time he was jumping far enough back not to be run over.

And on Sunday through the Square, the cut-out going full blast and Mr Buck Connors, the day marshal, hollering after him. And now he—Matt—had a girl with him, a country girl he had found somewhere, the racer rushing and roaring through the back streets into the last one, to rush slow and loud past Linda's house, as if the sole single symbol of frustrated love or anyway desire or maybe just frustration possible in Jefferson was an automobile cut-out; the sole single manifestation which love or anyway desire was capable of assuming in Jefferson, was rushing slow past the specific house with the cut-out wide open, so that he or she would have to know who was passing no matter how hard they worked at not looking out the window.

Though by that time Mr Connors had sent for the sheriff himself. He—Mr Connors—said his first idea was to wake up Otis Harker to come back to town and help him but when Otis heard that what Mr Connors wanted was to stop that racer, Otis wouldn't even get out of bed. Later, afterward, somebody asked Matt if he would have run over Mr Hampton too and Matt said—he was crying then, he was so mad—"Hit him? Hub Hampton? Have all them god-damn guts splashed over my paint job?" Though by then even Mr Hampton wasn't needed for the cut-out because Matt went right on out of town, maybe taking the girl back home; anyway about midnight that night they telephoned in for Mr Hampton to send somebody out to Caledonia where Matt had had a bad fight with Anse McCallum, one of Mr Buddy McCallum's boys, until Anse snatched up a fence rail or something and would have killed Matt except that folks caught and held them both while they telephoned for the sheriff and brought them both in to town and locked them in the jail and the next morning Mr Buddy McCallum came in on his cork leg and paid them both out and took them down to the lot behind I.O. Snopes's mule barn and told Anse:

"All right. If you cant be licked fair without picking up a fence rail, I'm going to take my leg off and whip you with it myself."

So they fought again, without the fence rail this time, with Mr Buddy and a few more men watching them now, and Anse still wasn't as good as Matt's Golden Gloves but he never quit until at last Mr Buddy himself said, "All right. That's enough," and told Anse to wash his face at the trough and then go and get in the car and then said to Matt: "And I reckon the time has come for you to be moving on too." Except that wasn't necessary now either; the garage said Matt was already fired and Matt said,

"Fired, hell. I quit. Tell that bastard to come down here and say that to my face." And Mr Hampton was there too by then, tall, with his big belly and his little hard eyes looking down at Matt. "Where the hell is my car?" Matt said.

"It's at my house," Mr Hampton said. "I had it brought in this morning."

"Well well," Matt said. "Too bad, aint it? McCallum came in and sprung me before you had time to sell it and stick the money in your pocket, huh? What are you going to say when I walk over there and get in it and start the engine?"

"Nothing, son," Mr Hampton said. "Whenever you want to leave."

"Which is right now," Matt said. "And when I leave your . . . .ing town, my foot'll be right down to the floor board on that cut-out too. And you can stick that too, but not in your pocket. What do you think of that?"

"Nothing, son," Mr Hampton said. "I'll make a trade with you. Run that cut-out wide open all the way to the county line and then ten feet past it, and I wont let anybody bother you if you'll promise never to cross it again."

And that was all. That was Monday, trade day; it was like the whole county was there, had come to town just to stand quiet around the Square and watch Matt cross it for the last time, the paper suitcase he had come to Jefferson with on the seat by him and the cut-out clattering and popping; nobody waving good-bye to him and Matt not looking at any of us: just that quiet and silent suspension for the little gaudy car to rush slowly and loudly through, blatant and noisy and defiant yet at the same time looking as ephemeral and innocent and fragile as a child's toy, a birthday favor, so that looking at it you knew it would probably never get as far as Memphis, let alone Ohio; on across the Square and into the street which would become the Memphis highway at the edge of town, the sound of the cut-out banging and clattering and echoing between the walls, magnified a thousand times now beyond the mere size and bulk of the frail little machine which produced it; and we—some of us—thinking how surely now he would rush slow and roaring for the last time at least past Linda Snopes's house. But he didn't. He just went on, the little car going faster and faster up the broad street empty too for the moment as if it too had vacated itself for his passing, on past where the last houses of town would give way to country, the vernal space of woods and fields where even the defiant uproar of the cut-out would become puny and fade and be at last absorbed.

So that was what Father called—said to Uncle Gavin—one down. And now it was May and already everybody knew that Linda Snopes was going to be the year's number-one student, the class's valedictorian; Uncle Gavin slowed us as we approached Wildermark's and nudged us in to the window, saying, "That one. Just behind the green one."

It was a lady's fitted travelling case.

"That's for travelling," Mother said.

"All right," Uncle Gavin said.

"For travelling," Mother said. "For going away."

"Yes," Uncle Gavin said. "She's got to get away from here. Get out of Jefferson."

"What's wrong with Jefferson?" Mother said. The three of us stood there. I could see our three reflections in the plate glass, standing there looking at the fitted feminine case. She didn't talk low or loud: just quiet. "All right," she said. "What's wrong with Linda then?"

Uncle Gavin didn't either. "I dont like waste," he said. "Everybody should have his chance not to waste."

"Or his chance to the right not to waste a young girl?" Mother said.

"All right," Uncle Gavin said. "I want her to be happy. Everybody should have the chance to be happy."

"Which she cant possibly do of course just standing still in Jefferson," Mother said.

"All right," Uncle Gavin said. They were not looking at one another. It was like they were not even talking to one another but simply at the two empty reflections in the plate glass, like when you put the written idea into the anonymous and even interchangeable empty envelope, or maybe into the sealed empty bottle to be cast into the sea, or maybe two written thoughts sealed forever at the same moment into two bottles and cast into the sea to float and drift with the tides and the currents on to the cooling world's end itself, still immune, still intact and inviolate, still ideas and still true and even still facts whether any eye ever saw them again or any other idea ever responded and sprang to them, to be elated or validated or grieved.

"The chance and duty and right to see that everybody is happy, whether they deserve it or not or even want it or not," Mother said.

"All right," Uncle Gavin said. "Sorry I bothered you. Come on. Let's go home. Mrs Rouncewell can send her a dozen sunflowers."

"Why not?" Mother said, taking his arm, already turning him, our three reflections turning in the plate glass, back toward the entrance and into the store, Mother in front now across to the luggage department.

"I think the blue one will suit her coloring, match her eyes," Mother said. "It's for Linda Snopes—her graduation," Mother told Miss Eunice Gant, the clerk.

"How nice," Miss Eunice said. "Is Linda going on a trip?"

"Oh yes," Mother said. "Very likely. At least probably to one of the Eastern girls' schools next year perhaps. Or so I heard."

"How nice," Miss Eunice said. "I always say that every young boy and girl should go away from home for at least one year of school in order to learn how the other half lives."

"How true," Mother said. "Until you do go and see, all you do is hope. Until you actually see for yourself, you never do give up and settle down, do you?"

"Maggie," Uncle Gavin said.

"Give up?" Miss Eunice said. "Give up hope? Young people should never give up hope."

"Of course not," Mother said. "They dont have to. All they have to do is stay young, no matter how long it takes."

"Maggie," Uncle Gavin said.

"Oh," Mother said, "you want to pay cash for it instead of charge? All right; I'm sure Mr Wildermark wont mind." So Uncle Gavin took two twenty-dollar bills from his wallet and took out one of his cards and gave it to Mother.

"Thank you," she said. "But Miss Eunice probably has a big one, that will hold all four names." So Miss Eunice gave her the big card and Mother held out her hand until Uncle Gavin uncapped his pen and gave it to her and we watched her write in the big sprawly hand that still looked like somebody thirteen years old in the ninth grade:

MR AND MRS CHARLES MALLISON
CHARLES MALLISON, JR
MR GAVIN STEVENS

and capped the pen and handed it back to Uncle Gavin and took the card between the thumb and finger of one hand and waved it dry and gave it to Miss Eunice.

"I'll send it out tonight," Miss Eunice said. "Even if the graduation isn't until next week. It's such a handsome gift, why shouldn't Linda have that much more time to enjoy it?"

"Yes," Mother said. "Why shouldn't she?" Then we were outside again, our three reflections jumbled into one walking now across the plate glass; Mother had Uncle Gavin's arm again.

"All four of our names," Uncle Gavin said. "At least her father wont know a white-headed bachelor sent his seventeen-year-old daughter a fitted travelling case."

"Yes," Mother said. "One of them wont know it."

FIFTEEN

GAVIN STEVENS

$\mathcal{T}$he difficulty was, how to tell her, explain to her. I mean, why. Not the deed, the act itself, but the reason for it, the *why* behind it—say point blank to her over one of the monstrous synthetic paradoxes which were her passion or anyway choice in Christian's drugstore, or perhaps out on the street itself: "We wont meet any more from now on because after Jefferson assimilates all the details of how your boyfriend tracked you down in my office and bloodied my nose one Saturday, and eight days later, having spent his last night in Jefferson in the county jail, shook our dust forever from his feet with the turbulent uproar of his racer's cut-out—after that, for you to be seen still meeting me in ice-cream dens will completely destroy what little was left of your good name."

You see? That was it: the very words *reputation* and *good name*. Merely to say them, speak them aloud, give their existence vocal recognition, would irrevocably soil and besmirch them, would destroy the immunity of the very things they represented, leaving them not just vulnerable but already doomed; from the inviolable and proud integrity of principles they would become, reduce to, the ephemeral and already doomed and damned fragility of human conditions; innocence and virginity become symbol and postulant of loss and grief, evermore to be mourned, existing only in the past tense *was* and *now is not, no more no more*.

That was the problem. Because the act, the deed itself, was simple enough. Luckily the affair happened late on a Saturday afternoon, which would give my face thirty-six hours anyway before it would have to make a public appearance. (It wouldn't have needed that long except for the ring he wore—a thing not quite as large as a brass knuckle and not really noticeably unlike gold if you didn't get too close probably, of a tiger's head gripping between its jaws what had been—advisedly—a ruby; advisedly because the fact that the stone was missing at the moment was a loss only to my lip.)

Besides, the drugstore meetings were not even a weekly affair, let alone daily, so even a whole week could pass before (1) it would occur to someone that we had not met in over a week, who (2) would immediately assume that we had something to conceal was why we had not met in over a week, and (3) the fact that we had met again after waiting over a week only proved it.

By which time I was even able to shave past my cut lip. So it was very simple; simple indeed in fact, and I the simple one. I had planned it like this: the carefully timed accident which would bring me out the drugstore door, the (say) tin of pipe tobacco still in plain sight on its way to the pocket, at the exact moment when she would pass on her way to school: "Good morning, Linda—" already stepping on past her and then already pausing: "I have another book for you. Meet me here after school this afternoon and we'll have a Coke over it."

Which would be all necessary. Because I was the simple one, to whom it had never once occurred that the blow of that ruby-vacant reasonably almost-gold tiger's head might have marked her too even if it didn't leave a visible cut; that innocence is innocent not because it rejects but because it accepts; is innocent not because it is impervious and invulnerable to everything, but because it is capable of accepting anything and still remaining innocent; innocent because it foreknows all and therefore doesn't have to fear and be afraid; the tin of tobacco now in my coat pocket because by this time even it had become noticeable, the last book-burdened stragglers now trotting toward the sound of the first strokes of the school bell and still she had not passed; obviously I had missed her somehow: either taken my post not soon enough or she had taken another route to school or perhaps would not leave home for school at all today, for whatever reasons no part of which were the middle-aged bachelor's pandering her to Jonson and Herrick and Thomas Campion; crossing—I— the now-unchildrened street at last, mounting the outside stairs since tomorrow was always tomorrow; indeed, I could even use the tobacco tin again, provided I didn't break the blue stamp for verity, and opened the screen door and entered the office.

She was sitting neither in the revolving chair behind the desk nor in the leather client's one before it but in a straight hard armless one against the bookcase as though she had fled, been driven until the wall stopped her, and turned then, her back against it, not quite sitting in the chair nor quite huddled in it because although her legs, knees were close and rigid and her hands were clasped tight in her lap, her head was still up watching the door and then me with the eyes the McCarron boy had marked her with which at a distance looked as black as her hair until you saw they were that blue so dark as to be almost violet.

"I thought . . ." she said. "They—somebody said Matt quit his job and left—went yesterday. I thought you might . . ."

"Of course," I said. "I always want to see you," stopping myself in time from *I've been waiting over there on the corner until the last bell rang, for you to pass* though this is what I really stopped from: *Get up. Get out of here quick. Why did you come here anyway? Dont you see this is the very thing I have been lying awake at night with ever since Saturday?* So I merely said that I had bought the can of tobacco which I must now find someone capable or anyway willing to smoke, to give it to, to create the chance to say: "I have another book for you. I forgot to bring it this morning, but I'll bring it at noon. I'll wait for you at Christian's after school and stand you a soda too. Now you'll have to hurry; you're already late."

I had not even released the screen door and so had only to open it again, having also in that time in which she crossed the room, space to discard a thousand frantic indecisions: to remain concealed in the office as though I had not been there at all this morning, and let her leave alone; to follow to the top of the stairs and see her down them, avuncular and fond; to walk her to the school itself and wait to see her through the actual door: the family friend snatching the neighbor's child from the rife midst of truancy and restoring it to duty— family friend to Flem Snopes who had no more friends than Blackbeard or Pistol, to Eula Varner who no more had friends than man or woman either would have called them that Messalina and Helen had.

So I did all three: waited in the office too long, so that I had to follow down the stairs too fast, and then along the street beside her not

far enough either to be unnoticed or forgotten. Then there remained
only to suborn my nephew with the dollar bill and the book; I dont
remember which one; I dont believe I even noticed.

"Sir?" Chick said. "I meet her in Christian's drugstore after school
and give her the book and tell her you'll try to get there but not to
wait. And buy her a soda. Why dont I just give her the book at school
and save time?"

"Certainly," I said. "Why dont you just give me back the dollar?"

"And buy her a soda," he said. "Do I have to pay that out of the
dollar?"

"All right," I said. "Twenty-five cents then. If she takes a banana
split you can drink water and make a nickel more."

"Maybe she'll take a Coke," he said. "Then I can have one too and
still make fifteen cents."

"All right," I said.

"Or suppose she dont want anything."

"Didn't I say all right?" I said. "Just dont let your mother hear you
say 'She dont.' "

"Why?" he said. "Father and Ratliff say 'she dont' all the time, and
so do you when you are talking to them. And Ratliff says 'taken' for
'took' and 'drug' for 'dragged' and so do you when you are talking
to country people like Ratliff."

"How do you know?" I said.

"I've heard you. So has Ratliff."

"Why? Did you tell him to?"

"No sir," he said. "Ratliff told me."

My rejoinder may have been Wait until you get as old as Ratliff
and your father and me and you can too, though I dont remember.
But then, inside the next few months I was to discover myself doing
lots of things he wasn't old enough yet for the privilege. Which was
beside the point anyway now; now only the afternoon remained: the
interminable time until a few minutes after half past three filled with
a thousand indecisions which each fierce succeeding harassment
would revise. You see? She had not only abetted me in making that
date with which I would break, wreck, shatter, destroy, slay something, she had even forestalled me in it by the simplicity of direct-
ness.

So I had only to pass that time. That is, get it passed, live it down; the office window as good as any for that and better than most since it looked down on the drugstore entrance, so I had only to lurk there. Not to hear the dismissal bell of course this far away but rather to see them first: the little ones, the infantile inflow and scatter of primer- and first-graders, then the middle-graders boisterous and horsing as to the boys, then the mature ones, juniors and seniors grave with weight and alien with puberty; and there she was, tall (no: not for a girl that tall but all right then: tall, like a heron out of a moil of frogs and tadpoles), pausing for just one quick second at the drugstore entrance for one quick glance, perhaps at the empty stairway. Then she entered, carrying three books any one of which might have been that book and I thought *He gave it to her at school; the damned little devil has foxed me for that odd quarter.*

But then I saw Chick; he entered too, carrying the book, and then I thought how if I had only thought to fill a glass with water, to count off slowly sixty seconds, say, to cover the time Skeets McGowan, the soda squirt, would need to tear his fascinations from whatever other female junior or senior and fill the order, then drink the water slowly to simulate the Coke; thinking *But maybe she did take the banana split; maybe there is still time,* already across the office, the screen door already in my hand before I caught myself: at least the County Attorney must not be actually *seen* running down his office stairs and across the street into a drugstore where a sixteen-year-old high-school junior waited.

And I was in time but just in time. They had not even sat down, or if they had she had already risen, the two of them only standing beside the table, she carrying four books now and looking at me for only that one last instant and then no more with the eyes you thought were just dark gray or blue until you knew better.

"I'm sorry I'm late," I said. "I hope Chick told you."

"It's all right," she said. "I have to go on home anyway."

"Without a Coke even?" I said.

"I have to go home," she said.

"Another time then," I said. "What they call a rain check."

"Yes," she said. "I have to go home now." So I moved so she could move, making the move first to let her go ahead, toward the door.

"Remember what you said about that quarter," Chick said.

And made the next move first too, opening the screen for her then stopping in it and so establishing severance and separation by that little space before she even knew it, not even needing to pause and half-glance back to prove herself intact and safe, intact and secure and unthreatened still, not needing to say Mister Stevens nor even Mister Gavin nor Good-bye nor even anything to need to say Thank you for, nor even to look back then although she did. "Thank you for the book," she said; and gone.

"Remember what you said about that quarter," Chick said.

"Certainly," I said. "Why the bejesus dont you go somewhere and spend it?"

Oh yes, doing a lot of things Chick wasn't old enough yet himself to do. Because dodging situations which might force me to use even that base shabby lash again was fun, excitement. Because she didn't know (Must not know, at least not now, not yet: else why the need for that base and shabby lash?), could not be certainly sure about that afternoon, that one or two or three (whatever it was) minutes in the drugstore; never sure whether what Chick told her was the truth: that I actually was going to be late and had simply sent my nephew as the handiest messenger to keep her company until or when or if I did show up, I so aged and fatuous as not even to realise the insult either standing her up would be, or sending a ten-year-old boy to keep her company and believing that she, a sixteen-year-old high-school junior, would accept him; or if I had done it deliberately: made the date then sent the ten-year-old boy to fill it as a delicate way of saying *Stop bothering me.*

So I must not even give her a chance to demand of me with the temerity of desperation which of these was right. And that was the fun, the excitement. I mean, dodging her. It was adolescence in reverse, turned upside down: the youth, himself virgin and—who knew?—maybe even more so, at once drawn and terrified of what draws him, contriving by clumsy and timorous artifice the accidental encounters in which he still would not and never quite touch, would not even hope to touch, really want to touch, too terrified in fact to touch; but only to breathe the same air, be laved by the same circumambience which laved the mistress's moving limbs; to whom the glove or the handkerchief she didn't even know she had lost, the flower she didn't even know she had crushed, the very ninth- or tenth-grade arithmetic or grammar or geography bearing her name in her own magical hand on the flyleaf, are more terrible and moving than ever will be afterward the gleam of the actual naked shoulder or spread of unbound hair on the pillow's other twin.

That was me: not to encounter; continuously just to miss her yet never be caught at it. You know: in a little town of three thousand people like ours, the only thing that could cause more talk and notice than a middle-aged bachelor meeting a sixteen-year-old maiden two or three times a week would be a sixteen-year-old maiden and a middle-aged bachelor just missing each other two or three times a week by darting into stores or up alleys. You know: a middle-aged lawyer, certainly the one who was County Attorney too, could always find enough to do even in a town of just three thousand to miss being on the one street between her home and the school house at eight-thirty and twelve and one and three-thirty oclock when the town's whole infant roster must come and go, sometimes, a few times even, but not forever.

Yet that's what I had to do. I had no help, you see; I couldn't stop her suddenly on the street one day and say, "Answer quickly now. Exactly how much were you fooled or not fooled that afternoon in the drugstore? Say in one word exactly what you believed about that episode." All I could do was leave well enough alone, even when the only well enough I had wasn't anywhere that well.

So I had to dodge her. I had to plan not just mine but Yoknapatawpha county's business too ahead in order to dodge a sixteen-year-old girl. That was during the spring. So until school was out in May it would be comparatively simple, at least for five days of the week. But in time vacation would arrive, with no claims of regimen or discipline on her; and observation even if not personal experience had long since taught me that anyone sixteen years old not nursing a child or supporting a family or in jail could be almost anywhere at any time during the twenty-four hours.

So when the time came, which was that last summer before her final year in high school when she would graduate, I didn't even have the catalogues and brochures from the alien and outland schools sent

first to me in person, to be handed by me to her, but sent direct to
her, to Miss Linda Snopes, Jefferson, Mississippi, the Mississippi to
be carefully spelt out in full else the envelope would go: first, to Jefferson, Missouri; second, to every other state in the forty-eight
which had a Jefferson in it, before: third, it would finally occur to
somebody somewhere that there might be someone in Mississippi
capable of thinking vaguely of attending an Eastern or Northern
school or capable of having heard of such or anyway capable of
enjoying the pictures in the catalogues or even deciphering the one-
syllable words, provided they were accompanied by photographs.

So I had them sent direct to her—the shrewd suave snob-entice-
ments from the Virginia schools at which Southern mothers seemed
to aim their daughters by simple instinct, I dont know why, unless
because the mothers themselves did not attend them, and thus
accomplishing by proxy what had been denied them in person since
they had not had mothers driven to accomplish vicariously what they
in their turn had been denied.

And not just the Virginia ones first but the ones from the smart
"finishing" schools north of Mason's and Dixon's too. I was being
fair. No: we were being fair, she and I both, the two of us who never
met any more now for the sake of her good name, in federation and
cahoots for the sake of her soul; the two of us together saying *in
absentia* to her mother: *There they all are: the smart ones, the snob ones.
We have been fair, we gave you your chance. Now, here is where we want
to go, where you can help us go, if not by approval, at least by not saying
no;* arranging for the other catalogues to reach her only then: the
schools which would not even notice what she wore and how she
walked and used her fork and all the rest of how she looked and acted
in public because by this time all that would be too old and fixed to
change, but mainly because it had not mattered anyway, since what
did matter was what she did and how she acted in the spirit's inviolable solitude.

So now—these last began to reach her about Christmas time of
that last year in high school—she would have to see me, need to see
me, not to help her decide which one of them but simply to discuss,
canvass the decision before it became final. I waited, in fact quite
patiently while it finally dawned on me that she was not going to

make the first gesture to see me again. I had avoided her for over six months now and she not only knew I had been dodging her since in a town the size of ours a male can no more avoid a female consistently for that long by mere accident than they can meet for that long by what they believed or thought was discretion and surreption, even she realised by this time that that business in Christian's drugstore that afternoon last April had been no clumsy accident. (Oh yes, it had already occurred to me also that she had no reason whatever to assume I knew she had received the catalogues, let alone had instigated them. But I dismissed that as immediately as you will too if we are to get on with this.)

So I must make that first gesture. It would not be quite as simple now as it had used to be. A little after half past three on any weekend afternoon I could see her from the office window (if I happened to be there) pass along the Square in the school's scattering exodus. Last year, in fact during all the time before, she would be alone, or seemed to be. But now, during this past one, particularly since the Levitt troglodyte's departure, she would be with another girl who lived on the same street. Then suddenly (it began in the late winter, about St. Valentine's Day) instead of two there would be four of them: two boys, Chick said the Rouncewell boy and the youngest Bishop one, the year's high-school athletic stars. And now, after spring began, the four of them would be on almost any afternoon in Christian's drugstore (at least there harbored apparently there no ghosts to make her blush and squirm and I was glad of that), with Coca-Colas and the other fearsome (I was acquainted there) messes which young people, young women in particular, consume with terrifying equanimity not only in the afternoon but at nine and ten in the morning too: of which—the four of them—I had taken to be two pairs, two couples in the steadfast almost uxorious fashion of high-school juniors and seniors, until one evening I saw (by chance) her going toward the picture show squired by both of them.

Which would make it a little difficult now. But not too much. In fact, it would be quite simple (not to mention the fact that it was already May and I couldn't much longer afford to wait): merely to wait for some afternoon when she would be without her convoy, when the Bishop and the Rouncewell would have to practice their dedications or maybe simply be kept in by a teacher after school. Which I did, already seeing her about a block away but just in time to see her turn suddenly into a street which would by-pass the Square itself: obviously a new route home she had adopted to use on the afternoons when she was alone, was already or (perhaps) wanted to be.

But that was simple too: merely to back-track one block then turn myself one block more to the corner where the street she was in must intercept. But quicker than she, faster than she, so that I saw her first walking fast along the purlieus of rubbish and ashcans and loading platforms until she saw me at the corner and stopped in dead mid-stride and one quick fleeing half-raised motion of the head. So that, who knows? At that sudden distance I might not have even stopped, being already in motion again, raising my hand and arm in return and on, across the alley, striding on as you would naturally expect a county attorney to be striding along a side street at forty-two min-utes past three in the afternoon; one whole block more for safety and then safe, inviolate still the intactness, unthreatened again.

There was the telephone of course. But that would be too close, too near the alley and the raised hand. And *grüss Gott* they had invented the typewriter; the Board of Supervisors could subtract the letterhead from my next pay check or who knows they might not even miss it; the typewriter and the time of course were already mine:

Dear Linda:
    When you decide which one you like the best, let's have a talk. I've seen some of them myself and can tell you more than the catalogue may have. We should have a banana split too; they may not have heard of them yet at Bennington and Bard and Swarthmore and you'll have to be a mis-sionary as well as a student.

Then in pencil, in my hand:

Saw you in the alley the other afternoon but didn't have time to stop. Incidentally, what were you doing in an alley?

You see? The *other afternoon*, so that it wouldn't matter when I mailed it: two days from now or two weeks from now; two whole weeks in which to tear it up, and even addressed the stamped envelope, knowing as I did so that I was deliberately wasting two—no, three, bought singly—whole cents, then tore them neatly across once and matched the torn edges and tore them across again and built a careful small tepee on the cold hearth and struck a match and watched the burn and uncreaked mine ancient knees and shook my trousers down.

Because it was May now; in two weeks she would graduate. But then Miss Eunice Gant had promised to send the dressing case yesterday afternoon and *grüss Gott* they had invented the telephone too. So once more (this would be the last one, the last lurk) to wait until half past eight o'clock (the bank would not open until nine but then even though Flem was not president of it you simply declined to imagine him hanging around the house until the last moment for the chance to leap to the ringing telephone) and then picked it up:

"Good morning, Mrs Snopes. Gavin Stevens. May I speak to Linda if she hasn't already . . . I see, I must have missed her. But then I was late myself this morning . . . Thank you. We are all happy to know the dressing case pleased her. Maggie will be pleased to have the note . . . If you'll give her the message when she comes home to dinner. I have some information about a Radcliffe scholarship which might interest her. That's practically Harvard too and I can tell her about Cambridge . . . Yes, if you will: that I'll be waiting for her in the drugstore after school this afternoon. Thank you."

And good-bye. The sad word, even over the telephone. I mean, not the word is sad nor the meaning of it, but that you really can say it, that the time comes always in time when you can say it without grief and anguish now but without even the memory of grief and anguish, remembering that night in this same office here (when was it? ten years ago? twelve years?) when I had said not just Good-bye but Get the hell out of here to Eula Varner, and no hair bleached, no bead of anguished sweat or tear sprang out, and what regret still stirred a little was regret that even if I had been brave enough not to say No then, even that courage would not matter now since even the cowardice was only thin regret.

At first I thought I would go inside and be already sitting at the table waiting. Then I thought better: it must be casual but not taken-for-granted casual. So I stood at the entrance, but back, not to impede the juvenile flood or perhaps rather not to be trampled by it. Because she must not see me from a block away waiting, but casual, by accident outwardly and chance: first the little ones, first- and second- and third-grade; and now already the larger ones, the big grades and the high school; it would be soon now, any time now. Except that it was Chick, with a folded note.

"Here," he said. "It seems to be stuck."

"Stuck?" I said.

"The record. The victrola. This is the same tune it was playing before, aint it? Just backward this time." Because she probably had insisted he read it first before she released it to him. So I was the second, not counting her:

Dear Mr Stevens
   I will have to be a little late if you can wait for me

                                                              Linda

"Not quite the same," I said. "I dont hear any dollar now."

"Okay," he said. "Neither did I. I reckon you aint coming home now."

"So do I," I said. So I went inside then and sat down at the table; I owed her that much anyway; the least I could give her was revenge, so let it be full revenge; full satisfaction of watching from wherever she would be watching while I sat still waiting for her long after even I knew she would not come; let it be the full whole hour then since "finis" is not "good-bye" and has no cause to grieve the spring of grief.

So when she passed rapidly across the plate-glass window, I didn't know her. Because she was approaching not from the direction of the school but from the opposite one, as though she were on her way to school, not from it. No: that was not the reason. She was already in the store now, rapidly, the screen clapping behind her at the same instant and in the same physical sense both running and poised motionless, wearing not the blouse and skirt or print cotton dress above the flat-heeled shoes of school; but dressed, I mean "dressed," in a hat and high heels and silk stockings and makeup who needed none and already I could smell the scent: one poised split-second of immobilised and utter flight in bizarre and paradox panoply of allure, like a hawk caught by a speed lens.

"It's all right," I said. Because at least I still had that much presence.

"I cant," she said. At least that much presence. There were not many people in the store but even one could have been too many, so I was already up now, moving toward her.

"How nice you look," I said. "Come on; I'll walk a way with you," and turned her that way, not even touching her arm, on and out, onto the pavement, talking (I presume I was; I usually am), speaking: which was perhaps why I did not even realise that she had chosen the direction, not in fact until I realised that she had actually turned toward the foot of the office stairs, only then touching her, her elbow, holding it a little, on past the stairs so that none (one hoped intended must believe) had marked that falter, on along the late spring storefronts—the hardware and farm-furnish stores cluttered with garden and farm tools and rolls of uncut plow-line and sample sacks of slag and fertilizer and even the grocery ones exposing neat cases of seed packets stencilled with gaudy and incredible vegetables and flowers—talking (oh ay, trust me always) sedate and decorous: the young girl decked and scented to go wherever a young woman would be going at four oclock on a May afternoon, and the gray-headed bachelor, avuncular and what old Negroes called "settled," incapable now of harm, slowed the blood and untroubled now the flesh by turn of wrist or ankle, faint and dusty-dry as memory now the hopes and anguishes of youth—until we could turn a corner into privacy or at least room or anyway so long as we did not actually stop.

"I cant," she said.

"You said that before," I said. "You cant what?"

"The schools," she said. "The ones you . . . the catalogues. From outside Jefferson, outside Mississippi."

"I'm glad you cant," I said. "I didn't expect you to decide alone. That's why I wanted to see you: to help you pick the right one."

"But I cant," she said. "Dont you understand? I cant."

Then I—yes, I—stopped talking. "All right," I said. "Tell me."

"I cant go to any of them. I'm going to stay in Jefferson. I'm going to the Academy next year." Oh yes, I stopped talking now. It wasn't what the Academy was that mattered. It wasn't even that the Academy was in Jefferson that mattered. It was Jefferson itself which was the mortal foe since Jefferson was Snopes.

"I see," I said. "All right. I'll talk to her myself."

"No," she said. "No. I dont want to go away."

"Yes," I said. "We must. It's too important. It's too important for even you to see now. Come on. We'll go home now and talk to your mother—" already turning. But already she had caught at me, grasping my wrist and forearm with both hands, until I stopped. Then she let go and just stood there in the high heels and the silk stockings and the hat that was a little too old for her or maybe I was not used to her in a hat or maybe the hat just reminded me of the one other time I ever saw her in a hat which was that fiasco of a Sunday dinner at home two years ago which was the first time I compelled, forced her to do something because she didn't know how to refuse; whereupon I said suddenly: "Of course I dont really need to ask you this, but maybe we'd better just for the record. You dont really want to stay in Jefferson, do you? You really do want to go up East to school?" then almost immediately said: "All right, I take that back. I cant ask you that; I cant ask you to say outright you want to go against your mother.—All right," I said, "you dont want to be there yourself when I talk to her: is that it?" Then I said: "Look at me," and she did, with the eyes that were not blue or gray either but hyacinthine, the two of us standing there in the middle of that quiet block in full view of at least twenty discreet window-shades; looking at me even while she said, breathed, again:

"No. No."

"Come on," I said. "Let's walk again," and she did so, docile enough. "She knows you came to meet me this afternoon because of course she gave you my telephone message.—All right," I said. "I'll come to your house in the morning then, after you've left for school. But it's all right; you dont need to tell her. You dont need to tell her anything—say anything—" Not even No No again, since she had said nothing else since I saw her and was still saying it even in the way she walked and said nothing. Because now I knew why the clothes, the scent, the makeup which belonged on her no more than the hat did. It was desperation, not to defend the ingratitude but at least to palliate the rudeness of it: the mother who said *Certainly, meet him by all means. Tell him I am quite competent to plan my daughter's education, and we'll both thank him to keep his nose out of it;* the poor desperate child herself covering, trying to hide the baseness of the one and the shame of the other behind the placentae of worms and the urine and vomit of cats and cancerous whales. "I'll come tomorrow morning, after you've gone to school," I said. "I know. I know. But it's got too important now for either of us to stop."

So the next morning: who—I—had thought yesterday to have seen the last of lurking. But I had to be sure. And there was Ratliff.

"What?" he said. "You're going to see Eula because Eula wont let her leave Jefferson to go to school? You're wrong."

"All right," I said. "I'm wrong. I dont want to do it either. I'm not that brave—offering to tell anybody, let alone a woman, how to raise her child. But somebody's got to. She's got to get away from here. Away for good from all the very air that ever heard or felt breathed the name of Snopes—"

"But wait, I tell you! Wait!" he said. "Because you're wrong—"

But I couldn't wait. Anyway, I didn't. I mean, I just deferred, marked time until at least nine oclock. Because even on a hot Mississippi May morning, when people begin to get up more or less with the sun, not so much in self-defense as to balance off as much as possible of the day against the hours between noon and four, a housewife would demand a little time to prepare (her house and herself or perhaps most of all and simply, her soul) for a male caller not only uninvited but already unwelcome.

But she was prepared, self, house and soul too; if her soul was ever in her life unready for anything that just wore pants or maybe if any woman's soul ever needed pre-readying and pre-arming against anything in pants just named Gavin Stevens, passing through the little rented (still looking rented even though the owner or somebody had painted it) gate up the short rented walk toward the little rented veranda and onto it, my hand already lifted to knock before I saw her through the screen, standing there quite still in the little hallway watching me.

"Good morning," she said. "Come in," and now with no screen between us still watching me. No: just looking at me, not brazenly, not with welcome, not with anything. Then she turned, the hair, where all the other women in Jefferson, even Maggie, had bobbed theirs now, still one heavy careless yellow bun at the back of her head, the dress which was not a morning gown nor a hostess gown nor even a house dress but just a simple cotton dress that was simply a dress and which, although she was thirty-five now—yes: thirty-six now by Ratliff's counting from that splendid fall like that one when she first crossed the Square that day sixteen years ago, appeared not so much as snatching in desperate haste to hide them but rather to spring in suppliance and adulation to the moving limbs, the very flowing of the fabric's laving folds crying *Evoe! Evoe!*

Oh yes, it was a sitting room, exactly like the hall and both of them exactly like something else I had seen somewhere but didn't have time to remember. Because she said, "Will you have some coffee?" and I saw that too: the service (not silver but the stuff the advertisements dont tell you is better than silver but simply newer. New: implying that silver is quite all right and even proper for people still thrall to gaslight and the horse-and-buggy) on a low table, with two chairs already drawn up and I thought *I have lost* even if she had met me wearing a barrel or a feed sack. Then I thought *So it really is serious*, since this—the coffee, the low table, the two intimate chairs was an assault not on the glands nor even just the stomach but on the civilized soul or at least the soul which believes it thirsts to be civilised.

"Thank you," I said and waited and then sat too. "Only, do you mind if I wonder why? We dont need an armistice, since I have already been disarmed."

"You came to fight then," she said, pouring.

"How can I without a weapon?" I said, watching: the bent head with the careless, almost untidy bun of hair, the arm, the hand which could have rocked a warrior-hero's cradle or even caught up its father's fallen sword, pouring the trivial (it would probably not even be very good coffee) fluid from the trivial spurious synthetic urn—

this, in that room, that house; and suddenly I knew where I had seen the room and hallway before. In a photograph, the photograph from say *Town and Country* labelled *American Interior*, reproduced in color in a wholesale furniture catalogue, with the added legend: *This is neither a Copy nor a Reproduction. It is our own Model scaled to your individual Requirements.* "Thank you," I said. "No cream. Just sugar.—Only it doesn't look like you."

"What?" she said.

"This room. Your house." And that was why I didn't even believe at first that I had heard her.

"It wasn't me. It was my husband."

"I'm sorry," I said.

"My husband chose this furniture."

"Flem?" I said, cried. "Flem Snopes?"—and she looking at me now, not startled, amazed: not anything or if anything, just waiting for my uproar to reach its end: nor was it only from McCarron that Linda got the eyes, but only the hair from him. "Flem Snopes!" I said. "Flem Snopes!"

"Yes. We went to Memphis. He knew exactly what he wanted. No, that's wrong. He didn't know yet. He only knew he wanted, had to have. Or does that make any sense to you?"

"Yes," I said. "Terribly. You went to Memphis."

"Yes," she said. "That was why: to find somebody who could tell him what he had to have. He already knew which store he was going to. The first thing he said was, 'When a man dont intend to buy anything from you, how much do you charge him just to talk?' Because he was not trading now, you see. When you're on a trade, for land or stock or whatever it is, both of you may trade or both of you may not, it all depends; you dont have to buy it or sell it; when you stop trading and part, neither of you may be any different from when you began. But not this time. This was something he had to have and knew he had to have: he just didn't know what it was and so he would not only have to depend on the man who owned it to tell him what he wanted, he would even have to depend on the man selling it not to cheat him on the price or the value of it because he wouldn't know that either: only that he had to have it. Do you understand that too?"

"All right," I said. "Yes. And then?"

"It had to be exactly what it was, for exactly what he was. That was when the man began to say, 'Yes, I think I see. You started out as a clerk in a country store. Then you moved to town and ran a café. Now you're vice president of your bank. A man who came that far in that short time is not going to stop just there, and why shouldn't everybody that enters his home know it, see it? Yes, I know what you want.' And Flem said No. 'Not expensive,' the man said. 'Successful.' and Flem said No. 'All right,' the man said. 'Antique then,' and took us into a room and showed us what he meant. 'I can take this piece here for instance and make it look still older.' And Flem said, 'Why?' and the man said, 'For background. Your grandfather.' And Flem said, 'I had a grandfather because everybody had. I dont know who he was but I know that whoever he was he never owned enough furniture for a room, let alone a house. Besides, I dont aim to fool anybody. Only a fool would try to fool smart people, and anybody that needs to fool fools is already one.' And that was when the man said wait while he telephoned. And we did, it was not long before a woman came in. She was his wife. She said to me: 'What are your ideas?' and I said, 'I dont care,' and she said 'What?' and I said it again and then she looked at Flem and I watched them looking at one another, a good while. Then she said, not loud like her husband, quite quiet: 'I know,' and now it was Flem that said, 'Wait. How much will it cost?' and she said, 'You're a trader. I'll make a trade with you. I'll bring the stuff down to Jefferson and put it in your house myself. If you like it, you buy it. If you dont like it, I'll load it back up and move it back here and it wont cost you a cent.' "

"All right," I said. "And then?"

"That's all," she said. "Your coffee's cold. I'll get another cup—" and began to rise until I stopped her.

"When was this?" I said.

"Four years ago," she said. "When he bought this house."

"Bought the house?" I said. "Four years ago? That's when he became vice president of the bank!"

"Yes," she said. "The day before it was announced. I'll get another cup."

"I dont want coffee," I said, sitting there saying *Flem Snopes Flem*

Snopes until I said, cried: "I dont want anything! I'm afraid!" until I finally said "What?" and she repeated:

"Will you have a cigarette?" and I saw that too: a synthetic metal box also and there should have been a synthetic matching lighter but what she had taken from the same box with the cigarette was a kitchen match. "Linda says you smoke a corncob pipe. Smoke it if you want to."

"No," I said again. "Not anything.—But Flem Snopes," I said. "Flem Snopes."

"Yes," she said. "It's not me that wont let her go away from Jefferson to school."

"But why?" I said. "Why? When she's not even his—he's not even her—I'm sorry. But you can see how urgent, how we dont even have time for. . . ."

"Politeness?" she said. Nor did I make that move either: just sitting there watching while she leaned and scratched the match on the sole of her side-turned slipper and lit the cigarette.

"For anything," I said. "For anything except her. Ratliff tried to tell me this this morning, but I wouldn't listen. So maybe that's what you were telling me a moment ago when I wouldn't or didn't listen? The furniture. That day in the store. Didn't know what he wanted because what he wanted didn't matter, wasn't important: only that he did want it, did need it, must have it, intended to have it no matter what cost or who lost or who anguished or grieved. To be exactly what he needed to exactly fit exactly what he was going to be tomorrow after it was announced: a vice president's wife and child along with the rest of the vice president's furniture in the vice president's house? Is that what you tried to tell me?"

"Something like that," she said.

"Just something like that," I said. "Because that's not enough. It's nowhere near enough. We wont mention the money because everybody who ever saw that bow tie would know he wouldn't pay out his own money to send his own child a sleeper-ticket distance to school, let alone another man's ba—" and stopped. But not she, smoking, watching the burning tip of cigarette.

"Say it," she said. "Bastard."

"I'm sorry," I said.

"Why?" she said.

"I'm trying," I said. "Maybe I could, if only you were. Looked like you were. Or even like you were trying to be."

"Go on," she said. 'Not the money."

"Because he—you—could get that from Uncle Will probably, not to mention taking it from me as a scholarship. Or is that it? He cant even bear to see the money of even a mortal enemy like old man Will Varner probably is to him wasted on sending a child out of the state to school when he pays taxes every year to support the Mississippi ones?"

"Go on," she said again. "Not the money."

"So it is that furniture catalogue picture after all, scaled in cheap color from the Charleston or Richmond or Long Island or Boston photograph, down to that one which Flem Snopes holds imperative that the people of Yoknapatawpha County must have of him. While he was just owner of a back-alley café it was all right for all French-man's Bend (and all Jefferson and the rest of the county too after Ratliff and a few others like him got through with it) to know the child who bore his name was really a—"

"Bastard," she said again.

"All right," I said. But even then I didn't say it: "—and even when he sold the café for a nice profit and was superintendent of the power-plant, it still wouldn't have mattered. And even after that when he held no public position but was simply a private usurer and property-grabber quietly minding his own business; not to mention the fact that ten or twelve years had now passed, by which time he could even begin to trust Jefferson to have enough tenderness for a twelve- or thirteen-year-old female child not to upset her life with that useless and gratuitous information. But now he is vice president of a bank and now a meddling outsider is persuading the child to go away to school, to spend at least the three months until the Christmas holidays among people none of whose fathers owe him money and so might keep their mouths shut, any one of whom might reveal the fact which at all costs he must now keep secret. So that's it," I said, and still she wasn't looking at me: just smoking quietly and steadily while she watched the slow curl and rise of the smoke. "So it's you, after all," I said. "He forbade her to leave Jefferson, and blackmailed you into supporting him by threatening you with what he himself is afraid of: that he himself will tell her of her mother's shame and her own illegitimacy. Well, that's a blade with three edges. Ask your father for the money, or take it from me, and get her away from Jefferson or I'll tell her myself who she is or is not."

"Do you think she will believe you?" she said.

"What?" I said. "Believe me? Believe me? Even without a mirror to look into, nothing to compare with and need to repudiate from, since all she needed was just to live with him for the seventeen years which she has. What more could she want than to believe me, believe anyone, a chance to believe anyone compassionate enough to assure her she's not his child? What are you talking about? What more could she ask than the right to love the mother who by means of love saved her from being a Snopes? And if that were not enough, what more could anybody want than this, that most never have the chance to be, not one in ten million have the right to be, deserve to be: not just a love child but one of the elect to share cousinhood with the world's immortal love-children—fruit of that brave virgin passion not just capable but doomed to count the earth itself well lost for love, which down all the long record of man the weak and impotent and terrified and sleepless that the rest of the human race calls its poets, have dreamed and anguished and exulted and amazed over—" and she watching me now, not smoking: just holding the poised cigarette while the last blue vapor faded, watching me through it.

"You dont know very much about women, do you?" she said. "Women aren't interested in poets' dreams. They are interested in facts. It doesn't even matter whether the facts are true or not, as long as they match the other facts without leaving a rough seam. She wouldn't even believe you. She wouldn't even believe him if he were to tell her. She would just hate you both—you most of all because you started it."

"You mean she will take . . . this—him—in preference to nothing? Will throw away the chance for school and everything else? I dont believe you."

"To her, this isn't nothing. She will take it before a lot of things. Before most things."

"I dont believe you!" I said, cried, or thought I did. But only thought it, until I said: "So there's nothing I can do."

"Yes," she said. And now she was watching me, the cigarette motionless, not even seeming to burn. "Marry her."

"What?" I said, cried. "A gray-headed man more than twice her age? Dont you see, that's what I'm after: to set her free of Jefferson, not tie her down to it still more, still further, still worse, but to set her free? And you talk about the reality of facts."

"The marriage is the only fact. The rest of it is still the poet's romantic dream. Marry her. She'll have you. Right now, in the middle of all this, she wont know how to say No. Marry her."

"Good-bye," I said. "Good-bye."

And Ratliff again, still in the client's chair where I had left him an hour ago.

"I tried to tell you," he said. "Of course it's Flem. What reason would Eula and that gal have not to jump at a chance to be shut of each other for nine or ten months for a change?"

"I can tell you that now myself," I said. "Flem Snopes is vice president of a bank now with a vice president's house with vice president's furniture in it and some of that vice president's furniture has got to be a vice president's wife and child."

"No," he said.

"All right," I said. "The vice president of a bank dont dare have it remembered that his wife was already carrying somebody else's bastard when he married her, so if she goes off to school some stranger that dont owe him money will tell her who she is and the whole playhouse will blow up."

"No," Ratliff said.

"All right," I said. "Then you tell a while."

"He's afraid she'll get married," he said.

"What?" I said.

"That's right," he said. "When Jody was born, Uncle Billy Varner made a will leaving half of his property to Miz Varner and half to Jody. When Eula was born, he made a new will leaving that same first half to Miz Varner and the other half split in two equal parts, one for Jody and one for Eula. That's the will he showed Flem that day him and Eula was married and he aint changed it since. That is, Flem

Snopes believed him when he said he wasn't going to change it, whether anybody else believed him or not—especially after Flem beat him on that Old Frenchman place trade."

"What?" I said. "He gave that place to them as Eula's dowry."

"Sho," Ratliff said. "It was told around so because Uncle Billy was the last man of all that would have corrected it. He offered Flem the place but Flem said he would rather have the price of it in cash money. Which was why Flem and Eula was a day late leaving for Texas: him and Uncle Billy was trading, with Uncle Billy beating Flem down to where he never even thought about it when Flem finally said all right, he would take that figger provided Uncle Billy would give him a option to buy the place at the same amount when he come back from Texas. So they agreed, and Flem come back from Texas with them paint ponies and when the dust finally settled, me and Henry Armstid had done bought that Old Frenchman place from Flem for my half of that restaurant and enough of Henry's cash money to pay off Uncle Billy's option, which he had done forgot about. And that's why Flem Snopes at least knows that Uncle Billy aint going to change that will. So he dont dare risk letting that girl leave Jefferson and get married, because he knows that Eula will leave him too then. It was Flem started it by saying No, but you got all three of them against you, Eula and that girl too until that girl finds the one she wants to marry. Because women aint interested—"

"Wait," I said, "wait. It's my time now. Because I dont know anything about women because things like love and morality and jumping at any chance you can find that will keep you from being a Snopes are just a poet's romantic dream and women aren't interested in the romance of dreams; they are interested in the reality of facts, they dont care what facts, let alone whether they are true or not if they just dovetail with all the other facts without leaving a saw-tooth edge. Right?"

"Well," he said, "I might not a put it jest exactly that way."

"Because I dont know anything about women," I said. "So would you mind telling me how the hell you learned?"

"Maybe by listening," he said. Which we all knew, since what Yoknapatawphian had not seen at some time during the past ten or fifteen years the tin box shaped and painted to resemble a house and containing the demonstrator machine, in the old days attached to the back of a horse-drawn buckboard and since then to the rear of a converted automobile, hitched or parked beside the gate to a thousand yards on a hundred back-country roads, while, surrounded by a group of four or five or six ladies come in sunbonnets or straw hats from anywhere up to a mile along the road, Ratliff himself with his smooth brown bland inscrutable face and his neat faded tieless blue shirt, sitting in a kitchen chair in the shady yard or on the gallery, listening. Oh yes, we all knew that.

"So I didn't listen to the right ones," I said.

"Or the wrong ones neither," he said. "You never listened to nobody because by that time you were already talking again."

Oh yes, easy. All I had to do was stand there on the street at the right time, until she saw me and turned, ducked with that semblance of flight, into the side street which would by-pass the ambush. Nor even then to back-track that one block but merely to go straight through the drugstore itself, out the back door, so that no matter how fast she went I was in the alley first, ambushed again behind the wall's angle in ample time to hear her rapid feet and then step out and grasp her arm just above the wrist almost before it began to rise in that reflex of flight and repudiation, holding the wrist, not hard, while she wrenched, jerked faintly at it, saying, "Please. Please."

"All right," I said. "All right. Just tell me this. When you went home first and changed before you met me in the drugstore that afternoon. It was your idea to go home first and change to the other dress. But it was your mother who insisted on the lipstick and the perfume, and the silk stockings and the high heels. Isn't that right?" And she still wrenching and jerking faintly at the arm I held, whispering:

"Please. Please."

SIXTEEN

CHARLES MALLISON

This is what Ratliff said happened up to where Uncle Gavin could see it.

It was January, a gray day though not cold because of the fog. Old Het ran in Mrs Hait's front door and down the hall into the kitchen, already hollering in her strong bright happy voice, with strong and childlike pleasure:

"Miss Mannie! Mule in the yard!"

Nobody knew just exactly how old old Het really was. Nobody in Jefferson even remembered just how long she had been in the poorhouse. The old people said she was about seventy, though by her own counting, calculated from the ages of various Jefferson ladies from brides to grandmothers that she claimed to have nursed from infancy, she would be around a hundred and, as Ratliff said, at least triplets.

That is, she used the poorhouse to sleep in or anyway pass most or at least part of the night in. Because the rest of the time she was either on the Square or the streets of Jefferson or somewhere on the mile-and-a-half dirt road between town and the poorhouse; for twenty-five years at least ladies, seeing her through the front window or maybe even just hearing her strong loud cheerful voice from the house next door, had been locking themselves in the bathroom. But even this did no good unless they had remembered first to lock the front and back doors of the house itself. Because sooner or later they would have to come out and there she would be, tall, lean, of a dark chocolate color, voluble, cheerful, in tennis shoes and the long rat-colored coat trimmed with what forty or fifty years ago had been fur, and the purple toque that old Mrs Compson had given her fifty years ago while General Compson himself was still alive, set on the exact

549

top of her headrag (at first she had carried a carpetbag of the same color and apparently as bottomless as a coal mine, though since the ten-cent store came to Jefferson the carpetbag had given place to a succession of the paper shopping bags which it gave away), already settled in a chair in the kitchen, having established already upon the begging visitation a tone blandly and incorrigibly social.

She passed that way from house to house, travelling in a kind of moving island of alarm and consternation as she levied her weekly toll of food scraps and cast-off garments and an occasional coin for snuff, moving in an urbane uproar and as inescapable as a tax-gatherer. Though for the last year or two since Mrs Hait's widowing, Jefferson had gained a sort of temporary respite from her because of Mrs Hait. But even this was not complete. Rather, old Het had merely established a kind of local headquarters or advanced foraging post in Mrs Hait's kitchen soon after Mr Hait and five mules belonging to Mr I. O. Snopes died on a sharp curve below town under the fast northbound through freight one night and even the folks at the poorhouse heard that Mrs Hait had got eight thousand dollars for him. She would come straight to Mrs Hait's as soon as she reached town, sometimes spending the entire forenoon there, so that only after noon would she begin her implacable rounds. Now and then when the weather was bad she spent the whole day with Mrs Hait. On these days her regular clients or victims, freed temporarily, would wonder if in the house of the man-charactered and man-tongued woman who as Ratliff put it had sold her husband to the railroad company for eight thousand percent profit, who chopped her own firewood and milked her cow and plowed and worked her own vegetable garden—they wondered if maybe old Het helped with the work in return for her entertainment or if even now she still kept the relationship at its social level of a guest come to divert and be diverted.

She was wearing the hat and coat and was carrying the shopping bag when she ran into Mrs Hait's kitchen, already hollering: "Miss Mannie! Mule in the yard!"

Mrs Hait was squatting in front of the stove, raking live ashes from it into a scuttle. She was childless, living alone now in the little wooden house painted the same color that the railroad company used on its stations and boxcars out of respect to and in memory of, we all said, that morning three years ago when what remained of Mr Hait had finally been sorted from what remained of the five mules and several feet of new manila rope scattered along the right-of-way. In time the railroad claims adjuster called on her, and in time she cashed a check for eight thousand five hundred dollars, since (as Uncle Gavin said, these were the halcyon days when even the railroad companies considered their Southern branches and divisions the rightful legitimate prey of all who dwelt beside them) although for several years before Mr Hait's death single mules and pairs (by coincidence belonging often to Mr Snopes too; you could always tell his because every time the railroad killed his mules they always had new strong rope on them) had been in the habit of getting themselves killed on that same blind curve at night, this was the first time a human being had—as Uncle Gavin put it—joined them in mutual apotheosis.

Mrs Hait took the money in cash; she stood in a calico wrapper and her late husband's coat sweater and the actual felt hat he had been wearing (it had been found intact) on that fatal morning and listened in cold and grim silence while the bank teller then the cashier then the president (Mr de Spain himself) tried to explain to her about bonds, then about savings accounts, then about a simple checking account, and put the money into a salt sack under her apron and departed; that summer she painted her house that serviceable and time-defying color which matched the depot and the boxcars, as though out of sentiment or (as Ratliff said) gratitude, and now she still lived in it, alone, in the calico wrapper and the sweater coat and the same felt hat which her husband had owned and worn until he no longer needed them; though her shoes by this time were her own: men's shoes which buttoned, with toes like small tulip bulbs, of an archaic and obsolete pattern which Mr Wildermark himself ordered especially for her once a year.

She jerked up and around, still clutching the scuttle, and glared at old Het and said—her voice was a good strong one too, immediate too—

"That son of a bitch," and, still carrying the scuttle and with old Het still carrying the shopping bag and following, ran out of the

kitchen into the fog. That's why it wasn't cold: the fog: as if all the
sleeping and breathing of Jefferson during that whole long January
night was still lying there imprisoned between the ground and the
mist, keeping it from quite freezing, lying like a scum of grease on
the wooden steps at the back door and on the brick coping and the
wooden lid of the cellar stairs beside the kitchen door and on
the wooden planks which led from the steps to the wooden shed in
the corner of the back yard where Mrs Hait's cow lived; when she
stepped down onto the planks, still carrying the scuttle of live ashes,
Mrs Hait skated violently before she caught her balance. Old Het in
her rubber soles didn't slip.

"Watch out!" she shouted happily. "They in the front!" One of
them wasn't. Because Mrs Hait didn't fall either. She didn't even
pause, whirling and already running toward the corner of the house
where, with silent and apparition-like suddenness, the mule
appeared. It belonged to Mr. I.O. Snopes too. I mean, until they
finally unravelled Mr Hait from the five mules on the railroad track
that morning three years ago, nobody had connected him with Mr
Snopes's mule business, even though now and then somebody did
wonder how Mr Hait didn't seem to need to do anything steady to
make a living. Ratliff said the reason was that everybody was wondering too hard about what in the world I.O. Snopes was doing in
the livestock business. Though Ratliff said that on second thought
maybe it was natural: that back in Frenchman's Bend I.O. had been
a blacksmith without having any business at that, hating horses and
mules both since he was deathly afraid of them, so maybe it was natural for him to take up the next thing he wouldn't have any business
in or sympathy or aptitude for, not to mention being six or eight or
a dozen times as scared since now, instead of just one horse or mule
tied to a post and with its owner handy, he would have to deal alone
with eight or ten or a dozen of them running loose until he could
manage to put a rope on them.

That's what he did though—bought his mules at the Memphis
market and brought them to Jefferson and sold them to farmers and
widows and orphans, black and white, for whatever he could get,
down to some last irreducible figure, after which (up to the night
when the freight train caught Mr Hait too and Jefferson made the

first connection between Mr Hait and Mr Snopes's livestock business) single mules and pairs and gangs (always tied together with that
new strong manila rope which Snopes always itemised and listed in
his claim) would be killed by night freight trains on that same blind
curve of Mr Hait's exit; somebody (Ratliff swore it wasn't him but the
depot agent) finally sent Snopes through the mail a printed train
schedule for the division.

Though after Mr Hait's misfortune (miscalculation, Ratliff said;
he said it was Mr Hait the agent should have sent the train schedule
to, along with a watch) Snopes's mules stopped dying of sudden
death on the railroad track. When the adjuster came to adjust Mrs
Hait, Snopes was there too, which Ratliff said was probably the most
terrible decision Snopes ever faced in his whole life: between the
simple prudence which told him to stay completely clear of the railroad company's investigation, and his knowledge of Mrs Hait which
had already told him that his only chance to get any part of that
indemnity would be by having the railroad company for his ally.

Because he failed. Mrs Hait stated calmly that her husband had
been the sole owner of the five mules; she didn't even have to dare
Snopes out loud to dispute it; all he ever saw of that money (oh yes,
he was there in the bank, as close as he dared get, watching) was
when she crammed it into the salt bag and folded the bag into her
apron. For five or six years before that, at regular intervals he had
passed across the peaceful and somnolent Jefferson scene in dust and
uproar, his approach heralded by forlorn shouts and cries, his passing
marred by a yellow cloud of dust filled with the tossing jug-shaped
heads and the clattering hooves, then last of all Snopes himself at a
panting trot, his face gaped with forlorn shouting and wrung with
concern and terror and dismay.

When he emerged from his conference with the adjuster he still
wore the concern and the dismay, but the terror was now blended
into an incredulous, a despairing, a shocked and passionate disbelief
which still showed through the new overlay of hungry hope it wore
during the next three years (again, Ratliff said, such a decision and
problem as no man should be faced with: who—Snopes—heretofore
had only to unload the mules into the receiving pen at the depot and
then pay a Negro to ride the old bell mare which would lead them

across town to his sales stable-lot, while now and single-handed he had to let them out of the depot pen and then force, herd them into the narrow street blocked at the end by Mrs Hait's small unfenced yard) when the uproar—the dust-cloud filled with plunging demonic shapes—would seem to be translated in one single burst across the peaceful edge of Jefferson and into Mrs Hait's yard, where the two of them, Mrs Hait and Snopes—Mrs Hait clutching a broom or a mop or whatever weapon she was able to snatch up as she ran out of the house cursing like a man, and Snopes, vengeance for the moment sated or at least the unbearable top of the unbearable sense of impotence and injustice and wrong taken off (Ratliff said he had probably long since given up any real belief of actually extorting even one cent of that money from Mrs Hait and all that remained now was the raging and baseless hope) who would now have to catch the animals somehow and get them back inside a fence—ducked and dodged among the thundering shapes in a kind of passionate and choreographic pantomime against the backdrop of that house whose very impervious paint Snopes believed he had paid for and within which its very occupant and chatelaine led a life of queenly and sybaritic luxury on his money (which according to Ratliff was exactly why Mrs Hait refused to appeal to the law to abate Snopes as a nuisance: this too was just a part of the price she owed for the amazing opportunity to swap her husband for eight thousand dollars)—this, while that whole section of town learned to gather—the ladies in the peignoirs and boudoir caps of morning, the children playing in the yards, and the people, Negro and white, who happened to be passing at the moment—and watch from behind neighboring shades or the security of adjacent fences.

When they saw it, the mule was running too, its head high too in a strange place it had never seen before, so that coming suddenly out of the fog and all, it probably looked taller than a giraffe rushing down at Mrs Hait and old Het with the halter-rope whipping about its ears.

"Dar hit!" old Het shouted, waving the shopping bag, "Hoo! Scat!" She told Ratliff how Mrs Hait whirled and skidded again on the greasy planks as she and the mule now ran parallel with one another toward the cowshed from whose open door the static and astonished face of the cow now looked out. To the cow, until a second ago standing peacefully in the door chewing and looking at the fog, the mule must have looked taller and more incredible than any giraffe, let alone looking like it aimed to run right through the shed as if it were straw or maybe even pure and simple mirage. Anyway, old Het said the cow snatched her face back inside the shed like a match going out and made a sound inside the shed, old Het didn't know what sound, just a sound of pure shock and alarm like when you pluck a single string on a harp or a banjo, Mrs Hait running toward the sound old Het said in a kind of pure reflex, in automatic compact of female with female against the world of mules and men, she and the mule converging on the shed at top speed, Mrs Hait already swinging the scuttle of live ashes to throw at the mule. Of course it didn't take this long; old Het said she was still hollering "Dar hit! Dar hit!" when the mule swerved and ran at her until she swung the shopping bag and turned it past her and on around the next corner of the house and back into the fog like a match going out too.

That was when Mrs Hait set the scuttle down on the edge of the brick coping of the cellar entrance and she and old Het turned the corner of the house in time to see the mule coincide with a rooster and eight white-leghorn hens coming out from under the house. Old Het said it looked just like something out of the Bible, or maybe out of some kind of hoodoo witches' Bible: the mule that came out of the fog to begin with like a hant or a goblin, now kind of soaring back into the fog again borne on a cloud of little winged ones. She and Mrs Hait were still running; she said Mrs Hait was now carrying the worn-out stub of a broom though old Het didn't remember when she had picked it up.

"There's more in the front!" old Het hollered.

"That son of a bitch," Mrs Hait said. There were more of them. Old Het said that little handkerchief-sized yard was full of mules and I. O. Snopes. It was so small that any creature with a stride of three feet could have crossed it in two paces, yet when they came in sight of it it must have looked like watching a drop of water through a microscope. Except that this time it was like being in the middle of the drop of water yourself. That is, old Het said that Mrs Hait and

I. O. Snopes were in the middle of it because she said she stopped against the house where she would be more or less out of the way even though nowhere in that little yard was going to be safe, and watched Mrs Hait still clutching the broom and with a kind of sublime faith in something somewhere, maybe in just her own invulnerability, though old Het said Mrs Hait was just too mad to notice, rush right into the middle of the drove, after the one with the flying halter-rein that was still vanishing into the fog still in that cloud of whirling loose feathers like confetti or the wake behind a speed boat.

And Mr Snopes too, the mules running all over him too, he and Mrs Hait glaring at each other while he panted:

"Where's my money? Where's my half of it?"

"Catch that big son of a bitch with the halter," Mrs Hait said. "Get that big son of a bitch out of here," both of them, old Het and Mrs Hait both, running on so that Snopes's panting voice was behind them now:

"Pay me my money! Pay me my part of it!"

"Watch out!" old Het said she hollered. "He heading for the back again!"

"Get a rope!" Mrs Hait hollered back at Snopes.

"Fore God, where is ere rope?" Snopes hollered.

"In the cellar, fore God!" old Het hollered. She didn't wait either. "Go round the other way and head him!" she said. And she said that when she and Mrs Hait turned that corner, there was the mule with the flying halter once more seeming to float lightly onward on a cloud of chickens with which, since the chickens had been able to go under the house and so along the chord while the mule had to go around on the arc, it had once more coincided. When they turned the next corner, they were in the back yard again.

"Fore God!" Het hollered. "He fixing to misuse the cow!" She said it was like a tableau. The cow had come out of the shed into the middle of the back yard; it and the mule were now facing each other about a yard apart, motionless, with lowered heads and braced legs like two mismatched book-ends, and Snopes was half in and half out of the now-open cellar door on the coping of which the scuttle of ashes still sat, where he had obviously gone seeking the rope; afterward old Het said she thought at the time an open cellar door wasn't a very good place for a scuttle of live ashes, and maybe she did. I mean, if she hadn't said she thought that, somebody else would, since there's always somebody handy afterward to prove their foresight by your hindsight. Though if things were going as fast as she said they were, I dont see how anybody there had time to think anything much.

Because everything was already moving again; when they went around the next corner this time, I.O. was leading, carrying the rope (he had found it), then the cow, her tail raised and rigid and raked slightly like the flagpole on a boat, and then the mule, Mrs Hait and old Het coming last and old Het told again how she noticed the scuttle of live ashes sitting on the curb of the now-open cellar with its accumulation of human refuse and Mrs Hait's widowhood—empty boxes for kindling, old papers, broken furniture and thought again that wasn't a very good place for the scuttle.

Then the next corner. Snopes and the cow and the mule were all three just vanishing on the cloud of frantic chickens which had once more crossed beneath the house just in time. Though when they reached the front yard there was nobody there but Snopes. He was lying flat on his face, the tail of his coat flung forward over his head by the impetus of his fall, and old Het swore there was the print of the cow's split foot and the mule's hoof too in the middle of his white shirt.

"Where'd they go?" she shouted at him. He didn't answer. "They tightening on the curves!" she hollered at Mrs Hait. "They already in the back again!" They were. She said maybe the cow had aimed to run back into the shed but decided she had too much speed and instead whirled in a kind of desperation of valor and despair on the mule itself. Though she said that she and Mrs Hait didn't quite get there in time to see it: only to hear a crash and clash and clatter as the mule swerved and blundered over the cellar entrance. Because when they got there the mule was gone. The scuttle was gone from the cellar coping too but old Het said she never noticed it then: only the cow in the middle of the yard where she had been standing before, her fore legs braced and her head lowered like somebody had passed and snatched away the other book-end. Because she and Mrs Hait didn't stop either, Mrs Hait running heavily now, old Het said, with her mouth open and her face the color of putty and one hand against her side. In fact she said they were both run out now, going so slow this time that the mule overtook them from behind and she said it jumped clean over them both: a brief demon thunder rank with the ammonia-reek of sweat, and went on (either the chickens had finally realised to stay under the house or maybe they were worn out too and just couldn't make it this time); when they reached the next corner the mule had finally succeeded in vanishing into the fog; they heard its hooves, brief, staccato and derisive on the hard street, dying away.

Old Het said she stopped. She said, "Well. Gentlemen, hush," she said. "Aint we had—" Then she smelled it. She said she stood right still, smelling, and it was like she was actually looking at that open cellar as it was when they passed it last time without any coal scuttle setting on the coping. "Fore God," she hollered at Mrs Hait, "I smell smoke! Child, run in the house and get your money!"

That was about nine oclock. By noon the house had burned to the ground. Ratliff said that when the fire engine and the crowd got there, Mrs Hait, followed by old Het carrying her shopping bag in one hand and a framed crayon portrait of Mr Hait in the other, was just coming out of the house carrying an umbrella and wearing the army overcoat which Mr Hait had used to wear, in one pocket of which was a quart fruit jar packed with what remained of the eighty-five hundred dollars (which would be most of it, according to how the neighbors said Mrs Hait lived) and in the other a heavy nickel-plated revolver, and crossed the street to a neighbor's house, where with old Het beside her in a second rocker, she had been sitting ever since on the gallery, the two of them rocking steadily while they watched the volunteer fire-fighters flinging her dishes and furniture up and down the street. By that time Ratliff said there were plenty of them interested enough to go back to the Square and hunt up I.O. and keep him posted.

"What you telling me for?" I.O. said. "It wasn't me that set that-ere scuttle of live fire where the first thing that passed would knock it into the cellar."

"It was you that opened the cellar door though," Ratliff said.

"Sho," Snopes said. "And why? To get that rope, her own rope, right where she sent me to get it."

"To catch your mule, that was trespassing on her yard," Ratliff said. "You cant get out of it this time. There aint a jury in the county that wont find for her."

"Yes," Snopes said. "I reckon not. And just because she's a woman. That's why. Because she is a durned woman. All right. Let her go to her durned jury with it. I can talk too; I reckon it's a few things I could tell a jury myself about—" Then Ratliff said he stopped. Ratliff said he didn't sound like I.O. Snopes anyway because whenever I.O. talked what he said was so full of mixed-up proverbs that you stayed so busy trying to unravel just which of two or three proverbs he had jumbled together that you couldn't even tell just exactly what lie he had told you until it was already too late. But right now Ratliff said he was too busy to have time for even proverbs, let alone lies. Ratliff said they were all watching him.

"What?" somebody said. "Tell the jury about what?"

"Nothing," he said. "Because why, because there aint going to be no jury. Me and Miz Mannie Hait? You boys dont know her if you think she's going to make trouble over a pure acci-dent couldn't me nor nobody else help. Why, aint a fairer, finer woman in Yokna-patawpha County than Mannie Hait. I just wish I had a opportunity to tell her so." Ratliff said he had it right away. He said Mrs Hait was right behind them, with old Het right behind her, carrying the shopping bag. He said she just looked once at all of them generally. After that she looked at I.O.

"I come to buy that mule," she said.

"What mule?" I.O. said. He answered that quick, almost automatic, Ratliff said. Because he didn't mean it either. Then Ratliff said they looked at one another for about a half a minute. "You'd like to own that mule?" he said. "It'll cost you a hundred and fifty, Miz Mannie."

"You mean dollars?" Mrs Hait said.

"I dont mean dimes nor nickels neither, Miz Mannie," Snopes said.

"Dollars," Mrs Hait said. "Mules wasn't that high in Hait's time."

"Lots of things is different since Hait's time," Snopes said. "Including you and me, Miz Mannie."

"I reckon so," she said. Then she went away. Ratliff said she turned without a word and left, old Het following.

"If I'd a been you," Ratliff said, "I dont believe I'd a said that last to her."

And now Ratliff said the mean harried little face actually blazed, even frothing a little. "I just wisht she would," Snopes said. "Her or anybody else, I dont care who, to bring a court suit about anything, jest so it had the name mule and the name Hait in it—" and stopped, the face smooth again. "How's that?" he said. "What was you saying?"

"That you dont seem to be afraid she might sue you for burning down her house," Ratliff said.

"Sue me?" Snopes said. "Miz Hait? If she was fixing to try to law something out of me about that fire, do you reckon she would a hunted me up and offered to pay me for it?"

That was about one oclock. Then it was four oclock; Aleck Sander and I had gone out to Sartoris Station to shoot quail over the dogs that Miss Jenny Du Pre still kept, I reckon until Benbow Sartoris got big enough to hold a gun. So Uncle Gavin was alone in the office to hear the tennis shoes on the outside stairs. Then old Het came in; the shopping bag was bulging now and she was eating bananas from a paper sack which she clamped under one arm, the half-eaten banana in that hand while with the other she dug out a crumpled ten-dollar bill and gave it to Uncle Gavin.

"It's for you," old Het said. "From Miss Mannie. I done already give him hisn"—telling it: waiting on the corner of the Square until it looked like sure to God night would come first, before Snopes finally came along, and she handed the banana she was working on then to a woman beside her and got out the first crumpled ten-dollar bill. Snopes took it.

"What?" he said. "Miz Hait told you to give it to me?"

"For that mule," old Het said. "You dont need to give me no receipt. I can be the witness I give it to you."

"Ten dollars?" Snopes said. "For that mule? I told her a hundred and fifty dollars."

"You'll have to contrack that with her yourself," old Het said. "She just give me this to hand to you when she left to get the mule."

"To get the—she went out there herself and taken that mule out of my lot?" Snopes said.

"Lord, child," old Het said she said. "Miss Mannie aint skeered of no mule. Aint you done found that out?—And now here's yourn," she said to Uncle Gavin.

"For what?" Uncle Gavin said. "I dont have a mule to sell."

"For a lawyer," old Het said. "She fixing to need a lawyer. She say for you to be out there at her house about sundown, when she had time to get settled down again."

"Her house?" Uncle Gavin said.

"Where it use to be, honey," old Het said. "Would you keer for a banana? I done et about all I can hold."

"No, much obliged," Uncle Gavin said.

"You're welcome," she said. "Go on. Take some. If I et one more, I'd be wishing the good Lord hadn't never thought banana One in all His life."

"No, much obliged," Uncle Gavin said.

"You're welcome," she said. "I dont reckon you'd have nothing like a extra dime for a little snuff."

"No," Uncle Gavin said, producing it. "All I have is a quarter."

"That's quality," she said. "You talk about change to quality, what you gets back is a quarter or a half a dollar or sometimes even a whole dollar. It's just trash that cant think no higher than a nickel or ten cents." She took the quarter; it vanished somewhere. "There's some folks thinks all I does, I tromps this town all day long from can-see to cant, with a hand full of gimme and a mouth full of much oblige. They're wrong. I serves Jefferson too. If it's more blessed to give than to receive like the Book say, this town is blessed to a fare-you-well because it's steady full of folks willing to give anything from a nickel up to a old hat. But I'm the onliest one I knows that steady receives. So how is Jefferson going to be steady blessed without me steady willing from dust-dawn to dust-dark, rain or snow or sun, to say much oblige? I can tell Miss Mannie you be there?"

"Yes," Uncle Gavin said. Then she was gone. Uncle Gavin sat there looking at the crumpled bill on the desk in front of him. Then he heard the other feet on the stairs and he sat watching the door until Mr Flem Snopes came in and shut it behind him.

"Evening," Mr Snopes said. "Can you take a case for me?"

"Now?" Uncle Gavin said. "Tonight?"

"Yes," Mr Snopes said.

"Tonight," Uncle Gavin said again. "Would it have anything to do with a mule and Mrs Hait's house?"

And he said how Mr Snopes didn't say What house? or What mule? or How did you know? He just said, "Yes."

"Why did you come to me?" Uncle Gavin said.

"For the same reason I would hunt up the best carpenter if I wanted to build a house, or the best farmer if I wanted to share-crop some land," Mr Snopes said.

"Thanks," Uncle Gavin said. "Sorry," he said. He didn't even have to touch the crumpled bill. He said that Mr Snopes had not only seen it the minute he entered, but he believed he even knew at that same moment where it came from. "As you already noticed, I'm already on the other side."

"You going out there now?" Mr Snopes said.

"Yes," Uncle Gavin said.

"Then that's all right." He began to reach into his pocket. At first Uncle Gavin didn't know why; he just watched him dig out an old-fashioned snap-mouth wallet and open it and separate a ten-dollar bill and close the wallet and lay the bill on the desk beside the other crumpled one and put the wallet back into the pocket and stand looking at Uncle Gavin.

"I just told you I'm already on the other side," Uncle Gavin said.

"And I just said that's all right," Mr Snopes said. "I dont want a lawyer because I already know what I'm going to do. I just want a witness."

"And why me for that?" Uncle Gavin said.

"That's right," Mr Snopes said. "The best witness too."

So they went out there. The fog had burned away by noon and Mrs Hait's two blackened chimneys now stood against what remained of the winter sunset; at the same moment Mr Snopes said, "Wait."

"What?" Uncle Gavin said. But Mr Snopes didn't answer, so they stood, not approaching yet; Uncle Gavin said he could already smell the ham broiling over the little fire in front of the still-intact cow-shed, with old Het sitting on a brand-new kitchen chair beside the fire turning the ham in the skillet with a fork, and beyond the fire Mrs Hait squatting at the cow's flank, milking into a new tin bucket.

"All right," Mr Snopes said, and again Uncle Gavin said What? because he had not seen I.O. at all: he was just suddenly there as though he had materialized, stepped suddenly out of the dusk itself into the light of the fire (there was a brand-new galvanised-iron coffee pot sitting in the ashes near the blaze and now Uncle Gavin said he could smell that too), to stand looking down at the back of Mrs Hait's head, not having seen Uncle Gavin and Mr Flem yet. But old Het had, already talking to Uncle Gavin while they were approaching:

"So this coffee and ham brought you even if them ten dollars couldn't," she said. "I'm like that, myself. I aint had no appetite in years it seems like now. A bird couldn't live on what I eats. But just let me get a whiff of coffee and ham together, now.—Leave that milk go for a minute, honey," she said to Mrs Hait. "Here's your lawyer."

Then I.O. saw them too, jerking quickly around over his shoulder his little mean harassed snarling face; and now Uncle Gavin could see inside the cowshed. It had been cleaned and raked and even swept; the floor was spread with fresh hay. A clean new kerosene stable lantern burned on a wooden box beside a pallet bed spread neatly on the straw and turned back for the night and now Uncle Gavin saw a second wooden box set out for a table beside the fire, with a new plate and knife and fork and spoon and cup and saucer and a still-sealed loaf of machine-made bread.

But Uncle Gavin said there was no alarm in I.O.'s face at the sight of Mr Flem though he said the reason for that was that he, Uncle Gavin, hadn't realised yet that I.O. had simply reached that stage where utter hopelessness wears the mantle of temerity. "So here you are," I.O. said. "And brung your lawyer too. I reckon you come now to get that-ere lantern and them new dishes and chair and that milk bucket and maybe the milk in too soon as she's done, hey? That's jest fine. It's even downright almost honest, coming right out in the open here where it aint even full dark yet. Because of course your lawyer knows all the rest all these here recent mulery and arsonery circumstances; likely the only one here that aint up to date is old Aunt Het there, and sholy she should be learned how to reco-nise a circumstance that even if she was to get up and run this minute, likely she would find she never had no shirt nor britches left neither by the time she got home, since a stitch in time saves nine lives for even a cat, as the feller says. Not to mention the fact that when you dines in Rome you durn sho better watch your overcoat.

"All right then. Now, jest exactly how much of them eight thousand and five hundred dollars the railroad company paid Miz Hait here for that husband of hern and them five mules of mine, do you reckon Miz Hait actively" (Uncle Gavin said he said actively for actually too, just like Ratliff. And Uncle Gavin said they were both right) "got? Well, in that case you will be jest as wrong as everybody else was. She got half of it. The reason being that the vice presi-dent here handled it for her. Of course, without a fi-nancial expert like the vice presi-dent to handle it for her, she wouldn't a got no more than that half nohow, if as much, so by rights she aint got nothing to complain of, not to mention the fact that jest half of even that half was rightfully hern, since jest Lonzo Hait was hern because them five mules was mine.

"All right. Now, what do you reckon become of the other half of them eight thousand and five hundred dollars? Then you'll be jest as wrong this time as you were that other one. Because the vice president here taken them. Oh, it was done all open and legal; he explained it: if Miz Hait sued the railroad, a lone lorn widder by herself, likely she wouldn't get more than five thousand at the most, and half of that she would have to give to me for owning the mules. And if me and her brought the suit together, with a active man on her side to compel them cold hard millionaire railroad magnits to do a lone woman justice, once I claimed any part of them mules, due to the previous bad luck mules belonging to me had been having on thatere curve, the railroad would smell a rat right away and wouldn't nobody get nothing. While with him, the vice presi-dent, handling it, it would be seventy-five hundred or maybe a even ten thousand, of which he would not only guarantee her a full half, he would even take out of his half the hundred dollars he would give me. All legal and open: I could keep my mouth shut and get a hundred dollars, where if I objected, the vice presi-dent his-self might accidently let out who them mules actively belonged to, and wouldn't nobody get nothing, which would be all right with the vice presi-dent since he would be right where he started out, being as he never owned Lonzo Hait nor the five mules neither.

"A pure and simple easy choice, you see: either a feller wants a hundred dollars, or either he dont want a hundred dollars. Not to mention, as the vice presi-dent his-self pointed out, that me and Miz Hait was fellow townsmen and you might say business acquaintances and Miz Hait a woman with a woman's natural tender gentle heart, so who would say that maybe in time it wouldn't melt a little more to where she might want to share a little of her half of them eight thousand and five hundred dollars. Which never proved much except that the vice presi-dent might know all there was to know about rail-road companies and eight thousand and five hundred dollars but he never knowed much about what Miz Hait toted around where other folks totes their hearts. Which is neither here nor there; water that's still under a bridge dont fill no oceans, as the feller says, and I was simply outvoted two to one, or maybe eight thousand and five hun-dred dollars to one hundred dollars; or maybe it didn't even take that much: jest Miz Hait's half of them eight thousand and five hundred, against my one hundred, since the only way I could a outvoted Miz Hait would a been with four thousand and two hundred and fifty-one dollars of my own, and even then I'd a had to split that odd dollar with her.

"But never mind. I done forgot all that now; that spilt milk aint going to help no ocean neither." Now Uncle Gavin said he turned rapidly to Mrs Hait with no break in the snarling and outraged bab-ble: "What I come back for was to have a little talk with you. I got something that belongs to you, and I hear you got something that belongs to me. Though naturally I expected to a-just it in private."

"Lord, honey," old Het said. "If you talking at me. Dont you mind me. I done already had so much troubles myself that listening to other folks even kind of rests me. You gawn talk what you wants to talk; I'll just set here and mind this ham."

"Come on," I.O. said to Mrs Hait. "Run them all away for a minute."

Mrs Hait had turned now, still squatting, watching him. "What for?" she said. "I reckon she aint the first critter that ever come in this yard when it wanted and went or stayed when it liked." Now Uncle Gavin said I.O. made a gesture, brief, fretted, and restrained.

"All right," he said. "All right. Let's get started then. So you taken the mule."

"I paid you for it," Mrs Hait said. "Het brought you the money."

"Ten dollars," I.O. said. "For a hundred-and-fifty-dollar mule."

"I dont know anything about hundred-and-fifty-dollar mules," Mrs Hait said. "All I know about mules is what the railroad pays for them. Sixty dollars a head the railroad paid that other time before that fool Hait finally lost all his senses and tied himself to that track too—"

"Hush!" I.O. said. "Hush!"

"What for?" Mrs Hait said. "What secret am I telling that you aint already blabbed to anybody within listening?"

"All right," I.O. said. "But you just sent me ten."

"I sent you the difference," Mrs Hait said. "The difference between that mule and what you owed Hait."

"What I owed Hait?" I.O. said.

"Hait said you paid him fifty dollars a trip, each time he got mules in front of the train in time, and the railroad had paid you sixty dollars a head for the mules. That last time, you never paid him because you never would pay him until afterward and this time there wasn't no afterward. So I taken a mule instead and sent you the ten dollars difference with Het here for the witness." Uncle Gavin said that actually stopped him. He actually hushed; he and Mrs Hait, the one standing and the other still squatting, just stared at one another while again old Het turned the hissing ham in the skillet. He said they were so still that Mr Flem himself spoke twice before they even noticed him.

"You through now?" he said to I.O.

"What?" I.O. said.

"Are you through now?" Mr Flem said. And now Uncle Gavin said they all saw the canvas sack—one of the canvas sacks stamped with the name of the bank which the bank itself used to store money in the vault—in his hands.

"Yes," I.O. said. "I'm through. At least I got one ten dollars out of the mule business you aint going to touch." But Mr Flem wasn't even talking to him now. He had already turned toward Mrs Hait when he drew a folded paper out of the sack.

"This is the mortgage on your house," he said. "Whatever the insurance company pays you now will be clear money; you can build it back again. Here," he said. "Take it."

But Mrs Hait didn't move. "Why?" she said.

"I bought it from the bank myself this afternoon," Mr Flem said. "You can drop it in the fire if you want to. But I want you to put your hand on it first." So she took the paper then, and now Uncle Gavin said they all watched Mr Flem reach into the sack again and this time draw out a roll of bills, I.O. watching too now, not even blinking.

" 'Fore God," old Het said. "You could choke a shoat with it."

"How many mules have you got in that lot?" Mr Flem said to I.O. Still I.O. just watched him. Then he blinked, rapid and hard.

"Seven," he said.

"You've got six," Mr Flem said. "You just finished selling one of them to Mrs Hait. The railroad says the kind of mules you deal in are worth sixty dollars a head. You claim they are worth a hundred and fifty. All right. We wont argue. Six times a hundred and fifty is—"

"Seven!" I.O. said, loud and harsh. "I aint sold Mrs Hait nor nobody else that mule. Watch." He faced Mrs Hait. "We aint traded. We aint never traded. I defy you to produce ara man or woman that seen or heard more than you tried to hand me this here same ten-dollar bill that I'm a handing right back to you. Here," he said, extending the crumpled bill, then jerking it at her so that it struck against her skirt and fell to the ground. She picked it up.

"You giving this back to me," she said, "before these witnesses?"

"You durn right I am," he said. "I jest wish we had ten times this many witnesses." Now he was talking to Mr Flem. "So I aint sold nobody no mule. And seven times a hundred and fifty dollars is ten hundred and fifty dollars—"

"Nine hundred dollars," Mr Flem said.

"Ten hundred and fifty," I.O. said.

"When you bring me the mule," Mr Flem said. "And on the main condition."

"What main condition?" I.O. said.

"That you move back to Frenchman's Bend and never own a business in Jefferson again as long as you live."

"And if I dont?" I.O. said.

"I sold the hotel this evening too," Mr Flem said. And now even I.O. just watched him while he turned toward the light of the fire and began to count bills—they were mostly fives and ones, with an occasional ten—from the roll. I.O. made one last effort.

"Ten hundred and fifty," he said.

"When you bring me the mule," Mr Flem said. So it was still only nine hundred dollars which I.O. took and counted for himself and folded away into his hip pocket and buttoned the pocket and turned to Mrs Hait.

"All right," he said, "where's Mister Vice Presi-dent Snopes's other mule?"

"Tied to a tree in the ravine ditch behind Mr Spilmer's house," Mrs Hait said.

"What made you stop there?" I.O. said. "Why didn't you take it right on up to Mottstown? Then you could a really enjoyed my time and trouble getting it back." He looked around again, snarling, sneering, indomitably intractable. "You're right fixed up here, aint you? You and the vice presi-dent could both save money if he jest kept that mortgage which aint on nothing now noway, and you didn't build no house atall. Well, good night, all. Soon as I get this-here missing extry mule into the lot with the vice presi-dent's other six, I'll do myself the honor and privilege of calling at his residence for them other hundred and fifty dollars since cash on the barrelhead is the courtesy of kings, as the feller says, not to mention the fact that beggars' choices aint even choices when he aint even got a roof to lay his head in no more. And if Lawyer Stevens has got ara thing loose about him the vice presi-dent might a taken a notion to, he better hold onto it since as the feller says even a fool wont tread where he jest got through watching somebody else get bit. Again, good night, all." Then he was gone. And this time Uncle Gavin said that Mr Flem had to speak to him twice before he heard him.

"What?" Uncle Gavin said.

"I said, how much do I owe you?" Mr Flem said. And Uncle Gavin said he started to say one dollar, so that Mr Flem would say One dollar? Is that all? And then Uncle Gavin could say Yes, or your knife or pencil or just anything so that when I wake up tomorrow I'll know I didn't dream this. But he didn't. He just said:

"Nothing. Mrs Hait is my client." And he said how again Mr Flem had to speak twice. "What?" Uncle Gavin said.

"You can send me your bill."

"For what?" Uncle Gavin said.

"For being the witness," Mr Snopes said.

"Oh," Uncle Gavin said. And now Mr Snopes was going and Uncle Gavin said how he expected he might even have said Are you going back to town now? or maybe even Shall we walk together? or maybe at last Good-bye. But he didn't. He didn't say anything at all. He simply turned and left and was gone too. Then Mrs Hait said:

"Get the box."

"That's what I been aiming to do soon as you can turn loose all this business and steady this skillet," old Het said. So Mrs Hait came and took the chair and the fork and old Het went into the shed and set the lantern on the ground and brought the box and set it at the fire. "Now, honey," she said to Uncle Gavin, "set down and rest."

"You take it," Uncle Gavin said. "I've been sitting down all day. You haven't." Though old Het had already begun to sit down on the box before he declined it; she had already forgotten him, watching now the skillet containing the still hissing ham which Mrs Hait had lifted from the fire.

"Was it you mentioned something about a piece of that ham," she said, "or was it me?" So Mrs Hait divided the ham and Uncle Gavin watched them eat, Mrs Hait in the chair with the new plate and knife and fork, and old Het on the box eating from the skillet itself since Mrs Hait had apparently purchased only one of each new article, eating the ham and sopping the bread into the greasy residue of its frying, and old Het had filled the coffee cup from the pot and produced from somewhere an empty can for her own use when I.O. came back, coming up quietly out of the darkness (it was full dark now), to stand holding his hands to the blaze as though he were cold.

"I reckon I'll take that ten dollars," he said.

"What ten dollars?" Mrs Hait said. And now Uncle Gavin expected him to roar, or at least snarl. But he did neither, just standing there with his hands to the blaze; and Uncle Gavin said he did look cold, small, forlorn somehow since he was so calm, so quiet.

"You aint going to give it back to me?" he said.

"Give what back to you?" Mrs Hait said. Uncle Gavin said he didn't seem to expect an answer nor even to hear her: just standing there musing at the fire in a kind of quiet and unbelieving amazement.

"I bear the worry and the risk and the agoment for years and years, and I get sixty dollars a head for them. While you, one time, without no trouble and risk a-tall, sell Lonzo Hait and five of my mules that never even belonged to him for eighty-five hundred dollars. Of course most of that-ere eighty-five hundred was for Lonzo, which I never begrudged you. Cant nere a man living say I did, even if it did seem a little strange that you should get it all, even my sixty standard price a head for them five mules, when he wasn't working for you and you never even knowed where he was, let alone even owned the mules; that all you done to get half of that money was jest to be married to him. And now, after all them years of not actively begrudging you it, you taken the last mule I had, not didn't jest beat me out of another hundred and forty dollars, but out of a entire another hundred and fifty."

"You got your mule back, and you aint satisfied yet?" old Het said. "What does you want?"

"Justice," I.O. said. "That's what I want. That's all I want: justice. For the last time," he said. "Are you going to give me my ten dollars back?"

"What ten dollars?" Mrs Hait said. Then he turned. He stumbled over something—Uncle Gavin said it was old Het's shopping bag—and recovered and went on. Uncle Gavin said he could see him for a moment—he could because neither Mrs Hait nor old Het was watching him any longer—as though framed between the two blackened chimneys, flinging both clenched hands up against the sky. Then he was gone; this time it was for good. That is, Uncle Gavin watched him. Mrs Hait and old Het had not even looked up.

"Honey," old Het said to Mrs Hait, "what did you do with that mule?" Uncle Gavin said there was one slice of bread left. Mrs Hait took it and sopped the last of the gravy from her plate.

"I shot it," she said.

"You which?" old Het said. Mrs Hait began to eat the slice of bread. "Well," old Het said, "the mule burnt the house and you shot the mule. That's what I calls more than justice: that's what I calls tit for tat." It was full dark now, and ahead of her was still the mile-and-a-half walk to the poorhouse with the heavy shopping bag. But the dark would last a long time on a winter night, and Uncle Gavin said the poorhouse too wasn't likely to move any time soon. So he said that old Het sat back on the box with the empty skillet in her hand and sighed with peaceful and happy relaxation. "Gentlemen, hush," she said. "Aint we had a day."

And there, as Uncle Gavin would say, was Ratliff again, sitting in the client's chair with his blue shirt neat and faded and quite clean and still no necktie even though he was wearing the imitation leather jacket and carrying the heavy black policeman's slicker which were his winter overcoat; it was Monday and Uncle Gavin had gone that morning over to New Market to the supervisors' meeting on some more of the drainage canal business and I thought he would have told Ratliff that when Ratliff came to see him yesterday afternoon at home.

"He might a mentioned it," Ratliff said. "But it dont matter. I didn't want nothing. I jest stopped in here where it's quiet to laugh a little."

"Oh," I said. "About I.O. Snopes's mule that burned down Mrs Hait's house. I thought you and Uncle Gavin laughed at that enough yesterday."

"That's right," he said. "Because soon as you set down to laugh at it, you find out it aint funny a-tall." He looked at me. "When will your uncle be back?"

"I thought he would be back now."

"Oh well," he said. "It dont matter." He looked at me again. "So that's two down and jest one more to go."

"One more what?" I said. "One more Snopes for Mr Flem to run out of Jefferson, and the only Snopes left will be him; or—"

"That's right," he said. "—one more uncivic ditch to jump like Montgomery Ward's photgraph studio and I.O.'s railroad mules, and there wont be nothing a-tall left in Jefferson but Flem Snopes." He looked at me. "Because your uncle missed it."

"Missed what?" I said.

"Even when he was looking right at it when Flem his—himself come in here the morning after them—those federals raided that studio and give your uncle that studio key that had been missing from the sheriff's office ever since your uncle and Hub found them—those pictures; and even when it was staring him in the face out yonder at Miz Hait's chimbley Saturday night when Flem give—gave her that mortgage and paid I.O. for the mules, he still missed it. And I cant tell him."

"Why cant you tell him?" I said.

"Because he wouldn't believe me. This here is the kind of a thing you—a man has got to know his—himself. He has got to learn it out of his own hard dread and skeer. Because what somebody else jest tells you, you jest half believe, unless it was something you already wanted to hear. And in that case, you dont even listen to it because you had done already agreed, and so all it does is make you think what a sensible feller it was that told you. But something you dont want to hear is something you had done already made up your mind against, whether you knowed—knew it or not; and now you can even insulate against having to believe it by resisting or maybe even getting even with that-ere scoundrel that meddled in and told you."

"So he wouldn't hear you because he wouldn't believe it because it is something he dont want to be true. Is that it?"

"That's right," Ratliff said. "So I got to wait. I got to wait for him to learn it his—himself, the hard way, the sure way, the only sure way. Then he will believe it, enough anyhow to be afraid."

"He is afraid," I said. "He's been afraid a long time."

"That's good," Ratliff said. "Because he had purely better be. All of us better be. Because a feller that jest wants money for the sake of money, or even for power, there's a few things right at the last that he wont do, will stop at. But a feller that come—came up from where he did, that soon as he got big enough to count it he thought he discovered that money would buy anything he could or would ever want, and shaped all the rest of his life and actions on that, trompling when and where he had to but without no—any hard feelings because he knowed—knew that he wouldn't ask nor expect no—any quarter his—himself if it had been him—to do all this and then find out at last, when he was a man growed—grown and it was maybe already too late, that the one thing he would have to have if there was to be any meaning to his life or even peace in it was not only something that jest money couldn't buy, it was something that not having money to begin with or even getting a holt of all he could count or imagine or even dream about and then losing it, couldn't even hurt or harm or grieve or change or alter—to find out when it was almost too late that what he had to have was something that any child was born having for free until one day he growed—grew up and found out when it was maybe too late that he had throwed—thrown it away."

"What?" I said. "What is it he's got to have?"

"Respectability," Ratliff said.

"Respectability?"

"That's right," Ratliff said. "When it's jest money and power a man wants, there is usually some place where he will stop; there's always one thing at least that ever—every man wont do for jest money. But when it's respectability he finds out he wants and has got to have, there aint nothing he wont do to get it and then keep it. And when it's almost too late when he finds out that's what he's got to have, and that even after he gets it he cant jest lock it up and set—sit down on top of it and quit, but instead he has got to keep on working with ever—every breath to keep it, there aint nothing he will stop at, aint nobody or nothing within his scope and reach that may not anguish and grieve and suffer."

"Respectability," I said.

"That's right," Ratliff said. "Vice president of that bank aint enough any more. He's got to be president of it."

"*Got* to be?" I said.

"I mean soon, that he dont dare risk waiting, putting it off. That girl of Miz Snopes's—Linda. She's going on—"

"She'll be nineteen the twelfth of April," I said.

"—nineteen now, over there— How do you know it's the twelfth?"

"That's what Uncle Gavin says," I said.

"Sho, now," Ratliff said. Then he was talking again. "—at the University at Oxford where there's a thousand extry young fellers all new and strange and interesting and male and nobody a-tall to watch her

except a hired dormitory matron that aint got no wife expecting to
heir half of one half of Uncle Billy Varner's money, when it was risky
enough at the Academy right here in Jefferson last year before your
uncle or her maw or whichever it was or maybe both of them
together, finally persuaded Flem to let her quit at the Academy and
go to the University after Christmas where he couldn't his—himself
supervise her masculine acquaintance down to the same boys she had
growed—grown up with all her life so at least their folks might have
kinfolk that owed him money to help handle them; not to mention
having her home ever—every night where he could reach out and
put his hand on her ever—every time the clock struck you might say.
So he cant, he dassent, risk it; any time now the telegram or the telephone might come saying she had jest finished running off to the
next nearest town with a j.p. in it that never give a hoot who Flem
Snopes was, and got married. And even if he located them ten minutes later and dragged her—"

"Drug," I said.

"—back, the—what?" he said.

"Drug," I said. "You said 'dragged.' "

Ratliff looked at me a while. "For ten years now, whenever he
would stop talking his-self long enough that is, and for five of them
I been listening to you too, trying to learn—teach myself to say
words right. And, jest when I call myself about to learn and I begin to
feel a little good over it, here you come, of all people, correcting me
back to what I been trying for ten years to forget."

"I'm sorry," I said. "I didn't mean it that way. It's because I like
the way you say it. When you say it, 'taken' sounds a heap more took
than just 'took,' just like 'drug' sounds a heap more dragged than just
'dragged.' "

"And not jest you neither," Ratliff said. "Your uncle too: me saying
'dragged' and him saying 'drug' and me saying 'dragged' and him
saying 'drug' again, until at last he would say, 'In a free country like
this, why aint I got as much right to use your *drug* for my *dragged* as
you got to use my *dragged* for your *drug*?' "

"All right," I said. " 'Even if he drug her back.' "

"—even if he drug—dragged—drug—You see?" he said. "Now

you done got me so mixed up until even I dont know which one I dont want to say?"

" '—it would be too late and the damage—' " I said.

"Yes," Ratliff said. "And at least even your Uncle Gavin knows this; even a feller as high- and delicate-minded as him must know that the damage would be done then and Miz Snopes would quit Flem too and he could kiss good-bye not jest to her share of Uncle Billy's money but even to the voting weight of his bank stock too. So Flem's got to strike now, and quick. He's not only got to be president of that bank to at least keep that much of a holt on that Varner money by at least being president of where Uncle Billy keeps it at, he's got to make his lick before the message comes that Linda's done got married or he'll lose the weight of Uncle Billy's voting stock."

S E V E N T E E N

ＧAVIN ＳTEVENS

*A*t last we knew why he had moved his money. It was as a bait.
Not putting it into the other bank, the old Bank of Jefferson, as the
bait, but for the people of Jefferson and Yoknapatawpha County to
find out that he had withdrawn his own money from the bank of
which he himself was vice president, and put it somewhere else.

But that wasn't first. At first he was simply trying to save it.
Because he knew no better then. His association with banks had been
too brief and humble for the idea even to have occurred to him that
there was a morality to banking, an inevictable ethics in it, else not
only the individual bank but banking as an institution, a form of
social behavior, could not endure.

His idea and concept of a bank was that of the Elizabethan tavern
or a frontier inn in the time of the opening of the American wilderness: you stopped there before dark for shelter from the wilderness;
you were offered food and lodging for yourself and horse, and a bed
(of sorts) to sleep in; if you waked the next morning with your purse
rifted or your horse stolen or even your throat cut, you had none to
blame but yourself since nobody had compelled you to pass that way
nor insisted on your stopping. So when he realised that the very circumstances which had made him vice president of a bank had been
born of the fact that the bank had been looted by an oaf with no
more courage or imagination than he knew his cousin Byron to possess, his decision to remove his money from it as soon as he could was
no more irrational than the traveller who, unsaddling in the inn yard,
sees a naked body with its throat cut being flung from an upstairs
window and re-cinches his saddle with no loss of time and remounts
and rides on again, to find another inn perhaps or if not, to pass the

night in the woods, which after all, Indians and bears and highwaymen to the contrary, would not be a great deal more unsafe.

It was simply to save his money—that money he had worked so
hard to accumulate, too hard to accumulate, sacrificed all his life to
gather together from whatever day it had been on whatever worn-
out tenant farm his father had moved from, onto that other worn-out
one of old Will Varner's at Frenchman's Bend which nobody else
except a man who had nothing would undertake, let alone hope, to
wrest a living from—from that very first day when he realised that he
himself had nothing and would never have more than nothing unless
he wrested it himself from his environment and time, and that the
only weapon he would ever have to do it with would be just money.

Oh yes, sacrificed all his life for, sacrificed all the other rights and
passions and hopes which make up the sum of a man and his life. Perhaps he would never, could never, have fallen in love himself and
knew it: himself constitutionally and generically unfated ever to
match his own innocence and capacity for virginity against the innocence and virginity of who would be his first love. But, since he was
a man, to do that was his inalienable right and hope. Instead, his was
to father another man's bastard on the wife who would not even
repay him with the passion of gratitude, let alone the passion of passion since he was obviously incapable of that passion, but merely with
her dowry.

Too hard for it, all his life for it, knowing at the same time that as
long as life lasted he could never for one second relax his vigilance,
not just to add to it but simply to keep, hang on to, what he already
had, had so far accumulated. Amassing it by terrible and picayune
nickel by nickel, having learned soon, almost simultaneously probably, that he would never have any other method of gaining it save
simple ruthless antlike industry, since (and this was the first time he
ever experienced humility) he knew now that he not only had not the
education with which to cope with those who did have education,
whom he must outguess and outfigure and despoil, but that he never
would have that education now, since there was no time now, since
his was the fate to have first the need for the money before he had
opportunity to acquire the means to get it. And, even having

acquired some of the money, he still had no place to put it down in safety while he did acquire the education which would enable him to defend it from those with the education who would despoil him of it in their turn.

Humility, and maybe a little even of regret—what little time there was to regret in—but without despair, who had nothing save the will and the need and the ruthlessness and the industry and what talent he had been born with, to serve them; who never in his life had been given anything by any man yet and expected no more as long as life should last; who had no evidence yet that he could cope with and fend off that enemy which the word Education represented to him, yet had neither qualm nor doubt that he was going to try.

So at first his only thought was to save that money which had cost him so dear, had in fact cost him everything since he had sacrificed his whole life to gain it and so it was his life, from the bank which his cousin had already proved vulnerable. That was it: a bank so vulnerable that someone like the one he himself knew his cousin Byron to be could have robbed it—an oaf without courage or even vision in brigandage to see further than the simple temptation of a few temporarily unguarded nickels and dimes and dollar bills of the moment, a feller, as Ratliff would have said, hardly bright enough to be named Snopes even, not even bright enough to steal the money without having to run immediately all the way to Texas before he could stop long enough to count it; having in fact managed to steal just about enough to buy the railroad ticket with.

Because remember, he didn't merely know that banks could be looted (*vide* his cousin Byron which he had witnessed himself), he believed, it was a tenet of his very being, that they were constantly looted; that the normal condition of a bank was a steady and decorous embezzlement, its solvency an impregnable illusion like the reputation of a woman who everybody knows has none yet which is intact and invulnerable because of the known (maybe proven) fact that every one of her male connections will spring as one man, not just to repudiate but to avenge with actual gunfire the slightest whisper of a slur on it. Because that—the looting of them—was the reason for banks, the only reason why anybody would go to the trouble and expense of organising one and keeping it running.

That was what Colonel Sartoris had done (he didn't know how yet, that was the innocence, but give him time) while he was president, and what Manfred de Spain would do as long as he in his turn could or did remain on top. But decently, with decorum, as they had done and would do: not reaved like a boy snatching a handful of loose peanuts while the vendor's back was turned, as his cousin Byron had done. Decently and peacefully and even more: cleverly, intelligently; so cleverly and quietly that the very people whose money had been stolen would not even discover it until after the looter was dead and safe. Nor even then actually, since by that time the looter's successor would have already shouldered the burden of that yet-intact disaster which was a natural part of his own heritage. Because, to repeat, what other reason was there to establish a bank, go to all the work and trouble to start one to be president of, as Colonel Sartoris had done; and to line up enough voting stock, figure and connive and finagle and swap and trade (not to mention digging into his own pocket—Ratliff always said De Spain borrowed some if not all of it on his personal note from old Will Varner—to replace the sum which Byron Snopes had stolen) to get himself elected president after the Colonel's death, as Manfred de Spain had done: who—De Spain—would have to be more clever even than the Colonel had been, since he—De Spain—must also contrive to cover up the Colonel's thievery in order to have any bank to loot himself.

He didn't—to repeat again—know how Colonel Sartoris had done it and how De Spain would continue to do it of course—how Colonel Sartoris had robbed it for twelve years yet still contrived to die and be buried in the odor of unimpugnable rectitude; and how De Spain would carry on in his turn and then quit his tenure (whenever that would be) not only with his reputation unimpaired but somehow even leaving intact that bubble of the bank's outward solvency. Or not yet, anyway. Which may have been when he first really tasted that which he had never tasted before—the humility of not knowing, of never having had any chance to learn the rules and methods of the deadly game in which he had gauged his life; whose fate was to have the dreadful need and the will and the ruthlessness, and then to have the opportunity itself thrust upon him before he had had any chance to learn how to use it.

So all he knew to do was to move his money out of the bank of which he was only vice president: not high enough in rank to rob it himself in one fell swoop which would net him enough to make it worth while fleeing beyond extradition for the rest of his life, nor even high enough in its hierarchy to defend himself from the inevitable next Byron Snopes who would appear at the book-keeper's desk, let alone from the greater hereditary predator who already ranked him.

And then he had nowhere to put it. If he could withdraw it from his own bank in utter secrecy, with no one ever to know it, he could have risked hiding it in his house or burying it in the back yard. But it would be impossible to keep it a secret; if no one else, the very book-keeper who recorded the transaction would be an automatic threat. And if word did spread that he had withdrawn his money from the bank in cash, every man and his cousin in the county would be his threat and enemy until every one of them was incontrovertibly convinced that the actual money actually was somewhere else, and exactly where that somewhere else was.

So he had no choice. It would have to be another bank, and done publicly. Of course he thought at once of the best bank he could find, the strongest and safest one: a big Memphis bank for instance. And here he had a new thought: a big bank where his (comparative) widow's mite would be safe because of its very minuscularity; but, believing as he did that money itself, cash dollars, possessed an inherent life of its mutual own like cells or disease, his minuscule sum would increment itself by simple parasitic osmosis like a leech or a goiter or cancer.

And even when he answered that thought immediately with *No. That wont do. The specific whereabouts of the money must be indubitably and incontrovertibly known. All Jefferson and Yoknapatawpha County must know by incontrovertible evidence that the money still is and will remain in Jefferson and Yoknapatawpha County, or I wont even dare leave my home long enough to go to the postoffice, for my neighbors and fellow citizens waiting to climb in the kitchen window to hunt for the sock inside the mattress or the coffee can beneath the hearth,* he did not yet realise what his true reason for moving the money was going to be. And even when he thought how by transferring it to the other Jefferson bank, he would simply be moving it from the frying pan into the fire itself by laying it vulnerable to whatever Byron Snopes the Bank of Jefferson contained, not to mention that one's own Colonel Sartoris or Manfred de Spain, and immediately rejected that by reminding himself that the Bank of Jefferson was older, had had a whole century since 1830 or so to adjust itself to the natural and normal thieving of its officers and employees which was the sole reason for a bank, and so by now its very unbroken longevity was a protection, its very unaltered walls themselves a guarantee, as the simple edifice of the longtime-standing church contains, diffuses and even compels a sanctity invulnerable to the human frailties and vices of parson or vestry or choir—even when he told himself this, his eyes had still not seen the dazzling vista composed not only of civic rectitude but of personal and private triumph and revenge too which the simple withdrawing of that first dollar had opened before him.

He was too busy; his own activity blinded him. Not just getting the money from one bank to the other, but seeing to it, making sure, that everyone in the town and the county knew that he was doing so, laboring under his preconception that the one universal reaction of every man in the county to the news that he had withdrawn his money from the Sartoris bank would be the determined intention of stealing it as soon as he put it down and turned his back; not for the county to know he had withdrawn it from a bank, but that he had put every cent of it into a bank.

It was probably days afterward, the money safe again or at least still again or at least for the moment still again; and I like to imagine it: one still in the overalls and the tieless shirt and still thrall, attached irrevocably by the lean umbilicus of bare livelihood which if it ever broke he would, solvently speaking, die, to the worn-out tenant farm which—the farm and the tieless shirt and the overalls—he had not wrenched free of yet as Snopes himself had, nor ever would probably and who for that very reason had watched the rise of one exactly like himself, from the overalls and the grinding landlord to a white shirt and a tie and the vice presidency of a bank; watched this not with admiration but simply with envy and respect (ay, hatred too), stopping Snopes on the street one day, calling him mister, servile and cringing because of the white shirt and the tie but hating them also because they were not his:

"Likely hit aint a thing to it, but I heerd tell you taken your money outen your bank."

"That's right," Snopes said. "Into the Bank of Jefferson."

"Outen the bank that you yourself are vice president of."

"That's right," Snopes said. "Into the Bank of Jefferson."

"You mean, the other one aint safe?" Which to Snopes was to laugh, to whom no bank was safe; to whom any bank was that clump of bushes at the forest's edge behind the one-room frontier cabin, which the pioneer had to use for outhouse since he had no other: the whole land, the whole dark wilderness (which meant the clump of bushes too) infested with Indians and brigands, not to mention bears and wolves and snakes. Of course it was not safe. But he had to go there. Because not until then did that vista, prospect containing the true reason why he moved his money, open before him. "Then you advise me to move mine too."

"No," Snopes said. "I just moved mine."

"Outen the bank that you yourself air vice president of."

"That's right," Snopes said. "What I myself am vice president of."

"I see," the other said. "Well, much oblige."

Because he saw it then, whose civic jealousy and pride four years later would evict and eliminate from Jefferson one of his own kinsmen who had set up a pay-as-you-enter peep show with a set of imported pornographic photographs, by planting in his place of business several gallons of untaxed homemade whiskey and then notifying the federal revenue people; the same civic jealousy and pride which six years later would evict and eliminate from Jefferson another (and the last) objectionable member of his tribe who had elevated into a profession the simple occupation of hitching mules between the rails at a strategic curve of the railroad where engine drivers couldn't see them in time, by the direct expedient of buying the kinsman's remaining mules at his—the kinsman's—own figure on condition that the kinsman never show his face in Jefferson again.

Civic jealousy and pride which you might say only discovered civic jealousy and pride at the same moment he realised that, in the simple

process of saving his own private money from rapine and ravage-
ment, he could with that same stroke evict and eliminate from his
chosen community its arch-fiend among sinners too, its supremely
damned among the lost infernal seraphim: a creature who was a living mockery of virtue and morality because he was a paradox: lately
mayor of the town and now president of one of its two banks and a
warden of the Episcopal church, who was not content to be a normal natural Saturday-night whoremonger or woman chaser whom
the town could have forgiven for the simple reason that he was natural and human and understandable and censurable, but instead must
set up a kind of outrageous morality of adultery, a kind of flaunted
uxoriousness in *paramours* based on an unimpugnable fidelity which
had already lasted flagrant and unimpugnable ever since the moment
the innocent cuckolded husband brought the female partner of it
into town twelve years ago and which promised, bade or boded,
whichever side you are on, to last another twelve unless the husband
found some way to stop it, and twice twelve probably if he—the husband—waited for the town itself to do anything about it.

Civic virtue which, like all virtue, was its own reward also. Because
in that same blinding flash he saw his own vengeance and revenge
too, as if not just virtue loved virtue but so did God since here He
was actually offering to share with virtue that quality which He had
jealously reserved solely to Himself: the husband's vengeance and
revenge on the man who had presented him with the badge of his
championship; vengeance and revenge on the man who had not
merely violated his home but outraged it—the home which in all
good faith he had tried to establish around a woman already irrevocably soiled and damaged in the world's (Frenchman's Bend's, which
was synonymous enough then) sight, and so give her bastard infant
a name. He had been paid for it, of course. That is, he had received
her dowry: a plantation of barely accessible worn-out land containing the weed-choked ruins of a formal garden and the remains (what
the neighbors had not pulled down plank by plank for firewood) of
a columned colonial house—a property so worthless that Will
Varner gave it away, since even as ruthless an old pirate as Will
Varner had failed in a whole quarter-century of ownership to evolve
any way to turn a penny out of it; so worthless in fact that even he,

Snopes, had been reduced to one of the oldest and hoariest expedients man ever invented: the salted gold mine: in order to sell the place to Henry Armstid and V. K. Ratliff, one of whom, Ratliff anyhow, should certainly have known better, for which reason he, Snopes, had no pity on him.

So in return for that worthless dowry (worthless since what value it had he had not found in it but himself had brought there) he had assumed the burden not only of his wife's moral fall and shame, but of the nameless child too; giving his name to it. Not much of a name maybe, since like what remained of the Old Frenchman's plantation, what value he found in it he himself had brought there. But it was the only name he had, and even if it had been Varner (ay, or Sartoris or De Spain or Compson or Grenier or Habersham or McCaslin or any of the other cognomens long and splendid in the annals of Yoknapatawpha County) he would have done the same.

Anyway, he gave the child a name and then moved the mother herself completely away from that old stage and scene and milieu of her shame, onto, into a new one, where at least no man could say *I saw that fall* but only *This is what gossip said*. Not that he expected gratitude from her, any more than he did from old Will Varner, who by his (Varner's) lights had already paid him. But he did expect from her the simple sense and discretion taught by hard experience: not gratitude toward him but simple sensibleness toward herself, as you neither expect nor care that the person you save from burning is grateful for being saved but at least you expect that from now on that person will stay away from fire.

But that was not the point, that maybe women are no more capable of sensibleness than they are of gratitude. Maybe women are capable only of gratitude, capable of nothing else but gratitude. Only, since the past no more exists for them than morality does, they have nothing which might have taught them sensibility with which to deal with the future and gratitude toward what or who saved them from the past; gratitude in them is a quality like electricity: it has to be produced, projected and consumed all in the same instant to exist at all.

Which was simply saying what any and every man whose fate— doom, destiny, call it whatever you will—finally led him into marriage, long since and soon learned the hard way: his home had been violated not because his wife was ungrateful and a fool, but simply because she was a woman. She had no more been seduced from the chastity of wifehood by the incorrigible bachelor flash and swagger of Manfred de Spain than she had been seduced from that of maidenhood by that same quality in that boy—youth—man—McCarron— back there in her virginity which he was convinced she no longer even remembered. She was seduced simply by herself: by a nymphomania not of the uterus: the hot unbearable otherwise unreachable itch and burn of the mare or heifer or sow or bitch in season, but by a nymphomania of a gland whose only ease was in creating a situation containing a recipient for gratitude, then supplying the gratitude.

Which still didn't exculpate Manfred de Spain. He didn't expect Manfred de Spain to have such high moral standards that they would forbid him seducing somebody else's wife. But he did expect him to have enough sense not to, since he wasn't a woman; to have too much sense this time, enough sense to look a little ahead into the future and refrain from seducing this wife anyway. But he hadn't. Worse: De Spain had even tried to recompense him for the privilege of that violation and defilement; out of base fear to pay him in base and niggling coin for what he, De Spain, juxtaposing De Spain against Snopes, considered his natural and normal *droit de seigneur*. True, old Will Varner had paid him for marrying his damaged daughter, but that was not the same. Old Will wasn't even trying to cover up, let alone liquidate, his daughter's shame. The very fact of what he offered for it—that ruined and valueless plantation of which even he, with a quarter of a century to do it in, had been able to make nothing, revealed what value he held that honor at; and as for liquidating the shame, he—old Will—would have done that himself with his pistol, either in his hand or in that of his oafish troglodyte son Jody, if he had ever caught McCarron. He—old Will—had simply used that forthrightness to offer what he considered a fair price to get out of his house the daughter who had already once outraged his fireside peace and in time would very likely do it again.

But not De Spain, who without courage at all had tried to barter and haggle, using his position as mayor of the town to offer the base coinage of its power-plant superintendency and its implied privileges of petty larceny, not only to pay for the gratification of his appetite but to cover his reputation, trying to buy at the same time the right to the wife's bed and the security of his good name from the husband who owned them both—this, for the privilege of misappropriating a handful of brass which he—Snopes—had availed himself of not for the petty profit it brought him but rather to see what depth De Spain's base and timorous fear would actually descend to.

He saw. They both did. It was not his—Snopes's—shame any more than it was De Spain's pride that when the final crisis of the brass came which could have destroyed him, De Spain found for ally his accuser himself. The accuser, the city official sworn and—so he thought until that moment—dedicated too, until he too proved to be vulnerable (not competent: merely vulnerable) to that same passion from which derived what should have been his—De Spain's—ruin and desolation; the sworn and heretofore dedicated city official who found too dangerous for breathing too that same air simply because she had breathed it, walked in it while it laved and ached; the accuser, the community's civic champion likewise blasted and stricken by that same lightning-bolt out of the old passion and the old anguish. But for him (the accuser) only the grieving without even the loss; for him not even ruin to crown the grieving: only the desolation, who was not competent for but merely vulnerable to, since it was not even for him to hold her hand.

So De Spain brazened that through too, abrogating to courage what had merely been his luck. And as if that were not temerity enough, effrontery enough: Colonel Sartoris barely dead of his heart attack in his grandson's racing automobile (almost as though he—De Spain—had suborned the car and so contrived the accident) and the presidency of the bank barely vacant, when here he—De Spain—was again not requesting or suggesting but with that crass and brazen gall assuming, taking it for granted that he, Snopes, was downright panting for the next new chance not merely to re-compound but publicly affirm again his own cuckolding, that mutual co-violating of his wife's bed—ay, publicly affirming her whoredom; the last clod still echoing as it were on Colonel Sartoris's coffin when De Spain approaches, figuratively rubbing his hands, already saying, "All right, let's get going. That little shirttail full of stock you own will help some of course. But we need a big block of it. You step out to French-man's Bend tomorrow—tonight if possible—and sew up Uncle Billy before somebody else gets to him. Get moving now." Or maybe even the true explicit words: *Your kinsman—cousin—has destroyed this bank by removing a link, no matter how small or large, in the chain of its cash integrity. Which means not just the value of the stock you own in it, but the actual dollars and cents which you worked so hard to acquire and deposit in it, and which until last night were available to you on demand, were still yours. The only way to anneal that chain is to restore that link to the last penny which your cousin stole. I will do that, but in return for it I must be president of the bank; anyone who restores that money will insist on being president in return, just as anyone to become president will have to restore that money first. That's your choice: keep the par of your stock and the full value of your deposit through a president that you know exactly how far you can trust him, or take your chance with a stranger to whom the value of your stock and deposit may possibly mean no more than they did to your cousin Byron.*

He obeyed. He had no choice. Because there was the innocence; ignorance, if you like. He had naturally taught himself all he could about banking, since he had to use them or something equivalent to keep his money in. But so far his only opportunities had been while waiting in line at a window, to peer through the grilled barricade which separated the money and the methods of handling it from the people to whom it belonged, who brought it in and relinquished it on that simple trust of one human being in another, since there was no alternative between that baseless trust and a vulnerable coffee can buried under a bush in the back yard.

Nor was it only to save his own money that he obeyed. In going out to Frenchman's Bend to solicit the vote of old Will Varner's stock for Manfred de Spain, he not only affirmed the fact that simple base-less unguaranteed unguaranteeable trust between man and man was solvent, he defended the fact that it not only could endure: it must endure, since the robustness of a nation was in the solvency of its economy, and the solvency of an economy depended on the rectitude of its banks and the sacredness of the individual dollars they con-tained, no matter to whom the dollars individually belonged, and that rectitude and sanctity must in the last analysis depend on the will of man to trust and the capacity of man to be trusted; in sacrificing the sanctity of his home to the welfare of Jefferson, he immolated the chastity of his wife on the altar of mankind.

And at what added price: not just humbling his pride but throwing it completely away to go out there and try to persuade, perhaps even plead and beg with that old pirate in his dingy country store at Varner's Crossroads—that tall lean choleric outrageous old brigand with his grim wife herself not church-ridden but herself running the local church she belonged to with the cold high-handedness of a ward-boss, and his mulatto concubines (Ratliff said he had three: the first Negroes in that section of the county and for a time the only ones he would permit there, by whom he now had grandchildren, this—the second—generation already darkening back but carrying intact still the worst of the new white Varner traits grafted onto the worst of their fatherless or two-fathered grandmothers' combined original ones), who was anything in the world but unmoral since his were the strictest of simple moral standards: that whatever Will Varner decided to do was right, and anybody in the way had damned well better beware.

Yet he went, to deal with the old man who despised him for having accepted an already-dishonored wife for a price no greater than what he, Varner, considered the Old Frenchman place to be worth; and who feared him because he, Snopes, had been smart enough to realise from it what he, Varner, had not been able to in twenty-five years; who feared him for what that smartness threatened and implied and therefore hated him because he had to fear.

And dealt with him too, persuaded or tricked or forced. Even Ratliff, whose Yoknapatawpha County reputation and good name demanded that he have an answer to everything, did not have that one, Ratliff himself knowing no more than the rest of us did, which was, one day there was a rumored coalition De Spain-Varner-Snopes; on the second day De Spain's own personal hand restored the money which Byron Snopes had absconded to Texas with; on the third day the stockholders elected De Spain president of the bank and Flem Snopes vice president.

That was all. Because there was the innocence. Not ignorance; he didn't know the inner workings of banks not because of ignorance but simply because he had not had opportunity and time yet to teach himself. Now he had only the need, the desperate necessity of having to save the entire bank in order to free his own deposit in it long enough to get the money out and into safety somewhere. And now that he was privileged, the actual vice president of it, from whom all the most secret mechanisms and ramifications of banking and the institution of banks, not only the terror and threat of them but the golden perquisites too, could no longer be hidden, he had less than ever of time. He had in fact time only to discover how simple and easy it was to steal from a bank since even a courageless unimaginative clod like his cousin Byron, who probably could not even conceive of a sum larger than a thousand or two dollars, had been able to do it with impunity; and to begin to get his own money out of it before all the rest of the employees, right on down to the Negro janitor who swept the floor every morning, would decide that the dust and alarm had settled enough to risk (or perhaps simply that the supply of loose money had built up enough again to make it worth while) emulating him.

That was it: the rush, the hurry, the harassment; it was probably with something very like shame that he remembered how it was not his own perspicuity at all but the chance meeting with an ignorant country man alarmed over his own (probably) two-figure bank balance, which opened to him that vista, that dazzling opportunity to combine in one single stroke security for himself and revenge on his enemy—that vengeance which had apparently been afoot for days and even weeks since a well-nigh nameless tenant farmer who probably never came to town four times a year had been his first notice of its existence; that revenge which he was not only unaware of, which he himself had not even planned and instigated, as if the gods or fates—circumstance—something—had taken up the cudgel in his behalf without even asking his permission, and naturally would some day send him a bill for it.

But he saw it now. Not to destroy the bank itself, wreck it, bring it down about De Spain's ears like Samson's temple; but simply to move it still intact out from under De Spain. Because the bank stood for money. A bank was money, and as Ratliff said, he would never injure money, cause to totter for even one second the parity and

immunity of money; he had too much veneration for it. He would
simply move the bank and the money it represented and stood for,
out from under De Spain, intact and uninjured and not even knowing it had been moved, into a new physical niche in the hegemony
and economy of the town, leaving De Spain high and dry with nothing remaining save the mortgage on his house which (according to
Ratliff) he had given old Will Varner for the money with which to
restore what Byron Snopes had stolen.

Only, how to do it. How to evict De Spain from the bank or
remove the bank from under De Spain without damaging it—snatch
it intact from under De Spain by persuading or frightening enough
more of the depositors into withdrawing their money; how to start
the avalanche of dollars which would suck it dry; persuade enough
of the depositors and stockholders to move their stock and funds
bodily out of this one and into a new set of walls across the Square,
or perhaps even (who knew) into the set of walls right next door to
De Spain's now empty ones without even breaking the slumber of the
bank's solvency.

Because even if every other one-gallused share-cropper in the
county whose sole cash value was the October or November sale of
the single bale of cotton which was his tithe of this year's work, withdrew his balance also, it would not be enough. Nor did he have
nature, biology, nepotism, for his weapon. Although there were
probably more people named Snopes or married to a Snopes or who
owed sums ranging from twenty-five cents to five dollars to a Snopes,
than any other name in that section of Mississippi, with one exception not one of them represented the equity of even one bale of
share-crop cotton, and that exception—Wallstreet Panic, the grocer—already banked with the other bank and so could not have been
used even if he—Flem—could have found any way to cope with the
fierce implacable enmity of his—Wallstreet's—wife.

And less than any did he possess that weapon which could have
served him best of all: friendship, a roster of people whom he could
have approached without fear or alarm and suggested or formed a
cabal against De Spain. He had no friends. I mean, he knew he didn't
have any friends because he had never (and never would) intended
to have them, be cluttered with them, be constantly vulnerable or

anyway liable to the creeping sentimental parasitic importunity which his observation had shown him friendship meant. I mean, this was probably when he discovered, for the first time in his life, that you needed friends for the simple reason that at any time a situation could—and in time would, no matter who you were—arise when you could use them; could not only use them but would have to, since nothing else save friendship, someone to whom you could say "Dont ask why; just take this mortgage or lien or warrant or distrainer or pistol and point it where I tell you, and pull the trigger," would do. Which was the innocence again: having had to scratch and scrabble and clutch and fight so soon and so hard and so unflaggingly long to get the money which he had to have, that he had had no time to teach himself how to hold onto it, defend and keep it (and this too with no regret either, since he still had no time to spend regretting). Yes, no regret for lack of that quantity which his life had denied him the opportunity to teach himself that he would need, not because he had no time for regret at this specific moment, but because that desperate crisis had not yet risen where even friendship would not have been enough. Even Time was on his side now; it would be five years yet before he would be forced to the last desperate win-all lose-all by the maturation of a female child.

Though he did have his one tool, weapon, implement—that nethermost stratum of unfutured, barely solvent one-bale tenant farmers which pervaded, covered thinly the whole county and on which in fact the entire cotton economy of the county was founded and supported; he had that at least, with running through his head probably all the worn platitudinous saws about the incrementation of the mere enoughs: enough grains of sand and single drops of water and pennies saved. And working underground now. He had always worked submerged each time until the mine was set and then blew up in the unsuspecting face. But this time he actually consorted with the moles and termites—not with Sartorises and Benbows and Edmondses and Habershams and the other names long in the county annals, which (who) owned the bank stock and the ponderable deposits, but with the other nameless tenants and croppers like his first interlocutor who as that one would have put it: "Knowed a rat when he smelt one."

He didn't proselytise among them. He was simply visible, depending on that first one to have spread the word, the idea, letting himself be seen going and coming out of the other bank, the Bank of Jefferson, himself biding until they themselves would contrive the accidental encounter for corroboration, in pairs or even groups, like a committee, straight man and clown, like this:

"Mawnin, Mister Snopes. Aint you strayed off the range a little, over here at this bank?"

"Maybe Mister Flem has done got so much money now that jest one bank wont hold it. "

"No, boys, it's like my old pappy used to say: Two traps will hold twice as many coons as one trap."

"Did your pappy ever ask that smart old coon which trap he would ruther be in, Mister Snopes?"

"No, boys. All that old coon ever said was, Just so it aint the wrong trap."

That would be all. They would guffaw; one might even slap the faded blue of his overall knee. But that afternoon (or maybe they would even wait a day or two days or even a week) they would appear singly at the teller's window of the old long-established Bank of Jefferson, the gnarled warped sunburned hands relinquishing almost regretfully the meagre clutch of banknotes; never to transfer the account by a simple check at the counter but going in person first to the bank which because of a whispered word supported by a clumsy parable they were repudiating, and withdraw the thin laborious sum in its actual cash and carry it across the Square to the other bank which at that same cryptic anonymous sourceless breath they would repudiate in its turn.

Because they were really neither moles nor termites. Moles can undermine foundations and the termites can reduce the entire house to one little pile of brown dust. But these had neither the individual determination of moles nor the communal determination of the termites even though they did resemble ants in numbers. Because like him, Snopes, they simply were trying to save their meagre individual dollars, and he—Flem—knew it: that another breath, word, would alarm them back into the other bank; that if De Spain himself only wanted to, with the judicious planting of that single word he could recover not merely his own old one-bale clients, but the Bank of Jefferson's entire roster too. Which he nor any other sane banker would want, since it would mean merely that many more Noes to say to the offers of galled mules and worn-out farm and household gear as security to make down payments on second-hand and worn-out automobiles.

It was not enough. It would be nowhere near enough. He recast his mind, again down the diminishing vain roster of names which he had already exhausted, as though he had never before weighed them and found them all of no avail: his nephew or cousin Wallstreet Panic the grocer, who less than ten years ago, by simple industry and honesty and hard work, plus the thousand-dollar compensation for his father's violent death, had gained an interest in a small side-street grocery store and now, in that ten years, owned a small chain of them scattered about north Mississippi, with his own wholesale warehouse to supply them; who—Wallstreet—would alone have been enough to remove De Spain's bank from under him except for two insurmountable obstacles: the fact that he already banked and owned stock in the other bank, and the implacable enmity of his wife toward the very word Snopes, who, it was said in Jefferson, was even trying to persuade her husband to change his own by law. Then the rest of his tribe of Snopes, and the other Snopeses about the county who were not Snopeses nor tenant farmers either, who had been paying him the usury on five- or ten- or twenty-dollar loans for that many years, who, even if he could have enrolled them at the price of individual or maybe lump remission, would have added no weight to his cause for the simple reason that anyone with any amount of money in a public institution anywhere would never have dared put his signature on any piece of paper to remain in his, Flem's, possession.

Which brought him back to where he had started, once more to rack and cast his mind down the vain and diminishing list, knowing that he had known all the while that one name to which he would finally be reduced, and had been dodging it. Old man Will Varner, his father-in-law, knowing all the time that in the end he would have to eat that crow: go back to the choleric irascible old man who never had and never would forgive him for having tricked him into selling him the Old Frenchman place for five hundred dollars, which he,

Flem, sold within two weeks for a profit of three or four hundred percent; go back again to the old man whom only five years ago he had swallowed his pride and approached and persuaded to use the weight of his stock and money to make president of the bank the same man he must now persuade Varner to dispossess.

You see? That was his problem. Probably, except for the really incredible mischance that the bastard child he had given his name to happened to be female, he would never have needed to surmount it. He may have contented himself with the drowsy dream of his revenge, himself but half awake in the long-familiar embrace of his cuckoldry as you recline in a familiar chair with a familiar book, if his wife's bastard had not been a girl.

But she was. Which fact (oh yes, men are interested in facts too, even ones named Flem Snopes) must have struck him at last, whatever the day, moment, was, with an incredible unanticipated shock. Here was this thing, creature, which he had almost seen born you might say, and had seen, watched, every day of its life since. Yet in all innocence, unsuspecting, unforewarned. Oh, he knew it was female, and, continuing to remain alive it must inevitably mature; and, being a human creature, on maturing it would have to be a woman. But he had been too busy making money, having to start from scratch (scratch? scratch was euphemism indeed for where he started from) to make money without owning or even hoping for anything to make it with, to have had time to learn or even to discover that he might need to learn anything about women. You see? A little thing, creature, is born; you say: It will be a horse or a cow, and in time it does become that horse or that cow and fits, merges, fades into environment with no seam, juncture, suture. But not that female thing or creature which becomes (you cannot stop it; not even Flem Snopes could) a woman—woman who shapes, fits herself to no environment, scorns the fixitude of environment and all the behavior patterns which had been mutually agreed on as being best for the greatest number, but on the contrary just by breathing, just by the mere presence of that fragile and delicate flesh, warps and wrenches milieu itself to those soft unangled rounds and curves and planes.

That's what he had. That's what happened to him. Because by that time he had probably resigned himself to no more than the vain and hopeless dream of vengeance and revenge on his enemy. I mean, to canvass and canvass, cast and recast, only to come always back to that one-gallused one-bale residuum which, if all their resources, including the price of the second-hand overalls too, could have been pooled, the result would not have shaken the economy of a country church, let alone a county-seat bank. So he probably gave up, not to the acceptance of his horns, but at least to living with them.

Then the bastard child to whom in what you might call all innocence he had given his name, not satisfied with becoming just *a* woman, must become or threaten to become this particular and specific woman. Being female, she had to become a woman, which he had expected of her and indeed would not have held against her, provided she was content to become merely an ordinary woman. If he had had choice, he naturally would have plumped for a homely one, not really insisting on actual deformity, but one merely homely and frightened from birth and hence doomed to spinsterhood to that extent that her coeval young men would as one have taken one glance at her and then forgot they had ever seen her; and the one who would finally ask for her hand would have one eye, probably both, on her (purported) father's money and so would be malleable to his hand.

But not this one, who was obviously not only doomed for marriage from the moment she entered puberty, but as obviously doomed for marriage with someone beyond his control, either because of geography or age or, worst, most outrageous of all: simply because the husband already had money and would neither need nor want his. *Vide* the gorilla-sized bravo drawn from as far away as Ohio while she was still only fifteen years old, who with his Golden Gloves fists or maybe merely his Golden Gloves reputation intimidated into a male desert except for himself her very surrounding atmosphere; until he was dispossessed by a fact which even his Golden Gloves could not cope with: that she was a woman and hence not just unpredictable: incorrigible.

You see? The gorilla already destined to own at least a Ford agency if not an entire labor union, not dispossessed by nor even superseded by, because they overlapped: the crown prince of the motor age merely on the way out because his successor was already in: the bachelor lawyer twice her age who, although apparently now fixed fast and incapable of harm in the matrix of the small town, bringing into her life and her imagination that same deadly whiff of outland, meeting her in the afternoon at soft-drink stands, not just to entice and corrupt her female body but far worse: corrupting her mind, inserting into her mind and her imagination not just the impractical and dreamy folly in poetry books but the fatal poison of dissatisfaction's hopes and dreams.

You see? The middle-aged (whiteheaded too even) small-town lawyer you would have thought incapable and therefore safe, who had actually served as his, Flem's champion in the ejection of that first, the Ohio gorilla, threat, had now himself become even more of a danger, since he was persuading the girl herself to escape beyond the range of his control, not only making her dissatisfied with where she was and should be, but even showing her where she could go to seek images and shapes she didn't know she had until he put them in her mind.

That was his problem. He couldn't even solve it by choosing, buying for her a husband whom he could handle and control. Because he dared not let her marry anybody at all until God or the devil or justice or maybe simple nature herself, wearied to death of him, removed old Will Varner from the surface at least of the earth. Because the moment she married, the wife who had taken him for her husband for the single reason of providing her unborn child with a name (a little perhaps because of old Will's moral outrage and fury, a good deal maybe just to escape the noise he was probably making at the moment, but mostly, almost all, for the child) would quit him too, either with her present lover or without; in any case, with her father's will drawn eighteen years before she married Flem Snopes and ten or twelve before she ever heard of him, still unchanged.

She must not marry at all yet. Which was difficult enough to prevent even while she was at home in Jefferson, what with half the football and baseball teams escorting her home from school in the afternoon and squiring her in gangs to the picture show during her junior and senior high-school years. Because at least she was living at home where her father could more or less control things either by being her father (oh yes, her father; she knew no different and in fact would have denied, repudiated the truth if anyone had tried to tell her it, since women are not interested in truth or romance but only in facts whether they are true or not, just so they fit all the other facts, and to her the fact was that he was her father for the simple fact that all the other girls, boys too of course, had fathers unless they were dead beneath locatable tombstones) or by threatening to call in or foreclose a usurious note or mortgage bearing the signature of the father or kin of the would-be bridegroom, or—if he, Flem, were lucky—that of the groom himself.

Then who must appear but this meddling whiteheaded outsider plying her with ice-cream sodas and out-of-state college catalogues and at last convincing her that not only her pleasure and interest but her duty too lay in leaving Jefferson, getting out of it the moment she graduated from high school. Upon which, she would carry that rich female provocation which had already drawn blood (ay, real blood once anyway) a dozen times in Jefferson, out into a world rifely teeming with young single men vulnerable to marriage whether they knew it or not before they saw her. Which he forestalled or rather stalled off for still another year which he compelled, persuaded (I dont know what he used; tears even perhaps; certainly tears if he could have found any to use) her to waste at the Academy (one of the last of those gentle and stubbornly fading anachronisms called Miss So-and-So's or The So-and-So Female Academy or Institute whose curriculum included deportment and china-painting, which continue to dot the South though the rest of the United States knows them no more); this, while he racked his brain for how to eliminate this menace and threat to his wife's inheritance which was the middle-aged country lawyer with his constant seduction of out-of-state school brochures. The same middle-aged lawyer in fact who had evicted the preceding menace of the Ohio garage mechanic. But none appeared to eliminate the lawyer save him, the embattled father, and the only tool he knew was money. So I can imagine this: Flem Snopes during all that year, having to remain on constant guard against any casual stranger like a drummer with a line of soap or hardware stopping off the train overnight, and at the same time wring and rack his harassed imagination for some means of compelling me to accept a loan of enough money at usurious enough interest to be under his control.

Which was what I expected of course. I had even reached the point of planning, dreaming what I would do with the money, what buy with the money for which I would continue to betray him. But he didn't do that. He fooled me. Or perhaps he did me that honor too: not just to save my honor for me by withholding the temptation to sully it, but assuming that I would even sell honor before I would sully it and so temptation to do the one would be automatically refused because of the other. Anyway, he didn't offer me the bribe. And I know why now. He had given up. I mean, he realised at last that he couldn't possibly keep her from marriage even though he kept her in Jefferson, and that the moment that happened, he could kiss good-bye forever to old Will Varner's money.

Because some time during that last summer—this last summer or fall rather, since school had opened again and she had even begun her second year at the Academy, wasting another year within the fading walls where Miss Melissa Hogganbeck still taught stubbornly to the dwindling few who were present, that not just American history but all history had not yet reached Christmas Day, 1865, since although General Lee (and other soldiers too, including her own grandfather) had surrendered, the war itself was not done and in fact the next ten years would show that even those token surrenders were mistakes— he sat back long enough to take stock. Indeed, he—or any other male—had only to look at her to know that this couldn't go on much longer, even if he never let her out of the front yard—that girl (woman now; she will be nineteen this month) who simply by moving, being, promised and demanded and would have not just passion, not her mother's fierce awkward surrender in a roadside thicket at night with a lover still bleeding from a gang fight; but love, something worthy to match not just today's innocent and terrified and terrifying passion, but tomorrow's strength and capacity for serenity and growth and accomplishment and the realisation of hope and at last the contentment of one mutual peace and one mutual conjoined old age. It—the worst, disaster, catastrophe, ruin, the last irrevocable chance to get his hands on any part of old Will Varner's money— could happen at any time now; and who knows what relief there might have been in the simple realization that at any moment now he could stop worrying not only about the loss of the money but having to hope for it, like when the receptionist opens the door to the dentist's torture-chamber and looks at you and says "Next" and it's too late now, simple face will not let you leap up and flee.

You see? Peace. No longer to have to waste time hoping or even regretting, having canvassed all the means and rejected all, since who knows too if during that same summer while he racked his harassed and outraged brain for some means to compel me to accept a loan at a hundred percent interest he had not also toyed with the possibility of finding some dedicated enthusiast panting for martyrdom in the simple name of Man who would shoot old Will some night through his kitchen window and then rejected that too, relinquishing not hope so much as just worry.

And not just peace, but joy too since, now that he could relinquish forever that will-o'-the-wisp of his father-in-law's money, he could go back to his original hope and dream of vengeance and revenge on the man responsible for the situation because of which he must give over all hope of his wife's inheritance. In fact he knew now why he had deferred that vengeance so long, dodged like a coward the actual facing of old Will's name in the canvass of possibilities. It was because he had known instinctively all the time that only Will could serve him, and once he had employed Will for his vengeance, by that same stroke he himself would have destroyed forever any chance of participating in that legacy.

But now that was all done, finished, behind him. He was free. Now there remained only the method to compel, force, cajole, persuade, trick—whichever was handiest or quickest or most efficient— the voting power of old Will's stock, plus the weight of that owned by others who were too afraid of old Will to resist him, in addition to his—Flem's—own stock and his corps of one-gallused depositors and their whispering campaign, to remove De Spain's bank from under him by voting him out of its presidency.

All that remained was how, how to handle in a word, lick—Will Varner. And who to dispute that he already knew that too, that plan already tested and retested back in the very time while he was still dodging the facing of old Will's name. Because apparently once his mind was made up and he had finally brought himself to cut out and cauterise with his own hand that old vain hope of his wife's inheritance, he didn't hesitate. Here was the girl, the one pawn which could wreck his hopes of the Varner money, whom he had kept at home where he could delay to that extent at least the inevitable marriage which would ruin him, keeping her at home not only against her own wishes but against those of her mother too (not to mention the meddling neighbor); keeping her at home even when to him too probably it meant she was wasting her time in that anachronistic vacuum which was the Female Academy. This for one entire year and up to the Christmas holidays in the second one; then suddenly, without warning, overnight, he gives his permission for her to go, leave Jefferson and enter the State University; only fifty miles away to be sure, yet they were fifty miles, where it would be impossible for her to report back home every night and where she would pass all her waking hours among a thousand young men, all bachelors and all male.

Why? It's obvious. Why did he ever do any of the things he did? Because he got something in return more valuable to him than what he gave. So you dont really need to imagine this: he and his wife talking together (of course they talked sometimes; they were married, and you have to talk some time to someone even when you're not married)—or four of them that is since there would be two witnesses waiting in the synthetic hall until she should take up the pen: *Sign this document guaranteeing me one half of whatever you will inherit under your father's will, regardless of whatever your and my status in respect to one another may be at that time, and I will give my permission for Linda to go away from Jefferson to school.* All right, granted it could be broken, abrogated, set aside, would not hold. She would not know that. And even if she had never doubted it would hold, had the actual inheritance in her hand at the moment, would she have refused to give him half of it for that in return? Besides, it wasn't her it was to alarm, spook out of the realm of cool judgment.

That was the "how." Now remained only the "when"; the rest of the winter and she away at the University now and he still about town, placid, inscrutable, unchanged, in the broad black planter's hat and the minute bow tie seen somewhere about the Square at least once during the day as regular as the courthouse clock itself; on through the winter and into the spring, until yesterday morning.

That's right. Just gone. So you will have to imagine this too since there would be no witnesses even waiting in a synthetic hall this time: once more the long, already summer-dusty gravel road (it had been simple dirt when he traversed it that first time eighteen years ago) out to Varner's store. And in an automobile this time, it was that urgent, "how" and "when" having at last coincided. And secret; the automobile was a hired one. I mean, an imported hired one. Although most of the prominent people in Jefferson and the county too owned automobiles now, he was not one of them. And not just because of the cost, of what more men than he in Yoknapatawpha County considered the foolish, the almost criminal immobilisation of that many dollars and cents in something which, even though you ran it for hire, would not pay for itself before it wore out, but because he was not only not a prominent man in Jefferson yet, he didn't even want to be: who would have defended as he did his life the secret even of exactly how solvent he really was.

But this was so urgent that he must use one for speed, and so secret that he would have hired one, paid money for the use of one, even if he had owned one, so as not to be seen going out there in his own; too secret even to have ridden out with the mail carrier, which he could have done for a dollar, too secret even to have commandeered from one of his clients a machine which he actually did own since it had been purchased with his money secured by one of his myriad usurious notes. Instead, he hired one. We would never know which one nor where: only that it would not bear Yoknapatawpha County license plates, and drove out there in it, out to Varner's Crossroads once more and for the last time, dragging, towing a fading cloud of yellow dust along the road which eighteen years ago he had travelled in the mule-drawn wagon containing all he owned: the wife and her bastard daughter, the few sticks of furniture Mrs Varner had given them, the deed to Ratliff's half of the little back-street Jefferson restaurant and the few dollars remaining from what Henry Armstid (now locked up for life in a Jackson asylum) and his wife had scrimped and hoarded for ten years, which Ratliff and Armstid had paid him for the Old Frenchman place where he had buried the twenty-five silver dollars where they would find them with their spades.

For the last time, completing that ellipsis which would contain those entire eighteen years of his life, since Frenchman's Bend and Varner's Crossroads and Varner's store would be one, perhaps *the* one, place to which he would never go again as long as he lived, since win or lose he would not need to, and win or lose he certainly would not dare to. And who knows, thinking even then what a shame that he must go to the store and old Will instead of to Varner's house where at this hour in the forenoon there would be nobody but Mrs Varner and the Negro cook,—must go to the store and beard and beat down by simple immobility and a scrap of signed and witnessed paper that violent and choleric old brigand instead. Because women are not interested in romance or morals or sin and its punishment, but only in facts, the immutable facts necessary to the living of life while you are in it and which they are going to damned well see themselves dont fiddle and fool and back and fill and mutate. How simple to have gone straight to her, a woman (the big hard cold gray woman who never came to town any more now, spending all her time between her home and her church, both of which she ran exactly alike: herself self-appointed treasurer of the collections she browbeat out of the terrified congregation, herself selecting and choosing and hiring the ministers and firing them too when they didn't suit her; legend was that she chose one of them out of a cotton field while passing in her buggy, hoicked him from between his plow-handles and ordered him to go home and bathe and change his clothes and followed herself thirty minutes later and ordained him).

How simple to ride up to the gate and say to the hired driver: "Wait here. I wont be long," and go up the walk and enter his ancestral halls (all right, his wife's; he was on his way now to dynamite his own equity in them) and on through them until he found Mrs Varner wherever she was, and say to her: "Good morning, Ma-in-law. I just found out last night that for eighteen years now our Eula's been sleeping with a feller in Jefferson named Manfred de Spain. I packed up and moved out before I left town but I aint filed the divorce yet because the judge was still asleep when I passed his house. I'll tend to that when I get back tonight," and turn and go back to the car and say to the driver: "All right, son. Back to town," and leave Mrs. Varner to finish it, herself to enter the lair where old Will sat among the symbolical gnawed bones—the racks of hames and plow-handles, the rank side meat and flour and cheap molasses and cheese and shoes and coal oil and work gloves and snuff and chewing tobacco and fly-specked candy and the liens and mortgages on crops and plow-tools and mules and horses and land—of his fortune. There would be a few loungers though not many since this was planting time and even the ones there should have been in the field, which they would realise, already starting in an alarmed surge of guilt when they saw her, though not fast enough.

"Get out of here," she would say while they were already moving. "I want to talk to Will.—Wait. One of you go to the sawmill and tell Jody I want his automobile and hurry." And they would say "Yessum, Miz Varner," which she would not hear either, standing over old Will now in his rawhide-bottomed chair. "Get up from there. Flem has finally caught Eula, or says he has. He hasn't filed the suit yet so you will have time before the word gets all over the county. I dont know what he's after, but you go in there and stop it. I wont have it. We had enough trouble with Eula twenty years ago. I aint going to have her back in my house worrying me now."

But he couldn't do that. It wasn't that simple. Because men, especially one like old Will Varner, were interested in facts too, especially a man like old Will in a fact like the one he, Flem, had signed and witnessed and folded inside his coat pocket. So he had to go, walk himself into that den and reach his own hand and jerk the unsuspecting beard and then stand while the uproar beat and thundered about his head until it spent itself temporarily to where his voice could be heard: "That's her signature. If you dont know it, them two witnesses do. All you got to do is help me take that bank away from Manfred de Spain—transfer your stock to my name, take my post-dated check if you want, the stock to be yourn again as soon as Manfred de Spain is out, or you to vote the stock yourself if you had druther—and you can have this paper. I'll even hold the match while you burn it."

That was all. And here was Ratliff again (oh yes, Jefferson could do without Ratliff, but not I—we—us; not I nor the whole damned tribe of Snopes could do without him), all neat and clean and tieless in his blue shirt, blinking a little at me. "Uncle Billy rid into town in Jody's car about four oclock this morning and went straight to Flem's. And Flem aint been to town today. What you reckon is fixing to pop now?" He blinked at me. "What do you reckon it was?"

"What what was?" I said.

"What he taken out there to Miz Varner yesterday that was important enough to have Uncle Billy on the road to town at four oclock this morning?"

"'To *Mrs* Varner?" I said. "He gave it to Will."

"No no," Ratliff said. "He never seen Will. I know. I taken him out there. I had a machine to deliver to Miz Ledbetter at Rockyford and he suh-jested would I mind going by Frenchman's Bend while he spoke to Miz Varner a minute and we did, he was in the house about a minute and come back out and we went on and et dinner with Miz Ledbetter and set up the machine and come on back to town." He blinked at me. "Jest about a minute. What do you reckon he could a said or handed to Miz Varner in one minute that would put Uncle Billy on the road to Jefferson that soon after midnight?

EIGHTEEN

$\mathcal{V}.\ \mathcal{K}.\ \mathcal{R}\!\mathit{ATLIFF}$

*N*o no, no no, no no. He was wrong. He's a lawyer, and to a lawyer, if it aint complicated it dont matter whether it works or not because if it aint complicated up enough it aint right and so even if it works, you dont believe it. So it wasn't that—a paper phonied up on the spur of the moment, that I dont care how many witnesses signed it, a lawyer not nowhere near as smart as Lawyer Stevens would a been willing to pay the client for the fun he would have breaking it wide open.

It wasn't that. I dont know what it was, coming up to me on the Square that evening and saying, "I hear Miz Ledbetter's sewing machine come in this morning. When you take it out to her, I'll make the run out and back with you if you wont mind going by Frenchman's Bend a minute." Sho. You never even wondered how he heard about things because when the time come around to wonder how he managed to hear about it, it was already too late because he had done already made his profit by that time. So I says,

"Well, a feller going to Rockyford could go by Frenchman's Bend. But then, a feller going to Memphis could go by Birmingham too. He wouldn't have to, but he could."—You know: jest to hear him dicker. But he fooled me.

"That's right," he says. "It's a good six miles out of your way. Would four bits a mile pay for it?"

"It would more than pay for it," I says. "To ride up them extra three dollars, me and you wouldn't get back to town before sunup Wednesday. So I'll tell you what I'll do. You buy two cigars, and if you'll smoke one of them yourself, I'll carry you by Frenchman's Bend for one minute jest for your company and conversation."

"I'll give them both to you," he says. So we done that. Oh sho, he beat me out of my half of that little café me and Grover Winbush owned, but who can say jest who lost then? If he hadn't a got it, Grover might a turned it into a French postcard peepshow too, and then I'd be out there where Grover is now: night watchman at that brick yard.

So I druv him by Frenchman's Bend. And we had the conversation too, provided you can call the monologue you have with Flem Snopes a conversation. But you keep on trying. It's because you hope to learn. You know silence is valuable because it must be, there's so little of it. So each time you think *Here's my chance to find out how a expert uses it.* Of course you wont this time and never will the next neither, that's how come he's a expert. But you can always hope you will. So we druv on, talking about this and that, mostly this of course, with him stopping chewing ever three or four miles to spit out the window and say "Yep" or "That's right" or "Sounds like it" until finally—there was Varner's Crossroads jest over the next rise—he says, "Not the store. The house," and I says,

"What? Uncle Billy wont be home now. He'll be at the store this time of morning."

"I know it," he says. "Take this road here." So we taken that road; we never even seen the store, let alone passed it, on to the house, the gate.

"You said one minute," I says. "If it's longer than that, you'll owe me two more cigars."

"All right," he says. And he got out and went on, up the walk and into the house, and I switched off the engine and set there thinking *What? What? Miz Varner. Not Uncle Billy: MIZ Varner.* That Uncle Billy jest hated him because Flem beat him fair and square, at Uncle Billy's own figger, out of that Old Frenchman place, while Miz Varner hated him like he was a Holy Roller or even a Baptist because he had not only condoned sin by marrying her daughter after somebody else had knocked her up, he had even made sin pay by getting the start from it that wound him up vice president of a bank. Yet it was *Miz* Varner he had come all the way out here to see, was willing to pay me three extra dollars for it (I mean, offered. I know now I could a asked him ten.)

No, not thinking *What? What?* because what I was thinking was

Who, who ought to know about this, trying to think in the little time
I would have, since his-self had volunteered that-ere one minute, so
one minute it was going to be, jest which who that was. Not me,
because there wasn't no more loose dangling Ratliff-ends he could
need; and not Lawyer Stevens and Linda and Eula and that going-
off-to-school business that had been the last what you might call
Snopes uproar to draw attention on the local scene, because that was
ended too now, with Linda at least off at the University over at
Oxford even if it wasn't one of them Virginia or New England colleges Lawyer was panting for. I didn't count Manfred de Spain
because I wasn't on Manfred de Spain's side. I wasn't against him neither, it was jest like Lawyer Stevens his-self would a said: the feller
that already had as much on his side as Manfred de Spain already had
or anyway as ever body in Jefferson whose business it wasn't neither,
believed he had, didn't need no more. Let alone deserve it.

Only there wasn't time. It wasn't one minute quite but it wasn't
two neither when he come out the door in that-ere black hat and his
bow tie, still chewing because I doubt if he ever quit chewing any
more than he probably taken off that hat while he was inside, back
to the car and spit and got in and I started the engine and says, "It
wasn't quite a full two, so I'll let you off for one," and he says,

"All right," and I put her in low and set with my foot on the clutch
and says,

"'In case she was out, you want to run by the store and tell Uncle
Billy you left a message on the hatrack for her?' and he chewed a lick
or two more and balled up the ambeer and leaned to the window and
spit again and set back and we went on to Rockyford and I set up the
machine for Miz Ledbetter and she invited us to dinner and we et
and come home and at four oclock this morning Uncle Billy druv
up to Flem's house in Jody's car with his Negro driver and I know
why four oclock because that was Miz Varner.

I mean Uncle Billy would go to bed soon as he et his supper,
which would be before sundown this time of year, so he would wake
up anywhere about one or two oclock in the morning. Of course he
had done already broke the cook into getting up then to cook his
breakfast but jest one Negro woman rattling pans in the kitchen
wasn't nowhere near enough for Uncle Billy, ever body else hadn't

jest to wake up then but to get up too: stomping around and banging doors and hollering for this and that until Miz Varner was up and
dressed too. Only Uncle Billy could eat his breakfast then set in a
chair until he smoked his pipe out and then he would go back to
sleep until daylight. Only Miz Varner couldn't never go back to sleep
again, once he had done woke her up good.

So this was her chance. I dont know what it was Flem told her or
handed her that was important enough to make Uncle Billy light out
for town at two oclock in the morning. But it wasn't no more important to Miz Varner than her chance to go back to bed in peace and
quiet and sleep until a decent Christian hour. So she jest never told
him or give it to him until he woke up at his usual two a.m.; if it was
something Flem jest handed her that she never needed to repeat,
likely she never had to get up a-tall but jest have it leaning against the
lamp when Uncle Billy struck a match to light it so he could see to
wake up the rest of the house and the neighbors.

So I dont know what it was. But it wasn't no joked-up piece of
paper jest in the hopes of skeering Uncle Billy into doing something
that until now he hadn't aimed to do. Because Uncle Billy dont skeer,
and Flem Snopes knows it. It had something to do with folks, people,
and the only people connected with Jefferson that would make Uncle
Billy do something he hadn't expected until this moment he would
do are Eula and Linda. Not Flem; Uncle Billy has knowed for twenty
years now exactly what he will do to Flem the first time Flem's eye
falters or his hand slips or his attention wanders.

Let alone going to Uncle Billy his-self with it. Because anything in
reference to that bank that Flem would know in advance that jest by
handing it or saying it to Miz Varner would be stout enough to move
Uncle Billy from Frenchman's Bend to Jefferson as soon as he heard
about it, would sooner or later have to scratch or leastways touch
Eula. And maybe Uncle Billy Varner dont skeer and Flem Snopes
knows it, but Flem Snopes dont skeer neither and most folks knows
that too. And it dont take no especial coward to not want to walk into
that store and up to old man Will Varner and tell him his daughter
aint reformed even yet, that she's been sleeping around again for
eighteen years now with a feller she aint married to, and that her husband aint got guts enough to know what to do about it.

N I N E T E E N

Charles Mallison

*I*t was like a circus day or the county fair. Or more: it was like the District or even the whole State field meet because we even had a holiday for it. Only it was more than just a fair or a field day because this one was going to have death in it too though of course we didn't know that then.

It even began with a school holiday that we didn't even know we were going to have. It was as if time, circumstance, geography, contained something which must, anyway was going to, happen and now was the moment and Jefferson, Mississippi, was the place, and so the stage was cleared and set for it.

The school holiday began Tuesday morning. Last week some new people moved to Jefferson, a highway engineer, and their little boy entered the second grade. He must have been already sick when his mother brought him because he had to go home; they sent for her and she came and got him that same afternoon and that night they took him to Memphis. That was Thursday but it wasn't until Monday afternoon that they got the word back that what he had was polio and they sent word around that the school would be closed while they found out what to do next or what to not do or whatever it was while they tried to learn more about polio or about the engineer's little boy or whatever it was. Anyhow it was a holiday we hadn't expected or even hoped for, in April; that April morning when you woke up and you would think how April was the best, the very best time of all not to have to go to school, until you would think *Except in the fall* with the weather brisk and not-cold at the same time and the trees all yellow and red and you could go hunting all day long; and then you would think *Except in the winter* with the Christmas holidays over and now nothing to look forward to until summer; and

609

you would think how no time is the best time to not have to go to school and so school is a good thing after all because without it there wouldn't be any holidays or vacations.

Anyhow we had the holiday, we didn't know how long; and that was fine too because now you never had to say *Only two days left* or *Only one day left* since all you had to do was just be holiday, breathe holiday, today and tomorrow too and who knows? tomorrow after that and, who knows? still tomorrow after that. So on Wednesday when even the children who would have been in school except for the highway engineer's little boy began to know that something was happening, going on inside the president's office of the bank—not the old one, the Bank of Jefferson, but the other, the one we still called the new bank or even Colonel Sartoris's bank although he had been dead seven years now and Mr de Spain was president of it—it was no more than we expected, since this was just another part of whatever it was time or circumstance or whatever it was had cleared the stage and emptied the school so it could happen.

No, to say that the stage was limited to just one bank; to say that time, circumstance, geography, whatever it was had turned school out in the middle of April in honor of something it wanted to happen inside just one set of walls was wrong. It was all of Jefferson. It was all the walls of Jefferson, the ground they stood on, the air they rose up in; all the walls and air in Jefferson that people moved and breathed and talked in; we were already at dinner except Uncle Gavin, who was never late unless he was out of town on county business, and when he did come in something was already wrong. I mean, I didn't always notice when something was wrong with him and it wasn't because I was only twelve yet, it was because you didn't have to notice Uncle Gavin because you could always tell from Mother since she was his twin; it was like when you said "What's the matter?" to Mother, you and she and everybody else knew you were saying What's wrong with Uncle Gavin?

But we could always depend on Father. Uncle Gavin came in at last and sat down and unfolded his napkin and said something wrong and father glanced at him and then went back to eating and then looked at Uncle Gavin again.

"Well," he said, "I hear they got old Will Vamer out of bed at two this morning and brought him all the way in to town to promote Manfred de Spain. Promote him where?"

"What?" Uncle Gavin said.

"Where do you promote a man that's already president of the bank?" Father said.

"Charley," Mother said.

"Or maybe promote aint the word I want," Father said. "The one I want is when you promote a man quick out of bed—"

"Charley!" Mother said.

"—especially a bed he never had any business in, not to mention having to send all the way out to Frenchman's Bend for your pa-in-law to pronounce that word—"

"Charles!" Mother said. That's how it was. It was like we had had something in Jefferson for eighteen years and whether it had been right or whether it had been wrong to begin with didn't matter any more now because it was ours, we had lived with it and now it didn't even show a scar, like the nail driven into the tree years ago that violated and outraged and anguished that tree. Except that the tree hasn't got much choice either: either to put principle above sap and refuse the outrage and next year's sap both, or accept the outrage and the sap for the privilege of going on being a tree as long as it can, until in time the nail disappears. It dont go away; it just stops being so glaring in sight, barked over, there is a lump, a bump of course, but after a while the other trees forgive that and everything else accepts that tree and that bump too until one day the saw or the axe goes into it and hits that old nail.

Because I was twelve then. I had reached for the second time that point in the looping circles children—boys anyway—make growing up when for a little while they enter, live in, the same civilisation that grown people use, when it occurs to you that maybe the sensible and harmless things they wont let you do really seem as silly to them as the things they seem either to want to do or have to do seem to you. No: it's when they laugh at you and suddenly you say, *Why, maybe I am funny*, and so the things they do are not outrageous and silly or shocking at all: they're just funny; and more than that, it's the same funny. So now I could ask. A few more years and I would know more than I knew then. But the loop, the circle, would be swinging

on away out into space again where you cant ask grown people
because you cant talk to anybody, not even the others your age
because they too are rushing on out into space where you cant touch
anybody, you dont dare try, you are too busy just hanging on; and
you know that all the others out there are just as afraid of asking as
you are, nobody to ask, nothing to do but make noise, the louder the
better, then at least the other scared ones wont know how scared
you are.

But I could still ask now, for a little while. I asked Mother.

"Why dont you ask Uncle Gavin?" she said.

She wanted to tell me. Maybe she even tried. But she couldn't. It
wasn't because I was only twelve. It was because I was her child, created by her and Father because they wanted to be in bed together
and nothing else would do, nobody else would do. You see? If Mrs
Snopes and Mr de Spain had been anything else but people, she
could have told me. But they were people too, exactly like her and
Father; and it's not that the child mustn't know that the same magic
which made him was the same thing that sent an old man like Mr
Will Varner into town at four oclock in the morning just to take
something as sorry and shabby as a bank full of money away from
another man named Manfred de Spain: it's because the child couldn't
believe that. Because to the child, he was not created by his mother's
and his father's passion or capacity for it. He couldn't have been
because he was there first, he came first, before the passion; he created the passion, not only it but the man and the woman who served
it; his father is not his father but his son-in-law, his mother not his
mother but his daughter-in-law if he is a girl.

So she couldn't tell me because she could not. And Uncle Gavin
couldn't tell me because he wasn't able to, he couldn't have stopped
talking in time. That is, that's what I thought then. I mean, that's
what I thought then was the reason why they—Mother—didn't tell
me: that the reason was just my innocence and not Uncle Gavin's too
and she had to guard both, since maybe she was my mother but she
was Uncle Gavin's twin and if a boy or a girl really is his father's and
her mother's father-in-law or mother-in-law, which would make the
girl her brother's mother no matter how much younger she was, then

a girl with just one brother and him a twin at that, would maybe be his wife and mother too.

So maybe that was why: not that I wasn't old enough to accept biology, but that everyone should be, deserves to be, must be, defended and protected from the spectators of his own passion save in the most general and unspecific and impersonal terms of the literary and dramatic lay-figures of the protagonists of passion in their bloodless and griefless posturings of triumph or anguish; that no man deserves love since nature did not equip us to bear it but merely to endure and survive it, and so Uncle Gavin's must not be watched where she could help and fend him, while it anguished on his own unarmored bones.

Though even if they had tried to tell me, it would have been several years yet, not from innocence but from ignorance, before I would know, understand, what I had actually been looking at during the rest of that Wednesday afternoon while all of Jefferson waited for the saw to touch that buried nail. No: not buried, not healed or annealed into the tree but just cysted into it, alien and poison; not healed over, but scabbed over with a scab which merely renewed itself, incapable of healing, like a signpost.

Because ours was a town founded by Aryan Baptists and Methodists, for Aryan Baptists and Methodists. We had a Chinese laundryman and two Jews, brothers with their families, who ran two clothing stores. But one of them had been trained in Russia to be a rabbi and spoke seven languages including classic Greek and Latin and worked geometry problems for relaxation and he was absolved, lumped in the same absolution with old Doctor Wyott, president emeritus of the Academy (his grandfather had founded it), who could read not only Greek and Hebrew but Sanskrit too, who wore two foreign decorations for (we, Jefferson, believed) having been not just a professing but a militant and even boasting atheist for at least six of his eighty years and who had even beaten the senior Mr Wildermark at chess; and the other Jewish brother and his family and the Chinese all attended, were members of, the Methodist church and so they didn't count either, being in our eyes merely non-white people, not actually colored. And although the Chinese was definitely a colored man even if not a Negro, he was only he, single peculiar and barren; not just kinless but even kindless, half the world or anyway half the continent (we all knew about San Francisco's Chinatown) sundered from his like and therefore as threatless as a mule.

There is a small Episcopal church in Jefferson, the oldest extant building in town (it was built by slaves and called the best, the finest too, I mean by the Northern tourists who passed through Jefferson now with cameras, expecting—we dont know why since they themselves had burned it and blown it up with dynamite in 1863—to find Jefferson much older or anyway older looking than it is and faulting us a little—because it isn't) and a Presbyterian congregation too, the two oldest congregations in the county, going back to the old days of Issetibbeha, the Chickasaw chief, and his sister's son Ikkemotubbe whom they called Doom, before the County was a county and Jefferson was Jefferson. But nowadays there wasn't much difference between the Episcopal and Presbyterian churches and Issetibbeha's old mounds in the low creek bottoms about the county because the Baptists and Methodists had heired from them, usurped and dispossessed; ours a town established and decreed by people neither Catholics nor Protestants nor even atheists but incorrigible nonconformists, nonconformists not just to everybody else but to each other in mutual accord; a nonconformism defended and preserved by descendants whose ancestors hadn't quitted home and security for a wilderness in which to find freedom of thought as they claimed and oh yes, believed, but to find freedom in which to be incorrigible and unreconstructible Baptists and Methodists; not to escape from tyranny as they claimed and believed, but to establish one.

And now, after eighteen years, the saw of retribution, which we of course called that of righteousness and simple justice, was about to touch that secret hidden unhealed nail buried in the moral tree of our community—that nail not only corrupted and unhealed but unhealable because it was not just sin but mortal sin—a thing which should not exist at all, whose very conception should be self-annihilative, yet a sin which people seemed constantly and almost universally to commit with complete impunity; as witness these two for eighteen years, not only flouting decency and morality but even compelling decency and morality to accept them simply by being discreet: nobody had actually caught them yet; outraging morality itself by allying economics on their side since the very rectitude and solvency of a bank would be involved in their exposure.

In fact, the town itself was divided into two camps, each split in turn into what you might call a hundred individual nonconforming bivouacs: the women who hated Mrs Snopes for having grabbed Mr de Spain first or hated Mr de Spain for having preferred Mrs Snopes to them, and the men who were jealous of De Spain because they were not him or hated him for being younger than they or braver than they (they called it luckier of course); and those of both sexes— no: the same sour genderless sex—who hated them both for having found or made together something which they themselves had failed to make, whatever the reason; and in consequence of which that splendor must not only not exist, it must never have existed—the females of it who must abhor the splendor because it was, had to be, barren; the males of it who must hate the splendor because they had set the cold stability of currency above the wild glory of blood: they who had not only abetted the sin but had kept alive the anguish of their own secret regret by supporting the sinners' security for the sake of De Spain's bank. Two camps: the one that said the sin must be exposed now, it had already lasted eighteen years too long; the other which said it dare not be exposed now and so reveal our own baseness in helping to keep it hidden all this long time.

Because the saw was not just seeking that nail. As far as Jefferson was concerned it had already touched it; we were merely waiting now to see in what direction the fragments of that particular tree in our wood (not the saw itself, never the saw: if that righteous and invincible moral blade flew to pieces at the contact, we all might as well give up, since the very fabric of Baptist and Methodist life is delusion, nothing) would scatter and disintegrate.

That was that whole afternoon while old Mr Varner still stayed hidden or anyway invisible in Mr Snopes's house. We didn't even know definitely that he was actually in town, nobody had seen him; we only had Ratliff's word that he had come in in his son's automobile at four oclock this morning, and we didn't know that for sure unless Ratliff had sat up all night watching the Snopes's front door. But then Mr Varner was there, he had to be or there wouldn't be any use for the rest of it. And Mr de Spain's bank continued its ordinary sober busy prosperous gold-auraed course to the closing hour at three oclock, when almost at once the delivery boy from Christian's drugstore knocked at the side door and was admitted with his ritual tray of four Coca-Colas for the two girl book-keepers and Miss Killebrew the teller and Mr Hovis the cashier. And presently, at his ordinary hour, Mr de Spain came out and got in his car as usual and drove away to look at one of the farms which he now owned or on which the bank held a mortgage, as he always did: no rush, no panic to burst upon the ordered financial day. And some time during the day, either forenoon or afternoon, somebody claimed to have seen Mr Snopes himself, unchanged too, unhurried and unalarmed, the wide black planter's hat still looking brand new (the tiny bow tie which he had worn for eighteen years now always did), going about his inscrutable noncommunicable affairs.

Then it was five oclock and nothing had happened; soon now people would begin to go home to eat supper and then it would be too late and at first I thought of going up to the office to wait for Uncle Gavin to walk home, only I would have to climb the stairs and then turn around right away and come back down again and I thought what a good name spring fever was to excuse not doing something you didn't want to do, then I thought maybe spring fever wasn't an excuse at all because maybe spring fever actually was.

So I just stood on the corner where he would have to pass, to wait for him. Then I saw Mrs Snopes. She had just come out of the beauty parlor and as soon as you looked at her you could tell that's where she had been and I remembered how Mother said once she was the only woman in Jefferson that never went to one because she didn't need to since there was nothing in a beauty shop that she could have lacked. But she had this time, standing there for a minute and she really did look both ways along the street before she turned and started toward me and then she saw me and came on and said, "Hello, Chick," and I tipped my cap, only she came up and stopped and I took my cap off; she had a bag on her arm like ladies do, already opening in to reach inside.

"'I was looking for you," she said. "Will you give this to your uncle when you go home?"

"Yessum," I said. It was an envelope.

"'Thank you,'" she said. "Have they heard any more about the little Riddell boy?"

"I dont know'm," I said. It wasn't sealed. It didn't have any name on the front either.

"Let's hope they got him to Memphis in time," she said. Then she said Thank you again and went on, walking like she does, not like a pointer about to make game like Linda, but like water moves somehow. And she could have telephoned him at home and I almost said *You dont want me to let Mother see it* before I caught myself. Because it wasn't sealed. But then, I wouldn't have anyway. Besides, I didn't have to. Mother wasn't even at home yet and then I remembered: Wednesday, she would be out at Sartoris at the meeting of the Byron Society though Mother said it had been a long time now since anybody listened to anybody read anything because they played bridge now but at least she said that when it met with Miss Jenny Du Pre they had toddies or juleps instead of just coffee or Coca-Colas.

So nothing had happened and now it was already too late, the sun going down though the pear tree in the side yard had bloomed and gone a month ago and now the mockingbird had moved over to the pink dogwood, already beginning where he had sung all night long all week until you would begin to wonder why in the world he didn't go somewhere else and let people sleep. And nobody at home at all yet except Aleck Sander sitting on the front steps with the ball and bat. "Come on," he said. "I'll knock you out some flies." Then he said, "All right, you knock out and I'll chase um."

So it was almost dark inside the house; I could already smell supper cooking and it was too late now, finished now: Mr de Spain gone out in his new Buick to watch how much money his cotton was making, and Mrs Snopes coming out of the beauty shop with her hair even waved or something or whatever it was, maybe for a party at her house tonight or maybe it hadn't even begun; maybe old Mr Varner wasn't even in town at all, not only wasn't coming but never had aimed to and so all the Riddell boy did by catching polio was just to give us a holiday we didn't expect and didn't know what to do with; until I heard Uncle Gavin come in and come up the stairs and I met him in the upstairs hall with the envelope in my hand: just the shape of him coming up the stairs and along the hall until even in that light I saw his face all of a sudden and all of a sudden I said:

"You're not going to be here for supper."

"No," he said. "Will you tell your mother?"

"Here," I said and held out the envelope and he took it.

TWENTY

GAVIN STEVENS

*T*hough you have to eat. So after I went back and unlocked the office and left the door on the latch, I drove out to Seminary Hill, to eat cheese and crackers and listen to old Mr Garraway curse Calvin Coolidge while he ran the last loafing Negroes out of the store and closed it for the night.

Or so I thought. Because you simply cannot go against a community. You can stand singly against any temporary unanimity of even a city full of human behavior, even a mob. But you cannot stand against the cold inflexible abstraction of a long-suffering community's moral point of view. Mr Garraway had been one of the first—no: the first— to move his account from Colonel Sartoris's bank to the Bank of Jefferson, even before Flem Snopes ever thought or had reason to think of his tenant-farmer panic. He had moved it in fact as soon as we—the town and county—knew that Manfred de Spain was definitely to be president of it. Because he—Mr Garraway—had been one of that original small inflexible unreconstructible Puritan group, both Baptist and Methodist, in the county who would have moved their fiscal allegiance also from Jefferson while De Spain was mayor of it, to escape the moral contamination and express their opinion of that liaison which he represented, if there had been another fiscal town in the county to have moved it to. Though later, a year or two afterward, he moved the account back, perhaps because he was just old or maybe he could stay in his small dingy store out at Seminary Hill and not have to come to town, have to see with his own eyes and so be reminded of his county's shame and disgrace and sin if he didn't want to be. Or maybe once you accept something, it doesn't really matter any more whether you like it or not. Or so I thought.

The note said ten oclock. That was all, *Please meet me at your office* *at ten tonigh*t. Not *if convenient*, let alone *when could you see me at your office?* but simply *at ten tonight please*. You see. Because in the first place, Why me? *Me?* To say that to all of them, all three of them— no, all four, taking De Spain with me: *Why cant you let me alone? What more can you want of me than I have already failed to do?* But there would be plenty of time for that; I would have plenty of time to eat the sardines and crackers and say What a shame to the account of whatever the recent outrage the President and his party had contrived against Mr Garraway, when he—Mr Garraway—said suddenly (an old man with an old man's dim cloudy eyes magnified and enormous behind the thick lenses of his iron-framed spectacles): "Is it so that Will Varner came in to town this morning?"

"Yes," I said.

"So he caught them." Now he was trembling, shaking, standing there behind the worn counter which he had inherited from his father, racked with tins of meat and spools of thread and combs and needles and bottles of cooking extract and malaria tonic and female compound some of which he had probably inherited too, saying in a shaking voice: "Not the husband! The father himself had to come in and catch them after eighteen years!"

"But you put your money back," I said. "You took it out at first, when you just heard at second hand about the sin and shame and outrage. Then you put it back. Was it because you saw her too at last? She came out here one day, into your store, and you saw her yourself, got to know her, to believe that she at least was innocent? Was that it?"

"I knew the husband," he said, cried almost, holding his voice down so the Negroes couldn't hear what we—he was talking about. "I knew the husband! He deserved it!"

Then I remembered. "Yes," I said. "I thought I saw you in town this afternoon." Then I knew. "You moved it again today, didn't you? You drew it out again and put it back into the Bank of Jefferson today, didn't you?" and he standing there, shaking even while he tried to hold himself from it. "Why?" I said. "Why again today?"

"She must go," he said. "They must both go—she and De Spain too."

"But why?" I said, muttered too, not to be overheard: two white men discussing in a store full of Negroes a white woman's adultery. More: adultery in the very top stratum of a white man's town and bank. "Why only now? It was one thing as long as the husband accepted it; it became another when somebody—how did you put it?—catches them, blows the gaff? They become merely sinners then, criminals then, lepers then? Nothing for constancy, nothing for fidelity, nothing for devotion, unpoliced devotion, eighteen years of devotion?"

"Is that all you want?" he said. "I'm tired. I want to go home." Then we were on the gallery where a few of the Negroes still lingered, the arms and faces already fading back into the darkness behind the lighter shades of shirts and hats and pants as if they were slowly vacating them, while his shaking hands fumbled the heavy padlock through the hasp and fumbled it shut; until suddenly I said, quite loud:

"Though if anything the next one will be worse because the next president will probably be Governor Smith and you know who Governor Smith is of course: a Catholic," and would have stopped that in time in very shame but could not, or maybe should have stopped it in time in very shame but would not. Since who was I, what anguish's missionary I that I must compound it blindly right and left like some blind unrational minor force of nature? Who had already spoiled supper and ruined sleep both for the old man standing there fumbling with his clumsy lock as if I had actually struck him—the old man who in his fashion, in a lot of people's fashion, really was a kindly old man who never in his life wittingly or unwittingly harmed anyone black or white, not serious harm: not more than adding a few extra cents to what it would have been for cash, when the article went on credit; or selling to a Negro for half-price or often less (oh yes, at times even giving it to him) the tainted meat or rancid lard or weevilled flour or meal he would not have permitted a white man—a Protestant gentile white man of course—to eat at all out of his store; standing there with his back turned fumbling at the giant padlock as though I had actually struck him, saying,

"They must go. They must go, both of them."

There is a ridge; you drive on beyond Seminary Hill and in time you come upon it: a mild unhurried farm road presently mounting to

cross the ridge and on to join the main highway leading from Jefferson to the world. And now, looking back and down, you see all Yoknapatawpha in the dying last of day beneath you. There are stars
now, just pricking out as you watch them among the others already
coldly and softly burning; the end of day is one vast green soundless
murmur up the northwest toward the zenith. Yet it is as though light
were not being subtracted from earth, drained from earth backward
and upward into that cooling green, but rather had gathered, pooling
for an unmoving moment yet, among the low places of the ground so
that ground, earth itself is luminous and only the dense clumps of
trees are dark, standing darkly and immobile out of it.

    Then, as though at signal, the fireflies—lightning-bugs of the
Mississippi child's vernacular—myriad and frenetic, random and
frantic, pulsing; not questing, not quiring, but choiring as if they
were tiny incessant appeaseless voices, cries, words. And you stand
suzerain and solitary above the whole sum of your life beneath that
incessant ephemeral spangling. First is Jefferson, the center, radiat-
ing weakly its puny glow into space; beyond it, enclosing it, spreads
the County, tied by the diverging roads to that center as is the rim
to the hub by its spokes, yourself detached as God Himself for this
moment above the cradle of your nativity and of the men and women
who made you, the record and chronicle of your native land proffered for your perusal in ring by concentric ring like the ripples on
living water above the dreamless slumber of your past; you to preside
unanguished and immune above this miniature of man's passions and
hopes and disasters—ambition and fear and lust and courage and
abnegation and pity and honor and sin and pride—all bound, precarious and ramshackle, held together by the web, the iron-thin warp
and woof of his rapacity but withal yet dedicated to his dreams.

    They are all held here, supine beneath you, stratified and super-
posed, osseous and durable with the frail dust and the phantoms—
the rich alluvial river-bottom land of Issetibbeha, the wild Chickasaw
king, with his Negro slaves and his sister's son called Doom who
murdered his way to the throne and, legend said (record itself said
since there were old men in the county of my own childhood who
had actually seen it), stole an entire steamboat and had it dragged
intact eleven miles overland to convert into a palace proper to

aggrandise his state; the same fat black rich plantation earth still synonymous of the proud fading white plantation names whether we—
I mean of course they—ever actually owned a plantation or not:
Sutpen and Sartoris and Compson and Edmonds and McCaslin and
Beauchamp and Grenier and Habersham and Holston and Stevens
and De Spain, generals and governors and judges, soldiers (even if
only Cuban lieutenants) and statesmen failed or not, and simple
politicians and over-reachers and just simple failures, who snatched
and grabbed and passed and vanished, name and face and all. Then
the roadless, almost pathless perpendicular hill-country of the
McCallum and Gowrie and Frazier and Muir translated intact with
their pot stills and speaking only the old Gaelic and not much of that,
from Culloden to Carolina, then from Carolina to Yoknapatawpha
still intact and not speaking much of anything except that they now
called the pots "kettles" though the drink (even I can remember this)
was still usquebaugh; then and last on to where Frenchman's Bend
lay beyond the southeastern horizon, cradle of Varners and ant-heap
for the northwest crawl of Snopes.

And you stand there—you, the old man, already whiteheaded
(because it doesn't matter if they call your gray hairs premature
because life itself is always premature which is why it aches and
anguishes) and pushing forty, only a few years from forty—while
there rises up to you, proffered up to you, the spring darkness, the
unsleeping darkness which, although it is of the dark itself, declines
the dark since dark is of the little death called sleeping. Because look
how, even though the last of west is no longer green and all of fir-
mament is now one unlidded studded slow-wheeling arc and the last
of earth-pooled visibility has drained away, there still remains one
faint diffusion, since everywhere you look about the dark panorama
you still see them, faint as whispers: the faint and shapeless lambence
of blooming dogwood returning loaned light to light as the phantoms of candles would.

And you, the old man, standing there while there rises to you,
about you, suffocating you, the spring dark peopled and myriad, two
and two seeking never at all solitude but simply privacy, the privacy
decreed and created for them by the spring darkness, the spring
weather, the spring which an American poet, a fine one, a woman and

so she knows, called girls' weather and boys' luck. Which was not the
first day at all, not Eden morning at all because girls' weather and
boys' luck is the sum of all the days: the cup, the bowl proffered once
to the lips in youth and then no more; proffered to quench or sip or
drain that lone one time and even that sometimes premature, too
soon. Because the tragedy of life is, it must be premature, inconclu-
sive and inconcludable, in order to be life; it must be before itself,
in advance of itself, to have been at all.

And now for truth was the one last chance to choose, decide:
whether or not to say *Why me? Why bother me? Why cant you let me
alone? Why must it be my problem whether I was right and your husband
just wants your lover's scalp, or Ratliff is right and your husband doesn't
care a damn about you or his honor either and just wants De Spain's
bank?*—the Square empty beneath the four identical faces of the
courthouse clock saying ten minutes to ten to the north and east and
south and west, vacant now beneath the arclight-stippled shadows
of fledged leaves like small bites taken out of the concrete paving, the
drugstores closed and all still moving now were the late last homeward stragglers from the second running of picture show. Or better
still, what she herself should have thought without my needing to say
it: *Take Manfred de Spain in whatever your new crisis is, since you didn't
hesitate to quench with him your other conflagration eighteen years ago. Or
do you already know in advance he will be no good this time, since a bank
is not a female but neuter?*

And of course Otis Harker. "Evening, Mr Stevens," he said.
"When you drove up I almost hoped maybe it was a gang come to
rob the postoffice or the bank or something to bring us a little excitement for a change."

"But it was just another lawyer," I said, "and lawyers dont bring
excitement: only misery?"

"I dont believe I quite said that, did I?" he said. "But leastways
lawyers stays awake, so if you're going to be around a while, maybe
I'll jest mosey back to the station and maybe take a nap while you
watch them racing clock-hands a spell for me." Except that he was
looking at me. No: he wasn't looking at me at all: he was watching
me, deferent to my white hairs as a "well-raised" Mississippian
should be, but not my representative position as his employer; not

quite servile, not quite impudent, waiting maybe or calculating
maybe.

"Say it," I said. "Except that—"

"Except that Mr Flem Snopes and Mr Manfred de Spain might
cross the Square any time now with old Will Varner chasing them
both out of town with that pistol."

"Good night," I said. "If I dont see you again."

"Good night," he said. "I'll likely be somewhere around. I mean
around awake. I wouldn't want Mr Buck himself to have to get up out
of bed and come all the way to town to catch me asleep."

You see? You cant beat it. Otis Harker too, who, assuming he
does keep awake all night as he is paid to do, should have been at
home all day in bed asleep. But of course, he was there; he actually
saw old Varner cross the Square at four this morning on his way to
Flem's house. Yes. You cant beat it: the town itself officially on
record now in the voice of its night marshal; the county itself had
spoken through one of its minor clowns; eighteen years ago when
Manfred de Spain thought he was just bedding another loose-
girdled bucolic Lilith, he was actually creating a piece of buffoon's
folklore.

Though there were still ten minutes, and it would take Otis
Harker at least twenty-five to "round up" the gin and compress and
their purlieus and get back to the Square. And I know now that I
already smelled tobacco smoke even before I put my hand on what I
thought was an unlocked door for the reason that I myself had made
a special trip back to leave it unlocked, still smelling the tobacco
while I still tried to turn the knob, until the latch clicked back from
inside and the door opened, she standing there against the dark interior in what little there was of light. Though it was enough to see her
hair, that she had been to the beauty parlor: who according to Maggie had never been to one, the hair not bobbed of course, not waved,
but something, I don't know what it was except that she had been to
the beauty parlor that afternoon.

"Good for you for locking it," I said. "We wont need to risk a light
either. Only I think that Otis Harker already—"

"That's all right," she said. So I closed the door and locked it again
and turned on the desk lamp. "Turn them all on if you want to," she

said. "I wasn't trying to hide. I just didn't want to have to talk to somebody."

"Yes," I said, and sat behind the desk. She had been in the client's chair, sitting in the dark, smoking; the cigarette was still burning in the little tray with two other stubs. Now she was sitting again in the client's chair at the end of the desk where the light fell upon her from the shoulder down but mostly on her hands lying quite still on the bag on her lap. Though I could still see her hair—no makeup, lips or nails either: just her hair that had been to the beauty shop. "You've been to the beauty shop," I said.

"Yes," she said. "That's where I met Chick."

"But not inside," I said, already trying to stop. "Not where water and soap are coeval, conjunctive," still trying to stop. "Not for a few years yet," and did. "All right," I said. "Tell me. What was it he took out there to your mother yesterday that had old Will on the road to town at two oclock this morning?"

"There's your cob pipe," she said. They were in the brass bowl beside the tobacco jar. "You've got three of them. I've never seen you smoke one. When do you smoke them?"

"All right," I said. "Yes. What was it he took out there?"

"The will," she said.

"No no," I said. "I know about the will; Ratliff told me. I mean, what was it Flem took out there to your mother yesterday morning—"

"I told you. The will."

"Will?" I said.

"Linda's will. Giving her share of whatever she would inherit from me, to her fa—him." And I sat there and she too, opposite one another across the desk, the lamp between us low on the desk so that all we could really see of either probably was just the hands: mine on the desk and hers quite still, almost as if two things asleep, on the bag in her lap, her voice almost as if it was asleep too so that there was no anguish, no alarm, no outrage anywhere in the little quiet dingy mausoleum of human passions, high and secure, secure even from any random exigency of what had been impressed on Otis Harker as his duty for which he was paid his salary, since he already knew it would be me in it: "The will. It was her idea. She did it herself. I mean, she believes she thought of it, wanted to do it, did it, herself. Nobody can tell her otherwise. Nobody will. Nobody. That's why I wrote the note."

"You'll have to tell me," I said. "You'll have to."

"It was the . . . school business. When you told her she wanted to go, get away from here; all the different schools to choose among that she hadn't even known about before, that it was perfectly natural for a young girl—young people to want to go to them and to go to one of them, that until then she hadn't even thought about, let alone known that she wanted to go to one of them. Like all she needed to do to go to one of them was just to pick out the one she liked the best and go to it, especially after I said Yes. Then her—he said No.

"As if that was the first time she ever thought of No, ever heard of No. There was a . . . scene. I dont like scenes. You dont have to have scenes. Nobody needs to have a scene to get what you want. You just get it. But she didn't know that, you see. She hadn't had time to learn it maybe, since she was just seventeen then. But then you know that yourself. Or maybe it was more than not knowing better. Maybe she knew too much. Maybe she already knew, felt even then that he had already beat her. She said: 'I will go! I will! You cant stop me! Damn your money; if Mama wont give it to me, Grandpa will—Mr Stevens' (oh yes, she said that too) 'will—' While he just sat there— we were sitting then, still at the table; only Linda was standing up— just sat there saying, 'That's right. I cant stop you.' Then she said, 'Please.' Oh yes, she knew she was beaten as well as he did. 'No,' he said. 'I want you to stay at home and go to the Academy.'

"And that was all. I mean . . . nothing. That was just all. Because you—a girl anyway—dont really hate your father no matter how much you think you do or should or should want to because people expect you to or that it would look well to because it would be romantic to—"

"Yes," I said, "—because girls, women, are not interested in romance but only facts. Oh yes, you were not the only one: Ratliff told me that too, that same day in fact."

"Vladimir too?" she said.

"No: Ratliff," I said. Then I said, "Wait." Then I said: "Vladimir? Did you say Vladimir? V.K. Is his name Vladimir?" And now she did sit still, even the hands on the bag that had been like things asleep and breathing their own life apart, seemed to become still now.

"I didn't intend to do that," she said.

"Yes," I said. "I know: nobody else on earth knows his name is Vladimir because how could anybody named Vladimir hope to make a living selling sewing machines or anything else in rural Mississippi? But he told you: the secret he would have defended like that of insanity in his family or illegitimacy. Why?—No, dont answer that. Why shouldn't I know why he told you; didn't I breathe one blinding whiff of that same liquor too? Tell me. I wont either. Vladimir K. What K.?"

"Vladimir Kyrilytch."

"Vladimir Kyrilytch what? Not Ratliff. Kyrilytch is only his middle name; all Russian middle names are itch or ovna. That's just son or daughter of. What was his last name before it became Ratliff?"

"He doesn't know. His . . . six or eight or ten times grandfather was . . . not lieutenant—"

"Ensign."

"—in a British army that surrendered in the Revolution—"

"Yes," I said. "Burgoyne. Saratoga."

"—and was sent to Virginia and forgotten and Vla—his grandfather escaped. It was a woman of course, a girl, that hid him and fed him. Except that she spelled it R-a-t-c-l-i-f-f-e and they married and had a son or had the son and then married. Anyway he learned to speak English and became a Virginia farmer. And his grandson, still spelling it with a c and an e at the end but with his name still Vladimir Kyrilytch though nobody knew it, came to Mississippi with old Doctor Habersham and Alexander Holston and Louis Grenier and started Jefferson. Only they forgot how to spell it Ratcliffe and just spelled it like it sounds but one son is always named Vladimir Kyrilytch. Except that like you said, nobody named Vladimir Kyrilytch could make a living as a Mississippi country man—"

"No," I said, cried. "Wait. That's wrong. We're both wrong. We're completely backward. If only everybody had known his name was really Vladimir Kyrilytch, he would be a millionaire by now, since any woman anywhere would have bought anything or everything he had to sell or trade or swap. Or maybe they already do?" I said, cried. "Maybe they already do?—All right," I said. "Go on."

"But one in each generation still has to have the name because Vla—V.K. says the name is their luck."

"Except that it didn't work against Flem Snopes," I said. "Not when he tangled with Flem Snopes that night in that Old Frenchman's garden after you came back from Texas.—All right," I said. " 'So that was all because you dont really hate your father—' "

"He did things for her. That she didn't expect, hadn't even thought about asking for. That young girls like, almost as though he had put himself inside a young girl's mind even before she thought of them. He gave me the money and sent us both to Memphis to buy things for her graduation from high school—not just a graduating dress but one for dancing too, and other things for the summer; almost a trousseau. He even tried—offered, anyway told her he was going to—to have a picnic for her whole graduating class but she refused that. You see? He was her father even if he did have to be her enemy. You know: the one that said 'Please' accepting the clothes, while the one that defied him to stop her refused the picnic.

"And that summer he gave me the money and even made the hotel reservations himself for us to go down to the coast—you may remember that—"

"I remember," I said.

"—to spend a month so she could swim in the ocean and meet people, meet young men; he said that himself: meet young men. And we came back and that fall she entered the Academy and he started giving her a weekly allowance. Would you believe that?"

"I do now," I said. "Tell me."

"It was too much, more than she could need, had any business with, too much for a seventeen-year-old girl to have every week just in Jefferson. Yet she took that too that she didn't really need just like she took the Academy that she didn't want. Because he was her father, you see. You've got to remember that. Can you?"

"Tell me," I said.

"That was the fall, the winter. He still gave her things—clothes she didn't need, had no business with, seventeen years old in Jefferson; you may have noticed that too; even a fur coat until she refused to let him, said No in time. Because you see, that was the You cant stop me again; she had to remind him now and then that she had defied him, she could accept the daughter's due but not the enemy's bribe.

"Then it was summer, last summer. That was when it happened. I saw it, we were all at the table again and he said, 'Where do you want to go this summer? The coast again? Or maybe the mountains this time? How would you like to take your mother and go to New York?' And he had her; she was already beat; she said, 'Wont that cost a lot of money?' and he said, 'That doesn't matter. When would you like to go?' and she said, 'No. It will cost too much money. Why dont we just stay here?' Because he had her, he had beat her. And the . . . terrible thing was, she didn't know it, didn't even know there had been a battle and she had surrendered. Before, she had defied him and at least she knew she was defying him even if she didn't know what to do with it, how to use it, what to do next. Now she had come over to his side and she didn't even know it.

"And that's all. Then it was fall, last October, she was at the Academy again and this time we had finished supper, we were in the living room before the fire and she was reading, sitting on one of her feet I remember and I remember the book too, the John Donne you gave her—I mean, the new one, the second one, to replace the one that boy—what was his name? the garage mechanic, Matt Something, Levitt—tore up that day in your office—when he said, 'Linda,' and she looked up, still holding the book (that's when I remember seeing what it was) and he said, 'I was wrong. I thought the Academy ought to be good enough, because I never went to school and didn't know any better. But I know better now, and the Academy's not good enough any more. Will you give up the Yankee schools and take the University at Oxford?'

"And she still sat there, letting the book come down slow onto her lap, just looking at him. Then she said, 'What?'

" 'Will you forget about Virginia and the Northern schools for this year, and enter the University after Christmas?' She threw the book, she didn't put it down at all: she just threw it, flung it as she stood up out of the chair and said:

" 'Daddy.' I had never seen her touch him. He was her father, she never refused to speak to him or to speak any way except respectfully.

But he was her enemy; she had to keep him reminded always that although he had beaten her about the schools, she still hadn't surrendered. But I had never seen her touch him until now, sprawled, flung across his lap, clutching him around the shoulders, her face against his collar, crying, saying, 'Daddy! Daddy! Daddy! Daddy!' "

"Go on," I said.

"That's all. Oh, that was enough; what more did he need to do than that? have that thing—that piece of paper—drawn up himself and then twist her arm until she signed her name to it? He didn't have to mention any paper. He probably didn't even need to see her again and even if he did, all he would have needed—she already knew about the will, I mean Papa's will leaving my share to just Eula Varner without even mentioning the word Snopes—all he would need would be just to say something like 'Oh yes, your grandfather's a fine old gentleman but he just never did like me. But that's all right; your mother will be taken care of no matter what happens to me myself; he just fixed things so I nor nobody else can take her money away from her before you inherit it'—something like that. Or maybe he didn't even need to do that much, knew he didn't have to. Not with her. He was her father, and if he wouldn't let her go off to school it was because he loved her, since that was the reason all parents seemed to have for the things they wont let their children do; then for him to suddenly turn completely around and almost order her to do the thing she wanted, which he had forbidden her for almost two years to do, what reason could that be except that he loved her still more: loved her enough to let her do the one thing in her life he had ever forbidden her?

"Or I dont know. He may have suggested it, even told her how to word it; what does it matter now? It's done, there: Papa storming into the house at four this morning and flinging it down on my bed before I was even awake—Wait," she said, "I know all that too; I've already done all that myself. It was legal, all regular—What do they call it?"

"Drawn up," I said.

"—drawn up by a lawyer in Oxford, Mr Stone—not the old one: the young one. I telephoned him this morning. He was very nice. He—"

"I know him," I said. "Even if he did go to New Haven."

"—said he had wanted to talk to me about it, but there was the . . ."

"Inviolacy," I said.

"Inviolacy—between client and lawyer. He said she came to him, it must have been right after she reached Oxford—Wait," she said. "I asked him that too: why she came to him, and he said—He said she was a delightful young lady who would go far in life even after she ran out of—of—"

"Contingencies," I said.

"—contingencies to bequeath people—she said that she had just asked someone who was the nicest lawyer for her to go to and they told her him. So she told him what she wanted and he wrote it that way; oh yes, I saw it: 'my share of whatever I might inherit from my mother, Eula Varner Snopes, as distinct and separate from whatever her husband shall share in her property, to my father Flem Snopes.' Oh yes, all regular and legal though he said he tried to explain to her that she was not bequeathing a quantity but merely devising a—what was it? contingency, and that nobody would take it very seriously probably since she might die before she had any inheritance or get married or even change her mind without a husband to help her or her mother might not have any inheritance beyond the one speci- fied or might spend it or her father might die and she would inherit half of his inheritance from herself plus the other half which her mother would inherit as her father's relict, which she would heir in turn back to her father's estate to pass to her mother as his relict to be inherited once more by her; but she was eighteen years old and com- petent and he, Mr Stone, was a competent lawyer or at least he had a license saying so, and so it was at least in legal language and on the right kind of paper. He—Mr Stone—even asked her why she felt she must make the will and she told him: Because my father has been good to me and I love and admire and respect him—do you hear that? Love and admire and respect him. Oh yes, legal. As if that mat- tered, legal or illegal, contingency or incontingency—"

Nor did she need to tell me that either: that old man seething out there in his country store for eighteen years now over the way his son-in-law had tricked him out of that old ruined plantation and then made a profit out of it, now wild with rage and frustration at the same

man who had not only out-briganded him in brigandage but since
then had even out-usury-ed him in sedentary usury, and who now
had wed the innocence of a young girl, his own granddaughter, who
could repay what she thought was love with gratitude and generosity at least, to disarm him of the one remaining weapon which he still
held over his enemy. Oh yes, of course it was worth nothing except
its paper but what did that matter, legal or valid either. It didn't even
matter now if he destroyed it (which of course was why Flem ever
let it out of his hand in the first place); only that he saw it, read it,
comprehended it: took one outraged incredulous glance at it, then
came storming into town—

"I couldn't make him hush," she said. "I couldn't make him stop,
be quiet. He didn't even want to wait until daylight to get hold of
Manfred."

"De Spain?" I said. "Then? At four in the morning?"

"Didn't I tell you I couldn't stop him, make him stop or hush? Oh
yes, he got Manfred there right away. And Manfred attended to
everything. It was quite simple to him. That is, when I finally made
him and Papa both believe that in another minute they would wake
up, rouse the whole neighborhood and before that happened I would
take Papa's—Jody's car and drive to Oxford and get Linda and none
of them would ever see us again. So he and Papa hushed then—"

"But Flem," I said.

"He was there for a little while, long enough—"

"But what was he doing?" I said.

'Nothing," she said. "What was he supposed to do? What did he
need to do now?"

"Oh," I said. " 'long enough' to—"

"—enough for Manfred to settle everything: we would simply
leave, go away together, he and I, which was what we should have
done eighteen years ago—"

"What?" I said, cried. "Leave—elope?"

"Oh yes, it was all fixed; he stopped right there with Papa still
standing over him and cursing him—cursing him or cursing Flem;
you couldn't tell now which one he was talking to or about or at—
and wrote out the bill of sale. Papa was—what's that word?—neutral.
He wanted both of them out of the bank, intended to have both of

them out of it, came all the way in from home at four oclock in the morning to fling both of them out of Jefferson and Yoknapatawpha County and Mississippi all three—Manfred for having been my lover for eighteen years, and Flem for waiting eighteen years to do anything about it. Papa didn't know about Manfred until this morning. That is, he acted like he didn't. I think Mamma knew. I think she has known all the time. But maybe she didn't. Because people are really kind, you know. All the people in Yoknapatawpha County that might have made sure Mamma knew about us, for her own good, so she could tell Papa for his own good. For everybody's own good. But I dont think Papa knew. He's like you. I mean, you can do that too."

"Do what?" I said.

"Be able to not have to believe something just because it might be so or somebody says it is so or maybe even it is so."

"Wait," I said. "Wait. What bill of sale?"

"For his bank stock. Manfred's bank stock. Made out to Flem. To give Flem the bank, since that was what all the trouble and uproar was about.—And then the check for Flem to sign to buy it with, dated a week from now to give Flem time to have the money ready when we cashed the check in Texas—when people are not married, or should have been married but aren't yet, why do they still think Texas is far enough? or is it just big enough?—or California or Mexico or wherever we would go."

"But Linda," I said. "Linda."

"All right," she said. "Linda."

"Dont you see? Either way she is lost? Either to go with you, if that were possible, while you desert her father for another man; or stay here in all the stink without you to protect her from it and learn at last that he is not her father at all and so she has nobody, nobody?"

"That's why I sent the note. Marry her."

"No. I told you that before. Besides, that wont save her. Only Manfred can save her. Let him sell Flem his stock, or give Flem the damned bank; is that too high a price to pay for what—what he—he—"

"I tried that," she said. "No."

"I'll talk to him," I said. "I'll tell him. He must. He'll have to; there's no other—"

"No," she said, "Not Manfred." Then I watched her hands, not fast, open the bag and take out the pack of cigarettes and the single kitchen match and extract the cigarette and put the pack back into the bag and close it and (no, I didn't move) strike the match on the turned sole of her shoe and light the cigarette and put the match into the tray and put her hands again on the bag. "Not Manfred. You dont know Manfred. And so maybe I dont either. Maybe I dont know about men either. Maybe I was completely wrong that morning when I said how women are only interested in facts because maybe men are just interested in facts too and the only difference is, women dont care whether they are facts or not just so they fit, and men dont care whether they fit or not just so they are facts. If you are a man, you can lie unconscious in the gutter bleeding and with most of your teeth knocked out and somebody can take your pocketbook and you can wake up and wash the blood off and it's all right; you can always get some more teeth and even another pocketbook sooner or later. But you cant just stand meekly with your head bowed and no blood and all your teeth too while somebody takes your pocketbook because even though you might face the friends who love you after-ward you never can face the strangers that never heard of you before. Not Manfred. If I dont go with him, he'll have to fight. He may go down fighting and wreck everything and everybody else, but he'll have to fight. Because he's a man. I mean, he's a man first. I mean, he's got to be a man first. He can swap Flem Snopes his bank for Flem Snopes's wife, but he cant just stand there and let Flem Snopes take the bank away from him."

"So Linda's sunk," I said. "Finished. Done. Sunk." I said, cried: "But you anyway will save something! To get away yourself at least, out of here, never again to . . . never again Flem Snopes, never again, never—"

"Oh, that," she said. "You mean that. That doesn't matter. That's never been any trouble. He . . . cant. He's—what's the word?—impo-tent. He's always been. Maybe that's why, one of the reasons. You see? You've got to be careful or you'll have to pity him. You'll have to. He couldn't bear that, and it's no use to hurt people if you dont get anything for it. Because he couldn't bear being pitied. It's like V.K.'s Vladimir. Ratliff can live with Ratliff's Vladimir, and you can live with Ratliff's Vladimir. But you mustn't ever have the chance to, the right to, the choice to. Like he can live with his impotence, but you mustn't have the chance to help him with pity. You promised about the Vladimir, but I want you to promise again about this."

"I promise," I said. Then I said: "Yes. You're going tonight. That's why the beauty parlor this afternoon: not for me but for Manfred. No: not even for Manfred after eighteen years: just to elope with, get on the train with. To show your best back to Jefferson. That's right, isn't it? You're leaving tonight."

"Marry her, Gavin," she said. I had known her by sight for eighteen years, with time out of course for the war; I had dreamed about her at night for eighteen years including the war. We had talked to one another twice: here in the office one night fourteen years ago, and in her living room one morning two years back. But not once had she ever called me even Mister Stevens. Now she said Gavin. "Marry her, Gavin."

"Change her name by marriage, then she wont miss the name she will lose when you abandon her."

"Marry her, Gavin," she said.

"Put it that I'm not too old so much as simply discrepant; that having been her husband once, I would never relinquish even her widowhood to another. Put it that way then."

"Marry her, Gavin," she said. And now I stopped, she sitting beyond the desk, the cigarette burning on the tray, balancing its muted narrow windless feather where she had not touched it once since she lit it and put it down, the hand still quiet on the bag and the face now turned to look at me out of the half-shadow above the rim of light from the lamp—the big broad simple still unpainted beautiful mouth, the eyes not the hard and dusty blue of fall but the blue of spring blooms, all one inextricable mixture of wistaria cornflowers larkspur bluebells weeds and all, all the lost girls' weather and boys' luck and too late the grief, too late.

"Then this way. After you're gone, if or when I become convinced that conditions are going to become such that something will have to be done, and nothing else but marrying me can help her, and she will have me, but have me, take me. Not just give up, surrender."

"Swear it then," she said.

"I promise. I have promised. I promise again."

"No," she said. "Swear."

"I swear," I said.

"And even if she wont have you. Even after that. Even if she w— you cant marry her."

"How can she need me then?" I said. "Flem—unless your father really does get shut of the whole damned boiling of you, runs Flem out of Jefferson too—will have his bank and wont need to swap, sell, trade her any more; maybe he will even prefer to have her in a New England school or even further than that if he can manage it."

"Swear," she said.

"All right," I said. "At any time. Anywhere. No matter what happens."

"Swear," she said.

"I swear," I said.

"I'm going now," she said and rose and picked up the burning cigarette and crushed it carefully out into the tray and I rose too.

"Of course," I said. "You have some packing to do even for an elopement, dont you? I'll drive you home."

"You dont need to," she said.

"A lady, walking home alone at—it's after midnight. What will Otis Harker say? You see, I've got to be a man too; I cant face Otis Harker otherwise since you wont stop being a lady to him until after tomorrow's southbound train; I believe you did say Texas, didn't you?" Though Otis was not in sight this time, though with pencil, paper and a watch I could have calculated about where he would be now. Though the figures could have been wrong and only Otis was not in sight, not we, crossing the shadow-bitten Square behind the flat rapid sabre-sweep of the headlights across the plate-glass storefronts, then into the true spring darkness where the sparse street lights were less than stars. And we could have talked if there had been more to talk about or maybe there had been more to talk about if we had talked. Then the small gate before the short walk to the small dark house not rented now of course and of course not vacant yet with a little space yet for decent decorum, and I wondered, thought

Will Manfred sell him his house along with his bank or just abandon both to him—provided of course old Will Varner leaves him time to collect either one? and stopped.

"Dont get out," she said and got out and shut the door and said, stooping a little to look at me beneath the top: "Swear again."

"I swear," I said.

"Thank you," she said. "Good night," and turned and I watched her, through the gate and up the walk, losing dimension now, onto or rather into the shadow of the little gallery and losing even substance now. And then I heard the door and it was as if she had not been. No, not that; not *not been*, but rather no more *is*, since *was* remains always and forever, inexplicable and immune, which is its grief. That's what I mean: a dimension less, then a substance less, then the sound of a door and then, not *never been* but simply *no more is* since always and forever that *was* remains, as if what is going to happen to one tomorrow already gleams faintly visible now if the watcher were only wise enough to discern it or maybe just brave enough.

The spring night, cooler now, as if for a little while, until tomorrow's dusk and the new beginning, somewhere had suspired into sleep at last the amazed hushed burning of hope and dream two-and-two engendered. It would even be quite cold by dawn, daybreak. But even then not cold enough to chill, make hush for sleep the damned mockingbird for three nights now keeping his constant racket in Maggie's pink dogwood just under my bedroom window. So the trick of course would be to divide, not him but his racket, the having to listen to him: one Gavin Stevens to cross his dark gallery too and into the house and up the stairs to cover his head in the bedclothes, losing in his turn a dimension of Gavin Stevens, an ectoplasm of Gavin Stevens impervious to cold and hearing too to bear its half of both, bear its half or all of any other burdens anyone wanted to shed and shuck, having only this moment assumed that one of a young abandoned girl's responsibility.

Because who would miss a dimension? Who indeed but would be better off for having lost it, who had nothing in the first place to offer but just devotion, eighteen years of devotion, the ectoplasm of devotion too thin to be crowned by scorn, warned by hatred, annealed by grief. That's it: unpin, shed, cast off the last clumsy and anguished dimension, and so be free. Unpin: that's the trick, remembering Vladimir Kyrilytch's "He aint unpinned it yet"—the twenty-dollar gold piece pinned to the undershirt of the country boy on his first trip to Memphis, who even if he has never been there before, has as much right as any to hope he can be, may be, will be tricked or trapped into a whorehouse before he has to go back home again. *He has unpinned it now* I thought.

TWENTY-ONE

CHARLES MALLISON

*Y*ou know how it is, you wake in the morning and you know at once that it has already happened and you are already too late. You didn't know what it was going to be, which was why you had to watch so hard for it, trying to watch in all directions at once. Then you let go for a second, closed your eyes for just one second, and bang! it happened and it was too late, not even time to wake up and still hold off a minute, just to stretch and think *What is it that makes today such a good one?* then to let it come in, flow in: *Oh yes, there's not any school today.* More: *Thursday and in April and still there's not any school today.*

But not this morning. And halfway down the stairs I heard the swish of the pantry door shutting and I could almost hear Mother telling Guster: "Here he comes. Quick. Get out," and I went into the dining room and Father had already had breakfast, I mean even when Guster has moved the plate and cup and saucer you can always tell where Father has eaten something; and by the look of his place Uncle Gavin hadn't been to the table at all and Mother was sitting at her place just drinking coffee, with her hat already on and her coat over Uncle Gavin's chair and her bag and gloves by her plate and the dark glasses she wore in the car whenever she went beyond the city limits as if light didn't have any glare in it except one mile from town. And I reckon she wished for a minute that I was about three or four because then she could have put one arm around me against her knee and held the back of my head with the other hand. But now she just held my hand and this time she had to look up at me. "Mrs Snopes killed herself last night," she said. "I'm going over to Oxford with Uncle Gavin to bring Linda home."

"Killed herself?" I said. "How?"

"What?" Mother said. Because I was only twelve then, not yet thirteen.

"What did she do it with?" I said. But then Mother remembered that too by that time. She was already getting up.

"With a pistol," she said. "I'm sorry, I didn't think to ask whose." She almost had the coat on too. Then she came and got the gloves and bag and the glasses. "We may be back by dinner, but I dont know. Will you try to stay at home, at least stay away from the Square, find something to do with Aleck Sander in the back yard? Guster's not going to let him leave the place today, so why dont you stay with him?"

"Yessum," I said. Because I was just twelve; to me that great big crepe knot dangling from the front door of Mr de Spain's bank signified only waste: another holiday when school was suspended for an indefinite time; another holiday piled on top of one we already had, when the best, the hardest holiday user in the world couldn't possibly use two of them at once, when it could have been saved and added on to the end of the one we already had when the little Riddell boy either died or got well or anyway they started school again. Or better still: just to save it for one of those hopeless days when Christmas is so long past you have forgotten it ever was, and it looks like summer itself has died somewhere and will never come again.

Because I was just twelve; I would have to be reminded that the longest school holiday in the world could mean nothing to the people which that wreath on the bank door freed for one day from work. And I would have to be a lot older than twelve before I realised that that wreath was not the myrtle of grief, it was the laurel of victory; that in that dangling chunk of black tulle and artificial flowers and purple ribbons was the eternal and deathless public triumph of virtue itself proved once more supreme and invincible.

I couldn't even know now what I was looking at. Oh yes, I went to town, not quite as soon as Mother and Uncle Gavin were out of sight, but close enough. So did Aleck Sander. We could hear Guster calling us both a good while after we had turned the corner, both of us going to look at the wreath on the closed bank door and seeing a lot of other people too, grown people, come to look at it for what I

know now was no braver reason than the one Aleck Sander and I had.
And when Mr de Spain came to town as he always did just before
nine o'clock and got his mail from the postoffice like he always did
and let himself into the back door of the bank with his key like he
always did because the back door always stayed locked, we—I—
couldn't know that the reason he looked exactly like nothing had
happened was because that was exactly the way he had to come to
town that morning to have to look. That he had to get up this morning and shave and dress and maybe practise in front of the mirror a
while in order to come to the Square at the time he always did so
everybody in Jefferson could see him doing exactly as he always did,
like if there was grief and trouble anywhere in Jefferson that morning, it was not his grief and trouble, being an orphan and unmarried;
even to going on into the closed bank by the back door as if he still
had the right to.

Because I know now that we—Jefferson—all knew that he had lost
the bank. I mean, whether old Mr Will Varner ran Mr Flem Snopes
out of Jefferson too after this, Mr de Spain himself wouldn't stay. In
a way, he owed that not just to the memory of his dead love, his dead
mistress; he owed that to Jefferson too. Because he had outraged us.
He had not only flouted the morality of marriage which decreed that
a man and a woman cant sleep together without a certificate from the
police, he had outraged the economy of marriage which is the production of children, by making public display of the fact that you can
be barren by choice with impunity; he had outraged the institution of
marriage twice: not just his own but the Flem Snopes's too. So they
already hated him twice: once for doing it, once for not getting
caught at it for eighteen years. But that would be nothing to the
hatred he would get if, after his guilty partner had paid with her life
for her share of the crime, he didn't even lose that key to the back
door of the bank to pay for his.

We all knew that. So did he. And he knew we knew. And we in
our turn knew he knew we did. So that was all right. He was finished,
I mean, he was fixed. His part was set. No: I was right the first time;
and now I know that too. He was done, ended. That shot had finished him too and now what he did or didn't do either didn't matter

any more. It was just Linda now; and when I was old enough I knew why none of us expected that day that old Mr Varner would come charging out of Mr Snopes's house with the same pistol maybe seeking more blood, if for no other reason than that there would have been no use in it. Nor were we surprised when (after a discreet interval of course, for decorum, the decorum of bereavement and mourning) we learned that "for business reasons and health" Mr de Spain had resigned from the bank and was moving out West (he actually left the afternoon of the funeral, appeared at the grave—alone and nobody to speak to him except to nod—with a crepe armband which was of course all right since the deceased was the wife of his vice president, and then turned from the grave when we all did except that he was the first one and an hour later that afternoon his Buick went fast across the Square and into the Memphis highway with him in it and the back full of baggage) and that his bank stock—not his house; Ratliff said that even Flem Snopes didn't have that much nerve: to buy the house too the same day he bought the bank stock— was offered for sale, and even less surprised that (even more discreetly) Mr Snopes had bought it.

It was Linda now. And now I know that the other people, the grown people, who had come to look at that wreath on the bank door for exactly the same reason that Aleck Sander and I had come to look at it, had come only incidentally to look at the wreath since they had really come for exactly the same reason Aleck Sander and I had really come: to see Linda Snopes when Mother and Uncle Gavin brought her home, even if mine and Aleck Sander's reason was to see how much Mrs Snopes's killing herself would change the way Linda looked so that we would know how we would look if Mother and Guster ever shot themselves. It was Linda because I know now what Uncle Gavin believed then (not knew: believed: because he couldn't have known because the only one that could have told him would have been Mrs Snopes herself and if she had told him in that note she gave me that afternoon before she was going to commit suicide, he would have stopped her or tried to because Mother anyway would have known it if he had tried to stop her and failed), and not just Uncle Gavin but other people in Jefferson too. So now they even forgave Mrs Snopes for the eighteen years of carnal sin, and now they could even forgive themselves for condoning adultery by forgiving it, by reminding themselves (one another too I reckon) that if she had not been an abomination before God for eighteen years, she wouldn't have reached the point where she would have to choose death in order to leave her child a mere suicide for a mother instead of a whore.

Oh yes, it was Linda. She had the whole town on her side now, the town and the county and everybody who ever heard of her and Mr de Spain or knew or even suspected or just guessed anything about the eighteen years, to keep any part of the guessing or suspecting or actual knowing (if there was any, ever was any) from ever reaching her. Because I know now that people really are kind, they really are; there are lots of times when they stop hurting one another not just when they want to keep on hurting but even when they have to; even the most Methodist and Baptist of the Baptists and Methodists and Presbyterians—all right, Episcopals too—the car coming at last with Linda in the front seat between Mother and Uncle Gavin; across the Square and on to Linda's house so that Aleck Sander and I had plenty of time to be waiting at the corner to nag Uncle Gavin when he came back.

"I thought Guster and your mother told both of you to stay home this morning," he said.

"Yes sir," we said. We went home. And he didn't eat any dinner either: just trying to make me eat, I dont know why. I mean, I dont know why all grown people in sight believe they have to try to persuade you to eat whether you want to or not or even whether they really want to try to persuade you or not, until at last even Father noticed what was going on.

"Come on," he told me. "Either eat it or leave the table. I dont want to lie to your mother when she comes home and asks me why you didn't eat it and I can always say you left suddenly for Texas." Then he said, "What's the matter, you too?" because Uncle Gavin had got up, right quick, and said,

"Excuse me," and went out; yes, Uncle Gavin too; Mr de Spain was finished now as far as Jefferson was concerned and now we—Jefferson—could put all our mind on who was next in sight, what else the flash of that pistol had showed up like when you set off a flashlight powder in a cave; and one of them was Uncle Gavin. Because I know now there were people in Jefferson then who believed that Uncle Gavin had been her lover too, or if he hadn't he should have been or else not just the whole Jefferson masculine race but the whole masculine race anywhere that called itself a man ought to be ashamed.

Because they knew about that old Christmas Ball older than I was then, and the whole town had seen and then heard about it so they could come, pass by accident and see for themselves Uncle Gavin and Linda drinking ice-cream sodas in Christian's with a book of poetry on the table between them. Except that they knew he really hadn't been Mrs Snopes's lover too, that not only if he had really wanted her, tried for her, he would have failed there too for simple consistency, but that even if by some incredible chance or accident he had beat Mr de Spain's time, it would have showed on the outside of him for the reason that Uncle Gavin was incapable of having a secret life which remained secret; he was, Ratliff said, "a feller that even his in-growed toenails was on the outside of his shoes."

So, since Uncle Gavin had failed, he was the pure one, the only pure one; not Mr Snopes, the husband, who if he had been a man, would have got a pistol even if he, Flem Snopes, had to buy one and blown them both, his wife and her fancy banker both, clean out of Jefferson. It was Uncle Gavin. He was the bereaved, the betrayed husband forgiving for the sake of the half-orphan child. It was that same afternoon, he had left right after he went out of the dining room, then Mother came back alone in the car, then about three oclock Uncle Gavin came back in a taxi and said (Oh yes, Aleck Sander and I stayed at home after Guster got hold of us, let alone Mother.):

"Four gentlemen are coming to see me. They're preachers so you'd better show them into the parlor." And I did: the Methodist, the Baptist, the Presbyterian and ours, the Episcopal, all looking like any other bankers or doctors or storekeepers except Mr Thorndyke and the only thing against him was his hind-part-before dog collar;

all very grave and long in the face, like horses; I mean, not looking
unhappy: just looking long in the face like horses, each one shaking
hands with me and kind of bumbling with each other while they were
getting through the door, into the parlor where Uncle Gavin was
standing too, speaking to each of them by name while they all shook
hands with him too, calling them all Doctor, the four of them bumbling again until the oldest one, the Presbyterian, did the talking:
they had come to offer themselves singly or jointly to conduct the
service; that Mr Snopes was a Baptist and Mrs Snopes had been born
a Methodist but neither of them had attended, been a communicant
of, any church in Jefferson; that Mr Stevens had assumed—offered
his—that is, they had been directed to call on Mr Stevens in regard
to the matter, until Uncle Gavin said:

"That is, you were sent. Sent by a damned lot of damned old
women of both sexes, including none. Not to bury her: to forgive
her. Thank you, gentlemen. I plan to conduct this service myself."
But that was just until Father came home for supper and Mother
could sic him on Uncle Gavin too. Because we had all thought, taken
it for granted, that the Varners (maybe Mr Flem too) would naturally
want her buried in Frenchman's Bend; that Mr Varner would pack
her up too when he went back home along with whatever else he had
brought to town with him (Ratliff said it wouldn't be much since the
only thing that travelled lighter than Uncle Billy Varner was a crow)
and take her back with him. But Uncle Gavin said No, speaking for
Linda—and there were people enough to say Gavin Stevens said No
speaking *to* the daughter. Anyway, it was No, the funeral to be tomorrow after Jody Varner's car could get back in from Frenchman's Bend
with Jody and Mrs Varner; and now Uncle Gavin had Father at him
too.

"Dammit, Gavin," he said. "You cant do it. We all admit you're a
lot of things but one of them aint an ordained minister."

"So what?" Uncle Gavin said. "Do you believe that this town
believes that any preacher that ever breathed could get her into
heaven without having to pass through Jefferson, and that even
Christ Himself could get her through on that route?"

"Wait," Mother said. "Both of you hush." She was looking at
Uncle Gavin. "Gavin, at first I thought I would never understand

why Eula did it. But now I'm beginning to believe that maybe I do. Do you want Linda to have to say afterward that another bachelor had to bury her?"

And that was all. And the next day Mrs Varner and Jody came in and brought with them the old Methodist minister who had christened her thirty-eight years ago—an old man who had been a preacher all his adult life but would have for the rest of it the warped back and the wrenched bitter hands of a dirt farmer—and we—the town—gathered at their little house, the women inside and the men standing around the little front yard and along the street, all neat and clean and wearing coats and not quite looking at each other while they talked quietly about crops and weather; then to the graveyard and the new lot empty except for the one raw excavation and even that not long, hidden quickly, rapidly beneath the massed flowers, themselves already doomed in the emblem-shapes—wreaths and harps and urns—of the mortality which they de-stingered, euphemised; and Mr de Spain standing there not apart: just solitary, with his crepe armband and his face looking like it must have when he was a lieutenant in Cuba back in that time, day, moment after he had just led the men that trusted him or anyway followed him because they were supposed to, into the place where they all knew some of them wouldn't come back for the reason that all of them were not supposed to come back which was all right too if the lieutenant said it was.

Then we came home and Father said, "Dammit, Gavin, why dont you get drunk?" and Uncle Gavin said,

"Certainly, why not?"—not even looking up from the paper. Then it was supper time and I wondered why Mother didn't nag at him about not eating. But at least as long as she didn't think about eating, her mind wouldn't hunt around and light on me. Then we—Uncle Gavin and Mother and I—went to the office. I mean that for a while after Grandfather died Mother still tried to make us all call it the library but now even she called it the office just like Grandfather did, and Uncle Gavin sitting beside the lamp with a book and even turning a page now and then, until the door bell rang.

"I'll go," Mother said. But then, nobody else seemed to intend to or be even curious. Then she came back down the hall to the office

door and said, "It's Linda. Come in, honey," and stood to one side
and beckoned her head at me as Linda came in and Uncle Gavin got
up and Mother jerked her head at me again and said, "Chick," and
Linda stopped just inside the door and this time Mother said,
"Charles!" so I got up and went out and she closed the door after us.
But it was all right. I was used to it by this time. As soon as I saw who
it was I even expected it.

TWENTY-TWO

GAVIN STEVENS

*T*hen Maggie finally got Chick out and closed the door.
I said, "Sit down, Linda." But she just stood there. "Cry," I said.
"Let yourself go and cry."

"I cant," she said. "I tried." She looked at me. "He's not my
father," she said.

"Of course he's your father," I said. "Certainly he is. What in the
world are you talking about?"

"No," she said.

"Yes," I said. "Do you want me to swear? All right. I swear he's
your father."

"You were not there. You dont know. You never even saw her until
she—we came to Jefferson."

"Ratliff did. Ratliff was there. He knows. He knows who your
father is. And I know from Ratliff. I am sure. Have I ever lied to
you?"

"No," she said. "You are the one person in the world I know will
never lie to me."

"All right," I said. "I swear to you then. Flem Snopes is your
father." And now she didn't move: it was just the tears, the water, not
springing, just running quietly and quite fast down her face. I moved
toward her.

"No," she said, "dont touch me yet," catching, grasping both my
wrists and gripping, pressing my hands hard in hers against her
breast. "When I thought he wasn't my father, I hated her and Manfred both. Oh yes, I knew about Manfred: I have . . . seen them look
at each other, their voices when they would talk to each other, speak
one another's name, and I couldn't bear it, I hated them both. But
now that I know he is my father, it's all right. I'm glad. I want her to
have loved, to have been happy.—I can cry now," she said.

649

TWENTY-THREE

V. K. RATLIFF

*I*t was like a contest, like Lawyer had stuck a stick of dynamite in his hind pocket and lit a long fuse to it and was interested now would or wouldn't somebody step in in time and tromple the fire out. Or a race, like would he finally get Linda out of Jefferson and at least get his-self shut forever of the whole tribe of Snopes first, or would he jest blow up his-self beforehand first and take ever body and ever thing in the neighborhood along with him.

No, not a contest. Not a contest with Flem Snopes anyway because it takes two to make a contest and Flem Snopes wasn't the other one. He was a umpire, if he was anything in it. No, he wasn't even a umpire. It was like he was running a little mild game against his-self, for his own amusement, like solitaire. He had ever thing now that he had come to Jefferson to get. He had more. He had things he didn't even know he was going to want until he reached Jefferson because he didn't even know what they was until then. He had his bank and his money in it and his-self to be president of it so he could not only watch his money from ever being stole by another twenty-two-calibre rogue like his cousin Byron, but nobody could ever steal from him the respectability that being president of one of the two Yoknapatawpha County banks toted along with it. And he was going to have one of the biggest residences in the county or maybe Mississippi too when his carpenters got through with Manfred de Spain's old home. And he had got rid of the only two downright arrant outrageous Snopeses when he run Montgomery Ward and I.O. finally out of town so that now, for the time being at least, the only other Snopes actively inside the city limits was a wholesale grocer not only as respectable but maybe even more solvent than jest a banker. So you would think he would a been satisfied now. But he wasn't. He had to make a young girl (woman now) that wasn't even his child, say "I humbly thank you, Papa, for being so good to me." That's right, a contest. Not even against Linda, and last of all against Lawyer Stevens, since he had already milked out of Lawyer Stevens all he needed from him, which was to get his wife buried all right and proper and decorous and respectable, without no uproarious elements making a unseemly spectacle in the business. His game of solitare was against Jefferson. It was like he was trying to see jest exactly how much Jefferson would stand, put up with. It was like he knowed that his respectability depended completely on Jefferson not jest accepting but finally getting used to the fact that he not only had evicted Manfred de Spain from his bank but he was remodeling to move into it De Spain's birthsite likewise, and that the only remaining threat now was what might happen if that-ere young gal that believed all right so far that he was her paw, might stumble onto something that would tell her different. That she might find out by accident that the man that was leastways mixed up somehow in her mother's suicide, whether he actively caused it or not, wasn't even her father, since if somebody's going to be responsible why your maw killed herself, at least let it be somebody kin to you and not jest a outright stranger.

So you would a thought that the first thing he would do soon as the dust settled after that funeral would be to get her clean out of Jefferson and as far away as he could have suh-jested into her mind she wanted to go. But not him. And the reason he give was that monument. And naturally that was Lawyer Stevens too. I mean, I dont know who delegated Lawyer into the monument business, who gave it to him or if he jest taken it or if maybe by this time the relationship between him and anybody named Snopes, or anyway maybe jest the Flem Snopeses (or no: it was that for him Eula Varner hadn't never died and never would because oh yes, I know about that too) was like that one between a feller out in a big open field and a storm of rain: there aint no being give nor accepting to it: he's already got it.

Anyway it was him—Lawyer—that helped Linda hunt through that house and her mother's things until they found the right photograph and had it—Lawyer still—enlarged, the face part, and sent it to Italy to be carved into a . . . yes, medallion to fasten onto the front of the monument, and him that the practice drawings would come back to to decide and change here and there and send back. Which would a been his right by his own choice even if Flem had tried to interfere in and stop him because he wanted that monument set up where Flem could pass on it more than anybody wanted it because then Flem would let her go. But it was Flem's monument; dont make no mistake about that. It was Flem that paid for it, first thought of it, planned and designed it, picked out what size and what was to be wrote on it—the face and the letters and never once mentioned price. Dont make no mistake about that. It was Flem. Because this too was a part of what he had come to Jefferson for and went through all he went through afterward to get it.

Oh yes, Lawyer had it all arranged for Linda to leave, get away at last; all they was hung on was the monument because Flem had give his word he would let her go then. It was to a place named Greenwich Village in New York; Lawyer had it all arranged, friends he knowed in Harvard to meet the train at the depot and take care of her, get her settled and ever thing.

"Is it a college?" I says. "Like out at Seminary Hill?"

"No no," he says. "I mean, yes. But not the kind you are talking about."

"I thought you was set on her going to a college up there."

"That was before," he says. "Too much has happened to her since. Too much, too fast, too quick. She outgrew colleges all in about twenty-four hours two weeks ago. She'll have to grow back down to them again, maybe in a year or two. But right now, Greenwich Village is the place for her."

"What is Greenwich Village?" I says. "You still aint told me."

"It's a place with a few unimportant boundaries but no limitations where young people of any age go to seek dreams."

"I never knowed before that place had no particular geography," I says. "I thought that-ere was a varmint you hunted anywhere."

"Not always. Not for her, anyway. Sometimes you need a favorable scope of woods to hunt, a place where folks have already successfully hunted and found the same game you want. Sometimes, some people even need help in finding it. The particular quarry they want to catch, they have to make first. That takes two."

"Two what?" I says.

"Yes," he says. "Two."

"You mean a husband," I says.

"All right," he says. "Call him that. It dont matter what you call him."

"Why, Lawyer," I says, "you sound like what a heap, a right smart in fact, jest about all in fact, unanimous in fact of our good God-fearing upright embattled Christian Jeffersons and Yoknapatawphas too that can proudly affirm that never in their life did they ever have one minute's fun that the most innocent little child couldn't a stood right there and watched, would call a deliberate incitement and pandering to the Devil his-self."

Only Lawyer wasn't laughing. And then I wasn't neither. "Yes," he says, "It will be like that with her. It will be difficult for her. She will have to look at a lot of them, a long time. Because he will face something almost impossible to match himself against. He will have to have courage, because it will be doom, maybe disaster too. That's her fate. She is doomed to anguish and to bear it, doomed to one passion and one anguish and all the rest of her life to bear it, as some people are doomed from birth to be robbed or betrayed or murdered."

Then I said it: "Marry her. Naturally you never thought of that."

"I?" he says. It was right quiet: no surprise, no nothing. "I thought I had just been talking about that for the last ten minutes. She must have the best. It will be impossible even for him."

"Marry her," I says.

"No," he says. "That's my fate: just to miss marriage."

"You mean escape it?"

"No no," he says. "I never escape it. Marriage is constantly in my life. My fate is constantly to just miss it or it to, safely again, once more safe, just miss me."

So it was all fixed, and now all he needed was to get his carved marble face back from Italy, nagging by long-distance telephone and telegraph dispatch ever day or so in the most courteous affable legal manner you could want, at the I-talian consul in New Orleans, so he could get it fastened onto the monument and then (if necessary) take a holt on Flem's coat collar and shove him into the car and take him out to the cemetery and snatch the veil offen it, with Linda's ticket to New York (he would a paid for that too except it wasn't necessary since the last thing Uncle Billy done before he went back home after the funeral was to turn over to the bank—not Flem: the bank, with Lawyer as one of the trustees—a good-size chunk of what would be Eula's inheritance under that will of hisn that he hadn't never changed to read Snopes) in his other hand.

So we had to wait. Which was interesting enough. I mean, Lawyer had enough to keep him occupied worrying the I-talian Government, and all I ever needed was jest something to look at, watch, providing of course it had people in it. They—Flem and Linda—still lived in the same little house that folks believed for years after he bought it that he was still jest renting it. Though pretty soon Flem owned a automobile. I mean, presently, after the polite amount of time after he turned up president of the bank; not to have Santy Claus come all at once you might say. It wasn't a expensive car: jest a good one, jest the right unnoticeable size, of a good polite unnoticeable black color and he even learned to drive it because maybe he had to because now ever afternoon after the bank closed he would have to go and watch how the carpenters was getting along with his new house (it was going to have colyums across the front now, I mean the extry big ones so even a feller that never seen colyums before wouldn't have no doubt a-tall what they was, like in the photographs where the Confedrit sweetheart in a hoop skirt and a magnolia is saying good-bye to her Confedrit beau jest before he rides off to finish tending to General Grant) and Flem would have to drive his-self because, although Linda could drive it right off and done it now and then and never mind if all women are naturally interested in the house-building or -remodeling occupation no matter whose it is the same as a bird is interested in the nesting occupation, although she druv him there the first afternoon to look at the house, she wouldn't go inside to look at it and after that one time she never even druv him back any more.

But like I said we was all busy or anyway occupied or at least interested, so we could wait. And sho enough, even waiting ends if you can jest wait long enough. So finally the medallion came. It was October now, a good time of year, one of the best. Naturally it was Lawyer went to the depot and got it though I'm sho Flem paid the freight on it for no other reason than Lawyer wouldn't a waited long enough for the agent to add it up, herding the two Negroes toting it all wrapped up in straw and nailed up in a wooden box, across the platform to his car like he was herding two geese. And for the next three days when his office seen him it was on the fly you might say, from a distance when he happened to pass it. Which was a good thing there wasn't no passel of brigands or highwaymen or contractors or jest simple lawyers making a concerted financial attack on Yoknapatawpha County at that time because Yoknapatawpha would a jest had to rock along the best it could without no help from its attorney. Because he had the masons already hired and waiting with likely even the mortar already mixed, even before the medallion come; one morning I even caught him, put my hand on the car door and says,

"I'll ride out to the cemetery with you," and he jest reached across, the car already in gear and the engine already racing, and lifted my hand off and throwed it away and says,

"Get out of the way," and went on and so I went up to the office, the door never was locked nohow even when he was jest normal and jest out of it most of the time, and opened the bottom drawer where he kept the bottle but it never even smelled like he used to keep whiskey in it. So I waited on the street until school let out and finally caught that boy, Chick, and says,

"Hasn't your uncle got some whiskey at home somewhere?" and he says,

"I don't know. I'll look. You want me to pour up a drink in something and bring it?" and I says,

"No. He dont need a drink. He needs a whole bottle, providing it's big enough and full enough. Bring all of it; I'll stay with him and watch."

Then the monument was finished, ready for Flem to pass on it, and he—Lawyer—sent me the word too, brisk and lively as a general jest getting ready to capture a town: "Be at the office at three-thirty so we can pick up Chick. The train leaves Memphis at eight oclock so we wont have any time to waste."

So I was there. Except it wasn't in the office at all because he was already in the car with the engine already running when I got there. "What train at eight oclock to where and whose?" I says.

"Linda's," he says. "She'll be in New York Saturday morning. She's all packed and ready to leave. Flem's sending her to Memphis in his car as soon as we are done."

"Flem's sending her?" I says.

"Why not?" he says. "She's his daughter. After all you owe something to your children even if it aint your fault. Get in," he says. "Here's Chick."

So we went out to the cemetery and there it was—another colyum not a-tall saying what it had cost Flem Snopes because what it was saying was exactly how much it was worth to Flem Snopes, standing in the middle of that new one-grave lot, at the head of that one grave that hadn't quite healed over yet, looking—the stone, the marble— whiter than white itself in the warm October sun against the bright yellow and red and dark red hickories and sumacs and gums and oaks like splashes of fire itself among the dark green cedars. Then the other car come up with him and Linda in the back seat, and the Negro driver that would drive her to Memphis in the front seat with the baggage (it was all new too) piled on the seat by him; coming up and stopping, and him setting there in that black hat that still looked brand new and like he had borrowed it, and that little bow tie that never had and never would look anything but new, chewing slow and steady at his tobacco; and that gal setting there by him, tight and still and her back not even touching the back of the seat, in a kind of dark suit for travelling and a hat and a little veil and her hands in white gloves still and kind of clenched on her knees and not once not never once ever looking at that stone monument with that marble medal-lion face that Lawyer had picked out and selected that never looked like Eula a-tall you thought at first, never looked like nobody nowhere you thought at first, until you were wrong because it never looked like all women because what it looked like was one woman that ever man that was lucky enough to have been a man would say, "Yes, that's her. I knowed her five years ago or ten years ago or fifty years ago and you would a thought that by now I would a earned the right not to have to remember her any more," and under it the carved letters that he his-self, and I dont mean Lawyer this time, had picked out:

EULA VARNER SNOPES
1889   1927
A Virtuous Wife Is a Crown to Her Husband
Her Children Rise and Call Her Blessed

and him setting there chewing, faint and steady, and her still and straight as a post by him, not looking at nothing and them two white balls of her fists on her lap. Then he moved. He leant a little and spit out the window and then set back in the seat.

"Now you can go," he says.

TWENTY-FOUR

CHARLES MALLISON

So the car went on. Then I turned and started walking back to ours when Ratliff said behind me: "Wait. You got a clean handkerchief?" and I turned and saw Uncle Gavin walking on away from us with his back to us, not going anywhere: just walking on, until Ratliff took the handkerchief from me and we caught up with him. But he was all right then, he just said:

"What's the matter?" Then he said, "Well, let's get on back. You boys are free to loaf all day long if you want to but after all I work for the County so I have to stay close enough to the office so that anybody that wants to commit a crime against it can find me."

So we got in the car and he started it and we drove back to town. Except that he was talking about football now, saying to me: "Why dont you wake up and get out of that kindergarten and into high school so you can go out for the team? I'll need somebody I know on it because I think I know what's wrong with football the way they play it now;" going on from there, talking and even turning loose the wheel with both hands to show us what he meant; how the trouble with football was, only an expert could watch it because nobody else could keep up with what was happening; how in baseball everybody stood still and the ball moved and so you could keep up with what was happening. But in football, the ball and everybody else moved at the same time and not only that but always in a clump, a huddle with the ball hidden in the middle of them so you couldn't even tell who did have it, let alone who was supposed to have it; not to mention the ball being already the color of dirt and all the players thrashing and rolling around in the mud and dirt until they were all that same color too; going on like that, waving both hands with Ratliff and me both hollering, "Watch the wheel! Watch the wheel!" and

Uncle Gavin saying to Ratliff, "Now you dont think so," or "You claim different of course," or "No matter what you say," and Ratliff saying, "Why, I never," or "No I dont," or "I aint even mentioned football," until finally he—Ratliff—said to me:

"Did you find that bottle?"

"No sir," I said. "I reckon Father drank it. Mr Gowrie wont bring the next kag until Sunday night."

"Let me out here," Ratliff said to Uncle Gavin. Uncle Gavin stopped talking long enough to say,

"What?"

"I'll get out here," Ratliff said. "See you in a minute."

So Uncle Gavin stopped long enough for Ratliff to get out (we had just reached the Square), then we went on, Uncle Gavin talking again or still talking since he had only stopped long enough to say What? to Ratliff, and parked the car and went up to the office and he was still talking that same kind of foolishness that you never could decide whether it didn't make any sense or not, and took one of the pipes from the bowl and begun to look around the desk until I went and shoved the tobacco jar up and he looked at the jar and said, "Oh yes, thanks," and put the pipe down, still talking. Then Ratliff came in and went to the cooler and got a glass and the spoon and sugar-bowl from the cabinet and took a pint bottle of white whiskey from inside of his shirt, Uncle Gavin still talking, and made the toddy and came and held it out.

"Here," he said.

"Why, much obliged," Uncle Gavin said. "That looks fine. That sure looks fine." But he didn't touch it. He didn't even take it while Ratliff set it down on the desk where I reckon it was still sitting when Clefus came in the next morning to sweep the office and found it and probably had already started to throw it out when he caught his hand back in time to smell it or recognise it or anyway drink it. And now Uncle Gavin took up the pipe again and filled it and fumbled in his pocket and then Ratliff held out a match and Uncle Gavin stopped talking and looked at it and said, "What?" Then he said, "Thanks," and took the match and scratched it carefully on the underside of the desk and blew it carefully out and put it into the tray and put the pipe into the tray and folded his hands on the desk and said to Ratliff:

"So maybe you can tell me because for the life of me I cant figure it out. Why did she do it? Why? Because as a rule women dont really care about facts just so they fit; it's just men that dont give a damn whether they fit or not, who is hurt, how many are hurt, just so they are hurt bad enough. So I want to ask your opinion. You know women, travelling around the country all day long right in the middle of them, from one parlor to another all day long all high and mighty, as dashing and smooth and welcome as if you were a damned rush—" and stopped and Ratliff said,

"What? What rush? Rush where?"

"Did I say rush?" Uncle Gavin said. "No no, I said Why? A young girl's grief and anguish when young girls like grief and anguish and besides, they can get over it. Will get over it. And just a week from her birthday too of course but after all Flem is the one to get the zero for that: for missing by a whole week anything as big as a young girl's nineteenth birthday. Besides, forget all that; didn't somebody just say that young girls really like grief and anguish? No no, what I said was, Why?" He sat there looking at Ratliff. "Why? Why did she have to? Why did she? The waste. The terrible waste. To waste all that, when it was not hers to waste, not hers to destroy because it is too valuable, belonged to too many, too little of it to waste, destroy, throw away and be no more." He looked at Ratliff. "Tell me, V.K. Why?"

"Maybe she was bored," Ratliff said.

"Bored," Uncle Gavin said. Then he said it again, not loud: "Bored." And that was when he began to cry, sitting there straight in the chair behind the desk with his hands folded together on the desk, not even hiding his face. "Yes," he said. "She was bored. She loved, had a capacity to love, for love, to give and accept love. Only she tried twice and failed twice to find somebody not just strong enough to deserve, earn it, match it, but even brave enough to accept it. Yes," he said, sitting there crying, not even trying to hide his face from us, "of course she was bored."

And one more thing. One morning—it was summer again now, July—the northbound train from New Orleans stopped and the first man off was usually the Negro porter—not the Pullman porters, they were always back down the track at the end; we hardly ever saw them, but the one from the day coaches at the front end—to get down and strut a little while he talked to the section hands and the other Negroes that were always around to meet the passenger trains. But this time it was the conductor himself, almost jumping down before the train stopped, with the white flagman at his heels, almost stepping on them; the porter himself didn't get off at all: just his head sticking out a window about half way down the car.

Then four things got off. I mean, they were children. The tallest was a girl though we never did know whether she was the oldest or just the tallest, then two boys, all three in overalls, and then a little one in a single garment down to its heels like a man's shirt made out of a flour- or meal-sack or maybe a scrap of an old tent. Wired to the front of each one of them was a shipping tag written in pencil:

FROM: BYRON SNOPES, EL PASO, TEXAS
TO: MR FLEM SNOPES, JEFFERSON, MISSISSIPPI

Though Mr Snopes wasn't there. He was busy being a banker now and a deacon in the Baptist church, living in solitary widowerhood in the old De Spain house which he had remodeled into an ante-bellum Southern mansion; he wasn't there to meet them. It was Dink Quistenberry. He had married one of Mr Snopes's sisters or nieces or something out at Frenchman's Bend and when Mr Snopes sent I.O. Snopes back to the country the Quistenberrys came in to buy or rent or anyway run the Snopes Hotel, which wasn't the Snopes Hotel any more now but the Jefferson Hotel though the people that stayed there were still the stock traders and juries locked up by the Circuit Court. I mean, Dink was old enough to be Mr Snopes's brother-in-law or whatever it was but he was the kind of man it just didn't occur to you to say Mister to.

He was there; I reckon Mr Snopes sent him. And when he saw them I reckon he felt just like we did when we saw them, and like the conductor and the flagman and the porter all looked like they had been feeling ever since the train left New Orleans, which was evidently where they got on it. Because they didn't look like people. They looked like snakes. Or maybe that's too strong too. Anyway, they didn't look like children; if there was one thing in the world they didn't look like it was children, with kind of dark pasty faces and black hair that looked like somebody had put a bowl on top of their heads and then cut their hair up to the rim of the bowl with a dull knife, and perfectly black perfectly still eyes that nobody in Jefferson (Yoknapatawpha County either) ever afterward claimed they saw blink.

I dont know how Dink talked to them because the conductor had already told everybody listening (there was a good crowd by that time) that they didn't talk any language or anything else that he had ever heard of and that to watch them because one of them had a switch knife with a six-inch blade, he didn't know which one and he himself wasn't going to try to find out. But anyway Dink got them into his car and the train went on.

Maybe it was the same thing they used in drugstores or at least with Skeets McGowan in Christian's because it wasn't a week before they could go into Christian's, all four of them (it was always all four of them, as if when the medicine man or whoever it was separated each succeeding one from the mother, he just attached the severed cord to the next senior child. Because by that time we knew who they were: Byron Snopes's children out of a Jicarilla Apache squaw in Old Mexico), and come out two minutes later all eating ice-cream cones.

They were always together and anywhere in town or near it at any time of day, until we found out it was any time of night too; one night at two oclock in the morning when Otis Harker caught them coming in single file from behind the Coca-Cola bottling plant; Otis said he didn't know how in the world they got into it because no door was open nor window broken, but he could smell warm Coca-Cola syrup spilled down the front of the little one's nightshirt or dressing-sacque or whatever it was from five or six feet away. Because that was as close as he got; he said he hollered at them to go on home to the Snopes, I mean the Jefferson Hotel but they just stood there looking at him and he said he never intended anything: just to get them moving since maybe they didn't understand what he meant yet. So he sort of flung his arms out and was just kind of jumping at them, hollering again, when he stopped himself just in time, the knife already in one of their hands with the blade open at least six inches long; so fast that he never even saw where it came from and in the next minute gone so fast he still didn't even know which one of the three in over-

alls—the girl or the two boys—had it; that was when Mr Connors
went to Dink Quistenberry the next morning and told him he would
have to keep them off the streets at night.

"Sure," Dink said. "You try it. You keep them off the streets or off
anywhere else. You got my full permission. You're welcome to it!"

So when the dog business happened, even Mr Hub Hampton
himself didn't get any closer than that to them. This was the dog
business. We were getting paved streets in Jefferson now and so
more new families, engineers and contractors and such like the little
Riddell boy's that gave us that holiday two years ago, had moved to
Jefferson. One of them didn't have any children but they had a Cadillac and his wife had a dog that they said cost five hundred dollars, the
only dog higher than fifty dollars except a field-trial pointer or set-
ter (and a part Airedale bear dog named Lion that Major de Spain,
Mr de Spain's father, owned once that hunting people in north Mississippi still talked about) that Jefferson ever heard of, let alone saw—
a Pekinese with a gold name-plate on its collar that probably didn't
even know it was a dog, that rode in the Cadillac and sneered
through the window not just at other dogs but at people too, and
even ate special meat that Mr Wall Snopes's butcher ordered special
from Kansas City because it cost too much for just people to buy and
eat it.

One day it disappeared. Nobody knew how, since the only time it
wasn't sneering out through the Cadillac window, it was sneering out
through a window in the house where it—they—lived. But it was
gone and I dont think anywhere else ever saw a woman take on over
anything like Mrs Widrington did, with rewards in all the Memphis
and north Mississippi and west Tennessee and east Arkansas papers
and Mr Hampton and Mr Connors neither able to sleep at night for
Mrs Widrington ringing their telephone, and the man from the
insurance company (its life was insured too so maybe there were
more people insured in Jefferson than there were dogs but then there
was more of them not insured in Jefferson than there was dogs too)
and Mrs Widrington herself likely at almost any time day or night
to be in your back yard calling what Aleck Sander and I thought was
Yow! Yow! Yow! until Uncle Gavin told us it was named Lao T'se for

a Chinese poet. Until one day the four Snopes Indians came out of Christian's drugstore and somebody passing on the street pointed his finger and hollered "Look!"

It was the collar with the gold name-plate. The little one was wearing it around its neck above the nightshirt. Mr Connors came quick and sent about as quick for Mr Hampton. And that was when Mr Hampton didn't come any closer either and I reckon we all were thinking about what he was: what a mess that big gut of his would make on the sidewalk if he got too close to that knife before he knew it. And the four Snopes Indians or Indian Snopeses, whichever is right, standing in a row watching him, not looking dangerous, not looking anything; not innocent especially and nobody would have called it affectionate, but not dangerous in the same sense that four shut pocket knives dont look threatening. They look like four shut pocket knives but they dont look lethal. Until Mr Hampton said:

"What do they do when they aint eating ice cream up here or breaking in or out of that bottling plant at two oclock in the morning?"

"They got a kind of camp or reservation or whatever you might call it in a cave they dug in the big ditch behind the school house," Mr Connors said.

"Did you look there?" Mr Hampton said.

"Sure," Mr Connors said. "Nothing there but just some trash and bones and stuff they play with."

"Bones?" Mr Hampton said. "What bones?"

"Just bones," Mr Connors said. "Chicken bones, spare ribs, stuff like that they been eating I reckon."

So Mr Hampton went and got in his car and Mr Connors went to his that had the red light and the sireen on it and a few others got in while there was still room, and the two cars went to the school house, the rest of us walking because we wanted to see if Mr Hampton with his belly really would try to climb down into that ditch and if he did how he was going to get out again. But he did it, with Mr Connors showing him where the cave was but letting him go first since he was the sheriff, on to where the little pile of bones was behind the fireplace and turned them over with his toe and then raked a few of them to one side. Because he was a hunter, a woodsman, a good one before his belly got too big to go through a thicket. "There's your dog," he said.

And I remember that time, five years ago now, we were all at the table and Matt Levitt's cut-out passing in the street and Father said at Uncle Gavin: "What's that sound I smell?" Except that Mr Snopes's brass business at the power-plant was before I was even born: Uncle Gavin's office that morning and Mrs Widrington and the insurance man because the dog's life had been insured only against disease or accident or acts of God, and the insurance man's contention (I reckon he had been in Jefferson long enough to have talked with Ratliff; any stranger in town for just half a day, let alone a week, would find himself doing that) was that four half-Snopeses and half-Jicarilla Apache Indians were none of them and so Jefferson itself was liable and vulnerable to suit. So I had only heard about Mr Snopes and the missing brass from Uncle Gavin, but I thought about what Father said that day because I had been there then: "What's that sound I smell?" when Mr Snopes came in, removing his hat and saying "Morning" to everybody without saying it to anybody; then to the insurance man: "How much on that dog?"

"Full pedigree value, Mr Snopes. Five hundred dollars," the insurance man said and Mr Snopes (the insurance man himself got up and turned his chair around to the desk for him) sat down and took a blank check from his pocket and filled in the amount and pushed it across the desk in front of Uncle Gavin and got up and said "Morning" without saying it to anybody and put his hat on and went out.

Except that he didn't quite stop there. Because the next day Byron Snopes's Indians were gone. Ratliff came in and told us.

"Sho," he said. "Flem sent them out to the Bend. Neither of their grandmaws, I mean I.O.'s wives, would have them but finally Dee-wit Binford"—Dewitt Binford had married another of the Snopes girls. They lived near Varner's store—"taken them in. On a contract, the Snopeses all clubbing together pro rata and paying Dee-wit a dollar a head a week on them, providing of course he can last a week. Though naturally the first four dollars was in advance, what you might call a retainer you might say."

It was. I mean, just about a week. Ratliff came in again; it was in the morning. "We jest finished using up Frenchman's Bend at noon yesterday, and that jest about cleans up the county. We're down at the dee-po now, all tagged and the waybill paid, waiting for Number Twenty-three southbound or any other train that will connect more or less or thereabouts for El Paso, Texas"—telling about that too: "A combination you might say of scientific interest and what's that word?" until Uncle Gavin told him anthropological "anthropological coincidence; them four vanishing Americans coming durn nigh taking one white man with them if Doris Snopes's maw and a few neighbors hadn't got there in time."

He told it: how when Dewitt Binford got them home he discovered they wouldn't stay in bed at all, dragging a quilt off onto the floor and lying in a row on it and the next morning he and his wife found the bedstead itself dismantled and leaned against the wall in a corner out of the way; and that they hadn't heard a sound during the process. He—Dewitt—said that's what got on his mind even before he began to worry about the little one: you couldn't hear them; you didn't even know they were in the house or not, when they had entered it or left it; for all you knew, they might be right there in your bedroom in the dark, looking at you.

"So he tried it," Ratliff said. "He went over to Tull's and borrowed Vernon's flashlight and waited until about midnight and he said he never moved quieter in his life, across the hall to the door of the room, trying to not even breathe if he could help it; he had done already cut out sighting notches in the door-frame so that when he laid the flashlight into them by feel it would be aimed straight at where the middle two heads would be on the pallet; and held his breath again, listening until he was sho there wasn't a sound, and snapped on the light. And them four faces and them eight black eyes already laying there wide open looking straight at him.

"And Dee-wit said he would like to a give up then. But by that time that least un wouldn't give him no rest a-tall. Only he didn't know what to do because he had done been warned about that knife even if he hadn't never seen it. Then he remembered them pills, that bottle of knock-out opium pills that Doc Peabody had give Miz Deewit that time the brooder lamp blowed up and burnt most of her front hair off, so he taken eight of them and bought four bottles of sody pop at the store and put two capsules into each bottle and druv the caps back on and hid the bottles jest exactly where he figgered they would have to hunt jest exactly hard enough to find them. And by dark the four bottles was gone and he waited again to be sho it had had plenty of time to work and taken Vernon's flashlight and went across the hall and got on his hands and knees and crawled across to the pallet—he knowed by practice now exactly where on the pallet that least un slept or anyway hid—and reached out easy and found the hem of that nightshirt with one hand and the flashlight ready to snap on in the other.

"And when he told about it, he was downright crying not with jest skeer so much as pure and simple unbelief. 'I wasn't doing nothing' he says. 'I wasn't going to hurt it. All in the world I wanted was jest to see which it was—' "

"Which is it?" Uncle Gavin said.

"That's what I'm telling you," Ratliff said. "He never even got to snap the flashlight on. He jest felt them two thin quick streaks of fire, one down either cheek of his face; he said that all that time he was already running backward on his hands and knees toward the door he knowed there wouldn't even be time to turn around, let alone get up on his feet to run, not to mention shutting the door behind him; and when he run back into his and Miz Deewit's room there wouldn't be no time to shut that one neither except he had to, banging it shut and hollering for Miz Dee-wit now, dragging the bureau against it while Miz Dee-wit lit the lamp and then come and holp him until he hollered at her to shut the windows first; almost crying with them two slashes running from each ear, jest missing his eye on one side, right down to the corners of his mouth like a great big grin that would bust scab and all if he ever let his face go, telling how they would decide that the best thing would be to put the lamp out too and set in the dark until he remembered how they had managed somehow to get inside that locked-up Coca-Cola plant without even touching the patented burglar alarm.

"So they jest shut and locked the windows and left the lamp burning, sitting there in that air-tight room on that hot summer night, until it come light enough for Miz Dee-wit to at least jump and dodge on the way back to the kitchen to start a fire in the stove and cook breakfast. Though the house was empty then. Not safe of course: jest empty except for themselves while they tried to decide whether to try to get word in to Flem or Hub Hampton to come out and get them, or jest pack up themselves without even waiting to wash up the breakfast dishes, and move over to Tull's. Anyhow Dee-wit said him and Miz Dee-wit was through and they knowed it, four dollars a week or no four dollars a week; and so, it was about nine oclock, he was on his way to the store to use the telephone to call Jefferson, when Miz I.O. Snopes, I mean the number-two one that got superseded back before she ever had a chance to move to town, saved him the trouble."

We all knew Doris Snopes. And even if we hadn't, we would have recognised him at first glance since he looked almost exactly like his older brother Clarence (Senator C. Eggleston Snopes, our—or Uncle Billy Varner's, Ratliff and Uncle Gavin said—member of the upper house of the state legislature) almost exactly alike, with (this is Uncle Gavin again) the same mentality of a child and the mutual moral principles of a woverine; younger than Clarence in years but not looking younger or more innocent so much as just newer, as the lesser-used axe or machine gun looks newer—a big hulking animal about seventeen years old, who like his brother Clarence was all one gray color: a grayish tinge already to his tow-colored hair, a grayish pasty look to his flesh, which looked as if it would not flow blood from a wound but instead a pallid fluid like thin oatmeal; he was the only Snopes or resident of Frenchman's Bend or Yoknapatawpha County either, for that matter, who made his Texas cousins welcome. "You might say he adopted them," Ratliff said. "Right from that first day. He even claimed he could talk to them and that he was going to train them to hunt in a pack; they would be better than any jest pack of dogs because sooner or later dogs always quit and went home, while it didn't matter to them where they was.

"So he trained them. The first way he done it was to set a bottle of sody pop on a stump in front of the store with a string running from it to where he would be setting on the gallery, until they would maneuver around and finally bushwack up to where one of them could reach for it, when he would snatch it off the stump with the string and drag it out of their reach. Only that never worked but once so then he would have to drink the bottles empty and fill them again

with muddy water or some such, or another good training method
was to gather up a few throwed-away candy-bar papers and wrap
them up again with mud inside or maybe jest not nothing a-tall
because it taken them a good while to give up then, especially if now
and then he had a sho enough candy bar or a sho enough bottle of
strawberry or orange shuffled into the other ones.

"Anyhow he was always with them, hollering at them and waving
his arms to go this way or that way when folks was watching, like
dogs; they even had some kind of a play house or cave or something
in another ditch about half a mile up the road. That's right. What
you think you are laughing at is the notion of a big almost growed
man like Clarence, playing, until all of a sudden you find out that
what you're laughing at is calling anything playing that them four
things would be interested in.

"So Dee-wit had jest reached the store when here come Doris's
maw, down the road hollering 'Them Indians! Them Indians!' jest
like that: a pure and simple case of mother love and mother instinct.
Because likely she didn't know anything yet and even if she had, in
that state she couldn't a told nobody: jest standing there in the road
in front of the store wringing her hands and hollering Them Indians until the men squatting along the gallery begun to get up and
then to run because about that time Dee-wit come up. Because he
knowed what Miz Snopes was trying to say. Maybe he never had no
mother love and mother instinct but then neither did Miz Snopes
have a last-night's knife-slash down both cheeks.

" 'Them Indians?' he says. 'Fore God, men, run. It may already be
too late.'

"But it wasn't. They was in time. Pretty soon they could hear
Doris bellowing and screaming and then they could line him out and
the fastest ones run on ahead and down into the ditch to where Doris
was tied to a blackjack sapling with something less than a cord of
wood stacked around him jest beginning to burn good.

"So they was in time. Jody telephoned Flem right away and in fact
all this would a formally took place yesterday evening except that
Doris's hunting pack never reappeared in sight until this morning
when Dee-wit lifted the shade enough to see them waiting on the
front gallery for breakfast. But then his house was barred in time

because he hadn't never unbarred it from last night. And Jody's car was already standing by on emergency alert as they say and it wasn't much trouble to toll them into it since like Doris said one place was jest like another to them.

"So they're down at the dee-po now. Would either of you gentlemen like to go down with me and watch what they call the end of a erea, if that's what they call what I'm trying to say? The last and final end of Snopes out-and-out unvarnished behavior in Jefferson, if that's what I'm trying to say."

So Ratliff and I went to the station while he told me the rest of it. It was Miss Eunice Habersham; she had done the telephoning herself: to the Travellers' Aid in New Orleans to meet the Jefferson train and put them on the one for El Paso, and to the El Paso Aid to get them across the border and turn them over to the Mexican police to send them back home, to Byron Snopes or the reservation or wherever it was. Then I noticed the package and said, "What's that?" but he didn't answer. He just parked the pickup and took the cardboard carton and we went around onto the platform where they were: the three in the overalls and what Ratliff called the least un in the night-shirt, each with the new shipping tag wired to the front of its garment, but printed in big block capitals this time, like shouting this time:

FROM: FLEM SNOPES, JEFFERSON, MISS.
TO: BYRON SNOPES
     EL PASO, TEXAS

There was a considerable crowd around them, at a safe distance, when we came up and Ratliff opened the carton; it contained four of everything: four oranges and apples and candy bars and bags of peanuts and packages of chewing gum. "Watch out, now," Ratliff said. "Maybe we better set it on the ground and shove it up with a stick or something." But he didn't mean that. Anyway, he didn't do it. He just said to me, "Come on; you aint quite growed so they may not snap at you," and moved near and held out one of the oranges, the eight eyes not once looking at it nor at us nor at anything that we could see; until the girl, the tallest one, said something, something quick and brittle that sounded quite strange in the treble of a child; whereupon the first hand came out and took the orange, then the next and the next, orderly, not furtive: just quick, while Ratliff and I dealt out the fruit and bars and paper bags, the empty hand already extended again, the objects vanishing somewhere faster than we could follow, except the little one in the nightshirt which apparently had no pockets: until the girl herself leaned and relieved the overflow.

Then the train came in and stopped; the day coach vestibule clanged and clashed open, the narrow steps hanging downward from the orifice like a narrow dropped jaw. Evidently, obviously, Miss Habersham had telephoned a trainmaster or a superintendent (maybe a vice president) somewhere too because the conductor and the porter both got down and the conductor looked rapidly at the four tags and motioned, and we—all of us; we represented Jefferson—watched them mount and vanish one by one into that iron impatient maw: the girl and the two boys in overalls and Ratliff's least un in its ankle-length single garment like a man's discarded shirt made out of flour- or meal-sacking or perhaps the remnant of an old tent. We never did know which it was.

OXFORD-CHARLOTTESVILLE-WASHINGTON-NEW YORK
NOVEMBER 1955—SEPTEMBER 1956

THE MANSION

TO PHIL STONE

CONTENTS

THE MANSION

This book is the final chapter of, and the summation of, a work conceived and begun in 1925. Since the author likes to believe, hopes that his entire life's work is a part of a living literature, and since "living" is motion, and "motion" is change and alteration and therefore the only alternative to motion is un-motion, stasis, death, there will be found discrepancies and contradictions in the thirty-four-year progress of this particular chronicle; the purpose of this note is simply to notify the reader that the author has already found more discrepancies and contradictions than he hopes the reader will— contradictions and discrepancies due to the fact that the author has learned, he believes, more about the human heart and its dilemma than he knew thirty-four years ago; and is sure that, having lived with them that long time, he knows the characters in this chronicle better than he did then.

W. F.

MINK

ONE

*T*he jury said "Guilty" and the Judge said "Life" but he didn't hear them. He wasn't listening. In fact, he hadn't been able to listen since that first day when the Judge banged his little wooden hammer on the high desk until he, Mink, dragged his gaze back from the far door of the courtroom to see what in the world the man wanted, and he, the Judge, leaned down across the desk hollering: "You, Snopes! Did you or didn't you kill Jack Houston?" and he, Mink, said, "Dont bother me now. Cant you see I'm busy?" then turned his own head to look again toward the distant door at the back of the room, himself hollering into, against, across the wall of little wan faces hemming him in: "Snopes! Flem Snopes! Anybody here that'll go and bring Flem Snopes! I'll pay you—Flem'll pay you!"

Because he hadn't had time to listen. In fact, that whole first trip, handcuffed to the deputy, from his jail cell to the courtroom, had been a senseless, a really outrageously foolish interference with and interruption, and each subsequent daily manacled trip and transference, of the solution to both their problems—his and the damned law's both—if they had only waited and let him alone: the watching, his dirty hands gripping among the grimed interstices of the barred window above the street, which had been his one, his imperious need during the long months between his incarceration and the opening of the Court.

At first, during the first few days behind the barred window, he had simply been impatient with his own impatience and—yes, he admitted it—his own stupidity. Long before the moment came when he had had to aim the gun and fire the shot, he knew that his cousin Flem, the only member of his clan with the power to and the reason to, or who could at least be expected to, extricate him from its consequences, would not be there to do it. He even knew why Flem would not be there for at least a year; Frenchman's Bend was too small: everybody in it knew everything about everybody else; they would all have seen through that Texas trip even without the hurrah

681

and hullabaloo that Varner girl had been causing ever since she (or whoever else it was) found the first hair on her bump, not to mention just this last past spring and summer while that durn McCarron boy was snuffing and fighting everybody else off exactly like a gang of rutting dogs.

So that long before Flem married her, he, Mink, and everybody else in ten miles of the Bend knew that old Will Varner was going to have to marry her off to somebody, and that quick, if he didn't want a woods colt in his back yard next grass. And when it was Flem that finally married her, he, Mink, anyway was not surprised. It was Flem, with his usual luck. All right, more than just luck then: the only man in Frenchman's Bend that ever stood up to and held his own with old Will Varner; that had done already more or less eliminated Jody, old Will's son, out of the store, and now was fixing to get hold of half of all the rest of it by being old Will's son-in-law. That just by marrying her in time to save her from dropping a bastard, Flem would not only be the rightful husband of that damn girl that had kept every man under eighty years old in Frenchman's Bend in an uproar ever since she was fifteen years old by just watching her walk past, but he had got paid for it to boot: not only the right to fumble his hand every time the notion struck him under that dress that rutted a man just thinking even about somebody else's hand doing it, but was getting a free deed to that whole Old Frenchman place for doing it.

So he knew Flem would not be there when he would need him, since he knew that Flem and his new wife would have to stay away from Frenchman's Bend at least long enough for what they would bring back with them to be able to call itself only one month old without everybody that looked at it dying of laughing. Only, when the moment finally came, when the instant finally happened when he could no longer defer having to aim the gun and pull the trigger, he had forgot that. No, that was a lie. He hadn't forgot it. He simply could wait no longer: Houston himself would not let him wait longer—and that too was one more injury which Jack Houston in the very act of dying, had done him: compelled him, Mink, to kill him at a time when the only person who had the power to save him and would have had to save him whether he wanted to or not because of the ancient immutable laws of simple blood kinship, was a thousand miles away; and this time it was an irreparable injury because in the very act of committing it, Houston had escaped forever all retribution for it.

He had not forgotten that his cousin would not be there. He simply couldn't wait any longer. He had simply had to trust *them*—the *Them* of whom it was promised that not even a sparrow should fall unmarked. By *them* he didn't mean that whatever-it-was that folks referred to as Old Moster. He didn't believe in any Old Moster. He had seen too much in his time that, if any Old Moster existed, with eyes as sharp and power as strong as was claimed He had, He would have done something about. Besides, he, Mink, wasn't religious. He hadn't been to a church since he was fifteen years old and never aimed to go again—places which a man with a hole in his gut and a rut in his britches that he couldn't satisfy at home, used, by calling himself a preacher of God, to get conveniently together the biggest possible number of women that he could tempt with the reward of the one in return for the job of the other—the job of filling his hole in payment for getting theirs plugged the first time the husband went to the field and she could slip off to the bushes where the preacher was waiting; the wives coming because here was the best market they knowed of to swap a mess of fried chicken or a sweet-potato pie; the husbands coming not to interrupt the trading because the husband knowed he couldn't interrupt it or even keep up with it, but at least to try and find out if his wife's name would come to the head of the waiting list today or if maybe he could still finish scratching that last forty before he would have to tie her to the bedpost and hide behind the door watching; and the young folks not even bothering to enter the church a-tall for already running to be the first couple behind the nearest handy thicket bush.

He meant, simply, that *them—they—it*, whichever and whatever you wanted to call it, who represented a simple fundamental justice and equity in human affairs, or else a man might just as well quit; the *they, them, it*, call them what you like, which simply would not, could not harass and harry a man forever without some day, at some moment, letting him get his own just and equal licks back in return. They could harass and worry him, or they could even just sit back and watch everything go against him right along without missing a lick, almost like there was a pattern to it; just sit back and watch and (all right, why not? he—a man—didn't mind, as long as he was a man and there was a justice to it) enjoy it too; maybe in fact They were even testing him, to see if he was a man or not, man enough to take a little harassment and worry and so deserve his own licks back when his turn came. But at least that moment would come when it was his turn, when he had earned the right to have his own just and equal licks back, just as They had earned the right to test him and even to enjoy the testing; the moment when they would have to prove to him that They were as much a man as he had proved to Them that he was; when he not only would have to depend on Them but had won the right to depend on Them and find Them faithful; and They dared not, They would not dare, to let him down, else it would be as hard for Them to live with themselves afterward as it had finally become for him to live with himself and still keep on taking what he had taken from Jack Houston.

So he knew that morning that Flem was not going to be there. It was simply that he could wait no longer; the moment had simply come when he and Jack Houston could, must, no longer breathe the same air. And so, lacking his cousin's presence, he must fall back on that right to depend on *them* which he had earned by never before in his life demanding anything of them.

It began in the spring. No, it began in the fall before. No, it began a long time before that even. It began at the very instant Houston was born already shaped for arrogance and intolerance and pride. Not at the moment when the two of them, he, Mink Snopes also, began to breathe the same north Mississippi air, because he, Mink, was not a contentious man. He had never been. It was simply that his own bad luck had all his life continually harassed and harried him into the constant and unflagging necessity of defending his own simple rights.

Though it was not until the summer before that first fall that Houston's destiny had actually and finally impinged on his, Mink's, own fate—which was another facet of the outrage: that nothing, not even *they*, least of all *they*, had vouchsafed him any warning of what that first encounter would end in. This was after Houston's young wife had gone into the stallion's stall hunting a hen nest and the horse had killed her and any decent man would have thought that any decent husband would never have had another stallion on the place as long as he lived. But not Houston. Houston was not only rich enough to own a blooded stallion capable of killing his wife, but arrogant and intolerant enough to defy all decency, after shooting the horse that killed her, to turn right around and buy another stallion exactly like it, maybe in case he did get married again; to act so grieving over his wife that even the neighbors didn't dare knock on his front door any more, yet two or three times a week ripping up and down the road on that next murderer of a horse, with that big Bluetick hound running like a greyhound or another horse along beside it, right up to Varner's store and not even getting down: the three of them just waiting there in the road—the arrogant intolerant man and the bad-eyed horse and the dog that bared its teeth and raised its hackles any time anybody went near it—while Houston ordered whoever was on the front gallery to step inside and fetch him out whatever it was he had come for like they were Negroes.

Until one morning when he, Mink, was walking to the store (he had no horse to ride when he had to go for a tin of snuff or a bottle of quinine or a piece of meat); he had just come over the brow of a short hill when he heard the horse behind him, coming fast and hard, and he would have given Houston the whole road if he had had time, the horse already on top of him until Houston wrenched it savagely off and past, the damn hound leaping so close it almost brushed his chest, snarling right into his face, Houston whirling the horse and holding it dancing and plunging, shouting down at him: "Why in hell didn't you jump when you heard me coming? Get off the road! Do you still want him to beat your brains out too before I can get him down again?"

Well, maybe that was what they call grieving for the wife that maybe you didn't actually kill her yourself and you even killed the horse that did it. But still arrogant enough or rich enough to afford to buy another one exactly like the one that did kill her. Which was all right with him, Mink, especially since all anybody had to do was just wait until sooner or later the son-of-a-bitching horse would kill Houston too; until the next thing happened which he had not counted on, planned on, not even anticipated.

It was his milk cow, the only one he owned, not being a rich man like Houston but only an independent one, asking no favors of any man, paying his own way. She—the cow—had missed some way, failed to freshen; and there he was, not only having gone a winter without milk and now faced with another whole year without it, he had also missed out on the calf for which he had had to pay a fifty-cents-cash bull fee, since the only bull in reach he could get for less than a dollar was the scrub bull belonging to a Negro who insisted on cash at the gate.

So he fed the cow all that winter, waiting for the calf which wasn't even there. Then he had to lead the cow the three miles back to the Negro's house, not to claim the return of the fifty cents but only to claim a second stand from the bull, which the Negro refused to permit without the payment in advance of another fifty cents, he, Mink, standing in the yard cursing the Negro until the Negro went back into the house and shut the door, Mink standing in the empty yard cursing the Negro and his family inside the blank house until he had exhausted himself enough to lead the still-barren cow the three miles again back home.

Then he had to keep the barren and worthless cow up under fence while she exhausted his own meager pasture, then he had to feed her out of his meager crib during the rest of that summer and fall, since the local agreement was that all stock would be kept up until all crops were out of the field. Which meant November before he could turn her out for the winter. And even then he had to divert a little feed to her from his winter's meat hogs, to keep her in the habit of coming more or less back home at night; until she had been missing three or four days and he finally located her in Houston's pasture with his beef herd.

In fact, he was already in the lane leading to Houston's house, the coiled plowline in his hand, when without even knowing he was going to and without even pausing or breaking stride he had turned about, already walking back toward home, rapidly stuffing the coiled rope inside his shirt where it would be concealed, not to return to the paintless repairless tenant cabin in which he lived, but simply to find privacy in which to think, stopping presently to sit on a log beside the road while he realised the full scope of what had just dawned before him.

By not claiming the worthless cow yet, he would not only winter her, he would winter her twice—ten times—as well as he himself could afford to. He would not only let Houston winter her (Houston, a man not only rich enough to be able to breed and raise beef cattle, but rich enough to keep a Negro to do nothing else save feed and tend them—a Negro to whom Houston furnished a better house to live in than the one that he, Mink, a white man with a wife and two daughters, lived in) but when he would reclaim the cow in the spring she would have come in season again and, running with Houston's beef herd-bull, would now be carrying a calf which would not only freshen her for milk but would itself be worth money as grade beef where the offspring of the Negro's scrub bull would have been worth almost nothing.

Naturally he would have to be prepared for the resulting inevitable questions; Frenchman's Bend was too little, too damn little for a man to have any privacy about what he did, let alone about what he owned or lacked. It didn't even take four days. It was at Varner's store, where he would walk down to the crossroads and back every day, giving them a chance to go ahead and get it over with. Until finally one said—he didn't remember who; it didn't matter: "Aint you located your cow yet?"

"What cow?" he said. The other said,

"Jack Houston says for you to come and get that bonerack of yours out of his feed lot; he's tired of boarding it."

"Oh, that," he said. "That aint my cow any more. I sold that cow last summer to one of the Gowrie boys up at Caledonia Chapel."

"I'm glad to hear that," the other said. "Because if I was you and my cow was in Jack Houston's feed lot, I would take my rope and go and get it, without even noticing myself doing it, let alone letting Jack Houston notice me. I don't believe I would interrupt him right now even to say Much obliged." Because all Frenchman's Bend knew Houston: sulking and sulling in his house all alone by himself since the stallion killed his wife four years ago. Like nobody before him had ever lost a wife, even when, for whatever incomprehensible reason the husband could have had, he didn't want to get shut of her. Sulking and sulling alone on that big place with two nigger servants, the man and the woman to cook, and the stallion and the big Bluetick hound that was as high-nosed and intolerant and surly as Houston himself—a durn surly sullen son of a bitch that didn't even know he was lucky: rich, not only rich enough to afford a wife to whine and nag and steal his pockets ragged of every dollar he made, but rich enough to do without a wife if he wanted: rich enough to be able to hire a woman to cook his victuals instead of having to marry her. Rich enough to hire another nigger to get up in his stead on the cold mornings and go out in the wet and damp to feed not only the beef cattle which he sold at the top fat prices because he could afford to hold them till then, but that blooded stallion too, and even that damn hound running beside the horse he thundered up and down the road on, until a fellow that never had anything but his own two legs to travel on, would have to jump clean off the road into the bushes or the son-of-a-bitching horse would have killed him too with its shod feet and left him laying there in the ditch for the son-of-a-bitching hound to eat before Houston would even have reported it.

All right, if Houston was in too high and mighty a mood to be said much obliged to, he, Mink, for one wasn't going to break in on him uninvited. Not that he didn't owe a much obliged to something somewhere. This was a week later, then a month later, then Christmas had passed and the hard wet dreary winter had set in. Each afternoon, in the slicker held together with baling wire and automobile tire patching which was the only winter outer garment he owned over his worn patched cotton overalls, he would walk up the muddy road in the dreary and fading afternoons to watch Houston's pedigree beef herd, his own sorry animal among them, move, not hurrying, toward and into the barn which was warmer and tighter against the weather than the cabin he lived in, to be fed by the hired Negro who wore warmer clothing than any he and his family possessed, cursing into the steamy vapor of his own breathing, cursing the Negro for his black skin inside the warmer garments than his, a white man's, cursing the rich feed devoted to cattle instead of humans even though his own animal shared it; cursing above all the unaware white man through or because of whose wealth such a condition could obtain, cursing the fact that his very revenge and vengeance—what he himself believed to be simple justice and inalienable rights—could not be done at one stroke but instead must depend on the slow incrementation of feed converted to weight, plus the uncontrollable, even unpredictable, love mood of the cow and the long subsequent nine months of gestation; cursing his own condition that the only justice available to him must be this prolonged and passive one.

That was it. Prolongation. Not only the anguish of hope deferred, not even the outrage of simple justice deferred, but the knowledge that, even when the blow fell on Houston, it would cost him, Mink, eight dollars in cash—the eight dollars which he would have to affirm that the imaginary purchaser of the cow had paid him for the animal in order to make good the lie that he had sold it, which, when he reclaimed the cow in the spring, he would have to give to Houston as an earnest that until that moment he really believed he had sold the animal—or at least had established eight dollars as its value—when he went to Houston and told him how the purchaser had come to him, Mink, only that morning and told him the cow had escaped from the lot the same night he had bought it and brought it home, and so reclaimed the eight dollars he had paid for it, thus establishing the cow not only in Houston's arrogant contempt but in the interested curiosity of the rest of Frenchman's Bend too, as having now cost him, Mink, sixteen dollars to reclaim his own property.

That was the outrage: the eight dollars. The fact that he could not even have wintered the cow for eight dollars, let alone put on it the weight of flesh he could see with his own eyes it now carried, didn't count. What mattered was, he would have to give Houston, who didn't need it and wouldn't even miss the feed the cow had eaten, the eight dollars with which he, Mink, could have bought a gallon of whiskey for Christmas, plus a dollar or two of the gewgaw finery his wife and his two daughters were forever whining at him for.

But there was no help for it. And even then, his pride was that he was not reconciled. Not he to be that meager and niggling and puny as meekly to accept something just because he didn't see yet how he could help it. More, since this too merely bolstered the

anger and rage at the injustice: that he would have to go fawning
and even cringing a little when he went to recover his cow; would
have to waste a lie for the privilege of giving eight dollars which he
wanted, must sacrifice to spare, to a man who didn't even need
them, would not even miss their lack, did not even know yet that
he was going to receive them. The moment, the day at last at the
end of winter when by local custom the livestock which had run
loose in the skeletoned cornfields since fall, must be taken up by
their owners and put inside fences so the land could be plowed and
planted again; one afternoon, evening rather, waiting until his cow
had received that final feeding with the rest of Houston's herd
before he approached the feed lot, the worn plowline coiled over his
arm and the meager lump of worn dollar bills and nickels and dimes
and quarters wadded into his overall pocket, not needing to fawn
and cringe yet because only the Negro with his hayfork would be
in the lot now, the rich man himself in the house, the warm kitchen,
with in his hand a toddy not of the stinking gagging homemade corn
such as he, Mink, would have had to buy with his share of the eight
dollars if he could have kept them, but of good red chartered
whiskey ordered out of Memphis. Not having to fawn and cringe
yet: just saying, level and white-man, to the nigger paused in the
door to the feeding shed to look back at him:

"Hidy. I see you got my cow there. Put this rope on her and I'll get
her outen your way," the Negro looking back at him a second longer
then gone, on through the shed toward the house; not coming back
to take the rope, which he, Mink, had not expected anyway, but gone
first to tell the white man, to know what to do. Which was exactly
what he, Mink, had expected, leaning his cold-raw, cold-reddened
wrists which even the frayed slicker sleeves failed to cover, on the top
rail of the white-painted fence. Oh yes, Houston with the toddy of
good red whiskey in his hand and likely with his boots off and his
stocking feet in the oven of the stove, warming for supper, who now,
cursing, would have to withdraw his feet and drag on again the cold
wet muddy rubber and come back to the lot.

Which Houston did: the very bang of the kitchen door and the
squish and slap of the gum boots across the back yard and into the lot
sounding startled and outraged. Then he came on through the shed

too, the Negro about ten feet behind him. "Hidy, Jack," Mink said. "Too bad to have to roust you out into the cold and wet again. That nigger could have tended to it. I jest learned today you wintered my cow for me. If your nigger'll put this plowline on her, I'll get her out of your way."

"I thought you sold that cow to Nub Gowrie," Houston said.

"So did I," Mink said. "Until Nub rid up this morning on a mule and said that cow broke out of his lot the same night he got her home and he aint seen her since, and collected back the eight dollars he paid me for her," already reaching into his pocket, the meager wad of frayed notes and coins in his hand. "So, since eight dollars seems to be the price of this cow, I reckon I owe you that for wintering her. Which makes her a sixteen-dollar cow now, dont it, whether she knows it or not. So here. Take your money and let your nigger put this plowline on her and I'll—"

"That cow wasn't worth eight dollars last fall," Houston said. "But she's worth a considerable more now. She's eaten more than sixteen dollars' worth of my feed. Not to mention my young bull topped her last week. It was last week, wasn't it, Henry?" he said to the Negro.

"Yes sir," the Negro said. "Last Tuesday. I put it on the book."

"If you had jest notified me sooner I'd have saved the strain on your bull and that nigger and his pitchfork too," Mink said. He said to the Negro: "Here. Take this rope—"

"Hold it," Houston said; he was reaching into his pocket too. "You yourself established the price of that cow at eight dollars. All right. I'll buy her."

"You yourself jest finished establishing the fact that she has done went up since then," Mink said. "I'm trying right now to give the rest of sixteen for her. So evidently I wouldn't take sixteen, let alone jest eight. So take your money. And if your nigger's too wore out to put this rope on her, I'll come in and do it myself." Now he even began to climb the fence.

"Hold it," Houston said again. He said to the Negro: "What would you say she's worth now?"

"She'd bring thirty," the Negro said. "Maybe thirty-five."

"You hear that?" Houston said.

"No," Mink said, still climbing the fence. "I dont listen to niggers:

I tell them. If he dont want to put this rope on my cow, tell him to get outen my way."

"Dont cross that fence, Snopes," Houston said.

"Well well," Mink said, one leg over the top rail, the coil of rope dangling from one raw-red hand, "dont tell me you bring a pistol along ever time you try to buy a cow. Maybe you even tote it to put a cottonseed or a grain of corn in the ground too?" It was tableau: Mink with one leg over the top rail, Houston standing inside the fence, the pistol hanging in one hand against his leg, the Negro not moving either, not looking at anything, the whites of his eyes just showing a little. "If you had sent me word, maybe I could a brought a pistol too."

"All right," Houston said. He laid the pistol carefully on the top of the fence post beside him. "Put that rope down. Get over the fence at your post. I'll back off one post and you can count three and we'll see who uses it to trade with."

"Or maybe your nigger can do the counting," Mink said. "All he's got to do is say Three. Because I aint got no nigger with me neither. Evidently a man needs a tame nigger and a pistol both to trade livestock with you." He swung his leg back to the ground outside the fence. "So I reckon I'll jest step over to the store and have a word with Uncle Billy and the constable. Maybe I ought to done that at first, saved a walk up here in the cold. I would a suh-gested leaving my plowline here, to save toting it again, only likely you would be charging me thirty-five dollars to get it back, since that seems to be your bottom price for anything in your lot that dont belong to you." He was leaving now. "So long then. In case you do make any eight-dollar stock deals, be sho you dont take no wooden nickels."

He walked away steadily enough but in such a thin furious rage that for a while he couldn't even see, and with his ears ringing as if someone had fired a shotgun just over his head. In fact he had expected the rage too and now, in solitude and privacy, was the best possible time to let it exhaust itself. Because he knew now he had anticipated something like what had happened and he would need his wits about him. He had known by instinct that his own outrageous luck would invent something like this, so that even the fact that going to Varner, the justice of the peace, for a paper for the constable to serve on Houston to recover the cow would cost him another two dollars and a half, was not really a surprise to him: it was simply *them* again, still testing, trying him to see just how much he could bear and would stand.

So, in a way, he was not really surprised at what happened next either. It was his own fault in a way: he had simply underestimated *them:* the whole matter of taking the eight dollars to Houston and putting the rope on the cow and leading it back home had seemed too simple, too puny for Them to bother with. But he was wrong; They were not done yet. Varner would not even issue the paper; whereupon two days later there were seven of them, counting the Negro—himself, Houston, Varner and the constable and two professional cattle buyers—standing along the fence of Houston's feed lot while the Negro led his cow out for the two experts to examine her.

"Well?" Varner said at last.

"I'd give thirty-five," the first trader said.

"Bred to a paper bull, I might go to thirty-seven and a half," the second said.

"Would you go to forty?" Varner said.

"No," the second said. "She might not a caught."

"That's why I wouldn't even match thirty-seven and a half," the first said.

"All right," Varner said—a tall, gaunt, narrow-hipped, heavily moustached man who looked like what his father had been: one of Forrest's cavalrymen. "Call it thirty-seven and a half then. So we'll split the difference then." He was looking at Mink now. "When you pay Houston eighteen dollars and seventy-five cents, you can have your cow. Only you haven't got eighteen dollars and seventy-five cents, have you?"

He stood there, his raw-red wrists which the slicker did not cover lying quiet on the top rail of the fence, his eyes quite blind again and his ears ringing again as though somebody had fired a shotgun just over his head, and on his face that expression faint and gentle and almost like smiling. "No," he said.

"Wouldn't his cousin Flem let him have it?" the second trader said. Nobody bothered to answer that at all, not even to remind them that Flem was still in Texas on his honeymoon, where he and his wife had been since the marriage last August.

"Then he'll have to work it out," Varner said. He was talking to Houston now. "What have you got that he can do?"

"I'm going to fence in another pasture," Houston said. "I'll pay him fifty cents a day. He can make thirty-seven days and from light till noon on the next one digging post holes and stringing wire. What about the cow? Do I keep her, or does Quick" (Quick was the constable) "take her?"

"Do you want Quick to?" Varner said.

"No," Houston said. "She's been here so long now she might get homesick. Besides, if she's here Snopes can see her every day and keep his spirits up about what he's really working for."

"All right, all right," Varner said quickly. "It's settled now. I don't want any more of that now."

That was what he had to do. And his pride still was that he would not be, would never be, reconciled to it. Not even if he were to lose the cow, the animal itself to vanish from the entire equation and leave him in what might be called peace. Which—eliminating the cow— he could have done himself. More: he could have got eighteen dollars and seventy-five cents for doing it, which, with the eight dollars Houston had refused to accept, would have made practically twenty-seven dollars, more cash at one time than he had seen in he could not remember when, since even with the fall sale of his bale or two of cotton, the subtraction of Varner's landlord's share, plus his furnish bill at Varner's store, barely left him that same eight or ten dollars in cash with which he had believed in vain that he could redeem the cow.

In fact, Houston himself made that suggestion. It was the second or third day of digging the post holes and setting the heavy locust posts in them; Houston came up on the stallion and sat looking down at him. He didn't even pause, let alone look up.

"Look," Houston said. "Look at me." He looked up then, not pausing. Houston's hand was already extended; he, Mink, could see the actual money in it. "Varner said eighteen seventy-five. All right, here it is. Take it and go on home and forget about that cow." Now he didn't even look up any longer, heaving onto his shoulder the post that anyway looked heavier and more solid than he did and dropping it into the hole, tamping the dirt home with the reversed shovel handle so that he only had to hear the stallion turn and go away. Then it was the fourth day; again he only needed to hear the stallion come up and stop, not even looking up when Houston said,

"Snopes," then again, "Snopes," then he said, "Mink," he—Mink—not even looking up, let alone pausing while he said:

"I hear you."

"Stop this now. You got to break your land for your crop. You got to make your living. Go on home and get your seed in the ground and then come back."

"I aint got time to make a living," he said, not even pausing. "I got to get my cow back home."

The next morning it was not Houston on the stallion but Varner himself in his buckboard. Though he, Mink, did not know yet that it was Varner himself who was suddenly afraid, afraid for the peace and quiet of the community which he held in his iron usurious hand, buttressed by the mortgages and liens in the vast iron safe in his store. And now he, Mink, did look up and saw money in the closed fist resting on Varner's knee.

"I've put this on your furnish bill for this year," Varner said. "I just come from your place. You aint broke a furrow yet. Pick up them tools and take this money and give it to Jack and take that damn cow on home and get to plowing."

Though this was only Varner; he could pause and even lean on the post-hole digger now. "Have you heard any complaint from me about that-ere cow court judgment of yourn?" he said.

"No," Varner said.

"Then get out of my way and tend to your business while I tend to mine," he said. Then Varner was out of the buckboard—a man already old enough to be called Uncle Billy by the debtors who fawned on him, yet agile too: enough so to jump down from the buckboard in one motion, the lines in one hand and the whip in the other.

"God damn you," he said, "pick up them tools and go on home. I'll be back before dark, and if I dont find a furrow run by then, I'm going to dump every sorry stick you've got in that house out in the road and rent it to somebody else tomorrow morning."

And he, Mink, looking at him, with on his face that faint gentle expression almost like smiling. "Likely you would do jest exactly that," he said.

"You're god-damned right I will," Varner said. "Get on. Now. This minute."

"Why, sholy," he said. "Since that's the next court judgment in this case, and a law-abiding feller always listens to a court judgment." He turned.

"Here," Varner said to his back. "Take this money."

"Aint it?" he said, going on.

By midafternoon he had broken the better part of an acre. When he swung the plow at the turn-row he saw the buckboard coming up the lane. It carried two this time, Varner and the constable, Quick, and it was moving at a snail's pace because, on a lead rope at the rear axle, was his cow. He didn't hurry; he ran out that furrow too, then unhitched the traces and tied the mule to the fence and only then walked on to where the two men still sat in the buckboard, watching him.

"I paid Houston the eighteen dollars and here's your cow," Varner said. "And if ever again I hear of you or anything belonging to you on Jack Houston's land, I'm going to send you to jail."

"And seventy-five cents," he said. "Or maybe them six bits evaporated. That cow's under a court judgment. I cant accept it until that judgment is satisfied."

"Lon," Varner said to the constable in a voice flat and almost gentle, "put that cow in the lot yonder and take that rope off it and get to hell back in this buggy."

"Lon," Mink said in a voice just as gentle and just as flat, "if you put that cow in my lot I'll get my shotgun and kill her."

Nor did he watch them. He went back to the mule and untied the lines from the fence and hooked up the traces and ran another furrow, his back now to the house and the lane, so that not until he swung the mule at the turn-row did he see for a moment the buckboard going back down the lane at that snail's pace matched to the plodding cow. He plowed steadily on until dark, until his supper of the coarse fatback and cheap molasses and probably weevilly flour which, even after he had eaten it, would still be the property of Will Varner until he, Mink, had ginned and sold the cotton next fall which he had not even planted yet.

An hour later, with a coal-oil lantern to light dimly the slow lift and thrust of the digger, he was back at Houston's fence. He had not lain down nor even stopped moving, working, since daylight this morning; when daylight came again he would not have slept in twenty-four hours; when the sun did rise on him he was back in his own field with the mule and plow, stopping only for dinner at noon, then back to the field again, plowing again—or so he thought until he waked to find himself lying in the very furrow he had just run, beneath the canted handles of the still-bedded plow, the anchored mule still standing in the traces and the sun just going down.

Then supper again like last night's meal and this morning's break-fast too, and carrying the lighted lantern he once more crossed Houston's pasture toward where he had left the post-hole digger. He didn't even see Houston sitting on the pile of waiting posts until Houston stood up, the shotgun cradled in his left arm. "Go back." Houston said. "Dont never come on my land again after sundown. If you're going to kill yourself, it wont be here. Go back now. Maybe I cant stop you from working out that cow by daylight but I reckon I can after dark."

But he could stand that too. Because he knew the trick of it. He had learned that the hard way; himself taught that to himself through simple necessity: that a man can bear anything by simply and calmly refusing to accept it, be reconciled to it, give up to it. He could even sleep at night now. It was not so much that he had time to sleep now, as because he now had a kind of peace, freed of hurry and haste. He broke the rest of his rented land now, then opened out the middles while the weather held good, using the bad days on Houston's fence, marking off one day less which meant fifty cents less toward the recovery of his cow. But with no haste now, no urgency; when spring finally came and the ground warmed for the reception of seed and he saw before him a long hiatus from the fence because of the compulsion of his own crop, he faced it calmly, getting his corn- and cotton-seed from Varner's store and planting his ground, making a better job of sowing than he had ever done before, since all he had to do now was to fill the time until he could get back to the fence and with his own sweat dissolve away another of the half-dollars. Because patience was his pride too: never to be reconciled since by this means he could beat Them; They might be stronger for a moment than he but nobody, no man, no nothing could wait longer than he could wait when nothing else but waiting would do, would work, would serve him.

Then the sun set at last on the day when he could put down patience also along with the digger and the stretchers and what remained of the wire. Houston would know it was the last day too of course. Likely Houston had spent the whole day expecting him to come trotting up the lane to get the cow the minute the sun was below the western trees; likely Houston had spent the whole day from sunrise on in the kitchen window to see him, Mink, show up for that last day's work already carrying the plowline to lead the cow home with. In fact, throughout that whole last day while he dug the last holes and tamped into them not the post at all but the last of that outrage which They had used old Will Varner himself as their tool to try him with, to see how much he really could stand, he could imagine Houston hunting vainly up and down the lane, trying every bush and corner to find where he must have hidden the rope.

Which—the rope—he had not even brought yet, working steadily on until the sun was completely down and no man could say the full day was not finished and done, and only then gathering up the digger and shovel and stretchers, to carry them back to the feed lot and set them neatly and carefully in the angle of the fence where the nigger or Houston or anybody else that wanted to look couldn't help but see them, himself not glancing even once toward Houston's house, not even glancing once at the cow which no man could now deny was his, before walking on back down the lane toward his cabin two miles away.

He ate his supper, peacefully and without haste, not even listening for the cow and whoever would be leading it this time. It might even

be Houston himself. Though on second thought, Houston was like
him; Houston didn't scare easy either. It would be old Will Varner's
alarm and concern sending the constable to bring the cow back, now
that the judgment was worked out to the last penny, he, Mink, chewing his fatback and biscuits and drinking his coffee with that same
gentle expression almost like smiling, imagining Quick cursing and
stumbling up the lane with the lead rope for having to do the job in
the dark when he too would rather be at home with his shoes off eating supper; Mink was already rehearsing, phrasing what he would tell
him: "I worked out eighteen and a half days. It takes a light and a
dark both to make one of them, and this one aint up until daylight
tomorrow morning. Just take that cow back where you and Will
Varner put it eighteen and a half days ago, and I'll come in the morning and get it. And remind that nigger to feed early, so I wont have to
wait."

But he heard nothing. And only then did he realise that he had
actually expected the cow, had counted on its return you might say.
He had a sudden quick light shock of fear, terror, discovering now
how spurious had been that peace he thought was his since his run-
in with Houston and the shotgun at the fence line that night two
months ago; so light a hold on what he had thought was peace that
he must be constantly on guard now, since almost anything apparently could throw him back to that moment when Will Varner had
told him he would have to work out eighteen dollars and seventy-five
cents at fifty cents a day to gain possession of his own cow. Now he
would have to go to the lot and look to make sure Quick hadn't put
the cow in it unheard and then run, fled; he would have to light a
lantern and go out in the dark to look for what he knew he would not
find. And as if that was not enough, he would have to explain to his
wife where he was going with the lantern. Sure enough, he had to
do it, using the quick hard unmannered word when she said, "Where
you going? I thought Jack Houston warned you,"—adding, not for
the crudeness but because she too would not let him alone:

"Lessen of course you will step outside and do it for me."

"You nasty thing!" she cried. "Using words like that in front of the
girls!"

"Sholy," he said. "Or maybe you could send them. Maybe both of them together could make up for one a-dult. Though from the way they eat, ara one of them alone ought to do hit."

He went to the barn. The cow was not there of course, as he had known. He was glad of it. The whole thing—realising that even if one of them brought the cow home, he would still have to go out to the barn to make sure—had been good for him, teaching him, before any actual harm had been done, just exactly what They were up to: to fling, jolt, surprise him off balance and so ruin him: Who couldn't beat him in any other way: couldn't beat him with money or its lack, couldn't outwait him; could beat him only by catching him off balance and so topple him back into that condition of furious blind earless rage where he had no sense.

But he was all right now. He had actually gained; when he took his rope tomorrow morning and went to get his cow, it wouldn't be Quick but Houston himself who would say, "Why didn't you come last night? The eighteenth-and-a-half day was up at dark last night"; it would be Houston himself to whom he would answer:

"It takes a light and a dark both to make a day. That-ere eighteen-and-a-half day is up this morning—providing that delicate nigger of yourn has done finished feeding her."

He slept. He ate breakfast; sunrise watched him walk without haste up the lane to Houston's feed lot, the plowline coiled on his arm, to lean his folded arms on the top rail of the fence, the coiled rope loosely dangling, watching the Negro with his pitchfork and Houston also for a minute or two before they saw him. He said:

"Mawnin, Jack. I come by for that-ere court-judgment cow if you'll kindly have your nigger to kindly put this here rope on her if he'll be so kindly obliging," then still leaning there while Houston came across the lot and stopped about ten feet away.

"You're not through yet," Houston said. "You owe two more days."

"Well well," he said, easily and peacefully, almost gently. "I reckon a man with a lot full of paper bulls and heifers, not to mention a half a mile of new pasture fence he got built free for nothing, might get mixed up about a little thing not no more important than jest dollars, especially jest eighteen dollars and seventy-five cents of them. But I

jest own one eight-dollar cow, or what I always thought was jest a
eight-dollar cow. I aint rich enough not to be able to count up to
eighteen seventy-five."

"I'm not talking about eighteen dollars," Houston said. "I'm—"

"And seventy-five cents," Mink said.

"—talking about nineteen dollars. You owe one dollar more."

He didn't move; his face didn't change; he just said: "What one
dollar more?"

"The pound fee," Houston said. "The law says that when anybody
has to take up a stray animal and the owner dont claim it before dark
that same day, the man that took it up is entitled to a one-dollar
pound fee."

He stood quite still; his hand did not even tighten on the coiled
rope. "So that was why you were so quick that day to save Lon the
trouble of taking her to his lot," he said. "To get that extra dollar."

"Damn the extra dollar," Houston said. "Damn Quick too. He
was welcome to her. I kept her instead to save you having to walk all
the way to Quick's house to get her. Not to mention I have fed her
every day, which Quick wouldn't have done. The digger and shovel
and stretchers are in the corner yonder where you left them last
night. Any time you want to—"

But he had already turned, already walking, peacefully and
steadily, carrying the coiled rope, back down the lane to the road, not
back toward his home but in the opposite direction toward Varner's
store four miles away. He walked through the bright sweet young
summer morning between the burgeoning woodlands where the
dogwood and redbud and wild plum had long since bloomed and
gone, beside the planted fields standing strongly with corn and cotton, some of it almost as good as his own small patches (obviously the
people who planted these had not had the leisure and peace he had
thought he had to sow in); treading peacefully the rife and vernal
earth boiling with life—the frantic flash and glint and crying of birds,
a rabbit bursting almost beneath his feet, so young and thin as to
have but two dimensions, unless the third one could be speed—on to
Varner's store.

The gnawed wood gallery above the gnawed wood steps should be
vacant now. The overalled men who after laying-by would squat or

stand all day against the front wall or inside the store itself, should be in the field too today, ditching or mending fences or running the first harrows and shovels and cultivators among the stalks. The store was too empty, in fact. He thought *If Flem was jest here*—because Flem was not there; he, Mink, knew if anyone did that that honeymoon would have to last until they could come back home and tell Frenchman's Bend that the child they would bring with them hadn't been born sooner than this past May *at* the earliest. But even if it hadn't been that, it would have been something else; his cousin's absence when he was needed was just one more test, harassment, enragement They tried him with, not to see if he would survive it because They had no doubt of that, but simply for the pleasure of watching him have to do something extra there was no reason whatever for him to have to do.

Only Varner was not there either. Mink had not expected that. He had taken it for granted that They certainly would not miss this chance: to have the whole store crammed with people who should have been busy in the field—loose idle ears all strained to hear what he had come to say to Will Varner. But even Varner was gone; there was nobody in the store but Jody Varner and Lump Snopes, the clerk Flem had substituted in when he quit to get married last summer.

"If he went in to town, he wont be back before night," Mink said.

"Not to town," Jody said. "He went over to look at a mill on Punkin Creek. He said he'll be back by dinner time."

"He wont be back until night," Mink said.

"All right," Jody said. "Then you can go back home and come back tomorrow."

So he had no choice. He could have walked the five miles back home and then the five more back to the store in just comfortable time before noon, if he had wanted a walk. Or he could stay near the store until noon and wait there until old Varner would finally turn up just about in time for supper, which he would do, since naturally They would not miss that chance to make him lose a whole day. Which would mean he would have to put in half of one night digging Houston's post holes since he would have to complete the two days by noon of day after tomorrow in order to finish what he would need to do since he would have to make one trip in to town himself.

Or he could have walked back home just in time to eat his noon meal and then walk back, since he would already have lost a whole day anyway. But They would certainly not miss that chance; as soon as he was out of sight, the buckboard would return from Punkin Creek and Varner would get out of it. So he waited, through noon when, as soon as Jody left to go home to dinner, Lump hacked off a segment of hoop cheese and took a handful of crackers from the barrel.

"Aint you going to eat no dinner?" Lump said. "Will wont miss it."

"No," Mink said.

"I'll put it on your furnish then, if you're all that tender about one of Will Varner's nickels," Lump said.

"I'm not hungry," he said. But there was one thing he could be doing, one preparation he could be making while he waited, since it was not far. So he went there, to the place he had already chosen, and did what was necessary since he already knew what Varner was going to tell him, and returned to the store and yes, at exactly midafternoon, just exactly right to exhaust the balance of the whole working day, the buckboard came up and Varner got out and was tying the lines to the usual gallery post when Mink came up to him.

"All right," Varner said. "Now what?"

"A little information about the Law," he said. "This here pound-fee law."

"What?" Varner said.

"That's right," he said, peaceful and easy, his face quiet and gentle as smiling. "I thought I had finished working out them thirty-seven and a half four-bit days at sundown last night. Only when I went this morning to get my cow, it seems like I aint done quite yet, that I owe two more days for the pound fee."

"Hell fire," Varner said. He stood over the smaller man, cursing. "Did Houston tell you that?"

"That's right," he said.

"Hell fire," Varner said again. He dragged a huge worn leather wallet strapped like a suitcase from his hip pocket and took a dollar bill from it. "Here," he said.

"So the Law does say I got to pay another dollar before I can get my cow."

"Yes," Varner said. "If Houston wants to claim it. Take this dollar—"

"I don't need it," he said, already turning. "Me and Houston don't deal in money, we deal in post holes. I jest wanted to know the Law. And if that's the Law, I reckon there aint nothing for a law-abiding feller like me to do but jest put up with it. Because if folks dont put up with the Law, what's the use of all the trouble and expense of having it?"

"Wait," Varner said. "Dont you go back there. Dont you go near Houston's place. You go on home and wait. I'll bring your cow to you as soon as I get hold of Quick."

"That's all right," he said. "Maybe I aint got as many post holes in me as Houston has dollars, but I reckon I got enough for just two more days."

"Mink!" Varner said. "Mink! Come back here!" But he was gone. But there was no hurry now; the day was already ruined; until tomorrow morning, when he was in Houston's new pasture until sundown. This time he hid the tools under a bush as he always did when he would return tomorrow, and went home and ate the sowbelly and flour gravy and undercooked biscuits; they had one timepiece, the tin alarm clock which he set for eleven and rose again then; he had left coffee in the pot and some of the meat cold in the congealed skillet and two biscuits so it was almost exactly midnight when the savage baying of the Bluetick hound brought the Negro to his door and he, Mink, said, "Hit's Mister Snopes. Reporting for work. Hit's jest gone exactly midnight for the record." Because he would have to do this in order to quit at noon. And They—Houston—were still watching him because when the sun said noon and he carried the tools back to the fence corner, his cow was already tied there in a halter, which he removed and tied his plowline around her horns and this time he didn't lead her but, himself at a trot, drove her trotting before him by lashing her across the hocks with the end of the rope.

Because he was short for time, to get her back home and into the lot. Nor would he have time to eat his dinner, again today, with five miles still to do, even straight across country, to catch the mail carrier before he left Varner's store at two oclock for Jefferson, since Varner did not carry ten-gauge buckshot shells. But his wife and

daughters were at the table, which at least saved argument, the necessity to curse them silent or perhaps even to have actually to strike, hit
his wife, in order to go to the hearth and dig out the loose brick and
take from the snuff tin behind it the single five-dollar bill which
through all vicissitudes they kept there as the boat owner will sell or
pawn or lose all his gear but will still cling on to one life preserver
or ring buoy. Because he had five shells for the ancient ten-gauge
gun, ranging from bird shot to one Number Two for turkey or geese.
But he had had them for years, he did not remember how long;
besides, even if he were guaranteed that they would fire, Houston
deserved better than this.

So he folded the bill carefully into the fob pocket of his overalls
and caught the mail carrier and by four that afternoon Jefferson was
in sight across the last valley and by simple precaution, a simple
instinctive preparatory gesture, he thrust his fingers into the fob
pocket, then suddenly dug frantically, himself outwardly immobile,
into the now vacant pocket where he knew he had folded and stowed
carefully the bill, then sat immobile beside the mail carrier while the
buckboard began to descend the hill. *I got to do it* he thought *so I
might as well* and then said quietly aloud, "All right. I reckon I'll take
that-ere bill now."

"What?" the carrier said.

"That-ere five-dollar bill that was in my pocket when I got in this
buggy back yonder at Varner's."

"Why, you little son of a bitch," the carrier said. He pulled the
buckboard off to the side of the road and wrapped the lines around
the whip stock and got out and came around to Mink's side of the
vehicle. "Get out," he said.

Now I got to fight him Mink thought *and I aint got no knife and likely
he will beat me to ere a stick I try to grab. So I might jest as well get it over
with* and got out of the buckboard, the carrier giving him time to get
his puny and vain hands up. Then a shocking blow which Mink
didn't even feel very much, aware instead rather merely of the hard
ungiving proneness of the earth, ground against his back, lying there,
peaceful almost, watching the carrier get back into the buckboard
and drive on.

Then he got up. He thought *I not only could a saved a trip, I might still had them five dollars.* But for only a moment; he was already in the road, already walking steadily on toward town as if he knew what he was doing. Which he did, he had already remembered: two, three years ago it was when Solon Quick or Vernon Tull or whoever it was had seen the bear, the last bear in that part of the county, when it ran across Varner's mill dam and into the thicket, and how the hunt had been organised and somebody rode a horse in to Jefferson to get hold of Ike McCaslin and Walter Ewell, the best hunters in the county, and they came out with their buckshot big-game shells and the bear and deer hounds and set the standers and drove the bottom where the bear had been seen but it was gone by then. So he knew what to do, or at least where to try, until he crossed the Square and entered the hardware store where McCaslin was junior partner and saw McCaslin's eyes. Mink thought quietly *Hit wont do no good. He has done spent too much time in the woods with deer and bears and panthers that either are or they aint, right quick and now and not no shades between. He wont know how to believe a lie even if I could tell him one.* But he had to try.

"What do you want with two buckshot shells?" McCaslin said.

"A nigger came in this morning and said he seen that bear's foot in the mud at Blackwater Slough."

"No," McCaslin said. "What do you want with buckshot shells?"

"I can pay you soon as I gin my cotton," Mink said.

"No," McCaslin said. "I aint going to let you have them. There aint anything out there at Frenchman's Bend you need to shoot buckshot at."

It was not that he was hungry so much, even though he hadn't eaten since midnight: it was simply that he would have to pass the time some way until tomorrow morning when he would find out whether the mail carrier would take him back to Varner's store or not. He knew a small dingy back-street eating place owned by the sewing-machine agent, Ratliff, who was well known in Frenchman's Bend, where, if he had a half a dollar or even forty cents, he could have had two hamburgers and a nickel's worth of bananas and still had twenty-five cents left.

For that he could have had a bed in the Commercial Hotel (an unpainted two-storey frame building on a back street also; in two years his cousin Flem would own it though of course Mink didn't know that now. In fact, he had not even begun to think about his cousin yet, not once again after that moment when he entered Varner's store yesterday morning, where until his and his wife's departure for Texas last August, the first object he would have seen on entering it would have been Flem) but all he had to do was to pass time until eight oclock tomorrow morning and if it cost cash money just to pass time he would have been in the poorhouse years ago.

Now it was evening, the lights had come on around the Square, the lights from the drugstore falling outward across the pavement, staining the pavement with dim rose and green from the red- and green-liquid-filled jars in the windows; he could see the soda fountain and the young people, young men and girls in their city clothes eating and drinking the gaudy sweet concoctions, and he could watch them, the couples, young men and girls and old people and children, all moving in one direction. Then he heard music, a piano, loud. He followed also and saw in a vacant lot the big high plank stockade with its entrance beside the lighted ticket window: the Airdome they called it; he had seen it before from the outside by day while in town for Saturdays, and three times at night too, lighted as now. But never the inside because on the three previous times he had been in Jefferson after dark he had ridden a mule in from Frenchman's Bend with companions of his age and sex to take the early train to a Memphis brothel with in his pocket the few meager dollars he had wrenched as though by main strength from his bare livelihood, as he had likewise wrenched the two days he would be gone from earning the replacement of them, and in his blood a need far more urgent and passionate than a moving-picture show.

Though this time he could have spared the dime it would cost. Instead he stood a little aside while the line of patrons crept slowly past the ticket window until the last one passed inside. Then the glare and glow of light from beyond the fence blinked out and into a cold flickering; approaching the fence and laying his eye to a crack he could see through the long vertical interstice a section, a fragment—the dark row of motionless heads above which the whirring cone of light burst, shattered into the passionate and evanescent posturings where danced and flickered the ephemeral hopes and dreams, tantalising and inconsequent since he could see only his narrow vertical strip of it, until a voice spoke from the ticket window behind him: "Pay a dime and go inside. Then you can see."

"No much obliged," he said. He went on. The Square was empty now, until the show would let out and once more the young people, young men and girls, would drink and eat the confections which he had never tasted either, before strolling home. He had hoped maybe to see one of the automobiles; there were two in Jefferson already: the red racer belonging to the mayor, Mr de Spain, and the White Steamer that the president of the old bank, the Bank of Jefferson, owned (Colonel Sartoris, the other rich bank president, president of the new bank, not only wouldn't own an automobile, he even had a law passed three years ago that no motor-driven vehicle could operate on the streets of Jefferson after the homemade automobile a man named Buffaloe had made in his back yard frightened the colonel's matched team into running away). But he didn't see either one; the Square was still empty when he crossed it. Then the hotel, the Holston House, the drummers sitting in leather chairs along the sidewalk in the pleasant night; one of the livery-stable hacks was already there, the Negro porter loading the grips and sample cases in it for the south-bound train.

So he had better walk on, to be in time, even though the four lighted faces of the clock on top of the courthouse said only ten minutes past eight and he knew by his own experience that the New Orleans train from Memphis Junction didn't pass Jefferson until two minutes to nine. Though he knew too that freight trains might pass at almost any time, let alone the other passenger train, the one his experience knew too, going north at half past four. So just by spending the night, without even moving, he would see certainly two and maybe five or six trains before daylight.

He had left the Square, passing the dark homes where some of the old people who didn't go to the picture show either sat in dim rocking chairs in the cool dark of the yards, then a section all Negro homes, even with electric lights too, peaceful, with no worries, no need to fight and strive single-handed, not to gain right and justice because they were already lost, but just to defend the principle of them, his rights to them, but instead could talk a little while and then

go even into a nigger house and just lay down and sleep in place of
walking all the way to the depot just to have something to look at
until the durn mail carrier left at eight oclock tomorrow. Then the
depot: the red and green eyes of the signal lamps, the hotel bus and
the livery-stable hacks and Lucius Hogganbeck's automobile jitney,
the long electric-lighted shed already full of the men and boys come
down to see the train pass, that were there the three times he had
got off of it, looking at him also like he had come from a heap further
than a Memphis whorehouse.

Then the train itself: the four whistle blasts for the north crossing,
then the headlight, the roar, the clanging engine, the engineer and
the fireman crouched dim and high above the hissing steam, slowing,
the baggage and day coaches then the dining car and the cars in
which people slept while they rode. It stopped, a Negro even more
uppity than Houston's getting out with his footstool, then the conductor, and the rich men and women getting gaily aboard where the
other rich ones were already asleep, followed by the nigger with his
footstool and the conductor, the conductor leaning back to wave at
the engine, the engine speaking back to the conductor, to all of them,
with the first deep short ejaculations of starting.

Then the twin ruby lamps on the last car diminished rapidly
together in one last flick! at the curve, the four blasts came fading
back from the south crossing and he thought of distance, of New
Orleans where he had never been and perhaps never would go, with
distance even beyond New Orleans, with Texas somewhere in it; and
now for the first time he began really to think about his absent
cousin: the one Snopes of them all who had risen, broken free, had
either been born with or had learned, taught himself, the knack or
the luck to cope with, hold his own, handle the They and Them
which he, Mink, apparently did not have the knack or the luck to do.
Maybe I ought to waited till he got back he thought, turning at last back
to the now empty and vacant platform, noticing only then that he
had thought, not *should* wait for Flem, but should *have* waited, it
already being too late.

The waiting room was empty too, with its hard wooden benches
and the cold iron tobacco-spattered stove. He knew about signs in
depots against spitting but he never heard of one against a man with-

out a ticket sitting down. Anyhow, he would find out—a small man anyway, fleshless, sleepless and more or less foodless too for going on twenty-two hours now, looking in the empty barren room beneath the single unshaded bulb as forlorn and defenseless as a child, a boy, in faded patched overalls and shirt, sockless in heavy worn iron-hard brogan shoes and a sweat-and-grease-stained black felt hat. From beyond the ticket window he could hear the intermittent clatter of the telegraph, and two voices where the night operator talked to somebody now and then, until the voices ceased and the telegraph operator in his green eyeshade was looking at him through the window. "You want something?" he said.

"No much obliged," Mink said. "When does the next train pass?"

"Four twenty-two," the operator said. "You waiting for it?"

"That's right," he said.

"That's six hours off yet. You can go home and go to bed and then come back."

"I live out at Frenchman's Bend," he said.

"Oh," the operator said. Then the face was gone from the window and he sat again. It was quiet now and he even began to notice, hear the katydids in the dark trees beyond the tracks buzzing and chirring back and forth, interminable and peaceful, as if they might be the sound of the peaceful minutes and seconds themselves of the dark peaceful summer night clicking to one another. Then the whole room shook and trembled, filled with thunder; the freight train was already passing and even now he couldn't seem to get himself awake enough to get outside in time. He was still sitting on the hard bench, cramped and cold while the ruby lights on the caboose flicked across the windows then across the open door, sucking the thunder behind them; the four crossing blasts came back and died away. This time the operator was in the room with him and the overhead bulb had been switched off. "You were asleep," he said.

"That's right," Mink said. "I nigh missed that un."

"Why don't you lay down on the bench and be comfortable?"

"You aint got no rule against it?"

"No," the operator said. "I'll call you when they signal Number Eight."

"Much obliged," he said, and lay back. The operator went back into the room where the telegraph was already chattering again. *Yes* he thought peacefully *if Flem had been here he could a stopped all this on that first day before it ever got started. Working for Varner like he done, being in with Houston and Quick and all the rest of them. He could do it now if I could jest a waited. Only it wasn't me that couldn't wait. It was Houston his-self that wouldn't give me time.* Then immediately he knew that that was wrong too, that no matter how long he had waited They Themselves would have prevented Flem from getting back in time. He must drain this cup too: must face, accept this last ultimate useless and reasonless risk and jeopardy too just to show how much he could stand before They would let his cousin come back where he could save him. This same cup also contained Houston's life but he wasn't thinking about Houston. In a way, he had quit thinking about Houston at the same moment when Varner told him he would have to pay the pound fee. "All right," he said peacefully, aloud this time, "if that's what They want, I reckon I can stand that too."

At half-past seven he was standing in the small lot behind the post office where the R.F.D. carriers' buckboards would stand until the carriers came out the back door with the bags of mail. He had already discerned the one for Frenchman's Bend and he stood quietly, not too near: simply where the carrier could not help but see him, until the man who had knocked him down yesterday came out and saw, recognised, him, a quick glance, then came on and stowed the mail pouch into the buckboard, Mink not moving yet, just standing there, waiting, to be refused or not refused, until the carrier got in and released the wrapped lines from the whip stock and said, "All right. I reckon you got to get back to your crop. Come on," and Mink approached and got in.

It was just past eleven when he got down at Varner's store and said Much obliged and began the five-mile walk home. So he was home in time for dinner, eating steadily and quietly while his wife nagged and whined at him (evidently she hadn't noticed the disturbed brick) about where he was last night and why, until he finished, drank the last of his coffee and rose from the table and with vicious and obscene cursing drove the three of them, his wife and the two girls, with the three hoes out to the patch to chop out his early cotton, while he lay on the floor in the cool draft of the dogtrot hall, sleeping away the afternoon.

Then it was tomorrow morning. He took from its corner behind the door the tremendous ten-gauge double-barrelled shotgun which had belonged to his grandfather, the twin hammers standing above the receiver almost as tall as the ears of a rabbit. "Now what?" his wife said, cried. "Where you fixing to go with that?"

"After a rabbit," he said. "I'm burnt out on sowbelly," and with two of the heaviest loads out of his meager stock of Number-Two and -Five and -Eight-shot shells, he went not even by back roads and lanes but by hedgerows and patches of woods and ditches and whatever else would keep him private and unseen, back to the ambush he had prepared two days ago while waiting for Varner to return, where the road from Houston's to Varner's store crossed the creek bridge—the thicket beside the road, with a log to sit on and the broken-off switches not yet healed over where he had opened a sort of port to point the gun through, with the wooden planks of the bridge fifty yards up the road to serve as an alert beneath the stallion's hooves in case he dozed off.

Because sometimes a week would pass before Houston would ride in to the store. But sooner or later he would do so. And if all he, Mink, needed to beat Them with was just waiting, They could have given up three months ago and saved Themselves and everybody else trouble. So it was not the first day nor the second either that he would go home with no rabbit, to eat his supper in quiet and inflexible silence while his wife nagged and whined at him about why there was none, until he would push away his empty plate and in a cold level vicious monotone curse her silent.

And it might not have been the third day either. In fact, he couldn't remember how many days it had been, when at last he heard the sudden thunder of the hooves on the bridge and then saw them: the stallion boring, frothing a little, wrenching its arrogant vicious head at the snaffle and curb both with which Houston rode it, the big lean hound bounding along beside it. He cocked the two hammers and pushed the gun through the porthole, and even as he laid the sight on Houston's chest, leading him just a little, his finger already

taking up the slack in the front trigger, he thought *And even now.*
They still aint satisfied yet as the first shell clicked dully without
exploding, his finger already moving back to the rear trigger, thinking *And even yet* as this one crashed and roared, thinking how if there
had only been time, space, between the roar of the gun and the
impact of the shot, for him to say to Houston and for Houston to
have to hear it: "I aint shooting you because of them thirty-seven and
a half four-bit days. That's all right; I done long ago forgot and forgive that. Likely Will Varner couldn't do nothing else, being a rich
man too and all you rich folks has got to stick together or else maybe
some day the ones that aint rich might take a notion to raise up and
take hit away from you. That aint why I shot you. I killed you
because of that-ere extry one-dollar pound fee."

TWO

*S*o the jury said "Guilty" and the Judge said "Life" but he wasn't even listening. Because something had happened to him. Even while the sheriff was bringing him in to town that first day, even though he knew that his cousin was still in Texas, he believed that at every mile post Flem or a messenger from him would overtake them or step into the road and stop them, with the money or the word or whatever it would be that would make the whole thing dissolve, vanish like a dream.

And during all the long weeks while he waited in jail for his trial, he would stand at the little window of his cell, his grimed hands gripped among the bars and his face craned and pressed against them, to watch a slice of the street before the jail and the slice of the Square which his cousin would have to cross to come to the jail and abolish the dream, free him, get him out. "Which is all I want," he would tell himself. "Jest to get out of here and go back home and farm. That dont seem like a heap to ask."

And at night too still standing there, his face invisible but his wan hands looking almost white, almost clean in the grimed interstices against the cell's darkness, watching the free people, men and women and young people who had nothing but peaceful errands or pleasures as they strolled in the evening cool toward the Square, to watch the picture show or eat ice cream in the drugstore or maybe just stroll peaceful and free because they were free, he beginning at last to call down to them, timidly at first, then louder and louder, more and more urgent as they would pause, almost as though startled, to look up at his window and then seem almost to hurry on, like they were trying to get beyond where he could see them; finally he began to offer, promise them money: "Hey! Mister! Missus! Somebody! Anybody that will send word out to Varner's store to Flem Snopes! He will pay you! Ten dollars! Twenty dollars!"

And even when the day finally came and they brought him hand-

cuffed into the room where he would face his jeopardy, he had not
even looked once toward the Bench, the dais which could well be
his Golgotha too, for looking, staring out over the pale identical
anonymous faces of the crowd for that of his cousin or at least the
messenger from him; right up to the moment when the Judge himself had to lean down from his high desk and say, "You, Snopes!
Look at me. Did you or didn't you kill Jack Houston?" and he
answered:
    "Dont bother me now. Cant you see I'm busy?"
    And the next day too, while the lawyers shouted and wrangled and
nagged, he hearing none of it even if he could have understood it, for
watching the door at the rear where his cousin or the messenger
would have to enter; and on the way back to the cell, still handcuffed,
his unflagging glance which at first had been merely fretted and
impatient but which now was beginning to be concerned, a little puzzled and quite sober, travelling rapid and quick and searching from
face to face as he passed them or they passed him, to stand again at
his cell window, his unwashed hands gripping the grimed bars and
his face wrenched and pressed against them to see as much as possible of the street and the Square below where his kinsman or the messenger would have to pass.
    So when on the third day, handcuffed again to the jailor, he
realised that he had crossed the Square without once looking at one
of the faces which gaped at him, and had entered the courtroom and
taken his accustomed place in the dock still without once looking out
over the massed faces toward that rear door, he still did not dare
admit to himself that he knew why. He just sat there, looking as small
and frail and harmless as a dirty child while the lawyers ranted and
wrangled, until the end of the day when the jury said Guilty and the
Judge said Life and he was returned, handcuffed, to his cell, and the
door clanged to and he sitting now, quiet and still and composed on
the mattress-less steel cot, this time only looking at the small barred
window where for months now he had stood sixteen or eighteen
hours a day in quenchless expectation and hope.
    Only then did he say it, think it, let it take shape in his mind: *He
aint coming. Likely he's been in Frenchman's Bend all the time. Likely he*

*heard about that cow clean out there in Texas and jest waited till the word
come back they had me safe in jail, and then come back to make sho they
would do ever thing to me they could now that they had me helpless. He
might even been hid in the back of that room all the time, to make sho
wouldn't nothing slip up before he finally got rid of me for good and all.*

So now he had peace. He had thought he had peace as soon as he
realised what he would have to do about Houston, and that Houston himself wasn't going to let him wait until Flem got back. But he
had been wrong. That wasn't peace then; it was too full of too many
uncertainties: such as if anybody would send word to Flem about his
trouble at all, let alone in time. Or even if the word was sent in time,
would the message find Flem in time. And even if Flem got the message in time, there might be a flood or a wreck on the railroad so he
couldn't get back in time.

But all that was finished now. He didn't have to bother and worry
at all now since all he had to do was wait, and he had already proved
to himself that he could do that. Just to wait: that's all he needed; he
didn't even need to ask the jailor to send a message since the lawyer
himself had said he would come back to see him after supper.

So he ate his supper when they brought it—the same sidemeat and
molasses and undercooked biscuits he would have had at home; this
in fact a little better since the meat had more lean in it than he could
afford to eat. Except that his at home had been free, eaten in freedom. But then he could stand that too if that was all *they* demanded
of him now. Then he heard the feet on the stairs, the door clashed,
letting the lawyer in, and clashed again on both of them—the lawyer
young and eager, just out of law school they told him, whom the
Judge had appointed for him—commanded rather, since even he,
Mink, busy as he was at the time, could tell that the man didn't really
want any part of him and his trouble—he never did know why then
because then he still thought that all the Judge or anybody else
needed to do to settle the whole business was just to send out to
Frenchman's Bend and get hold of his cousin.

Too young and eager in fact, which was why he—the lawyer—had
made such a hash of the thing. But that didn't matter now either; the
thing now was to get on to what came next. So he didn't waste any
time. "All right," he said. "How long will I have to stay there?"

"It's Parchman—the penitentiary," the lawyer said. "Cant you understand that?"

"All right," he said again. "How long will I have to stay?"

"He gave you life," the lawyer said. "Didn't you even hear him? For the rest of your life. Until you die."

"All right," he said for the third time, with that peaceful, that almost compassionate patience: "How long will I have to stay?"

By that time even this lawyer understood. "Oh. That depends on you and your friends—if you have any. It may be all your life, like Judge Brummage said. But in twenty or twenty-five years you will be eligible under the Law to apply for pardon or parole—if you have responsible friends to support your petition, and your record down there at Parchman dont hold anything against you."

"Suppose a man aint got friends," he said.

"Folks that hide in bushes and shoot other folks off their horses without saying Look out first or even whistling, don't have," the lawyer said. "So you wont have anybody left except you to get you out."

"All right," he said, with that unshakable, that infinite patience, "that's what I'm trying to get you to stop talking long enough to tell me. What do I have to do to get out in twenty or twenty-five years?"

"Not to try to escape yourself or engage in any plot to help anybody else escape. Not to get in a fight with another prisoner or a guard. To be on time for whatever they tell you to do, and do it without shirking or complaining or talking back, until they tell you to quit. In other words, to start right now doing all the things that, if you had just been doing them all the time since that day last fall when you decided to let Mr Houston winter your cow for nothing, you wouldn't be sitting in this cell here trying to ask somebody how to get out of it. But mainly, dont try to escape."

"Escape?" he said.

"Break out. Try to get away."

"Try?" he said.

"Because you cant," the lawyer said with a kind of seething yet patient rage. "Because you cant escape. You cant make it. You never can. You cant plan it without some of the others catching on to it and they always try to escape with you and so you all get caught. And even if they dont go with you, they tell the Warden on you and you are caught just the same. And even if you manage to keep everybody else from knowing about it and go alone, one of the guards shoots you before you can climb the fence. So even if you are not in the dead house or the hospital, you are back in the penitentiary with twenty-five more years added onto your sentence. Do you understand now?"

"That's all I got to do to get out in twenty or twenty-five years. Not try to escape. Not get in no fights with nobody. Do whatever they tell me to do, as long as they say to do it. But mainly not try to escape. That's all I got to do to get out in twenty or twenty-five years."

"That's right," the lawyer said.

"All right," he said. "Now go back and ask that judge if that's right, and if he says it is, to send me a wrote-out paper saying so."

"So you dont trust me," the lawyer said.

"I dont trust nobody," he said. "I aint got time to waste twenty or twenty-five years to find out whether you know what you're talking about or not. I got something I got to attend to when I get back out. I want to know. I want a wrote-out paper from that judge."

"Maybe you never did trust me then," the lawyer said. "Maybe you think I made a complete bust of your whole case. Maybe you think that if it hadn't been for me, you wouldn't even be here now. Is that it?"

And he, Mink, still with that inflexible and patient calm: "You done the best you knowed. You jest wasn't the man for the job. You're young and eager, but that wasn't what I needed. I needed a trader, a smart trader, that knowed how to swap. You wasn't him. Now you go get that paper from that judge."

Now he, the lawyer, even tried to laugh. "Not me," he said. "The Court discharged me from this case right after he sentenced you this afternoon. I just stopped in to say good-bye and to see if there was anything else I could do for you. But evidently folks that dont have friends dont need well-wishers either."

"But I aint discharged you yet," Mink said, rising now, without haste, the lawyer already on his feet, springing, leaping back against the locked door, looking at the small figure moving toward him as slight and frail and harmless-looking as a child and as deadly as a small viper—a half-grown asp or cobra or krait. Then the lawyer was shouting, bellowing, even while the turnkey's feet galloped on the stairs and the door clashed open and the turnkey stood in it with a drawn pistol.

"What is it?" the turnkey said. "What did he try to do?"

"Nothing," the lawyer said. "It's all right. I'm through here. Let me out." Only he was not through; he only wished he were. He didn't even wait until morning. Instead, not fifteen minutes later he was in the hotel room of the Circuit Judge who had presided on the case and pronounced the sentence, he, the lawyer, still breathing hard, still incredulous at his recent jeopardy and still amazed at his escape from it.

"He's crazy, I tell you!" he said. "He's dangerous! Just to send him to Parchman, where he will be eligible for parole and freedom in only twenty or twenty-five years, let alone if some of his kin—God knows he has enough—or someone with an axe to grind or maybe just some bleeding-heart meddler with access to the Governor's ear, doesn't have him out before that time even! He must go to Jackson, the asylum, for life, where he'll be safe. No: we'll be safe."

And ten minutes after that the District Attorney who had prosecuted the case was in the room too, saying (to the lawyer): "So now you want a suspended sentence, and a motion for a new trial. Why didn't you think of this before?"

"You saw him too," the lawyer said, cried. "You were in that courtroom with him all day long for three days too!"

"That's right," the District Attorney said. "That's why I'm asking you why now."

"Then you haven't seen him since!" the lawyer said. "Come up to that cell and look at him now, like I did thirty minutes ago!"

But the Judge was an old man, he wouldn't go then so it was the next morning when the turnkey unlocked the cell and let the three of them in where the frail-looking fleshless small figure in the patched and faded overalls and shirt and the sockless iron-stiff brogans got up from the cot. They had shaved him this morning and his hair was combed too, parted and flattened down with water across his skull.

"Come in, gentle-men," he said. "I aint got no chair but likely you aint fixing to stay long enough to set nohow. Well, Judge, you not only brought me my wrote-out paper, you brought along two witnesses to watch you hand it to me."

"Wait," the lawyer said rapidly to the Judge. "Let me." He said to Mink: "You wont need that paper. They—the Judge—is going to give you another trial."

Now Mink stopped. He looked at the lawyer. "What for?" he said. "I done already had one that I never got much suption out of."

"Because that one was wrong," the lawyer said. "That's what we've come to tell you about."

"If that un was wrong, what's the use of wasting time and money having another one? Jest tell that feller there to bring me my hat and open that door and I'll go back home and get back to my crop, providing I still got one."

"No, wait," the lawyer said. "That other trial was wrong because it sent you to Parchman. You wont have to go to Parchman now, where you'll have to work out in the hot sun all day long in a crop that isn't even yours." And now, with the pale faded gray eyes watching him as if not only were they incapable of blinking but never since birth had they ever needed to, the lawyer found himself babbling, not even able to stop it: "Not Parchman: Jackson, where you'll have a nice room to yourself—nothing to do all day long but just rest—doctors—" and stopped then; not he that stopped his babbling but the fixed unwinking pale eyes that did it.

"Doctors," Mink said. "Jackson." He stared at the lawyer. "That's where they send crazy folks."

"Hadn't you rather—" the District Attorney began. That was as far as he got too. He had been an athlete in college and still kept himself fit. Though even then he managed to grasp the small frantic creature only after it had hurled itself on the lawyer and both of them had gone to the floor. And even then it took him and the turnkey both to drag Mink up and away and hold him, frantic and frothing and hard to hold as a cat, panting,

"Crazy, am I? Crazy, am I? Aint no son a bitch going to call me crazy, I dont care how big he is or how many of them."

"You damn right, you little bastard," the District Attorney panted.

"You're going to Parchman. That's where they've got the kind of doctors you need."

So he went to Parchman, handcuffed to a deputy sheriff, the two of them transferring from smoking car to smoking car of local trains, this one having left the hills which he had known all his life, for the Delta which he had never seen before—the vast flat alluvial swamp of cypress and gum and brake and thicket lurked with bear and deer and panthers and snakes, out of which man was still hewing savagely and violently the rich ragged fields in which cotton stalks grew ranker and taller than a man on a horse, he, Mink, sitting with his face glued to the window like a child.

"This here's all swamp," he said. "It dont look healthy."

"It aint healthy," the deputy said. "It aint intended to be. This is the penitentiary. I cant imagine no more unhealth a man can have than to be locked up inside a bobwire pen for twenty or twenty-five years. Besides, a good unhealthy place ought to just suit you; you wont have to stay so long."

So that's how he saw Parchman, the penitentiary, his destination, doom, his life the Judge had said; for the rest of his life as long as he lived. But the lawyer had told him different, even if he couldn't really trust him: only twenty-five, maybe only twenty years, and even a lawyer a man couldn't trust could at least be trusted to know his own business that he had even went to special law school to be trained to know it, where all a judge had to do to get to be a judge was just to win a election vote-race for it. And even if the Judge hadn't signed a paper saying only twenty or twenty-five years, that didn't matter either since the Judge was on the other side and would naturally lie to a man coming up against him, where a lawyer, a man's own lawyer, wouldn't. More: his own lawyer couldn't lie to him, because there was some kind of rule somebody had told him about that if the client didn't lie to his lawyer, the Law itself wouldn't let the lawyer lie to his own client.

And even if none of that was so, that didn't matter either because he couldn't stay in Parchman all his life, he didn't have time, he would have to get out before then. And looking at the tall wire stockade with its single gate guarded day and night by men with shotguns, and inside it the low grim brick buildings with their barred windows, he thought, tried to remember, with a kind of amazement of the time when his only reason for wanting to get out was to go back home and farm, remembering it only for a moment and then no more, because now he had to get out.

He had to get out. His familiar patched faded blue overalls and shirt were exchanged now for the overalls and jumper of coarse white barred laterally with black which, according to the Judge, would have been his fate and doom until he died, if the lawyer hadn't known better. He worked now—gangs of them—in the rich black cotton land while men on horses with shotguns across the pommels watched them, doing the only work he knew how to do, had done all his life, in a crop which would never be his for the rest of his life if the Judge had his way, thinking *And that's all right too. Hit's even better. If a feller jest wants to do something, he might make it and he might not. But if he's GOT to do something, cant nothing stop him.*

And in the wooden bunk at night too, sheetless, with a cheap coarse blanket and his rolled-up clothing for a pillow, thinking, dinning it into himself since he was now having to change overnight and forever for twenty or twenty-five years his whole nature and character and being: *To do whatever they tell me to do. Not to talk back to nobody. Not to get into no fights. That's all I got to do for jest twenty-five or maybe even jest twenty years. But mainly not to try to escape.*

Nor did he even count off the years as they accomplished. Instead, he simply trod them behind him into oblivion beneath the heavy brogan shoes in the cotton middles behind the mule which drew the plow and then the sweep, then with the chopping and thinning hoe and at last with the long dragging sack into which he picked, gathered the cotton. He didn't need to count them; he was in the hands of the Law now and as long as he obeyed the four rules set down by the Law for his side, the Law would have to obey its single rule of twenty-five years or maybe even just twenty.

He didn't know how many years it had been when the letter came, whether it was two or three as he stood in the Warden's office, turning the stamped pencil-addressed envelope in his hand while the Warden watched him. "You cant read?" the Warden said.

"I can read reading, but I cant read writing good."

"You want me to open it?" the Warden said.

"All right," he said. So the Warden did.

"It's from your wife. She wants to know when you want her to come to see you, and if you want her to bring the girls."

Now he held the letter himself, the page of foolscap out of a school writing pad, pencilled over, spidery and hieroglyph, not one jot less forever beyond him than Arabic or Sanscrit. "Yettie cant even read reading, let alone write writing," he said. "Miz Tull must a wrote it for her."

"Well?" the Warden said. "What do you want me to tell her?"

"Tell her it aint no use in her coming all the way here because I'll be home soon."

"Oh," the Warden said. "You're going to get out soon, are you?" He looked at the small frail creature not much larger than a fifteen-year-old boy, who had been one of his charges for three years now without establishing an individual entity in the prison's warp. Not a puzzle, not an enigma: he was not anything at all; no record of run-in or reprimand with or from any guard or trusty or official, never any trouble with any other inmate. A murderer, in for life, who in the Warden's experience fell always into one of two categories: either an irreconcilable, with nothing more to lose, a constant problem and trouble to the guards and the other prisoners; or a sycophant, sucking up to whatever of his overlords could make things easiest for him. But not this one: who assumed his assigned task each morning and worked steady and unflagging in the cotton as if it was his own crop he was bringing to fruit. More: he worked harder for this crop from which he would not derive one cent of profit than, in the Warden's experience, men of his stamp and kind worked in their own. "How?" the Warden said.

Mink told him; it was automatic now after three years; he had only to open his mouth and breathe: "By doing what they tell me to. Not talking back and not fighting. Not to try to escape. Mainly that: not to try to escape."

"So in either seventeen or twenty-two years you'll go home," the Warden said. "You've already been here three."

"Have I?" he said. "I aint kept count.—No," he said. "Not right away. There's something I got to attend to first."

"What?" the Warden said.

"Something private. When I finish that, then I'll come on home. Write her that." *Yes sir* he thought. *It looks like I done had to come all the way to Parchman jest to turn right around and go back home and kill Flem.*

THREE

$\mathcal{V}.\ K\ \mathcal{R}ATLIFF$

$\mathcal{L}$ikely what bollixed Montgomery Ward at first, and for the next two or three days too, was exactly why Flem wanted him specifically in Parchman. Why wouldn't no other equally secure retired place do, such as Atlanta or Leavenworth or maybe even Alcatraz two thousand miles away out in California, where old Judge Long would a already had him on the first train leaving Jefferson while he was still looking at the top one of them French postcards; jest exactly why wouldn't no other place do Flem to have Montgomery Ward sent to but Parchman, Missippi.

Because even in the initial excitement, Montgomery Ward never had one moment's confusion about what was actively happening to him. The second moment after Lawyer and Hub walked in the door, he knowed that at last something was happening that he had been expecting ever since whenever that other moment was when Flem found out or suspected that whatever was going on up that alley had a money profit in it. The only thing that puzzled him was, why Flem was going to all that extra trouble and complication jest to usurp him outen that nekkid-picture business. That was like the story about the coon in the tree that asked the name of the feller aiming the gun at him and when the feller told him, the coon says, "Hell fire, is that who you are? Then you dont need to waste all this time and powder jest on me. Stand to one side and I'll climb down."

Not to mention reckless. Having Flem Snopes take his business away from him was all right. He had been expecting that: that sooner or later his turn would come too, running as he did the same risk with ever body else in Yoknapatawpha County owning a business solvent enough for Flem to decide he wanted it too. But to let the county attorney and the county sheriff get a-holt of them pictures, the two folks of all the folks in Yoknapatawpha County that not even Grover Winbush would a been innocent enough to dream would ever turn them loose again—Lawyer Stevens, so dedicated to civic improvement and the moral advancement of folks that his purest notion of duty was browbeating twelve-year-old boys into running five-mile foot races when all they really wanted to do was jest to stay at home and set fire to the barn; and Hub Hampton, a meat-eating Hard-Shell-Baptist deacon whose purest notion of pleasure was counting off the folks he personally knowed was already bound for hell.

Why, in fact, Montgomery Ward had to go anywhere, if all his uncle or cousin wanted was jest to take his business away from him, except maybe jest to stay outen sight for a week or maybe a month or two to give folks time to forget about them nekkid pictures, or anyway that anybody named Snopes was connected with them, Flem being a banker now and having to deal not jest in simple usury but in respectability too.

No, what really should a puzzled Montgomery Ward, filled him in fact with delighted surprise, was how he had managed to last even this long. It never needed the Law nor Flem Snopes neither to close out that studio, pull the blinds down (or rather up) for good and all on the French-postcard industry in Jefferson, Mississippi. Grover Winbush done that when he let whoever it was ketch him slipping outen that alley at two oclock that morning. No: Grover Winbush had done already wrecked and ruined that business in Jefferson at the same moment when he found out there was a side door in a Jefferson alley with what you might call a dry whorehouse behind it. No, that business was wrecked in Jefferson the same moment Grover Cleveland got appointed night marshal, Grover having jest exactly enough sense to be a night policeman providing the town wasn't no bigger and never stayed awake no later than Jefferson, Mississippi, since that would be the one job in all paid laborious endeavor—leaning all night against a lamppost looking at the empty Square—you would a thought he could a held indefinitely, providing the influence of whoever got it for him or give it to him lasted that long, without stumbling over anything he could do any harm with, to his-self or the job or a innocent bystander or maybe all three; and so naturally he would be caught by somebody, almost anybody, the second or third time he come slipping outen that alley. Which was jest a simple unavoidable occupational hazard of running a business like that in the same town where Grover Winbush was night marshal, which Montgomery Ward knowed as well as anybody else that knowed Grover. So when the business had been running over a year without no untoward interruption, Montgomery Ward figgered that whoever had been catching Grover slipping in and out of that alley after midnight once a month for the last nine or ten of them, was maybe business acquaintances Grover had made raiding crap games or catching them with a pint of moonshine whiskey in their hind pockets. Or who knows? Maybe even Flem hisself had got a-holt of each one of them in time, protecting not so much his own future interests and proposed investments, because maybe at that time he hadn't even found out he wanted to go into the a-teelyer (that's what Montgomery Ward called it; he had the name painted on the window: Atelier Monty) business, but simply protecting and defending solvency and moderate profit itself, not jest out of family loyalty to another Snopes but from pure and simple principle, even if he was a banker now and naturally would have to compromise, to a extent at least, profit with respectability, since any kind of solvency redounds to the civic interest providing it dont get caught, and even respectability can go hand in hand with civic interest providing the civic interest has got sense enough to take place after dark and not make no loud noise at it.

So when the county attorney and the county sheriff walked in on him that morning, Montgomery Ward naturally believed that pure and simple destiny was simply taking its natural course, and the only puzzling thing was the downright foolhardy, let alone reckless way Flem Snopes was hoping to take advantage of destiny. I mean, getting Lawyer Stevens and Sheriff Hampton into it, letting them get one whiff or flash of them nekkid pictures. Because of what you might call the late night shift his business had developed into, the Square never seen Montgomery Ward before noon. So until Lawyer and Hub told him about it, he hadn't had time yet to hear about them two fellers robbing Uncle Willy Christian's drug cabinet last night, that none of the folks watching the robbers through the front window could find hide nor hair of Grover Winbush to tell him about it until Grover finally come slipping back outen Montgomery Ward's alley, by which time even the robbers, let alone the folks watching them, had done all went home.

I dont mean Montgomery Ward was puzzled that Lawyer and Hub was the first ones there. Naturally they would a been when his a-teelyer business finally blowed up, no matter what was the reason for the explosion. He would a expected them first even if Yokna-patawpha County hadn't never heard the word Flem Snopes—a meal-mouthed sanctimonious Harvard- and Europe-educated lawyer that never even needed the excuse of his office and salaried job to meddle in anything providing it wasn't none of his business and wasn't doing him no harm; and old pussel-gutted Hampton that could be fetched along to look at anything, even a murder, once somebody remembered he was Sheriff and told him about it and where it was. No. What baffled Montgomery Ward was, what in creation kind of a aberration could Flem Snopes been stricken with to leave him believing he could use Lawyer Stevens and Hub Hampton to get them pictures, and ever dream of getting them away from them.

So for a moment his faith and confidence in Flem Snopes his-self wavered and flickered you might say. For that one horrid moment he believed that Flem Snopes could be the victim of pure circumstance compounded by Grover Winbush, jest like anybody else. But only a moment. If that durn boy that seen them two robbers in Uncle Willy's drug cabinet had to pick out to go to the late picture show that same one night in that whole week that Grover picked out to take jest one more slip up that alley to Montgomery Ward's back room; if Flem Snopes was subject to the same outrageous misfortune and coincidence that the rest of us was, then we all might jest as well pack up and quit.

So even after Lawyer and Hub told him about them two robbers in Uncle Willy's store, and that boy that his paw ought to burned his britches off for not being home in bed two hours ago, Montgomery Ward still never had one second's doubt that it had been Flem all the time—Flem his-self, with his pure and simple nose for money like a preacher's for sin and fried chicken, finding out fast and quick that profit of some degree was taking place at night behind that alley door, and enough of it to keep folks from as far away as three county seats sneaking up and down that alley at two and three oclock in the morning.

So all Flem needed now was to find out exactly what was going on up that alley that was that discreet and that profitable, setting his spies—not that Grover Winbush would a needed anybody calling his-self a respectable spy with pride in his profession to ketch him, since any little child hired with a ice-cream cone would a done for that—to watch who come and went around that corner; until sooner or later, and likely sooner than later, one turned up that Flem could handle. Likely a good deal sooner than later; even spread over four counties like that business was, there wasn't many among the set Montgomery Ward drawed his clientele from that hadn't at least offered to put his name onto a piece of paper to Flem at forty or fifty percent of three or four dollars, so that Flem could say to him: "About that-ere little note of yourn. I'd like to hold the bank offen you myself, but I aint only vice-president of it, and I cant do nothing with Manfred de Spain."

Or maybe it was Grover his-self that Flem caught, catching Grover his-self in the active flesh on that second or third time which was the absolute outside for Grover to slip outen that alley without somebody ketching him, long in fact before them two fellers robbing Uncle Willy Christian's store exposed him by rifling that prescription desk in plain sight of half Jefferson evidently going home from the late picture show except that couldn't nobody locate Grover to tell him about it. Anyway, Flem caught somebody he could squeeze enough to find out jest what Montgomery Ward was selling behind that door. So now all Flem had to do was move in on that industry too, move Montgomery Ward outen it or move it out from under Montgomery Ward the same way he had been grazing on up through Jefferson ever since he eased me and Grover Winbush outen that café we thought we owned back there when I never had no more sense neither than to believe I could tangle with Flem.

Only, a banker now, a vice-president, not to mention being the third man, after the Negro that fired the furnace and the preacher his-self, inside the Baptist Church ever Sunday morning, and the rest of his career in Jefferson doomed to respectability like a feller in his Sunday suit trying to run through a field of cuckleburs and beggarlice, naturally Flem not only couldn't show in it, it couldn't even have no connection with the word Snopes. So as far as Jefferson was concerned the Atelier Monty would be closed out, cleaned up and struck off the commercial register forevermore and the business moved into another alley that hadn't never heard of it before and under a management that, if possible, couldn't even spell Snopes. Or likely, if Flem had any sense, clean to another town in Montgomery Ward's old district, where it would be clean outen Grover Cleveland's reach until at least next summer when he taken his next two weeks' vacation.

So all Montgomery Ward had to do, all he could do in fact, was jest to wait until Flem decided the moment was ripe to usurp him outen his a-teelyer or usurp that a-teelyer out from under him, whichever Flem seen fittest. Likely Montgomery Ward had at least one moment or two of regretful musing that his business wasn't the kind where he could a held some kind of a quick fire sale before Flem would have time to hear about it. But his stock in trade being such a nebulous quantity that it never had no existence except during the moment when the customer was actively buying and consuming it, the only thing he could a sold would be his capital investment itself, which would not only be contrary to all the economic laws, he wouldn't even have no nebulous stock in trade to sell to nobody during whatever time he would have left before Flem foreclosed him, which might be weeks or even months yet. So all he could do was to apply whatever methods and means of speed-up and increased turnover was available while waiting for Flem to move, naturally speculating on jest what method Flem would finally use—whether Flem had done found some kind of handle or crowbar in his, Montgomery Ward's, own past to prize him out, or maybe would do something as crude and unimaginative as jest offering him money for it.

So he expected Flem. But he never expected Hub Hampton and Lawyer Stevens. So for what you might call a flashing moment or two after Hub and Lawyer busted in that morning, Montgomery Ward figgered it was this here new respectability Flem had done got involved with: a respectability that delicate and tetchous that wouldn't nothing else suit it but it must look like the Law itself had purified the Snopes a-teelyer industry outen Jefferson, and so Flem was jest using Lawyer Stevens and Hub Hampton for a cat's-paw. Of course another moment of thoughtful deliberation would a suhjested to him that once a feller dedicated to civic improvement and the moral advancement of youth like Lawyer Stevens, and a meat-eating Hard-Shell Baptist deacon like Hub Hampton got a-holt of them nekkid photographs, there wouldn't be nothing left of that business for Flem to move nowhere except the good will. Though them little hard pale-colored eyes looking down at him across the top of Hub Hampton's belly wasn't hardly the time for meditation and deliberation of any kind, thoughtful or not. In fact, Montgomery Ward was so far from being deliberate or even thinking a-tall for that matter, that it aint surprising if in that same flashing moment he likely cast on his cousin Flem the horrid aspersion that Flem had let Lawyer Stevens and Hub Hampton outfigger him; that Flem had merely aimed to close him, Montgomery Ward, out, and was innocent enough to believe he could get them nekkid pictures back outen Hub Hampton's hands once Hub had seen them, and that that cat's-paw's real name was Flem Snopes.

Though even in his extremity Montgomery Ward had more simple sense and judgment, let alone family pride and loyalty, than to actively believe that ten thousand Lawyer Stevenses and Hub Hamptons, let alone jest one each of them, could a diddled Flem Snopes. In fact, sooner than that foul aspersion, he would believe that Flem Snopes was subject to bad luck too, jest like a human being—not the bad luck of misreading Grover Winbush's character that Grover could slip up and down that alley two or three times a week for seven or eight months without ever body in Yoknapatawpha County ketching him at least once, but the bad luck of being unable to anticipate that them two robbers would pick out the same night to rob Uncle Willy Christian's drugstore that that Rouncewell boy would to climb down the drain pipe and go to the late picture show.

So all Montgomery Ward had to do now was set in his jail cell where Hub taken him and wait with what you might call almost professional detachment and interest to see how Flem was going to get them pictures back from Hub. It would take time of course; even with all his veneration and family pride for Flem Snopes, he knowed that even for Flem it wouldn't be as simple as picking up a hat or a umbrella. So when the rest of that day passed and hadn't nothing more happened, it was exactly as he had anticipated. Naturally he had toyed with the notion that, took by surprise too, Flem might call on him, Montgomery Ward, to pick up whatever loose useful ends of information he might have without even knowing he had none. But when Flem never showed up nor sent word, if anything his admiration and vindication for Flem jest increased that much more since here was active proof that Flem wasn't going to need even what little more, even if it wasn't no more than encouragement and moral support, that Montgomery Ward could a told him.

And he anticipated right on through that night and what you might call them mutual Yoknapatawpha County bedbugs, on into the next morning too. So you can imagine his interested surprise—not alarm yet nor even astonishment: jest interest and surprise—when whatever thoughtful acquaintance (it was Euphus Tubbs, the jailor; he was a interested party too, not to mention having spent most of his life being surprised) come in that afternoon and told him how Hub Hampton had went back to the studio that morning jest in case him and Lawyer had overlooked any further evidence yesterday, and instead captured five gallons of moonshine whiskey setting in the bottles on the shelf that Montgomery Ward his-self assumed never held nothing but photograph developer. "Now you can go to Parchman instead of Atlanta," Euphus says. "Which wont be so fur away. Not to mention being in Missippi, where a native Missippi jailor can get the money for your keep instead of these durn judges sending our Missippi boys clean out of the country where folks we never even heard of before can collect on them."

Not alarm, not astonishment: jest interest and surprise and even that mostly jest interest. Because Montgomery Ward knowed that them bottles never had nothing but developer in them when him and Hub and Lawyer left the a-teelyer yesterday morning, and he knowed that Hub Hampton and Lawyer Stevens both knowed that was all there was in them, because for a feller in the nekkid-photograph business in Jefferson, Missippi, to complicate it up with peddling whiskey, would be jest pleading for trouble, like the owner of a roulette wheel or a crap table dreaming of running a counterfeiting press in the same basement.

Because he never had one moment's doubt it was Flem that planted that whiskey where Hub Hampton would have to find it; and this time his admiration and veneration notched right up to the absolute top because he knowed that Flem, being a banker now and having to be as tender about respectability as a unescorted young gal waking up suddenly in the middle of a drummers' convention, not only couldn't a afforded to deal with no local bootlegger and so probably had to go his-self back out to Frenchman's Bend or maybe even all the way up into Beat Nine to Nub Gowrie to get it, he even had to pay twenty-five or thirty dollars of his own cash money to boot. And indeed for a unguarded fraction of the next moment the thought might a occurred to him how them twenty-five or thirty dollars revealed that Flem too in the last analysis wasn't immune neither to the strong and simple call of blood kinship. Though that was jest a fraction of a moment, if as much as that even, because even though Flem too at times might be victim of weakness and aberration, wouldn't none of them ever been paying even twenty dollars for a Snopes.

No, them twenty-five or thirty dollars simply meant that it was going to be a little harder than Flem had expected or figgered. But the fact that he hadn't hesitated even twenty-four hours to pay it, showed that Flem anyhow never had no doubts about the outcome. So naturally Montgomery Ward never had none neither, not even needing to anticipate no more but jest to wait, because by that time about half of Jefferson was doing the anticipating for him and half the waiting too, not to mention the watching. Until the next day we watched Flem cross the Square and go up the street to the jail and go into it and a half a hour later come out again. And the next day after that Montgomery Ward was out too with Flem for his bond. And the next day after that one Clarence Snopes was in town—Senator Clarence Egglestone Snopes of the state legislature now, that used to be Constable Snopes of Frenchman's Bend until he made the mistake of pistol-whipping in the name of the Law some feller that was spiteful and vindictive enough to object to being pistol-whipped jest because the one doing the whipping was bigger than him and wore a badge. So Uncle Billy Varner had to do something with Clarence so he got a-holt of Flem and both of them got a-holt of

Manfred de Spain at the bank and all three of them got a-holt of
enough other folks to get Clarence into the legislature in Jackson,
where he wouldn't even know nothing to do until somebody Uncle
Billy and Manfred could trust would tell him when to mark his name
or hold up his hand.

Except that, as Lawyer Stevens said, he seemed to found his true
vocation before that: finally coming in to town from Frenchman's
Bend one day and finding out that the country extended even on
past Jefferson, on to the northwest in fact until it taken in Mulberry
and Gayoso and Pontotoc streets in Memphis, Tennessee, so that
when he got back three days later the very way his hair still stood
up and his eyes still bugged out seemed to be saying, "Hell fire, hell
fire, why wasn't I told about this sooner? How long has this been
going on?" But he was making up fast for whatever time he had
missed. You might say in fact he had done already passed it because
now ever time he went or come between Frenchman's Bend and
Jackson by way of Jefferson he went by way of Memphis too, until
now he was what Lawyer Stevens called the apostolic venereal
ambassador from Gayoso Avenue to the entire north Mississippi
banloo.

So when on the fourth morning Montgomery Ward and Clarence
got on Number Six north-bound, we knowed Clarence was jest
going by Memphis to Jackson or Frenchman's Bend. But all we
thought about Montgomery Ward was, jest what could he a had in
that a-teelyer that even Hub never found, that was worth two thousand dollars of bond money to Flem Snopes to get him to Mexico
or wherever Montgomery Ward would wind up? So ours wasn't jest
interested surprise: ours was interested all right but it was astonishment and some good hard fast thinking too when two days later
Clarence and Montgomery Ward both got off of Number Five
south-bound and Clarence turned Montgomery Ward back over to
Flem and went on to Jackson or Frenchman's Bend or wherever he
would have to go to leave from to come back by Gayoso Street,
Memphis, next time. And Flem turned Montgomery Ward back over
to Euphus Tubbs, back into the cell in the jail, that two-thousand-
dollar bond of Flem's rescinded or maybe jest withdrawed for all time

like you hang your Sunday hat back on the rack until the next wedding or funeral or whenever you might need it again.

Who—I mean Euphus—apparently in his turn turned Montgomery Ward over to Miz Tubbs. We heard how she had even hung a old shade over the cell window to keep the morning sun from waking him up so early. And how any time Lawyer Stevens or Hub Hampton or any other such members of the Law would want a word with Montgomery Ward now, the quickest place to look for him would be in Miz Tubbs's kitchen with one of her aprons on, shelling peas or husking roasting ears. And we—all right, me then—would kind of pass along the alley by the jail and there Montgomery Ward would be, him and Miz Tubbs in the garden while Montgomery Ward hoed out the vegetable rows, not making much of a out at it maybe, but anyhow swinging the hoe as long as Miz Tubbs showed him where to chop next.

"Maybe she's still trying to find out about them pictures," Homer Bookwright says.

"What?" I says. "Miz Tubbs?"

"Of course she wants to know about them," Homer says. "Aint she human too, even if she is a woman?"

And three weeks later Montgomery Ward stood up in Judge Long's court and Judge Long give him two years in the state penitentiary at Parchman for the possession of one developer jug containing one gallon of moonshine whiskey herewith in evidence.

So ever body was wrong. Flem Snopes hadn't spent no two thousand dollars' worth of bond money to purify Montgomery Ward outen the U.S.A. America, and he hadn't spent no twenty-five or thirty dollars' worth of white-mule whiskey jest to purify the Snopes family name outen Atlanta, Georgia. What he had done was to spend twenty-five or thirty dollars to send Montgomery Ward to Parchman when the government would a sent him to Georgia free. Which was a good deal more curious than jest surprising, and a good deal more interesting than all three. So the next morning I happened to be on the depot platform when Number Eleven south-bound was due and sho enough, there was Montgomery Ward and Hunter Killegrew, the deputy, and I says to Hunter: "Dont you need to step into the washroom before you get on the train for such a long trip? I'll watch Montgomery Ward for you. Besides, a feller that wouldn't run off three weeks ago under a two-thousand-dollar bond aint likely to try it now with nothing on him but a handcuff."

So Hunter handed me his half of the handcuff and moved a little away and I says to Montgomery Ward:

"So you're going to Parchman instead. That'll be a heap better. Not only you wont be depriving no native-born Missippi grub contractor outen his rightful and natural profit on the native-born Missippi grub they'll be feeding a native-born Missippi convict, you wont be lonesome there neither, having a native-born Missippi cousin or uncle to pass the time with when you aint otherwise occupied with field work or something. What's his name? Mink Snopes, your uncle or cousin that got in that little trouble a while back for killing Jack Houston and kept trying to wait for Flem to come back from Texas in time to get him outen it, except that Flem was otherwise occupied too and so Mink acted kind of put out about it? Which was he, your uncle or your cousin?"

"Yeah?" Montgomery Ward says.

"Well, which?" I says.

"Which what?" Montgomery Ward says.

"Is he your uncle or is he your cousin?" I says.

"Yeah?" Montgomery Ward says.

FOUR

$\mathcal{M}$ONTGOMERY $\mathcal{W}$ARD $\mathcal{S}$NOPES

$\mathcal{S}$o the son of a bitch fooled you," I said. "You thought they were going to hang him but all he got was life."

He didn't answer. He just sat there in the kitchen chair—he had toted it up himself from Tubbs's kitchen. For me, there wasn't anything in the cell but the cot—for me and the bedbugs that is. He just sat there with the shadow of the window bars crisscrossing that white shirt and that damn little ten-cent snap-on bow tie; they said the same one he had worn in from Frenchman's Bend sixteen years ago. No: they said not the same one he took out of Varner's stock and put on the day he came in from that tenant farm and went to work as Varner's clerk and married Varner's whore of a daughter in and wore to Texas while the bastard kid was getting born and then wore back again; that was when he wore the cloth cap about the size for a fourteen-year-old child. And the black felt hat somebody told him was the kind of hat bankers wore, that he didn't throw away the cap: he sold it to a nigger boy for a dime that he took out in work and put the hat on for the first time three years ago and they said had never taken it off since, not even in the house, except in church, that still looked new. No, it didn't look like it belonged to anybody, even after day and night for three years, not even sweated, which would include while he was laying his wife too which would be all right with her probably since the sort of laying she was used to they probably didn't even take off their gloves, let alone their hats and shoes and overcoats.

And chewing. They said when he first came in to Frenchman's Bend as Varner's clerk it was tobacco. Then he found out about money. Oh, he had heard about money and had even seen a little of it now and then. But now he found out for the first time that there was more of it each day than you could eat up each day if you ate

twice as much fried sowbelly and white gravy. Not only that, but that
it was solid, harder than bones and heavy like gravel, and that if you
could shut your hands on some of it, there was no power anywhere
that could make you let go of more of it than you had to let go of,
so he found out that he couldn't afford to chew up ten cents' worth
of it every week because he had discovered chewing gum by then that
a nickel's worth of would last five weeks, a new stick every Sunday.
Then he came to Jefferson and he really saw some money, I mean
all at one time, and then he found out that the only limit to the
amount of money you could shut your hands on and keep and hold,
was just how much money there was, provided you had a good safe
place to put that other handful down and fill your fists again. And
then was when he found out he couldn't afford to chew even one cent
a week. When he had nothing, he could afford to chew tobacco;
when he had a little, he could afford to chew gum; when he found out
he could be rich provided he just didn't die beforehand, he couldn't
afford to chew anything, just sitting there in that kitchen chair with
the shadow of the cell bars crisscrossing him, chewing that and not
looking at me or not any more anyway.

"Life," I said. "That means twenty years, the way they figure it,
unless something happens between now and then. How long has it
been now? Nineteen eight, wasn't it, when he hung all day long
maybe in this same window here, watching the street for you to come
on back from Texas and get him out, being as you were the only
Snopes then that had enough money and influence to help him as
he figured it, hollering down to anybody that passed to get word out
to Varner's store for you to come in and save him, then standing up
there in that courtroom on that last day and giving you your last
chance, and you never came then either? Nineteen eight to nineteen
twenty-three from twenty years, and he'll be out again. Hell fire,
you've only got five more years to live, haven't you? All right. What
do you want me to do?"

He told me.

"All right," I said. "What do I get for it?"

He told me that. I stood there for a while leaning against the wall,
laughing down at him. Then I told him.

He didn't even move. He just quit chewing long enough to say, "Ten thousand dollars."

"So that's too high," I said. "All your life is worth to you is about five hundred, mostly in trade, on the installment plan." He sat there in that cross-barred shadow, chewing his mouthful of nothing, watching me or at least looking toward me. "Even if it works, the best you can do is get his sentence doubled, get twenty more years added onto it. That means that in nineteen forty-three you'll have to start all over again worrying about having only five years more to live. Quit sucking and smouching around for bargains. Buy the best: you can afford it. Take ten grand cash and have him killed. From what I hear, for that jack you could have all Chicago bidding against each other. Or ten grand, hell, and Chicago, hell too; for one you could stay right here in Mississippi and have a dozen trusties right there in Parchman drawing straws for him, for which one would shoot him first in the back."

He didn't even quit chewing this time.

"Well well," I said. "So there's something that even a Snopes wont do. No, that's wrong; Uncle Mink never seemed to have any trouble reconciling Jack Houston up in front of that shotgun when the cheese begun to bind. Maybe what I mean is, every Snopes has one thing he wont do to you—provided you can find out what it is before he has ruined and wrecked you. Make it five then," I said. "I wont haggle. What the hell, aint we cousins or something?"

This time he quit chewing long enough to say, "Five thousand dollars."

"Okay, I know you haven't got five grand cash either now," I said. "You dont even need it now. That lawyer says you got two years to raise it in, hock or sell or steal whatever you'll have to hock or sell or steal."

That got to him—or so I thought then. I'm a pretty slow learner myself sometimes, now and then, mostly now in fact. Because he said something: "You wont have to stay two years. I can get you out."

"When?" I said. "When you're satisfied? When I have wrecked the rest of his life by getting twenty more years hung onto it? Not me, you wont. Because I wont come out. I wouldn't even take the five grand; I was kidding you. This is how we'll do it. I'll go on down there and fix him, get him whatever additional time the traffic will bear. Only I wont come out then. I'll finish out my two years first; give you a little more time of your own, see. Then I'll come out and come on back home. You know: start a new life, live down that old bad past. Of course I wont have any job, business, but after all there's my own father's own first cousin every day and every way getting to be bigger and bigger in the bank and the church and local respectability and civic reputation and what the hell, aint blood thicker than just water even if some of it is just back from Parchman for bootlegging, not to mention at any minute now his pride might revolt at charity even from his respectable blood-kin banker cousin and he might decide to set up that old unrespectable but fairly damned popular business again. Because I can get plenty more stock-in-trade and the same old good will will still be here just waiting for me to tell them where to go and maybe this time there wont be any developer-fluid jugs sitting carelessly around. And suppose they are, what the hell? it's just two years and I'll be back again, already reaching to turn over that old new leaf—"

He put his hand inside his coat and he didn't say "Yep" in that tone because he didn't know how yet but if he had known he would. So he said, "Yep, that's what I figgered," and drew out the envelope. Oh sure, I recognised it. It was one of mine, with *Atelier Monty Jefferson Miss* in the left corner, all stamped and showing the cancellation clear as an etching and addressed to *G.C.Winbush, City* so I already knew what was in it before he even took it out: the photo that Winbush had insisted on buying for five bucks for his private files as they call it that I hadn't wanted to let him have it because anybody associating with him in anything was already in jeopardy. But what the hell, he was the Law, or what passed for it in that alley at one or two in the morning anyway. And oh yes, it had been through the mail all right even though I never mailed it and it hadn't been any further than through that damn cancelling machine inside the Jefferson post office. And with the trouble Winbush was already in from being in my back room instead of getting what he called his brains beaten out by old dope-eating Will Christian's burglars, it wouldn't have taken any Simon Legree to find out he had the picture and then to get it away from him; nor anything at all to make him swear or perjure to anything anybody suggested to him regarding it. Because he had a wife and all you'd need would be just to intimate to Winbush you were going to show it to her since she was the sort of wife that no power on earth would unconvince her that the girl in the photo—she happened to be alone in this one and happened not to be doing anything except just being buck-naked—was not only Winbush's private playmate but that probably only some last desperate leap got Winbush himself out of the picture without his pants on. And it wouldn't take any Sherlock Holmes to discern what that old sanctimonious lantern-jawed son of a bitch up there on that federal bench would do when he saw that cancelled envelope. So I said, "So it looks like I've been raised. And it looks like I wont call. In fact, it looks like I'm going to pass. After I go down there and get him fixed, you get me out. Then what?"

"A railroad ticket to wherever you want, and a hundred dollars."

"Make it five," I said. Then I said, "All right. I wont haggle. Make it two-fifty." And he didn't haggle either.

"A hundred dollars," he said.

"Only I'm going to cut the pot for the house kitty," I said. "If I've got to spend at least a year locked up in a god-damned cotton farm—" No, he didn't haggle; you could say that for him.

"I figgered that too," he said. "It's all arranged. You'll be out on bond tomorrow. Clarence will pick you up on his way through town to Memphis. You can have two days." And by God he had even thought of that too. "Clarence will have the money. It will be enough."

Whether what he would call enough or what I would call enough. So nobody was laughing at anybody any more now. I just stood there looking down at him where he sat in that kitchen chair, chewing, not looking at anything and not even chewing anything, that everybody that knew him said he never took a drink in his life yet hadn't hesitated to buy thirty or forty dollars' worth of whiskey to get me into Parchman where I could wreck Mink, and evidently was getting ready to spend another hundred (or more likely two if he intended to pay for Clarence too) to reconcile me to staying in Parchman long enough to do the wrecking that would keep Mink from getting out in five years; and all of a sudden I knew what it was that had bothered me about him ever since I got big enough to understand about such and maybe draw a conclusion.

"So you're a virgin," I said. "You never had a lay in your life, did you? You even waited to get married until you found a woman who not only was already knocked up, she wouldn't even have let you run your hand up her dress. Jesus, you do want to stay alive, don't you? Only, why?" And still he said nothing: just sitting there chewing nothing. "But why put out money on Clarence too? Even if he does prefer nigger houses where the top price is a dollar, it'll cost you something with Clarence as the operator. Give me all the money and let me go by myself." But as soon as I said it I knew the answer to that too. He couldn't risk letting me get one mile out of Jefferson without somebody along to see I came back, even with that cancelled envelope in his pocket. He knew better, but he couldn't risk finding out he was right. He didn't dare. He didn't dare at his age to find out that all you need to handle nine people out of ten is just to trust them.

Tubbs knew about the bond so he was all for turning me out that night so he could put the cost of my supper in his pocket and hope that in the confusion it wouldn't be noticed but I said Much obliged. I said: "Dont brag. I was in (on the edge of it anyway) the U.S. Army; if you think this dump is lousy, you should have seen some of the places I slept in," with Tubbs standing there in the open cell door with the key ring in one hand and scratching his head with the other. "But what you can do, go out and get me a decent supper; Mr Snopes will pay for it; my rich kinfolks have forgiven me now. And while you're about it, bring me the Memphis paper." So he started out until this time I hollered it: "Come back and lock the door! I dont want all Jefferson in here; one son of a bitch in this kennel is enough."

So the next morning Clarence showed up and Flem gave him the money and that night we were in Memphis, at the Teaberry. That was me. Clarence knew a dump where he was a regular customer, where we could stay for a dollar a day even when it wasn't even his money. Flem's money, that you would have thought anybody else named Snopes would have slept on the bare ground provided it just cost Flem twice as much as anywhere else would.

"Now what?" Clarence said. It was what they call rhetorical. He already knew what, or thought he did. He had it all lined up. One thing about Clarence: he never let you down. He couldn't; everybody that knew him knew he would have to be a son of a bitch, being my half-brother.

Last year Virgil (that's right. Snopes. You guessed it: Uncle Wesley's youngest boy—the revival song leader that they caught after church that day with the fourteen-year-old girl in the empty cotton house and tar-and-feathered him to Texas or anyway out of Yoknapatawpha County; Virgil's gift was inherited) and Fonzo Winbush, my patient's nephew I believe it is, came up to Memphis to enter a barbers' college. Somebody—it would be Mrs Winbush; she wasn't a Snopes—evidently told them never to rent a room to live in unless the woman of the house looked mature and Christian, but most of all motherly.

So they were probably still walking concentric circles around the railroad station, still carrying their suitcases, when they passed Reba Rivers's at the time when every afternoon she would come out her front door to exercise those two damn nasty little soiled white dogs that she called Miss Reba and Mr Binford after Lucius Binford who had been her pimp until they both got too old and settled down and all the neighborhood—the cop, the boy that brought the milk and collected for the paper, and the people on the laundry truck—called him landlord until he finally died.

She looked mature all right in anything, let alone the wrappers she wore around that time in the afternoon, and she would probably sound Christian all right whether religious or not, to anybody near enough to hear what she would say to those dogs at times when she had had a little extra gin; and I suppose anybody weighing two hundred pounds in a wrapper fastened with safety pins would look motherly even while she was throwing out a drunk, let alone to two eighteen-year-old boys from Jefferson, Mississippi.

Maybe she was motherly and Virgil and Fonzo, in the simple innocence of children, saw what us old long-standing mere customers and friends missed. Or maybe they just walked impervious in that simple Yoknapatawpha juvenile rural innocence where even an angel would have left his pocketbook at the depot first. Anyway, they asked if she had an empty room and she rented them one; likely they had already unpacked those paper suitcases before she realised they didn't even know they were in a whorehouse.

Anyhow, there she was, having to pay the rent and pay off the cops and the man that supplied the beer, and pay the laundry and Minnie, the maid, something on Saturday night, not to mention having to keep those big yellow diamonds shined and cleaned until they wouldn't look too much like big chunks of a broken beer bottle; and that Yoknapatawpha innocence right in the middle of the girls running back and forth to the bathroom in nighties and negligees or maybe not even that, and the customers going and coming and Minnie running stacks of towels and slugs of gin up the stairs and the women screaming and fighting and pulling each other's hair over their boys and clients and money, and Reba herself in the hall cursing a drunk while they tried to throw him out before the cops got there; until in less than a week she had that house as quiet and innocent as a girls' school until she could get Virgil and Fonzo upstairs into their room and in bed and, she hoped, asleep.

Naturally it couldn't last. To begin with, there was the barbers' college where they would have to listen to barbers all day long when you have to listen to enough laying just spending thirty minutes getting your hair cut. Then to come back there and get a flash of a leg or a chemise or maybe a whole naked female behind running through a door, would be bound to give them ideas after a time even though Virgil and Fonzo still thought they were all Reba's nieces or wards or something just in town maybe attending female equivalents of barbers' colleges themselves. Not to mention that pure instinct which Virgil and Fonzo (did I say he was Grover Winbush's nephew?) had inherited from the pure fountainheads themselves.

It didn't last past the second month. And since the Memphis redlight district is not all that big, it was only the course of time until they and Clarence turned up at the same time in the same place, especially as Virgil and Fonzo, still forced to devote most of their time to learning yet and not earning, had to hunt for bargains. Where right away Virgil showed himself the owner of a really exceptional talent—a capacity to take care of two girls in succession to their satisfaction or at least until they hollered quit, that was enough for two dollars, in his youthful enthusiasm and innocence not only doing it for pleasure but even paying for the chance until Clarence discovered him and put him into the money.

He—Clarence—would loaf around the poolrooms and the sort of hotel lobbies he patronised himself, until he would find a sucker who refused to believe his bragging about his—what's the word?—protégé's powers, and Clarence would bet him; the first time the victim would usually give odds. Of course Virgil would fail now and then—

"And pay half the bet," I said.

"What?" Clarence said. "Penalise the boy for doing his best? Besides, it dont happen once in ten times and he's going to get better and better as time goes on. What a future that little sod's got if the supply of two-dollar whores just holds out."

Anyway, that's what we were going to do tonight. "Much obliged," I said. "You go ahead. I'm going to make a quiet family call on an old friend and then coming back to bed. Let me have twenty-five—make it thirty of the money."

"Flem gave me a hundred."

"Thirty will do," I said.

"Be damned if that's so," he said. "You'll take half of it. I don't aim to take you back to Jefferson and have you tell Flem a god-damn lie about me. Here."

I took the money. "See you at the station tomorrow at train time."

"What?" he said.

"I'm going home tomorrow. You dont have to."

"I promised Flem I'd stay with you and bring you back."

"Break it," I said. "Haven't you got fifty dollars of his money?"

"That's it," he said. "Damn a son of a bitch that'll break his word after he's been paid for it."

Wednesday evenings were nearly always quiet unless there was a convention in town, maybe because so many of the women (clients too) came from little Tennessee and Arkansas and Mississippi country towns and Baptist and Methodist families, that they established among the joints and dives and cathouses themselves some . . . anal-

ogous? analogous rhythm to the midweek prayer-meeting night.
Minnie answered the bell. She had her hat on. I mean her whole
head was in it like a football helmet.

"Evening, Minnie," I said. "You going out?"

"No sir," she said. "You been away? We aint seen you in a long
time."

"Just busy," I answered. That was what Reba said too. The place
was quiet: nobody in the dining room but Reba and a new girl and
one customer, drinking beer, Reba in all her big yellow diamonds but
wearing a wrapper instead of the evening gown she would have had
on if it had been Saturday night. It was a new wrapper but it was
already fastened with safety pins. I answered the same thing too.
"Just busy," I said.

"I wish I could return the compliment," she said. "I might as well
be running a Sunday school. Meet Captain Strutterbuck," she said.
He was tall, pretty big, with a kind of roustabout's face; I mean, that
tried to look tough but wasn't sure yet how you were going to take it,
and hard pale eyes that looked at you hard enough, only he couldn't
seem to look at you with both of them at the same time. He was
about fifty. "Captain Strutterbuck was in both wars," Reba said.
"That Spanish one about twenty-five years ago, and the last one too.
He was just telling us about the last one. And this is Thelma. She just
came in last week."

"Howdy," Strutterbuck said. "Were you a buddy too?"

"More or less," I said.

"What outfit?"

"Lafayette Escadrille," I said.

"Laughing what?" he said. "Oh, La-Fayette Esker-Drill. Flying
boys. Dont know anything about flying, myself. I was cavalry, in
Cuba in '98 and on the Border in '16, not commissioned any longer,
out of the army in fact: just sort of a private citizen aide to Black Jack
because I knew the country. So when they decided to send him to
France to run the show over there, he told me if I ever got across to
look him up, he would try to find something for me. So when I heard
that Rick—Eddie Rickenbacker, the Ace," he told Reba and the new
girl, "the General's driver—that Rick had left him for the air corps,

I decided that was my chance and I managed to get over all right but he already had another driver, a Sergeant Somebody, I forget his name. So there I was, with no status. But I still managed to see a little of it, from the back seat you might say—Argonne, Showmont, Vymy Ridge, Shatter Theory; you probably saw most of the hot places yourself. Where were you stationed?"

"Y.M.C.A.," I said.

"What?" he said. He got up, slow. He was tall, pretty big; this probably wasn't the first time both his eyes had failed to look at the same thing at the same time. Maybe he depended on it. By that time Reba was up too. "You wouldn't be trying to kid me, would you?" he said.

"Why?" I said. "Dont it work?"

"All right, all right," Reba said. "Are you going upstairs with Thelma, or aint you? If you aint, and you usually aint, tell her so."

"I dont know whether I am or not," he said. "What I think right now is—"

"Folks dont come in here to think," Reba said. "They come in here to do business and then get out. Do you aim to do any business or dont you?"

"Okay, okay," he said. "Let's go," he told Thelma. "Maybe I'll see you again," he told me.

"After the next war," I said. He and Thelma went out. "Are you going to let him?" I said.

"He gets a pension from that Spanish war," Reba said. "It came today. I saw it. I watched him sign his name on the back of it so I can cash it."

"How much?" I said.

"I didn't bother with the front of it. I just made damn sure he signed his name where the notice said sign. It was a United States Government post-office money order. You dont fool around with the United States Government."

"A post-office money order can be for one cent provided you can afford the carrying charges," I said. She looked at me. "He wrote his name on the back of a piece of blue paper and put it back in his pocket. I suppose he borrowed the pen from you. Was that it?"

"All right, all right," she said. "What do you want me to do: lean over the foot of the bed and say, Just a second there, Buster?"—Minnie came in with another bottle of beer. It was for me. "I didn't order it," I said. "Maybe I should have told you right off. I'm not going to spend any money tonight."

"It's on me then. Why did you come here then? Just to try to pick a fight with somebody?"

"Not with him," I said. "He even got his name out a book. I dont remember what book right now, but it was a better book than the one he got his war out of."

"All right, all right," she said. "Why in hell did you tell him where you were staying? Come to think of it, why are you staying there?"

"Staying where?" I said.

"At the Y.M.C.A. I have some little squirts in here now and then that ought to be at the Y.M.C.A. whether they are or not. But I never had one of them bragging about it before."

"I'm at the Teaberry," I said. "I belonged to the Y.M.C.A. in the war."

"The Y.M.C.A.? In the war? They dont fight. Are you trying to kid me too?"

"I know they dont," I said. "That's why I was in it. That's right. That's where I was. Gavin Stevens, a lawyer down in Jefferson, can tell you. The next time he's in here ask him."

Minnie appeared in the door with a tray with two glasses of gin on it. She didn't say anything: she just stood in the door there where Reba could see her. She still wore the hat.

"All right," Reba said. "But no more. He never paid for that beer yet. But Miss Thelma's new in Memphis and we want to make her feel at home." Minnie went away. "So you're not going to unbutton your pocket tonight."

"I came to ask you a favor," I said. But she wasn't even listening.

"You never did spend much. Oh, you were free enough buying beer and drinks around. But you never done any jazzing. Not with any of my girls, anyway." She was looking at me. "Me neither. I've done outgrowed that too. We could get along." She was looking at me. "I heard about that little business of yours down there in the country. A lot of folks in business here dont like it. They figure you are cutting into trade un—un— What's that word? Lawyers and doctors are always throwing it at you."

"Unethical," I said. "It means dry."

"Dry?" she said.

"That's right. You might call my branch of your business the arid or waterproof branch. The desert-outpost branch."

"Yes, sure, I see what you mean. That's it exactly. That's what I would tell them: that just looking at pictures might do all right for a while down there in the country where there wasn't no other available handy outlet but that sooner or later somebody was going to run up enough temperature to where he would have to run to the nearest well for a bucket of real water, and maybe it would be mine." She was looking at me. "Sell it out and come on up here."

"Is this a proposition?" I said.

"All right. Come on up here and be the landlord. The beer and drinks is already on the house and you wouldn't need much but cigarettes and clothes and a little jack to rattle in your pocket and I can afford that and I wouldn't have to be always watching you about the girls, just like Mr Binford because I could always trust him too, always—" She was looking at me. There was something in her eyes or somewhere I never had seen before or expected either for that matter. "I nee— A man can do what a woman cant. You know: paying off protection, handling drunks, checking up on the son-a-bitching beer and whiskey peddlers that mark up prices and miscount bottles if you aint watching day and night like a god-damn hawk." Sitting there looking at me, one fat hand with that diamond the size of a piece of gravel holding the beer glass. "I need . . . I . . . not jazzing; I done outgrowed that too long a time ago. It's—it's . . . Three years ago he died, yet even now I still cant quite believe it." It shouldn't have been there: the fat raddled face and body that had worn themselves out with the simple hard physical work of being a whore and making a living at it like an old prize fighter or football player or maybe an old horse until they didn't look like a man's or a woman's either in spite of the cheap rouge and too much of it and the big diamonds that were real enough even if you just did not believe that color, and the eyes with something in or behind them that shouldn't have been there; that, as they say, shouldn't happen to a

dog. Minnie passed the door going back down the hall. The tray was
empty now. "For fourteen years we was like two doves." She looked
at me. Yes, not even to a dog. "Like two doves," she roared and lifted
the glass of beer then banged it down hard and shouted at the door:
"Minnie!" Minnie came back to the door. "Bring the gin," Reba said.
"Now, Miss Reba, you dont want to start that," Minnie said.
"Dont you remember, last time you started grieving about Mr Binford we had po-lice in here until four oclock in the morning. Drink
your beer and forget about gin."
    "Yes," Reba said. She even drank some of the beer. Then she set
the glass down. "You said something about a favor. It cant be
money—I aint talking about your nerve: I mean your good sense. So
it might be interesting—"
    "Except it is money," I said. I took out the fifty dollars and sepa-
rated ten from it and pushed the ten across to her. "I'm going away
for a couple of years. That's for you to remember me by." She didn't
touch it. She wasn't even looking at it though Minnie was. She just
looked at me. "Maybe Minnie can help too," I said. "I want to make
a present of forty dollars to the poorest son of a bitch I can find. Who
is the poorest son of a bitch anywhere at this second that you and
Minnie know?"
    They were both looking at me, Minnie too from under the hat.
"How do you mean, poor?" Reba said.
    "That's in trouble or jail or somewhere that maybe wasn't his
fault."
    "Minnie's husband is a son of a bitch and he's in jail all right,"
Reba said. "But I wouldn't call him poor. Would you, Minnie?"
    "Nome," Minnie said.
    "But at least he's out of woman trouble for a while," Reba told
Minnie. "That ought to make you feel a little better."
    "You dont know Ludus," Minnie said. "I like to see any place,
chain gang or not, where Ludus cant find some fool woman to
believe him."
    "What did he do?" I said.
    "He quit his job last winter and laid around here ever since, eat-
ing out of my kitchen and robbing Minnie's pocketbook every night
after she went to sleep, until she caught him actually giving the

money to the other woman, and when she tried to ask him to stop he snatched the flatiron out of her hand and damn near tore her ear off with it. That's why she has to wear a hat all the time even in the house. So I'd say if any—if anybody deserved them forty dollars it would be Minnie—"

A woman began screaming at the top of the stairs in the upper hall. Minnie and Reba ran out. I picked up the money and followed. The woman screaming the curses was the new girl, Thelma, standing at the head of the stairs in a flimsy kimono, or more or less of it. Captain Strutterbuck was halfway down the stairs, wearing his hat and carrying his coat in one hand and trying to button his fly with the other. Minnie was at the foot of the stairs. She didn't outshout Thelma nor even shout her silent: Minnie just had more volume, maybe more practice:

"Course he never had no money. He aint never had more than two dollars at one time since he been coming here. Why you ever let him get on the bed without the money in your hand first, I dont know. I bet he never even took his britches off. A man wont take his britches off, dont never have no truck with him a-tall; he done already shook his foot, no matter what his mouth still saying."

"All right," Reba told Minnie. "That'll do." Minnie stepped back; even Thelma hushed; she saw me or something and even pulled the kimono back together in front. Strutterbuck came on down the stairs, still fumbling at the front of his pants; maybe the last thing he did want was for both his eyes to look at the same thing at the same time. But I dont know; according to Minnie he had no more reason to be alarmed and surprised now at where he was than a man walking a tightrope. Concerned of course and damned careful, but not really alarmed and last of all surprised. He reached the downstairs floor. But he was not done yet. There were still eight or ten feet to the front door.

But Reba was a lady. She just held her hand out until he quit fumbling at his fly and took the folded money order out of whatever pocket it was in and handed it to her. A lady. She never raised her hand at him. She never even cursed him. She just went to the front door and took hold of the knob and turned and said, "Button yourself up. Aint no man going to walk out of my house at just eleven oclock at night with his pants still hanging open." Then she closed the door after him and locked it. Then she unfolded the money order. Minnie was right. It was for two dollars, issued at Lonoke, Arkansas. The sender's name was spelled Q'Milla Strutterbuck. "His sister or his daughter?" Reba said. "What's your guess?"

Minnie was looking too. "It's his wife," she said. "His sister or mama or grandma would sent five. His woman would sent fifty—if she had it and felt like sending it. His daughter would sent fifty cents. Wouldn't nobody but his wife sent two dollars."

She brought two more bottles of beer to the dining-room table. "All right," Reba said. "You want a favor. What favor?"

I took out the money again and shoved the ten across to her again, still holding the other forty. "This is for you and Minnie, to remember me until I come back in two years. I want you to send the other to my great-uncle in the Mississippi penitentiary at Parchman."

"Will you come back in two years?"

"Yes," I said. "You can look for me. Two years. The man I'm going to be working for says I'll be back in one but I dont believe him."

"All right. Now what do I do with the forty?"

"Send it to my great-uncle Mink Snopes in Parchman."

"What's he in for?"

"He killed a man named Jack Houston back in 1908."

"Did Houston deserve killing?"

"I dont know. But from what I hear, he sure worked to earn it."

"The poor son of a bitch. How long is your uncle in for?"

"Life," I said.

"All right," she said. "I know about that too. When will he get out?"

"About 1948 if he lives and nothing else happens to him."

"All right. How do I do it?" I told her, the address and all.

"You could send it From another prisoner."

"I doubt it," she said. "I aint never been in jail. I dont aim to be."

"Send it From a friend then."

"All right," she said. She took the money and folded it. "The poor son of a bitch," she said.

"Which one are you talking about now?"

"Both of them," she said. "All of us. Every one of us. The poor son of a bitches."

I hadn't expected to see Clarence at all until tomorrow morning. But there he was, a handful of crumpled bills scattered on the top of the dresser like the edge of a crap game and Clarence undressed down to his trousers standing looking at them and yawning and rooting in the pelt on his chest. This time they—Clarence—had found a big operator, a hot sport who, Virgil having taken on the customary two successfully, bet them he couldn't handle a third one without stopping, offering them the odds this time, which Clarence covered with Flem's other fifty since this really would be a risk; he said how he even gave Virgil a chance to quit and not hold it against him: " 'We're ahead now, you know; you done already proved yourself.' And do you know, the little sod never even turned a hair. 'Sure,' he says. 'Send her in.' And now my conscience hurts me," he said, yawning again. "It was Flem's money. My conscience says dont tell him a durn thing about it: the money just got spent like he thinks it was. But shucks, a man dont want to be a hog."

So we went back home. "Why do you want to go back to the jail?" Flem said. "It'll be three weeks yet."

"Call it for practice," I said. "Call it a dry run against my conscience." So now I had a set of steel bars between; now I was safe from the free world, safe and secure for a little while yet from the free Snopes world where Flem was parlaying his wife into the presidency of a bank and Clarence even drawing per diem as a state senator between Jackson and Gayoso Street to take the wraps off Virgil whenever he could find another Arkansas sport who refused to believe what he was looking at, and Byron in Mexico or wherever he was with whatever was still left of the bank's money, and mine and Clarence's father I.O. and all of our Uncle Wesley leading a hymn with one hand and fumbling the skirt of an eleven-year-old infant with the other; I dont count Wallstreet and Admiral Dewey and their father Eck, because they dont belong to us: they are only our shame.

Not to mention Uncle Murdering Mink six or seven weeks later (I had to wait a little while you see not to spook him too quick).

"Flem?" he said. "I wouldn't a thought Flem wanted me out. I'd a thought he'd been the one wanted to keep me here longest."

"He must have changed," I said. He stood there in his barred overalls, blinking a little—a damn little worn-out dried-up shrimp of a man not as big as a fourteen-year-old boy. Until you wondered how in hell anything as small and frail could have held enough mad, let alone steadied and aimed a ten-gauge shotgun, to kill anybody.

"I'm obliged to him," he said. "Only, if I got out tomorrow, maybe I wont done changed. I been here a long time now. I aint had much to do for a right smart while now but jest work in the field and think. I wonder if he knows to risk that? A man wants to be fair, you know."

"He knows that," I said. "He dont expect you to change inside here because he knows you cant. He expects you to change when you get out. Because he knows that as soon as the free air and sun shine on you again, you cant help but be a changed man even if you dont want to."

"But jest suppose I dont—" He didn't add *change in time* because he stopped himself.

"He's going to take that risk," I said. "He's got to. I mean, he's got to now. He couldn't have stopped them from sending you here. But he knows you think he didn't try. He's got to help you get out not only to prove to you he never put you here but so he can quit thinking and remembering that you believe he did. You see?"

He was completely still, just blinking a little, his hands hanging empty but even now shaped inside the palms like the handles of a plow and even his neck braced a little as though still braced against the loop of the plowlines. "I just got five more years, then I'll get out by myself. Then wont nobody have no right to hold expectations against me. l wont owe nobody no help then."

"That's right," I said. "Just five more years. That's practically nothing to a man that has already put in fifteen years with a man with a shotgun watching him plow cotton that aint his whether he feels like plowing that day or not, and another man with a shotgun standing over him while he eats grub that he either ate it or not whether he felt like eating or not, and another man with a shotgun to lock him up at night so he could either go to sleep or stay awake whether he felt like doing it or not. Just five years more, then you'll be out where the free sun and air can shine on you without any man with a shotgun's shadow to cut it off. Because you'll be free." "Free," he said, not loud: just like that: "Free." That was all. It was that easy. Of course the guard I welshed to cursed me; I had expected that: it was a free country; every convict had a right to try to escape just as every guard and trusty had the right to shoot him in the back the first time he didn't halt. But no unprintable stool pigeon had the right to warn the guard in advance.

I had to watch it too. That was on the bill too: the promissory note of breathing in a world that had Snopeses in it. I wanted to turn my head or anyway shut my eyes. But refusing to not look was all I had left now: the last sorry lousy almost worthless penny—the damn little thing looking like a little girl playing mama in the calico dress and sunbonnet that he believed was Flem's idea (that had been difficult; he still wanted to believe that a man should be permitted to run at his fate, even if that fate was doom, in the decency and dignity of pants; it took a little doing to persuade him that a petticoat and a woman's sunbonnet was all Flem could get). Walking; I had impressed that on him: not to run, but walk; as forlorn and lonely and fragile and alien in that empty penitentiary compound as a paper doll blowing across a rolling mill; still walking even after he had passed the point where he couldn't come back and knew it; even still walking on past the moment when he knew that he had been sold and that he should have known all along he was being sold, not blaming anybody for selling him nor even needing to sell him because hadn't he signed— he couldn't read but he could sign his name—that same promissory note too to breathe a little while, since his name was Snopes?

So he even ran before he had to. He ran right at them before I even saw them, before they stepped out of the ambush. I was proud, not just to be kin to him but of belonging to what Reba called all of us poor son of a bitches. Because it took five of them striking and slashing at his head with pistol barrels and even then it finally took the blackjack to stop him, knock him out.

The Warden sent for me. "Dont tell me anything," he said. "I wish I didn't even know as much already as I suspect. In fact, if it was left to me, I'd like to lock you and him both in a cell and leave you, you for choice in handcuffs. But I'm under a bond too so I'm going to move you into solitary for a week or so, for your own protection. And not from him."

"Dont brag or grieve," I said. "You had to sign one of them too."

"What?" he said. "What did you say?"

"I said you dont need to worry. He hasn't got anything against me. If you dont believe me, send for him."

So he came in. The bruises and slashes from the butts and the blades of the sights were healing fine. The blackjack of course never had showed. "Hidy," he said. To me. "I reckon you'll see Flem before I will now."

"Yes," I said.

"Tell him he hadn't ought to used that dress. But it dont matter. If I had made it out then, maybe I would a changed. But I reckon I wont now. I reckon I'll jest wait."

So Flem should have taken that suggestion about the ten grand. He could still do it. I could write him a letter: *Sure you can raise ten thousand. All you need to do is swap Manfred de Spain a good jump at your wife. No: that wont do: trying to peddle Eula Varner to Manfred de Spain is like trying to sell a horse to a man that's already been feeding and riding it for ten or twelve years. But you got that girl, Linda. She aint but eleven or twelve but what the hell, put smoked glasses and high heels on her and rush her in quick and maybe De Spain wont notice it.*

Except that I wasn't going to. But it wasn't that that worried me. It was knowing that I wasn't, knowing I was going to throw it away—I mean my commission of the ten grand for contacting the Chi syndicate for him. I dont remember just when it was, I was probably pretty young, when I realised that I had come from what you might call a family, a clan, a race, maybe even a species, of pure sons of bitches. So I said, *Okay, okay, if that's the way it is, we'll just show them. They call the best of lawyers, lawyers' lawyers and the best of actors an actor's actor and the best of athletes a ballplayer's ballplayer. All right, that's what we'll do: every Snopes will make it his private and personal aim to have the whole world recognise him as THE son of a bitch's son of a bitch.*

But we never do it. We never make it. The best we ever do is to be just another Snopes son of a bitch. All of us, every one of us— Flem, and old Ab that I dont even know exactly what kin he is, and Uncle Wes and mine and Clarence's father I.O., then right on down the line: Clarence and me by what you might call simultaneous bigamy, and Virgil and Vardaman and Bilbo and Byron and Mink. I dont even mention Eck and Wallstreet and Admiral Dewey because they dont belong to us. I have always believed that Eck's mother took some extracurricular night work nine months before he was born. So the one true bitch we had was not a bitch at all but a saint and martyr, the one technically true pristine immaculate unchallengeable son of a bitch we ever produced wasn't even a Snopes.

FIVE

*W*hen his nephew was gone, the Warden said, "Sit down." He did so. "You got in the paper," the Warden said. It was folded on the desk facing him:

TRIES PRISON BREAK
DISGUISED IN WOMEN'S CLOTHES

Parchman, Miss. Sept 8, 1923 M.C. "Mink" Snopes, under life sentence for murder from Yoknapatawpha County . . .

"What does the 'C' in your name stand for?" the Warden said. His voice was almost gentle. "We all thought your name was just Mink. That's what you told us, wasn't it?"

"That's right," he said. "Mink Snopes."

"What does the 'C' stand for? They've got it M.C. Snopes here."

"Oh," he said. "Nothing. Just M.C. Snopes like I. C. Railroad. It was them young fellers from the paper in the hospital that day. They kept on asking me what my name was and I said Mink Snopes and they said Mink aint a name, it's jest a nickname. What's your real name? And so I said M.C. Snopes."

"Oh," the Warden said. "Is Mink all the name you've got?"

"That's right. Mink Snopes."

"What did your mother call you?"

"I dont know. She died. The first I knowed my name was just Mink." He got up. "I better go. They're likely waiting for me."

"Wait," the Warden said. "Didn't you know it wouldn't work? Didn't you know you couldn't get away with it?"

"They told me," he said. "I was warned." He stood, not moving, relaxed, small and frail, his face downbent a little, musing, peaceful, almost like faint smiling. "He hadn't ought to fooled me to get caught in that dress and sunbonnet," he said. "I wouldn't a done that to him."

758

"Who?" the Warden said. "Not your . . . is it nephew?"

"Montgomery Ward?" he said. "He was my uncle's grandson. No. Not him." He waited a moment. Then he said again, "Well I better—"

"You would have got out in five more years," the Warden said. "You know they'll probably add on another twenty now, dont you?"

"I was warned of that too," he said.

"All right," the Warden said. "You can go."

This time it was he who paused, stopped. "I reckon you never did find out who sent me them forty dollars."

"How could I?" the Warden said. "I told you that at the time. All it said was From a Friend. From Memphis."

"It was Flem," he said.

"Who?" the Warden said. "The cousin you told me refused to help you after you killed that man? That you said could have saved you if he had wanted to? Why would he send you forty dollars now, after fifteen years?"

"It was Flem," he said. "He can afford it. Besides, he never had no money hurt against me. He was jest getting a holt with Will Varner then and maybe he figgered he couldn't resk getting mixed up with a killing, even if hit was his blood kin. Only I wish he hadn't used that dress and sunbonnet. He never had to do that."

They were picking the cotton now; already every cotton county in Mississippi would be grooming their best fastest champions to pick against the best of Arkansas and Missouri for the championship picker of the Mississippi Valley. But he wouldn't be here. No champion at anything would ever be here because only failures wound up here: the failures at killing and stealing and lying. He remembered how at first he had cursed his bad luck for letting them catch him but he knew better now: that there was no such thing as bad luck or good luck: you were either born a champion or not a champion and if he had been born a champion Houston not only couldn't, he wouldn't have dared, misuse him about that cow to where he had to kill him; that some folks were born to be failures and get caught always, some folks were born to be lied to and believe it, and he was one of them.

It was a fine crop, one of the best he remembered, as though everything had been exactly right: season: wind and sun and rain to

sprout it, the fierce long heat of summer to grow and ripen it. As
though back there in the spring the ground itself had said, *All right,
for once let's confederate instead of fighting*—the ground, the dirt which
any and every tenant farmer and sharecropper knew to be his sworn
foe and mortal enemy—the hard implacable land which wore out
his youth and his tools and then his body itself. And not just his
body but that soft mysterious one he had touched that first time
with amazement and reverence and incredulous excitement the
night of his marriage, now worn too to such leather-toughness that
half the time, it seemed to him most of the time, he would be too
spent with physical exhaustion to remember it was even female. And
not just their two, but those of their children, the two girls to watch
growing up and be able to see what was ahead of that tender and
elfin innocence; until was it any wonder that a man would look at
that inimical irreconcilable square of dirt to which he was bound
and chained for the rest of his life, and say to it: *You got me, you'll
wear me out because you are stronger than me since I'm jest bone and flesh.
I cant leave you because I cant afford to, and you know it. Me and what
used to be the passion and excitement of my youth until you wore out the
youth and I forgot the passion, will be here next year with the children of
our passion for you to wear that much nearer the grave, and you know it;
and the year after that, and the year after that, and you know that too.
And not just me, but all my tenant and cropper kind that have immolated
youth and hope on thirty or forty or fifty acres of dirt that wouldn't nobody
but our kind work because you're all our kind have. But we can burn you.
Every late February or March we can set fire to the surface of you until
all of you in sight is scorched and black, and there aint one god-damn thing
you can do about it. You can wear out our bodies and dull our dreams and
wreck our stomachs with the sowbelly and corn meal and molasses which
is all you afford us to eat but every spring we can set you afire again and
you know that too.*

It was different now. He didn't own this land; he referred of course
to the renter's or cropper's share of what it made. Now, what it produced or failed to produce—bumper or bust, flood or drouth, cotton at ten cents a pound or a dollar a pound—would make not one
tittle of difference in his present life. Because now (years had passed;

the one in which he would have been free again if he had not allowed his nephew to talk him into that folly which anybody should have known—even that young fool of a lawyer they had made him take back there at the trial when he, Mink, could have run his case much better, that didn't have any sense at all, at least knew this much and even told him so and even what the result to him would be—not only wouldn't work, it wasn't even intended to work, was now behind him) he had suddenly discovered something. People of his kind never had owned even temporarily the land which they believed they had rented between one New Year's and the next one. It was the land itself which owned them, and not just from a planting to its harvest but in perpetuity; not the owner, the landlord who evacuated them from one worthless rental in November, onto the public roads to seek desperately another similar worthless one two miles or ten miles or two counties or ten counties away before time to seed the next crop in March, but the land, the earth itself passing their doomed indigence and poverty from holding to holding of its thralldom as a family or a clan does a hopelessly bankrupt tenth cousin.

That was past now. He no longer belonged to the land even on those sterile terms. He belonged to the government, the state of Mississippi. He could drag dust up and down cotton middles from year in to year out and if nothing whatever sprang up behind him, it would make no difference to him. No more now to go to a commissary store every Saturday morning to battle with the landlord for every gram of the cheap bad meat and meal and molasses and the tumbler of snuff which was his and his wife's one spendthrift orgy. No more to battle with the landlord for every niggard sack of fertilizer, then gather the poor crop which suffered from that niggard lack and still have to battle the landlord for his niggard insufficient share of it. All he had to do now was just to keep moving; even the man with the shotgun standing over him neither knew nor cared whether anything came up behind him or not just so he kept moving, any more than he cared. At first he was ashamed, in shame and terror lest the others find that he felt this way; until one day he knew (he could not have said how) that all the others felt like this; that, given time enough, Parchman brought them all to this; he thought in a kind of musing amazement *Yes sir, a man can get used to jest anything, even to being in Parchman, if you jest give him time enough.*

But Parchman just changed the way a man looked at what he saw after he got in Parchman. It didn't change what he brought with him. It just made remembering easier because Parchman taught him how to wait. He remembered back there that day even while the Judge was still saying "Life" down at him, when he still believed that Flem would come in and save him, until he finally realised that Flem wasn't, had never intended to, how he had pretty near actually said it out loud: *Just let me go long enough to get out to Frenchman's Bend or wherever he is and give me ten minutes and I'll come back here and you can go on and hang me if that's what you want to do.* And how even that time three or five or eight years or whenever it was back there when Flem had used that nephew—what was his name? Montgomery Ward—to trick him into trying to escape in a woman's dress and sunbonnet and they had given him twenty years more exactly like that young fool lawyer had warned him they would at the very beginning, how even while he was fighting with the five guards he was still saying the same thing: *Just let me go long enough to reach Jefferson and have ten minutes and I will come back myself and you can hang me.*

He didn't think things like that any more now because he had learned to wait. And, waiting, he found out that he was listening, hearing too; that he was keeping up with what went on by just listening and hearing even better than if he had been right there in Jefferson because like this all he had to do was just watch them without having to worry about them too. So his wife had gone back to her people they said and died and his daughters had moved away too, grown girls now, likely somebody around Frenchman's Bend would know where. And Flem was a rich man now, president of the bank and living in a house he rebuilt that they said was as big as the Union Depot in Memphis, with his daughter, old Will Varner's girl's bastard, that was grown now, that went away and married and her and her husband had been in another war they had in Spain and a shell or cannon ball or something blew up and killed the husband but just made her stone deaf. And she was back home now, a widow, living with Flem, just the two of them in the big house where they claimed she couldn't even hear it thunder, the rest of the folks in Jefferson not

thinking much of it because she was already mixed up in a nigger
Sunday school and they said she was mixed up in something called
commonists, that her husband had belonged to and that in fact they
were both fighting on the commonist side in that war.

Flem was getting along now. They both were. When he got out in
1948 he and Flem would both be old men. Flem might not even be
alive for him to get out for in 1948 and he himself might not even
be alive to get out in 1948 and he could remember how at one time
that too had driven him mad: that Flem might die, either naturally or
maybe this time the other man wouldn't be second class and doomed
to fail and be caught, and it would seem to him that he couldn't bear
it: who hadn't asked for justice since justice was only for the best, for
champions, but at least a man might expect a chance, anybody had a
right to a chance. But that was gone too now, into, beneath the simple waiting; in 1948 he and Flem both would be old men and he even
said aloud: "What a shame we cant both of us jest come out two old
men setting peaceful in the sun or the shade, waiting to die together,
not even thinking no more of hurt or harm or getting even, not even
remembering no more about hurt or harm or anguish or revenge,"—
two old men not only incapable of further harm to anybody but even
incapable of remembering hurt or harm, as if whatever necessary
amount of the money which Flem no longer needed and soon now
would not need at all ever again, could be used to blot, efface, obliterate those forty years which he, Mink, no longer needed now and
soon also, himself too, would not even miss. *But I reckon not* he
thought. *Cant neither of us help nothing now. Cant neither one of us take
nothing back.*

So again he had only five more years and he would be free. And
this time he had learned the lesson which the fool young lawyer had
tried to teach him thirty-five years ago. There were eleven of them.
They worked and ate and slept as a gang, a unit, living in a detached
wire-canvas-and-plank hut (it was summer); shackled to the same
chain they went to the mess hall to eat, then to the field to work and,
chained again, back to the hut to sleep again. So when the escape was
planned, the other ten had to take him into their plot to prevent his
giving it away by simple accident. They didn't want to take him in;
two of them were never converted to the idea. Because ever since his

own abortive attempt eighteen or twenty years ago he had been known as a sort of self-ordained priest of the doctrine of non-escape.

So when they finally told him simply because he would have to be in the secret to protect it, whether he joined them or not, the moment he said, cried, "No! Here now, wait! Wait! Dont you see, if any of us tries to get out they'll come down on all of us and wont none of us ever get free even when our forty years is up," he knew he had already talked too much. So when he said to himself, "Now I got to get out of this chain and get away from them," he did not mean *Because if dark catches me alone in this room with them and no guard handy, I'll never see light again* but simply *I got to get to the Warden in time, before they try it maybe tonight even and wreck ever body.*

And even he would have to wait for the very darkness he feared, until the lights were out and they were all supposed to have settled down for sleep, so that his murderers would make their move, since only during or because of the uproar of the attack on him could he hope to get the warning, his message, to a guard and be believed. Which meant he would have to match guile with guile: to lie rigid on his cot until they set up the mock snoring which was to lull him off guard, himself tense and motionless and holding his own breath to distinguish in time through the snoring whatever sound would herald the plunging knife (or stick or whatever it would be) in time to roll, fling himself off the cot and in one more convulsive roll underneath it, as the men—he could not tell how many since the spurious loud snoring had if anything increased—hurled themselves onto the vacancy where a split second before he had been lying.

"Grab him," one hissed, panted. "Who's got the knife?" Then another:

"I've got the knife. Where in hell is he?" Because he—Mink—had not even paused; another convulsive roll and he was out from under the cot, on all-fours among the thrashing legs, scrabbling, scuttling to get as far away from the cot as he could. The whole room was now in a sort of sotto-voce uproar. "We got to have a light," a voice muttered. "Just a second of light." Suddenly he was free, clear; he could stand up. He screamed, shouted: no word, cry: just a loud human sound; at once the voice muttered, panted: "There. Grab him," but he had already sprung, leaped, to carom from invisible body to body, shouting, bellowing steadily even after he realised he could see, the air beyond the canvas walls not only full of searchlights but the siren too, himself surrounded, enclosed by the furious silent faces which seemed to dart like fish in then out of the shoulder-high light which came in over the plank half-walls, through the wire mesh; he even saw the knife gleam once above him as he plunged, hurling himself among the surging legs, trying to get back under a cot, any cot, anything to intervene before the knife. But it was too late, they could also see him now. He vanished beneath them all. But it was too late for them too: the glaring and probing of all the searchlights, the noise of the siren itself, seemed to concentrate downward upon, into the flimsy ramshackle cubicle filled with cursing men. Then the guards were among them, clubbing at heads with pistols and shotgun barrels, dragging them off until he lay exposed, once more battered and bleeding but this time still conscious. He had even managed one last convulsive wrench and twist so that the knife which should have pinned him to it merely quivered in the floor beside his throat.

"Hit was close," he told the guard. "But looks like we made hit."

But not quite. He was in the infirmary again and didn't hear until afterward how on the very next night two of them—Stillwell, a gambler who had cut the throat of a Vicksburg prostitute (he had owned the knife), and another, who had been the two who had held out against taking him into the plot at all but advocated instead killing him at once—made the attempt anyway though only Stillwell escaped, the other having most of his head blown off by a guard's shotgun blast.

Then he was in the Warden's office again. This time he had needed little bandaging and no stitches at all; they had not had time enough, and no weapons save their feet and fists except Stillwell's knife. "It was Stillwell that had the knife, wasn't it?" the Warden said.

He couldn't have said why he didn't tell. "I never seen who had it," he answered. "I reckon hit all happened too quick."

"That's what Stillwell seems to think," the Warden said. He took from his desk a slitted envelope and a sheet of cheap ruled paper, folded once or twice. "This came this morning. But that's right: you cant read writing, can you?"

"No," he said. The Warden unfolded the sheet.

"It was mailed yesterday in Texarkana. It says, 'He's going to have to explain Jake Barron' " (he was the other convict, whom the guard had killed) " 'to somebody someday so take good care of him. Maybe you better take good care of him anyway since there are some of us still inside.' " The Warden folded the letter back into the envelope and put it back into the drawer and closed the drawer. "So there you are. I cant let you go around loose inside here, where any of them can get at you. You've only got five more years; even though you didn't stop all of them, probably on a recommendation from me, the Governor would let you out tomorrow. But I cant do that because Stillwell will kill you."

"If Cap'm Jabbo" (the guard who shot) "had jest killed Stillwell too, I could go home tomorrow?" he said. "Couldn't you trace out where he's at by the letter, and send Cap'm Jabbo wherever that is?"

"You want the same man to kill Stillwell that kept Stillwell from killing you two nights ago?"

"Send somebody else then. It don't seem fair for him to get away when I got to stay here five more years." Then he said, "But hit's all right. Maybe we did have at least one champion here, after all."

"Champion?" the Warden said. "One what here?" But he didn't answer that. And now for the first time he began to count off the days and months. He had never done this before, not with that original twenty years they had given him at the start back there in Jefferson, nor even with the second twenty years they had added onto it after he let Montgomery Ward persuade him into that woman's mother hubbard and sunbonnet. Because nobody was to blame for that but himself; when he thought of Flem in connection with it, it was with a grudging admiration, almost pride that they were of the same blood; he would think, say aloud, without envy even: "That Flem Snopes. You cant beat him. There aint a man in Missippi nor the U.S. and A. both put together that can beat Flem Snopes."

But this was different. He had tried himself to escape and had failed and had accepted the added twenty years of penalty without protest; he had spent fifteen of them not only never trying to escape again himself, but he had risked his life to foil ten others who planned to: as his reward for which he would have been freed the next day, only a trained guard with a shotgun in his hands let one of the ten plotters get free. So these last five years did not belong to him at all. He had discharged his forty years in good faith; it was not his fault that they actually added up to only thirty-five, and these five extra ones had been compounded onto him by a vicious, even a horseplayish, gratuitor.

That Christmas his (now: for the first time) slowly diminishing sentence began to be marked off for him. It was a Christmas card, postmarked in Mexico, addressed to him in care of the Warden, who read it to him; they both knew who it was from: "Four years now. Not as far as you think." On Valentine's Day it was homemade: the coarse ruled paper bearing, drawn apparently with a carpenter's or a lumberman's red crayon, a crude heart into which a revolver was firing. "You see?" the Warden said. "Even if your five years were up . . ."

"It aint five now," he said. "Hit's four years and six months and nineteen days. You mean, even then you wont let me out?"

"And have you killed before you could even get home?"

"Send out and ketch him."

"Send where?" the Warden said. "Suppose you were outside and didn't want to come back and knew I wanted to get you back. Where would I send to catch you?"

"Yes," he said. "So there jest aint nothing no human man can do."

"Yes," the Warden said. "Give him time and he will do something else the police somewhere will catch him for."

"Time," he said. "Suppose a man aint got time jest to depend on time."

"At least you have got your four years and six months and nineteen days before you have to worry about it."

"Yes," he said. "He'll have that much time to work in."

Then Christmas again, another card with the Mexican postmark: "Three years now. Not near as far as you think." He stood there, fragile and small and durable in the barred overalls, his face lowered a little, peaceful. "Still Mexico, I notice," he said. "Maybe He will kill him there."

"What?" the Warden said. "What did you say?"

He didn't answer. He just stood there, peaceful, musing, serene.

Then he said: "Before I had that-ere cow trouble with Jack Houston, when I was still a boy, I used to go to church ever Sunday and Wednesday prayer meeting too with the lady that raised me until I—"

"Who were they?" the Warden said. "You said your mother died."

"He was a son of a bitch. She wasn't no kin a-tall. She was jest his wife.—ever Sunday until I—"

"Was his name Snopes?" the Warden said.

"He was my paw.—until I got big enough to burn out on God like you do when you think you are already growed up and dont need nothing from nobody. Then when you told me how by keeping nine of them ten fellers from breaking out I didn't jest add five more years to my time, I fixed it so you wasn't going to let me out a-tall, I taken it back."

"Took what back?" the Warden said. "Back from who?"

"I taken it back from God."

"You mean you've rejoined the church since that night two years ago? No you haven't. You've never been inside the chapel since you came here back in 1908." Which was true. Though the present Warden and his predecessor had not really been surprised at that. What they had expected him to gravitate to was one of the small violent irreconcilable nonconformist non-everything and -everybody else which existed along with the regular prison religious establishment in probably all Southern rural penitentiaries—small fierce cliques and groups (this one called themselves Jehovah's Shareholders) headed by self-ordained leaders who had reached prison through a curiously consistent pattern: by the conviction of crimes peculiar to the middle class, to respectability, originating in domesticity or anyway uxoriousness: bigamy, rifling the sect's funds for a woman: his wife or someone else's or, in an occasional desperate case, a professional prostitute.

"I didn't need no church," he said. "I done it in confidence."

"In confidence?" the Warden said.

"Yes," he said, almost impatiently. "You dont need to write God a letter. He has done already seen inside you long before He would even need to bother to read it. Because a man will learn a little sense in time even outside. But he learns it quick in here. That when a

Judgment powerful enough to help you, will help you if all you got to do is jest take back and accept it, you are a fool not to."

"So He will take care of Stillwell for you," the Warden said.

"Why not? What's He got against me?"

"Thou shalt not kill," the Warden said.

"Why didn't He tell Houston that? I never went all the way in to Jefferson to have to sleep on a bench in the depot jest to try to buy them shells, until Houston made me."

"Well I'll be damned," the Warden said. "I will be eternally damned. You'll be out of here in three more years anyway but if I had my way you'd be out of here now, today, before whatever the hell it is that makes you tick starts looking cross-eyed at me. I dont want to spend the rest of my life even thinking somebody is thinking the kind of hopes about me you wish about folks that get in your way. Go on now. Get back to work."

So when it was only October, no holiday valentine or Christmas card month that he knew of, when the Warden sent for him, he was not even surprised. The Warden sat looking at him for maybe half a minute, with something not just aghast but almost respectful in the look, then said: "I will be damned." It was a telegram this time. "It's from the Chief of Police in San Diego, California. There was a church in the Mexican quarter. They had stopped using it as a church, had a new one or something. Anyway it had been deconsecrated, so what went on inside it since, even the police haven't quite caught up with yet. Last week it fell down. They dont know why: it just fell down all of a sudden. They found a man in it—what was left of him. This is what the telegram says: 'Fingerprints F.B.I. identification your man Number 08213 Shuford H. Stillwell.' " The Warden folded the telegram back into the envelope and put it back into the drawer. "Tell me again about that church you said you used to go to before Houston made you kill him."

He didn't answer that at all. He just drew a long breath and exhaled it. "I can go now," he said. "I can be free."

"Not right this minute," the Warden said. "It will take a month or two. The petition will have to be got up and sent to the Governor. Then he will ask for my recommendation. Then he will sign the pardon."

"The petition?" he said.

"You got in here by law," the Warden said. "You'll have to get out by law."

"A petition," he said.

"That your family will have a lawyer draw up, asking the Governor to issue a pardon. Your wife—but that's right, she's dead. One of your daughters then."

"Likely they done married away too by now."

"All right," the Warden said. Then he said, "Hell, man, you're already good as out. Your cousin, whatever he is, right there in Jackson now in the legislature—Egglestone Snopes, that got beat for Congress two years ago?"

He didn't move, his head bent a little; he said, "Then I reckon I'll stay here after all." Because how could he tell a stranger: *Clarence, my own oldest brother's grandson, is in politics that depends on votes. When I leave here I wont have no vote. What will I have to buy Clarence Snopes's name on my paper?* Which just left Eck's boy, Wallstreet, whom nobody yet had ever told what to do. "I reckon I'll be with you them other three years too," he said.

"Write your sheriff yourself," the Warden said. "I'll write the letter for you."

"Hub Hampton that sent me here is dead."

"You've still got a sheriff, haven't you? What's the matter with you? Have forty years in here scared you for good of fresh air and sunshine?"

"Thirty-eight years this coming summer," he said.

"All right. Thirty-eight. How old are you?"

"I was born in eighty-three," he said.

"So you've been here ever since you were twenty-five years old."

"I dont know. I never counted."

"All right," the Warden said. "Beat it. When you say the word I'll write a letter to your sheriff."

"I reckon I'll stay," he said. But he was wrong. Five months later the petition lay on the Warden's desk.

"Who is Linda Snopes Kohl?" the Warden said.

He stood completely still for quite a long time. "Her paw's a rich banker in Jefferson. His and my grandpaw had two sets of chillen."

"She was the member of your family that signed the petition to the Governor to let you out."

"You mean the sheriff sent for her to come and sign it?"

"How could he? You wouldn't let me write the sheriff."

"Yes," he said. He looked down at the paper which he could not read. It was upside down to him, though that meant nothing either. "Show me where the ones signed to not let me out"

"What?" the Warden said.

"The ones that dont want me out."

"Oh, you mean Houston's family. No, the only other names on it are the District Attorney who sent you here and your Sheriff, Hubert Hampton, Junior, and V. K. Ratliff. Is he a Houston?"

"No," he said. He drew the slow deep breath again. "So I'm free."

"With one thing more," the Warden said. "Your luck's not even holding: it's doubling." But he handled that too the next morning after they gave him a pair of shoes, a shirt, overalls and jumper and a hat, all brand new, and a ten-dollar bill and the three dollars and eighty-five cents which were still left from the forty dollars Flem had sent him eighteen years ago, and the Warden said, "There's a deputy here today with a prisoner from Greenville. He's going back tonight. For a dollar he'll drop you off right at the end of the bridge to Arkansas, if you want to go that way."

"Much obliged," he said. "I'm going by Memphis first. I got some business to tend to there."

It would probably take all of the thirteen dollars and eighty-five cents to buy a pistol even in a Memphis pawn shop. He had planned to beat his way to Memphis on a freight train, riding the rods underneath a boxcar or between two of them, as he had once or twice as a boy and a youth. But as soon as he was outside the gate, he discovered that he was afraid to. He had been shut too long, he had forgotten how; his muscles might have lost the agility and co-ordination, the simple bold quick temerity for physical risk. Then he thought of watching his chance to scramble safely into an empty car and found that he didn't dare that either, that in thirty-eight years he might even have forgotten the unspoken rules of the freemasonry of petty lawbreaking without knowing it until too late.

So he stood beside the paved highway which, when his foot

touched it last thirty-eight years ago, had not even been gravel but instead was dirt marked only by the prints of mules and the iron tires of wagons; now it looked and felt as smooth and hard as a floor, what time you could see it or risk feeling it either for the cars and trucks rushing past on it. In the old days any passing wagon would have stopped to no more than his raised hand. But these were not wagons so he didn't know what the new regulations for this might be either; in fact if he had known anything else to do but this he would already be doing it instead of standing, frail and harmless and not much larger than a child in the new overalls and jumper still showing their off-the-shelf creases and the new shoes and the hat, until the truck slowed in toward him and stopped and the driver said, "How far you going, dad?"

"Memphis," he said.

"I'm going to Clarksdale. You can hook another ride from there. As good as you can here, anyway."

It was fall, almost October, and he discovered that here was something else he had forgotten about during the thirty-eight years: seasons. They came and went in the penitentiary too but for thirty-eight years the only right he had to them was the privilege of suffering because of them: from the heat and sun of summer whether he wanted to work in the heat of the day or not, and the rain and ice-like mud of winter whether he wanted to be out in it or not. But now they belonged to him again: October next week, not much to see in this flat Delta country which he had misdoubted the first time he laid eyes on it from the train window that day thirty-eight years ago: just cotton stalks and cypress needles. But back home in the hills, all the land would be gold and crimson with hickory and gum and oak and maple, and the old fields warm with sage and splattered with scarlet sumac; in thirty-eight years he had forgotten that.

When suddenly, somewhere deep in memory, there was a tree, a single tree. His mother was dead; he couldn't remember her nor even how old he was when his father married again. So the woman wasn't even kin to him and she never let him forget it: that she was raising him not from any tie or claim and not because he was weak and helpless and a human being, but because she was a Christian. Yet there was more than that behind it. He knew that at once—a gaunt harried slattern of a woman whom he remembered always either with a black eye or holding a dirty rag to her bleeding where her husband had struck her. Because he could always depend on her, not to do anything for him because she always failed there, but for constancy, to be always there and always aware of him, surrounding him always with that shield which actually protected, defended him from nothing but on the contrary seemed actually to invite more pain and grief. But simply to be there, lachrymose, harassed, yet constant.

She was still in bed, it was midmorning; she should have been hours since immolated into the ceaseless drudgery which composed her days. She was never ill, so it must have been the man had beat her this time even harder than he knew, lying there in the bed talking about food—the fatback, the coarse meal, the molasses which as far as he knew was the only food all people ate except when they could catch or kill something else; evidently this new blow had been somewhere about her stomach. "I cant eat hit," she whimpered. "I need to relish something else. Maybe a squirrel." He knew now; that was the tree. He had to steal the shotgun: his father would have beat him within an inch of his life—to lug the clumsy weapon even taller than he was, into the woods, to the tree, the hickory, to ambush himself beneath it and crouch, waiting, in the drowsy splendor of the October afternoon, until the little creature appeared. Whereupon he began to tremble (he had but the one shell) and he remembered that too: the tremendous effort to raise the heavy gun long enough, panting against the stock, "Please God please God," into the shock of the recoil and the reek of the black powder until he could drop the gun and run and pick up the still warm small furred body with hands that trembled and shook until he could barely hold it. And her hands trembling too as she fondled the carcass. "We'll dress hit and cook hit now," she said. "We'll relish hit together right now." The hickory itself was of course gone now, chopped into firewood or wagon spokes or single trees years ago; perhaps the very place where it had stood was eradicated now into plowed land—or so they thought who had felled and destroyed it probably. But he knew better: unaxed in memory and unaxeable, inviolable and immune, golden and splendid with October. *Why yes* he thought *it*

*aint a place a man wants to go back to; the place dont even need to be there
no more. What aches a man to go back to is what he remembers.*

Suddenly he craned his neck to see out the window. "Hit looks
like—" and stopped. But he was free; let all the earth know where
he had been for thirty-eight years. "—Parchman," he said.

"Yep," the driver said. "P.O.W. camp."

"What?" he said.

"Prisoners from the war."

"From the war?"

"Where you been the last five years, dad?" the driver said.
"Asleep?"

"I been away," he said. "I mind one war they fit with the Spaniards
when I was a boy, and there was another with the Germans after that
one. Who did they fight this time?"

"Everybody." The driver cursed. "Germans, Japanese, Congress
too. Then they quit. If they had let us lick the Russians too, we might
a been all right. But they just licked the Krauts and Japs and then
decided to choke everybody else to death with money."

He thought *Money.* He said: "If you had twenty-five dollars and
found thirty-eight more, how much would you have?"

"What?" the driver said. "I wouldn't even stop to pick up just
thirty-eight dollars. What the hell you asking me? You mean you got
sixty-three dollars and cant find nothing to do with it?"

Sixty-three he thought. *So that's how old I am.* He thought quietly
Not justice; I never asked that; jest fairness, that's all. That was all; not
to have anything for him: just not to have anything against him. That
was all he wanted, and sure enough, here it was.

LINDA

SIX

V. K. RATLIFF

Ｙou aint even going to meet the train?" Chick says. Lawyer never
even looked up, setting there at the desk with his attention (his nose
anyway) buried in the papers in front of him like there wasn't nobody
else in the room. "Not just a new girl coming to town," Chick says,
"but a wounded female war veteran. Well, maybe not a new girl," he
says. "Maybe that's the wrong word. In fact maybe 'new' is the wrong
word all the way round. Not a new girl in Jefferson, because she was
born and raised here. And even if she was a new girl in Jefferson or
new anywhere else once, that would be just once because no matter
how new you might have been anywhere once, you wouldn't be very
new anywhere any more after you went to Spain with a Greenwich
Village poet to fight Hitler. That is, not after the kind of Greenwich
Village poet that would get you both blown up by a shell anyhow.
That is, provided you were a girl. So just say, not only an old girl that
used to be new, coming back to Jefferson, but the first girl old or new
either that Jefferson ever had to come home wounded from a war.
Men soldiers yes, of course yes. But this is the first female girl soldier
we ever had, not to mention one actually wounded by the enemy.
Naturally we dont include rape for the main reason that we aint talking about rape." Still his uncle didn't move. "I'd think you'd have
the whole town down there at the depot to meet her. Out of simple
sympathetic interest, not to mention pity: a girl that went all the way
to Spain to a war and the best she got out of it was to lose her husband and have both eardrums busted by a shell. Mrs Cole," he says.

Nor did Lawyer look up even then. "Kohl," he says.

"That's what I said," Chick says. "Mrs Cole."

This time Lawyer spelled it. "K-o-h-l," he says. But even before
he spelled it, it had a different sound from the way Chick said it. "He

777

was a sculptor, not a poet. The shell didn't kill him. It was an aero-plane."

"Oh well, no wonder, if he was just a sculptor," Chick says. "Nat-urally a sculptor wouldn't have the footwork to dodge machine-gun bullets like a poet. A sculptor would have to stay in one place too much of his time. Besides, maybe it wasn't Saturday so he didn't have his hat on."

"He was in the aeroplane," Lawyer says. "It was shot down. It crashed and burned."

"What?" Chick says. "A Greenwich Village sculptor named K-o-h-l actually in an aeroplane where it could get shot down by an enemy?" He was looking more or less at the top of his uncle's head. "Not Cole," he says: "K-o-h-l. I wonder why he didn't change it. Dont they, usually?"

Now Lawyer closed the papers without no haste a-tall and laid them on the desk and pushed the swivel chair back and set back in it and clasped his hands behind his head. His hair had done already started turning gray when he come back from the war in France in 1919. Now it was pretty near completely white, and him setting there relaxed and easy in the chair with that white mop of it and the little gold key he got when he was at Harvard on his watch chain and one of the cob pipes stuck upside down in his shirt pocket like it was a pencil or a toothpick, looking at Chick for about a half a minute. "You didn't find that at Harvard," he says. "I thought that maybe after two years in Cambridge, you might not even recognise it again when you came back to Mississippi."

"All right," Chick says. "I'm sorry." But Lawyer just sat there easy in the chair, looking at him. "Damn it," Chick says, "I said I'm sorry."

"Only you're not sorry yet," Lawyer says. "You're just ashamed."

"Aint it the same thing?" Chick says.

"No," Lawyer says. "When you are just ashamed of something, you dont hate it. You just hate getting caught."

"Well, you caught me," Chick says. "I am ashamed. What more do you want?" Only Lawyer didn't even need to answer that. "Maybe I cant help it yet, even after two years at Harvard," Chick says. "Maybe I just lived too long a time among what us Mississippi folks call white people before I went there. You cant be ashamed of me for what I didn't know in time, can you?"

"I'm not ashamed of you about anything," Lawyer says.

"All right," Chick says. "Sorry, then."

"I'm not sorry over you about anything either," Lawyer says.

"Then what the hell is all this about?" Chick says.

So a stranger that never happened to be living in Jefferson or Yoknapatawpha County ten or twelve years ago might have thought it was Chick that was the interested party. Not only interested enough to be jealous of his uncle, but interested enough to already be jealous even when the subject or bone of contention not only hadn't even got back home yet, he wouldn't even seen her since ten years ago. Which would make him jealous not only over a gal he hadn't even seen in ten years, but that he wasn't but twelve or thirteen years old and she was already nineteen, a growed woman, when he seen her that last time—a insurmountable barrier of difference in age that would still been a barrier even with three or four more years added onto both of them, providing of course it was the gal that still had the biggest number of them. In fact you would think how a boy jest twelve or thirteen years old couldn't be man-jealous yet; wouldn't have enough fuel yet to fire jealousy and keep it burning very long or even a-tall over a gal nineteen years old or any other age between eight and eighty for that matter, except that how young does he have to be before he can dare to risk not having that fuel capable of taking fire and combusting? Jest how young must he be to be safe for a little while longer yet, as the feller says, from having his heart strangled as good as any other man by that one strand of Lilith's hair? Or how old either, for the matter of that. Besides, this time when she come back, even though she would still be the same six or seven years older, this time they would be jest six or seven years older than twenty-two or twenty-three instead of six or seven years older than twelve or thirteen, and that aint no barrier a-tall. This time he wouldn't be no innocent infantile bystanding victim of that loop because this time he would be in there fighting for the right and privilege of being lassoed; fighting not jest for the right and privilege of being strangled too, but of being strangled first.

Which was exactly what he looked like he was trying to do: nudg-

ing and whetting at his uncle, reaching around for whatever stick or
club or brickbat come to his hand like he was still jest twelve or thirteen years old or even less than that, grabbing up that one about
Linda's husband being a Jew for instance, because even at jest twelve,
if he had stopped long enough to think, he would a knowed that that
wouldn't even be a good solid straw as far as his present opponent
or rival was concerned.

Maybe that—swinging that straw at his uncle about how Lawyer
had been the main one instrumental in getting Linda up there in
New York where couldn't no homefolks look after her and so sho
enough she had went and married a Jew—was what give Chick away.
Because he aint even seen her again yet; he couldn't a knowed all that
other yet. I mean, knowed that even at jest twelve he already had all
the jealousy he would ever need at twenty-two or eighty-two either.
He would need to actively see her again to find out he had jest as
much right as any other man in it to be strangled to death by this
here new gal coming to town, and wasn't no man wearing hair going
to interfere in the way and save him. When he thought about her
now, he would have to remember jest what that twelve- or thirteen-
year-old boy had seen: not a gal but a woman growed, the same general size and shape of his own maw, belonging to and moving around
in the same alien human race the rest of the world except twelve-
year-old boys belonged to. And, if it hadn't been for his uncle finally
stopping long enough hisself to look at her and then you might say
ketching Chick by the scruff of the neck and grinding his attention
onto her by conscripting up half his out-of-school time toting notes
back and forth to her for them after-school ice-cream-parlor dates
her and Lawyer started to having, nowhere near as interesting.

So when Chick remembered her now, he would still have to see
what twelve or thirteen years old had seen: *Hell fire, she's durn nigh
old as maw.* He would have to actively look at her again to see what
twenty-two or twenty-three would see: *Hell fire, suppose she is a year
or two older than me, jest so it's me that's the man of the two of us.* So you
and that stranger both would a thought how maybe it taken a boy of
twelve or thirteen; maybe only a boy of twelve or thirteen is capable
of pure and undefiled, what you might call virgin, jealousy toward a
man of thirty over a gal of nineteen—or of any other age between

eight and eighty for that matter, jest as it takes a boy of twelve or thirteen to know the true anguish and passion and hope and despair of
love; you and that stranger both thinking that right up to that last final
moment when Chick give his-self away free-for-nothing by grabbing
up that one about Linda's husband being not only a poet but a Jew too
to hit at his uncle with. Then even that stranger would a realised
Chick wasn't throwing it at Linda a-tall: he was throwing it at his
uncle; that it wasn't his uncle he was jealous of over Linda Snopes:
he was jealous of Linda over his uncle. Then even that stranger would
a had to say to Chick in his mind: *Maybe you couldn't persuade me onto
your side at first, but we're sholy in the same agreement now.*

Leastways if that stranger had talked to me a little. Because I could
remember, I was actively watching it, that time back there when
Lawyer first got involved into Linda's career as the feller says. I dont
mean when Lawyer thought her career got mixed up into hisn, nor
even when he first thought he actively noticed her. Because she was
already twelve or thirteen herself then and so Lawyer had already
knowed her all her life or anyway since she was them one or two
years old or whenever it is when hit's folks begin to bring it out into
the street in a baby buggy or toting it and you first notice how it not
only is beginning to look like a human being, hit even begins to look
a little like some specific family of folks you are acquainted with. And
in a little town like Jefferson where not only ever body knows ever
body else but ever body has got to see ever body else in town at least
once in the twenty-four hours whether he wants to or not, except
for the time Lawyer was away at the war likely he had to see her at
least once a week. Not to mention having to know even before he
could recognise her to remember, that she was Eula Varner's daughter that all Jefferson and Yoknapatawpha County both that had ever
seen Eula Varner first, couldn't help but look at Eula Varner's child
with a kind of amazement, like at some minute-sized monster, since
anybody, any man anyhow, that ever looked at Eula once couldn't
help but believe that all that much woman in jest one simple normal-
sized chunk couldn't a possibly been fertilised by anything as frail and
puny in comparison as jest one single man, that it would a taken that
whole generation of young concentrated men to seeded them, as the
feller says, splendid—no: he would a said magnificent—loins.

And I dont mean when Lawyer voluntarily went outen his way and adopted Linda's career into a few spare extra years of hisn like he thought he was doing. What I mean is, when Eula Varner taken that first one look of hern at Lawyer—or let him take that first one look of hisn at her, whichever way you want to put it—and adopted the rest of his life into that of whatever first child she happened to have, providing of course it's a gal. Like when you finally see the woman that had ought to been yourn all the time, only it's already too late. The woman that ought to been sixteen maybe at this moment and you not more than nineteen (which at that moment when he first seen Eula Lawyer actively was; it was Eula that was out of focus, being as she was already a year older than Lawyer to start with) and you look at her that first one time and in the next moment says to her: "You're beautiful. I love you. Let's dont never part again," and she says, "Yes, of course"—no more concerned than that: "Of course I am. Of course you do. Of course we wont." Only it's already too late. She is already married to somebody else. Except it wasn't too late. It aint never too late and wont never be, providing, no matter how old you are, you still are that-ere nineteen-year-old boy that said that to that sixteen-year-old gal at that one particular moment outen all the moments you might ever call yourn. Because how can it ever be too late to that nineteen-year-old boy, because how can that sixteen-year-old gal you had to say that to ever be violated, it dont matter how many husbands she might a had in the meantime, providing she actively was the one that had to say "Of course" right back at you? And even when she is toting the active proof of that violation around in her belly or even right out in plain sight on her arm or dragging at the tail of her skirt, immolating hit and her both back into virginity wouldn't be no trick a-tall to that nineteen-year-old boy, since naturally that sixteen-year-old gal couldn't possibly be fertilised by no other seed except hisn, I dont care who would like to brag his-self as being the active instrument.

Except that Lawyer didn't know all that yet neither. Mainly because he was too busy. I mean, that day when Eula first walked through the Jefferson Square where not jest Lawyer but all Jefferson too would have to see her. That time back there when Flem had finally grazed up Uncle Billy Varner and Frenchman's Bend and so he would have to move on somewhere, and Jefferson was as good a place as any since, as the feller says, any spoke leads sooner or later to the rim. Or in fact maybe Jefferson was for the moment unavoidable, being as Flem had done beat me outen my half of that café me and Grover Winbush owned, and since there wasn't no easy quick practical way to get Grover out to Frenchman's Bend, Flem would simply have to make a stopover at least in Jefferson while he evicted Grover outen the rest of it.

Anyhow, Lawyer seen her at last. And there he was, entering not jest bare-handed but practically nekkid too, that engagement that he couldn't afford to do anything but lose it—Lawyer, a town-raised bachelor that was going to need a Master of Arts from Harvard and a Doctor of Philosophy from Heidelberg jest to stiffen him up to where he could cope with the natural normal Yoknapatawpha County folks that never wanted nothing except jest to break a few aggravating laws that was in their way or get a little free money outen the county treasury; and Eula Varner that never needed to be educated nowhere because jest what the Lord had already give her by letting her stand up and breathe and maybe walk around a little now and then was trouble and danger enough for ever male man in range. For Lawyer to win that match would be like them spiders, that the end of the honeymoon is when she finally finishes eating up his last drumstick. Which likely enough Lawyer knowed too, being nineteen years old and already one year at Harvard. Though even without Harvard, a boy nineteen years old ought to know that much about women jest by instinct, like a child or a animal knows fire is hot without having to actively put his hand or his foot in it. Even when a nineteen-year-old boy says "You're beautiful and I love you," even he ought to know whether it's a sixteen-year-old gal or a tiger that says "Certainly" back at him.

Anyhow, there Lawyer was, rushing headlong into that engagement that not only the best he could expect and hope for but the best he could want would be to lose it, since losing it wouldn't do nothing but jest knock off some of his hide here and there. Rushing in with nothing in his hand to fight with but that capacity to stay nineteen years old the rest of his life, to take on that McCarron boy that had not only cuckolded him before he ever seen Eula, but that was going to keep on cuckolding him in one or another different name and shape even after he would finally give up. Because maybe Flem never had no reason to pick out Jefferson to come to; maybe one spoke was jest the same as another to him since all he wanted was a rim. Or maybe he jest didn't know he had a reason for Jefferson. Or maybe married men dont even need reasons, being as they already got wives. Or maybe it's women that dont need reasons, for the simple reason that they never heard of a reason and wouldn't recognise it face to face, since they dont function from reasons but from necessities that couldn't nobody help nohow and that dont nobody but a fool man want to help in the second place, because he dont know no better; it aint women, it's men that takes ignorance seriously, getting into a skeer over something for no more reason than that they dont happen to know what it is.

So it wasn't Grover Winbush and what you might call that dangling other half of mine and his café that brought Miz Flem Snopes to Jefferson so she could walk across the Square whatever that afternoon was when Lawyer had to look at her. It wasn't even Eula herself. It was that McCarron boy. And I seen some of that too and heard about all the rest of it. Because that was about all folks within five miles of Varner's store talked about that spring. The full unchallenged cynosure you might say of the whole Frenchman's Bend section, from sometime in March to the concluding dee-neweyment or meelee which taken place jest beyond the creek bridge below Varner's house one night in the following July—that McCarron boy coming in to Frenchman's Bend that day without warning out of nowhere like a cattymount into a sheep pen among them Bookwrights and Binfords and Quicks and Tulls that for about a year now had been hitching their buggies and saddle mules to Will Varner's fence. Like a wild buck from the woods jumping the patch fence and already tromplng them tame domestic local carrots and squashes and eggplants that until that moment was thinking or leastways hoping that Eula's maiden citadel was actively being threatened and endangered, before they could even blench, let alone cover their heads. Likely—in fact, they had done a little local bragging to that effect—they called theirselves pretty unbitted too, until he come along that day, coming from nowhere jest exactly like a wild buck from the woods, like he had done located Eula from miles and even days away outen the hard unerring air itself and come as straight as a die to where she was waiting, not for him especially but maybe for jest any wild strong buck that was wild and strong enough to deserve and match her.

Yes sir. As the feller says, the big buck: the wild buck right off the mountain itself, with his tail already up and his eyes already flashing. Because them Bookwrights and Quicks and Tulls was pretty fair bucks theirselves, on that-ere home Frenchman's Bend range and reservation you might say, providing them outside boundary limits posted signs wasn't violated by these here footloose rambling uninvited strangers. In fact, they was pretty good at kicking and gouging and no holts barred and no bad feelings afterward, in all innocent friendliness and companionship not jest among one another but with that same friendly willingness to give and take when it was necessary to confederate up and learn him a lesson on some foreigner from four or five or six miles away that ought to stayed at home, had no business there, neither needed nor wanted, that had happened to see Eula somewhere once or maybe jest heard about her from somebody else that had watched her walk ten or fifteen feet. So he had to come crowding his buggy or mule up to Varner's picket fence some Sunday night, then coming innocently back down the road toward the gum and cypress thicket where the road crossed the creek bridge, his head still filled with female Varner dreams until the unified corporation stepped outen the thicket and bushwhacked them outen it and throwed creek water on him and put him back in the buggy or on the mule and wrapped the lines around the whipstock or the horn and headed him on toward wherever it was he lived and if he'd a had any sense he wouldn't a left it in the first place or at least in this direction.

But this here new one was a different animal. Because they— including them occasional volunteers—was jest bucks in the general—or maybe it's the universal—Frenchman's Bend pattern, while McCarron wasn't in nobody's pattern; he was unbitted not because he was afraid of a bit but simply because so fur he didn't prefer to be. So there not only wasn't nere a one of them would stand up to him alone, the whole unified confederated passel of them, that never hesitated one second to hide in that thicket against any other interloper that come sniffing at Varner's fence, never nerved theirselves up to him until it was already too late. Oh sho, they had chances. They had plenty of chances. In fact, he give them so many chances that by the end of May they wouldn't even walk a Frenchman's Bend road after dark, even in sight of one of their own houses, without they was at least three of them. Because this here was a different kind of a buck, coming without warning right off the big mountain itself and doing what Lawyer would call arrogating to his-self what had been the gynecological cynosure of a whole section of north Missippi for going on a year or two now. Not ravishing Eula away: not riding up on his horse and snatching her up behind him and galloping off, but jest simply moving in and dispossessing them; not even evicting them but like he was keeping them on hand for a chorus you might say, or maybe jest for spice, like you keep five or six cellars of salt setting handy while you are eating the watermelon, until it was already too late, until likely as not, as fur as they or Frenchman's Bend either knowed, Eula was already pregnant with Linda.

Except I dont think that was exactly it. I dont think I prefer it to happened that way. I think I prefer it to happened all at once. Or that aint quite right neither. I think what I prefer is, that them five timorous local stallions actively brought about the very exact thing they finally nerved their desperation up to try to prevent. There they all was, poised on the brink you might say of that-ere still intact maiden citadel, all seven of them: Eula and McCarron, and them five Tulls and Bookwrights and Turpins and Binfords and Quicks. Because what them Tulls and Quicks would a called the worst hadn't happened yet. I dont mean the worst in respects to Eula's chastity nor to the violated honor of Uncle Billy Varner's home, but in respects to them two years' investment of buggies and mules tied to the Varner fence when them and the five folks keeping them hitched there half the night both had ought to been home getting a little rest before going back to the field to plow at sunup, instead of having to live in a constantly shifting confederation of whatever four of them happened to believe that the fifth one was out in front in that-ere steeplechase, not to mention the need for all five of them having to gang up at a moment's notice maybe at almost any time on some stray interloper that turned up without warning with his head full of picket fence ideas too.

So I prefer to believe it hadn't happened yet. I dont know what
Eula and McCarron was waiting on. I mean, what McCarron was
waiting on. Eula never done no waiting. Likely she never even
knowed what the word meant, like the ground, dirt, the earth, whatever it is in it that makes seed sprout at the right time, dont know nor
need to know what waiting means. Since to know what waiting
means, you got to be skeered or weak or self-doubtful enough to
know what impatience or hurry means, and Eula never needed them
no more than that dirt does. All she needed was jest to be, like the
ground of the field, until the right time come, the right wind, the
right sun, the right rain; until in fact that-ere single unique big buck
jumped that tame garden fence outen the big woods or the high
mountain or the tall sky, and finally got through jest standing there
among the sheep with his head up, looking proud. So it was McCarron that put off that long what you might call that-ere inevitable.
Maybe that was why: having to jest stand there for a while looking
proud among the sheep. Maybe that was it: maybe he was jest simply having too much fun at first, playing with them Bookwright and
Quick sheep, tantalising them up maybe to see jest how much they
would have to stand to forget for a moment they was sheep, or to
remember that maybe they was sheep but at least there was five of
them, until at last they would risk him jest like he actively wasn't
nothing but jest one more of them natural occupational local hazards
Eula had done already got them accustomed to handling.
    So maybe you can figger what they was waiting on. They was
church folks. I mean, they went to church a heap of Sundays, and
Wednesday night prayer meeting too, unless something else come
up. Because church was as good a place as any to finish up one week
and start another, especially as there wasn't no particular other place
to go on Sunday morning; not to mention a crap game down back
of the spring while the church was busy singing or praying or listening; and who knowed but how on almost any Wednesday night you
might ketch some young gal and persuade her off into the bushes
before her paw or maw noticed she was missing. Or maybe they
never needed to ever heard it, since likely it wasn't even Samson and
Delilah that was the first ones to invent that hair-cutting
eupheemism neither. So the whole idea might be what you would call

a kind of last desperate instinctive hereditary expedient waiting
handy for ever young feller (or old one either) faced with some form
of man-trouble over his gal. So at least you knowed what they was
waiting for. Naturally they would preferred to preserve that-ere
maiden Varner citadel until one of them could manage to shake loose
from the other four by luck or expedient long enough to ravage it.
But now that this uninvited ringer had come in and wrecked ever
thing anyhow, at least they could use that violation and rapine not
only for revenge but to evict him for good from meddling around
Frenchman's Bend.

Naturally not jest laying cravenly back to ketch him at a moment
when he was wore out and exhausted with pleasure and success; they
wasn't that bad. But since they couldn't prevent the victory, at least
ketch him at a moment when he wasn't watching, when his mind was
still fondly distracted and divided between what you might call
bemusements with the recent past, which would a been last night,
and aspirations toward the immediate future, which would be in a
few minutes now as soon as the buggy reached a convenient place to
hitch the horse. Which is what they—the ambushment—done. They
was wrong of course; hadn't nothing happened yet. I mean, I prefer
that even that citadel was still maiden right up to this moment. No:
what I mean is, I wont have nothing else for the simple dramatic ver-
ities except that ever thing happened right there that night and all
at once; that even that McCarron boy, that compared to them other
five was a wild stag surrounded by a gang of goats—that even he
wasn't enough by his-self but that it taken all six of them even to ravage that citadel, let alone seed them loins with a child: that July night
and the buggy coming down the hill until they heard the horse's feet
come off the creek bridge and the five of them, finally nerved up to
even this last desperate gambit, piling outen that familiar bush-
whacking thicket that up to this time had handled them local trespassing rams so simple and easy you wouldn't hardly need to dust
off your hands afterward.

Naturally they never brought no bystanders with them and after
the first two or three minutes there wasn't no witness a-tall left, since
he was already laying out cold in the ditch. So my conjecture is jest as
good as yourn, maybe better since I'm a interested party, being as I

got what the feller calls a theorem to prove. In fact, it may not taken even three minutes, one of them jumping to ketch the horse's head and the other four rushing to snatch McCarron outen the buggy, providing of course he was still in the buggy by that time and not already blazing bushes up the creek, having chosen quick between discretion and valor, it dont matter a hoot who was looking, as had happened before with at least one of the invaders that had been quick enough.

Which, by the trompled evidence folks went to look at the next day, McCarron wasn't, though not for the already precedented reason. Nor did the evidence explain jest what the wagon spoke was doing there neither that broke McCarron's arm: only that McCarron had the wagon spoke now in his remaining hand in the road while Eula was standing up in the buggy with that lead-loaded buggy whip reversed in both hands like a hoe or a axe, swinging the leaded butt of it at whatever head come up next.

Not over three minutes, at the outside. It wouldn't needed more than that. It wouldn't wanted more: it was all that simple and natural—a pure and simple natural circumstance as simple and natural and ungreedy as a tide-wave or a cloudburst, that didn't even want but one swipe—a considerable of trompling and panting and cussing and nothing much to see except a kind of moil of tangled shadows around the horse (It never moved. But then it spent a good part of its life ever summer right in the middle of Will's sawmill and it stood right there in the yard all the time Will was evicting Ab Snopes from a house he hadn't paid no rent on in two years, which was the nearest thing to a cyclone Frenchman's Bend ever seen; it was said that Will could drive up to a depot and get outen the buggy and not even hitch it while a train passed, and only next summer it was going to be tied to the same lot gate that them wild Texas ponies Flem Snopes brought back from Texas demolished right up to the hinges when they run over Frenchman's Bend.) and buggy and the occasional gleam of that hickory wagon spoke interspersed among the mush-melon thumps of that loaded buggy whip handle on them French-man's Bend skulls.

And then jest the empty horse and buggy standing there in the road like the tree or rock or barn or whatever it was the tide-wave or cloudburst has done took its one rightful ungreedy swipe at and went away, and that-ere one remaining evidence—it was Theron Quick; for a week after it you could still see the print of that loaded buggy whip across the back of his skull; not the first time naming him Quick turned out to be what the feller calls jest a humorous allusion—laying cold in the weeds beside the road. And that's when I believe it happened. I dont even insist or argue that it happened that way. I jest simply decline to have it any other way except that one because there aint no acceptable degrees between what has got to be right and what jest can possibly be.

So it never even stopped. I mean, the motion, movement. It was one continuous natural rush from the moment five of them busted outen that thicket and grabbed at the horse, on through the cussing and trompling and hard breathing and the final crashing through the bushes and the last rapid and fading footfall, since likely the other four thought Theron was dead; then jest the peaceful quiet and the dark road and the horse standing quiet in the buggy in the middle of it and Theron Quick sleeping peacefully in the weeds. And that's when I believe it happened: not no cessation a-tall, not even no active pausing; not jest that maiden bastion capitulate and overrun but them loins themselves seeded, that child, that girl, Linda herself created into life right there in the road with likely Eula having to help hold him up offen the broke arm and the horse standing over them among the stars like one of them mounted big-game trophy heads sticking outen the parlor or the liberry or (I believe they call them now) den wall. In fact maybe that's what it was.

So in almost no time there was Will Varner with a pregnant unmarried daughter. I mean, there Frenchman's Bend was because even in them days when you said "Frenchman's Bend" you smiled at Uncle Billy Varner, or vice versa. Because if Eula Varner was a natural phenomenon like a cyclone or a tide-wave, Uncle Billy was one too even if he wasn't no more than forty yet: that had shaved notes and foreclosed liens and padded furnish bills and evicted tenants until the way Will Varner went Frenchman's Bend had done already left and the folks that composed it had damn sho better hang on and go too, unless they jest wanted to settle down in vacant space twenty-two miles southeast of Jefferson.

Naturally the McCarron boy was the man to handle the Varner family honor right there on the spot. After the first shock, folks all thought that's what he had aimed to do. He was the only child of a well-to-do widowed maw up in Tennessee somewhere until he happened to be wherever it was his fate arranged for him to have his look at Eula Varner like theirn would do for Lawyer Stevens and Manfred de Spain about a year later. And, being the only child of a well-to-do maw and only educated in one of them fancy gentleman's schools, you would naturally expect him to lit out without even stopping to have his broke arm splinted up, let alone waiting for Will Varner to reach for his shotgun.

Except you would be wrong. Maybe you not only dont run outen the middle of a natural catastrophe—you might be flung outen it by centrifugal force or, if you had any sense, you might tried to dodge it. But you dont change your mind and plans in the middle of it. Or he might in his case even wanted to stay in the middle of that particular one until it taken the rest of his arms and legs too, as likely any number of them other Quicks and Tulls and Bookwrights would elected to do. Not to mention staying in that select school that even in that short time some of them high academic standards of honor and chivalry rubbed off on him by jest exposure. Anyhow it wasn't him that left that-ere now-flyspecked Varner family honor high and dry. It was Eula herself that done it. So now all you can do is try to figger. So maybe it was the McCarron boy that done it, after all. Like maybe that centrifugal force that hadn't touched him but that one light time and he had already begun to crumple. That simple natural phenomenon that maybe didn't expect to meet another phenomenon, even a natural one, but at least expected or maybe jest hoped for something at least tough enough to crash back without losing a arm or a leg the first time they struck. Because next time it might be a head, which would mean the life along with it, and then all that force and power and unskeeredness and unskeerableness to give and to take and suffer the consequences it taken to be a female natural phenomenon in its phenomenal moment, would be wasted, throwed away. Because I aint talking about love. Natural phenomenons aint got no more concept of love than they have of the alarm and uncertainty and impotence you got to be capable of to know what waiting means. When she said to herself, and likely she did: *The next one of them creek-bridge episodes might destroy him completely*, it wasn't that McCarron boy's comfort she had in mind.

Anyhow, the next morning he was gone from Frenchman's Bend. I presume it was Eula that put what was left of the buggy whip back into the socket and druv the buggy back up the hill. Leastways they waked Will, and Will in his nightshirt (no shotgun: it would be anywhere up to twenty-eight days, give or take a few, before he would find out he needed the shotgun; it was jest his little grip of veterinary tools yet) patched up the arm to where he could drive on home or somewhere that more than a local cow-and-mule doctor could get a-holt of him. But he was back in Jefferson at least once about a month later, about the time when Eula likely found out if she didn't change her condition pretty quick now, it was going to change itself for her. And he even paid the mail rider extra to carry a special wrote-out private message to Eula. But nothing come of that neither, and at last he was gone. And sho enough, about sixty-five or seventy days after that-ere hors-de-combat creek-bridge evening—and if you had expected a roar of some kind to come up outen the Varner residence and environment, you would been wrong there too: it was jest a quick announcement that even then barely beat the wedding itself— Herman Bookwright and Theron Quick left Frenchman's Bend suddenly overnight too though it's my belief they was both not even bragging but jest wishing they had, and Eula and Flem was married; and after the one more week it taken Will to do what he thought was beating Flem down to accepting that abandoned Old Frenchman place as full receipt for Eula's dowry, Eula and Flem left for Texas, which was fur enough away so that when they come back, that-ere new Snopes baby would look at least reasonably legal or maybe what I mean is orthodox. Not to mention as Texas would be where it had spent the presumable most of its prenatal existence, wouldn't nobody be surprised if it was cutting its teeth at three months old. And when they was back in Frenchman's Bend a year later, anybody meddlesome enough to remark how it had got to be a pretty good-size gal in jest them three possible months, all he had to do was remind his-self that them three outside months had been laid in Texas likewise.

Jest exactly fourteen months since that McCarron boy started to crumple at the seams at that first encounter. But it wasn't waiting. Not a natural phenomenon like Eula. She was jest being, breathing, setting with that baby in a rocking chair on Varner's front gallery while Flem changed enough money into them sixty silver dollars and buried them in that Old Frenchman place rose garden jest exactly where me and Henry Armstid and Odum Bookwright couldn't help but find them. And still jest being and breathing, setting with the baby in the wagon that day they moved in to Jefferson so Flem could get a active holt on Grover Winbush to evict him outen the other half of that café me and Grover owned. And still jest being and breathing but not setting now because likely even the tide-wave dont need to be informed when it's on the right spoke to whatever rim it's due at next, her and Flem and the baby living in that canvas tent behind the cafe between when she would walk across the Square until finally Manfred de Spain, the McCarron that wouldn't start or break up when they collided together, would look up and see her. Who hadn't had none of them select advantages of being the only child of a well-to-do widowed maw living in Florida hotels while he was temporarily away at them select eastern schools, but instead had had to make out the best he could with jest being the son of a Confederate cavalry officer, that graduated his-self from West Point into what his paw would a called the Yankee army and went to Cuba as a lieutenant and come back with a long jagged scar down one cheek that the folks trying to beat him for mayor rumored around wasn't made by no Spanish bayonet a-tall but instead by a Missouri sergeant with a axe in a crap game: which, whether it was so or not, never stood up long between him and getting elected mayor of Jefferson, nor between him and getting to be president of Colonel Sartoris's bank when that come up, not to mention between him and Eula Varner Snopes when that come up.

I aint even mentioning Lawyer. It wasn't even his bad luck he was on that rim too because tide-waves aint concerned with luck. It was his fate. He jest got run over by coincidence, like a ant using the same spoke a elephant happened to find necessary or convenient. It wasn't that he was born too soon or too late or even in the wrong place. He was born at exactly the right time, only in the wrong envelope. It was his fate and doom not to been born into one of them McCarron sep-

arate covers too instead of into that fragile and what you might call
gossamer-sinewed envelope of boundless and hopeless aspiration
Old Moster give him.

So there he was, rushing headlong into that engagement that the
best he could possibly hope would be to lose it quick, since any semblance or intimation of the most minorest victory would a destroyed
him like a lightning bolt, while Flem Snopes grazed gently on up
them new Jefferson pastures, him and his wife and infant daughter
still living in the tent behind the café and Flem his-self frying the
hamburgers now after Grover Winbush found out suddenly one day
that he never owned one half of a café neither; then the Rouncewells
that thought they still owned what Miz Rouncewell called the Commercial Hotel against all the rest of Yoknapatawpha County calling it
the Rouncewell boarding house, found they was wrong too and the
Flem Snopeses lived there now, during the month or so it taken him
to eliminate the Rouncewells outen it, with the next Snopes from
Frenchman's Bend imported into the tent behind the café and frying the hamburgers because Flem his-self was now superintendent of
the power plant; Manfred de Spain had not only seen Eula, he was
already mayor of Jefferson when he done it.

And still Lawyer was trying, even while at least once ever day he
would have to see his mortal victorious rival and conqueror going
in and out of the mayor's office or riding back and forth across the
Square in that red brass-trimmed E.M.F. roadster that most of north
Missippi, let alone jest Yoknapatawpha County, hadn't seen nothing
like before; right on up and into that alley behind the Ladies' Cotillion Club Christmas ball where he tried to fight Manfred with his
bare fists until his sister's husband drug him up outen the gutter and
held him long enough for Manfred to get outen sight and then taken
him home to the bathroom to wash him off and says to him: "What
the hell do you mean? Dont you know you dont know how to fight?"
And Lawyer leaning over the washbowl trying to stanch his nose
with handfuls of tissue paper, saying, "Of course I know it. But can
you suh-jest a better way than this for me to learn?"

And still trying, on up to that last desperate cast going all the way
back to that powerhouse brass business. I mean, that pile of old
wore-out faucets and valves and pieces of brass pipe and old bear-

ings and such that had accumulated into the power plant until they all disappeared sometime during the second year of Flem's reign as superintendent, though there wasn't no direct evidence against nobody even after the brass safety valves vanished from both the boilers and was found to been replaced with screwed-in steel plugs; it was jest that finally the city auditors had to go to the superintendent and advise him as delicate as possible that that brass was missing and Flem quit chewing long enough to say "How much?" and paid them and then the next year they done the books again and found they had miscounted last year and went to him again and suh-jested they had made a mistake before and Flem quit chewing again long enough to say "How much?" and paid them that too. Going (I mean Lawyer) all the way back to them old by-gones even though Flem was not only long since resigned from being superintendent, he had even bought two new safety valves outen his own pocket as a free civic gift to the community; bringing all that up again, with evidence, in a suit to impeach Manfred outen the mayor's office until Judge Dukinfield recused his-self and appointed Judge Stevens, Lawyer's paw, to hear the case. Only we didn't know what happened then because Judge Stevens cleared the court and heard the argument in chambers as they calls it, jest Lawyer and Manfred and the judge his-self. And that was all; it never taken long; almost right away Manfred come out and went back to his mayor's office, and the tale, legend, report, whatever you want to call it, of Lawyer standing there with his head bent a lit-tle in front of his paw, saying, "What must I do now, Papa? Papa, what can I do now?"

But he was chipper enough the next morning when I seen him off on the train, that had done already graduated from Harvard and the University law school over at Oxford and was now on his way to a town in Germany to go to school some more. Yes sir, brisk and chip-per as you could want. "Here you are," he says. "This is what I want with you before I leave: to pass the torch on into your personal hand. You'll have to hold the fort alone now. You'll have to tote the load by yourself."

"What fort?" I says. "What load?"

"Jefferson," he says. "Snopeses. Think you can handle them alone for two years?" That's what he thought then: that he was all right now; he had done been disenchanted for good at last of Helen, and so now all he had to worry about was what them Menelaus-Snopeses might be up to in the Yoknapatawpha-Argive community while he had his back turned. Which was all right; it would ease his mind. He would have plenty of time after he come back to find out that aint nobody yet ever lost Helen, since for the rest of not jest her life but hisn too she dont never get shut of him. Likely it's because she dont want to.

Except it wasn't two years. It was nearer five. That was in the early spring of 1914, and that summer the war come, and maybe that—a war—was what he was looking for. Not hoping for, let alone expecting to have one happen jest on his account, since like most other folks in this country he didn't believe no war was coming. But looking for something, anything, and certainly a war would do as well as another, since no matter what his brains might a been telling him once he had that much water between him and Eula Snopes, even his instincts likely told him that jest two years wasn't nowhere near enough for him or Helen either to have any confidence in that disenchantment. So even if he couldn't anticipate no war to save him, back in his mind somewhere he was still confident that Providence would furnish something, since like he said, God was anyhow a gentleman and wouldn't bollix up the same feller twice with the same trick, at least in the same original package.

So he had his war. Only you would a wondered—at least I did—why he never went into it on the German side. Not jest because he was already in Germany and the Germans handy right there surrounding him, but because he had already told me how, although it was the culture of England that had sent folks this fur across the water to establish America, right now it was the German culture that had the closest tie with the modern virile derivations of the northern branch of the old Aryan stock. Because he said that tie was mystical, not what you seen but what you heard, and that the present-day Aryan, in America at least, never had no confidence a-tall in what he seen, but on the contrary would believe anything he jest heard and couldn't prove; and that the modern German culture since the revolutions of 1848 never had no concern with, and if anything a little contempt for, anything that happened to man on the outside, or through the eyes and touch, like sculpture and painting and civil laws for his social benefit, but jest with what happened to him through his ears, like music and philosophy and what was wrong inside of his mind. Which he said was the reason why German was such a ugly language, not musical like Italian and Spanish nor what he called the epicene exactitude of French, but was harsh and ugly, not to mention full of spit (like as the feller says, you speak Italian to men, French to women, and German to horses), so that there wouldn't be nothing to interfere and distract your mind from what your nerves and glands was hearing: the mystical ideas, the glorious music—Lawyer said, the best of music, from the mathematical inevitability of Mozart through the godlike passion of Beethoven and Bach to the combination bawdy-house street-carnival uproar that Wagner made—that come straight to the modern virile northern Aryan's heart without bothering his mind a-tall.

Except that he didn't join the German army. I dont know what lies he managed to tell the Germans to get out of Germany where he could join the enemy fighting them, nor what lies he thought up for the English and French to explain why a student out of a German university was a safe risk to have around where he might overhear somebody telling what surprise they was fixing up next. But he done it. And it wasn't the English army he joined neither. It was the French one: them folks that, according to him, spent all their time talking about epicene exactitudes to ladies. And I didn't know why even four years later when I finally asked him: "After all you said about that-ere kinship of German culture, and the German army right there in the middle of you, or leastways you in the middle of it, you still had to lie or trick your way out to join the French one." Because all he said was, "I was wrong." And not even another year after that when I said to him, "Even despite that splendid glorious music and them splendid mystical ideas?" he jest says:

"They are still glorious, still splendid. It's the word *mystical* that's wrong. The music and the ideas both come out of obscurity, darkness. Not out of shadow: out of obscurity, obfuscation, darkness. Man must have light. He must live in the fierce full constant glare of light, where all shadow will be defined and sharp and unique and personal: the shadow of his own singular rectitude or baseness. All human evils have to come out of obscurity and darkness, where there is nothing to dog man constantly with the shape of his own deformity."

In fact not until two or three years more and he was back home now, settled now; and Eula, still without having to do no more than jest breathe as far as he was concerned, had already adopted the rest of his life as long as it would be needed, into the future of that eleven- or twelve-year-old girl, and I said to him:

"Helen walked in light." And he says,

"Helen was light. That's why we can still see her, not changed, not even dimmer, from five thousand years away." And I says,

"What about all them others you talk about? Semiramises and Judiths and Liliths and Francescas and Isoldes?" And he says,

"But not like Helen. Not that bright, that luminous, that enduring. It's because the others all talked. They are fading steadily into the obscurity of their own vocality within which their passions and tragedies took place. But not Helen. Do you know there is not one recorded word of hers anywhere in existence, other than that one presumable Yes she must have said that time to Paris?"

So there they was. That gal of thirteen and fourteen and fifteen that wasn't trying to do nothing but jest get shut of having to go to school by getting there on time and knowing the lesson to make the rise next year, that likely wouldn't barely ever looked at him long enough to know him again except that she found out on a sudden that for some reason he was trying to adopt some of her daily life into hisn, or adopt a considerable chunk of his daily life into hern, whichever way you want to put it. And that bachelor lawyer twice her age, that was already more or less in the public eye from being county attorney, not to mention in a little town like Jefferson where ever time you had your hair cut your constituency knowed about it by suppertime. So that the best they knowed to do was to spend fifteen minutes after school one or two afternoons a week at a table in the window of Uncle Willy Christian's drugstore while she et a ice-cream sody or a banana split and the ice melted into the unteched Coca-Cola in front of him. Not jest the best but the only thing, not jest for the sake of her good name but also for them votes that two years from now might not consider buying ice cream for fourteen-year-old gals a fitting qualification for a county attorney.

About twice a week meeting her by that kind of purely coincidental accident that looked jest exactly as accidental as you would expect: Lawyer ambushed behind his upstairs office window across the street until the first of the let-out school would begin to pass, which would be the kindergarden and the first grade, then by that same accidental coincidence happening to be on the corner at the exact time to cut her outen the seventh or eighth or ninth grade, her looking a little startled and surprised the first time or two; not alarmed: jest startled a little, wondering jest a little at first maybe what he wanted. But not for long; that passed too and pretty soon Lawyer was even drinking maybe a inch of the Coca-Cola before it got too lukewarm to swallow. Until one day I says to him: "I envy you," and he looked at me and I says, "Your luck," and he says,

"My which luck?" and I says,

"You are completely immersed twenty-four hours a day in being busy. Most folks aint. Almost nobody aint. But you are. Doing the one thing you not only got to do, but the one thing in the world you want most to do. And if that wasn't already enough, it's got as many or maybe even more interesting technical complications in it than if you had invented it yourself instead of jest being discovered by it. For the sake of her good name, you got to do it right out in that very same open public eye that would ruin her good if it ever found a chance, but maybe wouldn't never even suspect you and she knowed one another's name if you jest kept it hidden in secret. Dont you call that keeping busy?"

Because he was unenchanted now, you see, done freed at last of that fallen seraphim. It was Eula herself had give him a salve, a ointment, for that bitter thumb the poets say ever man once in his life has got to gnaw at: that gal thirteen then fourteen then fifteen setting opposite him in Christian's drugstore maybe two afternoons a week in the intervals of them coincidental two or three weeks ever year while Miz Flem Snopes and her daughter would be on a holiday somewhere at the same coincidental time Manfred de Spain would be absent on hisn—not Mayor de Spain now but Banker de Spain

since Colonel Sartoris finally vacated the presidency of the bank him
and De Spain's paw and Will Varner had established, by letting his
grandson run the automobile off into a ditch on the way to town one
morning, and now Manfred de Spain was president of the bank,
moving outen the mayor's office into the president's office at about
the same more or less coincidental moment that Flem Snopes moved
outen being the ex-superintendent of the power plant, into being
vice-president of the bank, vacating simultaneously outen that little
cloth cap he come to Jefferson in (jest vacated, not abandoned it, the
legend being he sold it to a Negro boy for ten cents. Which wouldn't
be a bad price, since who knows if maybe some of that-ere financial
acumen might not a sweated off onto it.) into a black felt planter's hat
suitable to his new position and avocation.

Oh yes, Lawyer was unenchanted now, even setting alone now and
then in Christian's window while the ice melted into the Coca-Cola
until they would get back home, maybe to be ready and in practice
when them two simultaneous coincidences was over and school
would open again on a whole fresh year of two afternoons a week—
providing of course that sixteen- and seventeen-year-old gal never
run into a Hoake McCarron or a Manfred de Spain of her own
between two of them and Lawyer could say to you like the man in
the book: *What you see aint tears. You jest think that's what you're looking at.*

Sixteen and seventeen and going on eighteen now and Lawyer still
lending her books to read and keeping her stall-fed twice a week on
ice-cream sundaes and banana splits, so anyhow Jefferson figgered
it knowed what Lawyer was up to whether he admitted it out or not.
And naturally Eula had already knowed for five or six years what she
was after. Like there's a dog, maybe not no extra dog but leastways a
good sound what you might call a dog's dog, that dont seem to
belong to nobody else, that seems to show a preference for your
vicinity, that even after the five or six years you aint completely convinced there wont never be no other dog available, and that even
them five or six years back and even with another five or six years
added onto now, you never needed and you aint going to need that
dog personally, there aint any use in simply throwing away and wasting its benefits and accomplishments, even if they aint nothing but

fidelity and devotion, by letting somebody else get a-holt of it. Or say you got a gal child coming along, that the older and bigger she gets, the more of a nuisance she's bound to be on your time and private occupations: in which case not only wont that fidelity and devotion maybe come into handy use, but even the dog itself might that could still be capable of them long after even hit had give up all expectation of even one bone.

Which is what Jefferson figgered. But not me. Maybe even though she got rid of Hoake McCarron, even after she knowed she was pregnant, there is still moments when even female physical phenomenons is female first whether they want to be or not. So I believe that women aint so different from men: that if it aint no trouble nor shock neither for a man to father onto his-self the first child of the woman he loved and lost and still cant rid outen his mind, no matter how many other men holp to get it, it aint no trouble neither for that woman to father a dozen different men's chillen onto that man that lost her and still never expected nothing of her except to accept his devotion.

And since she was a female too, likely by the time Linda was thirteen or fourteen or even maybe as soon as she got over that first startle, which would a been at the second or third ice-cream sody, she taken for granted she knowed what he was aiming at too. And she would a been wrong. That wasn't Lawyer. Jest to train her up and marry her wasn't it. She wouldn't a been necessary for that—I mean, the simple natural normal following lifetime up to the divorce of steady uxorious hymeneal conflict that any female he could a picked outen that school crowd or from Christian's sody counter would been fully competent for. Jest that wouldn't a been worth his effort. He had to be the sole one masculine feller within her entire possible circumambience, not jest to recognise she had a soul still capable of being saved from what he called Snopesism: a force and power that stout and evil as to jeopardise it jest from her believing for twelve or thirteen years she was blood kin when she actively wasn't no kin a-tall, but that couldn't nobody else in range and reach but him save it—that-ere bubble-glass thing somewhere inside her like one of them shimmer-colored balls balanced on the seal's nose, fragile yet immune too jest that one constant fragile inch above the smutch and dirt of Snopes as long as the seal dont trip or stumble or let her attention wander. So all he aimed to do was jest to get her outen Jefferson or, better, safer still, completely outen Missippi, starting off with the nine months of the school year, until somebody would find her and marry her and she would be gone for good—a optimist pure and simple and undefiled if there ever was one since ever body knowed that the reason Flem Snopes was vice-president of De Spain's bank was the same reason he was ex-superintendent of the power plant: in the one case folks wanting to smile at Eula Varner had to at least be able to pronounce Flem Snopes, and in the other De Spain had to take Flem along with him to get the use of Will Varner's voting stock to get hisself president. And the only reason why Will Varner never used this chance to get back at Flem about that Old Frenchman homesite that Will thought wasn't worth nothing until Flem sold it to me and Odum Bookwright and Henry Armstid for my half of mine and Grover Winbush's café and Odum Bookwright's cash and the two-hundred-dollar mortgage on Henry's farm less them five or six dollars or whatever they was where Henry's wife tried to keep them buried from him behind the outhouse, was the same reason why Eula didn't quit Flem and marry De Spain: that staying married to Flem kept up a establishment and a name for that gal that otherwise wouldn't a had either. So once that gal was married herself or leastways settled for good away from Jefferson so she wouldn't need Flem's name and establishment no more, and in consequence Flem wouldn't have no holt over her any more, Flem his-self would be on the outside trying to look back in and Flem knowed it.

Only Lawyer didn't know it. He believed right up to the last that Flem was going to let him get Linda away from Jefferson to where the first strange young man that happened by would marry her and then Eula could quit him and he would be finished. He—I mean Lawyer—had been giving her books to read ever since she was fourteen and then kind of holding examinations on them while the Coca-Cola ice melted. Then she was going on seventeen, next spring she would graduate from the high school and now he was ordering off for the catalogues from the extra-select girls' schools up there close to Harvard.

Now the part comes that dont nobody know except Lawyer, who naturally never told it. So as he his-self would say, you got to surmise from the facts in evidence: not jest the mind-improving books and the school catalogues accumulating into a dusty stack in his office, but the ice-cream sessions a thing of the past too. Because now she was going to and from school the back way, up alleys. Until finally in about a week maybe Lawyer realised that she was dodging him. And she was going to graduate from high school in less than two months now and there wasn't no time to waste. So that morning Lawyer went his-self to talk to her maw and he never told that neither so now we got to presume on a little more than jest evidence. Because my childhood too come out of that same similar Frenchman's Bend background and mill-yew that Flem Snopes had lifted his-self out of by his own unaided bootstraps, if you dont count Hoake McCarron. So all I had to do was jest to imagine my name was Flem Snopes and that the only holt I had on Will Varner's money was through his daughter, and if I ever lost what light holt I had on the granddaughter, the daughter would be gone. Yet here was a durn meddling outsider with a complete set of plans that would remove that granddaughter to where I wouldn't never see her again, if she had any sense a-tall. And since the daughter had evidently put up with me for going on eighteen years now for the sake of that granddaughter, the answer was simple: all I needed to do was go to my wife and say, "If you give that gal permission to go away to school, I'll blow up this-here entire Manfred de Spain business to where she wont have no home to have to get away from, let alone one to come back to for Christmas and holidays."

And for her first eighteen years Eula breathed that same Frenchman's Bend mill-yew atmosphere too so maybe all I got to do is imagine my name is Eula Varner to know what she said back to Lawyer: "No, she cant go off to school but you can marry her. That will solve ever thing." You see? Because the kind of fidelity and devotion that could keep faithful and devoted that long without even wanting no bone any more, was not only too valuable to let get away, it even deserved to be rewarded. Because maybe the full rounded satisfaction and completeness of being Helen was bigger than a thousand Parises and McCarrons and De Spains could satisfy. I don't mean jest the inexhaustible capacity for passion, but of power: the power not jest to draw and enchant and consume, but the power and capacity to give away and reward; the power to draw to you, not more than you can handle because the words "cant-handle" and "Helen" aint even in the same language, but to draw to you so much more than you can possibly need that you could even afford to give the surplus away, be that prodigal—except that you are Helen and you cant give nothing away that was ever yourn: all you can do is share it and reward its fidelity and maybe even, for a moment, soothe and assuage its grief. And cruel too, prodigal in that too, because you are Helen and can afford it; you got to be Helen to be that cruel, that prodigal in cruelty, and still be yourself unscathed and immune, likely calling him by his first name for the first time too: "Marry her, Gavin."

And saw in his face not jest startlement and a little surprise like he seen in Linda's that time, but terror, fright, not at having to answer "No" that quick nor even at being asked it because he believed he had done already asked and decided that suh-jestion for-ever a long while back. It was at having it suh-jested to him by her. Like, since he hadn't been able to have no hope since that moment when he realised Manfred de Spain had already looked at her too, he had found out how to live at peace with hoping since he was the only one alive that knowed he never had none. But now, when she said that right out loud to his face, it was like she had said right out in public that he wouldn't a had no hope even if Manfred de Spain hadn't never laid eyes on her. And if he could jest get that "No" out quick enough, it would be like maybe she hadn't actively said what she said, and he would still not be destroyed.

At least wasn't nobody, no outsider, there to hear it so maybe even before next January he was able to believe hadn't none of it even been said, like miracle: what aint believed aint seen. Miracle, pure mira-cle anyhow, how little a man needs to outlast jest about anything. Which—miracle—is about what looked like had happened next Jan-uary: Linda graduated that spring from high school and next fall she entered the Seminary where she would be home ever night and all day Saturday and Sunday the same as before so Flem could keep his hand on her. Then jest after Christmas we heard how she had withdrawed from the Seminary and was going over to Oxford and enter the University. Yes sir, over there fifty miles from Flem day and night both right in the middle of a nest of five or six hundred bachelors under twenty-five years old any one of which could marry her that had two dollars for a license. A pure miracle, especially after I run into Eula on the street and says,

"How did you manage it?" and she says,

"Manage what?" and I says,

"Persuade Flem to let her go to the University," and she says,

"I didn't. It was his idea. He gave the permission without even consulting me. I didn't know he was going to do it either." Only the Frenchman's Bend background should have been enough, without even needing the sixteen or seventeen years of Jefferson environment, to reveal even to blind folks that Flem Snopes didn't deal in miracles: that he preferred spot cash or at least a signed paper with a X on it. So when it was all over and finished, Eula dead and De Spain gone from Jefferson for good too and Flem was now president of the bank and even living in De Spain's rejuvenated ancestral home and Linda gone with her New York husband to fight in the Spanish war, when Lawyer finally told me what little he actively knowed, it was jest evidence I had already presumed on. Because of course all Helen's children would have to inherit something of generosity even if they couldn't inherit more than about one millionth of their maw's bounty to be generous with. Not to mention that McCarron boy, that even if he wasn't durable enough to stand more than that-ere first creek bridge, was at least brave enough or rash enough to try to. So likely Flem already knowed in advance that he wouldn't have to bargain, swap, with her. That all he needed was jest to do what he probably done: ketching her after she had give up and then had had them three months to settle down into having give up, then saying to her: "Let's compromise. If you will give up them eastern schools, maybe you can go to the University over at Oxford." You see? Offering to give something that, in all the fourteen or fifteen years she could remember knowing him in, she had never dreamed he would do.

Then that day in the next April; she had been at the University over at Oxford since right after New Year's. I was jest leaving for

Rockyford to deliver Miz Ledbetter's new sewing machine when Flem stopped me on the Square and offered me four bits extra to carry him by Varner's store a minute. Urgent enough to pay me four bits when the mail carrier would have took him for nothing; secret enough that he couldn't risk either public conveyance: the mail carrier that would a took him out and back free but would a needed all day, or a hired automobile that would had him at Varner's front gate in not much over a hour.

Secret enough and urgent enough to have Will Varner storming into his daughter's and son-in-law's house in Jefferson before daylight the next morning loud enough to wake up the whole neighborhood until somebody (Eula naturally) stopped him. So we got to presume on a few known facts again: that Old Frenchman place that Will deeded to Flem because he thought it was worthless until Flem sold it to me and Odum Bookwright and Henry Armstid (less of course the active silver dollars Flem had had to invest into that old rose garden with a shovel where we—or any other Ratliffs and Bookwrights and Armstids that was handy—would find them). And that president's chair in the bank that we knowed now Flem had had his eye on ever since Manfred de Spain taken it over after Colonel Sartoris. And that gal that had done already inherited generosity from her maw and then was suddenly give another gob of it that she not only never in the world expected but that she probably never knowed how bad she wanted it until it was suddenly give to her free.

What Flem taken out to Frenchman's Bend that day was a will. Maybe when Linda finally got over the shock of getting permission to go away to school after she had long since give up any hope of it, even if no further away than Oxford, maybe when she looked around and realised who that permission had come from, she jest could not bear to be under obligations to him. Except I dont believe that neither. It wasn't even that little of bounty and generosity which would be all Helen's child could inherit from her, since half of even Helen's child would have to be corrupted by something less than Helen, being as even Helen couldn't get a child on herself alone. What Linda wanted was not jest to give. It was to be needed: not jest to be loved and wanted, but to be needed too; and maybe this was the first time in her life she ever had anything that anybody not jest wanted but needed too.

It was a will; Eula of course told Lawyer. Flem his-self could a suh-jested the idea to Linda; it wouldn't a been difficult. Which I don't believe neither. He didn't need to; he knowed her well enough to presume on that, jest like she knowed him enough to presume too. It was Linda herself that evolved the idea when she realised that as long as he lived and drawed breath as Flem Snopes, he wasn't never going to give her permission to leave Jefferson for any reason. And her asking herself, impotent and desperate: *But why? why?* until finally she answered it—a answer that maybe wouldn't a helt much water but she was jest sixteen and seventeen then, during which sixteen and seventeen years she had found out that the only thing he loved was money. Because she must a knowed something anyway about Manfred de Spain. Jefferson wasn't that big, if in fact any place is. Not to mention them two or three weeks of summer holiday at the seashore or mountains or wherever, when here all of a sudden who should turn up but a old Jefferson neighbor happening by accident to take his vacation too from the bank at the same time and place. So what else would she say? *It's grandfather's money, that his one and only chance to keep any holt on it is through mama and me so he believes that once I get away from him his holt on both of us will be broken and mama will leave too and marry Manfred and any hope of grandfather's money will be gone forever.*

Yet here was this man that had had sixteen or seventeen years to learn her he didn't love nothing but money and would do anything you could suh-jest to get another dollar of it, coming to her his-self, without no pressure from nobody and not asking for nothing back, saying, *You can go away to school if you still want to; only, this first time anyhow stay at least as close to home as Oxford;* saying in effect: *I was wrong. I wont no longer stand between you and your life, even though I am convinced I will be throwing away all hope of your grandpaw's money.*

So what else could she do but what she done, saying in effect back at him: *If you jest realised now that grandfather's money aint as important as my life, I could a told you that all the time; if you had jest told me two years ago that all you was was jest skeered, I would a eased you then—*

going (Lawyer his-self told me this) to a Oxford lawyer as soon as she was settled in the University and drawing up a will leaving whatever share she might ever have in her grandpaw's or her maw's estate to her father Flem Snopes. Sho, that wouldn't a held no water neither but she was jest eighteen and that was all she had to give that she thought anybody wanted or needed from her; and besides, all the water it would need to hold would be what old Will Varner would sweat out when Flem showed it to him.

So jest after ten that morning I stopped not at the store where Will would be at this hour but at his front gate jest exactly long enough for Flem to get out and walk into the house until he coincided with Miz Varner I reckon it was and turn around and come back out and get back into the pickup and presumably at their two oclock a.m. morning family breakfast it occurred to Miz Varner or anyway she decided to or anyhow did hand Will the paper his son-in-law left yestiddy for him to look at. And by sunup Will had that whole Snopes street woke up hollering inside Flem's house until Eula got him shut up. And by our normal ee-feet Jefferson breakfast time Manfred de Spain was there too. And that done it. Will Varner, that Flem had done already tricked outen that Old Frenchman place, then turned right around and used him again to get his-self and Manfred de Spain vice-president and president respectively of Colonel Sartoris's bank, and now Flem had done turned back around the third time and somehow tricked his granddaughter into giving him a quit-claim to half of his active cash money that so far even Flem hadn't found no way to touch. And Flem, that all he wanted was for Manfred de Spain to resign from the bank so he could be president of it and would jest as lief done it quiet and discreet and all private in the family you might say by a simple friendly suh-jestion from Will Varner to Manfred to resign from the bank, as a even swap for that paper of Linda's, which should a worked with anybody and would with anybody else except Manfred. He was the trouble; likely Eula could a handled them all except for him. Maybe he got thatere scar on his face by actively toting a flag up a hill in Cuba and running over a cannon or a fort with it, and maybe it come from the axe in that crap game that old mayor's-race rumor claimed. But leastways it was on his front and not on his back and so maybe a feller could knock him out with a piece of lead pipe and pick his pocket while he was laying there, but couldn't no Snopes nor nobody else pick it jest by pointing at him what the other feller thought was a pistol. And Eula in the middle of them, that likely could a handled it all except for Manfred, that had even made Will shut up but she couldn't make Manfred hush. That had done already spent lacking jest a week of nineteen years holding together a home for Linda to grow up and live in so she wouldn't never need to say, *Other children have got what I never had;* there was Eula having to decide right there right now, *If I was a eighteen-year-old gal, which would I rather have: my mother publicly notarised as a suicide, or publicly condemned as a whore?* and by noon the next day all Jefferson knowed how the afternoon before she come to town and went to the beauty parlor that hadn't never been in one before because she never needed to, and had her hair waved and her fingernails shined and went back home and presumably et supper or anyhow was present at it since it wasn't until about eleven oclock that she seemed to taken up the pistol and throwed the safety off.

And the next morning Lawyer and his sister drove over to Oxford and brought Linda home; a pure misfortunate coincidence that all this had to happen jest a week before her nineteenth birthday. But as soon as Flem received that will from her, naturally he figgered Will Varner would want to see it as soon as possible, being a interested party; it was Will that never had no reason a-tall to pick out that special day to come bellering in to town two hours after he first seen it. He could a jest as well waited two weeks or even a month to come in, since wasn't nobody hurrying him; Flem would certainly a waited on his convenience.

And Lawyer that tended to the rest of it too: arranged for the funeral and sent out to Frenchman's Bend for Miz Varner and the old Methodist preacher that had baptised Eula, and then seen to the grave. Because naturally the bereaved husband couldn't be expected to break into his grief jest to do chores. Not to mention having to be ready to take over the bank after a decent interval, being as Manfred de Spain his-self had packed up and departed from Jefferson right after the burying. And then, after another decorious interval, a little longer this time being as a bank aint like jest a house because a bank deals with active cash money and cant wait, getting ready to move into De Spain's house too since De Spain had give ever evident intention of not aiming to return to Jefferson from this last what you might still call Varner trip and there wasn't no use in letting a good sound well-situated house stand vacant and empty. Which—De Spain's house—was likely a part of that same swapping and trading between Flem and Will Varner that included Varner's bank-stock votes and that-ere financial Midsummer Night's Dream masque or rondeau that Linda and that Oxford lawyer composed betwixt them that had Linda's signature on it. Not to mention Lawyer being appointed by old man Will to be trustee of Linda's money since it was now finally safe from Flem until he thought up something that Lawyer would believe too this time, Will appointing Lawyer for the reason that likely he couldn't pass by Lawyer to get to no one else, Lawyer being not only in the middle of that entire monetary and sepulchrial crisis but all around ever part of it too, like one of them frantic water bugs skating and rushing immune and unwettable on top of a stagnant pond.

I mean, Lawyer was now busy over the headstone Flem had decided on. Because it would have to be made in Italy, which would take time, and so would demand ever effort on Lawyer's part before Linda could pack up and leave Jefferson too, being as Flem felt that that same filial decorum demanded that Linda wait until her maw's headstone was up and finished before leaving. Only I dont mean jest headstone: I mean monument: Lawyer combing and currying not jest Jefferson and Frenchman's Bend but most of the rest of Yoknapatawpha County too, hunting out ever photograph of Eula he could locate to send to Italy so they could carve Eula's face in stone to put on it. Which is when I noticed again how there aint nobody quite as temerious as a otherwise timid feller that finds out that his moral standards and principles is now demanding him to do something that, if all he had to depend on was jest his own satisfaction and curiosity, he wouldn't a had the brass to do, penetrating into ever house that not only might a knowed Eula but that jest had a Brownie Kodak, thumbing through albums and intimate photographic family records, courteous and polite of course but jest a man obviously not in no condition to be said No to, let alone merely Please dont.

He could keep busy now. Because he was contented and happy now, you see. He never had nothing to worry him now. Eula was safely gone now and now he could be safe forevermore from ever again having to chew his bitter poetic thumbs over the constant anticipation of who would turn up next named McCarron or De Spain. And now Linda was not only safe for good from Flem, he, Lawyer, even had the full charge and control of her money from her maw and grandpaw, so that now she could go anywhere she wanted—providing of course he could nag and harry them folks across the water to finish carving that face before the millennium or judgment day come, gathering up all the pictures of Eula he could find and sending them to Italy and then waiting until a drawing or a photograph of how the work was coming along would get back for him to see jest how wrong it was, and he would send me word to be at his office at a certain hour for the conference, with the newest fresh Italian sketch or photograph laid out on the desk with a special light on it and him saying, "It's the ear, or the line of the jaw, or the mouth—right here: see what I mean?" and I would say,

"It looks all right to me. It looks beautiful to me." And he would say,

"No. It's wrong right here. Hand me a pencil." Except he would already have a pencil, and he couldn't draw neither so he would have to rub that out and try again. Except that time was passing so he would have to send it back; and Flem and Linda living in De Spain's house now and now Flem had done bought a automobile that he couldn't drive but anyhow he had a daughter that could, leastways now and then; until at last even that was over. It was October and Lawyer sent me word the unveiling at the graveyard would be that afternoon. Except I had done already got word to Chick, since from the state of peace and contentment Lawyer had got his-self into by this time, it might take both of us. So Chick stayed outen school that afternoon so all three of us went out to the cemetery together in Lawyer's car. And there was Linda and Flem too, in Flem's car with the Negro driver that was going to drive her on to Memphis to take the New York train with her packed grips already in the car, and Flem leaning back in the seat with that black hat on that even after five years still didn't look like it actively belonged to him, chewing, and Linda beside him in her dark going-away dress and hat with her head bent a little and them little white gloves shut into fists on her lap. And there it was: that-ere white monument with on the front of it that face that even if it was carved outen dead stone, was still the same face that ever young man no matter how old he got would still never give up hope and belief that some day before he died he would finally be worthy to be wrecked and ruined and maybe even destroyed by it, above the motto that Flem his-self had picked:

A VIRTUOUS WIFE IS A CROWN TO HER HUSBAND
HER CHILDREN RISE AND CALL HER BLESSED

Until at last Flem leaned out the window and spit and then set back in the car and tells her: "All right. You can go now."

Yes sir, Lawyer was free now. He never had nothing to worry him now: him and Chick and me driving back to the office and him talking about how the game of football could be brought up to date in keeping with the progress of the times by giving ever body a football too so ever body would be in the game; or maybe better still, keep jest one football but abolish the boundaries so that a smart feller for instance could hide the ball under his shirttail and slip off into the bushes and circle around town and come in through a back alley and cross the goal before anybody even missed he was gone; right on into the office where he set down behind the desk and taken up one of the cob pipes and struck three matches to it until Chick taken it away from him and filled it from the tobacco jar and handed it back and Lawyer says, "Much obliged," and dropped the filled pipe into the wastebasket and folded his hands on the desk, still talking, and I says to Chick:

"Watch him. I won't be long," and went around into the alley; I never had much time so what was in the pint bottle was pretty bad but leastways it had something in it that for a moment anyhow would feel like alcohol. And I got the sugar bowl and glass and spoon from the cabinet and made the toddy and set it on the desk by him and he says,

"Much obliged," not even touching it, jest setting there with his hands folded in front of him, blinking quick and steady like he had sand in his eyes, saying: "All us civilised people date our civilisation from the discovery of the principle of distillation. And even though the rest of the world, at least that part of it in the United States, rates us folks in Mississippi at the lowest rung of culture, what man can deny that, even if this is as bad as I think it's going to be, we too grope toward the stars? Why did she do it, V.K.? That—all that—that she walked in, lived in, breathed in—it was only loaned to her; it wasn't hers to destroy and throw away. It belonged to too many. It belonged to all of us. Why, V.K.?" he says. "Why?"

"Maybe she was bored," I says, and he says:

"Bored. Yes, bored." And that was when he begun to cry. "She loved, had the capacity to love, to give and to take it. Only she tried twice and failed twice not jest to find somebody strong enough to deserve it but even brave enough to accept it. Yes," he says, setting there bolt upright with jest the tears running down his face, at peace now, with nothing nowhere in the world any more to anguish or grieve him. "Of course she was bored."

SEVEN

V. K. Ratliff

So he was free. He had not only got shut of his sireen, he had even got shut of the ward he found out she had heired to him. Because I says, "Grinnich Village?" and he says,

"Yes. A little place without physical boundaries located as far as she is concerned in New York City, where young people of all ages below ninety go in search of dreams." Except I says,

"Except she never had to leave Missippi to locate that place." And then I said it, what Eula herself must have, had to have, said to him that day: "Why didn't you marry her?"

"Because she wasn't but nineteen," he says.

"And you are all of thirty-five aint you," I says. "When the papers are full of gals still carrying a doll in one hand marrying folks of sixty and seventy, providing of course they got a little extra money."

"I mean, she's got too much time left to run into something where she might need me. How many papers are full of people that got married because someday they might need the other one?"

"Oh," I says. "So all you got to do now is jest stay around close where you can hear the long-distance telephone or the telegram boy can find you. Because naturally you wont be waiting for her to ever come back to Missippi. Or maybe you are?"

"Naturally not," he says. "Why should she?"

"Thank God?" I says. He didn't answer. "Because who knows," I says, "she may done already found that dream even in jest these . . . two days, aint it? three? Maybe he was already settled there when she arrived. That's possible in Grinnich Village, aint it?"

Then he said it too. "Yes," he says, "thank God." So he was free. And in fact, when you had time to look around a little, he never had nothing no more to do but jest rest in peace and quiet and content-

ment. Because not only him but all Jefferson was free of Snopeses;
for the first time in going on twenty years, Jefferson and Yoknapatawpha County too was in what you might call a kind of Snopes
doldrum.

Because at last even Flem seemed to be satisfied: setting
now at last in the same chair the presidents of the Merchants and
Farmers Bank had been setting in ever since the first one, Colonel
Sartoris, started it twenty-odd years ago, and actively living in the
very house the second one of it was born in, so that all he needed to
do too after he had done locked up the money and went home was to
live in solitary peace and quiet and contentment too, not only shut of
the daughter that had kept him on steady and constant tenterhooks
for years whether she might not escape at any moment to where he
couldn't watch her and the first male feller that come along would
marry her and he would lose her share of Will Varner's money, but
shut of the wife that at any time her and Manfred de Spain would
get publicly caught up with and cost him all the rest of Varner's
money and bank voting stock too.

In fact, for the moment Flem was the only true Snopes actively
left in Jefferson. Old man Ab never had come no closer than that hill
two miles out where you could jest barely see the water tank, where
he taken the studs that day back about 1910 and hadn't moved since.
And four years ago Flem had ci-devanted I.O. back to Frenchman's
Bend for good. And even before that Flem had eliminated Montgomery Ward into the penitentiary at Parchman where Mink
already was (Mink hadn't really resided in Jefferson nohow except
jest them few months in the jail waiting for his life sentence to be
awarded). And last month them four half-Snopes Indians that Byron
Snopes, Colonel Sartoris's bank clerk that resigned by the simple
practical expedient of picking up as much of the loose money he
could tote and striking for the nearest U.S. border, sent back collect from Mexico until somebody could get close enough to fasten
the return prepaid tags on them before whichever one had it at the
moment could get out that switch-blade knife. And as for Eck's
boys, Wallstreet Panic and Admiral Dewey, they hadn't never been
Snopeses to begin with, since all Wallstreet evidently wanted to do
was run a wholesale grocery business by the outrageous un-Snopesish method of jest selling ever body exactly what they thought they

was buying, for exactly what they thought they was going to pay for it.
Or almost satisfied that is. I mean Flem and his new house. It was jest a house: two-storey, with a gallery for Major de Spain, Manfred's paw, to set on when he wasn't fishing or hunting or practising a little law, and it was all right for that-ere second president of the Merchants and Farmers Bank to live in, especially since he had been born in it. But this was a different president. His road to that chair and that house had been longer than them other two. Likely he knowed he had had to come from too fur away to get where he was, and had to come too hard to reach it by the time he did. Because Colonel Sartoris had been born into money and respectability too, and Manfred de Spain had been born into respectability at least even if he had made a heap of the money since. But he, Flem Snopes, had had to earn both of them, snatch and tear and scrabble both of them outen the hard enduring resisting rock you might say, not jest with his bare hands but with jest one bare hand since he had to keep the other bare single hand fending off while he tore and scrabbled with the first one. So the house the folks owning the money would see Manfred de Spain walk into ever evening after he locked the money up and went home, wouldn't be enough for Flem Snopes. The house they would see him walk into ever evening until time to unlock the money tomorrow morning, would have to be the physical symbol of all them generations of respectability and aristocracy that not only would a been too proud to mishandle other folks' money, but couldn't possibly ever needed to.

So there was another Snopes in Jefferson after all. Not transplanted in from Frenchman's Bend: jest imported in for temporary use. This was Wat Snopes, the carpenter, Watkins Products Snopes his full name was, like it was painted on both sides and the back of Doc Meeks's patent-medicine truck; evidently there was a Snopes somewhere now and then that could read reading, whether he could read writing or not. So during the next nine or ten months anybody that had or could think up the occasion, could pass along the street and watch Wat and his work gang of kinfolks and in-laws tearing off Major de Spain's front gallery and squaring up the back of the house and building and setting up them colyums to reach all the way from

the ground up to the second-storey roof, until even when the painting was finished it still wouldn't be as big as Mount Vernon of course,
but then Mount Vernon was a thousand miles away so there wasn't
no chance of invidious or malicious eye-to-eye comparison.

So that when he locked up the bank and come home in the
evening he could walk into a house and shut the door that the folks
owning the money he was custodian of would some of them be jealous a little but all of them, even the jealous ones, would be proud and
all of them would approve, laying down to rest undisturbed at night
with their money that immaculate, that impeccable, that immune.
He was completely complete, as the feller says, with a Negro cook
and a yard boy that could even drive that-ere automobile now and
then since he no longer had a only daughter to drive it maybe once
a month to keep the battery up like the man told him he would have
to do or buy a new one.

But it was jest the house that was altered and transmogrified and
symbolised: not him. The house he disappeared into about four
p.m. ever evening until about eight a.m. tomorrow, might a been the
solid aristocratic ancestral symbol of Alexander Hamilton and
Aaron Burr and Astor and Morgan and Harriman and Hill and ever
other golden advocate of hard quick-thinking vested interest, but
the feller the owners of that custodianed money seen going and
coming out of it was the same one they had done got accustomed
to for twenty years now: the same little snap-on bow tie he had got
outen the Frenchman's Bend mule wagon in and only the hat was
new and different; and even that old cloth cap, that maybe was
plenty good enough to be Varner's clerk in but that wasn't to be seen
going in and out of a Jefferson bank on the head of its vice-president—even the cap not throwed away or even give away, but sold,
even if it wasn't but jest a dime because ten cents is money too
around a bank, so that all the owners of that money that he was
already vice-custodian of could look at the hat and know that, no
matter how little they might a paid for one similar to it, hisn had
cost him ten cents less. It wasn't that he rebelled at changing Flem
Snopes: he done it by deliberate calculation, since the feller you
trust aint necessarily the one you never knowed to do nothing
untrustable: it's the one you have seen from experience that he

knows exactly when being untrustable will pay a net profit and when it will pay a loss.

And that was jest the house on the outside too, up to the moment when he passed in and closed the front door behind him until eight oclock tomorrow. And he hadn't never invited nobody in, and so far hadn't nobody been able to invent no way in, so the only folks that ever seen the inside of it was the cook and the yardman and so it was the yardman that told me: all them big rooms furnished like De Spain left them, plus them interior-decorated sweets the Memphis expert learned Eula that being vice-president of a bank he would have to have; that Flem never even went into them except to eat in the dining room, except that one room at the back where when he wasn't in the bed sleeping he was setting in another swivel chair like the one in the bank, with his feet propped against the side of the fireplace: not reading, not doing nothing: jest setting with his hat on, chewing that same little mouth-sized chunk of air he had been chewing ever since he quit tobacco when he finally got to Jefferson and heard about chewing gum and then quit chewing gum too when he found out folks considered the vice-president of a bank rich enough not to have to chew anything. And how Wat Snopes had found a picture in a magazine how to do over all the fireplaces with colonial molding and colyums and cornices too and at first Flem would jest set with his feet propped on the white paint, scratching it a little deeper ever day with the pegs in his heels. Until one day about a year after the house was finished over, Wat Snopes was there to eat dinner and after Wat finally left the yardman said how he went into the room and seen it: not a defiance, not a simple reminder of where he had come from but rather as the feller says a reaffirmation of his-self and maybe a warning to his-self too: a little wood ledge, not even painted, nailed to the front of that hand-carved hand-painted Mount Vernon mantelpiece at the exact height for Flem to prop his feet on it.

And time was when that first president, Colonel Sartoris, had come the four miles between his ancestral symbol and his bank in a surrey and matched pair drove by a Negro coachman in a linen duster and one of the Colonel's old plug hats; and time aint so was when the second president still come and went in that fire-engine-colored E.M.F. racer until he bought that black Packard and a Negro too except in a white coat and a showfer's cap to drive it. This here new third president had a black automobile too even if it wasn't a Packard, and a Negro that could drive it too even if he never had no white coat and showfer's cap yet and even if the president didn't ride back and forth to the bank or at least not yet. Them two previous presidents would ride around the county in the evening after the bank closed and on Sunday, in that surrey and pair or the black Packard, to look at the cotton farms they represented the mortgages on, while this new president hadn't commenced that neither. Which wasn't because he jest couldn't believe yet that he actively represented the mortgages. He never doubted that. He wasn't skeered to believe it, and he wasn't too meek to nor doubtful to. It was because he was watching yet and learning yet. It wasn't that he had learned two lessons while he thought he was jest learning that single one about how he would need respectability, because he had done already brought that second lesson in from Frenchman's Bend with him. That was humility, the only kind of humility that's worth a hoot: the humility to know they's a heap of things you dont know yet but if you jest got the patience to be humble and watchful long enough, especially keeping one eye on your back trail, you will. So now on the evenings and Sundays there was jest that house where you wasn't invited in to see him setting in that swivel chair in that one room he used, with his hat on and chewing steady on nothing and his feet propped on that little wooden additional ledge nailed in unpainted paradox to that hand-carved and -painted mantel like one of them framed mottoes you keep hanging on the wall where you work or think, saying *Remember Death* or *Keep Smiling* or *-Working* or *God is Love* to remind not jest you but the strangers that see it too, that you got at least a speaking acquaintance with the fact that it might be barely possible it taken a little something more than jest you to get you where you're at.

But all that, footrest and all, would come later. Right now, Lawyer was free. And then—it wasn't no three days after Linda reached New York, but it wasn't no three hundred neither—he become, as the feller says, indeed free. He was leaning against the counter in the post-office lobby with the letter already open in his hand when I come in; it wasn't his fault neither that the lobby happened to be empty at the moment.

"His name is Barton Kohl," he says.

"Sho now," I says. "Whose name is?"

"That dream's name," he says.

"Cole," I says.

"No," he says. "You're pronouncing it Cole. It's spelled K-o-h-l."

"Oh," I says. "Kohl. That dont sound very American to me."

"Does Vladimir Kyrilytch sound very American to you?"

But the lobby was empty. Which, as I said, wasn't his fault. "Confound it," I says, "with one Ratliff in ever generation for them whole hundred and fifty years since your durn Yankee Congress banished us into the Virginia mountains, has had to spend half his life trying to live down his front name before somebody spoke it out loud where folks could hear it. It was Eula told you."

"All right," he says. "I'll help you bury your family shame.—Yes," he says. "He's a Jew. A sculptor, probably a damned good one."

"Because of that?" I says.

"Probably, but not exclusively. Because of her."

"Linda'll make him into a good sculptor, no matter what he was before, because she married him?"

"No. He would have to be the best of whatever he was for her to pick him out."

"So she's married now," I says.

"What?" he says. "No. She just met him, I tell you."

"So you aint—" I almost said *safe yet* before I changed it: "—sure yet. I mean, she aint decided yet."

"What the hell else am I talking about? Dont you remember what I told you last fall? that she would love once and it would be for keeps?"

"Except that you said 'doomed to.' "

"All right," he says.

"Doomed to fidelity and grief, you said. To love once quick and lose him quick and for the rest of her life to be faithful and to grieve. But leastways she aint lost him yet. In fact, she aint even got him yet. That's correct, aint it?"

"Didn't I say all right?" he says.

That was the first six months, about. Another year after that, that-ere little footrest ledge was up on that hand-painted Mount Vernon mantel—that-ere little raw wood step like out of a scrap pile, nailed by a country carpenter onto that what you might call respectability's virgin Matterhorn for the Al-pine climber to cling to panting, gathering his-self for that last do-or-die upsurge to deface the ultimate crowning pinnacle and peak with his own victorious initials. But not this one; and here was that humility again: not in public where it would be a insult to any and all that held Merchants and Farmers Bank Al-pine climbing in veneration, but in private like a secret chapel or a shrine: not to cling panting to it, desperate and indomitable, but to prop his feet on it while setting at his ease.

This time I was passing the office stairs when Lawyer come rushing around the corner as usual, with most of the law papers flying along loose in his outside pockets but a few of them still in his hand too as usual. I mean, he had jest two gaits: one standing more or less still and the other like his coattail was on fire. "Run back home and get your grip," he says. "We're leaving Memphis tonight for New York."

So we went up the stairs and as soon as we was inside the office he changed to the other gait as usual. He throwed the loose papers onto the desk and taken one of the cob pipes outen the dish and set down, only when he fumbled in his coat for the matches or tobacco or whatever it was he discovered the rest of the papers and throwed them onto the desk and set back in the chair like he had done already had all the time in the world and couldn't possibly anticipate nothing else happening in the next hundred years neither. "For the house-warming," he says.

"You mean the reception, dont you? Aint that what they call it after the preacher has done collected his two dollars?" He didn't say anything, jest setting there working at lighting that pipe like a jeweler melting one exact drop of platinum maybe into a watch. "So they aint going to marry," I says. "They're jest going to confederate. I've heard that: that that's why they call them Grinnich Village samples dreams: you can wake up without having to jump outen the bed in a dead run for the nearest lawyer."

He didn't move. He jest bristled, that lively and quick he never had time to change his position. He set there and bristled like a hedgehog, not moving of course: jest saying cold and calm, since even a hedgehog, once it has got itself arranged and prickled out, can afford a cold and calm collected voice too: "All right. I'll arrogate the term 'marriage' to it then. Do you protest or question it? Maybe you would even suggest a better one?—Because there's not enough time left," he says. "Enough left? There's none left. Young people today dont have any left because only fools under twenty-five can believe, let alone hope, that there's any left at all—for any of us, anybody alive today—"

"It dont take much time to say We both do in front of a preacher and then pay him whatever the three of you figger it's worth."

"Didn't I just say there's not even that much left if all you've had is just twenty-five or thirty years—"

"So that's how old he is," I says. "You stopped at jest twenty-five before."

He didn't stop at nowhere now: "Barely a decade since their fathers and uncles and brothers just finished the one which was to rid the phenomenon of government forever of the parasites—the hereditary proprietors, the farmers-general of the human dilemma who had just killed eight million human beings and ruined a forty-mile-wide strip down the middle of western Europe. Yet less than a dozen years later and the same old cynical manipulators not even bothering to change their names and faces but merely assuming a set of new titles out of the shibboleth of the democratic lexicon and its mythology, not even breaking stride to coalesce again to wreck the one doomed desperate hope—" *Now he will resume the folks that broke President Wilson's heart and killed the League of Nations* I thought, but he was the one that didn't even break stride: "That one already in Italy and one a damned sight more dangerous in Germany because all Mussolini has to work with are Italians while this other man has Germans. And the one in Spain that all he needs is to be let alone a little longer by the rest of us who still believe that if we just keep our eyes closed long enough it will all go away. Not to mention—"

"Not to mention the one in Russia," I said.

"—the ones right here at home: the organizations with the fine names confederated in unison in the name of God against the impure in morals and politics and with the wrong skin color and ethnology and religion: K.K.K. and Silver Shirts; not to mention the indigenous local champions like Long in Louisiana and our own Bilbo in Mississippi, not to mention our very own Senator Clarence Egglestone Snopes right here in Yoknapatawpha County—"

"Not to mention the one in Russia," I says.

"What?" he says.

"So that's why," I says. "He aint jest a sculptor. He's a communist too."

"What?" Lawyer says.

"Barton Kohl. The reason they didn't marry first is that Barton Kohl is a communist. He cant believe in churches and marriage. They wont let him."

"He wanted them to marry," Lawyer says. "It's Linda that wont." So now it was me that said What? and him setting there fierce and untouchable as a hedgehog. "You dont believe that?" he says.

"Yes," I says. "I believe it."

"Why should she want to marry? What could she have ever seen in the one she had to look at for nineteen years, to make her want any part of it?"

"All right," I says. "All right. Except that's the one I dont believe. I believe the first one, about there aint enough time left. That when you are young enough, you can believe. When you are young enough and brave enough at the same time, you can hate intolerance and believe in hope and, if you are sho enough brave, act on it." He still looked at me. "I wish it was me," I says.

"Not just to marry somebody, but to marry anybody just so it's marriage. Just so it's not adultery. Even you."

"Not that," I says. "I wish I was either one of them. To believe in intolerance and hope and act on it. At any price. Even at having to be under twenty-five again like she is, to do it. Even to being a thirty-year-old Grinnich Village sculptor like he is."

"So you do refuse to believe that all she wants is to cuddle up together and be what she calls happy."

"Yes," I says. "So do I." So I didn't go that time, not even when he said:

"Nonsense. Come on. Afterward we will run up to Saratoga and look at that ditch or hill or whatever it was where your first immi-grant Vladimir Kyrilytch Ratliff ancestor entered your native land."

"He wasn't no Ratliff then yet," I says. "We dont know what his last name was. Likely Nelly Ratliff couldn't even spell that one, let alone pronounce it. Maybe in fact neither could he. Besides, it wasn't even Ratliff then. It was Ratcliffe.—No," I says, "jest you will be enough. You can get cheaper corroboration than one that will not only need a round-trip ticket but three meals a day too."

"Corroboration for what?" he says.

"At this serious moment in her life when she is fixing to officially or leastways formally confederate or shack up with a gentleman friend of the opposite sex as the feller says, aint the reason for this trip to tell her and him at last who she is? or leastways who she aint?" Then I says, "Of course. She already knows," and he says,

"How could she help it? How could she have lived in the same house with Flem for nineteen years and still believe he could possi-bly be her father, even if she had incontrovertible proof of it?"

"And you aint never told her," I says. Then I says, "It's even worse than that. Whenever it occurs to her enough to maybe fret over it a little and she comes to you and says maybe, 'Tell me the truth now. He aint my father,' she can always depend on you saying, 'You're wrong, he is.' Is that the dependence and need you was speaking of?" Now he wasn't looking at me. "What would you do if she got it turned around backwards and said to you, 'Who is my father?'" No, he wasn't looking at me. "That's right," I says. "She wont never ask that. I reckon she has done watched Gavin Stevens too, enough to know there's some lies even he ought not to need to cope with." He wasn't looking at me a-tall. "So that there dependence is on a round-trip ticket too," I says.

He was back after ten days. And I thought how maybe if that sculptor could jest ketch her unawares, still half asleep maybe, and seduce her outen the bed and up to a altar or even jest a j.p. before she noticed where she was at, maybe he—Lawyer—would be free. Then I knowed that wasn't even wishful thinking because there wasn't nothing in that idea that could been called thinking a-tall. Because once I got rid of them hopeful cobwebs I realised I must a knowed for years what likely Eula knowed the moment she laid eyes on him: that he wouldn't never be free because he wouldn't never want to be free because this was his life and if he ever lost it he wouldn't have nothing left. I mean, the right and privilege and opportunity to dedicate forever his capacity for responsibility to something that wouldn't have no end to its appetite and that wouldn't never threaten to give him even a bone back in recompense. And I remembered what he said back there about how she was doomed to fidelity and monogamy—to love once and lose him and then to grieve, and I said I reckoned so, that being Helen of Troy's daughter was kind of like being say the ex-Pope of Rome or the ex-Emperor of Japan: there wasn't much future to it. And I knowed now he was almost right, he jest had that word "doomed" in the wrong place: that it wasn't her that was doomed, she would likely do fine; it was the one that was recipient of the fidelity and the monogamy and the love, and the one that was the proprietor of the responsibility that never even wanted, let alone expected, a bone back, that was the doomed one, and how even between them two the lucky one might be the one that had the roof fall on him while he was climbing into or out of the bed.

So naturally I would a got a fur piece quick trying to tell him that, so naturally my good judgment told me not to try it. And so partly by jest staying away from him but mainly by fighting like a demon, like Jacob with his angel, I finally resisted actively saying it—a temptation about as strong as a human man ever has to face, which is to deliberately throw away the chance to say afterward, "I told you so." So time passed. That little additional mantelpiece footrest was up now that hadn't nobody ever seen except that Negro yardman—a Jefferson legend after he mentioned it to me and him (likely) and me both happened to mention it in turn to some of our close intimates: a part of the Snopes legend and another Flem Snopes monument in that series mounting on and up from that water tank that we never knowed yet if they had got out of it all that missing Flem Snopes regime powerhouse brass them two mad skeered Negro firemen put into it.

Then it was 1936 and there was less and less of that time left: Mussolini in Italy and Hitler in Germany and sho enough, like Lawyer said, that one in Spain too; Lawyer said, "Pack your grip. We will take the airplane from Memphis tomorrow morning.—No no," he says, "you dont need to fear contamination from association this time. They're going to be married. They're going to Spain to join the Loyalist army and apparently he nagged and worried at her until at last she probably said, 'Oh hell, have it your way then.' "

"So he wasn't a liberal emancipated advanced-thinking artist after all," I says. "He was jest another ordinary man that believed if a gal was worth sleeping with she was worth deserving to have a roof over her head and something to eat and a little money in her pocket for the balance of her life."

"All right," he says. "All right."

"Except we'll go on the train," I says. "It aint that I'm jest simply skeered to go in a airplane: it's because when we go across Virginia I can see the rest of the place where that-ere first immigrant Vladimir Kyrilytch worked his way into the United States." So I was already on the corner with my grip when he drove up and stopped and opened the door and looked at me and then done what the moving pictures call a double take and says,

"Oh hell."

"It's mine," I says. "I bought it."

"You," he says, "in a necktie. That never even had one on before, let alone owned one, in your life."

"You told me why. It's a wedding."

"Take it off," he says.

"No," I says.

"I wont travel with you. I wont be seen with you."

"No," I says. "Maybe it aint jest the wedding. I'm going back to let all them V. K. Ratliff beginnings look at me for the first time. Maybe it's them I'm trying to suit. Or leastways not to shame." So we taken the train in Memphis that night and the next day we was in Virginia—Bristol then Roanoke and Lynchburg and turned northeast alongside the blue mountains and somewhere ahead, we didn't know jest where, was where that first Vladimir Kyrilytch finally found a place where he could stop, that we didn't know his last name or maybe he didn't even have none until Nelly Ratliff, spelled Ratcliffe then, found him, any more than we knowed what he was doing in one of them hired German regiments in General Burgoyne's army

that got licked at Saratoga except that Congress refused to honor the
terms of surrender and banished the whole kit-and-biling of them
to straggle for six years in Virginia without no grub nor money and
the ones like that first V.K. without no speech neither. But he never
needed none of the three of them to escape not only in the right
neighborhood but into the exact right hayloft where Nelly Ratcliffe,
maybe hunting eggs or such, would find him. And never needed no
language to eat the grub she toted him; and maybe he never knowed
nothing about farming before the day when she finally brought him
out where her folks could see him; nor never needed no speech to
speak of for the next development, which was when somebody—her
maw or paw or brothers or whoever it was, maybe jest a neighbor—
noticed the size of her belly; and so they was married and so that V.K.
actively did have a active legal name of Ratcliffe, and the one after
him come to Tennessee and the one after him moved to Missippi,
except that by that time it was spelled Ratliff, where the oldest son
is still named Vladimir Kyrilytch and still spends half his life trying
to keep anybody from finding it out.

   The next morning we was in New York. It was early; not even
seven oclock yet. It was too early. "Likely they aint even finished
breakfast yet," I says.

   "Breakfast hell," Lawyer says. "They haven't even gone to bed yet.
This is New York, not Yoknapatawpha County." So we went to the
hotel where Lawyer had already engaged a room. Except it wasn't a
room, it was three of them: a parlor and two bedrooms. "We can
have breakfast up here too," he says.

   "Breakfast?" I says.

   "They'll send it up here."

   "This is New York," I says. "I can eat breakfast in the bedroom
or kitchen or on the back gallery in Yoknapatawpha County." So we
went downstairs to the dining room. Then I says, "What time do
they eat breakfast then? Sundown? Or is that jest when they get up?"

   "No," he says. "We got a errand first.—No," he says, "we got two
errands." He was looking at it again, though I will have to do him the
justice to say he hadn't mentioned it again since that first time when
I got in the car back in Jefferson. And I remember how he told me
once how maybe New York wasn't made for no climate known to

man but at least some weather was jest made for New York. In which case, this was sholy some of it: one of them soft blue drowsy days in the early fall when the sky itself seems like it was resting on the earth like a soft blue mist, with the tall buildings rushing up into it and then stopping, the sharp edges fading like the sunshine wasn't jest shining on them but kind of humming, like wires singing. Then I seen it: a store, with a show window, a entire show window with not nothing in it but one necktie.

"Wait," I says.

"No," he says. "It was all right as long as just railroad conductors looked at it but you cant face a preacher in it."

"No," I says, "wait." Because I had heard about these New York side-alley stores too. "If it takes that whole show window to deserve jest one necktie, likely they will want three or four dollars for it."

"We cant help it now," he says. "This is New York. Come on."

And nothing inside neither except some gold chairs and two ladies in black dresses and a man dressed like a congressman or at least a preacher, that knowed Lawyer by active name. And then a office with a desk and a vase of flowers and a short dumpy dark woman in a dress that wouldn't a fitted nobody, with gray-streaked hair and the handsomest dark eyes I ever seen even if they was popped a little, that kissed Lawyer and then he said to her, "Myra Allanovna, this is Vladimir Kyrilytch," and she looked at me and said something; yes, I know it was Russian, and Lawyer saying: "Look at it. Just once if you can bear it," and I says,

"Sholy it aint quite as bad as that. Of course I had ruther it was yellow and red instead of pink and green. But all the same—" and she says,

"You like yellow and red?"

"Yessum," I says. Then I says, "In fact" before I could stop, and she says,

"Yes, tell me," and I says,

"Nothing. I was jest thinking that if you could jest imagine a necktie and then pick it right up and put it on, I would imagine one made outen red with a bunch or maybe jest one single sunflower in the middle of it," and she says,

"Sunflower?" and Lawyer says,

"Helianthe." Then he says, "No, that's wrong. Tournesol. Sonnenblume," and she says Wait and was already gone, and now I says
Wait myself.

"Even a five-dollar necktie couldn't support all them gold chairs. "
"It's too late now," Lawyer says. "Take it off." Except that when
she come back, it not only never had no sunflower, it wasn't even red.
It was jest dusty. No, that was wrong; you had looked at it by that
time. It looked like the outside of a peach, that you know that in a
minute, providing you can keep from blinking, you will see the first
beginning of when it starts to turn peach. Except that it dont do that.
It's still jest dusted over with gold, like the back of a sunburned gal.
"Yes," Lawyer says, "send out and get him a white shirt. He never
wore a white shirt before either."

"No, never," she says. "Always blue, not? And this blue, always?
The same blue as your eyes?"

"That's right," I says.

"But how?" she says. "By fading them? By just washing them?"

"That's right," I says. "I jest washes them."

"You mean, you wash them? Yourself?"

"He makes them himself too," Lawyer says.

"That's right," I says. "I sells sewing machines. First thing I
knowed I could run one too."

"Of course," she says. "This one for now. Tomorrow, the other
one, red with sonnenblume." Then we was outside again. I was still
trying to say Wait.

"Now I got to buy two of them," I says. "I'm trying to be serious.
I mean, please try to believe I am as serious right now as ere a man
in your experience. Jest exactly how much you reckon was the price
on that one in that window?"

And Lawyer not even stopping, saying over his shoulder in the
middle of folks pushing past and around us in both directions: "I
dont know. Her ties run up to a hundred and fifty. Say, seventy-five
dollars—" It was exactly like somebody had hit me a quick light lick
with the edge of his hand across the back of the neck until next I
knowed I was leaning against the wall back out of the rush of folks
in a fit of weak trembles with Lawyer more or less holding me up.
"You all right now?" he says.

"No I aint," I says. "Seventy-five dollars for a necktie? I cant! I wont!"

"You're forty years old," he says. "You should a been buying at the minimum one tie a year ever since you fell in love the first time. When was it? eleven? twelve? thirteen? Or maybe it was eight or nine, when you first went to school—provided the first-grade teacher was female of course. But even call it twenty. That's twenty years, at one dollar a tie a year. That's twenty dollars. Since you are not married and never will be and dont have any kin close enough to exhaust and wear you out by taking care of you or hoping to get anything out of you, you may live another forty-five. That's sixty-five dollars. That means you will have an Allanovna tie for only ten dollars. Nobody else in the world ever got an Allanovna tie for ten dollars."

"I wont!" I says. "I wont!"

"All right. I'll make you a present of it then."

"I cant do that," I says.

"All right. You want to go back there and tell her you dont want the tie?"

"Dont you see I cant do that?"

"All right," he says. "Come on. We're already a little late." So when we got to this hotel we went straight to the saloon.

"We're almost there," I says. "Cant you tell me yet who it's going to be?"

"No," he says. "This is New York. I want to have a little fun and pleasure too." And a moment later, when I realised that Lawyer hadn't never laid eyes on him before, I should a figgered why he had insisted so hard on me coming on this trip. Except that I remembered how in this case Lawyer wouldn't need no help since you are bound to have some kind of affinity of outragement anyhow for the man that for twenty-five years has been as much a part and as big a part of your simple natural normal anguish of jest having to wake up again tomorrow, as this one had. So I says,

"I'll be durned. Howdy, Hoake." Because there he was, a little gray at the temples, with not jest a sunburned outdoors look but a rich sunburned outdoors look that never needed that-ere dark expensive-looking city suit, let alone two waiters jumping around the table where he was at, to prove it, already setting there where Lawyer had drawed him from wherever it was out west he had located him, the same as he had drawed me for this special day. No, it wasn't Lawyer that had drawed McCarron and me from a thousand miles away and two thousand more miles apart, the three of us to meet at this moment in a New York saloon: it was that gal that done it—that gal that never had seen one of us and fur as I actively heard it to take a oath, never had said much more than good morning to the other two—that gal that likely not even knowed but didn't even care that she had inherited her maw's fatality to draw four men anyhow to that web, that one strangling hair; drawed all four of us without even lifting her hand—her husband, her father, the man that was still trying to lay down his life for her maw if he could jest find somebody that wanted it, and what you might call a by-standing family friend—to be the supporting cast while she said "I do" outen the middle of a matrimonial production line at the City Hall before getting on a ship to go to Europe to do whatever it was she figgered she was going to do in that war. So I was the one that said, "This is Lawyer Stevens, Hoake," with three waiters now (he was evidently that rich) bustling around helping us set down.

"What's yours?" he says to Lawyer. "I know what V.K. wants.—Bushmill's," he says to the waiter. "Bring the bottle.—You'll think you're back home," he says to me. "It tastes jest like that stuff Calvin Bookwright used to make—do you remember?" Now he was looking at it too. "That's an Allanovna, isn't it?" he says. "You've branched out a little since Frenchman's Bend too, haven't you?" Now he was looking at Lawyer. He taken his whole drink at one swallow though the waiter was already there with the bottle before he could a signalled. "Don't worry," he says. "You've got my word. I'm going to keep it."

"You stop worrying too," I says. "Lawyer's already got Linda. She's going to believe him first, no matter what anybody else might forget and try to tell her." And we could have et dinner there too, but Lawyer says,

"This is New York. We can eat dinner in Uncle Cal Bookwright's springhouse back home." So we went to that dining room. Then it was time. We went to the City Hall in a taxicab. While we was getting out, the other taxicab come up and they got out. He was not big, he jest looked big, like a football player. No: like a prize fighter. He didn't look jest tough, and ruthless aint the word neither. He looked like he would beat you or maybe you would beat him but you probably wouldn't, or he might kill you or you might kill him though you probably wouldn't. But he wouldn't never dicker with you, looking at you with eyes that was pale like Hub Hampton's but they wasn't hard: jest looking at you without no hurry and completely, missing nothing, and with already a pretty good idea beforehand of what he was going to see.

We went inside. It was a long hall, a corridor, a line of folks two and two that they would a been the last one in it except it was a line that never had no last: jest a next to the last and not that long: on to a door that said REGISTRAR and inside. That wasn't long neither; the two taxicabs was still waiting. "So this is Grinnich Village," I says. The door give right off the street but with a little shirttail of ground behind it you could a called a yard though maybe city folks called it a garden; it even had one tree in it, with three things on it that undoubtedly back in the spring or summer was leaves. But inside it was nice: full of folks of course, with two waiters dodging in and out with trays of glasses of champagne and three or four of the company helping too, not to mention the folks that was taking over the apartment while Linda and her new husband was off at the war in Spain— a young couple about the same age as them. "Is he a sculptor too?" I says to Lawyer.

"No," Lawyer says. "He's a newspaperman."

"Oh," I says. "Then likely they been married all the time."

It was nice: a room with plenty of window lights. It had a heap of stuff in it too but it looked like it was used—a wall full of books and a piano and I knowed they was pictures because they was hanging on the wall and I knowed that some of the other things was sculpture but the rest of them I didn't know what they was, made outen pieces of wood or iron or strips of tin and wires. Except that I couldn't ask then because of the rest of the poets and painters and sculptors and musicians, since he would still have to be the host until we—him and Linda and Lawyer and Hoake and me—could slip out and go down to where the ship was; evidently a heap of folks found dreams in Grinnich Village but evidently it was a occasion when somebody married in it. And one of them wasn't even a poet or painter or sculptor or musician or even jest a ordinary moral newspaperman but evidently a haberdasher taking Saturday evening off. Because we was barely in the room before he was not only looking at it too but rubbing it between his thumb and finger. "Allanovna," he says.

"That's right," I says.

"Oklahoma?" he says. "Oil?"

"Sir?" I says.

"Oh," he says. "Texas. Cattle then. In Texas you can choose your million between oil and cattle, right?"

"No sir," I says, "Missippi. I sell sewing machines."

So it was a while before Kohl finally come to me to fill my glass again.

"I understand you grew up with Linda's mother," he says.

"That's right," I says. "Did you make these?"

"These what?" he says.

"In this room," I says.

"Oh," he says. "Do you want to see more of them? Why?"

"I don't know yet," I says. "Does that matter?" So we shoved on through the folks—it had begun to take shoving by now—into a hall and then up some stairs. And this was the best of all: a loft with one whole side of the roof jest window lights—a room not jest where folks used but where somebody come off by his-self and worked. And him jest standing a little behind me, outen the way, giving me time and room both to look. Until at last he says,

"Shocked? Mad?" Until I says,

"Do I have to be shocked and mad at something jest because I never seen it before?"

"At your age, yes," he says. "Only children can stand surprise for the pleasure of surprise. Grown people cant bear surprise unless they are promised in advance they will want to own it."

"Maybe I aint had enough time yet," I says.

"Take it then," he says. So he leaned against the wall with his arms folded like a football player, with the noise of the party where he was still supposed to be host at coming up the stairs from below, while I taken my time to look: at some I did recognise and some I almost could recognise and maybe if I had time enough I would, and some

I knowed I wouldn't never quite recognise, until all of a sudden I knowed that wouldn't matter neither, not jest to him but to me too. Because anybody can see and hear and smell and feel and taste what he expected to hear and see and feel and smell and taste, and wont nothing much notice your presence nor miss your lack. So maybe when you can see and feel and smell and hear and taste what you never expected to and hadn't never even imagined until that moment, maybe that's why Old Moster picked you out to be the one of the ones to be alive.

So now it was time for that-ere date. I mean the one that Lawyer and Hoake had fixed up, with Hoake saying, "But what can I tell her—her husband—her friends?" and Lawyer says,

"Why do you need to tell anybody anything? I've attended to all that. As soon as enough of them have drunk her health, just take her by the arm and clear out. Just dont forget to be aboard the ship by eleven-thirty." Except Hoake still tried, the two of them standing in the door ready to leave, Hoake in that-ere dark expensive city suit and his derby hat in his hand, and Linda in a kind of a party dress inside her coat. And it wasn't that they looked alike, because they didn't. She was tall for a woman, so tall she didn't have much shape (I mean, the kind that folks whistle at), and he wasn't tall for a man and in fact kind of stocky. But their eyes was exactly alike. Anyhow, it seemed to me that anybody that seen them couldn't help but know they was kin. So he still had to try it: "A old friend of her mother's family. Her grandfather and my father may have been distantly related—" and Lawyer saying,

"All right, all right, beat it. Don't forget the time," and Hoake saying,

"Yes yes, we'll be at Twenty-One for dinner and afterward at the Stork Club if you need to telephone." Then they was gone and the rest of the company went too except three other men that I found out was newspapermen too, foreign correspondents; and Kohl his-self helped his new tenant's wife cook the spaghetti and we et it and drunk some more wine, red this time, and they talked about the war, about Spain and Ethiopia and how this was the beginning: the lights was going off all over Europe soon and maybe in this country too; until it was time to go to the ship. And more champagne in the bedroom there, except that Lawyer hadn't hardly got the first bottle open when Linda and Hoake come in.

"Already?" Lawyer says. "We didn't expect you for at least a hour yet."

"She—we decided to skip the Stork Club," Hoake says. "We took a fiacre through the Park instead. And now," he says, that hadn't even put the derby hat down.

"Stay and have some champagne," Lawyer says, and Kohl said something too. But Linda had done already held out her hand.

"Good-bye, Mr McCarron," she says. "Thank you for the evening and for coming to my wedding."

"Cant you say 'Hoake' yet?" he says.

"Good-bye, Hoake," she says.

"Wait in the cab then," Lawyer says. "We'll join you in a minute."

"No," Hoake says. "I'll take another cab and leave that one for you." Then he was gone. She shut the door behind him and came toward Lawyer, taking something outen her pocket.

"Here," she says. It was a gold cigarette lighter. "I know you wont ever use it, since you say you think you can taste the fluid when you light your pipe."

"No," Lawyer says. "What I said was, I know I can taste it."

"All right," she says. "Take it anyway." So Lawyer taken it. "It's engraved with your initials: see?"

"G L S," Lawyer says. "They are not my initials. I just have two: G S."

"I know. But the man said a monogram should have three so I loaned you one of mine." Then she stood there facing him, as tall as him almost, looking at him. "That was my father," she says.

"No," Lawyer says.

"Yes," she says.

"You dont mean to tell me he told you that," Lawyer says.

"You know he didn't. You made him swear not to."

"No," Lawyer says.

"You swear then."

"All right," Lawyer says. "I swear."

"I love you," she says. "Do you know why?"

"Tell me," Lawyer says.

"It's because every time you lie to me I can always know you will stick to it."

Then the second sentimental pilgrimage. No, something else come first. It was the next afternoon. "Now we'll go pick up the necktie," Lawyer says.

"No," I says.

"You mean you want to go alone?"

"That's right," I says. So I was alone, the same little office again and her still in the same dress that wouldn't fitted nobody already looking at my empty collar even before I put the necktie and the hundred and fifty dollars on the desk by the new one that I hadn't even teched yet because I was afraid to. It was red jest a little under what you see in a black-gum leaf in the fall, with not no single sunflower nor even a bunch of them but little yellow sunflowers all over it in a kind of diamond pattern, each one with a little blue center almost the exact blue my shirts gets to after a while. I didn't dare touch it. "I'm sorry," I says. "But you see I jest cant. I sells sewing machines in Missippi. I cant have it knowed back there that I paid seventy-five dollars apiece for neckties. But if I'm in the Missippi sewing-machine business and cant wear seventy-five dollar neckties, so are you in the New York necktie business and cant afford to have folks wear or order neckties and not pay for them. So here," I says. "And I ask your kindness to excuse me."

But she never even looked at the money. "Why did he call you Vladimir Kyrilytch?" she says. I told her.

"Except we live in Missippi now, and we got to live it down. Here," I says. "And I ask you again to ex—"

"Take that off my desk," she says. "I have given the ties to you. You cannot pay for them."

"Dont you see I cant do that neither?" I says. "No more than I could let anybody back in Missippi order a sewing machine from me and then say he had done changed his mind when I delivered it to him?"

"So," she says. "You cannot accept the ties, and I cannot accept the money. Good. We do this—" There was a thing on the desk that looked like a cream pitcher until she snapped it open and it was a cigarette lighter. "We burn it then, half for you, half for me—" until I says,

"Wait! Wait!" and she stopped. "No," I says, "no. Not burn money," and she says,

"Why not?" and us looking at each other, her hand holding the lit lighter and both our hands on the money.

"Because it's money," I says. "Somebody somewhere at some time went to—went through—I mean, money stands for too much hurt and grief somewhere to somebody that jest the money wasn't never worth—I mean, that aint what I mean . . ." and she says,

"I know exactly what you mean. Only the gauche, the illiterate, the frightened and the pastless destroy money. You will keep it then. You will take it back to—how you say?"

"Missippi," I says.

"Missippi. Where is one who, not needs: who cares about so base as needs? Who wants something that costs one hundred fifty dollar—a hat, a picture, a book, a jewel for the ear; something never never never anyhow just to eat—but believes he—she—will never have it, has even long ago given up, not the dream but the hope— This time do you know what I mean?"

"I know exactly what you mean because you jest said it," I says.

"Then kiss me," she says. And that night me and Lawyer went up to Saratoga.

"Did you tell Hoake better than to try to give her a lot of money, or did he jest have that better sense his-self?" I says.

"Yes," Lawyer says.

"Yes which?" I says.

"Maybe both," Lawyer says. And in the afternoon we watched the horses, and the next morning we went out to Bemis's Heights and Freeman's Farm. Except that naturally there wasn't no monument to one mercenary Hessian soldier that maybe couldn't even speak German, let alone American, and naturally there wasn't no hill or ditch or stump or rock that spoke up and said aloud: On this spot your first ancestral V.K. progenitor forswore Europe forever and entered the United States. And two days later we was back home, covering in two days the distance it taken that first V.K. four gener-

ations to do; and now we watched the lights go out in Spain and
Ethiopia, the darkness that was going to creep eastward across all
Europe and Asia too, until the shadow of it would fall across the
Pacific islands until it reached even America. But that was a little
while away yet when Lawyer says,

"Come up to the office," and then he says, "Barton Kohl is dead.
The airplane—it was a worn-out civilian passenger carrier, armed
with 1918 infantry machine guns, with homemade bomb bays
through which the amateur crew dumped by hand the homemade
bombs; that's what they fought Hitler's Luftwaffe with—was shot
down in flames so she probably couldn't have identified him even if
she could have reached the crash. She doesn't say what she intends to
do now."

"She'll come back here," I says.

"Here?" he says. "Back here?" then he says, "Why the hell
shouldn't she? It's home."

"That's right," I says. "It's doom."

"What?" he says. "What did you say?"

"Nothing," I says. "I jest said I think so too."

EIGHT

CHARLES MALLISON

*L*inda Kohl (Snopes that was, as Thackeray would say. Kohl that was too, since he was dead) wasn't the first wounded war hero to finally straggle back to Jefferson. She was just the first one my uncle bothered to meet at the station. I dont mean the railroad station; by 1937, it had been a year or so since a train had passed through Jefferson that a paid passenger could have got off of. And not even the bus depot because I dont even mean Jefferson. It was the Memphis airport we went to meet her, my uncle apparently discovering at the last minute that morning that he was not able to make an eighty-mile trip and back alone in his car.

She was not even the first female hero. For two weeks back in 1919 we had had a nurse, an authentic female lieutenant—not a denizen, citizen of Jefferson to be sure but at least kin to (or maybe just interested in a member of) a Jefferson family, who had been on the staff of a base hospital in France and—so she said—had actually spent two days at a casualty clearing station within sound of the guns behind Montdidier.

In fact, by 1919 even the five-year-old Jeffersonians like I was then were even a little blasé about war heroes, not only unscratched ones but wounded too getting off trains from Memphis Junction or New Orleans. Not that I mean that even the unscratched ones actually called themselves heroes or thought they were or in fact thought one way or the other about it until they got home and found the epithet being dinned at them from all directions until finally some of them, a few of them, began to believe that perhaps they were. I mean, dinned at them by the ones who organised and correlated the dinning—the ones who hadn't gone to that war and so were already on hand in advance to organise the big debarkation-port parades and the smaller county-seat local ones, with inbuilt barbecue and beer; the ones that hadn't gone to that one and didn't intend to go to the next one nor the one after that either, as long as all they had to do to stay out was buy the tax-free bonds and organise the hero-dinning parades so that the next crop of eight- and nine- and ten-year-old males could see the divisional shoulder patches and the wound- and service-stripes and the medal ribbons.

Until some of them anyway would begin to believe that that many voices dinning it at them must be right, and they were heroes. Because, according to Uncle Gavin, who had been a soldier too in his fashion (in the American Field Service with the French army in '16 and '17 until we got into it, then still in France as a Y.M.C.A. secretary or whatever they were called), they had nothing else left: young men or even boys most of whom had only the vaguest or completely erroneous idea of where and what Europe was, and none at all about armies, let alone about war, snatched up by lot overnight and regimented into an expeditionary force, to survive (if they could) before they were twenty-five years old what they would not even recognise at the time to be the biggest experience of their lives. Then to be spewed, again willy-nilly and again overnight, back into what they believed would be the familiar world they had been told they were enduring disruption and risking injury and death so that it would still be there when they came back, only to find that it wasn't there any more. So that the bands and the parades and the barbecues and all the rest of the hero-dinning not only would happen only that once and was already fading even before they could get adjusted to it, it was already on the way out before the belated last of them even got back home, already saying to them above the cold congealing meat and the flat beer while the last impatient brazen chord died away: "All right, little boys; eat your beef and potato salad and drink your beer and get out of our way, who are already up to our necks in this new world whose single and principal industry is not just solvent but dizzily remunerative peace."

So, according to Gavin, they had to believe they were heroes even though they couldn't remember now exactly at what point or by what action they had reached, entered for a moment or a second, that heroic state. Because otherwise they had nothing left: with only a third of life over, to know now that they had already experienced their greatest experience, and now to find that the world for which they had so endured and risked was in their absence so altered out of recognition by the ones who had stayed safe at home as to have no place for them in it any more. So they had to believe that at least some little of it had been true. Which (according to Gavin) was the why of the veterans' clubs and legions: the one sanctuary where at least once a week they could find refuge among the other betrayed and dispossessed reaffirming to each other that at least that one infinitesimal scrap had been so.

In fact (in Jefferson anyway) even the ones that came back with an arm or a leg gone, came back just like what they were when they left: merely underlined, italicised. There was Tug Nightingale. His father was the cobbler, with a little cubbyhole of a shop around a corner off the Square—a little scrawny man who wouldn't have weighed a hundred pounds with his last and bench and all his tools in his lap, with a fierce moustache which hid most of his chin too, and fierce undefeated intolerant eyes—a Hard-Shell Baptist who didn't merely have to believe it, because he knew it was so: that the earth was flat and that Lee had betrayed the whole South when he surrendered at Appomattox. He was a widower. Tug was his only surviving child. Tug had got almost as far as the fourth grade when the principal himself told Mr Nightingale it would be better for Tug to quit. Which Tug did, and now he could spend all his time hanging around the auction lot behind Dilazuck's livery stable, where he had been spending all his spare time anyhow, and where he now came into his own: falling in first with Lonzo Hait, our local horse and mule trader, then with Pat Stamper himself, who in the horse and mule circles not just in Yoknapatawpha County or north Mississippi but over most of Alabama and Tennessee and Arkansas too, was to Lonzo Hait what Fritz Kreisler would be to the fiddle player at a country picnic, and so recognised genius when he saw it. Because Tug didn't have any piddling mere affinity for and rapport with mules: he was an *homme fatal* to them, any mule, horse or mare either, being putty in his hands; he could do anything with them except buy and sell them for a profit. Which is why he never rose higher than a simple hostler and handy man and so finally had to become a house painter also to make a living: not a first-rate one, but at least he could stir the paint and put it on a wall or fence after somebody had shown him where to stop.

Which was his condition up to about 1916, when he was about thirty years old, maybe more, when something began to happen to him. Or maybe it had already happened and we—Jefferson—only noticed it then. Up to now he had been what you might call a standard-type provincial county-seat house painter: a bachelor, living with his father in a little house on the edge of town, having his weekly bath in the barbershop on Saturday night and then getting a little drunk afterward—not too much so: only once every two or three years waking up Sunday morning in the jail until they would release him on his own recognizance; this not for being too drunk but for fighting, though the fighting did stem from the whiskey, out of that mutual stage of it when the inevitable one (never the same one: it didn't need to be) challenged his old fixed father-bequeathed convictions that General Lee had been a coward and a traitor and that the earth was a flat plane with edges like the shed roofs he painted—then shooting a little dice in the big ditch behind the cemetery while he sobered up Sunday afternoon to go back to his turpentine Monday morning; with maybe four trips a year to the Memphis brothels.

Then it happened to him. He still had the Saturday-night barbershop bath and he still drank a little, though as far as Jefferson knew, never enough any more to need to go to combat over General Lee and Ptolemy and Isaac Newton, so that not only the jail but the harassed night marshal too who at the mildest would bang on the locked barbershop or poolroom door at two oclock Sunday morning, saying, "If you boys dont quiet down and go home," knew him no more. Nor did the dice game in the cemetery ditch; on Sunday morning now he would be seen walking with his scrawny fiercely moustached miniature father toward the little back-street Hard-Shell church, and that afternoon sitting on the minute gallery of their doll-sized house poring (whom the first three grades of school rotationally licked and the fourth one completely routed) over the newspapers and magazines which brought us all we knew about the war in Europe.

He had changed. Even we (Jefferson. I was only three then) didn't know how much until the next April, 1917, after the *Lusitania* and the President's declaration, and Captain (Mister then until he was elected captain of it) McLendon organised the Jefferson company to be known as the Sartoris Rifles in honor of the original Colonel Sartoris (there would be no Sartoris in it since Bayard and his twin brother John were already in England training for the Royal Flying Corps), and then we heard the rest of it: how Tug Nightingale, past thirty now and so even when the draft came would probably escape it, was one of the first to apply, and we—they— found out what his dilemma was: which was simply that he did not dare let his father find out that he planned to join the Yankee army, since if his father ever learned it, he, Tug, would be disinherited and thrown out. So it was more than Captain McLendon who said, "What? What's that?" and McLendon and another—the one who would be elected his First Sergeant—went home with Tug and the sergeant-to-be told it:

"It was like being shut up in a closet with a buzz saw that had jumped off the axle at top speed, or say a bundle of dynamite with the fuse lit and snapping around the floor like a snake, that you not only cant get close enough to step on it, you dont want to: all you want is out, and Mack saying, 'Wait, Mr Nightingale, it aint the Yankee army: it's the army of the United States: your own country,' and that durn little maniac shaking and seething until his moustache looked like it was on fire too, hollering, 'Shoot the sons of bitches! Shoot em! Shoot em!' and then Tug himself trying it: 'Papa, papa, Captain McLendon and Crack here both belong to it,' and old man Nightingale yelling, 'Shoot them then. Shoot all the blue-bellied sons of bitches,' and Tug still trying, saying, 'Papa, papa, if I dont join now, when they pass that draft they will come and get me anyway,' and still that little maniac hollering, 'Shoot you all! Shoot all you sons of bitches!' Yes sir. Likely Tug could join the German army or maybe even the French or British, and had his blessing. But not the one that General Lee betrayed him to that day back in 1865. So he threw Tug out. The three of us got out of that house as fast as we could, but before we even reached the sidewalk he was already in the room that was evidently Tug's. He never even waited to open the door: just kicked the window out, screen and all, and started throwing Tug's clothes out into the yard."

So Tug had crossed his Rubicon, and should have been safe now. I mean, Captain McLendon took him in. He—McLendon—was one of a big family of brothers in a big house with a tremendous mother weighing close to two hundred pounds, who liked to cook and eat both so one more wouldn't matter; maybe she never even noticed Tug. So he should have been safe now while the company waited for orders to move. But the others wouldn't let him alone; his method of joining the colors was a little too unique, not to mention *East Lynne;* there was always one to say:

"Tug, is it really so that General Lee didn't need to give up when he did?" and Tug would say,

"That's what papa says. He was there and seen it, even if he wasn't but seventeen years old." And the other would say:

"So you had to go clean against him, clean against your own father, to join the Rifles?" And Tug sitting there quite still now, the hands that never would be able to paint more than the roughest outhouse walls and finesseless fences but which could do things to the intractable and unpredictable mule which few other hands dared, hanging quiet too between his knees, because by now he would know what was coming next. And the other—and all the rest of them within range—watching Tug with just half an eye since the other three halves would be watching Captain McLendon across the room; in fact they usually waited until McLendon had left, was actually out.

"That's right," Tug would say; then the other:

"Why did you do it, Tug? You're past thirty now, safe from the draft, and your father's an old man alone here with nobody to take care of him."

"We cant let them Germans keep on treating folks like they're doing. Somebody's got to make them quit."

"So you had to go clean against your father to join the army to make them quit. And now you'll have to go clean against him again to go round to the other side of the world where you can get at them."

"I'm going to France," Tug would say.

"That's what I said: halfway round. Which way are you going? east or west? You can pick either one and still get there. Or better still, and I'll make you a bet. Pick out east, go on east until you find the war, do whatever you aim to do to them Germans and then keep right on going east, and I'll bet you a hundred dollars to one that when you see Jefferson next time, you'll be looking at it right square across Miss Joanna Burden's mailbox one mile west of the court-house." But by that time Captain McLendon would be there; probably somebody had gone to fetch him. He may have been such a bad company commander that he was relieved of his command long before it ever saw the lines, and a few years after this he was going to be the leader in something here in Jefferson that I anyway am glad I dont have to lie down with in the dark every time I try to go to sleep. But at least he held his company together (and not by the bars on his shoulders since, if they had been all he had, he wouldn't have had a man left by the first Saturday night, but by simple instinctive humanity, of which even he, even in the middle of that business he was going to be mixed up in later, seemed to have had a little, like now) until a better captain could get hold of it. He was already in uniform. He was a cotton man, a buyer for one of the Memphis export houses, and he spent most of his commissions gambling on cotton futures in the market, but he never had looked like a farmer until he put on the uniform.

"What the hell's going on here?" he said. "What the hell do you think Tug is? a damn ant running around a damn orange or something? He aint going *around* anything: he's going straight *across* it, across the water to France to fight for his country, and when they dont need him in France any longer he's coming back across the same water, back here to Jefferson the same way he went out of it, like we'll all be damn glad to get back to it. So dont let me hear any more of this" (excrement: my word) "any more."

Whether or not Tug would continue to need Captain McLendon, he didn't have him much longer. The company was mustered that week and sent to Texas for training; whereupon, since Tug was competent to paint any flat surface provided it was simple enough, with edges and not theoretical boundaries, and possessed that gift with horses and mules which the expert Pat Stamper had recognised at once to partake of that inexplicable quality called genius, naturally the army made him a cook and detached him the same day, so that he was not only the first Yoknapatawpha County soldier (the Sartoris boys didn't count since they were officially British troops) to go overseas, he was among the last of all American troops to get back home, which was in late 1919, since obviously the same military which would decree him into a cook, would mislay where it had sent him (not lose him; my own experience between '42 and '45 taught me that the military never loses anything: it merely buries it).

So now he was back home again, living alone now (old Mr Nightingale had died in that same summer of 1917, killed, Uncle Gavin said, by simple inflexibility, having set his intractable and contemptuous face against the juggernaut of history and science both that April day in 1865 and never flinched since), a barn and fence painter once more, with his Saturday-night bath in the barbershop and again drinking and gambling again within his means, only with on his face now a look, as V. K. Ratliff put it, as if he had been taught and believed all his life that the fourth dimension was invisible, then suddenly had seen one. And he didn't have Captain McLendon now. I mean, McLendon was back home too but they were no longer commander and man. Or maybe it was that even that natural humanity of Captain McLendon's, of which he should have had a pretty good supply since none of it seemed to be within his reach on his next humanitarian crises after that one when he shielded Tug from the harsh facts of cosmology, would not have sufficed here.

This happened in the barbershop too (no, I wasn't there; I still wasn't old enough to be tolerated in the barbershop at ten oclock on Saturday night even if I could have got away from Mother; this was hearsay from Ratliff to Uncle Gavin to me). This time the straight man was Skeets McGowan, Uncle Willy Christian's soda jerker—a young man with a swagger and dash to him, who probably smelled more like toilet water than just water, with a considerable following of fourteen- and fifteen-year-old girls at Uncle Willy's fountain, who we realised afterward had been just a little older than we always thought and, as Ratliff said, even ten years later would never know as much as he—Skeets—figured he had already forgotten ten years ago; he had just been barbered and scented, and Tug had finished his bath and was sitting quietly enough while the first drink or two began to take hold.

"So when you left Texas, you went north," Skeets said.

"That's right," Tug said.

"Come on," Skeets said. "Tell us about it. You left Texas going due north, to New York. Then you got on the boat, and it kept right on due north too."

"That's right," Tug said.

"But suppose they fooled you a little. Suppose they turned the boat, to the east or west or maybe right back south—"

"God damn it," Tug said. "Dont you think I know where north is? You can wake me up in the bed in the middle of the night and I can point my hand due north without even turning on the light."

"What'll you bet? Five dollars? Ten?"

"I'll bet you ten dollars to one dollar except that any dollar you ever had you already spent on that shampoo or that silk shirt."

"All right, all right," Skeets said. "So the boat went straight north, to France. And you stayed in France two years and then got on another boat and it went straight north too. Then you got off that boat and got on a train and it—"

"Shut up," Tug said.

"—went straight north too. And when you got off, you were back in Jefferson."

"Shut up, you goddam little bastard," Tug said.

"So dont you see what that means? Either one of two things: either they moved Jefferson—" Now Tug was on his feet though even now apparently Skeets knew no better: "—which all the folks that stayed around here and didn't go to that war can tell you they didn't. Or you left Jefferson going due north by way of Texas and come back to Jefferson still going due north without even passing Texas again—" It took all the barbers and customers and loafers too and finally the night marshal himself to immobilise Tug. Though by that time Skeets was already in the ambulance on his way to the hospital.

And there was Bayard Sartoris. He got back in the spring of '19 and bought the fastest car he could find and spent his time ripping around the county or back and forth to Memphis until (so we all believed) his aunt, Mrs Du Pre, looked over Jefferson and picked out Narcissa Benbow and then caught Bayard between trips with the other hand long enough to get them married, hoping that would save Bayard's neck since he was now the last Sartoris Mohican (John had finally got himself shot down in July of '18), only it didn't seem to work. I mean, as soon as he got Narcissa pregnant, which must have been pretty quick, he was back in the car again until this time Colonel Sartoris himself stepped into the breach, who hated cars yet gave up his carriage and pair to let Bayard drive him back and forth to the bank, to at least slow the car down during that much of the elapsed mileage. Except that Colonel Sartoris had a heart condition, so when the wreck came it was him that died: Bayard just walked out of the crash and disappeared, abandoned pregnant wife and all, until the next spring when he was still trying to relieve his boredom by seeing how much faster he could make something travel than he could invent a destination for; this time another aeroplane: a new experimental type at the Dayton testing field: only this one fooled him by shedding all four of its wings in midair.

"That's right: boredom, Uncle Gavin said—that war was the only civilised condition which offered any scope for the natural black-guardism inherent in men, that not just condoned and sanctioned it but rewarded it, and that Bayard was simply bored: he would never forgive the Germans not for starting the war but for stopping it, ending it. But Mother said that was wrong. She said that Bayard was frightened and ashamed: not ashamed because he was frightened but terrified when he discovered himself to be capable of, vulnerable to being ashamed. She said that Sartorises were different from other people. That most people, nearly all people, loved themselves first, only they knew it secretly and maybe even admitted it secretly; and so they didn't have to be ashamed of it—or if they were ashamed, they didn't need to be afraid of being ashamed. But that Sartorises didn't even know they loved themselves first, except Bayard. Which was all right with him and he wasn't ashamed of it until he and his twin brother reached England and got into flight training without parachutes in aeroplanes made out of glue and baling wire; or maybe not even until they were at the front, where even for the ones that had lived that far the odds were near zero against scout pilots sur-

viving the first three weeks of active service. When suddenly Bayard
realised that, unique in the squadron and, for all he knew, unique in
all the R.F.C. or maybe all military air forces, he was not one individual creature at all but there was two of him since he had a twin
engaged in the same risk and chance. And so in effect he alone out
of all the people flying in that war had been vouchsafed a double
indemnity against those odds (and vice versa of course since his twin
would enjoy the identical obverse vouchsafement)—and in the next
second, with a kind of terror, discovered that he was ashamed of the
idea, knowledge, of being capable of having thought it even.

That was what Mother said his trouble was—why he apparently
came back to Jefferson for the sole purpose of trying, in that sullen
and pleasureless manner, to find out just how many different ways he
could risk breaking his neck that would keep the most people
anguished or upset or at least annoyed: that completely un-Sartoris-
like capacity for shame which he could neither live with nor quit;
could neither live in toleration with it nor by his own act repudiate it.
That was why the risking, the chancing, the fatalism. Obviously the
same idea—twinship's double indemnity against being shot down—
must have occurred to the other twin at the same moment, since they
were twins. But it probably hadn't worried John any more than the
things he had done in his war (Uncle Gavin said—and in about five
years I was going to have a chance to test it myself—that no man ever
went to a war, even in the Y.M.C.A., without bringing back something he wished he hadn't done or anyway would stop thinking
about) worried that old original Colonel Sartoris who had been their
great-grandfather; only he, Bayard, of all his line was that weak, that
un-Sartoris.

So now (if Mother was right) he had a double burden. One was
anguish over what base depths of imagination and selfish hope he
knew himself to be, not so much capable of as doomed to be ashamed
of; the other, the fact that if that twinship double indemnity did work
in his favor and John was shot down first, he—Bayard—would, no
matter how much longer he survived, have to face his twin some day
in the omniscience of the mutual immortality, with the foul stain of
his weakness now beyond concealment. The foul stain being not the
idea, because the same idea must have occurred to his twin at the

same instant with himself although they were in different squadrons now, but that of the two of them, John would not have been ashamed of it. The idea being simply this: John had managed to shoot down three huns before he himself was killed (he was probably a better shot than Bayard or maybe his flight commander liked him and set up targets) and Bayard himself had racked up enough ninths and sixteenths, after the British method of scoring (unless somebody was incredible enough to say "Not me; I was too damn scared to remember to pull up the cocking handles") to add up to two and maybe an inch over; now that John was gone and no longer needed his, suppose, just suppose he could wangle, bribe, forge, corrupt the records and whoever kept them, into transferring all the Sartoris bumf under one name, so that one of them anyway could come back home an ace—an idea not base in itself, because John had not only thought of it too but if he had lived and Bayard had died, would have managed somehow to accomplish it, but base only after he, Bayard, had debased and befouled it by being ashamed of it. And he could not quit it of his own volition, since when he faced John's ghost some day in the course of simple fatality, John would be just amused and contemptuous; where if he did it by putting the pistol barrel in his mouth himself, that ghost would be not just risible and contemptuous but forever unreconciled, irreconcilable.

But Linda Snopes—excuse me: Snopes Kohl—would be our first female one. So you would think the whole town would turn out, or at least be represented by delegates: from the civic clubs and churches, not to mention the American Legion and the V.F.W., which would have happened if she had been elected Miss America instead of merely blown up by a Franco shell or land mine or whatever it was that went off in or under the ambulance she was driving and left her stone deaf. So I said, "What does she want to come back home for? There's nothing for her to join. What would she want in a Ladies' Auxiliary, raffling off homemade jam and lamp shades. Even if she could make jam, since obviously cooking is the last thing a sculptor would demand of his girl. Who was just passing time anyway between Communist meetings until somebody started a Fascist war he could get into. Not to mention the un-kosher stuff she would have had to learn in Jefferson, Mississippi. Especially if where she learned to cook was in that Dirty Spoon her papa beat Ratliff out of back there when they first came to town." But I was wrong. It wouldn't be municipal: only private: just three people only incidentally from Jefferson because they were mainly out of her mother's past: my uncle, her father, and Ratliff. Then I saw there would be only two. Ratliff wouldn't even get in the car.

"Come on," Uncle Gavin said. "Go with us."

"I'll wait here," Ratliff said. "I'll be the local committee. Until next time," he said at me.

"What?" Uncle Gavin said.

"Nothing," Ratliff said. "Jest a joke Chick told me that I'm reminding him of."

Then I saw it wasn't going to be even two out of her mother's past. We were not even going by the bank, let alone stop at it. I said, "What the hell would Mr Snopes want, throwing away at least six hours of good usury to make a trip all the way to Memphis to meet his daughter, after all the expense he had to go to get her out of Jefferson—not only butchering up De Spain's house, but all that imported Italian marble over her mother's grave to give her something worth going away from or not coming back to if you like that better."

I said: "So it's my fault I wasn't born soon enough either to defend Das Democracy in your war or Das Kapital in hers. Meaning there's still plenty of time for me yet. Or maybe what you mean is that Hitler and Mussolini and Franco all three working together cannot get an authentic unimpeachable paid-up member of the Harvard R.O.T.C. into really serious military trouble. Because I probably wont make Porcellian either; F.D.R. didn't."

I said: "That's it. That's why you insisted on me coming along this morning: although she hasn't got any eardrums now and cant hear you say No or Please No or even For God's sake No, at least she cant marry you before we get back to Jefferson with me right here in the car too. But there's the rest of the afternoon when you can chase me out, not to mention the eight hours of the night when Mother likes to believe I am upstairs asleep. Not to mention I've got to go back to Cambridge next month—unless you believe your . . . is it virginity or just celibacy? is worth even that sacrifice? But then why not,

since it was your idea to send me all the way to Cambridge, Mass, for
what we laughingly call an education. Being as Mother says she's
been in love with you all her life, only she was too young to know it
and you were too much of a gentleman to tell her. Or does Mother
really always know best?"

By this time we had reached the airport; I mean Memphis. Uncle
Gavin said, "Park the car and let's have some coffee. We've probably got at least a half-hour yet." We had the coffee in the restaurant;
I dont know why they dont call it the Skyroom here too. Maybe
Memphis is still off quota. Ratliff said she would have to marry somebody sooner or later, and every day that passed made it that much
sooner. No, that wasn't the way he put it: that he—Uncle Gavin—
couldn't escape forever, that almost any day now some woman would
decide he was mature and dependable enough at last for steady work
in place of merely an occasional chore; and that the sooner this happened the better, since only then would he be safe. I said, "How safe?
He seems to me to be doing all right; I never knew anybody that
scatheless."

"I dont mean him," Ratliff said. "I mean us, Yoknapatawpha
County; that he would maybe be safe to live with then because he
wouldn't have so much time for meddling."

In which case, saving us would take some doing. Because he—
Gavin—had one defect in his own character which always saved him,
no matter what jeopardy it left the rest of us in. I mean, the fact that
people get older, especially young girls of fifteen or sixteen, who
seem to get older all of a sudden in six months or one year than they
or anybody else ever does in about ten years. I mean, he always
picked out children, or maybe he was just vulnerable to female children and they chose him, whichever way you want it. That the selecting or victim-falling was done at an age when the oath of eternal
fidelity would have ceased to exist almost before the breath was dry
on it. I'm thinking now of Melisandre Backus naturally, before my
time and Linda Snopes's too. That is, Melisandre was twelve and
thirteen and fourteen several years before she vacated for Linda to
take her turn in the vacuum, Gavin selecting and ordering the books
of poetry to read to Melisandre or anyway supervise and check on,
which was maybe how by actual test, trial and error, he knew which

ones to improve Linda's mind and character with when her turn came, or anyway alter them.

Though pretty soon Melisandre committed the irrevocable error of getting a year older and so quitting forever that fey unworld of Spenser and the youth Milton, for the human race where even the sort of girl that he picked out or that picked out him, when a man talked about fidelity and devotion to her, she was in a position to tell him either to put up or shut up. Anyway, he was saved that time. Though I wasn't present to remember exactly what the sequence was: whether Gavin went off to Harvard first or maybe it was between Harvard and Heidelberg, or whether she got married first. Anyway, when he got back from his war, she was married. To a New Orleans underworld big shot named Harriss with two esses. And how in the world or where on earth she ever managed to meet him—a shy girl, motherless and an only child, who lived on what used to be one of our biggest plantations two or three miles from town but that for years had been gradually going to decay, with her widowed father who spent all his time on the front gallery in summer and in the library in winter with a bottle of whiskey and a volume of Horace. Who (Melisandre) had as far as we knew never been away from it in her life except to be driven daily in to town by a Negro coachman in a victoria while she graduated from the grammar school then the high school then the Female Academy. And a man about whom all we knew was what he said: that his name was Harriss with two esses, which maybe it was, and that he was a New Orleans importer. Which we knew he was, since (this was early 1919, before Uncle Gavin got back home) even Jefferson recognised when it saw one a bullet-proof Cadillac that needed two chauffeurs, both in double-breasted suits that bulged a little at the left armpit.

Not to mention the money. Mr Backus died about then and of course there were some to say it was with a broken heart over his only child marrying a bootleg czar. Though apparently he waited long enough to make sure his son-in-law was actually a czar or anyway the empire a going and solvent one, since the money had already begun to show a little before he died—the roofs and galleries patched and shored up even if Mr Backus evidently balked at paint on the house yet, and gravel in the drive so that when she came home to spend that first Christmas, she and the nurse and the czarevitch could go back and forth to town in an automobile instead of the old victoria drawn by a plow team. Then Mr Backus died and the house and outbuildings too got painted. And now Harriss with both his esses began to appear in Jefferson, making friends even in time though most of Yoknapatawpha County was unsold still, just neutral, going out there in the Model T's and on horses and mules, to stand along the road and watch what had been just a simple familiar red-ink north Mississippi cotton plantation being changed into a Virginia or Long Island horse farm, with miles of white panel fence where the rest of us were not a bit too proud for what we called bobwire and any handy sapling post, and white stables with electric light and steam heat and running water and butlers and footmen for the horses where a lot of the rest of us still depended on coal-oil lamps for light and our wives to tote firewood and water from the nearest woodlot and spring or well.

Then there were two children, an heir and a princess too, when Harriss died with his two esses in a New Orleans barber's chair of his ordinary thirty-eight-caliber occupational disease. Whereupon the horses and their grooms and valets became sold and the house closed except for a caretaker, vacant now of Mrs Harriss with her two esses and the two children and the five maids and couriers and nannies and secretaries, and now Mother and the other ones who had been girls with her in the old Academy days would get the letters and post cards from the fashionable European cities telling how just the climate at first but presently, in time, the climate and the schools both were better for the children and (on Mother's naturally) she hoped Gavin was well and maybe even married. "So at least he's safe from that one," I told Ratliff, who said,

"Safe?"

"Why the hell not? She not only got too big for the fairy tale, she's got two children and all that money: what the hell does she want to marry anybody for? Or not Gavin anyway; he dont want money: all he wants is just to meddle and change. Why the hell isn't he safe now?"

"That's right," Ratliff said. "It looks like he would almost have to be, dont it? At least until next time." Joke. And still worth repeating two hours ago when he declined to come with us. And Gavin sitting there drinking a cup of what whoever ran the airport restaurant called coffee, looking smug and inscrutable and arrogant and immune as a louse on a queen's arse. Because maybe Linda Kohl (pardon me, Snopes Kohl) had plenty of money too, not only what her mother must have left her but what Uncle Gavin, as her guardian, had managed to chisel out of old Will Varner. Not chiselled out of her father too because maybe old Snopes was glad to stump up something just to have what Gavin or Ratliff would call that reproachless virgin rectitude stop looking at him. But she didn't have two children so all Ratliff and I had to trust, depend on this time was that old primary condition founded on simple evanescence, that every time a moment occurred they would be one moment older: that they had to be alive for him to notice them, and they had to be in motion to be alive, and the only moment of motion which caught his attention, his eye, was that one at which they entered puberty like the swirl of skirt or flow or turn of limb when entering, passing through a door, slowed down by the camera trick but still motion, still a moment, irrevocable.

That was really what saved him each time: that the moment had to be motion. They couldn't stop in the door, and once through it they didn't stop either; sometimes they didn't even pause long enough to close it behind them before going on to the next one and through it, which was into matrimony—from maturation to parturition in one easy lesson you might say. Which was all right. Uncle Gavin wouldn't be at that next door. He would still be watching the first one. And since life is not so much motion as an inventless repetition of motion, he would never be at that first door long before there would be another swirl, another unshaped vanishing adolescent leg. So I should have thought to tell Ratliff that, while I was in Memphis helping Uncle Gavin say good-bye to this one, he might be looking around the Square to see who the next one was going to be, as Linda had already displaced Melisandre Backus probably before Melisandre even knew she had been dispossessed. Then in the next moment I knew that would not be necessary; obviously Uncle Gavin had already picked her out himself, which was why he could sit there placid and composed, drinking coffee while we waited for the plane to be announced.

Which it was at last. We went out to the ramp. I stopped at the rail. "I'll wait here," I said. "You'll want a little privacy while you can still get it even if it's only anonymity and not solitude. Have you got your slate ready? or maybe she'll already have one built in on her cuff, or maybe strapped to her leg like aviators carry maps." But he had gone on. Then the plane taxied up, one of the new DC 3's, and in time there she was. I couldn't see her eyes from this distance but then it wasn't them, it was just her ears the bomb or shell or mine or whatever it was blew up—the same tall girl too tall to have a shape but then I dont know: women like that and once you get their clothes off they surprise you even if she was twenty-nine years old now. Then I could see her eyes, so dark blue that at first you thought they were black. And I for one never did know how or where she got them or the black hair either since old Snopes's eyes were the color of stagnant pond water and his hair didn't have any color at all, and her mother had had blue eyes too but her hair was blond. So that when I tried to remember her, she always looked like she had just been raided out of a brothel in the Scandinavian Valhalla and the cops had just managed to fling a few garments on her before they hustled her into the wagon. Fine eyes too, that probably if you were the one to finally get the clothes off you would have called them beautiful too. And she even had the little pad and pencil in her hand while she was kissing Gavin. I mean, kissing him. Though evidently he would need a little time to get used to using it or depending on it because he said aloud, just like she was anybody else:

"Here's Chick too," and she remembered me; she was as tall as Gavin and damn near as tall as me, as well as a nail-biter though maybe that had come after the shell or perhaps after the bereavement. And when she shook hands she really had driven that ambulance and apparently changed the tires on it too, speaking not loud but in that dry harsh quacking voice that deaf people learn to use, even asking about Mother and Father as if she really cared, like any ordinary Jefferson woman that never dreamed of going to wars and getting blown up. Though Uncle Gavin remembered now, or at least was learning fast, taking the pad and pencil and scrawling something on it, baggage I reckon, since she said, "Oh yes," just like she could hear too, and got the checks out of her handbag.

I brought the car up while they untangled the bags. So she had lived with the guy for years before they married but it didn't show on her. And she had gone to Spain to the war and got blown up at the front, and that didn't show on her either. I said, "Why dont you let her drive? Then maybe she wont be so nervous because she cant talk to you."

"Maybe you'd better drive then," he said. So we did, and brought the hero home, the two of them in the back. And somebody may have said, "Why dont we all ride in front? the seat's wide enough." Though I dont remember it. Or at least nobody did. Or anyway at least they got into the back seat. So I dont remember that either: only Uncle Gavin: "You can relax now. You're quite safe. I'm holding her hand."

Which they were, she holding his hand in both hers on her lap and every mile or so the duck voice would say, "Gavin," and then after a mile or so, "Gavin." And evidently she hadn't had the pad and pencil long enough to get used to them either or maybe when you lose hearing and enter real silence you forget that everything does not take place in that privacy and solitude. Or maybe after he took the pencil from her to answer on the pad, she couldn't wait to get the pencil back so both should have had slates: "Yes it does. I can feel it, somewhere in my skull or the back of my mouth. It's an ugly sound. Isn't it?" But evidently Gavin was learning because it was still the duck voice: "Yes it is. I can feel it, I tell you." And still the duck voice: "How? If I try to practise, how can I know when it's right?" Which I agree with myself: if you're going to take time out from your law practice and being county attorney to restore to your deaf girl friend the lost bridehead of her mellifluity, how would you go about it. Though what a chance for a husband: to teach your stone-deaf wife that all she needed to make her tone and pitch beautiful was merely to hold her breath while she spoke. Or maybe what Uncle Gavin wrote next was simply Jonson (or some of that old Donne or Herrick maybe or even just Suckling maybe—any or all of them annotated to that one ear—eye now—by that old Stevens) *Vale not these cherry lips with vacant speech But let me drink instead thy tender Yes.* Or maybe what he wrote was simpler still: *Hold it till we get home. This is no place to restore your voice. Besides, this infant will have to go back to Cambridge next month and then we'll have plenty of time, plenty of privacy.*

Thus we brought the hero home. Now we could see Jefferson, the clock on the courthouse, not to mention her father's water tank, and now the duck voice was saying Ratliff. "Bart liked him. He said he hadn't expected to like anybody from Mississippi, but he was wrong." What Gavin wrote this time was obvious, since the voice said: "Not even you. He made me promise—I mean, whichever one of us it was, would give Ratliff one of his things. You remember it—the Italian boy that you didn't know what it was even though you had seen sculpture before, but Ratliff that had never even seen an Italian boy, nor anything else beyond the Confederate monument in front of the courthouse, knew at once what it was, and even what he was doing?" And I would have liked the pad myself long enough to write *What was the Italian boy doing?* only we were home now, the hero; Gavin said:

"Stop at the bank first. He should have some warning; simple decency commands it. Unless he has had his warning and has simply left town for a little space in which to wrestle with his soul and so bring it to the moment which it must face. Assuming of course that even he has realised by now that he simply cannot foreclose her out of existence like a mortgage or a note."

"And have a public reception here in the street before she has had a chance to fix her makeup?" I said.

"Relax," he said again. "When you are a little older you will discover that people really are much more gentle and considerate and kind than you want right now to believe."

I pulled up at the bank. But if I had been her I wouldn't even have reached for the pencil, duck quack or not, to say, "What the hell? Take me on home." She didn't. She sat there, holding his hand in both hers, not just on her lap but right against her belly, looking around at the Square, the duck voice saying, "Gavin. Gavin." Then: "There goes Uncle Willy, coming back from dinner." Except it wasn't old man Christian: he was dead. But then it didn't really matter whether anybody wrote that on the pad or not. And Gavin was right. Nobody stopped. I watched two of them recognise her. No, I mean they recognised juxtaposition: Gavin Stevens's car at the curb before the bank at twenty two minutes past one in the afternoon with me at the wheel and Gavin and a woman in the back seat. Who had all heard about Linda Kohl I mean Snopes Kohl, anyhow that she was female and from Jefferson and had gone near enough to a war for it to bust her eardrums. Because he is right: people are kind and gentle and considerate. It's not that you dont expect them to be, it's because you have already made up your mind they are not and so they upset you, throw you off. They didn't even stop, just one of them said Howdy Gavin and went on.

I got out and went into the bank. Because what would I do myself if I had a daughter, an only child, and her grandfather had plenty of money for it and I could have afforded myself to let her go away to school. Only I didn't and nobody knew why I wouldn't, until suddenly I let her go, but only as far as the University which was only fifty miles away; and nobody knew why for that either: only that I aimed to become president of the bank that the president of it now was the man everybody believed had been laying my wife ever since we moved to town. That is, nobody knew why until three months later, when my wife went to the beauty parlor for the first time in her life and that night shot herself carefully through the temple so as not to disarrange the new permanent, and when the dust finally settled sure enough that fornicating bank president had left town and now I was not only president of his bank but living in his house and you would have thought I wouldn't need the daughter any more and she could go wherever the hell she wanted provided it wasn't ever Jefferson, Mississippi, again. Except I wouldn't even let her do that until we could both sit in the car and see the monument over her mother's grave unveiled, sitting there defenseless before the carved face and the carved defenseless taunt:

A VIRTUOUS WIFE IS A CROWN TO HER HUSBAND
HER CHILDREN RISE AND CALL HER BLESSED

and then I said, "All right. You can go now." And I came back out.
"Mr Snopes has taken the afternoon off," I said. "To go home and wait there for his daughter." So we went there, on to the colonial monstrosity which was the second taunt. He had three monuments in Jefferson now: the water tank, the gravestone, and the mansion. And who knows at which of the windows he lurked his wait or waited

out his lurk, whichever way you prefer. "Maybe I should come in too," I said.

"Maybe we should each have a pad and pencil," Uncle Gavin said. "Then everybody could hear." We were expected. Almost at once the Negro yardman-chauffeur came out the front door. I got the luggage out onto the sidewalk while they still stood there, she as tall as him and Gavin in her arms just as much as she was in his, kissing right on the street in the broad daylight, the duck voice saying "Gavin Gavin" not so much as if she still couldn't believe it was him at last but as if she still hadn't got used to the new sound she was convinced she made. Then she turned him loose and he said, "Come on," and we got back in the car, and that was all. The hero was home. I turned in the middle of the block and looked not back, I would have liked to say, if it had been true: the houseman still scuttling up the walk with the bags and she still standing there, looking at us, a little too tall for my taste, immured, inviolate in silence, invulnerable, serene.

That was it: silence. If there were no such thing as sound. If it only took place in silence, no evil man has invented could really harm him: explosion, treachery, the human voice.

That was it: deafness. Ratliff and I couldn't beat that. Those others, the other times had flicked the skirt or flowed or turned the limb at and into mere puberty; beyond it and immediately, was the other door immediately beyond which was the altar and the long line of drying diapers: fulfillment, the end. But she had beat him. Not in motion continuous through a door, a moment, but immobilised by a thunderclap into silence, herself the immobile one while it was the door and the walls it opened which fled away and on, herself no mere moment's child but the inviolate bride of silence, inviolable in maidenhead, fixed, forever safe from change and alteration. Finally I ran Ratliff to ground; it took three days.

"Her husband is sending you a present," I said. "It's that sculpture you liked: the Italian boy doing whatever it was you liked that Gavin himself who has not only seen Italian boys before but maybe even one doing whatever this one is doing, didn't even know where first base was. But it's all right. You dont have a female wife nor any innocent female daughters either. So you can probably keep it right there in the house.—She's going to marry him," I said.

"Why not?" he said. "I reckon he can stand it. Besides, if somebody jest marries him, maybe the rest of us will be safe."

"The rest of them, you mean?" I said.

"I mean jest what I said," Ratliff answered. "I mean the rest of all of us."

NINE

CHARLES MALLISON

Gavin was right. That was late August. Three weeks later I was back in Cambridge again, hoping, I mean trying, or maybe what I mean is I belonged to the class that would or anyway should, graduate next June. But I had been in Jefferson three weeks, plenty long enough even if they had insisted on having banns read: something quite unnecessary for a widow who was not only a widow but a wounded war hero too. So then I thought maybe they were waiting until they would be free of me. You know: the old road-company drammer reversed in gender: the frantic child clinging this time to the prospective groom's coattail, crying "Papa papa papa" (in this case Uncle uncle uncle) "please don't make us marry Mrs Smith."

Then I thought (it was Thanksgiving now; pretty soon I would be going home for Christmas) *Naturally it wont occur to any of them to bother to notify me way up here in Massachusetts.* So I even thought of writing and asking, not Mother of course and certainly not Uncle Gavin, since if it had happened he would be too busy to answer, and if it hadn't he would still be too busy either dodging for his life if he was the one still saying No, or trying to learn her enough language to hear Please if he was the one saying Yes. But to Ratliff, who would be an interested bystander even if you couldn't call that much curiosity about other people's affairs which he possessed merely innocent— maybe even a wire: *Are they bedded formally yet or not? I mean is it rosa yet or still just sub, assuming you assume the same assumption they teach us up here at Harvard that once you get the clothes off those tall up-and-down women you find out they aint all that up-and-down at all.*

Then it was Christmas and I thought *Maybe I wronged them. Maybe they have been waiting for me all along, not to interrupt my education by an emergency call but for the season of peace and good will to produce me*

862

available to tote the ring or bouquet or whatever it is. But I didn't even see
her. Uncle Gavin and I even spent most of one whole day together.
I was going out to Sartoris to shoot quail with Benbow (he wasn't but
seventeen but he was considered one of the best bird shots in the
county, second only to Luther Biglin, a half farmer, half dog trainer,
half market hunter, who shot left-handed, not much older than Benbow, in fact about my age, who lived up near Old Wyottsport on the
river) and Uncle Gavin invited himself along. He—Gavin—wouldn't
be much of a gun even if he stopped talking long enough but now
and then he would go with me. And all that day, nothing; it was me
that finally said:

"How are the voice lessons coming?"

"Mrs Kohl? Fair. But your fresh ear would be the best judge," and
I said:

"When will that be?" and he said:

"Any time you're close enough to hear it." And again on Christmas day, it was me. Ratliff usually had Christmas dinner with us,
Uncle Gavin's guest though Mother liked him too, whether or not
because she was Uncle Gavin's twin. Or sometimes Uncle Gavin ate
with Ratliff and then he would take me because Ratliff was a damned
good cook, living alone in the cleanest little house you ever saw,
doing his own housework and he even made the blue shirts he always
wore. And this time too it was me.

"What about Mrs Kohl for dinner too?" I asked Mother, and
Uncle Gavin said:

"My God, did you come all the way down here from Cambridge
to spend Christmas too looking at that old fish-blooded son—" and
caught himself in time and said, "Excuse me, Maggie," and Mother
said:

"Certainly she will have to take her first Christmas dinner at home
with her father." And the next day I left. Spoade—his father had been
at Harvard back in 1909 with Uncle Gavin—had invited me to
Charleston to see what a Saint Cecilia ball looked like from inside.
Because we always broke up then anyway; the day after Christmas
Father always went to Miami to spend a week looking at horses and
Mother would go too, not that she was interested in running horses
but on the contrary: because of her conviction that her presence or

anyway adjacence or at least contiguity would keep him from buying one.

Then it was 1938 and I was back in Cambridge. Then it was September, 1938, and I was still or anyway again in Cambridge, in law school now. Munich had been observed or celebrated or consecrated, whichever it was, and Uncle Gavin said, "It wont be long now." But he had been saying that back last spring. So I said:

"Then what's the use in me wasting two or three more years becoming a lawyer when if you're right nobody will have time for civil cases any more, even if I'm still around to prosecute or defend them?" and he said:

"Because when this one is over, all humanity and justice will have left will be the law:" and I said:

"What else is it using now?" and he said:

"These are good times, boom halcyon times when what do you want with justice when you've already got welfare? Now the law is the last resort, to get your hand into the pocket which so far has resisted or foiled you."

That was last spring, in June when he and Mother (they had lost Father at Saratoga though he had promised to reach Cambridge in time for the actual vows) came up to see me graduate in Ack. And I said, "What? No wedding bells yet?" and he said:

"Not mine anyway:" and I said:

"How are the voice lessons coming? Come on," I said, "I'm a big boy now; I'm a Harvard A.M. too even if I wont have Heidelberg. Tell me. Is that really all you do when you are all cosy together? practise talking?" and he said:

"Hush and let me talk awhile now. You're going to Europe for the summer; that's my present to you. I have your tickets and your passport application; all you need do is go down to the official photographer and get mugged."

"Why Europe? and Why now? Besides, what if I dont want to go?" and he said:

"Because it may not be there next summer. So it will have to be this one. Go and look at the place; you may have to die in it."

"Why not wait until then, then?" and he said:

"You will go as a host then. This summer you can still be a guest."

There were three of us; by fast footwork and pulling all the strings we could reach, we even made the same boat. And that summer we— I: two of us at the last moment found themselves incapable of passing Paris—saw a little of Europe on a bicycle. I mean, that part still available: that presumable corridor of it where I might have to do Uncle Gavin's dying: Britain, France, Italy—the Europe which Uncle Gavin said would be no more since the ones who survived getting rid of Hitler and Mussolini and Franco would be too exhausted and the ones who merely survived them wouldn't care anyway.

So I did try to look at it, to see, since even at twenty-four I still seemed to believe what he said just as I believed him at fourteen and (I presume: I cant remember) at four. In fact, the Europe he remembered or thought he remembered was already gone. What I saw was a kind of composed and collected hysteria: a frenetic holiday in which everybody was a tourist, native and visitor alike. There were too many soldiers. I mean, too many people dressed as, and for the moment behaving like, troops, as if for simple police or temporary utility reasons they had to wear masquerade and add to the Maginot Line (so that they—the French ones anyway—seemed to be saying, "Have a heart; dont kid us. We dont believe it either.") right in the middle of the fight for the thirty-nine-hour week; the loud parliamentary conclaves about which side of Piccadilly or the Champs Elysées the sandbags would look best on like which side of the room to hang the pictures; the splendid glittering figure of Gamelin still wiping the soup from his moustache and saying, "Be calm. I am here"—as though all Europe (oh yes, us too; the place was full of Americans too) were saying, "Since Evil is the thing, not only *de rigueur* but successful too, let us all join Evil and so make it the Good."

Then me too in Paris for the last two weeks, to see if the Paris of Hemingway and the Paris of Scott Fitzgerald (they were not the same ones; they merely used the same room) had vanished completely or not too; then Cambridge again, only a day late: all of which, none of which that is, ties up with anything but only explains to me why it was almost a year and a half before I saw her again. And so we had Munich: that moment of respectful silence then once more about our affairs; and Uncle Gavin's letter came saying "It wont be long now." Except that it was probably already too late for me. When I had to go—no, I dont mean that: when the time came for me to go—I wanted to be a fighter pilot. But I was already twenty-four now; in six years I would be thirty and even now it might be too late; Bayard and John Sartoris were twenty when they went to England in '16 and Uncle Gavin told me about one R.F.C. (I mean R.A.F. now) child who was a captain with such a record that the British government sent him back home and grounded him for good so that he might at least be present on the day of his civilian majority. So I would probably wind up as a navigator or engineer on bombers, or maybe at thirty they wouldn't let me go up at all.

But still no wedding bells. Maybe it was the voice. My spies—I only needed one of course: Mother—reported that the private lessons were still going on, so maybe she felt that the Yes would not be dulcet enough yet to be legal. Which—legality—she would of course insist on, having tried cohabitation the first time *au naturel* you might say, and it blew up in her face. No, that's wrong. The cohabitation didn't blow up until after it became legal, until whichever one it was finally said, "Oh hell then, get the license and the preacher but please for sweet please sake shut up." So now she would fear a minister or a j.p. like Satan or the hangman, since to appear before one in the company of someone of the opposite sex would be the same as a death warrant. Which she certainly would not wish for Uncle Gavin, since not only was the Yes to him going to be tender enough to have brought her all the way back to Jefferson to say it, he wouldn't leave enough money to make it worth being his widow in case that Yes wasn't so tender.

No, that's wrong too. If she had to shack up with a man for five years before he would consent to marry her, I mean, with a sculptor so advanced and liberal that even Gavin couldn't recognise what he sculpted, made, he must have been pretty advanced in liberalism. And if he had to quit anything as safe and pleasant as being a Greenwich Village sculptor living with a girl that could afford and wanted to pay the rent and buy the grub whether he married her or not—if he had to quit all this to go to Spain to fight on what anybody could have told him would be the losing side, he must have been advanced even beyond just liberalism. And if she loved him enough to wait five

years for him to say All right, dammit, call the parson, and then went
to Spain to get blown up herself just to be with him, she must be one
of them too since apparently you cant even be moderate about communism: you either violently are or violently are not. (I asked him; I
mean of course Uncle Gavin. "Suppose she is," he said. "All right,"
I said. "So what the hell?" he said. "All right, all right," I said. "What
the hell's business is it of yours anyway?" he said. "All right, all right,
all right," I said.) And just being blown up wouldn't cure it. So there
would be no wedding bells; that other one had been a mere deviation
due to her youth, not to happen again; she was only for a moment
an enemy of the people, and paid quickly for it.

So there would be no preacher. They were just going to practise
people's democracy, where everybody was equal no matter what you
looked like when he finally got your clothes off, right here in Jefferson. So all you had to figure out was, how the bejesus they would
manage it in a town no bigger and equal than Jefferson. Or not they:
he, Gavin. I mean, it would be his trouble, problem, perhaps need.
Not hers. She was free, absolved of mundanity; who knows, who is
not likewise castrate of sound, circumcised from having to hear, of
need too. She had the silence: that thunderclap instant to fix her forever inviolate and private in solitude; let the rest of the world blun-
der in all the loud directions over its own feet trying to find first base
at the edge of abyss like one of the old Chaplin films.

He would have to find the ways and means; all she would bring
would be the capability for compliance, and what you might call a
family precedence. Except that she wasn't her mother, not to mention Gavin not being Manfred de Spain. I mean—I was only thirteen when Mrs Snopes shot herself that night so I still dont know
how much I saw and remembered and how much was compelled
onto or into me from Uncle Gavin, being, as Ratliff put it, as I had
spent the first eleven or twelve years of my existence in the middle
of Uncle Gavin, thinking what he thought and seeing what he saw,
not because he taught me to but maybe just because he let me,
allowed me to. I mean, Linda and Uncle Gavin wouldn't have that
one matchless natural advantage which her mother and Manfred de
Spain had, which was that aura, nimbus, condition, whatever the
word is, in which Mrs Snopes not just existed, lived, breathed, but

created about herself by just existing, living, breathing. I dont know what word I want: an aura not of license, unchastity, because (this may even be Ratliff; I dont remember now) little petty moral conditions like restraint and purity had no more connection with a woman like Mrs Snopes—or rather, a woman like her had no more concern with or even attention for them—than conventions about what force you use or when or how or where have to do with wars or cyclones. I mean, when a community suddenly discovered that it has the sole ownership of Venus for however long it will last, she cannot, must not be a chaste wife or even a faithful mistress whether she is or not or really wants to be or not. That would be not only intolerable, but a really criminal waste; and for the community so accoladed to even condone, let alone abet, the chastity, continence, would be an affront to the donors deserving their godlike vengeance. Like having all miraculous and matchless season—wind, sun, rain, heat and frost— concentrated into one miraculous instant over the county, then us to try to arrogate to ourselves the puny right to pick and choose and select instead of every man woman and child that could walk turning out to cultivate to the utmost every seed the land would hold. So we—I mean the men and the women both—would not even ask to escape the anguish and uproar she would cause by breathing and existing among us and the jealousy we knew ourselves to be unworthy of, so long as we did have one who could match and cope with her in fair combat and so be our champion and pride like the county ownership of the fastest horse in the country. We would all be on hers and De Spain's side; we would even engineer and guard the trysts; only the preachers would hate her because they would be afraid of her since the god she represented without even trying to, for the men to pant after and even the women to be proud that at least one of their sex was its ambassador, was a stronger one than the pale and desperate Galilean who was all they had to challenge with.

Because Linda didn't have that quality; that one was not transferable. So all that remained for her and Gavin was continence. To put it crudely, morality. Because where could they go. Not to her house because between her and her father, the wrong one was deaf. And not to his because the house he lived in wasn't his but Mother's and one of the earliest (when the time came of course) principles he taught me was that a gentleman does not bring his paramour into the home of: in this order: His wife. His mother. His sister. His mistress. And they couldn't make the coincidental trips to the available places in Memphis or New Orleans or maybe as far away as St Louis and Chicago that (we assumed) her mother and Manfred de Spain used to make, since even police morality, not to mention that of that semi-underworld milieu to which they would have had to resort, would have revolted at the idea of seducing a stone-deaf woman from the safety and innocence of her country home town, to such a purpose. So that left only his automobile, concealed desperately and franti-cally behind a bush—Gavin Stevens, aged fifty, M.A. Harvard, Ph.D. Heidelberg, LI.B. Mississippi, American Field Service and Y.M.C.A., France, 1915-1918, County Attorney; and Linda Kohl, thirty, widow, wounded in action with the communist forces in Spain, fumbling and panting in a parked automobile like they were seventeen years old.

Especially when the police found out (I mean if, of course, if somebody came and told them) that she was a communist. Or Jef-ferson either, for that matter. We had two Finns who had escaped by the skin of their teeth from Russia in 1917 and from Europe in 1919 and in the early twenties wound up in Jefferson; nobody knew why—one the cobbler who had taken over Mr Nightingale's little shop, the other a tinsmith—who were not professed communists nor confessed either since they still spoke too little English by the time Mr Roosevelt's N.R.A. and the labor unions had made "communist" a dirty word referring mostly to John L. Lewis's C.I.O. In fact, there was no need as they saw it to confess or profess either. They simply took it for granted that there was a proletariat in Jefferson as spe-cific and obvious and recognisable as the day's climate, and as soon as they learned English they would find it and, all being proletarians together, they would all be communists together too as was not only their right and duty but they couldn't help themselves. That was fif-teen years ago now, though the big one, the cobbler, the one slower at learning English, was still puzzled and bewildered, believing it was simply the barrier of language instead of a condition in which the Jef-ferson proletariat declined not only to know it was the proletariat but even to be content as the middle class, being convinced instead that it was merely in a temporary interim state toward owning in its turn

Mr Snopes's bank or Wallstreet Snopes's wholesale grocery chain or (who knows?) on the way to the governor's mansion in Jackson or even the White House in Washington.

The little one, the tinsmith, was quicker than that. Maybe, as distinct from the cobbler's sedentary and more meditative trade, he got around more. Anyway he had learned some time ago that any proletariat he became a member of in Jefferson he would have to manufacture first. So he set about it. The only means he had was to recruit, convert communists, and the only material he had were Negroes. Because among us white male Jeffersons there was one concert of unanimity, no less strong and even louder at the bottom, extending from the operators of Saturday curb-side peanut- and popcorn-vending machines, through the side-street and back-alley grocers, up to the department-store owners and automobile and gasoline agencies, against everybody they called communists now—Harry Hopkins, Hugh Johnson and everybody else associated with N.R.A., Eugene Debs, the I.W.W., the C.I.O.—any and everybody who seemed even to question our native-born Jefferson right to buy or raise or dig or find anything as cheaply as cajolery or trickery or threat or force could do it, and then sell it as dear as the necessity or ignorance or timidity of the buyer would stand. And that was what Linda had, all she had in our alien capitalist waste this far from home if she really was a communist and communism really is not just a political ideology but a religion which has to be practised in order to stay alive— two Arctic Circle immigrants: one practically without human language, a troglodyte, the other a little quick-tempered irreconcilable hornet because of whom both of them were already well advanced outside the Jefferson pale, not by being professed communists (nobody would have cared how much of a communist the little one merely professed himself to be so long as he didn't actually interfere with local wage scales, just as they could have been Republicans so long as they didn't try to interfere with our Democratic town and county elections or Catholics as long as they didn't picket churches or break up prayer meetings) but Negro lovers: consorters, political affiliators with Negroes. Not social consorters: we would not have put up with that from even them and the little one anyway knew enough Jefferson English to know it. But association of any sort was too much; the local police were already looking cross-eyed at them even though we didn't really believe a foreigner could do any actual harm among our own loyal colored. So, you see, all they—Gavin and Linda—had left now was marriage. Then it was Christmas 1938, the last one before the lights began to go out, and I came home for the holidays and she came to supper one night. Not Christmas dinner. I dont know what happened there: whether Mother and Gavin decided it would be more delicate to ask her and let her decline, or not ask her at all. No, that's wrong. I'll bet Mother invited them both—her and old Snopes too. Because women are marvellous. They stroll perfectly bland and serene through a fact that the men have been bloodying their heads against for years; whereupon you find that the fact not only wasn't important, it wasn't really there. She invited them both, exactly as if she had been doing it whenever she thought of it maybe at least once a month for the last hundred years, whenever she decided to give them a little pleasure by having them to a meal, or whenever she decided it would give her pleasure to have them whether they thought so or not; and Linda declined for both of them in exactly the same way.

So you can imagine that Christmas dinner in that house that nobody I knew had seen the inside of except Mother (oh yes, she would have by now, with Linda home again) and Uncle Gavin: the dining room—table chairs sideboard cabinets chandeliers and all— looking exactly as it had looked in the Memphis interior decorator's warehouse when he—Snopes—traded in Major de Spain's mother's furniture for it, with him at one end of the table and Linda at the other and the yardman in a white coat serving them—the old fish-blooded son of a bitch who had a vocabulary of two words, one being No and the other Foreclose, and the bride of silence more immaculate in that chastity than ever Caesar's wife because she was invulnerable too, forever safe, in that chastity forever pure, that couldn't have heard him if he had had anything to say to her, any more than he could have heard her, since he wouldn't even recognise the language she spoke in. The two of them sitting there face to face through the long excruciating ritual which the day out of all the days compelled; and nobody to know why they did it, suffered it, why she suffered and endured it, what ritual she served or compulsion expiated—or who knows? what portent she postulated to keep him reminded. Maybe that was why. I mean, why she came back to Jefferson. Evidently it wasn't to marry Gavin Stevens. Or at least not yet.

So it would be just an ordinary supper, though Mother would have said (and unshakably believed) that it was in honor of me being at home again. And didn't I just say that women are wonderful? She— Linda: a present from Guess Who—had a little pad of thin ivory leaves just about big enough to hold three words at a time, with gold corners, on little gold rings to turn the pages, with a little gold stylus thing to match, that you could write on and then efface it with a handkerchief or a piece of tissue or, in a mere masculine emergency, a little spit on your thumb and then use it again (sure, maybe he gave it to her in return for that gold cigarette lighter engraved G L S when he didn't have L for his middle initial or in fact any middle initial at all, that she gave him about five years ago that he never had used because nobody could unconvince him he could taste the fluid through his cob pipe). And though Mother used the pad like the rest of us, it was just coincidental, like any other gesture of the hands while talking. Because she was talking to Linda at the same time, not even watching her hand but looking at Linda instead, so that she couldn't have deciphered the marks she was making even provided she was making marks, just talking away at Linda exactly as she did to the rest of us. And be damned if Linda wouldn't seem to understand her, the two of them chattering and babbling away at one another like women do, so that maybe no women ever listen to the other one because they dont have to, they have already communicated before either one begins to speak.

Because at those times Linda would talk. Oh yes, Gavin's voice lessons had done some good because they must have, there had been too many of them or anyway enough of them, assuming they did spend some of the time together trying to soften down her voice. But it was still the duck's voice: dry, lifeless, dead. That was it: dead. There was no passion, no heat in it; and, what was worse, no hope. I mean, in bed together in the dark and to have more of love and excitement and ecstasy than just one can bear and so you must share it, murmur it, and to have only that dry and lifeless quack to murmur, whisper with. This time (there were other suppers during the next summer but this was the first one when I was at table too) she began to talk about Spain. Not about the war. I mean, the lost war. It was queer. She mentioned it now and then, not as if it had never happened but as if their side hadn't been licked. Some of them like Kohl had been killed and a lot of the others had had the bejesus blown out of the eardrums and arms and legs like her, and the rest of them were scattered (and in no time now would begin to be proscribed and investigated by the F.B.I., not to mention harried and harassed by the amateurs, but we hadn't quite reached that yet) but they hadn't been whipped and hadn't lost anything at all. She was talking about the people in it, the people like Kohl. She told about Ernest Hemingway and Malraux, and about a Russian, a poet that was going to be better than Pushkin only he got himself killed; and Mother scribbling on the pad but not paying any more attention to what she thought she was writing than Linda was, saying,

"Oh, Linda, no!"—you know: how tragic, to be cut off so young, the work unfinished, and Gavin taking the pad away from Mother but already talking too:

"Nonsense. There's no such thing as a mute inglorious Milton. If he had died at the age of two, somebody would still write it for him."

Only I didn't bother with the pad; I doubt if I could have taken it away from them. "Named Bacon or Marlowe," I said.

"Or maybe a good sound synthetic professional name like Shakespeare," Uncle Gavin said.

But Linda hadn't even glanced at the pad. I tell you, she and Mother didn't need it.

"Why?" she said. "What line or paragraph or even page can you compose and write to match giving your life to say No to people like Hitler and Mussolini?" and Gavin not bothering with the pad either now:

"She's right. She's absolutely right, and thank God for it. Nothing is ever lost. Nothing. Nothing." Except Linda of course. Gavin said how Kohl had been a big man, I dont mean just a hunk of beef, but virile, alive; a man who loved what the old Greeks meant by laughter, who would have been a match for, competent to fulfill, any woman's emotional and physical life too. And Linda was just thirty now and oh yes, the eyes were beautiful, and more than just the eyes; maybe it never mattered to Kohl what was inside her clothes, nor would to anyone else lucky enough to succeed him, including Uncle Gavin. So now I understood at last what I was looking at: neither Mother nor Linda either one needed to look at what Mother thought she was scribbling on that damned ivory slate, since evidently from the second day after Linda got home Mother had been as busy and ruthless and undevious as one of the old Victorian headhunting mamas during the open season at Bath or Tunbridge Wells in Fielding or Dickens or Smollett. Then I found out something else. I remembered how not much more than a year ago we were alone in the office and Ratliff said,

"Look-a-here, what you want to waste all this good weather being jealous of your uncle for? Somebody's bound to marry him sooner or later. Someday you're going to outgrow him and you'll be too busy yourself jest to hang around and protect him. So it might jest as well be Linda." You see what I mean? that evidently it was transferable. I mean, whatever it was her mother had had. Gavin had seen her once when she was thirteen years old, and look what happened to him. Then Barton Kohl saw her once when she was nineteen years old, and look where he was now. And now I had seen her twice, I mean after I was old enough to know what I was looking at: once at the Memphis airport last summer, and here tonight at the supper table, and now I knew it would have to be me to take Uncle Gavin off to the library or den or wherever such interviews happen, and say:

"Look here, young man. I know how dishonorable your intentions are. What I want to know is, how serious they are." Or if not him, at least somebody. Because it wouldn't be him. Ratliff had told me how Gavin said her doom would be to love once and lose him and then to mourn. Which could have been why she came back to Jefferson: since if all you want is to grieve, it doesn't matter where you are. So she was lost; she had even lost that remaining one who should have married her for no other reason than that he had done more than anybody else while she was a child to make her into what she was now. But it wouldn't be him; he had his own prognosis to defend, make his own words good no matter who anguished and suffered.

Yes, lost. She had been driving that black country-banker-cum-Baptist-deacon's car ever since she got home; apparently she had assumed at first that she would drive it alone, until old Snopes himself objected because of the deafness. So each afternoon she would be waiting in the car when the bank closed and the two of them would drive around the adjacent country while he could listen for the approaching horns if any. Which—the country drives—was in his character since the county was his domain, his barony—the acres, the farms, the crops—since even where he didn't already hold the mortgage, perhaps already in process of foreclosure even, he could measure and calculate with his eye the ones which so far had escaped him.

That is, except one afternoon a week, usually Wednesday. Old Snopes neither smoked nor drank nor even chewed tobacco; what his jaws worked steadily on was, as Ratliff put it, the same little chunk of Frenchman's Bend air he had brought in his mouth when he moved to Jefferson thirty years ago. Yes, lost: it wasn't even to Uncle Gavin: it was Ratliff she went to that afternoon and said, "I cant find who sells the whiskey now." No, not lost so much, she had just been away too long, explaining to Ratliff why she hadn't gone to Uncle Gavin: "He's the County Attorney; I thought—" and Ratliff patting her on the back right there in the street, saying for anybody to hear it since obviously she couldn't:

"You been away from home too long. Come on. We'll go git him."

So the three of them in Gavin's car drove up to Jakeleg Wattman's so-called fishing camp at Wyott's Crossing so she would know where and how herself next time. Which was to drive up to Jakeleg's little unpainted store (Jakeleg kept it unpainted so that whenever a recurrent new reform-administration sheriff would notify him he had to be raided again, Jakeleg wouldn't have a lot of paint to scratch up in drawing the nails and dismantling the sections and carrying them another mile deeper into the bottom until the reform reached its ebb and he could move back convenient to the paved road and the automobiles) and get out of the car and step inside where the unpainted shelves were crowded with fishhooks and sinkers and lines and tobacco and flashlight batteries and coffee and canned beans and shotgun shells and the neat row of United

States Internal Revenue Department liquor licenses tacked on the wall and Jakeleg in the flopping rubber hip boots he wore winter and summer with a loaded pistol in one of them, behind the chicken-wire-barricaded counter, and you would say, "Howdy, Jake. What you got today?" And he would tell you: the same one brand like he didn't care whether you liked that brand or not, and the same one price like he didn't give a damn whether that suited you either. And as soon as you said how many the Negro man (in the flopping hip boots Jakeleg had worn last year) would duck out or down or at least out of sight and reappear with the bottles and stand holding them until you had given Jakeleg the money and got your change (if any) back and Jakeleg would open the wicket in the wire and shove the bottles through and you would return to your car and that was all there was to it; taking (Uncle Gavin) Linda right on in with him, saying as likely as not: "Howdy, Jake. Meet Mrs Kohl. She cant hear but there's nothing wrong with her taste and swallowing." And maybe Linda said,

"What does he have?" and likely what Uncle Gavin wrote on the pad for that was *Thats fighting talk here This is a place where you take it or leave it Just give him eight dollars or sixteen if you want 2*. So next time maybe she came alone. Or maybe Uncle Gavin himself walked into the bank and on to that little room at the back and said, "Look here, you old fish-blooded son of a bitch, are you going to just sit here and let your only female daughter that wont even hear the trump of doom, drive alone up yonder to Jakeleg Wattman's bootleg joint to buy whiskey?" Or maybe it was simple coincidence: a Wednesday afternoon and he—Mr Snopes—cant say, "Here, hold on; where the hell you going? This aint the right road." Because she cant hear him and in fact I dont know how he did talk to her since I cant imagine his hand writing anything except adding a percent symbol or an expiration date; maybe they just had a county road map he could point to that worked up until this time. So now he had not one dilemma but three: not just the bank president's known recognisable car driving up to a bootleg joint, but with him in it; then the dilemma of whether to let every prospective mortgagee in Yoknapatawpha County hear how he would sit there in the car and let his only female child walk into a notorious river-bottom joint to buy whiskey, or go in himself and with his own Baptist deacon's hand pay out sixteen dollars' worth of his own life's blood.

Lost. Gavin told me how over a year ago the two Finn communists had begun to call on her at night (at her invitation of course) and you can imagine this one. It would be the parlor. Uncle Gavin said she had fixed up a sitting room for herself upstairs, but this would be in the parlor diagonally across the hall from the room where old Snopes was supposed to spend all his life that didn't take place in the bank. The capitalist parlor and the three of them, the two Finnish immigrant laborers and the banker's daughter, one that couldn't speak English and another that couldn't hear any language, trying to communicate through the third one who hadn't yet learned to spell, talking of hope, millennium, dream: of the emancipation of man from his tragedy, the liberation at last and forever from pain and hunger and injustice, of the human condition. While two doors away in the room where he did everything but eat and keep the bank's cash money, with his feet propped on that little unpainted ledge nailed to his Adam fireplace and chewing steadily at what Ratliff called his little chunk of Frenchman's Bend air—the capitalist himself who owned the parlor and the house, the very circumambience they dreamed in, who had begun life as a nihilist and then softened into a mere anarchist and now was not only a conservative but a tory too: a pillar, rock-fixed, of things as they are.

Lost. Shortly after that she began what Jefferson called meddling with the Negroes. Apparently she went without invitation or warning, into the different classrooms of the Negro grammar and high school, who couldn't hear thunder, mind you, and so all she could do was watch—the faces, expressions, gestures of the pupils and teachers both who were already spooked, perhaps alarmed, anyway startled and alerted to cover, by the sudden presence of the unexplained white woman who was presently talking to the teacher in the quacking duck's voice of the deaf and then holding out a tablet and pencil for the teacher to answer. Until presently, as quick as the alarmed messenger could find him I suppose, the principal was there—a college-bred man, Uncle Gavin said, of intelligence and devotion too—and then she and the principal and the senior woman teacher were in the principal's office, where it probably was not so much that she, the white woman, was trying to explain, as that they, the two Negroes, had already divined and maybe understood even if they did not agree with her. Because they, Negroes, when the problems are not from the passions of want and ignorance and fear—gambling, drink—but are of simple humanity, are a gentle and tender people, a little more so than white people because they have had to be; a little wiser in their dealings with white people than white people are with them, because they have had to survive in a minority. As if they already knew that the ignorance and superstition she would have to combat—the ignorance and superstition which would counteract, cancel her dream and, if she remained bullheaded enough in perseverance, would destroy her—would not be in the black race she proposed to raise but in the white one she represented.

So finally the expected happened, anticipated by everyone except her apparently, maybe because of the deafness, the isolation, the solitude of living not enclosed with sound but merely surrounded by gestures. Or maybe she did anticipate it but, having been through a war, she just didn't give a damn. Anyway, she bulled right ahead with her idea. Which was to establish a kind of competitive weekly test, the winners, who would be the top students for that week in each class, to spend the following week in a kind of academy she would establish, with white teachers, details to be settled later but for temporary they would use her sitting room in her father's house for a sort of general precept, the winners of each week to be replaced by next week's winners; these to embrace the whole school from kindergarden to seniors, her theory being that if you were old enough to be taught at eighteen you were old enough at eight too when learning something new would be even easier. Because she couldn't hear, you see, not just the words but the tones, over- and under-tones of alarm, fright, terror in which the black voice would have to say Thank you. So it was the principal himself who finally came to see Uncle Gavin at the office—the intelligent dedicated man with his composed and tragic face.

"I've been expecting you," Uncle Gavin said. "I know what you want to say."

"Thank you," the principal said. "Then you know yourself it wont work. That you are not ready for it yet and neither are we."

"Not many of your race will agree with you," Uncle Gavin said.
"None of them will," the principal said. "Just as none of them
agreed when Mr Washington said it."
"Mr Washington?"
"Booker T.," the principal said. "Mr Carver too."
"Oh," Uncle Gavin said. "Yes?"
"That we have got to make the white people need us first. In the
old days your people did need us, in your economy if not your culture, to make your cotton and tobacco and indigo. But that was the
wrong need, bad and evil in itself. So it couldn't last. It had to go.
So now you dont need us. There is no place for us now in your culture or economy either. We both buy the same installment-plan
automobiles to burn up the same gasoline in, and the same radios to
listen to the same music and the same iceboxes to keep the same beer
in, but that's all. So we have got to make a place of our own in your
culture and economy too. Not you to make a place for us just to get
us out from under your feet, as in the South here, or to get our votes
for the aggrandisement of your political perquisites, as in the North,
but us to make a place for ourselves by compelling you to need us,
you cannot do without us because nobody else but us can fill that
place in your economy and culture which only we can fill and so that
place will have to be ours. So that you will not just say Please to us,
you will need to say Please to us, you will want to say Please to us.
Will you tell her that? Say we thank her and we wont forget this. But
to leave us alone. Let us have your friendship all the time, and your
help when we need it. But keep your patronage until we ask for it."
"This is not patronage," Uncle Gavin said. "You know that too."
"Yes," the principal said. "I know that too. I'm sorry. I am ashamed
that I . . ." Then he said: "Just say we thank her and will remember
her, but to let us alone."
"How can you say that to someone who will face that much risk,
just for justice, just to abolish ignorance?"
"I know," the principal said. "It's difficult. Maybe we cant get
along without your help for a while yet, since I am already asking
for it.—Good day, sir," he said, and was gone. So how could Uncle
Gavin tell her either. Or anybody else tell her, everybody else tell her,
white and black both. Since it wasn't that she couldn't hear: she

wouldn't listen, not even to the unified solidarity of No in the Negro school itself—that massive, not resistance but immobility, like the instinct of the animal to lie perfectly still, not even breathing, not even thinking. Or maybe she did hear that because she reversed without even stopping, from the school to the board of education itself: if she could not abolish the ignorance by degrees of individual cases, she would attempt it wholesale by putting properly educated white teachers in the Negro school, asking no help, not even from Gavin, hunting down the school board then, they retreating into simple evaporation, the county board of supervisors in their own sacred lair, armed with no petty ivory tablet and gold stylus this time but with a vast pad of yellow foolscap and enough pencils for everybody. Evidently they committed the initial error of letting her in. Then Gavin said it went something like this:

The president, writing: *Assuming for the moment just for argument you understand that we substitute white teachers in the negro school what will become of the negro teachers or perhaps you plan to retire them on pensions yourself*

The duck's voice: "Not exactly. I will send them North to white schools where they will be accepted and trained as white teachers are."

The pencil: *Still assuming for the sake of argument we have got the negro teachers out where will you find white teachers to fill vacancies left by negroes in Mississippi and how long do you think they will be permitted to fill negro vacancies in Mississippi*

The duck's voice: "I will find them if you will protect them."

The pencil: *Protect them from who Mrs Kohl* Only she didn't need to answer that. Because it had already started: the words *Nigger Lover* scrawled huge in chalk on the sidewalk in front of the mansion the next morning for her father to walk steadily through them in his black banker's hat and his little snap-on bow tie, chewing his steady chunk of Frenchman's Bend air. Sure he saw it. Gavin said nobody could have helped seeing it, that by noon a good deal of the rest of Jefferson had managed to happen to pass by to look at it. But what else—a banker, THE banker—could he do? spit on his handkerchief and get down on his knees and rub it out? And later Linda came out on her way back to the courthouse to badger the rest of the county authorities back behind their locked doors. And maybe, very likely, she really didn't see it. Anyway, it wasn't either of them nor the cook nor the yardman either. It was a neighbor, a woman, who came with a broom and at least obscured it, viciously, angrily, neither to defend Linda's impossible dream nor even in instinctive female confederation with another female, but because she lived on this street. The words could have been the quick short primer-bald words of sex or excrement, as happened now and then even on sidewalks in this part of town, and she would have walked through them too since to pause would have been public admission that a lady knew what they meant. But nobody was going to write *Nigger Lover* nor *-Hater* either, delineate in visible taunting chalk that ancient subterrene atavistic ethnic fear on the sidewalk of the street she (and her husband of course) lived and owned property on.

Until at last the president of the board of supervisors crossed the Square to the bank and on to that back room where old Snopes sat with his feet propped on that mantelpiece between foreclosures, and I would have liked to hear that: the outsider coming in and saying, more or less: Cant you for God's sake keep your daughter at home or at least out of the courthouse. In desperation, because what change could he have hoped to get back, she was not only thirty years old and independent and a widow, she was a war veteran too who had actually—Ratliff would say, actively—stood gunfire. Because she didn't stop; it had got now to where the board of supervisors didn't dare unlock their door while they were in session even to go home at noon to eat, but instead had sandwiches from the Dixie Café passed in through the back window. Until suddenly you were thinking how suppose she were docile and amenable and would have obeyed him, but it was he, old Snopes, that didn't dare ask, let alone order, her to quit. You didn't know why of course. All you could do was speculate: on just what I.O.U. or mortgage bearing his signature she might have represented out of that past which had finally gained for him that back room in the bank where he could sit down and watch himself grow richer by lending and foreclosing other people's I.O.U.'s.

Because pretty soon he had something more than just that unsigned *Nigger Lover* to have to walk through practically any time

he came out his front door. One night (this was while I was in
Europe) a crude cross soaked in gasoline blazed suddenly on the lawn
in front of the mansion until the cops came and put it out, outraged
and seething of course, but helpless; who—the cops—would still
have been helpless even if they hadn't been cops. You know: if she
had only lived alone, or had been the daughter of a mere doctor or
lawyer or even a minister, it would have been one thing, and served
them both—her and her old man—right. Instead, she had to be the
daughter of not just *a* banker but THE banker, so that what the cross
really illuminated was the fact that the organisation which put it
there were dopes and saps: if the sole defense and protection of its
purity rested in hands which didn't—or what was worse, couldn't—
distinguish a banker's front yard, the white race was in one hell of a
fix.

   Then the next month was Munich. Then Hitler's and Stalin's pact
and now when he came out of his house in the morning in his black
banker's hat and bow tie and his little cud of Ratliff's Frenchman's
Bend air, what he walked through was no longer anonymous and
unspecific, the big scrawled letters, the three words covering the
sidewalk before the house in their various mutations and combina-
tions:

KOHL
COMMUNIST
JEW

JEW
KOHL
COMMUNIST

COMMUNIST
KOHL
JEW

and he, the banker, the conservative, the tory who had done more
than any other man in Jefferson or Yoknapatawpha County either to
repeal time back to 1900 at least, having to walk through them as if

they were not there or were in another language and age which he could not be expected to understand, with all Jefferson watching him at least by proxy, to see if his guard would ever drop. Because what else could he do. Because now you knew you had figured right and it actually was *durst not*, with that record of success and victory behind him which already had two deaths in it: not only the suicide which left her motherless, but if he had been another man except the one whose wife would finally have to shoot herself, he might have raised the kind of daughter whose Barton Kohl wouldn't have been a Jewish sculptor with that Spanish war in his horoscope. Then in the very next second you would find you were thinking the exact opposite: that those words on his sidewalk he had to walk through every time he left home were no more portents and threats of wreckage and disaster to him than any other loan he had guessed wrong on would be an irremediable disaster, as long as money itself remained unabolished. That the last thing in the world he was thinking to himself was *This is my cross; I will bear it* because what he was thinking was *All I got to do now is keep folks thinking this is a cross and not a gambit.*

Then Poland. I said, "I'm going now," and Gavin said, "You're too old. They wouldn't possibly take you for flight training yet," and I said, "Yet?" and he said, "Finish one more year of law. You dont know what will be happening then, but it wont be what you're looking at now." So I went back to Cambridge and he wrote me how the F.B.I. was investigating her now and he wrote me: *I'm frightened. Not about her. Not at what they will find out because she would tell them all that herself if it only occurred to them that the simple thing would be to come and ask her.* And told me the rest of it: how she had at last quit beating on the locked door behind which the board of supervisors and the school board crouched holding their breath, and now she was merely meeting a class of small children each Sunday at one of the Negro churches, where she would read aloud in the dry inflectionless quacking, not the orthodox Biblical stories perhaps but at least the Mesopotamian folklore and the Nordic fairy tales which the Christian religion has arrogated into its seasonal observances, safe now since even the white ministers could not go on record against this paradox. So now there was no more *Jew Communist Kohl* on the sidewalk and no more *Nigger Lover* either (you would like to think, from shame) to walk through in order to be seen daily on the Square: the bride of quietude and silence striding inviolate in the isolation of unhearing, immune, walking still like she used to walk when she was fourteen and fifteen and sixteen years old: exactly like a young pointer bitch just about to locate and pin down a covey of birds.

So that when I got home Christmas I said to Gavin: "Tell her to tear up that god-damn party card, if she's got one. Go on. Tell her. She cant help people. They are not worth it. They dont want to be helped any more than they want advice or work. They want cake and excitement, both free. Man stinks. How the hell can she have spent a year in a war that not only killed her husband and blew the bejesus out of the inside of her skull, but even at that price the side she was fighting for still lost, without finding that out? Oh sure, I know, I know, you and Ratliff both have told me often enough, if I've heard Ratliff one time I've heard him a hundred: 'Man aint really evil, he jest aint got any sense.' But so much the more reason, because that leaves him completely hopeless, completely worthless of anybody's anguish and effort and trouble." Then I stopped, because he had put his hand on my head. He had to reach up to do it now but he did it exactly as he used to when I was half as tall and only a third as old, gentle and tender and stroking it a little, speaking quiet and gentle too:

"Why dont you tell her?" he said. Because he is a good man, wise too except for the occasions when he would aberrate, go momentarily haywire and take a wrong turn that even I could see was wrong, and then go hell-for-leather, with absolutely no deviation from logic and rationality from there on, until he wound us up in a mess of trouble or embarrassment that even I would have had sense enough to dodge. But he is a good man. Maybe I was wrong sometimes to trust and follow him but I never was wrong to love him.

"I'm sorry," I said.

"Dont be," he said. "Just remember it. Dont ever waste time regretting errors. Just dont forget them."

So I ran Ratliff to earth again. No: I just took advantage of him. It was the regular yearly Christmas-season supper that Ratliff cooked himself at his house and invited Uncle Gavin and me to eat it with him. But this time Gavin had to go to Jackson on some drainage-district business so I went alone, to sit in Ratliff's immaculate little kitchen with a cold toddy of old Mr Calvin Bookwright's corn whiskey that Ratliff seemed to have no trouble getting from him, though now, in his old age, with anybody else Mr Cal might sell it to you or give it to you or order you off his place, you never knew which; sipping the cold toddy as Ratliff made them—first the sugar dissolved into a little water, then the whiskey added while the spoon still stirred gently, then rain water from the cistern to fill the glass—while Ratliff in a spotless white apron over one of the neat tieless faded blue shirts which he made himself, cooked the meal, cooking it damned well, not just because he loved to eat it but because he loved the cooking, the blending up to perfection's ultimate moment. Then he removed the apron and we ate it at the kitchen table, with the bottle of claret Uncle Gavin and I always furnished. Then with the coffee and the decanter of whiskey we moved (as always) to the little immaculate room he called his parlor, with the spotlessly waxed melodeon in the corner and the waxed chairs and the fireplace filled with fluted green paper in the summer but with a phony gas log in the winter, now that progress had reached, whelmed us, and the waxed table in the center of the room on which, on a rack under a glass bell, rested the Allanovna necktie—a rich not-quite-scarlet, not-quite-burgundy ground patterned with tiny yellow sunflowers each with a tiny blue center of almost the exact faded blue of his shirts, that he had brought home from New York that time three or four years ago when he and Gavin went to see Linda married and off to Spain, that I would have cut my tongue out before I would have told him it probably cost whoever (Gavin I suppose) paid for it around seventy-five dollars; until that day when I inadvertently said something to that effect and Ratliff said, "I know how much. I paid it. It was a hundred and fifty dollars." "What?" I said. "A hundred and fifty?" "There was two of them," he said. "I never saw but one," I said. "I doubt if you will," he said. "The other one is a private matter."—and beside it, the piece of sculpture that Barton Kohl had bequeathed him that, if Gavin was still looking for first base, I had already struck out because I didn't even know what it was, let alone what it was doing.

"All it needs is that gold cigarette lighter she gave him," I said. "The Linda Snopes room."

"No," he said. "The Eula Varner room. It ought to have more in it, but maybe this will do. Leastways it's something. When a community is lucky enough to be the community that every thousand years or so has a Eula Varner to pick it out to do her breathing in, the least we can do is for somebody to set up something; a . . . monument aint quite the word I want."

"Shrine," I said.

"That's it," he said. "A shrine to mark and remember it, for the folks that wasn't that lucky, that was already doomed to be too young . . ." He stopped. He stood there quite still. Except that you would think of him as being quizzical, maybe speculative, but not bemused. Then I said it:

"You were wrong. They aren't going to."

"What?" he said. "What's that?"

"She's not going to marry Gavin."

"That's right," he said. "It will be worse than that."

Now it was me that said, "What? What did you say?" But he was already himself again, bland, serene, inscrutable.

"But I reckon Lawyer can stand that too," he said.

TEN

GAVIN STEVENS

I could have suggested that, told her to do that, and she would have done it—torn the card up at once, quickly, immediately, with passion and exultation. She was like her mother in one thing at least: needing, fated to need, to find something competent enough, strong enough (in her case, this case, not tough enough because Kohl was tough enough: he happened to be mere flesh and bones and so wasn't durable enough) to take what she had to give; and at the same time doomed to fail, in this, her case, not because Barton failed her but because he also had doom in his horoscope. So if the Communist party, having already proved itself immune to bullets and therefore immortal, had replaced him, not again to bereave her, of course she would have torn her card up, with passion and exultation and joy too. Since what sacrifice can love demand more complete than abasement, abnegation, particularly at the price of what the unknowing materialist world would in its crass insensitive ignorance dub cowardice and shame? I have always had a sneaking notion that that old Christian martyr actually liked, perhaps even loved, his aurochs or his lion.

But I did suggest something else. It was 1940 now. The Nibelung maniac had destroyed Poland and turned back west where Paris, the civilised world's eternal and splendid courtesan, had been sold to him like any whore and only the English national character turned him east again; another year and Lenin's Frankenstein would be our ally but too late for her; too late for us too, too late for all the western world's peace for the next hundred years, as a tubby little giant of a man in England was already saying in private, but needs must when the devil etcetera.

It began in my office. He was a quiet, neat, almost negative man of no particular age between twenty-five and fifty, as they all appear, who showed me briefly the federal badge (his name was Gihon) and accepted the chair and said Thank you and opened his business quietly and impersonally, as they do, as if they are simply delivering a not-too-important message. Oh yes, I was doubtless the last, the very last on his list since he would have checked thoroughly on or into me without my knowing it as he had days and maybe months ago penetrated and resolved and sifted all there was to be learned about her.

"We know that all she has done, tried to do, has been done quite openly, where everybody would have a chance to hear about it, know about it—"

"I think you can safely say that," I said.

"Yes," he said. "—quite openly. Quite harmless. With the best of intentions, only not very . . . practical. Nothing in fact that a lady wouldn't do, only a little . . ."

"Screwy," I suggested.

"Thank you. But there you are. I can tell you in confidence that she holds a Communist party card. Naturally you are not aware of that."

Now I said, "Thank you."

"And, once a communist—I grant you, that's like the old saying (no imputation of course, I'm sure you understand that), Once a prostitute. Which anyone after calm reflection knows to be false. But there you are. This is not a time of calmness and reflection; to ask or expect, let alone hope, for that from the government and the people too, faced with what we are going to have to meet sooner probably than we realise—"

"Yes," I said. "What do you want me to do? What do you assume I can do?"

"She . . . I understand, have been informed, that you are her earliest and still are her closest friend—"

"No imputation of course," I said. But he didn't say Thank you in his turn. He didn't say anything, anything at all. He just sat there watching me through his glasses, gray, negative as a chameleon, terrifying as the footprint on Crusoe's beach, too negative and neuter in that one frail articulation to bear the terrible mantle he represented. "What you want then is for me to use my influence—"

"—as a patriotic citizen who is intelligent enough to know that we too will be in this war within five years—I set five years as an outside maximum since it took the Germans only three years before to go completely mad and defy us into that one—with exactly who for our enemy we may not know until it is already too late—"

"—to persuade her to surrender that card quietly to you and swear whatever binding oath you are authorised to give her," I said. "Didn't you just say yourself that Once a whore (with no imputations) always a whore?"

"I quite agree with you," he said. "In this case, not the one with the imputations."

"Then what do you want of me—her?"

He produced a small notebook and opened it; he even had the days of the week and the hours: "She and her husband were in Spain, members of the Loyalist communist army six months and twenty-nine days until he was killed in action; she herself remained, serving as an orderly in the hospital after her own wound, until the Loyalists evacuated her across the border into France—"

"Which is on record even right here in Jefferson."

"Yes," he said. "Before that she lived for seven years in New York City as the common-law wife—"

"—which of course damns her not only in Jefferson, Mississippi, but in Washington too." But he had not even paused.

"—of a known registered member of the Communist party, and the close associate of other known members of the Communist party, which may not be in your Jefferson records."

"Yes," I said. "And then?"

He closed the notebook and put it back inside his coat and sat looking at me again, quite cold, quite impersonal, as if the space between us were the lens of a microscope. "So she knew people, not only in Spain but in the United States too, people who so far are not even in our records—Communist members and agents, important people, who are not as noticeable as Jewish sculptors and Columbia professors and other such intelligent amateurs—" Because that was when I finally understood.

"I see," I said. "You offer a swap. You will trade her immunity for names. Your bureau will whitewash her from an enemy into a simple stool pigeon. Have you a warrant of any sort?"

"No," he said. I got up.

"Then good day, sir." But he didn't move yet.

"You wont suggest it to her?"

"I will not," I said.

"Your country is in danger, perhaps in jeopardy."

"Not from her," I said. Then he rose too and took his hat from the desk.

"I hope you wont regret this, Mr Stevens."

"Good day, sir," I said.

Or that is, I wrote it. Because it was three years now and she had tried, really tried to learn lip reading. But I dont know. Maybe to live outside human sound is to live outside human time too, and she didn't have time to learn, to bother to learn. But again I dont know. Maybe it didn't take even three years of freedom, immunity from it to learn that perhaps the entire dilemma of man's condition is because of the ceaseless gabble with which he has surrounded himself, enclosed himself, insulated himself from the penalties of his own folly, which otherwise—the penalties, the simple red ink—might have enabled him by now to have made his condition solvent, workable, successful. So I wrote it

Leave here Go away

"You mean, move?" she said. "Find a place of my own? an apartment or a house?"

I mean leave Jefferson I wrote. *Go completely away for good Give me that damn card & leave Jefferson*

"You said that to me before."

"No I didn't," I said. I even spoke it, already writing, already planning out the whole paragraph it would take: *We've never even mentioned that card or the Communist party either. Even back there three years ago when you first tried to tell me you had one and show it to me and I wouldn't let you, stopped you, refused to listen: dont you remember?* But she was already talking again:

"I mean back there when I was fifteen or sixteen and you said I must get away from Jefferson."

So I didn't even write the other; I wrote *But you couldnt then Now you can Give me the card & go* She stood quietly for a moment, a time. We didn't even try to use the ivory tablet on occasions of moment and crisis like this. It was a bijou, a gewgaw, a bangle, feminine; really almost useless: thin ivory sheets bound with gold and ringed together with more of it, each sheet about the size of a playing card so that it wouldn't really contain more than about three words at a time, like an anagram, an acrostic at the level of children—a puzzle say or maybe a continued story ravished from a primer. Instead, we were in her upstairs sitting room she had fitted up, standing at the mantel which she had designed at the exact right height and width to support a foolscap pad when we had something to discuss that there must be no mistake about or something which wasn't worth not being explicit about, like money, so that she could read the words as my hand formed them, like speech, almost like hearing.

"Go where?" she said. "Where could I go?"

Anywhere New York Back to Europe of course but in New York some of the people still you & Barton knew the friends your own age She looked at me. With the pupils expanded like this, her eyes looked almost black; blind too.

"I'm afraid," she said.

I spoke; she could read single words if they were slow: "You? Afraid?" She said:

"Yes. I dont want to be helpless. I wont be helpless. I wont have to depend."

I thought fast, like that second you have to raise or draw or throw in your hand, while each fraction of the second effaces another pip from your hole card. I wrote quite steadily while she watched *Then why am I here* and drew my hand back so she could read it. Then she said, in that dry, lifeless, what Chick calls duck's quack:

"Gavin." I didn't move. She said it again: "Gavin." I didn't move. She said: "All right. I lied. Not the depend part. I wont depend. I just must be where you are." She didn't even add *Because you're all I have now.* She just stood, our eyes almost level, looking at me out of, across, something—abyss, darkness; not abject, not questioning, not even hoping; in a moment I would know it; saying again in the quacking voice: "Gavin."

I wrote rapidly, in three- or four-word bursts, gaggles, clumps, whatever you want to call them, so she could read as I wrote *Its all right dont Be afraid I Refuse to marry you 20 years too much Difference for it To work besides I Dont want to*

"Gavin," she said.

I wrote again, ripping the yellow sheets off the pad and shoving them aside on the mantel *I dont want to*

"I love you," she said. "Even when I have to tell a lie, you have already invented it for me."

I wrote *No lie nobody Mentioned Barton Kohl*

"Yes," she said.

I wrote *No*

"But you can   me," she said. That's right. She used the explicit word, speaking the hard brutal guttural in the quacking duck's voice. That had been our problem as soon as we undertook the voice lessons: the tone, to soften the voice which she herself couldn't hear. "It's exactly backward," she told me. "When you say I'm whispering, it feels like thunder inside my head. But when I say it this way, I cant even feel it." And this time it would be almost a shout. Which is the way it was now, since she probably believed she had lowered her voice, I standing there while what seemed to me like reverberations of thunder died away.

"You're blushing," she said.

I wrote *that word*

"What word?"

that you just said

"Tell me another one to use. Write it down so I can see it and remember it."

I wrote *There is no other thats the right one only one I am old fashioned it still shocks me a little No what shocks is when a woman uses it & is not shocked at all until she realises I am* Then I wrote *thats wrong too what shocks is that all that magic passion excitement be summed up & dismissed in that one bald unlovely sound*

"All right," she said. "Dont use any word then."

I wrote *Do you mean you want to*

"Of course you can," she said. "Always. You know that." I wrote *Thats not what I asked you* She read it. Then she didn't move. I wrote *Look at me* She did so, looking at me from out or across what it was that I would recognise in a moment now.

"Yes," she said.

I wrote *Didnt I just tell you you dont ever have to be afraid* and this time I had to move the pad slightly to draw her attention to it, until she said, not looking up:

"I dont have to go away either?"

I wrote *No* under her eyes this time, then she looked up, at me, and I knew what it was she looked out of or across: the immeasurable loss, the appeaseless grief, the fidelity and the enduring, the dry quacking voice saying, "Gavin. Gavin. Gavin." while I wrote *because we are the 2 in all the world who can love each other without having to* the end of it tailing off in a sort of violent rubric as she clasped me, clinging to me, quite hard, the dry clapping voice saying, "Gavin. Gavin. I love you. I love you," so that I had to break free to reach the pad and write

Give me the card

She stared down at it, her hands arrested in the act of leaving my shoulders. "Card?" she said. Then she said, "I've lost it."

Then I knew: a flash, like lightning. I wrote *your father* even while I was saying out loud: "Oh the son of a bitch, the son of a bitch," saying to myself *Wait. Wait! He had to. Put yourself in his place. What else could he do, what other weapon did he have to defend his very existence before she destroyed it—the position he had sacrificed everything for—wife home friends peace—to gain the only prize he knew since it was the only one he could understand since the world itself as he understood it assured him that was what he wanted because that was the only thing worth having.* Of course: his only possible weapon: gain possession of the card, hold the threat of turning it in to the F.B.I. over her and stop her before she destroyed him. Yet all this time I was telling myself *You know better. He will use it to destroy her. It was he himself probably who scrawled Jew Communist Kohl on his own sidewalk at midnight to bank a reserve of Jefferson sympathy against the day when he would be compelled to commit his only child to the insane asylum.* I wrote

Ransacked your room drawers desk

"Somebody did," she said. "It was last year. I thought—" I wrote
It was your father
"Was it?" Yes, it was exactly that tone. I wrote
Dont you know it was
"Does it matter? They will send me another one I suppose. But that doesn't matter either. I haven't changed. I dont have to have a little printed card to show it."

This time I wrote slowly and carefully *You dont have to go I wont ask any more but when I do ask you again to go will you just believe me & go at once I will make all plans will you do that*
"Yes," she said.
I wrote *Swear*
"Yes," she said. "Then you can marry." I couldn't have written anyway; she had caught up both my hands, holding them between hers against her chest. "You must. I want you to. You mustn't miss that. Nobody must never have had that once. Nobody. Nobody." She was looking at me. "That word you didn't like. My mother said that to you once too, didn't she." It wasn't even a question. "Did you?"

I freed my hands and wrote You *know we didnt*
"Why didn't you?"

I wrote *Because she felt sorry for me when you do things for people just because you feel sorry for them what you do is probably not very important to you*
"I dont feel sorry for you. You know that. Dont you know it will be important to me?"

I wrote *Then maybe it was because l wasnt worthy of her & we both knew it but I thought if we didnt maybe she might always think maybe I might have been* and ripped the sheet off and crumpled it into my pocket and wrote *I must go now*
"Dont go," she said. Then she said, "Yes, go. You see, I'm all right now, I'm not even afraid any more."

I wrote *why should you ever have been* then on the same sheet *My hat* and she went and got it while I gathered up the rest of the used sheets into my pocket and took the hat and went toward the door, the quacking voice saying "Gavin" until I turned. "How did we say it? the only two people in the world that love each other and dont have to? I love you, Gavin," in that voice, tone which to her was whispering, murmuring perhaps but to anyone tragic enough to still have ears was as penetrating and shocking almost as an old-time klaxon automobile horn.

And out, fast and quick out of his house, his mansion, his palace, on to his bank fast and quick too, right on back into that little room and bump, nudge, startle the propped feet off the fireplace, my hand already out: "I will now take that card, if you please." Except that would be wantonly throwing away an opportunity, a gift actually; why let him pick his moment to surrender, produce the evidence on his side, to the F.B.I.? Why not strike first, sic the F.B.I. on him before he could, as Ratliff would say, snatch back: that mild neutral gray man flashing that badge on him, saying, "We have it on authority, Mr Snopes, that you have a Communist party card in your possession. Do you care to make a statement?"

But I didn't know where Gihon would be now and, his declared enemy, he wouldn't believe me. So the F.B.I. as represented by him was out; I would have to go straight to that vast Omnipotence called Govment; the stool-pigeoning itself must be unimpeachable; it must stem from the milieu and hold rigidly to the vernacular. A post card of course, a penny post card. I thought first of addressing it to the President of the United States but with the similar nut mail Mr Roosevelt was probably already getting, mine would be drowned in that flood. Which left the simple military. But although the military never loses any piece of paper once it has been written on and signed (anything else yes, it will abandon or give away or destroy, but a piece of signed paper never, though it have to subsidise and uniform a thousand people to do nothing else but guard it); it would inevitably reappear someday even if it took a hundred years, but that would be too long also. Whereupon I suddenly overheard myself asking, What's wrong with your first idea of the F.B.I.? to which the only answer was, Nothing. So I could even see the completed card. The vernacular was an informed one, it knew there were two Hoovers: one a carpet sweeper and the other had been President, and that the head of the F.B.I. was said to be named Hoover. So I could see it:

HERBERT HOOVER
F.B.I. DEPARTMENT

then paused, because not Washington; this vernacular was not only knowledgeable but consistent too so I thought first of Parchman, Mississippi, the State Penitentiary, except that the mail clerk there would probably be a trusty possibly in for life so what would a span of time computable in mere days, especially in regard to a piece of mail, be to him? and again it would be lost. Then I had the answer: Jackson, the Capital. It would be perfect: not really a big city, so that the agents there would be just bored and idle enough to leap at this opportunity; besides not being far. So that's what it would be:

> *Herbert Hoover*
> *F B & I Depment*
> *Jackson Miss*
> *If you will come up to Jefferson Miss and serch warant the bank and*
> *home of Flem Snopes you will fined a commonist party Card*
> > *Patriotic Citizen*

Whereupon you will object that "search warrant" is a little outside this writer's vernacular and that the spelling of "find" is really going a little too far. Whereupon I rebut you that this writer knows exactly what he is talking about; that "search warrant" and "fined" are the two words of them all which he would never make any mistake regarding, no matter how he might spell them: the one being constantly imminent in his (by his belief, in yours too) daily future and the other or its synonym "jailed" being its constant coadjutant.

If I only dared. You see? even if I burgled his house or bank vault and found the card and erased her name and substituted his to pass their gimlet muster, she herself would be the first to leap, spring, deny, refute, claim and affirm it for her own; she would probably have gone to Gihon or any else available before this and declared her convictions if it had occurred to her they might be interested. Whereupon, from then until even the stronger alliance of cosmic madmen had finally exhausted themselves into peace and oblivion, she would be harried and harassed and spied upon day and night, waking and eating and sleeping too. So finally I had to fall back, not on her innocent notion that it wasn't important, really wouldn't mat-

ter anyway, but on my own more evil or—and/or—legal conviction
that it was his only weapon of defense and he wouldn't use it until
he was frightened into it.

Or hope perhaps. Anyway, that's how it stood until in fact the Battle of Britain saved her; otherwise all that remained was simply to
go to him and say, "I want that card," which would be like walking up
to a stranger and saying Did you steal my wallet. So the Battle of
Britain saved her, him too for a time. I mean, the reports, stories now
coming back to us of the handful of children fighting it. Because during the rest of that spring and summer and fall of 1940 she was getting more and more restless. Oh, she was still doing her Negro
Sunday school classes, still "meddling" as the town called it, but after
a fashion condoned now, perhaps by familiarity and also that no one
had discovered yet any way to stop her.

This, until June when Chick came home from Cambridge.
Whereupon I suddenly realised—discovered—two things: that it was
apparently Chick now who was our family's representative in her
social pattern; and that she knew more than even he of the R.A.F.
names and the machines they flew: Malan and Aitken and Finucane
and Spitfire and Beaufighter and Hurricane and Buerling and Deere
and the foreigners too like the Americans who wouldn't wait and the
Poles and Frenchmen who declined to be whipped: Daymond and
Wzlewski and Clostermann; until that September, when we com-
promised: Chick agreed to take one more year of law and we agreed
to let it be the University over at Oxford instead of Cambridge.
Which was perhaps the reason: when he left, she no longer had anyone to swap the names with. So I should not have been surprised
when she came to the office. Nor did she say I must do something
to help, I've got to do something, I cant just sit here idle; she said:

"I'm going away. I've got a job, in a factory in California where
they make aircraft to be sent to Europe," and I scribbling, scrawling
Wait. "It's all right," she said. "It's all settled. I wrote them that I
couldn't hear but that I was familiar enough with truck engines and
gears to learn what they needed. And they said for me to come on
out, just bring a few papers with me. You know: letters saying you
have known me long enough to assure them she is moral and doesn't
get too tight and nobody has caught her stealing yet. That's what you

are to do because you can even sign them Chairman of the Yoknapatawpha County, Mississippi, Draft Board," and I still scrawling
Wait, or no, not writing it again because I already had: just gripping
her with one hand and holding the pad up with the other until she
read it and stopped or stopped long enough to read it or at least
hushed and I could write:

*at this factory all factories an individual of limitless power called Secu-
rity whose job position is the 1 thing on earth between him & being drafted
into the* and ripped that sheet off, already writing again, her hand, her
arm across my shoulder so I could feel her breathing and feel smell
her hair against my cheek *army which naturally he will defend with his
life by producing not too far apart provable subversives so that sooner or
later he will reach you & fire you you re* and ripped that one off, not
stopping *member the Mississippi coast Biloxi Ocean Springs you were there*
    "Yes. With Mother and"—and now I thought she would stop but
she didn't even pause—"Manfred. I remember."
    I wrote *Pascagoula a shipyard where they are building ships to carry
airplanes guns tanks if California will take you so will they will you go there*
    "Yes," she said. She said, "Russia." She drew a long breath. "But
the Security will be there too."
    I wrote *yes but thats close I could come there quick & even if Security I
could probably find you something else*
    "Yes," she said, breathing quiet and slow at my shoulder. "Close.
I could come home on week-ends."
    I wrote *you might have to work weekends they need ships*
    "Then you can come there. The draft board is closed on week-
ends, isn't it?"
    I wrote *we will see*
    "But together sometimes now and then. That's why I was afraid
about California, because it's so far. But Pascagoula is close. At least
occasionally now and then."
    I wrote *Of course*
    "All right," she said. "Of course I'll go."
    Which she did, right after New Year's, 1941 now. I knew a lawyer
there so she had a small apartment with its own entrance in a private home. And apparently her belief was that, once she was free of
Jefferson, at least twelve hours away from interdiction by Snopes or

me or either or both, nobody could challenge her intention to buy a
small car and run it herself, until I threatened to tell the Pascagoula
police myself that she was deaf the first time I heard about it. So she
agreed to refrain and my lawyer friend arranged for her in a car pool
and presently she was at work as a tool checker, though almost at
once she wrote that she had almost got them to agree to let her
become a riveter, where the deafness would be an actual advantage.
Anyway, she could wear overalls again, once more minuscule in that
masculine or rather sexless world engaged, trying to cope with the
lethal mechanical monstrosities which war has become now, and perhaps she was even at peace again, if peace is possible to anyone. Anyway, at first there were the letters saying *When you come we will* and
then *If you come dont forget* and then several weeks and just a penny
post card saying *I miss you* and nothing more—that almost inarticu-
late paucity of the picture cards saying *Wish you were here* or *This is
our room* which the semiliterate send back, until the last one, a letter
again. I mean, in an envelope: *It's all right. I understand. I know how
busy the draft board has to be. Just come when you can because I have something to ask you.* To which I answered at once, immediately (I was
about to add, Because I dont know what I thought. Only I know
exactly what I thought) *Ask me or tell me?* so that I already knew
beforehand what her answer would he: *Yes. Ask you.*

So (it was summer again now) I telegraphed a date and she
answered *Have booked room will meet what train love* and I answered
that (who had refused to let her own one) *Coming by car will pick you
up at shipyard Tuesday quitting time love* and I was there. She came out
with the shift she belonged in, in the overall, already handing me the
tablet and stylus before she kissed me, clinging to me, hard, saying,
"Tell me everything," until I could free myself to write, restricted
again to the three- or four-word bursts and gaggles before having to
erase:

You tell me what It is
"Let's go to the beach." And I:
You dont want to Go home first & Change
"No. Let's go to the beach." We did. I parked the car and it
seemed to me I had already written *Now tell me* but she was already
out of the car, already waiting for me, to take the tablet and stylus

from me and thrust them into her pocket, then took my near arm in both her hands, we walking so, she clinging with both hands to my arm so that we would bump and stagger every few steps, the sun just setting and our one shadow long along the tide-edge before us and I thinking *No no, that cant be it* when she said, "Wait," and released me, digging into the other overall pocket from the tablet. "I've got something for you. I almost forgot it." It was a shell; we had probably trodden on a million of them since we left the car two hundred yards back, I still thinking *It cant be that. That cant be so* "I found it the first day. I was afraid I might lose it before you got here, but I didn't. Do you like it?"

"It's beautiful," I said.

"What?" she said, already handing me the tablet and stylus. I wrote

Damn fine now Tell me

"Yes," she said. She clung, gripping my arm hard and strong in both hands again, we walking again and I thinking *Why not, why shouldn't it be so, why should there not be somewhere in the world at least one more Barton Kohl or at least a fair substitute, something to do, at least something a little better than grief* when she said, "Now," and stopped and turned us until we faced the moment's pause before the final plunge of the sun, the tall and ragged palms and pines fixed by that already fading explosion until the night breeze would toss and thresh them. Then it passed. Now it was just sunset. "There," she said. "It's all right now. We were here. We saved it. Used it. I mean, for the earth to have come all this long way from the beginning of the earth, and the sun to have come all this long way from the beginning of time, for this one day and minute and second out of all the days and minutes and seconds, and nobody to use it, no two people who are finally together at last after all the difficulties and waiting, and now they are together at last and are desperate because of all the long waiting, they are even running along the beach toward where the place is, not far now, where they will finally be alone together at last and nobody in the world to know or care or interfere so that it's like the world itself wasn't except you so now the world that wasn't even invented yet can begin." And I thinking *Maybe it's the fidelity and the enduring which must be so at least once in your lifetime, no matter who suf-*

fers. That you have heard of love and loss and grief and fidelity and endur-
ing and you have seen love and loss and maybe you have even seen love and
loss and grief but not all five of them—or four of them since the fidelity
and enduring I am speaking of were inextricable: one—this, even while
she was saying, "I dont mean just—" and stopped herself before I
could have raised the hand to clap to on her lips—if I had been going
to, saying: "It's all right, I haven't forgotten; I'm not going to say that
one any more." She looked at me. "So maybe you already know what
I'm going to ask you."

"Yes," I said; she could read that. I wrote *marriage*
"How did you know?"
What does it Matter I wrote *Im glad*
"I love you," she said. "Let's go eat. Then we will go home and I
can tell you."

I wrote *Not home first To change*
"No," she said. "I wont need to change where we're going."

She didn't. Among the other female customers, she could have
worn anything beyond an ear trumpet and a G-string, and even then
probably the ear trumpet would have drawn the attention. It was a
joint. By midnight on Saturday (possibly any other night in such
boom ship-building times) it would be bedlam, jumping as they say;
with the radio going full blast, it already was to me. But then, I was
not deaf. But the food—the flounder and shrimp—was first rate and
the waitress produced glasses and ice to match the flask I had
brought; and with all the other uproar her voice was not so noticeable. Because she used it, as if by premeditation, about things I would
need only Yes and No for, babbling actually, about the shipyard, the
work, the other people, sounding almost like a little girl home on her
first holiday from school, eating rapidly too, not chewing it enough,
until we had done and she said, "We can go now."

She hadn't told me yet where I was to stay, nor did I know where
her place was either. So when we were in the car again I snapped on
the dash light so she could see the tablet and wrote *Where.* "That
way," she said. It was back toward the center of town and I drove on
until she said, "Turn here," and I did; presently she said, "There it
is," so that I had to pull in to the curb to use the tablet
Which is

"The hotel," she said. "Right yonder." I wrote

We want to talk Havent you got a Sitting room your place Quiet & private

"We're going to both stay there tonight. It's all arranged. Our rooms are next door with just the wall between and I had both beds moved against it so after we talk and are in bed any time during the night I can knock on the wall and you can hear it and if I hold my hand against the wall I can feel you answer.—I know, I wont knock loud enough to disturb anybody, for anybody to hear it except you."

The hotel had its own parking lot. I took my bag and we went in. The proprietor knew her, perhaps by this time everybody in the town knew or knew of the young deaf woman working in the shipyard. Anyway, nobody stopped us, he called her by name and she introduced me and he gave me the two keys and still nobody stopped us, on to her door and unlocked it, her overnight bag was already in the room and there were flowers in a vase too and she said, "Now I can have a bath. Then I will knock on the wall," and I said,

"Yes," since she could read that and went to my room; yes, why should there have to be fidelity and enduring too just because you imagined them? If mankind matched his dreams too, where would his dreams be? Until presently she knocked on the wall and I went out one door, five steps, into the other one and closed it behind me. She was in bed, propped on both pillows, in a loose jacket or robe, her hair (evidently she had cut it short while she was driving the ambulance but now it was long enough again to bind in a ribbon dark blue like her eyes) brushed or dressed for the night, the tablet and stylus in one hand on her lap, the other hand patting the bed beside her for me to sit down.

"You wont really need this," she said, raising the tablet slightly then lowering it again, "since all you'll need is just to say Yes and I can hear that. Besides, since you already know what it is, it will be easy to talk about. And maybe if I tell you I want you to do it for me, it will be even easier for you to do. So I do say that. I want you to do it for me." I took the tablet

Of course I will Do what

"Do you remember back there at the beach when the sun finally went down and there was nothing except the sunset and the pines and the sand and the ocean and you and me and I said how that shouldn't be wasted after all that waiting and distance, there should be two people out of all the world desperate and anguished for one another to deserve not to waste it any longer and suddenly they were hurrying, running toward the place at last not far now, almost here now and no more the desperation and the anguish no more, no more—" when suddenly, as I watched, right under the weight of my eyes you might say, her face sprang and ran with tears, though I had never seen her cry before and apparently she herself didn't even know it was happening. I wrote

Stop it
"Stop what?" And I
youre crying
"No I'm not." And I
look at your Face
There was the customary, the standard, hand-glass and box of tissue on the table but instead I took my handkerchief and held it out. But instead she simply set the heels of her palms to her face, smearing the moisture downward and outward like you do sweat, even snapping, flicking the moisture away at the end of the movement as you do sweat.

"Dont be afraid," she said. "I'm not going to say that word. Because I dont even mean that. That's not important, like breathing's not important as long as you dont even have to think about it but just do it when it's necessary. It's important only when it becomes a question or a problem or an issue, like breathing's important only when it becomes a question or a problem of whether or not you can draw another one. It's the rest of it, the little things: it's this pillow still holding the shape of the head, this necktie still holding the shape of the throat that took it off last night even just hanging empty on a bedpost, even the empty shoes on the floor still sit with the right one turned out a little like his feet were still in them and even still walking the way he walked, stepping a little higher with one foot than the other like the old-time Negroes say a proud man walks—" And I
stop it stop It youre crying Again
"I cant feel it. I cant feel anything on my face since that day, not heat nor cold nor rain nor water nor wind nor anything." This time

she took the handkerchief and used it but when I handed her the mirror and even started to write *wheres your compact* she didn't even take the mirror. "I'll be careful now.—So that's what I want you to have too. I love you. If it hadn't been for you, probably I wouldn't have got this far. But I'm all right now. So I want you to have that too. I want you to do it for me." And I

But what for you You never have Told me yet

"Marry," she said. "I thought you knew. Didn't you tell me you knew what it was?" And I

Me marry You mean me

"Who did you think I meant? Did you think I was—Gavin."

"No," I said.

"I read that. You said No. You're lying. You thought I meant me."

"No," I said.

"Do you remember that time when I told you that any time you believed you had to lie for my sake, I could always count on you sticking to it, no matter how bad you were disproved?"

"Yes," I said.

"So that's settled, then," she said. "No, I mean you. That's what I want you to do for me. I want you to marry. I want you to have that too. Because then it will be all right. We can always be together no matter how far apart either one of us happens to be or has to be. How did you say it? the two people in all the earth out of all the world that can love each other not only without having to but we dont even have to not say that word you dont like to hear? Will you promise?"

"Yes," I said.

"I know you cant just step outdoors tomorrow and find her. It may take a year or two. But all you've got to do is just stop resisting the idea of being married. Once you do that it's all right because the rest of it will happen. Will you do that?"

"I swear," I said.

"Why, you said Swear, didn't you?"

"Yes," I said.

"Then kiss me." I did so, her arms quite hard, quite strong around my neck; a moment, then gone. "And early tomorrow morning, go back home." And I, writing

I was going to Stay all day

"No. Tomorrow. Early. I'll put my hand on the wall and when you're in bed knock on it and if I wake up in the night I can knock and if you're awake or still there you can knock back and if I dont feel you knock you can write me from Jefferson tomorrow or the next day. Because I'm all right now. Good night, Gavin."

"Good night, Linda," I said.

"I read that too. I love you."

"I love you," I said.

"I read that too but write it on the tablet anyway and I can have that for a—what do you call it?—eye opener in the morning."

"Yes," I said, extending my hand for the tablet.

ELEVEN

CHARLES MALLISON

This time, I was in uniform. So now all I need is to decide, find out, what this-time I mean or time for what I mean. It wasn't the next time I saw Linda, because she was still in Pascagoula building ships for Russia too now. And it wasn't the next time I was in Jefferson, because I passed through home en route to the brown suit. So maybe I mean the next time I ran Ratliff to earth. Though maybe what I really mean is that the next time I saw Uncle Gavin after his marriage, he was a husband.

Because it was 1942 and Gavin was married now, to Melisandre Harriss (Backus that was as Thackeray said); that pitcher had went to that well jest that one time too many, as Ratliff said, provided of course he had said it. One Sunday morning there was Pearl Harbor and I wired Gavin by return mail you might say from Oxford *This is it am gone now.* I wired Gavin because otherwise I would have had to talk to Mother on the telephone and on long distance Mother ran into money, so by wiring Gavin for forty-two cents the telephone call from Mother would be on Father's bill in Jefferson.

So I was at home in time to be actually present at the first innocent crumblings of what he had obviously assumed to be his impregnable bastions; to "stand up" with him, be groomsman to his disaster. It happened like this. I was unable to get into the government flight-training program course at the University but they told me that anybody with a college degree and any number of hours from one up of flying time, especially solo, would have about as good a chance of going straight into military training for a commission. So there was a professional crop-duster operating from the same field and he took me on as a student, on even bigger aircraft, one of (he claimed) the actual type of army primary training, than the little fifty h.p. popguns the official course used.

So when I sent Uncle Gavin the wire I had around fifteen logged hours, three of which were solo, and when Mother rang my telephone I was already packed up and the car already pointed toward Jefferson. So I was there to see the beginning of it whether Gavin recognised it as banns or not. I mean the Long Island horse farm that Miss Melisandre Harriss Backus that was used to bring the two children (they were grown now; Gavin was marrying not stepchildren but in-laws) back home to now and then from Europe until the Germans began to blow up Americans in actual sight of the Irish coast. So after that it had to be South America, this last time bringing the Argentine steeplechasing cavalry officer that that maniac boy of the two Harriss children (I dont mean that both Aunt Melisandre's children were maniacs but that only one of them was a boy) believed was trying to marry the money his mother was still trustee of instead of just his sister who just had an allowance like him. So he (the maniac of course) set out to murder the Argentine steeplechaser with that wild stallion of Rafe McCallum's that he (the maniac) bought or tricked or anyway got inside that stall where the innocent Argentine would have walked up in the dark and opened the door on what he (the innocent Argentine) thought was going to be not only a gentle horse but a partly blind one too. Except that Gavin read his tea leaves or used his second sight or divining rod or whatever it was he did in cases like this, and got hold of Rafe in time to reach the stall door first and stop him.

So the Argentine was saved, and that night the maniac took his choice between the army recruiting station in Memphis, and Uncle Gavin, and chose the army so he was safe, and that afternoon the Argentine and the maniac's sister were married and left Jefferson and they were safe. But Uncle Gavin remained, and the next day I had to go on to ground school, preflight, so when I got home next time I was in uniform and Gavin was not only a husband but father too of a stepson who would have been as neat a by-standing murderer as you could hope to see except for a stroke of arrant meddling which to a dog shouldn't happen, and a stepdaughter married to an Argen-

tine steeplechasing son-in-law. (By which time I was married too, to
a bombsight—I hadn't made pilot but at least I would be riding up
front—allotted to me by a government which didn't trust me with it
and so set spies to watch what I did with it, which before entrusting
it to me had trained me not to trust my spies nor anybody else
respecting it, in a locked black case which stayed locked by a chain
to me even while I was asleep—a condition of constant discomfort of
course but mainly of unflagging mutual suspicion and mutual dis-
trust and in time mutual hatred which you even come to endure,
which is probably the best of all training for successful matrimony.)

So when I saw Jefferson next I was in uniform, long enough to call
on the squire and his dame among his new ancestral white fences and
electric-lit stables and say Bless you my children and then run Ratliff
once more to earth.

"He cant marry her now," I said. "He's already got a wife."

And you never thought of *soberly* in connection with Ratliff either.
Anyway, not before now, not until this time. "That's right," he said.
"She aint going to marry him. It's going to be worse than that."

FLEM

TWELVE

*W*hen the pickup truck giving him the ride onward from Clarksdale turned off at a town called Lake Cormorant and he had to get out, he had to walk. And he was apparently still nowhere near Memphis. He was realising now that this was the biggest, in a way terrifying, thing that had happened to him in the thirty-eight years: he had forgotten distance. He had forgot how far one place could be from another. And now he was going to have to eat too. Because all he had was the ten-dollar bill they had given him along with the new overalls and hat and shoes at the Parchman gate, plus the three dollars and eighty-five cents still left out of the forty dollars his cousin Flem—it must have been Flem; after he finally realised that Flem wasn't going to come or even send in from Frenchman's Bend to help him and he quit calling down from the jail window to anybody passing that would send word out to Flem, nobody else but Flem and maybe the judge knew or even bothered to care what became of him, where he was—had sent him back there eighteen years ago just before Flem sent Montgomery Ward to trick him into trying to escape in that woman's wrapper and sunbonnet and he got caught of course and they gave him the other twenty years.

It was a small tight neatly cluttered store plastered with placards behind a gasoline pump beside the highway; a battered dust- and mud-stained car was parked beside it and inside were only the proprietor and a young Negro man in the remnants of an army uniform. He asked for a loaf of bread and suddenly he remembered sardines, the taste of them from almost forty years ago; he could afford another nickel one time, when to his shock and for the moment unbelief, possibly in his own hearing, he learned that the tin would now cost him twenty-six cents—the small flat solid-feeling tin ubiquitous for five cents through all his previous days until Parchman—and even while he stood in that incredulous shock the proprietor set another small tin before him, saying, "You can have this one for eleven."

"What is it?" he said.

"Lunch meat," the proprietor said.

"What is lunch meat?" he said.

"Dont ask," the proprietor said. "Just eat it. What else can you buy with eleven cents?"

Then he saw against the opposite wall a waist-high stack of soft-drink cases and something terrible happened inside his mouth and throat—a leap, a spring of a thin liquid like fire or the myriad stinging of ants all the way down to his stomach; with a kind of incredulous terror, even while he was saying *No! No! That will cost at least a quarter too*, his voice was saying aloud: "I reckon I'll have one of them."

"A whole case?" the proprietor said.

"You cant jest buy one bottle?" he said, counting rapidly, thinking *At least twenty bottles. That would take all the ten dollars. Maybe that will save me.* Nor, when the proprietor set the uncapped coldly sweating bottle on the counter before him, did he even have time to tell himself *I'm going to pick it up and put my mouth on it before I ask the price because otherwise I might not be able to touch it* because his hand had already picked up the bottle, already tilting it, almost ramming the neck into his mouth, the first swallow coldly afire and too fast to taste until he could curb, restrain the urgency and passion so he could taste and affirm that he had not forgot the taste at all in the thirty-eight years: only how good it was, draining that bottle in steady controlled swallows now and only then removing it and in horror hearing his voice saying, "I'll have another one," even while he was telling himself *Stop it! Stop it!* then stood perfectly calm and perfectly composed while the proprietor uncapped the second sweating bottle and took that one up and closed his eyes gently and drank it steadily empty and fingered one of the bills loose in the pocket where he carried the three dollar ones (the ten-dollar note was folded carefully beneath a wad of newspaper and safety-pinned inside the fob pocket of the overall bib and put it on the counter, not looking at it nor at anything while he waited for the proprietor to ask for a second bill or maybe two more; until the proprietor laid sixty-eight cents in coins on the counter and picked up the bill.

Because the two empty bottles were still sitting on the counter in plain sight; he thought rapidly *If I could jest pick up the change and git outside before he notices them*—if not an impossibility, certainly a gamble he dared not take, had not time to risk: to gamble perhaps two dollars against a shout, a leap over the counter to bar the door until another sheriff came for him. So he said, not touching the change: "You never taken out for the sody."

"What's that?" the proprietor said. He scattered the coins on the counter. "Lunch meat, eleven; bread—" He stopped and as suddenly huddled the coins into a pile again. "Where did you say you come from?"

"I never said," Mink said. "Down the road."

"Been away a long time, have you?"

"That's right," he said.

"Much obliged," the proprietor said. "I sure forgot about them two Cokes. Damn labor unions have even run Coca-Cola up out of sight like everything else. You had two of them, didn't you?" taking the half-dollar from the change and shoving the rest of it across to him. "I dont know what folks are going to do unless somebody stops them somewhere. Looks like we're going to have to get shut of these damn Democrats to keep out of the poorhouse. Where'd you say you were headed? Memphis?"

"I aint said," he started to say. But the other was already, or still, speaking to the Negro now, already extending toward the Negro another opened soda.

"This is on the house. Jump in your car and run him up to the crossroads; he'll have double chance to catch a ride there, maybe someone from the other highway."

"I wasn't fixing to leave yet," the Negro said.

"Yes you are," the proprietor said. "Just a half a mile? You got plenty of time. Dont let me see you around here until you get back. All right," he said to Mink. "You'll sure catch a ride there."

So he rode again, in the battered mud-stained car; just for a moment the Negro slid his eyes toward him, then away. "Where down the road did you come from?" the Negro said. He didn't answer. "It was Parchman, wasn't it?" Then the car stopped. "Here's the crossroads," the Negro said. "Maybe you can catch a ride."

He got out. "Much obliged," he said.

"You done already paid him," the Negro said. So now he walked again. But mainly it was to be out of the store; he must not stop at one again. If the bottles had been a dollar apiece, there was a definite limit beyond which temptation, or at least his lack of will power, could no longer harm him. But at only a quarter apiece, until he could reach Memphis and actually have the pistol in his hand, there was no foreseeable point within the twelve remaining dollars where he would have peace; already, before he was even outside the store, he was saying *Be a man, Be a man. You got to be a man, you got too much to do, too much to resk* and, walking again, he was still sweating a little, not panting so much as simply breathing deeply like one who has just blundered unwarned into then out of the lair, the arms, of Semiramis or Messalina, still incredulous, still aghast at his own temerity and still amazed that he has escaped with his life.

And now he was discovering something else. For most of the twenty-odd years before he went to Parchman, and during all the thirty-eight since, he had walked only on soft dirt. Now he walked on concrete; not only were his feet troubling him but his bones and muscles ached all the way up to his skull, until presently he found a foul puddle of water among rank shadeless weeds at the end of a culvert and removed the new stiff brogans they had given him with the new overalls and sat with his feet in the water, eating the tinned meat and the bread, thinking *I got to watch myself. Maybe I dassent to even go inside where they sell hit* thinking, not with despair really: still indomitable *Likely hit will cost the whole ten-dollar bill, maybe more. That jest leaves three dollars and eighty-five cents and I done already spent eighty-two of that* and stopped and took the handful of coins from his pocket and spread them carefully on the ground beside him; he had had three one-dollar bills and the eighty-five cents and he counted slowly the eighty-five cents, a half-dollar, a quarter, and two nickels, and set them aside. He had given the man at the store one of the dollar bills and the man had given him back change for bread, eleven cents, lunch meat eleven cents, which was twenty-two cents, then the man had taken up the half-dollar for the sodas, which was seventy-two cents, which should have left twenty-eight cents; counting what remained slowly over coin by coin again, then counting the coins he had already set aside to be sure they were right. And still it was only eighteen cents instead of twenty-eight. A dime was gone somewhere. And the lunch meat was just eleven cents, he remembered that because there had been a kind of argument about it. So it was the bread, it would have to be the bread. *It went up another dime right while I was standing there* he thought. *And if bread could jump up ten cents right while I was looking at it, maybe I cant buy a pistol even for the whole thirteen dollars. So I got to stop somewhere and find a job.*

The highway was dense with traffic, but going fast now, the automobiles big ones, brand new, and the trucks were big as railroad cars; no more the dusty pickups which would have offered him a lift, but vehicles now of the rich and hurried who would not even have seen a man walking by himself in overalls. Or probably worse: they probably would have hedged away with their own size and speed and shining paint any other one of them which might have stopped for him, since they would not have wanted him under their feet in Memphis either. Not that it mattered now. He couldn't even see Memphis yet. And now he couldn't even say when he was going to see it, thinking *So I may need as much as ten dollars more before I even get to where I can buy one.* But at least he would have to reach Memphis before that became an actual problem, obstacle; at least when he did reach Memphis the thirteen dollars and three cents he still had must be intact, no matter how much more he might have to add to it to get there. So he would have to get more money some way, who knew he could not be trusted in another roadside store where they sold soda pop. *So I will have to stop somewhere and ask for work and I aint never asked no man for work in my life so maybe I dont even know how* thinking *And that will add at least one more day, maybe even more than one* thinking quietly but still without despair *I'm too old for this. A feller sixty-three years old ought not to have to handle such as this* thinking, but without despair: quite indomitable still *But a man that's done already had to wait thirty-eight years, one more day or two or even three aint going to hurt.*

The woman was thick but not fat and not old, a little hard-looking, in a shapeless not very clean dress, standing in a small untidy yard pulling dead clematis vines from a frame beside a small house. "Are you a man of God?" she said.

"Ma'am?" he said.

"You look like a preacher."

"Nome," he said. "I been away."

"What kind of work can you do?"

"I kin do that. I kin rake the yard."

"What else?"

"I been a farmer. I reckon I can do most anything."

"I reckon first you want something to eat," she said. "All right. We're all God's creatures. Finish pulling down these vines. Then you'll find a rake by the kitchen door. And remember. I'll be watching you."

Perhaps she was, from behind the curtains. He couldn't tell. He didn't try to. Though evidently she was, already standing on the minuscule front gallery when he put the last rake-full on the pile, and told him where the wheelbarrow was and gave him three kitchen matches and stood watching while he wheeled the trash into the adjoining vacant lot and set fire to it. "Put the wheelbarrow and rake back where you got them and come in the kitchen," she said. He did so—a stove, sink, refrigerator, a table and chair set and on the table a platter of badly cooked greens with livid pork lumps in it and two slices of machine-made bread on a saucer and a glass of water; he standing for a time quite still, his hands hanging quietly at his sides, looking at it. "Are you too proud to eat it?" she said.

"It aint that," he said. "I aint hungry. I needed the money to get on. I got to get to Memphis and then back to Missippi."

"Do you want that dinner, or dont you?" she said.

"Yessum," he said. "Much obliged," and sat down, she watching him a moment, then she opened the refrigerator and took out an opened tin and set it on the table before him. It contained one half of a canned peach.

"Here," she said.

"Yessum," he said. "Much obliged." Perhaps she was still watching him. He ate what he could (it was cold) and had carried the plate and knife and fork to the sink to wash them when she came suddenly in again.

"I'll do that," she said. "You go on up the road four miles. You'll come to a mailbox with Brother Goodyhay on it. You can read, cant you?"

"I'll find it," he said.
"Tell him Beth Holcomb sent you."
He found it. He had to. He thought *I got to find it* thinking how maybe he would be able to read the name on the mailbox simply because he would have to read it, would have to penetrate through the inscrutable hieroglyph; thinking while he stood looking at the metal hutch with the words *Bro J C Goodyhay* not stencilled but painted on it, not sloven nor careless but impatiently, with a sort of savage impatience: thinking, either before or at least simultaneous with his realisation that someone nearby was shouting at him *Maybe I could read all the time and jest never knowed it until I had to.* Anyway, hearing the voice and looking up the tiny savagely untended yard, to another small frame house on that minuscule gallery of which a man stood waving one arm and shouting at him: "This is it. Come on."—a lean quick-moving man in the middle thirties with coldly seething eyes and the long upper lip of a lawyer or an orator and the long chin of the old-time comic-strip Puritan, who said,
"Hell, you're a preacher."
"No," he said. "I been away. I'm trying to get to—"
"All right, all right," the other said. "I'll meet you round back," and went rapidly back into the house. He, Mink, went around it into the back yard, which if anything was of an even more violent desolation than the front, since the back yard contained another house not dismantled so much as collapsed—a jumble of beams, joists, window- and door-frames and even still-intact sections of siding, among which moved or stood rather a man apparently as old as he, Mink, was, although he wore a battle jacket of the type which hadn't been copied from the British model until after Pearl Harbor, with the shoulder patch of a division which hadn't existed before then either, who when Mink came in sight began to chop rapidly with the axe in his hand among the jumble of lumber about him; barely in time as the back door of the house crashed open and the first man came out, carrying a buck saw; now Mink saw the sawbuck and a small heap of sawn lengths. "All right, all right," the first man said, handing Mink the saw. "Save all the sound pieces. Dont split the nails out, pull them out. Saw up all the scraps, same length. Dad is

in charge. I'll be in the house," and went back into it; even doors which he barely released seemed to clap to behind him violently, as though his passage had sucked them shut.

"So they caught you too did they, mac?" the man in the battle jacket (he would be Dad) said.

Mink didn't answer that. He said: "Is that the reverend?"

"That's Goodyhay," the other said. "I aint heard him preach yet but even if he hadn't opened his mouth he would be a better preacher than he is a cook. But then, somebody's got to scorch the biscuits. They claim his wife ran off with a sonabitching Four-F potato-chip salesman before he even got back from fighting in the Pacific. They were all doing it back then and what I notice, they aint quit, even without any war to blame it on. But what the hell, I always say there's still a frog in the puddle for every one that jumps out. So they caught you too, huh?"

This time he answered. "I got to get to Memphis and then back down to Missippi. I'm already behind. I got to get on tonight. How much does he pay here?"

"That's what you think," the other said. "That's what I thought three days ago: pick up a dollar or so and move on. Because you're building a church this time, bully boy. So maybe we both better hope the bastard can preach since we aint going to get our money until they take up the collection Sunday."

"Sunday?" he said.

"That's right," the other said. "This is Thursday; count it."

"Sunday," he said. "That's three days."

"That's right," the other said. "Sunday's always three days after Thursday around here. It's a law they got."

"How much will we get on Sunday?"

"It may be as much as a dollar cash; you're working for the Lord now, not mammon, jack. But anyway you'll be fed and slept—"

"I cant work that long for jest a dollar," he said. "I aint got the time."

"It may be more than a dollar. What I hear around here, he seems to have something. Anyway, he gets them. It seems he was a Marine sergeant on one of them landing barges out in the Pacific one day when a Jap dive bomber dove right at them and everybody tried to jump off into the water before the bomb hit, except one mama's boy that got scared or tangled up in something so he couldn't jump and the reverend (except he hadn't turned reverend then, not for the next few minutes yet) went back to try and untangle him, when the whole barge blew up and took the reverend and the mama's boy both right on down to the bottom with it before the reverend could get them both loose and up to the top again. Which is just the official version when they gave him the medal, since according to the reverend or leastways his congregation—What I hear, the rest of them are mostly ex-soldiers too or their wives or the other broads they just knocked up without marrying, mostly young, except for a few old ones that seem to got dragged in by the passing suction you might say; maybe the moms and pops of soldiers that got killed, or the ones like that Sister Holcomb one that caught you down the road, that probably never thawed enough to have a child of any kind and God help the husband either if she ever had one, that wasn't even sucked in but flagged the bus herself because the ride looked like it was free—" He stopped. Then he said: "No, I know exactly why she come: to listen to some of the words he uses doing what he calls preaching. Where was I? Oh yes: that landing barge. According to the reverend, he was already safe and dead and peacefully out of it at last on the bottom of the Pacific Ocean when all of a sudden Jesus Himself was standing over him saying Fall in and he did it and Jesus said Ten-SHUN, about-FACE and assigned him to this new permanent hitch right down here on the edge of Memphis, Tennessee. He's got something, enough of whatever it took to recruit this new-faith boot camp to need a church to hold it. And I be damned if I dont believe he's even going to get a carpenter to nail it together. What did he say when he first saw you?"

"What?" Mink said.

"What were his first words when he looked at you?"

"He said, 'Hell, you're a preacher.' "

"You see what I mean? He's mesmerised enough folks to scour the country for any edifice that somebody aint actually sitting on the front porch of, and knocking it down and hauling it over here to be broke up like we're doing. But he aint got a master carpenter yet to nail it together into a church. Because master carpenters belong to unions, and deal in cash money per diem on the barrel-head, where his assignment come direct from Jesus Christ Who aint interested in money or at least from the putting-out angle. So him and his outpost foxholes up and down the road like that Sister Holcomb that snagged you are sifting for one."

"Sifting?" he said.

"Sivving. Like flour. Straining folks through this back yard until somebody comes up that knows how to nail that church together when we get enough boards and planks and window frames ripped a-loose and stacked up. Which maybe we better get at it. I aint actually caught him spying behind a window shade yet but likely an ex-Marine sergeant even reformed into the ministry is no man to monkey with too far."

"You mean I cant leave?"

"Sure you can. All the outdoors is yours around here. You aint going to get any money until they take up that collection Sunday though. Not to mention a place to sleep tonight and what he calls cooking if you aint particular."

In fact, this house had no shades nor curtains whatever to be spied from behind. Indeed, as he really looked about it for the first time, the whole place had an air of violent transience similar to the indiscriminate jumble of walls and windows and doors among which he and the other man worked: merely still nailed together and so standing upright; from time to time, as the stack of reclaimed planks and the pile of fire-lengths to which his saw was reducing the spoiled fragments slowly rose, Mink could hear the preacher moving about inside the intact one, so that he thought *If he jest went back inside to compose up his sermon, it sounds like getting ready to preach takes as much activity and quickness as harnessing up a mule.* Now it was almost sunset; he thought *This will have to be at least a half a dollar. I got to have it. I got to get on. I cant wait till Sunday* when the back door jerked, burst open and the preacher said, "All right. Supper's ready. Come on."

He followed Dad inside. Nothing was said by anyone about washing. "I figgered—" he began. But it was already too late. This was a kitchen too but not Spartan so much as desolate, like a public camp site in a roadside park, with what he called another artermatic stove since he had never seen a gas or electric stove until he saw Mrs Holcomb's, Goodyhay standing facing it in violent immobility enclosed in a fierce sound of frying; Mink said again. "I figgered—" as Goodyhay turned from the stove with three platters bearing each a charred splat of something which on the enamel surfaces looked as alien and solitary and not for eating as the droppings of cows. "I done already et," Mink said. "I figgered I would jest get on."

"What?" Goodyhay said.

"Even after I get to Memphis, I still aint hardly begun," he said. "I got to get on tonight."

"So you want your money now," Goodyhay said, setting the platters on the table where there already sat a tremendous bottle of tomato ketchup and a plate of machine-sliced bread and a sugar bowl and a can of condensed milk with holes punched in the top. "Sit down," Goodyhay said, turning back to the stove, where Mink could smell the coffee overboiled too with that same violent impatience of the fried hamburger and the woodpiles in the yard and the lettering on the mailbox; until Goodyhay turned again with the three cups of coffee and said again, "Sit down." Dad was already seated. "I said, sit down," Goodyhay said. "You'll get your money Sunday after the collection."

"I cant wait that long."

"All right," Goodyhay said, dashing ketchup over his plate. "Eat your supper first. You've already paid for that." He sat down; the other two were already eating. In fact Goodyhay had already finished, rising in the same motion with which he put his fork down, still chewing, and went and swung inward an open door (on the back of which was hanging what Mink did not recognise to be a camouflaged battle helmet worn by Marine troops on the Pacific beach-heads and jungles because what he was looking at was the automatic-pistol butt projecting from its webbing belt beneath the helmet) and from the refrigerator behind it took a tin also of canned peach halves and brought it to the table and dealt, splashed the halves and the syrup with exact impartiality onto the three greasy plates and they ate that too, Goodyhay once more finishing first; and now, for the first time since Mink had known him, sitting perfectly motionless, almost as though asleep, until they had finished also. Then he said, "Police it," himself leading the way to the sink with his plate and utensils and cup and washed them beneath the tap, then stood and watched while the other two followed suit and dried and racked them as he had done. Then he said to Mink: "All right. You going or staying?"

"I got to stay," Mink said. "I got to have the money."

"All right," Goodyhay said. "Kneel down," and did so first again, the other two following, on the kitchen floor beneath the hard dim glare of the single unshaded low-watt bulb on a ceiling cord, Goodyhay on his knees but no more, his head up, the coldly seething desert-hermit's eyes not even closed, and said, "Save us, Christ, the poor sons of bitches," and rose and said, "All right. Lights out. The truck'll be here at seven oclock."

The room was actually a lean-to, a little larger than a closet. It had one small window, a door connecting with the house, a single bulb on a drop cord, a thin mattress on the floor with a tarpaulin cover but no pillows nor sheets, and nothing else, Goodyhay holding the door for them to enter and then closing it. They were alone.

"Go ahead," Dad said. "Try it."

"Try what?" Mink said.

"The door. It's locked. Oh, you can get out any time you want; the window aint locked. But that door leads back into the house and he dont aim to have none of us master-carpenter candidates maybe ramshagging the joint as a farewell gesture on the way out. You're working for the Lord now, buster, but there's still a Marine sergeant running the detail." He yawned. "But at least you will get your two dollars Sunday—three, if he counts today as a day too. Not to mention hearing him preach. Which may be worth even three dollars. You know: one of them special limited editions they can charge ten prices for because they never printed but two or three of." He blinked at Mink. "Because why. It aint going to last much longer." He blinked at Mink. "Because they aint going to let it."

"They wont even pay me two dollars?" Mink said.

"No no," the other said. "I mean the rest of the folks in the neighborhood he aint converted yet, aint going to put up with no such as this. The rest of the folks that already had to put up with that damn war for four-five years now and want to forget about it. That've already gone to all that five years of trouble and expense to get shut of it, only just when they are about to get settled back down again, be damned if here aint a passel of free-loading government-subsidised ex-drafted sons of bitches acting like whatever had caused the war not only actually happened but was still going on, and was going to keep on going on until somebody did something about it. A passel of mostly non-taxpaying folks that like as not would have voted for Norman Thomas even ahead of Roosevelt, let alone Truman, trying to bring Jesus Christ back alive in the middle of 1946. So it may be worth three dollars just to hear him in the free outside air. Because next time you might have to listen through a set of jail bars." He yawned again, prodigiously, beginning to remove the battle jacket. "Well, we aint got a book to curl up with in here even if we wanted to. So all that leaves is to go to bed."

Which they did. The light was off, he lay breathing quietly on his back, his hands folded on his breast. He thought *Sholy it will be three dollars. Sholy they will count today too* thinking *And Sunday will make three days lost because even if I got to Memphis Sunday after we are paid off the stores where I can buy one will still be closed until Monday morning* thinking *But I reckon I can wait three more days* a little wryly now *Likely because I cant figger out no way to help it* and almost immediately was asleep, peacefully, sleeping well because it was daylight when he knew next, lying there peacefully for a little time yet before he realised he was alone. It seemed to him afterward that he still lay there peaceful and calm, his hand still playing idly with the safety pin it had found lying open on his chest, for the better part of a minute after he knew what had happened; then sitting, surging up, not even needing to see the open window and the dangling screen, his now frantic hand scrabbling from the bib pocket of the overalls the wad of newspaper beneath which the ten-dollar bill had been pinned, his voice making a puny whimpering instead of the cursing he was trying for, beating his fists on the locked door until it jerked open and Goodyhay stood in it, also taking one look at the ravished window.

"So the son of a bitch robbed you," Goodyhay said.

"It was ten dollars," Mink said. "I got to ketch him. Let me out."

"Hold it," Goodyhay said, still barring the doorway. "You cant catch him now."

"I got to," he said. "I got to have that ten dollars."

"You mean you've got to have ten dollars to get home?"

"Yes!" he said, cursing again. "I cant do nothing without it. Let me out."

"How long since you been home?" Goodyhay said.

"Thirty-eight years. Tell me which way you figger he went."

"Hold it," Goodyhay said, still not moving. "All right," he said. "I'll see you get your ten dollars back Sunday. Can you cook?"

"I can fry eggs and meat," Mink said.

"All right. You cook breakfast and I'll load the truck. Come on." Goodyhay showed him how to light the stove and left him; he filled up last night's coffee pot with water as his tradition was until the grounds had lost all flavor and color too, and sliced the fatback and dusted it with meal into the skillet in his tradition also, and got eggs out to fry, standing for a while with the door in his hand while he looked, mused, at the heavy holstered pistol beneath the helmet, thinking quietly *If I jest had that for two days I wouldn't need no ten dollars* thinking *I done been robbed in good faith without warning; why aint that enough to free me to rob in my turn. Not to mention my need being ten times, a hundred times, a thousand times more despaired than ara other man's need for jest ten dollars* thinking quietly peacefully indeed now *No. I aint never stole. I aint never come to that and I wont never.*

When he went to the door to call them, Goodyhay and another man had the truck loaded with intact sections of wall and disassembled planks; he rode on top of the load, once more on the highway toward Memphis; he thought *Maybe they'll even go through Memphis and if I jest had the ten dollars* and then quit, just riding, in motion, until the truck turned into a side road; now they were passing, perhaps entering, already on, a big place, domain, plantation—broad cotton fields still white for the pickers; presently they turned into a farm road across a field and came to a willow-grown bayou and another pickup truck and another stack of dismembered walls and a group of three or four men all curiously similar somehow to Goodyhay and the driver of his—their—truck; he, Mink, couldn't have said how nor why, and not even speculating: remarking without attention another battle jacket, remarking without much attention either a rectangle of taut string between driven stakes in the dimensions of whatever it was they were going to build, where they unloaded the truck and Goodyhay said, "All right. You and Albert go back for another load."

So he rode in the cab this time, back to the parsonage or whatever it was, where he and Albert loaded the truck and they returned to the bayou, where by this time, with that many folks working—if any of the other four worked half as fast and as hard as Goodyhay did—they would probably have one wall already up. Instead, the other truck and Goodyhay and the stake-and-string rectangle were gone and only three men sat quietly beside the pile of lumber.

"Well?" Albert said.

"Yep," one of the others said. "Somebody changed his mind."

"Who?" Mink said. "Changed what? I got to get on. I'm already late."

"Fellow that owns this place," Albert said. "That gave us permission to put the chapel here. Somebody changed his mind for him. Maybe the bank that holds his mortgage. Maybe the Legion."

"What Legion?" he said.

"The American Legion. That's still holding the line at 1918. You never heard of it?"

"Where's Reverend Goodyhay?" he said. "I got to get on."

"All right," Albert said. "So long." So he waited. Now it was early afternoon when the other truck returned, being driven fast, Goodyhay already getting out of it before it stopped.

"All right," he said. "Load up." Then they were on the Memphis highway again, going fast now to keep at least in sight of Goodyhay, as fast as any of the traffic they dashed among, he thinking *If I jest had the ten dollars, even if we aint going all the way to Memphis this time neither.* They didn't. Goodyhay turned off and they ran again, faster than they dared except that Goodyhay in the front truck would have lost them, into a region of desolation, the lush Delta having played out now into eroded barren clay hills; into a final, the uttermost of desolation, where Goodyhay stopped—a dump, a jumbled plain of rusted automobile bodies and boilers and gin machinery and brick and concrete rubble; already the stakes had been re-driven and the rectangular string tautened rigid between them, Goodyhay standing beside his halter truck beckoning his arm, shouting, "All right. Here we are. Let's go."

So there was actual work again at last. But it was already late; most of the day was gone and tomorrow was Saturday, only one more full day. But Goodyhay didn't even give him a chance to speak. "Didn't I tell you you'd get your ten dollars Sunday? All right then." Nor did Goodyhay say, "Can you cook supper?" He just jerked, flung open the refrigerator door and jerked out the bloodstained paper of hamburger meat and left the kitchen. And now Mink remembered from somewhere that he had cooked grits once and found grits and the proper vessel. And tonight Goodyhay didn't lock the door; he, Mink, tried it to see, then closed it and lay down, again peacefully on his back, his hands folded on his breast like a corpse, until Goody-hay waked him to fry the side meat and the eggs again. The pickup truck was already there and a dozen men were on hand this time and now you could begin to see what the chapel (they called it) was going to look like; until dark. He said: "It aint cold tonight and besides I can lay under that-ere roofing paper and get started at daylight until the rest of them—"

"We dont work on Sunday," Goodyhay said. "Come on. Come on." Then it was Sunday. It was raining: the thin steady drizzle of early fall. A man and his wife called for them, not a pickup this time but a car, hard-used and a little battered. They turned again into a crossroad, not into desolate country this time but simply empty, coming at last to an unpainted box of a building which something somewhere back before the thirty-eight years in the penitentiary recognised, remembered. *It's a nigger schoolhouse* he thought, getting out among five or six other stained and battered cars and pickup trucks and a group of people already waiting, a few older ones but usually men and women about the age of Goodyhay or a little younger; again he sensed that identity, similarity among them even beyond the garments they wore—more battle jackets, green army slickers, one barracks cap still showing where the officer's badge had been removed; someone said, "Howdy," at his elbow. It was Albert and now he, Mink, recognised the Miss or Mrs Holcomb whose yard he had raked, and then he saw a big Negro woman—a woman no longer young, who looked at the same time gaunt yet fat too. He stopped, not quite startled: just watchful.

"You all take niggers too?" he said.

"We do this one," Albert said. Goodyhay had already entered the house. The rest of them now moved slowly toward the door, clotting a little. "Her son had it too just like she was a white woman, even if they didn't put his name on the same side of the monument with the others. See that woman yonder with the yellow hat?" The hat was soiled now but still flash, the coat below it had been white once too, a little flash too; the face between could have been twenty-five and probably at one time looked it, thin now, not quite raddled. "That's right," Albert said. "She still looks a little like a whore yet but you should have seen her last spring when she came out of that Catalpa Street house. Her husband commanded an infantry platoon back there when the Japs were running us out of Asia, when we were falling back all mixed up together—Aussies, British, French from IndoChina—not trying to hold anything any more except a line of foxholes after dark, fell long enough to get the stragglers up and move again tomorrow, including the ones in the foxholes too if any of them were still there by daylight. His platoon was the picket that night, him in one foxhole and his section strung out, when the nigger crawled up with the ammunition. He was new, you see. I mean, the nigger. This was as close as he had been to a Jap yet.

"So you know how it is: crouched in the stinking pitch dark in a stinking sweating hole in the ground with your eyes and ears both strained until in another minute they will pop right out of your head like marbles, and all around in front of you the chirping voices like crickets in a hayfield until you realise they aint crickets because pretty soon what they are chirping is English: 'Maline. Tonigh youdigh. Maline. Tonigh youdigh.' So here comes the nigger with his sack of grenades and Garand clips and the lieutenant tells him to get down into the hole and puts the nigger's finger on the trigger of the Garand and tells him to stay there while he crawls back to report to the p.c. or something.

"You know how it is. A man can stand just so much. He dont even know when it will be but all of a sudden a moment comes and he knows that's all, he's already had it; he hates it as much as you do but he didn't ask for it and he cant help it. That's the trouble; you dont know beforehand, there's nothing to warn you, to tell you to brace. Especially in war. It makes you think that just something no tougher

than men aint got any business in war, dont it? that if they're going
to keep on having them, they ought to invent something a little more
efficient to fight them with. Anyway, it's the next morning, first light,
when the first of the cut-off heads that maybe last night you split a
can of dog ration with, comes tumbling down among you like somebody throwing a basketball. Only this time it's that black head.
Because why not? a nigger bred up on a Arkansas plantation, that a
white man, not just a lieutenant but talking Arkansas to boot, says,
'Take a-holt of this here hoe or rifle and stay here till I get back.' So
as soon as we finished fighting the Japs far enough back to get organised to spend another day dodging the strafing planes, the lieutenant
goes around behind the dump of stuff we can tote with us and are
trying to set fire to it and make it burn—It's funny about jungles.
You're sweating all the time, even in the dark, and you are always
parched for water because there aint any in a jungle no matter what
you thought, and when you step into a patch of sun you blister before
you can even button your shirt. Until you believe that if you so much
as drop a canteen or a bayonet or even strike a boot calk against a
root a spark will jump out and set the whole country afire. But just
try to start one. Just try to burn something up and you'll see different. Anyway, the lieutenant went around behind the dump where he
would have a little privacy and put his pistol barrel in his mouth.
Sure, she can get in here."

Now they were all inside, and he recognised this from thirty-eight
years back too—how the smell of Negroes remained long after the
rooms themselves were vacant of them—the smell of poverty and
secret fear and patience and enduring without enough hope to
deodorise it—they (he supposed they would call themselves a congregation) filing onto the backless benches, the woman in the yellow hat on the front one, the big Negress alone on the back one,
Goodyhay himself facing them at the end of the room behind a plank
laid across two sawhorses, his hands resting, not clenched: just closed
into fists, on the plank until everybody was quiet.

"All right," Goodyhay said. "Anybody that thinks all he's got to
do is sit on his stern and have salvation come down on him like a
cloudburst or something, dont belong in here. You got to get up on
your feet and hunt it down until you can get a-hold of it and then

hold it, even fighting off if you have to. And if you cant find it, then by God make it. Make a salvation He will pass and then earn the right to grab it and hold on and fight off too if you have to but anyway hold it, hell and high water be damned—" when a voice, a man, interrupted:

"Tell it again, Joe. Go on. Tell it again."

"What?" Goodyhay said.

"Tell it again," the man said. "Go on."

"I tried to," Goodyhay said. "You all heard me. I cant tell it."

"Yes you can," the man said; now there were women's voices too: "Yes, Joe. Tell it," and he, Mink, still watching the hands not clenched but just closed on the plank, the coldly seething anchorite's eyes—the eyes of a fifth-century hermit looking at nothing from the entrance of his Mesopotamian cave—the body rigid in an immobility like a tremendous strain beneath a weight.

"All right," Goodyhay said. "I was laying there. I was all right, everything snafu so I was all right. You know how it is in water when you dont have any weight at all, just laying there with the light coming way down from up on top like them lattice blinds when they shake and shiver slow in a breeze without making any sound at all. Just laying there watching my hands floating along without me even having to hold them up, with the shadow of them lattice blinds winking and shaking across them, and my feet and legs too, no weight at all, nowhere to have to go or march, not even needing to breathe, not even needing to be asleep or nothing: just all right. When there He was standing over me, looking like any other shavetail just out of a foxhole, maybe a little older, except he didn't have a hat, bucket: just standing there bareheaded with the shadow of the lattice running up and down him, smoking a cigarette. 'Fall in, soldier,' He said.

" 'I cant,' I says. Because I knew that as long as I laid still, I would be all right. But that once I let myself start thinking about moving, or tried to, I would find out I couldn't. But what the hell, why should I? I was all right. I had had it. I had it made. I was sacked up. Let them do whatever they ....ing wanted to with their ....ing war up on top.

" 'That's once,' He said. 'You aint got but three times. You, the Top Soldier, saying cant. At Château-Thierry and St-Mihiel the company would have called you the Top Soldier. Do they still do that in the Corps on Guadalcanal?'

" 'Yes,' I says.

" 'All right, Top Soldier,' He said. 'Fall in.' So I got up. 'At ease,' He said. 'You see?' He said.

" 'I thought I couldn't,' I says. 'I didn't believe I could.'

" 'Sure,' He said. 'What else do we want with you. We're already full up with folks that know they can but dont, since because they already know they can, they dont have to do it. What we want are folks that believe they cant, and then do it. The other kind dont need us and we dont need them. I'll say more: we dont even want them in the outfit. They wont be accepted; we wont even have them under our feet. If it aint worth that much, it aint worth anything. Right?'

" 'Yes sir,' I says.

" 'You can say Sir up there too if you want,' He said. 'It's a free country. Nobody gives a damn. You all right now?'

" 'Yes sir,' I says.

" 'TenSHUN!' He said. And I made them pop, mud or no mud. 'About-FACE!' He said. And He never saw one smarter than that one neither. 'Forward MARCH!' He said. And I had already stepped off when He said, 'Halt!' and I stopped. 'You're going to leave him laying there,' He said. And there he was, I had forgot about him, laying there as peaceful and out of it too as you please—the damned little bastard that had gone chicken at the exact wrong time, like they always do, turned the wheel a-loose and tried to duck and caused the whole damn mess; lucky for all of us he never had a ....ing bar on his shoulder so he could have ....ed up the whole detail and done for all of us.

" 'I cant carry him too,' I says.

" 'That's two times,' He said. 'You've got one more. Why not go on and use it now and get shut of it for good?'

" 'I cant carry him too,' I says.

" 'Fine,' He said. 'That's three and finished. You wont ever have to say cant again. Because you're a special case; they gave you three times. But there's a general order coming down today that after this nobody has but one. Pick him up.' So I did. 'Dismiss,' He said. And that's all. I told you I cant tell it. I was just there. I cant tell it." He,

Mink, watching them all, himself alien, not only unreconciled but irreconcilable: not contemptuous, because he was just waiting, not impatient because even if he were in Memphis right this minute, at ten or eleven or whatever oclock it was on Sunday morning, he would still have almost twenty-four hours to get through somehow before he could move on to the next step. He just watched them: the two oldish couples, man and wife of course, farmers obviously, without doubt tenant farmers come up from the mortgaged bank- or syndicate-owned cotton plantation from which the son had been drafted three or four or five years ago to make that far from home that sacrifice, old, alien too, too old for this, unreconciled by the meager and arid tears which were less of tears than blisters; none of the white people actually watching as the solitary Negro woman got up from her back bench and walked down the aisle to where the young woman's soiled yellow hat was crushed into the crook of her elbow like a child in a child's misery and desolation, the white people on the bench making way for the Negro woman to sit down beside the young white woman and put her arm around her; Goodyhay still standing, his arms propped on the closed fists on the plank, the cold seething eyes not even closed, speaking exactly as he had spoken three nights ago while the three of them knelt on the kitchen floor: "Save us, Christ. The poor sons of bitches." Then Goodyhay was looking at him. "You, there," Goodyhay said. "Stand up." Mink did so. "He's trying to get home. He hasn't put in but one full day, but he needs ten dollars to get home on. He hasn't been home in thirty-eight years. He needs nine bucks more. How about it?"

"I'll take it," the man in the officer's cap said. "I won thirty-four in a crap game last night. He can have ten of that."

"I said nine," Goodyhay said. "He's got one dollar coming. Give him the ten and I'll give you one. He says he's got to go to Memphis first. Anybody going in tonight?"

"I am," another said.

"All right," Goodyhay said. "Anybody want to sing?"

That was how he saw Memphis again under the best, the matchless condition for one who hadn't seen it in . . . He could figure that. He was twenty years old when he got married. Three times before that he had wrenched, wrung enough money from the otherwise unpaid labor he did on the tenant farm of the kinsman who had raised him from orphanhood, to visit the Memphis brothels. The last visit was in the same year of his marriage. He was twenty-six years when he went to Parchman. Twenty dollars from twenty-six dollars was six dollars. He was in Parchman thirty-eight years. Six dollars and thirty-eight dollars was forty-four dollars to see Memphis again not only after forty-four years but under the matchless condition: at night, the dark earth on either hand and ahead already random and spangled with the neon he had never seen before, and in the distance the low portentous glare of the city itself, he sitting on the edge of the seat as a child sits, almost as small as a child, peering ahead as the car rushed, merging into one mutual spangled race bearing toward, as though by the acceleration of gravity or suction, the distant city; suddenly off to the right a train fled dragging a long string of lighted windows as rapid and ephemeral as dream; he became aware of a convergence like the spokes of a gigantic dark wheel lying on its hub, along which sped dense and undeviable as ants, automobiles and what they told him were called buses as if all the earth was hurrying, plunging, being sucked, decked with diamond and ruby lights, into the low glare on the sky as into some monstrous, frightening, unimaginable joy or pleasure.

Now the converging roads themselves were decked with globular lights as big and high in the trees as roosting turkeys. "Tell me when we get close," he said.

"Close to what?" the driver said.

"Close to Memphis."

"We're already in Memphis," the driver said. "We crossed the city limits a mile back." So now he realised that if he had still been walking, alone, with none to ask or tell him, his troubles would have really begun only after he reached Memphis. Because the Memphis he remembered from forty-four years back no longer existed; he thought *I been away too long; when you got something to handle like I got to handle, and by yourself and not no more to handle it with than I got, not to mention eighty more miles to go yet, a man jest cant afford to been away as long as I had to be.* Back then you would catch a ride in somebody's wagon coming in from Frenchman's Bend or maybe two or three of you would ride plow mules in to Jefferson, with a croker sack of corn behind the borrowed saddle, to leave the mules in the lot behind the Commercial Hotel and pay the nigger there a quarter to feed them until you got back, and get on the train at the depot and change at the Junction to one that went right into the middle of Memphis, the depot there almost in the center of town.

But all that was changed now. They had told him four days ago that most of the trains were gone, quit running, even if he had had that much extra money to spend just riding. They had told him how they were buses now but in all the four days he had yet to see anything that looked like a depot where he could buy a ticket and get on one. And as for the edge of Memphis that back there forty-four years ago a man could have walked in from in an hour, he, according to the driver, had already crossed it over a mile back yet still all he could see of it was just that glare on the sky. Even though he was actually in Memphis, he was apparently still as far from the goal he remembered and sought, as from Varner's store to Jefferson; except for the car giving him a ride and the driver of it who knew in general where he needed to go, he might have had to spend even the ten dollars for food wandering around inside Memphis before he ever reached the place where he could buy the pistol.

Now the car was wedged solid into a rushing mass of other vehicles all winking and glittering and flashing with colored lights; all circumambience in fact flashed and glared luminous and myriad with color and aloud with sound: suddenly a clutch of winking red green and white lights slid across the high night itself; he knew, sensed what they were but was much too canny to ask, telling, hissing to himself *Remember. Remember. It wont hurt you long as dont nobody find out you dont know it.*

Now he was in what he knew was the city. For a moment it merely stood glittering and serried and taller than stars. Then it engulfed him; it stooped soaring down, bearing down upon him like breathing the vast concrete mass and weight until he himself was breathless, having to pant for air. Then he knew what it was. *It's un-sleeping,* he thought. *It aint slept in so long now it's done forgot how to sleep and now there aint no time to stop long enough to try to learn how* again; the car rigid in its rigid mass, creeping then stopping then creeping again to the ordered blink and change of colored lights like the railroads used to have, until at last it drew out and could stop.

"Here's the bus station," the driver said. "This was where you wanted, wasn't it?"

"It's fine," he said.

"Buses leave here for everywhere. You want me to come in with you and find out about yours?"

"Much obliged," he said. "It's jest fine."

"So long then," the driver said.

"I thank you kindly," he said. "So long." Sure enough, it was a bus depot at last. Only if he went inside, one of the new laws he had heard about in Parchman—laws that a man couldn't saw boards and hammer nails unless he paid money to an association that would let him, couldn't even raise cotton on his own land unless the government said he could—might be that he would have to get on the first bus that left, no matter where it was going. So there was the rest of the night, almost all of it since it wasn't even late yet. But it would only be twelve hours and for that time he could at least make one anonymous more among the wan anonymous faces thronging about him, hurrying and myriad beneath the colored glare, passionate and gay and unsleeping. Then something happened. Without warning the city spun, whirled, vertiginous, infinitesimal and dizzying, then as suddenly braked and immobilised again and he not only knew exactly where he was, but how to pass the twelve hours. He would have to cross the street, letting the throng itself enclot and engulf him as the light changed; once across he could free himself and go on. And there it was: the Confederate Park they called it—the path- and flower-bed-crisscrossed vacancy exactly as he remembered it, the line of benches along the stone parapet in the gaps of which the old iron cannon from the War squatted and beyond that the sense and smell of the River, where forty-four and -five and -six years ago, having spent half his money in the brothel last night and the other half saved for tonight, after which he would have nothing left but the return ticket to Jefferson, he would come to watch the steamboats.

The levee would be lined with them bearing names like *Stacker Lee* and *Ozark Belle* and *Crescent Queen*, come from as far apart as

Cairo and New Orleans, to meet and pass while he watched them, the levee clattering with horse- and mule-drawn drays and chanting stevedores while the cotton bales and the crated machinery and the rest of the bags and boxes moved up and down the gangplanks, and the benches along the bluff would be crowded with other people watching them too. But now the benches were vacant and even when he reached the stone parapet among the old cannon there was nothing of the River but the vast and vacant expanse, only the wet dark cold blowing, breathing up from across the vast empty River so that already he was buttoning the cotton jumper over his cotton shirt; no sound here at all: only the constant unsleeping murmur of the city behind him, no movement save the minute crawl of the automobiles on the bridge far down the River, hurrying, drawn also toward and into that unceasing murmur of passion and excitement, into this backwash of which he seemed to have blundered, strayed, and then abandoned, betrayed by having had to be away from it so long. And cold too, even here behind one of the old cannon, smelling the cold aged iron too, huddled into the harsh cotton denim too new to have acquired his own body's shape and so warm him by contact; it was going to be too cold here before much longer even though he did have peace and quiet to pass the rest of the twelve hours in. But he had already remembered the other one, the one they called Court Square, where he would be sheltered from the River air by the tall buildings themselves provided he waited a little longer to give the people who might be sitting on the benches there time to get sleepy and go home.

So when he turned back toward the glare and the murmur, the resonant concrete hum, though unsleeping still, now had a spent quality like rising fading smoke or steam, so that what remained of it was now high among the ledges and cornices; the random automobiles which passed now, though gleaming with colored lights still, seemed now as though fleeing in terror, in solitude from solitude. It was warmer here. And after a while he was right: there was nobody here save himself; on a suitable bench he lay down, drawing and huddling his knees up into the buttoned jumper, looking no larger than a child and no less waif, abandoned, when something hard was striking the soles of his feet and time, a good deal of it, had passed and the night itself was now cold and vacant. It was a policeman; he recognised that even after the forty-four years of change and alteration.

"Damn Mississippi," the policeman said. "I mean, where are you staying in town here? You mean, you haven't got anywhere to sleep? You know where the railroad station is? Go on down there; you can find a bed for fifty cents. Go on now." He didn't move, waiflike and abandoned true enough but no more pitiable than a scorpion. "Hell, you're broke too. Here." It was a half-dollar. "Go on now. Beat it. I'm going to stand right here and watch you out of sight."

"Much obliged," he said. A half a dollar. So that was another part of the new laws they had been passing; come to remember, he had heard about that in Parchman too; they called it Relief or W P and A: the same government that wouldn't let you raise cotton on your own land would turn right around and give you a mattress or groceries or even cash money, only first you had to swear you didn't own any property of your own and even had to prove it by giving your house or land or even your wagon and team to your wife or children or any kinfolks you could count on, depend on, trust. And who knew? even if second-hand pistols had gone up too like everything else, maybe the one fifty cents more would be enough without another policeman.

Though he found another. Here was the depot. It at least hadn't changed: the same hollowly sonorous rotunda through which he had passed from the Jefferson train on the three other times he had seen Memphis—that first unforgettable time (he had figured it now: the last time had been forty-four years ago and the first time was three dollars onto that, which was forty-seven years) with the niggard clutch of wrenched and bitter dollars and the mentor and guide who had told him about the houses in Memphis for no other purpose, filled with white women any one of which he could have if he had the money: whose experiences until then had been furious unplanned episodes as violent as vomiting, with no more preparation than the ripping of buttons before stooping downward into the dusty roadside weeds or cotton middle where the almost invisible unwashed Negro girl lay waiting. But different in Memphis: himself and his guide stepping out into the street where the whole city lay supine to take him into itself like embrace, like arms, the very meager wad of bills in his pocket on fire too which he had wrung, wrested from between-crops labor at itinerant sawmills, or from the implacable rented ground by months behind a plow, his pittance of which he would have to fight his father each time to get his hands on a nickel of it. It was warm here too and almost empty and this time the policeman had jerked him awake before he even knew he was going to sleep. Though this one was not in uniform. But he knew about that kind too.

"I said, what train are you waiting for?" the policeman said.

"I aint waiting for no train," he said.

"All right," the policeman said. "Then get out of here. Go on home." Then, exactly like the other one: "You aint got anywhere to sleep? Okay, but you damn sure got some place to leave from, whether you go to bed or not. Go on now. Beat it." And then, since he didn't move: "Go on, I said. What're you waiting for?"

"The half a dollar," he said.

"The what?" the policeman said. "The half a— Why, you—" so that this time he moved, turned quickly, already dodging, not much bigger than a small boy and therefore about as hard for a man the size of the policeman to catch in a place as big as this. He didn't run: he walked, just fast enough for the policeman to be not quite able to touch him, yet still not have cause to shout at him, through the rotunda and out into the street, not looking back at the policeman standing in the doorway shouting after him: "And dont let me catch you in here again neither."

He was becoming more and more oriented now. There was another depot just down a cross street but then the same thing would happen there; evidently the railroad policemen who just wore clothes like everybody else didn't belong to the W P and A free-relief laws. Besides, the night was moving toward its end now; he could feel it. So he just walked, never getting very far away because he knew where he was now; and now and then in the vacant side streets and alleys he could stop and sit down, in a doorway or behind a cluster of garbage or trash cans and once more be waking up before he knew he had gone to sleep. Then he would walk again, the quiet and empty city—this part of it anyway—his impeachless own, thinking, with the old amazement no less fresh and amazed for being almost as old as he *A man can get through anything if he can jest keep on walking.*

Then it was day, not waking the city; the city had never slept, not resuming but continuing back into visibility the faces pallid and wan and unsleeping, hurrying, passionate and gay, toward the tremendous, the unimaginable pleasures. He knew exactly where he was now; this pavement could have shown his print from forty-four years ago; for the first time since he had come out the Parchman gate five mornings ago he was confident, invulnerable and immune. *I could even spend a whole dollar of it now and hit wouldn't stop me* he thought, inside the small dingy store where a few Negroes were already trafficking. A Negro man seemed to be running it or anyway serving the customers. Maybe he even owned it; maybe the new laws even said a nigger could even own a store, remembering something else from thirty-eight years back.

"Animal crackers," he said. Because he was there now, safe, immune and invulnerable. "I reckon they done jumped them up ten or fifteen cents too, aint they?" looking at the small cardboard box colored like a circus wagon itself and blazoned with beasts like a heraldry.

"Ten cents," the Negro said.

"Ten cents more than what?" he said.

"It's ten cents," the Negro said. "Do you want it or dont you?"

"I'll take two of them," he said. He walked again, in actual sunlight now, himself one with the hurrying throng, eating his minute vanilla menagerie; there was plenty of time now since he was not only safe but he knew exactly where he was; by merely turning his head (which he did not) he could have seen the street, the actual housefront (he didn't know it of course and probably wouldn't have recognised her either, but his younger daughter was now the madam of it) which he had entered with his mentor that night forty-seven years ago, where waited the glittering arms of women not only shaped like Helen and Eve and Lilith, not only functional like Helen and Eve and Lilith, but colored white like them too, where he had said No not just to all the hard savage years of his hard and barren life, but to Death too in the bed of a public prostitute.

The window had not changed: the same unwashed glass behind the wire grillework containing the same tired banjos and ornate clocks and trays of glass jewelry. "I want to buy a pistol," he said to one of the two men blue-jowled as pirates behind the counter.

"You got a permit?" the man said.

"A permit?" he said. "I jest want to buy a pistol. They told me before you sold pistols here. I got the money."

"Who told you we sold pistols here?" the man said.

"Maybe he dont want to buy one but just reclaim one," the second man said.

"Oh," the first said. "That's different. What sort of pistol do you want to reclaim, dad?"

"What?" he said.

"How much money have you got?" the first said. He removed the wadded paper from the bib of his overalls and took out the ten-dollar bill and unfolded it. "That all you got?"

"Let me see the pistol," he said.

"You cant buy a pistol for ten dollars, grandpaw," the first said. "Come on. Try them other pockets."

"Hold it," the second said. "Maybe he can reclaim one out of my private stock." He stooped and reached under the counter.

"That's an idea," the first said. "Out of your private stock, he wouldn't need a permit." The second man rose and laid an object on the counter. Mink looked at it quietly.

"Hit looks like a cooter," he said. It did: snub-nosed, short-barrelled, swollen of cylinder and rusted over, with its curved butt and flat reptilian hammer it did resemble the fossil relic of some small antediluvian terrapin.

"What are you talking about?" the first said. "That's a genuine bulldog detective special forty-one, the best protection a man could have. That's what you want, aint it—protection? Because if it's more than that; if you aim to take it back to Arkansaw and start robbing and shooting folks with it, the Law aint going to like it. They'll put you in jail for that even in Arkansaw. Even right down in Missippi you cant do that."

"That's right," Mink said. "Protection." He put the bill on the counter and took up the pistol and broke it and held the barrel up to the light. "Hit's dirty inside," he said.

"You can see through it, cant you?" the first said. "Do you think a forty-one-caliber bullet cant go through any hole you can see through?" Mink lowered the pistol and was in the act of closing it again when he saw that the bill was gone.

"Wait," he said.

"Sure, sure," the first said, putting the bill back on the counter. "Give me the pistol. We cant reclaim even that one to you for just ten dollars."

"How much will you have to have?"

"How much have you got?"

"I got jest three more. I got to get home to Jefferson."

"Sure he's got to get home," the second said. "Let him have it for eleven. We aint robbers."

"It aint loaded," he said.

"There's a store around the corner on Main where you can buy all the forty-ones you want at four dollars a box," the first said.

"I aint got four dollars," he said. "I wont have but two now. And I got to get—"

"What does he want with a whole box, just for protection?" the second said. "Tell you what. I'll let you have a couple out of my private stock for another dollar."

"I got to have at least one bullet to try it with," he said. "Unless you will guarantee it."

"Do we ask you to guarantee you aint going to rob or shoot anybody with it?" the first said.

"Okay, okay, he's got to try it out," the second said. "Give him another bullet for a— You could spare another quarter, couldn't you? Them forty-one bullets are hard to get, you know."

"Could it be a dime?" he said. "I got to get home yet."

"Okay, okay," the second said. "Give him the pistol and three bullets for twelve dollars and a dime. He's got to get home. To hell with a man that'll rob a man trying to get home."

So he was all right; he stepped out into the full drowsing sunlight of early fall, into the unsleeping and passionate city. He was all right now. All he had to do now was to get to Jefferson, and that wasn't but eighty miles.

THIRTEEN

$\mathcal{W}$hen Charles Mallison got home in September of 1945, there was a new Snopes in Jefferson. They had got shot down ("of course," Charles always added, telling it) though it wasn't a crash. Plexiglass was the pilot. Plex. His name was Harold Baddrington but he had an obsession on the subject of cellophane, which he called plexiglass, amounting to a phobia; the simple sight or even the mere idea of a new pack of cigarettes or a new shirt or handkerchief as you had to buy them now pre-encased in an invisible impenetrable cocoon, threw him into the sort of virulent almost hysterical frenzy which Charles had seen the idea of Germans or Japanese throw some civilians, especially ones around fifty years old. He—Plex—had a scheme for winning the war with cellophane: instead of bombs, the seventeens and twenty-fours and the British Lancasters and Blenheims would drop factory-vulcanised packs of tobacco and new shirts and underclothes, and while the Germans were queued up waiting turns at the ice pick, they could be strafed en masse or even captured without a shot by paratroop drops.

It wasn't even a bailout; Plex made a really magnificent one-engine landing. The trouble was, he picked out a farm that a German patrol had already selected that morning to practise a new occupation innovation or something whose directive had just come down, so in almost no time the whole crew of them were in the P.O.W. camp at Limbourg, which almost immediately turned out to be the most dangerous place any of them had been in during the war; it was next door to the same marshalling yard that the R.A.F. bombed regularly every Wednesday night from an altitude of about thirty or forty feet. They would spend six days watching the calendar creep inexorably toward Wednesday, when as regular as clockwork the uproar of crashes and thuds and snarling engines would start up, and the air full of searchlights and machine-gun bullets and whizzing fragments of AA, the entire barracks crouching under bunks or anything else that would interpose another inch of thickness, no matter

what, with that frantic desire, need, impulse to rush outdoors waving
their arms and shouting up at the pandemonium overhead: "Hey, fellows! For Christ's sake have a heart! It's us! It's us!" If it had been a
moving picture or a book instead of a war, Charles said they would
have escaped. But he himself didn't know and never knew anyone
who ever actually escaped from a genuine authentic stalag, so they
had to wait for regular routine liberation before he came back home
and found there was already another Snopes in Jefferson.

But at least they—Jefferson—were holding their own. Because in
that same summer, 1945, when Jefferson gained the new Snopes,
Ratliff eliminated Clarence. Not that Ratliff shot him or anything like
that: he just simply eliminated Clarence as a factor in what Charles's
Uncle Gavin also called their constant Snopes-fear and -dread, or you
might say, Snopes-dodging. It happened during the campaign which
ended in the August primary election; Charles hadn't got back home
yet by a month, nor was his Uncle Gavin actually present at the picnic
where it actually happened, where Clarence Snopes was actually
defeated in the race for Congress which, being a national election,
wouldn't even take place until next year. That's what he, Charles,
meant by Ratliff doing it. He was in the office when his Uncle Gavin
this time ran Ratliff to earth and bayed him and said, "All right. Just
exactly what did happen out there that day?"

Senator Clarence Egglestone Snopes, pronounced "Cla'nce" by
every free white Yoknapatawpha American whose right and duty it
was to go to the polls and mark his X each time old man Will Varner
told him to; just Senator Clarence Snopes for the first few years after
old Varner ordained or commanded—anyway, translated—him into
the upper house of the state legislature in Jackson; beginning
presently to put on a little flesh (he had been a big, hulking youth and
young man but reasonably hard and active in an awkward kind of way
until the sedentary brain work of being one of the elected fathers and
guardians and mentors of the parliamentary interests of Yoknapatawpha County began to redden his nose and pouch his eyes and
paunch his belt a little) until one hot July day in the middle twenties
when no other man in Jefferson or Yoknapatawpha County either
under sixty years of age had on a coat, Clarence appeared on the
Square in a complete white linen suit with a black Windsor tie, and

either just before or just after or maybe it was that same simultaneous start or shock brought it to their notice, they realised that he was now signing himself Senator C. E. Snopes, and Charles's Uncle Gavin said, "Where did the 'E' come from?" and Ratliff said,

"Maybe he picked it up along with that-ere white wedding suit going and coming through Memphis to get back and forth to Jackson to work. Because why not? Aint even a elected legislative senator got a few private rights like any free ordinary voter?"

What Charles meant was that Clarence already had them all a little off balance like a prize fighter does his opponent without really hitting him yet. So their emotion was simple docility when they learned that their own private Cincinnatus was not even C. any longer but was Senator Egglestone Snopes; his Uncle Gavin merely said, "Egglestone? Why Egglestone?" and Ratliff merely said,

"Why not?" and even his Uncle Gavin merely said,

"Yes, why not?" So they didn't really mark it when one day the C. was back again—Senator C. Egglestone Snopes now, with a definite belly and the pouched eyes and a lower lip now full from talking, forensic. Because Clarence was making speeches, anywhere and everywhere, at bond rallies and women's clubs, any place or occasion where there was a captive audience, because Charles was still in the German prison camp when his Uncle Gavin and Ratliff realised that Clarence intended to run for Congress in Washington and that old Will Varner might quite possibly get him elected to it—the same Clarence Snopes who had moved steadily onward and upward from being old Varner's privately appointed constable in Varner's own private Beat Two, then supervisor of the Beat and then elected out of the entire county by means of old Will's diffused usurious capacity for blackmail, to be the county representative in Jackson; and now, 1945, tapped by all the mutually compounding vote-swapping Varners of the whole congressional district for the House of Representatives in Washington itself, where in the clutches not of a mere neighborhood or sectional Will Varner but of a Will Varner of really national or even international scope, there would be no limit to what he might be capable of unless somebody did something about it. This, until that day in July at the annual Varner's Mill picnic where by custom and tradition not only the local candidates for county and state offices but even the regional and sectional ones for national offices, like Clarence, even though the election itself would not happen until next year, started the ball rolling. Whereupon Clarence not only failed to appear on the speakers' platform to announce his candidacy, he disappeared from the picnic grounds before the dinner was even served. And the next day word went over the county that Clarence had not only decided not to run for Congress, he was even withdrawing from public life altogether when his present term in the state senate was up.

So what Charles's Uncle Gavin really wanted to know was not so much what had happened to Clarence, as what had happened to old Will Varner. Because whatever eliminated Clarence from the congressional race would have to impact not on Clarence but on old Will; it wouldn't have needed to touch Clarence at all in fact. Because nobody really minded Clarence just as you dont mind a stick of dynamite until somebody fuses it; otherwise he was just so much sawdust and greasy paper that wouldn't even burn good set on fire. He was unprincipled and without morals of course but, without a guiding and prompting and absolving hand or intelligence, Clarence himself was anybody's victim since all he had was his blind instinct for sadism and overreaching, and was himself really dangerous only to someone he would have the moral and intellectual ascendency of, which out of the entire world's population couldn't possibly be anybody except another Snopes, and out of the entire Snopes population couldn't possibly be more than just one of them. In this case it was his youngest brother Doris—a hulking youth of seventeen who resembled Clarence not only in size and shape but the same mentality of a child and the moral principles of a wolverine, the only difference being that Doris hadn't been elected to the state legislature yet. Back in the late twenties Byron Snopes, who looted Colonel Sartoris's bank and fled to Texas, sent back C.O.D. four half-Snopes half-Apache Indian children which Clarence, spending the summer at home between two legislative sessions, adopted into a kind of peonage of practical jokes. Only, being a state senator now, Clarence had to be a little careful about his public dignity, not for the sake of his constituency but because even he knew a damn sight better than to take chances with old Will Varner's standards of *amour-propre*. So he

would merely invent the jokes and use his brother Doris to perpe-
trate them, until the four Indian children finally caught Doris alone
in no man's land and captured him and tied him to a stake in the
woods and even had the fire burning when someone heard his
screams and got there in time to save him.

But Clarence himself was in his late twenties then, already a state
senator; his career had begun long before that, back when he was
eighteen or nineteen years old out at Varner's store and became
leader of a subjugated (he was big and strong and Ratliff said really
liked fighting, provided the equality in size was enough in his favor)
gang of cousins and toadies who fought and drank and gambled and
beat up Negroes and terrified women and young girls around
Frenchman's Bend until (Ratliff said) old Varner became irritated and
exasperated enough to take him out of the public domain by ordering the local j.p. to appoint Clarence his constable. That was where
and when Clarence's whole life, existence, destiny, seemed at last to
find itself like a rocket does at the first touch of fire.

Though his career didn't go quite that fast, not at first anyway.
Or maybe it wasn't his career so much as his exposure, revealment.
At first it was almost like he was just looking around, orienting himself, learning just where he now actually was; and only then looking
in a sort of amazed incredulity at the vista opening before him.
Merely amazed at first, before the exultation began, at the limitless
prospect which nobody had told him about. Because at first he even
behaved himself. At first everybody thought that, having been as outrageous as he had been with no other backing than the unanimity of
his old lawless pack, he would be outrageous indeed now with the
challengeless majesty of organised law according to Will Varner to
back him. But he fooled them. Instead, he became the champion and
defender of the civic mores and the public peace of Frenchman's
Bend. Of course the first few Negroes who ran afoul of his new official capacity suffered for it. But there was now something impersonal
even to the savaging of Negroes. Previous to his new avatar, he and
his gang had beaten up Negroes as a matter of principle. Not chastis-
ing them as individual Negroes nor even, Charles's Uncle Gavin said,
warring against them as representatives of a race which was alien
because it was of a different appearance and therefore enemy *per se*,

but (and his Uncle Gavin said Clarence and his gang did not know this because they dared not know it was so) because they were afraid of that alien race. They were afraid of it not because it was black but because they—the white man—had taught the black one how to threaten the white economy of material waste, when the white man compelled the black man to learn how to do more with less and worse if the black man wanted to survive in the white economy—less and worse of tools to farm and work with, less of luxury to be content with, less of waste to keep alive with. But not any more now. Now when Clarence manhandled a Negro with the blackjack he carried or with the butt of the pistol which he now officially wore, it was with a kind of detachment, as if he were using neither the man's black skin nor even his human flesh, but simply the man's present condition of legal vulnerability as testing ground or sounding board on which to prove again, perhaps even reassure himself from day to day, just how far his official power and legal immunity actually went and just how physically strong, even with the inevitable passage of time, he actually remained.

Because they were not always Negroes. In fact, one of the first victims of Clarence's new condition was his lieutenant, his second-in-command, in the old gang; if anything, Clarence was even more savage this time because the man had tried to trade on the old relationship and the past; it was as if Clarence had now personally invested a kind of incorruptibility and integrity into his old natural and normal instinct and capacity for violence and physical anguish; had had to borrow them—the incorruptibility and the integrity—at so high a rate that he had to defend them with his life. Anyway, he had changed. And, Charles's Uncle Gavin said, since previous to his elevation to grace, everybody had believed Clarence incapable of change, now the same people believed immediately that the new condition was for perpetuity, for the rest of his life. They still believed this even after they found out—it was no rumor; Clarence himself bragged, boasted quietly of it—that he was a member of the Ku Klux Klan when it appeared in the county (it never got very far and didn't last very long; it was believed that it wouldn't have lasted at all except for Clarence), taken in because the Klan needed him or could use him, or, as Charles's Uncle Gavin said, probably because there was no way under heaven that they could have kept him out since it was his dish just as he was its. This was before he became constable of Frenchman's Bend; his virgin advent from private life you might say, his initial accolade of public recognition, comparatively harmless yet, since even a Ku Klux Klan would have more sense than to depend on Clarence very far; he remained just one more obedient integer, muscle man—what in a few more years people would mean by "goon"—until the day came when old Will Varner's irritation or exasperation raised him to constable, whereupon within the year it was rumored that he was now an officer in the Klavern or whatever they called it; and in two more years was himself the local Dragon or Kleagle: who having been designated by old Varner custodian of the public peace, had now decreed himself arbiter of its morals too.

Which was probably when he really discerned at last the breadth and splendor of his rising destiny; with amazement and incredulity at that apparently limitless expanse and, who knows? maybe even humility too that he should have been chosen, found worthy—that limitless field for his capacity and talents: not merely to beat, hammer men into insensibility and submission, but to use them; not merely to expend their inexhaustible numbers like ammunition or consume them like hogs or sheep, but to use, employ them like mules or oxen, with one eye constant for the next furrow tomorrow or next year; using not just their competence to mark an X whenever and wherever old Will Varner ordered them to, but their capacity for passion and greed and alarm as well, as though Clarence had been in the business of politics all his life instead of those few mere years as a hick constable. And, as Charles's uncle said, doing it all by simple infallible instinct, without preceptor or example. Because this was even before Huey Long had risen far enough to show their own Mississippi Bilbo just what a man with a little brass and courage and no inhibitions could really accomplish.

So when Clarence announced for the state legislature, they—the County—knew he would need no other platform than Uncle Billy Varner's name. In fact they decided immediately that his candidacy was not even Clarence's own idea but Uncle Billy's; that Uncle Billy's irritation had simply reached a point where Clarence must be removed completely from his sight. But they were wrong. Clarence had a platform. Which was the moment when some of them, a few of them like Charles's uncle and Ratliff and a few more of the young ones like Charles (he was only eight or ten then) who would listen (or anyway had to listen, like Charles) to them, discovered that they had better fear him, tremble and beware. His platform was his own. It was one which only his amoral temerity would have dared because it set him apostate to his own constituency; the thin deciding margin of his vote came from sources not only beyond the range of Will Varner's autocracy, it came from people who under any other conditions would have voted for almost any other member of the human race first: he came out publicly against the Ku Klux Klan. He had been the local Kleagle, Dragon, whatever the title was, right up to the day he announced his candidacy—or so the County thought. But now he was its mortal enemy, stumping the county apparently only coincidentally to win an office, since his dedication was to destroy a dragon, winning the race by that scant margin of votes coming mostly from Jefferson itself—schoolteachers, young professional people, women—the literate and liberal innocents who believed that decency and right and personal liberty would prevail simply because they were decent and right; who until Clarence offered them one, had had no political unanimity and had not even bothered always to vote, until at last the thing they feared and hated seemed to have produced for them a champion. So he went to Jackson not as the successful candidate for a political office but as the dedicated paladin of a cause, walking (Charles's uncle said) into the legislative halls in an aura half the White Knight's purity and half the shocked consternation of his own kind whom he had apparently wrenched himself from and repudiated. Because he did indeed destroy the Ku Klux Klan in Yoknapatawpha County; as one veteran klansman expressed it: "Durn it, if we cant beat a handful of schoolteachers and editors and Sunday-school superintendents, how in hell can we hope to beat a whole race of niggers and catholics and jews?"

So Clarence was in. Now he had it made, as Charles's generation would say. He was safe now for the next two years, when there would be another election, to look around, find out where to go next like the alpinist on his ledge. That's what Charles's uncle said it was: like the mountain climber. Except that the climber climbs the mountain not just to get to the top. He would try to climb it even if he knew he would never get there. He climbs it simply because he can have the solitary peace and contentment of knowing constantly that only his solitary nerve, will and courage stand between him and destruction, while Clarence didn't even know it was a mountain because there wasn't anything to fall off, you could only be pushed off; and anybody that felt himself strong enough or quick enough to push Clarence Snopes off anything was welcome to try it.

So at first what the County thought Clarence was doing now was simply being quiet while he watched and listened to learn the rules of the new trade. They didn't know that what he was teaching himself was how to recognise opportunities when they occurred; that he was still doing that even after he began at last to talk, address the House, himself still the White Knight who had destroyed bigotry and intolerance in Yoknapatawpha County in the eyes of the innocent illusionees whose narrow edge of additional votes had elected him, long after the rest of the County realised that Clarence was preaching the same hatred of Negroes and Catholics and Jews that had been the tenet of the organization by wrecking which he had got where he now was; when the Silver Shirts appeared, Clarence was one of the first in Mississippi to join it, joining, his uncle said, not because of the principles the Silver Shirts advocated but simply because Clarence probably decided that it would be more durable than the merely county-autonomous Klan which he had wrecked. Because by this time his course was obvious: to join things, anything, any organization to which human beings belonged, which he might compel or control or coerce through the emotions of religion or patriotism or just simple greed, political gravy-hunger; he had been born into the Baptist church in Frenchman's Bend; he was now affiliated in Jackson, where (he had been re-elected twice now) he now taught a Sunday-school class; in that same summer the County heard that he was contemplating resigning his seat in the legislature long enough to do a hitch in the army or navy to be eligible for the American Legion.

Clarence was in now. He had it made. He had—Charles was about to say "divided the county" except that "divided" implied balance or at least suspension even though the lighter end of the beam was irrevocably in the air. Where with Clarence and Yoknapatawpha County, the lesser end of that beam was not in suspension at all but rather in a condition of aerial banishment, making now only the soundless motions of vociferation in vacuum; Clarence had engorged the county whole as whales and owls do and, as owls do, disgorged onto that airy and harmless pinnacle the refuse of bones and hair he didn't need—the doomed handful of literate liberal underpaid white-collar illusionees who had elected him into the state senate because they thought he had destroyed the Ku Klux Klan, plus the other lesser handful of other illusionees like Charles's Uncle Gavin and Ratliff, who had voted for Clarence that time as the lesser of two evils because he had come out against the Klan and hence were even more doomed since where the school- and music-teachers and the other white-collar innocents who learned by heart President Roosevelt's speeches, could believe anew each time that honor and justice and decency would prevail just because they were honorable and just and decent, his uncle and Ratliff never had believed this and never would.

Clarence didn't destroy them. There were not enough of them. There were so few of them in fact that he could continue to send them year after year the mass-produced Christmas cards which it was said he obtained from the same firm he was instrumental in awarding the yearly contract for automobile license plates. As for the rest of the county voters, they only waited for Clarence to indicate where he wanted the X marked to elect him to any office he wanted, right up to the ultimate one which the County (including for a time even Charles's uncle's branch of the illusioned) believed was his goal: governor of the state. Huey Long now dominated the horizon of every Mississippi politician's ambition; it seemed only natural to the County that their own should pattern on him; even when Clarence took up Long's soak-the-rich battle cry as though he, Clarence, had invented it, even Charles's Uncle Gavin and Ratliff still believed that Clarence's sights were set no higher than the governor's mansion. Because, though at that time—1930–'35—Mississippi had no specific rich to soak—no industries, no oil, no gas to speak of—the idea of taking from anybody that had it that which they deserved no more than he did, being no more intelligent or industrious but simply luckier, struck straight to the voting competence of every sharecropper and tenant farmer not only in Yoknapatawpha County but in all the rest of Mississippi too; Clarence could have been elected governor of Mississippi on the simple platform of soaking the rich in Louisiana or Alabama, or for that matter in Maine or Oregon.

So their (his uncle's and Ratliff's little forlorn cell of unreconstructed purists) shock at the rumor that Clarence had contemplated for a moment taking over the American Legion in Mississippi was nothing to the one when they learned three years ago (Charles himself was not present; he had already departed from Yoknapatawpha County to begin training for his ten months in the German P.O.W. camp) that the most potent political faction in the state, the faction which was sure to bring their man in as governor, had offered to run Clarence for lieutenant governor, and Clarence had declined. He gave no reason but then he didn't need to because now all the county—not just Charles's uncle's little cell, but everybody—knew what Clarence's aim, ambition was and had been all the time: Washington, Congress. Which was horror only among the catacombs behind the bestiarium; with everyone else it was triumph and exultation: who had already ridden Clarence's coattails to the (comparatively) minor-league hog trough at Jackson and who saw now the clear path to that vast and limitless one in Washington.

And not just shock and horror, but dread and fear too of the man who had used the Ku Klux Klan while he needed it and then used their innocence to wreck the Klan when he no longer did, who was using the Baptist Church as long as he believed it would serve him; who had used W.P.A. and N.R.A. and A.A.A. and C.C.C. and all the other agencies created in the dream or hope that people should not suffer or, if they must, at least suffer equally in times of crisis and fear; being either for them or against them as the political breeze indicated, since in the late thirties he turned against the party which had fathered them, ringing the halls which at least occasionally had echoed the voices of statesmen and humanitarians, with his own voice full of racial and religious and economic intolerance (once the strongest plank in his political creed had been soaking the rich; now the loudest one was the menace of organised labor), with nothing to intervene between him and Congress but that handful of innocents still capable of believing that evil could be destroyed simply because it was evil, whom Clarence didn't even fear enough to stop sending them the cheap Christmas cards.

"Which wont be enough," Charles's uncle said, "as it never has been enough in the country, even if they could multiply themselves by the ten-thousand. Because he would only fool them again."

"Maybe," Ratliff said. (This was Charles's Uncle Gavin telling him what had happened when he got back home in September after it was all over and whatever it was had licked Clarence, caused him to withdraw from the race, at old Will Varner's annual picnic in July; this was back in April when his uncle and Ratliff were talking.) "What you need is to have the young folks back for at least a day or two between now and the seventeenth of next August. What a shame the folks that started this war and drafted all the young voters away never had sense enough to hold off at least long enough to keep Clarence Snopes outen Congress, aint it?"

"*You* need?" Charles's uncle said. "What do you mean, *you*?"

"I thought you jest said how the old folks like you and me cant do nothing about Clarence but jest fold our hands and feel sorry," Ratliff said.

"No more we can," his uncle said. "Oh, there are enough of us. It was the ones of your and my age and generation who carried on the good work of getting things into the shape they're in now. But it's too late for us now. We cant now; maybe we're just afraid to stick our necks out again. Or if not afraid, at least ashamed. No: not afraid: we are just too old. Call it just tired, too tired to be afraid any longer of losing. Just to hate evil is not enough. You—somebody—has got to do something about it. Only now it will have to be somebody else, and even if the Japs should quit too before the August primary, there still wont be enough somebody elses here. Because it wont be us."

"Maybe," Ratliff said. And his uncle was right. And then, maybe Ratliff was right too. One of the first to announce for the race to challenge Clarence from the district was a member of his uncle's somebody elses—a man from the opposite end of the district, who was no older than Charles: only—as Charles put it—braver. He announced for Congress even before Clarence did. The election for Congress wouldn't be until next year, 1946, so there was plenty of time. But then, Clarence always did it this way: waited until the other candidate or candidates had announced and committed or anyway indicated what their platforms would be. And Clarence had taught Yoknapatawpha County to know why: that by waiting to be the last, he didn't even need to invent a platform because by that time his chief, most dangerous opponent had supplied him with one. As happened now, Clarence using this one in his turn, using his valor as an instrument to defeat him with.

His name was Devries; Yoknapatawpha County had never heard of him before 1941. But they had since. In 1940 he had been Number One in his R.O.T.C. class at the University, had graduated with a regular army commission and by New Year's 1942 was already overseas; in 1943 when he was assigned back to the United States to be atmosphere in bond drives, he was a major with (this is Charles telling it) enough ribbons to make a four-in-hand tie which he had acquired while commanding Negro infantry in battle, having been posted to Negro troops by some brass-hatted theorist in Personnel doubtless on the premise that, being a Southerner, he would indubitably "understand" Negroes, and (Charles supposed) just as indubitably commanded them well for the same reason: that, being a Southerner, he knew that no white man understood Negroes and never would so long as the white man compelled the black man to be first a Negro and only then a man, since this, the impenetrable dividing wall, was the black man's only defense and protection for survival. Maybe he couldn't sell bonds. Anyway apparently he didn't really put his back into it. Because the story was that almost before his folks knew he was home he was on his way back to the war and when he came out this time, in 1944, he was a full bird colonel with next to the last ribbon and a tin leg; and while he was on his way to Washington to be given the last one, the top one, the story came out how he had finished the second tour up front and was already posted stateside when the general pinned the next to the last medal on him. But instead he dropped the medal into his foot locker and put back on the battle fatigues and worried them until they let him go back up the third time and one night he turned the rest of the regiment over to the second and with a Negro sergeant and a runner crawled out to where what was left of the other battalion had been trapped by a barrage and sent them back with the runner for guide, he and the sergeant holding off one attack single-handed until they were clear, then he, Devries, was carrying the sergeant back when he took one too and this time a hulking giant of an Arkansas Negro cotton-field hand crawled out and picked them both up and brought them in. And when he, Devries, came out of the ether with the remaining leg he worried enough people until they sent in the field hand and he, Devries, had the nurse dig the medal out of the foot locker and said to the field hand, "Lift me up, you big bastard," and pinned the medal on him.

That was Clarence's opponent for Congress. That is, even if the army hadn't anyone else at all for the experts to assume he understood Negroes, Devries (this is Charles talking) couldn't have talked himself back up front with one leg missing. So all he had now to try to persuade to send him somewhere were civilians, and apparently the only place he could think of was Congress. So (this is still Charles) maybe it would take somebody with no more sense than to volunteer twice for the same war, to have the temerity to challenge a long-vested interest like Clarence Snopes. Because even if they had arranged things better, more practical: either for 1944 to have happened in 1943 or have the election year itself moved forward one, or in fact if the Japs quit in 1945 too and all the ruptured ducks in the congressional district were back home in time, there still would not be enough of them and in the last analysis all Devries would have would be the heirs of the same uncoordinated political illusionees innocent enough to believe still that demagoguery and bigotry and intolerance must not and cannot and will not endure simply because they are bigotry and demagoguery and intolerance, that Clarence himself had already used up and thrown away twenty-odd years ago; Charles's uncle said to Ratliff:

"They'll always be wrong. They think they are fighting Clarence Snopes. They're not. They're not faced with an individual nor even a situation: they are beating their brains out against one of the foundation rocks of our national character itself. Which is the premise that politics and political office are not and never have been the method and means by which we can govern ourselves in peace and dignity and honor and security, but instead are our national refuge for our incompetents who have failed at every other occupation by means of which they might make a living for themselves and their families; and whom as a result we would have to feed and clothe and shelter out of our own private purses and means. The surest way to be elected to office in America is to have fathered seven or eight children and then lost your arm or leg in a sawmill accident: both of which—the reckless optimism which begot seven or eight children with nothing to feed them by but a sawmill, and the incredible ineptitude which would put an arm or a leg in range of a moving saw— should already have damned you from any form of public trust. They cant beat him. He will be elected to Congress for the simple reason that if he fails to be elected, there is nothing else he can do that anybody on earth would pay him for on Saturday night; and old Will Varner and the rest of the interlocked Snopes kin and connections have no intention whatever of boarding and feeding Clarence for the rest of his life. You'll see."

It looked like he was going to be right. It was May now, almost time for the political season to open; a good one again after four years, now that the Germans had collapsed too. And still Clarence hadn't announced his candidacy in actual words. Everybody knew why of course. What they couldn't figure out yet was just how Clarence planned to use Devries's military record for his, Clarence's, platform; exactly how Clarence intended to use Devries's military glory to beat him for Congress with it. And when the pattern did begin to appear at last, Yoknapatawpha County—some of it anyway—found out something else about the Clarence they had lived in innocence with for twenty and more years. Which was just how dangerous Clarence really was in his capacity to unify normal—you might even say otherwise harmless—human baseness and get it to the polls. Because this time he compelled them whose champion he was going to be, to come to him and actually beg him to be their champion; not just beg him to be their knight, but themselves to invent or anyway establish the cause for which they would need him.

Charles's Uncle Gavin told him how suddenly one day in that May or early June, the whole county learned that Clarence was not only not going to run for Congress, he was going to retire from public life altogether; this not made as a formal public announcement but rather breathed quietly from sheep to sheep of old Will Varner's vot-

ing flock which had been following Clarence to the polls for twenty-
five years now; gently, his Uncle Gavin said, even a little sadly, with a
sort of mild astonishment that it was not self-evident:

"Why, I'm an old man now," Clarence (he was past forty) said. "It's
time I stepped aside. Especially since we got a brave young man like
this Captain Devries—"

"Colonel Devries," they told him.

"Colonel Devries.—to represent you, carry on the work which I
tried to do to better our folks and our county—"

"You mean, you're going to endorse him? You going to support
him?"

"Of course," Clarence said. "Us old fellows have done the best we
could for you, but now the time has come for us to step down. What
we need in Congress now is the young men, especially the ones that
were brave in the war. Of course General Devries—"

"Colonel Devries," they told him.

"Colonel Devries.—is a little younger maybe than I would have
picked out myself. But time will cure that. Of course he's got some
ideas that I myself could never agree with and that lots of other old
fogies like me in Missippi and the South wont never agree with
either. But maybe we are all too old now, out of date, and the things
we believed in and stood up for and suffered when necessary, aint
true any more, aint what folks want any more, and his new ideas are
the right ones for Yoknapatawpha County and Missippi and the
South—"

And then of course they asked it: "What new ideas?"

And that was all. He told them: this man, Colonel Devries (no
trouble any more about the exactness of his rank), who had become
so attached to Negroes by commanding them in battle that he had
volunteered twice, possibly even having to pull a few strings (since
everyone would admit that he had more than done his share of fighting for his country and democracy and was entitled to—more: had
earned the right to—be further excused) to get back into the front
lines in order to consort with Negroes; who had there risked his life
to save one Negro and then had his own life saved by another Negro.
A brave man (had not his government and country recorded and
affirmed that by the medals it gave him, including that highest one in

its gift?) and an honorable one (that medal meant honor too; did not its very designation include the word?), what course would—could—dared he take, once he was a member of that Congress already passing legislation to break down forever the normal and natural (natural? God Himself had ordained and decreed them) barriers between the white man and the black one. And so on. And that was all; as his uncle said, Clarence was already elected, the county and the district would not even need to spend the money to have the ballots cast and counted; that Medal of Honor which the government had awarded Devries for risking death to defend the principles on which that government was founded and by which it existed, had destroyed forever his chance to serve in the Congress which had accoladed him.

"You see?" Charles's uncle said to Ratliff. "You cant beat him."

"You mean, even you cant think of nothing to do about it?" Ratliff said.

"Certainly," his uncle said. "Join him."

"Join him?" Ratliff said.

"The most efficacious, the oldest—oh yes, without doubt the first, the very first, back to the very dim moment when two cave men confederated against the third one—of all political maxims."

"Join—*him*?" Ratliff said.

"All right," his uncle said. "You tell me then. I'll join you."

His uncle told how Ratliff blinked at him awhile. "There must be some simpler way than that. It's a pure and simple proposition; there must be a pure and simple answer to it. Clarence jest purely and simply wants to get elected to Congress, he dont keer how; there must be some pure and simple way for the folks that purely and simply dont want him in Congress to say No to him, they don't keer how neither."

His uncle said again, "All right. Find it. I'll join you." But evidently it wasn't that pure and simple to Ratliff either: only to Clarence. His uncle said that after that Clarence didn't even need to make a campaign, a race; that all he would need to do would be to get up on the speakers' platform at the Varner's Mill picnic long enough to be sure that the people who had turned twenty-one since old Will Varner had last told them who to vote for, would know how to recognise the word Snopes on the ballot. In fact, Devries could have quit now, and his uncle said there were some who thought he ought to. Except how could he, with that medal—all five or six of them—for guts and valor in the trunk in the attic or wherever he kept them. Devries even came to Jefferson, into Clarence's own bailiwick, and made his speech as if nothing were happening. But there you were. There were not enough soldiers back yet who would know what the medal meant. And even though the election itself would not happen until next year, nobody could know now that the Japs would cave this year too. To the others, the parents and Four-F cousins and such to whom they had sent their voting proxies, Devries was a nigger lover who had actually been decorated by the Yankee government for it. In fact, the story now was that Devries had got his Congressional Medal by choosing between a Negro and a white boy to save, and had chosen the Negro and left the white boy to die. Though Charles's uncle said that Clarence himself did not start this one: they must do him that justice at least. Not that Clarence would have flinched from starting it: he simply didn't need that additional ammunition now, having been, not so much in politics but simply a Snopes long enough now to know that only a fool would pay two dollars for a vote when fifty cents would buy it.

It must have been even a little sad: the man who had already been beaten in advance by the very medal which wouldn't let him quit. It was more than just sad. Because his Uncle Gavin told him how presently even the ones who had never owned a mechanical leg and, if the odds held up, never would, began to realise what owning, having to live with one, let alone stand up and walk on it, must have meant. Devries didn't sit in the car on the Square or even halted on the road, letting the constituency, the votes, do the standing and walking out to the car to shake his hand and listen to him as was Clarence's immemorial and successful campaigning method. Instead, he walked himself, swinging that dead mechanical excrescence or bracing it to stand for an hour on a platform to speak, rationalising for the votes which he already knew he had lost, while trying to keep all rumor of the chafed and outraged stump out of his face while he did it. Until at last Charles's uncle said how the very ones who would still vote for him would dread having to look at him and keep the rumor of that stump out of their faces too; until they themselves began to wish the whole thing was over, the debacle accomplished, wondering (his uncle said) how they themselves might end it and set him free to go home and throw the tin leg away, chop it up, destroy it, and be just peacefully maimed.

Then the day approached for Uncle Billy Varner's election-year picnic, where by tradition all county aspirants for office, county state or national, delivered themselves and so Clarence too would have to announce formally his candidacy, his Uncle Gavin saying how they clutched even at that straw: that once Clarence had announced for Congress, Devries might feel he could withdraw his name and save his face.

Only he didn't have to. After the dinner was eaten and the speakers gathered on the platform, Clarence wasn't even among them; shortly afterward the word spread that he had even left the grounds and by the next morning the whole county knew that he had not only withdrawn from the race for Congress, he had announced his retirement from public life altogether. And that this time he meant it because it was not Clarence but old man Will Varner himself who had sent the word out that Clarence was through. That was July, 1945; a year after that, when the election for Congress finally came around, the Japanese had quit too and Charles and most of the rest of them who knew what Devries's medal meant, were home in person with their votes. But they merely increased Devries's majority; he didn't really need the medal because Ratliff had already beat Clarence Snopes. Then it was September, Charles was home again and the next day his uncle ran Ratliff to earth on the Square and brought him up to the office and said,

"All right. Tell us just exactly what did happen out there that day."

"Out where what day?" Ratliff said.

"You know what I mean. At Uncle Billy Varner's picnic when Clarence Snopes withdrew from the race for Congress."

"Oh, that," Ratliff said. "Why, that was what you might call a kind of a hand of God, holp a little of course by them two twin boys of Colonel Devries's sister."

"Yes," his uncle said. "That too: why Devries brought his sister and her family all the way over here from Cumberland County just to hear him announce for a race everybody knew he had already lost."

"That's that hand of God I jest mentioned," Ratliff said. "Because naturally otherwise Colonel Devries couldn't a possibly heard away over there in Cumberland County about one little old lonesome gum thicket behind Uncle Billy Varner's water mill now, could he?"

"All right, all right," his uncle said. "Thicket. Twin boys. Stop now and just tell us."

"The twin boys was twin boys and the thicket was a dog thicket," Ratliff said. "You and Chick both naturally know what twin boys is and I was about to say you and Chick both of course know what a dog thicket is too. Except that on second thought I reckon you dont because I never heard of a dog thicket neither until I seen this clump of gum and ash and hickory and pin-oak switches on the bank jest above Varner's millpond where it will be convenient for the customers like them city hotels that keeps a reservoy of fountain-pen ink open to anybody that needs it right next to the writing room—"

"Hold it," his uncle said. "Dog thicket. Come on now. I'm supposed to be busy this morning even if you're not."

"That's what I'm trying to tell you," Ratliff said. "It was a dog way-station. A kind of a dog post office you might say. Every dog in Beat Two uses it at least once a day, and every dog in the congressional district, let alone jest Yoknapatawpha County, has lifted his leg there at least once in his life and left his visiting card. You know: two dogs comes trotting up and takes a snuff and Number One says, 'I be dawg if here aint that old bobtail Bluetick from up at Wyott's Crossing. What you reckon he's doing away down here?' 'No it aint,' Number Two says. 'This here is that-ere fyce that Res Grier swapped Solon Quick for that half a day's work shingling the church that time, dont you remember?' and Number One says, 'No, that fyce come afterward. This here is that old Wyott's Crossing Bluetick. I thought he'd a been skeered to come back here after what that Littlejohn half-Airedale done to him that day.' You know: that sort of thing."

"All right," his uncle said. "Go on."

"That's all," Ratliff said. "Jest that-ere what you might call select dee-butant Uncle Billy Varner politics coming-out picnic and every voter and candidate in forty miles that owned a pickup or could bum a ride in one or even a span of mules either if wasn't nothing else handy, the sovereign votes theirselves milling around the grove

where Senator Clarence Egglestone Snopes could circulate among
them until the time come when he would stand up on the platform
and actively tell them where to mark the X. You know: ever thing
quiet and peaceful and ordinary and law-abiding as usual until this-
here anonymous underhanded son-of-a-gun—I wont say scoundrel
because evidently it must a been Colonel Devries his-self since
couldn't nobody else a knowed who them two twin boys was, let
alone what they was doing that far from Cumberland County; leastways not them particular two twin boys and that-ere local dog thicket
in the same breath you might say—until whoever this anonymous
underhanded feller was, suh-jested to them two boys what might
happen say if two folks about that size would shoo them dogs outen
that thicket long enough to cut off a handful of them switches well
down below the dog target level and kind of walk up behind where
Senator C. Egglestone Snopes was getting out the vote, and draw
them damp switches light and easy, not to disturb him, across the
back of his britches legs. Light and easy, not to disturb nobody,
because apparently Clarence nor nobody else even noticed the first
six or eight dogs until maybe Clarence felt his britches legs getting
damp or maybe jest cool, and looked over his shoulder to see the
waiting line-up of his political fate with one eye while already breaking for the nearest automobile or pickup you could roll the windows
up in with the other, with them augmenting standing-room-only
customers strung out behind him like the knots in a kite's tail until he
got inside the car with the door slammed and the glass rolled up,
them frustrated dogs circling round and round the automobile like
the spotted horses and swan boats on a flying jenny, except the dogs
was travelling on three legs, being already loaded and cocked and
aimed you might say. Until somebody finally located the owner of
the car and got the key and druv Clarence home, finally outdistanc-
ing the last dog in about two miles, stopping at last in the ex-Senator's yard where he was safe, the Snopes dogs evidently having went
to the picnic too, while somebody went into the house and fetched
out a pair of dry britches for the ex-Senator to change into in the
automobile. That's right. Ex-Senator. Because even with dry britches
he never went back to the picnic; likely he figgered that even then it
would be too much risk and strain. I mean, the strain of trying to

keep your mind on withdrawing from a political race and all the time having to watch over your shoulder in case some dog recollected your face even if your britches did smell fresh and uninteresting."

"Well I'll be damned," his uncle said. "It's too simple. I dont believe it."

"I reckon he figgered that to convince folks how to vote for him and all the time standing on one foot trying to kick dogs away from his other leg, was a little too much to expect of even Missippi voters," Ratliff said.

"I dont believe you, I tell you," his uncle said. "That wouldn't be enough to make him withdraw even if everybody at the picnic had known about it, seen it. Didn't you just tell me they got him into a car and away almost at once?" Then his uncle stopped. He looked at Ratliff, who stood blinking peacefully back at him. His uncle said: "Or at least—"

"That's right," Ratliff said. "That was the trade."

"What trade?" his uncle said.

"It was likely that same low-minded anonymous scoundrel again," Ratliff said. "Anyhow, somebody made the trade that if Senator Snopes would withdraw from this-here particular race for Congress, the folks that had seen them pro-Devries dogs would forget it, and the ones that hadn't wouldn't never need to know about it."

"But he would have beat that too," his uncle said. "Clarence Snopes stopped or even checked just because a few dogs raised their legs against him? Hell, he would have wound up having every rabies tag in Yoknapatawpha County counted as an absentee ballot."

"Oh, you mean Clarence," Ratliff said. "I thought you meant Uncle Billy Varner."

"Uncle Billy Varner?" his uncle said.

"That's right," Ratliff said. "It was Uncle Billy his-self that that low-minded rascal must a went to. Leastways Uncle Billy his-self sent word back that same afternoon that Senator Clarence Egglestone Snopes had withdrawed from the race for Congress; Uncle Billy never seemed to notified the ex-Senator a-tall. Oh yes, they told Uncle Billy the same thing you jest said: how it wouldn't hurt Clarence none in the long run; they even used your same words about the campaign tactics of the dogs, only a little stronger. But

Uncle Billy said No, that Clarence Snopes wasn't going to run for nothing in Beat Two.

" 'But he aint running in jest Beat Two,' they said. 'He aint even running in jest Yoknapatawpha County now. He's running in a whole one-eighth of the state of Missippi.' " And Uncle Billy said:

" 'Durn the whole hundred eighths of Missippi and Yoknapatawpha County too. I aint going to have Beat Two and Frenchman's Bend represented nowhere by nobody that ere a son-a-bitching dog that happens by cant tell from a fence post.' "

His uncle was looking at Ratliff. He had been looking at Ratliff for some time. "So this anonymous meddler you speak of not only knew the twin nephews and that dog thicket, he knew old Will Varner too."

"It looks like it," Ratliff said.

"So it worked," his uncle said.

"It looks like it," Ratliff said.

Both he and his uncle looked at Ratliff sitting neat and easy, blinking, bland and inscrutable in one of the neat blue shirts he made himself, which he never wore a tie with though Charles knew he had two at home he had paid Allanovna seventy-five dollars apiece for that time his uncle and Ratliff went to New York ten years ago to see Linda Snopes married, which Ratliff had never had on. "O Cincinnatus," his uncle said.

"What?" Ratliff said.

"Nothing," his uncle said. "I was just wondering who it was that told those twin boys about that dog thicket."

"Why, Colonel Devries, I reckon," Ratliff said. "A soldier in the war with all them medals, after three years of practice on Germans and I-talians and Japanese, likely it wasn't nothing to him to think up a little political strategy too."

"They were mere death worshippers and simple pre-absolved congenital sadists," his uncle said. "This was a born bred and trained American professional ward-level politician."

"Maybe aint neither of them so bad, providing a man jest keeps his eyes open and uses what he has, the best he knows," Ratliff said. Then he said, "Well," and rose, lean and easy, perfectly bland, perfectly inscrutable, saying to Charles now: "You mind that big oat field in the bend below Uncle Billy's pasture, Major? It stayed full of geese all last winter they say. Why dont you come out when the season opens and shoot a few of them? I reckon Uncle Billy will let us."

"Much obliged," Charles said.

"It's a trade then," Ratliff said. "Good day, gentlemen." Then Ratliff was gone. Now Charles was looking at his uncle, whereupon his uncle drew a sheet of paper to him and began to write on it, not fast: just extremely preoccupied, absorbed.

"So, quote," Charles said, "it will have to be you, the young people unquote. I believe that's about how it went, wasn't it?—that summer back in '37 when us moralists were even having to try to beat Roosevelt himself in order to get to Clarence Snopes?"

"Good day, Charles," his uncle said.

"Because quote it wont be us," Charles said. "We are too old, too tired, have lost the capacity to believe in ourselves—"

"Damn it," his uncle said, "I said good day."

"Yes sir," Charles said. "In just a moment. Because quote the United States, America: the greatest country in the world if we can just keep on affording it unquote. Only, let 'afford' read 'depend on God.' Because He saved you this time, using V. K. Ratliff of course as His instrument. Only next time Ratliff may be off somewhere selling somebody a sewing machine or a radio"—That's right, Ratliff now had a radio agency too, the radio riding inside the same little imitation house on the back of his pickup truck that the demonstrator sewing machine rode in; two years more and the miniature house would have a miniature TV stalk on top of it—"and God may not be able to put His hand on him in time. So what you need is to learn how to trust in God without depending on Him. In fact, we need to fix things so He can depend on us for a while. Then He wont need to waste Himself being everywhere at once." Now his uncle looked up at him and suddenly Charles thought *Oh yes, I liked Father too all right but Father just talked to me while Uncle Gavin listened to me, no matter how foolish what I was saying finally began to sound even to me, listening to me until I had finished, then saying, "Well, I dont know whether it will hold together or not but I know a good way to find out. Let's try it." Not* YOU *try it but* US *try it.*

"Yes," his uncle said. "So do I."

FOURTEEN

*T*hough by the time Ratliff eliminated Clarence back into private life in Frenchman's Bend, there had already been a new Snopes living in Jefferson for going on two years. So Jefferson was merely holding its own in what Charles's uncle would call the Snopes condition or dilemma.

This was a brand-new one, a bachelor named Orestes, called Res. That's right, Orestes. Even Charles's Uncle Gavin didn't know how either. His uncle told him how back in 1943 the town suddenly learned that Flem Snopes now owned what was left of the Compson place. Which wasn't much. The tale was they had sold a good part of it off back in 1909 for the municipal golf course in order to send the oldest son, Quentin, to Harvard, where he committed suicide at the end of his freshman year; and about ten years ago the youngest son, Benjy, the idiot, had set himself and the house both on fire and burned up in it. That is, after Quentin drowned himself at Harvard and Candace's, the sister's, marriage blew up and she disappeared, nobody knew where, and her daughter, Quentin, that nobody knew who her father was, climbed down the rainpipe one night and ran off with a carnival, Jason, the middle one, finally got rid of Benjy too by finally persuading his mother to commit him to the asylum only it didn't stick, Jason's version being that his mother whined and wept until he, Jason, gave up and brought Benjy back home, where sure enough in less than two years Benjy not only burned himself up but completely destroyed the house too.

So Jason took the insurance and borrowed a little more on the now vacant lot and built himself and his mother a new brick bungalow up on the main street to the Square. But the lot was a valuable location; Jefferson had already begun to surround it; in fact the golf links had already moved out to the country club back in 1929, selling the old course back to Jason Compson. Which was not surprising. While he was still in high school Jason had started clerking after school and on Saturdays in Uncle Ike McCaslin's hardware store,

which even then was run by a man named Earl Triplett that Uncle
Ike got from somewhere, everybody supposed off a deer stand or a
Delta fishing lake, since that was where Uncle Ike spent most of his
time. For which reason it was not surprising for the town to assume
presently that Triplett had long since gently eliminated Uncle Ike
from the business even though Uncle Ike still loafed in the store
when he wasn't hunting or fishing and without doubt Triplett still let
him have his rifle and shotgun ammunition and fishing tackle at cost.
Which without doubt the town assumed Jason did too when Jason
had eliminated Triplett in his turn back to his deer stand or trotline
or minnow bucket.

Anyhow, for all practical purposes Jason Compson was now the
McCaslin Hardware Company. So nobody was surprised when it was
learned that Jason had bought back into the original family holding
the portion which his father had sacrificed to send his older brother
to Harvard—a school which Jason held in contempt for the reason
that he held all schools beyond the tenth grade to be simply refuges
for the inept and the timid. Charles's uncle said that what surprised
him was when he went to the courthouse and looked at the records
and saw that, although Jason had apparently paid cash for the abandoned golf course, he had not paid off the mortgage on the other
part of the property on which he had raised the money to build his
new bungalow, the interest on which he had paid promptly in to
Flem Snopes's bank ever since, and apparently planned to continue.
This, right up to Pearl Harbor. So that you would almost believe
Jason had a really efficient and faithful spy in the Japanese Diet. And
then in the spring of 1942, another spy just as efficient and loyal in
the U.S. Cabinet too; his uncle said that to listen to Jason, you would
believe he not only had advance unimpeachable information that an
air-training field was to be located in Jefferson, he had an unimpeachable promise that it would be located nowhere else save on that
old golf links; his uncle said how back then nobody in Jefferson knew
or had thought much about airfields and they were willing to follow
Jason in that anything open enough to hit golf balls in was open
enough to land airplanes on.

Or anyway the right one believed him. The right one being Flem
Snopes, the president of the bank which held the mortgage on the

other half of Jason's property. His Uncle Gavin said it must have
been like a two-handed stud game when both have turned up a hole-
ace and by mutual consent decreed the other two aces dead cards.
Gavin said that of course nobody knew what really happened. All
they knew was what they knew about Jason Compson and Flem
Snopes; Gavin said there must have come a time when Flem, who
knew all along that he didn't know as much about airfields as Jason
did, must have had a terrifying moment when he believed maybe he
didn't know as much about money either. So Flem couldn't risk letting Jason draw another card and maybe raise him; Flem had to call.

Or (Gavin said) so Jason thought. That Jason was simply waving
that imaginary airfield around the Square to spook Mr Snopes into
making the first move. Which was evidently what Snopes did: he
called in the note his bank held on Jason's mortgage. All amicable
and peaceful of course, which was the way Jason expected it, inviting him (Jason) into that private back room in the bank and saying,
"I'm just as sorry about this as you can ever be, Mr Compson. But
you can see how it is. With our country fighting for its very life and
existence on both sides of the world, it's every man's duty and privilege too to add his little mite to the battle. So my board of directors
feel that every possible penny of the bank's resources should go into
matters pertaining directly to the war effort."

Which was just what Jason wanted: "Why certainly, Mr Snopes.
Any patriotic citizen will agree whole-heartedly with you. Especially
when there is a direct war effort right here in Jefferson, like this airfield I understand they have practically let the contract for, just as
soon as the title to the land is cleared:" naming his price for the ex-
golf course, out of which sum naturally the mortgage note would be
paid. Or, if Mr Snopes and his directors preferred, he, Jason, would
name a lump sum for the entire Compson property, including the
mortgage, and so leave the bank's directors or some patriotic civic
body representing the town itself to deal with the government for the
airfield; Jason reserving only the right to hope that the finished flying field might be christened Compson Field as a monument not to
him, Jason, but to the hope that his family had had a place in the history of Jefferson at least not to be ashamed of, including as it did one
governor and one brigadier general, whether it was worth commem-

orating or not. Because Charles's uncle said that Jason was shrewd too in his way, enough to speculate that the man who had spent as much as Snopes had to have his name on a marble monument over the grave of his unfaithful wife, might spend some more to have an airfield named for him too.

Or so Jason thought. Because in January '43 Jefferson learned that Mr Snopes—not the bank: Mr Private Individual Snopes—now owned the Compson place. And now his Uncle Gavin said how Jason exposed his hand a little from triumph. But then, who could really blame him since until now nobody but the Italian marble syndicate had ever managed to sell Flem Snopes anything as amorphous as prestige. And what the Italians had sold him was respectability, which was not a luxury but a necessity: referring (Jason did) to his old home property as Snopes Field, even (Charles's uncle said) waylaying, ambushing Mr Snopes himself now and then on the street when there was an audience, to ask about the progress of the project; this after even the ones who didn't know what an airfield really was, had realised there would not be one here since the government had already designated the flatter prairie land to the east near Columbus, and the perfectly flat Delta land to the west near Greenville, as the only acceptable terrain for flight training. Because then Jason began to commiserate with Mr Snopes in reverse, by delivering long public tirades on the government's stupidity; that Mr Snopes in fact was ahead of his time but that inevitably, in the course of time as the war continued and we all had to tighten our belts still further, the Snopes concept of a flying field composed of hills would be recognised as the only practical one and would become known throughout the world as the Snopes Airport Plan, since under it runways that used to have to be a mile long could be condensed into half that distance, since by simply bulldozing away the hill beneath it both sides of the runway could be used for each takeoff and landing, like a fly on a playing card wedged in a crack.

Or maybe Jason was whistling in the dark, Gavin said, saying No in terror to terrified realisation, already too late. Because Jason was shrewd in his way, having had to practise shrewdness pretty well to have got where he now was without any outside help and not much of a stake either. That maybe as soon as he signed the deed and before he even cashed the check, it may have occurred to him that Flem Snopes had practised shrewdness pretty well too, to be president of a bank now from even less of a stake than he, Jason, who at least had had a house and some land where Flem's had been only a wife. That Jason may have divined, as through some prescience bequeathed him by their mutual master, the Devil, that Flem Snopes didn't want and didn't intend to have a flying field on that property. That it was only Jason Compson who assumed that that by-product of war would go on forever which condemned and compelled real estate to the production and expension of airplanes and tanks and cannon, but that Flem Snopes knew better. Flem Snopes knew that the airplanes and tanks and guns were self-consuming in their own nihilism and inherent obsolescence, and that the true by-product of the war which was self-perpetuating and -compounding and would prevail and continue to self-compound into perpetuity, was the children, the birth rate, the space on which to build walls to house it from weather and temperature and contain its accumulating junk.

Too late. Because now Snopes owned it and all he had to do was just to sit still and wait while the war wore itself out. Since whether America, Jefferson, won it or lost it wouldn't matter; in either case population would compound and government or somebody would have to house it, and the houses would have to stand on something somewhere—a plot of land extending a quarter of a mile in both directions except for a little holding in one corner owned by a crotchety old man named Meadowfill, whom Flem Snopes would take care of in ten or fifteen minutes as soon as he got around to needing it, which even before Pearl Harbor had already begun to be by-passed and surrounded and enclosed by the town. So what Jason did next didn't surprise anyone; Charles's uncle said the only surprising thing was why Jason chose him, Gavin Stevens, to try to bribe either to find a flaw in the title he had conveyed to Mr Snopes; or if he, Stevens, couldn't find one, to invent one into it. His uncle said Jason answered that one himself: "Hell, aint you supposed to be the best-educated lawyer in this section? Not only Harvard but that German place too?"

"That is, if Harvard cant trick your property back from Flem Snopes, Heidelberg should," his uncle said. "Get out of here, Jason."

"That's right," Jason said. "You can afford virtue, now that you have married money, cant you?"

"I said get out of here, Jason," his uncle said.

"Okay, okay," Jason said. "I can probably find a lawyer somewhere that aint got enough money in Flem Snopes's bank to be afraid of him."

Except that Jason Compson shouldn't have needed anybody to tell him that Flem Snopes wasn't going to buy a title from anybody capable of having a flaw in it, or anything else in it to make it vulnerable. But Jason continued to try; Charles's uncle told him about it: Jason going about the business of trying to find some way, any way to overturn or even just shake Snopes's title, with a kind of coldly seething indefatigable outrage like that of a revivalist who finds that another preacher has stepped in behind his back and converted the client or patient he had been working on all summer, or a liar or a thief who has been tricked or robbed by another liar or thief. But he failed each time: Snopes's title to the entire old Compson place stood, so that even Jason gave up at last; and that same week the same Wat Snopes who had transformed the old De Spain house into Flem's antebellum mansion twenty years ago, came in again and converted the Compson carriage house (it was detached from the main house so Benjy had failed to burn it) into a small two-storey residence, and a month later the new Jefferson Snopes, Orestes, was living in it. And not merely as Flem Snopes's agent in actual occupation against whatever machinations Jason might still discover or invent. Because by summer Res had fenced up the adjacent ground into lots and was now engaged in the business of buying and selling scrubby cattle and hogs. Also, by that time he was engaged in an active kind of guerrilla feud with old man Meadowfill, whose orchard boundary was Res Snopes's hog-lot fence.

Even before the war old Meadowfill had a reputation in Jefferson: he was so mean as to be solvent and retired even from the savings on a sawmill. He had been active as a mill owner and timber dealer for a year or so after he bought his little corner of the Compson place and built his little unwired un-plumbing-ed house, until he sold his mill and retired into the house with his gray drudge of a wife and their one child; where, since it was obvious to anyone that a man

retiring still alive and with all his limbs from a sawmill could not possibly possess one extra dollar for anyone to borrow or sell him anything for, he could devote his full time to gaining and holding the top
name for curmudgeonry in all Jefferson and probably all Yoknapatawpha County too.

Charles remembered the daughter—a quiet modest mousy girl
nobody even looked at twice until suddenly in 1942 she graduated not
only valedictorian of her high school class but with the highest grades
ever made in it, plus a five-hundred-dollar scholarship offered by the
president of the Bank of Jefferson (not Snopes's bank: the other one)
as a memorial to his only son, a navy pilot who had been killed in one
of the first Pacific battles. She refused the scholarship. She went to Mr
Holland and told him she had already taken a job with the telephone
company and wouldn't need the scholarship but instead she wanted to
borrow five hundred dollars from the bank against her future salary,
and, pressed, finally divulged the reason for it: to put a bathroom in
her home; how once a week, on Saturday night, winter and summer,
the mother would heat water on the kitchen stove and fill a round gal-
vanised washtub in the middle of the floor, in which single filling all
three of them bathed in turn: the father, then the child, then last of
all the mother: at which point Mr Holland himself took over, had the
bathroom installed despite old Meadowfill's outraged fury (he didn't
intend to have his house meddled with at all by outsiders and
strangers but if it was he wanted the cash money instead) and gave
Essie a job for life in his bank.

Whereupon, now that the only child was not only secure but was
actually contributing to the family budget, old Meadowfill soared to
heights of outrageousness of which even he hadn't dreamed. Up to
this time he had done the grocery shopping himself, walking to town
each morning with an empty jute feed sack, to haggle in the small
dingy back- and side-street stores which catered mostly to Negroes,
for wilted and damaged leftovers of food which even Negroes would
have scorned. The rest of the day he would spend, not lurking exactly
but certainly in wait, ambushed, about his yard to shout and curse at
the stray dogs which crossed his unfenced property, and the small
boys who had a game of raiding the few sorry untended fruit trees
which he called his orchard. Now he stopped that. He waited exactly

one year, as though to be really sure Essie had her job for good. Then on the morning following the death of a paralytic old lady neighbor, he went and bought from the family the wheel chair she had inhabited for years, not even waiting until the funeral had left the house, and pushed the chair home along the street for his last appearance on it, and retired into the chair. Not completely at first. Although Charles's uncle said that Essie now did the daily shopping, Meadowfill could still be seen in the yard, still snarling and cursing at the small boys or throwing rocks (he kept a small pile handy, like the cannon balls of a war memorial) at the stray dogs. But he never left his own premises any more and presently he seemed to have retired permanently into the wheel chair, sitting in it like it was a rocking chair in a window which looked out over the vegetable patch he no longer worked at all now, and the scraggy fruit trees he had always been either too stingy or too perverse to spray and tend enough to produce even an edible crop, let alone a salable one.

Then Flem Snopes let Jason Compson overreach himself out of his ancestral acres, and Res Snopes built a hog lot along the boundary of old Meadowfill's orchard and made a new man of old Meadowfill. Because the trespassing of little boys merely broke a limb now and then, and stray dogs merely dug up flower beds if he had had flower beds. But one rooting hog could foul and sour and make sterile the very dirt itself. So now Meadowfill had a reason for staying alive. He even abandoned the wheel chair temporarily, it would have been in his way now, spending all day while Res and a hired Negro built the wire fence along his boundary, watching the digging of every post hole and the setting and tamping of the post, grasping the post in both hands to shake and test it, on the verge of apoplexy, a little mad by this time, shouting at Snopes and his helper as they stretched the wire: "Tighter! Tighter! Hell fire, what do you figger you're doing? hanging a hammock?" until Snopes—a lean gangling man with a cast in one sardonic eye—would say,

"Now, Mr Meadowfill, dont you worry a-tall. Before I would leave a old broke-down wheel-chair gentleman like you to have to climb this fence by hand, I aim to put slip bars in it that you could even get down and crawl under when you dont feel like opening them," with Meadowfill almost past speech now, saying,

"If ara one of them hogs—if jest ara durn one of then hogs—" and Snopes:

"Then all you got to do is jest ketch it and shut it up in your kitchen or bedroom or any other handy place and the pound law will make me pay you a dollar for it. In fact, that might even be good easy work for a retired wheel-chair old gentleman—" By which time Meadowfill would be in such a state that Snopes would call toward the kitchen, from the window or door of which by this time the gray wife would be watching or anyway hovering: "Maybe you better come and git him away from here."

Which she would do—until the next day. But at last the fence was finished. Or at least Snopes was no longer where Meadowfill could curse at him: only the hogs rooting and rubbing along the new fence which did hold them, or anyway so far. But only so far, only up to the moment it got too dark to see the orchard last night. So now he had something to stay alive for, to get up in the morning for, hurry out of bed and across to the window as soon as darkness thinned, to see if perhaps darkness itself hadn't betrayed him in which he couldn't have seen a hog in his orchard even if he had been able to stay awake twenty-four hours a day watching for it; to get into his chair and wheel himself across to the window and see his orchard for one more night anyway unravished; for one more night at least he had been spared. Then to begrudge the very time he would have to spend at table eating, since this would leave the orchard unguarded, unwatched of course he meant. Because, as Charles's uncle said, Meadowfill wasn't worrying at all about what he would do next when he did look out the window and actually see a hog on his property— an old bastard who, as Charles himself remembered, had already alienated all his neighbors before he committed himself to invalidism and the wheel chair, so that not one of them would have raised a hand to eject the hog for him or do anything else for him except maybe hide the body if and when his gray drab of a wife did what she should have done years ago: murdered him some night. Mead-owfill hadn't thought about what to do with the hog at all. He didn't need to. He was happy, for the first time in his life probably, Charles's Uncle Gavin said: that you are happy when your life is filled, and any life is filled when it is so busy living from moment to moment that it has no time over to remember yesterday or dread tomorrow. Which of course couldn't last, his uncle said. That in time Meadow-fill would reach the point where if he didn't look out that window some morning and see a hog in his orchard, he would die of simply hope unbearably deferred; and if he did some morning look out and see one, he would surely die because he would have nothing else left.

The atom bomb saved him. Charles meant that at last the Japs quit too and now the troops could come home from all directions, back to the women they had begun to marry before the echo of the first Pearl Harbor bomb had died away, and had been marrying ever since whenever they could get two days' leave, coming back home now either to already going families or to marry the rest of the women they hadn't got around to yet, the blood money already in the hands of the government housing loan (as his Uncle Gavin put it: "The hero who a year ago was rushing hand grenades and Garand clips up to front-line foxholes, is now rushing baskets of soiled didies out of side- and back-street Veterans Administration tenements.") and now Jason Compson was undergoing an anguish which he probably believed not only no human should suffer, but no human could really bear. Because when Charles reached home in September of '45, Jason's old lost patrimony was already being chopped up into a subdivision of standardised Veterans' Housing matchboxes; within the week Ratliff came to the office and told him and his uncle the official name of the subdivision: Eula Acres. Not Jason's old triumphant jeering gibe of Snopes Field, Snopes's Demolitional Jump-off, but Eula Acres, Eula's Uxorious Nest-place. And Charles didn't know whether old Flem Snopes had named it that himself or not but he would remember his uncle's face while Ratliff was telling them. But even without that he, Charles, would still prefer to believe it was not really Flem but his builder and (the town assumed) partner Wat Snopes who thought of it, maybe because Charles still wanted to believe that there are some things, at least one thing, that even Flem Snopes wouldn't do, even if the real reason was that Flem himself never thought of naming it anything because to him it couldn't matter whether it had a name or not. By Christmas it was already dotted over with small brightly painted pristinely new hutches as identical (and about as permanent) as squares of gingerbread or tea-

cakes, the ex-soldier or -sailor or -marine with his ruptured duck
pushing the perambulator with one hand and carrying the second (or
third) infant in the other arm, waiting to get inside almost before
the last painter could gather up his dropcloth. And by New Year's a
new arterial highway had been decreed and surveyed which would
run the whole length of Mr Snopes's subdivision, including the corner which old Meadowfill owned; whereupon there opened before
Meadowfill a prospect of excitement and entertainment beside which
the mere depredations of a hog would have been as trivial as the trespass of a frog or a passing bird. Because now one of the big oil companies wanted to buy the corner where Meadowfill's lot and the old
Compson (now Snopes) place joined—that is, a strip of Meadowfill's
orchard, with a contiguous strip of Res Snopes's hog lot—to build a
filling station on.

Because old Meadowfill didn't even own thirteen feet of the strip
of his land which the oil company wanted. In fact, as the town knew,
the title to none of his land vested in him. During the early second
Roosevelt days he had naturally been among the first to apply for
relief, learning to his outraged and incredulous amazement that a
finicking and bureaucratic federal government declined absolutely
and categorically to let him be a pauper and a property owner at the
same time. So he came to Gavin, choosing him from among the
other Jefferson lawyers for the simple reason that he, Meadowfill,
knew that in five minutes he would have Stevens so mad that very
likely Stevens would refuse to accept any fee at all for drawing the
deed transferring all his property to his nine-year-old (this was 1934)
daughter. He was wrong only in his estimate of the time, since it
required only two minutes for Stevens to reach the boil which carried him into the chancery clerk's vault, where he discovered that the
deed which Jason Compson's father had executed to Meadowfill read
"South to the road known as the Freedom Springs Road, thence East
along said Road . . ." The Freedom Springs road being, by the time
Meadowfill bought his corner, an eroded thicket-grown ditch ten
feet deep with only a footpath in it: as ponderable and inescapable a
geographical condition as the Grand Canyon, since this was before
the era when the bulldozer and the dragline would not only alter but
efface geography. Which was thirteen feet short of the actual survey-

line boundary which Mohataha, the Chickasaw matriarch, had granted to Quentin Compson in 1821, and Charles's uncle said his first impulse was the ethical one to tell old Meadowfill how he actually owned thirteen feet more of the surface of the earth than he thought he did, provided he did something about it before somebody else did. But if he, Stevens, did that, he would be ethically bound to accept Meadowfill's ten dollars for the title search, so he decided to let one ethic cancel the other and allow simple justice to prevail.

That was the situation when the survey line for the new highway was run to follow the old Chickasaw line, and Meadowfill discovered that his property only extended to the ditch which was thirteen feet short of it. But rage was a mild term for his condition when the oil company approached him to buy his part of the corner and he found that his mortal enemy, the hog-raising Snopes, owned the thirteen feet without a clear title to which the oil company would buy none of his, Meadowfill's, ground. There was rage in it too of course, since rage had been Meadowfill's normal condition for a year now. But now it was triumph too. More: it was vindication, revenge. Revenge on the Compsons who had uttered a false deed to him, allowing him to buy in good faith. Revenge on the community which had badgered him for years with small boys and stray dogs, by holding up a new taxpaying industry (if he could, by stopping the new highway itself). Revenge on the man who for a year now had ruined his sleep and his digestion too by the constant threat of that hog lot. Because he simply declined to sell any part of his property, under any conditions, to anyone: which, since his was in front of Snopes's, except for the thirteen-foot strip, would cut the oil company off from its proposed corner station as effectively as a toll gate, as a result of which the oil company declined to buy any part of Snopes's.

Of course, as the town knew, Snopes (Charles meant of course Res Snopes) had already approached Essie Meadowfill, in whose name the deed lay, who answered, as the town knew too: "You'll have to see papa." Because Snopes was under a really impossible handicap: his hog lot had forever interdicted him from approaching old Meadowfill in person, of having any sort of even momentary civilised contact with him. In fact, Snopes was under two insurmountable handicaps: the second one being the idea, illusion, dream that mere money could move a man who for years now had become so accustomed to not having or wanting one extra dollar, that the notion of a thousand could not even tempt him. So Snopes misread his man. But he didn't quit trying. (That's right. A stranger might have wondered what Flem Snopes was doing all this time, who owned the land in the first place. But they in the town were not strangers.) He went to the oil company's purchasing agent and said, "Tell him if he'll sign his deed, I'll give him ten percent of what you pay me for them thirteen feet." Then he said, "All right. Fifty percent then. Half of it." Then he said, "All right. How much will he take?" Then he said— and according to the oil company man, bland and affable and accommodating was no description for his voice: "All right. A good citizen cant stand in the way of progress, even if it does cost him money. Tell him if he will sign he can have them thirteen feet."

This time apparently Meadowfill didn't even bother to say No, sitting in his wheel chair at the window where he could look out upon the land which he wouldn't sell and the adjoining land which its owner couldn't sell because of him. So in a way, Snopes had a certain amount of local sympathy in his next move, which he made shortly before something happened to Essie Meadowfill which revealed her to be, underneath anyway, anything but mousy; and although demure might still be one word for her, the other wasn't quietness but determination.

One morning when Meadowfill wheeled his chair from the breakfast table to the window and looked out, he saw what he had been waiting to see for over a year now: a loose hog rooting among the worthless peaches beneath his worthless and untended trees; and even as he sat bellowing for Mrs Meadowfill, Snopes himself crossed the yard with an ear of corn and a loop of rope and snared the hog by one foot and half-drove half-led it back across the yard and out of sight, old Meadowfill leaning from the chair into the open window, bellowing curses at both of them even after they had disappeared.

The next morning he was already seated at the window when he actually saw the hog come at a steady trot up the lane and into his orchard; he was still leaning in the open window bellowing and cursing when the drab wife emerged from the house, clutching a shawl about her head, and hurried up the lane to knock at Snopes's locked front door until Meadowfill's bellowing, which had never stopped, drew her back home. By that time most of the neighbors were there watching what followed: the old man still bellowing curses from the wheel chair in the window while his wife tried single-handed to drive the hog out of the unfenced yard, when Snopes himself appeared (from where everybody knew now he had been concealed watching), innocent, apologetic and amazed, with his ear of corn and his looped plowline, and caught the hog and removed it.

Next, Meadowfill had the rifle—an aged, battered single-shot .22. That is, it looked second-hand simply by being in his possession, though nobody knew when he had left the wheel chair and the window (not to mention the hog) long enough to have hunted down the small boy owner and haggled or browbeat him out of it; the town simply could not imagine him ever having been a boy passionate and proud to own a single-shot .22 and to have kept it all these long years as a memento of that pure and innocent time. But he had it, cartridges too—not solid bullets but loaded with tiny shot such as naturalists use: incapable of killing the hog at all and even of hurting it much at this distance. In fact, Charles's uncle said Meadowfill didn't even really want to drive the hog away: he simply wanted to shoot it every day as other old people play croquet or bingo.

He would rush straight from the breakfast table, to crouch in his wheeled ambush at the window until the hog appeared. Then (he would have to rise from the chair to do this) he would stand up and slowly and quietly raise the window sash and the screen (he kept the grooves of both greased for speed and silence, and had equipped both of them with handles at the bottom so that he could raise either one with a single jerk) and deliver the shot, the hog giving its convulsive start and leap, until, forgetting, it would settle down again and receive the next shot, until at last its dim processes would connect the sting with the report and after the next shot it would go home, to return no more until tomorrow morning. Until finally it even connected the scattered peaches themselves with the general inimicality and for a whole week it didn't return at all; then the neighborhood legend rose that Meadowfill had contracted with the boy who delivered the Memphis and Jackson papers (he didn't take a paper himself, not being interested in any news which cost a dollar a month) to scavenge the neighborhood garbage cans and bait his orchard at night.

Now the town wondered more than ever just exactly what Snopes could be up to. That is, Snopes would naturally be expected to keep the hog at home after the first time old Meadowfill shot it. Or even sell it, which was Snopes's profession or trade, though probably no one would give the full market price per pound for a hog containing fourteen or fifteen months of Number Ten lead shot. Until finally Charles's uncle said they divined Snopes's intention: his hope that someday, by either error or mistake or maybe simple rage, swept beyond all check of morality or fear of consequences by his vice like a drunkard or gambler, Meadowfill would put a solid bullet in the gun; whereupon Snopes would not merely sue him for killing the hog, he would invoke the town ordinance against firing guns inside the city limits, and between the two of them somehow blackmail Meadowfill into making his, Snopes's, lot available to the oil company. Then the thing happened to Essie Meadowfill.

It was a Marine corporal. The town never did know how or where Essie managed to meet him. She had never been anywhere except occasionally for the day in Memphis, like everybody in north Mississippi went at least once a year. She had never missed a day from the bank except her summer vacations, which as far as anybody knew, she spent carrying her share of the burden of the wheel chair's occupation. Yet she met him, maybe through a lovelorn correspondence agency. Anyway, still carrying the parcels of the day's marketing, she was waiting at the station when the Memphis bus came in and he got out of it, whom Jefferson had never seen before, he carrying the grocery bag now along the street where Essie was now an hour late (people used to set their watches by her passing). And the town realised that "mousy" had been the wrong word for her for years evidently since obviously no girl deserving the word "mousy" could have bloomed that much, got that round and tender and girl-looking just in the brief time since the bus came up. And "quiet" was going to be the wrong word too; she was going to need the determination whether her Marine knew it yet or not, the two of them walking into the house and up to the wheel chair, into the point-blank range of that rage compared to which the cursing of small boys and throwing rocks at dogs and even shooting live ammunition at Snopes's hog was mere reflex hysteria, since this trespasser threatened the very system of peonage by which Meadowfill lived, and saying, "Papa, this is McKinley Smith. We're going to be married." Then walking back out to the street with him five minutes later and there, in full view of whoever wanted to look, kissing him—maybe not the first time she ever kissed him but probably the first time she ever kissed anyone without bothering (more, caring) whether or not it was a sin. And evidently McKinley had some determination too: son of an east Texas tenant farmer, who probably had barely heard of Mississippi until he met Essie wherever and however that was; who, once he realised that, because of the wheel chair and the gray mother, Essie was not going to cut away from her family and marry him regardless, should have given up and gone back to Texas by the next bus.

Or maybe what they had was a single determination held in collaboration, like they seemed to own everything else in common. They were indeed doomed and fated, whether they were star-crossed too or not. Because they even acted alike. It was obvious at once that he had cast his lot for keeps in Jefferson. Since for some time now (this was January, 1946, Charles was home now and saw the rest of it himself) the United States had been full of ex-G.I.'s going to school whether they were fitted for it or not or even really wanted to go, the obvious thing would be for him to enter the vocational school which had just been added to the Jefferson Academy, where at government expense he could hold her hand at least once every day while they waited for simple meanness finally to kill off old Meadowfill. But Essie's Marine dismissed higher education as immediately and firmly as Essie had, and for the same reason. He explained it: "I was a soldier for two years. The only thing I learned in that time was, the only place you can be safe in is a private hole, preferably with a iron lid you can pull down on top of you. I aim to own me a hole. Only I aint a soldier now and so I can pick where I want it, and even make it comfortable. I'm going to build a house."

He bought a small lot. In Eula Acres of course. And Essie selected it of course. It was not even very far from where she had lived most of her life; in fact, after the house began to go up, Meadowfill (he had to unless he gave the hog up and went back to bed) could sit right there in his window and watch every plank of its daily advancement: a constant reminder and warning that he dared not make the mistake of dying. Which at least was a valid reason for sitting in the wheel chair at the window, since he no longer had the hog. It anyway had given up—or anyway for the time being. Or Snopes had given up—for the time being. The hog had made its last sortie about the same day that Essie brought her Marine to the house for that first interview, and had not appeared in the orchard since. Snopes still owned it, or plenty of others (by the wind from that direction), or—since that was his business—he could have replaced it whenever he decided the time was right again. But for now at least he had desisted, patched his fence or (as the neighbors believed) simply stopped leaving the gate unfastened on what he considered strategic days. So now all old Meadowfill had to watch was the house.

McKinley built it himself, doing all the rough heavy work, with one professional carpenter to mark off the planks for him to saw, with the seething old man ambushed in the wheel chair behind the window without even the hog any more to vent his rage on. Obviously, as well as from habit, Meadowfill would have to keep the loaded rifle at hand. He could have no way whatever of knowing the hog would not come back; and now the town began to speculate on just how long it would be, how much he would be able to stand, before he fired the rifle at one of them—McKinley or the carpenter. Presently it would have to be the carpenter unless Meadowfill took to jacklighting, because one day (it was spring now) McKinley had a mule too and the town learned that he had rented a small piece of land two miles from town and was making a cotton crop on it. The house was about finished now, down to the millwork and trim which only the expert carpenter could do, so McKinley would depart on the mule each morning at sunrise, to be gone until nightfall. Which was when old Meadowfill probably touched the absolute of rage and impotence: McKinley might yet have been harried or frightened into selling his unfinished house and lot at any moment, possibly even for a profit. But no man in his senses would buy a cotton crop that hadn't even sprouted yet. Nothing could help him now but death—his own or McKinley's.

Then the hog came back. It simply reappeared; probably one

morning Meadowfill wheeled himself from the breakfast table to the window, expecting to face nothing save one more day of static outrage, when there was the hog again, rooting for the ghosts of last year's peaches as though it had never been away. In fact, maybe that's what Meadowfill wanted to believe at that moment: that the hog had never been away at all and so all that had happened since to outrage him had been only a dream, and even the dream to be exorcised away by the next shot he would deliver. Which was immediately; evidently he had kept the loaded rifle at his hand all the time; some of the neighbors said they heard the vicious juvenile spat while they were still in bed.

The sound of it had spread over the rest of town by noon, though Charles's Uncle Gavin was one of the few who actually felt the repercussion. He was just leaving the office to go home to dinner when he heard the feet on the stairs. Then Res Snopes entered, the five-dollar bill already in his hand. He laid it on the desk and said, "Good morning, Lawyer. I wont keep you long. I jest want a little advice—about five dollars' worth." Stevens didn't touch the bill yet: just looking from it to its owner who had never been known to pay five dollars for anything he didn't already know he could sell for at least twenty-five cents profit: "It's that hawg of mine that old gentleman—Mister Meadowfill—likes to shoot with them little bird shot."

"I heard about it," his uncle said. "Just what do you want for your five dollars?" Charles's uncle told it: Snopes standing beyond the desk, not secret: just polite and inscrutable. "For telling you what you already know? that once you sue him for injuring your hog, he will invoke the law against livestock running loose inside the city limits? For telling you what you already knew over a year ago when he fired the first shot at it? Either fix the fence or get rid of the hog."

"It costs a right smart to feed a hawg," Snopes said. "As for getting rid of it, that old gentleman has done shot it so much now, I doubt wouldn't nobody buy it."

"Then eat it," Stevens said.

"A whole hawg, for jest one man? Let alone with going on two years of bird shot in it?"

"Then give it away," Stevens said, and tried to stop himself but it was too late.

"That's your legal lawyer's advice then," Snopes said. "Give the hawg away. Much obliged," he said, already turning.

"Here," Stevens said, "wait;" holding out the bill.

"I come to you for legal lawyer's advice," Snopes said. "You give it to me: give the hawg away. I owe the fee for it. If five dollars aint enough, say so." Then he was gone. Stevens was thinking fast now, not *Why did he choose me?* because that was obvious: he had drawn Essie Meadowfill's deed to the property under dispute; he was the only person in Jefferson outside Meadowfill's family with whom old Meadowfill had had anything resembling human contact in almost twenty years. Nor even *Why did Snopes need to notify any outsider, lawyer or not, that he intended to give that hog away?* Nor even *Why did he lead me into saying the actual words first myself, technically constituting them paid-for legal advice?* Instead, what Stevens thought was *How, by giving that hog away, is he going to compel old Meadowfill to sell that lot?*

His Uncle Gavin always said he was not really interested in truth nor even in justice: that all he wanted was just to know, to find out, whether the answer was any of his business or not; and that all means to that end were valid, provided he left neither hostile witnesses nor incriminating evidence. Charles didn't believe him; some of his methods were not only too hard, they took too long; and there are some things you simply do not do even to find out. But his uncle said that Charles was wrong: that curiosity is another of the mistresses whose slaves decline no sacrifice.

The trouble in this case was, his uncle didn't know what he was looking for. He had two methods—inquiry and observation—and three leads—Snopes, the hog, and Meadowfill—to discover what he might not recognise in time even when he found it. He couldn't use inquiry, because the only one who might know the answer—Snopes—had already told all he intended for anyone to know. And he couldn't use observation on the hog because, like Snopes, it could move too. Which left only the one immobile: old Meadowfill. So he picked Charles up the next morning and at daylight they were ambushed also in his uncle's parked car where they could see the Meadowfill house and orchard and the lane leading to Snopes's house and, as the other point of the triangle, the little new house which

984   T H E   M A N S I O N

McKinley Smith had almost finished. They sat there for two hours. They watched McKinley depart on his mule for his cotton patch. Then Snopes himself came out of his yard into the lane and went on toward town, the Square. Presently it was time for even Essie Meadowfill to go to work. Then there remained only old Meadowfill ambushed behind his window. Only the hog was missing.

"If that's what we're waiting for," Charles said.

"I agree," his uncle said.

"I mean, to distract the eyes that have probably been watching us for the last two hours long enough for us to get away."

"I didn't want to come either," his uncle said. "But I had to or give that five dollars back."

And the next morning was the same. By then it was too late to quit; they both had too much invested now, not even counting Snopes's five dollars: two days of getting up before dawn, to sit for two hours in the parked car without even a cup of coffee, waiting for what they were not even sure they would recognise when they saw it. It was the third morning; McKinley and his mule had departed on schedule: so regular and normal that he and his uncle didn't even realise they had not seen Snopes yet until Essie Meadowfill herself came out of the house on her way to work. To Charles it was like one of those shocks, starts such as when you find yourself waking up without knowing until then you were asleep; his uncle was already getting out of the car to begin to run when they saw the hog. That is, it was the hog and it was doing exactly what they expected it to do: moving toward Meadowfill's orchard at that twinkling purposeful porcine trot. Only it was not where it should have been when it first became visible. It was going where they expected it to be going, but it was not coming from where it should have been coming from. It was coming not from the direction of Snopes's house but from that of McKinley Smith's. His uncle was already running, possibly from what Ratliff called his uncle's simple instinct or affinity for being where something was going to happen, even if he wasn't always quite on time, hurrying—Charles too of course—across the street and the little yard and into the house before old Meadowfill would see the hog through the window and make the shot.

His uncle didn't knock; they entered running, his uncle choosing by simple orientation the door beyond which old Meadowfill would have to be to use that particular window, and he was there, leaning forward in the wheel chair at the window, the glass sash of which was already raised though the screen was still down, the little rifle already half raised in one hand, the other hand grasping the handle to the screen to jerk it up. But he—Meadowfill—was just sitting there yet, looking at the hog. The town had got used to seeing meanness and vindictiveness and rage in his face; they were normal. But this time there was nothing in his face but gloating. He didn't even turn his head when Charles and his uncle entered: he just said, "Come right in; you got a grandstand seat." Now they could hear him cursing: not hard honest outdoors swearing but the quiet murmuring indoors obscenity which, Charles thought, if he ever had used it, his gray hairs should have forgot it now.

Then he began to stand up from the wheel chair and then Charles saw it too—a smallish lump a little longer than a brick, wrapped in a piece of gunny sack, bound in a crotch of the nearest peach tree about twenty feet from the house so that it pointed at the window, his uncle saying, "Stop! Stop! Dont raise it!" and even reaching for the screen, but too late; old Meadowfill, standing now, leaned the rifle beside the window and put both hands on the handle and jerked the screen up. Then the light sharp vicious spat of the .22 cartridge from the peach tree; his uncle said he was actually looking at the rising screen when the wire frayed and vanished before the miniature blast; Charles himself seemed actually to hear the tiny pellets hiss across old Meadowfill's belly and chest as the old man half-leaped half-fell backward into the chair which rushed from under him, leaving him asprawl on the floor, where he lay for a moment with on his face an expression of incredulous outrage: not pain, not anguish, fright: just outrage, already reaching for the rifle as he sat up.

"Somebody shot me!" he said.

"Certainly," his uncle said, taking the rifle away from him. "That hog did. Can you blame it? Just lie still now until we can see."

"Hog, hell," old Meadowfill said. "It was that blank blank blank McKinley Smith!"

He wasn't hurt: just burned, blistered, the tiny shot which had had to penetrate not only his pants and shirt but his winter underwear too, barely under his skin. But mad as a hornet, raging, bellowing and cursing and still trying to take the rifle away from Charles's uncle (Mrs Meadowfill was in the room now, the shawl already clutched about her head as if some fatalistic hopeless telepathy communicated to her the instant the hog crossed their unfenced boundary, like the electric eye that opens doors) until at last he exhausted himself into what would pass with him for rationality. Then he told it: how Snopes had told Essie two days ago that he had given the hog to McKinley as a housewarming present or maybe even—Snopes hoped—a wedding gift some day soon, with Charles's uncle saying, "Hold on a minute. Did Essie say Mr Snopes gave the hog to McKinley, or did she say Mr Snopes told her he had?"

"What?" Meadowfill said. "What?" Then he just began to curse again.

"Lie still," Charles's uncle said. "You've been shooting that hog for over a year now without hurting it so I reckon you can stand one shot yourself. But we'll have a doctor on your wife's account."

His uncle had the gun too: a very neat homemade booby trap: a cheap single-shot .22 also, sawed-off barrel and stock and fastened to a board, the whole thing wrapped in the piece of feed sack and bound in the crotch of the tree, a black strong small-gauge length of reel-backing running from the trigger through a series of screw eyes to the sash of the window screen, the muzzle trained at the center of the window about a foot above the sill.

"If he hadn't stood up before he raised that screen, the charge would have hit him square in the face," Charles said.

"So what?" his uncle said. "Do you think who put it there cared? Whether it merely frightened and enraged him into rushing at Smith with that rifle"—it had a solid bullet in it this time, the big one: the long rifle; this time old Meadowfill aimed to hurt what he shot—"and compelling Smith to kill him in self-defense, or whether the shot blinded him or killed him right there in his wheel chair and so solved the whole thing? Her father dead and her sweetheart in jail for murdering him, and only Essie to need to deal with?"

"It was pretty smart," Charles said.

"It was worse. It was bad. Nobody would ever have believed anyone except a Pacific veteran would have invented a booby trap, no matter how much he denied it."

"It was still smart," Charles said. "Even Smith will agree."

"Yes," his uncle said. "That's why I wanted you along. You were a soldier too. I may need an interpreter to talk to him."

"I was just a major," Charles said. "I never had enough rank to tell anything to any sergeant, let alone a Marine one."

"He was just a corporal," his uncle said.

"He was still a Marine," Charles said.

Only they didn't go to Smith first; he would be in his cotton patch now anyway. And, Charles told himself, if Snopes had been him, there wouldn't be anybody in Snopes's house either. But there was. Snopes opened the door himself; he was wearing an apron and carrying a frying pan; there was even a fried egg in it. But there wasn't anything in his face at all. "Gentle-men," he said. "Come in."

"No thanks," Charles's uncle said. "It wont take that long. This is yours, I think." There was a table; his uncle laid the sack-wrapped bundle on it and flipped the edge of the sacking, the mutilated rifle sliding across the table. And still there was nothing whatever in Snopes's face or voice:

"That-ere is what you lawyers call debatable, aint it?"

"Oh yes," Charles's uncle said. "Everybody knows about finger-prints now, just as they do about booby traps."

"Yes," Snopes said. "Likely you aint making me a present of it."

"That's right," his uncle said. "I'm selling it to you. For a deed to Essie Meadowfill for that strip of your lot the oil company wants to buy, plus that thirteen feet that Mr Meadowfill thought he owned." And now indeed Snopes didn't move, immobile with the cold egg in the frying pan. "That's right," his uncle said. "In that case, I'll see if McKinley Smith wants to buy it."

Snopes looked at his uncle a moment. He was smart; you would have to give him that, Charles thought. "I reckon you would," he said. "Likely that's what I would do myself."

"That's what I thought," his uncle said.

"I reckon I'll have to go and see Cousin Flem," Snopes said.

"I reckon not," his uncle said. "I just came from the bank."

"I reckon I would have done that myself too," Snopes said. "What time will you be in your office?"

And he and his uncle could have met Smith at his house at sundown too. Instead, it was not even noon when Charles and his uncle stood at the fence and watched McKinley and the mule come up the long black shear of turning earth like the immobilised wake of the plow's mold board. Then he was standing across the fence from them, naked from the waist up in his overalls and combat boots. Charles's uncle handed him the deed. "Here," his uncle said.

Smith read it. "This is Essie's."

"Then marry her," his uncle said. "Then you can sell the lot and buy a farm. Aint that what you both want? Haven't you got a shirt or a jumper here with you? Get it and you can ride back with me; the major here will bring the mule."

"No," Smith said; he was already shoving, actually ramming the deed into his pocket as he turned back to the mule. "I'll bring him in. I'm going home first. I aint going to marry nobody without a necktie and a shave."

Then they had to wait for the Baptist minister to wash his hands and put on his coat and necktie; Mrs Meadowfill was already wearing the first hat anybody had ever seen on her; it looked a good deal like the first hat anybody ever made. "But papa," Essie said.

"Oh," Charles's uncle said. "You mean that wheel chair. It belongs to me now. It was a legal fee. I'm going to give it to you and McKinley for a christening present as soon as you earn it."

Then it was two days later, in the office.

"You see?" his uncle said. "It's hopeless. Even when you get rid of one Snopes, there's already another one behind you even before you can turn around."

"That's right," Ratliff said serenely. "As soon as you look, you see right away it aint nothing but jest another Snopes."

FIFTEEN

$\mathcal{L}$inda Kohl was already home too when Charles got back. From her war also: the Pascagoula shipyard where she finally had her way and became a riveter; his Uncle Gavin told him, a good one. At least her hands, fingernails, showed it: not bitten, gnawed down, but worn off. And now she had a fine, a really splendid dramatic white streak in her hair running along the top of her skull almost like a plume. A collapsed plume; in fact, maybe that was what it was, he thought: a collapsed plume lying flat athwart her skull instead of cresting upward first then back and over; it was the fall of 1945 now and the knight had run out of tourneys and dragons, the war itself had slain them, used them up, made them obsolete.

In fact Charles thought how all the domestic American knights-errant liberal reformers would be out of work now, with even the little heretofore lost places like Yoknapatawpha County, Mississippi, fertilised to overflowing not only with ex-soldiers' blood money but with the two or three or four dollars per hour which had been forced on the other ex-riveters and -bricklayers and -machinists like Linda Kohl Snopes, he meant Linda Snopes Kohl, so fast that they hadn't had time to spend it. Even the two Finn communists, even the one that still couldn't speak English, had got rich during the war and had had to become capitalists and bull-market investors simply because they had not yet acquired any private place large enough to put that much money down while they turned their backs on it. And as for the Negroes, by now they had a newer and better high school building in Jefferson than the white folks had. Plus an installment-plan automobile and radio and refrigerator full of canned beer down-paid with the blood money which at least drew no color line in every unwired unscreened plumbingless cabin: double-plus the new social-revolution laws which had abolished not merely hunger and inequality and injustice, but work too by substituting for it a new self-compounding vocation or profession for which you would need no schooling at all: the simple production of children. So there was nothing for Linda to

tilt against now in Jefferson. Come to think of it, there was nothing
for her to tilt against anywhere now, since the Russians had fixed the
Germans and even they didn't need her any more. In fact, come to
think of it, there was really nothing for her in Jefferson at all any
more, now that his Uncle Gavin was married—if she had ever
wanted him for herself. Because maybe Ratliff was right and whatever she had ever wanted of him, it wasn't a husband. So in fact you
would almost have to wonder why she stayed in Jefferson at all now,
with nothing to do all day long but wait, pass the time somehow until
night and sleep came, in that Snopes-colonial mausoleum with that
old son of a bitch that needed a daughter or anybody else about as
much as he needed a spare bow tie or another hat. So maybe everybody was right this time and she wasn't going to stay in Jefferson
much longer, after all.

But she was here now, with her nails, his uncle said, not worn
down from smithing but scraped down to get them clean (and
whether his uncle added it or not: feminine) again, with no more
ships to rivet, and that really dramatic white plume collapsed in gallantry across her skull, with all the dragons dead. Only, even blacksmithing hadn't been enough. What he meant was, she wasn't any
older. No, that wasn't what he meant: not just older. Something had
happened to him during the three-plus years between December '41
and April '45 or at least he hoped it had or at least what had seemed
suffering and enduring to him at least met the standards of suffering
and enduring enough to enrich his spiritual and moral development
whether it did anything for the human race or not, and if it had purified his soul it must show on his outside too or at least he hoped it
did. But she hadn't changed at all, least of all the white streak in her
hair which it seemed that some women did deliberately to themselves. When he finally— All right, finally. So what if he did spend
the better part of his first three days at home at least hoping he didn't
look like he was hanging around the Square in case she did cross it or
enter it. There were towns bigger than Jefferson that didn't have a
girl—woman—in it that the second you saw her eight years ago getting out of an airplane you were already wondering what she would
look like with her clothes off except that she was too old for you, the
wrong type for you, except that that was exactly backward, you were

too young for her, the wrong type for her and so only your uncle that you had even spent some of the ten months in the Nazi stalag wondering if he ever got them off before he got married to Aunt Melisandre or maybe even after and if he didn't, what happened, what was wrong. Because his uncle would never tell him himself whether he ever did or not but maybe after three years and a bit he could tell by looking at her, that maybe a woman really couldn't hide that from another man who was . . . call it *simpatico*. Except that when he finally saw her on the street on the third day there was nothing at all, she had not changed at all, except for the white streak which didn't count anyway—the same one that on that day eight years ago when he and his uncle had driven up to the Memphis airport to get her, was at that first look a little too tall and a little too thin for his type so that in that same second he was saying *Well that's one anyway that wont have to take her clothes off on my account* and then almost before he could get it out, something else was already saying *Okay, buster, who suggested she was going to?* and he had been right: not her for him, but rather not him for her: a lot more might still happen to him in his life yet (he hoped) but removing that particular skirt wouldn't be one even if when you got the clothes off the too tall too thin ones sometimes they surprised you. And just as well; evidently his soul or whatever it was had improved some in the three years and a bit; anyway he knew now that if such had been his fate to get this particular one off, what would happen to him might, probably would, have several names but none of them would be surprise.

With no more ships to rivet now, and what was worse: no need any more for ships to rivet. So not just he, Charles, but all the town in time sooner or later would see her—or be told about it by the ones who had—walking, striding, most of the time dressed in what they presumed was the same army-surplus khaki she had probably riveted the ships in, through the back streets and alleys of the town or the highways and lanes and farm roads and even the fields and woods themselves within two or three miles of town, alone, walking not fast so much as just hard, as if she were walking off insomnia or perhaps even a hangover. "Maybe that's what it is," Charles said. Again his uncle looked up, a little impatiently, from the brief.

"What?" he said.

"You said maybe she has insomnia. Maybe it's hangover she's walking off."

"Oh," his uncle said. "All right." He went back to the brief. Charles watched him.

"Why dont you walk with her?" he said.

This time his uncle didn't look up. "Why dont you? Two ex-soldiers, you could talk about war."

"She couldn't hear me. I wouldn't have time to write on a pad while we were walking."

"That's what I mean," his uncle said. "My experience has been that the last thing two ex-soldiers under fifty years old want to talk about is war. You two even cant."

"Oh," he said. His uncle read the brief. "Maybe you're right," he said. His uncle read the brief. "Is it all right with you if I try to lay her?" His uncle didn't move. Then he closed the brief and sat back in the chair.

"Certainly," he said.

"So you think I cant," Charles said.

"I know you cant," his uncle said. He added quickly: "Dont grieve; it's not you. Just despair if you like. It's not anybody."

"So you know why," Charles said.

"Yes," his uncle said.

"But you're not going to tell me."

"I want you to see for yourself. You will probably never have the chance again. You read and hear and see about it in all the books and pictures and music, in Harvard and Heidelberg both. But you are afraid to believe it until you actually see it face to face, because you might be wrong and you couldn't bear that, and be happy. What you cant bear is to doubt it."

"I never got to Heidelberg," Charles said. "All I had was Harvard and Stalag umpty-nine."

"All right," his uncle said. "The high school and the Jefferson Academy then."

Anyway he, Charles, knew the answer now. He said so. "Oh, that. Even little children know all that nowadays. She's frigid."

"Well, that's as good a Freudian term as another to cover chastity or discretion," his uncle said. "Beat it now. I'm busy. Your mother invited me to dinner so I'll see you at noon."

So it was more than that, and his uncle was not going to tell him. And his uncle had used the word "discretion" also to cover something he had not said. Though Charles at least knew what that was because he knew his uncle well enough to know that the discretion applied not to Linda but to him. If he had never been a soldier himself, he would not have bothered, let alone waited, to ask his uncle's leave: he would probably already have waylaid her at some suitably secluded spot in the woods on one of her walks, on the innocent assumption of those who have never been in a war that she, having come through one, had been wondering for days now what in hell was wrong with Jefferson, why he or any other personable male had wasted all this time. Because he knew now why young people rushed so eagerly to war was their belief that it was one endless presanctioned opportunity for unlicensed rapine and pillage; that the tragedy of war was that you brought nothing away from it but only left something valuable there; that you carried into war things which, except for the war, you could have lived out your life in peace with without ever having to know they were inside you.

So it would not be him. He had been a soldier too even if he had brought back no wound to prove it. So if it would take physical assault on her to learn what his uncle said he didn't know existed, he would never know it; he would just have to make one more in the town who believed she was simply walking off one hangover to be ready for the next one, having evidence to go on, or at least a symptom. Which was that once a week, Wednesday or Thursday afternoon (the town could set its watches and calendars by this too) she would be waiting at the wheel of her father's car outside the bank when it closed and her father came out and they would drive up to what Jakeleg Wattman euphemiously called his fishing camp at Wyott's Crossing, and lay in her next week's supply of bootleg whiskey. Not her car: her father's car. She could have owned a covey of automobiles out of that fund his uncle was trustee of from her grandfather, old Will Varner rich out at Frenchman's Bend, or maybe from Varner and her father together as a part of or maybe a result

of that old uproar and scandal twenty years ago when her mother had
committed suicide and the mother's presumed lover had abandoned
the bank and his ancestral home both to her father, not to mention
the sculptor she married being a New York Jew and hence (as the
town was convinced) rich. And driven it—them—too, even stone
deaf, who could have afforded to hire somebody to sit beside her and
do nothing else but listen. Only she didn't. Evidently she preferred
walking, sweating out the hard way the insomnia or hangover or
whatever the desperate price she paid for celibacy—unless of course
Lawyer Gavin Stevens had been a slicker and smoother operator for
the last eight years than anybody suspected; though even he had a
wife now.

   And her supply: not her father's. Because the town, the county,
knew that too: Snopes himself never drank, never touched it. Yet he
would never let his daughter make the trip alone. Some were satisfied
with the simple explanation that Wattman, like everybody else nowadays, was making so much money that he would have to leave some
of it somewhere, and Snopes, a banker, figured it might as well be
in his bank and so he called on Jakeleg once a week exactly as he
would and did look in socially on any other merchant or farmer or
cotton ginner of the bank's profitable customers or clients. But there
were others, among them his Uncle Gavin and his uncle's special
crony, the sewing machine agent and rural bucolic grass-roots
philosopher and Cincinnatus, V. K. Ratliff, who went a little further:
it was for respectability, the look of things: that on those afternoons
Snopes was not just a banker, he was a leading citizen and father; and
even though his widowed only daughter was pushing forty and had
spent the four years of the war working like a man in a military shipyard where unspinsterish things had a way of happening to women
who were not even widows, he still wasn't going to let her drive alone
fifteen miles to a bootlegger's joint and buy a bottle of whiskey.

   Or a case of it; since it was hangover she walked off, she would
need, or anyway need to have handy, a fresh bottle every day. So
presently even the town would realise it wasn't just hangover since
people who can afford a hangover every day dont want to get rid of
it, walk it off, even if they had time to. Which left only jealousy and
rage; what she walked four or five miles every day to conquer or any-

way contain was the sleepless frustrated rage at his Uncle Gavin for having jilted her while she was away riveting ships to save Democracy, to marry Melisandre Harriss Backus that was as Thackeray says, thinking (Charles) how he could be glad it wasn't him that got the clothes off since if what was under them—provided of course his uncle had got them off—had driven his uncle to marry a widow with two grown children, one of them already married too, so that his Uncle Gavin might already have been a grandfather before he even became a bride.

Then apparently jealousy and frustrated unforgiving rage were wrong too. Christmas came and went and the rest of that winter followed it, into spring. His uncle was not only being but even acting the squire now. No boots and breeks true enough and although a squire might have looked like one behind a Phi Beta Kappa key even in Mississippi, he never could under a shock of premature white hair like a concert pianist or a Hollywood Cadillac agent. But at least he behaved like one, once each month and sometimes oftener, sitting at the head of the table out at Rose Hill with Charles's new Aunt Melisandre opposite him and Linda and Charles across from each other while his uncle interpreted for Linda from the ivory tablet. Or rather, interpreted for himself into audible English to Charles and his new Aunt Em. Because Linda didn't talk now any more than she ever had: just sitting there with that white streak along the top of her head like a collapsed plume, eating like a man; Charles didn't mean eating grossly: just soundly, heartily, and looking . . . yes, by God, that was exactly the word: happy. Happy, satisfied, like when you have accomplished something, produced, created, made something: gone to some—maybe a lot—trouble and expense, stuck your neck out maybe against your own better judgment; and sure enough, be damned if it didn't work, exactly as you thought it would, maybe even better than you had dared hope it would. Something you had wanted for yourself only you missed it so you began to think it wasn't so, was impossible, until you made one yourself, maybe when it was too late for you to want it any more but at least you had proved it could be.

And in the drawing room afterward also, with coffee and brandy for the ladies and port and a cigar for Charles though his uncle still stuck to the cob pipes which anyway used to cost only a nickel. Still happy, satisfied; and that other thing which Charles had sensed, recognised: proprietorial. As if Linda herself had actually invented the whole business: his Uncle Gavin, his Aunt Melisandre, Rose Hill—the old, once-small and -simple frame house which old Mr Backus with his Horace and Catullus and his weak whiskey-and-water would not recognise now save by its topographical location, transmogrified by the New Orleans gangster's money as old Snopes had tried to do to the De Spain house with his Yoknapatawpha County gangster's money and failed since here the rich and lavish cash had been spent with taste so that you didn't really see it at all but merely felt it, breathed it, like warmth or temperature; with, surrounding it, enclosing it, the sense of the miles of white panel fences marking the combed and curried acres and the electric-lighted and -heated stables and tack rooms and grooms' quarters and the manager's house all in one choral concord in the background darkness—and then invented him, Charles, to be present to at least look at her creation whether he approved of what she had made or not.

Then the hour to say Thank you and Good night and drive back to town through the April or May darkness and escort Linda home, back to her father's Frenchman's Bend–dreamed palace, to draw up at the curb, where she would say each time in the harsh duck voice (he, Charles, thinking each time too *Which maybe at least wouldn't sound quite so bad in the dark whispering after you finally got the clothes off* thinking *If of course it had been you*): "Come in for a drink." Nor enough light in the car for her to have read the ivory tablet if she had offered it. Because he would do this each time too: grin, he would hope loud enough, and shake his head—sometimes there would be moonlight to help—Linda already opening the door on her side so that Charles would have to get out fast on his to get around the car in time. Though no matter how fast that was, she would be already out, already turning up the walk toward the portico: who perhaps had left the South too young too long ago to have formed the Southern female habit-rite of a cavalier's unflagging constancy, or maybe the simple riveting of ships had cured the old muscles of the old expectation. Whichever it was, Charles would have to overtake, in effect outrun her already halfway to the house; whereupon she would check, almost pause in fact, to glance back at him, startled—not alarmed: just startled; merely what Hollywood called a double-take, still not so far dissevered from her Southern heritage but to recall that he, Charles, dared not risk some casual passerby reporting to his uncle that his nephew permitted the female he was seeing home to walk at least forty feet unaccompanied to her front door.

So they would reach that side by side anyway—the vast dim homemade columned loom of her father's dream, nightmare, monstrous hope or terrified placatement, whichever it was, whatever it had been; the cold mausoleum in which old Snopes had immolated that much of his money at least without grace or warmth, Linda stopping again to say, "Come in and have a drink," exactly as though she hadn't said it forty feet back at the car, Charles still with nothing but the grin and the shake of the head as if he had only that moment discovered his ability to do that too. Then her hand, hard and firm like a man's since after all it was a ship riveter's or at least an ex-ship riveter's. Then he would open the door, she would stand for an instant in it in the midst of motion against a faint light in the hall's depth; the door would close again.

Oh yes, it could have had several names but surprise would not have been one of them, thinking about his uncle, the poor dope, if his uncle really had got the clothes off once maybe. Whereupon he thought how maybe his uncle actually had, that once, and couldn't stand it, bear it, and ran, fled back those eighteen or twenty years to Melisandre Backus (that used to be), where he would be safe. So if the word wouldn't be surprise, maybe it wouldn't really have to be grief either: just relief. A little of terror maybe at how close the escape had been, but mainly relief that it had been escape under any condition, on any terms. Because he, Charles, had been too young at the time. He didn't know whether he actually remembered Linda's mother as his uncle and Ratliff obviously did, or not. But he had had to listen to both of them often enough and long enough to know that he surely did know all that they remembered, Ratliff especially; he could almost hear Ratliff saying again: "We was lucky. We not only had Helen of Argos right here in Jefferson, which most towns dont, we even knowed who she was and then we even had our own Paris to save us Argoses by jest wrecking Troy instead. What you want to

do is not to own Helen, but jest own the right and privilege of looking at her. The worst thing that can happen to you is for her to notice
you enough to stop and look back."

So, assuming that whatever made Helen was transferable or anyway inheritable, the word would not be grief at all but simple and
perhaps amazed relief; and maybe his uncle's luck and fate was simply to be cursed with less of fire and heat than Paris and Manfred de
Spain; to simply have taken simple fear from that first one time (if his
uncle really had got them off that first one time) and fled while he
still had life. You know: the spider lover wise enough with age or
cagey enough with experience or maybe just quick enough to spook
from sheer timid instinct, to sense, anticipate, that initial tender
caressing probe of the proboscis or suction tube or whatever it is his
gal uses to empty him of his blood too while all he thinks he is risking is his semen; and leap, fling himself free, losing of course the
semen and most of the rest of his insides too in the same what he
thought at first was just peaceful orgasm, but at least keeping his
husk, his sac, his life. Or the grape, say, a mature grape, a little on the
oversunned and juiceless side, but at least still intact enough even if
only in sapless hull after the spurting ejaculation of the nymphic kiss,
to retain at least the flattened semblance of a grape. Except that
about then you would have to remember what Ratliff said that time:
"No, she aint going to marry him. It's going to be worse than that,"
and you would wonder what in the world Helen or her inheritrix
could or would want with that emptied sac or flattened hull, and so
what in the hell could Ratliff have meant? Or anyway thought he
meant? Or at least was afraid he might have meant or mean?

Until it finally occurred to him to do the reasonable and logical
thing that anybody else would have thought about doing at first: ask
Ratliff himself what he meant or thought he meant or was afraid he
meant. So he did. It was summer now, June; McKinley Smith's cotton was not only up, Essie was pregnant. The whole town knew it;
she had made a public announcement in the bank one morning as
soon as the doors opened and the first depositors had lined up at the
windows; in less than two months she and McKinley had won old
Meadowfill's wheel chair.

"Because this aint enough," Ratliff said.

"Enough what?" Charles said.

"Enough to keep her busy and satisfied. No ships to rivet, and now she's done run out of colored folks too for the time being. This here is peace and plenty—the same peace and plenty us old folks like me and your uncle spent four whole years sacrificing sugar and beefsteak and cigarettes all three to keep the young folks like you happy while you was winning it. So much plenty that even the downtrod communist shoe patchers and tinsmiths and Negro children can afford to not need her now. I mean, maybe if she had asked them first they never actively needed her before neither, only they couldn't afford in simple dollars and cents to say so. Now they can." He blinked at Charles. "She has done run out of injustice."

"I didn't know you could do that," Charles said.

"That's right," Ratliff said. "So she will have to think of something, even if she has to invent it."

"All right," Charles said. "Suppose she does. If she was tough enough to stand what we thought up around here, she can certainly stand anything she can invent herself."

"I aint worried about her," Ratliff said. "She's all right. She's jest dangerous. I'm thinking about your uncle."

"What about him?" Charles said.

"When she finally thinks of something and tells him, he will likely do it," Ratliff said.

SIXTEEN

*T*hey met that morning in the post office, as they often did by complete uncalculation at morning mail time, she dressed as usual in the clothes she seemed to spend most of her time walking about the adjacent countryside in—the expensive English brogues scuffed and scarred but always neatly polished each morning, with wool stockings or socks beneath worn flannel trousers or a skirt or sometimes what looked like a khaki boiler-suit under a man's stained burberry; this in the fall and winter and spring; in the summer it would be cotton—dress or skirt or trousers, her head with its single white plume bare even in the worst weather. Afterward they would go to the coffee shop in the Holston House and drink coffee but this time instead Stevens took the gold-cornered ivory tablet he had given her eight years ago and wrote:

An appointment   At the office   To see me

"Shouldn't you make an appointment to see lawyers?" she said.

His next speech of course would be: "So it's as a lawyer you need me now." And if they both could have used speech he would have said that, since at the age of fifty-plus talking is no effort. But writing is still an effort at any age, so even a lawyer pauses at the obvious if he has got to use a pen or pencil. So he wrote *Tonight after supper At your house*

"No," she said.

He wrote *Why*

"Your wife will be jealous. I dont want to hurt Milly."

His next of course would be: "Melisandre, jealous? Of you and me? After all this, all this time?" Which of course was too long to write on a two-by-three-inch ivory tablet. So he had already begun to write *Nonsense* when he stopped and erased it with his thumb. Because she was looking at him, and now he knew too. He wrote *You want her To be jealous*

"She's your wife," she said. "She loves you. She would have to be jealous." He hadn't erased the tablet yet; he needed only to hold it up before her face until she looked at it again. "Yes," she said. "Being jealous is part of love too. I want you to have all of it too. I want you to have everything. I want you to be happy."

"I am happy," he said. He took one of the unopened envelopes just out of his mailbox and wrote on the back of it *I am happy I was given the privilege of meddling with impunity in other peoples affairs without really doing any harm by belonging to that avocation whose acolytes have been absolved in advance for holding justice above truth I have been denied the chance to destroy what I loved by touching it Can you tell me now what it is here or shall I come to your house after supper tonight*

"All right," she said. "After supper then."

At first his wife's money was a problem. In fact, if it hadn't been for the greater hysteria of the war, the lesser hysteria of that much sudden money could have been a serious one. Even four years later Melisandre still tried to make it a problem: on these warm summer evenings the Negro houseman and one of the maids would serve the evening meal on a flagged terrace beneath a wistaria arbor in the back yard, whereupon each time there were guests, even the same guest or guests again, Melisandre would say, "It would be cooler in the dining room" (in the rebuilt house the dining room was not quite as large as a basketball court) "and no bugs either. But the dining room makes Gavin nervous." Whereupon he would say, as he always did too, even before the same guest or guests again: "Dammit, Milly, nothing can make me nervous because I was already born that way."

They were sitting there now over the sandwiches and the iced tea. She said, "Why didn't you invite her out here." He merely chewed so she said, "But of course you did." So he merely chewed and she said, "So it must be something serious." Then she said, "But it cant be serious or she couldn't have waited, she would have told you right there in the post office." So then she said, "What do you suppose it is?" and he wiped his mouth and dropped the napkin, rising, and came around the table and leaned and kissed her.

"I love you," he said. "Yes. No. I dont know. Dont wait up."

Melisandre had given him a Cadillac roadster for her wedding present to him; this was during the first year of the war and God only knew where she had got a new Cadillac convertible and what she had paid for it. "Unless you really dont want it," she said.

"I do," he said. "I've always wanted a Cadillac convertible—provided I can do exactly what I want to with it."

"Of course you can," she said. "It's yours." So he drove the car back to town and arranged with a garage to store it for ten dollars a month and removed the battery and radio and the tires and the spare wheel and sold them and took the keys and the bill of sale to Snopes's bank and mortgaged the car for the biggest loan they would make on it. By that time progress, industrial renascence and rejuvenation had reached even rural Mississippi banks, so Snopes's bank now had a professional cashier or working vice-president imported from Memphis six months back to give it the New Look, that is, to bring rural banks abreast of the mental condition which accepted, could accept, the automobile as a definite ineradicable part of not only the culture but the economy also; where, as Stevens knew, Snopes alone would not lend God Himself one penny on an automobile. So Stevens could have got the loan from the imported vice-president on his simple recognizance, not only for the above reason but because the vice-president was a stranger and Stevens represented one of the three oldest families in the county and the vice-president would not have dared to say No to him. But Stevens didn't do it that way; this was to be, as the saying had it, Snopes's baby. He waylaid, ambushed, caught Snopes himself in public, in the lobby of his bank with not only all the staff but the moment's complement of customers, to explain in detail how he didn't intend to sell his wife's wedding gift but simply to convert it into war bonds for the duration of the war. So the loan was made, the keys surrendered and the lien recorded, which Stevens naturally had no intention whatever of ever redeeming, plus the ten dollars a month storage accrued to whatever moment when Snopes realised that his bank owned a brand-new though outdated Cadillac automobile complete except for battery and tires.

Though even with the six-year-old coupé which (as it were) he had got married from, the houseman still got there first to hold the door for him to get in and depart, down the long driveway lined immediately with climbing roses on the white-panelled fences where the costly pedigreed horses had once ranged in pampered idleness; gone now since there was no one on the place to ride them unless somebody paid him for it, Stevens himself hating horses even more than dogs, rating the horse an unassailable first in loathing since though both were parasites, the dog at least had the grace to be a sycophant too; it at least fawned on you and so kept you healthily ashamed of the human race. But the real reason was, though neither the horse nor the dog ever forgot anything, the dog at least forgave you, which the horse did not; and his, Stevens's, thought was that what the world needed was more forgiving: that if you had a good sensitive quick-acting capacity for forgiving, it didn't really matter whether you ever learned or even remembered anything or not.

Because he had no idea what Linda wanted either; he thought *Because women are wonderful: it doesn't really matter what they want or if they themselves even know what it is they think they want.* At least there was the silence. She would have to organise, correlate, tell him herself, rather than have whatever it was she wanted him to know dug out of her by means of the infinitesimal legal mining which witnesses usually required; he would need only write on the tablet *At least dont make me have to write out in writing whatever questions you want me to ask you so whenever you come to one of them just ask it yourself and go on from there.* Even as he stopped the car he could already see her, her white dress in the portico, between two of the columns which were too big for the house, for the street, for Jefferson itself; it would be dim and probably cooler and anyway pleasant to sit there. But there was the silence; he thought how there should be a law for everybody to carry a flashlight in his car or perhaps he could ask her with the tablet to get a flashlight from the house so she could read the first sentence; except that she couldn't read the request for the flashlight until she was inside the house.

She kissed him, as always unless they met on the street, almost as tall as he; he thought *Of course it will have to be upstairs, in her sitting room with the doors closed too probably; anything urgent enough to demand a private appointment* following her through the hall at the end of which was the door to the room where her father (he believed that out of all Jefferson only he and Ratliff knew better) sat, local legend had it not reading, not chewing tobacco: just sitting with his feet propped on the unpainted wooden ledge he had had his Frenchman's Bend carpenter-kinsman nail at the proper height across the Adam mantel; on up the stairs and, sure enough, into her sitting room whose own mantel had been designed to the exact height for them to stand before while he used the foolscap pad and pencil which was its fixture since she led him here only when there was more than the two-by-three ivory surface could hold. Though this time he hadn't even picked up the pencil when she spoke the eight or nine words which froze him for almost half that many seconds. He repeated one of them.

"Mink?" he said. "Mink?" He thought rapidly *Oh hell, not this* thinking rapidly *Nineteen . . . eight. Twenty years then twenty more on top of that. He will be out in two more years anyway. We had forgotten that. Or had we.* He didn't need to write *Tell me* either; she was already doing that; except for the silence he could, would have asked her what in the world, what stroke of coincidence (he had not yet begun to think chance, fate, destiny) had caused her to think of the man whom she had never seen and whose name she could have heard only in connection with a cowardly and savage murder. But that didn't matter now: which was the instant when he began to think destiny and fate.

With the houseman to do the listening, she had taken her father's car yesterday and driven out to Frenchman's Bend and talked with her mother's brother Jody; she stood now facing him beside the mantel on which the empty pad lay, telling him: "He had just twenty years at first, which would have been nineteen twenty-eight; he would have got out then. Only in nineteen twenty-three he tried to escape. In a woman's what Uncle Jody called mother hubbard and a sunbonnet. How did he get hold of a mother hubbard and a sunbonnet in the penitentiary."

Except for the silence he could have used gentleness. But all he had now was the yellow pad. Because he knew the answer himself now, writing *What did Jody tell you*

"That it was my . . . other cousin, Montgomery Ward, that had the dirty magic-lantern slides until they sent him to Parchman too, in nineteen twenty-three too, you remember?" Oh yes, he remembered: how he and the then sheriff, old Hub Hampton, dead now, both knew that it was Flem Snopes himself who planted the moonshine liquor in his kinsman's studio and got him sentenced to two years in Parchman, yet how it was Flem himself who not only had two private interviews with Montgomery Ward while he lay in jail waiting trial, but put up the money for his bond and surety which permitted Montgomery Ward a two-day absence from the jail and Jefferson too before returning to accept his sentence and be taken to Parchman to serve it, after which Jefferson saw him no more nor heard of him until eight or ten years ago the town learned that Montgomery Ward was now in Los Angeles, engaged in some quite lucrative adjunct or correlative to the motion-picture industry or anyway colony. *So that's why Montgomery Ward had to go to Parchman and nowhere else* he thought *instead of merely Atlanta or Leavenworth where only the dirty post cards would have sent him.* Oh yes, he remembered that one, and the earlier one too: in the courtroom also with the little child-sized gaunt underfed maniacal murderer, when the Court itself leaned down to give him his constitutional right to elect his plea, saying, "Dont bother me now; cant you see I'm busy?" then turning to shout again into the packed room: "Flem! Flem Snopes! Wont anybody here get word to Flem Snopes—" Oh yes, he, Stevens, knew now why Montgomery Ward had had to go to Parchman: Flem Snopes had bought twenty more years of life with that five gallons of planted evidence.

He wrote *You want me to get him out now*

"Yes," she said. "How do you do it?"

He wrote *He will be out in 2 more years why not wait till then* He wrote *He has known nothing else but that cage for 38 years He wont live a month free like an old lion or tiger At least give him 2 more years*

"Two years of life are not important," she said. "Two years of jail are."

He had even moved the pencil again when he stopped and spoke aloud instead; later he told Ratliff why. "I know why," Ratliff said. "You jest wanted to keep your own skirts clean. Maybe by this time she had done learned to read your lips and even if she couldn't you would at least been on your own record anyhow." "No," Stevens said. "It was because I not only believe in and am an advocate of fate and destiny, I admire them; I want to be one of the instruments too, no matter how modest." So he didn't write: he spoke:

"Dont you know what he's going to do the minute he gets back to Jefferson or anywhere else your father is?"

"Say it slow and let me try again," she said.

He wrote *I love you* thinking rapidly *If I say No she will find somebody else, anybody else, maybe some jackleg who will bleed her to get him out then continue to bleed her for what the little rattlesnake is going to do the moment he is free,* and wrote *Yes we can get him out it will take a few weeks a petition I will draw them up for you his blood kin the judge sheriff at the time Judge Long and old Hub Hampton are dead but Little Hub will do even if he wont be sheriff again until next election I will take them to the Governor myself*

Ratliff too he thought. Tomorrow the petition lay on his desk, Ratliff standing over it pen in hand. "Go on," Stevens said. "Sign it. I'm going to take care of that too. What do you think I am—a murderer?"

"Not yet anyway," Ratliff said. "How take care of it?"

"Mrs Kohl is going to," Stevens said.

"I thought you told me you never mentioned out loud where she could hear it what Mink would do as soon as he got back inside the same town limits with Flem," Ratliff said.

"I didn't need to," Stevens said. "Linda and I both agreed that there was no need for him to come back here. After forty years, with his wife dead and his daughters scattered God knows where; that in fact he would be better off if he didn't. So she's putting up the money. She wanted to make it a thousand but I told her that much in a lump would destroy him sure. So I'm going to leave two-fifty with the Warden, to be handed to him the minute before they unlock the gate to let him through it, with the understanding that the moment he accepts the money, he has given his oath to cross the Mississippi state line before sundown, and that another two-fifty will be sent every three months to whatever address he selects, provided he never again crosses the Mississippi line as long as he lives."

"I see," Ratliff said. "He cant tech the money a-tall except on the condition that he dont never lay eyes on Flem Snopes again as long as he lives."

"That's right," Stevens said.

"Suppose jest money aint enough," Ratliff said. "Suppose he wont take jest two hundred and fifty dollars for Flem Snopes."

"Remember," Stevens said. "He's going to face having to measure thirty-eight years he has got rid of, put behind him, against two more years he has still got to spend inside a cage to get rid of. He's selling Flem Snopes for these next two years, with a thousand dollars a year bonus thrown in free for the rest of his life. Sign it."

"Dont rush me," Ratliff said. "Destiny and fate. They was what you told me about being proud to be a handmaid of, wasn't they?"

"So what?" Stevens said. "Sign it."

"Dont you reckon you ought to maybe included a little luck into them too?"

"Sign it," Stevens said.

"Have you told Flem yet?"

"He hasn't asked me yet," Stevens said.

"When he does ask you?" Ratliff said.

"Sign it," Stevens said.

"I already did," Ratliff said. He laid the pen back on the desk. "You're right. We never had no alternative not to. If you'd a said No, she would jest got another lawyer that wouldn't a said No nor even invented that two-hundred-and-fifty-dollar gamble neither. And then Flem Snopes wouldn't a had no chance a-tall."

None of the other requisite documents presented any difficulty either. The judge who had presided at the trial was dead of course, as was the incumbent sheriff, old Hub Hampton. But his son, known as Little Hub, had inherited not only his father's four-year alternation as sheriff, but also his father's capacity to stay on the best of political terms with his alternating opposite number, Ephriam Bishop. So Stevens had those two names; also the foreman of the grand jury at the time was a hale (hence still quick) eighty-five, even running a small electric-driven corn mill while he wasn't hunting and fishing with Uncle Ike McCaslin, another octogenarian: plus a few other select signatures which Stevens compelled onto his petition as simply and ruthlessly as he did Ratliff's. Though what he considered his strongest card was a Harvard classmate, an amateur in state politics who had never held any office, who for years had been a sort of friend-of-the-court adviser to governors simply because all the state factions knew he was not only a loyal Mississippian but one already too wealthy to want anything.

So Stevens would have—indeed, intended to have—nothing but

progress to report to his client after he sent the documents in to the state capital and the rest of the summer passed toward and into fall— September, when Mississippi (including governors and legislatures and pardon boards) would put their neckties and coats back on and assume work again. Indeed, he felt he could almost select the specific day and hour he preferred to have the prisoner freed, choosing late September and explaining why to his client on the pad of yellow office foolscap, specious, voluble, convincing since he himself was convinced. September, the mounting apex of the cotton-picking season when there would be not only work, familiar work, but work which of all the freed man had the strongest emotional ties with, which after thirty-eight years of being compelled to it by loaded shotguns, he would now be paid by the hundredweight for performing it. This, weighed against being freed at once, back in June, with half a summer of idleness plus the gravitational pull back to where he was born; not explaining to Linda his reasons why the little child-size creature who must have been mad to begin with and whom thirty-eight years in a penitentiary could not have improved any, must not come back to Jefferson; hiding that too behind the rational garrulity of the pencil flying along the ruled lines—until suddenly he would look up (she of course had heard nothing) and Ratliff would be standing just inside the office door looking at them, courteous, bland, inscrutable, and only a little grave and thoughtful too now. So little in fact that Linda anyway never noticed it, at least not before Stevens, touching, jostling her arm or elbow as he rose (though this was never necessary; she had felt the new presence by now), saying, "Howdy, V.K. Come in. Is it that time already?"

"Looks like it," Ratliff would say. "Mawnin, Linda."

"Howdy, V.K.," she would answer in her deaf voice but almost exactly with Stevens's inflection: who could not have heard him greet Ratliff since, and even he could not remember when she could have heard him before. Then Stevens would produce the gold lighter monogrammed G L S though L was not his initial, and light her cigarette, then at the cabinet above the wash basin he and Ratliff would assemble the three thick tumblers and the sugar basin and the single spoon and a sliced lemon and Ratliff would produce from his clothing somewhere the flask of corn whiskey a little of which old Mr

Calvin Bookwright still made and aged each year and shared now and then with the few people tactful enough to retain his precarious irascible friendship. Then, Linda with her cigarette and Stevens with his cob pipe, the three of them would sit and sip the toddies, Stevens still talking and scribbling now and then on the pad for her to answer, until she would set down her empty glass and rise and say good-bye and leave them. Then Ratliff said:

"So you aint told Flem yet." Stevens smoked. "But then of course you dont need to, being as it's pretty well over the county now that Mink Snopes's cousin Linda or niece Linda or whichever it is, is getting him out." Stevens smoked. Ratliff picked up one of the toddy glasses. "You want another one?"

"No much obliged," Stevens said.

"So you aint lost your voice," Ratliff said. "Except, maybe back there in that vault in the bank where he would have to be counting his money, he cant hear what's going on. Except maybe that one trip he would have to make outside." Stevens smoked. "To go across to the sheriff's office." Stevens smoked. "You right sho you dont want another toddy?"

"All right," Stevens said. "Why?"

"That's what I'm asking you. You'd a thought the first thing Flem would a done would been to go to the sheriff and remind him of them final words of Mink's before Judge Long invited him to Parchman. Only he aint done that. Maybe because at least Linda told him about them two hundred and fifty dollars and even Flem Snopes can grab a straw when there aint nothing else in sight? Because naturally Flem cant walk right up to her and write on that tablet, The minute you let that durn little water moccasin out he's going to come straight back here and pay you up to date for your maw's grave and all the rest of it that these Jefferson meddlers have probably already persuaded you I was to blame for; naturally he dont dare risk putting no such idea as that in her head and have her grab a-holt of you and go to Parchman and take him out tonight and have him back in Jefferson by breakfast tomorrow, when as it is he's still got three more weeks, during which anything might happen: Linda or Mink or the Governor or the pardon board might die or Parchman itself might blow up. When did you say it would be?"

"When what will be?" Stevens said.

"The day they will let him out."

"Oh. Some time after the twentieth. Probably the twenty-sixth."

"The twenty-sixth," Ratliff said. "And you're going down there before?"

"Next week," Stevens said. "To leave the money and talk with the Warden myself. That he is not to touch the money until he promises to leave Mississippi before sundown and never come back."

"In that case," Ratliff said, "everything's all right. Especially if I—" He stopped.

"If you what?" Stevens said.

"Nothing," Ratliff said. "Fate, and destiny, and luck, and hope, and all of us mixed up in it—us and Linda and Flem and that durn little half-starved wildcat down there in Parchman, all mixed up in the same luck and destiny and fate and hope until cant none of us tell where it stops and we begin. Especially the hope. I mind I used to think that hope was about all folks had, only now I'm beginning to believe that that's about all anybody needs—jest hope. The pore son of a bitch over yonder in that bank vault counting his money because that's the one place on earth Mink Snopes cant reach him in, and long as he's got to stay in it he might as well count money to be doing something, have something to do. And I wonder if maybe he wouldn't give Linda back her two hundred and fifty dollars without even charging her no interest on it, for them two years of pardon. And I wonder jest how much of the rest of the money in that vault he would pay to have another twenty years added onto them. Or maybe jest ten more. Or maybe jest one more."

Ten days later Stevens was in the Warden's office at the state penitentiary. He had the money with him—twenty-five ten-dollar notes, quite new. "You dont want to see him yourself?" the Warden said.

"No," Stevens said. "You can do it. Anybody can. Simply offer him his choice: take the pardon and the two hundred and fifty dollars and get out of Mississippi as fast as he can, plus another two hundred and fifty every three months for the rest of his life if he never crosses the state line again; or stay here in Parchman another two years and rot and be damned to him."

"Well, that ought to do it," the Warden said. "It certainly would with me. Why is it whoever owns the two hundred and fifty dollars dont want him to come back home so bad?"

Stevens said rapidly, "Nothing to come back to. Family gone and scattered, wife died twenty-five or thirty years ago and nobody knows what became of his two daughters. Even the tenant house he lived in either collapsed of itself or maybe somebody found it and chopped it up and hauled it away for firewood."

"That's funny," the Warden said. "Almost anybody in Mississippi has got at least one cousin. In fact, it's hard not to have one."

"Oh, distant connections, relations," Stevens said. "Yes, it seems to have been the usual big scattered country clan."

"So one of these big scattered connections dont want him back home enough to pay two hundred and fifty dollars for it."

"He's mad," Stevens said. "Somebody here during the last thirty-eight years must have had that idea occur to them and suggested it to you even if you hadn't noticed it yourself."

"We're all mad here," the Warden said. "Even the prisoners too. Maybe it's the climate. I wouldn't worry, if I were you. They all make these threats at the time—big threats, against the judge or the prosecuting lawyer or a witness that stood right up in public and told something that any decent man would have kept to himself; big threats: I notice there's no place on earth where a man can be as loud and dangerous as handcuffed to a policeman. But even one year is a long time sometimes. And he's had thirty-eight of them. So he dont get the pardon until he agrees to accept the money. Why do you know he wont take the money and double-cross you?"

"I've noticed a few things about people too," Stevens said. "One of them is, how a bad man will work ten times as hard and make ten times the sacrifice to be credited with at least one virtue no matter how Spartan, as the upright man will to avoid the most abject vice provided it's fun. He tried to kill his lawyer right there in the jail during the trial when the lawyer suggested pleading him crazy. He will know that the only sane thing to do is to accept the money and the pardon, since to refuse the pardon because of the money, in two more years he not only wouldn't have the two thousand dollars, he might even be dead. Or, what would be infinitely worse, he would be alive and free at last and poor, and Fle—" and stopped himself.

"Yes?" the Warden said. "Who is Fleh, that might be dead himself in two more years and so out of reach for good? The one that owns the two hundred and fifty dollars? Never mind," he said. "I'll agree with you. Once he accepts the money, everything is jake, as they say. That's what you want?"

"That's right," Stevens said. "If there should be any sort of hitch, you can call me at Jefferson collect."

"I'll call you anyway," the Warden said. "You're trying too hard not to sound serious."

"No," Stevens said. "Only if he refuses the money."

"You mean the pardon, dont you?"

"What's the difference?" Stevens said.

So when about midafternoon on the twenty-sixth he answered his telephone and Central said, "Parchman, Mississippi, calling Mr Gavin Stevens. Go ahead, Parchman," and the faint voice said, "Hello. Lawyer?" Stevens thought rapidly *So I am a coward, after all. When it happens two years from now, at least none of it will spatter on me. At least I can tell her now because this will prove it* and said into the mouthpiece:

"So he refused to take the money."

"Then you already know," Ratliff's voice said.

". . . What?" Stevens said after less than a second actually. "Hello?"

"It's me," Ratliff said. "V.K. At Parchman. So they already telephoned you."

"Telephoned me what?" Stevens said. "He's still there? He refused to leave?"

"No, he's gone. He left about eight this morning. A truck going north—"

"But you just said he didn't take the money."

"That's what I'm trying to tell you. We finally located the money about fifteen minutes ago. It's still here. He—"

"Hold it," Stevens said. "You said eight this morning. Which direction?"

"A Negro seen him standing by the highway until he caught a ride on a cattle truck going north, toward Tutwiler. At Tutwiler he could have went to Clarksdale and then on to Memphis. Or he could have went from Tutwiler to Batesville and on to Memphis that-a-way. Except that anybody wanting to go from Parchman to Jefferson could go by Batesville too lessen he jest wanted to go by way of Chicago or New Orleans for the trip. Otherwise he could be in Jefferson pretty close to now. I'm leaving right now myself but maybe you better—"

"All right," Stevens said.

"And maybe Flem too," Ratliff said.

"Damn it, I said all right," Stevens said.

"But not her yet," Ratliff said. "Aint no need to tell her yet that likely she's jest finished killing her maw's husband—"

But he didn't even hear that, the telephone was already down; he didn't even have his hat when he reached the Square, the street below, the bank where Snopes would be in one direction, the court-house where the Sheriff would be in the other: not that it really mattered which one he saw first, thinking *So I really am a coward after all the talk about destiny and fate that didn't even sell Ratliff.*

"You mean," the Sheriff said, "he had already spent thirty-eight years in Parchman, and the minute somebody gets him out he's going to try to do something that will send him straight back even if it dont hang him first this time? Dont be foolish. Even a fellow like they say he was would learn that much sense in thirty-eight years."

"Ha," Stevens said without mirth. "You expressed it exactly that time. You were probably not even a shirttail boy back in 1908. You were not in that courtroom that day and saw his face and heard him. I was."

"All right," the Sheriff said. "What do you want me to do?"

"Arrest him. What do you call them? roadblocks? Dont even let him get into Yoknapatawpha County."

"On what grounds?"

"You just catch him, I'll furnish you with grounds as fast as you need them. If necessary we will hold him for obtaining money under false pretenses."

"I thought he didn't take the money."

"I dont know what happened yet about the money. But I'll figure out some way to use it, at least long enough to hold him on for a while."

"Yes," the Sheriff said. "I reckon you would. Let's step over to the bank and see Mr Snopes; maybe all three of us can figure out something. Or maybe Mrs Kohl. You'll have to tell her too, I reckon."

Whereupon Stevens repeated almost verbatim what Ratliff had said into the telephone after he had put it down: "Tell a woman that apparently she just finished murdering her father at eight oclock this morning?"

"All right, all right," the Sheriff said. "You want me to come to the bank with you?"

"No," Stevens said. "Not yet anyway."

"I still think you have found a booger where there wasn't one," the Sheriff said. "If he comes back here at all, it'll just be out at Frenchman's Bend. Then all we'll have to do is pick him up the first time we notice him in town and have a talk with him."

"Notice, hell," Stevens said. "Aint that what I'm trying to tell you? that you dont notice him. That was the mistake Jack Houston made thirty-eight years ago: he didn't notice him either until he stepped out from behind that bush that morning with that shotgun—if he even stepped out of the bushes before he shot, which I doubt."

He recrossed the Square rapidly, thinking *Yes, I really am a coward, after all* when that quantity, entity with which he had spent a great deal of his life talking or rather having to listen to (his skeleton perhaps, which would outlast the rest of him by a few months or years—and without doubt would spend that time moralising at him while he would be helpless to answer back) answered immediately *Did anyone ever say you were not?* Then he *But I am not a coward: I am a humanitarian.* Then the other *You are not even an original; that word is customarily used as a euphemism for it.*

The bank would be closed now. But when he crossed the Square to the sheriff's office the car with Linda behind the wheel had not been waiting so this was not the day of the weekly whiskey run. The shades were drawn but after some knob-rattling at the side door one of the bookkeepers peered out and recognised him and let him in; he passed on through the machine-clatter of the day's recapitulation—the machines themselves sounding immune and even inattentive to the astronomical sums they reduced to staccato trivia—and knocked at the door on which Colonel Sartoris had had the word PRIVATE lettered by hand forty years ago, and opened it. Snopes was sitting not at the desk but with his back to it, facing the cold now empty fireplace, his feet raised and crossed against the same heel scratches whose initial inscribing Colonel Sartoris had begun. He was not reading, he was not doing anything: just sitting there with his black planter's hat on, his lower jaw moving faintly and steadily as though he were chewing something, which as the town knew also he was not; he didn't even lower his feet when Stevens came to the desk (it was a broad flat table littered with papers in a sort of neat, almost orderly way) and said almost in one breath:

"Mink left Parchman at eight oclock this morning. I dont know whether you know it or not but we—I had some money waiting to be given to him at the gate, under condition that in accepting it he had passed his oath to leave Mississippi without returning to Jefferson and never cross the state line again. He didn't take the money; I dont know yet how since he was not to be given the pardon until he did. He caught a ride in a passing truck and has disappeared. The truck was headed north."

"How much was it?" Snopes said.

"What?" Stevens said.

"The money," Snopes said.

"Two hundred and fifty dollars," Stevens said.

"Much obliged," Snopes said.

"Good God, man," Stevens said. "I tell you a man left Parchman at eight oclock this morning on his way here to murder you and all you say is Much obliged?"

The other didn't move save for the faint chewing motion; Stevens thought with a kind of composed and seething rage *If he would only spit now and then.* "Then all he had was that ten dollars they give them when they turn them loose," Snopes said.

"Yes," Stevens said. "As far as we—I know. But yes." *Or even just go through the motions of spitting now and then* he thought.

"Say a man thought he had a grudge against you," Snopes said. "A man sixty-three years old now with thirty-eight of that spent in the penitentiary and even before that wasn't much, not much bigger than a twelve-year-old boy—"

That had to use a shotgun from behind a bush even then Stevens thought. *Oh yes, I know exactly what you mean: too small and frail even then, even without thirty-eight years in jail, to have risked a mere knife or bludgeon. And he cant go out to Frenchman's Bend, the only place on earth where someone might remember him enough to lend him one because even though nobody in Frenchman's Bend would knock up the muzzle aimed at you, they wouldn't lend him theirs to aim with. So he will either have to buy a gun for ten dollars, or steal one. In which case, you might even be safe: the ten-dollar one wont shoot and in the other some policeman might save you honestly.* He thought rapidly *Of course. North. He went to Memphis. He would have to. He wouldn't think of anywhere else to go to buy a gun with ten dollars.* And, since Mink had only the ten dollars, he would have to hitchhike all the way, first to Memphis, provided he got there before the pawnshops closed, then back to Jefferson. Which could not be before tomorrow, since anything else would leave simple destiny and fate too topheavy with outrageous hope and coincidence for even Ratliff's sanguine nature to pass. "Yes," he said. "So do I. You have at least until tomorrow night." He thought rapidly *And now for it. How to persuade him not to tell her without letting him know that was what he agreed to, promised, and that it was me who put it into his mind.* So suddenly he heard himself say: "Are you going to tell Linda?"

"Why?" Snopes said.

"Yes," Stevens said. Then heard himself say in his turn: "Much obliged." Then, suddenly indeed this time: "I'm responsible for this, even if I probably couldn't have stopped it. I just talked to Eef Bishop. What else do you want me to do?" *If he would just spit once* he thought.

"Nothing," Snopes said.

"What?" Stevens said.

"Yes," Snopes said. "Much obliged."

At least he knew where to start. Only, he didn't know how. Even if—when—he called the Memphis police, what would—could—he tell them: a city police force a hundred miles away, who had never heard of Mink and Flem Snopes and Jack Houston, dead these forty years now, either. When he, Stevens, had already failed to move very much the local sheriff who at least had inherited the old facts. How to explain what he himself was convinced Mink wanted in Memphis, let alone convince them that Mink was or would be in Memphis. And even if he managed to shake them that much, how to describe whom they were supposed to look for: whose victim forty years ago had got himself murdered mainly for the reason that the murderer was the sort of creature whom nobody, even his victim, noticed enough in time to pay any attention to what he was or might do.

Except Ratliff. Ratliff alone out of Yoknapatawpha County would know Mink on sight. To be unschooled, untravelled, and to an extent unread, Ratliff had a terrifying capacity for knowledge or local information or acquaintanceship to match the need of any local crisis. Stevens admitted to himself now what he was waiting, dallying, really wasting time for: for Ratliff to drive back in his pickup truck from Parchman, to be hurried on to Memphis without even stopping, cutting the engine, to reveal Mink to the Memphis police and so save Mink's cousin, kinsman, whatever Flem was, from that just fate; knowing—Stevens—better all the while: that what he really wanted with Ratliff was to find out how Mink had not only got past the Parchman gate without that absolutely contingent money, but had managed it in such a way that apparently only the absolutely unpredicted and unwarranted presence of Ratliff at a place and time that he had no business whatever being, revealed the fact that he hadn't taken it.

It was not three oclock when Ratliff phoned; it would be almost nine before he reached Jefferson. It was not that the pickup truck wouldn't have covered the distance faster. It was that no vehicle owned by Ratliff (provided he was in it and conscious, let alone driving it) was going to cover it faster. Besides, at some moment not too long after six oclock he was going to stop to eat at the next dreary repetitive little cotton-gin hamlet, or (nowadays) on the highway itself, drawing neatly in and neatly parking before the repetitive Dixie Cafés or Mac's or Lorraine's, to eat, solitary, neatly and without haste the meat a little too stringy to chew properly and too overcooked to taste at all, the stereotyped fried potatoes and the bread you didn't chew but mumbled, like one of the paper napkins, the machine-chopped prefrozen lettuce and tomatoes like (except for the tense inviolate color) something exhumed by paleontologists from tundras, the machine-made prefrozen pie and what they would call coffee—the food perfectly pure and perfectly tasteless except for the dousing of machine-made tomato ketchup.

He (Stevens) could, perhaps should, have had plenty of time to drive out to Rose Hill and eat his own decent evening meal. Instead, he telephoned his wife.

"I'll come in and we can eat at the Holston House," she said.

"No, honey. I've got to see Ratliff as soon as he gets back from Parchman."

"All right. I think I'll come in and have supper with Maggie" (Maggie was his sister) "and maybe we'll go to the picture show and I'll see you tomorrow. I can come in to town, cant I, if I promise to stay off the streets?"

"You see, you dont help me. How can I resist togetherness if you wont fight back?"

"I'll see you tomorrow then," she said. "Good night." So they ate at the Holston House; he didn't feel quite up to his sister and brother-in-law and his nephew Charles tonight. The Holston House still clung to the old ways, not desperately nor even gallantly: just with a cold and inflexible indomitability, owned and run by two maiden sisters (that is, one of them, the younger, had been married once but so long ago and so briefly that it no longer counted) who were the last descendants of the Alexander Holston, one of Yoknapatawpha County's three original settlers, who had built the log ordinary which the modern edifice had long since swallowed, who had had his part—been in fact the catalyst—in the naming of Jefferson over a century ago; they still called the dining room simply the dining room and (nobody knew how) they still kept Negro men waiters, some of whose seniority still passed from father to son; the guests still ate the table d'hôte meals mainly at two long communal tables at the head of each of which a sister presided; no man came there without a coat and necktie and no woman with her head covered (there was a dressing room with a maid for that purpose), not even if she had a railroad ticket in her hand.

Though his sister did pick his wife up in time for the picture show. So he was back in the office when a little after eight-thirty he heard

Ratliff on the stairs and said, "All right. What happened?" Then he said, "No. Wait. What were you doing at Parchman?"

"I'm a—what do you call it? optimist," Ratliff said. "Like any good optimist, I dont expect the worst to happen. Only, like any optimist worth his salt, I like to go and look as soon as possible afterward jest in case it did. Especially when the difference between the best and the worst is liable to reach all the way back up here to Jefferson. It taken a little doing, too. This was about ten oclock this morning; he had been gone a good two hours by then, and they was a little impatient with me. They had done done their share, took him and had him for thirty-eight years all fair and regular, like the man said for them to, and they felt they had done earned the right to be shut of him. You know: his new fresh pardon and them new fresh two hundred and fifty dollars all buttoned up neat and safe and secure in his new fresh overhalls and jumper and the gate locked behind him again jest like the man said too and the official Mink Snopes page removed outen the ledger and officially marked Paid in Full and destroyed a good solid two hours back, when here comes this here meddling out-of-town son-of-a-gun that aint even a lawyer saying Yes yes, that's jest fine, only let's make sho he actively had that money when he left.

"The Warden his-self had tended to the money in person: had Mink in alone, with the table all ready for him, the pardon in one pile and them two hundred and fifty dollars that Mink hadn't never seen that much at one time before in his life, in the other pile; and the Warden his-self explaining how there wasn't no choice about it: to take the pardon he would have to take the money too, and once he teched the money he had done give his sworn word and promise and Bible oath to strike for the quickest place outside the state of Mississippi and never cross the line again as long as he lived. 'Is that what I got to do to get out?' Mink says. 'Take the money?' 'That's it,' the Warden says, and Mink reached and taken the money and the Warden his-self helped him button the money and the pardon both inside his jumper and the Warden shaken his hand and the trusty come to take him out to where the turnkey was waiting to unlock the gate into liberty and freedom—"

"Wait," Stevens said. "Trusty."

"Aint it?" Ratliff said with pleased, almost proud approval. "It was so simple. Likely that's why it never occurred to none of them, especially as even a Parchman deserving any name a-tall for being well conducted, aint supposed to contain nobody eccentric and antisocial enough to behave like he considered anything like free-will choice to even belong in the same breath with two hundred and fifty active dollars give him free for nothing so he never even had to say Much obliged for them. That's what I said too: 'That trusty. He left here for the gate with them two hundred and fifty dollars. Let's jest see if he still had them when he went outen it.' So that's what I said too: 'That trusty.'

" 'A lifer too,' the Warden says. 'Killed his wife with a ball-peen hammer, was converted and received salvation in the jail before he was even tried and has one of the best records here, is even a lay preacher.'

" 'Than which, if Mink had had your whole guest list to pick from and time to pick in, he couldn't a found a better feller for his purpose,' I says. 'So it looks like I'm already fixing to begin to have to feel sorry for this here snatched brand even if he was too impatient to think of a better answer to the enigma of wedlock than a garage hammer. That is, I reckon you still got a few private interrogation methods for reluctant conversationalists around here, aint you?'

"That's why I was late calling you: it taken a little time too, though I got to admit nothing showed on his outside. Because people are funny. No, they aint funny: they're jest sad. Here was this feller already in for life and even if they had found out that was a mistake or somebody even left the gate unlocked, he wouldn't a dast to walk outen it because the gal's paw had done already swore he would kill him the first time he crossed the Parchman fence. So what in the world could he a done with two hundred and fifty dollars even if he could ever a dreamed he could get away with this method of getting holt of it."

"But how, dammit?" Stevens said. "How?"

"Why, the only way Mink could a done it, which was likely why never nobody thought to anticipate it. On the way from the Warden's office to the gate he jest told the trusty he needed to step into the gentlemen's room a minute and when they was inside he give the trusty the two hundred and fifty dollars and asked the trusty to hand it back to the Warden the first time the trusty conveniently got around to it, the longer the better after he, Mink, was outside the gate and outen sight, and tell the Warden Much obliged but he had done changed his mind and wouldn't need it. So there the trusty was: give Mink another hour or two and he would be gone, likely forever, nobody would know where or care. Because I dont care where you are: the minute a man can really believe that never again in his life will he have any use for two hundred and fifty dollars, he's done already been dead and has jest this minute found it out. And that's all. I dont—"

"I do," Stevens said. "Flem told me. He's in Memphis. He's too little and frail and old to use a knife or a club so he will have to go to the nearest place he can hope to get a gun with ten dollars."

"So you told Flem. What did he say?"

"He said, Much obliged," Stevens said. After a moment he said, "I said, when I told Flem Mink had left Parchman at eight oclock this morning on his way up here to kill him, he said Much obliged."

"I heard you," Ratliff said. "What would you a said? You would sholy be as polite as Flem Snopes, wouldn't you? So maybe it's all right, after all. Of course you done already talked to Memphis."

"Tell them what?" Stevens said. "How describe to a Memphis policeman somebody I wouldn't recognise myself, let alone that he's actually in Memphis trying to do what I assume he is trying to do, for the simple reason that I dont know what to do next either?"

"What's wrong with Memphis?" Ratliff said.

"I'll bite," Stevens said. "What is?"

"I thought it would took a heap littler place than Memphis not to have nobody in it you used to go to Harvard with."

"Well I'll be damned," Stevens said. He put in the call at once and presently was talking with him: the classmate, the amateur Cincinnatus at his plantation not far from Jackson, who had already been instrumental in getting the pardon through, so that Stevens needed merely explain the crisis, not the situation.

"You dont actually know he went to Memphis, of course," the friend said.

"That's right," Stevens said. "But since we are forced by emergency to challenge where he might be, at least we should be permitted one assumption in good faith."

"All right," the friend said. "I know the mayor and the commissioner of police both. All you want—all they can do really—is check any places where anyone might have tried to buy a gun or pistol for ten dollars since say noon today. Right?"

"Right," Stevens said. "And ask them please to call me collect here when—if they do."

"I'll call you myself," the friend said. "You might say I also have a small equity in your friend's doom."

"When you call me that to Flem Snopes, smile," Stevens said.

That was Thursday; during Friday Central would run him to earth all right no matter where he happened to be about the Square. However, there was plenty to do in the office if he composed himself to it. Which he managed to do in time and was so engaged when Ratliff came in carrying something neatly folded in a paper bag and said, "Good mawnin," Stevens not looking up, writing on the yellow foolscap pad, steadily, quite composed in fact even with Ratliff standing for a moment looking down at the top of his head. Then Ratliff moved and took one of the chairs beyond the desk, the one against the wall, then half rose and placed the little parcel neatly on the filing case beside him and sat down, Stevens still writing steadily between pauses now and then to read from the open book beneath his left hand; until presently Ratliff reached and took the morning Memphis paper from the desk and opened it and rattled faintly the turn of the page and after a while rattled that one faintly, until Stevens said,

"Dammit, either get out of here or think about something else. You make me nervous."

"I aint busy this mawnin," Ratliff said. "If you got anything to tend to outside, I can set here and listen for the phone."

"I have plenty I can do here if you'll just stop filling the damned air with—" He flung, slammed the pencil down. "Obviously he hasn't reached Memphis yet or anyway hasn't tried to buy the gun, or we would have heard. Which is all we want: to get the word there first. Do you think that any reputable pawnshop or sporting-goods store that cares a damn about its license will sell him a gun now after the police—"

"If my name was Mink Snopes, I dont believe I would go to no place that had a license to lose for selling guns or pistols."

"For instance?" Stevens said.

"Out at Frenchman's Bend they said Mink was a considerable hell-raiser when he was young, within his means of course, which wasn't much. But he made two or three of them country-boy Memphis trips with the young bloods of his time—Quicks and Tulls and Turpins and such: enough to probably know where to begin to look for the kind of places that dont keep the kind of licenses to have police worrying them ever time a gun or a pistol turns up in the wrong place or dont turn up in the right one."

"Dont you think the Memphis police know as much about Memphis as any damned little murdering maniac, let alone one that's been locked up in a penitentiary for forty years? The Memphis police, that have a damned better record than a dozen, hell, a hundred cities I could name—"

"All right, all right," Ratliff said.

"By God, God Himself is not so busy that a homicidal maniac with only ten dollars in the world can hitchhike a hundred miles and buy a gun for ten dollars then hitchhike another hundred and shoot another man with it."

"Dont that maybe depend on who God wants shot this time?" Ratliff said. "Have you been by the sheriff's this mawnin?"

"No," Stevens said.

"I have. Flem aint been to him either yet. And he aint left town neither. I checked on that too. So maybe that's the best sign we want: Flem aint worried. Do you reckon he told Linda?"

"No," Stevens said.

"How do you know?"

"He told me."

"Flem did? You mean he jest told you, or you asked him?"

"I asked him," Stevens said. "I said, 'Are you going to tell Linda?' "

"And what did he say?"

"He said, 'Why?' " Stevens said.

"Oh," Ratliff said.

Then it was noon. What Ratliff had in the neat parcel was a sand-

wich, as neatly made. "You go home and eat dinner," he said. "I'll
set here and listen for it."

"Didn't you just say that if Flem himself dont seem to worry, why
the hell should we?"

"I wont worry then," Ratliff said. "I'll jest set and listen."

Though Stevens was back in the office when the call came in
midafternoon. "Nothing," the classmate's voice said. "None of the
pawnshops nor any other place a man might go to buy a gun or pistol of any sort, let alone a ten-dollar one. Maybe he hasn't reached
Memphis yet, though it's more than twenty-four hours now."

"That's possible," Stevens said.

"Maybe he never intended to reach Memphis."

"All right, all right," Stevens said. "Shall I write the commissioner
myself a letter of thanks or—"

"Sure. But let him earn it first. He agreed that it not only wont
cost much more, it will even be a good idea to check his list every
morning for the next two or three days, just in case. I thanked him
for you. I even went further and said that if you ever found yourselves
in the same voting district and he decided to run for an office instead
of just sitting for it—" as Stevens put the telephone down and turned
to Ratliff again without seeing him at all and said,

"Maybe he never will."

"What?" Ratliff said. "What did he say?" Stevens told, repeated,
the gist. "I reckon that's all we can do," Ratliff said.

"Yes," Stevens said. He thought *Tomorrow will prove it. But I'll wait
still another day. Maybe until Monday.*

But he didn't wait that long. On Saturday his office was always,
not busy with the county business he was paid a salary to handle, so
much as constant with the social coming and going of the country-
men who had elected him to his office. Ratliff, who knew them all
too, as well or even better, was unobtrusive in his chair against the
wall where he could reach the telephone without even getting up;
he even had another neat homemade sandwich, until at noon Stevens
said,

"Go on home and eat a decent meal, or come home with me. It
wont ring today."

"You must know why," Ratliff said.

"Yes. I'll tell you Monday. No: tomorrow. Sunday will be appropriate. I'll tell you tomorrow."

"So you know it's all right now. All settled and finished now. Whether Flem knows it yet or not, he can sleep from now on."

"Dont ask me yet," Stevens said. "It's like a thread; it's true only until I—something breaks it."

"You was right all the time then. There wasn't no need to tell her."

"There never has been," Stevens said. "There never will be."

"That's jest what I said," Ratliff said. "There aint no need now."

"And what I just said was there never was any need to tell her and there never would have been, no matter what happened."

"Not even as a moral question?" Ratliff said.

"Moral hell and question hell," Stevens said. "It aint any question at all: it's a fact: the fact that not you nor anybody else that wears hair is going to tell her that her act of pity and compassion and simple generosity murdered the man who passes as her father whether he is or not or a son of a bitch or not."

"All right, all right," Ratliff said. "This here thread you jest mentioned. Maybe another good way to keep it from getting broke before time is to keep somebody handy to hear that telephone when it dont ring at three oclock this afternoon."

So they were both in the office at three oclock. Then it was four. "I reckon we can go now," Ratliff said.

"Yes," Stevens said.

"But you still wont tell me now," Ratliff said.

"Tomorrow," Stevens said. "The call will have to come by then."

"So this here thread has got a telephone wire inside of it after all."

"So long," Stevens said. "See you tomorrow."

And Central would know where to find him at any time on Sunday too and in fact until almost half past two that afternoon he still believed he was going to spend the whole day at Rose Hill. His life had known other similar periods of unrest and trouble and uncertainty even if he had spent most of it as a bachelor; he could recall one or two of them when the anguish and unrest were due to the fact that he was a bachelor, that is, circumstances, conditions insisted on his continuing celibacy despite his own efforts to give it up. But back then he had had something to escape into: nepenthe, surcease: the

project he had decreed for himself while at Harvard of translating the
Old Testament back into the classic Greek of its first translating;
after which he would teach himself Hebrew and really attain to
purity; he had thought last night *Why yes, I have that for tomorrow; I
had forgotten about that.* Then this morning he knew that that would
not suffice any more, not ever again now. He meant of course the
effort: not just the capacity to concentrate but to believe in it; he was
too old now and the real tragedy of age is that no anguish is any
longer grievous enough to demand, justify, any sacrifice.

So it was not even two-thirty when with no surprise really he
found himself getting into his car and still no surprise when, entering
the empty Sunday-afternoon Square, he saw Ratliff waiting at the
foot of the office stairs, the two of them, in the office now, making no
pretence as the clock crawled on to three. "What happened that we
set exactly three oclock as the magic deadline in this here business?"
Ratliff said.

"Does it matter?" Stevens said.

"That's right," Ratliff said. "The main thing is not to jar or otherwise startle that-ere thread." Then the courthouse clock struck its
three heavy mellow blows into the Sabbath somnolence and for the
first time Stevens realised how absolutely he had not just expected,
but known, that his telephone would not ring before that hour. Then
in that same second, instant, he knew why it had not rung; the fact
that it had not rung was more proof of what it would have conveyed
than the message itself would have been.

"All right," he said. "Mink is dead."

"What?" Ratliff said.

"I dont know where, and it doesn't matter. Because we should
have known from the first that three hours of being free would kill
him, let alone three days of it." He was talking rapidly, not babbling:
"Dont you see? a little kinless tieless frail alien animal that never
really belonged to the human race to start with, let alone belonged in
it, then locked up in a cage for thirty-eight years and now at sixty-
three years old suddenly set free, shoved, flung out of safety and
security into freedom like a krait or a fer-de-lance that is quick and
deadly dangerous as long as it can stay inside the man-made man-
tended tropic immunity of its glass box, but wouldn't live even

through the first hour set free, flung, hoicked on a pitchfork or a pair
of long-handled tongs into a city street?"

"Wait," Ratliff said, "wait."

But Stevens didn't even pause. "Of course we haven't heard yet
where he was found or how or by whom identified because nobody
cares; maybe nobody has even noticed him yet. Because he's free. He
can even die wherever he wants to now. For thirty-eight years until
last Thursday morning he couldn't have had a pimple or a hangnail
without it being in a record five minutes later. But he's free now.
Nobody cares when or where or how he dies provided his carrion
doesn't get under somebody's feet. So we can go home now, until
somebody does telephone and you and Flem can go and identify
him."

"Yes," Ratliff said. "Well—"

"Give it up," Stevens said. "Come on out home with me and have
a drink."

"We could go by first and kind of bring Flem up to date," Ratliff
said. "Maybe even he might take a dram then."

"I'm not really an evil man," Stevens said. "I wouldn't have loaned
Mink a gun to shoot Flem with; I might not even have just turned my
head while Mink used his own. But neither am I going to lift my
hand to interfere with Flem spending another day or two expecting
any moment that Mink will."

He didn't even tell the Sheriff his conviction that Mink was dead.
The fact was, the Sheriff told him; he found the Sheriff in his courthouse office and told him his and Ratliff's theory of Mink's first
objective and the reason for it and that the Memphis police would
still check daily the places where Mink might try to buy a weapon.

"So evidently he's not in Memphis," the Sheriff said. "That's how
many days now?"

"Since Thursday."

"And he's not in Frenchman's Bend."

"How do you know?"

"I drove out yesterday and looked around a little."

"So you did believe me, after all," Stevens said.

"I get per diem on my car," the Sheriff said. "Yesterday was a nice
day for a country drive. So he's had four days now, to come a hundred

miles. And he dont seem to be in Memphis. And I know he aint in
Frenchman's Bend. And according to you, Mr Snopes knows he aint
in Jefferson here. Maybe he's dead." Whereupon, now that another
had stated it, spoke it aloud, Stevens knew that he himself had never
believed it, hearing without listening while the Sheriff went on: "A
damned little rattlesnake that they say never had any friends to begin
with and nobody out at the Bend knows what became of his wife and
his two girls or even when they disappeared. To be locked up for
thirty-eight years and then suddenly turned out like you do a cat at
night, with nowhere to go and nobody really wanting him out.
Maybe he couldn't stand being free. Maybe just freedom killed him.
I've known it to happen."

"Yes," Stevens said, "you're probably right," thinking quietly *We
wont stop him. We cant stop him—not all of us together, Memphis police
and all. Maybe even a rattlesnake with destiny on his side dont even need
luck, let alone friends.* He said: "Only we dont know yet. We cant
count on that."

"I know," the Sheriff said. "I deputised two men at Varner's store
yesterday that claim they remember him, would know him again.
And I can have Mr Snopes followed, watched back and forth to the
bank. But dammit, watch for who, what, when, where? I cant put a
man inside his house until he asks for it, can I? His daughter. Mrs
Kohl. Maybe she could do something. You still dont want her to
know?"

"You must give me your word," Stevens said.

"All right," the Sheriff said. "I suppose your Jackson buddy will let
you know the minute the Memphis police get any sort of a line, wont
he?"

"Yes," Stevens said. Though the call didn't come until Wednesday.
Ratliff had rung him up a little after ten Tuesday night and told him
the news, and on his way to the office this morning he passed the
bank whose drawn shades would not be raised today, and as he stood
at his desk with the telephone in his hand he could see through his
front window the somber black-and-white-and-violet convolutions
of tulle and ribbon and waxen asphodels fastened to the locked front
door.

"He found a ten-dollar pistol," the classmate's voice said. "Early

Monday morning. It wasn't really a properly licensed pawnshop, so they almost missed it. But under a little . . . persuasion the proprietor recalled the sale. But he said not to worry, the pistol was only technically still a pistol and it would require a good deal more nourishment than the three rounds of ammunition they threw in with it to make it function."

"Ha," Stevens said without mirth. "Tell the proprietor from me he doesn't know his own strength. The pistol was here last night. It functioned."

SEVENTEEN

*W*hen he reached the Junction a little before eleven oclock Monday morning, he was in the cab of another cattle truck. The truck was going on east into Alabama but even if it had turned south here actually to pass through Jefferson, he would have left it at this point. If it had been a Yoknapatawpha County truck or driven by someone from the county or Jefferson, he would not have been in it at all.

Until he stepped out of the store this morning with the pistol actually in his pocket, it had all seemed simple; he had only one problem: to get the weapon; after that, only geography stood between him and the moment when he would walk up to the man who had seen him sent to the penitentiary without raising a finger, who had not even had the decency and courage to say No to his bloodcry for help from kin to kin, and say, "Look at me, Flem," and kill him.

But now he was going to have to do what he called "figger" a little. It seemed to him that he was confronted by an almost insurmountable diffusion of obstacles. He was in thirty miles of Jefferson now, home, one same mutual north Mississippi hill-country people even if there was still a trivial county line to cross; it seemed to him that from now on anyone, everyone he met or who saw him, without even needing to recognise or remember his specific face and name, would know at once who he was and where he was going and what he intended to do. On second thought—an immediate, flashing, almost simultaneous second thought—he knew this to be a physical impossibility, yet he dared not risk it; that the thirty-eight years of being locked up in Parchman had atrophied, destroyed some quality in him which in people who had not been locked up had very likely got even sharper, and they would recognise, know, divine who he was without his even knowing it had happened. *It's because I done had to been away so long* he thought. *Like now I'm fixing to have to learn to talk all over again.*

He meant not talk, but think. As he walked along the highway (blacktop now, following a graded survey line, on which automobiles sped, which he remembered as winding dirt along which slow mules and wagons, or at best a saddle horse, followed the arbitrary and random ridges) it would be impossible to disguise his appearance— change his face, his expression, alter his familiar regional clothes or the way he walked; he entertained for a desperate and bizarre moment then dismissed it the idea of perhaps walking backward, at least whenever he heard a car or truck approaching, to give the impression that he was going the other way. So he would have to change his thinking, as you change the color of the bulb inside the lantern even though you cant change the lantern itself; as he walked he would have to hold himself unflagging and undeviating to *thinking* like he was someone who had never heard the name Snopes and the town *Jefferson* in his life, wasn't even aware that if he kept on this road he would have to pass through it; to think instead like someone whose destination and goal was a hundred and more miles away and who in spirit was already there and only his carcass, his progressing legs, walked this particular stretch of road.

Also, he was going to have to find somebody he could talk with without rousing suspicion, not to get information so much as to validate it. Until he left Parchman, was free at last, the goal for which he had bided patiently for thirty-eight years now practically in his hand, he believed he had got all the knowledge he would need from the, not day-to-day of course and not always year-to-year, but at least decade-to-decade trickling which had penetrated even into Parchman—how and where his cousin lived, how he spent his days, his habits, what time he came and went and where to and from; even who lived in or about his house with him. But now that the moment was almost here, that might not be enough. It might even be completely false, wrong; he thought again *It's having to been away so long like I had to been; having to been in the place I had to been* as though he had spent those thirty-eight years not merely out of the world but out of life, so that even facts when they finally reached him had already ceased to be truth in order to have penetrated there; and, being inside Parchman walls, were *per se* inimical and betraying and fatal to him if he attempted to use them, depend on them, trust them.

Third, there was the pistol. The road was empty now, running between walls of woods, no sound of traffic and no house or human in sight and he took the pistol out and looked at it again with something like despair. It had not looked very much like a pistol in the store this morning; here, in the afternoon's sunny rural solitude and silence, it looked like nothing recognisable at all; looking, if anything, more than ever like the fossilised terrapin of his first impression. Yet he would have to test it, spend one of his three cartridges simply to find out if it really would shoot and for a moment, a second something nudged at his memory. *It's got to shoot* he thought. *It's jest got to. There aint nothing else for hit to do. Old Moster jest punishes; He dont play jokes.*

He was hungry too. He had not eaten since the animal crackers at sunrise. He had a little money left and he had already passed two gasoline station-stores. But he was home now; he dared not stop in one and be seen buying the cheese and crackers which he could still afford. Which reminded him of night also. The sun was now less than three hours high; he could not possibly reach Jefferson until tomorrow so it would have to be tomorrow night so he turned from the highway into a dirt crossroad, by instinct almost since he could not remember when he had begun to notice the wisps of cotton lint snared into the roadside weeds and brambles from the passing gin-bound wagons, since this type of road was familiar out of his long-ago tenant-farmer freedom too: a Negro road, a road marked with many wheels and traced with cotton wisps, yet dirt, not even gravel, since the people who lived on and used it had neither the voting power to compel nor the money to persuade the Beat supervisor to do more than scrape and grade it twice a year.

So what he found was not only what he was hunting for but what he had expected: a weathered paintless dog-trot cabin enclosed and backed by a ramshackle of also-paintless weathered fences and out-houses—barns, cribs, sheds—on a rise of ground above a creek-bottom cotton patch where he could already see the whole Negro family and perhaps a neighbor or so too dragging the long stained sacks more or less abreast up the parallel rows—the father, the mother, five children between five or six and twelve, and four girls and young men who were probably the neighbors swapping the work, he, Mink, waiting at the end of the row until the father, who would be the boss, reached him.

"Hidy," Mink said. "Looks like you could use another hand in here."

"You want to pick?" the Negro said.

"What you paying?"

"Six bits."

"I'll help you a spell," Mink said. The Negro spoke to the twelve-year-old girl beside him.

"Hand him your sack. You go on to the house and start supper." He took the sack. There was nothing unfamiliar about it. He had been picking cotton at this time of the year all his life. The only difference was that for the last thirty-eight years there had been a shotgun and a bull whip at the end of the row behind him as a promise for lagging, where here again were the weighing scales and the money they designated as a reward for speed. And, as he had expected, his employer was presently in the row next him.

"You dont stay around here," the Negro said.

"That's right," he said. "I'm jest passing through. On my way down to the Delta where my daughter lives."

"Where?" the Negro said. "I made a Delta crop one year myself." It wasn't that he should have expected this next question and would have avoided it if he knew how. It was rather that the question would not matter if he only didn't forget to think himself someone else except who he was. He didn't hesitate; he even volunteered: "Doddsville," he said. "Not fur from Parchman." And he knew what the next question would have been too, the one the Negro didn't ask and would not ask, answering that one too: "I been over a year in a hospital up in Memphis. The doctor said walking would be good for me. That's why I'm on the road instead of the train."

"The Vetruns Hospital?" the Negro said.

"What?" he said.

"The Govment Vetruns Hospital?"

"That's right," he said. "The govment had me. Over a year."

Now it was sundown. The wife had gone to the house some time ago. "You want to weigh out now?" the Negro said.

"I aint in no rush," he said. "I can give you a half a day tomorrow; jest so I knock off at noon. If your wife can fix me a plate of supper and a pallet somewhere, you can take that out of the weighing."

"I don't charge nobody to eat at my house," the Negro said.

The dining room was an oilcloth-covered table bearing a coal-oil lamp in the same lean-to room where the wood-burning stove now died slowly. He ate alone, the family had vanished, the house itself might have been empty, the plate of fried sidemeat and canned corn and tomatoes stewed together, the pale soft barely cooked biscuits, the cup of coffee already set and waiting for him when the man called him to come and eat. Then he returned to the front room where a few wood embers burned on the hearth against the first cool of autumn night; immediately the wife and the oldest girl rose and went back to the kitchen to set the meal for the family. He turned before the fire, spreading his legs; at his age he would feel the cool tonight. He spoke, casual, conversational, in the amenities, idly; at first, for a little while, you would have thought inattentively:

"I reckon you gin and trade in Jefferson. I used to know a few folks there. The banker. Dee Spain his name was, I remember. A long time back, of course."

"I dont remember him," the Negro said. "The main banker in Jefferson now is Mr Snopes."

"Oh yes, I heard tell about him. Big banker, big rich. Lives in the biggest house in town with a hired cook and a man to wait on the table for jest him and that daughter is it that makes out she's deaf."

"She is deaf. She was in the war. A cannon broke her eardrums."

"So she claims." The Negro didn't answer. He was sitting in the room's—possibly the house's—one rocking chair, not moving anyway. But now something beyond just stillness had come over him: an immobility, almost like held breath. Mink's back was to the fire, the light, so his face was invisible; his voice anyway had not altered. "A woman in a war. She must have ever body fooled good. I've knowed them like that myself. She jest makes claims and ever body around is too polite to call her a liar. Likely she can hear ever bit as good as you and me."

Now the Negro spoke, quite sternly. "Whoever it was told you she is fooling is the one that's lying. There are folks in more places than right there in Jefferson that know the truth about her whether the word has got up to that Vetrun Hospital where you claim you was at or not. If I was you, I don't believe I would dispute it. Or leastways I would be careful who I disputed it to."

"Sho, sho," Mink said. "You Jefferson folks ought to know. You mean, she can't hear nothing? You could walk right up behind her, say, into the same room even, and she wouldn't know it?"

"Yes," the Negro said. The twelve-year-old girl now stood in the kitchen door. "She's deaf. You dont need to dispute it. The Lord touched her, like He touches a heap of folks better than you, better than me. Dont worry about that."

"Well, well," Mink said. "Sho, now. Your supper's ready." The Negro got up.

"What you going to do tonight?" he said. "I aint got room for you."

"I dont need none," Mink said. "That doctor said for me to get all the fresh air I can. If you got a extry quilt, I'll sleep in the cotton truck and be ready for a early start back in that patch tomorrow."

The cotton which half-filled the bed of the pickup truck had been covered for the night with a tarpaulin, so he didn't even need the quilt. He was quite comfortable. But mainly he was off the ground. That was the danger, what a man had to watch against: once you laid flat on the ground, right away the earth started in to draw you back down into it. The very moment you were born out of your mother's body, the power and drag of the earth was already at work on you; if there had not been other womenfolks in the family or neighbors or even a hired one to support you, hold you up, keep the earth from touching you, you would not live an hour. And you knew it too. As soon as you could move you would raise your head even though that was all, trying to break that pull, trying to pull erect on chairs and things even when you still couldn't stand, to get away from the earth, save yourself. Then you could stand alone and take a step or two but even then during those first few years you still spent half of them on the ground, the old patient biding ground saying to you, "It's all right, it was just a fall, it dont hurt, dont be afraid." Then you are a man grown, strong, at your peak; now and then you can deliberately risk laying down on it in the woods hunting at night; you are too far from home to get back so you can even risk sleeping the rest of the night on it. Of course you will try to find something, anything—a plank, boards, a log, even brush tops—something, anything to intervene between your unconsciousness, helplessness, and the old patient ground that can afford to wait because it's going to get you someday, except that there aint any use in giving you a full mile just because you dared an inch. And you know it; being young and strong you will risk one night on it but even you wont risk two nights in a row. Because even, say you take out in the field for noon and set under a tree or a hedgerow and eat your lunch and then lay down and you take a short nap and wake up and for a minute you dont even know where you are, for the good reason that you aint all there; even in that short time while you wasn't watching, the old patient biding unhurried ground has already taken that first light holt on you, only you managed to wake up in time. So, if he had had to, he would have risked sleeping on the ground this last one night. But he had not had to chance it. It was as if Old Moster Himself had said, "I aint going to help you none but I aint going to downright hinder you neither."

Then it was dawn, daybreak. He ate again, in solitude; when the sun rose they were in the cotton again; during these benisoned harvest days between summer's dew and fall's first frost the cotton was moisture-free for picking as soon as you could see it; until noon. "There," he told the Negro. "That ought to holp you out a little. You got a good bale for that Jefferson gin now so I reckon I'll get on down the road while I can get a ride for a change."

At last he was that close, that near. It had taken thirty-eight years and he had made a long loop down into the Delta and out again, but he was close now. But this road was a new approach to Jefferson, not the old one from Varner's store which he remembered. These new iron numbers along the roads were different too from the hand-lettered mile boards of recollection and though he could read figures all right, some, most of these were not miles because they never got any smaller. But if they had, in this case too he would have had to make sure:

"I believe this road goes right through Jefferson, dont it?"

"Yes," the Negro said. "You can branch off there for the Delta."

"So I can. How far do you call it to town?"

"Eight miles," the Negro said. But he could figger a mile whether he saw mileposts or not, seven then six then five, the sun only barely past one oclock; then four miles, a long hill with a branch bottom at the foot of it and he said,

"Durn it, let me out at that bridge. I aint been to the bushes this morning." The Negro slowed the truck toward the bridge. "It's all right," Mink said. "I'll walk on from here. In fact I'd pure hate for that-ere doctor to see me getting out of even a cotton truck or likely he'd try his durndest to collect another dollar from me."

"I'll wait for you," the Negro said.

"No no," Mink said. "You want to get ginned and back home before dark. You aint got time." He got out of the cab and said, in the immemorial country formula of thanks: "How much do I owe you?" And the Negro answered in it:

"It aint no charge. I was coming anyway."

"Much obliged," Mink said. "Jest dont mention to that doctor about it if you ever run across him. See you in the Delta someday."

Then the truck was gone. The road was empty when he left it. Out of sight from the road would be far enough. Only, if possible, nobody must even hear the sound of the trial shot. He didn't know why; he could not have said that, having had to do without privacy for thirty-eight years, he now wanted, intended to savor, every minuscule of it which freedom entitled him to; also he still had five or six hours until dark, and probably even less than that many miles, following the dense brier-cypress-willow jungle of the creek bottom for perhaps a quarter of a mile, maybe more, when suddenly he stopped dead with a kind of amazed excitement, even exhilaration. Before him, spanning the creek, was a railroad trestle. Now he not only knew how to reach Jefferson without the constant risk of passing the people who from that old Yoknapatawpha County affinity would know who he was and what he intended to do, he would have something to do to pass the time until dark when he could go on.

It was as though he had not seen a railroad in thirty-eight years. One ran along one entire flank of the Parchman wire and he could see trains on it as far as he recalled every day. Also, from time to time gangs of convicts under their shotgun guards did rough construction or repair public works jobs in sight of railroads through the Delta where he could see trains. But even without the intervening wire, he looked at them from prison; the trains themselves were looked at, seen, alien in freedom, fleeing, existing in liberty and hence unreal, chimaeras, apparitions, without past or future, not even going anywhere since their destinations could not exist for him: just in motion a second, an instant, then nowhere; they had not been. But now it would be different. He could watch them, himself in freedom, as they fled past in freedom, the two of them mutual, in a way even interdependent: it to do the fleeing in smoke and noise and motion, he to do the watching; remembering how thirty-eight or forty years ago, just before he went to Parchman in fact—this occasion connected also with some crisis in his affairs which he had forgotten now; but then so were all his moments: connected, involved in some crisis of the constant outrage and injustice he was always having to drop everything to cope with, handle, with no proper tools and equipment for it, not even the time to spare from the unremitting work it took to feed himself and his family; this was one of those moments or maybe it had been simply the desire to see the train which had brought him the twenty-two miles in from Frenchman's Bend. Anyway, he had had to pass the night in town whatever the reason was and had gone down to the depot to see the New Orleans-bound passenger train come in—the hissing engine, the lighted cars each with an uppity impudent nigger porter, one car in which people were eating supper while more niggers waited on them, before going back to the sleeping cars that had actual beds in them; the train pausing for a moment then gone: a long airtight chunk of another world dragged along the dark earth for the poor folks in overalls like him to gape at free for a moment without the train itself, let alone the folks in it, even knowing he was there.

But as free to stand and watch it as any man even if he did wear overalls instead of diamonds; and as free now, until he remembered something else he had learned in Parchman during the long tedious years while he prepared for freedom—the information, the trivia he had had to accumulate since when the time, the freedom came, he might not know until too late what he lacked: there had not been a passenger train through Jefferson since 1935, that the railroad which old Colonel Sartoris (not the banker they called Colonel but his father, the real colonel, that had commanded all the local boys in the

old slavery war) had built, which according to the old folks whom
even he, Mink, knew and remembered, had been the biggest thing to
happen in Yoknapatawpha County, that was to have linked Jefferson
and the county all the way from the Gulf of Mexico in one direction
to the Great Lakes in the other, was now a fading weed-grown
branch line knowing no wheels any more save two local freight trains
more or less every day.

In which case, more than ever would the track, the right-of-way
be his path into town where the privacy of freedom it had taken him
thirty-eight years to earn would not be violated, so he turned and
retraced his steps perhaps a hundred yards and stopped; there was
nothing: only the dense jungle dappled with September-afternoon
silence. He took out the pistol. *Hit does look like a cooter* he thought,
with what at the moment he believed was just amusement, humor,
until he realised it was despair because he knew now that the thing
would not, could not possibly fire, so that when he adjusted the
cylinder to bring the first of the three cartridges under the hammer
and cocked it and aimed at the base of a cypress four or five feet away
and pulled the trigger and heard the faint vacant click, his only emotion was calm vindication, almost of superiority, at having been right,
of being in an unassailable position to say I told you so, not even
remembering cocking the hammer again since this time he didn't
know where the thing was aimed when it jerked and roared, incredible with muzzle-blast because of the short barrel; only now, almost
too late, springing in one frantic convulsion to catch his hand back
before it cocked and fired the pistol on the last remaining cartridge
by simple reflex. But he caught himself in time, freeing thumb and
finger completely from the pistol until he could reach across with his
left hand and remove it from the right one which in another second
might have left him with an empty and useless weapon after all this
distance and care and time. *Maybe the last one wont shoot neither* he
thought, but for only a moment, a second, less than a second, thinking *No sir. It will have to. It will jest have to. There aint nothing else for
it to do. I dont need to worry. Old Moster jest punishes; He dont play jokes.*

And now (it was barely two oclock by the sun, at least four hours
till sundown) he could even risk the ground once more, this late, this
last time, especially as he had last night in the cotton truck on the

credit side. So he moved on again, beneath and beyond the trestle this time, just in case somebody had heard the shot and came to look, and found a smooth place behind a log and lay down. At once he began to feel the slow, secret, tentative palping start as the old biding unimpatient unhurried ground said to itself, "Well, well, be dawg if here aint one already laying right here on my doorstep so to speak." But it was all right, he could risk it for this short time.

It was almost as though he had an alarm clock; he woke exactly in time to see through a leafed interstice overhead the last of sun drain, fade from the zenith, just enough light left to find his way back through the jungle to the railroad and mount onto it. Though it was better here, enough of day left to see him most of the last mile to town before it faded completely, displaced by darkness random with the sparse lights of the town's purlieus, the beginning, the first quiet edge-of-town back street beneath the rigid semaphore arms of the crossing warning and a single lonely street light where the Negro boy on the bicycle had ample time to see him standing in the center of the crossing and brake to a stop. "Hidy, son," he said, using the old country-Negroid idiom for "live" too: "Which-a-way from here does Mr Flem Snopes stay?"

By now, since the previous Thursday night in fact, from about nine-thirty or ten each night until daybreak the next morning, Flem Snopes had had a bodyguard, though no white person in Jefferson, including Snopes himself, except the guard's wife, knew it. His name was Luther Biglin, a countryman, a professional dog trainer and market hunter and farmer until the last sheriff's election. Not only was his wife the niece of the husband of Sheriff Ephriam Bishop's wife's sister, Biglin's mother was the sister of the rural political boss whose iron hand ruled one of the county divisions (as old Will Varner ruled his at Frenchman's Bend) which had elected Bishop sheriff. So Biglin was now jailor under Bishop's tenure. Though with a definite difference from the standard nepotic run. Where as often as not, the holders of such lesser hierarchic offices gave nothing to the position they encumbered, having not really wanted it anyway but accepting it merely under family pressure to keep some member of the opposite political faction out of it, Biglin brought to his the sort of passionate enthusiastic devotion and fidelity to the power and immaculacy and integrity of his kinsman-by-marriage's position as say Murat's orderly corporal might have felt toward the symbology of his master's baton.

He was not only honorable (even in his market hunting of venison and duck and quail, where he broke only the law: never his word), he was brave too. After Pearl Harbor, although his mother's brother might, probably could and would, have found or invented for him absolution from the draft, Biglin himself volunteered for the Marine Corps, finding to his amazement that by military standards he had next to no vision whatever in his right eye. He had not noticed this himself. He was a radio man, not a reading man, and in shooting (he was one of the best wing shots in the county though in an exuberant spendthrift southpaw fashion—he was left-handed, shooting from his left shoulder; in the course of two of his three previous vocations he shot up more shells than anyone in the county; at the age of thirty he had already shot out two sets of shotgun barrels) the defect had been an actual service to him since he had never had to train himself to keep both eyes open and see the end of the gun and the target at the same instant, or half-close the right one to eliminate parallax. So when (not by curiosity but by simple bureaucratic consanguinity) he learned—even quicker than the Sheriff did because he, Biglin, immediately believed it—that with Mink Snopes free at last from the state penitentiary, his old threats against his cousin, even though forty years old, durst not be ignored, let alone dismissed as his patron and superior seemed inclined to do.

So his aim, intent, was still basically to defend and preserve the immaculacy of his kinsman-by-marriage's office, which was to preserve the peace and protect human life and well-being, in which he modestly shared. But there was something else too, though only his wife knew it. Even the Sheriff didn't know about his plan, campaign; he only told his wife: "There may be nothing to it, like Cousin Eef says: just another of Lawyer Stevens's nightmares. But suppose Cousin Eef is wrong and Lawyer is right; suppose—" He could visualise it: the last split second, Mr Snopes helpless in bed beneath his doom, one last hopeless cry for the help which he knew was not there, the knife (hatchet, hammer, stick of stovewood, whatever the vengeance-ridden murderer would use) already descending when he,

Biglin, would step, crash in, flashlight in one hand and pistol in the other: one single shot, the assassin falling across his victim, the expression of demonic anticipation and triumph fading to astonishment on his face—"Why, Mr Snopes will make us rich! He'll have to! There wont be nothing else he can do!"

Since Mr Snopes mustn't know about it either (the Sheriff had explained to him that in America you cant wet-nurse a free man unless he requests it or at least knowingly accepts it), he could not be inside the bedroom itself, where he should be, but would have to take the best station he could find or contrive outside the nearest window he could enter fastest or at least see to aim through. Which meant of course he would have to sit up all night. He was a good jailor, conscientious, keeping his jail clean and his prisoners properly fed and tended; besides the errands he did for the Sheriff. Thus the only time he would have to sleep in during the twenty-four hours would be between supper and the latest imperative moment when he must be at his station outside Snopes's bedroom window. So each night he would go to bed immediately after he rose from the supper table, and his wife would go to the picture show, on her return from which, usually about nine-thirty, she would wake him. Then, with his flashlight and pistol and a sandwich and a folding chair and a sweater against the chill as the late September nights cooled toward midnight, he would stand motionless and silent against the hedge facing the window where, as all Jefferson knew, Snopes spent all his life outside the bank, until the light went out at last; by which time, the two Negro servants would have long since left. Then he would move quietly across the lawn and open the chair beneath the window and sit down, sitting so immobile that the stray dogs which roamed all Jefferson during the hours of darkness, would be almost upon him before they would sense, smell, however they did it, that he was not asleep, and crouch and whirl in one silent motion and flee; until first light, when he would fold up the chair and make sure the crumpled sandwich wrapping was in his pocket, and depart; though by Sunday night, if Snopes had not been asleep and his daughter not stone deaf, now and then they could have heard him snoring—until, that is, the nocturnal dog crossing the lawn this time would sense, smell—

however they did it—that he was asleep and harmless until actually touched by the cold nose. Mink didn't know this. But even if he had, it probably would have made little difference. He would simply have regarded the whole thing—Biglin, the fact that Snopes was now being guarded—as just one more symptom of the infinite capacity for petty invention of the inimical forces which had always dogged his life. So even if he had known that Biglin was already on station under the window of the room where his cousin now sat (He had not hurried. On the contrary: once the Negro boy on the bicycle had given him directions, he thought *I'm even a little ahead. Let them eat supper first and give them two niggers time to be outen the way.*) he would have behaved no differently: not hiding, not lurking: just unseen unheard and irrevocably alien like a coyote or a small wolf; not crouching, not concealed by the hedge as Biglin himself would do when he arrived, but simply squatting on his hams—as, a countryman, he could do for hours without discomfort—against it while he examined the house whose shape and setting he already knew out of the slow infinitesimal Parchman trickle of facts and information which he had had to garner, assimilate, from strangers yet still conceal from them the import of what he asked; looking in fact at the vast white columned edifice with something like pride that someone named Snopes owned it; a complete and absolute unjealousy: at another time, tomorrow, though he himself would never dream nor really ever want to be received in it, he would have said proudly to a stranger: "My cousin lives there. He owns it."

It looked exactly as he had known it would. There were the lighted rear windows of the corner room where his cousin would be sitting (they would surely have finished supper by now; he had given them plenty of time) with his feet propped on the little special ledge he had heard in Parchman how another kinsman Mink had never seen, Wat Snopes having been born too late, had nailed onto the hearth for that purpose. There were lights also in the windows of the room in front of that one, which he had not expected, knowing also about the special room upstairs the deaf daughter had fixed up for herself. But no light showed upstairs at all, so evidently the daughter was still downstairs too. And although the lights in the kitchen indicated that the two Negro servants had not left either, his impulse was so strong that he had already begun to rise without waiting longer, to cross to the window and see, if necessary begin now: who had had thirty-eight years to practise patience in and should have been perfect. Because if he waited too long, his cousin might be in bed, perhaps even asleep. Which would be intolerable and must not be: there must be that moment, even if it lasted only a second, for him to say, "Look at me, Flem," and his cousin would do so. But he restrained himself, who had had thirty-eight years to learn to wait in, and sank, squatted back again, easing the hard lump of the pistol which he now carried inside the bib front of his overalls; her room would be on the other side of the house where he couldn't see the lighted windows from here, and the lights in the other room meant nothing since if he was big rich like his cousin Flem, with a fine big house like that, he would have all the lights on downstairs too.

Then the lights went off in the kitchen; presently he could hear the Negro man and the woman still talking as they approached and (he didn't even hold his breath) passed within ten feet of him and went through the gate in the hedge, the voices moving slowly up the lane beyond it until they died away. Then he rose, quietly, without haste, not furtive, not slinking: just small, just colorless, perhaps simply too small to be noticed, and crossed the lawn to the window and (he had to stand on tiptoe) looked into it at his cousin sitting in the swivel chair like in a bank or an office, with his feet propped against the chimney and his hat on, as he, Mink, had known he would be sitting, looking not too different even though Mink hadn't seen him in forty years; a little changed of course: the black planter's hat he had heard about in Parchman but the little bow tie might have been the same one he had been wearing forty years ago behind the counter in Varner's store, the shirt a white city shirt and the pants dark city pants too and the shoes polished city shoes instead of farmer's brogans. But no different, really: not reading, just sitting there with his feet propped and his hat on, his jaw moving faintly and steadily as if he were chewing.

Just to be sure, he would circle the house until he could see the lighted upper windows on the other side and had already started around the back when he thought how he might as well look into the other lighted room also while he was this close to it and moved, no less quiet than a shadow and with not much more substance, along the wall until he could stand on tiptoe again and look in the next window, the next room. He saw her at once and knew her at once—a room walled almost to the ceiling with more books than he knew existed, a woman sitting beneath a lamp in the middle of the room reading one, in horn-rim glasses and that single white streak through the center of her black hair that he had heard about in Parchman too. For a second the old helpless fury and outrage possessed him again and almost ruined, destroyed him this time—the rage and fury when, during the first two or three years after he learned that she was back home again apparently for good and living right there in the house with Flem, he would think *Suppose she aint deaf a-tall; suppose she's jest simply got ever body fooled for whatever devilment of her own she's up to* since this—the real truth of whether she was deaf or just pretending—was one gambit which he would not only have to depend on somebody else for, but on something as frail and undependable as second- or third-hand hearsay. Finally he had lied, tricked his way in to the prison doctor but there he was again: daring not to ask what he wanted to know, had to know, find out, learn: only that even the stone-deaf would—could—feel the concussion of the air if the sound were loud enough or close enough. "Like a—" Mink said before he could stop himself. But too late; the doctor finished it for him: "That's right. A shot. But even if you could make us believe you are, how would that get you out of here?" "That's right," Mink said. "I wouldn't need to hear that bull whip: jest feel it."

But that would be all right; there was that room she had fixed up for herself upstairs, while every word from home that trickled down to him in Parchman—you had to believe folks sometimes, you had to, you jest had to—told how his cousin spent all his time in the one downstairs cattycorner across that house that was bigger they said than even the jail. Then to look in the window and find her, not upstairs and across the house where she should have been, where in a way it had been promised to him she would be, but right there in the next room. In which case everything else he had believed in and depended on until now was probably trash and rubble too; there didn't even need to be an open door between the two rooms so she could be sure to feel what the prison doctor had called the concussion because she wasn't even deaf. Everything had lied to him; he thought quietly *And I aint even got but one bullet left even if I would have time to use two before somebody come busting in from the street. I got to find a stick of stovewood or a piece of ahrn somewhere*—that close, that near to ruination and destruction before he caught himself back right on the brink, murmuring, whispering, "Wait now, wait. Aint I told you and told you Old Moster dont play jokes; He jest punishes? Of course she's deaf: aint all up and down Missippi been telling you that for ten years now? I dont mean that durn Parchman doctor nor all the rest of them durn jailbird son of a bitches that was all I had to try to find out what I had to know from, but that nigger jest yestiddy evening that got almost impident, durn nigh called a white man a liar to his face the least suh-jestion I made that maybe she was fooling folks. Niggers that dont only know all the undercover about white folks, let alone one that they already claim is a nigger lover and even one of them commonists to boot, until all the niggers in Yoknapatawpha County and likely Memphis and Chicago too know the truth about whether she is deaf or not or ever thing else about her or not. Of course she's deaf, setting there with her back already to the door where you got to pass and they's bound to be a back door too that all you got to do is jest find it and walk right on out," and moved on, without haste: not furtive, just small and light-footed and invisible, on around the house and up the steps and on between the soaring columns of the portico like any other guest, visitor, caller, opening the screen door quietly into the hall and through it, passing the open door beyond which the woman sat, not even glancing toward it, and went on to the next one and drew the pistol from his overall bib; and, thinking hurriedly, a little chaotically, almost like tiny panting *I aint got but one bullet so it will have to be in the face, the head; I cant resk jest the body with jest one bullet* entered the room where his cousin sat and ran a few more steps toward him.

He didn't need to say, "Look at me, Flem." His cousin was already doing that, his head turned over his shoulder. Otherwise he hadn't moved, only the jaws ceased chewing in midmotion. Then he moved, leaned slightly forward in the chair and he had just begun to lower his propped feet from the ledge, the chair beginning to swivel around, when Mink from about five feet away stopped and raised the toad-shaped iron-rust-colored weapon in both hands and cocked and steadied it, thinking *Hit's got to hit his face:* not *I've got to* but *It's got to* and pulled the trigger and rather felt than heard the dull foolish almost inattentive click. Now his cousin, his feet now flat on the floor and the chair almost swiveled to face him, appeared to sit immobile and even detached too, watching too Mink's grimed shaking child-sized hands like the hands of a pet coon as one of them lifted the hammer enough for the other to roll the cylinder back one notch so that the shell would come again under the hammer; again that faint something out of the past nudged, prodded: not a warning nor even really a repetition: just faint and familiar and unimportant still since, whatever it had been, even before it had not been strong enough to alter anything nor even remarkable enough to be remembered; in the same second he had dismissed it. *Hit's all right* he thought *Hit'll go this time: Old Moster dont play jokes* and cocked and steadied the pistol again in both hands, his cousin not moving at all now though he was chewing faintly again, as though he too were watching the dull point of light on the cock of the hammer when it flicked away.

It made a tremendous sound though in the same instant Mink no longer heard it. His cousin's body was now making a curious half-stifled convulsive surge which in another moment was going to carry the whole chair over; it seemed to him, Mink, that the report of the pistol was nothing but that when the chair finished falling and crashed to the floor, the sound would wake all Jefferson. He whirled; there was a moment yet when he tried to say, cry, "Stop! Stop! You got to make sho he's dead or you will have throwed away ever thing!" but he could not, he didn't remember when he had noticed the other door in the wall beyond the chair but it was there; where it led to didn't matter just so it led on and not back. He ran to it, scrabbling at the knob, still shaking and scrabbling at it even after he realised it was locked, still shaking the knob, quite blind now, even after the voice spoke behind him and he whirled again and saw the woman standing in the hall door; for an instant he thought *So she could hear all the time* before he knew better: she didn't need to hear; it was the same power had brought her here to catch him that by merely pointing her finger at him could blast, annihilate, vaporise him where he stood. And no time to cock and aim the pistol again even if he had had another bullet so even as he whirled he flung, threw the pistol at her, nor even able to follow that because in the same second it seemed to him she already had the pistol in her hand, holding it toward him, saying in that quacking duck's voice that deaf people use:

"Here. Come and take it. That door is a closet. You'll have to come back this way to get out."

EIGHTEEN

"*S*top the car," Stevens said. Ratliff did so. He was driving though it was Stevens's car. They had left the highway at the crossroads— Varner's store and gin and blacksmith shop, and the church and the dozen or so dwellings and other edifices, all dark now though it was not yet ten oclock, which composed the hamlet—and had now traversed and left behind the rest of the broad flat rich valley land on which old Varner—in his eighties now, his hair definitely gray, twelve years a widower until two years ago when he married a young woman of twenty-five or so who at the time was supposed to be engaged to, anyway courted by, his grandson—held liens and mortgages where he didn't own it outright; and now they were approaching the hills: a section of small worn-out farms tilted and precarious among the eroded folds like scraps of paper. The road had ceased some time back to be even gravel and at any moment now it would cease to be passable to anything on wheels; already, in the fixed glare (Ratliff had stopped the car) of the headlights, it resembled just one more eroded ravine twisting up the broken rise crested with shabby and shaggy pine and worthless blackjack. The sun had crossed the equator, in Libra now; and in the cessation of motion and the quiet of the idling engine, there was a sense of autumn after the slow drizzle of Sunday and the bright spurious cool which had lasted through Monday almost; the jagged rampart of pines and scrub oak was a thin dike against the winter and rain and cold, under which the worn-out fields overgrown with sumac and sassafras and persimmon had already turned scarlet, the persimmons heavy with fruit waiting only for frost and the baying of potlicker possum hounds. "What makes you think he will be there even if we can get there ourselves?" Stevens said.

"Where else would he be?" Ratliff said. "Where else has he got to go? Back to Parchman, after all this recent trouble and expense it taken him to get out? What else has he got but home?"

"He hasn't even got that home any more," Stevens said. "When was it—three years ago—that day we drove out here about that boy—what was his name?—"

"Turpin," Ratliff said.

"—that didn't answer his draft call and we came out looking for him. There wasn't anything left of the house then but the shell. Part of the roof, and what was left of the walls above the height convenient to pull off for firewood. This road was better then too."

"Yes," Ratliff said. "Folks kept it kind of graded and scraped up dragging out that kindling."

"So there's not even the shell any more."

"There's a cellar under it," Ratliff said.

"A hole in the ground?" Stevens said. "A den like an animal?"

"He's tired," Ratliff said. "Even if he wasn't sixty-three or -four years old. He's been under a strain for thirty-eight years, let alone the last—this is Thursday, aint it?—seven days. And now he aint got no more strain to prop him up. Jest suppose you had spent thirty-eight years waiting to do something, and sho enough one day you finally done it. You wouldn't have much left neither. So what he wants now is jest to lay down in the dark and the quiet somewhere for a spell."

"He should have thought of that last Thursday," Stevens said. "It's too late to do that now."

"Aint that exactly why we're out here?" Ratliff said.

"All right," Stevens said. "Drive on." Instead, Ratliff switched off the engine. Now indeed they could sense, feel the change of the season and the year. Some of the birds remained but the night was no longer full of the dry loud cacophony of summer nocturnal insects. There were only the crickets in the dense hedgerows and stubble of mown hayfields, where at noon the dusty grasshoppers would spurt, frenetic and random, going nowhere. And now Stevens knew what was coming, what Ratliff was going to talk about.

"You reckon she really never knowed what that durn little rattlesnake was going to do the minute they turned him loose?" Ratliff said.

"Certainly not," Stevens said, quickly, too quickly, too late. "Drive on."

But Ratliff didn't move. Stevens noticed that he still held his hand over the switch key so that Stevens himself couldn't have started the engine. "I reckon she'll stop over in Memphis tonight," Ratliff said. "With that-ere fancy brand-new automobile and all."

Stevens remembered all that. His trouble was, to forget it. She had told him herself—or so he believed then—this morning after she had given him the necessary information to draw the deed: how she wasn't going to accept her so-called father's automobile either but instead had ordered a new one from Memphis, which would be delivered in time for her to leave directly after the funeral; he could bring the deed to the house for her signature when they said good-bye, or what they—she and he—would have of good-bye.

It was a big funeral: a prominent banker and financier who had not only died in his prime (financial anyway) of a pistol wound but from the wrong pistol wound, since by ordinary a banker dying of a pistol in his own bedroom at nine oclock in the evening should have just said good night to a state or federal (maybe both) bank inspector. He (the deceased) had no auspices either: fraternal, civic, nor military: only finance; not an economy—cotton or cattle or anything else which Yoknapatawpha County and Mississippi were established on and kept running by, but belonging simply to Money. He had been a member of a Jefferson church true enough, as the outward and augmented physical aspect of the edifice showed, but even that had been not a subservience nor even an aspiration nor even really a confederation nor even an amnesty, but simply an armistice temporary between two irreconcilable tongues.

Yet not just the town but the county too came to it. He (Stevens) sat, a member of the cast itself, by the (sic) daughter's request, on the front row in fact and next her by her insistence: himself and Linda and her Uncle Jody, a balding man who had added another hundred pounds of jowl and belly to his father's long skeleton; and yes, Wallstreet Snopes, Wallstreet Panic Snopes, who not only had never acted like a Snopes, he never had even looked like one: a tall dark man except for the eyes of an incredible tender youthful periwinkle blue, who had begun as the delivery boy in a side-street grocery to carry himself and his younger brother, Admiral Dewey, through school, and went from there to create a wholesale grocery supply house in Jefferson serving all the county; and now, removed with his family to Memphis, owned a chain of wholesale grocery establishments blanketing half of Mississippi and Tennessee and Arkansas too; all of them facing the discreetly camouflaged excavation beside the other grave over which not her husband (who had merely ordained and paid for it) but Stevens himself had erected the outrageous marble lie which had been the absolution for Linda's freedom nineteen years ago. As it would be he who would erect whatever lie this one would postulate; they—he and Linda—had discussed that too this morning.

"No. Nothing," she said.

Yes he wrote.

"No," she said. He merely raised the tablet and held the word facing her; he could not have written *Its for your sake* Then he didn't need to. "You're right," she said. "You will have to do another one too."

He wrote *We will*

"No," she said. "You will. You always have for me. You always will for me. I know now I've never really had anybody but you. I've never really even needed anybody else but you."

Sitting there while the Baptist minister did his glib and rapid office, he (Stevens) looked around at the faces, town faces and country faces, the citizens who represented the town because the town should be represented at this obsequy; the ones who represented simply themselves because some day they would be where Flem Snopes now lay, as friendless and dead and alone too; the diffident anonymous hopeful faces who had owed him or his bank money and, as people will and can, hoped, were even capable of believing that, now that he was dead, the debt might, barely might become lost or forgotten or even simply undemanded, uncollected. Then suddenly he saw something else. There were not many of them: he distinguished only three, country faces also, looking no different from the other country faces diffident, even effacing, in the rear of the crowd; until suddenly they leaped, sprang out, and he knew who they were. They were Snopeses; he had never seen them before but they were incontrovertible: not alien at all: simply identical, not so much in expression as in position, attitude; he thought rapidly, in something like that second of simple panic when you are violently wakened *They're like wolves come to look at the trap where another bigger wolf, the boss wolf, the head wolf, what Ratliff would call the bull wolf, died; if maybe there was not a shred or scrap of hide still snared in it.* Then that was gone. He could not keep on looking behind him and now the minister had finished and the undertaker signalled for the select, the publicly bereaved, to depart; and when he looked, could look again, the faces were gone. He left Linda there. That is, her uncle would drive her home, where by this time the new automobile she had told him she had telephoned to Memphis for after she decided yesterday afternoon to drive alone to New York as soon as the funeral was over, would be waiting; she would probably be ready to leave, the new car packed and all, by the time he got there with the deed for her to sign.

So he went to the office and picked it up—a deed of gift (with the usual consideration of one dollar) returning the house and its lot to the De Spains. She had done it all herself, she hadn't even informed him in the process, let alone beforehand. She had been unable to locate Manfred, whom Snopes had dispossessed of it along with the bank and the rest of his, Manfred's, name and dignity in Jefferson, but she had found at last what remained of his kin—the only sister of old Major de Spain, Manfred's father, and her only child: a bedridden old woman living in Los Angeles with her spinster daughter of sixty, the retired principal of a suburban Los Angeles grammar school; she, Linda, tracing, running them down herself without even consulting her lawyer: an outrage really, when the Samaritan, the philanthropist, the benefactor, begins not only to find but even to invent his own generosities, not only without recourse to but even ignoring the lawyers and secretaries and public relations counsellors; outrageous, antisocial in fact, taking the very cake out of that many mouths.

The papers wanted only her signature; it had not been fifteen minutes yet when he slowed his car in toward the curb before the house, not even noticing the small group—men, boys, a Negro or so—in front of him except to say, "The local committee validating her new automobile," and parked his own and got out with the briefcase and had even turned, his glance simply passing across the group because it was there, when he said with a quick, faint, not really yet surprise, "It's a British Jaguar. It's brand new," and was even walking on when suddenly it was as if a staircase you are mounting becomes abruptly a treadmill, you still walking, mounting, expending energy and motion but without progress; so abrupt and sudden in fact that you are only your aura, your very momentum having carried your corporeality one whole step in advance of you; he thought *No place on earth from which a brand-new Jaguar could be delivered to Jefferson, Mississippi, since even noon yesterday, let alone not even telephoned for until last night* thinking, desperately now *No! No! It is possible! They could have had one, found one in Memphis last night or this morning— this ramshackle universe which has nothing to hold it together but coincidence* and walked smartly up and paused beside it, thinking *So she knew she was going to leave after last Thursday; she just didn't know until Tuesday night exactly what day that would be.* It was spanking unblemished new, the youngish quite decent-looking agent or deliverer stood beside it and at that moment the Negro houseman came out the front door carrying some of her luggage.

"Afternoon," Stevens said. "Damned nice car. Brand new, isn't it?"

"That's right," the young man said. "Never even touched the ground until Mrs Kohl telephoned for it yesterday."

"Lucky you had one on hand for her," Stevens said.

"Oh, we've had it since the tenth of this month. When she ordered it last July she just told us to keep it when it came in, until she wanted it. I suppose her father's . . . death changed her plans some."

"Things like that do," Stevens said. "She ordered it in July."

"That's right. They haven't caught the fellow yet, I hear."

"Not yet," Stevens said. "Damned nice car. Would like to afford one myself," and went on, into the open door and up the stairs which knew his feet, into the sitting room which knew him too. She stood watching him while he approached, dressed for the drive in a freshly laundered suit of the faded khaki coveralls, her face and mouth heavily made up against the wind of motion; on a chair lay the stained burberry and her purse and heavy gloves and a scarf for her head; she said, At least I didn't lie to you. I could have hidden it in the garage until you had come and gone, but I didn't. Though not in words: she said,

"Kiss me, Gavin," taking the last step to him herself and taking

him into her arms, firm and without haste and set her mouth to his,
firmly and deliberately too, and opened it, he holding her, his hand
moving down her back while the dividing incleft outswell of her buttocks rose under the harsh khaki, as had happened before now and
then, the hand unchallenged—it had never been challenged, it would
never be, the fidelity unthreatened and secure even if there had been
nothing at all between the hand and the inswelling incleft woman
flesh, he simply touching her, learning and knowing not with despair
or grief but just sorrow a little, simply supporting her buttocks as you
cup the innocent hipless bottom of a child. But not now, not this
time. It was terror now; he thought with terror *How did it go? the man
"whose irresistible attraction to women was that simply by being in their
presence he gave them to convince themselves that he was capable of any sacrifice for them." Which is backward, completely backward; the poor dope not
only didn't know where first base was, he didn't even know he was playing
baseball. You dont need to tempt them because they have long since already
selected you by that time, choosing you simply because they believe that in the
simple act of being selected you have at once become not merely willing and
ready but passionately desirous of making a sacrifice for them just as soon
as the two of you can think of one good enough, worthy.* He thought *Now
she will realise that she cannot trust me but only hoped she could so now the
thrust of hips, gripping both shoulders to draw me into the backward-falling
even without a bed* and was completely wrong; he thought *Why should
she waste her time trusting me when she has known all her life that all she
has to do is just depend on me.* She just stood holding him and kissing
him until he himself moved first to be free. Then she released him
and stood looking at his face out of the dark blue eyes not secret, not
tender, perhaps not even gentle.

"Your mouth is a mess," she said. "You'll have to go to the bathroom.—You are right," she said. "You always are right about you and
me." They were not secret: intent enough yes, but not secret; someday perhaps he would remember that they had never been really tender even. "I love you," she said. "You haven't had very much, have
you. No, that's wrong. You haven't had anything. You have had nothing."

He knew exactly what she meant: her mother first, then her; that
he had offered the devotion twice and got back for it nothing but

the privilege of being obsessed, bewitched, besotted if you like; Ratliff certainly would have said besotted. And she knew he knew it; that was (perhaps) their curse: they both knew any and every mutual thing immediately. It was not because of the honesty, nor because she believed she had been in love with him all her life, that she had let him discover the new Jaguar and what it implied in the circumstances of her so-called father's death. It was because she knew she could not have kept concealed from him the fact that she had ordered the car from New York or London or wherever it came from, the moment she knew for sure he could get Mink the pardon.

She had pockets in all her clothes into which the little ivory tablet with its clipped stylus exactly fitted. He knew all of them, the coveralls too, and reached his hand and took it out. He could have written *I have everything. You trusted me. You chose to let me find you murdered your so-called father rather than tell me a lie.* He could, perhaps should have written *I have everything. Haven't I just finished being accessory before a murder.* Instead, he wrote *We have had everything*

"No," she said.

He wrote *Yes*

"No," she said.

He printed *YES* this time in letters large enough to cover the rest of the face of the tablet and erased it clean with the heel of his palm and wrote *Take someone with You to hear you Will be killed*

She barely glanced at it, nowhere near long enough, anyone would have thought, to have read it, then stood looking at him again, the dark blue eyes that whether they were gentle or not or tender or not or really candid or not, it didn't matter. Her mouth was smeared too behind the faint smiling, itself—the smiling—like a soft smear, a drowsing stain. "I love you," she said. "I have never loved anybody but you."

He wrote *No*

"Yes," she said.

He wrote *No* again and even while she said "Yes" again he wrote *No No No No* until he had completely filled the tablet and erased it and wrote *Deed* And, standing side by side at the mantel where they transacted all her business which required communication between them, he spread the document and uncapped his pen for her to sign it and folded the paper and was putting it back into the briefcase when she said, "This too." It was a plain long envelope, he had noticed it on the mantel. When he took it he could feel the thick sheaf of banknotes through the paper, too many of them; a thousand dollars would destroy him in a matter of weeks, perhaps days, as surely as that many bullets. He had been tempted last night to tell her so: "A thousand dollars will kill him too. Will you be satisfied then?" even though he was still ignorant last night how much truth that would be. But he refrained. He would take care of that himself when the time came. "Do you know where you can find him?"

Ratliff does he wrote and erased it and wrote *Go out 2 minutes Bathroom your Mouth too* and stood while she read it and then herself stood a moment longer, not moving, her head bent as if he had written perhaps in cryptogram. "Oh," she said. Then she said: "Yes. It's time," and turned and went to the door and stopped and half-turned and only then looked at him: no faint smile, no nothing: just the eyes which even at this distance were not quite black. Then she was gone.

He already had the briefcase in his hand. His hat was on the table. He put the envelope into his pocket and scrubbed at his mouth with his handkerchief, taking up the hat in passing, and went on, down the stairs, wetting the handkerchief with spittle to scrub his mouth. There would be a mirror in the hall but this would have to do until he reached the office; there would be, was a back door of course but there was the houseman somewhere and maybe even the cook too. Besides, there was no law against crossing the front lawn itself from the front entrance and so through the side gate into the lane, from which he could reach the street without even having to not look at the new car again. Until Ratliff, happening to be standing by chance or coincidence near the foot of the office stairs, said, "Where's your car? Never mind, I'll go pick it up. Meantime you better use some water when you get upstairs."

He did, and locked the stained handkerchief into a drawer and sat in the office. In time he heard Ratliff's feet on the stairs though Ratliff shook the locked door only; here was another time when he could have worked at his youthful dream of restoring the Old Testament to its virgin's pristinity. But he was too old now. Evidently it takes more than just anguish to be all that anguishing. In time the telephone rang. "She's gone," Ratliff said. "I've got your car. You want to come and eat supper with me?"

"No," he said.

"You want me to telephone your wife that's what you're doing?"

"Dammit, I told you No," he said. Then he said, "Much obliged."

"I'll pick you up at eight oclock say," Ratliff said.

He was at the curb waiting; the car—his—moved immediately he was in it. "I'm not safe," he said.

"I reckon so," Ratliff said. "It's all over now, soon that is as we get used to it."

"I mean, you're not safe. Nobody is, around me. I'm dangerous. Cant you understand I've just committed murder?"

"Oh, that," Ratliff said. "I decided some time back that maybe the only thing that would make you safe to have around would be for somebody to marry you. That never worked but at least you're all right now. As you jest said, you finally committed a murder. What else is there beyond that for anybody to think up for you to do?" Now they were on the highway, the town behind them and they could pick up a little speed to face the twenty miles out to Varner's store. "You know the one in this business I'm really sorry for? It's Luther Biglin. You aint heard about that and likely wouldn't nobody else if it hadn't kind of come out today in what you might call a private interview or absolvement between Luther and Eef Bishop. It seems that ever night between last Thursday and the following Tuesday, Luther has been standing or setting guard as close as he could get outside that window from as soon as he could get there after Miz Biglin would get back from the picture show and wake him up, to daylight. You know: having to spend all day long taking care of his jail and prisoners in addition to staying close to the sheriff's office in case Eef might need him, he would have to get some rest and the only way he could work it in would be after he et supper until Miz Biglin, who acted as his alarm clock, got back from the picture show, which would be from roughly seven oclock to roughly more or less half-past nine or ten oclock, depending on how long the picture show was, the balance of the night standing or setting in a folding chair jest outside Flem's window, not for a reward or even glory, since nobody but Miz Biglin knowed it, but simply outen fidelity to Eef

Bishop's sworn oath to defend and protect human life in Jefferson even when the human life was Flem Snopes's. Yet outen the whole twenty-four hours Mink could a picked, he had to pick one between roughly seven oclock and roughly nine-thirty to walk in on Flem with that thing whoever sold it to him told him was a pistol, almost like Mink done it outen pure and simple spite—a thing which, as the feller says, to a dog shouldn't happen."

"Drive on," Stevens said. "Pick it up."

"Yes," Ratliff said. "So this is what it all come down to. All the ramshacking and foreclosing and grabbling and snatching, doing it by gentle underhand when he could but by honest hard trompling when he had to, with a few of us trying to trip him and still dodge outen the way when we could but getting overtrompled too when we couldn't. And now all that's left of it is a bedrode old lady and her retired old-maid schoolteacher daughter that would a lived happily ever after in sunny golden California. But now they got to come all the way back to Missippi and live in that-ere big white elephant of a house where likely Miss Allison will have to go back to work again, maybe might even have to hump and hustle some to keep it up since how can they have mere friends and acquaintances, let alone strangers, saying how a Missippi-born and -bred lady refused to accept a whole house not only gift-free-for-nothing but that was actively theirn anyhow to begin with, without owing even Much obliged to nobody for getting it back. So maybe there's even a moral in it somewhere, if you jest knowed where to look."

"There aren't any morals," Stevens said. "People just do the best they can."

"The pore sons of bitches," Ratliff said.

"The poor sons of bitches," Stevens said. "Drive on. Pick it up."

So somewhere about ten oclock he sat beside Ratliff in the dark car on a hill road that had already ceased to be a road and soon would cease to be even passable, while Ratliff said, "So you think she really didn't know what he was going to do when he got out?"

"Yes I tell you," Stevens said. "Drive on."

"We got time," Ratliff said. "He aint going nowhere. Talking about that thing he used for a pistol, that he dropped or throwed it away while he was running through that back yard. Eef Bishop let me look at it. That Memphis feller was right. It didn't even look like a pistol. It looked like a old old mud-crusted cooter. It had two shells in it, the hull and another live one. The cap of the hull was punched all right, only it and the live one both had a little nick jest outside the cap, both of the nicks jest alike and even in the same place, so that when Eef taken the live one out and turned the hull a little and set it back under the hammer and cocked it and snapped it and we opened the cylinder, there was another of them little nicks in the case jest outside the cap, like sometimes that mossback firing pin would hit the cap and sometimes it wouldn't. So it looks like Mink either tried out both of them shells beforehand for practice test and both of them snapped once, yet he still walked in there to kill Flem jest hoping one of them would go off this time, which dont sound reasonable; or that he stood there in front of Flem and snapped maybe both of them at him and then turned the cylinder back to try again since that was all he had left he could do at that moment, and this time one of them went off. In that case, what do you reckon Flem's reason was for setting there in that chair letting Mink snap them two shells at him until one of them went off and killed him?"

"I dont know," Stevens said harshly. "Drive on!"

"Maybe he was jest bored too," Ratliff said. "Like Eula. Maybe there was two of them. The pore son of a bitch."

"He was impotent," Stevens said.

"What?" Ratliff said.

"Impotent. When he got in bed with a woman all he could do was go to sleep.—Yes!" Stevens said. "The poor sons of bitches that have to cause all the grief and anguish they have to cause! Drive on!"

"But suppose it was more than that," Ratliff said. "You was town-raised when you was a boy; likely you never heard of Give-me-lief. It was a game we played. You would pick out another boy about your own size and you would walk up to him with a switch or maybe a light stick or a hard green apple or maybe even a rock, depending on how hard a risk you wanted to take, and say to him, 'Gimme lief,' and if he agreed, he would stand still and you would take one cut or one lick at him with the switch or stick, as hard as you picked out, or back off and throw at him once with the green apple or the rock. Then you would stand still and he would take the same switch or stick or apple or rock or anyways another one jest like it, and take one cut or throw at you. That was the rule. So jest suppose—"

"Drive on!" Stevens said.

"—Flem had had his lief fair and square like the rule said, so there wasn't nothing for him to do but jest set there, since he had likely found out years back when she finally turned up here again even outen a communist war, that he had already lost—"

"Stop it!" Stevens said. "Dont say it!"

"—and now it was her lief and so suppose—"

"No!" Stevens said. "No!" But Ratliff was not only nearer the switch, his hand was already on it, covering it.

"—she knowed all the time what was going to happen when he got out, that not only she knowed but Flem did too—"

"I wont believe it!" Stevens said. "I wont! I cant believe it," he said. "Dont you see I cannot?"

"Which brings up something else," Ratliff said. "So she had a decision to make too that once she made it, it would be for good and all and too late to change it. She could a waited two more years and God His-self couldn't a kept Mink in Parchman without He killed him, and saved herself not jest the bother and worry but the moral responsibility too, even if you do say they aint no morals. Only she didn't. And so you wonder why. If maybe, if there wasn't no folks in heaven, it wouldn't be heaven, and if you couldn't recognise them as folks you knowed, wouldn't nobody want to go there. And that some-day her maw would be saying to her, 'Why didn't you revenge me and my love that I finally found it, instead of jest standing back and blind hoping for happen-so? Didn't you never have no love of your own to learn you what it is?'—Here," he said. He took out the immaculately clean, impeccably laundered and ironed handkerchief which the town said he not only laundered himself but hemstitched himself too, and put it into Stevens's blind hand and turned the switch and flicked on the headlights. "I reckon we'll be about right now," he said.

Now the road even ceased to be two ruts. It was a gash now, choked with brier, still mounting. "I'll go in front," Ratliff said. "You growed up in town. I never even seen a light bulb until after I could handle a straight razor." Then he said, "There it is"—a canted roof line where one end of the gable had collapsed completely (Stevens did not recognise, he simply agreed it could once have been a house) above which stood one worn gnarled cedar. He almost stumbled through, across what had been a fence, a yard fence, fallen too, choked fiercely with rose vines long since gone wild again. "Walk behind me," Ratliff said. "They's a old cistern. I think I know where it is. I ought to brought a flashlight."

And now, in a crumbling slant downward into, through, what had been the wall's old foundation, an orifice, a black and crumbled aperture yawned at their feet as if the ruined house itself had gaped at them. Ratliff had stopped. He said quietly: "You never seen that pistol. I did. It didn't look like no one-for-ten-dollars pistol. It looked like one of a two-for-nine-and-a-half pistols. Maybe he's still got the other one with him," when Stevens, without stopping, pushed past him and, fumbling one foot downward, found what had been a step; and, taking the gold initialled lighter from his pocket, snapped it on and by the faint wavered gleam continued to descend, Ratliff, behind now, saying, "Of course. He's free now. He wont never have to kill nobody else in all his life," and followed, into the old cellar—the cave, the den where on a crude platform he had heaped together, the man they sought half-squatted half-knelt blinking up at them like a child interrupted at its bedside prayers: not surprised in prayer: interrupted, kneeling in the new overalls which were stained and foul now, his hands lying half-curled on the front of his lap, blinking at the tiny light which Stevens held.

"Hidy," he said.

"You cant stay here," Stevens said. "If we knew where you were, dont you know the Sheriff will think of this place too by tomorrow morning?"

"I aint going to stay," he said. "I jest stopped to rest. I'm fixing to go on pretty soon. Who are you fellers?"

"Never mind that," Stevens said. He took out the envelope containing the money. "Here," he said. It was two hundred and fifty dollars again. The amount was indubitable out of the whole thousand it had contained. Stevens had not even troubled to rationalise his decision of the amount. The kneeling man looked at it quietly.

"I left that money in Parchman. I had done already got shut of it before I went out the gate. You mean a son of a bitch stole that too?"

"This is not that money," Stevens said. "They got that back. This is new money she sent you this morning. This is different."

"You mean when I take it I aint promised nobody nothing?"

"Yes," Stevens said. "Take it."

He did so. "Much obliged," he said. "That other time they said I would get another two hundred and fifty again in three months if I went straight across Missippi without stopping and never come back again. I reckon that's done stopped this time."

"No," Stevens said. "That too. In three months tell me where you are and I'll send it."

"Much obliged," Mink said. "Send it to M. C. Snopes."

"What?" Stevens said.

"To M. C. Snopes. That's my name: M. C."

"Come on," Ratliff said, almost roughly, "let's get out of here," taking him by the arm even as Stevens turned, Ratliff taking the burning lighter from him and holding it up while Stevens found the fading earthen steps again, once more up and out into the air, the night, the moonless dark, the worn-out eroded fields supine beneath the first faint breath of fall, waiting for winter. Overhead, celestial and hierarchate, the constellations wheeled through the zodiacal pastures: Scorpion and Bear and Scales; beyond cold Orion and the Sisters the fallen and homeless angels choired, lamenting. Gentle and tender as a woman, Ratliff opened the car door for Stevens to get in. "You all right now?" he said.

"Yes I tell you, goddammit," Stevens said.

Ratliff closed the door and went around the car and opened his and got in and closed it and turned the switch and snapped on the lights and put the car in gear—two old men themselves, approaching their sixties. "I dont know if she's already got a daughter stashed out somewhere, or if she jest aint got around to one yet. But when she does I jest hope for Old Lang Zyne's sake she dont never bring it back to Jefferson. You done already been through two Eula Varners and I dont think you can stand another one."

When the two strangers took the light away and were gone, he didn't lie down again. He was rested now, and any moment now the time to go on again would come. So he just continued to kneel on the crude platform of old boards he had gathered together to defend himself from the ground in case he dropped off to sleep. Luckily the man who robbed him of his ten dollars last Thursday night hadn't taken the safety pin too, so he folded the money as small as it would fold into the bib pocket and pinned it. It would be all right this time; it made such a lump that even asleep he couldn't help but feel anybody fooling with it.

Then the time came to go on. He was glad of it in a way; a man can get tired, burnt out on resting like on anything else. Outside it was dark, cool and pleasant for walking, empty except for the old ground. But then a man didn't need to have to keep his mind steadily on the ground after sixty-three years. In fact, the ground itself never let a man forget it was there waiting, pulling gently and without no hurry at him between every step, saying, Come on, lay down; I aint going to hurt you. Jest lay down. He thought *I'm free now. I can walk any way I want to.* So he would walk west now, since that was the direction people always went: west. Whenever they picked up and moved to a new country, it was always west, like Old Moster Himself had put it into a man's very blood and nature his paw had give him at the very moment he squirted him into his maw's belly.

Because he was free now. A little further along toward dawn, any time the notion struck him to, he could lay down. So when the notion struck him he did so, arranging himself, arms and legs and back, already feeling the first faint gentle tug like the durned old ground itself was trying to make you believe it wasn't really noticing itself doing it. Only he located the right stars at that moment, he was not laying exactly right since a man must face the east to lay down; walk west but when you lay down, face the exact east. So he moved, shifted a little, and now he was exactly right and he was free now, he could afford to risk it; to show how much he dared risk it, he even would close his eyes, give it all the chance it wanted; whereupon as if believing he really was asleep, it gradually went to work a little harder, easy of course, not to really disturb him: just harder, increasing. Because a man had to spend not just all his life but all the time of Man too guarding against it; even back when they said man lived in caves, he would raise up a bank of dirt to at least keep him that far off the ground while he slept, until he invented wood floors to protect him and at last beds too, raising the floors storey by storey until they would be laying a hundred and even a thousand feet up in the air to be safe from the earth.

But he could risk it, he even felt like giving it a fair active chance just to show him, prove what it could do if it wanted to try. And in fact, as soon as he thought that, it seemed to him he could feel the Mink Snopes that had had to spend so much of his life just having unnecessary bother and trouble, beginning to creep, seep, flow easy as sleeping; he could almost watch it, following all the little grass blades and tiny roots, the little holes the worms made, down and down into the ground already full of the folks that had the trouble but were free now, so that it was just the ground and the dirt that had to bother and worry and anguish with the passions and hopes and skeers, the justice and the injustice and the griefs, leaving the folks themselves easy now, all mixed and jumbled up comfortable and easy so wouldn't nobody even know or even care who was which any more, himself among them, equal to any, good as any, brave as any, being inextricable from, anonymous with all of them: the beautiful, the splendid, the proud and the brave, right on up to the very top itself among the shining phantoms and dreams which are the milestones of the long human recording—Helen and the bishops, the kings and the unhomed angels, the scornful and graceless seraphim.

Charlottesville, Virginia
9 March 1959